
The Annotated

Huckleberry Finn

OTHER ANNOTATED BOOKS FROM W. W. NORTON & COMPANY

The Annotated Alice in Wonderland
by Lewis Carroll, edited with notes
and an introduction by Martin Gardner

The Annotated Wizard of Oz
by L. Frank Baum, edited with notes
and an introduction by Michael Patrick Hearn

"Mark Twain"
Samuel Langhorne Clemens
(1835–1910)
Courtesy Library of Congress.

W. W. Norton & Company
New York • London

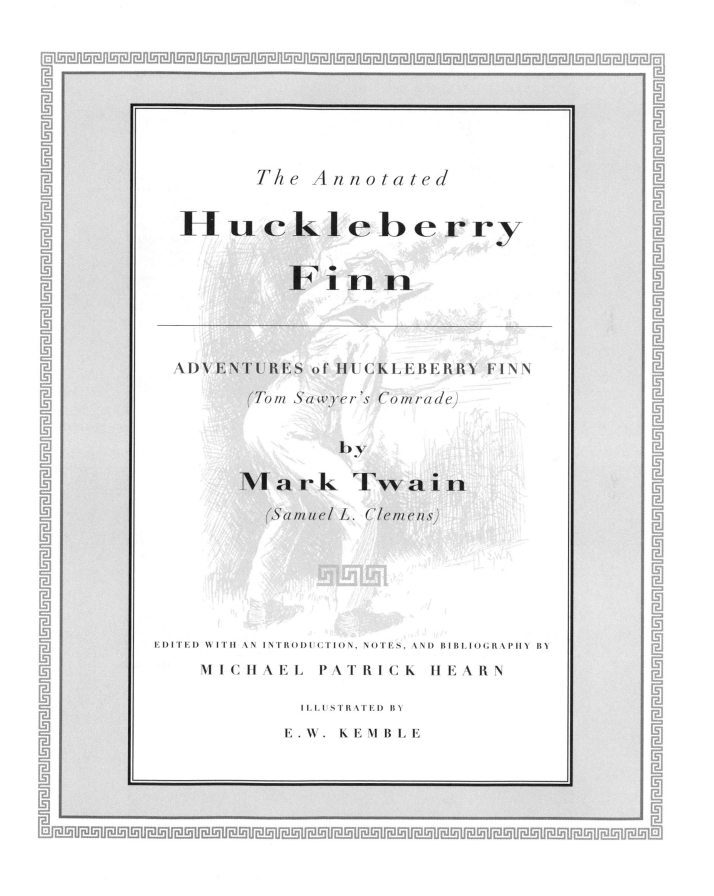

The Annotated

Huckleberry Finn

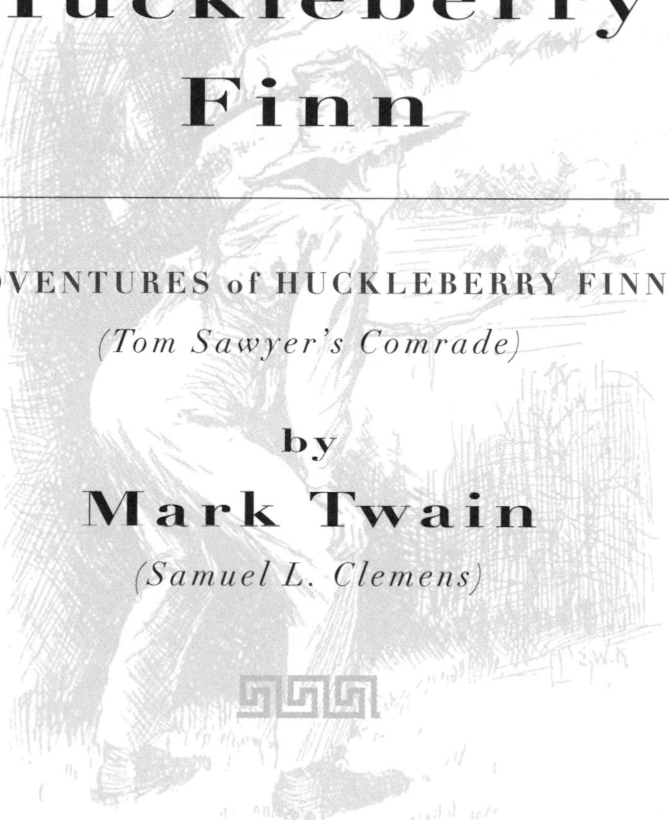

ADVENTURES of HUCKLEBERRY FINN

(Tom Sawyer's Comrade)

by

Mark Twain

(Samuel L. Clemens)

EDITED WITH AN INTRODUCTION, NOTES, AND BIBLIOGRAPHY BY

MICHAEL PATRICK HEARN

ILLUSTRATED BY

E.W. KEMBLE

Printed in the United States of America

The text of this book is composed in Didot LH with the
display set in Didot LH Bold
Composition by Sue Carlson/Jo Anne Metsch
Manufacturing by The Courier Companies, Inc.
Book design by JAM Design
Production manager: Andrew Marasia

Library of Congress Cataloging-in-Publication Data

Twain, Mark, 1835–1910.
[Adventures of Huckeberry Finn]
The annotated Huckleberry Finn : Adventures of Huckleberry Finn
(Tom Sawyer's comrade) / by Mark Twain ; illustrated by E. W. Kemble ;
edited with an introduction, notes, and bibliography
by Michael Patrick Hearn.
p. cm.
Includes bibliographical references.
ISBN 0-393-02039-8
1. Finn, Huckleberry (Fictitious character)—Fiction.
2. Twain, Mark, 1835–1910. Adventures of Huckleberry Finn.
3. Mississippi River—Fiction. 4. Missouri—Fiction.
5. Boys—Fiction. I. Hearn, Michael Patrick. II. Title.

PS1305.A2 H43 2001
813'.4-dc21 2001031507

W. W. Norton & Company, Inc.
500 Fifth Avenue, New York, N.Y. 10110
www.wwnorton.com

W. W. Norton & Company Ltd.
Castle House, 75/76 Wells Street,
London W1T 3QT

1 2 3 4 5 6 7 8 9 0

In Memory of

Ada Fear Fisk.

—M.P.H.

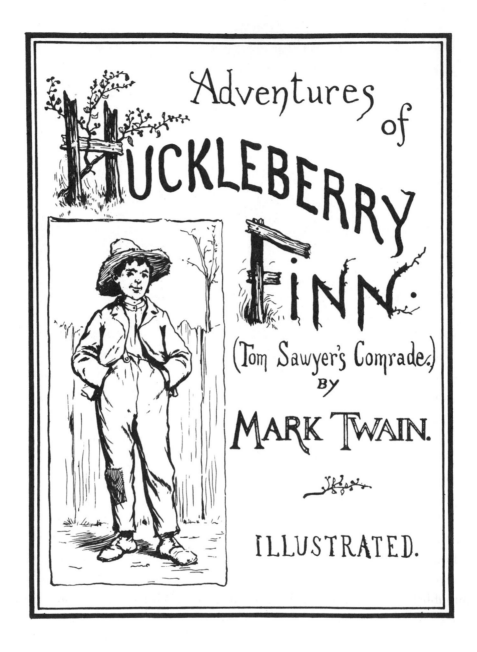

Adventures of Huckleberry Finn.

(Tom Sawyer's Comrade.)

BY

MARK TWAIN.

ILLUSTRATED.

Acknowledgments

Anyone who dares write about *Adventures of Huckleberry Finn* must consider the vast and rich critical heritage of Mark Twain and his work. I am no exception. I am merely building on the labors of my distinguished predecessors, everyone from William Dean Howells to Toni Morrison. Fortunately, Samuel L. Clemens saved correspondence, working notes, galleys, and reading copies of his most famous novel; and his only surviving daughter, Clara Clemens Samossoud, in establishing a center for Mark Twain scholarship, deposited this priceless literary archive in the Bancroft Library at the University of California. I could not have done *The Annotated Huckleberry Finn* without the generous support of the staff of the Mark Twain Project. Robert H. Hirst, Victor Fischer, Lin Salamo, Neda Salem, and the others at the Bancroft Library are a scholar's scholars, and have greatly enriched my and every other researcher's efforts. They provided unlimited access to both published and unpublished material in the Mark Twain Papers. With the permission of the Mark Twain Project and the University of California Press, I have quoted from the galleys and copies of the book annotated by Mark Twain for his 1884–1885 and 1895–1896 reading tours and reproduced in facsimile in the 1988 University of California edition of *Adventures of Huckleberry Finn*.

The discovery in 1990 of the first half of the manuscript of *Adventures of Huckleberry Finn* necessitated a rethinking of the composition of the novel. Random House published most of this new material in the 1996 "Comprehensive Edition" of the novel and kindly granted me permission to quote from the manuscript now housed in the Buffalo and Erie County Public Library. I am also grateful to William H. Loos, curator of the Rare Book Room, Buffalo and Erie County Public Library, for providing photographs (by Joseph Hryvniak) of pages of the manuscript; to the New-York Historical Society for copies of pictures from their collection; to Sidney Shiff of the Limited Editions Club for permission to reproduce an E. W. Kemble drawing from the 1933 edition of *Adventures of Huckleberry Finn*; and to the directors of the Berg Collection, the New York Public Library, Astor, Lenox and Tilden Foundations, for allowing me to quote from a letter from Twain to Walter Besant. Another important source has been the Jean Webster McKinney Family Papers, Special Collections, in the Vassar College Libraries, which houses Charles L. Webster's papers and many of the original drawings by E. W. Kemble for *Adventures of Huckleberry Finn*. And as always, I have drawn heavily on the enormous collections of the New York Public Library and the Library of Congress.

I would also like to thank Alex Cardona, Roberta Certner, Jocelyn A. Chadwick, Beverly R. David, Cynthia Hearn Dorfman, Victor Doyno, Karl Michael Emyrs, Deborah Foley, Martin Gardner, Peter E. Hanff, William White Howells, Jeanne Lamb, Sasha Lurie, Frances MacDonnell, Francis Martin, Jr., Patrick and Rita Maund, Daniel A. Menaker, David Moyer, Dean M. Roger, Mitchell Rose, Victoria Sabelli, Barbara Seaman, Bob Slotta, Thomas A. Tenney, Richard A. Watson, Nancy Willard, and my late father, who in different ways helped in the preparation of this book. I am especially indebted to Patrick Martin for his invaluable advice on all matters pertaining to Twain. *The Annotated Huckleberry Finn* could not have been possible without the hard work and infinite patience of the people at W. W. Norton. Robert Weil, my visionary editor, and his gifted assistants Neil Giordano and Jason Baskin squired the bulky manuscript through completion. Copyeditors Don Rifkin and Ted Johnson prevented me from making more blunders than I might otherwise have. Norton's miracle worker Andrew Marasia heroically saw this complex book through production, and Sue Carlson orchestrated the beautiful layout. I am thankful too for Nancy Palmquist's enormous contribution and to Aimee Bianca in publicity and Bill Rusin in sales for their support. I was again fortunate to have as the book's designer Jo Anne Metsch, who did similar honors to *The Annotated Wizard of Oz*. They are the ones who deserve the credit for making this the impressive volume that it is. Thank you all, and I do apologize for any inconvenience I may have caused along the way. All errors are purely my own.

M. P. H.

CONTENTS

INTRODUCTION TO
The Annotated Huckleberry Finn

This is Huck Finn, a child of mine of shady reputation.
Be good to him for his parent's sake.

—MARK TWAIN, in a presentation copy of
Adventures of Huckleberry Finn[1]

I

MARK TWAIN once sarcastically defined a classic as "a book which people praise and don't read."[2] However, his *Adventures of Huckleberry Finn* is the exception to his rule: It is a classic which is both praised and still read. It has also been condemned and banned. No other living work of American literature has suffered so contradictory a history as the autobiography of Tom Sawyer's comrade. It has been called both a literary masterpiece and racist trash. It has been marketed as a gift book for boys and girls; it has been removed from the children's rooms of public libraries across the country. It is required reading in universities both in America and abroad; it is banned from the curricula of elementary and high school systems.

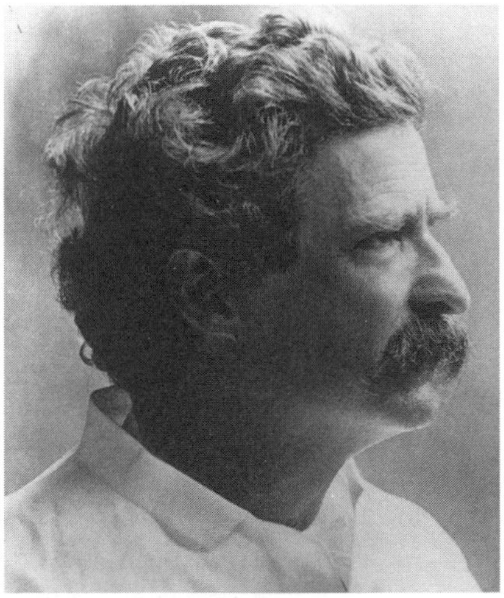

Mark Twain, 1885.
Courtesy Library of Congress.

1. From a note in the Mark Twain Papers, Bancroft Library, University of California at Berkeley. Due to the enormous volume of references in this introduction, footnotes have been kept to a minimum. Often-quoted works, particularly collections of correspondence, are mentioned once in the footnotes; page numbers are included in parenthesis at the end of each subsequent quotation in the text. Sources for quotations from short articles are generally indicated by author and title with page numbers within the body of the introduction.

2. Aphorism from "Pudd'nhead Wilson's Calendar," Chapter 25, *Following the Equator* (1897).

William Dean Howells, 1875.
Private collection.

Like Huckleberry Finn on his fateful journey down the Mississippi, the novel has seemed to be many things to many people. "It is by no means an easy matter, at this late date, to say anything new or fresh about Huckleberry Finn," said Twain's friend Laurence Hutton in *Harper's Magazine* (September 1896). Over a century later, *Huckleberry Finn* remains one of the most beloved and hated and consequently the most frequently discussed of American classics.

Its author never understood the controversy about "Huck, that abused child of mine who has had so much unfair mud flung at him."[3] When he began the novel in July 1876, Twain considered "Huck Finn's Autobiography" to be merely "a kind of companion" to the recently completed *The Adventures of Tom Sawyer* (1876). He had originally intended to carry the hero of that book into manhood; but, he wrote William Dean Howells, the eminent novelist and his literary confidant, "I believe it would be fatal to do it in any shape but autobiography—like *Gil Blas*. I perhaps made a mistake in not writing it in the first person. If I went on, now, and took him into manhood, he would just be like all the one-horse men in literature and the reader would conceive a hearty contempt for him."[4] So in his "Conclusion" to *Tom Sawyer*, Twain left open the possibility of a picaresque sequel by suggesting that "some day it may seem worth while to take up the story of the younger ones again and see what sort of men and women they turned out to be." He told Howells he might "take a boy of twelve and run him

3. In a letter to Joel Chandler Harris, November 29, 1885, *Mark Twain to Uncle Remus*, edited by Thomas H. English (Atlanta, Ga: Emory University Library, 1953), p. 20.

4. In a letter to William Dean Howells, July 5, 1875, *Mark Twain–Howells Letters*, vol. 1, edited by Henry Nash Smith, William M. Gibson, and Frederick Anderson (Cambridge, Mass.: Harvard University Press, 1960), p. 91. Unless otherwise indicated, all quotations from correspondence between Twain and Howells are from this book.

through life (in the first person) but not Tom Sawyer—he would not be a good character for it" (p. 92).

By August 9, 1876, Twain had found his proper spokesman. He wrote Howells that he had reluctantly begun "another boys' book—more to be at work than anything else. I have written 400 pages on it—therefore it is very nearly half done. It is 'Huck Finn's Autobiography'" (p. 144).[5] The new novel developed directly from *Tom Sawyer*, from a final chapter that Howells had advised Twain to delete, it being out of character with the rest of the story. Twain admitted to "the strong temptation to put Huck's life at the widow's into detail, instead of generalizing it in a paragraph" (p. 113), but he accepted his friend's suggestion to drop the episode, and then reworked it as the opening of the sequel.

Soon the original scheme to run Huck Finn through life was abandoned, and Twain grew weary of the new effort. "I like it only tolerably well," he wrote Howells, "and may possibly pigeonhole or burn the manuscript when it is done"(p. 144). Fortunately, he merely put it aside; and for the next six years, he intermittently pulled it out to work in additional episodes. "I don't write the book," he once told the New York *Times* (December 10, 1889). "A book writes itself." While working on *Tom Sawyer*, Twain found that "a book is pretty sure to get tired, along about the middle, and refuse to go on with its work until its powers and its interest should have been refreshed by a rest and its depleted stock of raw materials reinforced by lapse of time."[6] The cause of the delay was simple: "My tank had run dry." However, after it had been neglected for two years, he took it out and reread the last chapter and discovered that "when the tank runs dry you've only to leave it alone and it will fill up again in time. . . . There was plenty of material now and the book went on and finished itself without any trouble." So too it was with *Huckleberry Finn*.

Tom Sawyer was not only Twain's first novel, but also his first children's book.[7] It was a far more ambitious book than *Sketches, New and Old,* which also

5. The manuscript, now in the Buffalo and Erie County Public Library, Buffalo, New York, consists of 1,361 holograph pages. Twain wrote with remarkable haste, sometimes not even pausing to lift pen from paper from word to word. He then made his major revisions on various typescripts, which do not survive. The second part of the manuscript was published as *Adventures of Huckleberry Finn (Tom Sawyer's Comrade): A Facsimile of the Manuscript* (Detroit: Gale Research Co., 1983); and the rediscovered first half was the basis for the "Comprehensive Edition" of *Huckleberry Finn*, published by Random House in 1996.

6. In *Mark Twain in Eruption*, edited by Bernard DeVoto (New York and London: Harper & Bros., 1940), p. 196.

7. Twain cowrote *The Gilded Age* (1873) with his friend Charles Dudley Warner, editor of the Hartford *Courant*, but he began *Tom Sawyer* a year before commencing that book.

Mark Twain. Frontispiece in *The Galaxy*, August 1870.
Courtesy Library of Congress.

came out in 1876. Samuel Langhorne Clemens affectionately recalled in his semiautobiographical story people, places, and incidents from his boyhood of thirty years before in Hannibal, Missouri. While it received little critical notice, it immediately captured the public's affection. Sales were not as great as hoped: Although he arranged a concurrent English edition with Chatto & Windus in London and a Continental one with Tauchnitz in Leipzig, he could not prevent a Canadian publisher from pirating the book and unloading about 100,000 cheap copies on the American market. Thereafter, Twain was careful to cross into Canada for a few weeks to fulfill the then residency requirement to protect his subsequent copyrights.

Demand for a sequel to *Tom Sawyer*, however, was so swift and strong that Twain had to print up a form letter in 1877: "I have the honor to reply to your letter just received, that it is my purpose to write a continuation of Tom Sawyer's history, but I am not able at this time to determine when I shall begin the work. You will excuse this printed form, in consideration of the fact that the inquiry which you have made recurs with sufficient frequency to warrant this method of replying."[8] As he hoped one day to finish the boy's story, Twain must have been encouraged that some reviews of *Tom Sawyer* referred to Huckleberry Finn as worthy of special mention. The New York *Times* noted on January 13, 1877, "One admirable character in the book and touched with the hand of the master is that of Huckleberry Finn. There is a reality about the boy which is striking." Howells said in his notice in *The Atlantic Monthly* (May 1876), "The worthless vagabond, Huck Finn, is entirely delightful throughout" (p. 621).

Twain briefly pulled out the manuscript in 1879, after a trip to Europe. He added a few more chapters up to the shooting of Boggs by Sherburn in Chapter 22, and then put it aside again. The spring of 1882 saw him back in Missouri

[8] Copy in the Jean Webster McKinney Family Papers, Vassar College Library.

to gather material for the expansion of seven articles, "Old Times on the Mississippi," first published in *The Atlantic Monthly* (January–August 1875), into *Life on the Mississippi* (1883). "By way of illustrating keelboat talk and manners, and that now-departed and hardly-remembered raft-life," Twain padded the new book by throwing into Chapter 3 an episode from Huck Finn's autobiography, "a book which I have been working at, by fits and starts, during the past five or six years, and may possibly finish in the course of five or six more."

Fortunately, he got back to it the following summer in Elmira, where the Clemenses always spent the season. "We have been here on the hill a week or more," he reported to friends on July 2, 1883, "and I am deep in my work and grinding out manuscript by the acre—stick to it the whole day, and allowing myself only time to scratch off two or three brief letters *after* they yell for me to come down to supper."[9] He ecstatically told Howells on July 20, "I haven't piled up manuscript so in years as I have done since we came here to the farm three weeks and a half ago. Why, it's like old times, to step straight into the study, damp from the breakfast table, and sail right in and sail right on, the whole day long, without thought of running short of stuff or words. I wrote 4,000 words today and I touch 3,000 and upwards pretty often, and don't fall below 2,600 on any working day. And when I get fagged out, I lie abed a couple of days and read and smoke, and then go it again for six or seven days and am away along in a big one that I half-finished two or three years ago" (p. 435). Nothing could stop him as he confessed that "once or twice I smouched a Sunday when the boss wasn't looking. Nothing is half so good as literature hooked on Sunday on the sly" (p. 438). He proudly wrote his family in Illinois, "I haven't had such booming writing-days for many years. I am piling up manuscript in a really astonishing way. I believe I shall complete, in two months, a book which I have been going over for seven years. This summer is no more trouble to me to write than it is to lie."[10] Even then he was unsure of the book's merits. "And *I* shall *like* it," he promised Howells, "whether anybody else does or not" (p. 435).

By September the book was done. As he informed his publisher James R. Osgood, he "had written 50,000 words on it before; and this summer it took 70,000 to complete it."[11] He was feeling cocky about the final work when he told his British publishers, Chatto & Windus, on September 1 that "modesty

9. In a letter to Karl and Josephine Gerhardt, July 2, 1883, transcript courtesy the Mark Twain Papers.

10. In a letter to Jane Lampton Clemens and others, July 21, 1871, *Mark Twain's Letters*, vol. 1, edited by Albert Bigelow Paine (New York: Harper & Bros., 1935), p. 434.

11. Quoted in Walter Blair and Victor Fischer, Introduction, *Adventures of Huckleberry Finn* (Berkeley and Los Angeles: University of California, 1988), p. 432.

Susy Clemens.
Courtesy the Mark Twain Papers, Bancroft Library, University of California at Berkeley.

compels me to say it's a rattling good one, too—*Adventures of Huckleberry Finn (Tom Sawyer's Comrade)*."[12] They anxiously wrote back the popular writer on October 23, "We are all agog for the promised *Adventures of Huckleberry Finn* and hope you will be able to publish it by next year." Twain replied on November 12 that he would be ready "to talk business and make contracts with you on the new book pretty soon now—possibly a month hence." But he was being overly optimistic.[13]

The many years during which Twain composed *Huckleberry Finn* were perhaps the happiest and most productive of the author's long troubled life. To his vast public, the famous humorist "Mark Twain" seemed to be exactly as one twelve-year-old admirer described him: "He is jolly; I imagine him to be a funny man . . . who always keeps every body laughing and who is happy as the Man in the Moon looks. . . . he makes so much money. . . . he is worth millions. . . . he has a beautiful wife and children. . . . he has everything a man could have."[14] This appraisal of the public man matches the impressions Samuel Langhorne Clemens gave another child, his fourteen-year-old daughter, Susy, in the 1885 "biography" she wrote of her celebrated father. "We are a very happy family," she explained. "We consist of Papa, Mamma, Jean, Clara,

12. In a letter to Andrew Chatto, September 1, 1883, quoted in Dennis Welland, *Mark Twain in England* (London: Chatto & Windus, 1978), p. 116. Unless otherwise indicated, all quotations from Chatto & Windus correspondence are from this book.

13. Twain and the American publisher tried to keep Chatto & Windus up to date on the book's numerous delays: First it was spring, then fall, then Christmas of 1884, then "late in the fall," and finally December 10, 1885. It was necessary to bring out the English and Canadian editions a day or two in advance of the American edition to secure copyright outside the United States. See Welland, pp. 116–17.

14. In a composition by David Watt Bowser, March 16, 1880, "Dear Master Wattie: The Mark Twain–David Watt Bowser Letters," edited by Pascal Covici, Jr., *Southwest Review*, Spring 1960, p. 106.

Olivia, Clara, Jean, and Susy Clemens on the porch of their Hartford home, 1885.
Courtesy the Mark Twain Papers, Bancroft Library, University of California at Berkeley.

and me."[15] The adored and adoring child described him in her biography at age fifty, with his "beautiful gray hair, not any too thick or any too long, but just right; a Roman nose, which greatly improves the beauty of his features; kind blue eyes and a small mustache. He has a wonderfully shaped head and profile. He has a very good figure. . . . All his features are perfect, except that he hasn't extraordinary teeth. His complexion is very fair. . . . He is a very good man and a very funny man. He *has* got a temper, but we all of us have in this family. He is the loveliest man I ever saw or hope to see—and oh, so absent-minded" (p. 709).

The Clemenses of Hartford, Connecticut, were indeed prosperous and content. They had settled in the booming, handsome state capital to be near his publishers as well as a congenial circle of writers at Nook Farm, on the city's

15. In "Chapters from My Autobiography," *North American Review*, October 19, 1906, p. 707. "The spelling is frequently desperate," Twain admitted of his daughter's biography, "but it was Susy's and it shall stand" (p. 706). And his wishes have been followed in subsequent quotations from her biography.

"Yours truly, Mark Twain." Engraved frontispiece, *A Tramp Abroad*, 1880.

Courtesy Picture Collection, New York Public Library, Astor, Lenox, and Tilden Foundations.

Caricature of Mark Twain by Kendrick, *Life*, March 22, 1883.
Courtesy Library of Congress.

western edge. "There was a constant running in and out of friendly houses where the lively hosts and guests called one another by their Christian names or nicknames," Howells recalled a visit in *My Mark Twain*, "and no such vain ceremony as knocking or ringing at doors" (p. 7). Here, where also resided Charles Dudley Warner as well as Harriet Beecher Stowe, the author of *Uncle Tom's Cabin* (1852), the Clemenses built a magnificent mansion Twain thought worthy of a successful author. Financed largely by the inheritance of his wealthy wife, the former Olivia L. Langdon of Elmira, New York, and profits of his best-selling books, the Mark Twain house reflected the former Mississippi riverboat pilot's personality as much as that of its architect, Edward Potter. It was the most eccentric home in wealthy Hartford, a nineteen-room, five-bath structure sporting a porch shaped like a steamboat deck and a balcony like a pilothouse. The mansion's Gothic turrets and polychromatic bricks and roof tiles, along with interiors designed by Louis J. Tiffany of New York and "aesthetic" wallpaper by English artist Walter Crane, reflected his wife's taste for what Potter defined as the currently fashionable "English violet order of architecture."[16] "There are nineteen different styles in it and folks can take their pick," Twain told the Rochester (N.Y.) *Herald* (December 8, 1884). "It wouldn't do to call it 'mongrel' for that would be offensive to some. I guess we'll call it 'eclectic'—the word describes everything that can't be otherwise described." This bizarre, yet comfortable, combination of Mississippi steamboat, English castle, and Victorian church took three years to complete, with further renovations and extensions in 1881. In all, the Clemenses spent nearly $200,000, a

16. In *My Mark Twain* (New York and London: Harper & Bros., 1910), p. 7.

The Clemens home in Hartford, Connecticut,
Scribner's Monthly Magazine, November 1876.
Courtesy Library of Congress.

fortune at the time, to buy the land and erect and furnish the main building and carriage house.

This remarkable residence was built as much for hospitality as for show; and being conveniently situated between Boston and New York, the household entertained a steady stream of visitors traveling between these two major literary centers of the country. Constant entertaining and the general upkeep of the house (which required at least six servants) strained the family's finances; in one year the costs were as high as $100,000. "I have a badgered, harassed feeling, a good part of the time," Clemens wrote his mother in 1878. "It comes mainly of business responsibilities and annoyances. . . . There are other things also that help to consume my time and defeat my projects. Well, the consequence is, I cannot write a book at home. This cuts my income down."[17] In desperate attempts to economize, he took his family to Europe, where he resolved to "budge no more until I shall have completed one of the half dozen books that lie begun, up stairs."

His study in Hartford was never the most convenient place to work. One reporter noted how the "floor was littered up with a confusion of newspapers, newspaper cuttings, books, children's toys, pipes, models of machinery, and cigar ends. Twain's method is to drop everything when he's done using it, but he will let nobody else interfere with the arrangements of his study."[18] And Twain's mind was as cluttered as his studio with new ideas and unfinished projects. With so many distractions at home, he rarely got any writing done "Work?" he replied to a friend's inquiry in 1881. "One *can't*, you know, to any purpose. I don't really get anything done worth speaking of, except during the three or four months that we are away in the Summer. I keep three or four books on the stocks all the time, but I seldom add a satisfactory chapter to one of them at home."[19] Nevertheless, during the seven years that *Huckleberry Finn* was "on the stocks," Twain produced *A Tramp Abroad* (1880), an account of his walking tour of Europe; *The Prince and the Pauper* (1882), a novel set in sixteenth-century London; and *Life on the Mississippi* (1883), partially a record of his recent return down the great river that he had navigated as a young steamboat pilot before the Civil War.

It was not in Hartford but in more remote Elmira that Twain did most of his writing. He admitted to Edwin J. Park in "A Day with Mark Twain" (Chicago *Tribune*, September 19, 1886) that this quiet upstate New York community "may be called the home of *Huckleberry Finn* and other books of mine, for they were written here." For years, the Clemenses spent their summers at Quarry Farm, the home of Olivia's adopted sister, Susan Langdon Crane, about three miles outside of Elmira and perched on a high hill; it was a glorious summer camp for the girls, and for Livy a needed refuge from the exhausting responsibilities of running the Hartford house. "There is too much social life in my city for a literary man," he told the Bombay *Gazette* (January 23, 1896) about life in Hartford. "It has only been during the three months that I have annually been on

17. In a letter to Jane Lampton Clemens and others, July 21, 1871, *Mark Twain's Letters*, vol. 1, pp. 319–20.

18. Quoted in Milton Meltzer, *Mark Twain Himself* (New York: T. Y. Crowell, 1960), p. 141.

19. In a letter to Charles Warren Stoddard, October 26, 1881, *Mark Twain's Letters*, vol. 1, p. 405.

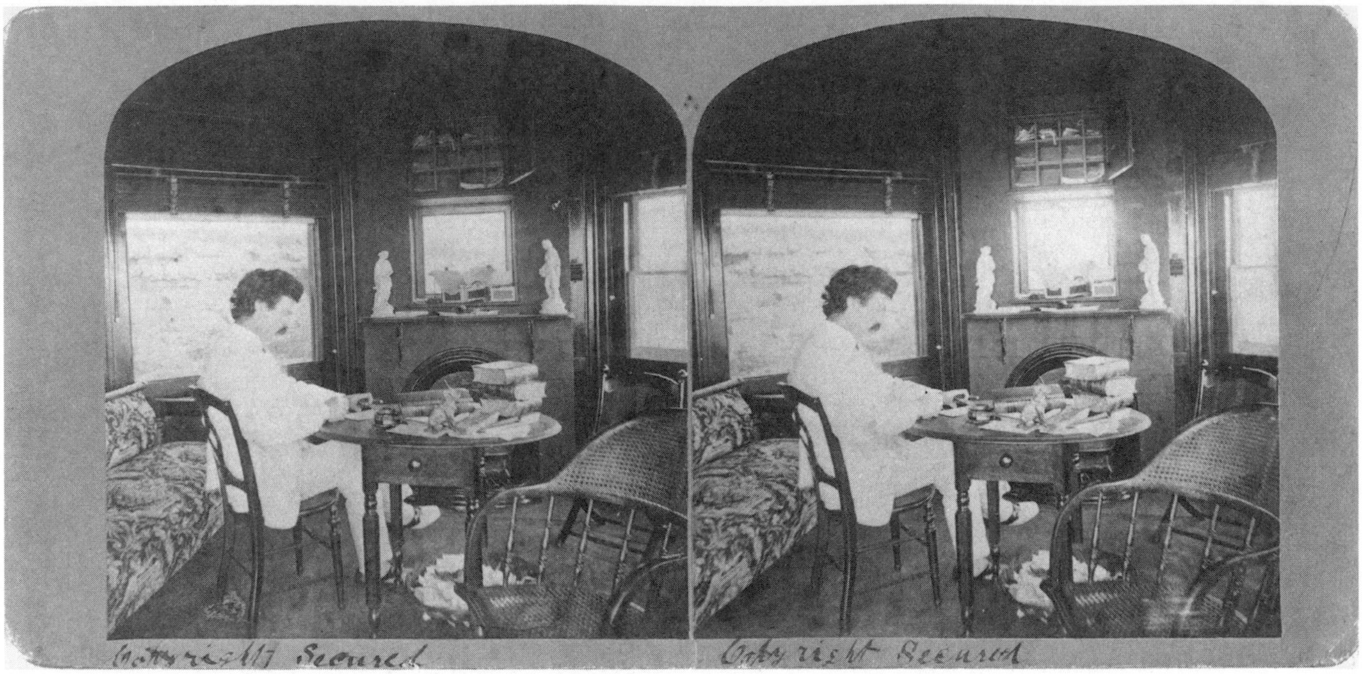

Mark Twain in his study at Quarry Farm, 1874.

Courtesy the Mark Twain Papers, Bancroft Library, University of California at Berkeley.

Mark Twain returns to his study at Quarry Farm, where he wrote *Adventures of Huckleberry Finn*, 1903.

Courtesy Library of Congress.

vacation, and have been supposed to be holiday-making that I have written anything." Only in seclusion did Twain work best; and his sister-in-law thoughtfully built for him a lovely little studio, a summer house shaped like a pilothouse, that overlooked the countryside. "It is octagonal, with a peaked roof," he informed friends, "each octagon filled with a spacious window, and it sits perched in complete isolation on top of an elevation that commands leagues of valley and city and retreating ranges of distant blue hills. It is a cosy nest, with just room in it for a sofa and a table and three or four chairs—and when the storms sweep down the remote valley and the lightning flashes above the hills below and the rain beats upon the roof over my head, imagine the luxury of it! . . . On the hot days I spread the study wide open, anchor my papers with brickbats and write in the midst of hurricanes, clothed in the same thin linen we make shirts of."[20]

Mark Twain at work. Frontispiece by True W. Williams, *A Tramp Abroad*, 1880. *Private collection.*

But Twain did not spend all of his time at Quarry Farm writing. In her biography, Susy carefully recorded his summer routine: "Papa rises about 1/2 past 7 in the morning, breakfasts at eight, writes, plays tennis with Clara and me and tries to make the donkey go . . . ; does various things in the P. M., and in the evening plays tennis with Clara and me and amuses Jean and the donkey." And during that productive summer of 1883 that saw the completion of *Huckleberry Finn*, he was also preoccupied with the possibilities of manufacturing a pair of grape scissors invented by Howells's father, marketing a history game created to amuse his daughters, and

20. In a letter to the Rev. and Mrs. Joseph Twichell, June 11, 1874, *Mark Twain's Letters*, vol. 1, p. 220.

preparing a play or two with Howells. He also wrote a tiresome 18,000-word burlesque "1002d Arabian Night" which nobody wanted to publish, and finished that year a four-act dramatization of *Tom Sawyer* that nobody wanted to produce. As he busied himself with various fruitless projects, he may very well have been unaware of exactly what he had achieved in the new novel.

Immediately he turned the manuscript over to his "faithful, judicious and painstaking editor," his wife, Olivia Clemens. He often read what he had just completed to the family and friends, to mixed reactions. "All my daughters ought to be pretty familiar with my works, seeing that they have edited my manuscript since they were seven years old," he told the Helena (Mont.) *Daily Herald* (August 3, 1895). "They always sided with me when Mrs. Clemens thought I had used some sentence or word that was a little too strong. But we never stood on that because Madame was always in the majority anyway." It was no different with *Huckleberry Finn*. Susy noted in the biography, "Ever since papa and mama were married papa has written his books . . . and she has expergated them. Papa read *Huckleberry Finn* to us in manuscript . . . , and then he would leave parts of it for mama to expergate, while he went off to the study to work, and sometimes Clara and I would be sitting with mama while she was looking the manuscript over, and I remember so well . . . one part perticularly which was perfectly fascinating it was so terrible, that Clara and I used to delight in and oh, with what despair we saw mama turn down the leaf on which it was written, we thought the book would be almost ruined without it. But we generally come to think as mama did."[21] Clemens was not above a little perverse teasing of his intrepid reader's genteel sensibilities. "For my own entertainment, and to enjoy the protests of the children," he confessed in "Chapters from My Autobiography" (*North American Review*, November 2, 1906), "I often abused my editor's innocent confidence. I often interlarded remarks of a studied and felicitously atrocious character purposely to achieve the children's brief delight, and then see the

Olivia Langdon Clemens, 1885.
Courtesy the Mark Twain Papers, Bancroft Library, University of California at Berkeley.

21. In "Chapters from My Autobiography," *North American Review*, June 7, 1907, p. 243. "He liked to exaggerate her fierceness just as the lion tamer likes to pretend his tame cats are all ready to tear him to bits," explained his grandnephew Samuel Charles Webster in *Mark Twain, Business Man* (Boston: Little, Brown, 1946). "When she was alive Aunt Livy kept him from publishing any second-rate stuff" (p. 285).

remorseless pencil do its fatal work. I often joined my supplications to the children's for mercy . . . and pretended to be in earnest. They were deceived and so was their mother. . . . But it was very delightful, and I could not resist the temptation. . . . Then I privately struck the passage out myself" (p. 837). Censorship is too strong a word. "We write frankly and fearlessly," Twain admitted in Chapter 14 of *Life on the Mississippi*, "but then we 'modify' before we print." If Twain did not entirely approve of this practice of self-censorship, he still allowed it to be done. Once he had finished writing something, he took little further interest in it. And he rarely reread his books.

Much has been made of Olivia Clemens's "expergating" her husband's work. Van Wyck Brooks in *The Ordeal of Mark Twain* (1920) went so far as to accuse Twain of having compromised his artistic integrity through his wife's misguided attempt "to turn Caliban into a gentleman" (p. 116). Olivia Langdon's refined upbringing was far removed from that of Sam Clemens, it is true: A semi-invalid from the age of sixteen, she had been trained in a respectable upper-middle-class home where piety, comfort, and morality were valued; her sheltered life knew none of the roughness and violence native to the American Southwest before the Civil War in which her husband grew up. It was a liberal household of abolitionists and Congregationalists, who welcomed social reformers like William Garrison, Gerritt Smith, and Frederick Douglass to their parlor. "For my part," suggested Max Eastman in "Mark Twain of Elmira" (*Harper's Monthly*, May 1938), "having grown up in the very same environment and with her family among my dear friends, I think that the Elmira influence was a vitally liberating one to Mark Twain, and that he actively, and with judgement as well as joy, absorbed it" (p. 632). Eastman called *The Ordeal of Mark Twain* "Mr. Brooks' historical novel."

When they met in 1867, through her brother, young lovesick Sam Clemens yearned to do anything to win his beloved Livy. He was willing to swear off liquor and tobacco just for her sake, and, he admitted, "not that I believed there was the faintest *reason* in the matter, but just as I would deprive myself of sugar in my coffee if she wished it, or quit wearing socks if she thought them immoral."[22] As further proof of his devotion, Clemens promised Olivia's

22. In a letter to Twichell, quoted in Meltzer, p. 144. "Papa uses very strong language," Susy Clemens observed in her biography of her father, "but I have an idea not nearly so strong as when he first married mamma" (quoted in "Chapters from My Autobiography," *North American Review*, October 19, 1906, p. 716). The Langdons, Olivia's family, could be intimidating. "I myself, much as I admired and loved her family, was always a little frightened by their refinement," admitted Eastman in "Mark Twain's Elmira." "I was tongue-tied and troubled by the discovery that I had hands and feet whenever I entered the serene door of the stately dark-brown mansion where they lived" (p. 629).

mother that he would try to "earn enough money some way or other, to buy a remunerative share in a newspaper of high standing, and then instruct and elevate and civilize the public through its columns, and my wife (to be) will superintend the domestic economy, furnish ideas and sense, erase improprieties from the manuscript, and read proof."[23]

One of his habits she could not abide was his swearing. "All through the first ten years of my married life," he continued in "Chapters from My Autobiography," "I kept a constant and discreet watch upon my tongue while in the house, and went outside and to a distance when circumstances were too much for me and I was obliged to seek relief. I prized my wife's respect and approval above all the rest of the human race's respect and approval" (*North American Review*, November 2, 1906, p. 833). But Mrs. Clemens succeeded no better in reforming her husband than did Widow Douglas in "sivilizing" Huck Finn. "His profanity," Howells explained in *My Mark Twain*, "was the heritage of his boyhood and young manhood in social conditions and under the duress of exigencies in which everybody swore about as impersonally as he smoked" (p. 76). It was a part of his nature; it could be arrested temporarily but never eradicated from his character.

Twain was generally open-minded about criticism of his writing. "If you wanted a thing changed," Howells recalled, "very good, he changed it; if you suggested that a word or a sentence or a paragraph had better be struck out, very good, he struck it out" (p. 19). Twain had complete faith in Howells's literary advice. Twain once described the process his manuscripts went through to an editor of *Century Magazine*: "Mrs. Clemens will edit it tonight; I will re-edit it tomorrow, and then send it. I have made so many little alterations that I must ask you . . . to read the *whole* of it anew, page by page. Then tell me what to strike out; also what to add, if anything occurs to you."[24] Some people actually thought it was a good thing she did take a look at his work. "What a noble woman she is!" recalled Twain's lecture manager Major James B. Pond. "It is Mark Twain's wife who makes his works so great. She edits everything and brings, purity, dignity, and sweetness to his writings."[25]

Twain relied as much on Howells as he did on Mrs. Clemens for refined opinion of his work from the time of *Tom Sawyer*. "I do not know what his mis-

23. In a letter to Olivia L. Langdon, February 13, 1869, in *The Love Letters of Mark Twain*, edited by Dixon Wecter (New York: Harper & Bros., 1949), p. 67. Unless otherwise indicated, all quotations from correspondence between Twain and Olivia Clemens are from this book.

24. Letter to Robert Underwood Johnson, August 15, 1885, "Twain to R. U. Johnson," *Mark Twain Quarterly*, Winter/Spring 1945, p. 23.

25. In *Eccentricities of Genius* (New York: G. W. Dillingham Co., 1900), p. 223.

ADVENTURES

OF

HUCKLEBERRY FINN

Tom Sawyer's Comrade

[OVER]

By Mark Twain.

New York

Chas. L. Webster & Co.

1885

Title page of the manuscript of
Adventures of Huckleberry Finn, 1884.
Courtesy Buffalo and Erie County Public Library, Buffalo, New York.

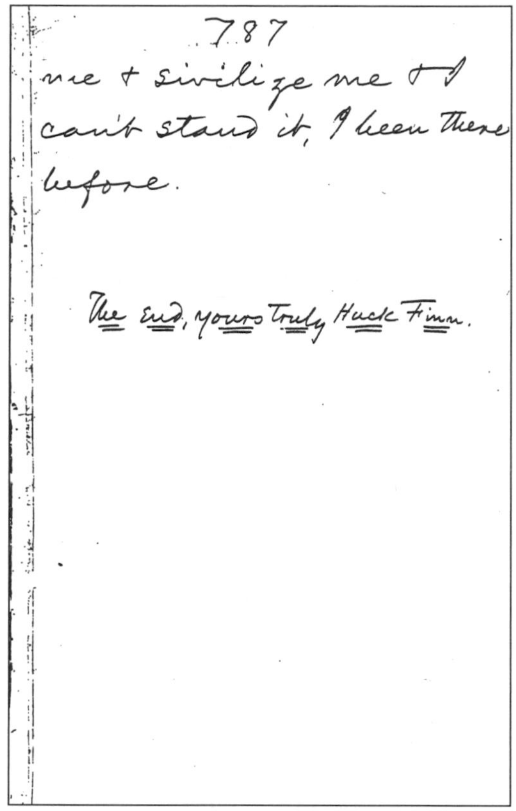

787

me & sivilize me & I can't stand it, I been there before.

The end, yours truly Huck Finn.

The final page of the manuscript of
Adventures of Huckleberry Finn, 1884.
Courtesy Buffalo and Erie County Public Library, Buffalo, New York.

givings were," Howells wrote in *My Mark Twain*, "perhaps they were his wife's misgivings, for she wished him to be known not only for the wild and boundless humor that was in him, but for the beauty and tenderness and 'natural piety'; and she would not have had him judged by a too close fidelity to the rude conditions of Tom Sawyer's life" (p. 48). He could not have been happier when Howells offered to read the galleys of the new book, something Twain himself loathed. "My new book is draining me day by day, and will continue the drain several months yet," he whined to Howells. "My days are given up to cursings—both loud and deep—for I am reading the *Huckleberry Finn* proofs. They don't make a very great many mistakes; but those that do occur are of a nature to make a man curse his teeth loose" (p. 493). But Howells was eager to help his friend just for "the pleasure of admiring a piece of work I like under the microscope" (p. 484). Twain apologized for "doing a most criminal and outrageous thing—for I am sending you these infernal *Huck Finn* proofs—but the very last vestige of my patience has gone to the devil, and I cannot bear the sight of another slip of them. My hair turns white with rage, at the sight of the mere outside of the package" (p. 497). He had such faith in his friend's critical ability that he readily gave Howells "*carte blanche* in making corrections."[26] He appreciated all the help Howells gave him. "It was a relief and a respite," he said, "and I cursed my way through the rest and survived. I was most heavenly glad to get done with it. The sight of a proof-slip is always exasperating to me; but on this book it was maddeningly" (p. 500). Howells graciously assured him, "If I had written half as good a book as *Huck Finn*, I shouldn't ask anything better than to read the proofs" (p. 499).

Oddly, Howells could be as much of a prude as, if not more of one than, Mrs. Clemens. Although he and Clemens "were natives of the same vast Mississippi Valley; and Missouri was not so far from Ohio," his friend's ribaldry shocked Howells. "Throughout my long acquaintanceship with him," Howells wrote in *My Mark Twain*, "his graphic touch was always allowing itself a freedom which I cannot bring my fainter pencil to illustrate. He had the Southwestern, the Lincolnian, the Elizabethan breadth of parlance, which I suppose one ought not to call coarse without calling one's self prudish; and I was often hiding away in discreet holes and corners the letters in which he had loosed his bold fancy to stoop on rank suggestion; I could not bear to burn them, and I could not, after the first reading, quite bear to look at them" (pp. 3–4). Twain could be uninhibitedly vulgar; and Howells once admitted that his friend's "humor was not for most women."[27] And not for all men either. Nevertheless, the reticent Howells found little in the proofs of *Huckleberry Finn* so offensive that it needed to be struck out.

26. Letter to Charles L. Webster, April 22, 1884, *Mark Twain, Business Man*, p. 250. "It took my breath away," Twain gushed to Howells, "and I haven't recovered it yet, entirely—I mean the generosity of your proposal to read the proofs of *Huck Finn*. Now if you *mean* it, old man—if you are in *earnest*—proceed, in God's name, and be by me forever blest. I cannot conceive of a rational man deliberately piling such an atrocious job upon himself; but if there is such a man, and you be that man, why then *pile it on*. . . . Herr, I would not read the proof of one of my books for any fair and reasonable sum whatever, if I could get out of it. The proof-reading on *The Prince and the Pauper* cost me the last rags of my religion" (pp. 482–83). Twain exaggerated, because Howells was offended that Twain was communicating with him only through his agent and nephew, Charles L. Webster. Unless otherwise indicated, all quotations from Webster correspondence are from this book.

27. In "Mark Twain: An Inquiry," *North American Review*, February 1901, p. 314. For example, he delivered a risqué lecture, "Some Thoughts on the Science of Onanism," at the Stomach Club, Paris, in the spring of 1879; and his notorious 1876 Elizabethan parody *1601* (in which the queen, Francis Bacon, Sir Walter Raleigh, and other notables of the English court discuss such indelicate subjects as who "did breake wind" in the royal presence) was composed

Richard Watson Gilder, the editor of *Century*, was another matter. In the three excerpts from *Huckleberry Finn* that he serialized in the magazine before the book's publication in the United States, Gilder deleted references to nakedness, offensive smells, and the blowing of noses; such a phrase as "both of them took on like they'd lost the twelve apostles" was suppressed, perhaps for fear of being perceived as blasphemous. Under Gilder's blue pencil, "such a sweat" became "such a hurry," "wet cloth" became "shroud." He thus left nothing in the text that might make Miss Watson blush. Oddly, no one thought of deleting the vulgar word "nigger." "Mr. Clemens has great faults," the cautious editor admitted; "at times he is inartistically and indefensibly coarse . . . there is much of his writing that we would not print for a miscellaneous audience. If you should ever carefully compare the chapters of *Huckleberry Finn*, as we printed them, with the same as they appear in his book, you will see the most decided difference. These extracts were carefully edited for a magazine audience with his full consent."[28] Yet Gilder was astute enough to recognize

---

to entertain the Rev. John Twichell, a Congregational minister, and has since become an underground classic of ribaldry.

28. In a letter to Clemens, January 8, 1886, *Letters of Richard Watson Gilder*, edited by Rosamund Gilder (Boston and New York: Houghton Mifflin, 1916), pp. 398–99. "There are some few expressions 'not adapted to our audience' (I do not find many) that we would wish the liberty of expunging," Gilder wrote Twain on October 10, 1884, "and a good deal would have to be omitted on account of space—and in omitting we might also have a regard for our audience. But I have a pretty 'robustuous taste' (for a pharisaical dude), and wouldn't mutilate your book you may be sure. I can only think of one expression that would be of the kind that I would expunge—as far as I have read—the two lines . . . about navigation." The offending lines appear in Chapter 5: "And when they come to look at that spare room, they had to take soundings before they could navigate it." He considered "the old daddie's talk about the mullatoes" in the same chapter to be "one of your best things"; but he did not use it. Gilder originally wanted four excerpts for January, February, March, and April; but he settled for three: "An Adventure of Huckleberry Finn: With an Account of the Famous Grangerford–Shepherdson Feud" (December 1884), pp. 268–78; "Jim's Investments, and King Sollermun" (January 1885), pp. 456–58; "Royalty on the Mississippi: As Chronicled by Huckleberry Finn" (February 1885), pp. 544–67. He wrote Twain on October 17, "[I] have only omitted the poem, and a few cuss words—about the fog" from Chapters 17 and 18, published as "An Adventure of Huckleberry Finn: With an Account of the Famous Grangerford–Shepherdson Feud." In letters to Samuel L. Clemens, October 10, 11, and 17, 1885, Mark Twain Papers. But a comparison between the book and the excerpts in *Century Magazine* demonstrates that Gilder did considerably more than that. "There is restraint about writing for *The Century*, somehow," Twain admitted to Gilder's colleague Richard Underwood Johnson on August 15, 1885. "It is not intemperate language to say it is the best magazine that was ever printed; and so, what would read quite fairly elsewhere, loses force and grace in the company of so much derned good writing" ("Twain to R. U. Johnson," p. 23). *Century* also syndicated "Jim's Investments" and "Royalty on the Mississippi" in several papers in January, and the Chicago *Herald* reprinted the episode about Jim and his deaf daughter from Chapter 23 on both February 20 and 22, 1885. See the 1988 University of California edition of *Huckleberry Finn*, p. 523.

the novel's exceptional artistic value and catholic enough in his tastes to include "Royalty on the Mississippi," the final excerpt from *Huckleberry Finn*, in the same issue as his serializations of *The Rise of Silas Lapham* by Howells and *The Bostonians* by Henry James.[29]

There is little evidence to support the popular assumption that but for Olivia Clemens, Mark Twain might have been a nineteenth-century Henry Miller or J. D. Salinger. As DeLancey Ferguson was the first to point out, in "Huck Finn Aborning" (*Colophon*, Spring 1938), of the hundreds of changes within the portion of the holograph manuscript of *Huckleberry Finn* that he was able to examine, none significantly alters the character of the story. Even the recently discovered first part of the manuscript does not correct Ferguson's original observation. What Livy, Howells, and Twain himself altered in the cause of propriety is minimal.[30] Some indiscretions were slips of the pen and had to come out, while others apparently had been thrown in by Sam Clemens merely to torment his long-suffering wife. But, as George Orwell observed, "no writer is really the intellectual slave of his wife. Mrs. Clemens could not have stopped Mark Twain writing any book he really wanted to write. She may have made his surrender to society easier, but the surrender happened because of that flaw in his own nature, his inability to despise success."[31]

Richard Watson Gilder.
Courtesy Picture Collection, New York Public Library, Astor, Lenox, and Tilden Foundations.

Even in the relatively unfettered *Huckleberry Finn*, Twain was generally conscious of what was

29. "As an account of literature," Bernard DeVoto argued in *Mark Twain's America* (Boston and New York: Houghton Mifflin, 1932), "American journalism attained its highest reach in the February or Midwinter number of *The Century Magazine* of 1885" (p. 308). Twain himself was not impressed with the company. "And as for *The Bostonians*," he wrote Howells on July 21, 1885, "I would rather be damned to John Bunyan's heaven than read that" (p. 534).

30. Blasphemies were tempered: "Damn" became "dern" or "blame," "Judas Iscariot" is merely "Judas," "as mild as a Sunday School" now is "as mild as goose milk," and a character turns "up towards the sky" rather than "towards the throne." Some indelicacies were excised: "Iron-rust and spit" was changed to "iron-rust and tears," and the comment that a conscience "takes up more room than all the rest of a person's bowels" was dropped. See Bernard DeVoto, *Mark Twain at Work*, pp. 82–84.

31. In *The Collected Essays, Journalism and Letters of George Orwell*, edited by Sonia Orwell and Ian Angus, vol. 2 (New York: Harcourt, Brace & World, Inc., 1968), p. 328.

appropriate and inappropriate in then contemporary literature. In private he might revel in "the frank indelicacies of speech permissible among ladies and gentlemen in . . . ancient times," but in print he abided by the current taste: "Many of the terms used in the most matter-of-fact way by . . . the first ladies and gentlemen in the land would have made a Comanche blush. Indelicacy is too mild a term to convey the idea. However, I had read *Tom Jones* and *Roderick Random*, and other books of that kind, and knew that the highest and first ladies and gentlemen in England had remained little or no cleaner in their talk, and in the morals and conduct which such talk implies, clear . . . into our nineteenth century—in which century, broadly speaking, the earliest samples of the real lady and real gentleman discoverable in English history—or in European history . . . may be said to have made their appearance."[32] Even profane Clemens acknowledged limitations to strong speech: He did not approve of swearing before women and children.[33] He also recognized that "in certain trying circumstances, desperate circumstances, urgent circumstances, profanity furnishes a relief even to prayer."[34] The same was true of blasphemy. However, only once in the manuscript of *Huckleberry Finn* did he insist on his original phrase: In Chapter 23, when Jim cries "de Lord God Almighty" on realizing what he had done to his little girl, Twain wrote boldly in the margin, "This expression shall not be changed."

Suggestion is an important element of humor, and Twain knew just how far he could go with implied vulgarity.[35] In Chapter 24 of *Huckleberry Finn*, he cuts Huck short before he can say "hawking and spitting"; in Chapter 23, Huck

32. In Chapter 4 of *A Connecticut Yankee in King Arthur's Court* (1889).

33. Twain could be as prudish as Lewis Carroll, who once proposed a bowdlerized edition of Shakespeare that might be suitable for little girls. "It pains me to think of your reading that book just as it is," Twain warned his fiancée about *Don Quixote* in a letter of March 1, 1869. "You are as pure as snow, and I would have you always so—untaunted, untouched even by the impure thoughts of others. . . . Read nothing that is not *perfectly* pure . . . but neither it nor Shakespeare are proper books for virgins to read until some hand has culled them of their grossness" (p. 76). He also discouraged Olivia from reading *Gil Blas*: "It would sadly offend your delicacy" (p. 132).

34. Quoted by Mrs. Thomas Bailey Aldrich, *Crowding Memories* (Boston and New York: Houghton Mifflin, 1916), pp. 150–51.

35. Twain devised all sorts of ways of suggesting profanity in his writing. In Chapter 4 of *Roughing It* (1872), he digressed when someone is called "you son of a skunk": "No, I forget—skunk was not the word; it seems to me it was still stronger than that; I know it was, in fact. . . . However, it is no matter—probably it was too strong for print, anyway." In Chapter 22 of *A Connecticut Yankee in King Arthur's Court*, Sir Madok yells, "Blank-blank-blank him!"; in Chapter 27, the Yankee delivers "a hair-lifting soul scorching thirteen-jointed insult." Also, in Chapter 13 of that novel, when describing the outrages inflicted upon freemen by the nobles of the Middle Ages, Twain continued that "if a freeman's daughter—but no, that last infamy of monarchical government is unprintable." The sounds may not be the same, but the sense is still there.

stops before revealing exactly what the king's phallic costume looks like. The child never dwells on detailed descriptions of all the gore he encounters on his trip down the Mississippi. When Twain resorted to "damned" for accuracy in earlier work, it was generally printed "d——d"; but there was no need to resort to that genteel device in *Huckleberry Finn*, for Twain through Huck was a master of the euphemism. John Seelye's *The True Adventures of Huckleberry Finn* (1970) meticulously provided all the possible profanity, but what was gained by the young hero's describing the wildest part of the king's outfit as "a lit candle that was stuck upright in his ass"? That may be an accurate description of his costume, but it is not true to Huck's character to describe it. The voice of the narrator, and thus the tone of the novel, is so distorted by these "improvements" that Seelye has violated the integrity of Twain's novel. Maybe Sam Clemens swore, but it is not in Huck Finn's nature as drawn in *Huckleberry Finn* to use profanity. Good-hearted Huck is uncomfortable around people who use foul language, such as pap and the man on the ferry landing in Chapter 7; the boy does have his bad habits, but swearing is not one of them. Men who use the Lord's name in vain in *Huckleberry Finn* are to be scorned, not admired, no matter how much Clemens reveled in the practice in private. Although the boy disdains conventional religion, Heaven and Hell are ever present to superstitious Huck; only in a moment of overwhelming emotional crisis, in Chapter 31, does the boy vow to "*go* to hell." Twain knew exactly what he was doing in replacing common profanities with colorful, and sometimes ingenious, euphemisms. After all it is Huck speaking, not Mark Twain or Sam Clemens. Only the most uncompromising of critics would prefer to exchange one of Huck's "derns" or "blames" for a single good "goddamn."[36]

On completing the manuscript in September 1883, Twain cautiously consid-

36. He confessed to Howells on January 18, 1876, "I tamed the various obscenities until I judged that [they] no longer curried offense" (p. 120). Twain was surprised, in going over the "expergated" manuscript of *Tom Sawyer*, that neither his wife nor Howells caught the phrase "they comb me all to hell" in Chapter 35, in Huck's description of his new life at the widow's. Twain admitted to Howells that that was "the most natural remark for that boy to make (and he had been allowed few privileges of speech in the book)" (p. 122). Nevertheless, he wondered, "Did you question the propriety of it? Since the book is now professedly and confessedly a boy's and girl's book, that darn word bothers me some, nights, but it never did until I had ceased to regard the volume as being for adults." He said he read it to Olivia, who let it pass; then he tried her aunt and mother, "(both sensitive and loyal subjects of the kingdom of heaven, so to speak)," and they said nothing. "I'd have out that swearing in an instant," Howells advised. "I suppose I didn't notice it because the location was so familiar to my Western sense, and so exactly the thing that Huck would say. But it won't do for the children." When Olivia saw his letter, she demanded of her husband, "Where is the profanity Mr. Howells speaks of?" Then he confessed he left it out when he read her the manuscript, and he dutifully changed it to "they comb me all to thunder." Upton Sinclair got this incident all mixed

ered the best way to publish *Huckleberry Finn*. His early books, *The Innocents Abroad* (1869) and *Roughing It* (1870), established his reputation as one of the country's best-selling writers. The extraordinary sale of 100,000 copies of *The Innocents Abroad* in two years was the work of Elisha Bliss and his American Publishing Company of Hartford, Connecticut, the most aggressive subscription house in the country, which marketed its wares not in bookstores but door-to-door by an army of "broken-down clergymen, maiden ladies, grass widows, and college students" all over the nation.[37] Within a decade, works by Mark Twain, "the people's author," were as common in rural parlors as the family Bible and Webster's Dictionary. However, convinced that the American Publishing Company was cheating him, Twain abruptly broke with the firm in 1881 and gave his new books, *The Stolen White Elephant, Etc.* and *The Prince and the Pauper*, to a reputable Boston trade house, James R. Osgood and Company, the publishers of William Dean Howells, Walt Whitman, and Henry James. "Heretofore," noted Joel Chandler Harris in his review of *The Stolen White Elephant* in the Atlanta *Constitution* (June 11, 1882), "Mr. Clemens, who is in

James R. Osgood.
Courtesy Library of Congress.

---

up with Olivia and *Huckleberry Finn*: "Mrs. Clemens came home from church one day, horrified by a rumor that her husband had put some swear words into a story; she made him produce the manuscript, in which poor Huck, telling how he can't live in the respectable world, exclaims: 'They comb me all to hell.' Now when you read *Huckleberry Finn* you read: 'They comb me all to thunder!'" (*Mammonart: An Essay in Economic Interpretation*, Pasadena, California: privately printed, 1924, p. 330).

37. Quoted in Meltzer, *Mark Twain Himself*, p. 194. "Books were bought by the pound," explained George Ade in "Mark Twain and the Old Time Subscription Book" (*American Review of Reviews*, June 1910). "Sometimes the agent was a ministerial person in black clothes and a stove-pipe hat. Modern ladies and widows, who supplemented their specious arguments with tales of woe, moved from one town to another feeding upon prominent citizens. Occasionally the prospectus was unfurled by an undergraduate of a freshwater college working for the money to carry him another year" (p. 703). Children too on occasion canvassed subscription books like *Huckleberry Finn*: Webster advertised for agents in *The Youth's Companion* and elsewhere.

Mark Twain copyrights *The Prince and the Pauper* in Canada.
Caricature by Thomas Nast, *Harper's Weekly*, 1882.
Courtesy Library of Congress.

the habit of looking keenly after his interests, has not displayed any fondness for publishers. He has been inclined to look upon them as the inventors of a new and profitable method of highway robbery, and he has had a theory that a man who writes a book ought to secure at least as large a share of the profits as the man who prints it."

Unfortunately for Twain, the reviews of *The Prince and the Pauper* were excellent and the sales disappointing. "Anything but subscription publishing is printing for private circulation," he told Howells in *My Mark Twain* (p. 8). Osgood pleaded with Twain to let him try again, so he reluctantly gave him *Life on the Mississippi,* which was manufactured at the author's expense and sold by subscription. It did not do much better than *The Prince and the Pauper* did. "I changed publishers once—and just as sure as death and taxes I never *will* again," he vowed.[38]

The only answer was to issue *Huckleberry Finn* as a subscription book and for Twain to publish it himself. Twain never liked the way Osgood handled *The Prince and the Pauper* and *Life on the Mississippi*, and he did not like Osgood's conservative terms for *Huckleberry Finn*. "*The Prince and [the] Pauper* and [*Life on*] *the Mississippi* are the only books of mine which have ever failed," he reminded the publisher. "The first failure was not unbearable—but this second one is so nearly so that it is not a calming subject for me to talk upon. I am out $50,000 on this last book—that is to say, the sale which should have been 80,000 (seeing that the Canadians were for the first out of competition) is only 30,000." He insisted "that the publisher who sells less than 50,000 copies of a book for me has merely injured me, he has not benefited me. Legally one pays the same rate for an injury as for a benefit, but not morally. In the beginning, you may have contemplated the possibility of a sale which should fall short of 50,000; but I had had no experience of that kind and never once thought of it. I could not have engaged to pay any royalty at all on 30,000, and would not have engaged to pay much on 50,000 if the sale stopped at that."[39] Osgood was shocked. "We are deeply conscious of having done everything anybody could have done for this book," he wrote Twain about *Life on the Mississippi* in a letter of December 8, 1883 (now in the Mark Twain Papers). "We have worked harder over it and had more anxiety in connection with it than any book we ever had to do with. So far from being a source of undue profit to us, we have done the business at an unprecedentedly low commission. If it is a failure it is not due to lack of intelligent, conscientious and energetic effort on our part." It was just as well he dropped the firm, for Osgood went bankrupt in 1885. Twain admitted to Webster on February 28, 1885, "Glad to be of rid of Osgood" (p. 300).

Twain briefly toyed with the idea of returning to the American Publishing Company, and issuing *Huckleberry Finn* as early as May 20 or 25, 1884. But they could not agree on terms: According to the New York *World* (November 27, 1884), the Hartford publisher offered Twain 50 percent of the proceeds from *Huckleberry Finn*, but the author wanted 60. In February 1884, he set up his nephew-in-law in two offices in New York as Charles L. Webster and Company. The young man had already proven himself to be energetic and effective in straightening out some of his uncle's many business problems. Although he

38. In a letter to Frank Fuller, October 18, 1884, transcript courtesy the Mark Twain Papers.

39. Letter to James R. Osgood, December 21, 1883, in *Mark Twain's Letters to His Publishers*, edited by Hamlin Hill (Berkeley and Los Angeles: University of California Press, 1967), p. 165.

had served as general agent for Osgood in distributing *Life on the Mississippi*, Webster was a novice in subscription publishing, so Twain immediately hired a veteran in the trade to teach Webster all he knew about book canvassing. Naively, the writer believed that these two men and a secretary and a clerk, plus his capital, both literary and financial, were all that were needed to run a profitable publishing house.

Twain suggested to Webster that they offer *Tom Sawyer* and *Huckleberry Finn* together, "selling both books for $4.50 where a man orders both, and arranging with the [American] Publishing Company that I shall have half the profits on all *Sawyers* so sold, and also upon all that they sell while our canvas lasts." Another possibility was canvassing *Tom Sawyer* and *Huckleberry Finn* with *The Prince and the Pauper* "all at once—a reduced price where a man orders the three. It's a good idea—*don't forget to arrange for it*" (pp. 239–40). They finally abandoned the idea in September, for they never could come to terms with Bliss and Twain was not on the best terms with Osgood. "*The book is to be issued when a big edition has been sold—and not before*," he insisted to Webster on April 12. "There is no date for the book. It can issue the 1st of December if 40,000 have been sold. It must wait till they *are* sold, if it is seven years." He reminded Webster on April 14, "Bliss never issued with less than 43,000 orders on hand, except in one case—and it usually took him five or six months' canvassing to get them" (p. 248).

Charles L. Webster.
Courtesy the Mark Twain Papers, Bancroft Library, University of California at Berkeley.

Since *Huckleberry Finn* was designed as "a companion to *Tom Sawyer*," it had to have the same format as the earlier book. Webster was concerned that the sequel was much longer than the first one, so Twain agreed to drop from the new story the "raft episode" he had included in *Life on the Mississippi*.[40] "Be particular," he warned Webster, "and don't get any of that *old* matter into your canvassing book—(the *raft* episode)" (p. 249). A necessary feature of subscription books was that they be crammed with pictures and often of the crudest sort.

[40] His break with Osgood may have influenced his decision *not* to include the "raft episode" in *Huckleberry Finn*. See Chapter 16, note 4; and Appendix B.

"Some Uses for Electricity."
Cartoon by E. W. Kemble, *Life*, March 13, 1884.
Courtesy Library of Congress.

They generally cost more than regular trade books, so the salesmen had to offer buyers more for their money. *Huckleberry Finn* had to look like *Tom Sawyer*, but there is no evidence that Twain or Webster ever considered True (Truman) W. Williams for the new book. Although he was Twain's most prolific illustrator, having drawn pictures for *The Innocents Abroad*; *Roughing It*; *The Gilded Age*; *Sketches, New and Old*; and *A Tramp Abroad* as well as *Tom Sawyer*, Williams drank and was generally unreliable. He was an indifferent draftsman, his pictures varying from the coarse to the highly sentimental. Also, he was now living in Chicago and had not illustrated anything by Twain in years. The new book needed someone fresh. Webster originally suggested "a *very* cheap man" named Hooper for *Huckleberry Finn*. However, Twain enjoyed a cartoon by another artist in a recent issue of *Life* (March 13, 1884), the humor weekly, and told Webster he "wanted the man who illustrated the applying of electrical protectors to the door-knobs, door-mats, etc., and electrical hurriers to messengers, waiters, etc. . . . *That* is the man I want to try" (p. 246).

Edward Windsor Kemble.
Courtesy Francis Martin, Jr.

But Edward Windsor Kemble (1861–1933) was not cheap: Although he had been illustrating professionally for only two years and had never done a book before, the twenty-three-year-old artist was so in demand as a cartoonist that he asked for $2,000 to make 174 pen-and-ink drawings for *Huckleberry Finn*. Webster agreed to $1,200, and later got him to lower his fee to $1,000. He was an odd choice, for he knew nothing about the Mississippi Valley. Born in Sacramento, California, Kemble was largely self-taught, though he did attend the Art Students League in New York for a year. "I don't know what good it did," he admitted, "for no one ever looked at what I drew."[41] Undaunted by his lack of training, he sold several drawings to *Harper's Bazaar* (September and October

41. Quoted in his obituary, New York *Times*, September 20, 1933. Twain may not have known that his father was Edward Cleveland Kemble, founder of the *Alta California*, for which Twain was a traveling correspondent and in which first appeared the letters that became *The Innocents Abroad*. "Is that artist's name *Kemble*?" he asked Webster on March 31. "I *can*not recall that man's name. Is that it?" (p. 246). On another occasion, he thought it was "Kendall."

1880) and secured a job as staff cartoonist on the New York *Daily Graphic* in 1881; and when *Life* was founded in 1883, Kemble became one of its early contributors.

Kemble never met with Twain to discuss his work on the new novel. All negotiations were done through Webster. "I am not going to tell you what to draw," Twain told another of his artists. "If a man comes to me and says, 'Mr. Clemens, I want you to write me a story,' I'll write it for him; but if he undertakes to tell me what to write, I'll say, 'Go hire a typewriter.'"[42] But Twain did not hesitate to tell an illustrator what *not* to draw. Webster kept Twain informed of every step of the artist's progress on the pictures. Then, if anything displeased Twain, Webster reported it back to Kemble.

Self-caricature of E. W. Kemble at work on his illustrations for *Adventures of Huckleberry Finn*, from a letter to Charles L. Webster, May 1, 1884. *Courtesy Library of Congress.*

Because the book had to be out in time for the Christmas season of 1884, Kemble immediately set to work. He followed the same procedure as many illustrators, doing a preliminary sketch in pencil and then inking it in. He was at a disadvantage in not being able to read the entire story before beginning his work. Twain fed him manuscript (through Webster) as it was being typed, so the illustrations too were delivered piecemeal but consecutively. Then there was an unforeseeable delay. "I cannot have many of the illustrations finished until the latter part of next week," he warned Webster on May 1, "as we all have the moving craze and experiencing such little delights as eating our meals off the mantle shelf, bathing in a coal scuttle behind a fire screen, etc., etc. I have tried to work but cannot make it go." The artist then appended his note with a sketch of "a faint idea of my condition" (pp. 251–52).

42. In a letter to Dan Beard, quoted in Albert Bigelow Paine, *Mark Twain: A Biography*, vol. 2 (New York and London: Harper & Bros., 1912), p. 888.

The first sketch to come in was for the "book back" or cover design; and Twain told Webster on May 7 that it was "all right and good, and will answer; although the boy's mouth is a trifle more Irishy than necessary" (p. 253). In spite of his distractions, Kemble did deliver the first batch as promised; but they must have been hurried, and Twain was not pleased with the results. "Some of the pictures are good," he wrote Webster on May 24, "but none of them are very *very* good. The faces are generally ugly, and wrenched into over-expression amounting sometimes to distortion. As a rule (though not always) the people in these pictures are forbidding and repulsive. Reduction will modify them, no doubt, but it can hardly make them pleasant folk to look at" (p. 255). But Kemble depicted only what he found in the text: Many of the people in *Huckleberry Finn* are forbidding and repulsive, and he showed considerable restraint in avoiding the numerous corpses along the way. Letter-perfect accuracy was not what Twain expected from his illustrators. "An artist shouldn't follow a book too literally, perhaps," he explained to Webster; "if this be the necessary result. And mind you, much of the drawing in these pictures is careless and bad."

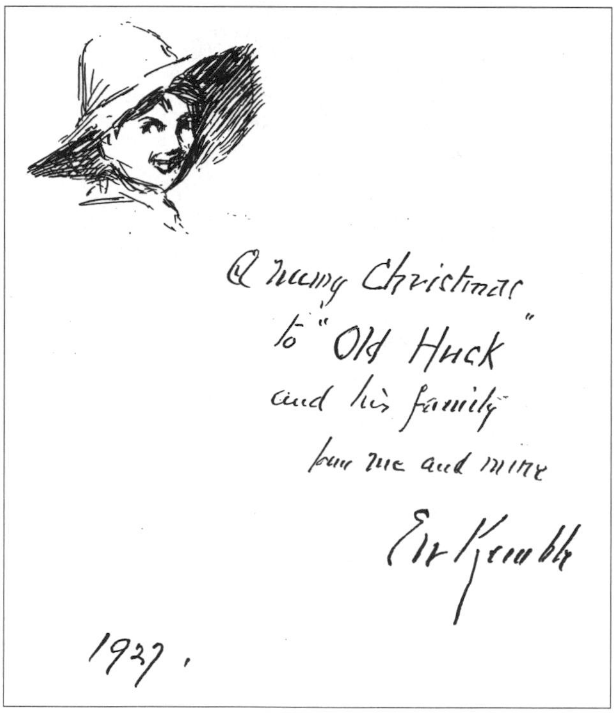

A merry Christmas
to "Old Huck"
and his family
from me and mine
E W Kemble
1927.

Christmas greetings from E. W. Kemble to Courtland Morris, his model for Huckleberry Finn, December 1927.
Private collection.

Kemble worked with several disadvantages. Although the artist was in great demand as a cartoonist, *Huckleberry Finn* was the first novel he ever illustrated. His household was disrupted at the time, and he worked on the book in sections as Howells went over the galley proofs.[43] Also, Kemble used the same model for all of the story's many characters. Cort Morris, the sixteen-year-old New York City boy Kem-

43. In a letter from Kemble to Webster, June 2, 1884, quoted in Beverly R. David, "The Pictorial *Huck Finn*: Mark Twain and His Illustrator, E. W. Kemble," *American Quarterly*, October 1974, in which the artist asked the publisher to "send me the manuscript from XIII Chapter on . . . as these are illustrations here which are described minutely and I am afraid to touch them without the reading matter to refer to" (p. 336). Kemble also apparently worked from portions of the uncorrected typed manuscript rather than from galleys, for there are details in the drawings not in the published text; for example, two Phelps children depicted in Chapter 32 are described in the manuscript but not in the book.

ble chose for Huck Finn, doubled for everyone else from Mrs. Judith Loftus to the "late Dauphin." Kemble recalled in "Illustrating *Huckleberry Finn*" (*Colophon*, February 1930) that his young model posed as the king in "an old frock coat and padded his waistline with towels until he assumed the proper rotundity. Then he would mimic the sordid old reprobate and twist his boyish face into the most outlandish expressions. If I could have drawn his grimaces as they were, I would have had a convulsing collection of comics, but these would not have jibed with the text and I was forced to forgo them." Certain problems in the sketches may be traced to Kemble's having to interpret the figures rather than draw directly from life. The child was not perfect even for Huck Finn. "He was a bit tall for the ideal boy," Kemble admitted, "but I could jam him down a few pegs in my drawing." Twain found even this character wanting at first. "The frontispiece has the usual blemish—an ugly, ill-drawn face," he complained to his nephew on May 24. "Huck Finn is an exceedingly good-hearted boy, and should carry a good and good-looking face." Only reluctantly did Twain add, "The pictures will *do*—they will just barely do—and that is the best I can say for them." Nevertheless, Kemble's depiction of Huck Finn was an improvement over True W. Williams's riverfront ragamuffin in *Tom Sawyer*.

Twain was as cautious about certain subjects in the story as he was about the general style and personality of the drawings. Some details could not be depicted: Huck confesses in Chapter 19 that "we was always naked, day and night," but Kemble never portrayed the fugitives nude; and Twain suppressed a drawing of the "lecherous old rascal kissing the girl at the campmeeting" in Chapter 20. "It is powerful good," he wrote Webster on June 11, "but it mustn't go in—don't forget it. Let's not make *any* pictures of the campmeeting. The subject won't *bear* illustrating. It is a disgusting thing, and pictures are sure to tell the truth about it plainly" (p. 260). Again, suggestion was as important in the illustrations as in the text; and Kemble came up with two pictures for the chapter, the girl and boy "courting on the sly" and the king dressed as a pirate. Twain warned Webster, "Don't dishearten the artist—show him where he has *improved*, rather than where he has failed, and punch him up to improve more" (p. 256). Happily, on receipt of more illustrations, Twain wrote Webster on June 11, "I *knew* Kemble had it *in* him, if he would only modify his violences and come down to careful, painstaking work. This batch of pictures is most rattling good. They please me exceedingly" (p. 260). He evidently did as his uncle asked, for on July 1, Twain wrote Webster, "Kemble's pictures are mighty good, now" (p. 263). Webster was encouraged when one of his agents assured him on seeing the pictures, "That looks more like the old Twain books and will make 'em go."[44] He delivered the last batch on July 12, in plenty of time to get the book out by Christmas.

Because the book was designed as "a companion to *The Adventures of Tom Sawyer*," Kemble followed the general design of the True W. Williams illustrations for that book. At first glance, the two books do look alike with their myriads of spot line drawings darting in and out of the type, but the differences between the two artists' work are greater than their similarities. Kemble was the better of the two draftsmen, but the pictures in *Tom Sawyer* are much prettier than those in *Huckleberry Finn*. Williams, as much as the author himself, idealized "St. Petersburg," the riverfront town of Hannibal, Missouri, where Sam Clemens grew up; the artist captured the nostalgic view of childhood immortalized in what Twain himself called "simply a hymn, put into prose to give it a worldly air."[45] The abrupt change in atmosphere between the books is established in the opening illustration for each novel: Williams made Tom Sawyer's humble home into a mansion; the Widow's mansion looks like any other backwoods dwelling in Kemble's picture. Kemble was a less self-conscious stylist than Williams was; and his strong, matter-of-fact drawings are free of the sweet fussiness of his predecessor's designs. Even when depicting violence like Dr. Robinson's murder, Williams emphasized the romance and melodrama of the occasion; but Kemble depicted the shooting of Old Boggs by Colonel Sherburn as coolly and directly as Huck describes the crime.

Self-caricature of True W. Williams.
Illustration in *Roughing It*, 1872.
Private collection.

Kemble was by profession a cartoonist, so humor generated most of his pictures in *Huckleberry Finn*. What is most remarkable about these illustrations is the way the artist extended even the minor comedy suggested by the text: With tongue firmly in cheek, he interpreted some little ludicrous statement, whether it concerned Solomon and his million wives, the king dressed as Juliet, or poor

44. Quoted by Webster in letter to Clemens, May 29, 1884, Mark Twain Papers.

45. In an unmailed letter, September 8, 1887, *Mark Twain's Letters*, vol. 2, 1917, p. 477.

Huckleberry Finn. Illustration by True W. Williams,
The Adventures of Tom Sawyer, 1876.
Private collection.

Hannah with her "dreadful pluribus-unum mumps," mentioned in just a passing phrase. He was generally allowed extraordinary freedom in what subjects to illustrate. Further levity came from the captions, provided by the artist and then revised by the author and the publisher; particularly effective are the sardonic puns, such as "Falling from Grace" in Chapter 5 and "A Dead Head" in Chapter 22. Twain left the writing of the running heads to Webster.

E. W. Kemble was not strictly a caricaturist: His comedy arose from the situation being illustrated rather than from stylistic tricks of depiction. Whatever he may have lacked in technical grace (and some of the pictures *are* poorly drawn, as Twain said), Kemble shared with the greatest illustrators the uncanny ability to give even an insignificant individual in a text a distinct visual personality; just as Twain so deftly defined a full-rounded character in a

THE ADVENTURES OF TOM SAWYER.

CHAPTER I.

"TOM!"

No answer.

"TOM!"

No answer.

"What's gone with that boy, I wonder? You TOM!"

No answer.

The old lady pulled her spectacles down and looked over them about the room; then she put them up and looked out under them. She seldom or never looked *through* them for so small a thing as a boy; they were her state pair, the pride of her heart, and were built for "style," not service—she could have seen through a pair of stove lids just as well. She looked perplexed for a moment, and then said, not fiercely, but still loud enough for the furniture to hear:

TOM AT HOME.

Opening page, with illustration
by True W. Williams,
The Adventures of Tom Sawyer, 1876.
Private collection.

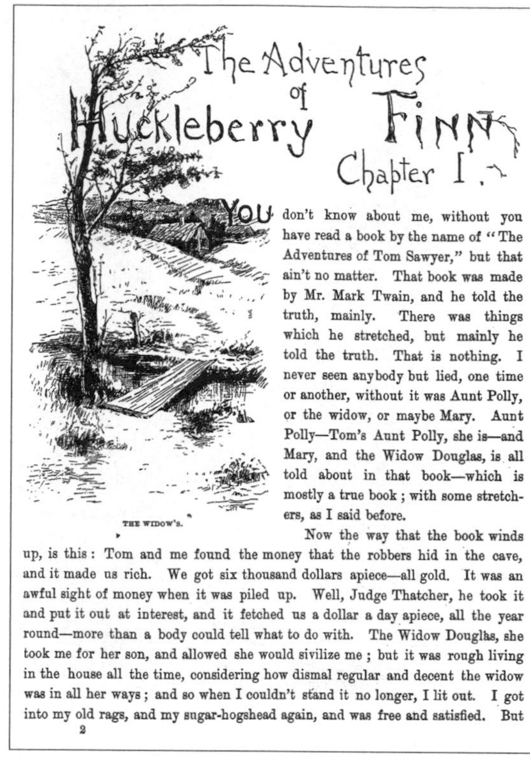

The Adventures of Huckleberry Finn

Chapter I.

YOU don't know about me, without you have read a book by the name of "The Adventures of Tom Sawyer," but that ain't no matter. That book was made by Mr. Mark Twain, and he told the truth, mainly. There was things which he stretched, but mainly he told the truth. That is nothing. I never seen anybody but lied, one time or another, without it was Aunt Polly, or the widow, or maybe Mary. Aunt Polly—Tom's Aunt Polly, she is—and Mary, and the Widow Douglas, is all told about in that book—which is mostly a true book; with some stretchers, as I said before.

THE WIDOW'S.

Now the way that the book winds up, is this: Tom and me found the money that the robbers hid in the cave, and it made us rich. We got six thousand dollars apiece—all gold. It was an awful sight of money when it was piled up. Well, Judge Thatcher, he took it and put it out at interest, and it fetched us a dollar a day apiece, all the year round—more than a body could tell what to do with. The Widow Douglas, she took me for her son, and allowed she would sivilize me; but it was rough living in the house all the time, considering how dismal regular and decent the widow was in all her ways; and so when I couldn't stand it no longer, I lit out. I got into my old rags, and my sugar-hogshead again, and was free and satisfied. But

2

Opening page, with illustration
by E. W. Kemble,
Adventures of Huckleberry Finn, 1885.
Private collection.

few phrases, so too did Kemble depict with a few strokes of his pen that same entire personage. Kemble may have initially depended on the way Williams depicted the characters in *Tom Sawyer*, but he made them his own in his lively drawings for *Huckleberry Finn.* Although many other artists have reillustrated *Huckleberry Finn* innumerable times, no one other artist has captured the atmosphere and characters of Twain's novel, whether pious Miss Watson, drunken pap Finn, the blubbering king, or the bombastic duke, so convincingly as did the original illustrator.[46] E. W. Kemble will forever be attached to

46. The majority of illustrated editions of *Huckleberry Finn*, usually gift books for boys and girls, have been undistinguished. The most likely candidate to do the great American novel was Norman Rockwell, famous for his folksy *Saturday Evening Post* covers; however, although he was perfect for *Tom Sawyer*, his coy pictures in the 1940 Heritage Press edition failed to capture the bitter satire of *Huckleberry Finn*. Modern American painter Thomas Hart Benton, in his lean, muscular drawings for the 1942 Limited Editions Club edition, was tougher than Rockwell; but Benton's burlesque is more exaggerated than Kemble's. English artist Edward Ardizzone supplied elegant pen-and-ink drawings for the 1961 Heinemann edition, as did American Warren Chappell for *The Complete Adventures of Tom Sawyer and Huckleberry Finn*

Tom Sawyer whitewashing the fence.
Illustration by True W. Williams,
The Adventures of Tom Sawyer, 1876.
Private collection.

Tom Sawyer whitewashing the fence.
Illustration by E. W. Kemble,
Mark Twain's Library of Humor, 1888.
Private collection.

Mark Twain's *Huckleberry Finn* as firmly as John Tenniel is to Lewis Carroll's *Alice in Wonderland* not merely for having been the first, but for being the best. Huck Finn himself is perhaps best remembered as much from Kemble's image of the good-hearted boy as from Twain's description. "Certainly there is some-

(New York: Harper & Row, 1978). Barry Moser's wood engravings for the 1985 Pennyroyal Press edition are portraits of the actors who appeared in the 1995 PBS *American Playhouse* television production of *Huckleberry Finn*; he himself played backwoods store owner "Hank."

From time to time, Kemble returned to his first success to draw new pictures for the story. He provided four pen-and-wash illustrations for the 1899 "Autograph Edition" of Twain's collected works; and for a special number of the Sunday comic section "The Funny Side" in the New York *World* (December 10, 1899), Kemble contributed three new pen-and-ink sketches of incidents from Twain's greatest book. One of the last drawings of the artist's long career was made for the 1933 Limited Editions Club edition of *Huckleberry Finn*: When the publisher George Macy learned that the original illustrator of the book lived nearby, in Ridgefield, Connecticut, he asked Kemble to add something new to his edition of the book; the artist provided a new picture of Huck, Tom, and Jim reading the famous story of their Mississippi adventures. All of these supplemental illustrations are reprinted for the first time in any edition in *The Annotated Huckleberry Finn*.

"Huck Finn." Lithograph of a detail of the mural in the Missouri State Capitol by Thomas Hart Benton, 1936.
© T. H. Benton and R. P. Benton,
Testamentary Trusts/Licensed by VAGA, New York, New York.

thing lacking in *Huckleberry Finn* when it appears without the capital drawings of Kemble," suggested H. L. Mencken in "Mark Twain" (*Smart Set,* October 1919, p. 138). Thomas Hart Benton, who himself took on the book for the Limited Editions Club in 1942, thought Kemble did a fine job. "No illustrator who has tackled the book since," wrote Benton in the club newsletter, "has in any way approached his delicate fantasy, his great humor, or his ability to produce an atmosphere of pathos."

Even before the book came out, editors were noticing Kemble's sizable contribution to *Huckleberry Finn*. "We are not only indebted to you for a good chapter [from *Huckleberry Finn*] for our next number," Gilder told Twain, "but are profoundly indebted to you for unearthing a gem of an artist for us. As soon as we saw Kemble's pictures in your proofs, we recognized the fact that was a find for us and so we went for him and we've got him."[47] Gilder immediately sent him off to New Orleans to draw pictures for another article, and he illustrated Twain's "The History of a Private Campaign That Failed," which appeared in *Century Magazine* in December 1885. *Huckleberry Finn* made Kemble's reputation as one of the most important American illustrators of the late nineteenth century. It also determined the course of his career. Jim was the character everyone noticed in *Huckleberry Finn*. Ironically, although he had never been farther south than Sandy Hook when Twain hired him for *Huckleberry Finn*, the book made Kemble famous as a depicter of the rural South. Now whenever an editor needed pictures for a story or article about that part of the country, he usually went to Kemble first. He was so in demand that not only *Century* but also *Harper's*, *Collier's*, *St. Nicholas*, and many other major magazines competed for his services to illustrate work by such popular Southern writers as Joel Chandler Harris, George W. Cable, Thomas Nelson Page, and Paul Lawrence Dunbar. Hoosier poet James Whitcomb Riley admired how Kemble illustrated "mainly with a simple homely dignity."[48] Kemble did visit the South and filled his sketchbooks with sensitive studies of African-American life; these drawings were particularly helpful for his fine illustrations for *Uncle Tom's Cabin* (1892). Kemble's Jim, while not ideal, is far more sympathetic than Kemble's caricatures of other African-Americans. He earned his widest popularity for the embarrassing "Kemble's Coons" and "Blackberries"; he also drew the famous "Gold Dust Twins," and his current reputation suffers from all these dreadfully dated stereotypes. He was one of countless American cartoonists who exploited racial and ethnic slurs after the failure of Reconstruction; late-nineteenth-century magazines, newspapers, and books were a national cesspool of xenophobia and bigotry. Kemble said that the character Cort Morris most liked posing for was Jim. "He would jam his little black wool cap over his head, shoot out his lips and mumble coon talk all the while he was posing," Kemble recalled. Consequently, the stain of racism harms the pictures in *Huckleberry Finn*, but they are tame when compared to Kemble's drawings

47. Quoted by Twain in a letter to Webster, *Mark Twain, Business Man*, p. 282.

48. Quoted in Francis Martin, Jr., "Edward Windsor Kemble, A Master of Pen and Ink," *American Art Review*, January/February 1976, p. 62. Not everyone cared for his work, however. "For a man who has no conception whatever of human nature," Harris complained, "Kemble does very well. But he is too doggoned flip to suit me." Harris disapproved of the dependence upon stock characters like those Kemble used in his cartoons. "Neither fictive nor illustrative art," argued the author of *Uncle Remus, His Songs and His Sayings* (1880), "has any business with types. It must address itself to life, to the essence of life, which is character, which is individuality." See Beverly R. David, "Visions of the South: Joel Chandler Harris and His Illustrators," *American Literary Realism*, Summer 1976, p. 198.

for Henry Guy Carleton's *The Thompson Street Poker Club* (1884), then appearing in *Life* and probably known to Twain. "It all seems so strange to me now," Kemble said in "Illustrating *Huckleberry Finn*," "that a single subject, a Negro, drawn from a pose given me by a lanky white schoolboy, should have started me on a career that has lasted for forty-five years, especially as I had no more desire to specialize in that subject than I had in the Chinaman or the Malay pirate." Strange indeed.

Huckleberry Finn may have made Kemble's career, but he illustrated only one other book by Twain and published by Webster, *Mark Twain's Library of Humor* (1888). Twain hated these drawings and hoped Dan Beard would do better with *A Connecticut Yankee in King Arthur's Court* (1889). "I prefer this time to contract for the very best an artist can do," he insisted. "This time I want pictures, not black-board outlines and charcoal sketches. If Kemble's illustrations for my last book were handed to me today, I could understand how tiresome to me that sameness would get to be, when distributed through a whole book, and I would put them promptly in the fire."[49] But Kemble's reputation could not be ignored: Harper & Brothers brought him back in 1899 to illustrate both *Huckleberry Finn* and *Pudd'nhead Wilson* for the "Autograph Edition" of Mark Twain's collected works.

About the time *Huckleberry Finn* was going to the press, Twain hastily inserted another picture into this already well-illustrated novel. That summer in Elmira he posed for a plaster portrait by his young protégé Karl Gerhardt, whose studies in Paris the author had subsidized since 1881. "The resemblance is not the superficial one of the photograph," insisted Charles Dudley Warner in the Hartford *Courant*; "it gives the character of the sitter, his peculiarities, and we may say the nature and the temperament of the man."[50] Twain agreed. "Gerhardt is completing a most excellent bust of me," he reported to Webster on August 19, 1884; and he had it photographed for use in *Huckleberry Finn*. Therefore the first edition of the novel contained two frontispieces, the heliotype of this rather Germanic sculpture being out of character with Kemble's clean, crisp pen-and-ink portrait of grinning Huck Finn. So carelessly was the heliotype prepared for the book that it exists in varying states and has become a bibliographic thorn in the side of collectors and librarians. Chatto & Windus, however, rejected it for the London edition, informing Webster on November 25 "that it does not do the author justice" (p. 118).

49. In a draft of a letter to Frederick J. Hall of Charles L. Webster and Company, after July 19, 1889, *Mark Twain's Letters to His Publishers*, p. 254.

50. Quoted in "Mark Twain in Bronze," *The Critic*, October 18, 1884, p. 185.

When the book finally went to the printers the fall of 1884, Twain was looking forward to a most prodigious success. "*Tom Sawyer* has been steadily climbing for years—and now at last . . . has achieved second place in the list of my old books," he proudly reported to Howells on October 15. Only *The Innocents Abroad* was doing better. "I think that this promises pretty well for *Huck Finn*. Although I mean to publish *Huck* in a volume by itself, I think I will also jam it and *Sawyer* into a volume *together* at the same time, since *Huck* is in some sense a continuation of the former story" (pp. 445–46). Despite the nation's recent economic crisis, orders for *Huckleberry Finn* were coming in steadily from all over the country. Twain too had been hit by the Panic of 1884; and to correct some recent financial setbacks, he decided to "stump the Union" on a four-month public reading tour, his first since 1874. He originally envisioned an ambitious series of traveling lectures by his friends William Dean Howells, Charles Dudley Warner, Thomas Bailey Aldrich, Joel Chandler Harris, and Southern novelist George Washington Cable; but only Cable accepted his invitation.

Twain had first heard him read in Atlanta in 1882, while researching *Life on the Mississippi*; and Cable had recently completed a successful tour of his own, stopping on the way in Hartford to see the Clemenses. "He is a marvelous speaker on a deep subject," Twain reported to Howells on November 4, 1882. "You know when it comes to moral honesty, limpid innocence, and utterly blemishless piety, the Apostles were mere policemen to Cable" (p. 419). Twain turned to Cable's manager, Major James B. Pond, to handle all the business arrangements of the tour. At first Pond urged Twain to go solo; he was the one everyone wanted to hear. "I did not feel equal to the strain of a full evening's programme," he recalled in an interview, "Twain Brands a Fake" (Seattle *Post-Intelligencer*, August 14, 1895). "I

Bust of Mark Twain by Karl Gerhardt, 1884. Frontispiece from *Adventures of Huckleberry Finn*, 1885. *Courtesy Library of Congress.*

Frontispiece by Gustave Doré, *Aventures du Baron de Munchhausen*, 1862. *Courtesy Library of Congress.*

wanted some one to relieve me of part of the burden." Then, when Thomas Nast, the famous *Harper's Weekly* cartoonist, wanted to team with another lecturer, Pond suggested that he and Twain would make a wonderful bill with Nast illustrating Twain's work and Twain describing Nast's pictures.[51] But Cable seemed a perfect partner for Twain, an experienced public speaker with a different aesthetic sensibility from Twain's. Cable would provide the pathos and Twain the comedy. "We are exactly opposite temperaments," Twain admitted, "and on that account perhaps became not only close friends, but the most congenial of traveling companions."

Back in September 1883, Twain met with both Richard Watson Gilder of *Century Magazine* and Charles A. Dana of the New York *Sun* to discuss the possibility of serializing the book. But he dropped the possibility of magazine or newspaper publication when he decided to issue it by subscription, fearing that printing it elsewhere in any other form might hurt sales. Gilder, however, desperately wanted *Huckleberry Finn*. Reminding Twain "that you have the largest audience of any English writer above ground," he suggested that "the advertising and notoriety of the serial publication could not *hurt* and might *help* your winter readings. You could, *moreover, as did Cable* . . . run ahead of the serial publication in your readings and thereby secure greater novelty and freshness for these."[52] Twain did bend his rule and promised to provide Gilder with an excerpt from the novel. Gilder proposed that since "Huckleberries won't be ripe for the public for a month or two," Twain let *Century* publish one half or three quarters of the novel with pictures in the Christmas issue. "We could just skim through that book," he said, "make up a jolly thing of it for four or five numbers—conservative, interesting and in every way credible to you and the magazine—then you could in announcing your book through agents etc. say that the book version contained twice as much matter—or one third—or one fourth as much. It would not kill the sale in book form for two reasons—one is that it would not all be in the magazine and the second is that a very large part of your audience lies outside of the magazine's regular readers." But Twain did not like serializing so much in a magazine and agreed to just three excerpts, and *Century* paid him the same money as for entirely original material. The excerpts were therefore shrewdly planned to run concurrent with Twain's public readings.

The "Twins of Genius" tour (as Pond billed it) proved to be a long and arduous journey for Twain. With only ten days off to spend the Christmas holidays

51. In letters to Samuel L. Clemens, July 3 and 6, 1884, Mark Twain Papers.

52. In a letter to Clemens, October 10, 1884, Mark Twain Papers.

with their families, Twain and Cable were on the road from November 5, 1884, through February 18, 1885, covering ten thousand miles through seventy cities from Washington, D.C., to Toronto, and as far west as Minnesota. (Twain told Pond *not* to schedule readings in Elmira or Hartford, where he would no doubt be too distracted to give a good performance.)[53] The two men alternated between their brief readings, Cable always appearing first and Twain topping off the program with the famous African-American folk tale "The Golden Arm." But Twain changed his selections at will and without announcement, much to the annoyance of the press. It was also a promotional tour, so Twain read from "advance sheets" of *Huckleberry Finn*. At the time that was considered a novel way of advertising a book and not appreciated by everyone. "The unbecomingness and the charlatanism of an author's going around the country reading from the proofs of a book he is about to publish are degrading to literature," complained the Pittsburgh *Dispatch* on December 30, 1884. "How Mr. Clemens could allow himself to do it is past comprehension." But that reporter was in the minority. Most papers praised "this literary conspiracy" (as Twain called it) that produced equally tears and laughter. "Twain's voice has the resonance of a cracked steamboat whistle," said the St. Louis *Globe Democrat* on January 10, 1885. "He enunciates slowly, gesticulates with his head, and keeps either hand in a pants pocket during his stay on the stage." And he never smiled. The New York *Times* was less than enthusiastic about his performance. "The management, in its newspaper advertisements, spoke of the entertainment as a 'combination of genius and versatility,'" it noted on November 18, 1884, "but neglected to say which of the gentleman had the genius and which the versatility. Some of those who were present last evening may have felt justified in coming to the conclusion that Mr. Cable represented both those elements, while Mr. Clemens was simply man, after the fashion of that famous hunting animal one-half of which was pure Irish setter and the other half 'just plain

Mark Twain and George W. Cable on the "Twins of Genius" tour, 1884–1885.
Negative Number 1670 © Collection of The New-York Historical Society.

53. In a letter to James B. Pond, July 1884, Berg Collection, New York Public Library.

dog.' Mr. Cable was humorous, pathetic, weird, grotesque, tender, and melodramatic by turns, while Mr. Clemens confined his efforts to the ridicule of such ridiculous matters as aged colored gentlemen, the German language, and himself."

But audiences loved him, particularly women and children. "Oh, Auntie! Oh, Auntie!" cried one little boy. "It was better than Buffalo Bill!"[54] Black and white both came to hear them. "Mark is on the platform," Cable wrote his wife from backstage in Philadelphia on November 21, 1884, "there goes a roar of applause! . . . There goes another round of applause. . . . There they go again! . . . There they go again!"[55] Western writer Hamlin Garland, then a student of "dramatic expression," was among the fortunate ones to attend a reading in Boston at the Music Hall in November. "Twain appears on the stage with a calm face and easy homelike style that puts all at ease," he jotted in his notebook. "His voice is flexible and with a fine compass. Running to very fine deep notes easily. He hits off his most delicious things with a raspy, dry, 'rosen' voice. He has a habit of coughing drily that adds to his quizzical wit. Passes his hands through his hair and wrings them. Never the ghost of a smile. Is an excellent elocutionist. Sighs deeply at times, with an irresistibly comic effect. . . . Is altogether a man whom you would take for any thing but the funny man he is."[56] Howells was there too and assured Twain the next day, "I thought that the bits from *Huck Finn* told the best—at least I enjoyed them the most. That is a mighty good book, and I should like to hear you read it all. But *everything* of yours is good for platform reading. You can't go amiss" (p. 513). President-elect Grover Cleveland, then governor of New York, requested an audience when the "Twins of Genius" were passing through Albany. President Chester A. Arthur and Frederick Douglass went backstage when Twain and Cable were in Washington, D.C., on November 30. "They met as acquaintances," Cable wrote his wife the very next day. "Think of it! A runaway slave!"[57]

The tour started off well in November 1884. "For the first time in years," Twain wrote his English publishers on December 4, from Muskegon, Michi-

54. Quoted in George Washington Cable's speech, *Public Meeting under the Auspices of the American Academy and the National Institute of Arts and Letters at Carnegie Hall, New York, November 3, 1910, in Memory of Samuel Langhorne Clemens (Mark Twain)* (New York: American Academy of Arts and Letters, 1922), p. 77.

55. Quoted in Arlin Turner, *Mark Twain and George W. Cable* (East Lansing: University of Michigan Press, 1960), p. 60.

56. Quoted in James B. Stronks, "Mark Twain's Stage Debut as Seen by Hamlin Garland," *The New England Quarterly*, March 1963, p. 86.

57. Quoted in Lucy Leffingwell Cable Bickle, *George W. Cable: His Life and Letters* (New York: Russell & Russell, 1928), p. 134.

gan, "I am on the Highway, i. e. the platform, giving readings from *Huck Finn*, and other of my books, and am having a jolly good time. Tell me, shall I come over and try it in London in the Spring in the West End? I am tempted to venture it. Would I draw; do you think? . . . Would the people come to hear me?"[58] Twain considered going to Europe and Australia; then he decided not to, because Olivia did not want to disrupt the children's schooling and he would not go without his family.[59] It was just as well, for the readings soon proved to be exhausting. "I ought to have staid at home and written another book," he confided in Webster on January 25. "It pays better than the platform" (p. 297).

The truth was Cable grated on Twain's nerves. Particularly irritating was his partner's cheapness and pious refusal to perform or even travel on Sundays. Remarkably, they were sometimes booked in churches. Also, Cable had the bad habit of lengthening his selections, which cut into Twain's time on the platform. "His body is small," Twain complained with his usual invective and exaggeration to Olivia on February 17, "but it is much too large for his soul. He is the pitifulest human louse I have ever known" (p. 237). Traveling from one place to another by train during a particularly rough winter was stressful enough, but Twain and Cable often gave two performances on the same day. And then there were all the reporters who loitered backstage during the readings in search of interviews. "On a day like this, when we give two performances, I feel like all burnt out after the first performance," Twain told the New York *World* (November 20, 1884). "As soon as I get back to the hotel I go to bed. I must get some sleep somehow. If I don't I will not be able to go through with the evening performance the way I want to."

" 'Mark Twain,' America's Best Humorist."
Color lithograph by J. Keppler,
Puck, December 16, 1885.
Courtesy Picture Collection, New York Public Library, Astor, Lenox, and Tilden Foundations.

The tour did have its diversions, however. "Each was familiar with all the plantation songs

58. Transcript courtesy the Mark Twain Papers.

59. In a letter to Orion and Mollie Clemens, March 5, 1885, *Mark Twain, Business Man*, p. 305; and one to Reginald Cholmondeley, March 28, 1885, Mark Twain Papers.

and Mississippi River chanties of the negro," Major Pond recalled in *Eccentricities of Genius*, "and they would often get to singing these together when by themselves, or with their manager for sole audience" (p. 231). The two spent Thanksgiving at Thomas Nast's home in Morristown, New Jersey; and they stopped in Hannibal in early 1885. "You can never imagine the infinite great deeps of pathos that have rolled their tides over me," Clemens wrote his wife on January 14. "I shall never see another such day. I have carried my heart in my mouth for twenty-four hours" (p. 229). He went on to Keokuk, Illinois, to see his mother and brother Orion during one of the worst snowstorms of the season. He arrived on the train from Hannibal just moments before the performance, so he just caught his mother as she was leaving the theater and gave her a kiss and a hug. "Why, Sam," she said, "I didn't know you." "That's because I'm getting so good-looking," he replied.[60] He informed his wife on January 14 that he had spent "a beautiful evening with ma and she is her old beautiful self; a nature of pure gold—one of the purest and finest and highest this land has produced" (p. 229). He told his brother and sister-in-law, "I had a *perfect* twenty-four hours there, with the sort of social activity which produces rest instead of fatigue."[61]

George W. Cable and Mark Twain. Caricature by Thomas Nast, Thanksgiving, 1884. *Courtesy Library of Congress.*

Everyone seemed to respond well to the readings, regardless of locale or class. "Whenever we strike a Southern audience," Twain proudly reported back to Olivia from Paris, Kentucky, on New Year's Day, "they laugh themselves all to pieces. They catch a point before you can get it out—and then, if you are not a muggins, you *don't* get it out; you leave it unsaid. It is a great delight to talk to such folks" (p. 224). Cable recalled how the citizens of Paris "applauded [Twain] until their palms were sore and until their feet were tired, and . . . laughed as

60. Quoted in "Twain-Cable," Keokuk *Daily Gate City*, January 16, 1885.

61. In a letter to Orion Clemens, January 17, 1885, *Mark Twain Business Man*, p. 292.

he came forward for the fourth alternation of our reading together—the one side of him dragging, one foot limping after the other . . . the house burst into such a storm of laughter, coming from so crowded a house, that Mark Twain himself, grim controller of his emotions at all times, burst into laughter and had to acknowledge to me, as he came off the platform: 'Yes, yes'—still laughing with joy of it himself—'yes; they got me off my feet that time.' "[62] But Twain and Cable wisely did not swing into the Deep South after Cable's essay "The Freedman's Case in Equity" appeared in the January *Century*. Many Southerners did not appreciate his liberal views on racial equality, and Cable was forced to eventually move North to escape their wrath.

"The 'Mark Twain'-Cable Readings" were an enormous success, grossing $46,201, with Twain himself taking about $15,000 after expenses (including $6,750 to Cable). It also proved to be a great advertisement for *Huckleberry Finn*. His presentation distressed him at first. "Written things are not for speech," he admitted in 1907; "their form is literary; they are stiff, inflexible, and will not lend themselves to happy and effective delivery with the tongue—where their purpose is to merely entertain, not instruct; they have to be limbered up, broken up, colloquialized, and turned into the common forms of unpremeditated talk—otherwise they will bore the house, not entertain it."[63] Within a week, he put the texts aside and memorized the passages; and "in delivering them from the platform they soon transformed themselves into flexible talk, with all their obstructing precisenesses and formalities gone out of them for good."

It required considerable work to make them sound spontaneous and effortless. Twain heavily revised the proof sheets of "King Sollermun" from Chapter 14 and "Huck Finn and Tom Sawyer's Brilliant Achievement" from the last chapters of the book (now in the Mark Twain Papers) for use on the road. Changes were made for greater clarity when recited or to enhance the humor; others show how Twain was rethinking crucial passages in the novel while it was in the press. He was not always content with his performance and questioned the wisdom of his going on the road at all. "Oh, Cable," he turned to his companion one night, "I am demeaning myself. I am allowing myself to be a mere buffoon. It's ghastly. I can't endure it any longer."[64] When it was all over, in Washington, D.C., on February 28, 1885, he decided that he would never

62. Quoted in George Washington Cable's speech, *Public Meeting under the Auspices of the American Academy and the National Institute of Arts and Letters*, 1922, pp. 75–76.

63. *The Autobiography of Mark Twain*, edited by Charles Neider (New York: Harper & Row, 1959), p. 231.

64. See *Mark Twain's Love Letters*, pp. 231–32.

read in public again unless forced to do it.[65] But at the request of Charles Dudley Warner, John H. Twichell, and other members of the Art Society of Hartford, Twain came out of retirement briefly to give two readings for charity at Unity Hall, on the evening of June 5, 1885, and the following afternoon. This time he did not share the bill so he started off with "King Sollermun" and finished with the old reliable "The Golden Arm." The Hartford *Courant* reported on June 6 that his appearance "was most heartily enjoyed by an audience which included many of the best-known and most intelligent and cultivated people in the city. They were untiring in their demands for more, and called out Mark Twain after each reading and were slow to let him retire from the stage when the end of the entertainment was reached."

An especially gnawing anxiety on the tour was the approaching publication of *Huckleberry Finn*. Twain hoped Webster had everything under control, but he never really trusted his nephew. The touchy young man resented his uncle's outbursts and insisted on defending his actions rather than just waiting for the storms to pass. Twain suffered from violent mood swings all his life. He has been accused of being a paranoid, of suffering from a persecution complex; perhaps today he would be diagnosed a manic-depressive. "He possesses some of the frontier traits—a fierce spirit of retaliation and the absolute confidence that life-long 'partners,' in the Western sense, develop," Major Pond explained in *Eccentricities of Genius*. "Injure him, and he is merciless, especially if you betray his confidence" (p. 197). Daughter Clara recalled that her father "could be forbiddingly reserved and locked away from the most vivacious attempts of visitors to enter his personality ever so tiny a distance. He was a constant surprise in his varied moods, which dropped unheralded upon him, creating day or night for those about him by his twinkling eyes or his clouded brows. How he would be affected by this or that no one could ever foresee."[66] Only Olivia seemed to be able to assuage his darker periods.

Twain was merciless to his nephew's memory. "I handed Webster a competent capital and along with it I handed him the manuscript of *Huckleberry Finn*," he recalled in 1906. "He was coldly and wisely discounting all my prophecies about *Huckleberry Finn*'s high commercial value."[67] But Mark Twain

65. Twain facetiously referred to these readings with Cable as his "farewell" tour. He suggested in the New York *World* (November 20, 1884) that "when this tour was over I would not appear again at least, say, not for nine years. . . . I have known people to give farewell tours for fifty years in succession. Now, that I would call stretching a thing a little too far."

66. In Clara Clemens Gabrilowitsch, "My Father," *The Mentor*, May 1924, p. 21.

67. In *Mark Twain in Eruption*, edited by Bernard DeVoto (New York and London: Harper & Bros., 1940), p. 167.

was largely the architect of his own misery. His ambition and greed in establishing the publishing company in the first place and the disastrous investment in James W. Paige's compositor, a miraculous typesetting machine which promised to revolutionize the printing industry and which nobody wanted, were his own undoing, not Webster's. He needed a scapegoat and convinced himself that the cause of his troubles could be traced to one individual, Charles L. Webster. "I have never hated any creature with a one hundred thousandth fraction of the hatred I bear that human louse, Webster," Twain wrote Orion in 1889. He told his sister Pamela, Webster's mother-in-law, that Charley was "not a man but a hog."[68] Twain eventually froze him out of Charles L. Webster and Company, and replaced him with another man. When Webster died on April 26, 1891, at age forty, Twain abstained from attending the funeral. Webster could be arrogant, but he was neither fool nor villain as Twain painted him. He tried to conscientiously keep his uncle informed of various business details, but Twain resented the imposition on his valuable time. Webster's sin was in considering himself to be an equal partner in the firm when Twain thought of him as no more than his employee. And he treated him like an errand boy.

Trying to oversee the book's publication from hotel rooms was frustrating and the cause of considerable misjudgment. Twain turned over to Webster the responsibility of manufacturing, distributing, and selling the book while he stumped the country with Cable. His uncle was particularly abusive about the galley proofs. "Charley, your proofreader is an idiot," he informed him; "and not only an idiot but blind; and not only blind, but partly dead. Some of the spacing—*most* of it, in fact—is absolutely disgraceful; but this goddamned ass never sees it. By God he can't see *anything*; he is blind and dead and rotten, and ought to be thrown into the sewer.... The compositor ... is not a compositor at all, he is a three-weeks apprentice."[69]

Twain had intended to publish *Huckleberry Finn* in America in late September or early October 1884, but his troubles were just beginning. Webster

68. Quoted in Charles H. Gold, "What Happened to Charley Webster?," *Mark Twain Journal*, Fall 1994, p. 20. "All the Webster matter is biased," noted Albert Bigelow Paine, "the result of misunderstanding and disagreement. Webster was probably vainglorious and irritating but in all the letters and records there is nothing to show that he was not working for the best interests of the firm, or that he was ever unfair in his mistakes. He was very industrious—in fact literally worked himself to death" (p. 17).

69. Transcript of undated note courtesy the Mark Twain Papers. Even Webster's son Samuel L. Webster had to admit in *Mark Twain, Business Man*, "The reader must understand that when Uncle Sam calls a man a damned fool it doesn't mean that there is any friction between them" (p. 266). But knowing that did not make it any easier for thin-skinned Charley Webster.

dutifully sent him an advertisement appearing in the New York *World*, *Frank Leslie's Illustrated Newspaper*, and elsewhere, stating that the Frank Coker News Company of Talladega, Alabama, was offering paper-covered editions of seven of Twain's books, including *The Innocents Abroad*, *The Prince and the Pauper*, and *Tom Sawyer,* for fifty cents each. But it only agitated Twain. "When you send me pirate ads which are calculated to enrage me," he informed his nephew on September 1, "I wish you would send me a form for a letter for the American Publishing Company to fit the case. You lay me liable to make trouble under a sudden and frantic impulse when there is no occasion for it. Besides, the episode unfits me for work for a week afterward. I have lost $3,000 worth of time over this pirate business, and I do not see where any good has been done, unless the erection of a quarrel with the Publishing Company can come under that head" (pp. 273–74). He wanted them to "smash these pirates" (p. 262). And if the American Publishing Company refused to do anything, he threatened to find some way to take his copyrights back (p. 264). Sam Clemens was not only paranoid but litigious, a deadly combination. According to the New York *Times* (January 10, 1883), Twain had already lost one case that year: He brought suit against Belford, Clarke & Co. of Chicago to prevent them from republishing his works; he thought that registering "Mark Twain" as a trademark would protect him, but the judge decided that pseudonyms could not be construed as trademarks. He immediately got his lawyers, Alexander & Green of New York, after the pirates and considered sending Anthony Comstock of the infamous Society for the Suppression of Vice to investigate the charge that Coker was publishing obscene literature. But the American Publishing Company judiciously contacted an attorney in Alabama who stopped Coker from issuing Twain's books.[70]

And that was not the only lawsuit that aggravated Twain that year. He was so angry when he came across a booksellers' holiday catalog advertising *Huckleberry Finn* for sale at a reduced price, from $2.75 to $2.15, even before his salesmen had copies in hand, that he tore out the page and sent it to Webster. "Charley," he scrawled across it, "if this is a lie, let Alexander & Green sue them for damages instantly. And if we have no chance at them in law, tell me at once and I will publish them as thieves and swindlers" (p. 284). He enclosed an announcement he wanted Webster "to print . . . in *facsimile* of my handwriting, and put a copy in every canvasser's hands":

70. In letters from the lawyers Alexander & Green to Samuel L. Clemens, October 20, 23, and 31, 1884, Mark Twain Papers.

> *Huckleberry Finn.*
>
> My new book is not out of the press; no man has a copy of it; yet Estes & Lauriat, of Boston announce it as "now ready," and for sale by them—and at a reduced price. These people deliberately lied when they made that statement. Since it was a lie which could in no possible way advantage them, it was necessarily a purely malicious lie, whose only purpose was to injure me, who have in no way harmed them.
>
> They will have an immediate opportunity to explain, in court, and pay for the opportunity of explaining.
>
> MARK TWAIN (pp. 284–85)

Webster did not follow through on this proposal, perhaps at Aunt Olivia's urging.

Twain already knew this firm, having done business with them before. According to the Boston *Daily Advertiser* (January 7, 1885), Estes & Lauriat had bought Twain's books at a considerable discount from agents in the past without complaint and arranged to buy at least one hundred of *Huckleberry Finn* from at least one of Webster's salesmen. But the company said it tore out the offending page from the catalog as soon as the trouble began and promised not to circulate any more containing it. "I saw one of Estes & Lauriat's chief men on the train," Twain reported back to Webster on December 28, "and he said the firm supposed my book was coming out before the holidays, or they would not have put in that ad. I said we couldn't help what they 'supposed,' and we should have to require them to pay for supposing such injurious things" (p. 289). On December 30, 1884, Twain filed a suit in the United States Circuit Court in Boston to restrain Estes & Lauriat from further distribution of the disputed catalog. Apparently, the booksellers tried to bring him to reason and settle the matter out of court, but Twain would not budge. "I assuredly have no quarrel against you for selling at any price any book of mine which you have 'bought and paid for,'" he wrote back. "My quarrel is that you advertise for sale at a low price, a book of mine which you have *not bought, and do not possess*. Such an advertisement necessarily works me injury. It puts a prohibitory obstruction in the path of my canvassers."[71] Twain was also worried that through collusion the booksellers might get his agents to break their contracts with Webster and supply Estes & Lauriat with books at a considerable dis-

71. Transcript of a letter from Samuel L. Clemens to Estes & Lauriat, January 7, 1885, Mark Twain Papers.

count in direct competition with the subscription price. The affair was making Olivia "sick." "Youth dear," she wrote him on January 2, 1885. "How I wish you were less ready to fight, and more ready to see other people's side of things. . . . If you write, write civilly."[72] But even she could not prevent him from seeing the matter through.

The case was finally heard on January 14, and the judgment went against Twain. He was furious that "a Massachusetts judge has just decided in open court that a Boston publisher may sell, not only his own property in a free and unfettered way, but also may as freely sell property which does not belong to him, but to me—property which he has not bought, and which I have not sold." He therefore proposed "advertising that judge's homestead for sale, and if I make as good a sum out of it as I expect, I shall go on and sell out the rest of his property."[73] His appeal was denied in February, and then this tempest too passed: He wrote Webster in a postscript, "I forgot to say I've made up with Estes & Lauriat and ended that quarrel" (pp. 303 and 318).

There was one other problem. The American, English, and Canadian editions were all in place when Webster made a terrible discovery. While the publisher was in San Francisco on business, an agent showed him a queer detail in one of the cuts in his prospectus: In "Who Do You Reckon 'T Is?," prophetically beneath the running head "In a Dilemma" in Chapter 32, there was something peculiar protruding from Uncle Silas's pants like an erect penis. Webster immediately returned to New York and offered a $500 reward for the apprehension and conviction of the person responsible for this obscene alteration of the engraving. No one was ever caught.

Webster also demanded that each agent remove the offensive page from every copy of the prospectus or face immediate dismissal; and all released copies were recalled for correction of the unsightly error. Webster frantically contacted the English and Canadian publishers to stop the presses and correct the plate.[74] "The book was examined by W. D. Howells, Mr. Clemens, the proofreader and myself," Webster told the New York *Herald* (November 29, 1884). "Nothing improper was discovered." But they did not examine press proofs, so the damage was probably done while the book was being printed. "By the

72. Quoted in Kaplan, *Mr. Clemens and Mark Twain* (New York: Simon & Schuster, 1966), p. 264.

73. In a letter to Frank A. Nichols, Secretary, Concord Free-Trade Club, March 1885, Mark Twain Papers. See also "Mark Twain *vs.* Estes & Lauriat," *Publishers' Weekly*, January 3, 1885, p. 9, and January 17, 1885, pp. 52–53.

74. See Gordon Roper, "Mark Twain and His Canadian Publishers," *American Book Collector*, June 1960, p. 27.

punch of an awl or graver, the illustration became an immoral one," Webster reported. "But 250 copies left the office . . . before the mistake was discovered. Had the first edition been run off our loss would have been $250,000. Had the mistake not been discovered, Mr. Clemens' credit for decency and morality would have been destroyed." The company then tore out the offending page and tipped in a corrected one; the entire signature with the final plate was reprinted for later copies. "This cost me plenty," admitted J. J. Little, the printer, many years later; but so thoroughly did the firm tend to the problem that no known copies of the first edition survive with the obscene plate intact. No one thought of saving one as a souvenir. Publication had to be postponed. The initial investment in *Huckleberry Finn* and Twain's reputation were saved, but the important Christmas season was lost. Also, despite the author's valiant attempts to rid his novel of any improprieties, the news item describing the obscene plate was widely reprinted in the papers and tainted the book's reputation long before it came out.

Twain made sure the route of his reading tour put him in Toronto on December 10, 1884, where he remained from noon to five o'clock, so that he was legally "domiciled" on British soil to protect his copyright when Chatto & Windus released the British edition concurrently with the Canadian issue of Dawson Brothers in Montreal. "You want to look out for the Canadian pirates," Twain warned Webster on July 1, 1884. "Bliss used to swear that they laid in with pressmen and printing office boys and bought advance sheets of one of my books and got the book out before we did. They could play mischief with us now, if they should beat us out a month or two with this book" (p. 263). According to *Mark Twain in England*, Chatto & Windus arranged for an unillustrated European edition to be brought out by Bernhard Tauchnitz of Leipzig, whose clientele (according to Twain) "are mainly traveling Englishmen and native Germans" (pp. 125–26). "The orders we have already in advance for [*Huckleberry Finn*] are much greater than previously received for any of his other volumes," Chatto & Windus happily informed the German publisher on December 3.[75] They also negotiated translations of the new novel. Anna C. Hamilton-Geete of Stockholm agreed to pay £15 "for the authorization of and exclusive rights to a [Swedish] translation from the said proofs" of *Huckleberry Finn*. But the Danish publisher of *Life on the Mississippi* was not interested in Twain's new novel. "We regret sincerely—after a perusal of the book—that we can not join your opinion regarding the quality of it," they replied; "quite on

75. Transcript of a letter from Chatto & Windus to Bernhard Tauchnitz, Jr., December 3, 1884, Mark Twain Papers.

the contrary we must presume that the sale of the work will not exceed that of Mr. Clemens' last book . . . from which our benefits have only been very small." Consequently, they offered even less for the Danish-Norwegian edition than the Swedes did for theirs.[76]

On December 3, 1884, the title of the work was deposited with the Librarian of Congress in Washington, D.C., to secure copyright, and on December 13 the Copyright Office received its two required copies of the American edition (now lost). These were among the handful Webster had hastily bound up in green before the holidays, and he kept back one for his father and another for his son as Christmas presents. "Sam," he warned him, "you must not lend that copy of *Huck Finn* until it is published which will not be until some time in February. That copy is one of ten which we have got out privately in advance to save our copyright, and we don't want any of them to get out. Don't show it to any agent at present."[77] Kemble asked for a copy he inscribed to "Huckleberry" Cort, for the model for Huck Finn; and Twain sent Howells three of them in time for Christmas. "Thank you heartily for the books," Howells wrote back. "They have made two boys enormously happy, and one old fellow of my name has been reading *Huckleberry Finn* nearly all through again for the fifth time. When do you publish? I might like to write about the book."[78]

Twain made sure that his friend John Hay, the author of *Pike County Ballads* (1871), got a copy; after all, Hay knew many of the same scenes, events, and characters growing up on the Mississippi in Warsaw, Illinois. Hay wrote Twain "to thank you most sincerely for the pleasure you have given me. . . . Huck Finns and Tom Sawyers were my admired and trusted friends—though I had to cultivate them as the early Christians did their religion—in out of the way places. I am glad to meet them again in your luminous pages." Twain sent another to Oliver Wendell Holmes, that other master of colloquial American English, who assured Twain, "I expect great pleasure from it, as I have always found from your books, ever since I began with 'The Jumping Frog,' and I believe I have smoothed many wrinkles by the inward delight and the outward relaxation of features they have never failed to produce."[79]

76. Transcripts of letters from Anna C. Hamilton-Geete to Chatto & Windus, November 17, and C. With to Chatto & Windus, December 2, 1884, Mark Twain Papers.

77. In a letter to Pamela and Samuel Charles Webster, December 18, 1884, Jean Webster McKinney Family Papers, Vassar College Libraries.

78. In Cyril Clemens, "The Model for Huckleberry Finn," *Hobbies*, February 1955, p. 107; and letter to Charles L. Webster, December 27, 1885, Jean Webster McKinney Family Papers, Vassar College Libraries.

79. In a letter from John Hay to Samuel L. Clemens, April 14, 1885; and one from Oliver Wendell Holmes to Clemens, March 16, 1885, both in the Mark Twain Papers. Twain kept several

Twain also supplied his family with advance copies. "It simply amazes me," his sister-in-law Mollie wrote back, "to see how you kept up the dialects and the underlying moral lesson without a particle of apparent effort. *It is real*, to me."[80] What exactly Orion thought of his brother's masterpiece is not known, but he paid Sam a fine backhand compliment. The leading lawyer in town told Orion that he thought *Huckleberry Finn* "is as distinctly a created character as Falstaff. The dialogues between him and Jim are inimitable, and the dialect perfect. How you could get down to their ideas, especially Jim's of King Sollermun, and manage so many dialects he does not see. His boys lie on the floor and read it, and race over, and laugh. *Tom Sawyer* was read and loaned till it had to be re-covered; and *Huckleberry Finn* will soon start on the same journey. He regards Jim as a very clear-cut character, standing out with Huckleberry [in] natural distinctness. He can see them. To him they are real characters. The feud is a perfect picture."[81] For Christmas, Twain presented a copy to his editor and censor, "Livy L. Clemens with the matured and perfect love of the Author."[82]

On the eve of the book's American release, Twain was surprisingly gloomy about its prospects. "I am not able to see that anything can save *Huck Finn* from being another defeat, unless you are expecting to do it by tumbling books into the trade," he complained to Webster on February 10, "and I suppose you are not calculating upon any sale there worth speaking of, since you are not binding much of an edition of the book" (p. 300). The publisher was far more optimistic than the author was. "I am not afraid of *Huck Finn*," Webster replied on February 14; "it is going to sell, but you must remember it is awful hard times and I am starting in under *very* trying circumstances. However, *we will sell that book*. . . . Huck is a good book and I am working intelligently and *hard* and if it don't sell it won't be your fault or mine but the extreme hard times. It *shall* sell however" (p. 303).

---

cranky responses to the new novel he received from various correspondents. Old friends in San Francisco saw little value in *Huckleberry Finn*. "I am tempted to take the liberty and the occasion to say, that when all your other published works shall be forgotten (if that can ever be) [*The*] *Prince and* [*the*] *Pauper* will live," wrote the Fitches on May 27, 1885. "You have money enough. Instead of 'potboilers' why don't you write another such a book as [*The*] *Prince and* [*the*] *Pauper*?" "For God's sake give the suffering public a rest on your labored wit," wrote an irate reader in Cleveland on a postcard on March 10, 1885. "Shoot your trash and quit it. You are only an *imitator of Artemus Ward* and a sickening one at that and we are *all sick of you*. For God's sake take a tumble and give U. S. a rest." Twain must have been amused by a long, rambling, and incoherent letter to him and Cable about *Huckleberry Finn* and the "Twins of Genius" tour from an inmate at the Pennsylvania Hospital for the Insane in West Philadelphia, George Farquhar Marstmont, dated March 11, 1885, for he kept that one, too. All of these letters are preserved in the Mark Twain Papers.

80. In a letter to Samuel L. Clemens, January 17, 1885, Mark Twain Papers.

81. In a letter to Samuel L. Clemens, January 8, 1885, Mark Twain Papers.

82. Transcript courtesy the Mark Twain Papers.

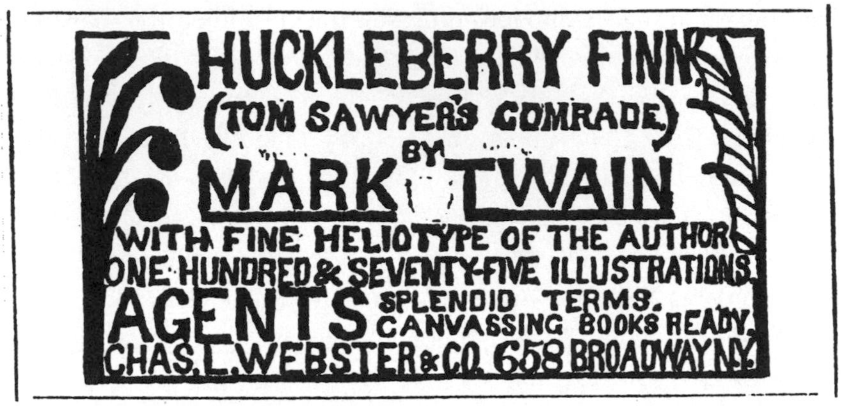

Charles L. Webster and Company advertisement for agents to sell *Adventures of Huckleberry Finn*, *The Youth's Companion*, November 20, 1884. *Courtesy Library of Congress.*

II

Despite Twain's misgivings, *Huckleberry Finn* was one of the most eagerly anticipated books of the season. The San Francisco *Morning Call* noted on March 17 that "it is fair to say that Clemens needs less advertising than almost any living author. The announcement that Mark Twain is going to write a book is sufficient. The report spreads like an epidemic disease, and from that moment everybody is waiting for it." Agents were ordering hundreds more copies of *Huckleberry Finn* than they had of *Life in the Mississippi*. Webster finally released the first edition of 30,000 copies on February 18, 1885. It was available in three formats—blue or olive-green cloth with plain edges at $2.75; leather (sheepskin) library binding with sprinkled edges at $3.25; and half morocco with marbled edges at $4.25. The publisher's prospectus noted that in the case of the regular cloth binding, "green will be sent unless otherwise ordered."[83]

Charles L. Webster and Company assured the public that *Huckleberry Finn* was "written in Mark Twain's old style" and was "a cure for melancholy." Although the book was being sold as "a companion to *The Adventures of Tom Sawyer*" and as a *humorous* book with "side-splitting stories, sly hints at differ-

83. *Tom Sawyer* had been bound in blue cloth; but Webster warned Twain on April 13, 1884, that "there is a growing dislike to that color." He said that customers asked for "*any color but blue*." Consequently, copies of *Huckleberry Finn* in olive green are far more common than those in blue. See letter to Samuel L. Clemens, April 13, 1884, Mark Twain Papers.

ent weaknesses of society, and adventures of the most humorous description," the prospectus did contain bits of the Grangerford–Shepherdson feud and Colonel Sherburn's shooting of Boggs. However, the publisher's write-up sounded like a patent medicine testimonial: "Nine-tenths of our ills are due to an over-burdened mind and overtaxed brain, or imaginary troubles that never come. An amusing book is a panacea more agreeable than medicine and less expensive than doctors' bills." Advertised as "a book for the young and the old, the rich and the poor," it inaccurately summarized the novel as "the adventures of Huckleberry Finn, Tom Sawyer and a negro named Jim, who in their travels fall in with two tramps engaged in *taking in* the different country towns through which they pass, by means of the missionary dodge, the temperance crusade, or under any pretext that offers to *easily* raise a dishonest dollar . . . until finally, we find the tramps properly and warmly clothed,—*with a coat of tar and feathers*." Despite the gold on the cover, there was nothing pretty about Kemble's pictures or Twain's story. *Huckleberry Finn* was not the usual book for babes or a proper parlor companion.

Charles L. Webster and Company advertisement for *Adventures of Huckelberry* [*sic*] *Finn*, *Life*, December 11, 1884. *Courtesy Library of Congress.*

On January 23 and again on the 26th, Twain instructed Webster to get advance copies to the magazines and then to the newspapers in time for publication. But he had little confidence in reviews and never had to depend on them. "The public is the only critic whose judgement is worth anything at all," he said in "A General Reply" (*Galaxy*, November 1870, p. 733). The press rarely noticed subscription books, and the public loved his books. "I found that the latest review of a book is pretty sure to be just a reflection of the *earliest* review of it," he confessed; "that whatever the first reviewer found to praise or censure in the book would be repeated in the latest reviewer's report, with nothing fresh added."[84] He had had a miserable experience when *The Gilded Age* came out, and the New York *Daily Graphic* jumped publication date and printed a blistering review that was

84. In "Chapters from My Autobiography," *North American Review*, October 19, 1906, p. 707.

picked up everywhere. Thereafter Twain was careful always to give William Dean Howells first crack at his next book in the pages of *The Atlantic Monthly*. Twain instructed Webster on January 27 not to send any advance copies of *Huckleberry Finn* to the papers until *after* they had lined up a notice in either *The Atlantic* or *Century Magazine*. "What we want is a favorable review, by an authority," he said to Webster, "then immediately distribute the book among the press" (p. 298). "You seem to have a mighty poor opinion of my business capacity," Webster answered him on January 30, in a letter in the Mark Twain Papers, but he did exactly as Twain demanded. Howells was eager to do something, but it was just too late to synchronize *The Atlantic* or *Century Magazine* with the book's publication.

It was almost a miracle *Huckleberry Finn* was reviewed at all.[85] "Heavens and earth!" Twain wrote Webster on February 8, "the book ought to have been reviewed in the March *Century* and *Atlantic*!—how have we been dull enough to go and overlook that? It is an irreparable blunder. It should have been attended to, weeks ago, when we named the day of publication. If we had done *that,* we could flood the country with press copies the 25th of February, for then the magazines would already have given the keynote to the reviews" (p. 299). He wailed that they also forgot to lace the American papers before publication with excerpts from the English reviews. The damage was repairable, however. "Send immediately, copies (bound and unbound)," he instructed Webster on February 10, "to the [New York] *Evening Post, Sun*, *World,* and *The Nation*; the Hartford *Courant*, *Post* and *Times*; and the principal Boston dailies, Baltimore *American*. (Never send any to *The New York Graphic*.) Keep a sharp outlook, and if the general tone of the resulting notices is favorable, then send out your 300 press copies over the land, for that may *possibly* float a further canvas and at least create a bookstore demand. No use to wait for the magazines—how in *hell* we overlooked that unspeakably important detail, utterly beats my time" (p. 300). Webster reminded him in a letter of February 14 (in the Mark Twain Papers) that he had *not* overlooked this point: "You remember you told me in the start that press notices *hurt* the last book before it was out and that this year we would send *none* until the book was out. I have sent the notices [from Chatto & Windus] that you have sent."

Most of these publications did in the end review the book, and the immediate reaction was an odd mixture of hostility and praise.[86] By odd coincidence,

85. See Victor Fischer, "Huck Finn Reviewed: The Reception of *Huckleberry Finn* in the United States, 1884–1897," *American Literary Realism: 1870–1900*, Spring 1983, pp. 1–57.

86. Many of these reviews are reprinted in full in *Mark Twain: The Contemporary Reviews*, edited by Louis J. Budd (Cambridge, England: Cambridge University Press, 1999), pp. 259–80.

Charles L. Webster and Company advertisement for *Adventures of Huckleberry Finn*, *The Youth's Companion*, February 26, 1885.
Courtesy Library of Congress.

Twain had largely predicted the response to *Huckleberry Finn* years before in his review of the long-forgotten *Sut Lovingood* (1867) by George Harris. "The book abounds in humor, and is said to represent the Tennessee dialect correctly," he wrote in the San Francisco *Alta California* (July 14, 1867). "It will sell well in the West, but the Eastern people will call it coarse and possibly taboo it."

Contradictory opinion could be found within the papers of the same city. For example, the San Francisco *Examiner* said on March 9 that the book's picture of the Southwest "is very much of the same character as many of the author's Pacific Coast sketches, in the utter absence of truth and being unlike anything that ever existed in the earth, above the earth, or in the waters under the earth." But the *Sunday Chronicle* countered on March 15 that "anyone who has ever lived in the Southwest, or who has visited that section, will recognize the truth of all these sketches and the art with which they are brought into this story." "Everybody will want to see *Huckleberry Finn*," predicted the Hartford *Times* on March 9. "As to stirring incidents, the story is full of them. It will hugely please the boys, and also interest people of more mature years." "The story is so interesting, so full of life and dramatic force," said the Hartford

Courant on March 19, "that the reader will be carried along irresistibly, and the time he loses in laughing he will make up in diligence to hurry along and find out how things come out."

Charles A. Dana bore no grudge that his paper had not serialized *Huckleberry Finn*. On the contrary, he published a lengthy review of the book, one of the first of the few, in the New York *Sun* on February 15. Mark Twain, "the greatest living authority on the Mississippi River and on juvenile cussedness," offered "no end of stirring incident, river lore, human nature, philology, and fun" in his new book; and the paper supported its points with pithy excerpts from the text. "Who on earth except Mark Twain would ever cotton to a youth like Huckleberry Finn for the hero of what is neither a boys' book nor a grown-up novel?" the *Sun* asked. "And who else . . . could so present his character and misdeeds as to hold the reader through four hundred pages and then dismiss him Huck's friend for life? We want to say something, too, about Mark Twain's good English. His book, for the most part, is made up of words of one syllable."

As if in response to the *Sun*'s shining tribute, the New York *World* attacked *Huckleberry Finn* on March 2 as "cheap and pernicious stuff," supported by lengthy quotes from the book. It wondered, "But what can be said of a man of Mr. Clemens' wit, ability, and position deliberately imposing upon the unoffending public a piece of careless hackwork in which a few good things are dropped amid a mass of rubbish." Joseph Pulitzer was then in the middle of a fierce campaign against the evil influence of dime novels on young readers, and his *World* thought Twain's "wretchedly low, vulgar, sneaking and lying Southern country boy of forty years ago" belonged in one of these books. The paper said that Twain as humorist was inferior to Artemus Ward, Sydney Smith, and John Hay, that *Huckleberry Finn* belonged with George W. Peck's *Peck's Bad Boy and His Pa* (1883). "There is an abundance of moving accidents by fire and flood," it went on, "a number of situations more or less unpleasant in which he involves his dramatis personae and then leaves them to lie themselves out of it, a series of episodes and digressions apparently introduced to give Mr. Twain's peculiar sense of humor a breathing spell, and finally two or three unusually atrocious murders in cold blood, thrown in by way of incidental diversion." It sneered that "the 'Royal Nonesuch' should find a favored place in the list of parlor entertainments."

Twain took particular exception to the *World*'s objection to "two or three unusually atrocious murders." After all, Pulitzer was already engaged in the sensationalism named "yellow journalism" at century's end. Twain planned revenge by jotting in his notebook all the reports of murders, rapes, suicides, and other lurid news printed in just one issue of the New York *World*, April 9, 1885, for an article he intended to write to challenge the integrity of the paper's publisher and editors. "In a week," he observed, "they spread a full *Huck* before 1,000,000 families—4,000,000 a month they say. The same bulk is furnished to more than 50,000,000 people by that paper in a year—while 100,000,000 have read *Huckleberry Finn* and forgotten him. *Moral.* If you want to rear a family just right for sweet and pure society here and Paradise hereafter, banish Huck Finn from the home circle and introduce the New York *World* in its place."[87] Again, Olivia or Howells likely advised him against seeking retribution.

"There is very little of literary art in the story," sniffed the San Francisco *Bulletin* in its review of March 14. Much of the humor was "of the more dreary sort, as if the author was subjected to a pretty hard strain at times to work his facetious vein." It warned that Huck Finn represents a type of child character who "is not all together desirable, nor is it one that most parents who want a future of promise for their young folks would select without some hesitation." The paper recognized Twain's satire, but "whether young people who read this volume will be better for it will be an open question." The most sarcastic attack, however, came from Kemble's magazine, *Life* (February 21, 1885). Robert Bridges said that the book contained "a very refined and delicate piece of narration by Huck Finn, describing his venerable and dilapidated 'pap' as afflicted with delirium tremens, rolling over and over, . . . is especially suited to amuse children on long, rainy afternoons"; "an elevating and laughable description of how Huck killed a pig, smeared its blood on an axe and mixed in a little of his own hair, and then ran off, setting up a job on the old man and the community, and leading them to believe him murdered . . . can be repeated by any smart boy for the amusement of his fond parents"; and "a graphic and romantic tale of a Southern family feud . . . resulted in an elopement and from six to eight corpses." Bridges had failed to mention Kemble's contribution, but made up for it on March 12: His "clever illustrations . . . enliven many a page of coarse and dreary fun. His sketches of Huck Finn and the Negro (Jim) are carried through the series with a wonderful variety of laughable expressions, attitudes, and costumes."[88]

87. See *Mark Twain's Notebooks and Journals*, vol. 3, edited by Robert Park Browning, Michael B. Frank, and Lin Salamo (Berkeley and Los Angeles: University of California Press, 1979), pp. 128 and 130.

88. Reactions to Kemble's illustrations were generally good. Brander Matthews in the London *Saturday Review* (January 31, 1885) thought that the pictures, "although slight and unpretending, are far better than those to be found in most of Mark Twain's books. For one thing, they actually illustrate—and this is a rare quality in illustrations nowadays." The Montreal *Star* (February 21, 1885) said that "we can give them no higher praise than by saying that the artist has thoroughly understood the conceptions of the author, and has embodied them in forms which appeal to the reader's eyes as strongly as the pictures presented by Mark Twain

The worst reviews originated in Massachusetts, the heartland of Yankee respectability. The Boston Brahmins had never embraced Twain; they considered him rude, crude, and lewd when compared to their own Henry James. Boston was the home of the respectable trade houses while Hartford was famous for low-brow subscription publishing. Books came from Hartford, but literature came from Boston. Twain got his first taste of what was to come when the *Morning Journal* (January 16, 1885), in reaction to the recent lawsuit, noted, "If the extracts from *Huckleberry Finn* already published [in *Century Magazine*] are fair samples of the whole book, we cannot see why Estes & Lauriat want to sell it less than the subscription price. A man ought to pay $2.75 for the privilege of reading the book. It will teach him a lesson." The *Herald* on February 1, 1885, accused the excerpt "Royalty on the River" in the new *Century* of being "pitched in one key, and that is the key of a vulgar and abhorrent life."

Twain believed his battle with Boston went back to December 17, 1877, when Howells innocently asked him to speak at the dinner honoring John Greenleaf Whittier's seventieth birthday. Twain took the occasion to spoof the grand old men of American letters, Ralph Waldo Emerson, Henry Wadsworth Longfellow, and Oliver Wendell Holmes, all of whom were present at this august gathering. He proceeded to describe in great detail an absurd meeting of these gentlemen in a log cabin in the foothills of the Sierras. "Mr. Emerson was a seedy little bit of a chap—red-headed," he said. "Mr. Holmes was as fat as a balloon—he weighed as much as three hundred, and had double chins all the way down to his stomach. Mr. Longfellow was built like a prizefighter. His head was cropped and bristly—like as if he had a wig made of hair-brushes. His nose lay straight down his face, like a finger with the end joint tilted up. They had been drinking—I could see that. And what queer talk they used!"[89] He went on and on and on with "the amazing mistake, the bewildering blun-

---

possess the mind." "Many of the designs are drawn with spirit," said the San Francisco *Bulletin* on March 14, "and are all executed well enough for the plan of the book." The Hartford *Evening Post* (February 17, 1885) considered the pictures to be "well designed and executed. They are on the average very expressive and calculated to explain the text to a nicety." The San Francisco *Alta California*, founded by Kemble's father, had little good to say about its former reporter Twain's story; but it did acknowledge on March 29, that the pictures "are cleverly executed, and the book is gotten up in good style." Although Franklin B. Sanborn in the Springfield (Mass.) *Daily Republican* (April 27, 1885) admired Twain's sense of humor, he thought "it is very little helped by the so-called illustrations of his book. These throw some light on the housing, dress and external circumstances of the personages, but seldom reproduce, as the author does, their internal struggles and entanglements."

89. See "Twain at the Whittier Dinner," New York *Times*, December 20, 1877.

der, the cruel catastrophe," as Howells described the incident in *My Mark Twain*. When Twain finally finished, "There fell a silence, weighing many tons to the square inch, which deepened from moment to moment, and was broken only by the hysterical and blood-curdling laughter of a single guest, whose name shall not be handed down to infamy. Nobody knew whether to look at the speaker or down at his plate" (p. 60). It may not really have been as bad as all that, but Twain was mortified. He never quite comprehended all the scorn thrown at him. "It is amazing, it is incredible," he wondered in 1906, "that they didn't shout with laughter, and those deities the loudest of them all."[90]

He lost no time in writing Emerson, Longfellow, and Holmes each a letter of apology, admitting that he was a fool, but God's fool. Emerson's hearing was so bad that he could hardly hear Twain's speech, so he was not offended. The only thing Longfellow said to Howells was "Ah, he is a *wag!*" and left it at that.[91] Holmes assured Twain that no offense was taken and he need not think of the matter again. They remained friends, and Holmes wrote a light-hearted tribute to Twain in the occasion of his fiftieth birthday, published in *The Critic* (November 28, 1885):

I know whence all your magic came, —
Your secret I've discovered, —
The source that fed your inward flame
The dreams that round you hovered:

Before you learned to bite or munch
Still kicking in your cradle,
The Muses mixed a bowl of punch
And Hebe seized the ladle. (p. 253)

While the three injured parties apparently forgave and forgot Twain, the Boston press did not. They branded the speaker as uncouth and not worthy of serious consideration. They generally ignored subscription books, but were ready to pounce on *Huckleberry Finn*. The *Evening Traveller* (March 5, 1885) called it "singularly flat, stale, and unprofitable." The *Advertiser* (March 12, 1885) thought the book was "wearisome and labored" and criticized its "coarse-

90. Quoted in Justin Kaplan, *Mr. Clemens and Mark Twain*, p. 211.

91. See Howells, *My Mark Twain*, pp. 61–62.

ness and bad taste."[92] The *Transcript* said on March 17 that it was "so flat, as well as coarse, that nobody wants to read it after a taste in *The Century*."

Some cynical reviewers resented all the recent printer's ink devoted to the new book. They considered it nothing more than some cheap publicity stunt. "It is little wonder that Mr. Samuel L. Clemens, otherwise Mark Twain, resorted to real or mock lawsuits, as may be, to restrain some real or imaginary selling of *The Adventures of Huckleberry Finn* as a means of advertising that extraordinary senseless publication," snapped the Boston *Evening Traveller* (March 5). "Before the work is disposed of, Mr. Mark Twain will probably have to resort to law to compel some to sell it by any sort of bribery or corruption. It is doubtful if the edition could be disposed of to people of average intellect at anything short of the point of the bayonet." "No book has been put on the market with more advertising," sniffed the San Francisco *Bulletin* (March 14). "When it was given out that some one had tampered with the engravings in the printing office, in a mysterious way, that accounted for the delay in bringing out the book, it secured at the same time many thousand dollars' worth of free advertising. Then the *Century* gave the enterprise a lift by publishing a chapter [*sic*] of the book in advance, which, while an advertisement, was still a readable article. *Huckleberry Finn* has been introduced to the world as it were, with the blare of trumpets." The Boston *Daily Globe* suggested on April 2 that Twain "has consented to convert himself into a walking sign, a literary sandwich, placarded all over with advertisements of his wares." Even Twain's old paper the San Francisco *Alta California* (March 24) admitted that *Huckleberry Finn* "has been probably the best advertised book of the present age. . . . As a self-advertiser, Mark Twain has become more of a success than as a humorist, as is shown by the *Adventures of Huckleberry Finn*." Of course, all of these complaints were self-defeating, for they gave the book even more publicity.

The viciousness of the attack in America was all the more surprising because the book was so warmly received in England. "For sometime past Mr. Clemens has been carried away by the ambition of seriousness and fine writing," said the *Athenæum* (December 27, 1884). "In *Huckleberry Finn* he returns to his right

92. Twain thought the editor had it in for him. "The severest censor has been the Boston *Advertiser*," he noted in his journal. "He is merely taking what he imagines is legitimate revenge upon me for what was simply and solely by an accident. I had the misfortune to catch him in a situation which will not bear describing. He probably thinks I have told that thing all around. It is an error. I have never told it, except to one man, and he came so near absolutely dying with laughter that I judged it best to take no more chances with that narrative." He contemplated various forms of torture for his critics: "The accident of a sitz-bath with a steel-trap" to the editor of the Springfield *Daily Republican*; and how the editor of the *Daily Republican* or *Advertiser* "got his *Nüsse* [nuts] caught in the steel trap." See *Mark Twain's Notebooks and Journals*, vol. 3, pp. 132, 135–36, 234, and 356.

mind and is again the Mark Twain of old time. It is such a book as he and he alone, could have written. It is meant for boys; but there are few men (we should hope) who, once they take it up, will not delight in it." The *Westminster Review* said in April that *Huckleberry Finn* was characterized by "abundance of American humour of the best sort; plenty of incident, sometimes thrilling, at others, extravagantly burlesque; charming descriptions of scenery, and admirable sketches of character." Although the *British Quarterly Review* (April 1, 1885) admitted that Twain "is sometimes a little coarse, sometimes a little irreverent, and inclined to poke fun at the Old Testament," *Huckleberry Finn* was nevertheless "lively and fresh, and proves that Mark Twain's vein, if not quite inexhaustible, is abundant." Perhaps the best of the British reviews was by an American, Brander Matthews, in the London *Saturday Review* (January 31, 1885). "Sequels of stories which have been widely popular are not a little risky," he admitted. "*Huckleberry Finn* is a sharp exception." He said Huck was "a walking repository of the juvenile folklore of the Mississippi Valley—a folk-lore partly traditional among the white settlers, but largely influenced by intimate association with the negroes." Matthews also thought that "perhaps, in no other book has the humourist shown so much artistic restraint, for there is in *Huckleberry Finn* no mere 'comic copy,' no straining after effect; one might almost say that there is no waste word in it." Canadians too liked the book. "All, or nearly all, who have laughed over Tom Sawyer," said the Montreal *Star* (February 21, 1885), "will not fail to heartily enjoy the predicaments of vagabond 'Huck,' and . . . rarely have they read a more thoroughly interesting and mirth-provoking book, or one that so entirely satisfied their anticipation."

Huckleberry Finn was one of the most talked-about American books in English literary circles since *Uncle Remus, His Songs and Sayings* (1880). "Huck Finn is a kind of boyish, semi-savage Gil Blas, of the low—the lowest—Transatlantic life, living by his wits on the Mississippi," Cambridge professor Henry Sidgwick jotted in his journal. "The novelty of the scene heightens the romantic *imprévu* of his adventures: and the comic *imprévu* of his reflections is—about once every three times—irresistibly laughable."[93] Socialist reformer Henry Carpenter quoted a passage from *Huckleberry Finn* as an epigraph in *England's Ideal* (1887). Brander Matthews recalled spending an afternoon with Robert Louis Stevenson in the smoking room of the Savoy Club, discussing *Tom Sawyer* and its sequel. "We agreed in praise," he said; "we agreed in thinking that either of these books was far better than that established favorite of the eighteenth century, *Gil Blas*, and . . . we agreed . . . that *Huckleberry Finn* was the

93. Quoted in Arthur and Eleanor Mildred Sidgwick, *Henry Sidgwick: A Memoir* (London and New York: Macmillan, 1906), p. 406.

The Concord Public Library, *Harper's Monthly*, December 1876.
Courtesy Library of Congress.

better book of the two, not solely because it had a larger field, not solely because it was the *Odyssey* of the Mississippi, not solely because it was the picture of a vanished civilization, but mainly because there is a finer, a stronger, a more strenuous moral decorum." Stevenson considered it to be "the strongest book which had appeared in our language in its decade."[94] Juliana Horatia Ewing, the author of *Jackanapes* (1879) and other children's books, remarkably asked for *Huckleberry Finn* on her deathbed.[95]

But *Huckleberry Finn* seemed to be cursed from the start. In March, the Concord Free Library was the first institution to ban the book. "While I do not wish to state it as my opinion that the book is absolutely immoral in its tone,"

94. Quoted in "Mark Twain's 70th Birthday," *Harper's Weekly*, December 23, 1905, p. 1886; and "American Fiction Again," *Cosmopolitan*, March 1892, p. 638.

95. See Henry M. Alden, "Mark Twain—An Appreciation," *The Bookman*, June 1910, p. 367.

explained one cautious member of the Concord Library Committee, "still it seems to me that it contains but very little humor; and that little is of a very coarse type. If it were not for the author's reputation the book would undoubtedly meet with severe criticism. I regard it as the veriest trash." Another rather redundantly described similar reasons for dismissing the book: "It deals with a series of adventures of a very low grade of morality; it is couched in the language of a rough, ignorant dialect, and all through its pages there is a systematic use of bad grammar and an employment of rough, coarse, inelegant expressions. It is also very irreverent. To sum up, the book is flippant and irreverent in its style. It deals with a series of experiences that are certainly not elevating. The whole book is of a class that is more profitable for the slums than it is for respectable people, and it is trash of the veriest sort."[96]

The story of the ban was immediately picked up by the papers all over the country, most of which had not reviewed the book. "Strange to say," reported the Boston *Daily Advertiser* on March 23, "few if any editors of these journals find any reason to differ from the book judges of Concord. Probably the editors have all tried to read the book." The Springfield (Mass.) *Daily Republican* immediately threw its support behind the library's action. "It is time," the paper editorialized on March 17, "that this influential pseudonym should cease to carry into homes and libraries unworthy productions. Mr. Clemens is a genuine and powerful humorist, with a bitter vein of satire on the weaknesses of humanity which is sometimes wholesome, sometimes only grotesque, but in certain of his works degenerates into a gross trifling with every fine feeling. The trouble with Mr. Clemens is that he has no reliable sense of propriety." His boy's books, *Tom Sawyer* and *Huckleberry Finn*, "are no better than the dime novels which flood the blood-and-thunder reading population. Mr. Clemens has made them smarter, for he has an inexhaustible fund of 'quips and cranks and wanton wiles,' and his literary skill is, of course, superior; but their moral level is low, and their perusal cannot be anything less than harmful." "*Huckleberry Finn* cannot be said to have a very high moral tone," said the Cleveland *Leader and Herald* on April 19, "but records the adventures of a lot of fishy people who try to outdo each other in mischievousness; very amusing, no doubt, but hardly suitable for a Sunday school as Horace Greeley remarked about Byron's poems." The paper added that the Gerhardt bust looked like Gustave Doré's portrait of Baron von Munchausen, "the champion liar of the world." Bridges likewise gloated on April 9, "It is a pleasure to note that the Concord

96. Quoted in the St. Louis *Globe-Democrat*, March 17, 1885; and New York *Herald*, March 18, 1885. The Boston *Transcript* (which Twain must have seen first) published a shorter report on March 17.

Library Committee agrees with *Life*'s estimate of Mark Twain's 'blood-curdling humor,' and have banished *Huckleberry Finn* to limbo." The most damning comment came from an unexpected source, Louisa May Alcott, the author of *Little Women* (1868) and one of Concord's prominent literary figures. "If Mr. Clemens cannot think of something better to tell our pure-minded lads and lasses," she advised, "he had best stop writing for them."[97]

The Sacramento *Daily Record-Union* astutely suggested on March 26, "If the Concord people are not in league with Mark Twain to advertise the book, they should have kept their proceedings profoundly secret." Even the Concord *Freeman*, which supported the library's decision, noted the inconsistency in the library's actions on March 20, for "the sale of the proscribed book has largely increased in Concord this week." The New York *Sun* suggested on March 18 that Twain "ought to send them a small check in acknowledgement of the compliment and the advertising they have given him."

The Boston *Commonwealth* suggested on March 21 that Twain "is probably laughing in his sleeves at the advertisement his book has received." He was offended, but not greatly worried by the ban. As Chicago's *Literary Life* (July 1885) observed, "When a book is pronounced irreverent or indecent, there will always be people anxious to read it on account of the very qualities which offend the moral sense" (p. 198). Twain told Webster on March 18 that those fools in Concord "have given us a rattling tiptop puff which will go into every paper in the country. They have expelled *Huck* from their library as 'trash and suitable only for the slums.' That will sell 25,000 copies for us sure."[98] Being banned in Boston or Concord did have its advantages. "This generous action of theirs," he said, "must necessarily benefit me in one or two additional ways. For instance, it will deter other libraries from buying the book; and you are doubtless aware that one book in a public library prevents the sale of a sure ten and a possible hundred of its mates. And, secondly, it will cause the purchasers of the book to read it, out of curiosity, instead of merely intending to do so, after the usual way of the world and library committees; and they will discover, to my great advantage and their own indignant disappointment, that there is nothing objectionable in the book after all."[99]

Twain assured his sister Pamela on April 15 that "those idiots in Concord are not a court of last resort, and I am not disturbed by their moral gymnastics. No

97. Quoted in Kaplan, *Mr. Clemens and Mark Twain*, p. 268. Twain was no admirer of Alcott either: He wrote *The Gilded Age* in part as an answer to popular contemporary novels such as her *Little Women*.

98. In *Mark Twain's Letters*, vol. 2, 1917, pp. 452-53.

99. Letter to Nichols, March 1885, Mark Twain Papers.

other book of mine has sold so many copies within two months after issue as this one has done."[100] Nevertheless, the insult festered in the wound. When invited to speak at the Cornell alumni dinner in New York on April 29, he contemplated using the occasion to publicly get back at the Concord Library Committee. But Howells advised against it. "That Concord Library Committee is game too small for you," he wrote Clemens on April 20, "and you can't stir it up without seeming to care more than you ought for it. You have done enough" (p. 526). Then out of the blue the Concord Free-Trade Club elected Twain an honorary member, and the writer capitalized on the irony of the situation by releasing his thank-you letter to the press after Howells called it "capital" (p. 525). He felt vindicated by this distinction, for, as he wrote Frank A. Nichols, secretary of the Concord Free-Trade Club, in March, "it endorses me as worthy to associate with certain gentleman whom even the moral icebergs of the Concord Library Committee are bound to respect." (He considered calling them "glaciers" or "icicles" before deciding on "icebergs.") Even that was criticized: The Boston *Globe* said on April 2 that the writer of the letter "is a man who can guy justice without pleasantry, and return thanks for favors in a paragraph that has no object except to advertise himself." The Springfield *Daily Republican* said on April 3 that the letter demonstrates how Twain "carefully avoids defending himself from the criticism justly made upon his latest book, and simply rejoices in the fact that he is going to make money out of it. Mr. Clemens has found that vulgarity pays, and he proposes to reap the benefits of his discovery. . . . He ought to be ashamed of *Huckleberry Finn*, but he boastfully declares that he is not in this extraordinary communication." On April 2, the Boston *Advertiser* objected to "his impudent intimations that a larger sale and larger profits are a satisfactory recompense to him for the unfavorable judgment of honest critics." That was "a true indication of the standard by which he measures success in literature." Twain took all this criticism to heart, complaining to Webster on April 4 that those two last papers in particular "still go for me daily. All right, we may as well get the benefit of such advertising as can be drawn from it."[101] He seriously thought of publishing a sarcastic "Prefatory Remark" to *Huckleberry Finn*, attacking the editors of both the Boston *Advertiser* and Springfield *Daily Republican*; but Olivia forbade it.[102]

He also had his defenders. "The action of the Concord Public Library in

100. In *Mark Twain, Business Man*, p. 317.

101. Quoted in Fischer, "Huck Finn Reviewed," p. 152.

102. In a note to *Mark Twain–Howells Letters*, p. 527. See Twain's "Explanatory" introducing *Huckleberry Finn*, note 5.

Heavyweight boxing champion John L. Sullivan addresses the Concord School of Philosophy with Mark Twain asleep far right in the front row. Cartoon by Kendrick, *Life*, August 9, 1883.
Courtesy Library of Congress.

excluding Mark Twain's new book, *Huckleberry Finn*, on the ground that it is flippant and irreverent, is absurd," said the San Francisco *Chronicle*. "There is a large class of people who are impervious to a joke, even when told by as consummate a master of the art of narration as Mark Twain. For all these the book will be dreary, flat, stale, and unprofitable. But for the great body of readers it will furnish much hearty, wholesome laughter." The Boston *Morning Journal* of March 17 called Concord's male librarian "a woman who prefers a book of purity rather than of fame."

Some took aim at Concord's reputation for philosophical obtuseness. The St. Louis *Post-Dispatch* reported on March 17, "Concord keeps up its recent reputation of being the home of speculative philosophy and practical nonsense."[103]

[103] As Fischer noted in "Huck Finn Reviewed" (pp. 142–43), some critics of *Huckleberry Finn* enjoyed poking fun at Transcendental thought and the Concord School of Philosophy, the only summer school of philosophy anywhere in the world. "When Mark writes another book," suggested the Boston *Globe* on March 17, "he should think of the Concord School of Philosophy and put in a little more whenceness of the hereafter among his nowness of the here." The New York *World* suggested on March 18 that the book should be "immensely pop-

W. E. Pankhurst, editor of the Clinton (Mass.) *Courant*, sent Twain "a copy of my paper, by which you will see that our library directors have decided to help your sale of *Huckleberry Finn* by *refusing* it a place in our library. I can assure you, that the anxiety to see and read *Huckleberry* is on the increase here; the adults are daily inquiring where *Finn* can be had, and even the children are crying for "Huckleberries"; the only way by which we can preserve some of our young lads in the path of moral rectitude is to promise to give them a copy of Mark Twain's rejected *Huckleberry Finn*. Both as an *incentive* and as an *opiate* the *promise* of a copy of this work is a marked success."[104]

People all over the country assured Twain he really had nothing to be afraid of. The San Francisco *Chronicle* replied in its editorial on March 29, "In regard to the charge of grossness, there is not a line in it which cannot be read by a pure-minded woman." In its regular review of the book on March 15, the *Chronicle* called Twain "the Edison of our literature" and *Huckleberry Finn* "the most amusing book Mark Twain has written for years." The San Francisco *Morning Call* reported that *Huckleberry Finn* "is a story that every one may read and at least be entertained. It is at times immensely amusing, and fully sustains Mr. Clemens' well-earned reputation as a humorous writer." "It is by all odds the most humorous of all Mr. Clemens' writings," insisted the Sacramento *Daily Record-Union*; "not such elevated humor, of course, as the literary student cares to spend much time upon, but for all that, a humor full of caustic truth and that reveals broad originality. Indeed, it is the most original of all Mark Twain's efforts." The Napa (Calif.) *Register* (May 8, 1885) predicted that *Huckleberry Finn* "will amuse and interest you, where other books prove insipid. . . . Your library is not complete without it."

The Concord Public Library clumsily tried to explain its reasons for removing *Huckleberry Finn* in a vain attempt to correct the accusation of censorship that was rapidly spreading across the country. One of the trustees told the Hartford *Courant* (April 4, 1885) that it was not the Concord Public Library policy to permit fiction on its shelves and someone had mistaken *Adventures of Huckleberry Finn* for a biography. The New York *Herald* (March 18, 1885) told a different story: "Knowing the author's reputation," the committee considered

---

ular with the Concord School of Philosophy, which will find in it no end of Henceness of the Which and Thingness of the Unknowable." The Augusta (Ga.) *Chronicle and Constitutionalist* suggested with Southern pride on March 22 that Twain's "exaggerated waggeries are not near so dangerous to faith and morals as are the agnostic speculations of New England pundits, who have learned how to suppress population and refine God out of his own universe."

104. Letter to Samuel L. Clemens, Mark Twain Papers.

it "totally unnecessary to make a careful examination of *Huckleberry Finn* before sending it to Concord." (Had none of them read *The Innocents Abroad* or *Roughing It* or even *Tom Sawyer*?) The librarian, however, "was not particularly pleased with it" and protested to the committee who finally read and condemned it.

The mighty *Century*, too, had to defend its having published excerpts from the offensive book. When a superintendent of schools out West angrily wrote the magazine that this material was "destitute of a single redeeming quality" and "hardly worth a place in the columns of the average county newspaper which never assumes any literary airs," Gilder cautiously replied, "At least, as a picture of the life which he describes, his *Century* sketches are of decided force and worth. Mark Twain is not a giber at religion or morality. He is a good citizen and believes in the best things." *Century Magazine* answered the criticism in May with a full-length review by Boston scholar and historian Thomas Sergeant Perry, the only full-length review of *Huckleberry Finn* to appear in any major national magazine that year. Perry said that the novel "has the great advantage of being written in autobiographical form. This secures a unity that is most valuable; every scene is given, not described; and the result is a vivid picture of Western life forty or fifty years ago." As for the humor being coarse, Perry said, "It lends vividness to every page." He agreed with Twain that "literature is at its best when it is an imitation of life and not an excuse for instruction." He praised Huck's "undying fertility of invention, his courage, his manliness in every trial" as being "an incarnation of the better side of ruffianism that is one result of the independence of Americans, just as hypocrisy is one result of the English respect for civilization."

When the Springfield *Daily Republican* finally got around to publishing a proper review of the book on April 27, it turned out to be an unexpectedly strong defense against the recent Concord controversy. "I cannot subscribe," declared Prof. Franklin B. Sanborn, "to the extreme censor passed upon this volume, which is no coarser than Mark Twain's books usually are, while it has a vein of deep morality beneath its exterior of falsehood and vice, that will redeem it in the eyes of mature persons." He admitted that it might not be right for "Sunday-school libraries, and should perhaps be left unread by growing boys; but the mature in mind may read it, without distinction of age or sex, and without material harm." Nevertheless, it offered "an argument against negro-slavery, lynching, whisky-drinking, family feuds, promiscuous shooting, and nearly all the vices of Missouri in the olden time." It was a historical novel that "goes farther to explain the political history of the United States from 1854 to 1860 than any other work I have seen." He also considered the philo-

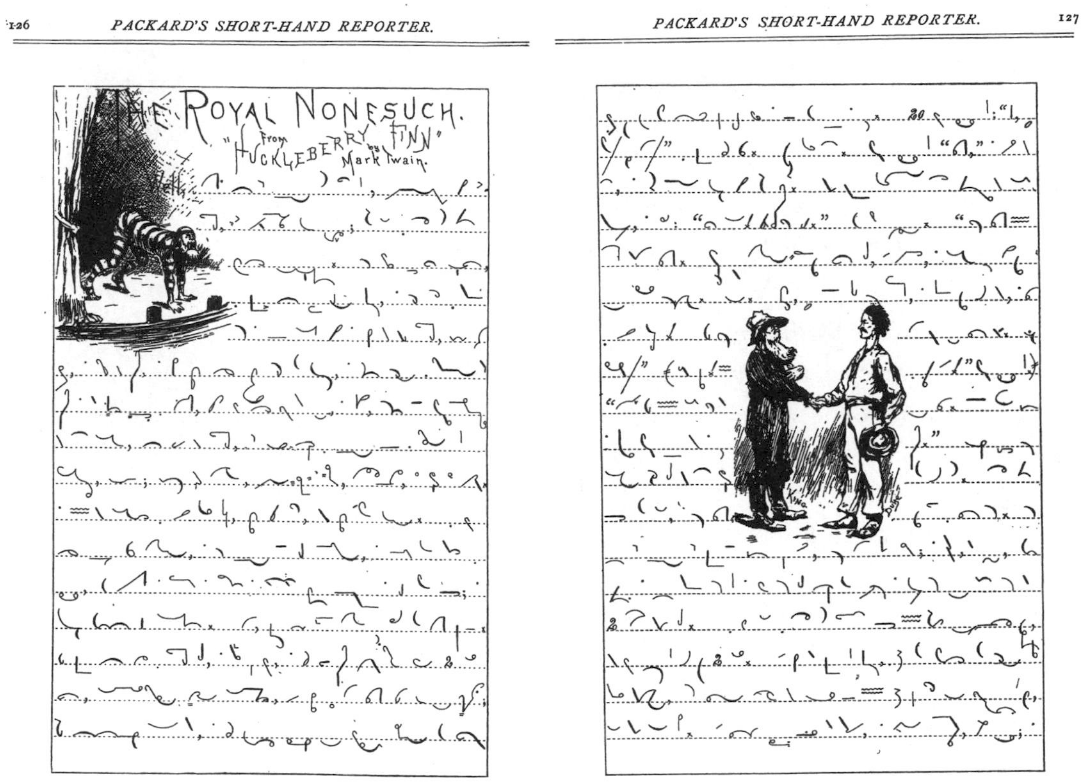

Excerpt from *Adventures of Huckleberry Finn* retold in shorthand,
Packard's Short-hand Reporter and Amanuensis, April 1885.
Courtesy Library of Congress.

sophical and psychological depths to the novel: "There is hardly anything so true to human nature in the whole realm of casuistry as the young hero's meditations with himself over his duty regarding the runaway slave, Jim, when it first dawns upon the boy that he is an accomplice in the escape from slavery."

Later, when the superintendent of the New York State Reformatory asked Prof. Sanborn about the book, he replied, "I have read *Huckleberry Finn*, and I do not see any reason why it should not go into your Reference Library, at least, and form the subject of a debate in your Practical Morality Class. I am serious about this."[105] *Packard's Short-hand Reporter and Amanuensis* (April 1885) reprinted the Royal Nonesuch episode from Chapter 23 of the "trashy" book in shorthand and with the Kemble pictures, adding that it was not hard

105. Quoted in *The Critic*, May 30, 1885, p. 264.

to see "why the authorities of the transcendental town of Concord should tumble the book off the shelves of their school [*sic*] library, thereby inducing every smart boy and girl in the town to buy it and read it on the sly. . . . That is just the kind of book that young people are reaching for, and Mark knows it" (pp. 105–6). Poet and critic Edmund Charles Stedman wrote Twain that he thought the description of the Grangerford–Shepherdson feud "is not only the most finished and condensed thing you have done, but as dramatic and powerful an episode as I know in modern literature."[106] He asked Twain if he might reprint it in his *Library of American Literature* (1887–1890), and Twain happily agreed. Charles L. Webster and Company eventually published Stedman and Ellen Mackay Hutchinson's eleven-volume anthology, with disastrous results for the firm.

Twain had perhaps no greater champion than Joel Chandler Harris. "I know that some professionals critics will not agree with me," he wrote *The Critic* (November 28, 1885) on the occasion of Twain's fiftieth birthday, "but there is not in our fictive literature a more wholesome book than *Huckleberry Finn*. It is history, it is romance, it is life. Here we behold human character stripped of all tiresome details; we see people growing and living; we laugh at their humor, share their griefs; and, in the midst of it all, behold we are taught the lesson of honesty, justice and mercy" (p. 253). The trouble was not with Mark Twain or Huck Finn. "From the artistic point of view," Harris explained in an editorial in the Atlanta *Constitution* (May 6, 1885), "there is not a coarse nor vulgar suggestion from the beginning to the end of the book. Whatever is coarse and crude is the life that is pictured, and the picture is perfect. It may be said that the humor is sometimes excessive, but it is genuine humor." Harris apologized to Twain that his notice "fails to express half my admiration for the book, for I think that its value as a picture of life and as a study of philology will yet come to be recognized by those whose recognition is worth anything. It is the most original contribution that has yet been made to American literature." Twain was deeply touched by his friend's kind and sincere support of Huck Finn. "Somehow, *I* can't help believing in him," he told Harris, "and it's a great refreshment to my faith to have a man back me up who has been where such boys live, and knows what he is talking about."[107] Conspicuously missing from the debate was William Dean Howells. *The Atlantic* published no more than a

106. Quoted in Paine, *Mark Twain: A Biography*, vol. 2, p. 793. It was reprinted in vol. 9 of Stedman and Ellen Mackay Hutchinson, *A Library of American Literature* (1891), pp. 200–307.

107. Letters from Harris to Clemens, June 1, 1885; and from Clemens to Harris, November 29, 1885, *Mark Twain to Uncle Remus*, p. 20.

brief notice of "Mark Twain's new book for young folks" in the April issue; all *The Nation* did was list it among books received on February 26, 1885.

Harris's review of *Huckleberry Finn* was practically the only major notice in any Southern publication. It was not that the South ignored Twain but that Twain ignored the South. He and Webster never bothered to send many review copies below the Mason-Dixon Line, recognizing the volatile and potentially offensive subject matter of the novel. "Possibly," noted the Augusta (Ga.) *Chronicle and Constitutionalist* (March 22, 1884), "Mark Twain's later books are coarse and dime-novelish. We do not know. We have not read them." Nor had many other Southern journalists. "Mark Twain's latest book is condemned, American critics say, because it is vulgar and coarse," declared the *Arkansaw Traveler* (April 25, 1885). "The days of vulgar humor are over in this country. There was a time when a semi-obscene joke would find admirers, but the reading public is becoming more refined. Exaggerated humor will also pass away. The humorist must be chaste and truthful." But this critic never actually said that he had read *Huckleberry Finn*.

The book was selling so well so quickly that Webster had to go back to press within the first month of publication with a second printing of 10,000 copies. There was now no need to canvass the country with 300 press copies of *Huckleberry Finn* as once planned. Webster had good news to report on March 14: He had already sold 39,000 copies, more than any of Twain's earlier books had done in so short a period. "Your news is splendid," he replied to Webster on March 16. "*Huck* certainly *is* a success, and from the standpoint of my own requirement. . . . Every time you sell a thousand *Huck*s, let me know. It's a handsome success" (p. 307). His mood changed radically. Success made him cocky. "I am frightened at the proportions of prosperity," he bragged. "It seems to me that whatever I touch turns to gold."[108]

Hopes for the English edition had also run high. "The orders we have already in advance for it are much greater than previously received for any of his other volumes," Chatto & Windus reported to Tauchnitz on December 13, 1884.[109] Unfortunately, sales in England did not live up to expectations. "It is true that *Huck Finn* has not treated you kindly," Twain admitted to Chatto & Windus on September 8, 1885, "but it must be because the English people do not understand the dialect; for here, where the people do understand it, the book has sold more than 60,000 copies, at my usual high prices. . . . Times have been harder

108. Quoted by Paine, *Mark Twain: A Biography*, p. 831.

109. Transcript of letter from Chatto & Windus to Bernhard Tauchnitz, Jr., December 3, 1884, Mark Twain Papers.

than anywhere else in the book-reading world, I suppose—in fact they have been unspeakably bad—so it was doubtless not your hard times, but that unchristian dialect that modified the sale." Evidently the book did not appeal much to English tourists and Germans. "That dialect," he suggested to Chatto & Windus, "would give these latter the belly-ache every time" (pp. 125–26). His English publishers eventually sold 43,500 copies of *Huckleberry Finn* between 1884 and 1902, not a bad sum but 2,500 fewer than *Life on the Mississippi*.[110]

Having been bruised by the Concord controversy, Twain was flattered when James Fraser Glück, one of the curators of the Young Men's Association of Buffalo, wrote him to request a manuscript for the library's autograph collection. Twain had not lived in Buffalo for fourteen years, but the library's current superintendent was Josephus N. Larned, Twain's coeditor at the Buffalo *Express* soon after the Clemenses married. Unfortunately, Twain was in the habit of discarding his manuscripts or giving them away and could not find a complete one on hand, only portions of *Life on the Mississippi* and *Huckleberry Finn*. He therefore hastily contacted friends to see if any of them might have something else he could donate to the collection. The frantic, rude tone of his request must have irritated his friend, the famous preacher Henry Ward Beecher, who had some of his manuscripts. "Brother Clemens," he replied, "sit down and be silent! You speak after the manner of the foolish. I *do* know where the manuscripts are. They are safe, and will soon be on their way home. Were it not for these wanton aspersions on my habits, I should say how much they helped me, and how much I am obliged for your generous pains to aid me, but you have forfeited these sentiments, until I hear that you wash with ashes and sit in sackcloth." Benjamin H. Ticknor of Ticknor & Company wrote back, "I am very sorry for Mr. Glück, but I fear I cannot gratify him. If you remember I made an appeal to your generosity after *The Prince and the Pauper* manuscript was returned to you and you gave it to me, sending it back from Elmira. It is not in a glass case, but it does me, at least, lots of good, and . . . it [is] prized more, if exhibited less, than in a big public library"[111]

No one apparently came through, so Twain halfheartedly offered the second half of *Huckleberry Finn* to Buffalo. "I have hunted the house over," he reported to Glück on November 12, "and that is all I can find, except half of *Life on the Mississippi*—in mixed and shabby condition and not worth expressage."[112] He

110. See Welland, *Mark Twain in England*, pp. 125–26 and 231.

111. Letters to Samuel L. Clemens, November 9 and 16, 1885, Mark Twain Papers.

112. Letter to James Fraser Glück, November 12, 1885, Mark Twain Papers. Glück also wanted manuscripts from Twain's neighbors Charles Dudley Warner and Harriet Beecher Stowe, but he said they had saved nothing.

had no clue where the first part was. "Half of the Finn book is extant because *that* half was written after the typewriter came into general use," he tried to explain to Glück. "Before that, it was my custom (and everybody's in my line, no doubt) to have my books copied with pen and ship the original to the printers, who never returned it. As soon as the book was printed, the copy made by the amanuensis was no longer valuable, and was destroyed; it was only made, in the first place, as a precautionary measure." Later "the *last* half was copied on the typewriter, and the copy went to the printer instead of the less-readable original—and thus the original was preserved." But Twain must have confused *Huckleberry Finn* with another book: Twain gave both portions of the holograph manuscript to different typists, and theirs were the copies that went to the printer. Twain had simply misplaced the first part.

Glück happily accepted the hefty fragment of *Huckleberry Finn*, hoping that Twain might also send the incomplete *Life on the Mississippi* manuscript. "I hope when you next come to Buffalo," he replied on November 12, "you will allow me to show you in our library how pleasant an abiding place we have given the much-abused Huckleberry Finn. When Boston and Concord desert him then the home of the Presidents shall take him up." He immediately placed the precious parcel in the library's vault, but promised on November 14 that "Mr. Finn's resurrection will take place when, unlike most instances, a case—of glass and velvet—has been secured for the remains."[113] It was not until 1887 that Twain stumbled on the first half of the manuscript, and happily had it sent to Buffalo. Glück was delighted and assured Twain on July 11, "The whole can now be bound and placed on exhibition."[114] But he never got around to doing it. The first half of the manuscript disappeared for over one hundred years until Glück's granddaughters happened to find it in an old trunk; and the two parts were finally reunited in Buffalo in 1992.[115]

It is clear from the reviews of *Huckleberry Finn* how little Twain's contemporaries understood his work. "Why don't people understand that Mark Twain is not merely a great humorist?" Thomas Hardy once asked Howells. "He's a very remarkable fellow in a very different way."[116] Twain was not merely a humorist with a talent for local color; he was an important social critic. "I cannot recall to

113. Letters to Samuel L. Clemens. November 12 and 14, 1885, Mark Twain Papers. The manuscript of *Life on the Mississippi* is now in the J. Pierpont Morgan Library, New York City.

114. Letters from J. N. Larned to Franklin G. Whitmore, July 5, 1887; and from James F. Glück to Samuel L. Clemens, July 11, 1887, Mark Twain Papers.

115. See Dorothy S. Gelatt, "Huck Finn Ms., Lost 100 Years, Turns Up in Hollywood Attic," *Maine Antiques Digest*, April 1991, pp. 30A–31A.

116. Quoted in a letter from Howells to Clemens, July 10, 1883, *Mark Twain–Howells Letters*, p. 434

The Young Men's Association of Buffalo.
Courtesy Buffalo and Erie County Public Library, Buffalo, New York.

mind a single instance where I have ever been irreverent," Twain said, "except towards the things which were sacred to other people."[117] Twain described his own struggle with his Protestant upbringing in the struggle between the heart and the conscience in *Huckleberry Finn*. In Huck Finn, he created the natural man, the ideal romantic hero, unfettered by middle-class conventions, who in the end must run off to the wilderness to escape being "sivilized." "All details of 'civilization' are legitimate matters for jeering," Twain believed. "It is made up of about three tenths of reality and sincerity, and seven tenths of wind and humbug."[118] *Huckleberry Finn* is, as Lionel Trilling argued in *The Liberal Imagi-*

117. In *Is Shakespeare Dead?* (New York and London: Harper & Bros., 1909), p. 134.

118. Quoted in Walter Blair, *Mark Twain and Huck Finn* (Berkeley and Los Angeles: University of California Press, 1960), p. 339.

nation (1950), "a subversive book—no one who reads thoughtfully the dialectic of Huck's great moral crisis will ever again be wholly able to accept without some question and some irony the assumptions of the respectable morality by which he lives, nor will ever again be certain that what he considers the clear dictates of moral reason are not merely the engrained customary beliefs of his time and place" (p. 112).

Not even Twain's family was in complete sympathy with the novel. Susy in particular was distressed when a reader wrote her father, "I enjoyed *Huckleberry Finn* immensely and am glad to see that you have returned to your old style." "That enoyed me," she wrote in her biography, "that enoyed me greatly, because it trobles me to have so few know papa, I mean realy know him, they think of Mark Twain as a humorist joking at everything."[119] What the little girl demanded from her father was a more self-consciously serious work which would "reveal something of his kind sympathetic nature." Susy was likely paraphrasing her mother; as Howells noted in *My Mark Twain* (p. 48), Olivia Clemens too wished her famous husband might "be known not only for the world and boundless humor that was in him but for the beauty and tenderness and 'natural piety' " (p. 48). But some writers write primarily out of revenge, and Twain needed something that so vexed him to send him storming back to pen and paper. Susy must have been expressing the family's opinion (and many of their contemporaries') when she argued that *The Prince and the Pauper*, not *Huckleberry Finn*, was her father's finest effort. "The book is full of charming ideas," she said, "and oh the language! It is perfect."

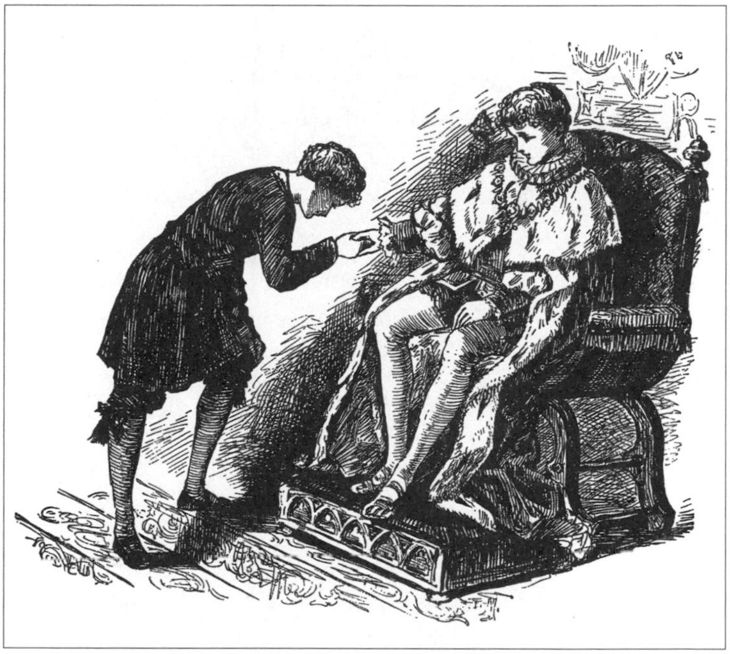

Tom Canty and Edward Tudor. Illustration by Frank T. Merrill, *The Prince and the Pauper*, 1882. *Courtesy Library of Congress.*

Susy Clemens was raised within the conventions upheld by the policies of the Concord Library Committee. *The Prince and the Pauper* could have sat

119. Quoted in "Chapters from My Autobiography," *North American Review*, November 2, 1906, p. 836.

safely on the shelf of any well-bred institution like that and in any genteel American parlor, for it was everything *Huckleberry Finn* was not: a refined historical romance larded with elegant archaic phrases and anchored to an obviously moral scrutiny of the men and manners of sixteenth-century England. Concord, as much as Boston, was a great defender of New England's genteel traditions. It was also the home of Emerson and Thoreau, the home of American "civil disobedience," so it is ironic that Huck Finn should have offended anyone there. The citizens of this former hotbed of abolitionism should have championed Huck's determination to free Jim from bondage. But there is rarely much sense in censorship. Twain's critics were more concerned with the style and spirit of a work of literature than with intellectual content. Irony was wasted on them and other literalists.

Twain told the New York *Times* (December 10, 1889) that he believed in "maintaining in America a national literature, of preserving national sentiment, national politics, national thought, and national morals." Americans were not quite ready to throw off the yoke of European influence. "We are fed on foreign literature, and imbibe foreign ideas," Twain complained. It is remarkable how few American books are referred to in *Huckleberry Finn*. Ever since the Revolutionary War, American writers suffered from an artistic inferiority complex. The young nation, in denying the grand traditions of Europe, had little left on which to build its reputation. Consequently, written American English (unlike speech) became more formal, more artificial, more ornate than its British counterpart. What was most admired in New England was self-consciously literary or "bookish" prose. Then came self-made Mark Twain out of the great Western wilderness, the first important American novelist born west of the Mississippi. "Of all the literary men I have known," Howells confessed in *My Mark Twain*, "he was the most unliterary in his make and manner. . . . he used English in all its alien derivations as if it were native to his own air, as if it had come up out of American, out of Missourian ground" (p. 17). Traditional Yankee critics did not know what to make of Twain's methods and generally failed to recognize this truly original voice crying out of the West. He spoke another language.

Those who might accept local color as literature did so only reluctantly and only when written by respectable and genteel writers like James Russell Lowell, Joel Chandler Harris, John Hay, and Harriet Beecher Stowe. When compared to their studied dialect, Twain's deliberately bad grammar and slang did seem merely coarse and inelegant; there was nothing quaint about Huck Finn's contemporary colloquialisms. Artemus Ward, Josh Billings, Petroleum V. Nasby, Mark Twain, and other humorists were not for the American intelligentsia. Sadly, Twain's critics then and now skimmed the surface but missed the substance. Dialect was suitable only for humorous writing, and then as now, the literary world, E. B. White observed, "decorates its serious writers with laurel and its wags with Brussels sprouts."[120] Comedy was inferior to tragedy; critics agreed with Howells that "American humorists formerly chose the wrong in public matters; they were on the side of slavery, of drunkenness, and of irreligion; the friends of civilization were their prey; their spirit was thoroughly vulgar and base."[121] Twain appeared no different to many in America. But Howells at least thought his dear friend's work deviated from that of his fellow comic writers. "There is still sufficient flippancy and brutality in it," he acknowledged; "but there is no longer the stupid and monkeyish cruelty of motive and intention which once disgraced and insulted us."

Perhaps what so enraged the critics about American humor was its lack of earnestness: It did not elevate, it only entertained. Twain, however, always had a purpose within the levity. "I have always preached," he insisted. "If the humor came of its own accord and uninvited I have allowed it a place in my sermon, but I was not writing the sermon for the sake of the humor."[122] And his secular preaching was not aimed at such as the Concord Library Committee. "Indeed I have been misjudged from the very first," he wrote in 1889. "I have never tried in even one single little instance, to help cultivate the cultivated classes. I was not equipped for it, either by nature gifts or training. And . . . honestly, I never cared what became of the cultivated classes; they could go to the theater and the opera. They had no use for me and the melodeon."[123] Instead, Twain "always hunted for the bigger game—the masses." How could so popular a writer be worthy of serious critical consideration? Could someone so widely read be a true artist?

Another problem with *Huckleberry Finn* was that, as Louisa May Alcott indicated, it was generally marketed, reviewed, and read as just another boy's book. The publishers encouraged this perception by advertising it as uniform with *Tom Sawyer*, but even that novel, Twain told Howells, "is *not* a boy's book, at all. It will only be read by adults. It is only for adults" (p. 91). But Howells thought otherwise: "It's altogether the best boy's story I ever read. . . . But I think you ought to treat it explicitly *as* a boy's story. Grown-ups will enjoy it just as much

120. In "Some Remarks on Humor," *Essays of E. B. White* (New York: Harper and Row, 1977), p. 244.

121. In "Mark Twain," *Century Magazine*, September 1882, p. 781.

122. In *Mark Twain in Eruption*, p. 202.

123. In a letter to Andrew Lang, *Mark Twain's Letters*, vol. 2, pp. 527–28.

Tom Sawyer. Illustration by True W. Williams,
The Adventures of Tom Sawyer, 1876.
Private collection.

if you do; and if you should put it forth as a study of boy character from the grown-up point of view, you'd give the wrong key to it" (pp. 110–11). Half-heartedly Twain gave in to his advisers. "Mrs. Clemens decides with you," he informed Howells, "that the book should issue as a book for boys, pure and simple—and so do I. It is surely the correct idea" (p. 112). However, so that his initial purpose should not be lost, Twain apologized in the preface, "Although my book is intended mainly for the entertainment of boys and girls, I hope it will not be shunned by men and women on that account, for part of my plan has been to try to pleasantly remind adults of what they once were themselves."

Tom Sawyer belongs to the subgenre of the "bad boy's book."[124] Thomas Bai-

124. See Joseph Hinz, "Huck and Pluck: 'Bad' Boys in American Fiction," *The South Atlantic Quarterly*, January 1952, pp. 120–29.

ley Aldrich established this tradition in nineteenth-century American literature with *The Story of a Bad Boy* (1870), a rambling series of thinly disguised autobiographical sketches told by the grown-up "Tom Bailey." "I call my story the story of a bad boy," he explained, "partly to distinguish myself from those faultless young gentlemen who generally figure in narratives of this kind, and partly because I really was *not* a cherub. I may truthfully say I was an amiable, impulsive lad, blessed with fine digestive powers and no hypocrite. . . . In short, I was a real human boy, such as you may meet anywhere in New England, and no more like the impossible boy in a story-book than a sound orange is like one that has been sucked dry." Although Howells found in Tom Bailey "a new thing . . . in American literature, an absolute novelty," others had already explored the "bad boy" in fiction; for example, Benjamin Penhollow Shillaber introduced Ike, a mischievous foster child, in *Life and Sayings of Mrs. Partington* (1854). Twain himself had parodied the countless Sunday-school tracts about disobedient boys who came to suffer for their sins, in "Story of the Bad Boy Who Didn't Come to Grief" (San Francisco *Alta California*, December 23, 1865). He confessed that he found little to admire in his friend's *The Story of a Bad Boy*. He likely wrote *Tom Sawyer* in part to correct what he considered Aldrich's misconceptions of boy life.[125]

Tom Bailey, the bad boy. Illustration by Sol Eytinge, Jr., *The Story of a Bad Boy* by Thomas Bailey Aldrich, 1869.
Courtesy Library of Congress.

Although *Tom Sawyer* was initially ignored by the majority of critics as just another subscription book, Howells championed his friend's first children's book in *The Atlantic Monthly* (May 1876) as "a wonderful study of the boy-mind, which inhabits a world quite distinct from that in which he is bodily present with his elders, and in this lies its great charm and its universality, for boy nature, however human nature varies, is the same everywhere" (p. 621). To Howells, Tom Sawyer was the archetypal boy: "He is mischievous, but not vicious; he is ready for almost any

125. Parallels between *Tom Sawyer* and *The Story of a Bad Boy* have been discussed by Blair in *Mark Twain and Huck Finn* (pp. 64–65) and in the introduction and explanatory notes in *The Adventures of Tom Sawyer; Tom Sawyer Abroad; Tom Sawyer, Detective*, edited by John C. Gerber, Paul Baender, and Terry Furkins (Berkeley and Los Angeles: University of California Press, 1980).

depredation that involves the danger and honor of adventure, but profanity he knows may provoke a thunderbolt upon the heart of the blasphemer, and he almost never swears; he resorts to any stratagem to keep out of school, but he is not a downright liar. . . . He is cruel, as all children are, but chiefly because he is ignorant; he is not mean, but there are definite bonds to his generosity. . . . In a word, he is a boy, and merely and exactly an ordinary boy on the moral side."

"The Story of the Bad Little Boy."
Illustration by True W. Williams,
Mark Twain's Sketches, New and Old, 1875.
Courtesy Library of Congress.

The reviewers may have shunned Twain's hymn to boyhood, but not so his fellow writers. Soon it must have seemed, if one assumes literature to be merely a mirror held up to life, that the self-contradictory "bad boy" was indeed "located in every city, village, and country hamlet throughout the land. He is wide awake, full of vinegar, and ready to crawl under the canvas of a circus or repeat a hundred verses of the New Testament in Sunday School. He knows where every melon patch in the neighborhood is located, and at what hours the dog is chained up. He will tie an oyster can to a dog's tail to give the dog exercise, or will fight at the drop of a hat to protect the smaller boy or a school girl."[126] Aldrich's *The Story of a Bad Boy* encouraged such inferior works of literature as *Peck's Bad Boy and His Pa* and its numerous sequels, and *A Bad Boy's Diary* (1880) and other "bad boy" books by "Walter T. Gray" (Maetta Victoria Victor).[127] Twain's novel inspired a succession of imitations, mostly transparent autobiographical tales of rural boyhoods: Charles Dudley Warner's *Being a Boy* (1878), B. P. Shillaber's *Ike*

126. George W. Peck in his preface to *Peck's Bad Boy and His Pa* (Chicago: C. B. Beach, 1883).

127. Twain hated the anonymous *A Bad Boy's Diary* and wanted to take legal action against the publishers. "They are using my name," he wrote Webster on September 19, 1882, "to sell stuff which I never wrote. I would not be the author of that witless stuff . . . for a million dollars" (p. 197). They implied in their advertising that *A Bad Boy's Diary* was written by the author of *Tom Sawyer*.

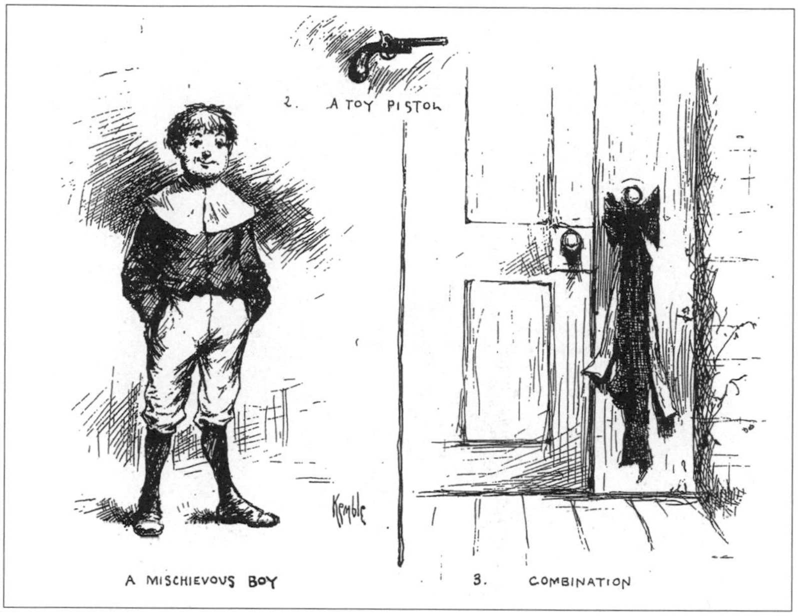

"A Mischievous Boy." Cartoon by E. W. Kemble, *Life*, March 27, 1884.
Courtesy Library of Congress.

Peck's bad boy and his pa. Illustration by True W. Williams,
Peck's Bad Boy and His Pa by George W. Peck, 1893 edition.
Courtesy Library of Congress.

Little Lord Fauntleroy. Illustration by Reginald Birch,
Little Lord Fauntleroy by Frances Hodgson Burnett, 1886.
Courtesy Library of Congress.

Partington (1879), and Edward Eggleston's *The Hoosier Schoolboy* (1883). The book most clearly indebted to *Tom Sawyer* was *A Boy's Town* (1890) by William Dean Howells.[128] But these sentimentalized accounts of a boy's paradise lost lacked the vitality of Twain's story and generally appealed more to nostalgic adults than to children.

Then there was Huckleberry Finn. He was not like any other character in children's books of the day: He was the first antihero in the American nursery. "Huck is the child of neglect and acquainted with cold, hunger, privation, humiliation, and with the unearned aversion of the upper crust of the commu-

128. Howells recalled a sentimentalized version of Huck Finn in *A Boy's Town*: The protagonist's "closest friend was a boy who was probably never willingly at school in his life, and who had no more relish of literature or learning in him than the open fields, or the warm air of an early spring day. . . . He was like a piece of the genial earth, with no more hint of toiling or spinning in him; willing for anything, but passive and without force or aim. He lived in a belated log cabin that stood . . . on the river-bank" (p. 191).

nity," Twain explained. "The respectable boys were not allowed to play with him—so they played with him all the time—preferred his company to any other. There was nothing against him but his rags, and to a boy's untutored eye rags don't count if the person in them is satisfactory."[129] In its uncompromising scrutiny of a society now past, where everyone was either a scoundrel or a fool, the sequel declared the idyll of *Tom Sawyer* over. Naked Huck Finn on the river raft shocked a public who so readily clasped Frances Hodgson Burnett's Little Lord Fauntleroy in golden curls, lace collar, and velvet suit to its ample breast within the year.[130] Huck Finn was of a lower caste than even that of "bad boy" Tom Sawyer, but not mere class prejudice expelled Twain's waif from respectable parlors. Other street Arabs populated boy's books by Horatio Alger, Jr., and "James Otis" (James Otis Kaler) without any great outcry. However, these shoeshines and newsboys adhered to the virtues of thrift, cheerfulness, and industry in their "rags-to-riches" stories. But Huck Finn never trades in his tatters or respectability; he cannot wait to get back to his hogshead or return to the raft. Instead, he follows the dictates of his own boy heart rather than the demands of a corrupt and corrupting society by not only helping a slave to run away but vowing to "*go* to hell" rather than to betray him to his owner. As T. S. Eliot observed, there is no more solitary figure in fiction than good-hearted Huck Finn.[131]

Even if he is, as Brander Matthews argued in the London *Saturday Review*, "neither a girl in boy's clothes like many of the modern heroes of juvenile fiction, nor is he a 'little man,' a full-grown man cut down; he is a boy, just a boy, only

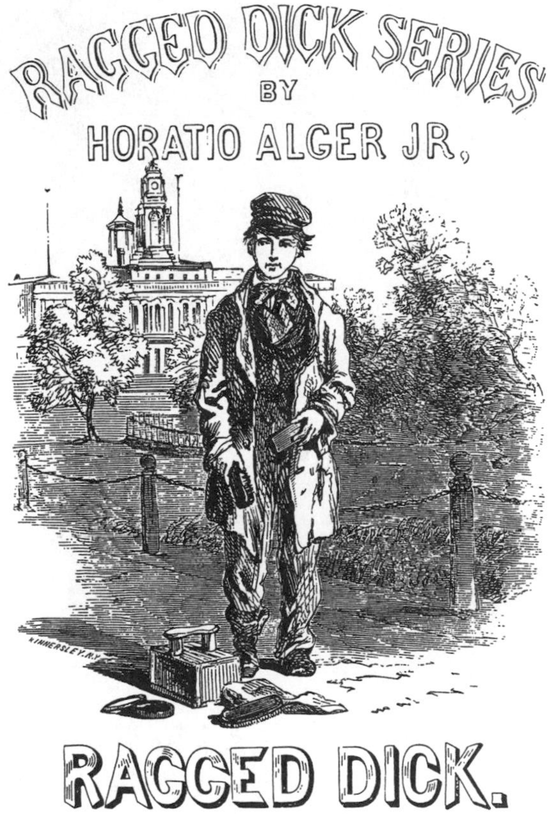

Pictorial half-title page from Ragged Dick series by Horatio P. Alger, 1867.
Courtesy Library of Congress.

129. Notes for the 1895 "Tour Around the World," quoted by Blair and Fischer in the 1988 University of California edition of *Huckleberry Finn*, p. 806.

130. Twain thought Burnett took the idea of *Little Lord Fauntleroy* (1886) from *The Prince and the Pauper*; he had unwittingly sent her a complimentary copy in 1881. See *Mark Twain's Letters*, vol. 2, 1917, p. 814.

131. In the introduction to the 1950 edition of *Huckleberry Finn*, published in London by the Crest Press and in New York by Chanticleer Press.

Illustration by Thomas Nast,
Hans Brinker or the Silver Skates
by Mary Mapes Dodge, 1865.
Courtesy Library of Congress.

a boy," there was much more in the novel to threaten even the most liberal of late-nineteenth-century households. Its vivid descriptions of family feuds and lynchings and the thirteen corpses which litter the story like snags on the great Mississippi itself were strong meat for babes weaned on Mary Mapes Dodge's *Hans Brinker or the Silver Skates* (1865) and Louisa May Alcott's *Little Men* (1871). Twain's violences were indeed the stuff of dime novels, the comic books of their day, so eagerly read by thrill-seeking boys like Tom Sawyer and loathed by all the Aunt Pollys who had to raise them. Their exciting Indian attacks and street gang brawls anticipated the more sensational events of *Huckleberry Finn*. There are grisly details in *Tom Sawyer*, too, such as Doc Robinson's murder in the graveyard and Injun Joe's threat to slit the widow's nostrils like a sow's; but whitewashing Aunt Polly's fence and the schoolyard romances and the bucolic exile on Jackson's Island temper the more alarming events of this bad boy's book. However, in having the ignorant boy tell his own story in his own words in his own time, Twain left little place for nostalgic revery in *Huckleberry Finn*.

Those memorable comic and pastoral interludes which do appear in Huck Finn's autobiography were introduced for a specific dialectical purpose, as contrast to and to strengthen the horrific events in the story. "It is a law that humor is created by contrasts," Twain told the New York *World* (May 31, 1891). "It is the legitimate child of contrast." At work on his travelogue *A Tramp Abroad*, Twain described a specific satiric method which served him well in his fiction. He explained that the burlesque "Gambetta Duel" in Chapter 7 "will follow a perfectly serious description of five very bloody student duels which I witnessed in Heidelberg one day—a description which simply *describes* the terrific spectacle, with no jests interlarded and no comments added. The contrast between that chapter and the next one (the Gambetta duel) will be silent but eloquent comment."[132] However, in the as-yet-unfinished-and-unpublished

132. In a letter to Mary Fairbanks, quoted in Blair, *Mark Twain and Huck Finn*, p. 236.

Huckleberry Finn, Twain also reversed the order of contrasting scenes; and the effect is even more disturbing than in *A Tramp Abroad*. Huck's petty thefts in Chapter 17 anticipate an encounter with murderous river pirates on a sinking steamboat; in Chapter 19, the boy's blissful description of life on the Mississippi acts as an ironic introduction to the outrageous frauds perpetuated by the king and duke on the land; the burlesque of the existential "Hamlet's Soliloquy" in Chapter 21 offers a sly contrast to the cold-blooded killing of Boggs by Colonel Sherburn. The finest example of unexpected juxtaposition is Huck's enraptured description of the absurdly and hypocritically decorated Grangerford parlor in Chapter 17, with the no-nonsense account of all the carnage left by the feud in the subsequent chapter. Such bitter, uncompromising satire would have been wasted in a book just for boys.

Had Twain intended the novel for children, as his critics maintained, would it not have been wiser to publish excerpts from *Huckleberry Finn* in *St. Nicholas* rather than in *Century*? Not everyone saw it as a children's book. The San Francisco *Chronicle* suggested in its March 29, 1885, review "that upon nine boys out of ten much of the humor, as well as the pathos, would be lost. The more general knowledge one has the better he is fitted to appreciate this book, which is a remarkably careful sketch of life along the Mississippi river forty years ago." It did not provide what children usually expected of their reading. "When a boy under 16 reads a book he wants adventure and plenty of it," the *Chronicle* insisted. "He doesn't want any moral thrown in or even implied; the elaborate jokes worked out with so much art, which are Mark Twain's specialty, are wasted upon him. All the character sketches go for nothing with this eager reader, who demands a story."

Frontispiece from *Little Men* by Louisa May Alcott, 1871. *Courtesy Library of Congress.*

Twain, however, was delighted when children did read and enjoy the story, and he never hesitated to pass it on to young people. He readily presented little Elsie Leslie, the child actress who played the Prince *and* the Pauper onstage in 1889, with an autographed copy of

Huckleberry Finn, assuring her that it was "one of the stateliest poems of modern times."[133] If it was good enough for his own girls, it was good enough for others. "When *Huck Finn* was flung out of the Concord Public Library twenty-one years ago," he proudly recalled in 1906, "a number of letters of sympathy and indignation reached me—mainly from children, I am obliged to admit—and I kept some of them so that I might reread them now and then and apply them as a salve to my soreness." He was amused in particular by one little girl's remarks:

> I am eleven years old, and I live on a farm near Rockville, Maryland. Once this winter we had a boy to work for us named John. We lent him *Huck Finn* to read, and one night he let his clothes out of the window and left in the night. The last we heard from him he was out in Ohio; and father says if we had lent him *Tom Sawyer* to read he would not have stopped on this side of the ocean.

Twain happily reported that the child "gives me something more of a dig than even the library had done."[134] Not even the censors could keep *Huckleberry Finn* out of the hands of children. Twain felt vindicated when Webster gave him a year after its publication a check for $54,500 in royalties for *Huckleberry Finn*, including his original $1,500 investment in the project. "Once more I experienced a new birth," he said. "I have been born more times than anybody except Krishna, I suppose."[135] Or Huck Finn.

Twain eventually came to think as his public did about the book. In July 1889, he jotted in his notebook an idea for a story, "Creatures of Fiction," in which Mother Goose, Hans Brinker, Tom Bailey, Uncle Remus's Little Boy, Mowgli the Jungle Boy, the Prince and the Pauper, and other prominent children's book characters would join Tom and Huck in some unnamed storybook land.[136] It is not known what form this tale might have taken, for Twain never wrote it. Nevertheless, this winsome picture of the two boys as classic children's book characters persists, and particularly with people who have never read *Huckleberry Finn*.[137] However true this popular image may be to *Tom Sawyer*, it is false to *Huckleberry Finn*.

133. Quoted in Jane Douglass, *Trustable and Preshus Friends* (New York: Harcourt Brace Jovanovich, 1977), p. 53.

134. Dictated April 10, 1906, Mark Twain Papers.

135. *Mark Twain in Eruption*, pp. 169–70.

136. See *Mark Twain's Hannibal, Huck and Tom*, edited by Walter Blair (Berkeley and Los Angeles: University of California, 1969), p. 113.

137. James Joyce, for example. While working on *Finnegans Wake* (1939), the Irish author instructed his brother's stepson to take some notes on *Huckleberry Finn* for use in the new

Even when some critics abandoned the boy, Twain remained loyal to poor abused Huck. "The only one of my own books that I can ever read with pleasure," he told the New York *World* (May 31, 1891), "is . . . *Huck Finn*, and partly because I know the dialect is true and good. I didn't know I could read even that till I read it aloud last Summer to one of my little ones who was sick. My children all read *The Prince and the Pauper*, but none of the others." He admitted to the Johannesburg (South Africa) *Star* (May 18, 1896) that he was having such a good time reading *Huckleberry Finn* aloud that his daughter Jean scolded him for laughing at something he had written himself.

Not all of the adventures of Huckleberry Finn made it into *Adventures of Huckleberry Finn*. Twain was correcting proofs for the novel when he began a sequel describing Tom and Huck's "howling adventures amongst the Indians, over in the Territory." On July 6, 1884, he instructed Webster to send him "several other *personal narratives* of life and adventure out yonder on the plains and in the mountains, if you can run across them—especially life among the Indians. Send what you can find. I mean to send Huck Finn out there" (p. 265). He worked from time to time on "Huck Finn and Tom Sawyer Among the Indians" during the summers at Quarry Farm between 1884 and 1889, and went so far as to have what he had finished of the story typeset on the Paige compositor and printed; then he abruptly stopped. He had written 18,000 words, but could not bear to explain the exact meaning of four pegs in the ground and a bloody scrap of a woman's gown in an abandoned Indian camp. It was hard enough to describe the Grangerford–Shepherdson feud, but rape was something he just could not handle.[138] Other ideas for further adventurers came to him on the journey back to Hannibal in January 1885 on his "Twins of Genius" tour, inspired by the "slathers of ancient friends, and such worlds of talk, and such

---

novel. "I need to know something about it," he wrote on August 8, 1937. "I never read it and have nobody to read it to me and it takes too much time with all I am doing"; in *Selected Letters of James Joyce*, edited by Richard Ellmann (New York: Viking, 1975), p. 387. Not only the similarity between the names "Finnegan" and "Finn" but also the river and the raft appealed to the novelist as appropriate symbols to be worked into his stream-of-unconsciousness narrative. However, the young man did not do exactly as Joyce asked; the references to Twain, Tom, and Huck in *Finnegans Wake* suggest *Tom Sawyer* rather than Huckleberry Finn.

138. Almost at the last moment on July 24, 1884, Twain instructed Webster to change the title page of *Huckleberry Finn* from "Time, forty years ago" to "Time, forty or fifty years ago" (p. 271). He wanted the date to conform with that of the new story. "Huck Finn and Tom Sawyer Among the Indians" was first published in *Life* (December 20, 1968), pp. 33–48; and later in Blair's *Mark Twain's Hannibal, Huck and Tom*, and in *Huck Finn and Tom Sawyer Among the Indians and Other Unfinished Stories*, edited by Walter Blair and Dahlia Armon (Berkeley and Los Angeles: University of California Press, 1989). This story should not be confused with Clement Wood's *More Adventures of Huckleberry Finn* (New York and Cleveland: World, 1940), which is a completely original novel about the boys' travels in Indian Territory.

deep enjoyment of it!"[139] He thought of having Tom and Huck steal a ride on a steamboat all the way downriver to New Orleans; Tom's brother Sid and Jim's little deaf-mute daughter were to be in it, too, as well as an old liar who was to tell impossible tales about his world travels. He also considered "a kind of Huck Finn narrative—let him ship as cabin boy and another boy as cub pilot—and so put the great river and its bygone ways into history in form of a story." He also wanted to "put Huck and Tom and Jim through my Missouri campaign, and give a chapter to *The Century*. Union soldier accosts Tom and says his name is U. S. Grant."[140] Of all of these notes, the only one that became a finished tale was the latter one, as the straightforwardly autobiographical "The Private History a Campaign That Failed," published in *Century Magazine* (December 1885) with pictures by Kemble.

Twain really had no idea what direction another book about Tom and Huck might take. When Rudyard Kipling interviewed him at Quarry Farm the summer of 1889, Twain mentioned, "I have had a notion of writing the sequel to *Tom Sawyer* in two ways. In one I would make him rise to great honor and go to Congress, and in the other I should hang him. Then the friends and enemies of the book could take their choice." He told Kipling that "that would be a good way of ending the book, because, when you come to think of it, neither religion, training, nor education avails anything against the force of circumstances that drive a man. Suppose we took the next four-and-twenty years of Tom Sawyer's life, and gave a little joggle to the circumstances that controlled him. He would, logically and according to the joggle, turn out a rip or an angel." But Kipling protested this double-barreled scheme, insisting that Tom Sawyer "isn't your property any more. He belongs to us."[141]

Not until 1893 did Twain finally publish another Tom Sawyer story. He was now friends with Mary Mapes Dodge, the author of *Hans Brinker* and editor of *St. Nicholas*, the most prestigious children's magazine of its day; and when she asked him for a book she might serialize in her monthly, he immediately began *Tom Sawyer Abroad*. He needed the money, and he finished the story in two months, because "the humor flows as easily as the adventures and surprises."[142]

139. In a letter to Olivia L. Clemens, January 14, 1885, *The Love Letters of Mark Twain*, p. 228.

140. In *Mark Twain's Notebooks and Journals*, vol. 3, pp. 88–91 and 105.

141. See "Rudyard Kipling on Mark Twain," New York *Herald*, August 17, 1890; reprinted as "An Interview with Mark Twain," *From Sea to Sea* (New York: Doubleday & McClure, 1899), pp. 174–75.

142. In a letter to Mary Mapes Dodge, quoted in *The Adventures of Tom Sawyer; Tom Sawyer Abroad; Tom Sawyer, Detective*, p. 246. See also O. M. Brack, Jr., "Mark Twain in Knee Pants: The Expurgation of *Tom Sawyer Abroad*," *Proof*, 1972, pp. 145–51.

And there was no question that it, unlike *Huckleberry Finn*, was written specifically for boys and girls. "I tried to leave the improprieties all out," he proudly said; "if I didn't Mrs. Dodge can scissor them out." Twain even thought that should *Tom Sawyer Abroad* prove successful, then he could easily turn out a long line of Tom Sawyer books by just "adding 'Africa,' 'England,' 'Germany,' etc., to the title page of each successive volume of the series," in the manner of such popular boys' travelogues as those about Horace Scudder's Bodleys, Hezekiah Butterworth's Zig-Zag Club, and Charles Asbury's Young Yachters and Knockabout Club, all undistinguished literature but best-sellers in their day.

Twain, however, was not prepared to limit the appeal of *Tom Sawyer Abroad* to children only. It was coyly advertised as suitable for any boy from eight to

Tom, Huck, and Jim. Illustration by Dan Beard,
Tom Sawyer Abroad, *St. Nicholas*, February 1894.
Courtesy Library of Congress.

eighty. "I conceive that the right way to write a story for boys," he argued, "is to write so that it will not only interest boys but will strongly interest any man who has ever been a boy. That immensely enlarges the audience." Mrs. Dodge serialized the book in *St. Nicholas*, from November 1893 through April 1894, with drawings by Twain's favorite illustrator, Dan Beard, who had so successfully drawn the controversial pictures for *A Connecticut Yankee in King Arthur's Court,* but only after she had "scissored out" what she considered the story's numerous improprieties for a juvenile audience. Not even the prissy Gilder was as cautious as this lady editor: Drunkenness, death, and religious slurs were not allowed; Tom and Huck could not swear, slobber, or even sicken in her respectable journal. Dodge removed a long passage from Chapter 8, about Roman Catholic priests' "cussing." And she did not stop there. She even demanded that Beard put shoes on the characters! Miss Watson or Olivia Clemens could not have been a more demanding editor than Mrs. Dodge was. She did not merely censor, she rewrote the text. Beard recalled that Twain was furious with the results and stormed into the *St. Nicholas* office. "Any editor to whom I submit my manuscripts has an undisputed right to delete anything to which he objects," he cried, "but God Almighty Himself has no right to put words in my mouth that I never used!" [143] The resulting book of *Tom Sawyer Abroad* (1894) was a hodgepodge of Dodge's edited and Twain's approved texts.

The emasculation of Tom, Huck, and Twain did nothing for the already puerile narrative. Just as "Huck Finn and Tom Sawyer Among the Indians" made fun of James Fenimore Cooper's romantic idea of the Indian as the "noble savage," *Tom Sawyer Abroad* burlesqued Jules Verne's *Five Weeks in a Balloon* (1869), and both stories were wearying fun. Tom, Huck, and Jim's encounters with lions and Arabs in unlikely locales for these Missourians are as absurd as any of Tom Sawyer's "stretchers." Even Twain recognized how flat the writing was, how uninspired and hopeless the tale was: Without warning, he arbitrarily ended the intended world tour when Aunt Polly demands they come back home to St. Petersburg.

Having satirized Verne's science fiction in *Tom Sawyer Abroad*, Twain was ready to capitalize on the current craze for Arthur Conan Doyle's Sherlock Holmes stories in "Tom Sawyer, Detective."[144] "It is delightful work and a delightful subject," he bragged about the new story to Olivia on November 10,

143. Daniel Carter Beard, *Hardly a Man Is Now Alive* (New York: Doubleday, Doran, 1939), p. 344.

144. Back in 1876, Twain parodied both Jules Verne and detective stories in *A Murder, a Mystery, and a Marriage* (New York: W. W. Norton, 2001).

1893. "The story tells itself" (p. 277). Again Twain was cautious about his audience; he said the new tale "is really written for grown folk, though I expect young folk to read it, too." However, he had learned his lesson: He published "Tom Sawyer, Detective" in *Harper's Magazine* (August and September 1896) with pictures by Arthur Burdett Frost, rather than in *Harper's Round Table*, the firm's children's magazine. It was based on the mystery of a seventeenth-century pastor who had been falsely accused and executed for the murder of a servant from Denmark. Twain merely transferred it to the banks of the Mississippi of the 1840s. Unfortunately, the story had little to recommend it beyond the encouraging opportunity of having Huck play Dr. Watson to Tom's Sherlock Holmes, much as they were Sancho Panza and Don Quixote in *Huckleberry Finn*. The basic problem with stories like *Tom Sawyer Abroad* and "Tom Sawyer, Detective" was Twain's injudicious attempts to capitalize on currently popular forms by forcing his well-known characters to adapt to genres with which they are not compatible. Why were Tom, Huck, and Jim wandering off to Egypt in a balloon?

Huck, Tom, and Aunt Polly. Illustration by A. B. Frost, "Tom Sawyer, Detective," *Harper's Monthly*, August 1896.
Courtesy Library of Congress.

Not surprisingly, the reviews of *Tom Sawyer Abroad* were generally poor. "This book has a lame and impotent conclusion, and is far from showing its author at his best," said the London *Literary World* (May 4, 1894). "The humour is genuine and characteristic, but it is thin," judged the London *Saturday Review* (May 19, 1894). "*Tom Sawyer Abroad* will come as a grievous disappointment to admirers of *The Adventures of Tom Sawyer* or his friend Huckleberry Finn," warned the *Athenaeum* (May 26, 1895). "Mark Twain has often proved that he has the gift of being amusing; it is a pity that he should squander himself on such a book as this." Later Twain combined the two stories with some old material to make the one-volume *Tom Sawyer Abroad; Tom Sawyer, Detective; and Other Stories* (1896); and the reviews were just as bad as before. *St. James' Gazette* (December 31, 1896) called the book "a vastly unpleasing tale—extravagant, incredible, not at all amusing."

Before the century was up, Twain was a victim of his own success. He had given his novice publishing house an enormous boost by beating out the Century Company for the opportunity to publish the *Personal Memoirs of Ulysses S. Grant*, issued as a subscription book in two volumes in 1885 and 1886. It was an enormous success: Twain bragged that his firm paid the largest royalty check up to that time, made out for $200,000 to Grant's widow; he later framed it with another for $150,000 and hung them up in his home. Mrs. Grant's entire earnings from the book reached $400,000, far greater than Twain earned from any of his books. It was obvious to Twain that being a publisher was far more lucrative than being a writer. The April 1887 profit statement from Charles L. Webster and Company showed that Twain was entitled to $93,481.34 for Grant's memoirs, but only $3,227.44 for *Huckleberry Finn*.[145] Ironically, although *Huckleberry Finn* was a national bestseller, none of the books that Twain wrote *and* published himself did any better financially than did those issued by other houses.

Mark Twain. Wood-engraved frontispiece, *The Book Buyer*, October 1890.
Courtesy Picture Collection, New York Public Library, Astor, Lenox, and Tilden Foundations.

The history of Charles L. Webster and Company was an embarrassment of miscalculations. And Twain was as much to blame as Webster. Hoping to strike oil again and again and again in the same field, they put out a steady stream of memoirs by Civil War generals. They also got Mrs. George Armstrong Custer to write about her late husband, but their biggest blunder was an authorized biography of Pope Leo XIII. Twain recklessly believed that every Roman Catholic would have to buy a copy. It barely broke even. Leo Tolstoy and Walt Whitman shared space with Twain on the Webster list, and Robert Louis Stevenson approached Twain about becoming his publisher, too; but most of the Webster writers and books have long been forgotten. The business expanded far too quickly and wasted its capital in such dubious projects as Stedman's *Library of American Literature*. They paid Henry Ward Beecher a hefty advance for an autobiography

145. See Frederick Anderson and Hamlin Hill, "How Sam Clemens Became Mark Twain's Publisher: A Study of the James R. Osgood Contracts," *Proof*, 1972, p. 143.

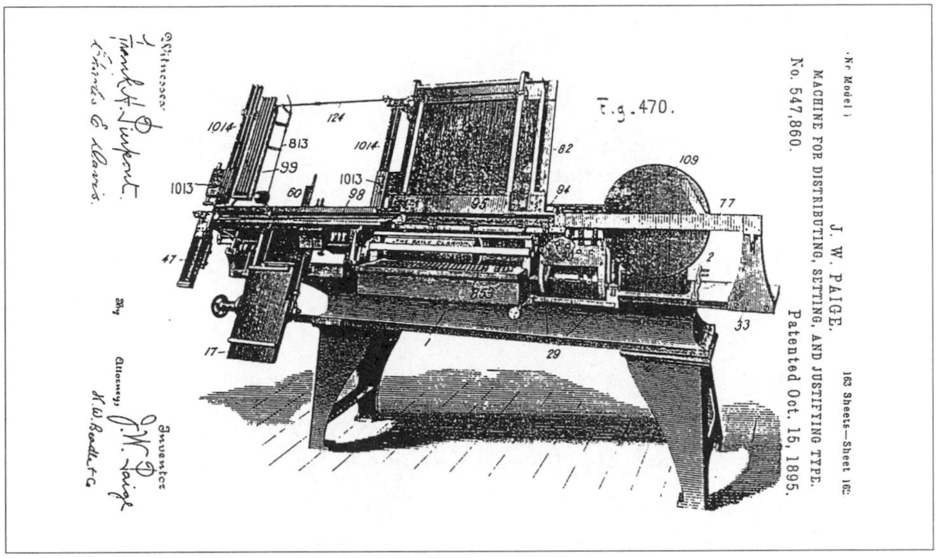

J. W. Paige's patent drawing for a machine for distributing, setting, and justifying type, October 15, 1895.
Courtesy Library of Congress.

he never lived to finish, and a bookkeeper embezzled $25,000 from the firm. Also, the country was moving away from subscription books. A new director of Webster and Company unloaded that portion of the business in 1893 and steered it into traditional trade publishing.

Nothing helped. The stock market crash of June 1893 sent the country again into economic panic. The bank finally called in its loans on April 18, 1894, and Webster and Company went into voluntary bankruptcy. The firm owed $160,000. The collapse of the publishing house as well as the depletion of $100,000 through his disastrous investments in the impractical Paige compositor left Twain broke. "I had two-thirds interest in the publishing firm, whose capital I furnished," he explained to his nephew Samuel E. Moffett in "Mark Twain to Pay All" (San Francisco *Examiner*, August 17, 1895), "and if the firm had prospered I should have expected to collect two-thirds of the profits. As it is I expect to pay all the debts. My partner has no resources, and I don't look for assistance from him." He said that the company's chief creditor was Olivia Clemens; the firm owed her $70,000. "In satisfaction of this great claim," her husband told Moffett, "she has taken nothing, except to avail herself of the opportunity of retaining control of the copyrights of my books, which for many easily understood reasons of which financial ones are the least we do not desire to see in the hands of strangers."

A new friend, Henry H. Rogers, the ruthless vice-president of the Standard

Oil Company and one of the wealthiest men in the world, was a great admirer of Twain's work and offered to straighten out his finances. But Twain refused to declare bankruptcy. He was determined to do exactly as Sir Walter Scott had done in his day and pay back every penny. "The law recognizes no mortgage on a man's brain, and the merchant who has given up all he has may take advantage of the rules of insolvency and start again for himself," he explained to Moffett. "But I am not a businessman, and honor is a harder master than the law. It cannot compromise for less than one hundred cents on the dollar, and its debts never outlaw."

Twain now identified his relationship with Webster and Company with that between Sir Walter Scott and Ballantyne Brothers. "In his successful effort to pay off the vast debt of $600,000," Twain mentioned to the Seattle *Post-Intelligencer* (August 14, 1895), "he killed himself by overwork. No other author could have accomplished such a feat, even at the sacrifice of his own life." Twain had other plans. "Apparently I've got to mount the lecture platform next fall or starve," he reluctantly admitted to Rogers in February 1895.[146] He turned to Major Pond to handle all the negotiations as he had done back in 1884 and 1885. Twain estimated that it would take him four years to pay off his debts, requiring two lecture seasons in America, one in Europe, and another around the world. Advertised as the "greatest lecture tour of the century," it kept him, now a man nearing sixty, on the road from July 1895 to July 1896, five of these months traveling through Australia, New Zealand, India, and South Africa. This time, however, he took his wife and daughter Clara to keep him company. In all he gave 140 performances, and the tour was a triumph. As many as 4,200 people saw him in a night, as they did in Cleveland. The Portland *Oregonian* (August 11, 1895) said that young and old were eager to hear Mark Twain, because "the name is as familiar to the rising generation as it was when he first made his appearance to the literary world." They also feared this might well be their last opportunity to see him in person. He was not in the best of health, because of his recent troubles, but his spirits were good. He even granted interviews to reporters, often in bed. "Lecturing is gymnastics, chest-expander, medicine, mind healer, blues destroyer, all in one," he wrote Moffett as he sailed off for Europe. "I am twice as well as I was when I started out."[147] After the American leg of his travels, he realized that it might take him only three years to get out of debt; and the journey yielded his final travel book, *Following the Equator* (1897). The New York *Times* reported on March 12, 1898, that Twain had successfully paid all his creditors in full.

146. In *Mark Twain's Correspondence with Henry Huttleston Rogers 1893–1909*, edited by Lewis Leary (Berkeley and Los Angeles: University of California Press, 1969), p. 129.

147. Quoted in Pond, *Eccentricities of Genius*, p. 225.

The "Tour Around the World" was a financial success and increased Mark Twain's international prestige a thousandfold. Not only was he in the press constantly, but the papers turned him into a hero. The New York *Times* (October 13, 1900) called him "the bravest author in all literature." Since this time he did not have to share the platform with anyone else, Twain devised the "Morals Lecture," pulling together several selections from various works which reflected on the same theme. At first it contained nothing from *Huckleberry Finn*, just an excerpt from Chapter 1 of his new book *Tom Sawyer Abroad*, the discussion between Tom, Huck, and Jim about the crusades. Reporters cautiously suggested that the program did not quite live up to their expectations, and Twain too was unhappy with his performance. Then Olivia Clemens mentioned to Pond "that too much humor tired an audience with laughing." Her husband "took the hint and worked in three or four pathetic stories that made the entertainment perfect."

He made revisions of several chapters in the first volume of the new 1893 printing of the Tauchnitz Continental edition of *Huckleberry Finn*, a smaller, more compact version than the American.[148] He settled on including "Smallpox and a Lie Save Jim" from Chapter 16 of *Huckleberry Finn*, as an example of how early training shapes one's conscience. He then tried out "a new entertainment, blending pathos with humor with unusual continuity," on July 23, at the Metropolitan Opera House in Minneapolis. "It was about as big a night as 'Mark' ever had to my knowledge," said Pond in *Eccentricities of Genius*. "The 'show' is a triumph, and 'Mark' will never again need a running mate to make him satisfactory to everybody" (p. 206). The Minneapolis *Tribune* reported the next day that "without doubt the best story, and the one which the audience listened to with hushed attention, was the pathetic struggle with [Huck's] conscience over his aiding to liberty runaway Darky Jim. . . . one of the prettiest pictures of ante-emancipation life on the Mississippi that has ever been penned." The Minneapolis *Journal* (July 24, 1895) agreed: "Possibly the best of all was the story of Huck Finn helping the negro Jim to escape from slavery. There was a humorously pathetic tone to the story of Huck Finn's struggles with his conscience which would not let him rest easy either when he was endeavoring to hide or betray the slave whom he was aiding to escape to freedom." The Bombay *Gazette* (January 25, 1895) said that Twain demonstrated in *Huckleberry Finn* "the Virgilian sense of tears in human things, and he knows the acute suffering of the soul." "The manner in which the flight of Huck from the brutalities of his drunken father, and of Jim from slavery, on a raft floating

148. The edited pages are reproduced in the 1988 University of California edition of *Huckleberry Finn*, pp. 809–41.

down the Mississippi, as recounted was initmitable," reported the Calcutta *Statesman* (February 11, 1896); "and it was easy to see that when Mark Twain had once thoroughly launched his listeners into the subject, he might, if the tale had taken that direction, moved some of them, at least, to tears as well as laughter. For, though the incident was presented to them by one who is a professed jester, the humour of it was strictly subordinated to its pathos." On July 27, in Winnipeg, Manitoba, he tried "King Sollermun," which had been so popular back on the "Twins of Genius" tour; but he never read it again on or off the tour. He vowed never again to go on the road. Relieved to be finally out of debt, he turned down Major Pond's offer of $50,000 to give another 125 lectures across America the following year.

Mark Twain may have retired from the lecture circuit, but Huck Finn was soon on the boards. On January 28, 1902, Twain contracted with the powerful theatrical syndicate Klaw & Erlanger, who had so successfully staged *Ben Hur* in 1899, to produce a lavish musical dramatization of *Huckleberry Finn*. Twain had been trying to get *Tom Sawyer* on the stage ever since he wrote the story. Twain was not really a playwright and had some peculiar ideas for a production, such as having Tom and Huck played by young women. Webster failed to place the four-act dramatization Twain had been working on in 1884, while *Huckleberry Finn* was in production. On May 28, 1900, Twain contracted with Paul Kester and his brother Vaughan to dramatize and stage *Tom Sawyer* by June 1, 1900, but their play was never produced in Twain's lifetime and not registered for copyright until 1914. Frustrated with their failure to come through on time, Twain put his faith in Klaw & Erlanger. They paid him an advance of $1,500 with 10 percent of the net receipts of the show, and assigned Charles B. Dillingham to produce it.[149] Although advertised as *Mark Twain's Huckleberry Finn*, it was neither Mark Twain's nor *Huckleberry Finn*. The producers hired a minor Southern playwright, Lee Arthur, to write the script. "It was love's labor," he told the St. Louis *Republic* (October 12, 1902). "The manuscript wrote itself, and the only thing I regret was that I was not able to incorporate in it all the good things in the book. . . . I defy any one not thoroughly acquainted with the book to tell which belong in the manuscript and which I put in there." And he put plenty of his own things in it. The three-act production was notable less for its story than for its elaborate scenes, including the whitewashing of Aunt Polly's fence, the raid on a temperance picnic by Tom Sawyer's Gang, a swimming-hole scene, and a boys' circus with Tom Sawyer as ringmas-

149. See Brooks McNamara, "*Huckleberry Finn* on Stage: A Mark Twain Letter in the Shubert Archive," *The Passing Show*, Fall 1991, p. 2.

THE CAST

No. 70 Tuesday Night. Nov. 11

MESSRS. KLAW & ERLANGER

Present a Dramatization of Mark Twain's Famous Story

"Huckleberry Finn"

By Mark Twain and Lee Arthur.

With music, except otherwise indicated, composed, selected and arranged by Frederick Solomon.

Staged under direction of Ben Teal.

Business direction of Edwin H. Price.

Program Continued.

CAST OF CHARACTERS.

Huckleberry Finn, known as "Huck"	Arthur Dunn
Tom Sawyer, Huck's Pal	Jack Slavin
Joe Harper, the Cry Baby	Master Jack Ryan
Ben Rogers, the Smart Aleck	James Devlin
Billy Fisher, known as "Fatty"	Master Archie Anderson
Sid Sawyer, the tattle-tale	Master Webb Raum
Judge Thatcher	Charles W. Stokes
Mr. Walters	Samuel Reed
The Duke { Two Crooks }	Chas. Stanley
The Dauphin { Two Crooks }	Wm. Sampson
Mr. Doughton	W. C. Kelley
Silas Finn, Huck's father	A. T. Earnest
Hannibal Johnson, known as " No 'count Johnson"	E. J. Connelly
Mr. Lawrence	Robert Harold
Jim, a negro slave	Charles K. French
Pete, a negro boy	H. Van Cleve

Program Continued

Johnnie Russell	Hughie Flaherty
Amy Lawrence	Flora Parker
Becky Thatcher, the Judge's niece	Leonie Darmon
Mary Ann	Julie A. Herne
Aunt Polly	Marie Bingham
Widow Douglass	Mrs. Weston
Palmyra { Reception Committee of Ladies Temperance Union. }	Virginia Ross
Agatha	Lizette LeBaron
Cresy	Jane Dara
Mrs. Lawrence	Mabelle de Rham

Playmates of Huck and Tom.
Members of the Temperance Union and Villagers.

N. B. The dramatists have drawn on the stories of "Huckleberry Finn" and "Tom Sawyer" for the scenes, incidents and characters of this play.

Program Continued

Act I—Scene I—REAR OF AUNT POLLY'S HOME,

Musical Numbers—A—Entrance of Pierrots (Galop). B—Pierrot Dance. C—"I want to be a drummer in the Band." (Words by Matt. C. Woodward. Music by Silvio Heine)—Mr. Dunn, assisted by the Misses Beatrice Walsh, Lillian Rice, Edna McClure, Florence Carette, Nellie Harris, Lucille de Mendz, Angie Wiemars, Louise Elton, Lola Merrill, Babe Adams, Sallie Bergere, May O'Neill, Norine Williams, Geraldine Royal, Sadie Haynes, Edith Williams, Mabel Mordaunt. D—Stanton, the Giant Rooster. E—"When Little Tommy Sawyer saw The Circus." (Words by Matt. C. Woodward, Music by Ben. M Jerome) Mr. Slavin.

Scene II—THE OLD HAUNTED HOUSE, EVENING SAME DAY.

Musical Number—Serenade, "Good night, Lucindy."—Mr. Slavin and full Chorus.

Act II—Scene I—THE PICNIC GROUNDS, NOON, NEXT DAY.

Musical Numbers—Opening Chorus. The Temperance Union Band. Quartette "Courting".—Misses Parker and Darmon, Messrs. Dunn and Slavin. A—Children's Temperance Glee. B—Madrigal. A—Chorus of Flower Girls. B—Song—"The Sunflower and the Violet."—Miss Flora Parker and Chorus.

Act III—Scene I—McDOWELL'S CAVE. EVENING SAME DAY.

Musical Numbers—Opening Chorus and Tarantella. "Oh, Isn't It Fine to be Robbers." Specialties. "Animal's Convention." (Words and Music by Cole and Johnson)—Charles K. French and Chorus.

Scene II—COURT HOUSE SQUARE, NEXT MORNING.

Locale of Scenes and time of action, St. Petersburg, Mo. (now known as (Hannibal) sixty years ago.

Scenery by Ernest Gros. Mechanical Construction by P. J. McDonald. Light Effects by Harry Bissing. Dresses Designed by F. Richard Anderson. Wigs by Wm. Hepner.

EXECUTIVE STAFF FOR KLAW & ERLANGER

Frank Martineau,	Advance Representative	Wm. Hoover,	Mechanical Department
John Harding,	Musical Director	Wm. Price,	Master of Properties
Robert Harold,	Stage Manager	E. A. Weed,	Electrician
Julian Myers,	Assistant Stage Manager	Mrs. S. Sherwood.	Wardrobe Mistress

BEGINNING TUESDAY NIGHT, NOV. 11.
for balance of week,
Matinees Wednesday and Saturday.

MARK TWAIN'S "Huckleberry Finn"

Stage Version by Mark Twain and Lee Arthur.
Magnificently produced by Klaw and Erlanger.

ACTED BY A GREAT COMPANY OF 80 PEOPLE.

A NEW DEPARTURE IN THEATRICAL ENTERTAINMENT.

Seats on sale Friday, Nov. 7th. Applications for seats from out of town patrons will be filled in the order of their receipt.

WEDNESDAY AND THURSDAY, NOV. 19-20.

Francis Wilson in the Toreador.

From the program of the Klaw & Erlanger musical production of *Mark Twain's "Huckleberry Finn"* by Mark Twain and Arthur Lee, 1902.

Courtesy Billy Rose Theatre Collection, New York Public Library for the Performing Arts, Astor, Lenox, and Tilden Foundation.

ter. Huck and Tom were played by adults, Arthur Dunn and Jack Slavin (who earlier in the summer created the role of the Wizard in the 1902 musical extravaganza *The Wizard of Oz*); and to balance Tom's romance with Becky Thatcher, Huck was matched with Amy Lawrence. Although Jim had a part in the play, the script resembled *Tom Sawyer* more than it did *Huckleberry Finn* and took vast liberties with both. The contrived plot revolved around the suspicion that Huck and his father, "Silas Finn," are responsible for all the recent burglaries in town; after Tom and Huck thwart a scheme to kidnap the girls,

Amy Lawrence (Flora Parker) and chorus singing
"The Sunflower and the Violet" in the Klaw & Erlanger musical
production of *Mark Twain's "Huckleberry Finn,"* 1902.
Courtesy Billy Rose Theatre Collection, New York Public Library for the Performing Arts, Astor, Lenox, and Tilden Foundations.

the real crooks, the King and the Dauphin, are exposed. At least one member of the cast realized at the reading of the play "the ghastly proof that Mr. Erlanger had decided to debauch this classic by making it the frame on which to hang a musical comedy. Even with my vague knowledge of the theatre, I marvelled at the inconsistency of a chorus of forty white-satined pierrots assisting Huck Finn to sing a march entitled 'I Want to be a Drummer in the Band.' There were at least a dozen such assaults on dramatic license."[150]

Although credited as coauthor of the play with Arthur, Twain had little to do with it. He first heard the script in July 1902, and seemed happy enough with it to give Klaw & Erlanger permission to announce it as "Mark Twain's 'Huckleberry Finn' adapted for the stage by Mark Twain and Lee Arthur."[151] But one thing bothered him, and he advised Dillingham "that we must transpose Huck

150. Walter C. Kelly, *Of Me I Sing* (New York: Dial Press, 1953), p. 46. There were also several children in the cast, including Webb Raum as Sid Sawyer; he later changed his name to Clifton Webb.

151. In a letter to Klaw & Erlanger, July 27, 1902, *Mark Twain Journal*, Winter 1974.

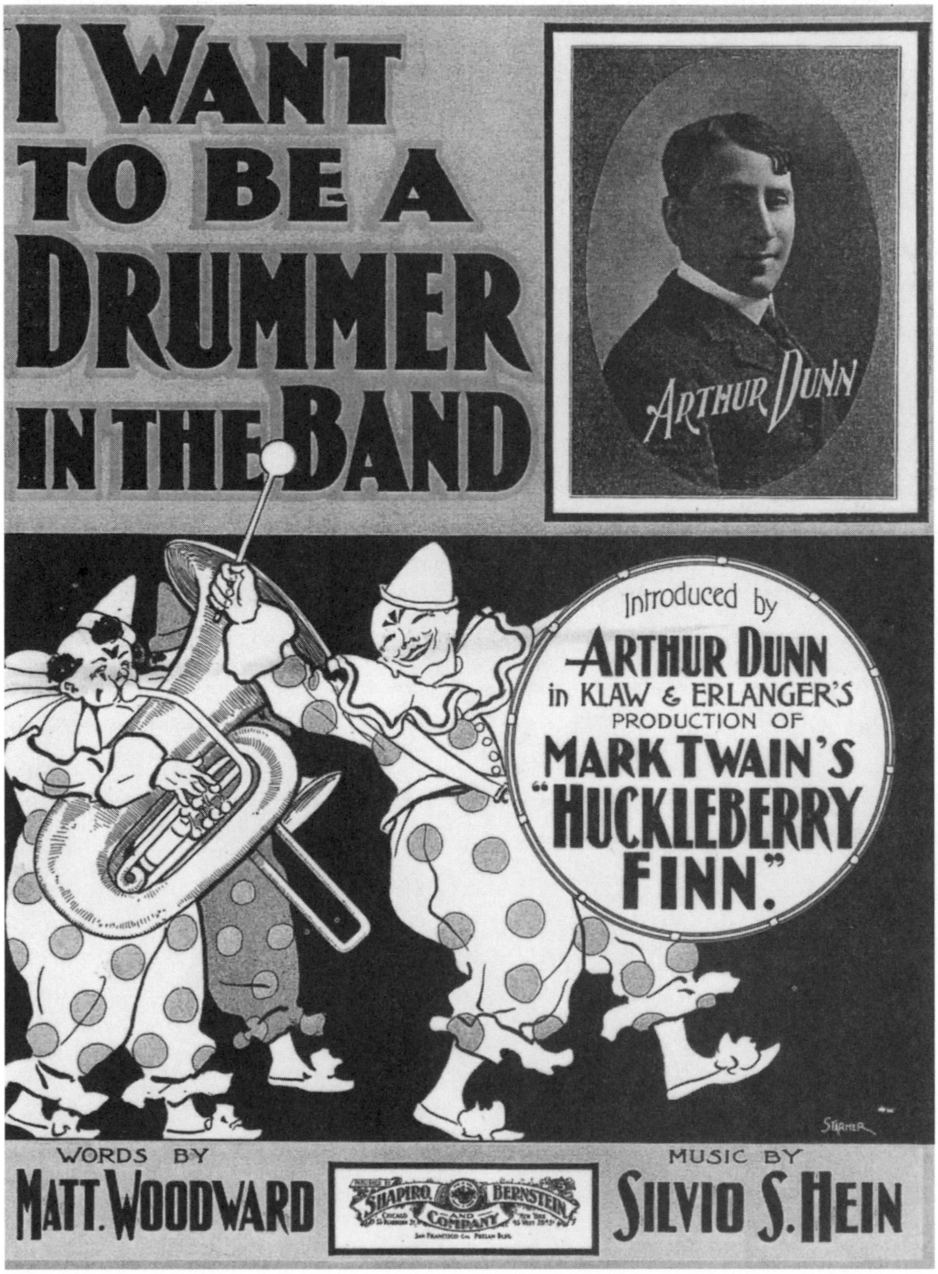

Sheet music cover of "I Want to be a Drummer in the Band," words by Matt Woodward, music by Silvio S. Hein. A song in the musical production of *Huckleberry Finn*, 1902.

Courtesy Music Division, Library of Congress.

and Tom and give each his own name and character." He said that the audience and the papers would object to seeing Tom dressed up like Huck and saying and doing things Huck should be saying and doing and vice versa. "There is no need to change the *title* of the play," he added. "In the books Huck is quite as important as Tom. They are foils to show each other off." Dillingham reminded him "that plays made from books have little in common with the book excepting the title," and he saw no advantage in rewriting the script at that late date. He did ask Twain to attend a rehearsal in October, but the writer was too preoccupied with Olivia's failing health to take him up on the invitation. The play opened in Hartford at the Parson's Theatre on November 11, 1902, to generally favorable reviews. Twain conveniently declined attending, again owing to the illness of his wife. Howells too was scheduled to appear, but he did not show up either. There is no record that Twain ever saw the play. He did ask Dillingham to correct the impression in the press that *he* wrote the play. The lavish production with eighty people in the cast, advertised as the largest company of the season, was far too expensive to maintain long. It closed in Baltimore after less than forty performances and before ever reaching Broadway.[152]

During the last years of his life, Twain had increasing difficulty completing anything. Much of his writing became therapy, never intended to be published or even finished. Certain things troubled him so that he had to get them out of his system. He intermittently worked on his autobiography. This long and rambling exercise in recollection and revenge begain as a collection of miscellaneous sketches in the 1870s; he dictated other memories to a series of secretaries in the latter part of his life. In a sense, he had been writing his autobiography all his life, inventing some incidents as he went along and perhaps

152. The influential trade paper the New York *Dramatic News* (November 29, 1902) condemned it as "a dreadful fiasco, the universal verdict of the entire press, as also the few patrons that paid their money in anticipation of witnessing a meritorious play from a noted author. 'It is a little bit of everything and not much of anything,' besides being extremely tiresome, without one redeeming feature." Twain could not have said it better himself. In 1951, Joshua Logan announced a Broadway musical, "Huck and Jim," with book and lyrics by Maxwell Anderson and music by Kurt Weill, to be directed by Reuben Mamoulian; when Weill died, he and Anderson had finished only five songs. Frank Loesser was then signed to provide the score; but the backers probably felt intimidated by a proposed but never produced MGM movie musical, so nothing came of the stage production. *Big River*, a musical comedy of *Huckleberry Finn* with songs by Roger Miller, opened on Broadway in 1984 and starred Daniel H. Jenkins as Huck and Ron Richardson as Jim. This respectful adaptation won seven Tony Awards including Best Musical. An opera based on *Huckleberry Finn*, composed by Hall Overton with librettist Judah Stampfer, was performed by the Juilliard Opera Center in New York in May 1971, with David Hall as Huck, John Seabury as Tom, and Willard White as Jim.

eventually actually believing them himself. He swore he would tell the truth, the whole truth, and nothing but the truth; but it was the autobiography of Mark Twain, after all, not that of Samuel Langhorne Clemens.[153] He informed the New York *Times* (May 27, 1899) that he intended the book to be published one hundred years after his death, as if he were literally speaking "from the grave," because he wanted to talk as freely and frankly as possible and there were plenty of old scores he wanted to settle. Some passages were too explosive for his contemporaries; but he published selections as "Chapters from My Autobiography" in *The North American Review* (September 7, 1906–December 1907) shortly before his death. Albert Bigelow Paine compiled *Mark Twain's Autobiography* from this mass of material after using what he wanted for his 1912 biography, and he published it posthumously in two volumes in 1924. Bernard DeVoto, Paine's successor as editor of the Mark Twain Estate, pulled together a good deal of previously unpublished material as *Mark Twain in Eruption* (1940). Twain's daughter Clara was cautious and protective of this material, but gave Charles Neider permission to prepare *The Autobiography of Mark Twain* (1959) from both published and unpublished sources in a conventionally chronological order. Michael J. Kiskis collected the *North American* articles in 1990 as *Mark Twain's Own Autobiography*.

Illness and loss kept Twain from writing. Even more painful than his economic disasters was the sudden death of his beloved Susy, at age twenty-four, of spinal meningitis, on August 18, 1896. Her father could not bear to live in the place where she died, so the Clemenses closed up the Hartford house and eventually sold it in 1903. "No," he said, "I don't want to see it. It is peopled with spirits, not only of my own family, but of the old friends whose faces I used to see so often and who are now gone. Strangers come in with roughshod feet and walk over holy ground. No, I don't want to see inside the old house now."[154] When Susy died, he angrily wrote her mother, "You want me to believe it is a judicious, a charitable God that runs this world. Why, I could run it better."[155] The same bitterness tainted his later efforts, particularly his last major novel, *The Mysterious Stranger* (1916).

153. Not to be confused with *Mark Twain's (Burlesque) Autobiography* (1871).

154. Quoted in William A. Graham, "Mark Twain—Dean of Our Humorists," *Human Life*, May 1906, p. 1.

155. "It is an odious world," he wrote Olivia on August 29, 1896,"a horrible world—it is Hell; the true one, not the lying invention of the superstitious; and we have come to it from elsewhere to expiate our sins" (*Mark Twain's Letters*, vol. 2, p. 328).

The original chronicle of Young Satan little resembled the published version. Remarkably, what became *The Mysterious Stranger* was at first intended to be a Tom Sawyer story. It took place in St. Petersburg in the 1840s, not "Eseldorf" (literally "Assville"), Austria, in 1409; Satan Jr. was a chum of Tom and Huck Finn. "He was always doing miracles," Twain noted; "his pals knew they were miracles, the others thought them mysteries. . . . He is a good little devil; but swears, and breaks the Sabbath."[156] Among the proposed incidents in this late "bad boy's book" was the devil's conquest of the school bully, his romance with the town tomboy "Hellfire Hotchkiss," and his showing Tom and Huck around Hell one Sunday. The fragment that survives is a cross between an allegory and a parody of *Tom Sawyer*; only slowly, after a couple of false starts, did Twain reform this burlesque into his never-completed nihilistic fable *The Mysterious Stranger*.

Mark Twain. Color wood engraving by William Nicholson, *Twelve Portraits*, Second Series, 1902.
Courtesy Picture Collection, New York Public Library, the Astor, Lenox, and Tilden Foundations.

The pessimism of his later life may be found in nearly everything he wrote at this time. He did not care what he said or whom he told. He raged at the injustices of Man and God. "The contemplation of injustice in the world, whether from individual toward individual or country toward country, gradually modified his capacity to enjoy the bright side of life," his daughter Clara Clemens Gabrilowitsch confessed in "My Father," "and more and more he fell to brooding until his voice came to be 'a wail for the world's wrong'" (p. 22). He shocked Alice Hegan Rice, the author of *Mrs. Wiggs of the Cabbage Patch* (1901), with his ranting about the inequities of the universe while visiting Richard Watson Gilder in 1909. Their host felt obligated to take Rice aside and whisper, "Don't listen to that blasphemous and unhappy old man!"[157] Twain lost Livy and then

156. In a notebook entry of November 1898, quoted in Gibson, *The Mysterious Stranger* (Berkeley and Los Angeles: University of California Press, 1969), p. 428.

157. Quoted in Alice Hegan Rice, *The Inky Way* (New York: Appleton-Century, 1940), p. 80.

Jean. His wife had always been frail, and much of their wandering about the world in her final years was for her health. In April 1902, they bought a house in Tarrytown, New York, their first permanent residence in thirteen years; but the Clemenses never occupied it. They left for Italy in late 1903 in search of a warmer climate. Olivia died in Florence on June 5, 1904. It was a loss from which her husband never recovered. It may also have contributed to their daughter Jean's worsening epilepsy. She died suddenly in her morning bath at Stormfield, the mansion Twain built in Redding, Connecticut, of an apparent heart attack during a seizure. The last chapter he dictated for his autobiography was on Christmas Day 1909, the day after his daughter died.

Mark Twain died on April 21, 1910. He had become a wealthy man, leaving his daughter Clara his entire estate, said to be worth a half million dollars. He came to believe, as he wrote in Chapter 34 of *The Mysterious Stranger* (1916), "There is no God, no universe, no human race, no earthly life, no heaven, no hell. It is all a Dream—a grotesque and foolish dream. Nothing exists but You. And You are but a *Thought*—a vagrant Thought, a useless Thought, a homeless Thought, wandering forlorn among the empty eternities!" Yet to the public at large Mark Twain remained even in his last sad years the "Dean of American Humor," the "Prince of American Humorists," the celebrated creator of Tom Sawyer and Huckleberry Finn. He seemed always ready to give some bright, clever quip to the papers as he pursued a second career as an after dinner speaker. But his most bitter remarks about the "damned human race" he generally reserved only for private circulation.

He wrote in his notebook in March 1891, a few months after his mother died, the scheme for another book: "Huck comes back, sixty years old, from nobody knows where—and crazy. Thinks he is a boy again, and scans always every face for Tom and Becky, etc. Tom comes at last from . . . wandering the world and tends Huck, and together they talk of the old times, both are desolate, life has been a failure, all that was lovable, all that was beautiful is under the mold. They die together."[158] He revived this idea briefly in 1902, after his final trip to Hannibal. When the University of Missouri invited him to receive an honorary degree at the June commencement, he took advantage of the invitation as the perfect opportunity for him to go back home to gather more material for this story. The visit profoundly affected the town's most famous native son: He talked with old friends and countless reporters and stood "in the door of the old house I lived in when I whitewashed the fence fifty-three years ago . . . was photographed, with the crowd looking on"; and when he

158. In *Mark Twain's Notebooks and Journals*, vol. 3, p. 606.

spoke before a local club about his boyhood, he broke into tears when he mentioned his mother.[159] He made notes for a story set "fifty years later": "The Cold Spring—Jim has gone home—they can't find him—all railway tracks."[160] It may have been planned in two parts, the old times of Tom Sawyer's Gang contrasted with the reality of their failed lives on their reunion a half-century later. "I carried it as far as thirty-eight thousand words four years ago," he explained in 1906, "then destroyed it for fear I might some day finish it. Huck Finn was the teller of the story, and of course Tom Sawyer and Jim were the heroes of it. But I believed that that trio had done work enough in this world and were entitled to a permanent rest."[161]

Although Twain never recaptured the brilliance of *Huckleberry Finn* in any other story about Tom and Huck, the original sold handsomely into the twentieth century.[162] Critical recognition of the novel's importance was slow and steady, despite reluctance from some literary circles. "Although his name is a household word in all places where the English language is spoken, and in many where it is not," said Charles Miner Thompson in "Mark Twain as an Interpreter of American Character" (*Atlantic Monthly*, April 1897), "he has never been accorded any serious critical notice" (p. 447). That was no surprise, if one is to believe Thompson's comments: "But his style,—which he has improved steadily,—even when correct, is technically without distinction. . . . he is singularly devoid of any aptitude for construction. . . . No, he is not a great or skillful writer. . . . Neither is Mark Twain—bold as the assertion may seem—a great humorist or a great wit." However, Huck Finn was "the best of Mark Twain's creations" who "has the good fortune . . . of being the hero of his originator's best book. In that wild, youthful, impossible Odyssey, the record of his voyage on a frail raft down the strong Mississippi, he assumes in a manner epic proportions" (p. 446).

"The great American novel" was what Scottish writer Andrew Lang, now known for his fairy books, called *Huckleberry Finn* in "The Art of Mark Twain"

159. See Meltzer, *Mark Twain Himself*, p. 233; and Blair, *Mark Twain's Hannibal, Huck and Tom*, p. 17.

160. Quoted in Blair, *Mark Twain's Hannibal, Huck and Tom*, p. 17.

161. In *Mark Twain in Eruption*, p. 199. Howells hazily recollected in *My Mark Twain* that, although Twain later denied it, he showed Howells a few chapters of a story "laid in a Missouri town, and the characters such as he had known in boyhood" (p. 90). Their letters suggest that this uncompleted work was the half-finished novel mentioned in 1906, and in *Mark Twain's Hannibal, Huck and Tom*, pp. 18–20.

162. According to Blair in *Mark Twain and Huck Finn* (p. 371), more than 10 million copies of *Huckleberry Finn* had been sold by 1960. That estimate did not include the sales of foreign editions, in at least thirty languages, which have appeared since 1885.

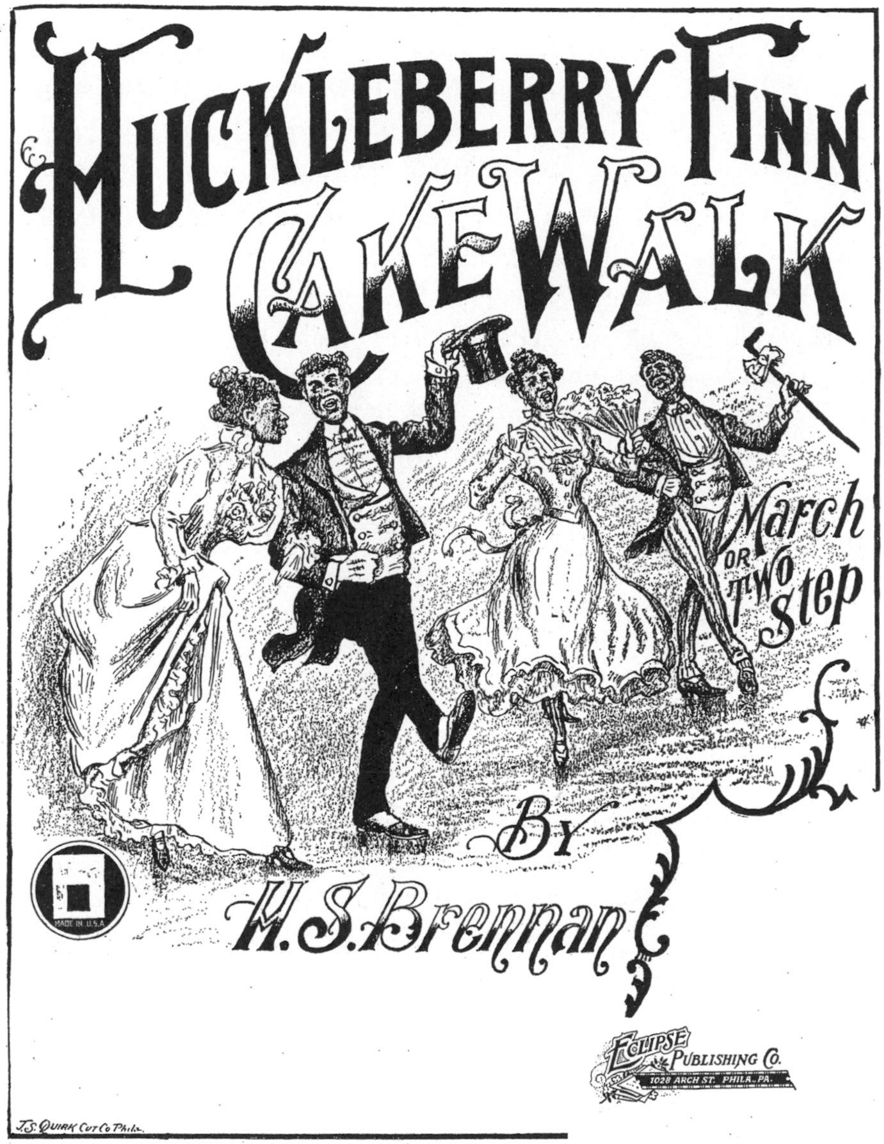

Sheet music cover of "Huckleberry Finn Cake Walk"
by H. S. Brennan, 1900.
Private collection.

(*Illustrated London News*, February 14, 1891, p. 222). *The Independent* (July 23, 1896) agreed that it was Twain's "masterpiece" (p. 19). "We are suspicious of the middle-aged person who has not read *Huckleberry Finn*," said the Philadelphia *Public Ledger* on June 16, 1896; "we envy the young person who has it still in store." Brander Matthews predicted in *The Book Buyer* (January 1897), "I do not think it will take a century or take three generations before we Americans generally discover how great a book *Huckleberry Finn* really is, how keen its vision of character, how close its observations of life, how sound its philosophy" (pp. 978–79). William Archer declared in his study *America Today: Observations and Reflections* (New York: Charles Scribners' Sons, 1899), "If any work of incontestable genius, and plainly predestined to immortality, has been issued in the English language in the past quarter century, it is that brilliant romance of the Great Rivers, *The Adventures of Huckleberry Finn*" (pp. 212–13). "I pin my faith on *Huckleberry Finn*," said music critic J. G. Hunecker in the *Musical Courier* (June 28, 1899). "For me it is the great American novel, even if it is written for boys" (p. 23). On the contrary, Henry C. Vedder suggested in *American Writers of To-Day* (1894), "It is only when, as 'Mark Twain,' he writes some trash as *The Adventures of Huckleberry Finn* that this really capable writer can make sure of an appreciative hearing" (p. 94). Vedder preferred *The Prince and the Pauper*.

Twain's friends on occasion made extravagant claims for his literary achievement in their eager and earnest effort to lift Mark Twain to the pantheon of American, if not world, letters. As the New York *Times* (February 21, 1906) reported, Prof. Brander Matthews taught his American literature class at Columbia that Twain was "the greatest figure in English literature." "When we look back over our literature, and see what savage and stupid and pitiless things have passed for humor, and then open his page, we seem not only to have invented the only true humorist, but to have invented humor itself," said Howells at the Lotus Club dinner given in Twain's honor on his return to America in 1900. "We do not know by what mystery his talent sprang from our soil and flowered in our air, but we know that no such talent has been known to any other; and if we set any bounds to our joy in him, it must be from that innate American modesty, not always perceptible to the alien eye, which forbids us to keep throwing bouquets at ourselves."[163]

Huckleberry Finn was perhaps even more admired abroad than at home. A story (probably apocryphal) goes that an Englishman stopped Twain in a train to tell him, "Mr. Clemens, I would give £10 not to have read your *Huckleberry Finn*." "Why so?" asked the baffled writer. "So that I could again have the pleasure of reading it for the first time," was the reply.[164] English novelist Walter Besant chose Twain and *Huckleberry Finn* for the article "My Favorite Novelist and His Best Book" in *Munsey's Magazine* (February 1898). Copies of *Huckle-*

163. Quoted in "Mark Twain: The Lotus Club Dinner—His Speech and the Others—Those Present," New York *Times*, November 17, 1900.

164. See James O'Donnell Bennett, *Much Loved Books* (New York: Boni & Liveright, 1927), p. 220.

Sheet music cover of "Huckleberry Finn: A Missouri Intermezzo"
by Aubrey Stauffer, 1904.
Courtesy Music Division, Library of Congress.

berry Finn were spotted in such unexpected places as Bismarck's writing desk, the private parlor of the President of Chile, and the Czarina's boudoir.[165] By the time of his death, according to Archibald Henderson, "Mark Twain vied with Tolstoy for the place of the most widely read and most genuinely popular author in the world."[166]

165. See Kaplan, *Mr. Clemens and Mark Twain*, p. 325.

166. In *Mark Twain* (New York: Frederick Stokes, 1912), p. 5.

"It would probably be difficult to find many cultured people who have not read the story," insisted *The Critic* (June 20, 1896), "but it would be even more difficult, we opine, to find many cultured people who do not desire to read it again" (p. 446). But Twain objected to this misconception about the author of *Huckleberry Finn*. "The thin top crust of humanity—the cultivated—are worth pacifying, worth pleasing, worth coddling, worth nourishing and preserving with dainties and delicacies, it is true," he wrote Andrew Lang in 1889; "but to be caterer to that little faction is no very dignified or valuable occupation, it seems to me; it is merely feeding the overfed, and there must be small satisfaction in that. It is not that little minority who are already saved that are best worth trying to uplift, I should think, but the mighty mass of the uncultivated who are underneath."[167]

Uncultivated Huck Finn was still far from respectable, when the Denver Public Library banned the book in August 1902. "*Huck Finn* was turned out of a New England library seventeen years ago—ostensibly on account of his morals," Twain wrote the Denver *Post* on August 14; "really to curry favor with a personage. There has been no instance until now."[168] This time he suspected that the reason was political. He said the library was retaliating to his scathing attack on Medal of Honor winner Frederick Funston, "In Defense of Funston" (*North American Review*, May 1902), calling into question American military policy in the Philippines. He thought the villains in the Denver matter were "a few persons who wish to curry favor with Funston, and whom God has not dealt kindly with in the matter of wisdom. Everybody in Denver knows this, even the dead people in the cemetery. It may be that Funston has wit enough to know that these good idiots are adding another howling absurdity to his funny history; it may be that God has charitably spared him that degree of penetration, slight as it is. In any case, he is—as usual—a proper object of compassion, and the bowels of my sympathy are moved toward him." This scatological detail would not have been appreciated in Denver, but Twain dealt his most sarcastic blow at the people in Colorado who he thought started it all. "There's nobody for me to attack in this matter even with soft and gentle ridicule—and I shouldn't think of using a grown up weapon in this kind of nursery. Above all, I couldn't venture to attack the clergymen whom you mention, for I have their habits and live in the same glass house which they are occupying. I am always reading immoral books on the sly, and then selfishly trying to prevent other people from having the same wicked good time." But he was clearly hurt by this censorship

167. *Mark Twain's Letters*, vol. 2, 1917, p. 527.

168. See "Mark Twain on 'Huck Finn,'" New York *Tribune*, August 22, 1902.

of his book. "No, if Satan's morals and Funston's are preferable to Huck's," he concluded, "let Huck's take a back seat; they can stand any ordinary competition, but not a combination like that. And I'm not going to defend them, anyway."

Almost simultaneously with Denver's library, the Omaha Public Library condemned *Huckleberry Finn* in 1902 as a pernicious influence on young people; and the Omaha *World-Herald* contacted Twain for his reaction. He was weary of it all, but wrote back, "I am fearfully afraid this noise is doing much harm. It has started a number of hitherto spotless people to reading *Huck Finn*, out of a natural human curiosity to learn what this is all about—people who had not heard of him before; people whose morals will go to wreck and ruin now. The publishers are glad, but it makes me want to borrow a handkerchief and cry. I should be sorry to think it was the publishers themselves that got up this entire little flutter to enable them to unload a book that was taking too much room in their cellars, but you never can tell what a publisher will do. I have been one myself."[169]

He never understood the antagonism to his book. "The truth is," he added on another occasion, "that when a library expels a book of mine and leaves an unexpurgated Bible lying around where unprotected youth and age can get hold of it, the deep unconscious irony of it delights me and doesn't anger me."[170] He relished the rich irony when the librarian of the Sunday School Library of the Central Baptist Church of Elizabeth, New Jersey, wrote to assure him that this institution at least had a complete set of his works. He said that "it squares an old account, heals an old sore, banishes an old grievance: the turning of Huck Finn out of the Concord (Massachusetts) circulating library seventeen years ago because he was immoral and said he would stand by Jim and *go* to hell if he must."[171]

But that was hardly the end of the troubles. The Emmetsburg (Iowa) *Democrat* reported on December 7, 1904, that both *Huckleberry Finn* and *Tom Sawyer* were banned from the juvenile department of the local library, because they

169. See "Mark Twain on 'Huck Finn,'" *The Canadian Bookseller*, September 1902, p. 56.

170. In a letter to Mrs. F. G. Whitmore, February 7, 1907, *Mark Twain's Letters*, vol. 2, 1917, p. 805.

171. Transcript of letter to L. Fred Silvers, July 31, 1902, Mark Twain Papers. Item 297, sold at Sotheby's auction house in New York on October 29, 1996, was a letter from Twain to a little girl from Greely, Nebraska, named Gertrude Swain, who confessed to him that she had read *Huckleberry Finn* no less than fifty times. "I would rather have your judgement of the moral quality of the Huck Finn book, after your fifty re-readings of it than that of fifty clergymen after reading it once apiece," he wrote her on October 16, 1902. "I should have confidence in your moral vision, but not so much in theirs, because it is limited in the matter of distance, pretty much out of focus." He added that he knew this to be true, "because I used to study for the ministry myself."

were "too strenuous and work a wrong influence on readers." Then in late 1905 the head librarian of the Brooklyn Public Libraries put *Tom Sawyer* and *Huckleberry Finn* on the "restricted list" of the children's rooms after the children's librarians complained "that Huck was a deceitful boy; that he not only itched but scratched; and that he said *sweat* when he should have said *perspiration*."[172] Only one of the librarians objected and privately wrote Twain in the hope that a word from him might persuade his colleagues to keep the books. "I am greatly troubled by what you say," he replied. "I wrote *Tom Sawyer* and *Huck Finn* for adults exclusively, and it always distresses me when I find that boys and girls have been allowed access to them. The mind that becomes soiled in youth can never again be washed clean; I know this by my own experience, and to this day I cherish an unappeasable bitterness against the unfaithful guardians of my young life, who not only permitted but compelled me to read an unexpurgated Bible through before I was fifteen years old. None can do that and ever draw a clean sweet breath again this side of the grave."

The librarian was young and inexperienced and did not know exactly what to make of Twain's irreverent answer, so he read the letter to his colleagues at their next meeting. "Most honestly do I wish I could say a softening word or two in defence of Huck's character, since you wish it," Twain continued, "but really in my opinion it is no better than God's (in the Ahab chapter and 97 others) and those of Solomon, David, Satan, and the rest of the sacred brotherhood. If there is an unexpurgated [Bible] in the Children's Department, won't you please help that young woman remove Huck and Tom from that questionable companionship?" The ladies were shocked, but agreed to let the matter drop.

The press somehow got word of the letter, however, and went after Twain to release it. They even pestered his secretary, but Twain would not budge. "That letter would be a bombshell for me if it got out," he realized. And for the librarian as well. But it amused Twain how the reporters would not give up. He told his secretary "to never mind—human nature would win the victory for us. There would be an earthquake somewhere, or a municipal upheaval *here*, or a threat of war in Europe—something would be sure to happen in the way of a big excitement that would call the boys away from No. 21 Fifth Avenue for twenty-four hours, and . . . they wouldn't think of that letter again." He released enigmatic messages to the press and got back in touch with the librarian. "Be wise as a serpent and wary as a dove!" Twain advised him. "The newspaper boys want that letter—don't you let them get hold of it. They say you refuse to

172. In Asa Don Dickinson, "Huckleberry Finn Is Fifty Years Old—Yes; But Is He Respectable?," *Wilson Bulletin for Librarians*, November 1935, p. 183.

let them see it without my consent. Keep on refusing, and I'll take care of this end of the line." The young man assured Twain that the book remained on the open shelves in the adult sections and that any child could read it there. The letter was never released in Twain's lifetime.

E. L. Pearson of the Library of the Military Information Division, Washington, D.C., came to Twain's defense in "The Children's Librarian *versus* Huckleberry Finn: A Brief for the Defence" (*Library Journal*, July 1907). He facetiously suggested that the prevalent cause of genteel female children's librarians' antagonism to Twain's characters was snobbery: "But you—you naughty, bad boys, your faces aren't washed, and your clothes are all covered with dirt. I do not believe that either of you brushed his hair this morning, and Tom Sawyer, I saw you yawn in church last Sunday. As for you, Huckleberry, you haven't any shoes or stockings at all, and every one knows what your father is. . . . Now, both of you run right away as fast as you can, or I will call the policeman and have him attend to you!" (p. 312). The magazine, however, did not entirely support Pearson's position on *Huckleberry Finn*. In an editorial, *The Library Journal* expressed its doubts "whether prejudice against Mark Twain's famous story exists to quite such a degree as is indicated in Mr. Pearson's amusing 'brief for the defence'; in many children's departments, assuredly, it finds its place as a matter of course, and its popularity with boys goes unrebuked. On the other hand, it is true that there have been cases where children's librarians have committed themselves to the policy of establishing what the newspapers love to call a 'ban' upon this particular book; but the criticism and comment evoked by such decision have generally been more extended and caustic than seem reasonable" (p. 302).

It was not really a man-versus-woman dispute, as Pearson suggested, for some gentlemen were as ardently opposed to the books as the lady librarians were. At the second annual conference for teachers and others interested in children's reading held at the Grand Rapids Public Library on May 15, 1906, Dr. J.R.T. Lothrop replied to the question "Are the writings of Mark Twain wholesome for children?" that both "*Tom Sawyer* and *Huckleberry Finn* were lacking in moral tone, and likely to foster lawlessness and disrespect of sacred things."[173] Twain, however, never understood the problem. "When people let Huck alone he goes peacefully along, damaging a few children here and there and yonder," he explained, "but there will be plenty of children in heaven without those, so it is no great matter. It is only when well-meaning people expose him that he gets his real chance to do harm. Temporarily, then, he spreads

173. See *The Library Journal*, June 1906, pp. 288–89.

Mark Twain at the dinner given in honor of his seventieth birthday at Delmonico's, December 5, 1905.
Courtesy Library of Congress.

havoc all around in the nurseries and no doubt does prodigious harm while he has his chance. By and by, let us hope, people that really have the best interests of the rising generation at heart will become wise and stir Huck up" (p. 185).

Remarkably, Twain bore no grudge against these mighty institutions in theory. "Books are the liberated spirits of men," he wrote on the dedication of the Millicent Library, Fairhaven, Connecticut, on February 22, 1894, "and should be bestowed in a heaven of light and grace and harmonious comfort . . . instead of the customary kind of public library, with its depressing austerities and severities of form and furniture and decoration. A public library is the most enduring of memorials, the trustiest monument for the preservation of an event or a name or an affection; for it, and it only, is respected by wars and revolutions and survives them. Creed and opinion change with time, and their symbols perish; but Literature and its temples are sacred to all creeds, and inviolate."[174] In gratitude, the library hung on the south wall of its reading and reference room a bronze tablet of Mark Twain, flanked by Tom Sawyer and Huckleberry Finn.

174. Letter to the Officers of the Millicent Library, February 22, 1894, quoted in Earl J. Davis, "Mark Twain in Fairhaven," *Mark Twain Journal*, Summer 1967, p. 15.

When he heard of all the public libraries his friend Andrew Carnegie was planning to build, Twain asked the industrialist if the books he was going to put in them would be "on a high moral plane." "If they are not," he quipped, "he had better build the libraries and I would write the books. With the wealth I would get out of writing the books, I could build libraries and then he could write books."[175] If public servants refused to put *Huckleberry Finn* in their libraries, then Twain just had to build one that would. Shortly before he died, he gave $6,000 toward the erection of the Mark Twain Free Library in Redding, Connecticut; and his daughter Clara donated 2,500 books, nearly his entire library, to this institution.[176]

Mark Twain returns to his boyhood home, Hannibal, Missouri, 1902.
Courtesy Library of Congress.

Mark Twain felt vindicated as the most beloved and reviled American author of his day. Besides the University of Missouri honorary degree in literature in 1902, Yale made him a master of arts in 1888 and a doctor of literature in 1901; but this ornery old self-taught backwoodsman was most touched by the honorary doctorate of laws degree bestowed upon him by Oxford University in 1907. Not only did he go to England to receive it, he proudly wore his academic robe and mortarboard around the house. He celebrated his seventieth birthday on December 5, 1905, at a gala dinner at Delmonico's in New York, surrounded by family, friends, and celebrities. England sent a cablegram bearing the congratulations of James M. Barrie, G. K. Chesterton, Arthur Conan Doyle, W. S. Gilbert, Thomas Hardy, Rudyard Kipling, John Tenniel, and other famous well-wishers. President Theodore Roosevelt honored Twain by calling him "one of the citizens whom all Americans should delight to honor, for he has rendered a great and peculiar service to America, and his writings, though such as no one

175. Quoted in "Mark Twain on Training That Pays: Speaks at a Supper of the Male Teachers' Association," New York *Times*, March 17, 1901.

176. See *The Library Journal*, July 1910, p. 344.

but an American could have written, yet emphatically come within that small list which are written for no particular country, but for all countries, and which are not merely written for the time being, but have an abiding and permanent value."[177]

Twain knew his place in American letters, and how it frustrated and disgusted him that he never saw the recognition he felt he so rightly deserved. "Privately I am quite well aware that for a generation I have been as widely celebrated a literary person as America has ever produced," he said in 1907, "and I am also privately aware that in my own peculiar line I have stood at the head of my guild during all that time, with none to dispute the place with me." It troubled him how the universities honored "persons of small and temporary consequence—persons of local and evanescent notoriety, persons who drift into obscurity and are forgotten inside of ten years—and never a degree offered to me! Of all those thousands, not fifty are known outside of America, and not a hundred are still famous in it."[178] Who among all those once hallowed guests at the Delmonico's birthday dinner (other than Willa Cather) is still read today? Surely, Twain in his time was not considered as a serious artist within the illustrious brotherhood of Emerson, Longfellow, Lowell, and Holmes; even Howells in his time was more admired as a man of letters than Twain was. But Howells knew the truth, as he wrote in *My Mark Twain*: "Emerson, Longfellow, Lowell, Holmes—I knew them all and all the rest of our sages, poets, seers, critics, humorists; they were like one another and like other literary men; but Clemens was sole, incomparable, the Lincoln of our literature" (p. 101).

His peers and not just Howells appreciated him, particularly English, Scottish, and Irish writers. Rudyard Kipling idolized "the great and God-like Clemens." "He is the biggest man you have on your side of the water by a damn sight, and don't you forget it," the author of *The Jungle Book* (1894) and *Kim* (1901) informed an American friend. "Cervantes was a relation of his." Robert Louis Stevenson, who wrote *Treasure Island* (1883), told Twain that he had read *Huckleberry Finn* four times "and am quite ready to begin again tomorrow." According to George Bernard Shaw, William Morris, who should have been offended by *A Connecticut Yankee in King Arthur's Court*, was "an incurable Huckofinomaniac"; he told his Irish friend that Twain was "a greater master of English" than even Thackeray. Shaw himself said, "Mark Twain is the greatest American writer"; and the playwright wrote the Missouri sage that "the future

177. Quoted in "Mark Twain's 70th Birthday," *Harper's Weekly*, December 23, 1905, p. 1884.

178. In *The Autobiography of Mark Twain*, edited by Charles Neider, p. 457.

historian of America will find your works as indispensable to him as a French historian finds the political tracts of Voltaire."[179]

Weary of all the controversy the book generated, Twain vacillated as to which of his books was his personal favorite. He once said he preferred the historical romance *Personal Recollections of Joan of Arc* (1896) to all the others; but in 1900, when asked to state which was his favorite novel, he replied, "*Huckleberry Finn*."[180] At his death in 1910, critics disagreed as to what his legacy might be. For the American *Bookman*'s Mark Twain memorial issue of May 1910, long-forgotten Harry Thurston Peck predicted with a shocking lack of foresight in "Mark Twain a Century Hence" that *Tom Sawyer* and *Huckleberry Finn* "will remain for perhaps two decades. All the rest of Mr. Clemens' books may perhaps be sold by subscription agents among his 'complete works' for a certain time, but they will not be read" (p. 389). He thought that Twain's immortality lay with "The Jumping Frog of Calaveras County" and *A Tramp Abroad*. "It is only short-sighted persons who talk of Mark Twain's profound 'philosophy of life,' " Peck insisted. "He had no philosophy of life, any more than Fielding had or Steele or Harte. But like them he had an instinct for pure humor, which was most effective when it was unconscious" (p. 393). American critic Waldo Frank disagreed. "Out of the bitter wreckage of his long life, one great work emerges by whose contrasting fire we can observe the darkness," he wrote in *Our America* (1919). "This work is *Huckleberry Finn*. It must go down in history, not as the expression of a rich natural culture like the books of Chaucer, Rabelais, Cervantes, but as the voice of American chaos, the voice of a pre-cultural epoch."[181] But Frank rather harshly concluded that "the balance of his literary life, before and after, went mostly to the wastage of half-baked, half-believed, half-clownish labor." "Mark Twain has the very marrow of Americanism," said Brander Matthews in "Tribute to Mark Twain" (New York *Times*, December 3, 1910), and *Huckleberry Finn* was "the story in which that life has

179. Stevenson quoted in Meltzer, pp. 179 and 277; Kipling and Shaw in George Sanderlin, *Mark Twain: As Others Saw Him* (New York: Coward, McCann & Geoghegan, 1978), pp. 115 and 117–18.

180. See special cable from Berlin, New York *Times*, April 23, 1910; and "Literary Gossip," *The Athenæum*, April 30, 1910, p. 527. "I like the *Joan of Arc* best of all my books," Twain wrote on November 30, 1908, "and it *is* the best; I know it perfectly well. And besides, it furnished me seven times the pleasure afforded me by any of the others: twelve years of preparation and two years of writing. The others needed no preparation, and got none" (quoted in Paine, *Mark Twain: A Biography*, vol. 3, 1912, p. 1034). Twain once asked critic William Lyon Phelps which of his novels he liked best; when he said *Huckleberry Finn*, Twain added, "That is undoubtedly my best work." See Cyril Clemens, "Mark Twain's Favorite Book," *Overland Monthly*, May 1930, p. 157.

181. Waldo Frank, *Our America* (New York: Boni & Liveright, 1919), pp. 38 and 40.

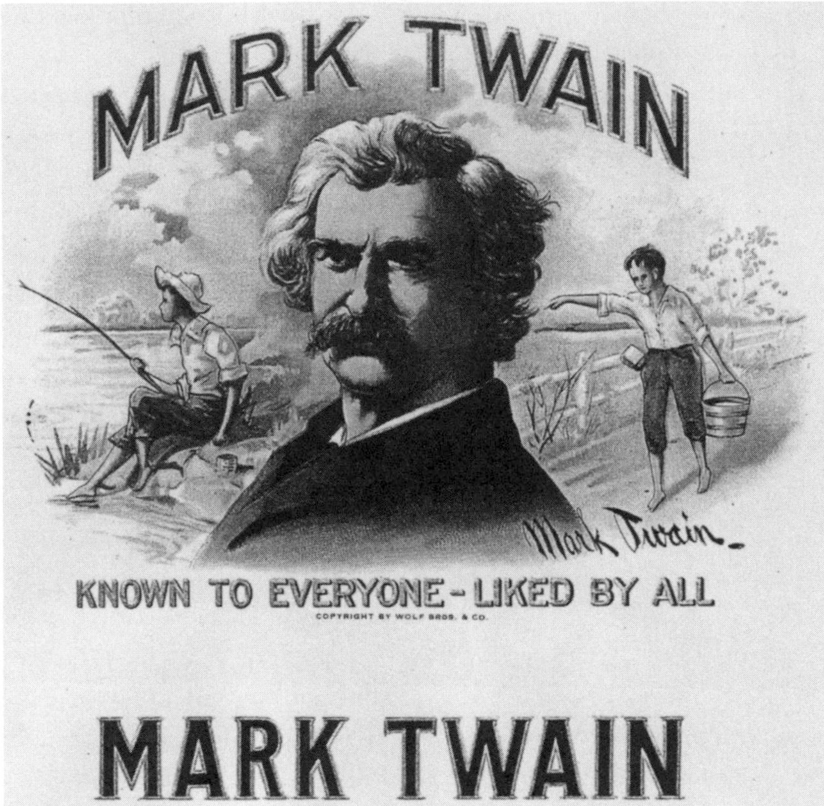

Chromolithographed box label for "Mark Twain" cigars.
Private collection.

been crystallized forever . . . the Odyssey of the Mississippi, the finest of his books, the deepest in its insight, and the widest in its appeal." H. L. Mencken declared in "Oyez! Oyez! All Ye Who Read Books" (*Smart Set*, December 1908) simply that *Huckleberry Finn* was "the greatest work of fiction yet produced by an American" (p. 153). "However his work may be judged by impartial and unprejudiced generations," observed the New York *Times* (April 22, 1910) in its editorial on his death, "his fame is imperishable."

III

THERE WAS A slow and deliberate effort to change the writer's rough-hewn image after his death, to make him acceptable in the parlor, bedroom, and nursery. Harper & Brothers described the "Author's National Edition" of Twain's works in their 1912 catalog as "go-to-bed books," ones which "you can dip into lazily, even sleepily, and enjoy the sweet whimsicality of a kindred soul." His ideal reader was "a boy full of the fresh animal spirits of his years, full of activity, imagination, enthusiasm." As for the adult, "You can renew your youth by rereading them or, what is better, make it possible for the rising generation to make the acquaintance of these greatest of children's books." Most people agreed with Fred Lewis Pattee's *A History of American Literature Since 1870* (1915) that the Mark Twain who would survive was "the romancer, who in boyhood had dreamed by the great river, and who later caught the romance of a period of American life." That and nothing more. Tom Sawyer and Huckleberry Finn were worth remembering for their nostalgic picture of America's lost innocence. Clara Clemens Gabrilowitsch and the Mark Twain Company

"Huckleberry Finn," song tribute to
the Mark Twain character by Sam M. Lewis,
Joe Young, and Cliff Hess, 1918.
Private collection.

"Tom Sawyer and Huck Finn." Comic strip drawn by Clare Victor Dwiggins, March 2, 1919.
Courtesy Library of Congress.

further exploited this popular image of Huck and Tom as riverfront scamps in 1918, by authorizing the McClure newspaper syndicate to produce a daily and Sunday "Tom Sawyer and Huck Finn" comic strip drawn by Clare Victor Dwiggins. It survived until 1946, when "Dwig" retired from the funny papers to devote his time to illustration and painting.[182] Unfortunately, "Tom Sawyer and Huck Finn" bore little resemblance to *The Adventures of Tom Sawyer* and none to *Adventures of Huckleberry Finn*. Hollywood has done its share of damage, too. No motion picture or television production has yet retained the spirit of the novel or explored the depths of Twain's vision.[183]

Color lithographed poster by Anton Levinskii for the Russian release of the 1920 Paramount motion picture *Huckleberry Finn*.
Courtesy Sasha Lurie.

Soon after Twain's death, the once reviled *Tom Sawyer* and *Huckleberry Finn* became national treasures, the fictional equivalents of the Declaration of Independence and the Emancipation Proclamation. Hannibal, Missouri, was already eagerly engaged in the cult of celebrity even before Twain died. He described in *Is Shakespeare Dead?* (1909) how he received a recent clipping from the Hannibal *Courier-Post*, which described how the name "Mark Twain" "is associated with every old building that is torn down to make way for the modern structures

182. See Richard Marschall, "An American Classic and a Classic Comic Strip," *Nemo*, December 1985, pp. 19–33; and M. Thomas Inge, "Mark Twain and the Comics," *Mark Twain Journal*, Fall 1990, pp. 30–39.

183. Although *Huckleberry Finn* has been filmed many times, Hollywood has not yet produced a definitive version of Twain's classic. Most screenwriters have tried to turn *Huckleberry Finn* into *Tom Sawyer*; many have combined elements from both stories. Some have been better than others: 1920, Paramount, a silent film with Lewis Sargent (Huck), Gordon Griffith (Tom), and George Reed (Jim); 1931, Paramount, sound film with Junior Durkin (Huck), Jackie Coogan (Tom), Clarence Muse (Jim), Mitzi Green (Becky), and Jackie Searl (Sid); 1939, MGM with Mickey Rooney (Huck), Rex Ingram (Jim), Walter Connolly (the king), and William Frawley (the duke); 1960, MGM, with Samuel Goldwyn, Jr., a Technicolor production with four songs by Alan Jay Lerner and Burton Lane, with Eddie Hodges (Huck), Archie Moore (Jim), Tony Randall (the king), and Buster Keaton, Andy Divine, Judy Canova, Sterling Holloway, and John Carradine; 1974, United Artists–Reader's Digest, with a script and ten songs by Richard M. and Robert B. Sherman, with Jess East (Huck), Paul Winfield (Jim), Harvey Corman (the king), and David Wayne (the duke); 1978, Schick Sunn, with Kurt Ida (Huck), Brock Peters (Jim), Dan Monahan (Tom), Forrest Tucker (the duke), and Larry Storch (the dauphin); 1993, Walt Disney Pictures, with Elijah Wood (Huck), Courtney Vance (Jim), Jason Robards (the king), and Anne Heche (Mary Jane Wilks). Georgii Daneliya directed a 1973 Russian picture with Roma Modyanov (Huck) and Felix Immokuede (Jim). There have also been several television productions: 1955, CBS-TV *Climax* series, with Charles Taylor

demanded by a rapidly growing city, and with every hill or cave over or through which he might by any possibility have roamed, while the many points of interest which he wove into his stories, such as Holliday Hill, Jackson's Island, or Mark Twain Cave, are now monuments to his genius. Hannibal is glad of any opportunity to do him honor as he has honored her" (p. 146). Hannibal erected a statue of Mark Twain in Mark Twain Memorial Park, and another of Tom and Huck at the foot of Cardiff Hill. Albert Bigelow Paine objected to putting "Humorist" on Twain's base; they settled for "Citizen of the World." Likewise, his birthplace—Florida, Missouri—placed a bronze bust of the village's most famous native son at the crossroads. Hannibal became "Tom Sawyer's Town," a national shrine where tourists could visit the actual homes of fictional characters. The building that Sam Clemens grew up in was donated to the town in 1912 and became known as the "Tom Sawyer House." Where Laura Hawkins spent her childhood became the "Becky Thatcher House." Every fence in town seemed to be the "original" one that every boy in town whitewashed for Tom Sawyer. But the place where Tom Blankenship, the model for Huck Finn, lived burned down and was razed. This was the town of Tom Sawyer, not Huckleberry Finn and Jim. It seemed that memories of slavery had been conveniently expunged from the town's history.[184]

(Huck), Thomas Mitchell (the king), and John Carradine (the duke); 1957, *U. S. Steel Hour*, with Jimmy Boyd (Huck), Earle Hyman (Jim), Basil Rathbone (the king), Jack Carson (the duke), and Florence Henderson (Mary Jane Wilks); 1975, ABC-TV special, with Ron Howard (Huck), Donny Most (Tom), Antonio Fargas (Jim), and Howard's father, mother, and brother in the cast; and 1985, PBS *American Playhouse*, with Patrick Day (Huck), Samm-Art Williams (Jim), and Jim Dale, Lillian Gish, Barnard Hughes, Richard Kiley, Butterfly McQueen, Sada Thompson, and Geraldine Page. In 1952, MGM announced (but never produced) a Technicolor musical with Dean Stockwell (Huck), Gene Kelly (the king), Danny Kaye (the duke), and Margaret O'Brien (Mary Jane Wilks); and in 1969, Universal bought the rights to the unfinished "Tom Sawyer and Huck Finn Among the Indians." In the late 1990s, Spike Lee also considered making a more promising film of *Huckleberry Finn*, but it was never produced.

Paramount sent its crew for the 1920 silent picture on location on the Mississippi, but Southern California cannot duplicate the Mississippi Valley. The scripts have demonstrated little respect for Twain's story by concentrating on the initial flight of the fugitives and the episodes with the king and the duke. The casts have been generally uninspired, and most versions soften the bitter satire of the original with light or broad comedy and musical numbers. The 1974 United Artists–Reader's Digest film courageously included the Grangerford–Shepherdson feud, but its message was lost in all the singing and dancing of the rest of the film; also, Paul Winfield was closer to Nat Turner than to Miss Watson's Jim. The most ambitious and faithful production was the 1985 four-hour miniseries on PBS *American Playhouse* with an all-star cast; unfortunately, it has been aired in its entirety only once, in 1986, perhaps because it was darker than the others.

184. See William Zinsser, *American Places: A Writer's Pilgrimage to 15 of This Country's Most Visited and Cherished Sites* (New York: HarperCollins, 1992); and Shelley Fisher Fishkin, *Lighting Out for the Territory: Reflections on Mark Twain and American Culture* (New York and Oxford: Oxford University Press, 1997).

Despite the whitewashing of his image, the name "Mark Twain" still carried the taint of scandal in some circles late into the twentieth century. "I went stark mad for Mark Twain," admitted William Allen White in his autobiography. "My mother was shocked, for Mark Twain was accounted to an atheist."[185] Upton Sinclair recalled in *Mammonart* (1925), "When I was a boy we all read *Tom Sawyer* and *Huckleberry Finn* and 'laughed our heads off' over them; but if anybody had suggested to us that Mark Twain might be one of the world's great writers, we should have thought it a Mark Twain joke" (pp. 90–91). T. S. Eliot missed *Huckleberry Finn* during his childhood in St. Louis. "I suspect that a fear on the part of my parents lest I should acquire a premature taste for tobacco, and perhaps other habits of the hero of the story, kept the book out of my way," he suggested in his introduction to the 1950 Cresset/Chanticleer edition. When Edmund Wilson suggested that Vladimir Nabokov, the author of *Lolita* (1955), introduce his fourteen-year-old son to Mark Twain's works, Véra Nabokov was shocked. She considered *Tom Sawyer* "an immoral book that teaches bad behavior and suggests to little boys the idea of taking an interest in little girls too young."[186]

The literary canonization of Mark Twain produced its heretics; and after World War I, when his reputation was ready for revision, modernists generally acknowledged that Twain was greatly overrated. William Faulkner considered Twain to be no more than "a hack writer who would not have been considered fourth rate in Europe, who tricked out a few of the old proven 'sure fire' literary skeletons with sufficient local color to intrigue the superficial and the lazy."[187] D. H. Lawrence failed to recognize Twain in *Studies in Classic American Literature* (1923) as did F. O. Matthiessen many years later in *The American Renaissance* (1957). While the defender of nineteenth-century genteel tradition had chastised him for his lack of restraint, the social Freudian critics of the Roaring Twenties, led by Van Wyck Brooks in *The Ordeal of Mark Twain*, attacked him for not going far enough.[188] He was too vulgar *and* not vulgar

185. In *The Autobiography of William Allen White* (New York: Macmillan, 1946), pp. 60–61.

186. See Stacy Schiff, *Véra (Mrs. Vladimir Nabokov)* (New York: Random House, 1999), p. 136.

187. Quoted in Sanderlin, *Mark Twain: As Others Saw Him,* p. 129. Even Faulkner eventually came to acknowledge Twain as "the father of American literature, though he is not the first one." "In my opinion," the novelist from Mississippi told an interviewer, "Mark Twain was the first truly American writer, and all of us since are his heirs. . . . Before him the writers who were considered American were not, really; their tradition, their culture was European culture. It was only with Twain, Walt Whitman, there became a true indigenous American culture." See James B. Meriweather and Michael Millgate, *Lion in the Garden: Interviews with William Faulkner 1926–1962* (New York: Random House, 1968), p. 137.

188. Critic Alexander Nicolas DeMenil still maintained in "A Century of Missouri Literature" (*Missouri Historical Review*, October 1920) that Twain "is often coarse" and "irreverent, if not

enough. From a cursory reading of Paine's biography, Brooks invented a new myth to explain Mark Twain, his Oedipal struggle with first Jane Clemens and then Olivia Langdon in bridling his artistic potential. Short-story writer Sherwood Anderson may have suggested this theory to Brooks. "I can't help wishing Twain hadn't married such a good woman," he wrote Brooks in 1918. "There was such a universal inclination to tame the man—to save his soul, as it were. Left alone, I fancy Mark might have been willing to throw his soul overboard and then—ye gods, what a fellow he might have been, what poetry might have come from him."[189] The legend of the evil Olivia took various forms in contemporary criticism. "His one masterpiece, *Huckleberry Finn*, he wrote secretly at odd moments, taking many years at the task, and finally publishing it with anxiety," social reformer Upton Sinclair carelessly recounted the book's evolution in *Mammonart*. "We understand how he poured his soul into Huck Finn; this poor henpecked genius, dressed up and made to go through the paces of a literary lion, yearns back to the days when he was a ragged urchin and was happy; Huck Finn and Tom Sawyer represent all that daring, that escape from the bourgeois world, which Sam Clemens dreamed but never achieved" (pp. 330–31). American poet Edgar Lee Masters said in *Mark Twain: A Portrait* (1938) that Twain was able to so effectively describe "the psychology and the ideas for Huck Finn's disgust with the régime of the Widow Douglas' house," because "Olivia had given him the understanding of what it is to be watched and dominated" (p. 88).

But reports of his literary demise were greatly exaggerated. The New Deal, a phrase taken from *A Connecticut Yankee in King Arthur's Court*, ushered in a new era for Mark Twain and *Huckleberry Finn*. America was now building grand cultural monuments to itself; and, according to Theodore Dreiser in "Mark the Double Twain" (*English Journal*, October 1935), Twain "remains to this hour, in the minds of most Americans, not the powerful and original and amazingly pessimistic thinker that he really was, and that several of his most distinguished contributions to American letters prove—but rather, and to this hour, the incorrigible and prolific joker, and, at best, humorist who, up to the time of his death and since, has kept the world chuckling so continuously that it has

---

blasphemous" and "lacks the education absolutely necessary to be a great writer; he lacks refinement which would render it impossible for him to create such coarse characters as Huckleberry Finn; furthermore, he is absolutely unconscious of almost all the canons of literary art" (p. 97).

189. In a letter from Sherwood Anderson, early April 1918, *Letters of Sherwood Anderson*, edited by Howard Mumford Jones and Walter B. Rideout (Boston: Little, Brown, 1953), p. 32.

not even now sobered sufficiently to detect in him the gloomy and wholly mechanistic thinker" (p. 615). Dreiser knew what it meant to be censored. While Marxist critics like Granville Hicks in *The Great Tradition* (1933) dismissed Twain for never writing the great American socialist novel, a simple declaration from Ernest Hemingway made *Huckleberry Finn* the official Great American Novel. He thought the great American writers were Henry James, Stephen Crane, and Mark Twain. "All modern American literature comes from one book by Mark Twain called *Huckleberry Finn*," he wrote in *The Green Hills of Africa* (1935). "All American writing comes from that. There was nothing before. There has been nothing as good since" (p. 22). He probably picked up his opinion from H. L. Mencken, who said in "Mark Twain" (*Smart Set*, October 1919) that *Huckleberry Finn* is "perhaps the greatest novel ever written in English. . . . the greatest work of the imagination that These States have yet seen" (pp. 142–43). F. Scott Fitzgerald supported his friend Hemingway's assertion that *Huckleberry Finn* was indeed a great book. "Huckleberry Finn took the first journey *back*," Fitzgerald noted also in 1935. "He was the first to look *back* at the republic from the perspective of the West. His eyes were the first eyes that ever looked at us objectively that were not the eyes from overseas. There were mountains at the frontier but he wanted more than mountains to look at with his restless eyes—he wanted to find out about men and how they lived together. And because he turned back we have him forever."[190] Argentinian writer Jorge Luis Borges replied in "Una Vindication de Mark Twain" (*Sur*, November 1935) to two "insults" propagated by Van Wyck Brooks in *The Ordeal of Mark Twain*: "first, . . . that in his happy works the moments of lament and sarcasm are the fundamental ones; second, that of reducing him to a mere symbol of the artist frustrated and mutilated by the arid nineteenth century and by a brutal continent" (p. 40). Borges insisted that *Huckleberry Finn* is "a book neither burlesque nor tragic: simply a happy book." Theodore Dreiser was not so sure: He argued in "Mark the Double Twain" that "the best he did for the Negro at any time was to set over against Harriet Beecher Stowe's Uncle Tom, the more or less Sambo portrait of the Negro Jim who, with Huckleberry Finn, occupied the raft that was the stage of that masterly record of youthful life, *Huckleberry Finn*" (p. 622).

Hemingway's opinion carried more weight than any other contemporary writer's in 1935, and his statement happened to conveniently coincide with Twain's centenary. It was also the fiftieth anniversary of *Huckleberry Finn*. The nation's schools designated November 1 as Mark Twain Day. Centennial din-

190. See *Fitzgerald Newsletter*, Winter 1960, pp. 1–2.

ners were held in New York, Bermuda (where he often vacationed), San Francisco, and Honolulu on November 18. Clara Clemens Gabrilowitsch went to Hannibal to dedicate the Mark Twain Museum. Eddie Guest, then America's most popular poet, wrote a poem in honor of Mark Twain's hundredth birthday: "Down in Hannibal, Missouri, they're living once again/All the countless happy memories of a boy they called Mark Twain." Guest forgot that they called him Sam Clemens in Hannibal; he called himself Mark Twain after he left town. President Franklin D. Roosevelt officially opened the year-long centennial celebration in Hannibal on November 30, by pressing a key from the White House that turned on the Mark Twain Memorial Lighthouse on Cardiff Hill. "The perpetuation of Mark Twain's name, birthplace and the haunts of his youth are very dear to me," the president said, "especially because I myself, as a boy, had the happy privilege of shaking hands with him. That was a day I shall never forget." He further legitimized the Tom Sawyer myth by dedicating the Mark Twain Memorial Bridge in Hannibal on September 4, 1936. "No American youth," he said in his speech, "has knowingly or willingly escaped the lessons, the philosophy and the spirit which beloved Mark Twain wove out of the true life of which he was a part along this majestic river. Abroad, too, this peaceful valley is known around the world as the cradle of the chronicles of buoyant boyhood. Mark Twain and his tales live, though the years have passed and time has wrought its changes on the Mississippi."[191] The Soviet Union too honored one of the most beloved writers in Russia the year of his centennial with an impressive exhibition of Mark Twainiana at the House of Culture Library in Leningrad, largely amassed by the Queens Borough Public Library, Jamaica, New York, and shipped by the International Exchange of the Smithsonian Institution.

Twain would have appreciated the irony of all this attention to his once shunned novel. "I believe that the trade of critic, in literature, music and the drama, is the most degraded of all trades and that it has no real value—certainly no large value," he wrote in "Chapters from My Autobiography" (*North American Review*, October 19, 1906). "However, let it go. It is the will of God that we must have critics, and missionaries, and Congressmen, and humorists, and we must bear the burden" (pp. 707–8). So venerated did *Huckleberry Finn* become after World War II that a vast academic industry surrounded and threatened to engulf the study and appreciation of the novel. Lionel Trilling in

191. "Roosevelt's Speech at Twain Bridge," New York *Times*, September 5, 1936. Presidents John F. Kennedy and William Jefferson Clinton repeated switching on the lighthouse from the White House in May 1963 and July 1994.

his introduction to the 1948 Holt, Rinehart & Winston edition of *Huckleberry Finn* recognized it as "one of the world's great books and one of the central documents of American culture." T. S. Eliot read it for the first time to write his introduction to the 1950 Cresset/Chanticleer edition, and he pronounced it a masterpiece. With the weight of these critical heavyweights behind it, the novel's dominance over American literature was challenged but rarely swayed. "*Huckleberry Finn* is now read as a key to the very essence of the American imagination, a central document of our most primitive impulses," declared Norman Podhoretz in "The Literary Adventures of Huck Finn" (New York *Times*, December 6, 1959). The book has been debated and reinterpreted according to every current critical trend, so much so that one would hardly think that anything new could possibly be said about it. Unfortunately, not all the sage critics have kept in mind Twain's sane advice, "Don't explain your author, read him right and he explains himself."[192]

There have also been vain attempts to rewrite the author. Twain himself made countless changes in the text for his public readings of the novel. Bernard DeVoto, as editor of the Mark Twain Papers, put the "raft episode" that Twain had taken out for use in *Life on the Mississippi* back into the 1942 Limited Editions Club edition of *Huckleberry Finn*. Walter Blair and Victor Fischer followed this model in their meticulously edited "Mark Twain Library" edition published by the University of California in 1985 and again in 1988 and 2001 with an exhaustive scholarly apparatus. This was the text used in the 1985 Pennyroyal Press edition, illustrated by Barry Moser, as well as that of the 1999 third edition of the Norton Critical Edition. Having read all the best authorities on the book, John Seelye was not content with what Twain himself had written and rewrote the story as *The True Adventures of Huckleberry Finn* to appease all the complaints hurled at the book over the years; sadly, Seelye is a scholar, not a novelist, and violated the spirit of Twain's original by killing off Jim at the end. Charles Neider, who made a long and lucrative career out of refashioning Twain's work, revised *Huckleberry Finn* by including the "raft episode" and

192. Quoted by Sanderlin, *Mark Twain: As Others Saw Him*, p. 89. Too often these studies reveal more about the the critic's particular preoccupations than anything pertinent about Twain's art. For example, Charles E. May explored what he considered the "latent sexuality" of the novel in "Literary Masters and Masturbators: Sexuality, Fantasy, and Reality in *Huckleberry Finn*," *Literature and Psychology*, no. 2 (1978), pp. 85–92. Even more notorious than this psychoanalytic interpretation was Leslie Fielder's essay, "Come Back to the Raft Ag'in, Huck Honey!" in *The End of Innocence* (1955): Perhaps there is evidence to make a case for an alleged sexual affair between Ishmael and Queequeg in *Moby-Dick*, but Fiedler's unconvincing gropings for proof of an implicit homosexual liaison between Huck and Jim on their Mississippi raft are irrelevant to *Huckleberry Finn*.

condensing the last chapters to coincide with the book's centennial in 1985. After the first half of the manuscript was discovered in 1990, Random House issued its "comprehensive" edition in 1996 to include passages that Twain himself had revised or deleted. There have also been numerous other edited, revised, expurgated, and rewritten versions of *Huckleberry Finn*, usually for the juvenile market.

The New Critics, like T. S. Eliot and Lionel Trilling, tried to analyze *Huckleberry Finn* purely as literature, but one cannot remove the history from the story. Mark Twain was above all an autobiographical writer; one cannot divorce the art of Mark Twain from the life of Sam Clemens. "Experience is an author's most valuable asset," he said, "experience is the thing that puts the muscle and the breath and the warm blood into the book he writes."[193] Twain recalled and reshaped many of the people and places of the novel from his boyhood in Hannibal, which Howells called "a loafing, out-at-the-elbows, down-at-the-heels, slave-holding Mississippi River town" before the Civil War.[194] "I confine myself to life with which I am familiar, when pretending to portray life," Twain explained in a letter of 1890. "But I confined myself to the boy-life out on the Mississippi because that had a peculiar charm for me and not because I was not familiar with other phases of life. . . . *Now* then: as the most valuable capital, or culture, or education usable in the building of novels is personal experience, I ought to be well-equipped for that trade." However, he appended to the letter, "And yet I can't go away from the boyhood period and write novels because *capital* (that is, personal experience) is not sufficient by itself and I lack the other essential: interest in handling the men and experiences of later life."[195] Invention was never enough for Twain; he had to reflect the life around him. "If you attempt to create a wholly imaginary incident, adventure or situation," he jotted in his notebook in the late 1880s, "you will go astray and the artificiality of the thing will be detectable, but if you found on a *fact* in your personal experience it is as an acorn, a root, and every created adornment that grows up out of it, and spreads its foliage and blossom to the sun will seem reality, not inventions."[196] Any writer who thinks he is inventing really draws on some forgotten individual or experience. "I don't think an author . . . ever lived,

193. In *Is Shakespeare Dead?* (New York and London: Harper & Bros., 1909), p. 39.

194. In "Mark Twain," *Century Magazine*, September 1882, p. 780.

195. In a letter quoted by Bernard DeVoto in *The Portable Mark Twain* (New York: Viking, 1946), pp. 773–75 and 9.

196. In *Mark Twain's Notebook*, edited by Albert Bigelow Paine (New York and London: Harper & Bros., 1935), pp. 192–93.

who created a character," he told Lute Pease in "Mark Twain Talks" (Portland *Sunday Oregonian*, August 9, 1895). "It was always drawn from his recollection of someone he had known. Sometimes, like a composite photograph, an author's presentation of a character may possibly be from the blending of more than two or more real characters in his recollection. But, even when he is making no attempt to draw his character from life . . . , he is yet unconsciously drawing from memory." In a sense, *Huckleberry Finn* summarized and crystallized not only the author's experience but his earlier work as well. "It was a book," DeVoto argued in *Mark Twain's America*, that Twain "was foreordained to write: it brought harmoniously to a focus everything that had a basic reality in his mind" (p. 311). His other books may be seen to be as mere apprentice work in preparation for his one masterpiece, *Huckleberry Finn*.[197]

IV

The year 1985 marked not only the centenary of the publication of *Huckleberry Finn* in the United States, but also Mark Twain's sesquicentennial and the seventy-fifth anniversary of his death. Some people preferred celebrating one hundred years of *Huckleberry Finn* a bit earlier in 1984, the year the book was released in England and Canada. Hannibal, Elmira, and Hartford all had centennial celebrations. President Ronald Reagan declared November 30, Twain's birthday, Mark Twain Day. The Modern Language Association sponsored a special session devoted to the book at its annual convention, and symposiums on *Huckleberry Finn* were held at universities around the country. *Mark Twain Journal* (Fall 1984) devoted an entire issue to reevaluations of the novel by prominent African-American scholars.

Not everyone found reason to celebrate Mark Twain and *Huckleberry Finn*. Charges of racism had been thrown at the book for years. In September 1957, the New York City Board of Education removed *Huckleberry Finn* from the approved textbook lists in the elementary and junior high schools for being

197. For example, the opening chapters are reworkings of sections of *Tom Sawyer*; the Grangerford parlor is "The House Beautiful" and the Grangerford–Shepherdson feud the same as that between the Darnells and Watsons in *Life on the Mississippi*; Bricksville is Obedstown, Tennessee, in *The Gilded Age*; the king's and the duke's false histories parody Mules Hendon's lineage as well as the mistaken identities of Tom Canty and Prince Edward in *The Prince and the Pauper*; even the novel's form imitates that of *The Innocents Abroad*, *A Tramp Abroad*, and *Life on the Mississippi*, travelogues describing the people and manners of picturesque parts of the world.

"racially offensive." Editorials and angry letters appeared in the New York papers and elsewhere, deriding this censorship; and the New York *Herald-Tribune* offered a prize for the best essay on *Huckleberry Finn* written by a high school student. Even former president Harry S. Truman, a Missourian, came to the book's defense. He thought that those "who would edit Mark Twain's *Tom Sawyer* and *Huckleberry Finn*" were "misguided people." "What a distortion of literature and history we would have," he said at a dinner in his honor held at the Lotus Club on September 14, 1957, "if each succeeding generation sought to edit what was set down by others in the past in order to make it fit the momentary picture and the language of the present."[198]

Trying to duck the accusation of censorship, Ethel F. Huggard, Associate Superintendent and Chairman of the Committee on Textbooks and Supplies, wrote the *Herald-Tribune* (November 11, 1957) that *Huckleberry Finn* "has not been banned nor barred from use in the New York public schools." She insisted that it was available in the school system through the libraries and appeared on supplemental reading lists. "This kind of academic double-talk is typical of what's wrong with our schools," replied the paper. "Who in his right mind would presume to 'adapt' *Huckleberry Finn*?" The local NAACP denied having any hand in the book's removal, but the organization did take the opportunity to voice its strong opposition to the "racial slurs" and "belittling racial designations" in Twain's work. The objection to the textbook version then in use was not that it used "nigger," but that it did not capitalize "Negro."[199]

But no other case of censoring *Huckleberry Finn* received the same national attention as the case in Fairfax County, Virginia, as the book approached its centenary. Taking the advice of its Human Rights Committee, the principal at the the Mark Twain Intermediate School removed the book from the required reading list in 1982. The irony of the Mark Twain Intermediate School's "banning" Mark Twain's masterpiece was not lost on the public. As the history of the American press proves, the more extreme the rhetoric the more likely it will be quoted. Moderation is never news. "The book is poison," an administra-

198. See "Truman Predicts Income Tax Raise," New York *Times*, November 15, 1957.

199. The New York City school system was one of many that bought the 1951 Scott, Foresman & Co. edition adapted by Verne B. Brown. Designed for "the student who doesn't read well," this rewriting of the novel followed a teacher-approved two-thousand-word vocabulary list. "Idiot" turned into "fool," and even "Jew's harp" was now "mouth organ." The very first sentence in the book, "You don't know about me, without you have read a book by the name of 'The Adventures of Tom Sawyer,' but that ain't no matter" was reduced to "You don't know about me unless you have read 'The Adventures of Tom Sawyer.' " See Arthur M. Louis, "'Huck Finn' Expelled by City Schools," Philadelphia *Inquirer*, April 17, 1963.

tive aide, John H. Wallace, told Mike Sager in "Mark Twain School Trying to Censor Huck" (Washington *Post,* April 8, 1982). "It is anti-American; it works against the melting pot theory of our country; it works against the idea that all men are created equal; it works against the 14th Amendment to the Constitution and against the preamble that guarantees all men life, liberty and the pursuit of happiness." He told Ted Koppel on *Nightline* on February 4, 1985, that *Huckleberry Finn* "is the most grotesque example of racist trash ever written." Where might he put the writings of avowed bigots like Thomas A. Dixon and Adolf Hitler? "You don't ban Mark Twain—you explain Mark Twain!" replied sensible NAACP Education Director Beverly P. Cole in "NAACP on Huck Finn: Teach Teachers to Be Sensitive; Don't Censor . . . " (*Crisis*, October 1982). "To study an idea is not necessarily to endorse an idea. Mark Twain's satirical novel, *Huckleberry Finn*, accurately portrays a time in history—the mid-nineteenth century and one of its evils, slavery. . . . Before a book such as *Huckleberry Finn* is placed on a required reading list, some type of in-service training should be provided the teachers, with *concrete* guidelines that relate to the presentation and discussion" (p. 33).[200] Because of the national outcry, a Fairfax County school superintendent finally ruled that the book could be taught, but only with "appropriate planning."

Twain would certainly have been amused to know that Wallace self-published his own "adaptation" of *Huckleberry Finn* for use in schools at the height of the controversy in 1983. Wallace now summarized the story in his foreword as "Huck and his friend, Tom Sawyer, have lots of fun playing tricks on Jim and on several other characters in the novel." His bowdlerization of "the most grotesque example of racist trash ever written" is mild compared to even Olivia Clemens's and William Dean Howells's tinkering. Now he told *Jet* (July 26, 1982), "I think the book is great and should be enjoyed by all children" (p. 22). How did Wallace transform *Huckleberry Finn* from "racist trash" to a book every child should read? By merely replacing "nigger" with "slave," and removing some of the stronger material like the "Killed a nigger" exchange from Chapter

200. According to Larry Marshburne, "The NAACP and Mark Twain" (*Mark Twain Journal*, Spring 1998, pp. 2–7), *The Crisis*, the official journal of the organization, has never officially condemned the book or its author. On the contrary, almost from the beginning of its history, it has favored them. The NAACP has responded differently to *Huckleberry Finn* in different parts of the country, often being the catalyst behind its removal from required reading lists. J. Wyatt Mondesire, president of the Philadelphia NAACP, opposed the group's campaign to file grievances with the state Human Rights Commission against district superintendents and local school boards who kept *Huckleberry Finn* on mandatory reading lists. According to Robert Moran and Connie Langland ("Pennsylvania NAACP Opposes 'Huck Finn' Requirement," Buffalo *News*, February 2, 1998), Mondesire reminded his colleagues, "You're not going to learn anything by closing your eyes and not reading."

32. He also kept most of Jim's dialect and retained the plot largely as Twain wrote it. But by soft-pedaling the language, one softens the discourse. In this version, Huck is not true to his time and place and class. "Ultimately," suggested Kenny J. Williams in "*Adventures of Huckleberry Finn*, or, Mark Twain's Racial Ambiguity" (*Mark Twain Journal*, Fall 1984), "*Adventures of Huckleberry Finn* as a 'classic' may tell us more about the nation than many Americans want to know" (p. 42).

African-Americans were not entirely neglectful of Mark Twain or *Huckleberry Finn* over the years. Some recognized the book's importance in the development of American culture and their place within it. "His interest in the negro race is perhaps expressed best in one of his most delightful stories, *Huckleberry Finn*," Booker T. Washington recalled of his friend Mark Twain in *The North American Review* (June 1910). "It is possible the ordinary reader of this story has been so absorbed in the adventures of the two white boys that he did not think much about the part 'Jim' . . . played in all these adventures" (pp. 828–29). "In this book," Prof. Sterling Brown referred to *Huckleberry Finn* in his landmark study *The Negro in American Fiction* (1937), "Twain deepens the characterization of Jim, who, like Tom and Huck and the rest of that fine company, was drawn from life." Brown praised "the tenderness and truth of this portrayal."[201] Ralph Ellison noted in "Light on *Invisible Man*" (*Crisis*, March 1953) that "something vital had gone out of American prose after Mark Twain," as well as the African American as "gauge of the human condition as it waxed and waned in our democracy" (p. 158). Langston Hughes too recognized the advance of Twain's characters in American literary history. "Mark Twain, in his presentation of Negroes as human beings, stands head and shoulders above the other Southern writers of his times, even such distinguished ones as Joel Chandler Harris, F. Hopkins Smith, and Thomas Nelson Page," Hughes acknowledged in his preface to the 1959 Bantam Books edition of *Pudd'nhead Wilson*. "It was a period when most writers who included Negro characters in their work at all, were given to presenting the slave as ignorant and happy, the freed men of color as ignorant and miserable, and all Negroes as either comic servants on the one hand or dangerous brutes on the other." Some actually read and enjoyed *Huckleberry Finn*. "I loved the book, I just loved it," Dr. Kenneth B. Clark, cited in the case of *Brown v. Board of Education* before the Supreme Court, told journalist Nat Hentoff in "Huck Finn Better Get Out of Town by Sundown" (*Village Voice*, May 4, 1982). "Especially the relationship

201. Sterling Brown, *The Negro in American Fiction* (Washington, D.C.: Associates of American Folk Education, 1937), pp. 67–68.

between Huck and Jim. It was such an easy, *understanding* relationship. The kind a boy wishes he could have." But he warned, "The last damn thing blacks should do is get into the vanguard of banning books. The next step is banning blacks."

Wallace knew otherwise. "My own research," he said, "indicates that the assignment and reading aloud of *Huckleberry Finn* in our classrooms is humiliating and insulting to black students. It contributes to their feelings of low self-esteem and to the white students' disrespect for black people. It constitutes mental cruelty, harassment, and outright racial intimidation to force black students to sit in the classroom with their white peers and read *Huckleberry Finn*. The attitudes developed by the reading of such literature can lead to tensions, discontent, and even fighting."[202] Not everyone has found this to be the case. "When my African-American students felt free to voice their most urgent concerns validated by their white classmates, it was not long before their underlying affection for the book became apparent," reported Kay Puttock in "Many Responses to the Many Voices of *Huckleberry Finn*" (*Lion and the Unicorn*, June 1992). "Moreover, their evident involvement raised the quality of the discussion, and caused the whole class to become engaged with the book on a deeper level than would have happened without them" (p. 79). Peaches Henry cited in "The Struggle for Tolerance: Race and Censorship in *Huckleberry Finn*" two independent studies which came to the opposite conclusion to Wallace's.[203] Herbert Lewis Frankel discovered for his 1972 Temple University dissertation, "The Effects of Reading *The Adventures of Huckleberry Finn* on the Racial Attitudes of Selected Ninth Grade Boys," that white students, after reading the book in the class, had "reduce[d] hostile or unfavorable feelings . . . and increase[d] favorable feelings toward members of another race" and that "black students tended to identify more strongly and positively with other members of their race." Another study, *The Effects of Reading "Huckleberry Finn" on the Racial Attitudes of Ninth Grade Students,* conducted by the State College Area School of District and the Forum on Black Affairs of Pennsylvania State University in 1983, reported that "the preponderance of our data suggests that, if anything, it lessens such stereotyping." Nevertheless, the committee recommended that the book be removed from the ninth-grade curriculum and placed in the eleventh- or twelfth-grade syllabus. Evidently the statements in

202. In "The Case Against *Huck Finn*," *Satire or Evasion?: Black Perspectives on "Huckleberry Finn*," edited by James S. Leonard, Thomas A. Tenney, and Thadious M. Davis (Durham, N.C. and London: Duke University Press, 1992), pp. 39–43.

203. Also in *Satire or Evasion?*, pp. 39–43.

Huckleberry Finn, like those Huck found in *Pilgrim's Progress*, were interesting, but tough.

While the book has been challenged all over the country, one of the few recorded instances in which an African-American child was verbally and physically harassed by white classmates after reading *Huckleberry Finn* occurred in Warrington, Pennsylvania, in 1982.[204] His parents did not object to *Huckleberry Finn* or Mark Twain but to the wisdom of putting the book in the hands of ignorant eighth-graders. "To miss that teaching opportunity, to not confront what happened to that black kid in Warrington head-on by really exploring this book," observed Dr. Clark, "is to underestimate every child in that classroom. And by underestimating them—while also 'protecting' the black child from this book—you deprive them all of what they should know. And what they can especially learn from *Huckleberry Finn*."[205] In 1996, Kathy Monteiro, an elementary-school teacher in Phoenix, Arizona, challenged the teaching of *Huckleberry Finn* as a hate crime when she sued the Tempe Union School on behalf of her teenage daughter for "egregious public racial harassment." The suit claimed that assigning *Huckleberry Finn* and William Faulkner's short story "A Rose for Emily" as part of the mandatory curriculum with their "repeated use of the profane, insulting and racially derogatory term 'nigger' . . . created and contributed to a racially hostile educational environment" and encouraged racial harassment by other students; and when the school refused to act on their complaints, it violated provisions of the Civil Rights Act of 1964. Assuming that these works were indeed "racist" as alleged, the Ninth U.S. Circuit Court of Appeals ruled on October 18, 1998, that it was not the function of the courts to "ban books or other literary works from school curricula on the basis of their content." The judges were aware of recent attempts by white parents and students to suppress works by Maya Angelou, Langston Hughes, Toni Morrison, Alice Walker, and Richard Wright. Monteiro had failed to show that the usage of "the most noxious racial epithet in the contemporary American

204. The American Library Association has designated Mark Twain and *Huckleberry Finn* as among the top ten of the most challenged authors and books in America. According to reports in *Newsletter on Intellectual Freedom* and elsewhere, communities which have objected to *Huckleberry Finn* in the classroom in recent years have included Mesa, Arizona; San Jose, California; Deland and Miami, Florida; Indianapolis; Rockford, Springfield, and Winnetka, Illinois; Caddo Parish and Houma, Louisiana; Berrien Springs and Portage, Michigan; Cherry Hill, New Jersey; Enid, Oklahoma; Erie, Philadelphia, and State College, Pennsylvania; Sevierville, Tennessee; and Houston, Lewisville, and Plano, Texas. The issue was also explored in the PBS documentary "Born to Trouble: Adventures of Huckleberry Finn," part of the *Culture Shock* series, aired on January 26, 2000.

205. Quoted in Nat Hentoff, "Huck Finn and the Shortchanging of Black Kids," *The Village Voice*, May 18, 1982.

lexicon" in both *Huckleberry Finn* and "A Rose for Emily" on its own led to increased racial tension within school. "We view with considerable skepticism charges that reading books causes evil conduct," replied Judge Stephen Reinhardt in the opinion. It further noted "that a student is required to read a book does not mean that he is being asked to agree with what is in it. It cannot be disputed that a necessary component of any education is learning to think critically about offensive ideas—without that ability one can do little to respond to them." But it reprimanded the school for failing to respond properly to complaints from parents and students about the racially hostile environment. Toni Morrison, like Dr. Clark, suspected that these attempts to remove *Huckleberry Finn* were based "on a narrow notion of how to handle the offense Mark Twain's use of the term 'nigger' would occasion for black students and the corrosive effect it would have on white ones. It struck me as a purist yet elementary kind of censorship designed to appease adults rather than educate children. Amputate the problem, band-aid the solution."[206]

This dispute sometimes sounds like a reworking of the "King Sollermun" dialogue in Chapter 14, with Jim speaking from the heart while Huck quotes the "authorities," the man's personal experience challenging the boy's schooling. The introduction of American slavery into the classroom has always been a volatile issue, but the anxiety and anger *Huckleberry Finn* engenders in some students has rarely been addressed. Margot Allen, academic coordinator for Penn State's Office of Academic Assistance Program, spoke for many African-American children when she described her introduction to *Huckleberry Finn* in school in Portland, Oregon, in 1957, when she was thirteen years old. "I was the only Black student in the class," she recalled in "*Huck Finn*: Two Generations of Pain" (*Interracial Books for Children Bulletin*, no. 5, 1984). "When *Huck Finn* was assigned, there was no advance preparation; we simply started to read the book, a classic whose name held a familiar—and friendly—ring for most students. As we began to get into the story, however, the dialect alone made me feel uneasy. And as we continued, I began to be apprehensive, to fear being singled out, being put on the spot, being ridiculed or made fun of because of my color, and only because of my color!" (p. 9). And then there was that word.

Her son suffered the same "tension, discomfort and hurt" when the book was read in class years later. "I read *Huck Finn* when I was in high school—and I can remember feeling betrayed by the teacher," Wallace recounted in "*Huckleberry Finn* Is Offensive" (Washington *Post*, April 11, 1982). "I felt humiliated and embarrassed. Ten years ago, my oldest son went through the same experi-

206. In her introduction to the 1996 Oxford University Press edition of *Huckleberry Finn*.

ence in high school, until I went to talk to the teachers about it; and he lost interest in English classes." The same pattern was repeated in schools across the country: The lone sensitive child of color forced to read a book that demeaned that student among one's peers. The agony arose from the perception of what the others might be thinking or might be capable of doing. The pain resulted more from apprehensiveness of classmates rather than from the book itself. "Fear and alarm are what I remembered most about my first encounter with Mark Twain's *Adventures of Huckleberry Finn*," Toni Morrison testified in her introduction to the 1996 Oxford University Press edition of *Huckleberry Finn*. "Palpable alarm. Unlike the treasure-island excursion of *Tom Sawyer*, at no point along Huck's journey was a happy ending signaled or guaranteed. Reading *Huckleberry Finn*, chosen randomly without guidance or recommendation, was deeply disturbing. My second reading of it, under the supervision of an English teacher in junior high school, was no less uncomfortable—rather more. It provoked a feeling I can only describe now as muffled rage, as though appreciation of the work required my complicity and sanction of something shaming." But was the book at fault or the circumstances under which it was presented in class?

The rage must be addressed. "Unless *Huck Finn*'s racist *and* anti-racist messages are considered, the book can have racist results," warned the Council of Interracial Books in an editorial in its *Bulletin* in 1984. However, after one hundred years of *Huckleberry Finn*, no one seems to agree on what those messages might be. "Irony, as all students of literature know," explained Richard K. Barsdale in "History, Slavery, and Thematic Irony in *Huckleberry Finn*" (*Mark Twain Journal*, Fall 1984), "involves a deliberate misstatement—a misstatement designed to highlight the longtime adverse effects of a grossly immoral act or a blatantly dishonest deed or an inhumane or unchristian practice. If the ironic statement made by an author in a work of fiction is too subtly wrought, it will not be effectively communicated to the average reader" (p. 20). Little was achieved in calling the book's opponents "know-nothings and noise-makers," as British critic Christopher Hitchens did in "American Notes" (*TLS*, March 8, 1985, p. 258). Jonathan Arac made the extravagant accusation in *Huckleberry Finn as Idol and Target* (1997) that "the idolatry of the book has served, and—remarkably—continues to serve, as an excuse for well-meaning white people to use the term *nigger* with the good conscience that comes from believing that their usage is sanctioned by their idol (whether Twain, or his book, or Huck) and is made safe by the technique of irony" (p. 16). But there is nothing safe about the word "nigger." As Arac himself observed, "talking about *Huckleberry Finn* has made many smart people to say foolish things" (p. 77). The same "well-meaning white people" have also called Jim "saint," "one of the noblest characters in American literature," "adult guide and protector," even "hero." Oddly, white supremacists have yet to claim *Huckleberry Finn* as a cornerstone of their odious philosophy. The book seems to be an equal opportunity offender.

Some of the recent complaints about the book are reminiscent of the Concord Library Committee's ban. "Twain's notion of freedom is the simplistic one of freedom from restraint and responsibility," complained Julius Lester in "Morality and *Adventures of Huckleberry Finn*" (*Mark Twain Journal*, Fall 1984). "It is an adolescent vision of life, an exercise in nostalgia for the paradise that never was" (p. 46). Jane Smiley's angry reaction to the novel, "Say It Ain't So, Huck" (*Harper's Magazine*, January 1996), unleashed a howl of protest.[207] She argued that "the entry of *Huck Finn* into classrooms sets the terms of the discussion of racism and American history, and sets them very low: all you have to do to be a hero is to acknowledge that your poor sidekick is human; you don't actually have to act in the interests of his humanity" (p. 67). Yet in the book Huck does act: He sacrifices everything to help Jim escape. The thrust of her attack, however, was not so much to knock Twain (although she did that quite soundly) as to boost Harriet Beecher Stowe in a vain feminist campaign to restore *Uncle Tom's Cabin* to the American literary canon. (Arac's vote was for something by James Fenimore Cooper.) The positioning of *Uncle Tom's Cabin* and *Huckleberry Finn* in literary importance was not the result of some deadly white men's conspiracy, as she (as well as Arac) implied. While Stowe's moral stance conforms to Smiley's political agenda, Stowe still falls short of Twain's verbal invention and philosophical depth. Smiley's novel *The All-True Travels and Adventures of Lidie Newton* (1998), set in pre–Civil War Kansas, was a mere-

207. "That any dunce," wrote Alexander Theroux in a letter to the editor of *Harper's* in April, 1996 "would presume to criticize Mark Twain's masterpiece, *Huckleberry Finn*, on such lame topical and political grounds, never mind a working novelist and Pulitzer Prize winner for fiction (!), and then be allowed to publish such tripe in any magazine, never mind a reputable one, is proof positive not only that the barbarians are at the gate but that they have already poured through, with howls, with knives, with rattling fishhorns, and somehow, all in the form of Jane Smiley" (p. 7). Justin Kaplan, Twain's biographer, replied in "Selling 'Huck Finn' Down the River" (*The New York Times Book Review*, March 10, 1996), that "Mark Twain was writing a historical, not a reformist, novel. Instead of being issue driven, a cry for action, as Stowe's book was, his was autobiographical and nostalgic. Perhaps he had set out to do something not altogether possible, to meld a tenderly remembered boyhood with a profoundly troubled adult recognition that the same white, riverine society that allowed Huck his brief rafting idyll was also heartless and greedy, a league of swindlers, drunks, hypocrites, lunkheads, bounty hunters, and trigger-happy psychopaths" (p. 27). Smiley apparently forgot what "Uncle Tom" came to mean, as Arnold Rampersad said, "a byword among blacks for unmanly compromise." See "*Adventures of Huckleberry Finn* and Afro-American Literature," *Mark Twain Journal*, Fall 1984, p. 49.

tricious attempt to dislodge *Huckleberry Finn* and its dead white male author from the hierarchy of American letters. Smiley was guilty of the same sin she accused Twain of committing: She gave Lidie a voice but not a novel.

Howells insisted in *My Mark Twain* that his friend "was the most desouthernized Southerner I ever knew. No man more perfectly sensed and more entirely abhorred slavery" (p. 35). Joel Chandler Harris referred to him in the Atlanta *Constitution* (June 11, 1882) as a "reconstructed Missourian." Twain proudly insisted that (besides the French) "I have no race prejudices, and I think I have no color prejudices. . . . All that I care to know is that a man is a human being—that is enough for me; he can't be worse."[208] One of his most scathing attacks on racism was "King Leopold's Soliloquy," an enraged protest against the atrocities the king of Belgium committed against the people of the Congo. It was so advanced for its time that *The North American Review* refused to publish it, and Twain issued it in a short pamphlet in 1905. He did not attack injustice only abroad, but another angry essay, "The United States of Lyncherdom," had to be published posthumously. "Huck Finn's acceptance of the evil implicit in his 'emancipation' of Jim," suggested Ralph Ellison, "represents Twain's acceptance of his personal responsibility in the condition of Society. This was the tragic face behind the comic mask."[209] However, just as Huck seems indifferent to Jim's needs, Twain did not write *Huckleberry Finn* for the African-American audience. The black press did not review the book when it came out and was conspicuously silent about it for decades.

W.E.B. Du Bois, who admired Twain, argued in *The Souls of Black Folk* (1903) that the African-American inhabits "a world which yields him no true self-consciousness, but only lets him see himself through the revelation of the other world. It is a peculiar sensation, this double-consciousness, this sense of always looking at one's self through the eyes of others, of measuring one's soul by the tape of a world that looks on in amused contempt and pity" (pp. 16–17). Remarkably, much of the recent discussion of *Huckleberry Finn* among African-American scholars has been a reclaiming of Jim. "At a time when both political and literary forces seem determined to turn the nation's attention away from racist maltreatment of black people, and blacks to 'true scholarship'—the study of white people and their public fictions—Twain deserves a careful reading as a white person who almost, but not quite, publicly emancipated himself from racism," Richard K. Barsdale proposed in "History, Slavery,

208. Quoted in E. Burleson Stevenson, "Mark Twain's Attitude Toward the Negro," *The Quarterly Review of Higher Education Among Negroes*, October 1945, p. 342.

209. In *Shadow and Act* (New York: Random House), p. 33.

and Thematic Irony in *Huckleberry Finn*" (*Mark Twain Journal*, Fall 1984). "He and his books cry out for reflective careful study, not angry efforts to prohibit the readings of his work" (p. 37). These critics have reconsidered Twain's place within American literature and culture, particularly in regard to African-American writers. Arnold Rampersad saw Twain's importance as an even broader and richer influence than did Hemingway, Eliot, and their disciples. "In his stress on folk culture, on dialect, and on American humor," Rampersand argued in "*Adventures of Huckleberry Finn* and Afro-American literature," "Mark Twain anticipated Dunbar, Hughes . . . , Hurston, Fisher, Thurman, Ellison, Gaines, Childress, Reed, and Alice Walker. In his depiction of alienation in an American context, prominently including race, Mark Twain anticipates other aspects of most of these writers' work and also Richard Wright, Chester Himes, Ann Petry, James Baldwin, and Toni Morrison" (p. 52). And they have redefined the meaning of the novel. It is no longer Huck's story, but Jim's as well. "Whenever Huck is inclined to let the baseness of his human condition assume control, it is Jim who guides him," observed Williams in "*Adventures of Huckleberry Finn*, or, Mark Twain's Racial Ambiguity." "The bond between the two characters is so strong that if one takes Jim away, Huck—as we know him—ceases to exist" (p. 40).[210]

One consequence of reading *Huckleberry Finn* that Twain's critics fail to consider is that the book may actually *discourage* racism. Norman Frank, the son of Hans Frank, the goveror-general of Poland who was executed at Nuremberg for crimes committed against humanity under Hitler, recalled that *Huckleberry Finn* "ruined me for the rest of the Third Reich. My mind was always with Jim and the Mississippi River. It was so special to me, had such an impact on me. It was such a different world than the one I knew. . . . I read it at nine and I still

210. Recently there has emerged a rich subgenre of literary criticism devoted to the racial controversies surrounding the novel, particularly Twain's portrayal of Jim: Tom Quirk, *Coming to Grips with Huckleberry Finn: Essays on a Book, a Boy, and a Man* (Columbia: University of Missouri Press, 1993); Shelley Fisher Fishkin, *Was Huck Black?: Mark Twain and African American Voices* (New York and Oxford: Oxford University Press, 1993); Gerald Graff and James Phelan, *Adventures of Huckleberry Finn: A Case Study in Critical Controversy* (Boston and New York: Bedford Books for St. Martin's Press, 1995); Claudia D. Johnson, *Understanding Adventures of Huckleberry Finn: A Student Casebook to Issues, Sources, and Historical Documents* (Westport, Conn.: Greenwood Press, 1996); Jonathan Arac, *Huckleberry Finn as Idol and Target: The Functions of Criticism in Our Time* (Madison: University of Wisconsin Press, 1997); Joselyn Chadwick-Joshua, *The Jim Dilemma: Reading Race in Huckleberry Finn* (Jackson: University Press of Mississippi, 1998); James S. Leonard, *Making Mark Twain Work in the Classroom* (Durham, N.C.: Duke University Press, 1999); Elaine Mensh and Harry Mensh, *Black, White, & Huckleberry Finn: Re-Imagining the American Dream* (Tuscaloosa: University of Alabama Press, 2000); and Carl F. Wieck, *Refiguring Huckleberry Finn* (Athens, Ga. and London: University of Georgia Press, 2000).

remember it clearly. . . . I would rather have been there than in Berlin."[211] The same may well be true of American, Russian, Chinese, and other children around the world: They would rather be with Jim on the Mississippi River.

Huckleberry Finn has not remained just an American classic. Russian poet Yevgeny Yevtushenko and Nobel Prize winner Kenzabure Ōe of Japan are among the many writers who have acknowledged the influence of *Huckleberry Finn* on their work. "Mark Twain is not a humorist," said Jean Cocteau in *Mark Twain Journal* (Spring and Summer 1958). "He is a poet and I love him." In 1982, Jorge Luis Borges agreed to lecture on Walt Whitman at Washington University in St. Louis, only on the condition that he could make a side trip to Hannibal, the hometown of the author of *Huckleberry Finn*. Nearly blind at the time, he was unimpressed with the Mark Twain Museum; and over lunch, he asked the curator to take him to the river. "The Mississippi River is the source of Mark Twain's strength," he said. "I want to touch the river." So they went down to the waterfront, and Borges squatted on the cobblestones to let the water run through his fingers. "Now my journey is complete," he said.[212]

V

FROM THE mighty Mississippi the book draws its strengths and its weaknesses. *Huckleberry Finn* is a historical novel set in a specific time and place, and yet it resonates far beyond the early nineteenth century and far beyond the banks of the Big Muddy. First, there is the voice of Huckleberry Finn. Twain beautifully succeeded in his artifice that here was exactly how such a boy would speak. Remarkably, he was also able to sustain at least seven different variants of American English throughout the story. Twain seemed as much at ease with the Missouri slave lingo and the duke's extravagant gibberish as he was with the ordinary "Pike County" idiom of the young narrator. Rarely does Huck fall from character; only in Chapter 22 is it apparent that Mark Twain is speaking rather than Colonel Sherburn when he quells the Bricksville mob. Despite the deliberate care taken in the book's composition, one of the great-

211. Quoted in Wieck, *Refiguring Huckleberry Finn*, p. ix. According to Edgar H. Hemminghaus, *Mark Twain in Germany* (New York: Columbia University Press, 1939, p. 142), 190,000 copies of *Huckleberry Finn* sold in Germany between 1890 and 1937; but sales of all his books declined under the Third Reich due to the accusation that Mark Twain was a Jewish writer. For example, in Theodor Fritsch, *Handbuch der Judenfrage* (1933), Alfred Eisenmenger suggested, "You don't want to believe that Mark Twain is a Jew, but his way of writing is Jewish" (p. 144).

212. See Zinsser, *American Places*, pp. 63–64.

est powers of *Huckleberry Finn* lies in how effortless it all appears. Huck's voice is, as DeVoto argued in *Mark Twain's America*, "a sensitive, subtle, and versatile instrument—capable of every effect it is called upon to manage" (p. 318). To Dwight Macdonald in "Mark Twain: An Unsentimental Journey" (*New Yorker*, April 9, 1960), Twain in this instance "was able to raise the vernacular to a great style" (p. 174). There is a lyricism in his speech which avoids "the gaudiness and inane phraseology of many modern writers" that William Wordsworth wished to strip from contemporary poetry through his *Lyrical Ballads* (1798); nearly a century later, Huck's colloquial description of the sunrise on the river in Chapter 19 served as the climax of the nineteenth-century American attempt through local color to invent a contemporary style in the manner of Wordsworth from what the poet described as "a selection of the real language of men in a state of vivid sensation." As T. S. Eliot suggested, Twain through Huck Finn brought the language up to date.

Sam Clemens, printer's apprentice, 1850.
Courtesy the Mark Twain Papers, Bancroft Library, University of California at Berkeley.

However, Twain's mastery of dialect does not fully account for the greatness of the style of *Huckleberry Finn*. Actually, although he may have been (as Eliot said) the first author to use natural speech through the entirety of a novel, Samuel L. Clemens as "Mark Twain" wrote within a long tradition of American humor. Well-known *noms de guerre* such as "Artemus Ward" (Charles Farrar Browne), "Petroleum V. Nasby" (David Ross Locke), and "Josh Billings" (Henry Wheeler Shaw) preceded him. These comic writers, all forgotten now, formed a school of seemingly illiterate backwoodsmen whose common sense exposed the stupidities of contemporary American life; and also, in the Huck Finn manner, each spoke in his natural idiom. Twain, however, unlike the others, did not indulge, as Howells argued in "Mark Twain" (*Century Magazine*, September 1882), "in literary attitude, in labored dictionary funning, in affected quaintness, in dreary dramatization, in artificial 'dialect' " (p. 781).

Twain stands head and shoulders above writers like Nasby and Billings as much for his purpose as for his prose style. "Humor is only a fragrance, a decoration," he said. "Often it is merely an odd trick of speech and of spelling, as in the case of Ward and Billings and Nasby . . . , and presently the fashion passes and the fame along with it." For the work to survive, it must teach and preach as well as amuse. "The proper office of humor," Twain wryly explained, "is to reflect, to put you in a pensive mood of deep thought, to make you think of your sins."[213] With these ambitious intentions, Twain transformed mere humor into enduring satire.

Petroleum V. Nasby, Mark Twain, and Josh Billings.
Courtesy Library of Congress.

Twain went even further than his predecessors in exploring a comic vernacular by making his narrator a boy rather than a grown man. "It wasn't Huck who wrote *Huckleberry Finn*," insisted British critic F. R. Leavis in "The Americanness of American Literature" (*Commentary*, November 1952); "the mind that conceived *him* was mature, subtle, and sophisticated. Mark Twain had had very wide and varied experience of men and the world, and he was a shrewd observer; he observed out of a ripe wisdom" (pp. 471–72). He drew on this vast knowledge and experience to create the semiliterate son of the town drunk. Huck is from the lowest level of St. Petersburg society, and yet he (like his Hannibal prototype, Tom Blankenship) is the only really independent person in the community. Therefore, unlike Tom Sawyer, he owes nothing to anyone—not to pap Finn, who beats him, and not to the Widow Douglas, who befriends him. He can thus tell the truth, the whole truth, and nothing but the truth denied to bookish, romantic Tom Sawyer. Through his ignorance, his lack of "sivilizing," he views the world through the clear eyes of a true innocent. Huck Finn is an American of the Romantic ideal of the divine fool. He is Twain's wild boy of Aveyron, Twain's Kaspar Hauser.

He is also related to Southwestern folk heroes. He is a direct descendant of Mike Fink, the Mississippi River boatman, so suspicious of progress that he keeps moving west to stay ahead of civilization; he is a cousin of Mike Shuck, "a white-headed, hardy urchin, who nobody claimed kin to, and who disclaimed

213. In *Mark Twain in Eruption*, p. 202; and the lecture "Theoretical and Practical Morals," delivered in London, July 8, 1899, *Mark Twain's Speeches* (New York: Harper & Bros., 1910), p. 131.

connexion with all mankind," who too fled to the great American wilderness.[214] There is much of Shuck and Fink in Huck Finn: Like Hank Morgan in Chapter 39 of *A Connecticut Yankee in King Arthur's Court*, the boy is "the champion of hard, unsentimental common-sense and reason." Whether describing the carnage left by the Grangerford–Shepherdson feud or Sherburn's killing Boggs, the boy records all the horrible events he witnesses free of any sentimental or intellectual elaboration. He merely observes, he does not judge. He does briefly break down in Chapter 18, on the discovery of the corpse of a murdered friend, but he pulls back on describing the aftermath: "I ain't agoing to tell *all* that happened—it would make me sick again if I was to do it. . . . I ain't ever going to get shut of them—lots of times I dream about them." What is most chilling in this passage is what is implied.

Unlike Twain in his other work, Huck never digresses into diatribes: The Connecticut Yankee in King Arthur's Court, for example, is often more Sam Clemens than Hank Morgan. In Chapter 38 of *Life on the Mississippi*, Twain gave a straight description of a typical interior of the period similar to the Grangerford parlor in Chapter 17 of *Huckleberry Finn*, but this sarcastic account of "The House Beautiful" lacks the subtle irony of Huck's version; the effect in the latter is far more telling, far sharper, for the ignorant boy so admires every detail of the Grangerford décor. As Walter Besant suggested in "My Favorite Novelist and His Best Book" (*Munsey's Magazine*, February 1898), Huck is so often unconsciously humorous because he rarely sees the comedy in anything. Twain snickers behind the boy's back.

But Huck does comment on the stupidities and cruelties he observes after Boggs's murder. It does not take long for him to recognize the king and the duke for the frauds they are; later he condemns the mob's tarring and feathering the two scoundrels. "It was a dreadful thing to see," Huck says. "Human beings *can* be awful cruel to one another." Huck himself has one flaw: a conscience deformed from being trained within a slave state. Under his shiftless father's tutelage, he believes that though he be white trash he is better than any person of color, whether slave or free.

Ironically, the boy's companion down the river is Miss Watson's Jim, a fugitive slave; and this unfortunate soul, like Huck, has had plenty of unfair mud flung at him. The story starts inauspiciously by making Jim the butt of Tom Sawyer's cruel jokes. Only slowly does the man's dignity and the depth of his humanity emerge, all the time testing and conquering Huck's prejudices and

214. See "Aurora Borealis" (Capt. Alphonso Wetmore), "The Beaver Hunter," Franklin *Missouri Intelligencer*, October 29, 1822.

assumptions about his race. Jim's very presence in the novel challenges the validity of American republicanism that allowed so pernicious an institution as slavery to thrive under the laws of the South and Southwest. Just as Jim challenges Huck's conscience, so too was slavery the persistent threat to Western democracy.

Particularly offensive to Twain's detractors are the minstrel-show-like exchanges between Jim in a role similar to that of "Mr. Bones," the comic, and Huck as "Mr. Interlocutor," the straight man. But it is not so simple as that. One must read between the lines to get to the core of the deceptively comic discourse. Jim belongs to the tradition of Ward, Billings, and other once prominent figures of American humor. After all, Jim wins the argument of whether King Solomon should or should not have killed that child, through his common sense. Jim always wins, because he speaks from the heart and not just from the head. He may be illiterate, but he is not ignorant. He knows all the signs of Nature and the ways of the river; he acts as a protector, as an "elder brother," to Huck just as Miles Hendon does to Edward Tudor in *The Prince and the Pauper*.

Jim does have a level head, as Huck must admit at the beginning of Chapter 16. One need only look at all the skills he demonstrates on the journey down the Mississippi when he and Huck are left to their own devices. It is only when they pick up passengers or return to the land that he becomes degraded, forced to play the subservient role again. Of course, his knowledge and opinions are not the conventional kind, and that may be why he so fascinated Twain. He also has a good heart, probably the only adult who does within the whole novel. He is by nature both wise and kind. This black brother is not only the "other," but the "better." Ralph Ellison admitted in "Change the Yoke and Slip the Yoke" (*Partisan Review*, Spring 1958), "I could imagine myself as Huck Finn (I so nicknamed my brother) but not, though I racially identified with him, as Nigger Jim, who struck me as a white man's inadequate portrait of a slave" (p. 222). But it is wrong to view Jim as either a stereotype or an archetype. He is a man, just a man, and a good man. His virtues far outweigh his faults. He sacrifices his own freedom to help Tom Sawyer not because he is Julius Lester's "good nigger," but because he is a good human being, perhaps the only truly decent person in the entire novel.

The raft is a great equalizer. Huck admits in Chapter 19 that "what you want, above all things, on a raft, is for everybody to be satisfied, and feel right and kind towards the others." Only on the river can such harmony be found in the novel. Conflicts arise only when the fugitives come ashore or encounter other men on the water. To Huck and Jim, Hell is other people. The constant threat to their peaceful existence is "sivilization," what Twain called "a shoddy, poor thing and full of cruelties, vanities, and arrogances, meannesses, and hypocrisies."[215] Everyone they meet wants either to imprison or to steal Huck's "nigger"; whenever the boy goes ashore and leaves Jim alone, the man must be either tied up or disguised to protect him from thieves. When the king and the duke join them, they establish aristocracy on the raft and make Huck a servant and Jim a slave again. Nothing civilization provides the fugitives is worthwhile. Its religion teaches brotherly love on Sundays and good churchgoers like the Grangerfords and Shepherdsons slaughter one another; preachers like Uncle Silas own slaves. Close family ties inspire the stupidities of the Southern feud, one careless insult ends in Sherburn shooting Boggs. The slave system reveals all the ugliest qualities not only in the South, but of humanity.

During the 1840s, the supposed period of the novel, American culture was in transition. The Mississippi Valley was still largely untouched, largely a Jeffersonian agrarian society removed from the Industrial Revolution, still free of railroads; even steam power was then just some marvelous toy. Progress invades the American Eden in *Huckleberry Finn* when a steamship wrecks Huck's raft. Greed too shatters the delicate balance on the river. Nineteenth-century progress meant merely materialism to Twain.[216] The Mississippi Valley was never the same after the California Gold Rush of 1849. Before that craze, Twain believed, "'rich' men were not worshipped, and not envied. They were not arrogant, not assertive, nor tyrannical, nor exigent."[217] The Gold Rush with its "get-rich-quick" schemes "begat the lust for money which is the rule today, and the hardness and the cynicism which is the spirit of today." Although not mentioned specifically in the text, 1849, the year both Sam Clemens and Huck Finn were fourteen, may well be the date of *Huckleberry Finn*. The lust for money pollutes the life on the river with the introduction of the shiftless king and duke, two professional swindlers, who sell Jim for "forty dirty dollars."

Huck's only defense against a deceptive society is deception. Paradoxically, although he vows to tell the truth in the novel's very first paragraph, Huck Finn is an incurable liar. *Huckleberry Finn* is as much a confession as a story. At

215. Quoted in Paine, *Mark Twain: A Biography*, vol. 2, p. 1906.

216. "Prodigious acquisitions," he argued in a letter to Twichell, March 14, 1905, "were made in things which add to the comfort of the many and make life harder for as many more. . . . Money is the supreme ideal—all others take tenth place. . . . Money-lust has always existed, but not in the history of the world was it ever a craze, a madness, until your time and mine. This lust will rot these nations; it has made them hard, sordid, ungentle, dishonest, oppressive" (*Mark Twain's Letters*, vol. 2, pp. 769–70).

217. In "Villagers of 1840–3," *Tom Sawyer and Huck Finn Among the Indians*, p. 100.

every stop along the river, he takes on a new alias; and he succeeds so effortlessly in outwitting others on the water and land by appealing to their cowardice, sentimentality, vanity, cruelty, and greed as well as their good qualities. "All men are liars," Twain insisted, "partial or hiders of facts, half tellers of truth, shirks, moral sneaks. When a merely honest man appears he is a comet—his fame is eternal—needs no genius, no talent—mere honesty."[218] Twain must have thought *he* was that man. Huck too is a liar. He is really no different than anyone else, surely no different than those two great pretenders the king and the duke. However, the boy never lies or steals for self-gain, only for self-preservation. And he never deceives himself: In his agonizing wrestling with his unrelenting conscience, he follows the honest dictates of his good heart.

A common complaint against *Huckleberry Finn* is that as a novel it is as formless as the mighty Mississippi itself. Critics have failed to heed Twain's warning that "any persons attempting to find a plot in it will be shot" seriously and deplored its apparent lack of design. "Episodically, both *Huckleberry Finn* and *Tom Sawyer* are magnificent," said English novelist Arnold Bennett in the London *Bookman* (June 1910), "but as complete works of art they are of quite inferior quality. Mark Twain was always a divine amateur, and he never would or never could appreciate the fact . . . that the most important thing in any work of art is its construction. He had no notion of construction, and very little power of self-criticism. He was great in the subordinate business of decoration, as distinguished from construction; but he would mingle together the very best and the very worst decorations. The praise poured out on his novels seems to me exceedingly exaggerated" (p. 118). *Huckleberry Finn* is, as T. S. Eliot noted, "not the kind of story which the author knows, from the beginning, what is going to happen." Twain's working notes support this assertion; they contain such unappetizing possibilities as "turn Jim into an Injun" and "then exhibit him for a gorrilla—then wild Arab etc., using him for two shows same day" and Huck escaping the circus on the back of an elephant.[219] Twain was an intuitive writer; he composed, as Howells explained in *My Mark Twain*, "as he thought, and as all men think, without sequence, without an eye to what went before or should come after" (p. 17).

Twain told Howells that he was thinking of Lesage's *Gil Blas* (1715) when he began *Huckleberry Finn*. Although he informed Brander Matthews that he had never really read the Lesage novel, he was nevertheless acquainted with it and

218. In *Mark Twain's Notebook* (1935), p. 181.

219. See the 1988 University of California edition of *Huckleberry Finn*, pp. 728 and 757.

other picaresque novels such as *Tom Jones* and *Roderick Random*.[220] Huck Finn is a *pícaro*, a rogue or roguish wanderer, a type introduced in eighteenth-century Spanish literature as the antithesis of the medieval hero. While the courtly knight is of noble birth and character, dedicated to the rules of chivalry, the *pícaro* is low and immoral by the usual standards of civilization; the hero goes on a quest for something admirable, but *pícaro* escapes, often from the law. The medieval knight, because of his virtue, generally embodies superhuman strength and ideals; the rogue is often physically weak and must survive by his wits through deception, stealth, and theft. A picaresque novel is also generally told in the first person, has an episodic plot, and satirizes several levels of society. In *Huckleberry Finn*, Twain replaced the road with the river; and in so doing, he abandoned all semblance of a motive, a moral, and a plot. What was sacrificed in the incoherent construction was gained in the introduction of a series of repetitions and variations on a set of contrasting themes.

"People will read *Huck Finn* for a long time," Faulkner admitted. "Twain has never really written a novel, however. His work is too loose. We'll assume that a novel has set rules. His work is a mass of stuff—just a series of events."[221] "He wrote by whim," suggested E. L. Doctorow in "Huck, Continued" (*New Yorker*, June 26/July 3, 1995), "without plan, giving himself totally to the pleasures of improvisation and the music he heard in speech" (p. 132). Twain admitted in some introductory remarks in *Pudd'nhead Wilson and Those Extraordinary Twins* he often began with "no clear idea of his story . . . merely . . . some people in his mind, and an incident or two, also a locality." He followed the method that was later defined as stream of consciousness. As he suggested in his *Autobiography* (vol. 1, 1924), "narrative should flow as flows the brook down through the hills and the leafy woodlands, its course changed by every boulder it comes across and by every grass-clad gravelly spur that projects in its path; its surface broken, but its course not stayed by rocks and gravel on the bottom of the shoal places; a brook that never goes straight for a minute, but *goes*, and goes briskly, sometimes ungrammatically, and sometimes fetching a horseshoe three quarters of a mile around, and at the end of the circuit flowing within a yard of the path it traversed an hour before; but always *going*, and always following at least

220. To Matthews, *The Tocsin of Revolt*, p. 267; Matthews noticed that Hucklebery Finn shared with Gil Blas "an unheroic hero who is not the chief actor in the chief episodes he sets forth and who is often little more than a recording spectator, before whose tolerant eyes the panorama of human vicissitude is unrolled." Matthews was recalling Huck's reaction to the Grangerford–Shepherdson feud and Sherburn's shooting of Boggs in Twain's novel. See also Charles E. Metzger, "*The Adventures of Huckleberry Finn* as Picaresque," *The Midwest Quarterly*, April 1964, pp. 249–56.

221. Quoted in Meriweather and Millgate, *Lion in the Garden*, p. 56.

one law, always loyal to that law, the law of *narrative*, which *has no law*" (pp. 237–38). He compared it to a canal which "moves slowly, smoothly, decorously, sleepily, it has no blemish except that it is all blemish. It is too literary, too prim, too nice; the gait and the style and movement are not suited to narrative. That canal stream is always reflecting; it is its nature; it can't help it. Its slick shiny surface is interested in everything it passes along the banks—cows, foliage, flowers, everything. And so it wastes a lot of time in reflections." It is clear from the start of *Huckleberry Finn* that Twain never knew beforehand exactly where that stream might lead him.

The inconsistencies and other problems within the narrative may be traced in part to the fits and starts the novel underwent during its seven years of composition. Just as Huck's adventures are a series of deaths and rebirths on the river, the manuscript went through several reincarnations of its own. The early chapters pick up where *Tom Sawyer* left off. "Widow Douglas takes Huck into her family, and distresses the life out of the vagabond with her cleanly, systematic, and pious ways," Twain recounted.[222] Under her roof and out in the woods with pap Finn, Huck learns to reject St. Petersburg religion, morality, and law before fleeing that society. He must say "goodbye to all that" to escape his past; only through his "death" can he truly be free. The plot is further complicated by the entrance of the runaway slave: Jim is necessary to provide the boy with a protector, and he instigates events not just by his prophecies but also by his mere presence on the river. He is a valuable piece of property that everyone covets. Jim and Huck head off for Cairo, south of Hannibal, where they might find passage into the free states; but in Chapter 18, after the raft is lost and Jim with it, Twain suddenly stopped when Huck asks Buck Grangerford what a feud is. Obviously, Twain had no interest in taking the two up the Ohio into territory with which he was unfamiliar; he had to send them south, but that compromised Jim's escape from bondage. The deeper they traveled in slave country, the harder his chances of getting to freedom. Twain really did not know what to do next.

It was two years before he described the carnage of the Grangerford–Shepherdson feud and Sherburn's killing of Boggs. This brief interlude introduced a new purpose to the text: He would satirize various classes of Southern society. He filled his notes with later abandoned ideas for subsequent chapters, describing such typical Southern rural scenes as a backwoods cotillion, a village fire, a candy-pulling, a house-raising, a quilting, a horse trade, and a country funeral. The writing picked up considerably with the introduction of the

222. See Blair, *Mark Twain's Hannibal, Huck and Tom*, p. 245.

most famous con artists in American literature, the king and the duke. But he hit another snag when he had Colonel Sherburn murder Boggs.

Twain had been reading all sorts of Southern humor for consideration in *Mark Twain's Library of Humor* (1888), an American imitation of William E. Burton's *Cyclopedia of Wit and Humor* (1858). Here he included excerpts from William Tappan Thompson's *Chronicles of Pineville* (1853), Johnson Jones Hooper's *Adventures of Captain Simon Suggs* (1845), and Richard Malcolm Johnston's *Dukesborough Tales* (1871). These long-forgotten books were filled with shifty confidence men, and Twain transformed them into his king and duke. "In attempting to represent some character which he cannot recall, which he draws from what he thinks is his imagination," Twain told the Portland *Oregonian* (August 9, 1895), "an author may often fall into the error of copying in part a character already drawn by another, a character which impressed itself upon his memory from some book. . . . We mortals can't create, we can only copy." References to and variants of characters and events in many of the books he read for the *Library of Humor* pop up regularly in *Huckleberry Finn*. "Mark Twain had a very good memory," an acquaintance told Matthews in *The Tocsin of Revolt*, "and that's where he gets most of his best stories" (p. 268). Although the least admiring critic might call it nothing but a soft name for "stealing," Twain did not think this "borrowing" from other books was plagiarism. After all, he explained, "Shakespeare took other people's quartz and extracted gold from it—it was a nearly valueless commodity before."[223]

The trip back down the river in 1882 for *Life on the Mississippi* reinvigorated him for the writing of *Huckleberry Finn* on his return to Elmira. Not only did the journey refresh his memory of those old days, but Twain went through all sorts of contemporary accounts of Mississippi life. The journey was a revelation: "The world which I knew in its blossoming youth," he wrote Livy after visiting Hannibal on May 17, 1882, "is old and bowed and melancholy, now; its soft cheeks are leathery and wrinkled, the fire is gone out of its eyes, and the spring from its step. It will be dust and ashes when I come again" (*Mark Twain's Letters*, vol. 1, 1917, p. 419). This disillusionment as well as the realization that the good old days were not so good after all, only old, further transformed the character of the novel.

The final portion of the novel, the "evasion" on Phelps farm, was written during Twain's final burst of inspiration, but how inspired this section actually is still troubles critics. DeVoto declared in *Mark Twain at Work* that there was "no more abrupt or more chilling descent" in the whole range of the novel in

223. Quoted in Blair, *Mark Twain and Huck Finn*, p. 60.

English than Tom Sawyer's attempt to free Jim (p. 92). "The greatest picaresque since Cervantes and Diderot is thrown away in doddering schtick," complained E. L. Doctorow in "Huck, Continued" (*New Yorker*, June 26/July 3, 1995, p. 132). "If you read it you must stop when the Nigger Jim is stolen from the boys," was Hemingway's advice. "That is the real end. The rest is just cheating." Even when the book came out in 1885, there were some objections to the ending. "Like all professed humorists, he carries the joke too far, and 'runs it into the ground,'" said Sanborn in the Springfield *Republican*. "It is possible to feel," T. S. Perry wrote in his original review of the book in *Century Magazine*, "that the fun in the long account of Tom Sawyer's artificial imitation of escapes from prison is somewhat forced; everywhere simplicity is a good rule, and while the account of the Southern *vendetta* is a masterpiece, the caricature of books of adventure leaves us cold. In one we have a bit of life; in the other Mark Twain is demolishing something that has a place in the book." The Cleveland *Leader and Herald* said, "The concluding chapters drag considerably, and are very 'talky,' as is said of certain plays." "The story, to be sure," Lang admitted in "The Art of Mark Twain," "ends by lapsing into burlesque, when Tom Sawyer insists on freeing the slave whom he knows to be free already, in a manner accordant with 'the best authorities.' But even the burlesque is redeemed by Tom's real unconscious heroism" (p. 222). But dissenters were few until Hemingway published his manifesto in *The Green Hills of Africa* extolling all of *Huckleberry Finn* but the "evasion."

People laugh differently in different ages. Audiences actually *liked* this selection from *Huckleberry Finn* at one time. "King Sollermun," which offends many people today, also was an enormous success with the public when Twain read it on the "Twins of Genius" tour in 1884 and 1885.[224] Cable picked the selection

224. It seemed to be popular everywhere they read. The Philadelphia *Inquirer* (November 22, 1885) said that "tears ran down his listeners' cheeks" as Twain read "King Sollermun." The Buffalo *Times* of December 11 said that this brief episode "was sufficient proof to show that in this, Mark Twain's latest literary effort, his fund of humor has not yet left him." The Cleveland *Leader* insisted on December 18 that it "was the best effort of the evening." "There were a hundred ludicrous incidents in it," said the Pittsburgh *Dispatch* (December 30), "which could but stir the risibilities of a very appreciative audience. In his second call he continued the story of the boys' comical tricks and perplexities, which in spite of his inanimate recital, kept the hearers in a smile all the while he spoke." Twain "kept his listeners in a roar all through" his reading of it, according to the South Bend (Ind.) *Daily Tribune* of February 5, 1885. The Cincinnati *Enquirer* (January 4) concurred that it "created roars of laughter." "Mr. Clemens convulsed the house with uncontrollable mirth," said the Chicago *Tribune* (February 3). "His account of the runaway slave's escape from the log cabin under the auspices of Tom Sawyer and Huckleberry Finn was irresistible." The Indianapolis *Journal* (February 8) said that the audience was "tickled to death with the story of Huck Finn and Tom Sawyer in their arrangement of Jim's escape from the cabin in accordance with the dramatic unities of history and romance."

from *Huckleberry Finn* for Twain to read, assuring him that "'King Sollermun' is enough by itself to immortalize its author."[225]

"The Escape" (as Twain called it on the road) was not only popular but *the* highlight of Twain's public readings. When Twain introduced "the episode where Tom and Huck stock Jim's cabin with reptiles, and then set him free, in the night, with the crowd of farmers after them," on his and George W. Cable's stop in Pittsburgh on December 29, 1884, it proved to be, as he wrote Olivia, "the biggest card I've got in my whole repertoire. . . . It went a-booming" (p. 223). Even his fellow lecturer loved it. "Cable's praises are not merely loud, they are boisterous," Clemens proudly wrote his wife. "Says its literary quality is high and fine—and great; its truth to boy nature unchallengeable; its humor constant and delightful; and its dramatic close full of stir, and boom, and *go*. Well, he has stated it very correctly." Although it took twenty-five minutes to tell, "Tom and Huck setting Jim free from prison" "just went with a long roll of artillery-laughter all down the line, interspersed with Congreve rockets and bombshell explosions, from the first word to the last" (pp. 230–31). But its success must have been due more to the manner in which Twain told it from the platform than the content of the selection.

More seems to have been written about the "evasion" than any other portion of the novel and more in *defense* of it than against it. But none of this discussion makes it any easier to read. It goes on too long, and seems mere padding to make the story a proper subscription book. Readers complained that *Tom Sawyer* was a bit thin for one of these publications, and Twain was not prepared to repeat this error in *Huckleberry Finn*. "Exaggeration is ludicrous, but it is not genuine humor," argued Joel Chandler Harris in his review of *The White Elephant*; "and the difference between Mark Twain and those who give forth exaggerations only is the fundamental difference that exists between emptiness and pungency. It is the difference that makes trash of one and literature of the other." Sadly, exaggeration seems at times all that is there in the evasion. Leo Marx feared in "Mr. Eliot, Mr. Trilling and *Huckleberry Finn*" (*The American Scholar*, Autumn 1953) that the two boys' mindless abuse of the slave compromises the total integrity of the novel.

"Literature is an *art*, not an inspiration," Twain insisted. "And its capital is *experience*." He advised writers to "live within your literary means, and don't borrow. Whatever you have *lived*, you can write—and by hard work and a genuine apprenticeship, you can learn to write well; but what you have not lived you cannot write, you can only pretend to write—you will merely issue a

225. In a letter to Samuel L. Clemens, October 25, 1884, Mark Twain Papers.

plausible-looking bill which will be pronounced spurious at the first counter." He warned that "the moment you venture outside your *own* experience, you are in peril—don't ever do it."[226] It is a shame he did not follow his own sound advice in the final chapters of *Huckleberry Finn*.

Twain returned to the mood of the opening of the novel by reviving his attack on the romantic mentality that he felt so corrupted Southern society not only in the 1840s of the story but in the 1880s as well. He thought "the most insidious manipulator of the imagination" to be "the felicitously written romance." He complained in "International Copyright" (*Century Magazine*, February 1886) that these novels "fill the imagination with an unhealthy fascination for foreign life, with its dukes and earls and kings, its fuss and feathers, its graceful immoralities, its sugar-coated injustices and oppressions" (p. 634). Tom Sawyer has fallen under the evil influence of these romances and hard, not only *The Count of Monte Cristo* and *The Man in the Iron Mask* but also the indiscreet memoirs of the most notorious roués in European history, Cellini, Casanova, and Baron von Trenck; and to free Jim he devises an absurd scheme drawing on the events of these books. Huck vainly protests this foolishness, but Tom silences him just as effectively as the king does the duke during the Wilks family swindle. Tom and Huck are playing their own elaborate con game at the Phelps farm.

Twain personally hated another of Tom's favorite authors, Sir Walter Scott. "Lord, it's all so juvenile!" he complained to Brander Matthews, who admired the Scottish novelist. "And oh, the poverty of the invention! Not poverty in inventing situations, but poverty in furnishing reasons for them. Sir Walter . . . elaborates, and elaborates, and elaborates, til if you live to get to it you don't believe it when it happens."[227] Unfortunately, the same can be said of the "evasion": Twain elaborates, and elaborates, and elaborates until the situation is no longer plausible. Unlike the rest of the novel, the artifice here is so obvious and tedious. "Where he lacked the support of the solid fact and had to rely on his own fantastic imagination," observed Brander Matthews of his friend in *The Tocsin of Revolt*, "his whimsicality was likely to betray him disastrously. . . . He needed to have the sustaining solidity of the concrete fact, which he could deal with at will, bringing out its humor, its latent beauty, and its human significance" (p. 270). The most disappointing aspect of this portion of the story is how cruelly the boys treat Jim. All the noble characteristics revealed on the

226. In a letter to Mrs. Whiteside, quoted in one to Olivia Clemens, January 10(?), 1885, in *The Love Letters of Mark Twain*, p. 228.

227. In a letter to Brander Matthews, May 4, 1904, *Mark Twain's Letters*, vol. 2, p. 738.

river are drained out of him when he is returned to bondage. The "evasion" so disappoints in the end, as do "Tom Sawyer and Huck Finn Among the Indians," *Tom Sawyer Abroad*, and "Tom Sawyer, Detective," because they derive their humor from literature and not from life.

For parody to succeed, the reader must be familiar with what is being burlesqued. More than a century has passed since *Huckleberry Finn* was published; and even at that date, it was a historical novel. The life it portrayed was already part of the nation's long-dead past. *The Annotated Huckleberry Finn* attempts not only to recount what has been forgotten but also to clarify the elusive subtleties within Mark Twain's grand fiction, his great flawed masterpiece. The customs, the language, the literature, the law, even the terrain have changed. *Huckleberry Finn* is indeed a vivid picture of a time and a place long gone, but it has entered the world's literature. Mark Twain endures because of what Howells in *My Mark Twain* called "the self-lawed genius of a man who will be remembered with the great humorists of all time, with Cervantes, with Swift, or with any others worthy his company; none of them was his equal in humanity" (p. 13). *Huckleberry Finn* continues to challenge readers for what it reveals about the American character, the good, the bad, and the ugly, and about the author himself. Like America itself, Twain was growing and maturing. Perhaps there will be no need for Twain or his masterpiece once it is a better country. And the damned human race is better, too.

Huck, Jim, and Tom. Drawing by E. W. Kemble,
Adventures of Huckleberry Finn, 1932.
Courtesy Limited Editions Club.

The Annotated

Huckleberry Finn

HUCKLEBERRY FINN.

ADVENTURES

OF

HUCKLEBERRY FINN

(TOM SAWYER'S COMRADE).

SCENE: THE MISSISSIPPI VALLEY.
TIME: FORTY TO FIFTY YEARS AGO.

BY

MARK TWAIN.

WITH ONE HUNDRED AND SEVENTY-FOUR ILLUSTRATIONS.

NEW YORK:
CHARLES L. WEBSTER AND COMPANY.
1885.

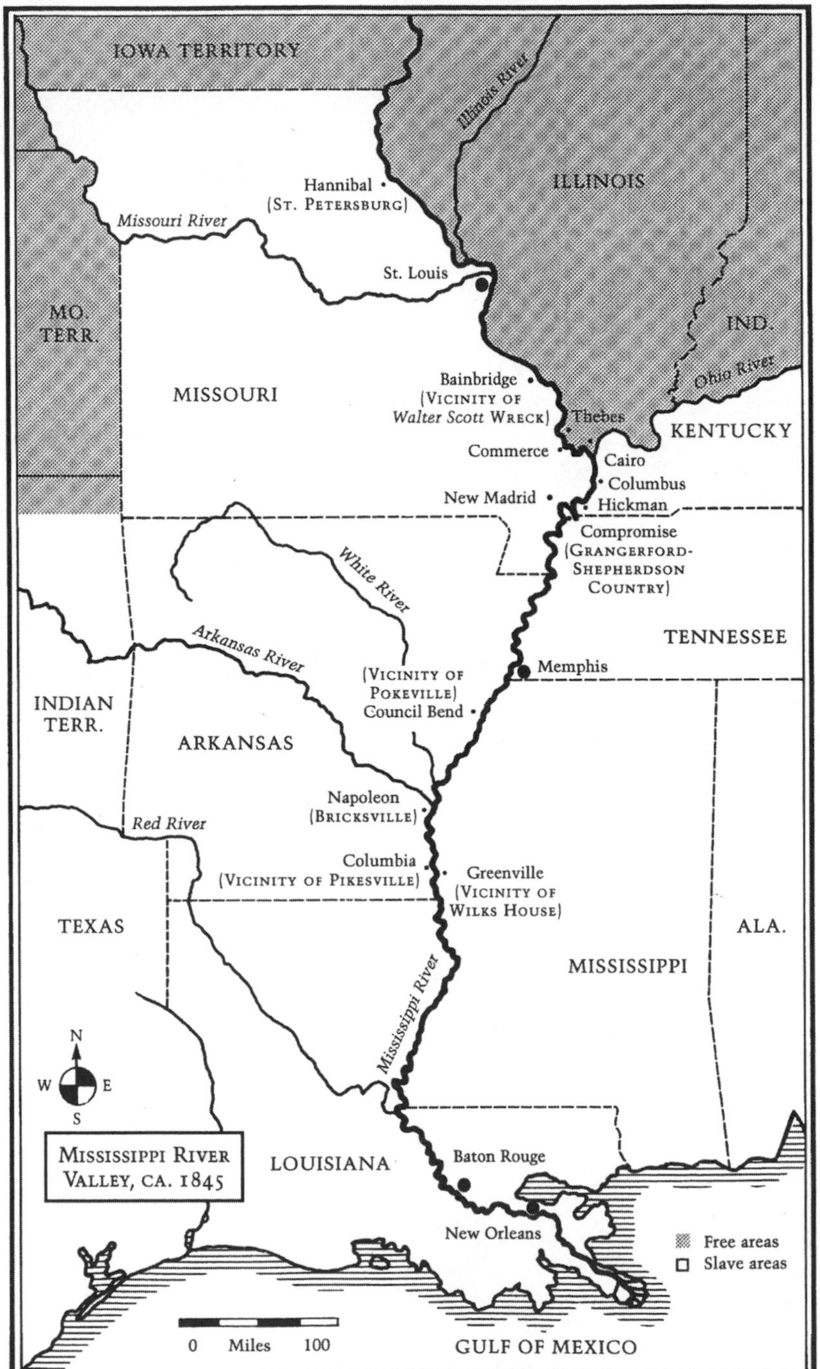

Map of the Mississippi River Valley, circa 1845.

Reprinted with permission from the Mark Twain Project's Adventures of Huckleberry Finn, *edited by Victor Fischer and Lin Salamo (University of California, 2001). Copyright © 1985 and 2001 by the Regents of the University of California Press.*

NOTICE[1]

PERSONS attempting to find a motive in this narrative[2] will be prosecuted; persons attempting to find a moral in it will be banished;[3] persons atempting to find a plot in it will be shot.

BY ORDER OF THE AUTHOR
PER G. G.,[4] CHIEF OF ORDNANCE.

1. *NOTICE.* According to Victor Fischer and Lin Salamo in their introduction to the 2001 University of California edition of *Huckleberry Finn*, Twain originally intended to dedicate the novel to his childhood friends:

> *To the Once Boys and Girls*
> who comraded with me in the
> morning of time
> and the youth of antiquity, in the village of
> *Hannibal, Missouri,*
> this book is inscribed, with affection for
> themselves,
> respect for their virtues, and reverence for
> their honorable gray hairs.
> The Author.

He may have been inspired by seeing so many of his old playmates in 1883 while back in Hannibal, researching material for *Life on the Mississippi*. He finally decided against it; the story is not always flattering to the town and its residents. He replaced it with his famous ironic "Notice." As disclosed in "A Little Note to M. Paul Bourget" in *Tom Sawyer, Detective* (1897), it was meant to "playfully warn the public against taking us seriously" (p. 232). Robert Bridges, in his review of the novel in *Life* (February 26, 1885), accurately characterized this "Notice" as "a nice little artifice to scare off the critics—a kind of 'trespassers on these grounds will be dealt with according to law'" (p. 119).

2. *narrative.* Twain had originally written "book" (**MS**), but probably changed it to reinforce the illusion that the text is "Huck Finn's Autobiography" as "recorded by Mark Twain." He may have altered it once he recognized the importance that Jim brought to the story. "Narrative" came to mean an account of a slave's flight to freedom, as in *The Interesting Narrative of the Life of Olaudah Equiano, or Gustavus Vassa, the African* (1814) and *Narrative of the Life of Frederick Douglass, an American Slave* (1845).

See *The Classic Slave Narratives*, edited by Henry Louis J. Gates, Jr. (New York: Mentor, 1987).

3. *persons attempting to find a moral in it will be banished.* This warning was an afterthought, for it does not appear in Twain's manuscript, now in the Buffalo and Erie County Public Library. This little threat did not discourage Twain's contemporaries from suggesting one or another lesson in *Huckleberry Finn*. The reviewer for the New York *Sun* (February 15, 1885) noted that "a beautiful moral decorates nearly every one of its shining pages, namely that it is better and nobler to lie simply and directly to the purpose than to put on frills of over elaborate mendacity, or to wander from the main chance into the byways of unnecessary prevarication." The San Francisco *Morning Call* (March 17) disagreed: "The motive is the author's, a financial consideration; the plot—well, even omnipotence has not yet created a wretch of a boy who was not pregnant with plots; the moral every reader must draw for himself." The Hartford *Times* (March 9) said that the novel "teaches, without seeming to do it, the virtue of honest simplicity, directness, truth." Joel Chandler Harris insisted in his editorial "Huckleberry Finn and His Critics" (Atlanta *Constitution*, May 26, 1885) that "the moral of the book, though it is not scrawled across every page, teaches the necessity of manliness and self-sacrifice."

4. *G. G.* Possibly General (Ulysses S.) Grant (1822–1885), commander of the Union Armies during the Civil War and former President of the United States, whose memoirs Twain was then arranging for publication. Grant rose from foot soldier to Commander of the Union Army during the Civil War to eighteenth President of the United States. But scandal rocked his administration, and he failed in his bid for a third term. He entered a brokerage firm in New York, but an unscrupulous partner sent it into bankruptcy. The former Civil War hero was broke. He tried to pull himself out of debt by producing articles about his war experiences for *Century Magazine*, and Twain convinced Grant to write his memoirs for the new subscription publishing house Twain founded to publish *Huckleberry Finn*, Charles L. Webster and Company, rather than for the Century Company. Although now suffering with throat cancer, Grant finished the two-volume work just before he died. *Personal Memoirs of U. S. Grant* (1885–1886) was a best-seller, and Twain always boasted how he was able to give the general's widow the biggest royalty check issued up to that time—for $200,000. The summer of the general's death, Twain thought of a story about Tom Sawyer and Huck Finn and the Civil War and Grant during his Missouri campaign. Instead he wrote "The Private History of a Campaign That Failed" for *Century Magazine* (December 1885), illustrated by E. W. Kemble. Twain considered replacing "Ordnance" with "Artillery" (**MS**) here, but that would have made the joke too obvious. Walter Blair and Victor Fischer noted in the 1988 University of California edition of *Huckleberry Finn* that "Grant never signed himself in this way, nor was he ever chief of ordnance, the high-ranking officer responsible for the army's supplies and weaponry" (pp. 372–73). However, Twain generally called him General Grant. Fischer and Salamo in the 2001 revised University of California edition suggested that "G. G." might stand for George Griffin, Twain's butler. "Chief of Ordnance" may refer to Twain's putting Griffin in charge of security at the Hartford house when the Clemenses were out of town; one night in July 1877, he shot at some rowdies who were yelling insults at Twain. See also Chapter 2, note 3.

EXPLANATORY.

In this book a number of dialects[1] are used, to wit: the Missouri negro dialect;[2] the extremest form of the backwoods South-Western dialect; the ordinary "Pike-County"[3] dialect; and four modified varieties of this last. The shadings have not been done in a hap-hazard fashion, or by guess-work;[4] but pains-takingly, and with the trustworthy guidance and support of personal familiarity with these several forms of speech.

I make this explanation for the reason that without it many readers would suppose that all these characters were trying to talk alike and not succeeding.

THE AUTHOR.[5]

1. *a number of dialects*. David Carkeet in "The Dialects in *Huckleberry Finn*" (*American Literature*, November 1979, pp. 315–32) distinguished the various ones spoken by the characters in the novel as (1) Missouri Negro: Jim and the other slaves; (2) backwoods Southwestern: the Grangerfords in Chapters 17 and 18, and the various Arkansas townspeople; (3) the "Ordinary Pike County": Huckleberry Finn, Tom Sawyer, Ben Rogers, pap Finn, Judith Loftus in Chapter 11, and Aunt Polly; and (4) four variants of modified "Pike County": (*a*) the robbers on the *Walter Scott* in Chapter 13; (*b*) the king; (*c*) the Bricksville loafers; and (*d*) Aunt Sally and Uncle Silas Phelps and their neighbors.

2. *the Missouri negro dialect*. Twain traced his firsthand knowledge of this speech back to his uncle John A. Quarles's place near Florida, Missouri. "Yes," he told Raymond Blaithwait in "Mark Twain on Humor" (New York *World*, May 31, 1891), "I was born in one of those [slave] States and I lived a great deal of my childhood on a plantation of my uncle's, where forty or fifty negroes lived belonging to him, and who had been drawn from two or three States and so I gradually absorbed their different dialects which they had brought with them." His first important experiment with dialect was "A True Story" (*Atlantic Monthly*, November 1874), a transcription of a former slave's terrible memories of her children being sold at auction. "The rugged truth of the sketch leaves all other stories of slave life infinitely far behind," said William Dean Howells in *The Atlantic* (December 1875), "and reveals a gift in the author for the simple, dramatic report of reality which we have seen equalled in no other American writer (pp. 750–51)." But Howells was appalled when many people mistook this disturbing tale as "humorous." Twain began *Huckleberry Finn* several years before Joel Chandler Harris published *Uncle Remus, His Songs and Sayings* (1880); and this book may have been in part responsible for the extensive revisions of Jim's dialogue in the manuscript. Twain said in Chapter 47 of *Life on the Mississippi* (1883) that Harris "is the only master the country has produced." He admitted to Harris on August 10, 1881, that although he wrote African-American dialect, "I can't spell it in your matchless way. It is marvelous the way you and [George Washington] Cable spell the negro and creole dialects" (*Mark Twain's Letters*, edited by Albert Bigelow Paine, vol. 1, 1917, p. 402).

3. *"Pike-County."* Pike County was the original home of the "Piker," a stock character in Western folk balladry of the 1850s, usually a Missourian or any other "squatter" who went west during the Gold Rush. "In '49, when the gold seekers on the way to California were streaming through our little town, many of the men and boys, including Sam [Clemens], got the gold fever," Laura Hawkins (Frazer), "Becky Thatcher" of *Tom Sawyer*, recalled Hannibal at the time to Aretta L. Watts, "Mark Twain's Gay Mother" (New York *Times*, February 5, 1928). "Mrs. [Jane] Clemens excitedly watched the covered wagon processions go through. Sam, not content with mere watching, expended his energy with the gang playing at mining; they borrowed skiffs and went down the river three miles to the cave where they would stake their claims and pretend to dig gold." The vogue for original "Pike County ballads" written in the squatter dialect began in 1871, with the publication of John Hay's collection; it was soon followed by Bret Harte's "Plain Language from Truthful James" and other verses. In an open letter to *Harper's Weekly* (October 21, 1905, p. 1530), Twain corrected the common assumption that Harte, and not his friend Hay, was the legitimate father of the genre. Hay himself called Twain "the finest living delineator of the true Pike accent" ("Mark Twain at Steinway Hall," New York *Tribune*, January 25, 1872). He was greatly impressed with Twain's achievement in *Huckleberry Finn*. "It is a strange life you have described, one which I imagine must be already pretty nearly obsolete in most respects," Hay wrote him in a letter of April 14, 1885 (now in the Mark Twain Papers, Bancroft Library, University of California at Berkeley). "I, who grew up in the midst of it, have almost forgotten it, except when I read of it in your writings—the only place, I think, where a faithful record of it survives. To me the great interest of this, and your other like books, independent of their wit and humor and pathos, which every body can see, is 'documentary.' Without them I should not know today, the speech and the way of living, with which I was familiar as a child."

4. *The shadings have not been done in a hap-hazard fashion, or by guess-work.* "Spoken speech is one thing, written speech is quite another," Twain admitted to *Ladies' Home Journal* editor Edward Bok. "The moment 'talk' is put into print you recognize that it is not what it was when you heard it; you perceive that an immense something has disappeared from it. That is its very soul" (*Mark Twain's Letters,* vol. 2, 1917, p. 504). But that did not prevent him from trying to capture the elusive nuances of the various voices in *Huckleberry Finn*. "I amend dialect stuff by talking and talking and *talking* it till it sounds right," Twain wrote William Dean Howells about composing "A True Story," "and I had difficulty with this negro talk because a negro sometimes (rarely) says 'goin' and sometimes 'gwyne,' and they make just such discrepancies in other words—and when you come to reproduce them on paper they look as if the variation resulted from the writer's carelessness" (*Mark Twain–Howells Letters*, 1960, p. 26). Twain fel that a writer had to grow up with the dialect to get it just right. "It must be exceedingly difficult to acquire a dialect by study or observation," he suggested to Raymond Blaithwait in "Mark Twain on Humor" (New York *World*, May 31, 1891). "In the vast majority of cases it probably can be done, as in my case, only by absorption. So a child might pick up the differences in dialect by means of that unconscious absorbtion when a practised writer could not do it twenty years later by closest observation." Twain insisted in "Fenimore Cooper's Literary Offenses" (*North American Review*, July 1895) that "when the personages of a tale deal in conversation, the talk shall sound like human talk, and be talk such as human beings would be likely to talk in the given circumstances, and have a discoverable meaning, also a discoverable purpose, and a show of relevancy, and remain in the neighborhood of the subject in hand, and be interesting to the reader, and help out the tale, and stop when the people cannot think of anything more to say" (p. 2).

Not everyone was impressed with his efforts in *Huckleberry Finn*. Edgar Lee Masters, author of *Spoon River Anthology* (1915), grew up in Petersburg, Illinois, amid the same boy lingo as Sam Clemens of Hannibal, Missouri; he argued in *Mark Twain: A Portrait* (1938) that Huck should have said "feller" not "fellow," "terbacker" not "tobacco," "et" not "eat" (pp. 130–31). Even Twain's friend and biographer Albert Bigelow Paine had to admit that the dialects "are not always maintained" (*Mark Twain: A Biography*, vol. 2, 1912, p. 794). Nevertheless, most readers agree with Southern poet and novelist James Dickey, in his introduction to the 1979 New American Library edition, that *Huckleberry Finn* "is the only book I have ever read which used dialect in a manner not offensive to me."

5. *THE AUTHOR.* When the Boston *Transcript* and Springfield (Mass.) *Daily Republican* (both March 17, 1885) published items in support of the Concord Public Library's banning of *Huckleberry Finn*, Twain instructed Charles L. Webster to insert the following "Prefatory Remark" in all subsequent editions of the novel:

> Huckleberry Finn is not an imaginary person. He still lives; or rather, *they* still live; for Huckleberry Finn is two persons in one—namely, the author's two uncles, the present editors of the Boston *Transcript* and the Springfield *Republican*. In character, language, clothing, education, instinct, and origin, he is the painstakingly and truthfully drawn photograph and counterpart of these two gentlemen as they were in the time of their boyhood, forty years ago. The work has been most carefully and conscientiously done, and is exactly true to the originals, in even the minutest particulars, with but one exception, and that a trifling one: this boy's language has been toned down and softened, here and there, in deference to the taste of a more modern and fastidious day.

Fortunately, Olivia Clemens objected to this notice, and it was never added. In the case of the *Transcript*, Twain was merely blaming the messenger; and this "Prefatory Remark" was obsolete by April 27, when the *Daily Republican* published Franklin B. Sanborn's *positive* review of *Huckleberry Finn*. Oddly, although the 1932 Limited Editions Club, both 1985 and 1988 University of California, Random House's 1995 "Comprehensive," the 1999 Norton Critical, and other editions of *Huckleberry Finn* have restored the "Raft Episode" (see Appendix B) as well as other suppressed passages to their original positions in the novel, none of them includes the "Prefatory Remark."

The Adventures of Huckleberry Finn[1]

Chapter I.

THE WIDOW'S.

YOU DON'T know about me,[2] without you have read a book by the name of "The Adventures of Tom Sawyer,"[3] but that ain't no matter.[4] That book was made by Mr. Mark Twain,[5] and he told the truth, mainly. There was things which he stretched, but mainly he told the truth. That is nothing. I never seen anybody but lied, one time or another, without it was Aunt Polly,[6] or the widow,[7] or maybe Mary.[8] Aunt Polly—Tom's Aunt Polly, she is—and Mary, and the Widow Douglas, is all told about in that book—which is mostly a true book; with some stretchers,[9] as I said before.

Now the way that the book winds up, is this: Tom and me found the money that the robbers hid in the cave, and it made us rich. We got six thousand dollars apiece—all gold. It was an awful sight of money when it was piled up. Well, Judge Thatcher,[10] he took it and put it out at interest, and it fetched us a dollar a day apiece, all the year round—more than a body could tell what to do with. The Widow Douglas, she took me for her son, and allowed she would sivilize me; but it was rough living in the house all the time, considering how dismal regular and decent the widow was in all her ways; and so when I couldn't stand it no longer, I lit out. I got into my old rags, and my sugar-hogshead[11] again, and was free and satis-

1. *Huckleberry Finn.* The huckleberry is a kind of blueberry, is not native to Missouri, and was at the time considered a particularly inferior fruit. Samuel Clemens discovered huckleberries one afternoon in Hartford, Connecticut, when he spotted some children gathering them. "They are a new beverage to me," he admitted in "Morality and Huckleberries" (San Francisco *Alta California*, September 6, 1868). "They are excellent. I had always thought a huckleberry was something like a turnip. On the contrary, they are no larger than buckshot. They are better than buckshot, though, and more digestible." The word indicated something small and of little consequence. Twain was aware of this meaning when he said in Chapter 26 of *A Connecticut Yankee in King Arthur's Court* (1889), "Sir Palamides the Saracen . . . is no huckleberry himself."

"Huckleberry Finn, indeed!" says a character in Chapter 29 of *The Adventures of Tom Sawyer* (1876). "It ain't a name to open many doors, I judge!" Twain took the surname from Jimmy Finn, the town drunkard of Hannibal, Missouri. "There was something about the name 'Finn' that suited," Twain admitted to Lute Pease in "Mark Twain Speaks" (Portland *Oregonian*, August 11, 1895), "and 'Huck Finn' was all that was needed to somehow describe another kind of a boy than 'Tom Sawyer,' a boy of lower extraction or degree. Now, 'Arthur Van de Vanter Montague' would have sounded ridiculous, applied to characters like either 'Tom Sawyer' or 'Huck Finn.'" Twain reminisced in a letter to childhood friend Will Bowen on February 6, 1870, how "we stole [Jim Finn's] dinner while he slept in the vat and fed it to the hogs in order to keep them still till we could mount them and have a ride" (*Huck Finn and Tom Sawyer Among the Indians*, 1989, p. 20). When he sent him a copy of *Huckleberry Finn*, another old friend,

Thomas S. Nash, wrote back, "The mere mention of the book takes me back in memory to 'old Jim Finn of Craig's Alley,' who if I remember right perished with the burning of the old calabose on Front Street" (in a letter of April 23, 1885, Mark Twain Papers). Actually, he confused Finn with another drunk, Dennis McDermid, who died in a fire on January 23, 1853. Twain recalled in Chapter 56 of *Life on the Mississippi* that he innocently gave the "whiskey-sodden tramp" the matches that caused the blaze and that Finn "died a natural death in a tan vat, of a combination of delirium tremens and spontaneous combustion."

As the abandoned son of the town drunkard, Huckleberry Finn is of a lower order than Tom Sawyer: The schoolmaster switches Tom for just stopping to talk to him. He does not show up until Chapter 6 of *Tom Sawyer*, inauspiciously dragging a dead cat. He is the prototypical "bad boy" of American children's literature, "the juvenile pariah of the village," "the romantic outcast." "Huckleberry was cordially hated and dreaded by all the mothers of the town," Twain wrote, "because he was idle, and lawless, and vulgar and bad—and because all their children admired him so, and delighted in his forbidden society, and wished they dared to be like him.... Huckleberry was always dressed in the cast-off clothes of full-grown men, and they were in perennial bloom and fluttering with rags. . . . Huckleberry came and went, at his own free will. He slept on door-steps in fine weather and in empty hogsheads in wet; he did not have to go to school or to church, or call any being master or obey anyone; he could go fishing or swimming when and where he chose, and stay as long as it suited him; nobody forbade him to fight; he could sit up as late as he pleased; he was always the first boy that went barefoot in the spring and the last to resume leather in the fall; he never had to wash, nor put on clean clothes; he could swear wonderfully. In a word, everything that goes to make life precious, that boy had. So thought every harassed, hampered, respectable boy." Of course, his social status rises dramatically when the Widow Douglas takes him in at the end of *Tom Sawyer*.

"Huck Finn is drawn from life," Twain insisted in his preface to *Tom Sawyer*. "There is nothing disrespectful nor even irreverent in my confessing that, up to date, more than a dozen real Tom Sawyers and Huckleberry Finns have succumbed in the past twenty years," he reported in "Huckleberry Finn's End Disap-

fied. But Tom Sawyer, he hunted me up and said he was going to start a band of robbers, and I might join if I would go back to the widow and be respectable. So I went back.

The widow she cried over me, and called me a poor lost lamb, and she called me a lot of other names, too, but she never meant no harm by it. She put me in them new clothes again,[12] and I couldn't do nothing but sweat and sweat, and feel all cramped up. Well, then, the old thing commenced again. The widow rung a bell for supper, and you had to come to time. When you got to the table you couldn't go right to eating, but you had to wait for the widow to tuck down her head and grumble a little over the victuals, though there warn't really anything the matter with them.[13] That is, nothing only everything was cooked by itself. In a barrel of odds and ends[14] it is different; things get mixed up, and the juice kind of swaps around, and the things go better.

LEARNING ABOUT MOSES AND THE "BULRUSHERS."

After supper she got out her book and learned me about Moses and the Bulrushers;[15] and I was in a sweat to find out all about him; but by-and-by she let it out that Moses had been dead a considerable long time; so then I didn't care no more about him; because I don't take no stock in dead people.[16]

Pretty soon I wanted to smoke, and asked the widow to let me. But she wouldn't. She said it was a mean practice and wasn't clean, and I must try to not do it any more. That is just the way with some people. They get down on a thing when they don't know nothing about it.[17] Here she was a bothering about Moses, which was no kin to her, and no use to anybody, being gone, you see, yet finding a power of fault with me for doing a thing that had some good in it. And she took snuff too;[18] of course that was all right, because she done it herself.

Her sister, Miss Watson,[19] a tolerable slim old maid,[20] with goggles[21] on, had just come to live with her, and took a set at me now, with a spelling-book.[22] She worked me middling hard for about an hour, and then the widow made her ease up. I couldn't stood it much longer. Then for an hour it was deadly dull, and I was fidgety. Miss Watson would say,

Miss Watson

"Dont put your feet up there, Huckleberry;" and "dont scrunch up like that, Huckleberry—set up straight;" and pretty soon she would say, "Don't gap and stretch[23] like that, Huckleberry—why don't you try to behave?" Then she

points Mark Twain" (New York *American-Journal*, March 18, 1906). "I wonder how many times the originals of Hamlet or Tom Brown or Robinson Crusoe or Gulliver or David Copperfield or any of the great tragic characters of history were buried and resurrected?" He was particularly amused by an obituary for Captain Alexander C. Toncray that claimed that this native of Hannibal and former Mississippi and Missouri river pilot had inspired Huckleberry Finn. "So Huck Finn has died again?" he laughed. "Well, now that's too bad—too bad! To think that a boy who had so many hair-breadth escapades at an age when life was worth living adventurously, should calmly go West and have heart failure! I am disappointed, besides being distressed. I always had a sneaking idea that Huck would come to a more artistic end, such as hanging, though he was always more practical than Tom Sawyer, his companion in crime." Jim's hair ball predicts in Chapter 4 of *Huckleberry Finn* that Huck will be hanged one day. "Now," Twain added, "Jim knew Huckleberry Finn pretty well, and there is nothing in the verdict that coincides with the death of Captain Toncray. Did I know Captain Toncray? Maybe so, but my memory is not as good as it was. It seems likely that any one with the reputation that Huck Finn had round Hannibal would change his name."

Another rumor said that someone else, Barney Farthing of Paris, Kentucky, was the "real" Huckleberry Finn. He denied it while Twain was alive but later did little to discourage it. The story may have been sparked by an incident on Twain's final visit to Hannibal in June 1902. When he ran into Farthing on the street, Clemens greeted his old friend, "Old Huck, how well I remember when you and I frequently robbed the Richmond peach orchard and stole watermelons from John Fry's patch when we were kids together. To this day I have never regretted our wrong doings on those occasions" ("Sermon by Mark Twain," Chicago *Daily Tribune*, June 8, 1902). Since Sam Clemens and the other boys nicknamed Farthing "Huck," many believed *he* was the original Huckleberry Finn. And he liked telling reporters that yes, indeed, he *was* Huckleberry Finn (as in Homer Croy, "The Originals of Mark Twain's Characters," *The Bellman*, June 25, 1910, p. 804). The grown "Old Huck" (as he became known) was a poor candidate for Huckleberry Finn, because Colonel Barnett Noran Coffee Farthing, as Clerk of the Missouri House in Monroe County, was an active segregationist who said he "don't like a nigger much nohow." See David E. E. Sloane and Sherri Farley, " 'My Uncle B.C.M. Farthing, the *Original* Huckleberry Finn': The Sherri Farley and David L. Rittershouse Documents," *Mark Twain Journal*, Fall 1995, pp. 31–40.

The Captain Toncray story so bothered Twain that on March 8, 1906, he dictated in "Chapters from My Autobiography" that once and for all Huckleberry Finn was based on another Hannibal boy, Tom Blankenship. Oddly, when Twain published "Chapters from My Autobiography" (*North American Review*, August 2, 1907), he discreetly referred to him as "Frank F." (p. 691), not sure whether Tom Blankenship was alive or dead. But by October, he had no qualms about

The home of Tom Blankenship, Hannibal, Missouri.
Courtesy the Mark Twain Papers, Bancroft Library, University of California at Berkeley.

mentioning "Tom Blankenship ('Huck Finn')" (p. 164). "In *Huckleberry Finn*," he said, "I have drawn Frank [Tom] exactly as he was. He was ignorant, unwashed, insufficiently fed; but he had as good a heart as ever any boy had. His liberties were totally unrestricted. He was the only really independent person—boy or man—in the community, and by consequence he was tranquilly and continuously happy, and was envied by all the rest of us. We liked him; we enjoyed his society. And as his society was forbidden us by our parents, the prohibition trebled and quadrupled its value, and therefore we sought and got more of his society than of any other boy's" (p. 692). When he wrote to Toncray's brother on March 8, 1906, he reminisced about Tom Blankenship and the old days in

told me all about the bad place,[24] and I said I wished I was there. She got mad,[25] then, but I didn't mean no harm. All I wanted was to go somewheres; all I wanted was a change, I warn't particular. She said it was wicked to say what I said; said she wouldn't say it for the whole world; *she* was going to live so as to go to the good place. Well, I couldn't see no advantage in going where she was going, so I made up my mind I wouldn't try for it. But I never said so, because it would only make trouble, and wouldn't do no good.

Now she had got a start, and she went on and told me all about the good place. She said all a body would have to do there was to go around all day long with a harp and sing, forever and ever.[26] So I didn't think much of it. But I never said so. I asked her if she reckoned Tom Sawyer would go there, and, she said, not by a considerable sight. I was glad about that, because I wanted him and me to be together.[27]

Miss Watson she kept pecking at me, and it got tiresome and lonesome. By-and-by they fetched the niggers[28] in and had prayers,[29] and then everybody was off to bed. I went up to my room with a piece of candle and put it on the table. Then I set down in a chair by the window and tried to think of something cheerful, but it warn't no use. I felt so lonesome I most wished I was dead.[30] The stars was shining, and the leaves rustled in the woods ever so mournful; and I heard an owl, away off, who-whooing about somebody that was dead,[31] and a whippowill[32] and a dog crying about somebody that was going to die;[33] and the wind was trying to whisper something to me and I couldn't make out what it was, and so it made the cold shivers run over me. Then away out in the woods I heard that kind of a sound that a ghost makes when it wants to tell about something that's on its mind[34] and can't make itself understood, and so can't rest easy in its grave and has to go about that way every night grieving. I got so down-hearted and scared, I did wish I had some company. Pretty soon a spider[35] went crawling up my shoulder, and I flipped it off and it lit in the candle; and before I could budge it was all shriveled up. I didn't need anybody to tell me that that was an awful bad sign and would fetch me some bad luck, so I was scared and most shook the clothes off of me. I got up and turned around in my tracks three times and crossed my breast every time;[36] and then I tied up a little lock of my hair with a thread to keep witches away.[37] But I hadn't no confidence. You do that when you've lost a horse-shoe that you've found, instead of nailing it up over the door,[38] but I hadn't ever heard anybody say it was any way to keep off bad luck when you'd killed a spider.

I set down again, a shaking all over, and got out my pipe for a smoke; for the house was all as still as death, now, and so the widow wouldn't know. Well, after a long time I heard the clock away off in the town go boom—boom—boom—twelve licks—and all still again—stiller than ever. Pretty soon I heard a twig snap,[39] down in the dark amongst the trees—something was a stirring. I set still and listened. Directly I could just barely hear a *"me-yow! me-yow!"*[40] down there. That was good! Says I, *"me-yow! me-yow!"* as soft as I could, and then I put out the light and scrambled out of the window onto the shed. Then I slipped down to the ground and crawled in amongst the trees, and sure enough there was Tom Sawyer[41] waiting for me.

HUCK STEALING AWAY.

Hannibal. "You may remember that Tom was a good boy, notwithstanding his circumstances," he said. "To my mind he was a better boy than Henry Beebe and John Reagan put together, those swells of the ancient days" (quoted in *Huck Finn and Tom Sawyer Among the Indians*, 1989, p. 302). Twain recalled Beebe as a bully; and he must have been thinking of *Jimmy* Reagan, the model for "the Model Boy of the Village" in Chapter 1 of *Tom Sawyer*.

Others had revealed Huck Finn's true identity even earlier, and not everyone shared Twain's veneration of Tom Blankenship. "He was nothing more than a plain reprobate," complained an old Hannibal resident to Elizabeth Davis Fiedler in "Familiar Haunts of Mark Twain" (*Harper's Weekly*, December 16, 1899). "I knew him, and I could never see anything picturesque about him. The principal exploit of his which I now recall is the fact that he once stole a prized kite of mine. He had been regarding it with envious eyes for days, and at last, when he knew I was not at home, he went around and told my mother that I had sent him for the kite. Of course he got it, and that was the last I ever saw of it; but I had my satisfaction . . . I punched his head!" (p. 10). Tom's sister Rebecca Blankenship was not that impressed with her brother's posthumous notoriety. "Yes, I reckon it was him [in *Huckleberry Finn*]," she admitted in "Familiar Haunts of Mark Twain." "Sam and our boys run together considerable them days, and I reckon it was Tom or Ben . . . ; it don't matter which, for both of 'ems dead" (p. 10). There was some confusion whether the "real" Huck Finn was Tom or his older brother Benson. When the writer returned to Hannibal for the last time, the New York *Herald* in "Mark Twain's Reunion" (June 15, 1902) identified him as Benson Blankenship. See also Chapter 8, note 25.

Tom Blankenship was one of eight children of Woodson and Mahala Blankenship, and four years older than Clemens. "The parents paupers and drunkards," Twain recalled in 1897 in "Villagers of 1840–43," "the girls charged with prostitution—not proven. Tom, a kindly young heathen. . . . These children were never sent to school or church. Played out and disappeared" (*Huck Finn and Tom Sawyer Among the Indians*, p. 96). Their origins too are unknown. "I remember all about the Blankenships," Jimmie McDaniel told Keene Abbott in "Tom Sawyer's Town" (*Harper's Weekly*, August 9, 1913). "The whole family—father, mother, two boys, and a girl—came down the river in a 'dugout.' Know what a 'dugout' is? Well, it's a boat or canoe made of a big tree hollowed out. They came from up river some place, and they landed at the foot of North Street" (p. 16). According to Barney Farthing (in Sloane and Farley, " 'My Uncle B.C.M. Farthing, the *Original* Huckleberry Finn,' " p. 39), the Blankenships owned a fishing boat, and Tom and his father caught catfish in a nearby creek. McDaniel added that Tom Blankenship "was too harum-scarum even to trot in our class of society. Tom—dead long ago—Tom was the original for Huck Finn."

Another neighbor, J. W. Ayres, confirmed what Twain had said about their boyhood friend. "My grandmother told us that Tom Blankenship was a bad boy and we were forbidden to play with him," Ayres wrote in "Recollections of Hannibal" (Palmyra *Spectator*, August 22, 1917), "but when we went on a rabbit chase he joined us. Tom Blankenship was in fact 'some kid.' He was not subject to laws of conventionality and did not have to go to school and 'behave himself' as the rest of us boys did, and therefore he was much envied." Twain also said to the *Herald* reporter in "Mark Twain's Reunion," "Huckleberry Finn was the son of the town drunkard, but it could not be said that literally he was the boy I had in view." Yet so vivid and accurate is Twain's portrait of his old Hannibal friend that when his sister Pamela read a few pages to their mother, Pamela exclaimed, "Why that's Tom Blankenship!" See Samuel Charles Webster, *Mark Twain, Business Man* (Boston: Little, Brown, 1946), p. 265.

What exactly happened to the fellow is not known. Twain heard on his return to Hannibal in 1902, that Tom Blankenship "was justice of the peace in a remote village in the state of [Montana] and was a good citizen and was greatly respected" ("Chapters from My Autobiography," *North American Review*, August 2, 1902, p. 691). He never confirmed this rumor, but another of Tom's boyhood companions told Clifton Johnson in *Highways and Byways of the Mississippi Valley* (1906, p. 162) that when Tom Blankenship left town, it was to go to the penitentiary. Another childhood friend, Hedrick Smith, reported in "He Returns" (Hannibal *Journal*, April 18, 1889) that Tom Blankenship died of cholera. "I never knew Sam Clemens well enough to be able to make any comments worthy of record," admitted Ayres, "but I feel justified in saying that from my childhood standards Tom Blankenship was possessed with the innate qualities, the 'immortal timber,' to entitle him to be made the hero of boyish adventures around Hannibal in those early days." It may have just been wishful thinking on Twain's part or a private joke when he said that Tom ended up a justice of the peace. In his draft for "Tom Sawyer: A Drama," deposited for copyright July 21, 1875 (and reprinted in *Mark Twain's Hannibal, Huck and Tom*, 1969, p. 245), Twain predicted, "Fifty Years Later . . . General Sawyer, Bishop Finn."

Edward Windsor Kemble (1861–1933) based his characterization on a sixteen-year-old New York City boy named Courtland P. Morris. The two met around 1878 at the New York Athletic Club Boathouse, where the boy ran errands for and fished with the artist. "Being a nimrod and fisherman just like Huck, landed me the job which lasted from May 1st to October 1st, 1884," Morris recounted in "The Model for Huck Finn" (*Mark Twain Quarterly*, Summer/Fall 1938). "And was I gloriously interested in being Huckleberry Finn? No, but in the $4.00 a week. Yes, tremendously. . . . Huckleberry Finn was not known at that time. He was not established, nobody knew him or ever heard of him" (p. 23). But Morris forgot about *Tom Sawyer*, where the character was introduced. "He was always grinning," Kemble recalled his model in "Illustrating Huckleberry Finn" (*Colophon*, February 1930), "and one side of his cheek was usually well padded with a 'sour ball' or a huge wad of molasses taffy. Throwing his wool cap and muslin-covered schoolbooks on a lounge, he would ask what was wanted at this session. I would designate the character." And he posed for everyone else in the book, from the most insignificant to Jim, his favorite. That is why Jim is dressed in the very first picture of him in Chapter 2 exactly like Huck in the frontispiece, complete with the straw hat. Morris dressed up in old clothes of his own or belonging to his parents that he found up in his attic. "The battered old straw hat, which was so much a part of Huck Finn, was mine," he told Cyril Clemens in "The Model for Huckleberry Finn" (*Hobbies*, February, 1955). "I used to wear it when I went fishing along the Harlem River in the summertime. The old single-barreled shotgun, another of Huck's treasured possessions, was a gun my aunt had given me a few years before" (p. 107). Kemble let Morris read the manuscript as it arrived. "From the very first page, the story appealed to my youthful imagination," he told Cyril Clemens, "and then and there, I became an ardent admirer of Mark Twain's work" (p. 106). At first Twain was disappointed with Kemble's interpretation (he complained that Huck Finn looked too "Irishy"), but the author came to accept his illustrator's sizeable contribution to the novel.

2. *You don't know about me. Huckleberry Finn* was the first important novel in Western literature to be told entirely from a child's viewpoint, but Twain was ambiguous as to whether "Huck Finn's Autobiography" was written or dictated. He noted on the first page of the manuscript "Reported by Mark Twain" (**MS**), but Huck confesses in Chapter the Last that "there ain't nothing left to write about." "I begin to write incidents out of real life," he explained his method of composition in "Mark Twain Tells the Secrets of Novelists" (New York *American*, May 26, 1907). "One of the persons I wrote about begins to talk this way and another, and pretty soon I find that these creatures of the imagination have developed into characters, and have for me a distinct personality. They are not 'made,' they just grow naturally out of the subject. That was the way Tom Sawyer, Huck Finn and other characters came to exist."

Twain had been extolling the virtues of children as writers for years before beginning *Huckleberry Finn*. "They write simply and naturally and without strain for effect," he reported in "An Open Letter to the American People" (New York *Weekly Review*, February 17, 1866). "They tell all they know, and stop. They seldom deal in abstractions or homilies." In "Miss Clapp's School" (Virginia City [Nev.] *Territorial Enterprise*, January 19–20, 1864), Twain described a visit to an elementary school in Carson City, Nevada, where student compositions were read aloud. He admired greatly their simple, direct manner of expression: "the cutting to the bone of the subject with the very first gash, without any preliminary foolishness in the way of a gorgeous introductory; the inevitable and persevering tautology; the brief monosyllabic sentences (beginning, as a very general thing, with the pronoun 'I'); the penchant for presenting rigid, uncompromising facts for the consideration of the hearer, rather than ornamental fancies; the depending for the success of the composition upon its general merits, without tacking artificial aids to the end of it, in the shape of deductions, or conclusions, or claptrap climaxes." Huckleberry Finn follows much the same rules in telling his story. Twain was also fond of the juvenilia penned by a six-year-old Scottish prodigy whose work he discovered about 1873 and honored in "Marjorie Fleming, the Wonder Child" (*Harper's Bazaar*, December 1909, pp. 1182–83, 1229). In August 1876, about a month after commencing "Huck Finn's Autobiography," Twain began a private journal of his own children's remarks captured offhand in "A Record of the Small Foolishnesses of Susie and 'Bay' [Clara] Clemens (Infants)" (now in the Clifton Waller Barrett Collection, University of Virginia).

Twain's first extensive attempt to employ the voice of a child was a short story written about 1868 that Albert Bigelow Paine called "Boy's Manuscript" and Bernard DeVoto published in *Mark Twain at Work* (1942). It was also his first attempt to exploit his boyhood experiences in Hannibal in fiction. Twain must have realized how flat a boy's diary reads, for he never published it. Instead, he reworked some of the incidents in *Tom Sawyer*. Twain may have been familiar with *The William Henry Letters* (1870) by Abby Morton Diaz, a once-popular epistolary novel purportedly written and illustrated by a mischievous redheaded ten-year-old away at a New England boarding school. Twain also read Thomas Bailey Aldrich's *The Story of a Bad Boy* (1869), but he did not care for it.

He was also experimenting with dialect, notably in "A True Story, Repeated Word for Word as I Heard It" (*Atlantic Monthly*, November 1874), told to him by Mary Ann Cord, a former slave who worked for his in-laws at Quarry Farm in Elmira, New York. Twain was proud of "A True Story" not only as "a shameful tale of wrong and hardship," but also as "a curiously strong piece of literary work to come unpremeditated from the lips untrained in the literary art" (quoted in Shelley Fisher Fishkin, *Was Huck Black?*, 1993, p. 99). He could have been speaking of *Huckleberry Finn*. As Fishkin demonstrated in *Was Huck Black?*, the first piece Twain published that was written largely in the voice of a child was a sketch "Sociable Jimmy" (New York *Times*, November 29, 1874). Loquacious boys and girls appeared briefly in earlier work, but this "bright, simple, guileless little darky" who waited on him in a hotel proved to be "the most artless, sociable, and exhaustless talker I ever came across." Twain was likewise impressed with the writing of Wattie Bowser, a twelve-year-old schoolboy who wrote him a fan letter in 1880. "I notice you use plain, simple language, short words and brief sentences," Twain replied on March 20, 1880. "That is the way to write English—it is the modern way, and the best way. Stick to it; don't let fluff and flowers and verbosity creep in. When you catch an adjective, kill it. No, I don't mean utterly, but kill most of them—then the rest will be valuable. They weaken when they are close together. They give strength when they are wide apart. An adjective habit, or a wordy, diffuse, flowery habit, once fastened upon a person, is as hard to get rid of as any other vice" (quoted in Pascal Covici, Jr., "Dear Master Wattie: The Mark Twain–David Watt Bowser Letters," *Southwest Review*, Spring 1960, pp. 108–9). That is the style of *Huckleberry Finn*.

3. *"The Adventures of Tom Sawyer."* Many of the introductory incidents in *Huckleberry Finn* are reworkings of material in the last chapter of the earlier book. Even before completing that story, Twain was already planning to describe in detail Huck's life at the widow's. Walter Blair proposed in "When Was *Huckleberry Finn* Written?" (*Mark Twain Journal*, Summer 1979, pp. 1–3) contradictions evident in the narrator's evoking the earlier book at the opening of his "autobiography." Is Huck Finn recalling something that happened "forty or fifty years ago" from the publication of *Huckleberry Finn* in 1884 or from 1876, the year *Tom Sawyer* came out? Or is he recounting his adventures sometime between 1835 and 1845, right after they occurred? The final paragraph of the novel suggests that Huck is all ready to head off on his new adventures out West.

4. *but that ain't no matter*. This casual aside does not appear in the manuscript. Victor Doyno suggested in the 1996 Random House "Comprehensive Edition" of *Huckleberry Finn* that this phrase may have been Twain's way of assuring the public that one need not have read the earlier book to enjoy the sequel.

5. *Mark Twain*. Famous pseudonym of Samuel Langhorne Clemens (1835–1910), born in Florida, Missouri, but raised on the Mississippi River in nearby Hannibal. It was not his first and only pen name: He signed his earliest juvenilia "W. Epaminondas Adrastus Blab." In 1877, he explained "Mark Twain" or "two marks" as "a leadsman's term and signifies a depth of two fathoms [twelve feet] of water"; it indicates "safe water." Clemens often heard the call of "by the mark twain" as he piloted up and down the Mis-

"Mark Twain!" Wood engraving from *The Gilded Age*, 1873.
Courtesy Library of Congress.

sissippi when a young man. Helen Keller thought that his name's "nautical significance suggests the deep and beautiful things he has written" (*The Story of My Life* [New York: Doubleday, Page & Co.], 1903, p. 228). By the time of his death in 1910, "Mark Twain" was probably the most famous pseudonym in the world. Among the various objects named in his honor during his lifetime were a cigar, a shirt collar, and a Mississippi steamboat.

As early as 1873, in a note to Charles Dudley Warner, editor of the Hartford *Courant*, Twain said that he took the famous pen name from another pilot, Captain Isaiah Sellers. "The old gentleman was not of a literary turn or capacity," he wrote in Chapter 50 of *Life in the Mississippi* (1883), "but he used to jot down brief paragraphs of plain practical information about the river, and sign them 'Mark Twain,' and give them to the New Orleans *Picayune*." Clemens said that he wrote a parody of one of them and published it in the New Orleans *True Delta* under the name "Mark Twain." And it so infuriated Sellers that he never wrote anything again. When he heard that Sellers had died, Clemens felt free to use Mark Twain as his pen name. Many critics have viewed this account as just another one of Twain's tall tales. He published his burlesque in the New Orleans *Daily Crescent* (May 17, 1859), and there is no proof that Captain Sellers ever signed his work "Mark Twain" in the New Orleans *Picayune* or any other paper. The earliest time Clemens used it was in a letter sent from Carson City, Nevada, and printed in the Virginia City *Territorial Enterprise* (February 3, 1863), at least a year *before* Sellers died; but he may have confused him with another riverboat captain, Isaiah Russell, who died in 1862. The one column by Captain Sellers that he was able to get his hands on when preparing *Life on the Mississippi* was signed "I. Sellers," which he discreetly excised when he reprinted the item in his book. He may have confused his memory of "Mark Twain" with that of "Sergeant Fathom," the name he gave Sellers in his parody. Twain knew all of this when he wrote *Life on the Mississippi*, because friends provided him with all the documentation in actual clippings from the papers. The best examination of this story is in Horst H. Kruse, "Mark Twain's *Nom de Plume*: Some Mysteries Resolved," *Mark Twain Journal*, 1994, pp. 1–33.

Albert Bigelow Paine, the author's handpicked biographer and first executor of his estate, insisted that "it is incorrect to refer to Mark Twain as 'Twain.' Twain was not his name, but only a part of his nom de plume. Without the first part it has no meaning, and he himself would have resented it. . . . He was often called 'Mark,' and sometimes signed himself that way, but that somehow was different. 'Twain' alone has in it a suggestion of illiteracy" (quoted in "Letters to Cyril Clemens," *Mark Twain Journal*, Spring/Fall 1999, p. 78). Samuel Langhorne Clemens was the private persona, Mark Twain the public one; therefore, it is as "Twain" that he is best remembered.

6. *Aunt Polly*. Tom Sawyer's aunt, based in part on Twain's mother, Jane Lampton Clemens (1803–1890). "I fitted her out with a dialect," he explained in "Chapters from My Autobiography" (*North American Review*, March 1, 1907), "and tried to think up other improvements for her, but did not find any" (p. 455). He said shortly after his mother died in 1890, "She had a slender small body, but a large heart; a heart so large that everybody's griefs and everybody's joys found welcome in it and hospitable accommodation" ("Jane Lampton Clemens," *Huck Finn and Tom Sawyer Among the Indians*, 1989, p. 83). Many of the things that happened to Tom Sawyer happened to Sam Clemens, but Jane Clemens told Thomas W. Handford in *Pleasant Hours with Illustrious Men and Women* (1885) that she thought her son "was more like Huckleberry Finn than Tom Sawyer" (p. 308).

Joshua T. Tucker, pastor of the Hannibal Presbyterian Church, recalled her as "a woman of the sunniest temperament, lively, affable, a general favorite" (Henry H. Sweets II, *The Hannibal, Missouri Presbyterian Church: A Sesquicentennial History*, 1984, p. 17). "Mark Twain inherited the humor and the talents which have made him famous from his mother," his sister-in-law Mollie Stotts Clemens informed Handford. "He is all 'Lampton,' and resembles her as strongly in person as in mind. Tom Sawyer's Aunt Polly and Mrs. Hawkins, in *The Gilded Age* (1874), are direct portraits of his mother" (p. 308). "She was very bright, and was fond of banter and playful

Aunt Polly. Illustration by True W. Williams, *The Adventures of Tom Sawyer*, 1876. *Private collection.*

duets of wits," Twain admitted in "Jane Lampton Clemens," a sketch he wrote after her death in 1890, "and she had a sort of ability which is rare in men and hardly ever existent in women—the ability to say a humorous thing with the perfect air of not knowing it to be humorous." He had been a sickly child, and years later asked his mother how she felt about him in those early days. "All along at first I was afraid you would die," she replied frankly, "and after that I was afraid you wouldn't" (*Huck Finn and Tom Sawyer Among the Indians*, 1989, p. 91). Her son cultivated this skill. His father was different. "He never laughed aloud, and seldom smiled," Orion Clemens recalled in Richard I. Holcombe, *History of Marion County, Missouri* (St. Louis: E. F. Perkins, 1884). "He seldom indulged in joking. If he did the subject was pure and clean, and accompanied with a little twinkle at the corner of the eye, and only a perceptible smile" (p. 915). See Chapter 4, note 17.

7. *the widow.* The Widow Douglas, Huck Finn's foster mother, described in Chapter 5 of *Tom Sawyer* as "fair, smart, and forty, a generous and good-hearted soul and well-to-do, her hill mansion the only place in town, and the most hospitable and much the most lavish in the matter of festivities that St. Petersburg could boast." Since she is one of the few people in town who has ever been kind to him, he warns her in Chapter 29 of Injun Joe's threat to "slit her nostrils . . . notch her ears, like a sow's" as payment for a public horsewhipping her late husband, a justice of the peace, once gave the villain. Out of gratitude for the boy's heroism, she opens her heart and home to the outcast Huck. However, she is less affectionately portrayed in *Huckleberry Finn* than in *Tom Sawyer*.

The Widow Douglas. Illustration by True W. Williams, *The Adventures of Tom Sawyer*, 1876.
Private collection.

She was based on twice-widowed Melicent S. Holliday: "Lived on Holliday's Hill. Well off. Hospitable. Fond of having parties of young people. Widow. Old, but anxious to marry" ("Villagers of 1840–43," *Huck Finn and Tom Sawyer Among the Indians*, 1989, pp. 95–96).

8. *Mary.* Tom Sawyer's cousin, the only member of his family who is fully sympathetic toward the boy; Huck gets a glimpse of her in Chapter 8 of *Huckleberry Finn*. She was based on the author's sister Pamela Ann

Mary. Illustration by True W. Williams, *The Adventures of Tom Sawyer*, 1876.
Private collection.

Clemens (1827–1904), eight years his senior but one of his closest allies. "Her character was without blemish, and she was of a most kindly and gentle disposition," her brother recalled (quoted in *Huck Finn and Tom Sawyer Among the Indians*, 1989, p. 313).

9. *stretchers.* Exaggerations or lies, as in stretching the truth.

10. *Judge Thatcher.* Father of Becky Thatcher, Tom Sawyer's sweetheart in *Tom Sawyer*. He visits the Sunday school in Chapter 4, "a prodigious personage—no less a one than the county judge—altogether the most august creation these children had ever looked upon—and they wondered what kind of material he was made of." Although Kemble used *Tom Sawyer* here and there as a guide for his pictures for *Huckleberry Finn*, his Judge Thatcher in Chapter 4 is not the "fine, portly, middle-aged gentleman with iron-gray hair" Twain described in the earlier book.

11. *my sugar-hogshead.* An enormous barrel, used to store a ship's cargo of sugar and holding from sixty-three to 140 gallons, and big enough for a vagrant boy to sleep in. In Chapter 35 of *Tom Sawyer*, Huck lives "among some old empty hogsheads behind the abandoned slaughterhouse."

Huck in his sugar-hogshead. Illustration by True W. Williams, *The Adventures of Tom Sawyer*, 1876.
Private collection.

12. *She put me in them new clothes again.* In his copy of the 1893 Tauchnitz edition of *Huckleberry Finn* that he marked for his 1895–1896 "Tour Around the World" (now in the Mark Twain Papers), Twain reworked this line by adding a particularly sharp simile: "She crowded me in them new clothes—they make you feel all cramped up and uncomfortable like a bee that's busted through a spider's web and wisht he'd gone *around*."

13. *there warn't really anything the matter with them.* "As far as I could see," Twain added to his 1895–1896 public reading copy .

14. *a barrel of odds and ends.* Originally the more vulgar "swill barrel" in the manuscript (**MS**), indicating that Huck's diet once consisted of what the pigs in the tanyard ate.

15. *Moses and the Bulrushers.* The widow wishes Huck to identify her with the Pharaoh's daughter who adopted the baby Moses. This casual reference to Exodus 2:3–10 introduces a central theme to the novel: Like Moses who freed the Israelites from bondage in Egypt, so too does Huck Finn aid a Southern slave in his flight from his master. Both outlawed boys escape by a river: Moses in an ark of bulrushes on the Nile, Huck by raft down the Mississippi. And both are wards of women of the upper class, the slave-owning class. This scripture especially appealed to slaves who knew that one day they too would be liberated. "Go down, Moses!" they sang. "Tell old Pharaoh, let my people go!" Ironically, although he led his own people out of bondage, Moses provided for slavery among the Israelites in Exodus 21; and it was this holy ordinance that Southern slaveholders clung to as proof that God not only sanctioned but ordered their system of servitude.

In "Annie and Huck: A Note on *The Adventures of Huckleberry Finn*" (*American Literature*, May 1967), Horst H. Kruse suggested that Twain was likely recalling the religious instruction he received from his nine-year-old niece, Annie E. Moffett. "She used to try to teach me lessons from the Bible," he wrote his mother on April 2, 1862, "but I never could understand them. Don't she remember telling me the story of Moses, one Sunday, last Spring, and how hard she tried to explain it and simplify it so that I could understand it—but I *couldn't*? And how she said it was strange that while her ma and her grandma and her uncle Orion could understand anything in the world, I was so dull that I couldn't understand the '*ea-siest* thing'?" (p. 210). Annie reminded him of it later in a letter: "Uncle Mark, if you was here I could tell you about Moses and the Bulrushers again. I know it better, now" (quoted by Twain, "An Open Letter to the American Public," New York *Weekly Review*, February 17, 1866).

16. *I don't take no stock in dead people.* I don't think much of dead people.

17. *They get down on a thing when they don't know nothing about it.* Blair and Fischer in the 1988 University of California edition compared

Huck's reasoning here to Sam Clemens's response to his future in-laws' objection to his smoking. "I cannot attach any weight to either the arguments or the evidence of those who know nothing about the matter personally and so must simply theorize," he wrote his beloved Olivia Langdon on January 13, 1870. "Theorizing has no effect on me. I have smoked habitually for twenty-six of my thirty-four years, and I am the only healthy member our family has. . . . There *is* no argument that can have even a feather's weight with me against smoking . . . for I *know*, and others merely *suppose*" (pp. 374–75).

18. *And she took snuff too.* It was proper in this part of the country for women and girls of all classes and ages to take snuff; men and boys generally smoked or chewed their tobacco. In "Chapters from My Autobiography" (*North American Review*, March 1, 1907), Twain recalled his first visit to a country school near Florida, Missouri, where an older girl asked him if he "used tobacco." When he said no, she told all the other children with scorn, "Here is a boy seven years old who can't chaw tobacco" (p. 459). Everybody used it then. "Some people take it in snuff," humorist Benjamin Penhallow Shillaber explained in "Tobacco" (*Knitting-Work*, 1859), "by holding the snuff between the thumb and finger, and drawing it up into the nose. This is an exciting operation with elderly females, and it is interesting to watch its effects when the nose is fully charged and primed, before it sneezes off" (p. 380). The widow's chastisement of Huck for smoking is reminiscent of another episode by Shillaber, "Mrs. Partington on Tobacco" (*Life and Sayings of Mrs. Partington*, 1854), in which the old woman after dipping into her snuffbox decries "the body and soul destroying nature of the weed" and then stops "a moment to lecture Ike who was enjoying a sugar cigar upon the front door-step" (p. 285). Twain knew Shillaber, whose Boston paper *The Carpet-Bag* was the first journal outside of Hannibal to publish anything by Samuel L. Clemens. Shillaber's Mrs. Ruth Partington and her foster son, Ike, served as sources for Twain's Aunt Polly and her foster son, Tom Sawyer. See Walter Blair, *Mark Twain and Huck Finn*, 1960, pp. 62–63.

19. *Miss Watson.* The model for this spinster was Mary Ann Newcomb (later Bangs), one of Sam's schoolteachers in Hannibal, who lived and took her meals with the Clemenses. Kemble's picture looks remarkably like Twain's description of this "devoutly pious Calvinist" in his unfinished burlesque "Autobiography of a Damned Fool" (1877), down to her "spit curls": "She had ringlets, and a long sharp nose, and thin colorless lips, and you could not tell her breast from her back if she had her head up a stove-pipe hole looking for something in the attic. . . . She had her share of vinegar" (*Mark Twain's Satires and Burlesques*, 1968, pp. 140 and 163). There might never have been Mark Twain if not for this schoolmarm. "I owe a great deal to Mary Newcomb," he confessed on his return to Hannibal in 1902, "she compelled me to learn to read" (quoted in "Former Florida Neighbor of Clemens Family Head of School Attended Here by Mark Twain," Hannibal *Evening Courier-Post*, March 6, 1935). Miss Watson shows up alive and well in the unfinished story "Tom Sawyer's Conspiracy" (in *Huck Finn and Tom Sawyer Among the Indians*, 1989, pp. 134–213), Twain having forgotten he killed her off in *Huckleberry Finn*.

Ike and Mrs. Partington. Wood engraving from *Life and Sayings of Mrs. Partington* by B. P. Shillaber, 1854.
Courtesy Library of Congress.

20. *a tolerable slim old maid.* Twain also called her "lanky" (**MS**) in the manuscript. In his 1895–1896 public reading copy of *Huckleberry Finn*, Twain made her "an old maid and wonderful lean and long-legged and slim like a hairpin." He also called her "sour and moral," but crossed that out.

21. *goggles.* Glasses.

22. *a spelling-book.* Twain added in his 1895–1896 public reading copy, "Drat a spelling book, I don't see no use in 'em." Huck does not attend school in *Tom Sawyer.* "There were no public schools in Missouri in those early days," Twain recalled in 1906, "but there were two private schools—terms twenty-five cents per week per pupil and collect it if you can" (*Mark Twain in Eruption*, p. 107). These were known as "subscription schools." Huck is so illiterate that in Chapter 10, when he and Tom decide to sign an oath to "keep mum" about Doc Robinson's murder, Tom must show Huck "how to make an H and F."

23. *gap and stretch.* Gape or yawn and stretch; Twain first wrote in the manuscript "yawn and stretch and gap" (**MS**), but he quickly recognized the redundancy. Widow Douglas and not her sister Miss Watson was the one who told Huck not to "gape, nor stretch, nor scratch, before folks" in Chapter 35 of *Tom Sawyer.*

24. *the bad place.* Miss Watson is so pious that she cannot even say the word Hell—nor can she say Heaven (the "good place").

25. *mad.* Twain considered "huffy" (**MS**) in the manuscript, but that is not a word Huck Finn might likely use, so he changed it back.

26. *all a body would have to do there was to go around all day long with a harp and sing, forever and ever.* Miss Watson describes the popular Protestant view of Paradise, probably picked up from the pulpit and from such books as John Bunyan's *Pilgrim's Progress* (see Chapter 17, note 31). Huck's resistance to this vision of Eternity was shared by Old Taggart in *History of the Big Bonanza* (1876) by "Dan De Quille," Twain's friend William Wright. On his deathbed, Old Taggart confesses to Deacon Dudley that he will not feel at home in Heaven. "I'm surprised, my good friend," replies the deacon, "to hear that you don't want to be one of that heavenly band that sit before the throne, playing on golden harps, and singing praises forever and forever!" "Me play on a harp, Deacon?" says Old Taggart, smiling. "It's all nonsense to talk about me playin' a harp. I tell you plainly, Deacon, that I don't want to go among the musicians up there. It wouldn't suit me!" (pp. 368–69).

Twain no more looked forward to such an afterlife than do Huck or Old Taggart. "The Presbyterian hell is all misery," he complained in "Reflections on the Sabbath" (*Golden Era*, March 18, 1866); "the heaven is all happiness—nothing to do." In "Letters from the Earth" of 1909, he attacked what he thought were the inanities of Miss Watson's literal interpretation of Paradise:

> In man's heaven *everybody* sings! . . . the man who did not sing on earth, . . . is able to do it there. This universal singing is not casual, not occasional, not relieved by intervals of quiet, it goes on, all day long, and every day, during a stretch of twelve hours. . . . The singing is of hymns alone. Nay, it is of *one* hymn alone. The words are always the same, in number they are only about a dozen, there is no rhyme, there is no poetry; "Hosannah, hosannah, hosannah, Lord God of Sabaoth, 'rah, 'rah, 'rah!—ssht!—boom! . . . a-a-ah!"
>
> Meantime, *every person* is playing on a harp—those millions and millions! whereas not more than twenty in a thousand of them could play an instrument in the earth, or ever *wanted* to. (*What Is Man?*, edited by Paul Baender [Berkeley and Los Angeles: University of California Press, 1973], p. 409)

The most elaborate of Twain's burlesques of the "pearly gate" vision of the "World to Come" is *Extract from Captain Stormfield's Visit to Heaven* (1909), a work he began in 1868 and left unfinished. "People take the figurative language of the Bible and the allegories for literal, and the first thing they ask for when they get here is a halo and a harp, and so on," he complained. "They go and sing and play just about one day, and that's the last you'll ever see them in the choir. They didn't need anybody to tell them that that sort of thing wouldn't make a heaven—at least not a heaven that a sane man could stand a week and remain sane" (p. 40). But by the time this "extract" came out, few Protestants still believed in Miss Watson's simplistic vision of the "good place."

27. *I wanted him and me to be together.* Huck explains his reasons in the manuscript in words that did not make it into the book: "and I knowed I would be lonesome with angels, not being used to them, and they not being used to my kind, but I could get along anywheres with Tom Sawyer" (**MS**).

28. *the niggers.* Coarse, vulgar word for slaves and other people of African descent, derived from the Latin *niger* (black) or an English or Irish dialectical pronunciation of the French *negre* or the Spanish and Portuguese *negro*. It is a relatively recent epithet; *The Oxford English Dictionary* located it no earlier than the eighteenth century. Even in the slave South, only the lowest of the low used the word. Hannibal papers (including that run by Orion Clemens) rarely printed "nigger." It was not part of the vocabulary of properly brought-up Southern belles. "There," Scarlet O'Hara reminds herself in Chapter 24 of Margaret Mitchell's *Gone with the Wind* (1936), "I've said 'nigger' and Mother wouldn't like that." Samuel Langhorne Clemens was born and raised in a slave state, and his use of the word at least 211 times in *Adventures of Huckleberry Finn* reflects his upbringing. To replace the word with "African-American" or "Black" instead of "nigger" is anachronistic and untrue to Huck's upbringing, class, and rhetoric, and it is not enough to merely replace the epithet with "slave." That word, William Styron explained in "Huck Continued" (*New Yorker*, June 26/July 3, 1995), "was generally confined to government proclamations, religious discussions, and legal documents" (p. 133). Stryon concluded that "'nigger' remains our most powerful secular blasphemy." But Huck says it out of habit, not malice.

When Missouri (originally part of the Louisiana Purchase) was admitted to the Union in 1820 by the infamous Missouri Compromise, slavery was preserved in the new state but forever prohibited in territory north of latitude 36° 30' N. The Clemenses of Hannibal were slaveholders, and Twain's social awakening was not an epiphany but as slow and painful as Huck Finn's in the novel. From childhood through early manhood, he used "nigger" as mindlessly as Huck does. "Nigger" appears in other work, but Twain generally put it in quotes when not in direct discourse.

It *was* vile in 1884 when *Huckleberry Finn* was in the press. George Washington Cable strongly objected to Twain's calling a selection from Chapter 14 for their public reading tour "Can't learn a nigger to argue." "When we consider the programme is advertised and becomes cold-blooded newspaper reading," Cable wrote him on October 25, "I think we should avoid any risk of appearing—even to the most thin-skinned and supersensitive and hypocritical matrons and misses—the faintest bit gross. In the text, whether on the printed page or in the readers' utterances, the phrase is absolutely without a hint of grossness; but alone on a published programme, it invites discreditable conjectures of what the content may be, from that portion of our public who cannot live without aromatic vinegar" (quoted in Guy L. Cardwell, *Twins of Genius*, p. 105). Twain readily changed it to "King Sollermun."

Since the days of Reconstruction, the epithet has taken on layer on layer of meaning through constant and pernicious usage. "The word *nigger* to colored people of high and low degree is like a red flag to a bull," Langston Hughes explained in *The Big Sea* (New York: Thunder Mouth's Press, 1940). "Used rightly or wrongly, ironically or seriously, of necessity for the sake of realism, or impishly for the sake of comedy, it doesn't matter. Negroes do not like it in any book or play whatsoever, be the book or play ever so sympathetic in its treatment of the basic problems of the race. Even though the book or play is written by a Negro, they still do not like it. The word *nigger*, you see, sums up for us who are colored all the bitter years of insult and struggle in America" (pp. 268–69). For years local branches of the NAACP have challenged the use of *Huckleberry Finn* in their schools primarily for the story's frequent use of that word. In 1985, the year of the book's centenary, a member of the Chicago School Board said it "ought to be burned." Not everyone within the NAACP agreed. Larry Marshaburne pointed out in "The NAACP and Mark Twain" (*Mark Twain Journal*, Spring 1998, pp. 2–7) that *The Crisis*, the official journal of the national organization, has never condemned the book. "Parents have the right to question book selection but not the right to demand their removal," argued Prof. Kenneth A. Dunn in "Backsliding on Free Speech" (*Crisis*, April/May 1998). "To restrict access to information, whether it is contained in classic literature or recently published novels, dilutes a critical thinking approach. The definition of freedom in America is a work in progress. The struggle continues" (p. 13).

Everyone in *Huckleberry Finn* says the word, even slaves. There is a long history of African-Americans, whether Bert Williams or modern rap artists, employing the word satirically and ironically. "The use of the word 'nigger,' which no white man must use, is coupled with innuendo and suggestion which brings irresistible gales of laughter," W.E.B. Du Bois explained in "The Humor of Negroes" (*Mark Twain Quarterly*, Fall/Winter, 1943). "They imitate the striver, the nouveau riche, the partially educated man of large words and the entirely untrained" (p. 12). Its use is in part an attempt to demystify the term, to reclaim and redefine it among one's peers, to dull its sting. But the extensive use of the word throughout *Huckleberry Finn* has kept the novel at the center of modern freedom-of-speech disputes. Can a book which uses racist language, however subtly, be a great work of literature? Should it have a place in the public school curriculum or library? Remarkably, the Board of Education of the District of Columbia removed *The Crisis* from its approved list of periodicals for use in public schools in 1936, because it occasionally printed what the group called "N——." "Any consideration of the use of this term should take in account, not simply the word, but the way in which it is used," replied Acting Editor Roy Wilkins in the May issue. "To classify this word as it is used in a literary sense with its use as an editorially derogatory epithet, is, in our opinion, an error which the Board of Education ought not commit, even in its concern for the understandably sensitive feelings of colored people. The use of this word in the columns of *The Crisis* has always driven home to Negro readers the insulting and contemptible characterization involved; to any literate white person its use in our columns has made clear the resentment of colored people over the term" (p. 138). The same argument should apply to *Huckleberry Finn*.

29. *prayers*. God-fearing Southern slave owners, who believed that the Bible sanctioned the "peculiar institution," considered it their responsibility to provide their servants with some religious instruction. The more pious among them held both morning and evening services, but generally slaves attended only vespers after the day's work was done. "My master had family worship, night and morning," disclosed a runaway in *The Narrative of William W. Brown, a Fugitive Slave* (1848). "At night the slaves were called in to attend; but in the mornings they had to be at their work, and master did all the praying" (quoted by Lyrae Van Clief-Stefanon, New Riverside Edition edition of *Adventures of Huckleberry Finn*, p. 72). Sometimes they were taken to church, where they were segregated from their owners. "They had one corner where they sat with the slaves of other people, " recalled Missouri slave Malinda Discus. "There was always something about that I couldn't understand. They treated the colored folks like animals and would not hesitate to sell and separate them, yet they seemed to think they had souls and tried to make Christians of them" (quoted by Lorenzo J. Greene, Gary R. Kremer, and Antonio F. Holland, New Riverside Editions edition, *Adventures of Huckleberry Finn*, p. 25). "Along with all of that piety, most of which was doubtless sincere, one would naturally expect to hear many a human voice raised in behalf of the unfortunate slave," Twain observed in a suppressed passage from Chapter 40 of *Life on the Mississippi*; "on the contrary, where one such voice was lifted, there were ten thousand that remained discreetly quiet, or else twaddled the ever-handy Scripture-texts in justification of the institution" (Limited Editions Club edition, 1944, p. 407).

30. *I felt so lonesome I most wished I was dead.* Tom Sawyer suffers much the same melancholy in Chapter 9 of *Tom Sawyer* from reading "signs" of the night, just before he and Huck run off to the graveyard. In Chapter 1 of "Tom Sawyer, Detective," Huck defines his feelings as "spring fever," which "sets him to sighing and saddening around, and there's something the matter with him, he don't know what. But anyway, he gets out by himself and mopes and thinks; and mostly he hunts for a lonesome place high up on the hill in the edge of the woods and sets there and looks away off on the big Mississippi down there a-reading miles and miles around the points where the timber looks smoky and dim it's so fur off and still, and everything's so solemn it seems like everything you've loved is dead and gone and you most wish you was dead and gone too, and done with it all."

These sentiments are the first indication of Huck's great preoccupation with death, a trait he shared with Mark Twain. The high infant mortality rate of the Mississippi Valley must have contributed to his excessive morbidity. "One quarter of the children born," Dixon Wecter quoted the Hannibal *Gazette* (June 3, 1847) in *Sam Clemens of Hannibal* (1952), "die before they are one year old; one half die before they are twenty-one, and not one quarter reach the age of forty" (p. 80). Few families in Hannibal were spared: Sam's brother Pleasant Hannibal Clemens died at three months; another brother, Benjamin, at ten years; and a sister, Margaret, at just under four. And his firstborn and only son, Langdon Clemens, was less than two when he died from diphtheria on June 2, 1872, in Hartford, Connecticut.

31. *an owl . . . who-whooing about somebody that was dead.* Being a nocturnal creature with a mournful hoot, the owl ever since antiquity has been said to possess the power to predict the death of a loved one. Pliny called it "the funerel bird of the night"; Edmund Spenser in *The Faerie Queene* called it "death's dreadful messenger." "A screech owl flapping its wings against the windows of a sick person's chamber, or screeching at them," explained Francis Grose in *A Provincial Glossary* (1787), "portends the same." "Madison Tensas" (Henry Clay Lewis) in "My First Call in the Swamp" in *Odd Leaves from the Life of a Louisiana "Swamp Doctor"* (1846) also played with the folk belief: "The screech-owl has hollered, and she is boun' to die—it's a sure sign, and can't fail!" (p. 154). And Uncle Remus tells the little boy in *Uncle Remus, His Songs and Sayings* (1880) by Joel Chandler Harris, "Squinch-owl holler ev'ry time he see a witch" (p. 133).

In his preface to *Tom Sawyer*, Twain explained, "The odd superstitions touched upon were all prevalent among children and slaves in the West at the period of this story." In Chapter 9 of that novel, Tom and Huck acknowledge that one of their "signs" comes from the slaves, "and they know all about these kinds of things." Frederick Douglass speculated in Chapter 8 of his *Narrative* (1845) why these superstitions meant so much to slaves, particularly to the mother whose young ones were torn from her. "The hearth is desolate," he said. "Instead of the voices of her children, she hears by day the moans of the dove, and by night the screams of the hideous owl. All is gloom."

Brander Matthews in his review of the novel in London *Saturday Review* (January 31, 1885) called *Huckleberry Finn* "a walking repository of the juvenile folklore of the Mississippi Valley—a folklore partly traditional among the white settlers, but largely influenced by intimate association with the negroes." However, most of these beliefs came from their white masters; Daniel G. Hoffman argued in "Black Magic—and White—in *Huckleberry Finn*" (*Form and Fable in American Literature*, 1961, pp. 317–42) that the majority of these signs are actually of European, and not of African, origin. "Huck's superstitions (and Jim's, and Twain's, for that matter) are not at all African-American," explained Harold Bloom in *Major Literary Characters: Huck Finn* (1990), "but go back to the Thracian, shamanistic origins of Western folk-religion, to what can be regarded as the Orphic traditions. As befits an American Orphic, Huck's Orphism bears a marked difference from the ancient variety. The emphasis is not upon the survival of an occult self, but upon survival plain and simple, upon the continuity of the self" (p. 2). This boy who had nothing until the widow took him in has learned in his short life to rely on luck and fortune-telling signs. And his wits, of course.

32. *a whippowill.* Or "whip-poor-will," the popular name in the United States and Canada for a species of goatsucker, which has a low, plaintive call. Twain played with a popular superstition associated with this creature in Chapter 10 of *Tom Sawyer*: Huck tells Tom that two weeks ago "a whipporwill come in [a friend's house] and lit on the bannisters and sung," but "there ain't anybody dead there yet."

33. *a dog crying about somebody that was going to die.* An ancient superstition of Europe and parts of the Near East; according to Grose's *A Provincial Glossary*, dogs "have the faculty of seeing spirits," but "they usually shew signs of terror by whining and creeping to their masters for protection"; and their howling is a certain sign that someone in the family is going to die. The death of Maximus is said to have been predicted by the baying of dogs; in Book XV of the *Odyssey*, the dogs of Eumaeus are terrified by the presence of the goddess Minerva. William Dean Howells mentioned in *A Boy's Town* (1890) that he too knew this omen growing up in the Ohio River valley: "He shuddered when he heard a dog howling in the night, for that was a sign that somebody was going to die" (p. 199). Discussing witches in his book of songs and sayings, Uncle Remus warned that "w'en you hear a dog howlin' in de middle er de night, one un um's mighty ap' ter be prowlin' 'roun'" (p. 135). Likewise in Chapter 10 of *Tom Sawyer*, Huck reports that "they say a stray dog come howling around Johnny Miller's house, 'bout midnight, as much as two weeks ago," but "there ain't nobody dead there yet." Although these signs have all proven to be ineffectual in the earlier novel, Huck is not ready to deny his pagan beliefs so quickly as he has Miss Watson's Sunday-school teachings.

34. *the kind of a sound that a ghost makes when it wants to tell about something that's on its mind.* Blair and Fischer in their notes to the 1988 University of California edition (p. 377) said that this superstition can be traced as far back as the tenth century; they cited Hamlet's father's ghost as an eminent example of this tradition.

35. *a spider*. To see a spider in the evening signifies peace, but to kill it is a bad omen. An English nursery rhyme goes:

> *If you wish to live and thrive,*
> *Let the spider walk alive.*

In the 1988 University of California edition, Blair and Fischer quoted another belief from *Kentucky Superstitions* (1920), compiled by Daniel Lindsay Thomas and Lucy Blayney Thomas: "If a spider is consumed through falling into a lamp, witches are near" (p. 377).

36. *turned around in my tracks three times and crossed my breast every time*. Nearly every culture has a ritual that must be performed in threes to ward off evil spirits; crossing one's breast is equivalent to making the sign of the cross, the symbol of Christ, and doing it three times invokes the protection of the Holy Trinity.

37. *I tied up a little lock of my hair with a thread to keep witches away*. "Niggers tie wool up with thread," Twain noted in 1866, "to keep witches from riding them" (*Notebooks and Journals*, vol. 1 [Berkeley and Los Angeles: University of California Press, 1975], p. 160). Clemens learned this custom from "Aunt" Hannah, a slave owned by his uncle John A. Quarles. "Whenever witches were around," he recalled in "Chapters from My Autobiography" (*North American Review*, March 1, 1907), "she tied up the remnant of her wool in little tufts, with white thread, and this promptly made the witches impotent" (p. 454). Another slave named Nat, in Chapter 34 of *Huckleberry Finn*, wears his hair "all tied up in little bunches with thread. That was to keep witches off." And like most of the superstitions Huck mentions here, this one is of European origin. See Chapter 2, note 9.

38. *lost a horse-shoe that you've found, instead of nailing it up over the door*. It is good luck to find a horseshoe, bad luck to lose one. It is said that when a witch spies one nailed over a door, she must ride every road that that horsehoe has traveled; and by that time, it will be morning and her wicked powers will cease. Although this belief can be traced back to antiquity, it is credited in England to Saint Dunstan, the patron saint of goldsmiths: He drove the devil off with hot pincers, and ever since then, evil spirits avoid any place in Britain where a horseshoe is hung.

39. *I heard a twig snap*. One of the most frequently employed devices to introduce a character in James Fenimore Cooper's romantic "Leatherstocking Tales" is by the sound of a twig snapping. Twain despised this cliché. He complained in "Fenimore Cooper's Literary Offenses" (*North American Review*, July 1895) that his predecessor "prized his broken twig above all the rest of his effects, and worked it the hardest. It is a restful chapter in any book of his when somebody doesn't step on a dry twig and alarm all the reds and whites for two hundred yards around. . . . In fact, the Leatherstocking Series ought to have been called the Broken Twig Series" (pp. 3–4). Then why did Twain himself use it here? Roger B. Bailey in *The Explicator* (September 1967) suggested that it is a particularly apt way of introducing Tom Sawyer as a descendant of Cooper's romantic heroes in *Huckleberry Finn*. It serves as a good contrast to Huck's tripping over a root in the next chapter, what Twain considered one of "a hundred handier things to step on" than a dry twig. From the very first, Twain distinguishes pragmatic Huck from romantic Tom.

40. *I could just barely hear a* "me-yow! me-yow!" Huck uses the same signal when he calls Tom to his window at night, in Chapter 9 of *Tom Sawyer*. Their roles have been reversed: In the first novel Huck inaugurates the adventures, but in the sequel Tom is the instigator.

41. *Tom Sawyer*. " 'Tom Sawyer' and 'Huckleberry Finn' were both real characters," Twain told Lute Pease in "Mark Twain Speaks" (Portland *Oregonian*, August 11, 1895), "but 'Tom Sawyer' was not the real name of the former, nor the name of any person I knew, so far as I can remember, but the name was an ordinary one—just the sort that seemed to fit the boy, some way, by its sound, and so I used it." When a reporter from the New York *Herald* asked an old Hannibal resident who the "real" Tom Sawyer was, he replied, "Town's full of 'em" ("Mark Twain's Reunion," June 15, 1902). "They are not absolute portraits of any one person," Twain told the same reporter. "Some of the incidents accredited to Tom Sawyer happened to one and some to another, and some not at all." Twain admitted in his preface to *Tom Sawyer* that Tom, like Huck, was "drawn from life . . . but not from an individual—he is a combination of the characteristics of three boys whom I knew, and therefore belongs to the composite order of architecture." The three were John Briggs, Will Bowen, and Sam Clemens himself. Jane Clemens, however, thought her son "was more like Huckleberry Finn than Tom Sawyer" (quoted in Thomas W. Handford, *Pleasant Hours with Illustrious Men and Women*, 1885, p. 307). Twain admitted, "My mother had a good deal of trouble with me, but I think she enjoyed it" ("Chapters from My Autobiography," *North American Review*, November 2, 1906, p. 54).

Chapter II.

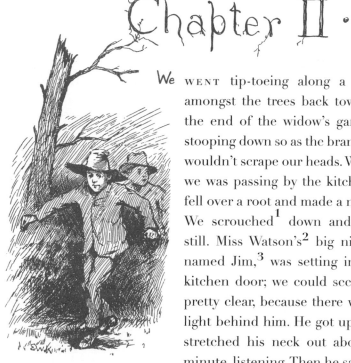

THEY TIP-TOED ALONG.

WE WENT tip-toeing along a path amongst the trees back towards the end of the widow's garden, stooping down so as the branches wouldn't scrape our heads. When we was passing by the kitchen I fell over a root and made a noise. We scrouched[1] down and laid still. Miss Watson's[2] big nigger, named Jim,[3] was setting in the kitchen door; we could see him pretty clear, because there was a light behind him. He got up and stretched his neck out about a minute, listening. Then he says,

"Who dah?"

He listened some more; then he come tip-toeing down and stood right between us; we could a touched him, nearly. Well, likely it was minutes and minutes that there warn't a sound, and we all there so close together. There was a place on my ankle that got to itching;[4] but I dasn't scratch it; and then my ear begun to itch; and next my back, right between my shoulders. Seemed like I'd die if I couldn't scratch. Well, I've noticed that thing plenty of times since. If you are with the quality,[5] or at a funeral, or trying to go to sleep when you ain't sleepy—if you are anywheres where it won't do for you to scratch, why you will itch all over in upwards of a thousand places. Pretty soon Jim says:

1. *scrouched*. Crouched.

2. *Miss Watson's*. Jim was originally "the Widow's" (**MS**) in the manuscript, but Twain changed it to "Miss Watson's" when he realized that she was more likely to abuse a slave than her sister was. This change must have been made relatively late in the book's composition, because Twain noted in his introductory remarks to the "Raft Episode" (see Appendix B) from *Huckleberry Finn* he published in Chapter 3 of *Life on the Mississippi* (1883) that Huck ran away with "a slave of the widow's."

3. *Jim*. Not to be confused with another Jim, "the small colored boy" who cuts wood and totes water for Aunt Polly in Chapter 2 of *Tom Sawyer*. He was based on Sandy, the young slave the Clemenses hired from a man in Hannibal when Sam was a boy. Miss Watson's Jim was

Jim. Illustration by E. W. Kemble, *Mark Twain's Library of Humor*, 1889. *Courtesy Library of Congress.*

based in large part on Uncle Dan'l, "a faithful and affectionate good friend, ally and advisor . . . , a middle-aged slave whose head was the best one in the Negro quarter, whose sympathies were wide and warm and whose heart was honest and simple and knew no guile" ("Chapters from My Autobiography," *North American Review*, March 1, 1907, p. 454). Twain knew Uncle Dan'l on his uncle John A. Quarles's farm near Florida, Missouri. "He has served me well, these many, many years," the writer admitted. "I have not seen him for more than half a century, and yet spiritually I have had his welcome company a good part of that time, and have staged him in books under his own name [in *The Gilded Age*, 1874] and as 'Jim,' and carted him all around—to Hannibal, down the Mississippi on a raft, and even across the Desert of Sahara in a balloon—and he has endured it all with patience and friendliness and loyalty which were his birthright." According to Blair and Fischer in the 1988 University of California edition (p. 378), Quarles freed Uncle Dan'l in 1855, when he was fifty years old. "It was on the farm," Twain confessed, "that I got my strong liking for his race and my appreciation of certain of its fine qualities. This feeling and this estimate have stood the test of sixty years and more and have suffered no impairment. The black face is as welcome to me now as it was then."

Other qualities of Jim have been traced to John Lewis, a farmer at Quarry Farm, near Elmira, New York, where Sam Clemens and his family spent their summers, and George Griffin, the butler in Hartford, Connecticut, whom Twain described as "handsome, . . . well-built,

Mark Twain and John Lewis, 1903.
Courtesy Library of Congress.

"Say—who is you? Whar is you? Dog my cats[6] ef I didn' hear sumf'n. Well, I knows what I's gwyne to do. I's gwyne to set down here and listen tell I hears it agin."[7]

So he set down on the ground betwixt me and Tom. He leaned his back up against a tree, and stretched his legs out till one of them most touched one of mine. My nose begun to itch. It itched till the tears come into my eyes. But I dasn't scratch. Then it begun to itch on the inside. Next I got to itching underneath. I didn't know how I was going to set still. This miserableness went on as much as six or seven minutes; but it seemed a sight longer than that. I was itching in eleven different places now. I reckoned I couldn't stand it more'n a minute longer, but I set my teeth hard and got ready to try. Just then Jim begun to breathe heavy; next he begun to snore—and then I was pretty soon comfortable again.

Tom he made a sign to me—kind of a little noise with his mouth—and we went creeping away on our hands and knees. When we was ten foot off, Tom whispered to me and wanted to tie Jim to the tree for fun; but I said no;[8] he might wake and make a disturbance, and then they'd find out I warn't in. Then Tom said he hadn't got candles enough, and he would slip in the kitchen and get some more. I didn't want him to try. I said Jim might wake up and come. But Tom wanted to resk it; so we slid in there and got three candles, and Tom laid five cents on the table for pay. Then we got out, and I was in a sweat to get away; but nothing would do Tom but he must crawl to where Jim was, on his hands and knees, and play something on him. I waited, and it seemed a good while, everything was so still and lonesome.

As soon as Tom was back, we cut along the path, around the garden fence, and by-and-by fetched up on the steep top of the hill the other side of the house. Tom said he slipped Jim's hat off of his head and hung it on a limb right over him, and Jim stirred a little, but he didn't wake. Afterwards Jim said the witches bewitched him and put him in a trance, and rode him all over the State,[9] and then set him under the trees again and hung his hat on a limb to show who done it. And next time Jim told it he said they rode him down to New Orleans;[10] and after that, every time he told it he spread it more and more,[11] till by-and-by he said they rode him all over the world, and tired him most to death,

JIM.

and his back was all over saddle-boils. Jim was monstrous proud about it, and he got so he wouldn't hardly notice the other niggers. Niggers would come miles to hear Jim tell about it, and he was more looked up to than any nigger in that country. Strange niggers[12] would stand with their mouths open and look him all over, same as if he was a won-der. Niggers is always talking about witches in the dark by the kitchen fire;[13] but whenever one was talking and let-ting on to know all about such things, Jim would happen in and say, "Hm! What you know 'bout witches?" and that nig-ger was corked up and had to take a back seat. Jim always kept that five-center piece[14] around his neck with a string and said it was a charm the devil give to him with his own hands[15] and told him he could cure anybody with it and fetch witches whenever he wanted to, just by saying some-thing to it; but he never told what it was he said to it. Nig-

shrewd, wide, polite, always good-natured, cheerful to gaiety, honest, religious, a cautious truth-speaker, devoted friend to the family, champion of its interests." See Arthur G. Pettit, *Mark Twain and the South*, 1974, pp. 95–106. Twain may have been familiar with the friendship between Grandmother Richmond's "Black John" and Tom Blankenship, the model for Huckleberry Finn. "Black John and Tom Blankenship were naturally leading spirits," reported J. W. Ayres in "Recollections of Hannibal" (Palmyra *Spectator*, August 22, 1917), "and they led us younger 'weaker' ones through our sports. Both were 'talented,' bold, kind, and just and we all 'liked' them both and were easily led by them."

It should be noted that Huck Finn never once calls him "Nigger Jim" in the novel. He is "Miss Watson's Jim" or just "Jim." In Chapter 9 of *The Tragedy of Pudd'nhead Wilson* (1894), Roxy informs her son that he, a Southern slave, "ain't *got* no fambly name, beca'se niggers don't *have* 'em!" Twain discussed an oddity of this custom in a note to Chapter 10 in *Tom Sawyer*: Miss Watson's slave named Jim was commonly known as "Miss Watson's Jim," but a son or a dog by that name would have been "Jim Watson." (Ironically, emancipated slaves often took the surnames of their former owners as their "family" names.) Royalty are no better than slaves: When talking about "that old hump-backed" Richard III in Chapter 25 of *Tom Sawyer*, Tom tells Huck, "Kings don't have any but a given name." "Well, if they likes it, Tom, all right," replies Huck; "but I don't want to be a king and have only a given name, like a nigger."

In *The Mark Twain Forum* (February 11, 1993), scholar Taylor Roberts traced the earliest use of "Nigger Jim" to "Fun at the Opera House: 'Mark Twain' and Geo. W. Cable Entertain a Large Audience," a report of a recent public reading in the Ottawa *Free Press* (February 18, 1885). But Twain did not employ that phrase when he introduced the character in his public reading in Toronto two months before. Albert Bigelow Paine used "Nigger Jim" in his 1912 Twain biography; and consequently everyone from Ernest Hemingway to Norman Mailer—even Ralph Ellison—has used it indiscriminately.

In "Morality and *Adventures of Huckleberry Finn*" (*Mark Twain Journal*, Fall 1984), Julius Lester accused Twain of depicting "the only kind of black that whites have ever truly liked—faithful, tending sick whites, not speaking, not causing trouble, and totally passive. He is the archetypal 'good nigger,' who lacks self-respect, dignity, and a sense of self separate from the ones whites want him to have. A century of white readers have accepted this characterization because it permits their own 'humanity' to shine with more luster" (p. 44). This is "The Jim Dilemma," as Jocelyn Chadwick-Joshua called her 1998 study of *Huckleberry Finn*. David Lionel Smith noted in "Black Critics and Mark Twain" (*The Cambridge Companion to Mark Twain*, edited by Forrest G. Robinson, 1995) that many critics, both black and white, "have rejected realism—some realities are embarrassing, after all—insisting instead on idealism, propriety, and the depiction of only what they consider complimentary to the race" (p. 120). "Like all Clemens' blacks, Jim is a *pre-war* slave," reminded Naneolia S. Doughty in "Realistic Negro Characterization of Postbellum Fiction" (*Negro American Literature Forum*, Summer 1957). "His submissiveness is the necessary bearing of the wholly-owned chattel—*not* a synthetic attitude decreed by the author" (p. 57).

Although the novel was ignored in the Black press when it came out in 1885, some African-Americans have recognized the importance of Jim to the development of American literature. "I do not believe anyone can read this story closely without becoming aware of the deep sympathy of the author for 'Jim,'" Booker T. Washington said in *North American Review* (June 1910). "In fact, before one gets through the book, one cannot fail to observe that in some way or other the author, without making any comment and without going out of his way, has somehow succeeded in making his readers feel a genuine respect for 'Jim,' in spite of the ignorance he displays. I cannot help feeling that in this character Mark Twain has, perhaps unconsciously, exhibited his sympathy and interest in the masses of the negro people" (p. 828). Sterling Brown in his pioneering study *The Negro in American Fiction* (1937) considered Jim to be "the best example in nineteenth century fiction of the average Negro slave (not the tragic mulatto or the noble savage), illiterate, superstitious, yet clinging to his hope for freedom, for his love for his own. And he is completely believable" (p. 62). Langston Hughes acknowledged with Milton Meltzer and C. Eric Lincoln in *A Pictorial History of Black Americans* (1968) that Jim "is considered one of the best portraits in American fiction of an unlettered slave clinging to the hope of freedom" (p. 235). Even John H. Wallace, one of Twain's most vitu-

gers would come from all around there and give Jim anything they had, just for a sight of that five-center piece; but they wouldn't touch it, because the devil had had his hands on it. Jim was most ruined, for a servant,[16] because he got so stuck up on account of having seen the devil and been rode by witches.

Well, when Tom and me got to the edge of the hill-top, we looked away down into the village[17] and could see three or four lights twinkling, where there was sick folks, may be; and the stars over us was sparkling ever so fine; and down by the village was the river, a whole mile broad, and awful still and grand. We went down the hill and found Jo Harper, and Ben Rogers,[18] and two or three more of the boys, hid in the old tanyard. So we unhitched a skiff[19] and pulled down the river two mile and a half, to the big scar on the hillside,[20] and went ashore.

We went to a clump of bushes, and Tom made everybody swear to keep the secret, and then showed them a hole in the hill, right in the thickest part of the bushes. Then we lit the candles and crawled in on our hands and knees. We went about two hundred yards, and then the cave opened up. Tom poked about amongst the passages and pretty soon ducked under a wall where you wouldn't a noticed that there was a hole. We went along a narrow place and got into a kind of room, all damp and sweaty and cold, and there we stopped. Tom says:

"Now we'll start this band of robbers and call it Tom Sawyer's Gang.[21] Everybody that wants to join has got to take an oath, and write his name in blood."

Everybody was willing. So Tom got out a sheet of paper that he had wrote the oath on, and read it. It swore every boy to stick to the band, and never tell any of the secrets; and if anybody done anything to any boy in the band, whichever boy was ordered to kill that person and his family must do it, and he mustn't eat and he mustn't sleep till he had killed them and hacked a cross in their breasts,[22] which was the sign of the band.[23] And nobody that didn't belong to the band could use that mark, and if he did he must be sued;[24] and if he done it again he must be killed.

TOM SAWYER'S BAND OF ROBBERS.

And if anybody that belonged to the band told the secrets, he must have his throat cut,[25] and then have his carcass burnt up and the ashes scattered all around, and his name blotted off of the list with blood and never mentioned again by the gang, but have a curse put on it and be forgot, forever.

Everybody said it was a real beautiful oath, and asked Tom if he got it out of his own head. He said, some of it, but the rest was out of pirate books, and robber books,[26] and every gang that was high-toned[27] had it.

Some thought it would be good to kill the *families* of boys that told the secrets.[28] Tom said it was a good idea, so he took a pencil and wrote it in. Then Ben Rogers says:

"Here's Huck Finn, he hain't got no family—what you going to do 'bout him?"[29]

"Well, hain't he got a father?" says Tom Sawyer.

"Yes, he's got a father, but you can't never find him, these days. He used to lay drunk with the hogs in the tanyard, but he hain't been seen in these parts for a year or more."

They talked it over, and they was going to rule me out, because they said every boy must have a family or somebody to kill, or else it wouldn't be fair and square for the others. Well, nobody could think of anything to do—everybody was stumped, and set still. I was most ready to cry; but

perative critics, described Jim in the foreword to his 1983 "adaptation" of *Huckleberry Finn* as simply "a mature, insightful older man seeking his freedom from the cruel and peculiar institution of slavery."

4. *got to itching*. "Like sin" (**MS**) in the manuscript.

5. *the quality*. "At the social summit stood the 'quality,'" Twain explained in his uncompleted "Indiantown," 1899. "This word was used by the commoner folk of the South and the Southwest, and was the equivalent of 'aristocracy'" (in *Which Was the Dream?*, 1967, p. 157).

6. *Dog my cats*. "*Blame* my cats" (**MS**) in the manuscript, but changed when Twain decided to soften some of the oaths in the story. And of course, "dog" goes better with "cats."

7. *I's gwyne to set down here and listen tell I hears it agin*. Is it possible that Jim knows all along exactly who the culprits are and is just playing a trick on those merry pranksters, Tom and Huck? Why else would he announce out loud what he is going to do unless he is teasing the boys? He then goes to such great lengths to make them feel uncomfortable.

8. *Tom . . . wanted to tie Jim to the tree for fun; but I said no*. It is not part of Huck's character to play such a mean joke on Jim. In Chapter 28 of *Tom Sawyer*, Huck mentions his ambiguous relationship with another slave, Ben Roger's father's slave: "I tote water for Uncle Jake whenever he wants me to, and any time I ask him he gives me a little something to eat if he can spare it. That's a mighty good nigger, Tom. He likes me, becuz I don't ever act as if I was above him. Sometimes, I've set right down and eat *with* him. But you needn't tell that. A body's got to do things when he's awful hungry he wouldn't want to do as a steady thing." These contradictory feelings of affection and disdain toward Uncle Jack anticipate the boy's attitudes toward Miss Watson's Jim.

9. *Jim said the witches . . . rode him all over the State*. A common superstition among Southern slaves, apparently of European origin. Evidence that one had been ridden by witches were feeling "down and out" the next morning; sores on the sides of the mouth from the witches' bridling; and "witches' stirrups," tangles in the hair. Being ridden by witches was also said to induce nightmares.

10. *down to New Orleans.* Slaves in Missouri were more often domestics or worked the fields side by side with their masters, and thus were known to be better treated by their owners; but in the Deep South, many toiled on the plantations as field hands under the supervision of cruel overseers. Many tales of how men and women were beaten, overworked, chained, disfigured, and sometimes murdered traveled up the river; and nothing was more feared by those in the border states than to be sold south. So Jim's statement that witches rode him down to New Orleans, the point farthest south in the slave states, is equivalent to his saying he was taken to Hell. See Chapter 8, note 29.

11. *he spread it more and more.* Jim is nearly as inventive a storyteller as Tom or Huck—or Mark Twain.

12. *Strange niggers.* Meaning strangers from other parts.

13. *Niggers is always talking about witches in the dark by the kitchen fire.* It was in Uncle Dan'l's kitchen on Uncle John A. Quarles's farm that young Sam Clemens first heard similar tales, "the white and black children grouped on the hearth, with the firelight playing on their faces and the shadows flickering upon the walls, clear back toward the cavernous gloom of the rear, and I can hear Uncle Dan'l telling the immortal tales which Uncle Remus Harris was to gather into his books and charm the world with, by and by; and I can feel again the creepy joy which quivered through me when the time for the ghost story of the 'Golden Arm' [retold in "How to Tell a Story," *The Youth's Companion*, October 3, 1895] was reached—and the sense of regret, too, which came over me, for it was always the last story of the evening" ("Chapters from My Autobiography," *North American Review*, March 1, 1907, p. 461).

14. *five-center piece.* An anachronism: Nickels were not minted until after the Civil War.

15. *it was a charm the devil give to him with his own hands.* Coins (usually silver) were worn by Southern slaves as protection against hoodoo, or evil magic. In Chapter 35 of *Uncle Tom's Cabin* (1852), Harriet Beecher Stowe described a simi-

all at once I thought of a way, and so I offered them Miss Watson—they could kill her.[30] Everybody said:

"Oh, she'll do, she'll do. That's all right. Huck can come in."

Then they all stuck a pin in their fingers to get blood to sign with, and I made my mark on the paper.

"Now," says Ben Rogers,[31] "what's the line of business of this Gang?"[32]

"Nothing only robbery and murder," Tom said.

"But who are we going to rob? houses—or cattle—or—"

"Stuff![33] stealing cattle and such things ain't robbery, it's burglary," says Tom Sawyer. "We ain't burglars. That ain't no sort of style. We are highwaymen. We stop stages and carriages on the road, with masks on, and kill the people and take their watches and money."

"Must we always kill the people?"

"Oh, certainly. It's best. Some authorities think different, but mostly it's considered best to kill them. Except some that you bring to the cave here and keep them till they're ransomed."

"Ransomed? What's that?"

"I don't know.[34] But that's what they do. I've seen it in books; and so of course that's what we've got to do."[35]

"But how can we do it if we don't know what it is?"

"Why blame[36] it all, we've *got* to do it. Don't I tell you it's in the books? Do you want to go to doing different from what's in the books, and get things all muddled up?"

"Oh, that's all very fine to *say*, Tom Sawyer, but how in the nation[37] are these fellows going to be ransomed if we don't know how to do it to them? that's the thing *I* want to get at. Now what do you *reckon* it is?"

"Well I don't know. But per'aps if we keep them till they're ransomed, it means that we keep them till they're dead."

"Now, that's something *like*. That'll answer. Why couldn't you said that before? We'll keep them till they're ransomed to death—and a bothersome lot they'll be, too, eating up everything and always trying to get loose."

"How you talk, Ben Rogers. How can they get loose when

there's a guard over them, ready to shoot them down if they move a peg?"

"A guard. Well, that *is* good. So somebody's got to set up all night and never get any sleep, just so as to watch them. I think that's foolishness. Why can't a body take a club and ransom them as soon as they get here?"

"Because it ain't in the books so—that's why. Now Ben Rogers, do you want to do things regular, or don't you?—that's the idea. Don't you reckon that the people that made the books knows what's the correct thing to do? Do you reckon *you* can learn 'em anything? Not by a good deal. No, sir, we'll just go on and ransom them in the regular way."

"All right. I don't mind; but I say it's a fool way, anyhow. Say—do we kill the women, too?"

"Well, Ben Rogers, if I was as ignorant as you I wouldn't let on. Kill the women? No—nobody ever saw anything in the books like that.[38] You fetch them to the cave, and you're always as polite as pie[39] to them; and by-and-by they fall in love with you and never want to go home any more."

"Well, if that's the way, I'm agreed, but I don't take no stock in it. Mighty soon we'll have the cave so cluttered up with women, and fellows waiting to be ransomed, that there won't be no place for the robbers. But go ahead, I ain't got nothing to say."

Little Tommy Barnes was asleep, now, and when they waked him up he was scared, and cried, and said he wanted to go home to his ma, and didn't want to be a robber any more.[40]

So they all made fun of him, and called him cry-baby, and that made him mad, and he said he would go straight and tell all the secrets. But Tom give him five cents to keep quiet, and said we would all go home and meet next week and rob somebody and kill some people.

Ben Rogers said he couldn't get out much, only Sundays, and so he wanted to begin next Sunday; but all the boys said it would be wicked to do it on Sunday,[41] and that settled the thing. They agreed to get together and fix a day as soon as they could, and then we elected Tom Sawyer first

lar witch's talisman worn by slaves around the neck with black string which "keeps 'em from feelin' when they's flogged." The potency of Jim's charm derives from its having been touched by the devil.

16. *Jim was most ruined, for a servant.* Slaveholders were obsessed about "ruining" slaves for servitude. Any small thing could do it. Frederick Douglass said in Chapter 9 of his *Narrative* (1845) that one of his masters complained that the time he spent in the city "had a very pernicious effect upon me. It had almost ruined me for every good purpose, and fitted me for everything which was bad." Harriet Jacobs recalled in Chapter 2 of *Incidents in the Life of a Slave Girl* (1861) that her owners thought that her father "spoiled his children, by teaching them to feel that they were human beings. This was blasphemous doctrine for a slave to teach; presumptuous in him, and dangerous to the masters."

17. *the village.* Hannibal, Missouri, the little riverside town where Samuel Clemens lived from his third to seventeenth year, and renamed by Twain in *Tom Sawyer* "St. Petersburg"—literally "Heaven." The name was appropriate for the locale of that novel, which Twain called his "hymn to boyhood." Also he may have had in mind as an ironic reference to his burlesque verse "To Miss Katie of H—l" ("Hannibal" or "Hell"?), which he published in

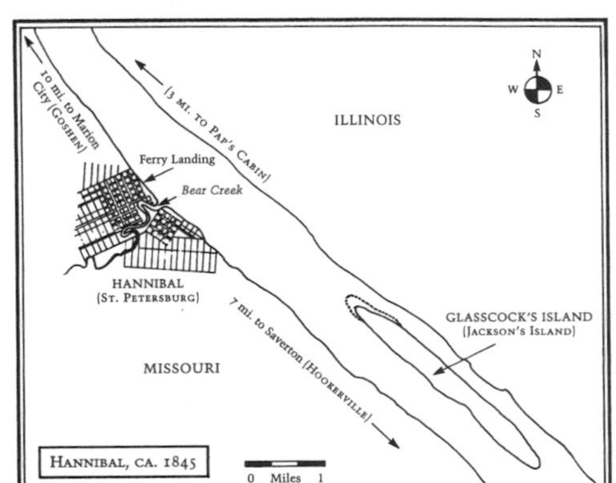

Map of Hannibal, Missouri, circa 1845.
Reprinted with permission from the Mark Twain Project's Adventures of Huckleberry Finn, *edited by Victor Fischer and Lin Salamo (University of California, 2001). Copyright © 1985 and 2001 by the Regents of the University of California Press.*

his brother Orion's paper, the Hannibal *Journal* (May 6, 1853). Twain's contemporary Ben Ezra Stiles Ely recalled the Hannibal of their childhood in the 1830s:

> At that time the country was but sparsely settled and one might ride for miles through the primeval forests and over the wide, rolling prairies covered with tall prairie grass, flowers, and in the season so plentiful of dewberries and strawberries so numerous that sometimes in riding over them the hoofs of the horses would be stained red. I have seen the deer in droves, coming up from the forests in single file from their watering places or licks, and at night sitting in the doorway. I have heard the prairie wolves howling around the house. (Quoted in Curtis Dahl, "Mark Twain and Ben Ely: Two Missouri Boyhoods," *Missouri Historical Review*, July 1972, p. 552)

"In the small town of Hannibal, Missouri, when I was a boy," Twain recalled in the memorial sketch "Jane Lampton Clemens" of 1890,

Hannibal, Missouri. Color lithograph by Henry Lewis, *Das illustrirte Mississippithal*, 1857.
Courtesy Rare Books Division, New York Public Library, Astor, Lenox, and Tilden Foundations.

"everybody was poor but didn't know it; and everybody was comfortable, and did know it. And there were grades of society; people of good family, people of unclassified family, people of no family. Everybody knew everybody, and was affable to everybody, and nobody put on any visible airs; yet the class lines were quite

captain and Jo Harper second captain of the Gang, and so started home.

I clumb up the shed and crept into my window[42] just before day was breaking. My new clothes was all greased up and clayey, and I was dog-tired.

HUCK CREEPS INTO HIS WINDOW.

clearly drawn, and the familiar social life of each class was restricted to that class" (*Huck Finn and Tom Sawyer Among the Indians*, p. 85). The Clemenses were lower-middle-class, neither rich nor poor.

18. *Jo Harper, and Ben Rogers.* Tom Sawyer's "bosom" friends who were based respectively on Twain's "first, and oldest, and dearest friend" Will Bowen (1836–1893) and John B. Briggs (1837–1907). Bowen was also one of the models for Tom Sawyer.

19. *a skiff.* A flat-bottomed open boat.

20. *the big scar on the hillside.* A large, bare place on the side of the hill like a scar on a face.

21. *Tom Sawyer's Gang.* As explained in Chapter 33 of *Tom Sawyer*, the immediate inspiration for this band of robbers is Injun Joe and his cohorts. However, Tom's plans rival those of John A. Murrell, the notorious land pirate who terrorized the Mississippi Valley from 1826 to 1834. Twain mentioned him in passing in Chapter 26 of *Tom Sawyer* and in his working notes for *Huckleberry Finn*; he described "Murrell's Gang" in detail in Chapter 29 of *Life on the Mississippi* as "a colossal combination of robbers, horse thieves, Negro-stealers, and counterfeiters engaged in business along the river some fifty or sixty years ago." The area was full of tales about the exploits of this remarkable scoundrel. "Murrell projected negro insurrections and the capture of New Orleans," said Twain; "and furthermore, on occasion, this Murell could go into the pulpit and edify the congregation." He was finally captured and imprisoned for stealing slaves.

22. *hacked a cross in their breasts.* Tom has been reading Robert Montgomery Bird's *Nick of the Woods* (1837), in which an evil spirit called "Jabbenainsay" (the Spirit-that-walks) by the Indians and "Nick of the Woods" by the white settlers leaves its victims with "a knife cut, or brace of 'em, over the ribs in the shape of a cross." Blair and Fischer noted in the 1988 University of California edition that Twain recalled this book in an 1859 sketch, "The Mysterious Murders in Risse," in which an assassin marks his victim "bearing upon the centre of his forehead the form of a cross, apparently cut with a knife" (*Early Tales and Sketches*, vol. 1, 1979, p. 140).

23. *the sign of the band.* This too has been borrowed from Injun Joe: In Chapter 33 of *Tom Sawyer*, Tom and Huck find the robber's gold buried beneath a cross carved into the wall of the cave. See Chapter 4, note 5.

24. *nobody that didn't belong to the band could use that mark, and if he did he must be sued.* Just like a trademark? Clemens registered "Mark Twain" as a trademark; and this may be an inside joke intended as a little warning to anyone who might try to "pirate" his work.

25. *he must have his throat cut.* This punishment originally contained other details "and his bowels took out and burnt up before his face" (**MS**), but they were likely too outrageous to survive Olivia Clemens's "expergating." This may be the very phrase that little Susy Clemens wrote in her biography of her father "was perfectly fascinating it was dreadful, that Clara and I used to delight in, and oh with what dispair we saw mamma turn down the leaf on which it was written, we thought the book would be almost ruined without it." "I do not remember what the condemned phrase was," Twain confessed in "Chapters from My Autobiography" (*North American Review*, June 7, 1907). "It had much company, and they all went to the gallows; but it is possible that that specially dreadful one which gave those little people so much delight was cunningly devised and put in the book for just that function, and not with any hope or expectation that it would get by the 'expergator' alive" (pp. 243–44).

26. *pirate books, and robber books.* No matter how sensational the reading matter of the day, there was always something noble behind the slaughter. Twain noted in "Villagers of 1840–43," written in 1897, that of the literature at the time, "Pirates and knights [were] preferred to other society" (*Huck Finn and Tom Sawyer Among the Indians*, 1989, p. 99). Besides popular histories of Murrell's gang and Bird's *Nick of the Woods*, Tom was likely reading "dime novels" by "Ned Buntline" (Edward Zane Carroll Judson). *The Black Avenger; or, The Fiend of Blood* (1847) provides Tom with his alias as pirate chief in Chapter 8 of *Tom Sawyer*. Just the titles of these lurid books (for example, *The Last Days of Callao; or, The Doomed Sea of Sin!*, 1847; and *The King of the Sea; A Tale of the Fearless and Free*, 1847) promise the reader that each is "a story of thrilling scenes, daring deeds and stirring times," or "a tale of love, strife, and chivalry." Judson continued to grind out potboilers far into the century, but he eventually turned from pirates and highwaymen to Western heroes like "Wild Bill" Hickock and "Buffalo Bill" Cody. He helped establish their legends through his dime novels.

When *Huckleberry Finn* came out, there was a national campaign led by Joseph Pulitzer's New York *World* and Anthony Comstock's Society for the Prevention of Vice against the distribution of this sensationalistic literature to impressionable young readers. It was similar to the modern attacks on comic books, rock and roll, and video games. According to Albert E. Stone, Jr., *The Innocent Eye* (1961), the most notorious juvenile deliquent of the age was Jesse Pomeroy, a fourteen-year-old Boston newsboy. Accused of murdering at least three children and torturing many others, he confessed that he got all his ideas from dime novels. Of course, Twain was in part burlesquing these books in *Tom Sawyer* and *Huckleberry Finn*, but not everyone got the joke. The Springfield *Daily Republican* (March 17, 1885) accused Twain's books of being "no better in tone than the dime novels which flood the blood-and-thunder reading population," and the Concord Public Library banned *Huckleberry Finn* when it came out. "Much of it is so improbable as to become at times wholly unconvincing on one level of understanding," complained critic Joseph Wood Krutch in "Bad Novels and Good Novels" (*New York Times Book Review*, May 23, 1954). "It is also episodic, clumsily plotted, and sometimes as crudely melodramatic as a dime novel" (p. 2).

27. *high-toned*. Aristocratic, stylish.

28. *Some thought it would be good to kill the* families *of boys that told the secrets*. Such wisdom from the mouths of babes! These vendettas were the common stuff of nineteenth-century popular fiction. Twain admitted in Chapter 55 of *Life on the Mississippi* that while he was growing up in Hannibal, he was fascinated with a local carpenter's exciting tales of how "he had killed his victims in every quarter of the globe, and . . . these victims were always named Lynch" in revenge for the muder of his sweetheart by a "base hireling" by the name of Archibald Lynch; Sam Clemens was crestfallen when he learned that this self-proclaimed murderer of thirty human beings was "a romantic, sentimental, melodramatic fraud." "This ass had been reading the *Jibbenainosay*, no doubt, and had had his poor romantic head turned by it," Twain recalled in disgust; "but as I had not seen the book then, I took his inventions for truth, and did not suspect that he was a plagiarist." See note 22 above.

29. *Huck Finn . . . hain't got no family—what you going to do 'bout him?* Huck is even an outcast among his peers; this statement can only reinforce his deep feeling of loneliness described in the previous chapter. However, Tom Blankenship, the real Huck, was a leader of the Hannibal boys. See Dixon Wector, *Sam Clemens of Hannibal*, 1952, p. 149.

30. *I offered them Miss Watson—they could kill her*. Not only is this remark a splendid joke, but it also sets up Miss Watson as a moral foil for the boy's wastrel father, the town drunk pap Finn.

31. *Ben Rogers*. Twain originally had "Jo Harper" (**MS**) grill Tom about the gang in the manuscript; but he may have remembered that Joe had been "General" of one of the armies of boys in Chapter 3 of *Tom Sawyer* and so less likely to question Tom than Ben Rogers might.

32. *what's the line of business of this Gang?* This exchange is largely a rephrasing of Tom's discussion with Huck in Chapter 33 of *Tom Sawyer*.

33. *Stuff!* Twain originally wrote "Bosh!" (**MS**) in the manuscript, but "Stuff!" is a better word for a backwoods boy like Tom Sawyer.

34. *Ransomed? . . . I don't know*. Tom has a short memory: He told Huck in Chapter 33 in *Tom Sawyer* that a ransom is "money. You make them raise all they can, off'n their friends; and after you've kept them a year, if it ain't raised then you kill them. That's the general way."

35. *I've seen it in books; and so of course that's what we've got to do*. Tom Sawyer is one of those sad, trusting, naive souls who believes that just because he has seen it in print, it must be true. Because he does not trust in either instinct or experience, he cannot really distinguish fact from fiction.

36. *blame*. Euphemism for "damn"—from "blasphemous."

37. *the nation*. Euphemism for "damnation."

38. *Kill the women? No—nobody ever saw anything in the books like that.* In the dime novels Tom has read, even the criminals follow a chivalrous code. "The heroes of these young people—even the pirates—were moved by lofty impulses," Twain recalled in "Villagers 1840–43" of 1897: "they waded in blood, in distant fields of war and adventure and upon the pirate deck, to rescue the helpless, not to make money; they spent their blood and made their self-sacrifice for 'honor's' sake, not to capture a giant fortune; they married for love, not for money and position. It was an intensely sentimental age, but it took no sordid form" (*Huck Finn and Tom Sawyer Among the Indians*, p.100).

39. *polite as pie*. Polite as can be. See Chapter 5, note 16.

40. *Little Tommy Barnes . . . cried, and said he wanted to go home to his ma, and didn't want to be a robber any more.* Tom's wild dreams of glory are undercut by this reminder that his band of cutthroats is a mere bunch of children, and no danger to anyone. "Boys will be boys," after all. "A boy hardly knows what harm is," Howells observed in Chapter 18 of *A Boy's Town*, "and he does it mostly without realizing that it hurts. He cannot invent anything, he can only imitate; and it is easier to imitate evil than good." Their play therefore is an accurate reflection of adult society; they can only be as good as their parents are.

But Twain was not fooled by the veneer of "innocence." In Chapter 31 of *A Connecticut Yankee in King Arthur's Court*, he presented a bleak picture of how far they might go: "A small mob of half-naked boys and girls came tearing out of the woods, scared and shrieking. The eldest among them were not more than twelve or fourteen years. They implored help, but they were so beside themselves that we couldn't make out what the matter was. However, we plunged into the wood, they scurrying in the lead, and the trouble was quickly revealed: they had hanged a little fellow with a bark rope, and he was kicking and struggling, in the process of choking to death. We rescued him, and fetched him around." And these children are no older than Tom and Huck, "admiring little folk imitating their elders . . . playing mob." Remarkably these crimes that Tom wishes his gang to commit are chillingly carried out by their elders later in the novel. The boy's seemingly absurd fantasies accurately anticipate the violent realities of life on the Mississippi that Huck encounters on his flight from civilization.

41. *all the boys said it would be wicked to do it on Sunday*. Sam Clemens was brought up among pious Presbyterians, so he knew that it was sacrilegious to do anything on the day of rest except go to church or read one's Bible. "We didn't break the Sabboth often enough to signify—once a week perhaps," he facetiously recalled in an address presented at the Metropolitan Club, New York, on November 28, 1902 (*Mark Twain's Speeches*, 1910, p. 371). American blue laws as well as the dictates of the pulpit were so rigid at the time that one was always breaking the Sabbath. Twain never reconciled himself to this taboo. "God runs this worldly business," he once complained, "just the same on Sundays as on weekdays, but if you break the Sabboth we get damned for it" (quoted in Caroline Thomas Harnsberger, *Mark Twain's View of Religion*, 1961, p. 6).

42. *I . . . crept into my window*. Notice that Kemble's tailpiece is an exact mirror image of that titled "Huck Stealing Away" in Chapter 1. No doubt the American artist was aware that John Tenniel drew a similar pair of pictures to illustrate Chapter 1 of *Through the Looking-Glass* (1872), as the girl pierces through the mirror and the page.

Chapter III.

MISS WATSON'S LECTURE.

WELL I GOT a good going-over in the morning, from old Miss Watson, on account of my clothes; but the widow she didn't scold, but only cleaned off the grease and clay and looked so sorry that I thought I would behave a while if I could. Then Miss Watson she took me in the closet and prayed,[1] but nothing come of it. She told me to pray every day, and whatever I asked for I would get it.[2] But it warn't so. I tried it. Once I got a fish-line, but no hooks. It warn't any good to me without hooks. I tried for the hooks three or four times, but somehow I couldn't make it work. By-and-by, one day, I asked Miss Watson to try for me, but she said I was a fool.[3] She never told me why, and I couldn't make it out no way.

I set down, one time, back in the woods, and had a long think about it. I says to myself, if a body can get anything they pray for, why don't Deacon Winn get back the money he lost on pork? Why can't the widow get back her silver snuff-box that was stole? Why can't Miss Watson fat up? No, says I to myself, there ain't nothing in it. I went and told the widow about it, and she said the thing a body could get by praying for it was "spiritual gifts."[4] This was too many for me, but she told me what she meant—I must help other people, and do everything I could for other people, and look out for them all the time, and never think about myself.

1. *Miss Watson . . . took me in the closet and prayed.* This pious woman literally interprets Matthew 6:6: "But thou, when thou prayest, enter thy closet." Similarly, in Chapter 30 of *The Prince and the Pauper*, the grimly holy Lady Mary so offends Tom Canty as King Edward VI that he commands her "to go to her closet, and beseech God to take away the stone that was in her breast, and give her a human heart."

2. *whatever I asked for I would get it.* The young Sam Clemens was more successful with childish experiments with answered prayers than poor Huckleberry Finn. He recalled in 1906 how his teacher Elizabeth Horr once lectured on the text "Ask and ye shall receive" (Matthew 7:7), reassuring the children that "whosoever prayed for a thing with earnestness and strong desire need not doubt that his prayer would be answered." He decided on gingerbread, which the baker's daughter routinely brought to school every morning. He recalled that "she had always kept it out of sight before but when I finished my prayer and glanced up, there it was in easy reach and she was looking the other way. In all my life I believe I never enjoyed an answer to prayer more than I enjoyed that one; and I was a convert, too. I had no ends of wants and they had always remained unsatisfied up to that time, but I meant to supply them and extend them now that I had found out how to do it" (*Mark Twain in Eruption*, 1940, pp. 108–9). Unfortunately, none of his other prayers was ever answered. "When we pray, when we beg, when we implore, does He listen? Does He answer?" Twain asked on July 23, 1906. "There is not a single authentic instance of it in human history" ("Reflections on Religion," *Hudson Review*, Autumn 1963, pp. 344–45)

This was including Miss Watson, as I took it. I went out in the woods and turned it over in my mind a long time, but I couldn't see no advantage about it—except for the other people—so at last I reckoned I wouldn't worry about it any more, but just let it go. Sometimes the widow would take me one side and talk about Providence in a way to make a body's mouth water; but maybe next day Miss Watson would take hold and knock it all down again. I judged I could see that there was two Providences,[5] and a poor chap would stand considerable show with the widow's Providence, but if Miss Watson's got him there warn't no help for him any more.[6] I thought it all out, and reckoned I would belong to the widow's, if he wanted me, though I couldn't make out how he was agoing to be any better off then than what he was before,[7] seeing I was so ignorant and so kind of low-down and ornery.

Pap he hadn't been seen for more than a year, and that was comfortable for me; I didn't want to see him no more. He used to always whale me when he was sober and could get his hands on me; though I used to take to the woods most of the time when he was around. Well, about this time he was found in the river drowned, about twelve mile above town, so people said. They judged it was him, anyway; said this drowned man was just his size, and was ragged, and had uncommon long hair—which was all like pap—but they couldn't make nothing out of the face, because it had been in the water so long it warn't much like a face at all. They said he was floating on his back in the water. They took him and buried him on the bank. But I warn't comfortable long, because I happened to think of something. I knowed mighty well that a drownded man don't float on his back, but on his face.[8] So I knowed, then, that this warn't pap, but a woman dressed up in a man's clothes. So I was uncomfortable again. I judged the old man would turn up again by-and-by,[9] though I wished he wouldn't.

We played robber now and then about a month, and then I resigned. All the boys did. We hadn't robbed nobody, we hadn't killed any people, but only just pretended. We used to hop out of the woods and go charging down on hog-

3. *she said I was a fool.* Miss Watson constantly uses her narrow knowledge to put ignorant Huck in his place. Twain had no sympathy for such false notions of superiority. A man named Macfarlane, whom Clemens knew in a Cincinnati boardinghouse when a young man, told him that "man's intellect was a brutal addition to him and degraded him to a rank far below the plane of the other animals, and that there was never a man who did not use his intellect daily all his life to advantage himself at other people's expense" ("Macfarlane," 1896, in *What Is Man?*, 1973, p. 78). See also Chapter 14, note 9.

4. *"spiritual gifts."* In his 1895–1896 public reading copy, he added "that's what she said" to explain the quotes around this phrase.

5. *two Providences.* In "The Two Providences" (*College English*, January 1950, pp. 188–95), Edgar M. Branch argued that the widow's morality is intuitive and based upon example while Miss Watson's is conventional and derived from fear. The Widow Douglas encourages unselfish aid to others through "good works," but her sister is merely selfish in her terror of the "bad place." Walter Blair in *Mark Twain and Huck Finn* (pp. 135–36) pointed to the similarity between Huck's internal debate and the conflict between two opposing philosophies in W.E.H. Lecky, *History of European Morals from Augustus to Charlemagne* (1869), a two-volume book Twain admired. The first is "the stoical, the intuitive, the independent, or the sentimental"; the second "the epicurean, the inductive, the utilitarian, or the selfish." "The moralists of the former school," Lecky explained, "believe that we have a natural power of perceiving that some qualities such as benevolence, chastity, or veracity, are better than others, and that we ought to cultivate them, and to repress their opposites." The follower of the other school "maintains that we have by nature absolutely no knowledge of merit and demerit, of the comparative excellence of our feelings and actions, and that we derive these notions solely from an observation of the course of life which is conducive to human happiness. That which makes actions good, is that they increase the happiness or diminish the pains of mankind." Blair reported that Twain underlined other passages in the book in which Lecky applied his theory to the Greek philosophers: The Stoics abstained from sin "not through fear of punishment" but "from the desire and obli-

drovers and women in carts taking garden stuff to market, but we never hived[10] any of them. Tom Sawyer called the hogs "ingots," and he called the turnips and stuff "julery" and we would go to the cave[11] and pow-wow[12] over what we had done and how many people we had killed and marked.[13] But I couldn't see no profit in it. One time Tom sent a boy to run about town with a blazing stick, which he called a slogan[14] (which was the sign for the Gang to get together), and then he said he had got secret news by his spies that next day a whole parcel of Spanish merchants and rich A-rabs was going to camp in Cave Hollow[15] with two hundred elephants, and six hundred camels, and over a thousand "sumter" mules,[16] all loaded down with di'-monds, and they didn't have only a guard of four hundred soldiers, and so we would lay in ambuscade,[17] as he called it, and kill the lot and scoop the things. He said we must slick up[18] our swords and guns, and get ready. He never could go after even a turnip-cart but he must have the swords and guns all scoured up for it; though they was only lath and broom-sticks, and you might scour at them till you rotted and then they warn't worth a mouthful of ashes more than what they was before. I didn't believe we could lick

THE ROBBERS DISPERSED.

gation of what is just and good," while the general populace followed another order, for the Greek word for superstition signified "fear of gods" or daemons; and "the philosophers sometimes represented the vulgar as shuddering at the thoughts of death, through dread of certain endless sufferings to which it will lead them."

According to Lecky's theory, Huck's thinking is muddled: He exhibits both selfish and unselfish reasons for choosing one philosophy over the other. Arguably, no matter what he does in seeking either the widow's or Miss Watson's Providence, Huck does so selfishly. He has no choice. "From his cradle to his grave," Twain insisted in *What Is Man?* (1973), "a man never does a single thing which has any *first and foremost* object but one—to secure peace of mind, spiritual comfort, for *himself*" (p. 163). Huck never neatly works out his philosophy.

6. *if Miss Watson's got him there warn't no help for him any more.* Twain struggled with this phrase. He originally wrote in the manuscript, "if Miss Watson took him into camp he was a goner" (**MS**). It became "if Miss Watson took him you bet you 'twas all day with him" in Twain's 1895–1896 public reading copy.

7. *I couldn't make out how he was agoing to be any better off then than what he was before.* Twain added "it 'uz hark from the tomb for *him*" in his 1895–1896 public reading copy. See Chapter 26, note 13.

8. *a drownded man don't float on his back, but on his face.* "You will always find the body of a drowned woman floating face up," reported Harry Middleton Hyatt in *Folk-Lore of Adams County, Illinois* (Hannibal, Mo.: Western Printing and Publishing Co., 1965); "the body of a drowned man, face down. Although these positions are occasionally reversed in some sayings, this is the general belief—they are the normal positions in coitus" (p. 697). Fischer and Salamo in the 2001 University of California edition suggested that Twain likely knew this superstition from one of his favorite books, W.E.H. Lecky's *History of European Morals* (vol. 2, 1874): "It was said that drowned men floated on their backs, and drowned women on their faces; and this, in the opinion of Roman naturalists, was due to the superior purity of the latter" (p. 318).

9. *I judged the old man would turn up again by-and-by.* Huck makes the same prediction in such a crowd of Spaniards and A-rabs, but I wanted to see the camels and elephants, so I was on hand next day, Saturday, in the ambuscade; and when we got the word, we rushed out of the woods and down the hill. But there warn't no Spaniards and A-rabs, and there warn't no camels nor no elephants. It warn't anything but a Sunday-school picnic, and only a primer-class[19] at that. We busted it up, and chased the children up the hollow; but we never got anything but some doughnuts and jam, though Ben Rogers got a rag doll, and Jo Harper got a hymn-book and a tract;[20] and then the teacher charged in and made us drop everything and cut. I didn't see no di'monds, and I told Tom Sawyer so. He said there was loads of them there, anyway; and he said there was A-rabs there, too, and elephants and things. I said, why couldn't we see them, then? He said if I warn't so ignorant, but had read a book called "Don Quixote,"[21] I would know without asking. He said it was all done by enchantment. He said there was hundreds of soldiers there, and elephants and treasure, and so on, but we had enemies which he called magicians, and they had turned the whole thing into an infant Sunday school, just out of spite. I said, all right, then the thing for us to do was to go for the magicians. Tom Sawyer said I was a numskull.[22]

"Why," says he, "a magician could call up a lot of genies, and they would hash you up like nothing before you could say Jack Robinson.[23] They are as tall as a tree and as big around as a church."[24]

"Well," I says, "s'pose we got some genies to help *us*—can't we lick the other crowd then?"

"How you going to get them?"

"I don't know. How do *they* get them?"

"Why they rub an old tin lamp or an iron ring, and then the genies come tearing in,[25] with the thunder and lightning a-ripping around and the smoke a-rolling, and everything they're told to do they up and do it. They don't think nothing of pulling a shot tower[26] up by the roots, and belting a Sunday-school superintendent[27] over the head with it—or any other man."

Chapter 25 of *Tom Sawyer*, when he and Tom contemplate what they might do should they discover any buried treasure: "Pap would come back thish-yer town some day and get his claws on it." This chapter is a reworking of themes first explored in Chapter 25 of *Tom Sawyer*. Pap Finn never appears in the earlier book.

10. *hived*. Robbed. Describing the old days in "Hannibal—By a Native Historian" (*Alta California*, May 26, 1867), Twain made an atrocious pun by saying that "the scarlet fever came, and the hives, and between them they came near hiving all the children in the camp."

11. *the cave*. In his 1895–1896 public reading copy, Twain changed this to "our cave in the hills" in accordance with the habits of other robbers.

12. *pow-wow*. Discuss, usually noisily; an American Indian word for feasts, dances, and other public celebrations, originally preliminary to a hunt, a council, or a war expedition.

13. *marked*. Twain added the following explanation to his 1895–1896 public reading copy: "becuz always we uz goin' to *mark* 'em, so's they'd know who *done* it, and we'd git a ruputation." Desperadoes often "marked," or scarred, their victims with a signature; the most famous example of this habit in modern literature is the "Z" that Johnston McCulley's "Zorro" slashes on his enemies.

14. *Tom sent a boy to run about town with a blazing stick, which he called a slogan*. Leo Marx suggested in his notes to the 1967 Bobbs-Merrill edition of *Huckleberry Finn* that Tom confuses two passages from Sir Walter Scott's work: In *The Lady of the Lake* (Canto Third), the "fiery cross" is carried throughout the countryside to call the Scottish clans together; in *The Lay of the Last Minstrel* (Canto Four, xxvii), "slogan" has its earliest meaning as a Scottish war cry. For Twain's opinion of Scott as a writer, see Chapter 13, note 10.

15. *Cave Hollow*. Twain identified this term as "Missourian for 'valley'" ("Chapters from My Autobiography," *North American Review*, October 1907, p. 165). "On the Saturday holidays in summer-time," Twain recalled, "we used to borrow skiffs whose owners were not present and go down the river three miles [from Hannibal] to the cave hollow." It led to MacDowell's (later

"Who makes them tear around so?"

"Why, whoever rubs the lamp or the ring. They belong to whoever rubs the lamp or the ring, and they've got to do whatever he says. If he tells them to build a palace forty miles long, out of di'monds, and fill it full of chewing gum,[28] or whatever you want, and fetch an emperor's daughter from China for you to marry,[29] they've got to do it—and they've got to do it before sun-up next morning, too. And more—they've got to waltz that palace around over the country wherever you want it, you understand."

"Well," says I, "I think they are a pack of flatheads[30] for not keeping the palace themselves 'stead of fooling them away like that. And what's more—if I was one of them I would see a man in Jericho[31] before I would drop my business and come[32] to him for the rubbing of an old tin lamp."

"How you talk, Huck Finn. Why, you'd *have* to come when he rubbed it, whether you wanted to or not."

"What, and I as high as a tree and as big as a church? All right, then; I *would* come; but I lay I'd make that man climb the highest tree there was in the country."[33]

RUBBING THE LAMP.

McDougal's) cave, where Tom and Becky get lost and Injun Joe's treasure is hidden in *Tom Sawyer*.

16. *"sumter" mules*. "Sumptor," or pack, mules; Tom appropriately uses an archaic eighteenth-century spelling of the term, found somewhere in his eclectic reading.

17. *lay in ambuscade*. Another archaic term, for "lay in ambush."

18. *slick up*. Colloquial for polish, make elegant, from to "sleek."

19. *primer-class*. Reading class of the youngest group of schoolchildren, now equivalent of a kindergarten.

20. *tract*. Likely one of the pious little pamphlets issued by the American Tract Society. This prolific publisher equipped Sunday schools with booklets of short stories and verse of religious and moral instruction, which were given as rewards to boys and girls for regular attendance, punctuality, good conduct, and success in exams. This cheap literature was the most common reading matter for backwoods children at this time. Sam Clemens and his fellow Sunday-school pupils in Hannibal earned the privilege of borrowing such books by reciting verses in class. Five verses entitled one to three blue tickets, which could be redeemed for the chance to take out anything in the school's bookcase. "They were pretty dreary books," Twain recalled in "Chapters from My Autobiography" (*North American Review*, October 1907), "for there was not a bad boy in the entire bookcase. They were *all* good boys and good girls and drearily uninteresting, but they were better society than none, and I was glad to have company and disapprove of it" (p. 165).

21. *"Don Quixote."* Tom recalls Chapter 18 of Part I of the Cervantes novel, wherein the delusional don explains to his servant Sancho Panza, after they have been driven off by an irate herdsman, that his mortal enemy, a magician, has transformed an army of knights into a flock of sheep. Tom is a literalist: He reads only for story, so he cannot distinguish between burlesque and true romance. Several critics have noted similarities between bookish Tom Sawyer and Don Quixote, and matter-of-fact Huckleberry Finn and Sancho Panza, particularly in

"Shucks, it ain't no use to talk to you, Huck Finn.[34] You don't seem to know anything, somehow—perfect saphead."[35]

I thought all this over for two or three days, and then I reckoned I would see if there was anything in it. I got an old tin lamp and an iron ring and went out in the woods and rubbed and rubbed till I sweat like an Injun,[36] calculating to build a palace and sell it; but it warn't no use, none of the genies come. So then I judged that all that stuff was only just one of Tom Sawyer's lies. I reckoned he believed in the A-rabs and the elephants, but as for me I think different. It had all the marks of a Sunday school.[37]

Tom's condecending attitude toward Huck. "Much of the dialogue between Tom and Huck over the matter of books is almost *verbatim* the regular argument between Don Quixote and his squire," explained Olin Harris Moore in "Mark Twain and Don Quixote" (*Publications of the Modern Language Association*, June 1922, p. 336). For example, Tom says, "You don't seem to know anything, somehow"; and Don Quixote says, "How little thou knowest about it."

Twain admired *Don Quixote*—but with certain reservations. He recommended it to his wife-to-be, Olivia Langdon, but not before he expurgated it for her. "*Don Quixote* is one of the most exquisite books that was ever written," he wrote her, "and to lose it from the world's literature would be as the wresting of a constellation from the symmetry and perfection of the firmament—but neither it nor Shakespeare are proper books for virgins to read until some hand has culled them of their grossness" (*Love Letters of Mark Twain*, 1949, pp. 76–77). A less prudish Twain praised it in Chapter 46 of *Life on the Mississippi* for having "swept the world's admiration for the medieval chivalry-silliness out of existence"; then, he lamented, Sir Walter Scott's *Ivanhoe* restored it.

Tom's Quixotean raid on the Sunday-school class is only one of Twain's frequent attacks upon such romantic deceptions in his fiction. Hank Morgan plays Sancho Panza to the Don Quixote of Demoiselle Allisande la Carteloise, "Sandy," in Chapter 20 of *A Connecticut Yankee in King Arthur's Court*. The lady gets him to take her on a quest to a castle where (she says) three ogres have imprisoned her mistress and forty-four other princesses; but when they come upon the object of their search, it turns out to be nothing but a pigsty. And even then Sandy convinces herself that the castle must be under a wicked enchantment. Morgan pities the girl, but her kissing and caressing the hogs while addressing them as princesses is too much for the Connecticut Yankee. "I was ashamed of her," he admits (just like Huck Finn at the end of Chapter 24), "ashamed of the human race."

22. *numbskull.* Tom calls him "puddn'head" in Twain's 1895–1896 public reading copy; he published *Pudd'nhead Wilson* just the year before.

23. *before you could say Jack Robinson.* Fischer and Salamo revealed in the 2001 University of California edition that Twain marked this phrase in his copy of Francis Grose's *Classical Dictionary of the Vulgar Tongue* (1785): "A saying to express a very short time, originating from a very volatile gentleman of that appellation, who would call on his neighbours, and be gone before his name could be announced." Known in both Great Britain and the United States, it appears in the last line of a popular song, "And he was off before he could say Jack Robinson."

24. *as big around as a church.* Churches were often the largest and most impressive structures in these rural towns, sometimes big enough to hold the entire populace of a settlement.

25. *they rub an old tin lamp or an iron ring, and then the genies come tearing in.* Tom Sawyer is trying to recall "Aladdin and His Wonderful Lamp" in *The Arabian Nights.* "Those stories are renowned the world over," reported Orion Clemens's Hannibal *Journal* (November 6, 1851); "they have amused the great and the small, the learned and unlearned; the old man and the child. The invention of the writer was wonderful, though his stories were extravagant." And probably no one else in Hannibal loved the book more than Sam Clemens did. "He used to tell us tales," a childhood friend recalled, "and we loved to listen at him. His father had a book—*The Arabian Nights*—that no one else had in town, and Sam would get us boys together of evenings and tell us stories from that book, and we was glad to listen as long as he'd talk" (quoted in Clifton Johnson, *Highways and Byways of the Mississippi Valley*, 1906, p. 181). When Harper & Brothers asked several leading men of letters and other prominent public figures to suggest selections for its *Favorite Fairy Tales* (1907), Twain chose "Aladdin and His Wonderful Lamp." See also Chapter 40, note 22.

26. *a shot tower.* A tall, round tower where buckshot was made; molten lead was dropped from the top and formed spherical balls as it fell into a tank of cold water below.

27. *a Sunday-school superintendent.* One of the most formidable and intimidating adults to small town boys, often held up to them as a model deserving great respect and an example of impeccable character. In "A Little Pilgrimage" in *Whilomville Stories* (1900), Stephen Crane characterizes the "ideal Sunday-School superintendent" as "one who had never felt hunger or thirst or the wound of the challenge of dishonor."

St. Louis shot tower.
Courtesy Library of Congress.

28. *chewing gum.* Twain added "and doughnuts or fish-hooks" to his 1895–1896 public reading copy.

29. *an emperor's daughter from China for you to marry.* It should be noted that although *The Arabian Nights* is of Persian origin, the story of Aladdin takes place in China; he marries the Chinese princess, and the genie carries a palace wherever Aladdin wishes.

30. *flatheads.* Twain had difficulty choosing this word: he also considered "chuckleheads" and "softies" (**MS**) in the manuscript.

31. *Jericho.* Euphemism for Hell; "to see a man in Jericho" is to see him damned. The phrase derives from II Samuel 10:1–5: Suspecting David's ambassadors to be spies, Hunan seizes them, cuts their beards and robes, and sends them back in disgrace; David then tells them to stay in Jericho until their beards have grown back. Twain changed it to "Halifax" in the

1895–1896 public reading copy; another word for Hell, dating from the sixteenth century when Halifax, England, was notorious for its thieves and other criminals.

32. *I would drop my business and come.* Twain added "a rumbling and a thundering" in his 1895–1896 public reading copy, after crossing out "a-trotting."

33. *country.* Twain changed this to "county" in the 1895–1896 public reading copy.

34. *it ain't no use to talk to you, Huck Finn.* In a letter to theatrical producer Charles Dillingham of August 2, 1902, Twain described the differences in personality between the two boys: Tom Sawyer is "ostentatiously smart and inventive and always *boss*," while Huckleberry Finn is "humble, timid, ignorant, uninventive, Tom's willing slave and enthusiastic admirer" (quoted in Brooks McNamara, "*Huckleberry Finn* on Stage: A Mark Twain Letter in the Shubert Archive," *The Passing Show*, Fall 1991, p. 3). Huck is far less tolerant in *Tom Sawyer Abroad* when Tom flings his knowledge in his friend's face. In Chapter 1, when Tom asks him if he knows what a Crusade is, Huck replies, "No . . . I don't. And I don't care, nuther. I've lived till now and done without it, and had my health, too. But as soon as you tell me, I'll know, and that's soon enough. I don't see no use in finding out things and clogging my head up with them when I mayn't ever have any occasion for them." Unlike bookish Tom, Huck has no interest in knowledge for its own sake; it must have some practical application to be of any worth to him.

In Chapter 13 of *Tom Sawyer Abroad*, in another parody of *The Arabian Nights*, Huck wonders whether knowledge or instinct determines Tom's delusions. When they arrive in Egypt, Tom is certain that they have found the very house described in one of the tales in *The Arabian Nights*; however, the only evidence he has is a single brick. Huck is baffled as to how Tom can be so certain with so little to go by. "Is it knowledge, or is it instink?" Huck ponders; "it's my opinion that some of it is knowledge but the main bulk of it is instink." To test his friend's claim, Huck puts "another brick considerable like it in its place, and [Tom] didn't know the difference—but there was a difference, you see. . . . Instink tells him where the exact *place* is for the brick to be in, and so he recognized it by the place it's in, not by the look of the brick. If it was knowledge, not instink, he would know the brick again by the look of it the next time he seen it—which he didn't. So it shows that for all the brag you hear about knowledge being such a wonderful thing, instink is worth forty of it for real unerringness." Here, as throughout *Huckleberry Finn*, pragmatic Huck prefers the proven to the hypothetical; again he will trust his own heart rather than what others tell him.

Huck descends from the anti-intellectual backwoodsman common to Southern and Southwestern literature. "Well," Simon Suggs explains in Johnson Jones Hooper's *Some Adventures of Captain Simon Suggs* (1845), "mother-wit kin beat book larnin', at *any* game! . . . Human natur' and the human family is *my* books, and I've never seed many but what I could hold my own with. . . . Books ain't fitten for nothin' but jist to give to children goin' to school, to keep 'em outen mischief" (pp. 53–54). Twain seemed to share this contempt for "book-larnin'." "The most valuable capital or culture or education usable in the building of novels is personal experience," he wrote in a letter of 1891. "I surely have the equipment, a wide culture, and all of it real, none of it artificial, for I don't know anything about books" (*Letters*, vol. 2, p. 543). However, just a cursory glance through *Huckleberry Finn* reveals countless references to other books and authors, proving how widely read rough-hewn Twain actually was.

35. *sap-head.* A fool; Tom's conclusion confirms Miss Watson's opinion, expressed in the beginning of the chapter. Edward Eggleston defined this term in his notes to the 1890 edition of *The Hoosier School-Boy* as "a nickname having reference to the sap or soft wood in timber" (p. 11).

36. *sweat like an Injun.* As noted by John S. Farmer in *Americanisms Old and New* (1889), American Indians were known for their "sweat-houses" or "sweat-lodges," "half a religious temple, . . . half a sanitary asylum," where braves sweltered all night by smothered fires and in the morning plunged still perspiring into ice-cold water.

37. *It had all the marks of a Sunday school.* Literally and figuratively. Thus Tom's boyish fantasies are no different from Miss Watson's pious teachings. By aligning his friend's fancy with the old maid's morality, Huck slides closer to the widow's Providence. In an address delivered at the New Vagabonds Club in London on July 8, 1899, Twain distinguished between theoretical and practical morals, between those espoused by Miss Watson and those by the Widow Douglas: "Theoretical morals are the sort you get on your mother's knee, in good books, and from the pulpit. You gather them in your head, and not in your heart; they are theory without practice" (*Mark Twain's Speeches*, 1910, p. 132). Only through experience, in practicing what he preaches, can Huck gain a set of useful morals.

Chapter IV.

!!!!!

WELL, THREE or four months run along, and it was well into the winter, now. I had been to school most all the time, and could spell, and read, and write just a little,[1] and could say the multiplication table up to six times seven is thirty-five, and I don't reckon I could ever get any further than that if I was to live forever. I don't take no stock in mathematics, anyway.

At first I hated the school,[2] but by-and-by I got so I could stand it. Whenever I got uncommon tired I played hookey, and the hiding I got next day done me good and cheered me up. So the longer I went to school the easier it got to be. I was getting sort of used to the widow's ways, too, and they warn't so raspy on me. Living in a house, and sleeping in a bed, pulled on me pretty tight, mostly, but before the cold weather I used to slide out and sleep in the woods, sometimes, and so that was a rest to me. I liked the old ways best, but I was getting so I liked the new ones, too, a little bit. The widow said I was coming along slow but sure, and doing very satisfactory. She said she warn't ashamed of me.

One morning I happened to turn over the salt-cellar at breakfast. I reached for some of it as quick as I could, to throw over my left shoulder and keep off the bad luck,[3] but

1. *and write just a little*. Twain inserted this phrase as an afterthought to the manuscript, perhaps to account for the possibility of Huck's being able to write his story rather than merely to dictate it to "Mark Twain."

2. *At first I hated the school*. Twain originally wrote "like sin" (**MS**) in the manuscript; but even if Sam Clemens believed that, it seems a bit harsh for Huck Finn. Well he might hate it, if one is to believe Twain's bitter recollection of a typical school of the period in Chapter 5 of *The Gilded Age* (1874): "a place where tender young humanity devoted itself for eight or ten hours a day to learning incomprehensible rubbish by heart out of books and reciting it by rote, like parrots; so that a finished education consisted simply of a permanent headache and the ability to read without stopping to spell the words or take breath." He was likely describing his own experience at J. D. Dawson's school in Hannibal, depicted so vividly as that run by Mr. Dobbins in *Tom Sawyer*. It was an era when corporal punishment was not only condoned but frequently administered; nearly every schoolmaster or schoolmarm was quick to use the hickory stick on a disobedient or inattentive pupil.

"Sam was always a good-hearted boy," his mother told Thomas W. Handford in *Pleasant Hours with Illustrous Men and Women* (1885), "but he was a very wild and mischievous one, and do what we would we could never make him go to school. This used to trouble his father and me dreadfully, and we were convinced that he would never amount to as much in the world as his brothers, because he was not near so steady and sober-minded as they were" (p. 306). Perhaps no other child in Hannibal hated school more than Sam Clemens did. "Went to school with him," John A. Fry recalled after Twain's death in Keene Abbott; "Tom Sawyer's Town"

Miss Watson was in ahead of me, and crossed me off. She says, "Take your hands away, Huckleberry—what a mess you are always making." The widow put in a good word for me, but that warn't going to keep off the bad luck, I knowed that well enough. I started out, after breakfast, feeling worried and shaky, and wondering where it was going to fall on me, and what it was going to be. There is ways to keep off some kinds of bad luck, but this wasn't one of them kind; so I never tried to do anything, but just poked along low-spirited and on the watch-out.

I went down the front garden and clumb over the stile,[4] where you go through the high board fence. There was an inch of new snow on the ground, and I seen somebody's tracks. They had come up from the quarry and stood around the stile a while, and then went on around the garden fence. It was funny they hadn't come in, after standing around so. I couldn't make it out. It was very curious, somehow. I was going to follow around, but I stooped down to look at the tracks first. I didn't notice anything at first, but next I did. There was a cross in the left boot-heel made with big nails, to keep off the devil.[5]

I was up in a second and shinning[6] down the hill. I looked over my shoulder every now and then, but I didn't see nobody. I was at Judge Thatcher's as quick as I could get there. He said:

"Why, my boy, you are all out of breath. Did you come for your interest?"

"No sir," I says; "is there some for me?"

"Oh, yes, a half-yearly is in, last night. Over a hundred and fifty dollars. Quite a fortune for you. You better let me invest it along with your six thousand, because if you take it you'll spend it."

"No sir," I says, "I don't want to spend it. I don't want it at all—nor the six thousand, nuther. I want you to take it; I want to give it to you—the six thousand and all."

He looked surprised. He couldn't seem to make it out. He says:

"Why, what can you mean, my boy?"

I says, "Don't you ask me no questions about it, please.

(*Harper's Weekly*, April 9, 1913), "and I'm bound to say that he did keep up with us, but nobody ever knew how he managed to learn anything. Shiftless, lazy, and dadblasted tired—born tired! No study in him. All the time too busy getting up some new kind of devilment. And he sure was a boy, Sam was, who knew how to entertain himself" (p. 17). "And we know papa played 'Hookey' all the time," Susy Clemens confirmed in her biography of her father (quoted in "Chapters from My Autobiography," *North American Review*, November 2, 1906). "And how readily would papa pretend to be dying so as not to have to go to school!" (p. 839). He so despised it that, when his mother summoned him to his father's deathbed, the boy begged, "I will promise anything, if you won't make me go to school! Anything!" (quoted in Paine, *Mark Twain: A Biography*, vol. 1, 1912, p. 75). And his mother finally gave in. But, as his daughter Susy soberly reported, "He . . . gradually picked up enough education to enable him to do about as well as those who were more studious in early life." Indeed he did.

3. *I happened to turn over the salt-cellar at breakfast. I reached for some of it as quick as I could, to throw over my left shoulder and keep off the bad luck*. "To scatter salt, by overturning the vessel in which it is contained, is very unlucky," Francis Grose reported in *A Provincial Glossary* (1787), "and portends quarreling with a friend, or fracture of a bone, sprain, or other bodily misfortune. Indeed this may in some measure be averted, by throwing it over one's head." When salt was precious, it was given as a token of friendship; but when spilled, it was said to be an omen of a rift between friends. It was also believed that the devil lingers on the left side of the body and watches at the table to cause mischief; the spilling of salt thus gives him reason to provoke a fight, unless one throws some over the left shoulder and hits him in the eye. Leonardo da Vinci's fresco *The Last Supper* refers to this superstition, for spilled salt on the table indicates which one is Judas Iscariot among the disciples.

4. *the stile*. "The pyramid of large blocks," as Twain called it in Chapter 1of *The Gilded Age*.

5. *a cross in the left boot-heel made with big nails, to keep off the devil*. The cross, the symbol of Christ, is a common protection against demons. Tom Sawyer repeats this belief in Chapter 33 of *Tom Sawyer*, "Lookyhere, Huck. . . . Injun Joe's

You'll take it—won't you?"

He says:

"Well I'm puzzled. Is something the matter?"

"Please take it," says I, "and don't ask me nothing—then I won't have to tell no lies."[7]

He studied a while, and then he says:

"Oho-o. I think I see. You want to *sell* all your property to me—not give it. That's the correct idea."

JUDGE THATCHER SURPRISED.

Then he wrote something on a paper and read it over, and says:

"There—you see it says 'for a consideration.' That means I have bought it of you and paid you for it. Here's a dollar for you. Now, you sign it."

So I signed it, and left.

Miss Watson's nigger, Jim, had a hair-ball[8] as big as your fist, which had been took out of the fourth stomach of an ox, and he used to do magic with it. He said there was a spirit inside of it, and it knowed everything. So I went to him that night and told him pap was here again, for I found his tracks in the snow. What I wanted to know, was, what he

ghost ain't a-going to come around where there's a cross!" Nails were used because iron was said to be a protection against witches and other evil spirits thanks to St. Dunstan of England; and it is in the left heel, because the devil is said to lurk on that side.

6. *shinning*. Moving as fast as his legs could carry him.

7. *don't ask me nothing—then I won't have to tell no lies*. Huck is trying to remember the old English proverb "Ask me no questions and I'll tell you no lies" (as in Oliver Goldsmith's *She Stoops to Conquer*, 1773, Act III, scene i).

8. *a hair-ball*. When an ox licks his hair, it goes down into the left side of the pouch where it forms a ball. It was believed that a hair ball not only could tell the future but might also be used to bewitch others. Ever since ancient times, visceral objects have been thought to possess soothsaying powers; and while hair-ball divination is a voodoo practice (and one of the few examples of Jim's "magic" which is of African origin), it is also a German tradition.

9. *Irish potato*. Term used in the South to distinguish the white from the sweet potato. Discovered in Peru and imported first to Spain, the potato was brought over to Ireland by Sir Walter Raleigh in 1610, and it quickly became the staple crop of the people; however, not until the nineteenth century was it widely accepted elsewhere as a food.

10. *next morning you couldn't see no brass, and it wouldn't feel greasy no more*. Remarkably, the white of the potato can clean tarnish off brass.

11. *Sometimes he spec he'll go 'way, en den agin he spec he'll stay*. Twain, of course, is playing with the duplicity of fortune-tellers. By nature a skeptic, he nevertheless frequently subjected himself to palmists, phrenologists, and spiritualists, but tried to conceal his identity in most cases; and astonishingly, he slyly reported in Chapter 13 of *The Autobiography of Mark Twain* (1959), they all concurred that "the evidence that I do not possess the sense of humor is overwhelming, satisfying, convincing, incontrovertible—at last I believe it myself."

12. *Dey's two angels hoverin' 'roun 'bout him. . . . De white one gits him to go right, a little while, den* *de black one sail in en bust it all up*. The same is true for Huck Finn. There are always two forces hovering about him, one good one and one bad, whether they are the Widow Douglas and Miss Watson or Judge Thatcher and pap Finn or his temperament and his training. Some people believe that every person has two guardian angels, one good and one bad, influencing one's actions. Life is therefore a never-ending moral struggle between these contrary forces. Twain considered this belief as it applied to the "sensible religion" of Indians in the unfinished "Huck Finn and Tom Sawyer Among the Indians":

> . . . the Injuns hadn't only but two Gods, a good one and a bad one, and they never paid no attention to the good one, nor ever prayed to him or worried about him at all, but only tried their level best to flatter up the bad god and keep on the good side of him; because the good one loved him and wouldn't ever think of doing them any harm, and so there warn't any occasion to be bothering him with prayers and things, because he was always doing the very best he could for them, anyway, and prayers couldn't better it; but all the trouble come from the bad god, who was setting up nights to think up ways to bring them bad luck and bust up all their plans, and never fooled away a chance to do them all the harm he could; and so the sensible thing was to keep praying and fussing around him all the time, and get him to let up. (*Huck Finn and Tom Sawyer Among the Indians*, 1989, p. 61)

Jim says it simpler in Chapter 8 of *Huckleberry Finn*: "What you want to know good luck's a-comin' for?" Huck is torn between two other forces, Christianity and paganism. "If he has no religion, however, he has plenty of superstition," noted Walter Besant in "My Favorite Novelist and His Best Book" (*Munsey's Magazine*, February 1898); "he believes all the wonderful things 'nigger' Jim tells him: the ghosts and the signs of bad luck and good luck" (p. 664).

Twain was brought up on the Presbyterian catechism which declared that there is but one God the Almighty who decides all, both the good and the bad. No matter what happens, whether blessing or curse, it is always an act of divine Providence. Man is always at the mercy of this mysterious plan. Twain, however, considered it mere ornery whim and never could accept this concept of a single omnipotent godhead. "To trust the God of the Bible," he com-

was going to do, and was he going to stay? Jim got out his hair-ball, and said something over it, and then he held it up and dropped it on the floor. It fell pretty solid, and only rolled about an inch. Jim tried it again, and then another time, and it acted just the same. Jim got down on his knees and put his ear against it and listened. But it warn't no use; he said it wouldn't talk. He said sometimes it wouldn't talk without money. I told him I had an old slick counterfeit quarter that warn't no good because the brass showed

JIM LISTENING.

through the silver a little, and it wouldn't pass nohow, even if the brass didn't show, because it was so slick it felt greasy, and so that would tell on it every time. (I reckoned I wouldn't say nothing about the dollar I got from the judge.) I said it was pretty bad money, but maybe the hair-ball would take it, because maybe it wouldn't know the difference. Jim smelt it, and bit it, and rubbed it, and said he would manage so the hair-ball would think it was good. He said he would split open a raw Irish potato[9] and stick the quarter in between and keep it there all night, and next morning you couldn't see no brass, and it wouldn't feel greasy no more,[10] and so anybody in town would take it in a minute, let alone a hair-ball. Well, I knowed a potato would do that, before, but I had forgot it.

Jim put the quarter under the hair-ball and got down and listened again. This time he said the hair-ball was all right.

He said it would tell my whole fortune if I wanted it to. I says, go on. So the hair-ball talked to Jim, and Jim told it to me. He says:

"Yo' ole father doan' know, yit, what he's a-gwyne to do. Sometimes he spec he'll go 'way, en den agin he spec he'll stay.[11] De bes' way is to res' easy en let de ole man take his own way. Dey's two angels hoverin' roun' 'bout him. One uv 'em is white en shiny, en 'tother one is black. De white one gits him to go right, a little while, den de black one sail in en bust it all up.[12] A body can't tell, yit, which one gwyne to fetch him at de las'. But you is all right. You gwyne to have considable trouble in yo' life, en considable joy.[13] Sometimes you gwyne to git hurt, en sometimes you gwyne to git sick; but every time you's gwyne to git well agin. Dey's two gals flyin' 'bout you in yo' life. One uv 'em's light en 'tother one is dark. One is rich en 'tother is po'. You's gwyne to marry de po' one fust en de rich one by-en-by. You wants to keep 'way fum de water[14] as much as you kin, en don't run no resk, 'kase it's down in de bills[15] dat you's gwyne to git hung."[16]

When I lit my candle and went up to my room that night, there set pap,[17] his own self!

plained, "is to trust in an irascible, vindictive, fierce and ever fickle and changeful master" (quoted in Paine, *Mark Twain: A Biography*, vol. 1, 1912, p. 412).

13. *You gwyne to have considable trouble in yo' life, en considable joy*. These are nearly the same words spoken by ex-slave "Aunty Rachel" at the end of "A True Story" (*Atlantic Monthly*, November 1874), "Oh no, Misto C[lemens], *I* hain't had no trouble. An' no *joy!*" (p. 594). She was Mary Ann Cord, the cook at Quarry Farm, near Elmira, New York, where the Clemenses spent their summers; and Twain wrote down verbatim her memories of how she and her family were sold at auction one by one. "A True Story" was Twain's first important use of dialect, and the pathos of this powerful story resonates through *Huckleberry Finn*.

14. *You wants to keep 'way fum de water*. In his 1895–1896 public reading copy, Twain added new emphasis to this prediction: "Now de main thing, de *main* thing. . . ." He may have been recalling the advice given him by a long-winded fortune-teller in 1861: At the urging of Melicent S. Holliday, the model for Widow Douglas, he finally visited Madam Caprell while he was in New Orleans; and she told him, "*don't* go *near* the water—I will *not* tell you why, but by all that is true and good, I charge you, while that month lasts, keep away from water (which she repeated several times, with much show of earnestness . . .)" (*Mark Twain's Letters*, vol. 1, 1988, p. 109).

15. *down in de bills*. Leo Marx explained this phrase in his notes to the 1967 Bobbs-Merrill edition: "Written down in the specifications (bills, as in the phrase, fill the bill); thus, foreordained."

16. *you's gwyne to git hung*. Jim's nebulous prophecy must be playing with the old saying "He that is born to be hanged shall never be drowned." Twain told Paine that a pet motto of his mother's was "People born to be hanged are safe in water" (*Mark Twain: A Biography*, vol. 1, 1912, p. 35).

17. *pap*. Twain admitted in "Chapters from My Autobiography" (*North American Review*, August 2, 1907) that Jimmy Finn "slept in the deserted tan-yard with the hogs" (p. 692). Everyone in Hannibal knew him. "Now, I never read any of

Sam's books," childhood friend Jimmie McDaniel told Keene Abbott in "Tom Sawyer's Town" (*Harper's Weekly*, April 9, 1913), "but from what I hear I reckon that his description of Huck Finn's old rip of a father was pretty much on the order of old Jim Finn. One morning he was found dead in Jim Craig's tanyard, that used to be up there at Main and North streets, but it's gone long ago" (p. 16).

Although few critics have mentioned it, pap Finn is the stereotypical Irish drunk of American humor. According to Hugh J. Dawson in "The Ethnicity of Huck Finn—and the Difference It Makes" (*American Literary Realism*, Winter 1998), he is "lazy, dirty, brutal, swinish, superstitious, bigoted, lying, illiterate, antireligious, foul-mouthed, financially irresponsible and destructive" (p. 9). Huck and his pap are the only characters in the entire novel without a recognizable Anglo-Saxon surname. (Brief mention is made toward the end of Chapter 6 of profane Sowberry Hagan, obviously another Irish drunk.) Sometimes called "white niggers," the Irish were mercilessly caricatured by American writers and artists during the great wave of nineteenth-century immigration. Pap Finn is most likely *not* an immigrant, for he speaks in a more extreme form of Pike County dialect than Huck does, but one associated with Irish-Americans at the time of the story.

W. H. Auden considered pap Finn to be "a greater and more horrible monster than almost any I can think of in fiction" ("Huck and Oliver," *Listener*, October 1, 1953, p. 540). Through his white Anglo-Saxon Protestant upbringing, Twain was as ambivalent about the Irish as he was about other minorities: He freely played with stereotypes for both laughs and pathos. Chapter 33 of *The Gilded Age* touches on contemporary prejudices against the ambitious "shanty" Irish in America. One of the worst traits of the Irish drunk was domestic violence. The only reference to Huck's mother appears in Chapter 25 of *Tom Sawyer*. "Look at pap and my mother," says Huck. "Fight!? Why they used to fight all the *time*. I remember, mighty well." Pap Finn is reminiscent of another old sot, Londoner John Canty, the abusive father in *The Prince and the Pauper*. Of course, Twain did not feel the same about all Irishmen. He told the New York *Times* (March 5, 1906) that Patrick McAleer, his Irish coachman, "was as beautiful in his graces as he was in his spirit, and he was as honest a man as ever lived . . . and if I were to describe a gentleman in detail I would describe Patrick."

Chapter V.

"PAP."

I HAD shut the door to. Then I turned around, and there he was. I used to be scared of him all the time, he tanned me so much. I reckoned I was scared now, too; but in a minute I see I was mistaken. That is, after the first jolt, as you may say, when my breath sort of hitched—he being so unexpected; but right away after, I see I warn't scared of him worth bothering about.

He was most fifty, and he looked it. His hair was long and tangled and greasy, and hung down, and you could see his eyes shining through like he was behind vines. It was all black, no gray; so was his long, mixed-up whiskers. There warn't no color in his face, where his face showed; it was white;[1] not like another man's white, but a white to make a body sick, a white to make a body's flesh crawl—a tree-toad white, a fish-belly white. As for his clothes—just rags, that was all. He had one ankle resting on 'tother knee; the boot on that foot was busted, and two of his toes stuck through, and he worked them now and then. His hat was laying on the floor; an old black slouch[2] with the top caved in, like a lid.

I stood a-looking at him; he set there a-looking at me, with his chair tilted back a little. I set the candle down. I noticed the window was up; so he had clumb in by the

1. *it was white.* By emphasizing the old man's pallid complexion, Twain contrasts pap Finn with Miss Watson's Jim. By contrasting the nobility of one race, in this case a slave, with the degradation of another in the town drunkard, the author shows the futility in judging a person's character solely on the color of one's skin. The two spirits the hair ball mentioned may indeed be black and white, Jim and pap.

2. *an old black slouch.* A soft felt hat with a broad floppy brim, "worn gallusly" (according to "Villagers of 1840–43," *Huck Finn and Tom Sawyer Among the Indians*, 1989, p. 99). Twain wore one himself, admitting that "it identifies me." On their "Twins of Genius" tour, Cable told a reporter from the Paris (Ky.) *Kentuckian* (January 3, 1885) that "the man you see with the worst hat on is Mark Twain."

shed. He kept a-looking me all over. By-and-by he says:

"Starchy clothes—very. You think you're a good deal of a big-bug,[3] *don't* you?"

"Maybe I am, maybe I ain't," I says.

"Don't you give me none o' your lip," says he. "You've put on considerable many frills[4] since I been away. I'll take you down a peg before I get done with you. You're educated, too, they say; can read and write. You think you're better'n your father,[5] now, don't you, because he can't? *I'll* take it out of you. Who told you you might meddle with such hifalut'n foolishness, hey?—who told you you could?"

"The widow. She told me."

"The widow, hey?—and who told the widow she could put in her shovel[6] about a thing that ain't none of her business?"

"Nobody never told her."

"Well, I'll learn her how to meddle. And looky here—you drop that school, you hear? I'll learn people to bring up a boy to put on airs over his own father and let on to be better'n what *he* is. You lemme catch you fooling around that school again, you hear? Your mother couldn't read, and she couldn't write, nuther, before she died. None of the family couldn't, before *they* died. *I* can't; and here you're a-swelling yourself up like this. I ain't the man to stand it—you hear? Say—lemme hear you read."

I took up a book and begun something about General Washington and the wars.[7] When I'd read about a half a minute, he fetched the book a whack with his hand and knocked it across the house. He says:

"It's so. You can do it. I had my doubts when you told me. Now looky here; you stop that putting on frills. I won't have it. I'll lay for you,[8] my smarty; and if I catch you about that school I'll tan you good. First you know you'll get religion, too. I never see such a son."

He took up a little blue and yaller picture of some cows and a boy, and says:

"What's this?"

"It's something they give me for learning my lessons good."[9]

3. *a big-bug.* A "big shot," a person of consequence, used contemptuously.

4. *put on . . . frills.* Put on airs, have affectations in manners. Frills are purely ornamental and useless; they are there only for "show" or "style." "They don't put ruffles on a shirt to help keep a person warm, do they?" Tom asks in Chapter 5 of *Tom Sawyer Abroad*.

5. *You think you're better'n your father.* This was years before mandatory public education in Missouri, so pap Finn was never required, and likely never had the opportunity, to read; the only reason Huck can do it now is that the Widow Douglas pays to have him attend classes.

Pap Finn's abuse of Huck may originate with Charles Dickens. Blair suggested in *Mark Twain and Huck Finn* (p. 128) that Twain may have recalled how Jerry Cruncher abuses his wife in front of their son in Book 2, Chapter 1, of *A Tale of Two Cities* (1859). "You're at it agin, are you?" he complains, throwing a muddy boot at her. "Saying your prayers. You're a nice woman! What do you mean by flopping yourself down and praying agin me? . . . I'm not a going to be made unlucky by *your* sneaking. If you must go flopping yourself down, flop in favour of your husband and child, and not in opposition to 'em." Twain told Raymond Blaithwait in "Mark Twain on Humor" (New York *World*, May 31, 1891) that he thought *A Tale of Two Cities* "a beautiful work spoilt for me by that ostensibly humorous character, Jerry. I would improve that book, I would make it all a book should be by leaving out Jerry." But a closer analogy to pap's ravings, according to Joseph H. Gardner, "Gaffer Hexam and Huck Finn" (*Modern Philology*, November 1968, pp. 155–56), may be found in Book 2, Chapter 6 of *Our Mutual Friend* (1864–1865) where Gaffer Hexam chastises his son when he learns the boy can read and write. "Let him never come within sight of my eyes, nor within reach of my arm," he says. "His own father ain't good enough for him. He disowns his own father. His own father, therefore, disowns him for ever and ever, as a unnat'ral young beggar. . . . Now I see why them men yonder held aloof from me. They says to one another, 'Here comes the man as ain't good enough for his own son!' " Another possible model for pap was William Brown, the steamboat pilot under whom Twain cubbed in 1858. "My, what a fine bird we are!" he berates the young man in

HUCK AND HIS FATHER.

He tore it up, and says—

"I'll give you something better—I'll give you a cowhide."[10]

He set there a-mumbling and a-growling a minute, and then he says—

"*Ain't* you a sweet-scented dandy, though? A bed; and bedclothes; and a look'n-glass; and a piece of carpet on the floor—and your own father got to sleep with the hogs in the tanyard. I never see such a son. I bet I'll take some o' these frills out o' you before I'm done with you. Why there ain't no end to your airs—they say you're rich. Hey?—how's that?"

"They lie—that's how."

"Looky here—mind how you talk to me; I'm a-standing about all I can stand, now—so don't gimme no sass. I've been in town two days, and I hain't heard nothing but about you bein' rich. I heard about it away down the river, too. That's why I come. You git me that money to-morrow—I want it."

"I hain't got no money."

"It's a lie. Judge Thatcher's got it. You git it. I want it."

"I hain't got no money, I tell you. You ask Judge Thatcher; he'll tell you the same."

"All right. I'll ask him; and I'll make him pungle,[11] too, or

Chapter 18 of *Life on the Mississippi*. "We must have *orders*! Our father was a *gentleman*—owned slaves—and *we've* been to school. Yes, *we* are a gentleman, *too*, and got to have *orders*! ORDERS, is it? ORDERS is what you want! Dod dern my skin, *I'll* learn you to swell yourself up and blow around *here* about your dod-derned *orders*! G' way from the wheel!"

6. *put in her shovel*. Or "put in one's oar," take an active interest in something, butt in.

7. *I took up a book and begun something about General Washington and the wars*. He could have picked up almost any of his schoolbooks, like the McGuffey's Eclectic Readers, which always contained something about George Washington, the "Father of Our Country," in their lessons.

8. *I'll lay for you*. I'll lay in wait for you, I'll ambush you.

9. *It's something they give me for learning my lessons good*. Called "a reward of merit," a cheaply and gaudily printed card with a blank space across it for the child's name. But Huck's lessons have not stuck: He makes a classic mistake in grammar by saying he learned them "good" rather than "well."

10. *give you a cowhide*. Give you a whipping. Twain originally wrote "rawhide" (**MS**); a cowhide was a strong hide whip often used on slaves.

11. *pungle*. Pay, hand over (usually money), from the Spanish *pongálo*: out with it, let's have it.

I'll know the reason why. Say—how much you got in your pocket? I want it."

"I hain't got only a dollar, and I want that to—"

"It don't make no difference what you want it for—you just shell it out."

He took it and bit it to see if it was good, and then he said he was going down town to get some whisky; said he hadn't had a drink all day. When he had got out on the shed, he put his head in again, and cussed me for putting on frills and trying to be better than him; and when I reckoned he was gone, he come back and put his head in again, and told me to mind about that school, because he was going to lay for me and lick me if I didn't drop that.

Next day he was drunk, and he went to Judge Thatcher's and bullyragged[12] him and tried to make him give up the money, but he couldn't, and then he swore he'd make the law force him.

The judge and the widow went to law to get the court to take me away from him and let one of them be my guardian; but it was a new judge that had just come, and he didn't know the old man; so he said courts mustn't interfere and separate families if they could help it; said he'd druther not take a child away from its father. So Judge Thatcher and the widow had to quit on the business.

That pleased the old man till he couldn't rest. He said he'd cowhide me till I was black and blue if I didn't raise some money for him. I borrowed three dollars from Judge Thatcher,[13] and pap took it and got drunk and went a-blowing around and cussing and whooping and carrying on; and he kept it up all over town, with a tin pan, till most midnight; then they jailed him, and next day they had him before court, and jailed him again for a week. But he said *he* was satisfied; said he was boss of his son, and he'd make it warm for *him.*

When he got out the new judge[14] said he was agoing to make a man of him.[15] So he took him to his own house, and dressed him up clean and nice, and had him to breakfast and dinner and supper with the family, and was just old pie to him,[16] so to speak. And after supper he talked to him

12. *bullyragged.* Vehemently badgered, scolded.

13. *I borrowed three dollars from Judge Thatcher.* Twain changed this in his 1895–1896 public reading copy to "I got three dollars out of my pile from Judge Thatcher."

14. *the new judge.* Twain originally had Judge Thatcher try to reform pap Finn, but Twain noted in the margin of the manuscript, "Better make this the *new* judge? That other has known him too long" (**MS**).

15. *he was agoing to make a man of him.* Twain admitted in "Chapters from My Autobiography" (*North American Review*, August 2, 1907, p. 692) that his father, Justice John M. Clemens, tried once to reform Jimmy Finn, the town drunkard of Hannibal; he failed as dismally as the good citizens of St. Petersburg. In a letter to the *Alta California* (May 26, 1867), Twain described how local temperance advocates "made much of Jimmy Finn—dressed him up in new clothes, and had him out to breakfast and to dinner, and so forth, and showed him off as a great living curiosity—a shining example of the power of temperance doctrines when earnestly and eloquently set forth. . . . [B]ut Jimmy Finn couldn't stand it. He got remorseful of his liberty; and then he got melancholy from thinking about it so much; and after that, he got . . . awfully drunk in the chief citizen's house, and the next morning the house was as if the swine had tarried in it." Although outraged by his behavior, these total abstainers from alcoholic drink did not give up: They "rallied and reformed Jim once more, but in an evil hour temptation came upon him and he sold his body to a doctor for a quart of whiskey, and that ended all his earthly troubles. He drank it all at one sitting, and his soul went to its long account and his body went to Dr. [Orville] Grant."

16. *just old pie to him.* As pleasant to him as could be, just the best. Pie, then a luxury, referred to anything especially good, particularly for Huck. In Twain's unproduced 1884 play of *Tom Sawyer*, when Huck and Tom make plans for the buried treasure they hope to find, Huck says, "Well, I'll have a pie and a glass of soda every *day*, and I'll go to every circus that comes along. . . . This county's 40 mile wide; and day after tomorrow when they want to find out who's bought up all the *pie*, you take and send 'em to Huck *Finn*. . . . If I don't eat up'ards of a about temperance and such things till the old man cried, and said he'd been a fool, and fooled away his life; but now he was agoing to turn over a new leaf and be a man nobody wouldn't be ashamed of, and he hoped the judge would help him and not look down on him. The judge said he could hug him for them words; so *he* cried, and his wife she cried again; pap said he'd been a man that had always been misunderstood before, and the judge said he believed it. The old man said that what a man wanted that was down, was sympathy; and the judge said it was so; so they cried again. And when it was bedtime, the old man rose up and held out his hand, and says:

"Look at it gentlemen, and ladies all; take ahold of it; shake it. There's a hand that was the hand of a hog;[17] but it ain't so no more; it's the hand of a man that's started in on a new life, and 'll die before he'll go back. You mark them words—don't forget I said them. It's a clean hand now; shake it—don't be afeard."

REFORMING THE DRUNKARD.

So they shook it, one after the other, all around, and cried. The judge's wife she kissed it. Then the old man he signed a pledge[18]—made his mark.[19] The judge said it was the holiest time on record, or something like that. Then they tucked the old man into a beautiful room, which was the spare room, and in the night sometimes he got powerful

mile and a half of pie every day for seven *year*, I wish I may *bust*" (*Mark Twain's Hannibal, Huck and Tom*, 1969, pp. 286 and 289–90).

17. *There's a hand that was the hand of a hog.* A reminder that pap Finn usually sleeps with the hogs in the tanyard.

18. *signed a pledge.* Converts to the temperance movement signed written oaths to abstain from all intoxicating beverages. Hannibal formed a Cadets of Temperance under the banner of "Love, Purity, and Fidelity"; and the very first name on the roll was "Samuel L. Clemens," but he soon withdrew. (See Keene Abbot, "Tom Sawyer's Town," *Harper's Weekly*, April 9, 1913, p. 16.) Twain described his experiences with the organization in Chapter 22 of *Tom Sawyer*. "Hannibal always had a weakness for the Temperance cause," he admitted in "Hannibal—By a Native Son" (*Alta Californian*, May 26, 1867). "I joined the Cadets myself, although they didn't allow a boy to smoke, or drink or swear, but I never thought I could be truly happy till I wore one of those stunning red scarfs and walked in procession when a distinguished citizen died. I stood it four months, but never an infernal distinguished citizen died during the whole time; and when they finally pronounced old Dr. Norton convalescent (a man I had been depending on for seven or eight weeks), I just drew out. I drew out in disgust, and pretty much all the other distinguished citizens in the camp died within the next three weeks." His friend Jimmie McDaniel was the official "Patriarch" of the cadets until he was expelled. "You see, we weren't allowed to smoke any, and maybe I smoked a little," he told Abbott; "we weren't allowed to chew [tobacco], and maybe I chewed a little; we weren't allowed to drink any cider or wine or beer or whisky, and maybe I—well, I reckon they sort o' lost confidence in me." Tom Blankenship, however, "could never get in." According to his working notes reproduced in the 1988 University of California edition (p. 753), Twain considered writing something about the Cadets of Temperance (along with the Masons, Oddfellows, and Militia) later in the Phelps farm episode of *Huckleberry Finn*.

19. *made his mark.* Because he can neither read nor write, pap Finn makes an "X" in front of witnesses to legalize the document.

thirsty and clumb out onto the porch-roof and slid down a stanchion and traded his new coat for a jug of forty-rod,[20] and clumb back again and had a good old time; and towards daylight he crawled out again, drunk as a fiddler, and rolled off the porch and broke his left arm in two places and was most froze to death when somebody found him after sun-up. And when they come to look at that spare room, they had to take soundings before they could navigate it.[21]

The judge he felt kind of sore. He said he reckoned a body could reform the ole man with a shot-gun, maybe, but he didn't know no other way.[22]

FALLING FROM GRACE.

20. *forty-rod*. Cheap, vile whiskey, so strong that it was warranted to knock down or kill a man at forty rods. Chester L. Davis estimated in *The Twainian* (September/October 1961, p. 4) that the distance is a remarkable 660 feet or an eighth of a mile. But "forty" is used in the biblical sense of a great amount, as in forty days and forty nights.

21. *take soundings before they could navigate it*. Riverboat slang, meaning to proceed cautiously. Chapter 12 of *Life on the Mississippi* gives a detailed description of a "sounding": While the ship is tied up in a shallow crossing, the pilot not on watch takes some of the crew in a yawl to hunt the deepest water; once found, this pilot "sounds" its depth by measuring it with a pole ten or twelve feet long, so the pilot on watch can navigate the boat safely into the deep water beyond.

22. *but he didn't know no other way*. "And right he *was*, every time," Twain added to his 1895–1896 public reading copy.

Chapter VI

GETTING OUT OF THE WAY.

Well pretty soon the old man was up and around again, and then he went for Judge Thatcher in the courts to make him give up that money, and he went for me, too, for not stopping school. He catched me a couple of times and thrashed me, but I went to school just the same, and dodged him or out-run him most of the time. I didn't want to go to school much, before, but I reckoned I'd go now to spite pap. That law trial was a slow business; appeared like they warn't ever going to get started on it; so every now and then I'd borrow two or three dollars off of the judge for him, to keep from getting a cowhiding. Every time he got money he got drunk; and every time he got drunk he raised Cain around town; and every time he raised Cain he got jailed. He was just suited—this kind of thing was right in his line.

He got to hanging around the widow's too much, and so she told him at last, that if he didn't quit using around there[1] she would make trouble for him. Well, *wasn't* he mad? He said he would show who was Huck Finn's boss. So he watched out for me one day in the spring, and catched me, and took me up the river about three mile, in a skiff, and crossed over to the Illinois shore[2] where it was woody

1. *if he didn't quit using around there.* If he didn't stop hanging around.

2. *crossed over to the Illinois shore.* That side of the Mississippi was out of the jurisdiction of "St. Petersburg" (Hannibal), Missouri.

SOLID COMFORT.

and there warn't no houses but an old log hut[3] in a place where the timber was so thick you couldn't find it if you didn't know where it was.

He kept me with him all the time, and I never got a chance to run off. We lived in that old cabin, and he always locked the door and put the key under his head, nights. He had a gun which he had stole, I reckon, and we fished and hunted, and that was what we lived on. Every little while he locked me in and went down to the store, three miles, to the ferry, and traded fish and game for whisky and fetched it home and got drunk and had a good time, and licked me. The widow she found out where I was, by-and-by, and she sent a man over to try to get hold of me, but pap drove him off with the gun, and it warn't long after that till I was used to being where I was, and liked it, all but the cowhide part.

It was kind of lazy and jolly, laying off comfortable all day, smoking and fishing, and no books nor study. Two months or more run along, and my clothes got to be all rags and dirt, and I didn't see how I'd ever got to like it so well at the widow's, where you had to wash, and eat on a plate, and comb up,[4] and go to bed and get up regular, and be forever bothering over a book and have old Miss Watson pecking at you all the time. I didn't want to go back no more. I had stopped cussing, because the widow didn't like it; but now I

3. *an old log hut.* Backwoodsmen often lived in log cabins at this time. "The spaces between the logs were chinked up with clay and stones or chips," Ben Ezra Stiles Ely recalled of one of these typical rude huts. "The chimney with its great wide fireplace into which you could roll an immense backlog was built of logs and large stones at the bottom and topped off with sticks laid across each other at the corners and plastered over with clay. Most of the cabins had but one room, which served for a kitchen, dining room, parlor and bedroom" (quoted in Curtis Dahl, "Mark Twain and Ben Ely: Two Missouri Boyhoods," *Missouri Historical Review*, July 1972, p. 554).

4. *comb up.* Make oneself presentable, spruce up, brush up. "Combing up" was not an easy or pleasant task for young red-haired Sam Clemens. Boyhood friend Barney Farthing said that Sam's hair "looked more like the mane of a lion in texture and tangled luxuriance than anything else; and more distinctly than anything I remember on that subject was that it was some remark I chanced to make about its appearance which occasioned our acquaintance and necessitated my going home with a bloody nose" (quoted in Wilfred R. Hollister and Harry Norman, *Five Famous Missourians*, 1900, p. 28).

took to it again because pap hadn't no objections. It was pretty good times[5] up in the woods there, take it all around.

But by-and-by pap got too handy with his hick'ry,[6] and I couldn't stand it. I was all over welts. He got to going away so much, too, and locking me in. Once he locked me in and was gone three days. It was dreadful lonesome. I judged he had got drowned and I wasn't ever going to get out any more. I was scared. I made up my mind I would fix up some way to leave there. I had tried to get out of that cabin many a time, but I couldn't find no way. There warn't a window to it big enought for a dog to get through. I couldn't get up the chimbly, it was too narrow. The door was thick solid oak slabs.[7] Pap was pretty careful not to leave a knife or anything in the cabin when he was away; I reckon I had hunted the place over as much as a hundred times; well, I was 'most all the time at it, because it was about the only way to put in the time. But this time I found something at last; I found an old rusty wood-saw without any handle; it was laid in between a rafter and the clapboards of the roof. I greased it up and went to work. There was an old horse-blanket nailed against the logs at the far end of the cabin behind the table, to keep the wind from blowing through the chinks and putting the candle out. I got under the table and raised the blanket and went to work to saw a section of the big bottom log out, big enough to let me through. Well, it was a good long job, but I was getting towards the end of it when I heard pap's gun in the woods. I got rid of the signs of my work, and dropped the blanket and hid my saw, and pretty soon pap come in.

Pap warn't in a good humor—so he was his natural self. He said he was down to town, and everything was going wrong. His lawyer said he reckoned he would win his lawsuit and get the money, if they ever got started on the trial; but then there was ways to put it off a long time, and Judge Thatcher knowed how to do it. And he said people allowed[8] there'd be another trial to get me away from him and give me to the widow for my guardian, and they guessed it would win, this time. This shook me up considerable, because I didn't want to go back to the widow's any

5. *pretty good times*. Twain originally wrote "much bullier" (**MS**), but that made them sound far more fun than they were.

6. *too handy with his hick'ry*. Too quick to administer a beating; parents and teachers often whipped disobedient children with hickory switches. Sam and Olivia Clemens approved of spanking children if adminstered "on purely business principles—disciplinary principles—and with hearts totally free from temper." He explained in "What Ought He to Have Done?" (*Christian Union*, July 16, 1885) that "whippings are not given in our house for revenge; they are not given for spite, nor ever in anger; they are given partly for punishment, but mainly by way of impressive reminder, and protector against the repetition of the offense" (p. 5). It followed a strict but fair procedure in the Clemens household. "The interval between the promise of a whipping and its infliction is usually an hour or two," he explained. "By that time both parties are calm, and the one is judicial, the other receptive. The child never goes from the scene of punishment until it has been loved back into happy-heartedness and a joyful spirit. The spanking is never a cruel one, but it's always an honest one. It hurts." And he left the discipline up to his wife even when the child offended him. "If it hurts the child, imagine how it must hurt the mother," he added. "Her spirit is serene, tranquil. She has not the support which is afforded by anger. Every blow she strikes the child bruises her own heart."

7. *The door was thick solid oak slabs*. Twain originally wrote that the door also had "a heavy chain" (**MS**), but cut it when he decided on Huck's means of escape from the shack.

8. *allowed*. Or "'lowed," meaning "guessed" in the Middle States, "reckoned" in the South; it has no kinship to the usual meaning of "allowed."

more and be so cramped up and sivilized,[9] as they called it. Then the old man got to cussing, and cussed everything and everybody he could think of, and then cussed them all over again to make sure he hadn't skipped any, and after that he polished off with a kind of a general cuss all round, including a considerable parcel of people[10] which he didn't know the names of, and so called them what's-his-name, when he got to them, and went right along with his cussing.

He said he would like to see the widow get me. He said he would watch out, and if they tried to come any such game on him he knowed of a place six or seven mile off, to stow me in, where they might hunt till they dropped and they couldn't find me. That made me pretty uneasy again, but only for a minute; I reckoned I wouldn't stay on hand till he got that chance.[11]

The old man made me go to the skiff and fetch the things he had got. There was a fifty-pound sack of corn meal, and a side of bacon, ammunition, and a four-gallon jug of whisky,

THINKING IT OVER.

and an old book and two newspapers for wadding,[12] besides some tow.[13] I toted up a load, and went back and set down on the bow of the skiff to rest. I thought it all over, and I reckoned I would walk off with the gun and some

9. *sivilized.* Twain originally wrote "civilized" (**MS**) in the manuscript, but decided instead on eye dialect, one of the few instances in the book.

10. *a considerable parcel of people.* A particularly large number of people.

11. *I reckoned I wouldn't stay on hand till he got that chance.* Huck, who so readily shed the widow's influences, now quickly regresses to his old ways; although he may prefer the freedom of life in the wilderness to the confines of the "sivilizing" town, he decides to run away only when his life is threatened. He now denies the guardianship of either the widow or his father.

12. *an old book and two newspapers for wadding.* Paper was often made of old rags at the time, so it was good for packing powder and shot in rifles. Illiterate pap Finn would have little other use for newspapers than for wadding.

13. *tow.* Rope made from strands of flax or hemp.

lines,[14] and take to the woods when I run away. I guessed I wouldn't stay in one place, but just tramp right across the country, mostly night times, and hunt and fish to keep alive, and so get so far away that the old man nor the widow couldn't ever find me any more. I judged I would saw out and leave that night if pap got drunk enough, and I reckoned he would. I got so full of it I didn't notice how long I was staying, till the old man hollered and asked me whether I was asleep or drownded.

I got the things all up to the cabin, and then it was about dark. While I was cooking supper the old man took a swig or two and got sort of warmed up, and went to ripping again. He had been drunk over in town, and laid in the gutter all night, and he was a sight to look at. A body would a thought he was Adam, he was just all mud.[15] Whenever his liquor begun to work,[16] he most always went for the govment.[17] This time he says:[18]

"Call this a govment! why, just look at it and see what it's like. Here's the law a-standing ready to take a man's son away from him—a man's own son, which he has had all the trouble and all the anxiety and all the expense of raising. Yes, just as that man has got that son raised at last, and ready to go to work and begin to do suthin' for *him* and give him a rest, the law up and goes for him. And they call *that* govment! That ain't all, nuther. The law backs that old Judge Thatcher up and helps him to keep me out o' my property.[19] Here's what the law does. The law takes a man worth six thousand dollars and upards, and jams him into an old trap of a cabin like this, and lets him go round in clothes that ain't fitten for a hog. They call that govment! A man can't get his rights in a govment like this. Sometimes I've a mighty notion to just leave the country for good and all. Yes, and I *told* 'em so; I told old Thatcher so to his face. Lots of 'em heard me, and can tell what I said. Says I, for two cents I'd leave the blamed country and never come anear it agin.[20] Them's the very words. I says, look at my hat—if you call it a hat—but the lid raises up and the rest of it goes down till it's below my chin, and then it ain't rightly a hat at all, but more like my head was shoved up through a

14. *lines*. "Fishing lines" (**MS**), as Twain noted in the manuscript but dropped from the finished book.

15. *A body would a thought he was Adam, he was just all mud*. Huck originally said "he was whitewashed with mud" (**MS**) in the manuscript; a joke on Genesis 1:8, which tells how God created Adam out of the dust of the earth. In the advance sheets of *Huckleberry Finn* used for the 1884–1885 lecture tour (now in the Mark Twain Papers, University of California at Berkeley), Twain greatly expanded this metaphor: "A body just glancing at him would a thought he was Adam, if a body'd struck him in the Garden of Eden he'd just say 'Adam, I presume,' he was just all mud—it was caked on him and dried, so'st he looked solid." Twain made a similar joke in a suppressed passage from Chapter 38 of *Life on the Mississippi*, in which he said a Cincinnati steamer was so filthy that "it would have attracted the attention of Adam himself, while his own dirt was still damp."

16. *his liquor begun to work*. Or "he was a-souring after a spree," as in Twain's revisions of this passage in the advance sheets of *Huckleberry Finn* he prepared for his 1884–1885 reading tour.

17. *he most always went for the govment*. Pap Finn's rantings about government intervention may seem absurd coming from the town drunkard, but many of his opinions were shared by sober God-fearing Americans before—and after—the Civil War. "There is but one sound and patriotic position to be taken on the subject—that of noninterference with the question of slavery," wrote Sam Clemens's boss Joseph P. Ament in an editorial, "Missouri and Slavery in the Territiories" (Hannibal *Missouri Courier*, April 19, 1849). "It is the only one that can save the Union from violent disorder, from convulsion, and perhaps from dissolution itself." The Emancipation Proclamation of 1863 and the Reconstruction following did nothing to ensure in America that all men—and women—are created equal. Violence and other manifestations of racism made sure that not all citizens would reap the full rewards of citizenship. The Jim Crow laws effectively restricted voting privileges in the South until the civil rights movement. Even today in parts of the country—Florida, for instance—racism persists at the polls.

18. *This time he says*. In the advance sheets he used for his 1884–1885 reading tour, Twain revealed that "he went a-swellin' around the old sugar-house."

19. *The law backs that old Judge Thatcher up and helps him to keep me out o' my property*. At this time, a boy's property belonged to his parents; but because he suspects that his pap has returned, Huck wisely transfers the money to the judge for $1.

20. *for two cents I'd leave the blamed country and never come anear it again*. Pap Finn expresses the arrogance of democracy. Why anyone should care whether or not this drunkard leaves the country never occurs to him, because he believes that he is just as important as any other citizen of the country. Twain apparently agreed with Captain Frederick Marryat's evaluation of the failure of the American republic. This English writer argued that New World democracy took the power out of the few of the noble aristocracy and put it into the morally corrupt crowd, which led to "the total extinction, or if not extinction, absolute bondage, of the aristocracy of the country, both politically and as well as socially." He attributed the transformation to the Revolutionary War. "There was an aristocracy at the time of independence—not an aristocracy of title, but a much superior one," Marryat explained in Chapter 14 of the second series of his American diaries of 1840; "an aristocracy of great, powerful, and leading men, who were looked up to and imitated; . . . but although a portion of it remains, it may be said to have been almost altogether smothered, and in society it no longer exists." Clemens identified with this American aristocracy; after all, he descended from the First Families of Virginia. He did not entirely believe that all men are created equal, spiritually, morally, or intellectually. "I am an aristocrat (in the aristocracy of the mind of achievement)," he wrote in a copy of Sarah Grand, *The Heavenly Twins* (Item 195 in *Catalogue of the Library and Manuscripts of Samuel L. Clemens*, New York: Anderson Auction Company, 1911), "and from my Viscountship look reverently up at all earls, marquises and dukes above me, and superciliously down upon the barons, baronets, and knights below me." As *Huckleberry Finn* proves, he had little sympathy for popular opinion. "Whenever you find that you are on the side of the majority," he warned

jint o' stove-pipe.[21] Look at it, says I—such a hat for me to wear—one of the wealthiest men[22] in this town, if I could git my rights.

"Oh, yes, this is a wonderful govment, wonderful. Why, looky here. There was a free nigger there, from Ohio;[23] a mulatter, most as white as a white man.[24] He had the whitest shirt on you ever see, too, and the shiniest hat; and there ain't a man in that town that's got as fine clothes as what he had; and he had a gold watch and chain, and a silver-headed cane—the awfulest old gray-headed nabob[25] in the State. And what do you think? they said he was a p'fessor in a college, and could talk all kinds of languages,[26] and knowed everything. And that ain't the wust. They said he could *vote*, when he was at home.[27] Well, that let me out. Thinks I, what is the country a-coming to?[28] It was 'lection day, and I was just about to go and vote, myself, if I warn't too drunk to get there; but when they told me there was a State in this country where they'd let that nigger vote, I drawed out.[29] I says I'll never vote agin. Them's the very words I said; they all heard me; and the country may rot for all me—I'll never vote agin as long as I live. And to see the cool way of that nigger—why, he wouldn't a give me the road if I hadn't shoved him out o' the way. I says to the people, why ain't this nigger put up at auction and sold?—that's what I want to know. And what do you reckon they said? Why, they said he couldn't be sold till he'd been in the State six months,[30] and he hadn't been there that long yet. There, now—that's a specimen. They call that a govment that can't sell a free nigger till he's been in the State six months. Here's a govment that calls itself a govment, and lets on to be a govment, and thinks it is a govment, and yet's got to set stock-still for six whole months before it can take ahold of a prowling, thieving, infernal, white-shirted free nigger, and——"

Pap was agoing on so, he never noticed where his old limber legs was taking him to, so he went head over heels over the tub of salt pork,[31] and barked both shins,[32] and the rest of his speech was all the hottest kind of language[33]—mostly hove at the nigger and the govment, though he give the tub some, too, all along, here and there. He hopped around the cabin considerable, first on one leg and then on the other, holding first one shin and then the other one, and at last he let out with his left foot all of a sudden and fetched the tub a rattling kick. But it warn't good judgment, because that was the boot that had a couple of his toes leaking out of the front end of it; so now he raised a howl that fairly made a body's hair raise, and down he went in the dirt, and rolled there, and held his toes; and the cussing he done then laid over anything he had ever done previous. He said so his own self, afterwards. He had heard old Sowberry Hagan in his best days, and he said it laid over him, too; but I reckon that was sort of piling it on, maybe.

After supper pap took the jug, and said he had enough whisky there for two drunks and one delirium tremens.[34] That was always his word.[35] I judged he would be blind drunk in about an hour, and then I would steal the key, or saw myself out, one or 'tother. He drank, and drank, and

RAISING A HOWL.

tumbled down on his blankets, by-and-by; but luck didn't run my way. He didn't go sound asleep, but was uneasy. He groaned, and moaned, and thrashed around this way and

in his *Notebook* (1935), "it is time to reform—(or pause and reflect)" (p. 393).

21. *like my head was shoved up through a jint o' stove-pipe*. Huck makes the same silly simile when he puts on the sun-bonnet in Chapter 10.

22. *wealthiest men*. Twain changed this to the equally sarcastic but more accurate "oldes' citizens" in the advance sheets he used for his 1884–1885 reading tour, then deleted the whole passage about pap's hat.

23. *There was a free nigger there, from Ohio*. Slavery was abolished in Ohio when it joined the Union in 1803; this free state became a hotbed of Abolitionism and a major link on the Underground Railroad. Some freedmen did actually reside in Hannibal, Missouri, by the 1840s, but under severe restrictions. Donald H. Walsh reported in "Sam Clemens' Hannibal, 1836–1838" (*Midcontinent American Studies*, Spring 1962) that city ordinances in Hannibal "provided that no free Negro or mulatto could reside within the city without securing a license from the mayor, and that to secure this permit he must show evidence of good moral character and behavior, pay $5 annually for the use of the city, and give a maximum bond of $1,000 for his good behavior. Any unlicensed Negro without proof of freedom might be jailed as a runaway slave, and any Negro going out after 9 p.m. without a pass was subject to fine. Nor were Negroes allowed to hold an assemblage at night or remain at any ball or meeting after 11 p.m. without the major's permission. The ordinances further decreed that any white person over the age of ten who was found at any Negro social affair should be fined $50, that anyone giving a slave a pass illegally should be fined $20 to the value of the slave, and that a master allowing his slave to hire out to others should be fined from $5 to $20" (p. 38). Huck Finn reveals in the unfinished "Tom Sawyer's Conspiracy" that when abolitionists were suspected in the area, the town "tightened up the rules, and a nigger couldn't be out after dark at night, pass or no pass. And all the young men was parceled into paterollers, and they watched the streets all night, ready to stop any stranger that come along" (*Huck Finn and Tom Sawyer Among the Indians*, 1989, pp. 143). It would seem that only freedmen of the social and financial status of the college professor from Ohio could reside in Hannibal, but the *Gazette* complained on October 14, 1847, that "our streets are lined with negroes loafing and rowdying every Saturday. Crowds of them occupy the street corners, and fill the kitchens of our citizens, and have become a real annoyance." Twain's brother Orion bravely opposed Hannibal's "special and onerous tax" of $10 imposed on freedmen in 1852. "Many of them, with the utmost industry, and with what would be most rigid economy, even in a negro family, can scarcely save more than the tax out of their hard earnings, particularly if they have large families," he wrote in "Free Negro Tax" (Hannibal *Journal*, July 8, 1852). "But this tax is only imposed upon negroes of good character for quiet and orderly behavior, sobriety and honesty, and (the council must be satisfied) that he or she will in no wise be a tax on the city; for unless the council can be convinced of these facts, freed negroes will not be allowed to stay in the city. But this is not all; they must procure surety for good behavior, to the amount of $100. How many of them, with the best character, can obtain such security?" Instead, he insisted, "every slaveholder must make his own kitchen laws and force his slaves to abide by them." But Orion Clemens did not speak for the rest of Hannibal. "Born and reared among slaves and slaveholders," Twain explained in "Chapters from My Autobiography" (*North American Review*, January 18, 1907), "he was yet an abolitionist from his boyhood to his death" (p. 115). Sam Clemens, however, had no such sympathies while he was growing up in Hannibal.

24. *a mulatter, most as white as a white man.* This important distinction was an afterthought, inserted in the first draft of the manuscript some time after the rest. Mulattoes, being "persons of color," were considered equal to Negroes under Southern law. In the advance sheets of *Huckleberry Finn* used in preparing his 1884–1885 lecture tour, Twain increased the irony of this diatribe by changing this phrase to "most as white as *I'd* be—if I was washed." Again Twain attacks the absurdity of judging a person's character by his color or any other aspect of his outward appearance. "If the color of one's skin is important (as some Americans believe), then readers need to look carefully at the description of Huck's father's face [in the last chapter] which contains a very specific reference to a white man," suggested Kenny J. Williams in "*Adventures of Huckleberry Finn*; or, Mark Twain's Racial Ambiguity" (*Mark Twain Journal*, Fall 1984). "If one compares this

that, for a long time. At last I got so sleepy I couldn't keep my eyes open, all I could do, and so before I knowed what I was about I was sound asleep, and the candle burning.

I don't know how long I was asleep, but all of a sudden there was an awful scream and I was up. There was pap, looking wild and skipping around every which way and yelling about snakes.[36] He said they was crawling up his legs; and then he would give a jump and scream, and say one had bit him on the cheek—but I couldn't see no snakes. He started and run round and round the cabin, hollering "take him off! take him off! he's biting me on the neck!" I never see a man look so wild in the eyes. Pretty soon he was all fagged out, and fell down panting; then he rolled over and over, wonderful fast, kicking things every which way, and striking and grabbing at the air with his hands, and screaming, and saying there was devils ahold of him. He wore out, by-and-by, and laid still a while, moaning. Then he laid stiller, and didn't make a sound. I could hear the owls and the wolves, away off in the woods, and it seemed terrible still. He was laying over by the corner. By-and-by he raised up, part way, and listened, with his head to one side. He says very low:

"Tramp—tramp—tramp;[37] that's the dead; tramp—tramp—tramp; they're coming after me; but I won't go—Oh, they're here! don't touch me—don't! hands off—they're cold; let go—Oh, let a poor devil alone!"

Then he went down on all fours and crawled off begging them to let him alone, and he rolled himself up in his blanket and wallowed in under the old pine table, still a-begging; and then he went to crying. I could hear him through the blanket.

By-and-by he rolled out and jumped up on his feet looking wild, and he see me and went for me. He chased me round and round the place, with a clasp-knife,[38] calling me the Angel of Death[39] and saying he would kill me and then I couldn't come for him no more. I begged, and told him I was only Huck, but he laughed *such* a screechy laugh, and roared and cussed, and kept on chasing me up. Once when I turned short and dodged under his arm he made a grab and got me by the jacket between my shoulders, and I thought I was gone; but I slid out of the jacket quick as lightning, and saved myself. Pretty soon he was all tired out, and dropped down with his back against the door, and said he would rest a minute and then kill me. He put his knife under him, and said he would sleep and get strong, and then he would see who was who.

So he dozed off, pretty soon. By-and-by I got the old split-bottom chair[40] and clumb up, as easy as I could, not to make any noise, and got down the gun.[41] I slipped the ramrod down it to make sure it was loaded, and then I laid it across the turnip barrel,[42] pointing towards pap, and set down behind it to wait for him to stir. And how slow and still the time did drag along.

description of pap with that of the free black man from Ohio who so angered Huck's father that he refused to vote again or with the presentation of the noble qualities of Jim, 'white' does not appear to have any particular advantage" (p. 41).

25. *nabob*. A prominent member of the community; *New York Times* columnist William Safire briefly resurrected this archaic word in 1970, with the phrase "nattering nabobs of negativism" in a speech delivered by Vice-President Spiro T. Agnew in response to his critics.

A nabob. Illustration by Roswell Morse Shurtleff, *Roughing It*, 1872.
Private collection.

26. *a p'fessor in a college, and could talk all kinds of languages*. According to Chapter 23 of *The Innocents Abroad,* Twain experienced an epiphany similar to pap Finn's, but with vastly different consequences, when he met a remarkable man in Venice in 1867 who was born of slaves in South Carolina but raised in Europe:

> He is well educated. He reads, writes, and speaks English, Italian, Spanish, and French, with perfect facility; is a worshipper of art and thoroughly conversant with it; knows the history of Venice by heart and never tires of talking of her illustrious career. He dressed better than any of us, I think, and is daintily polite. Negroes are deemed as good as white people in Venice, and so this man feels no desire to go back to his native land. His judgement is correct.

William Baker suggested in "Mark Twain and the Shrewd Ohio Audiences" (*American Literary Realism*, Spring and Autumn 1985, p. 17) that a possible model for the remarkable gentleman who inspired pap Finn's diatribe was the Rev. John G. Mitchell. Born in Indiana and one of several African-Americans to graduate from Oberlin College before the Civil War, he was professor of Greek, Latin, and mathematics at Wilberforce University near Xenia, Ohio; the school was named for the British antislavery leader William Wilberforce. Mitchell attended Oberlin from 1853 to 1857, and was a teacher as well as pastor of the African Methodist Episcopal Church in Georgia, Indiana, Kentucky, Ohio, Pennsylvania, Virginia, and Washington, D.C. He was part of the Wilberforce faculty from 1863 to 1870, in 1883 and 1884, and from 1891 until his death in 1900.

Do not think that only "poor white trash" like pap Finn held such contempt for educated freedmen. When reporting on an item in the Boston *Commonwealth* that two "colored lawyers" were "regarded with as much deference as any in the assembly" as they sat in the United States Circuit Court with several judges "and a long train of other notables in the law," the Hannibal *Missouri Courier* (November 18, 1852) added, "Surely, 'there's no accounting for tastes!'"

27. *They said he could* vote, *when he was at home*. Blair and Fischer pointed out in the 1988 University of California edition that pap Finn is mistaken: "Actually, free blacks were not allowed to vote in Ohio. Like most states outside the Northeast, Ohio limited the 'elective franchise to white male persons' " (pp. 382–83).

28. *what is the country a-coming to?* But why does pap Finn so hate this man who has done him no harm? Why is he, a poor white, so in favor of slavery, which does not personally benefit him? "That this sentiment should exist among slave-owners," Twain explained in an 1895 notebook entry, "is comprehensible—there were good commercial reasons for it—but that it should exist and did exist among the paupers, the loafers, the rag-tag and bobtail of the community, and in a passionate and uncompromising form, is not in our remote day realizable. It seemed natural enough that Huck and his father, the worthless loafer, should feel it and approve it, though it now seems absurd" (quoted in Philip S. Foner, *Mark Twain: Social Critic*, 1958, p. 206). It baffled Harriet Jacobs too, as she wrote in Chapter 12 of *Incidents in the Life of a Slave Girl* (1861), that "the low whites" failed to realize "that the power which trampled on the colored people also kept themselves in poverty, ignorance, and moral degradation." Why did poor whites feel so threatened by people of color? Twain believed that education was at fault here. As indicated by the boy's detached, uneditorialized recording of his father's unbridled rantings in this chapter, it is obvious from whom Huck learned his racist attitudes toward people of color. "It shows," Twain argued, "that that strange thing, the conscience—the unerring monitor—can be trained to approve any wild thing you want it to approve if you begin its education early and stick to it."

Twain also recognized that "poor whites" did have call for their resentment of their social "inferiors," even if it was provided by the slave owners. Ironically, because slaves were valuable property, they were sometimes treated to certain courtesies not granted to other laborers. Because nothing was invested in unskilled Irish and German immigrants, they were considered an expendable commodity. "There was much said before the election about 'Irishmen' and 'Germans,' " observed the Hannibal *Missouri Courier* (December 9, 1852). "Now, they are all 'Paddies' and 'Dutchmen.' " On steamboats, the heavier labor often fell to foreigners, while slaves were not always so overworked, could be well fed and clothed and granted limited hours of work, and were tended to when sick or injured. And unconditional obedience was demanded in return for such treatment. It is no surprise then that some slaves greatly resented other workers; "poor white trash" was the contemptuous term they applied to their "inferiors." Such animosity between groups who do not profit from the system that oppresses them and who therefore should be working together to fight its injustices persists as long as those in power provide special privileges to one faction while denying them to others. Twain admitted in "Goldsmith's Friend Abroad Again" (*Galaxy*, November 1870) that "misery and hardship do not make their victims gentle or charitable toward each another" (p. 729). Instead they blame each other for their misfortune rather than the true source of their oppression (see Chapter 32, note 14).

Twain acknowledged in Chapter 30 of *A Connecticut Yankee in King Arthur's Court* a final paradox of the attitude of pap Finn's class toward that of the slave in that "the 'poor whites' of our South who were always despised, and frequently insulted, by the slave lords around them, and who owed their base condition simply to the presence of slavery in their midst, were yet pusillanimously ready to side with the slave lords in all political moves for the upholding and perpetuating of slavery, and did also finally shoulder their muskets and pour out their lives in an effort to prevent the destruction of the very institution which degraded them. And there was only one redeeming feature connected with this pitiful piece of history . . . that secretly the 'poor white' did detest the slave-lord, and did feel his own shame." Sam Clemens was among the poor fools who went to war to protect American slavery. Racism is, alas, a too common pathology that bears no relation to logic or compassion, to either head or heart.

29. *when they told me there was a State in this country where they'd let that nigger vote, I drawed out.* Pap Finn expresses the view generally held in the South at the time that all men are not created equal and thus they do not all deserve the same rights under the law. Twain himself believed that intelligence above all other considerations should determine one's right to vote. In his lecture "Universal Suffrage," delivered on February 15, 1875 (and discussed by Blair in *Mark Twain and Huck Finn*), he disapproved of equating the vote of "a consummate scoundrel" with that of "a president, a bishop, a college professor, a merchant prince" (p. 132). In his study of Utopia, the article "The Curious Republic of Gondour" (*Atlantic Monthly*, October 1875), Twain agreed that universal suffrage, giving "every citizen, howsoever poor or ignorant," one vote, should be preserved, "but if a man possessed a good common-school education and no money, he had two votes; a high school education gave him four; if he had property likewise, to the value of three thousand *sacos*, he wielded one vote; for every fifty thousand *sacos* a man added to his property, he was entitled to another vote; a university education entitled a man to nine votes, even if he owned no property" (p. 461). (And this from the man who said in the aphorism to Chapter 5 of *Pudd'nhead Wilson* that a "cauliflower is nothing but cabbage with a college education"!) Twain suffered from the nineteenth-century misassumption that wealth and education were the natural rewards of superior intelligence. In Gondour, he explained, "learning being more prevalent and more easily acquired than riches, educated men became a wholesome check upon wealthy men, since they could outvote them. Learning goes usually with uprightness, broad views, and humanity; so the learned voters, possessing the balance of power, became the vigilant and efficient protectors of the great lower rank of society." It never occurred to him that "the great lower rank of society" did not want protection or that a college education did not necessarily ensure "uprightness, broad views, and humanity." Twain may well have believed that this college professor, no matter what his color, was more worthy of the vote than pap Finn. Yet Twain shared some of the drunkard's twisted logic: While the squatter hates the gentleman from Ohio for his race, the writer admires him for his accomplishments. Neither one judges him by the quality of his character.

30. *they said they couldn't be sold till he'd been in the State six months.* "And might as well say six years," pap Finn sarcastically adds in the advance sheets Twain used for his 1884–1885 reading tour. The Missouri constitution of 1820 provided that it was the responsibility of the legislature to protect slave owners' property rights by passing laws to prevent free Negroes and mulattoes from entering the state. It was commonly assumed in the slave states that just the appearance of freedmen would incite slaves to overthrow their masters. The Missouri Code of 1825 stated that any Negro traveler, even the citizen of another state with proof of his freedom, was prohibited to stay there more than six months. "De law kin sell me now," realizes the now freed Roxy in Chapter 16 of *Pudd'nhead Wilson*, "if dey tell me to leave de State in six months en I don't go." Anyone had the right to apprehend a slave, but the person risked being fined $100 plus all costs if a nonfugitive was arrested. By February 16, 1847, the law was changed to read: "No free negro or mulatto shall, under any pretext, emigrate to this State, from any other State or territory."

31. *he went head over heels over the tub of salt pork.* Twain is reminding the reader that pap Finn sleeps with the hogs in the tanyard while implying that all of his provisions, including this salt pork, have been stolen. In preparing the advance sheets of the book for his 1884–1885 public reading tour, Twain wrote an entirely new incident here: " . . . he went head over heels into a vat of molasses, head over heels and was most drownded. We fished him out and stood him up. It was the first time I ever see him stuck. He couldn't say a word. Just stood there and dripped—stood there and looked oncomfortable; I never see a man look so oncomfortable over a little thing." "To be stuck" is a colloquial expression meaning "to be speechless," making this accident even more outrageous than in the original. Pap has been anything but "stuck" at any point in his diatribe against "the govment and the nigger."

32. *barked both shins.* Scraped the skin off both shins.

33. *language.* Twain originally said in the manuscript "cussing" (**MS**), but must have softened it for propriety's (or Livy's) sake.

34. *delirium tremens.* Commonly called the "DTs," hallucinations with loss of muscular control brought on by heavy drinking. Twain revealed in Chapter 56 of *Life on the Mississippi* that that man's namesake, Jimmy Finn, "died a natural death in a tan vat, of a combination of delirium tremens and spontaneous combustion." Edgar M. Branch in "Mark Twain: Newspaper Reading and the Writer's Creativity" (*Nineteenth-Century Fiction*, March 1983) quoted another account, "The Horrors of Delirium Tremens" (St. Louis *Missouri Democrat*, June 11, 1861), that is remarkably like pap Finn's attack: "raving of devils and snakes, as he expressed it, creeping things innumerable, both small and great; his face flushed, his eyes bloodshot and glistening. . . . He was struggling with imaginary demons, and shouting at the top of his voice that he was devil possessed, and that his time was come to go to utter darkness. 'Oh, devils of the air, how they glare on me! Messengers of Satan, sent to buffet me, I'll have it out yet! Off, off, I say! Crawl, crawl, creep, creep!' Then would ensue a fearful paroxysm, and he would make snatches at the bed clothes, or cower beneath them, or peep over the edge of the bed, with an expression . . . murderous in its terror/ . . . His screams and yells were awful, and when they ceased he gabbled incessantly . . . to the imaginary beings who crowded his chamber, imploring their pity" (p. 577). It took four men to subdue him.

35. *That was always his word.* An afterthought in the manuscript, Twain realizing that "delirium tremens" was likely not part of a backwoods boy's vocabulary.

36. *snakes.* A common hallucination of heavy drinkers; "seeing snakes" is another way of referring to delirium tremens.

37. *Tramp—tramp—tramp.* Paul Baender located this line in the refrain of a temperance song, "The Dead March," included in *The Treasury of Song for the Home* (1882), which Twain owned, and reported it to Blair and Fischer for the 1988 University of California edition:

Tramp, tramp, tramp, in the drunkard's way
March the feet of a million men.
If none shall pity and none shall save,
Where will all this marching end?
The young, the strong, and the old are there,
In woeful ranks as they hurry past,
With not a moment to think or care
What the fate that comes at last.

Tramp, tramp, tramp . . .
They are rushing madly on,
Tramp, tramp, tramp . . .
What a fearful ghostly throng;
Rouse, Christian rouse ere it be too late,
Rescue these souls from the drunkard's fate. (pp. 383–84)

38. *a clasp-knife.* A jackknife with a large blade; Twain mentioned in the manuscript a far more terrifying "butcher knife" (**MS**). See Chapter 7, note 14.

39. *the Angel of Death.* The belief that this spirit comes to people who are about to die comes from the Bible. Pap Finn may have berated his son's "getting religion" before, but the old drunk follows his own superstitious beliefs in Heaven and Hell.

40. *split-bottom chair.* Splint-bottomed chair, a cheap homemade piece of furniture with a cane seat and common to homes in this part of the country.

41. *the gun.* Twain originally wrote "one of the guns" (**MS**) in the manuscript, forgetting that earlier in the chapter pap only had the one which Huck "reckoned" he stole.

42. *the turnip barrel.* Twain changed from "the table" (**MS**) to this in the manuscript, perhaps because a turnip barrel provides a higher level from which to aim than the table could.

CHAPTER VII.

"GIT UP!"

UP! what you 'bout!"

I opened my eyes and looked around, trying to make out where I was. It was after sun-up, and I had been sound asleep. Pap was standing over me, looking sour—and sick, too. He says—

"What you doin' with this gun?"

I judged he didn't know nothing about what he had been doing, so I says:

"Somebody tried to get in, so I was laying for him."

"Why didn't you roust me out?"

"Well I tried to, but I couldn't; I couldn't budge you."

"Well, all right. Don't stand there palavering[1] all day, but out with you and see if there's a fish on the lines for breakfast. I'll be along in a minute."

He unlocked the door and I cleared out, up the river bank. I noticed some pieces of limbs and such things floating down, and a sprinkling of bark; so I knowed the river had begun to rise. I reckoned I would have great times, now, if I was over at the town. The June rise[2] used to be always luck for me; because as soon as that rise begins, here comes cord-wood[3] floating down, and pieces of log rafts—sometimes a dozen logs together; so all you have to do is to catch them and sell them to the wood yards and the sawmill.

I went along up the bank with one eye out for pap and

1. *palavering*. Jabbering, from the Spanish *palabra*, "words."

2. *June rise*. The spring flooding of the river, when (as Twain explained) "the snows melted in the mountains at the head waters of the mighty Missouri river some thousands of miles to the north and west and delivered the result into the Mississippi" ("Indiantown," *Mark Twain's Which*

The Mississippi at low water.
Illustration from *Harper's Monthly*,
December 1855.
Private collection.

The same scene during the June rise.
Illustration from *Harper's Monthly*,
December 1855.
Private collection.

Was the Dream?, 1967, p. 154). He explained in Chapter 3 of *Life on the Mississippi* that the time of *Huckleberry Finn* was "high water and dead summer time." He further described the June rise in Chapter 10: "The whole vast face of the stream was black with drifting dead logs, broken boughs, and great trees that had caved in and been washed away."

This annual flooding hit Hannibal especially hard the spring of 1851, when Sam Clemens was working for his brother Orion in the Hannibal *Western Union* office. "The great river is pitching, roaring and tumbling through the streets, as if wholly unconscious of being an intruder!" the paper reported on May 29. "There is a skiff moored to a post opposite this office—river rising rapidly as ever. Altogether things look squally all about here—so much so, that if you don't get any paper next week, you may set it down that we are in the Mississippi! If there is a room to rent on the second or third story of any good business house on Main street, we should be glad to be informed of the fact." It was even worse by June 5: "The water here, night before last, rose through the night at the rate of more than half an inch an hour! The same quantity of water added to the Mississippi at an ordinary stage of water, would, in the same time, (ten hours) have raised the river three feet, supposing it is now six miles wide, though by many it is supposed to be eight. The Mississippi, thus spread out like a sea, and encroaching upon us continually, has come up considerably beyond the alley between Water street and Main. There is now enough water in the alley to float a flatboat, twenty or thirty feet from Bird or Hill street." The rival Hannibal *Missouri Courier* added on June 12: "With a few exceptions, every town on the river is more or less under water, and many of them are completely submerged to the depth of several feet. All the bottoms, and of course all the bottom farms are overflown—in some instances greatly injuring them, and in all cases completely destroying the crops for the present season. Fences, and houses without number, and large quantities of cordwood have been swept off."

'tother one out for what the rise might fetch along. Well, all at once, here comes a canoe; just a beauty, too, about thirteen or fourteen foot long,[4] riding high like a duck. I shot head first off of the bank, like a frog, clothes and all on, and struck out for the canoe. I just expected there'd be somebody laying down in it, because people often done that to fool folks, and when a chap had pulled a skiff out most to it they'd raise up and laugh at him. But it warn't so this time. It was a drift-canoe, sure enough, and I clumb in and paddled her ashore. Thinks I, the old man will be glad when he sees this—she's worth ten dollars. But when I got to shore pap wasn't in sight yet, and as I was running her into a little creek like a gully, all hung over with vines and willows, I struck another idea; I judged I'd hide her good, and then, stead of taking to the woods when I run off, I'd go down the river about fifty mile and camp in one place for good, and not have such a rough time tramping on foot.

It was pretty close to the shanty, and I thought I heard the old man coming, all the time; but I got her hid; and then I out and looked around a bunch of willows, and there was the old man down the path apiece just drawing a bead on a bird with his gun.[5] So he hadn't seen anything.

When he got along, I was hard at it taking up a "trot" line.[6] He abused me a little for being so slow, but I told him

THE SHANTY.

I fell in the river and that was what made me so long. I knowed he would see I was wet, and then he would be asking questions. We got five cat-fish off of the lines and went home.

While we laid off, after breakfast, to sleep up, both of us being about wore out, I got to thinking that if I could fix up some way to keep pap and the widow from trying to follow me, it would be a certainer thing than trusting to luck to get far enough off before they missed me; you see, all kinds of things might happen. Well, I didn't see no way for a while, but by-and-by pap raised up a minute, to drink another barrel of water, and he says:

"Another time a man comes a-prowling round here, you roust me out, you hear? That man warn't here for no good. I'd a shot him. Next time, you roust me out, you hear?"

Then he dropped down and went to sleep again—but what he had been saying give me the very idea I wanted. I says to myself, I can fix it now so nobody won't think of following me.

About twelve o'clock we turned out and went along up the bank. The river was coming up pretty fast, and lots of drift-wood going by on the rise. By-and-by, along comes part of a log raft[7]—nine logs fast together. We went out with the skiff and towed it ashore. Then we had dinner. Anybody but pap would a waited and seen the day through, so as to catch more stuff; but that warn't pap's style. Nine logs was enough for one time; he must shove right over to town and sell. So he locked me in and took the skiff and started off towing the raft about half-past three. I judged he wouldn't come back that night. I waited till I reckoned he had got a good start, then I out with my saw and went to work on that log again. Before he was 'tother side of the river I was out of the hole; him and his raft was just a speck on the water away off yonder.

I took the sack of corn meal and took it to where the canoe was hid, and shoved the vines and branches apart and put it in; then I done the same with the side of bacon; then the whisky jug;[8] I took all the coffee and sugar there was, and all the ammunition; I took the wadding; I took the

Cord-wood. Illustration from *Harper's Monthly*, December 1855.
Private collection.

3. *cord-wood.* Wood for fuel; a cord is a stack, eight feet long by four feet high, each billet of the pile being four feet long.

4. *thirteen or fourteen foot long.* Twain originally said in the manuscript that the canoe is only "twelve foot long" (**MS**), but changed it when he realized how many provisions it would have to hold.

5. *drawing a bead on a bird with his gun.* Taking aim at the bird, by gradually raising the front sight, or "bead," to a level with the hindsight of the rifle.

6. *a "trot" line.* "A very long fishing-line attached to the shore at one end and perma-

A "trot" line. Illustration from *Every Saturday*, September 30, 1871.
Courtesy Library of Congress.

bucket and gourd, I took a dipper and a tin cup, and my old saw and two blankets, and the skillet and the coffee-pot. I took fish-lines and matches[9] and other things—everything that was worth a cent. I cleaned out the place. I wanted an axe, but there wasn't any, only the one out at the wood pile, and I knowed why I was going to leave that. I fetched out the gun, and now I was done.

I had wore the ground a good deal, crawling out of the hole and dragging out so many things. So I fixed that as good as I could from the outside by scattering dust on the place, which covered up the smoothness and the sawdust. Then I fixed the piece of log back into its place, and put two rocks under it and one against it to hold it there,—for it was bent up at that place, and didn't quite touch ground.[10] If you stood four or five foot away and didn't know it was sawed, you wouldn't ever notice it; and besides, this was the back of the cabin and it warn't likely anybody would go fooling around there.

It was all grass clear to the canoe; so I hadn't left a track. I followed around to see. I stood on the bank and looked out over the river. All safe. So I took the gun and went up a piece into the woods and was hunting around for some birds, when I see a wild pig; hogs soon went wild in them

SHOOTING THE PIG.

nently anchored in the water at the other. Little gangs or branch lines are attached to it at frequent intervals, and each of these has a hook at the end of it. Usually the line is examined every day by drawing a boat along under the line, which passes over the boat and falls back into the water. The fish are thus removed from the hooks, which are baited again" (Edward Eggleston in a note to the 1890 edition of *The Hoosier School-Boy*, p. 83).

7. *a log raft.* Also known as a "crib." "Beginning in the 1840s," explained Sherwood Cummings in "Mark Twain's Moveable Farm and the Evasion" (*American Literature,* September 1991), "cribs were assembled at sawmills on the banks of Wisconsin's forested rivers by layering boards, each layer at right angles to the previous one, three feet high. 'Binding planks' on top were fastened to 'foundation planks' at the bottom with 'grub pins,' and the crib was set afloat. Once such narrows and rapids as might occur in the upper rivers were negotiated, cribs were fastened together in 'strings' of six or more, and on the Mississippi before 1860 in rafts of as many as forty or fifty cribs" (p. 443). See Chapter 16 and Appendix B for one of these massive rafts.

8. *then the whisky jug.* An afterthought, probably inserted in the manuscript when Twain realized he would need it later in Chapter 10.

9. *matches.* Blair and Fisher explained in the 1988 University of California edition that "these new fangled things they call matches" (as Tom refers to them in Chapter 33 of *Tom Sawyer*) were also known as "lucifer" matches and had been patented in the United States only in 1836.

10. *for it was bent up at that place, and didn't quite touch ground.* Another afterthought, needed to explain exactly why Huck needed to put the rocks there.

bottoms[11] after they had got away from the prairie farms. I shot this fellow and took him into camp.

I took the axe and smashed in the door—I beat it and hacked it considerable, a-doing it. I fetched the pig in and took him back nearly to the table and hacked into his throat with the axe, and laid him down on the ground to bleed—I say ground, because it *was* ground—hard packed, and no boards. Well, next I took an old sack and put a lot of big rocks in it,—all I could drag—and I started it from the pig and dragged it to the door and through the woods down to the river and dumped it in, and down it sunk, out of sight. You could easy see that something had been dragged over the ground. I did wish Tom Sawyer was there,[12] I knowed he would take an interest in this kind of business, and throw in the fancy touches. Nobody could spread himself[13] like Tom Sawyer in such a thing as that.

Well, last I pulled out some of my hair, and bloodied the ax good, and stuck it on the back side, and slung the axe in the corner. Then I took up the pig and held him to my breast with my jacket (so he couldn't drip) till I got a good piece below the house and then dumped him into the river. Now I thought of something else. So I went and got the bag of meal and my old saw out of the canoe and fetched them to the house. I took the bag to where it used to stand, and ripped a hole in the bottom of it with the saw, for there warn't no knives and forks on the place—pap done everything with his clasp-knife, about the cooking.[14] Then I carried the sack about a hundred yards across the grass and through the willows east of the house, to a shallow lake that was five mile wide and full of rushes—and ducks too, you might say, in the season. There was a slough[15] or a creek leading out of it on the other side, that went miles away, I don't know where, but it didn't go to the river. The meal sifted out and made a little track all the way to the lake. I dropped pap's whetstone there too, so as to look like it had been done by accident. Then I tied up the rip in the meal sack with a string, so it wouldn't leak no more, and took it and my saw to the canoe again.

11. *bottoms*. Or "bottomlands," Western term for the rich flatlands along riverbanks.

12. *I did wish Tom Sawyer was there*. Huck may have rejected his wild fantasies in Chapter 3, but he nevertheless venerates Tom in much the same manner that Tom envies Huck in *Tom Sawyer*. He cannot help but invoke his friend's spirit of adventure throughout the progress of the novel. Nevertheless, Huck proves that he is perfectly capable of thinking for himself and getting out of "scrapes" without the aid of Tom's "fancy touches."

13. *spread himself*. Exert or display himself ostentatiously.

14. *pap done everything with his clasp-knife, about the cooking*. Twain reminded himself in the margin of the manuscript "Back yonder is mention of a butcher knife," but then he changed it to "clasp-knife." See Chapter 6, note 38.

15. *a slough*. A comparatively narrow stretch of backwater; a sluggish channel or inlet.

It was about dark, now; so I dropped the canoe down the river under some willows that hung over the bank, and waited for the moon to rise. I made fast to a willow; then I took a bite to eat, and by-and-by laid down in the canoe to smoke a pipe and lay out a plan. I says to myself, they'll follow the track of that sackful of rocks to the shore and then drag the river for me.[16] And they'll follow that meal track to the lake and go browsing down the creek that leads out of it to find the robbers that killed me and took the things. They won't ever hunt the river for anything but my dead carcass.[17] They'll soon get tired of that, and won't bother no more about me. All right; I can stop anywhere I want to. Jackson's Island[18] is good enough for me; I know that island pretty well, and nobody ever comes there. And then I can paddle over to town, nights, and slink around and pick up things I want. Jackson's Island's the place.

I was pretty tired, and the first thing I knowed, I was asleep. When I woke up I didn't know where I was, for a minute. I set up and looked around, a little scared. Then I remembered. The river looked miles and miles across. The moon was so bright I could a counted the drift logs that went a slipping along, black and still, hundred of yards out from shore. Everything was dead quiet, and it looked late, and *smelt* late. You know what I mean—I don't know the words to put it in.

I took a good gap and a stretch, and was just going to unhitch and start, when I heard a sound away over the water. I listened. Pretty soon I made it out. It was that dull kind of a regular sound that comes from oars working in rowlocks when it's a still night. I peeped out through the willow branches, and there it was—a skiff, away across the water. I couldn't tell how many was in it. It kept a-coming, and when it was abreast of me I see there warn't but one man in it. Thinks I, maybe it's pap, though I warn't expecting him. He dropped below me, with the current, and by-and-by he come a-swinging up shore in the easy water,[19] and he went by so close I could a reached out the gun and touched him. Well, it *was* pap, sure enough—and sober, too, by the way he laid to his oars.

16. *drag the river for me.* The same procedure is followed in Chapter 35 of *Tom Sawyer*, when Huck disappears after just three weeks at the widow's. "At the end of two or more lines," Harry Middleton Hyatt described the procedure in *Folk-Lore of Adams County, Illinois* (1965), "grapnel or similar hooks are attached. and these are sometimes weighted by pieces of iron slipped through the lines" (pp. 696–97).

17. *They won't ever hunt the river for anything but my dead carcass.* The first of Huck's symbolic "deaths" in the novel.

18. *Jackson's Island.* The bucolic refuge of Tom Sawyer's gang of "pirates" in Chapters 13–16 of *Tom Sawyer*; appropriately, Huck returns to the scene of his previous escape from "sivilization" when he and his companions were thought to be dead. This is Glasscock's Island, once about three miles downstream from Hannibal but now long eroded away by the river. For Twain, it always remained a sanctuary from the strains of adult life. He confessed to British novelist Walter Besant in a letter of February 22, 1898 (now in the Berg Collection, New York Public Library), "I suppose we all have a Jackson's Island somewhere, and dream of it when we are tired." Twain's boyhood friend Barnett C. Farthing recalled that it was also a haven for runaway slaves "who sometmes 'twas said lurked in the dense thickets of trees and brush which then covered the island" (quoted in David E. E. Sloane and Sherri Farley, " 'My Uncle B.C.M. Farley, the *Original* Huckleberry Finn,' " *Mark Twain Journal*, Fall 1994, p. 38).

19. *the easy water.* "Not much current," Twain noted in Chapter 9 of *Life on the Mississippi*.

I didn't lose no time. The next minute I was a-spinning down stream soft but quick in the shade of the bank. I made two mile and a half, and then struck out a quarter of a mile or more towards the middle of the river, because pretty soon I would be passing the ferry landing and people might see me and hail me. I got out amongst the drift-wood and then laid down in the bottom of the canoe and let her float. I laid there and had a good rest and a smoke out of my pipe, looking away into the sky, not a cloud in it. The sky looks ever so deep when you lay down on your back in the moonshine; I never knowed it before. And how far a body can hear on the water such nights! I heard people talking at the ferry landing. I heard what they said, too, every word of it. One man said it was getting towards the long days and the short nights, now. 'Tother one said *this* warn't one of the short ones, he reckoned—and then they laughed, and he said it over again and they laughed again; then they waked up another fellow and told him, and laughed, but he didn't laugh; he ripped out something brisk[20] and said let him alone. The first fellow said he 'lowed to tell it to his old woman—she would think it was pretty good; but he said that warn't nothing to some things he had said in his time. I heard one man say it was nearly three o'clock, and he hoped daylight wouldn't wait more than about a week

20. *ripped out something brisk.* Uttered violently, swore.

TAKING A REST.

21. *a ripping rate*. An especially rapid rate.

22. *the dead water*. Calm, without any current.

23. *stabboard*. Or "starboard," the right-hand side of a vessel.

longer. After that, the talk got further and further away, and I couldn't make out the words any more, but I could hear the mumble; and now and then a laugh, too, but it seemed a long ways off.

I was away below the ferry now. I rose up and there was Jackson's Island, about two mile and a half down stream, heavy-timbered and standing up out of the middle of the river, big and dark and solid, like a steamboat without any lights. There warn't any signs of the bar at the head—it was all under water, now.

It didn't take me long to get there. I shot past the head at a ripping rate,[21] the current was so swift, and then I got into the dead water[22] and landed on the side towards the Illinois shore. I run the canoe into a deep dent in the bank that I knowed about; I had to part the willow branches to get in; and when I made fast nobody could a seen the canoe from the outside.

I went up and set down on a log at the head of the island and looked out on the big river and the black driftwood, and away over to the town, three mile away, where there was three or four lights twinkling. A monstrous big lumber raft was about a mile up stream, coming along down, with a lantern in the middle of it. I watched it come creeping down, and when it was most abreast of where I stood I heard a man say, "Stern oars, there! heave her head to stabboard!"[23] I heard that just as plain as if the man was by my side.

There was a little gray in the sky, now; so I stepped into the woods and laid down for a nap before breakfast.

Chapter VIII

IN THE WOODS.

The SUN was up so high when I waked,[1] that I judged it was after eight o'clock. I laid there in the grass and the cool shade, thinking about things and feeling rested and ruther comfortable and satisfied. I could see the sun out at one or two holes, but mostly it was big trees all about, and gloomy in there amongst them. There was freckled places on the ground where the light sifted down through the leaves, and the freckled places swapped about a little, showing there was a little breeze up there. A couple of squirrels set on a limb and jabbered at me very friendly.

I was powerful lazy and comfortable—didn't want to get up and cook breakfast. Well, I was dozing off again, when I thinks I hears a deep sound of "boom!" away up the river. I rouses up and rests on my elbow and listens; pretty soon I hears it again. I hopped up and went and looked out at a hole in the leaves, and I see a bunch of smoke laying on the water a long ways up—about abreast the ferry. And there was the ferry-boat full of people, floating along down. I knowed what was the matter, now. "Boom!" I see the white smoke squirt out of the ferry-boat's side. You see, they was firing cannon over the water, trying to make my carcass come to the top.[2]

1. *The sun was up so high when I waked.* This chapter is reminiscent of Chapter 14 of *Tom Sawyer*: Both open with a sunrise on Jackson Island and describe the firing of cannon over the water to raise the bodies of boys who have *not* drowned. Also, Kemble's picture for the chapter opening looks remarkably like True W. Williams's in *Tom Sawyer*.

CHAPTER XIV.

WHEN Tom awoke in the morning, he wondered where he was. He sat up and rubbed his eyes and looked around. Then he comprehended. It was the cool gray dawn, and there was a delicious sense of repose and peace in the deep pervading calm and silence of the woods. Not a leaf stirred; not a sound obtruded upon great Nature's meditation. Beaded dew-drops stood upon the leaves and grasses. A white layer of ashes covered the fire, and a thin blue breath of smoke rose straight into the air. Joe and Huck still slept.

Now, far away in the woods a bird called; another answered; presently the hammering of a woodpecker was heard. Gradually the cool dim gray of the morning whitened, and as gradually sounds multiplied and life manifested itself. The marvel of Nature shaking off

121

Opening page of Chapter 14, with illustration by True W. Williams, *The Adventures of Tom Sawyer*, 1876. *Private collection.*

2. *they was firing cannon over the water, trying to make my carcass come to the top.* According to British superstition, the explosion from a can-

The search for the drowned. Illustration by True W. Williams, *The Adventures of Tom Sawyer*, 1876.
Private collection.

I was pretty hungry, but it warn't going to do for me to start a fire, because they might see the smoke. So I set there and watched the cannon-smoke and listened to the boom. The river was a mile wide, there, and it always looks pretty on a summer morning—so I was having a good enough time seeing them hunt for my remainders, if I only had a bite to eat. Well, then I happened to think how they always put quicksilver in loaves of bread and float them off because they always go right to the drownded carcass and stop there.[3] So says I, I'll keep a lookout, and if any of them's floating around after me, I'll give them a show. I

WATCHING THE BOAT.

changed to the Illinois edge of the island to see what luck I could have, and I warn't disappointed. A big double loaf come along, and I most got it, with a long stick, but my foot slipped and she floated out further. Of course I was where the current set in the closest to the shore—I knowed enough for that. But by-and-by along comes another one, and this time I won. I took out the plug and shook out the

non causes a concussion that breaks the gall-bladder and causes the body to float. Sam Clemens witnessed this procedure when the people of Hannibal thought he had drowned. "I jumped overboard from the ferry boat in the middle of the river that stormy day to get my hat," he wrote in a letter of February 6, 1870, to a childhood friend Will Bowen, "and swam two or three miles after it (and *got* it), while all the town collected on the wharf and for an hour or so looked out across the angry waste of 'white caps' toward where people said Sam Clemens was last seen before he went down" (*Huck Finn and Tom Sawyer Among the Indians*, 1989, p. 21). Another boy died in the river, for Twain noted in 1902 that they "fired cannon to raise drowned bodies of Clint Levering and me—when I escaped from the ferry boat" (University of California edition, 1988, p. 385). He was apparently the boy who Twain called "Lem Hackett" in Chapter 54 of *Life on the Mississippi*. Twain also recalled the custom in Chapter 14 of *Tom Sawyer*, when Huck, Tom, and Joe Harper run off to Jackson's Island to play pirates. It was a foregone conclusion along the river that if someone was missing, the person obviously had drowned and sunk to the bottom. "There was a foolish superstition of some little prevalence in that day," Twain explained in a note to Chapter 27 of *Life on the Mississippi*, "that the Mississippi would neither buoy up a swimmer, nor permit a drowned person's body to rise to the surface."

3. *they always put quicksilver in loaves of bread and float them off because they always go right to*

little dab of quicksilver, and set my teeth in. It was "baker's bread"[4]—what the quality eat—none of your low-down corn-pone.[5]

I got a good place amongst the leaves, and set there on a log, munching the bread[6] and watching the ferry-boat, and very well satisfied. And then something struck me. I says, now I reckon the widow or the parson or somebody prayed that this bread would find me,[7] and here it has gone and done it. So there ain't no doubt but there is something in that thing. That is, there's something in it when a body like the widow or the parson prays, but it don't work for me, and I reckon it don't work for only just the right kind.

I lit a pipe and had a good long smoke and went on watching. The ferry-boat was floating with the current, and I allowed I'd have a chance to see who was aboard when she come along, because she would come in close, where the bread did. When she'd got pretty well along down towards me, I put out my pipe and went to where I fished out the bread, and laid down behind a log on the bank in a little open place. Where the log forked I could peep through.

By-and-by she come along, and she drifted in so close that they could a run out a plank and walked ashore. Most everybody was on the boat.[8] Pap, and Judge Thatcher, and Bessie Thatcher,[9] and Jo Harper, and Tom Sawyer, and his old Aunt Polly, and Sid[10] and Mary, and plenty more. Everybody was talking about the murder, but the captain broke in and says:

"Look sharp, now; the current sets in the closest here, and maybe he's washed ashore and got tangled amongst the brush at the water's edge. I hope so, anyway."

I didn't hope so. They all crowded up and leaned over the rails, nearly in my face, and kept still, watching with all their might. I could see them first-rate, but they couldn't see me. Then the captain sung out:

"Stand away!" and the cannon let off such a blast right before me that it made me deef with the noise and pretty near blind with the smoke, and I judged I was gone. If they'd a had some bullets in, I reckon they'd a got the corpse they was after. Well, I see I warn't hurt, thanks to

the drownded carcass and stop there. Another British superstition was that a hollowed-out loaf of bread, filled with mercury (which is insoluble in water) and blessed by clergy, would float to where a body lay. H. M. Belden in "Scyld Scefing and Huck Finn" (*Modern Language Notes*, May 1918, p. 315) traced this practice to an ancient British rite of divination by shield, sheaf, and candle: "It is precisely the bread, the staff of life, the modern representative of the medieval sheaf, by which the divination is wrought. The quicksilver in place of the candle seems to be the case of metallurgy displacing medieval devotion" (p. 315). However, in Chapter 14 of *Tom Sawyer*, Tom argues just the opposite: "'Oh, it ain't the bread, so much,' said Tom; 'I reckon its mostly what they *say* over it before they start it out.' 'But they don't say anything over it,' said Huck. 'I've seen 'em, and they don't.' 'Well, that's funny,' said Tom. 'But maybe they say it to themselves. Of *course* they do. Anybody might know that.' The other boys agreed that there was reason in what Tom said, because an ignorant lump of bread, uninstructed by incantation, could not be expected to act very intelligently when sent upon an errand of such gravity." Edgar M. Branch in "Mark Twain: Newspaper Reading and Creativity" (*Nineteenth-Century Fiction*, March 1983) quoted an article about this practice, "Finding Drowned Persons by Quicksilver" (St. Louis *Missouri Democrat*, August 16, 1859): "After a long and almost hopeless search after the body, a very novel idea was suggested. . . . About three ounces of quicksilver were put into a loaf of *brown bread*, well baked, and thrown out into the lake. The loaf was discovered to move directly *against the wind*; soon it stopped, whirled round several times and sank" (p. 579). And there the body of the young man was found seventy feet below the water. As late as September 15, 1926, the New York *Times* reported how the Connecticut State Police successfully located the body of a drowned woman by floating loaves of bread on Lake Zoar, near Newtown.

4. *"baker's bread."* Or "store-bought bread" made from white wheat flour, then a luxury.

5. *low-down corn-pone*. Cornmeal mixed with a tablespoon of salt and water, then baked in a skillet or small oven; an Indian dish which was particularly meager fare. Remarkably, John Russell Bartlett in his *Dictionary of Americanisms* defined this as "a superior kind of corn goodness. The boat floated on and went out of sight around the shoulder of the island. I could hear the booming, now and then, further and further off, and by-and-by after an hour, I didn't hear it no more. The island was three mile long. I judged they had got to the foot, and was giving it up. But they didn't yet a while. They turned around the foot of the island and started up the channel on the Missouri side, under steam, and booming once in a while as they went. I crossed over to that side and watched them. When they got abreast the head of the island they quit shooting and dropped over to the Missouri shore and went home to the town.

I knowed I was all right now. Nobody else would come a-hunting after me. I got my traps[11] out of the canoe and made me a nice camp in the thick woods. I made a kind of a tent out of my blankets to put my things under so the rain couldn't get at them. I catched a cat-fish and haggled him open[12] with my saw, and towards sundown I started my camp fire and had supper. Then I set out a line to catch some fish for breakfast.

When it was dark I set by my camp fire smoking, and feeling pretty satisfied; but by-and-by it got sort of lonesome, and so I went and set on the bank and listened to the currents washing along, and counted the stars and drift-logs and rafts that come down, and then went to bed; there ain't no better way to put in time when you are lonesome; you can't stay so, you soon get over it.

And so for three days and nights. No difference—just the same thing. But the next day I went exploring around down through the island. I was boss of it; it all belonged to me, so to say, and I wanted to know all about it; but mainly I wanted to put in the time. I found plenty strawberries, ripe and prime; and green summer-grapes,[13] and green razberries; and the green blackberries was just beginning to show. They would all come handy by-and-by,[14] I judged.

Well, I went fooling along in the deep woods till I judged I warn't far from the foot of the island. I had my gun along, but I hadn't shot nothing; it was for protection; thought I would kill some game nigh home. About this time

bread" (p. 148). It was a staple of a slave's diet at the time, as basic as baked bread. One of the sermons delivered by "a gay and impudent and satirical and delightful young black man" fifteen-year-old Sam Clemens knew back in Hannibal was based on the text "You tell me whar a man gits his corn-pone, en I'll tell you what his 'pinions is." This pragmatic aphorism evolved into "Corn-Pone Opinions," an essay embodying one of Twain's central beliefs, "that a man is not independent, and cannot afford views which might interfere with his bread and butter." It was first printed as Twain wrote it in *What Is Man?*, edited by Paul Baender, 1973, pp. 92–97.

6. *munching the bread.* Another idea Twain jotted down in his notes but later abandoned concerned Huck's "reflections upon the satisfaction of being a guest at one's own funeral and with such prime refreshments furnished free" (Blair and Fischer, University of California edition, 1988, p. 752). He probably dropped it because it was too similar to incidents in Chapter 17 of *Tom Sawyer*.

7. *the widow or the parson or somebody prayed that this bread would find me.* A reference to Ecclesiastes 11:1: "Cast thy bread upon the waters: for thou shalt find it after many days." The allusion is more evident in some commentary in his notes for the novel which did not make it into the finished book: "And bread cast *returns*—which it don't and can't, less'n you heave it upstream—you cast your bread downstream once, and see. It can't stem the current; so it can't come back no more. But the widow she didn't know no better than to believe it, and it warn't my business to correct my betters. There's a heap of ignorance like that, around" (Blair and Fischer, University of California edition, 1988, p. 752). Twain probably intended this to go in Chapter 1 as an alternative lesson to the one about Moses and the bulrushes, to foreshadow the floating bread filled with quicksilver in search of Huck.

8. *Most everybody was on the boat.* Nearly the entire cast of *Tom Sawyer*, in fact. Huck seems to be symbolically saying goodbye to his past, to both St. Petersburg and the former novel.

9. *Bessie Thatcher.* Confused, Twain scribbled in his notes to the novel, " 'Bessie' or 'Becky'?" (University of California edition, 1988, p. 751).

I mighty near stepped on a good sized snake, and it went sliding off through the grass and flowers, and I after it, trying to get a shot at it. I clipped along, and all of a sudden I bounded right on to the ashes of a camp fire that was still smoking.[15]

My heart jumped up amongst my lungs. I never waited for to look further, but uncocked my gun and went sneaking back on my tip-toes as fast as ever I could. Every now and then I stopped a second, amongst the thick leaves, and listened; but my breath come so hard I couldn't hear nothing else. I slunk along another piece further, then listened again; and so on, and so on; if I see a stump, I took it for a

DISCOVERING THE CAMP FIRE.

man; if I trod on a stick and broke it, it made me feel like a person had cut one of my breaths in two and I only got half, and the short half, too.

When I got to camp I warn't feeling very brash, there warn't much sand in my craw;[16] but I says, this ain't no time to be fooling around. So I got all my traps into my canoe again so as to have them out of sight, and I put out

Becky Thatcher. Illustration by True W. Williams, *The Adventures of Tom Sawyer*, 1876.
Private collection.

Carelessly, he never bothered to check *Tom Sawyer*, where she is introduced as Tom Sawyer's childhood sweetheart. But no matter: Huck Finn probably does not know the girl well, and could easily get her name wrong. He also misspells "Joe Harper." Becky Thatcher was modeled on Anna Laura Hawkins (later Frazer; 1837–1928), always known as Laura Hawkins and Sam Clemens's "first sweetheart," who lived across the street from him in Hannibal. He recalled her in "Villagers of 1840–43" of 1897 as a "pretty little creature" (*Huck Finn and Tom Sawyer Among the Indians*, 1989, p. 95). "We were boy and girl sweethearts, Sam Clemens and I," she said in "Mark Twain's Childhood Sweetheart Recalls Their Romance" (*Literary Digest*, March 23, 1918). "I think I must have liked Sam Clemens the very first time I saw him. He was different from the other boys. I didn't know then, of course, what it was that made him different, but afterward, when my knowledge of the world and its people grew, I realized that it was his natural refinement" (p. 73). Clemens dined with her on his last visit to Hannibal in 1902; and she and her granddaughter came out to see him at Stormfield in Redding, Connecticut, in 1908, two years before his the fire and scattered the ashes around to look like an old last year's camp, and then clumb a tree.

I reckon I was up in the tree two hours; but I didn't see nothing, I didn't hear nothing—I only *thought* I heard and seen as much as a thousand things. Well, I couldn't stay up there forever; so at last I got down, but I kept in the thick woods and on the lookout all the time. All I could get to eat was berries and what was left over from breakfast.

By the time it was night I was pretty hungry. So when it was good and dark, I slid out from shore before moonrise and paddled over to the Illinois bank—about a quarter of a mile. I went out in the woods and cooked a supper, and I had about made up my mind I would stay there all night, when I hear a *plunkety-plunk, plunkety-plunk,* and says to myself, horses coming; and next I hear people's voices. I got everything into the canoe as quick as I could, and then went creeping through the woods to see what I could find out. I hadn't got far when I hear a man say:

"We better camp here, if we can find a good place; the horses is about beat out. Let's look around."

I didn't wait, but shoved out and paddled away easy. I tied up in the old place, and reckoned I would sleep in the canoe.

I didn't sleep much. I couldn't, somehow, for thinking. And every time I waked up I thought somebody had me by the neck. So the sleep didn't do me no good. By-and-by I says to myself, I can't live this way; I'm agoing to find out who it is that's here on the island with me; I'll find it out or bust. Well, I felt better, right off.

So I took my paddle and slid out from shore just a step or two, and then let the canoe drop along down amongst the shadows. The moon was shining, and outside of the shadows it made it most as light as day. I poked along well onto an hour, everything still as rocks and sound asleep.[17] Well by this time I was most down to the foot of the island. A little ripply, cool breeze begun to blow, and that was as good as saying the night was about done. I give her a turn with the paddle and brung her nose to shore; then I got my gun and slipped out and into the edge of the woods. I set down

Joe Harper. Illustration by True W. Williams, *The Adventures of Tom Sawyer*, 1876. *Private collection.*

death. His daughter Clara Clemens greeted her, "You are *Becky Thatcher*, and I'm happy to see you" (p. 74). There he presented her with his photograph, signed "To Laura Fraser [*sic*], with the love of her earliest sweetheart" (now at the Mark Twain Shrine, Mark Twain State Park, Florida, Missouri). The place where she grew up is now the Becky Thatcher House in Hannibal.

10. *Sid.* Tom Sawyer's "younger brother (or rather, half-brother)," in Chapter 1 of *Tom Sawyer*; based on Sam Clemens's brother Henry (1838–1858). "He is 'Sid' in *Tom Sawyer*," Twain admitted in "Chapters from My Autobiography" (*North American Review*, November 2, 1906). "But Sid was not Henry. Henry was a very much finer and better boy than ever Sid was" (p. 838). Henry Clemens died after the steamboat he was working on blew up; whether he died from his injuries or a carelessly injected dose of morphine is not known for certain. See also Chapter 32, note 16.

11. *traps.* Trappings, belongings.

12. *haggled him open.* Cut him open.

13. *summer-grapes.* North American wild grapes.

there on a log and looked out through the leaves. I see the moon go off watch and the darkness begin to blanket the river. But in a little while I see a pale streak over the tree-tops, and knowed the day was coming. So I took my gun and slipped off towards where I had run across that camp fire, stopping every minute or two to listen. But I hadn't no luck, somehow; I couldn't seem to find the place. But by-and-by, sure enough, I catched a glimpse of fire, away through the trees. I went for it, cautious and slow. By-and-by I was close enough to have a look, and there laid a man on the ground. It most give me the fan-tods.[18] He had a blanket around his head, and his head was nearly in the fire.[19] I set there behind a clump of bushes, in about six foot of him, and kept my eyes on him steady. It was getting gray daylight, now. Pretty soon he gapped, and stretched himself, and hove off the blanket, and it was Miss Watson's Jim! I bet I was glad to see him. I says:

"Hello, Jim!" and skipped out.

He bounced up and stared at me wild. Then he drops down on his knees, and puts his hands together and says:

"Doan' hurt me—don't! I hain't ever done no harm to a ghos'. I awluz liked dead people, en done all I could for 'em. You go en git in de river agin, whah you b'longs,[20] en doan' do nuffn to Ole Jim, 'at 'uz awluz yo' fren'."

Sid Sawyer. Illustration by True W. Williams, *The Adventures of Tom Sawyer*, 1876.
Private collection.

14. *They would all come handy by-and-by.* Evidently Huck intends to hide out on the island for some time.

15. *all of a sudden I bounded right on to the ashes of a camp fire that was still smoking.* Huck's fears on discovering the traces of other human life on what he thinks is a deserted island were

JIM AND THE GHOST.

"He bounced up and stared at me." Illustration by E. W. Kemble, New York *World*, December 10, 1899.
Private collection.

apparently inspired by Daniel Defoe's *Robinson Crusoe* (1719), in which the hero stumbles on "the print of a man's naked foot on the shore" on *his* island: "I stood like one thunder-struck . . . ; I listened, I looked round me, I could hear nothing, nor see . . . no other impression but that one. . . . But after innumerable fluttering thoughts, like a man perfectly confused and out of my self, I came home to my fortification, not feeling, as we say, the ground I went on, but terrify'd to the last degree, looking behind me at every two or three steps, mistaking every bush and tree, and fancying every stump at a distance to be a man; nor is it possible to describe how many various shapes affrighted imagination represented things to me in, how many wild ideas were found every moment in my fancy, and what strange unaccountable whimsies came into my thoughts by the way." Twain noted in Chapter 2 of *Life on the Mississippi* that the early French explorers "one day came upon the footprints of men in the mud of the western bank—a Robinson Crusoe experience which carries an electric shiver with it yet, when one stumbles upon it in print." He used a similar device earlier in Chapter 31 of *Tom Sawyer*. "We have always thought," Brander Matthews admit-

Robinson Crusoe finds the footprint in the sand. Illustration by George Cruikshank, *The Life and Times of Robinson Crusoe* by Daniel Defoe, 1831.
Courtesy Library of Congress.

Well, I warn't long making him understand I warn't dead. I was ever so glad to see Jim. I warn't lonesome, now. I told him I warn't afraid of *him* telling the people where I was. I talked along, but he only set there and looked at me; never said nothing. Then I says:

"It's good daylight. Le's get breakfast. Make up your camp fire good."

"What's de use er makin' up de camp fire to cook strawbries en sich truck?[21] But you got a gun, hain't you? Den we kin git sumfn better den strawbries."

"Strawberries and such truck," I says. "Is that what you live on?"

"I couldn' git nuffn else," he says.

"Why, how long you been on the island, Jim?"

"I come heah de night arter you's killed."

"What, all that time?"

"Yes-indeedy."

"And ain't you had nothing but that kind of rubbage[22] to eat?"

"No, sah—nuffn else."

"Well, you must be most starved, ain't you?'

"I reck'n I could eat a hoss. I think I could. How long you ben on de islan'?"

"Since the night I got killed."

"No! W'y, what has you lived on? But you got a gun. Oh, yes, you got a gun. Dat's good. Now you kill sumfn en I'll make up de fire."

So we went over to where the canoe was, and while he built a fire in a grassy open place amongst the trees, I fetched meal and bacon and coffee, and coffee-pot and frying-pan, and sugar and tin cups, and the nigger was set back considerable, because he reckoned it was all done with witchcraft. I catched a good big cat-fish, too, and Jim cleaned him with his knife, and fried him.

When breakfast was ready, we lolled on the grass and eat it smoking hot. Jim laid it in with all his might, for he was most about starved. Then when we had got pretty well stuffed, we laid off and lazied.

By-and-by Jim says:

"But looky here, Huck, who wuz it dat 'uz killed in dat shanty, ef it warn't you?"

Then I told him the whole thing, and he said it was smart. He said Tom Sawyer couldn't get up no better plan than what I had.[23] Then I says:

"How do you come to be here, Jim, and how'd you get here?"

He looked pretty uneasy, and didn't say nothing for a minute. Then he says:

"Maybe I better not tell."

"Why, Jim?"

"Well, dey's reasons. But you wouldn' tell on me ef I 'uz to tell you, would you, Huck?"

"Blamed if I would, Jim."

"Well, I b'lieve you, Huck. I—I *run off.*"[24]

"Jim!"

"But mind, you said you wouldn't tell—you know you said you wouldn't tell, Huck."

"Well, I did. I said I wouldn't, and I'll stick to it.[25] Honest *injun*[26] I will.[27] People would call me a low down Ablitionist and despise me for keeping mum[28]—but that don't make no difference. I ain't agoing to tell, and I ain't agoing back there anyways. So now, le's know all about it."

"Well, you see, it 'uz dis way. Ole Missus—dat's Miss Watson—she pecks on me all de time, en treats me pooty rough, but she awluz said she wouldn' sell me down to Orleans.[29] But I noticed dey wuz a nigger trader[30] roun' de place considable, lately, en I begin to git oneasy. Well, one night I creeps to de do', pooty late, en de do' warn't quite shet, en I hear ole missus tell de widder she gwyne to sell me down to Orleans, but she didn' want to, but she could git eight hund'd dollars for me,[31] en it 'uz sich a big stack o' money she couldn' resis'. De widder she try to git her to say she wouldn' do it,[32] but I never waited to hear de res'. I lit out mighty quick, I tell you.

"I tuck out en shin down de hill en 'spec to steal a skift 'long de sho' som'ers 'bove de town, but dey wuz people a-stirrin' yit, so I hid in de ole tumble-down cooper shop[33] on de bank to wait for everybody to go 'way. Well, I wuz dah

ted in his review of *Huckleberry Finn* in London *Saturday Review* (January 31, 1885), "that the vision of the hand in the cave in *Tom Sawyer* is one of the very finest things in the literature of adventure since Robinson Crusoe first saw a single footprint in the sand of the seashore."

It is appropriate that Twain should evoke the very first sign of Friday on Crusoe's island while introducing the fugitive slave Jim. Also, although *Robinson Crusoe* takes place somewhere off the coast of South America, Friday was often depicted in nineteenth-century American popular culture (and still is) as being African rather than Native American. Huck feels the same great pangs of loneliness that Crusoe does on his deserted island until he bonds with Friday, a brotherly union between an Englishman and a man of another race which like Huck and Jim's would be sneered at back in "sivilization." See also Chapter 9, note 20.

16. *there warn't much sand in my craw.* I didn't have much courage left.

17. *I poked along well onto an hour, everything still as rocks and sound asleep.* Twain originally had in the manuscript "I drifted well onto an hour, and everything still as death, except that kind of creatures that always making noises in the night" (**MS**); but he may have thought the sentiment too poetic for a semiliterate backwoods boy.

18. *give me the fan-tods.* Give me the fidgets, the "creeps," the "jimjams"; made me nervous; supposedly from "fantasy." Macabre artist Edward Gorey appropriately named his press "The Fantod Press."

19. *He had a blanket around his head, and his head was nearly in the fire.* Harold Beaver in "Run, Nigger, Run: *Adventures of Huckleberry Finn* as a Fugitive Slave Narrative" (*Journal of American Studies*, December 1974) suggested that Jim must have grown up on a farm, because of this custom of the country slave to sleep with a blanket around the head and near the fire; Beaver said that Indians slept with their feet to the heat. "Negroes glory in a close, hot atmosphere," insisted race theorist Dr. Samuel A. Cartwright in *Natural History of the Prognathous Species of Man* (1857); "they instinctively cover their head and faces with a blanket at night, and prefer laying with their heads to the fire instead of their feet" (p. 342).

all night. Dey wuz somebody roun' all de time. 'Long 'bout six in de mawnin', skifts begin to go by, en 'bout eight er nine every skift dat went 'long wuz talkin' 'bout how yo' pap come over to de town en say you's killed. Dese las' skifts wuz full o' ladies en genlmen agoin' over for to see de place.[34] Sometimes dey'd pull up at de sho' en take a res' b'fo' dey started acrost, so by de talk I got to know all 'bout de killin'. I 'uz powerful sorry you's killed, Huck, but I ain't no mo', now.

"I laid dah under de shavins all day. I 'uz hungry, but I warn't afeared; bekase I knowed ole missus en de widder wuz goin' to start to de camp-meetn'[35] right arter breakfas' en be gone all day, en dey knows I goes off wid de cattle 'bout daylight, so dey wouldn' 'spec to see me roun' de place, en so dey wouldn' miss me tell arter dark in de evenin'. De yuther servants wouldn' miss me, kase dey'd shin out en take holiday, soon as de ole folks 'uz out'n de way.

"Well, when it come dark I tuck out up de river road, en went 'bout two mile er more to whah dey warn't no houses. I'd made up my mine 'bout what I's agwyne to do. You see ef I kep' on tryin' to git away afoot, de dogs 'ud track me; ef I stole a skift to cross over, dey'd miss dat skift, you see, en dey'd know 'bout whah I'd lan' on de yuther side en whah to pick up my track. So I says, a raff is what I's arter; it doan' *make* no track.

"I see a light a-comin' roun' de p'int, bymeby, so I wade' in en shove' a log ahead o' me, en swum more'n half-way acrost de river, en got in 'mongst de drift-wood, en kep' my head down low, en kinder swum agin de current tell de raff come along. Den I swum to de stern uv it, en tuck aholt. It clouded up en 'uz pooty dark for a little while. So I clumb up en laid down on de planks. De men 'uz all 'way yonder in de middle, whah de lantern wuz. De river wuz arisin' en dey wuz a good current; so I reck'n'd 'at by fo' in de mawnin' I'd be twenty-five mile down de river, en den I'd slip in, jis' b'fo' daylight, en swim asho' en take to de woods on de Illinoi side.[36]

"But I didn' have no luck. When we 'uz mos' down to de

20. *You go en git in de river agin, whah you b'longs.* Because they were not properly buried with benefit of clergy, ghosts of the unrecovered bodies of the drowned were said to be restless and wander aimlessly along riverbanks. "The Ancients [in Greece and Rome] believed that Charon was not permitted to ferry over the Ghosts of unburied persons," Francis Grose explained in *A Provincial Glossary* (1787), "but that they wandered up and down the banks of the river Styx for an hundred years."

21. *truck.* Stuff, market produce, "garden-truck," "market-truck"; groceries.

22. *rubbage.* An unintended portmanteau word combining "rubbish" and "garbage."

23. *He said Tom Sawyer couldn't get up no better plan than what I had.* Remarkably, Jim venerates Tom Sawyer's ingenuity as much as Huck does.

24. *I—I* run off. Twain reminded himself in his 1895–1896 public reading copy: "Pantomime of looking around for listeners."

25. *I said I wouldn't, and I'll stick to it.* It was not Tom Blankenship, the model for Huckleberry Finn, but rather his big brother Benson whose history Twain recalled in Huck's promise not to tell on Jim. As reported in Dixon Wecter, *Sam Clemens of Hannibal* (1952, p. 148), Benson befriended a runaway slave whom he came across while fishing off an island opposite Hannibal, Missouri, in Pike County, Illinois, the summer of 1847. Ignoring a posted reward of $50 and defying possible conviction for aiding a fugitive, he brought him food and remained silent for days about the man's hideout; then some woodchoppers flushed him out, and he disappeared in the swamp. "While some of our citizens were fishing a few days since on Sny Island," reported the Hannibal *Journal* on August 9, "they discovered in what is called Bird Slough the body of a negro man. On examination of the body, they found it to answer the description of a runaway from Neriam Todd, of Howard County. . . . The body when discovered was much mutilated." One of "our citizens" was young Sam Clemens: Twain told Albert Bigelow Paine in *Mark Twain: A Biography* (vol. 1, 1912, p. 64) that he and some friends had been exploring in the area, perhaps looking for berries or pecans, when suddenly rose a man about half head er de islan', a man begin to come aft wid de lantern. I see it warn't no use fer to wait, so I slid overboad, en struck out fer de islan'. Well, I had a notion I could lan' mos' anywhers, but I couldn't—bank too bluff. I 'uz mos' to de foot er de islan' b'fo' I foun' a good place. I went into de woods en jedged I wouldn' fool wid raffs no mo', long as dey move de lantern roun' so. I had my pipe en a plug er dog-leg,[37] en some matches in my cap, en dey warn't wet, so I 'uz all right."

"And so you ain't had no meat nor bread to eat all this time? Why didn't you get mud-turkles?"

"How you gwyne to git'm? You can't slip up on um en grab um; en how's a body gwyne to hit um wid a rock? How could a body do it in de night? en I warn't gwyne to show mysef on de bank in de daytime."

"Well, that's so. You've had to keep in the woods all the time, of course. Did you hear 'em shooting the cannon?"

"Oh, yes. I knowed dey was arter you. I see um go by heah; watched um thoo de bushes."

Some young birds come along, flying a yard or two at a time and lighting. Jim said it was a sign it was going to rain. He said it was a sign when young chickens flew that way,[38] and so he reckoned it was the same way when young birds done it. I was going to catch some of them, but Jim wouldn't let me. He said it was death. He said his father laid mighty sick once, and some of them catched a bird, and his old granny said his father would die, and he did.[39]

And Jim said you musn't count the things you are going to cook for dinner,[40] because that would bring bad luck. The same if you shook the table-cloth after sundown.[41] And he said if a man owned a bee-hive, and that man died, the bees must be told about it before sun-up next morning,[42] or else the bees would all weaken down and quit work and die. Jim said bees wouldn't sting idiots;[43] but I didn't believe that, because I had tried them lots of times myself, and they wouldn't sting me.

I had heard about some of these things before, but not all of them. Jim knowed all kinds of signs. He said he knowed most everything. I said it looked to me like all the signs was

length out of the water. Terrified that the dead man might be after them, the boys tore back to town.

26. *Honest* injun. Although originally a sarcastic allusion to the Indian's purported propensity for thievery, it acquired its meaning from the myth of the "noble savage," popularized by Jean-Jacques Rousseau, Chateaubriand, and James Fenimore Cooper. In the unfinished "Huck Finn and Tom Sawyer Among the Indians," Tom Sawyer, who has been reading such fictions, tells Huck the romantic white man's view of the "Injun": "They're the noblest human beings that's ever been in the world. . . . [I]f an Injun tells you a thing, you can bet on it every time for the petrified fact; because you can't get an Injun to lie, he would cut his tongue out first. If you trust to a white man's honor, you better look out; but you trust to an Injun's honor, and nothing in the world can make him betray you—he would die first, and be glad to. An Injun is *all* honor. It's what they're *made* of" (*Huck Finn and Tom Sawyer Among the Indians*, 1989, p. 35). But Twain did not believe in this popular notion: Soon after the boy makes this statement, the Indians massacre a band of settlers who trusted them. Twain wrote a scathing rebuttal to the romantic notion of "The Noble Red Man" in *The Galaxy* (September 1870) polluted with such racist phrases as "nothing but a poor, filthy, naked scurvy vagabond," "base and treacherous, and hateful in every way," "a skulking coward and windy braggart, who strikes without warning," and "the skum of the earth!" (pp. 427–28). Injun Joe, the grave robber and murderer in *Tom Sawyer*, embodies all that Twain hated about native people. He later modified his opinions. "In Canada the Indians are peaceful and contented enough," he told the Calcutta *Englishman* (February 8, 1896). "In the United States there are continual rows with the Government, which invariably end with the red men being shot down. . . . I attribute it to the greater humanity with which the Indians are treated in Canada. In the States we shut them off into a reservation, which we frequently encroached upon. Then ensued trouble. The red men killed settlers, and of course the Government had to order our troops and put them down. If an Indian kills a white man he is sure to lose his life, but if a white man kills a redskin he never suffers according to law." Even then he had far to go toward full tolerance. See Helen L. Harris, "Mark Twain's Responses to the Native

American," *American Literature* (January 1975), pp. 495–505.

27. *I will.* Huck originally added here, "There—shake on it" (**MS**); but that was something no white boy, not even good-hearted Huck Finn, was likely to do at this time in this part of the country. The shaking of hands represents a bond between equals, and even Huck is not yet ready to acknowledge equality with a slave at this point in the story.

28. *People would call me a low down Ablitionist and despise me for keeping mum.* "All you had to do was to slip up behind a man and say Abolitionist if you wanted to see him jump, and see the cold sweat come," Huck says in the unfinished story "Tom Sawyer's Conspiracy" (in *Huck Finn and Tom Sawyer Among the Indians*, 1989, p. 143). The growth of abolitionism in the 1830s called for the total eradication of human slavery in America. Southern slaveholders particularly hated the radical wing that called for this reform by any means possible, regardless of political results or of constitutional guarantees to slaveholders. "It is our opinion that the emissaries of negro-stealing societies are prowling about the country, exciting the slave population to insubordination, and enticing them away

Abolitionists and runaways in jail in Palmyra, Missouri, 1841. Wood engraving in George Thompson's *Prison Life and Reflections*, 1897.
Courtesy Library of Congress.

from their masters," warned the Hannibal *Missouri Courier* (November 10, 1853). "It would be well for everybody to keep a good look-out for such characters; but, at the same time, due care

about bad luck, and so I asked him if there warn't any good-luck signs. He says:

"Mighty few—an' *dey* ain' no use to a body. What you want to know when good luck's a-comin' for?[44] want to keep it off?" And he said: "Ef you's got hairy arms en a hairy breas', it's a sign dat you's agwyne to be rich.[45] Well, dey's some use in a sign like dat, 'kase it's so fur ahead. You see, maybe you's got to be po' a long time fust, en so you might git discourage' en kill yo'sef 'f you did n' know by de sign dat you gwyne to be rich bymeby."

"Have you got hairy arms and a hairy breast, Jim?"

"What's de use to ax dat question? don' you see I has?"

"Well, are you rich?"

"No, but I ben rich wunst, and gwyne to be rich agin. Wunst I had foteen dollars, but I tuck to specalat'n', en got busted out."[46]

"What did you speculate in, Jim?"

"Well, fust I tackled stock."

"What kind of stock?"

"Why, live stock. Cattle, you know. I put ten dollars in a cow. But I ain' gwyne to resk no mo' money in stock. De cow up 'n' died on my han's."

"So you lost the ten dollars."

"No, I didn' lose it all. I on'y los' 'bout nine of it. I sole de hide en taller[47] for a dollar en ten cents."

"You had five dollars and ten cents left. Did you speculate any more?"

"Yes. You know dat one-laigged nigger[48] dat b'longs to old Misto Bradish?[49] well, he sot up a bank, en say anybody dat put in a dollar would git fo' dollars mo' at de en' er de year. Well, all de niggers went in, but dey didn' have much. I wuz de on'y one dat had much. So I stuck out for mo' dan fo' dollars, en I said 'f I didn' git it I'd start a bank mysef. Well o' course dat nigger want' to keep me out er de business, bekase he say dey warn't business 'nough for two banks, so he say I could put in my five dollars en he pay me thirty-five at de en' er de year.

"So I done it. Den I reck'n'd I'd inves' de thirty-five dollars right off en keep things a-movin'. Dey wuz a nigger

MISTO BRADISH'S NIGGER.

name' Bob, dat had ketched a wood-flat,[50] en his marster didn' know it;[51] en I bought it off'n him en told him to take de thirty-five dollars when de en' er de year come; but somebody stole de wood-flat dat night, en nex' day de one-laigged nigger say de bank 's busted. So dey didn' none uv us git no money."

"What did you do with the ten cents, Jim?"

"Well, I 'uz gwyne to spen' it, but I had a dream, en de dream tole me to give it to a nigger name' Balum—Balum's Ass[52] dey call him for short, he's one er dem chuckle-heads, you know. But he's lucky, dey say,[53] en I see I warn't lucky. De dream say let Balum inves' de ten cents en he'd make a raise for me. Well, Balum he tuck de money, en when he wuz in church he hear de preacher say dat who-ever give to de po' len' to de Lord, en boun' to git his money back a hund'd times.[54] So Balum he tuck en give de ten cents to de po,' en laid low to see what wuz gwyne to come of it."

"Well, what did come of it, Jim?"

should be taken to avoid punishing the innocent for the sins of the guilty. Several stampedes among the negroes have taken place recently in this vicinity. . . . and there is no doubt at all but they were aided in making their escape by Northern Abolitionists." Antislavery advocates believed that a "higher law" guided them in breaking the law of the land. "In those old slave-holding days," Twain wrote in his notebook in 1895 (quoted in Foner, *Mark Twain: Social Critic*, 1958), "the whole community was agreed as to one thing—the awful sacredness of slave property. To steal a horse or a cow was a low crime, but to help a hunted slave, or feed him or shelter him, or hide him, or comfort him, in his trouble, his terrors, his despair, or hesitate to promptly betray him to the slave-catcher when opportunity offered was a much baser crime, and carried with it a stain, a moral smirch which nothing could wipe away" (p. 206). Frederick Douglass recognized in Chapter 10 of his *Narrative* that for white men to stand up for a slave "required a degree of courage unknown to them to do so; for just at that time, the slightest manifestation of humanity toward a colored person was denounced as abolitionism, and that name subjected its bearer to frightful liabilities. The watchwords of the bloody-minded in that region, in those days, were, 'Damn the abolitionists!' and 'Damn the niggers!' "

Twain recalled that when he was ten years old, he saw the execution of Robert Hardy, an abolitionist from Marion City, a small town near Hannibal. "People came for miles around to see the hanging, " he recalled, "they brought cakes and cider, also the women and children, and made a picnic of the matter. It was the largest crowd the village had ever seen. The rope that hanged Hardy was eagerly bought up, in inch samples, for everybody wanted a memento of the memorable event" (quoted in DeVoto, *Mark Twain's America*, 1932, p. 64). It was supposed to have occurred in Palmyra, but Frank H. Sosey proved in "Palmyra and Its Historical Environment" (*Missouri Historical Review*, April 1929, pp. 361–62) that Hardy was not hanged there; either it happened somewhere else or Twain made up the incident.

The case of Northern abolitionist aggression that most infuriated the town of Hannibal was the famous "Jerry Rescue" in far-off Syracuse, New York. On October 1, 1851, a mob of two to three thousand antislavery advocates in black-face and armed with clubs, axes, and crowbars

"Nuffn' never come of it. I couldn' manage to k'leck dat money no way; en Balum he couldn'. I ain' gwyne to len' no mo' money 'dout I see de security. Boun' to git yo' money back a hund'd times, de preacher says! Ef I could git de ten *cents* back, I'd call it squah, en be glad er de chanst."

"Well, it's all right, anyway, Jim, long as you're going to be rich again some time or other."

"Yes—en I's rich now, come to look at it. I owns mysef, en I's wuth eight hund'd dollars. I wisht I had de money, I wouldn' want no mo'."[55]

stormed the local jail and released a runaway who had been recently arrested under the Fugitive Slave Act of 1850. Hannibal was interested in the incident, because Jerry McHenry had once been owned by John McReynolds, a wealthy landowner who lived in the area. Jerry ran away from Marion County about ten years before, settled in Syracuse under the name "Henry," and worked as a carpenter. A Missourian recognized him one day and reported back to McReynolds, who then sent his agent to Syracuse to bring his "property" back to Marion County. "From the formidable number engaged in this mob," Orion Clemens editorialized in the Hannibal *Journal and Union* (October 16, 1851), "it is natural to infer that the sentiment in the region of Syracuse is both bitter and unanimous against the Fugitive Slave Law, and that there is a disposition prevailing the entire community, hostile to extending the Southern men rights guaranteed to them by the constitution and laws of the land. . . . Slaveholders may now set it down as an established fact, that their chance of recovering a fugitive slave is almost as good in Canada, a foreign country, as in the Northern States of the Union, though in the latter, the people call us brethren, in liberty, religion and law. The slaveholder may calculate on recovering his lost property, in those States, if at all, at the imminent risk or failure, after incurring heavy expense, and at the hazard of his life." The local militia was called together at the sheriff's request, but the commander refused to intervene. Jerry McHenry escaped to Canada on the Underground Railroad.

29. *sell me down to Orleans.* "That selling to the south is set before the negro from childhood as the last severity of punishment," Harriet Beecher Stowe explained in Chapter 10 of *Uncle Tom's Cabin.* "The threat that terrifies more than whipping or torture of any kind is the threat of being sent down river. We have ourselves heard this feeling expressed by them, and seen the unaffected horror with which they will sit in their gossiping hours, and tell frightful stories of that 'down river.'" Because Missouri slaves were primarily household or familial servants, they greatly feared the horrors suffered by field hands on the large, overseered Southern plantations. "It was the mild domestic slavery," Twain recalled of the system in Hannibal, "not the brutal plantation article. Cruelties were very rare and exceedingly and wholesomely unpopular. . . . If the threat to sell an incorrigible slave 'down the river' would not reform him, nothing would—his case was past cure" ("Jane Lampton Clemens," *Huck Finn and Tom Sawyer Among the Indians*, 1989, p. 88). His mother kept the family's slave Jenny under control by threatening to "rent her to the Yankees"; they eventually sold her to a man in Hannibal, who then sold her "down the river" (*Huck Finn and Tom Sawyer Among the Indians*, p. 327.) He saw few public acts of cruelty to slaves when a boy in Hannibal, but one incident he never did forget. "I vividly remember seeing a dozen black men and women chained to each other, once, and lying in a group on the pavement, awaiting shipment to the southern slave market," Twain wrote in "Jane Lampton Clemens." "Those were the saddest faces I ever saw" (p. 88). In a sense, Jim's nightmare in Chapter 2 has come true; as Twain noted in Chapter 2 of *Pudd'nhead Wilson*, the threat of selling slaves down the river "was equivalent to condemning them to hell!"

30. *a nigger trader*. "The 'nigger trader' was loathed by everybody," Twain explained in "Jane Clemens" (1890). "He was regarded as a sort of human devil who bought and conveyed poor helpless creatures to hell—for to our whites and blacks alike the southern plantation was simply hell; no milder name could describe it" (*Huck Finn and Tom Sawyer Among the Indians*, 1989, p. 88). Sam Clemens was not the only one in Hannibal who felt this way. "Let me say here that no character was more thoroughly despised among southern people than a Negro-trader," wrote Ben Ezra Stiles Ely. "I am confidently persuaded that if the people of the North and the South had known one another better than they did, the bitter acrimonies that characterized the past would not have existed and that slavery would eventually have been abolished without the fearful expenditure of blood and treasure resulting from the War" (quoted in Curtis Dahl, "Mark Twain and Ben Ely: Two Missouri Boyhoods," *Missouri Historical Review*, July 1972, pp. 560–61).

31. *she could git eight hund'd dollars for me*. Twain originally wrote "five or six hundred" (**MS**), then "seven or eight hundred" (**MS**), before settling on the final figure. Miss Watson has been offered more than the average price for Jim. Twain recalled in Chapter 54 of *Life on the Mississippi* that a family of slaves "in my time . . . would have been worth no less than five hundred dollars apiece." With the abolition of the importation of African slaves into the United States in 1808 and the increase in cotton production with the invention of the cotton gin, the interstate traffic in slave trading increased enormously as did the value of this "property"; by 1860, the same slave might command $1,300 on the open market.

32. *De widder she try to git her to say she wouldn' do it*. Although slaveholders in Hannibal often threatened to sell disobedient slaves "down the river," it was not often done; the "quality" like the Widow Douglas greatly frowned upon it.

33. *cooper shop*. Place where they made barrels.

34. *Dese las' skifts wuz full o' ladies en genlmen agoin' for to see de place*. Curiosity seekers are off on a pleasure excursion to visit the scene of the crime.

35. *de camp-meetn'*. A congress held in the open air under tents in the wilderness, usually for religious services and chiefly among the Methodists; Jim probably feels safe to run off now, for these gatherings often went on for days. Huck attends a camp meeting in Chapter 20.

36. *swim asho' en take to de woods on de Illinoi side*. Abolitionists from Illinois often raided the Missouri side of the Mississippi to help runaways escape on the Underground Railroad. "They are as thick down here in the bottoms," one woman in nearby Palmyra, Missouri, described the abolitionists of Quincy, Illinois, "as maggots in a dead horse, watching for slaves." In the unfinished story "Tom Sawyer's Conspiracy," which takes place after *Huckleberry Finn*, Huck tells how "two weeks past there was whispers going around about strangers being seen in the woods over on the Illinois side, and then disappearing, and then seen again; and everybody reckoned it was ablitionists laying for a chance to run off with some of our niggers to freedom" (*Huck Finn and Tom Sawyer Among the Indians*, 1989, p. 142). Twain likely recalled the famous 1841 case in Marion City when three abolitionist "liberators" tried to persuade two slaves to escape across the river with them to Canada, where slavery had already been abolished. But slaves were constantly warned that abolitionists were their worst enemies and reminded how Murrell's Gang would deceive them and then sell them "down the river." Frederick Douglass admitted in Chapter

7 of his *Narrative*, "White men have been known to encourage slaves to escape, and then, to get the reward, catch them and return them to their masters." It may have been out of loyalty that the two men told their owners, and the three abolitionists were captured. Despite the constant threat of a lynching, they were tried (Judge Clemens was on the jury) and then sentenced to twelve years in prison at hard labor. They were released before their term expired; and one of them, George Thompson, wrote an impassioned account of their failed plot and imprisonment in *Prison Life and Reflections* (1897).

Many critics of the novel have objected with DeVoto in *Mark Twain at Work* to Twain's "lordly disregard of the fact that Jim . . . could have reached free soil by simply paddling to the Illinois shore from Jackson's Island" (p. 54). But that may not have been so easy. The Hannibal papers contained accounts of the apprehension of fugitives in Illinois. "Emigrants from slave States, who hold large property in slaves," Orion Clemens noted in the Hannibal *Western Union* (May 29, 1851), "imagine that their property cannot be safe anywhere near the Mississippi. This is a mistake. Ten slaves run away from the Missouri river, where one leaves this section. The negroes in this part of the State, hardly ever run off, because they are well acquainted with the difficulty of getting away." Although Illinois was technically free, it was also a border state. Although it was on the route of the Underground Railroad, it did not automatically recognize a runaway as a freedman: Being separated from slave states only by the Mississippi and Ohio rivers, it upheld the Fugitive Slave Law. Illinois law considered any person of color without freedom papers to be a fugitive and thus subject to arrest and, upon conviction, to sentencing to a system of indentured servitude. "Rewards were offered for runaways," DeLancey Ferguson replied to the criticism in *The Explicator* (April 1946); "capturing and returning them was a profitable business. Jim would have had a much better chance of staying free had he entered free soil at a remote point, instead of right opposite the place where the alarm had already been raised." Julius Lester complained in "Morality and *Adventures of Huckleberry Finn*" (*Mark Twain Journal*, Fall 1984), "The novel plays with black reality from the moment Jim runs away and does not immediately seek freedom. It defies logic that Jim did not know Illinois was a free state" (p. 44). But Jim is wiser than that. He is fully aware of the dangers of swimming off to Illinois: He thinks of taking a raft to throw off the dogs tracking him and the tracing of the stolen skiff; and he has already been thwarted in his attempt to cross the river. Frederick Douglass explained in Chapter 10 of his *Narrative* that even if one did make it to the North, the fugitive would not entirely be free but instead would "be forever harassed with the frightful liability of being returned to slavery." He knew the terrible risks the runaway had to face: "At every gate through which we were to pass, we saw a watchman—at every ferry a guard—on every bridge a sentinel—in every wood a patrol. We were hemmed in on every side." In the end, Jim must choose the river over the shore, because (as Douglass explained), "if we should take the land route, we should be subjected to interruptions of almost every kind. Any one having a white face, and being so disposed, could stop us, and subject us to examination."

37. *a plug er dog-leg*. A tightly twisted stick or cake of cheap tobacco.

38. *it was a sign when young chickens flew that way*. A popular superstition in this part of the country warned that when chickens flocked together, it was going to rain.

39. *his old granny said his father would die, and he did*. Jim is likely recalling the superstition that if a bird entered the home of sick person and then died, the patient would die too.

40. *you mustn't count the things you are going to cook for dinner*. Counting was often associated with bad luck in this part of the country: Never count stars, cars in a funeral cortège, followers to a funeral, or the graves in a churchyard.

41. *shook the table-cloth after sundown*. Blair and Fischer in the 1988 University of California Edition (p. 387) identified this as another European superstition.

42. *the bees must be told about it before sun-up next morning*. A European superstition; bees were said to be the messengers of the gods in ancient Greece and Rome. "A remarkable custom, brought from the Old Country, formerly prevailed in the rural districts of New England," John Greenleaf Whittier prefaced his 1858 poem "Telling the Bees." "On the death of a member of the family, the bees were at once informed of the event, and their hives dressed in mourning. This ceremonial was supposed to be necessary to prevent the swarms from leaving their hives and seeking a new home." Another Missourian, Eugene Field, used this superstition in his 1893 poem also called "Telling the Bees."

43. *bees wouldn't sting idiots*. The handicapped were once believed to be "God's Poor" and thus blessed and protected by Him. Twain made a similar joke in "Chapters from My Autobiography" (*North American Review*, July 5, 1907): "The proverb says that Providence protects children and idiots. This is really true. I know it because I have tested it" (p. 471). Fischer and Salamo reported in the 2001 University of California edition that Twain knew this superstition from letter 27 in George White's *The Natural History and Antiquities of Selborne* (1789), about an idiot boy who never got stung despite his obsession with bees.

44. *What you want to know when good luck's a-comin' for?* Jim agrees with a Native American belief that one need only concern oneself with bad spirits, never good. See Chapter 4, note 12.

45. *Ef you's got hairy arms en a hairy breas', it's a sign dat you's agwyne to be rich.* The belief that a person with a hairy body will always have money exists as well in parts of Great Britain. It may go back to the tradition that the beautiful Queen of Sheba had legs as hairy as an ape's; therefore it was believed that a hairy woman will always marry a rich man.

46. *I tuck to specalat'n', en got busted out.* Jim's story about his investments is similar to an exchange between a Piute guide named Captain Juan and "Dan De Quille," Twain's friend William Wright, who recorded it in his *History of the Big Bonanza* (1870), recollections of the early Nevada mining days. "I was pretty well off once," Captain Juan explains. "I had *fifty dollars*." Wright continues: "And what became of all this wealth?"

"Me burst all to smash."

"Well, that was bad. In kind of speculation?"

"Me not understand spectoolation. What you call um spectoolation?"

"Well, it's when you . . . plant your money in some speculation to get more money."

"Yes; well, me make one bad plant."

Captain Juan, in contrast to Jim, lost his money to a demanding Spanish wife who threw him out when he ran out of cash. By refashioning Wright's Piute as "Mr. Bones" in the minstrel show, Twain played with the dialectical conflict between the nonwhite and mainstream American culture, a theme widely exploited in nineteenth-century humor. However, Twain greatly transformed Wright's original by reworking the exchange as an ironic introduction of contradictions in the slave system and its treatment of people as merely chattel.

Victor Doyno observed in the 1996 Oxford University edition of *Huckleberry Finn* that this consideration of investments and bank failures is "quite an odd topic for these two characters to be discussing in, say, 1845. But many Americans knew in 1876 and in 1885 . . . that the Freedman's Bank that was set up after the Civil War had failed, costing Black depositors about $27 million in very hard earned nickels and dimes. Jim's talk about the dangers of 'specalat'n' must have sounded a bittersweet note when written in 1876 or read in 1885, because there had been no federal reimbursement to the Black depositors. Indeed, many white readers may have lost money themselves . . . because at least ninety-eight banks had failed in the 1873 panic, and even more would do so over the next few years" (p. 11).

47. *taller*. Tallow, cow's fat.

48. *dat one-laigged nigger*. Blair and Fischer in the 1988 University of California edition identified him as the local Hannibal character Higgins, the "one-legged mulatto, who belonged to Mr. Garth" (p. 388). Twain reminded his boyhood friend Will Bowen on February 6, 1870, of how they "taught that one-legged nigger, Higgins," to harass another citizen. He may have been referring to the time in 1851 that the slave pestered a woman wearing the new and notorious "Bloomer costume." "Higgins (everybody knows Higgins)," reported the Hannibal *Western Union* (July 10, 1851), "plied his single leg with amazing industry and perseverance, keeping up a running fire of comment not calculated to initiate him in the good graces of the person addressed. When the leg became tired, its owner would seat himself and recover a little breath, after which, the indomitable leg would drag off persevering Higgins at an accelerated pace."

49. *Misto Bradish.* In the uncompleted story "Tom Sawyer's Conspiracy" of 1897, Huck reveals that Tom Sawyer has discovered that Bat Bradish, "a nigger trader in a little small way," was "at the bottom of it the time old Miss Watson come so near selling Jim down the river and Jim heard about it and run away and me and him floated down to Arkansaw on the raft. It was Bradish that persuaded her to sell Jim and give him the job of doing it for her" (*Huck Finn and Tom Sawyer Among the Indians*, 1989, p. 187). When Bradish is found murdered, the newly freed Jim is arrested for the crime and accused of doing it out of revenge for his betrayal by this "nigger trader."

50. *a wood-flat.* A raft or flat-bottomed boat for transporting timber.

51. *his marster didn' know it.* He does not bother to tell his owner about it, because a slave was forbidden by law to own personal property; everything he may find automatically belongs to his master.

52. *Balum's Ass.* In Numbers 22:7–35, Balaam's ass three times protects his master from the Avenging Angel in the road, and each time his master beats him. The Lord then causes the animal to speak to ask why he has been so abused. Balaam replies that he has been made to look like a fool. And the Lord opens his eyes, so he can see the Avenging Angel before him; and Balaam confesses he has sinned. It is an apt lesson on the way American slave owners regularly mistreated loyal servants. Balaam was one of the Lord's prophets, and Twain is burlesquing Jim's powers as a seer himself. Twain, like other nineteenth-century American humorists, was fond of the name: He said in his *Burlesque Autobiography* (1871) that Balaam's Ass was one of his ancestors; a pompous ass named the Rev. Orson Balaam who exploits the Indians appears in Chapter 31 of *The Gilded Age*. Twain described in *The Innocents Abroad* (Chapters 43 and 44) the absurdity of visiting a fountain in Figia, Syria, where Balaam's Ass ("the patron saint of all pilgrims like us") refreshed himself. Joel Chandler Harris may have recalled this discussion in *Huckleberry Finn* when he named another abused slave "Balaam" in *Balaam and His Master and Other Sketches and Stories* (1891).

53. *he's one er dem chuckle-heads. . . . But he's lucky, dey say.* As mentioned in note 43 above, idiots were believed to be blessed by God.

54. *de preacher say dat whoever give to de po' len' to de Lord, en boun' to git his money back a hund'd times.* Jim's preacher repeats much the same lesson that Miss Watson tried to teach Huck in the opening of Chapter 3; Jim and Huck come to the same conclusion, that there is no reason to "take stock" in religious investments. This skepticism establishes another affinity between the boy and the runaway slave.

55. *I wisht I had de money, I wouldn't want no mo'.* Twain seems not to have been entirely happy with the punchline. He evidently replaced it himself in the serialization of this chapter as "Jim's Investments, and King Sollermun" in *Century Magazine* (January 1885) with this other one: "But live stock's too resky, Huck;—I wisht I had de eight hund'd dollars en somebody else had de nigger" (p. 457). Blair and Fischer mentioned in the 1988 University of California edition another rethinking of this phrase for use in his 1884–1885 public reading tour he jotted in his notebook in December 1884: "Hang it, Huck, ef I could ony c'leck de *int*rust I would let the *princi*pal go" (p. 528). In his 1895–1896 public reading copy, Twain added a new punchline: "Cuz niggers is mighty resky property." Actually insurance on slaves was available in Hannibal when Sam Clemens was a boy; his boss, Joseph P. Ament, editor and publisher of the *Missouri Courier*, offered this service from November 20, 1850, as agent for the Boston Union Mutual Insurance Company.

Chapter IX.

EXPLORING THE CAVE.

I WANTED to go and look at a place right about the middle of the island, that I'd found when I was exploring; so we started, and soon got to it, because the island was only three miles long and a quarter of a mile wide.

This place was a tolerable long steep hill or ridge, about forty foot high. We had a rough time getting to the top, the sides was so steep and the bushes so thick. We tramped and clumb around all over it, and by-and-by found a good big cavern in the rock, most up to the top on the side towards Illinois. The cavern was as big as two or three rooms bunched together, and Jim could stand up straight in it. It was cool in there. Jim was for putting our traps in there, right away, but I said we didn't want to be climbing up and down there all the time.

Jim said if we had the canoe hid in a good place, and had all the traps in the cavern, we could rush there if anybody was to come to the island, and they would never find us without dogs. And besides, he said them little birds had said it was going to rain, and did I want the things to get wet?

So we went back and got the canoe and paddled up

1. *a perfect ripper of a gust*. An especially powerful gust.

abreast the cavern, and lugged all the traps up there. Then we hunted up a place close by to hide the canoe in, amongst the thick willows. We took some fish off of the lines and set them again, and begun to get ready for dinner.

The door of the cavern was big enough to roll a hogshead in, and on one side of the door the floor stuck out a little bit and was flat and a good place to build a fire on. So we built it there and cooked dinner.

We spread the blankets inside for a carpet, and eat our dinner in there. We put all the other things handy at the back of the cavern. Pretty soon it darkened up and begun to thunder and lighten; so the birds was right about it. Directly it begun to rain, and it rained like all fury, too, and I never see the wind blow so. It was one of these regular summer storms. It would get so dark that it looked all blue-black outside, and lovely; and the rain would thrash along by so thick that the trees off a little ways looked dim and spider-webby; and here would come a blast of wind that would bend the trees down and turn up the pale underside of the leaves; and then a perfect ripper of a gust[1] would follow along and set the branches to tossing their arms as if they was just wild; and next, when it was just about the bluest and blackest—*fst!* it was as bright as glory and you'd

IN THE CAVE.

have a little glimpse of tree-tops a-plunging about, away off yonder in the storm, hundreds of yards further than you could see before; dark as sin[2] again in a second, and now you'd hear the thunder let go with an awful crash and then go rumbling, grumbling, tumbling down the sky towards the under side of the world, like rolling empty barrels down stairs, where it's long stairs and they bounce a good deal, you know.

"Jim, this is nice," I says. "I wouldn't want to be nowhere else but here. Pass me along another hunk of fish and some hot corn-bread."

"Well, you wouldn't a ben here, 'f it hadn't a ben for Jim.[3] You'd a ben down dah in de woods widout any dinner, en gittn' mos' drownded, too, dat you would, honey.[4] Chickens knows when its gwyne to rain, en so do de birds, chile."

The river went on raising and raising[5] for ten or twelve days, till at last it was over the banks. The water was three or four foot deep on the island in the low places and on the Illinois bottom. On that side it was a good many miles wide; but on the Missouri side it was the same old distance across—a half a mile—because the Missouri shore was just a wall of high bluffs.

Daytimes we paddled all over the island in the canoe. It was mighty cool and shady in the deep woods even if the sun was blazing outside. We went winding in and out amongst the trees; and sometimes the vines hung so thick we had to back away and go some other way. Well, on every old broken-down tree, you could see rabbits, and snakes, and such things; and when the island had been overflowed a day or two, they got so tame, on account of being hungry, that you could paddle right up and put your hand on them if you wanted to; but not the snakes and turtles—they would slide off in the water. The ridge our cavern was in, was full of them. We could a had pets enough if we'd wanted them.[6]

One night we catched a little section of a lumber raft—nice pine planks. It was twelve foot wide and about fifteen or sixteen foot long, and the top stood above water six or seven inches, a solid level floor. We could see saw-logs go by

2. *as bright as glory . . . dark as sin.* Huck may violently resist the Widow Douglas and Miss Watson's Sunday-school teachings, but these similes nevertheless betray the boy's deep unconscious religious convictions.

3. *you wouldn't a ben here, 'f it hadn't a ben for Jim.* Truer words were never spoken. This is only the first instance of many in which the slave aids the boy in his flight from civilization. Jim possesses enormous common sense; his knowledge of the river is immense, and he is skilled in surviving in the wilderness. Many of their best schemes are Jim's. He may be as much a fugitive as Huck, but he acts as the boy's protector on their journey down the river and acts (like Miles Hendon to Edward in Twain's *The Prince and the Pauper*, 1882) as elder brother to Huck.

4. *honey.* Much has been made of this word, particularly by Leslie Fiedler in "Come Back to the Raft Ag'in, Huck Honey!" (*Partisan Review*, June 1948, pp. 664–71), as proof of an implicit homosexual relationship between Huck and Jim. But "honey" is no more than a universal Southern term of endearment, used by Jim, Mrs. Judith Loftus, and others in the novel toward Huck. No more so than "chile."

5. *The river went on raising and raising.* When the long lost first half of the holograph manuscript of *Huckleberry Finn* resurfaced in 1990, it revealed a suppressed passage that appears nowhere else in Twain's work. It was published in *The New Yorker* (June 26/July 3, 1995) as "Jim and the Dead Man" and as the "cadaver episode" in the 1996 Random House "Comprehensive Edition." It is reprinted in *The Annotated Huckleberry Finn* as Appendix A.

6. *We could a had pets enough if we'd wanted them.* The June rise has made companions of creatures that otherwise would be natural enemies through their shared misery. Only the intrusion of the floating house disrupts this delicate balance. Twain explored a similar situation in "Man's Place in the Animal World" of 1897: "In truth, man is incurably foolish. Simple things which the other animals easily learn, he is incapable of learning. . . . In an hour I taught a cat and a dog to be friends. I put them in a cage. In another hour I taught them to be friends with a rabbit. In the course of two days I was able to find a fox, a goose, a squirrel and some doves. Finally a monkey. They lived in

peace; even affectionately" (*What Is Man?*, 1973, p. 85). However, not so with man, for "man's heart was the only bad heart in the animal kingdom." Twain agreed with a Scotsman he knew back in Cincinnati in his youth, who argued that "man was the only animal capable of feeling malice, envy, vindictiveness, vengefulness, hatred, selfishness, the only animal that loved drunkenness, almost the only animal that could endure personal uncleanliness and a filthy habitation . . . the sole animal that robs, persecutes, oppresses, and kills members of his own immediate tribe, the sole animal that steals and enslaves the members of *any* tribe" ("Macfarlane," *What Is Man?*, p. 78). This seemingly gratuitous adventure in an uprooted house of thieves and murderers, which proves to be Huck and Jim's first encounter with civilization after they have fled St. Petersburg, introduces an important underlying theme of the novel: What Is Man?

7. *So Jim says.* Twain originally had Huck rather than Jim call into the floating house in the manuscript, which explains "again" when the boy hollers later. The Twain had a second thought of letting Jim conceal the identity of the murdered man until the very end of the story, but forgot to drop "again." Did Twain at one time consider Huck to be the Angel of Death as pap accuses him of being in Chapter 6? He takes on various aliases and encounters corpses and murders along the Mississippi: the robbers stuck on the *Walter Scott* in Chapter 12; the slaughter in Chapter 18; the shooting of Boggs by Smarr in Chapter 21.

8. *gashly.* Jim has unconsciously invented a particularly apt portmanteau word from "gash" (as in the dead man's wounds) and "ghastly."

in the daylight, sometimes, but we let them go; we didn't show ourselves in daylight.

Another night, when we was up at the head of the island, just before daylight, here comes a frame house down, on the west side. She was a two-story, and tilted over, considerable. We paddled out and got aboard—clumb in at an upstairs window. But it was too dark to see yet, so we made the canoe fast and set in her to wait for daylight.

The light begun to come before we got to the foot of the island. Then we looked in at the window. We could make out a bed, and a table, and two old chairs, and lots of things

JIM SEES A DEAD MAN.

around about on the floor; and there was clothes hanging against the wall. There was something laying on the floor in the far corner that looked like a man. So Jim says:[7]

"Hello, you!"

But it didn't budge. So I hollered again, and then Jim says:

"De man ain't asleep—he's dead. You hold still—I'll go en see."

He went and bent down and looked, and says:

"It's a dead man. Yes, indeedy; naked, too. He's ben shot in de back. I reck'n he's ben dead two er three days. Come in, Huck, but doan' look at his face—it's too gashly."[8]

I didn't look at him at all. Jim throwed some old rags over him, but he needn't done it; I didn't want to see him. There was heaps of old greasy cards scattered around over the floor, and old whisky bottles, and a couple of masks made out of black cloth;[9] and all over the walls was the ignorantest kind of words and pictures, made with charcoal.[10] There was two old dirty calico[11] dresses, and a sun-bonnet, and some women's under-clothes, hanging against the wall, and some men's clothing, too.[12] We put the lot into the canoe; it might come good. There was a boy's old speckled straw hat on the floor; I took that too. And there was a bottle that had had milk in it; and it had a rag stopper[13] for a baby to suck. We would a took the bottle, but it was broke. There was a seedy old chest, and an old hair trunk[14] with the hinges broke. They stood open, but there warn't nothing left in them that was any account. The way things was scattered about, we reckoned the people left in a hurry and warn't fixed so as to carry off most of their stuff.

We got an old tin lantern, and a butcher knife without any handle, and a bran-new Barlow knife[15] worth two bits[16] in any store, and a lot of tallow candles, and a tin candlestick, and a gourd, and a tin cup, and a ratty old bed-quilt off the bed, and a reticule[17] with needles and pins and beeswax[18] and buttons and thread and all such truck in it, and a hatchet and some nails, and a fish-line as thick as my little finger, with some monstrous hooks on it, and a roll of buckskin, and a leather dog-collar, and a horse-shoe, and some vials of medicine that didn't have no label on them; and just as we was leaving I found a tolerable good curry-comb,[19] and Jim he found a ratty old fiddle-bow, and a wooden leg. The straps was broke off of it, but barring that, it was a good enough leg, though it was too long for me and not long enough for Jim, and we couldn't find the other one, though we hunted all around.

And so, take it all around, we made a good haul.[20] When we was ready to shove off, we was a quarter of a mile below the island, and it was pretty broad day; so I made Jim lay down in the canoe and cover up with the quilt, because if

9. *and a couple of masks made out of black cloth.* An afterthought added in the manuscript to clarify in what line of business the residents of this house were engaged.

10. *all over the walls was the ignorantest kind of words and pictures, made with charcoal.* Originally "*vulgarest* words" (**MS**), but that sounds more like Widow Douglas or Miss Watson than Huck Finn. These crude decorations are reminiscent of others in another thief's den, that of the late Tom Sheppard, in Chapter 1 of William Harrison Ainsworth's *Jack Sheppard* (1839), a novel Twain owned and enjoyed: "The bare walls were scored all over with grotesque designs, the chief of which represented Nebuchadnezzar. The rest were hieroglyphic characters, executed in red chalk and charcoal." Likely Twain is suggesting that the owners of this dwelling are so poor that they cannot afford even the cheapest print for the walls. However, Thomas Hart Benton in his illustration of this scene in the 1942 Limited Editions Club edition (and John Seelye in *The True Adventures of Huckleberry Finn*, 1970) interpreted "ignorantest kind of words" as "shit," "piss," "fuck," and other vulgarities.

11. *calico.* Brightly printed cheap cotton cloth, coarser than muslin. Referring to the typical backwoodsmen of Obedstown, East Tennessee, Twain said in Chapter 1 of *The Gilded Age* that wearing coats and vests "made of tolerably fanciful patterns of *calico*" was "a fashion which prevails there to this day among those of the community who have tastes above the common level and are able to afford style."

12. *some women's under-clothes, hanging against the wall, and some men's clothing, too.* These details suggested to V. S. Pritchett ("Current Literature," *New Statesman and Nation*, August 2, 1941) that this frame house was "evidently some sort of brothel" (p. 113). The man must have been in bed with the prostitute when he was murdered.

13. *rag stopper.* Twain had originally called it "sugar teat" (**MS**) in the manuscript, but the phrase was probably too vulgar to survive his personal censors, Olivia Clemens and William Dean Howells. See also Chapter 21, Note 22.

he set up, people could tell he was a nigger a good ways off. I paddled over to the Illinois shore, and drifted down most a half a mile doing it. I crept up the dead water under the bank, and hadn't no accidents and didn't see nobody. We got home all safe.

14. *hair trunk.* A trunk made from an untanned hide, still with the hair on it. Twain found much to joke about in this ugly article. For example, in Chapter 20 of *A Tramp Abroad*, while complaining how slow German "slow freight" was, he observed, "The hair on my trunk was soft and thick and youthful, when I got it ready for shipment in Hamburg; it was baldheaded when it reached Heidelburg."

15. *Barlow knife.* A single-bladed jackknife, named for its eighteenth-century English inventor, Russell Barlowe. Tom Sawyer's cousin Mary in Chapter 4 of *Tom Sawyer* "gave him a bran-new 'Barlow' knife worth twelve and a half cents; and the convulsion of delight that swept his system shook him to his foundations. True, the knife would not cut anything, but it was a 'sure-enough' Barlow, and there was inconceivable grandeur in that—though where the western boys ever got the idea that such a weapon could possibly be counterfeited to its injury, is an imposing mystery and will always remain so, perhaps."

Tom Sawyer tries out his new Barlow knife.
Illustration by True W. Williams,
The Adventures of Tom Sawyer, 1876.
Private collection.

16. *two bits.* Twice what Tom Sawyer's "Barlow" cost, being twenty-five cents in American currency, based on the Spanish milled dollar of eight reals, or "bits," known as "pieces of eight."

17. *a reticule.* A handbag, here a sewing bag. Edgar Lee Masters complained in *Mark Twain: A Portrait* (1938) that this word was inappropriate for a boy of Huck's class and region; he should have said something like "one of them things they keep needles in, ratacoul or something" (p. 130).

18. *beeswax.* Used by seamstresses to wax their thread.

19. *curry-comb.* A metal comb, usually used for grooming horses.

20. *And so, take it all around, we made a good haul.* This inventory of what Huck and Jim took from the floating house back to Jackson's Island is reminiscent of how Robinson Crusoe salvaged whatever he could from the shipwreck to sustain his living on the desert island. T. S. Eliot was particularly impressed with this passage of *Huckleberry Finn.* "This is the sort of list a boy reader should pore over with delight," the poet wrote in his introduction to the 1950 Cresset/Chanticleer edition of *Huckleberry Finn*; "but the paragraph performs other functions of which the boy reader would be unaware. It provides the right counterpoise to the horror of the wrecked house and the corpse; it has a grim precision which tells the reader all he needs to know about the way of life of the human derelicts who had used the house; and (especially the wooden leg, and the fruitless search for its mate) reminds us at the right moment of the kinship of mind and sympathy between the boy outcast from society and the negro fugitive from the injustice of society."

Chapter X.

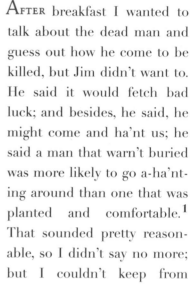

THEY FOUND EIGHT DOLLARS.

After breakfast I wanted to talk about the dead man and guess out how he come to be killed, but Jim didn't want to. He said it would fetch bad luck; and besides, he said, he might come and ha'nt us; he said a man that warn't buried was more likely to go a-ha'nting around than one that was planted and comfortable.[1] That sounded pretty reasonable, so I didn't say no more; but I couldn't keep from studying over it and wishing I knowed who shot the man, and what they done it for.

We rummaged the clothes we'd got, and found eight dollars in silver sewed up in the lining of an old blanket overcoat.[2] Jim said he reckoned the people in that house stole the coat, because if they'd a knowed the money was there they wouldn't a left it. I said I reckoned they killed him, too; but Jim didn't want to talk about that. I says:

"Now you think it's bad luck; but what did you say when I fetched in the snake-skin that I found on the top of the ridge day before yesterday? You said it was the worst bad luck in the world to touch a snake-skin with my hands.[3] Well, here's your bad luck! We've raked in all this truck and eight dollars besides. I wish we could have some bad luck like this every day, Jim."

1. *a man that warn't buried was more likely to go a-ha'nting around than one that was planted and comfortable*. It was not only bad luck to speak ill of the dead, but it was also commonly believed that the spirit of a dead person cannot rest in peace until it has been buried in hallowed ground.

2. *blanket over-coat*. Or "wrap-rascal," a cheap coat common to itinerants of the West, made from a heavy blanket and often with the stripe of the border crossing various parts of the garment; it served two functions, coat during the day and blanket at night. The silver was sewn in the lining because the coat lacked pockets, a luxury in that neck of the woods.

A blanket overcoat. Wood engraving by F.O.C. Darley, *Some Adventures of Captain Simon Suggs* by Johnson Jones Hooper, 1845. *Courtesy Library of Congress.*

"Never you mind, honey, never you mind. Don't you git too peart.[4] It's a-comin'. Mind I tell you, it's a-comin'."

It did come, too. It was a Tuesday that we had that talk. Well, after dinner Friday, we was laying around in the grass at the upper end of the ridge, and got out of tobacco. I went to the cavern to get some, and found a rattlesnake in there. I killed him, and curled him up on the foot of Jim's blanket, ever so natural, thinking there'd be some fun when Jim found him there. Well, by night I forgot all about the snake, and when Jim flung himself down on the blanket while I struck a light, the snake's mate was there, and bit him.

He jumped up yelling, and the first thing the light

JIM AND THE SNAKE.

showed was the varmint curled up and ready for another spring. I laid him out in a second with a stick, and Jim grabbed pap's whisky jug and begun to pour it down.[5]

He was barefooted, and the snake bit him right on the heel.[6] That all comes of my being such a fool as to not remember that wherever you leave a dead snake its mate

3. *the worst bad luck in the world to touch a snake-skin with my hands.* A popular superstition in this part of the country, said to originate with the Indians, warned that anyone who touches a snakeskin will be bitten by a snake within three days. Mary Ann Cord, a former slave who was the cook at Quarry Farm in Elmira, New York, where the Clemenses spent their summers, told the children that "snakes must be killed on sight, even the harmless ones; and the discoverer of a sloughed snake-skin lying in the road was in for all kinds of calamities" (quoted in Arthur G. Pettit, *Mark Twain and the South*, 1974, pp. 53–54). Slaves also used snakeskins as protection against evil spirits and in the treatment of such ills as rheumatism, headache, and fits. See Note 8 below.

4. *peart.* Also spelled "pert," fresh, smart.

5. *Jim grabbed pap's whisky jug and begun to pour it down.* Blair and Fischer disclosed in the 1988 University of California edition that the 1867 edition of *Gunn's New Family Physician*, one of the books owned by the Grangerfords in Chapter 17, prescribed this very treatment for snakebite:

> Internally, give the patient *all the Whisky he can drink*. From a quart to a gallon should be drunk in six or eight hours. No fears need be entertained of making the patient drunk. . . . It should be drunk like water for a few hours, and continued, at short intervals, until the patient gives signs of intoxication, when the quantity should gradually be diminished, as the disease is beginning to recede. Keep him "under the influence of liquor," however, until you are sure he is out of danger. (p. 388)

Edgar M. Branch located in "Mark Twain: Newspaper Reading and the Writer's Creativity" (*Nineteenth-Century Fiction*, March 1983) another description from "Remarkable Case of a Rattlesnake Bite" (St. Louis *Missouri Democrat*, June 11, 1861), in which the victim consumes "a full quart of strong whisky and ninety drops of hartshorn" in three doses every five minutes. Soon he "commenced to laugh, then to whistle, next to sing, and finally tried to dance. . . . the whisky had got head of the poison, and had reached his vitals first. In five minutes more he was as drunk as Bacchus, sprawled out on the floor, slept half a day, and next morning was at work as well as ever" (p. 578). Actually, this treatment is dangerous for the victim: Alcohol dilates the blood vessels and therefore facilitates the flow of venom rather than slows it down.

6. *the snake bit him right on the heel.* Twain may be referring to the superstition that Charles Dudley Warner mentioned in Chapter 13 of *The Gilded Age*, when he described how an Easterner buys leather top boots, "a perfect protection against prairie rattle-snakes, which never strike above the knee."

7. *and he eat it.* Many folk cures like this one for snakebite derive from the medical theory of *similia similibus curantur*, "like cures like."

8. *He made me take off the rattles and tie them around his wrist, too. He said that would help.* This custom of wearing a necklace or bracelet of rattlesnake rattles to cure or ward off various ills (including snakebite) originated with Southern slaves. In Chapter 16 of *Tom Sawyer*, Tom, in throwing off his trousers to take a swim, "had kicked his string of rattlesnake rattles off his ankle, and he wondered how he had escaped cramp so long without the protection of this mysterious charm."

9. *see the new moon over his left shoulder.* To look at the new moon over the right shoulder was said to be good luck, but to view it over the left (where the devil waits) could prove fatal.

10. *Old Hank Bunker done it once.* The sad fate of reckless Hank Bunker is typical of the extravagantly violent slapstick, once common to Southwestern tall tales, which survives in contemporary comic strips and animated cartoons. Twain was fond of this exaggerated gallows humor and inserted examples of it everywhere in his early writing. Hank Bunker's tragedy is of the same sort as that of William Wheeler (Chapter 53, *Roughing It*), who "got nipped by the machinery in a carpet factory and went through in less than a quarter of a minute; his widder bought the piece of carpet that had his remains wove in, and people come a hundred mile to 'tend the funeral. There was fourteen yards in the piece. She wouldn't let them roll him up, but planted him just so—full length. . . . and let him stand up, same as a monument. And they nailed a sign on it and . . . put on it: [Sacred to the Memory of Fourteen Yards of Three-Ply Carpet Containing All That Was Mortal of William Wheeler]."

always comes there and curls around it. Jim told me to chop off the snake's head and throw it away, and then skin the body and roast a piece of it. I done it, and he eat it[7] and said it would help cure him. He made me take off the rattles and tie them around his wrist, too. He said that that would help.[8] Then I slid out quiet and throwed the snakes clear away amongst the bushes; for I warn't going to let Jim find out it was all my fault, not if I could help it.

Jim sucked and sucked at the jug, and now and then he got out of his head and pitched around and yelled; but every time he come to himself he went to sucking at the jug again. His foot swelled up pretty big, and so did his leg; but by-and-by the drunk begun to come, and so I judged he was all right; but I'd druther been bit with a snake than pap's whisky.

Jim was laid up for four days and nights. Then the swelling was all gone and he was around again. I made up my mind I wouldn't ever take aholt of a snake-skin again with my hands, now that I see what had come of it. Jim said he reckoned I would believe him next time. And he said that handling a snake-skin was such awful bad luck that maybe we hadn't got to the end of it yet. He said he druther see the new moon over his left shoulder[9] as much as a thousand times than take up a snake-skin in his hand. Well, I was getting to feel that way myself, though I've always reckoned that looking at the new moon over your left shoulder is one of the carelessest and foolishest things a body can do. Old Hank Bunker done it once,[10] and bragged about it; and in less than two years he got drunk and fell off of the shot tower and spread himself out so that he was just a kind of a layer, as you may say; and they slid him edgeways between two barn doors for a coffin, and buried him so, so they say, but I didn't see it. Pap told me. But anyway, it all come of looking at the moon that way, like a fool.

Well, the days went along, and the river went down between its banks again; and about the first thing we done was to bait one of the big hooks with a skinned rabbit and set it and catch a cat-fish that was as big as a man, being six

OLD HANK BUNKER.

foot two inches long, and weighed over two hundred pounds.[11] We couldn't handle him, of course; he would a flung us into Illinois. We just set there and watched him rip and tear around till he drownded. We found a brass button in his stomach, and a round ball, and lots of rubbage. We split the ball open with the hatchet, and there was a spool in it. Jim said he'd had it there a long time, to coat it over so and make a ball of it. It was as big a fish as was ever catched in the Mississippi, I reckon. Jim said he hadn't ever seen a bigger one. He would a been worth a good deal over at the village. They peddle out such a fish as that by the pound in the market house there; everybody buys some of him; his meat's as white as snow and makes a good fry.

Next morning I said it was getting slow and dull, and I wanted to get a stirring up, some way. I said I reckoned I would slip over the river and find out what was going on. Jim liked that notion; but he said I must go in the dark and look sharp. Then he studied it over and said, couldn't I put on some of them old things and dress up like a girl? That

11. *a cat-fish that was as big as a man, being six foot two inches long, and weighed over two hundred pounds*. This might be just another "fish story" except that Twain admitted in Chapter 2 of *Life on the Mississippi*, "I have seen a Mississippi catfish that was more than six feet long, and weighed two hundred and fifty pounds." Blair and Fischer reported in the 1988 University of California edition (p. 389) that Twain associated the "big catfish" in a note written about 1897 with Bence Blankenship, whose benevolence toward a fugitive slave in part inspired the events on Jackson's Island.

12. *you couldn't start a face in that town that I didn't know*. You couldn't introduce me to anyone in that town I didn't know.

"I practiced around all day." Illustration by E. W. Kemble, "Autograph Edition" of *The Collected Works of Mark Twain*, 1899. *Private collection.*

was a good notion, too. So we shortened up one of the calico gowns and I turned up my trowser-legs to my knees and got into it. Jim hitched it behind with the hooks, and it was a fair fit. I put on the sun-bonnet and tied it under my chin, and then for a body to look in and see my face was like looking down a joint of stove-pipe. Jim said nobody would know me, even in the daytime, hardly. I practiced around all day to get the hang of the things, and by-and-by I could do pretty well in them, only Jim said I didn't walk like a girl; and he said I must quit pulling up my gown to get at my britches pocket. I took notice, and done better.

I started up the Illinois shore in the canoe just after dark.

I started across to the town from a little below the ferry

"A FAIR FIT."

landing, and the drift of the current fetched me in at the bottom of the town. I tied up and started along the bank. There was a light burning in a little shanty that hadn't been lived in for a long time, and I wondered who had took up quarters there. I slipped up and peeped in at the window. There was a woman about forty year old in there, knitting by a candle that was on a pine table. I didn't know her face; she was a stranger, for you couldn't start a face in that town that I didn't know.[12] Now this was lucky, because I was weakening; I was getting afraid I had come; people might know my voice and find me out. But if this woman had been in such a little town two days she could tell me all I wanted to know; so I knocked at the door, and made up my mind I wouldn't forget I was a girl.

Chapter XI.

"COME IN."

"COME IN," says the woman, and I did. She says:

"Take a cheer."

I done it. She looked me all over with her little shiny eyes, and says:

"What might your name be?"

"Sarah Williams."

"Where 'bouts do you live? In this neighborhood?"

"No'm. In Hookerville, seven mile below.[1] I've walked all the way and I'm all tired out."

"Hungry, too, I reckon. I'll find you something."

"No'm, I ain't hungry. I was so hungry I had to stop two mile below here at a farm; so I ain't hungry no more. It's what makes me so late. My mother's down sick, and out of money and everything, and I come to tell my uncle Abner Moore. He lives at the upper end of the town, she says. I hain't ever been here before. Do you know him?"

"No; but I don't know everybody yet. I haven't lived here quite two weeks. It's a considerable ways to the upper end of the town. You better stay here all night. Take off your bonnet."

"No," I says, "I'll rest a while, I reckon, and go on. I ain't afeard of the dark."

She said she wouldn't let me go by myself, but her husband would be in by-and-by, maybe in a hour and a half,

1. *Hookerville, seven mile below.* According to Dahlia Armon and Walter Blair in *Huck Finn and Tom Sawyer Among the Indians* (1989, p. 291), Twain's working notes for "Tom Sawyer, Conspirator" of 1897 indicate that this is Saverton, Missouri, a small town seven miles south of Hannibal.

and she'd send him along with me. Then she got to talking about her husband, and about her relations up the river, and her relations down the river, and about how much better off they used to was, and how they didn't know but they'd made a mistake coming to our town, instead of letting well alone—and so on and so on, till I was afeard *I* had made a mistake coming to her to find out what was going on in the town; but by-and-by she dropped onto pap and the murder, and then I was pretty willing to let her clatter right along. She told about me and Tom Sawyer finding the six thousand dollars[2] (only she got it ten) and all about pap and what a hard lot he was, and what a hard lot I was, and at last she got down to where I was murdered. I says:

"Who done it? We've heard considerable about these goings on, down in Hookerville, but we don't know who 'twas that killed Huck Finn."

"Well, I reckon there's a right smart chance of people[3] *here* that 'd like to know who killed him. Some thinks old Finn done it himself."

"No—is that so?"

"Most everybody thought it at first. He'll never know how nigh he come to getting lynched.[4] But before night they changed around and judged it was done by a runaway nigger named Jim."

"Why *he*——"

I stopped. I reckoned I better keep still. She run on, and never noticed I had put in at all.

"The nigger run off the very night Huck Finn was killed. So there's a reward out for him—three hundred dollars. And there's a reward out for old Finn too—two hundred dollars.[5] You see, he come to town the morning after the murder, and told about it, and was out with 'em on the ferry-boat hunt, and right away after he up and left. Before night they wanted to lynch him, but he was gone, you see. Well, next day they found out the nigger was gone; they found out he hadn't ben seen sence ten o'clock[6] the night the murder was done. So then they put it on him, you see, and while they was full of it, next day back comes old Finn and went boo-hooing to Judge Thatcher to get money to

2. *me and Tom Sawyer finding the six thousand dollars*. The editors of the 1977 Norton Critical Edition of *Huckleberry Finn* suggested that Huck must mean six thousand dollars *apiece*; Twain said in Chapter 34 of *Tom Sawyer,* "The sum amounted to little over twelve thousand dollars." Huck reported in Chapter 1 of *Huckleberry Finn*, "We got six thousand dollars apiece—all gold."

3. *a right smart chance of people*. A particularly great number of people. "No phrase of the . . . Southern dialect is such a stumbling block to the outsider as right smart," Edward Eggleston explained in the 1913 annotated edition of *The Hoosier Schoolmaster*. "The writer from the North or East will generally use it wrongly. Mrs. Stowe says, 'I sold right smart of eggs,' but the Hoosier woman as I knew her would have said 'a right smart lot of eggs' or 'a right smart of eggs,' using the article and understanding the noun. A farmer omitting the preposition boasts of having 'raised right smart corn' this year. No expression could have a more vague sense than this" (p. 71).

4. *getting lynched*. Vigilantism, known as "lynch law," was widespread throughout the South and Southwest at the time of the story. "I believe it originated in one of the Southern States," Charles Augustus Murray explained in vol. 2, Chapter 5, of *Travels in North America* (1839), "where a body of farmers, unable to bring some depredators to justice, according to legal form, chose one of their number, named Lynch, judge; from the rest they selected a jury, and from this self-constituted court they issued and enforced sundry whippings, and other punishments. During the last few years the settlements in the Mississippi valley have increased so fast, that the number of law courts have been found too few and dilatory; and the inhabitants have, in many places assembled together, assumed the sovereign authority of the law, appointed a judge Lynch and a jury from among themselves, and have punished, and frequently hanged, those brought before them." Originally, "lynching" referred to any punishment executed by these false courts, but the term soon became synonymous with "hanging."

Orion Clemens reprinted a report of the execution of an accused murderer "by a decree of Judge Lynch's court" in the Hannibal *Journal* (May 27, 1852):

> Great excitement pervaded the town, and it was suggested that the prisoner be *lynched.* But he was taken to the Court House and confined in the upper room and ironed. The examination proceeded. For a time the people . . . were quiet. The Sheriff addressed the crowd, and they agreed not to be guilty of any violence. After a while, however, and when the body was disposed for the enquiry, the officers were alarmed by the appearance of a party who demanded the possession of the prisoner. The Sheriff remonstrated, but to no purpose. The emigrants took the man in custody, and proceeded to try him. A judge, jury, and officers were appointed; and despite the remonstrances of the District Attorney, and others, the trial was proceeded with. At the conclusion of the examination, the jury declared the prisoner guilty, and sentenced him to execution at 5 o'clock that evening, at or near the spot where the murder was committed. Clergymen were admitted to him, but he protested his innocence of this crime, though guilty of others. At the hour appointed, the man was taken to the spot, a rope thrown over the limb of a tree, and adjusted round his neck—the prisoner then mounted on a mule, which was driven from under him, and the fall broke his neck. To the last, he protested his innocence of the crime.

In a suppressed chapter on Southern violence for *Life on the Mississippi* (but published in the 1944 Limited Editions Club edition), Twain argued that the chief cause of vigilantism was that "it is not the rule for courts to hang murderers. . . . Their juries fail to convict, even in the clearest cases. That this is not agreeable to the public, is shown by the fact that very frequently such a miscarriage of justice so rouses the people that they rise, in a passion, and break into the jail, drag out their man and lynch him. . . . But this hundred or two hundred men usually do this act of public justice with masks on. They go to their grim work with clear consciences, but with their faces disguised. They know that the law will not meddle with them—otherwise, at least, than by empty form—and they know that the community will applaud their act" (p. 414).

And lynching was hardly the only form of lawlessness common to the South and Southwest. "Never, perhaps, in the records of nations," wrote Englishman Captain Marryat in

hunt for the nigger all over Illinois with.[7] The judge give him some, and that evening he got drunk and was around till after midnight with a couple of mighty hard looking strangers, and then went off with them. Well, he hain't come back sence, and they ain't looking for him back till this thing blows over a little, for people thinks now that he killed his boy and fixed things so folks would think robbers done it, and then he'd get Huck's money without having to bother a long time with a lawsuit. People do say he warn't any too good to do it. Oh, he's sly, I reckon. If he don't come back for a year, he'll be all right. You can't prove anything on him, you know; everything will be quieted down then, and he'll walk into Huck's money as easy as nothing."

"Yes, I reckon so, 'm. I don't see nothing in the way of it. Has everybody quit thinking the nigger done it?"

"Oh, no, not everybody. A good many thinks he done it. But they'll get the nigger pretty soon, now, and maybe they can scare it out of him."

"Why, are they after him yet?"

"Well, you're innocent, ain't you! Does three hundred dollars lay round every day for people to pick up? Some folks thinks the nigger ain't far from here. I'm one of them—but I hain't talked it around. A few days ago I was talking with an old couple that lives next door in the log shanty, and they happened to say hardly anybody ever goes to that island over yonder that they call Jackson's Island. Don't anybody live there? says I. No, nobody, says they. I didn't say any more, but I done some thinking. I was pretty near certain I'd seen smoke over there, about the head of the island, a day or two before that, so I says to myself, like as not that nigger's hiding over there; anyway, says I, it's worth the trouble to give the place a hunt. I hain't seen any smoke sence, so I reckon maybe he's gone, if it was him; but husband's going over to see—him and another man. He was gone up the river; but he got back to-day and I told him as soon as he got here two hours ago."

I had got so uneasy I couldn't set still. I had to do some-

"HIM AND ANOTHER MAN."

thing with my hands; so I took up a needle off of the table and went to threading it. My hands shook, and I was making a bad job of it. When the woman stopped talking, I looked up, and she was looking at me pretty curious, and smiling a little. I put down the needle and thread and let on to be interested—and I was, too—and says:

"Three hundred dollars is a power[8] of money. I wish my mother could get it. Is your husband going over there to-night?"

"Oh, yes. He went up town with the man I was telling you of, to get a boat and see if they could borrow another gun. They'll go over after midnight."

"Couldn't they see better if they was to wait till day-time?"

"Yes. And couldn't the nigger see better, too? After mid-night he'll likely be asleep, and they can slip around through the woods and hunt up his camp fire all the better for the dark, if he's got one."

"I didn't think of that."

The woman kept looking at me pretty curious, and I didn't feel a bit comfortable. Pretty soon she says:

Chapter 8 of the second of his American diaries (1840), "was there an instance of a century of such unvarying and unmitigated crime as is to be collected from the history of the turbulent and bloodstained Mississippi." Understandably, Twain was defensive. "It is imagined in the North," he wrote in the suppressed passage, "that the South is one vast and gory murder-field, and that every man goes armed, and has at one time or another taken a neighbor's life. . . . There is a superstition, current everywhere, that the Southern temper is peculiarly hot; whereas, in truth, the temper of the average Southerner is no hotter than that of the average Northerner (413)." And yet even a quiet little town like St. Petersburg could quickly and easily turn ugly when its citizens too followed mob rule. Local abolitionist George Thompson wrote in his memoirs, *Prison Life and Reflections* (1847), that during his trial, a mob formed in Palmyra and "had erected a gallows, provided ropes, blackened their faces, and were ever ready to take us at a moment's notice, in case we were acquitted, and hang us on the spot!" (p. 91). Reconstruction did nothing to correct the situation. Twain wrote a scathing attack on the recent lynching of an innocent man, falsely accused of raping a white woman in Memphis, in "Only a Nigger" (Buffalo *Express*, August 26, 1869). Twain quoted a contemporary article from Louisville, Kentucky, in the suppressed chapter for *Life on the Mississippi*: "The social condition of the State is worse than we have ever known it. Murders are more frequent, punishment is lighter, pardons more numerous, and abuses more flagrant than at any period within our recollection, dating back fifteen years" (p. 415). And consequently, lynching was rampant in the South. The numerous references to lynchings and other examples of violent social injustice throughout *Huckleberry Finn* reflected as much the time in which it was published as the historical period in which the story is set. Forty to fifty years might have passed, but nothing had changed.

5. *there's a reward out for him—three hundred dollars. And there's a reward out for old Finn too—two hundred dollars.* Although each man is accused of the same crime, Jim is such valuable property that the bounty on his head is higher than that for worthless pap Finn.

"What did you say your name was, honey?"

"M—Mary Williams."

Somehow it didn't seem to me that I said it was Mary before, so I didn't look up; seemed to me I said it was Sarah; so I felt sort of cornered, and was afeared maybe I was looking it, too. I wished the woman would say something more; the longer she set still, the uneasier I was. But now she says:

"Honey, I thought you said it was Sarah when you first come in?"

"Oh, yes'm, I did. Sarah Mary Williams. Sarah's my first name. Some calls me Sarah, some calls me Mary."[9]

"Oh, that's the way of it?"

"Yes'm."

I was feeling better, then, but I wished I was out of there, anyway. I couldn't look up yet.

Well, the woman fell to talking about how hard times was, and how poor they had to live, and how the rats was as free as if they owned the place, and so forth, and so on, and then I got easy again. She was right about the rats. You'd see one stick his nose out of a hole in the corner every little while. She said she had to have things handy to throw at them when she was alone, or they wouldn't give her no peace. She showed me a bar of lead, twisted up into a knot, and said she was a good shot with it generly, but she'd wrenched her arm a day or two ago, and didn't know whether she could throw true, now. But she watched for a chance, and directly she banged away at a rat, but she missed him wide, and said "Ouch!" it hurt her arm so. Then she told me to try for the next one. I wanted to be getting away before the old man got back, but of course I didn't let on. I got the thing, and the first rat that showed his nose I let drive, and if he'd a stayed where he was he'd a been a tolerable sick rat. She said that that was first-rate, and she reckoned I would hive the next one.[10] She went and got the lump of lead and fetched it back and brought along a hank of yarn, which she wanted me to help her with. I held up my two hands and she put the hank over them and went on talking about her and her husband's matters. But she broke off to say:

6. *he hadn't ben seen sence ten o'clock.* The curfew for slaves in Hannibal was nine o'clock, so it took only about an hour for people to notice Jim was gone.

7. *to hunt for the nigger all over Illinois with.* According to the Fugitive Slave Act of 1850, runaways could be pursued into free soil.

8. *a power.* Or "powerful lot," a great deal.

9. *some calls me Sarah, some calls me Mary.* Twain was caught in a similar fix while traveling in Europe, when a pretty woman greeted him and he just did not remember her. In Chapter 25 of *A Tramp Abroad*, he described how she plied him with questions for which he struggled to contrive acceptable replies. They get on to discussing a supposed mutual friend's child who has died, and the woman says:

> "And what a pretty little thing his child was! . . . What *was* that name? I can't call it to mind."
>
> It appeared to me that ice was getting pretty thin, here. . . . I thought I might risk a name for it and trust to luck. Therefore I said,—
>
> "I called that one Thomas Henry."
>
> She said, musingly,—
>
> "That is very singular . . . very singular."

She then went on to other topics; and still Twain did not know what she was talking about, and yet he would not confess that he did not know her. Finally she said:

> "But there is one thing that is ever so puzzling me."
>
> "Why what is that?"
>
> "That dead child's name. What did you say it was?"
>
> Here was another balmy place for to be in: I had forgotten the child's name. . . . However, I had to pretend to know, anyway, so I said,
>
> "Joseph William."
>
> The youth at my side corrected me, and said,—
>
> "No,—Thomas Henry."
>
> I thanked him. . . . "Thomas Henry—yes, Thomas Henry was the poor child's name . . . for Thomas—er,—Thomas Carlyle, the great author, you know,—and Henry—er,—er—Henry the Eighth. The parents were very grateful to have a child named Thomas Henry."
>
> "That makes it more singular than ever," murmured my beautiful friend.

"Keep your eye on the rats. You better have the lead in your lap, handy."

So she dropped the lump into my lap, just at that moment, and I clapped my legs together on it and she went on talking. But only about a minute. Then she took off the hank and looked me straight in the face, but very pleasant, and says:

"Come, now—what's your real name?"

"Wh-what, mum?"

"What's your real name? Is it Bill, or Tom, or Bob?—or what is it?"

I reckon I shook like a leaf, and I didn't know hardly what to do. But I says:

"Please to don't poke fun at a poor girl like me, mum. If I'm in the way, here, I'll——"

"No, you won't. Set down and stay where you are. I ain't going to hurt you, and I ain't going to tell on you, nuther. You just tell me your secret, and trust me. I'll keep it; and what's more, I'll help you. So'll my old man, if you want him to. You see, you're a runaway 'prentice—that's all. It ain't anything. There ain't any harm in it. You've been treated bad, and you made up your mind to cut. Bless you, child, I wouldn't tell on you. Tell me all about it, now—that's a good boy."

So I said it wouldn't be no use to try to play it any longer, and I would just make a clean breast and tell her everything,[11] but she mustn't go back on her promise. Then I told her my father and mother was dead, and the law had bound me out to a mean old farmer[12] in the country thirty mile back from the river, and he treated me so bad I couldn't stand it no longer; he went away to be gone a couple of days, and so I took my chance and stole some of his daughter's old clothes, and cleared out, and I had been three nights coming the thirty miles; I traveled nights, and hid day-times and slept, and the bag of bread and meat I carried from home lasted me all the way and I had a plenty. I said I believed my uncle Abner Moore would take care of me, and so that was why I struck out for this town of Goshen."[13]

"Does it? Why?"

"Because when the parents speak of that child now, they always call it Susan Amelia."

10. *I would hive the next one*. I would get (or hit) the next one.

11. *I would just make a clean breast and tell her everything*. "Readers who have met Huck Finn before (in *Tom Sawyer*)," Twain prefaced "An Adventure of Huckleberry Finn" (*Century Magazine*, December 1884), "will not be surprised to note that whenever Huck is caught in a close place and is obliged to explain, the truth gets well crippled before he gets through" (p. 268). Twain must have been recalling Chapter 30 in *Tom Sawyer*, where the boy blurts more information than he should: "Huck had made another terrible mistake! He was trying his best to keep the old man from getting the faintest hint of who the Spaniard might be, and yet his tongue seemed determined to get him into trouble in spite of all he could do. He made several efforts to creep out of his scrape, but the old man's eye was upon him and he made blunder after blunder." But Huck's nimble brain also has extraordinary recuperative powers, as in the second "stretcher" he contrives for Mrs. Judith Loftus.

12. *my father and mother was dead, and the law had bound me out to a mean old farmer*. A male orphan, as a ward of the state and with few rights of his own, could by law be bound as an apprentice from the age of fourteen until he reached twenty-one years of age. Their appointed masters often abused these boys, so there were about as many runaway apprentices in the country as fugitive slaves. These boys were always at the mercy of the whims of their employers. A year after his father died in 1847, Sam Clemens was apprenticed to Joseph Ament, publisher of the Hannibal *Missouri Courier*, whose chief competition briefly was the *Western Union*, run by Sam's brother Orion. His boss paid him "the usual emolument of the office of apprentice—that is to say board and clothes, and no money. The clothes consisted of two suits a year, but one of the suits always failed to materialize and the other suit was not purchased so long as Mr. [Ament]'s old clothes held out. I was only about half as big as Mr. [Ament], consequently his shirts gave me the uncomfortable sense of living in a circus tent, and I had to turn up his pants to my ears to make them short enough" ("Chapters from My Autobiography," *North American Review*, January 18, 1907, p. 118).

13. *Goshen.* The biblical Land of Plenty, a fitting neighboring town for "St. Petersburg"; actually Marion City, ten miles upriver from Hannibal. Twain noted in Chapter 57 of *Life on the Mississippi* that Marion City, at this time, "contained one street, and nearly or quite six houses."

"Goshen, child? This ain't Goshen. This is St. Petersburg. Goshen's ten mile further up the river. Who told you this was Goshen?"

"Why, a man I met at day-break this morning, just as I was going to turn into the woods for my regular sleep. He told me when the roads forked I must take the right hand, and five mile would fetch me to Goshen."

"He was drunk I reckon. He told you just exactly wrong."

"Well, he did act like he was drunk, but it ain't no matter now. I got to be moving along. I'll fetch Goshen before day-light."

SHE PUTS UP A SNACK.

"Hold on a minute. I'll put you up a snack to eat. You might want it."

So she put me up a snack, and says:

"Say—when a cow's laying down, which end of her gets up first? Answer up prompt, now—don't stop to study over it. Which end gets up first?"

"The hind end, mum."

"Well, then, a horse?"

"The for'rard end, mum."

"Which side of a tree does the most moss grow on?"

"North side."

"If fifteen cows is browsing on a hillside, how many of them eats with their heads pointed the same direction?"

"The whole fifteen, mum."

"Well, I reckon you *have* lived in the country. I thought maybe you was trying to hocus me[14] again. What's your real name, now?"

"George Peters, mum."

"Well, try to remember it, George. Don't forget and tell me it's Elexander before you go, and then get out by saying it's George-Elexander when I catch you. And don't go about women in that old calico. You do a girl tolerable poor, but you might fool men, maybe. Bless you, child, when you set out to thread a needle, don't hold the thread still and fetch the needle up to it; hold the needle still and poke the thread at it—that's the way a woman most always does; but a man always does 'tother way.[15] And when you throw at a rat or anything, hitch yourself up a tip-toe, and fetch your hand up over your head as awkard as you can, and miss your rat about six or seven foot. Throw stiff-armed from the shoulder, like there was a pivot there for it to turn on—like a girl; not from the wrist and elbow, with your arm out to one side, like a boy. And mind you, when a girl tries to catch anything in her lap, she throws her knees apart; she don't clap them together,[16] the way you did when you catched the lump of lead. Why, I spotted you for a boy when you was threading the needle; and I contrived the other things just to make certain.[17] Now trot along to your uncle, Sarah Mary Williams George Elexander Peters, and if you get into trouble you send word to Mrs. Judith Loftus, which is me, and I'll do what I can to get you out of it. Keep the river road, all the way, and next time you tramp, take shoes and socks with you. The river road's a rocky one, and your feet 'll be in a condition when you get to Goshen,[18] I reckon."

I went up the bank about fifty yards, and then I doubled on my tracks and slipped back to where my canoe was, a good piece below the house. I jumped in and was off in a hurry. I went up stream far enough to make the head of the

14. *hocus me*. Play a trick on me; from "hoax" or "hocus-pocus."

15. *a man always does 'tother way*. And yet Miles Hendon does it exactly the opposite way in Chapter 13 of *The Prince and the Pauper*: "He did as men have always done, and probably always will do, to the end of time—held the needle still, and tried to thrust the thread through the eye, which is the opposite of a woman's way." Obviously Twain did not really know which was the true "woman's way."

16. *when a girl tries to catch anything in her lap, she throws her knees apart; she don't clap them together*. Blair in *Mark Twain and Huck Finn* (p. 400) mentioned a similar incident in an obscure romance by George Payne Ramsford James, *One in a Thousand* (1836): A guard unmasks a woman, disguised as a page, when he throws a knife in her lap and she spreads her legs to catch it. And Philip H. Highfill, Jr., in *Mark Twain Journal* (Fall 1961, p. 6) suggested another possible source in "The Two Thieves," an anecdote in Edmund H. Barker's *Literary Anecdotes and Contemporary Reminiscences* (vol. 1, 1852): "Two thieves, disguised as country-girls, obtained admittance at a farmhouse, which they intended to rob. In the course of the evening, the farmer began to entertain suspicion of their sex. To settle the point, he tossed into their laps shells of some nuts he had been cracking. The pretended females immediately closed their knees to prevent the shells from falling through, forgetting that women never do so, because their petticoats accomplish that purpose for them. The farmer secretly left the house and returned with assistance to capture his deceitful guests" (p. 282).

However, the most likely model for this scene appears in Charles Reade's *The Cloister and the Hearth* (1861), a romance set in Rome in the age of Lorenzo de Medici and a book which Twain greatly enjoyed. In Chapter 63, two ladies, jealous of all the attention lavished on a newcomer introduced as "Marcia," conspire against the creature:

> "Signora, do you love almonds?"
> The speaker had a lapful of them.
> "Yes, I love them; when I can get them," said Marcia, pettishly, and eying the fruit with ill-concealed desire; "but yours is not the hand to give me any, I trow."
> "You are much mistook," said the other. "Here, catch!"

island, and then started across. I took off the sun-bonnet, for I didn't want no blinders[19] on, then. When I was about the middle, I hear the clock begin to strike; so I stops and listens; the sound come faint over the water, but clear—eleven. When I struck the head of the island I never waited to blow, though I was most winded, but I shoved right into the timber where my old camp used to be, and started a good fire there on a high-and-dry spot.

Then I jumped in the canoe and dug out for our place a mile and a half below, as hard as I could go. I landed, and slopped through the timber and up the ridge and into the cavern. There Jim laid, sound asleep on the ground. I roused him out and says:

"Git up and hump yourself,[20] Jim! There ain't a minute to lose. They're after us!"

Jim never asked no questions, he never said a word; but the way he worked for the next half an hour showed about how he was scared. By that time everything we had in the world was on our raft and she was ready to be shoved out from the willow cove where she was hid. We put out the camp fire at the cavern the first thing, and didn't show a candle outside after that.

"HUMP YOURSELF!"

And suddenly threw a double handful into Marcia's lap.

Marcia brought her knees together by an irresistible instinct.

"Aha! you are caught, my lad," cried she of the nuts. "'Tis a man, or a boy. A woman still parteth her knees to catch the nuts the surer in her apron; but a man closeth his for fear they shall fall between his hose."

17. *I contrived the other things just to make certain.* Mrs. Judith Loftus is one of those clever housewives in Twain's fiction, whose cunning interrogations of boys owe something to the contrivances of Shillaber's Mrs. Partington (see Chapter 1, note 18) and of Jane Clemens, the author's mother. A neighbor once asked her, "Do you ever believe anything that that boy says?" "He is the well-spring of truth, but you can't bring up the whole truth with one bucket," Jane Clemens said of her mischievous boy. "I know his average, therefore he never deceives me. I discount him thirty per cent for embroidery, and what is left is perfect and priceless truth, without a flaw in it anywhere" ("Chapters from My Autobiography," *North American Review*, April 19, 1907, pp. 785–86).

Another kindhearted farm wife who shares this "pet vanity" is the woman who befriends the fugitive Edward in Chapter 19 of *The Prince and the Pauper*. Curious about the stranger's origins, she "set herself to contriving devices to surprise the boy into betraying his real secret." And unlike Judith Loftus, she fails; she suspects he is a cow-boy, a shepherd, a servant, or an apprentice, but never the rightful King of England. Of course, the most famous of these women is Tom Sawyer's Aunt Polly. "Like many other simple-hearted souls," Twain said in Chapter 1 of *Tom Sawyer*, "it was her pet vanity to believe she was endowed with a talent for dark and mysterious diplomacy, and she loved to contemplate her most transparent devices as marvels of low cunning."

18. *The river road's a rocky one . . . to Goshen.* An unintended pun? The proverbial road to "Goshen" (Heaven) is said to be a rocky one. Note that Huck Finn characteristically takes the opposite route.

19. *blinders.* Or blinkers; flaps on a horse's bridle to prevent it from seeing distracting objects

I took the canoe out from shore a little piece and took a look, but if there was a boat around I couldn't see it, for stars and shadows ain't good to see by. Then we got out the raft and slipped along down in the shade, past the foot of the island dead still, never saying a word.

at its sides. Twain reminds the reader that the sunbonnet so hid Huck's face that it "was like looking down a joint of stove-pipe."

20. *hump yourself.* "Be sharp!"; "Look alive!"

Chapter XII

ON THE RAFT.

MUST a been close onto one o'clock when we got below the island at last, and the raft did seem to go mighty slow. If a boat was to come along, we was going to take to the canoe and break for the Illinois shore; and it was well a boat didn't come, for we hadn't ever thought to put the gun into the canoe, or a fishing-line or anything to eat. We was in ruther too much of a sweat to think of so many things. It warn't good judgment to put *everything* on the raft.

If the men went to the island, I just expect they found the camp fire I built, and watched it all night for Jim to come. Anyways, they stayed away from us, and if my building the fire never fooled them it warn't no fault of mine. I played it as low-down on them as I could.

When the first streak of day begun to show, we tied up to a tow-head[1] in a big bend on the Illinois side, and hacked off cotton-wood branches with the hatchet and covered up the raft with them so she looked like there had been a cave-in in the bank there. A tow-head is a sand-bar that has cotton-woods on it as thick as harrow-teeth.[2]

We had mountains on the Missouri shore and heavy timber on the Illinois side, and the channel was down the Missouri shore at that place, so we warn't afraid of anybody running across us. We laid there all day and watched the

1. *a tow-head.* "'Tow-head' means infant, an infant island, a growing island" (*Mark Twain's Notebook*, 1935, p. 161).

2. *as thick as harrow-teeth.* As numerous as the blades on a peg-toothed cultivating machine.

rafts and steamboats spin down the Missouri shore, and up-bound steamboats[3] fight the big river in the middle. I told Jim all about the time I had jabbering with that woman; and Jim said she was a smart one, and if she was to start after us herself *she* wouldn't set down and watch a camp fire—no, sir, she'd fetch a dog.[4] Well, then, I said, why couldn't she tell her husband to fetch a dog? Jim said he bet she did think of it by the time the men was ready to start, and he believed they must a gone up town to get a dog and so they lost all that time, or else we wouldn't be here on a tow-head sixteen or seventeen mile below the village—no, indeedy, we would be in that same old town again. So I said I didn't care what was the reason they didn't get us, as long as they didn't.

When it was beginning to come on dark, we poked our heads out of the cottonwood thicket and looked up, and down, and across; nothing in sight; so Jim took up some of the top planks of the raft and built a snug wigwam to get under in blazing weather and rainy, and to keep the things dry. Jim made a floor for the wigwam, and raised it a foot or more above the level of the raft, so now the blankets and all the traps was out of the reach of steamboat waves. Right in the middle of the wigwam we made a layer of dirt about five or six inches deep with a frame around it for to hold it to its place; this was to build a fire on in sloppy weather or chilly; the wigwam would keep it from being seen. We made an extra steering oar, too, because one of the others might get broke, on a snag[5] or something. We fixed up a short forked stick to hang the old lantern on; because we must always light the lantern whenever we see a steamboat coming down stream,[6] to keep from getting run over; but we wouldn't have to light it for up-stream boats unless we see we was in what they call a "crossing;"[7] for the river was pretty high yet, very low banks being still a little under water; so up-bound boats didn't always run the channel, but hunted easy water.

This second night we run between seven and eight hours, with a current that was making over four mile an hour. We catched fish, and talked, and we took a swim now

3. *up-bound steamboats.* Ships heading up-stream against the current.

4. *she'd fetch a dog.* Twain wondered how practical this might be; he jotted in the margin of the manuscript, "Dog no good if island still overflowed" (**MS**).

5. *a snag.* An obstruction in the water; floods tear out trees and branches, which then accumulate sand and other refuse and pose a constant danger to navigation. Undetected snags caused the most frequent damage to steamboats, flatboats, and other vessels along the Mississippi.

Snags. Illustration from *Harper's Monthly*, December 1855.
Private collection.

6. *we must always light the lantern whenever we see a steamboat coming down stream.* Twain noted in Chapter 10 of *Life on the Mississippi* that the "law required all such helpless traders to keep a light burning, but it was a law that was often broken." "Like the raft, downstream boats followed the current in the river's natural channel, where water was fastest and safest," Blair and Fischer explained in the 1988 University of California edition. "Since such boats operated under power, there was always some danger of their overtaking and colliding with the raft, especially at night. Upstream boats, on the other hand, at least during high water, deliberately avoided the resistance of the channel, seeking out 'easy water' near the banks. Since the channel itself meandered from one side of the river to the other . . . , upstream boats were sometimes obliged to cross in the opposite direction to avoid it. Huck reasons that upstream boats posed a danger of collision

only when their paths intersected the channel" (p. 390).

7. *a "crossing."* A place in the river where steamboats, seeking the safest current, cross from one side to the other.

8. *twenty or thirty thousand people in St. Louis.* Twain originally wrote "15 or 20,000 people" (**MS**); but he must have checked the number later. In Chapter 22 of *Life on the Mississippi*, he quoted Marryat's 1839 American diary as confirming the population of St. Louis at the time as being 20,000. Huck and Jim are now about 170 miles south of "St. Petersburg" (Hannibal).

St. Louis, Missouri. Lithograph by J. S. Wild, *The Valley of the Mississippi* by J. E. Thomas, 1841.
Courtesy General Research and Humanities Division, New York Public Library, Astor, Lenox, and Tilden Foundations.

and then to keep off sleepiness. It was kind of solemn, drifting down the big still river, laying on our backs looking up at the stars, and we didn't ever feel like talking loud, and it warn't often that we laughed, only a little kind of a low chuckle. We had mighty good weather, as a general thing, and nothing ever happened to us at all, that night, nor the next, nor the next.

Every night we passed towns, some of them away up on black hillsides, nothing but just a shiny bed of lights, not a house could you see. The fifth night we passed St. Louis, and it was like the whole world lit up. In St. Petersburg they used to say there was twenty or thirty thousand people in St. Louis,[8] but I never believed it till I see that wonderful spread of lights at two o'clock that still night. There warn't a sound there; everybody was asleep.

HE SOMETIMES LIFTED A CHICKEN.

Every night, now, I used to slip ashore, towards ten o'clock, at some little village, and buy ten or fifteen cents' worth of meal or bacon or other stuff to eat; and sometimes I lifted a chicken that warn't roosting comfortable, and took him along. Pap always said, take a chicken when you get a chance, because if you don't want him yourself you can easy find somebody that does, and a good deed ain't ever forgot. I never see pap when he didn't want the chicken himself, but that is what he used to say, anyway.

Mornings, before daylight, I slipped into corn fields and borrowed a watermelon, or a mushmelon, or a punkin,[9] or some new corn, or things of that kind. Pap always said it warn't no harm to borrow things, if you was meaning to pay them back, sometime; but the widow said it warn't anything but a soft name for stealing, and no decent body would do it. Jim said he reckoned the widow was partly right and pap was partly right;[10] so the best way would be for us to pick out two or three things from the list and say we wouldn't borrow them any more—then he reckoned it wouldn't be no harm to borrow the others. So we talked it over all one night, drifting along down the river, trying to make up our minds whether to drop the watermelons, or the cantelopes, or the mushmelons, or what. But towards daylight we got it all settled satisfactory, and concluded to drop crabapples and p'simmons.[11] We warn't feeling just right, before that, but it was all comfortable now. I was glad the way it come out, too, because crabapples ain't ever good, and the p'simmons wouldn't be ripe for two or three months yet.

We shot a water-fowl, now and then, that got up too early in the morning or didn't go to bed early enough in the evening. Take it all around, we lived pretty high.

The fifth night below St. Louis we had a big storm after midnight,[12] with a power of thunder and lightning, and the rain poured down in a solid sheet. We stayed in the wigwam and let the raft take care of itself. When the lightning glared out we could see a big straight river ahead, and high rocky bluffs on both sides. By-and-by says I, "Hel-*lo,* Jim, looky yonder!" It was a steamboat that had killed herself on a rock.[13] We was drifting straight down for her. The lightning showed her very distinct. She was leaning over, with part of her upper deck above water, and you could see every little chimbly-guy[14] clean and clear, and a chair by the big bell, with an old slouch hat hanging on the back of it[15] when the flashes come.

9. *a mushmelon, or a punkin.* A muskmelon, or a pumpkin.

10. *the widow was partly right and pap was partly right.* Two angels, one black and the other white, as Jim predicted back in Chapter 4, are still hovering over Huck Finn. Along the river the theft of edibles was not considered stealing, while taking money was. It was commonly assumed that one had the right to take whatever one needed to feed oneself—if one could get away with it. "'Stole' is a strong word," Twain said of his theft of a watermelon back in Hannibal, in a talk titled "Morals and Memory" delivered at Barnard College, March 7, 1906. "Stole? Stole? No, I don't mean that. It was the first time I ever withdrew a watermelon. It was the first time I ever *ex*tracted a watermelon. That is exactly the word I want—'extracted.' It is definite. It is precise" (*Mark Twain's Speeches*, 1910, p. 228).

Fred W. Lorch reported in "A Note on Tom Blankenship (Huckleberry Finn)" (*American Literature*, November 1940, pp. 351–53) that the real Huckleberry Finn was a notorious local thief. According to the Hannibal *Daily Messenger* (April 21, 1861), the boy spent thirty days in the county jail for stealing turkeys; and after he was out, he took some onions from a garden the next Sunday night. "What is it that Tom wouldn't steal?" the paper asked on June 4. "We expect next to hear of his 'cabbaging' all the garden vegetables in town, after which he will probably go out in the country and 'hook' a few wheat and oat fields." So wide was his reputation that when anything was reported missing in Hannibal, Tom was the usual suspect. The *Daily Messenger* reported on the current increase in stealing in town in "Wholesale Thievery" (June 12), when two horses, a large lot of bacon, a six-gallon jug of butter, a washtubful of clothes, a large quantity of sugar, ten gallons of molasses, and some chickens all disappeared. "Tom Blankenship must have concluded to make another descent," the paper speculated, "and effectually clean out the Bay; or at least the surplus products of the inhabitants." He may well have left town and ended up in the penitentiary as reported in Chapter 1, note 1.

11. *p'simmons.* Persimmons, the American date plum, an orange-colored fruit common to Missouri and the South; although astringent when unripe, they were popular with slaves, who brewed "persimmon beer."

Well, it being away in the night, and stormy, and all so mysterious-like, I felt just the way any other boy would a felt when I see that wreck laying there so mournful and lonesome in the middle of the river. I wanted to get aboard of her and slink around a little, and see what there was there. So I says:

"Le's land on her, Jim."

But Jim was dead against it, at first. He says:

"I doan' want to go fool'n 'long er no wrack. We's doin' blame' well, en we better let blame' well alone, as de good book says.[16] Like as not dey's a watchman on dat wrack."

"Watchman your grandmother," I says; "there ain't nothing to watch but the texas[17] and the pilot-house; and do you reckon anybody's going to resk his life for a texas and a pilot-house such a night as this, when it's likely to break up and wash off down the river any minute?"[18] Jim couldn't say nothing to that, so he didn't try. "And besides," I says, "we might borrow something worth having, out of the captain's stateroom.[19] Seegars, *I* bet you—and cost five cents apiece,[20] solid cash. Steamboat captains is always rich, and get sixty dollars a month,[21] and *they* don't care a cent what a thing costs, you know, long as they want it. Stick a candle in your pocket; I can't rest, Jim, till we give her a rummaging. Do you reckon Tom Sawyer would ever go by this thing? Not for pie,[22] he wouldn't. He'd call it an adventure—that's what he'd call it; and he'd land on that wreck if it was his last act. And wouldn't he throw style into it?—wouldn't he spread himself, nor nothing? Why, you'd think it was Christopher C'lumbus discovering Kingdom-Come. I wish Tom Sawyer *was* here."

Jim he grumbled a little, but give in. He said we mustn't talk any more than we could help, and then talk mighty low. The lightning showed us the wreck again, just in time, and we fetched the starboard derrick, and made fast there.[23]

The deck was high out, here. We went sneaking down the slope of it to labboard,[24] in the dark, towards the texas, feeling our way slow with our feet, and spreading our hands out to fend off the guys,[25] for it was so dark we couldn't see no sign of them. Pretty soon we struck the forward end of the

12. *The fifth night below St. Louis we had a big storm after midnight.* The remainder of this chapter and the two subsequent ones were an afterthought, written in a burst of activity in the summer of 1883 when Twain finally completed the book. These pages introduce themes, including the influence of Sir Walter Scott on the Mississippi River Valley culture and the absurdity of kings, developed further in the story.

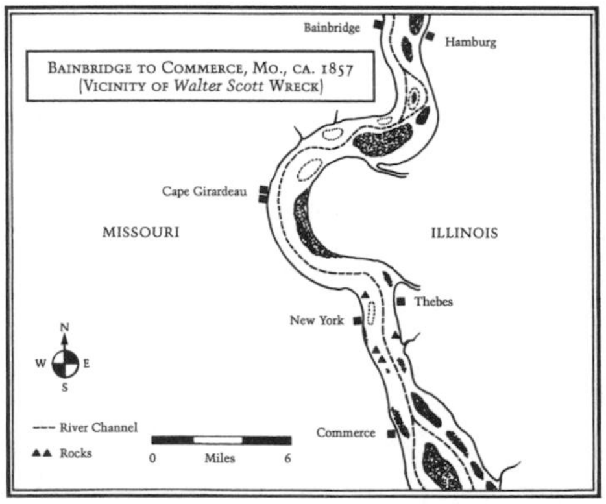

Map of the vicinity of the *Walter Scott* wreck, circa 1857.
Reprinted with permission from the Mark Twain Project's Adventures of Huckleberry Finn, edited by Victor Fischer and Lin Salamo (University of California, 2001). Copyright © 1985 and 2001 by the Regents of the University of California Press.

13. *a steamboat that had killed herself on a rock.* No matter what the name of the vessel, *Paul Jones* or *Sir Walter Scott* or even *Mark Twain*, a steamboat like other ships is traditionally called "she." Blair and Fischer suggested in the 1988 University of California edition that Twain may well have been thinking of "the Grand Chain," between Thebes, Illinois, and Commerce, Missouri, which he described in Chapter 25 of *Life on the Mississippi* as "a chain of sunken rocks admirably arranged to capture and kill steamboats on bad nights. A good many steamboat corpses lie buried there, out of sight." Twain's "first friend," the *Paul Jones*, "knocked her bottom out and went down like a pot, so the historian told me." Michael G. Miller suggested in "Geography and Structure" (*Studies in the Novel*, February 1980, p. 199) that another possibility for the location is that part of the river a few miles above Thebes, between Bainbridge, Mis-

skylight, and clumb onto it; and the next step fetched us in front of the captain's door, which was open, and by Jimminy, away down through the texas-hall we see a light! and all in the same second we seem to hear low voices in yonder!

Jim whispered and said he was feeling powerful sick, and told me to come along. I says, all right; and was going to start for the raft; but just then I heard a voice wail out and say:

"Oh, please don't, boys; I swear I won't ever tell!"

Another voice said, pretty loud:

"It's a lie, Jim Turner. You've acted this way before. You always want more'n your share of the truck, and you've always got it, too, because you've swore 't if you didn't you'd tell. But this time you've said it jest one time too many. You're the meanest, treacherousest hound in this country."

By this time Jim was gone for the raft. I was just a-biling[26] with curiosity; and I says to myself, Tom Sawyer wouldn't back out now, and so I won't either; I'm agoing to see what's going on here. So I dropped on my hands and knees, in the little passage, and crept aft in the dark, till there warn't but about one stateroom betwixt me and the cross-hall of the texas. Then, in there I see a man stretched on the floor and tied hand and foot, and two men standing over him, and one of them had a dim lantern in his hand, and the other one had a pistol. This one kept pointing the pistol at the man's head on the floor and saying—

"I'd *like* to! And I orter, too, a mean skunk!"

The man on the floor would shrivel up, and say: "Oh, please don't, Bill—I hain't ever goin' to tell."

And every time he said that, the man with the lantern would laugh, and say:

"'Deed you *ain't!* You never said no truer thing 'n that, you bet you." And once he said: "Hear him beg! and yit if we hadn't got the best of him and tied him, he'd a killed us both. And what *for?* Jist for noth'n. Jist because we stood on our *rights*—that's what for. But I lay you ain't agoin' to threaten nobody any more, Jim Turner. Put *up* that pistol, Bill."

Bill says:

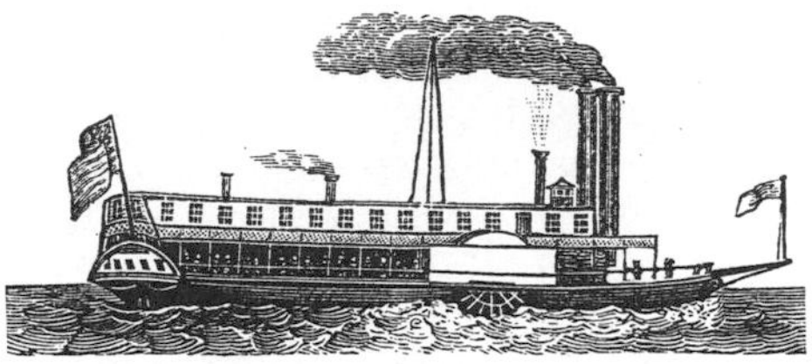

A Mississippi steamboat.
Courtesy Library of Congress.

souri, and Hamburg, Illinois, upstream and Cape Girardeau, Missouri, downstream, on the rocks of Grand Tower and Devil's Bake Oven or Devil's Tea Table. Twain explained in Chapter 25 of *Life on the Mississippi* that Grand Tower "gets its name from a huge, squat pillar of rock, which stands up out of the water on the Missouri side of the river—a piece of nature's fanciful handiwork—and is one of the most picturesque features of the scenery of that region. For nearer or remoter neighbors, the Tower has the Devil's Bake Oven—so called, perhaps, because it does not powerfully resemble anybody else's bake oven; and the Devil's Tea Table—this latter a great smooth-surfaced mass of rock, with diminishing wine-glass stem, perched some fifty or sixty feet above the river, beside a beflowered and garlanded precipice, and sufficiently like a tea-table to answer for anybody, Devil or Christian."

14. *chimbly-guy.* Chimney-guy, a steel cable used to fix and hold a smokestack in place.

15. *a chair by the big bell, with an old slouch hat hanging on the back of it.* Either the pilot was away from his watch, causing the wreck of the steamboat, or he had to abandon the boat so quickly that he left his hat. "'The big bell' was used to signal arrivals and departures as well as various alarms," explained Blair and Fischer in the 1988 University of California edition. "It was a standard fixture on the roof of the upper (hurricane) deck. The captain would routinely 'come on the roof' and stand beside the three-foot fixed bell, briefly resuming command from his pilot until the boat was again under way. . . . The captain might also take up this post during any hazardous maneuver" (p. 390). They also quoted Dickens's observation in *American Notes* (1842) that "when the nights are very dark, the look-out, stationed in the head of the boat, knows by the ripple of the water if any great impediment be at hand, and rings a bell beside him, which is the signal for the engine to be stopped."

16. *let blame' well alone, as de good book says.* The maxim "Let well enough alone" is not biblical; it has been traced as far back as 161 B.C., to Terence's *Phormio*, and even there is said to be an "old saying." A common device in Southern and Southwestern humor was crediting any old proverb to the Bible (or to Shakespeare).

17. *the texas.* The officers' quarters, the largest cabin, occupying the upper deck of the river steamer, with the pilot house located before or on top. According to John S. Farmer's *Americanisms—Old and New* (1889), this open deck was originally "frequented by the personal friends of the pilot, . . . men of great daring, . . . and expert in the use of the bowie-knife and pistol, but as little desirable as the first settlers of the Republic of Texas, which attracted all the lawless and desperate characters of the Union." However, the most common theory of the etymology of the name is that the cabins of Mississippi steamboats were named for the states (see note 19 below), and in the 1840s, after Texas entered the Union, the largest of the rooms became known as "the texas" after the largest of the states. See also Chapter 13, note 19.

18. *do you reckon anybody's going to resk his life for a texas and a pilot-house such a night as this, when it's likely to break up and wash off down the river any minute?* Huck Finn displays an extraordinarily extensive knowledge of river wisdom as the son of the town drunkard. These terms and descriptions, provided by former Mississippi pilot Sam Clemens, were not common knowledge of most of Twain's readers.

19. *stateroom.* An individual sleeping room on a passenger steamer, originally named for the states of the Union. The earliest riverboats contained only one large cabin for men and a smaller one for women; but about 1817, Henry M. Shreve, captain of the *Washington*, broke these up into separate quarters and named them after the states. Captain Isaiah Sellers, another pilot (and the author of a newspaper column that Clemens burlesqued in 1859

"PLEASE DON'T, BILL."

"I don't want to, Jake Packard. I'm for killin' him—and didn't he kill old Hatfield jist the same way—and don't he deserve it?"

"But I don't *want* him killed, and I've got my reasons for it."

"Bless yo' heart for them words, Jake Packard! I'll never forgit you, long's I live!" says the man on the floor, sort of blubbering.

Packard didn't take no notice of that, but hung up his lantern on a nail, and started towards where I was, there in the dark, and motioned Bill to come. I crawfished[27] as fast as I could, about two yards, but the boat slanted so that I couldn't make very good time; so to keep from getting run over and catched I crawled into a stateroom on the upper side. The man come a-pawing along in the dark, and when Packard got to my stateroom, he says:

"Here—come in here."

And in he come, and Bill after him. But before they got in, I was up in the upper berth, cornered, and sorry I come. Then they stood there, with their hands on the ledge of the berth, and talked. I couldn't see them, but I could tell where they was,[28] by the whisky they'd been having. I was glad I didn't drink whisky; but it wouldn't made much difference, anyway, because most of the time they couldn't a treed[29] me because I didn't breathe. I was too scared. And besides, a body *couldn't* breathe, and hear such talk. They talked low and earnest. Bill wanted to kill Turner. He says:

"He's said he'll tell, and he will. If we was to give both our shares to him *now*, it wouldn't make no difference after the row, and the way we've served him. Shore's you're born, he'll turn State's evidence;[30] now you hear *me*. I'm for putting him out of his troubles."

"So'm I," says Packard, very quiet.

"Blame it, I'd sorter begun to think you wasn't. Well, then, that's all right. Les' go and do it."

"Hold on a minute; I hain't had my say yit. You listen to

"IT AIN'T GOOD MORALS."

me. Shooting's good, but there's quieter ways if the thing's *got* to be done. But what *I* say, is this; it ain't good sense to go court'n around after a halter,[31] if you can git at what you're up to in some way that's jist as good and at the same time don't bring you into no resks. Ain't that so?"

"You bet it is. But how you goin' to manage it this time?"

"Well, my idea is this: we'll rustle around and gether up

Inside a stateroom.
Courtesy Picture Collection, New York Public Library, Astor, Lenox, and Tilden Foundations.

under the name "Sergeant Fathom") is credited with having given the term "stateroom" to these cabins.

20. *Seegars . . . cost five cents apiece*. Quite a price for a cigar at the time. Twain noted in "Villagers of 1840–43" (1897) that a wealthy merchant in Hannibal smoked fancy cigars, "regalias," that cost five cents apiece (*Huck Finn and Tom Sawyer Among the Indians*, 1989, p. 101). As for "long yards," a cheaper kind he smoked when a riverboat pilot, he recalled in "Chapters from My Autobiography" (*North American Review*, April 19, 1907) that "you could get a basketful of them for a cent—or a dime, they didn't use cents out there in those days" (p. 787).

21. *Steamboat captains . . . get sixty dollars a month*. Huck underestimates a captain's salary: Twain said in Chapter 4 of *Life on the Mississippi*, that "the pilot, even in those days of trivial wages, had a princely salary—from a hundred and fifty to two hundred and fifty dollars a month, and no board to pay." Perhaps sixty dollars is synonymous with "princely salary" for destitute Huck.

22. *Not for pie*. Not for the best thing there is, not for anything. See Chapter 2, note 39.

whatever pickins we've overlooked in the staterooms, and shove for shore and hide the truck. Then we'll wait. Now I say it ain't agoin' to be more 'n two hours befo' this wrack breaks up and washes off down the river. See? He'll be drownded, and won't have nobody to blame for it but his own self. I reckon that's a considerble sight[32] better'n killin' of him. I'm unfavorable to killin' a man as long as you can git around it; it ain't good sense, it ain't good morals.[33] Ain't I right?"

"Yes—I reck'n you are. But s'pose she *don't* break up and wash off?"

"Well, we can wait the two hours, anyway, and see, can't we?"[34]

"All right, then; come along."

So they started, and I lit out, all in a cold sweat, and scrambled forward. It was dark as pitch there; but I said in a kind of a coarse whisper,[35] "Jim!" and he answered up, right at my elbow, with a sort of a moan, and I says:

"Quick, Jim, it ain't no time for fooling around and moaning; there's a gang of murderers in yonder, and if we don't hunt up their boat and set her drifting down the river so these fellows can't get away from the wreck, there's one of 'em going to be in a bad fix. But if we find their boat we can put *all* of 'em in a bad fix—for the Sheriff 'll get 'em. Quick—hurry! I'll hunt the labboard side, you hunt the stabboard. You start at the raft, and—"

"Oh, my lordy, lordy! *Raf*? Dey ain' no raf' no mo', she done broke loose en gone!—'en here we is!"

"O MY LORDY, LORDY!"

23. *we fetched the starboard derrick, and made fast there.* "The steamboat is pointed upstream, listing to port, with only her hurricane deck, texas and pilothouse above water," explained Blair and Fischer in the 1988 University of California edition. "Huck and Jim tie the raft to 'the starboard derrick,' an upright pole that passes just in front of the hurricane deck, onto which they climb. They move across this sloping surface, fending off the chimney guy wires, toward the officers' cabin, or 'texas.' They first reach a slight upward step in the deck, the front end of the skylight roof (also called the texas deck). Climbing onto this roof, they find themselves in front of the 'captain's door,' at the head of the 'texas hall,' which bisects the cabin and gives access to the staterooms on either side of it" (p. 391).

24. *labboard.* Larboard, the left side of the boat, looking toward the bows; now called the port. "The term 'larboard,'" Twain explained in Chapter 12 of *Life on the Mississippi*, "is never used at sea, now, to signify the left hand; but was always used on the river in my time."

25. *the guys.* The ropes fastened aloft for hoisting or dropping cargo.

26. *a-biling.* Boiling.

27. *crawfished.* Crawled backward, like a crawfish. Missourian Charles L. Davis in *The Twainian* (September–October 1961) explained "crawfished" as "an expression we used when we were touching bottom with our hands or feet in the water and not actually swimming . . . and to some youngster just learning to swim but not actually doing so we would jokingly say, 'Ah! he's just crawfishing.' Later in life in many encounters whether in business deal or in a law suit . . . we often hear of one who backs out of a deal as one who 'crawfished' out. Of course the main direction of travel of a crawfish or a crawdad as we used to call the miniature lobsters, is backwards" (p. 3).

28. *I could tell where they was.* Fischer and Blair suggested in the 1988 University of California edition that the typist of the manuscript missed a phrase, "and how close they was" (p. 529).

29. *treed.* Literally chased up a tree, but here merely cornered.

30. *he'll turn State's evidence.* Remarkably this criminal knows the letter of the law: To avoid prosecution himself, Jim Parker could make a deal with the state prosecutor to testify in court against his former partners.

31. *to go court'n around after a halter.* To risk getting hanged. Packard too knows the law: The sentence in Missouri at the time for killing a man, even another thief, was public hanging.

32. *a considerble sight.* Euphemism for "a damned sight," as suggested by H. L. Mencken in *The American Language* (New York: Random House, 1963, p. 396).

33. *it ain't good sense, it ain't good morals.* But what does morality have to do with killing a man? By allowing selfish interests to shape what he says is a moral decision, Packard follows the same line of reasoning Huck used earlier in the chapter when he rationalized stealing only the good fruit but leaving the bad and unripe.

34. *Well, we can wait the two hours, anyway, and see, can't we?* The manuscript reveals that Bill had other plans for Jim Turner: "*Then*, if the thing don't work, it'll still be long enough befo' daylight, and we'll come back and do the next *best* thing—tie a rock to him and dump him into the river" (quoted in Ferguson, "Huck Finn Aborning," *Colophon*, Spring 1938, p. 177). They gag him, but he works himself free and his cries call them back just as Huck and Jim are making their getaway. But Twain dropped the passage, likely because, as Ferguson argued, "it merely complicated the action without intensifying it."

35. *coarse whisper.* Or "stage whisper," speaking just loud enough and clearly and distinctly to be heard.

Chapter XIII

IN A FIX.

Well, I catched my breath and most fainted. Shut up on a wreck with such a gang as that! But it warn't no time to be sentimentering.[1] We'd *got* to find that boat, now—had to have it for ourselves. So we went a-quaking and shaking down the stabboard side, and slow work it was, too—seemed a week before we got to the stern. No sign of a boat. Jim said he didn't believe he could go any further—so scared he hadn't hardly any strength left, he said. But I said come on, if we get left on this wreck, we are in a fix, sure. So on we prowled, again. We struck for the stern of the texas, and found it, and then scrabbled[2] along forwards on the skylight, hanging on from shutter to shutter, for the edge of the skylight was in the water. When we got pretty close to the cross-hall door, there was the skiff, sure enough! I could just barely see her. I felt ever so thankful. In another second I would a been aboard of her; but just then the door opened. One of the men stuck his head out, only about a couple of foot from me, and I thought I was gone; but he jerked it in again, and says:

"Heave that blame lantern out o' sight, Bill!"

He flung a bag of something into the boat, and then got

1. *sentimentering*. Sentimentalizing.

2. *scrabbled*. Scrambled on hands and feet. Blair and Fischer explained in the 1988 University of California edition that Huck and Jim "scramble forward on the left side of the texas, walking on the narrow and sloping skylight roof (or texas roof), holding onto the stateroom shutters because the edge of this deck 'is in water'" (p. 391).

in himself, and set down. It was Packard. Then Bill *he* come out and got in. Packard says, in a low voice:

"All ready—shove off!"

I couldn't hardly hang onto the shutters, I was so weak. But Bill says:

"Hold on—'d you go through him?"

"No. Didn't you?"

"No. So he's got his share o' the cash, yet."

"Well, then, come along—no use to take truck and leave money."

"Say—won't he suspicion what we're up to?"

"Maybe he won't. But we got to have it anyway. Come along."

So they got out and went in.

The door slammed to, because it was on the careened side; and in a half second I was in the boat, and Jim come a tumbling after me. I out with my knife and cut the rope, and away we went!

We didn't touch an oar, and we didn' speak nor whisper, nor hardly even breathe. We went gliding swift along, dead silent, past the tip of the paddle-box, and past the stern; then in a second or two more we was a hundred yards below the wreck, and the darkness soaked her up, every last sign of her, and we was safe, and knowed it.

When we was three or four hundred yards down stream, we see the lantern show like a little spark at the texas door, for a second, and we knowed by that that the rascals had missed their boat, and was beginning to understand that they was in just as much trouble, now, as Jim Turner was.

Then Jim manned the oars, and we took out after our raft. Now was the first time that I begun to worry about the men—I reckon I hadn't had time to before. I begun to think how dreadful it was, even for murderers, to be in such a fix. I says to myself, there ain't no telling but I might come to be a murderer myself, yet, and then how would *I* like it? So says I to Jim:

"The first light we see, we'll land a hundred yards below it or above it, in a place where it's a good hiding-place for you and the skiff, and then I'll go and fix up some kind of a yarn, and get somebody to go for that gang and get them out of their scrape, so they can be hung when their time comes."[3]

But that idea was a failure; for pretty soon it begun to storm again, and this time worse than ever. The rain poured down, and never a light showed; everybody in bed, I reckon. We boomed along[4] down the river, watching for lights and watching for our raft. After a long time the rain let up, but the clouds staid,[5] and the lightning kept whimpering, and by-and-by a flash showed us a black thing ahead, floating, and we made for it.

It was the raft, and mighty glad was we to get aboard of it again. We seen a light, now, away down to the right, on shore. So I said I would go for it. The skiff was half full of plunder which that gang had stole, there on the wreck. We hustled it onto the raft in a pile, and I told Jim to float along down, and show a light when he judged he had gone about two mile, and keep it burning till I come; then I manned my oars and shoved for the light. As I got down towards it, three or four more showed—up on a hillside. It was a village. I closed in above the shore-light, and laid on my oars and floated. As I went by, I see it was a lantern hanging on the jackstaff[6] of a double-hull ferry-boat.[7] I skimmed around for the watchman, a-wondering whereabouts he slept; and by-and-by I found him roosting on the bitts,[8] forward, with his head down between his knees. I give his shoulder two or three little shoves, and begun to cry.

He stirred up, in a kind of a startlish way; but when he see it was only me, he took a good gap and stretch, and then he says:

"Hello, what's up? Don't cry, bub. What's the trouble?"

I says:

"Pap, and mam, and sis, and——"

Then I broke down. He says:

"Oh, dang it, now, *don't* take on so, we all has to have our troubles and this'n 'll come out all right. What's the matter with 'em?"

"They're—they're—are you the watchman of the boat?"

"Yes," he says, kind of pretty-well-satisfied like. "I'm the

3. *get them out of their scrape, so they can be hung when their time comes.* Another example of Twain's playing with the maxim "He that is born to be hanged shall never drown." See Chapter 4, note 16.

4. *boomed along.* Moved swiftly right along without any obstructions.

5. *staid.* "The spelling of 'staid' is one of Mark Twain's idiosyncrasies," explained Paul Fatout in *Mark Twain Speaks for Himself* (1978). "Although allowed by *Webster's Unabridged* as a variant of 'stayed,' the latter is customary, but Mark Twain, who prided himself on his spelling, consistently used 'staid'" (p. 28).

6. *the jackstaff.* A short staff, usually set upon the bowsprit or at the bow of a ship, on which the "jack" or flag, is hoisted.

7. *a lantern hanging on the jackstaff of a double-hull ferry-boat.* Blair and Fischer persuasively argued in the 1988 University of California edition that the typist skipped two sentences which should be here: "Everything was dead still, nobody stirring. I floated in under the stern, made fast, and clumb aboard." That explains "exactly where Huck was when he 'skimmed around' in search of the watchman: he was on the deck of the ferryboat, not in the skiff" (p. 505).

8. *the bitts.* Short posts with ropes strung between and fastened in pairs above the deck, to which lines or cables can be secured.

"HELLO, WHAT'S UP?"

captain and the owner, and the mate, and the pilot, and watchman, and head deck-hand; and sometimes I'm the freight and passengers. I ain't as rich as old Jim Hornback, and I can't be so blame' generous and good to Tom, Dick and Harry as what he is, and slam around money the way he does; but I've told him a many a time 't I wouldn't trade places with him; for, says I, a sailor's life's the life for me, and I'm derned if *I'd* live two mile out o' town, where there ain't nothing ever goin' on, not for all his spondulicks[9] and as much more on top of it. Says I—"

I broke in and says:

"They're in an awful peck of trouble, and—"

"*Who* is?"

"Why, pap, and mam, and sis, and Miss Hooker; and if you'd take your ferry-boat and go up there—"

"Up where? Where are they?"

"On the wreck."

"What wreck?"

"Why, there ain't but one."

"What, you don't mean the *Walter Scott?*"[10]

"Yes."

"Good land! what are they doin' *there,* for gracious sakes?"

9. *spondulicks*. Or "spondulix," cash, money.

10. *the* Walter Scott. According to *Merchant Steam Vessels of the United States 1807–1868* (1952), compiled by William M. Lytle and edited by Forrest R. Holdcamper, a side-wheeler named *Walter Scott*, whose home port was New Orleans, traveled up and down the Mississippi from 1829 until it was "lost" in 1838. Several other steamships of the period took their names (such as *Ivanhoe*, *Waverley*, and *Lady of the Lake*) from Scott's popular romances and poems. (Frederick Douglass revealed in Chapter 11 of his *Narrative* that his surname came from *The Lady of the Lake.*) Appropriately, Twain calls the floundering ship after a writer whose work he hated. He contends in "Enchantments and Enchanters" (Chapter 46, *Life on the Mississippi*) that the novelist "sets the world in love with dreams and phantoms; with decayed and degraded systems of government; with the sillinesses and emptinesses, sham grandeurs, sham gauds, and sham chivalries of a brainless and worthless long-vanished society. He did measureless harm; more real and lasting harm, perhaps, than any other individual that ever wrote. Most of the world has now outlived a good part of these harms . . . ; but in our South they flourish pretty forcefully still. . . . Sir Walter had so large a hand

Sir Walter Scott.
Courtesy Library of Congress.

in making Southern character, as it existed before the war, that he is in great measure responsible for the war." Twain further argued that the residue of this "Sir Walter disease" kept the South from progressing after the Civil War. In Chapter 4 of *The American Claimant* (1892), he continues his attack upon the "Walter Scott disease" by inventing Rowena-Ivanhoe College, "the selectest and most aristocratic seat of learning for young ladies in our country. . . . Castellated college-buildings—towers and turrets and an imitation moat—and everything about the place named out of Sir Walter Scott's books and redolent of royalty and state and style," where "the girls don't learn a blessed thing . . . but showy rubbish and unamerican pretentiousness." The accuracy of Twain's accusations was considered by Hamilton James Eckenrode in "Sir Walter Scott and the South," *The North American Review*, October 1917, pp. 595–603; Grace Warren Landram in "Sir Walter Scott and His Literary Rivals in the Old South," *American Literature*, vol. 2 (1930–1931), pp. 256–76; and G. Harrison Orians in "Walter Scott, Mark Twain, and the Civil War," in *The South Atlantic Quarterly*, October 1941, pp. 342–59.

11. *the horse-ferry.* A ferry which carried horses and carriages across the water.

A horse-ferry. Illustration from *Emerson's Magazine and Putnam's Monthly*, October 1857. *Courtesy Library of Congress.*

12. *saddle-baggsed.* Caught on the wreck and doubled around like a saddlebag.

"Well, they didn't go there a-purpose."

"I bet they didn't! Why, great goodness, there ain't no chance for 'em if they don't git off mighty quick! Why, how in the nation did they ever git into such a scrape?"

"Easy enough. Miss Hooker was a-visiting, up there to the town—"

"Yes, Booth's Landing—go on."

"She was a-visiting, there at Booth's Landing, and just in the edge of the evening she started over with her nigger woman in the horse-ferry,[11] to stay all night at her friend's house, Miss What-you-may-call-her, I disremember her name, and they lost their steering-oar, and swung around and went a-floating down, stern-first, about two mile, and saddle-baggsed[12] on the wreck, and the ferry man and the nigger woman and the horses was all lost, but Miss Hooker she made a grab and got aboard the wreck. Well, about an hour after dark, we come along down in our trading-scow,[13] and it was so dark we didn't notice the wreck till we was right on it; and so *we* saddle-baggsed; but all of us was saved but Bill Whipple—and oh, he *was* the best cretur!—I most wish't it had been me, I do."

"My George! It's the beatenest thing I ever struck. And *then* what did you all do?"

"Well, we hollered and took on, but it's so wide there, we couldn't make nobody hear. So pap said somebody got to get ashore and get help somehow. I was the only one that could swim, so I made a dash for it, and Miss Hooker she said if I didn't strike help sooner, come here and hunt up her uncle, and he'd fix the thing. I made the land about a mile below, and been fooling along ever since, trying to get people to do something, but they said, 'What, in such a night and such a current? there ain't no sense in it; go for the steam-ferry.' Now if you'll go, and—"

"By Jackson,[14] I'd *like* to, and blame it I don't know but I will; but who in the dingnation's agoin' to *pay* for it? Do you reckon your pap—"

"Why *that's* all right. Miss Hooker she told me, *particular*, that her uncle Hornback—"

"Great guns! is *he* her uncle? Looky here, you break for that light over yonder-way, and turn out west when you git there, and about a quarter of a mile out you'll come to the tavern; tell 'em to dart you out[15] to Jim Hornback's and he'll foot the bill. And don't you fool around any, because he'll want to know the news. Tell him I'll have his niece all safe before he can get to town. Hump yourself, now; I'm agoing up around the corner here, to roust out my engineer."

I struck for the light, but as soon as he turned the corner I went back and got into my skiff and bailed her out and then pulled up shore in the easy water about six hundred yards, and tucked myself in among some woodboats; for I couldn't rest easy till I could see the ferry-boat start. But take it all around, I was feeling ruther comfortable on accounts of taking all this trouble for that gang, for not many would a done it. I wished the widow knowed about it. I judged she would be proud of me for helping these rapscallions,[16] because rapscallions and dead beats[17] is the kind the widow and good people takes the most interest in.[18]

Well, before long, here comes the wreck,[19] dim and dusky, sliding along down! A kind of cold shiver went through me, and then I struck out for her. She was very deep, and I see in a minute there warn't much chance for anybody being alive in her. I pulled all around her and

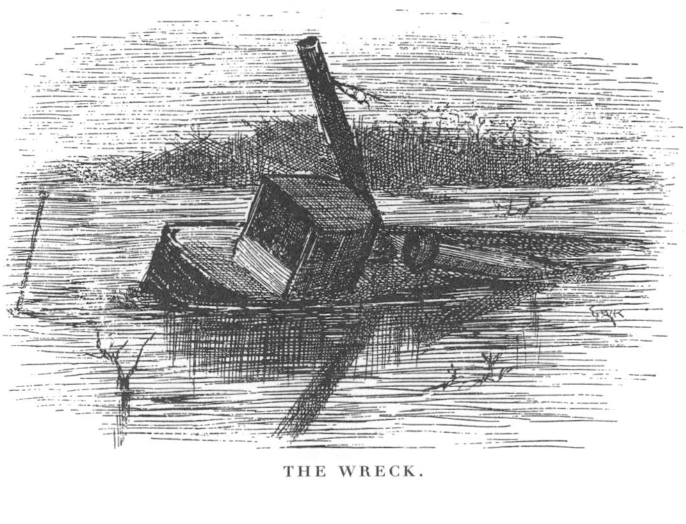

THE WRECK.

13. *trading-scow*. Riverboat for carrying cargo.

14. *My George! . . . By Jackson*. These interjections may suggest to Huck the alias he adopts in Chapter 17.

15. *to dart you out.* To send you forth.

16. *rapscallions*. Rascals, scamps.

17. *dead beats*. Loafers, spongers, good-for-nothings.

18. *the kind the widow and good people takes the most interest in*. For example, Huckleberry Finn. The widow and the other pious people believe in the parable of the prodigal son in Luke 15:11–32, who is of more concern to the father than the other, obedient child. Twain rather contemptuously recounted in Chapter 33 of *Tom Sawyer* that after Injun Joe's funeral, all the do-gooders in town decide to pressure the governor to pardon the late murderer. "The petition had been largely signed," he explained; "many tearful and eloquent meetings had been held and a committee of sappy women been appointed to go in deep mourning and wail around the governor and implore him to be a merciful ass and trample his duty under foot. Injun Joe was believed to have killed five citizens of the village, but what of it? If he had been Satan himself there would have been plenty of weaklings ready to scribble their names to a pardon-petition and drop a tear on it from their permanently impaired and leaky water-works."

19. *the wreck*. Hurrying to get the next batch of illustrations in, Kemble misread "the stern of the texas" and carelessly labeled the boat in the picture *Texas* rather than *Walter Scott* as in the text. Twain immediately jumped on the error when he saw the proof and told Webster in a letter of June 25, 1884, "that on the pilot house of that steamboat-wreck the artist has put *Texas*—having been misled by some of Huck's remarks about the boat's 'texas'—a thing which is part of *every* boat. That word had better be removed from that pilot house" (quoted in Samuel Charles Webster, *Mark Twain, Business Man*, 1946, p. 262). The offending detail was dutifully corrected before publication.

hollered a little, but there wasn't any answer; all dead still. I felt a little bit heavy-hearted about the gang, but not much, for I reckoned if they could stand it, I could.

Then here comes the ferry-boat; so I shoved for the middle of the river on a long down-stream slant; and when I judged I was out of eye-reach, I laid on my oars, and looked back and see her go and smell around the wreck for Miss Hooker's remainders, because the captain would know her uncle Hornback would want them; and then pretty soon the ferry-boat give it up and went for shore, and I laid into my work and went a-booming down the river.

It did seem a powerful long time before Jim's light showed up; and when it did show, it looked like it was a thousand mile off. By the time I got there the sky was beginning to get a little gray in the east; so we struck for an island, and hid the raft, and sunk the skiff, and turned in and slept like dead people.

WE TURNED IN AND SLEPT.

Chapter XIV.

TURNING OVER THE TRUCK.

BY-AND-BY, when we got up, we turned over the truck the gang had stole off of the wreck, and found boots, and blankets, and clothes, and all sorts of other things, and a lot of books, and a spyglass, and three boxes of seegars. We hadn't ever been this rich before, in neither of our lives.[1] The seegars was prime. We laid off all the afternoon in the woods talking, and me reading the books, and having a general good time. I told Jim all about what happened inside the wreck, and at the ferry-boat; and I said these kinds of things was adventures; but he said he didn't want no more adventures. He said that when I went in the texas and he crawled back to get on the raft and found her gone, he nearly died; because he judged it was all up with *him,* anyway it could be fixed; for if he didn't get saved he would get drownded; and if he did get saved, whoever saved him would send him back home so as to get the reward, and then Miss Watson would sell him South, sure. Well, he was right; he was most always right; he had an uncommon level head, for a nigger.

I read considerable to Jim about kings, and dukes, and earls,[2] and such, and how gaudy they dressed, and how much style they put on, and called each other your majesty, and your grace, and your lordship, and so on, 'stead of mis-

1. *We hadn't ever been this rich before, in neither of our lives* And yet Huckleberry Finn is worth $6,000—at least on paper. Since he has had so little experience with money, the boy defines wealth in the accumulation of objects and cold cash rather than in the relative abstract of capital. "Money, in truth, is almost a perfectly unknown commodity in their midst," Daniel R. Hundley in *Social Relations in Our Southern States* (1860), explained the squatter's attitude toward currency, "and nearly all of their trafficking is carried on by means of barter alone. . . . Dollars and dimes . . . they never bother their brains any great deal about" (p. 262).

2. *I read considerable to Jim about kings, and dukes, and earls.* When he started this chapter in 1883, probably the last one written for the book, Twain reminded himself in the margin to have Huck "read astronomy from book, to Jim." But he decided to go into another direction when he wrote in some notes for the novel, "Back yonder, Huck reads and tells about monarchies and kings etc. So Jim stares when he learns the rank of these two." This chapter sets the tone for the introduction of the duke and the king in Chapter 19.

Twain was particularly fond of this chapter. At Cable's suggestion, he included it on their 1884–1885 public reading tour; and *Century Magazine* (January 1885) serialized it by combining it with the episode about Balum's Ass of Chapter 8 as "Jim's Investments, and King Sollermun." Cable called the "King Sollermun" selection "one of his best things" on the program. "I hear the ladies laughing at the tops of their voices," he wrote his wife on January 29, from Milwaukee, "and whenever they do that the encore is certain to come" (quoted in Arlin Turner, *Mark Twain and George W. Cable: The Record of a Literary Friendship*, 1960, p. 92). And audiences *did* love it. The Keokuk (Iowa) *Daily Gate City* (January 15) said that Twain "caused many a laugh by his funny description of the discussion of the merits of and demerits of 'King Sollermun' between the darkey Jim and Huckleberry Finn." The St. Paul *Daily Dispatch* (January 24) reported that Twain "went on to relate 'King Sollermun,' with which the public is already familiar with from having seen the anecdote in print in *The Century Magazine* and various newspapers. The audience laughed and laughed and applauded heartily again at the close of the reading."

Modern readers, particularly African-American readers, have not been so amused by this chapter. "Writing at a time when the blackfaced minstrel was still popular, and shortly after a war which left even the abolitionists weary of those problems associated with the Negro," Ralph Ellison explained in "Change the Joke and Slip the Yoke" (*Partisan Review*, Spring 1958), "Twain fitted Jim out with the outlines of the minstrel tradition, and it is from behind this stereotype mask that we see Jim's dignity and human capacity—and Twain's complexity—emerge" (p. 215). Twain loved the minstrel show, "the show which to me had no peer and whose peer has not yet arrived, in my experience" (*Mark Twain in Eruption*, 1940, p. 110). He enjoyed the minstrel's "very broad negro dialect; he used it competently and with easy facility and it was funny—delightfully and satisfyingly funny." Anthony J. Berret argued in "Huckleberry Finn and the Minstrel Show" (*American Studies*, Fall 1986, p. 38) that the structure of *Huckleberry Finn* follows that of the traditional minstrel show: opening comic dialogues like this one about "King Sollermun"; the "olio" of novelty acts like those put on by the king and duke; and an extravagant burlesque like Tom Sawyer's "evasion." Twain was particularly fond of the heated exchanges between the two vernacular endmen Bones and Banjo, stock minstrel characters. "Sometimes the quarrel would last five minutes," he recalled; "the two contestants shouting deadly threats in each other's faces with their noses not six inches apart, the house shrieking with laughter all the while at this happy and accurate imitation of the usual and familiar negro quarrel" (p. 113). He greatly enjoyed the often heated disputes (usually over religion) between Mary Ann Cord, a cook, and John T. Lewis, a farmer, at Quarry Farm, where he wrote *Huckleberry Finn*, because they reminded him of the old

ter; and Jim's eyes bugged out, and he was interested. He says:

"I didn' know dey was so many un um. I hain't hearn 'bout none un um, skasely, but ole King Sollermun,[3] onless you counts dem kings dat's in a pack er k'yards. How much do a king git?"

"Get?" I says; "why, they get a thousand dollars a month if they want it; they can have just as much as they want; everything belongs to them."

"*Ain'* dat gay? En what dey got to do, Huck?"

"*They* don't do nothing! Why how you talk. They just set around."

"No—is dat so?"

"Of course it is. They just set around. Except maybe when there 's a war; then they go to the war. But other times they just lazy around; or go hawking—just hawking and sp—[4] Sh!—d' you hear a noise?"

We skipped out and looked; but it warn't nothing but the flutter of a steamboat's wheel, away down coming around the point; so we come back.

"Yes," says I, "and other times, when things is dull, they fuss with the parlyment; and if everybody don't go just so he whacks their heads off.[5] But mostly they hang round the harem."[6]

"Roun' de which?"

"Harem."

"What's de harem?"

"The place where he keep his wives. Don't you know about the harem? Solomon had one; he had about a million wives."[7]

"Why, yes, dat's so; I—I'd done forgot it. A harem's a bo'd'n-house, I reck'n. Mos' likely dey has rackety times in de nussery. En I reck'n de wives quarrels considable; en dat 'crease de racket. Yit dey say Sollermun de wises' man dat ever live'. I doan' take no stock in dat. Bekase why: would a wise man want to live in de mids' er sich a blimblammin' all de time? No—'deed he wouldn't. A wise man 'ud take en buil' a biler-factry;[8] en den he could shet *down* de biler-factry when he want to res'."

SOLOMON AND HIS MILLION WIVES.

"Well, but he *was* the wisest man, anyway; because the widow she told me so, her own self."[9]

"I doan k'yer what de widder say, he *warn't* no wise man, nuther. He had some er de dad-fetchedes' ways I ever see. Does you know 'bout dat chile dat he 'uz gwyne to chop in two?"[10]

"Yes, the widow told me all about it."

"*Well*, den! Warn' dat de beatenes' notion in de worl'? You jes' take en look at it a minute. Dah's de stump,[11] dah—dat's one er de women; heah's you—dat's de yuther one; I's Sollermun; en dish-yer dollar bill's de chile. Bofe un you claims it. What does I do? Does I shin aroun' mongs' de neighbors en fine out which un you de bill *do* b'long to, en han' it over to de right one, all safe en soun', de way dat anybody dat had any gumption[12] would? No—I take en whack de bill in *two*, en give half un it to you, en de yuther half to de yuther woman. Dat's de way Sollermun was gwyne to do wid de chile. Now I want to ast you: what's de use er dat half a bill?—can't buy noth'n wid it. En what use is a half a chile? I would'n give a dern for a million un um."

"But hang it, Jim, you've clean missed the point—blame it, you've missed it a thousand mile."

"Who? Me? Go 'long. Doan' talk to *me* 'bout yo' pints. I

minstrel-show debates. Huck and Jim's exchange corresponds to the straight-man-and-comic dialogue between the genteel interlocutor and the extravagant endman Bones or Banjo. However, although Twain made use of the conventions of the minstrel show, he transformed the quarrel into a deeper philosophical discussion that resonates throughout the novel.

3. *ole King Sollermun*. King Solomon of Israel, whose reign is described in the First Book of Kings, was considered in his day to be the wisest man in the world. This amusing exchange is reminiscent of another between Uncle Dan'l and Clay Hawkins in Chapter 3 of *The Gilded Age*, in which the throwing of the "he-brew" and "she-brew chil'en" in the fiery furnace (Daniel 3:1–10) is discussed. Twain may also have introduced Solomon here because, as the author of the erotic Song of Solomon and a famed lover, he shared an interest with other sexually active royalty burlesqued in the story.

4. *hawking and sp—*. "Hawking and spitting," a British vulgarism for noisily clearing the throat of phlegm; the interruption of the steamboat leaves one to think that Huck is referring to falconry. Twain weakened this joke in his 1895–1896 public reading copy by changing it to "hawking and hogging or whatever it is." It is clear in the earlier version that Huck knows the exact phrase. Howard G. Baezhold suggested in *Mark Twain and John Bull* (1970) that Twain might have picked up this pun from Sir Walter Scott's *The Fortunes of Nigel* (1822), which Twain consulted while writing *The Prince and the Pauper*: Lord Dalgarno tells Dame Nelly, "You shall ride a hunting and hawking with a lord, instead of waiting upon an old ship-chandler, who could hawk and spit" (p. 94). It was not a word one heard in more genteel nineteenth-century society. Twain noted in Chapter 29 of *Life on the Mississippi* that English tourist Frances Trollope was so uncomfortable with saying "spitting" that she preferred using "etc." wherever she could in *Domestic Manners of the Americans* (1831). "The 'etc.,' " Twain said, "stands for an unpleasant word there, a word which she does not always charitably cover up, but sometimes prints."

5. *they fuss with the parlyment; and if everybody don't go just so he whacks their heads off*. Huck is thinking of Henry VIII (1491–1547), who ruled England from to 1509 to 1547 and spent much reck'n I knows sense when I sees it; en dey ain' no sense in sich doin's as dat. De 'spute warn't 'bout a half a chile, de 'spute was 'bout a whole chile; en de man dat think he kin settle a 'spute 'bout a whole chile wid a half a chile, doan' know enough to come in out'n de rain. Doan' talk to me 'bout Sollermun, Huck, I knows him by de back."[13]

"But I tell you you don't get the point."

"Blame de pint! I reck'n I knows what I knows. En mine you, de *real* pint is down furder—it's down deeper. It lays in de way Sollermun was raised. You take a man dat's got on'y one er two chillen;[14] is dat man gwyne to be waseful o'

THE STORY OF "SOLLERMUN."

chillen? No, he ain't; he can't 'ford it. *He* know how to value 'em. But you take a man dat's got 'bout five million chillen runnin' roun' de house, en it's diffunt. *He* as soon chop a chile in two as a cat. Dey's plenty mo'. A chile er two, mo'er less, warn't no consekens to Sollermun, dad fetch him!"

I never see such a nigger. If he got a notion in his head once, there warn't no getting it out again. He was the most down on Solomon of any nigger I ever see. So I went to talking about other kings, and let Solomon slide. I told about Louis Sixteenth that got his head cut off in France long time age; and about his little boy the dolphin,[15] that would a been a king, but they took and shut him up in jail, and some say he died there.

of his time battling Parliament and whacking off people's heads.

6. *they hang round the harem.* Twain originally wrote "wallow," but this word was a bit too suggestive, so he replaced it with the innocuous "hang." Huck may be thinking of Henry VIII, who had six wives, as much as of Solomon. Twain noted in Chapter 1 of *Life on the Mississippi* that the year the river was being explored by Hernando de Soto, Henry VIII "was getting his English reformation and his harem effectively started." The irony seems to be lost on Huck that Southern plantations were often run like harems, with nighttime visits by the masters to the slave quarters.

7. *he had about a million wives.* According to the Bible, King Solomon had seven hundred wives who were princesses and another three hundred concubines. Many were not Jews; and because the Lord forbade Israelites from marrying gentiles, these unions led to the downfall of his great kingdom. American humor is full of jokes about all the troubles Solomon must have had with so many wives and lovers.

8. *a biler-factry.* Robert L. Ramsay and Guthrie Emberson in "A Mark Twain Lexicon" (*University of Missouri Studies*, January 1, 1938) explained that Twain used "biler-factry" as "a synonym for noise or pandemonium."

9. *the widow she told me so, her own self.* Huck exploits the widow's religious instruction, which he had previously scorned, when it serves his purpose in trying to win the argument with Jim. Like Miss Watson, he uses his knowledge of the Bible to put an "inferior" in his place. Although this episode at first glance may seem to be gratuitous to the action of the story, it nevertheless repeats an important theme of the novel, that one's morality must come naturally from within oneself (as it does with Jim here) and not from some abstract set of values or from some "authority" (as with Huck).

10. *Does you know 'bout dat chile dat he 'uz gwyne to chop in two?* According to I Kings 3:16–28, two harlots came before King Solomon, each claiming that the other was the mother of a child who had died in the night. When he threatened to cut the surviving baby in two so that each might have one half, the true mother revealed herself by offering to give the child to the other woman

"Po' little chap."

"But some says he got out and got away, and come to America."

"Dat's good! But he'll be pooty lonesome—dey ain' no kings here, is dey, Huck?"

"No."

"Den he cain't git no situation. What he gwyne to do?"

"Well, I don't know. Some of them gets on the police,[16] and some of them learns people how to talk French."[17]

"Why, Huck, doan' de French people talk de same way we does?"

"*No*, Jim; you couldn't understand a word they said[18]—not a single word."

"Well, now, I be ding-busted! How do dat come?"

"*I* don't know; but it's so. I got some of their jabber out of a book. Spose a man was to come to you and say *Polly-voo-franzy*[19]—what would you think?"

"I wouldn' think nuff'n; I'd take en bust him over de head. Dat is, if he warn't white.[20] I wouldn't 'low no nigger to call me dat."

"Shucks, it ain't calling you anything. It's only saying do you know how to talk French."

"Well, den, why couldn't he *say* it?"

"Why, he *is* a-saying it. That's a Frenchman's *way* of saying it."

"Well, it's a blame' ridicklous way, en I doan' want to hear no mo' 'bout it. Dey ain' no sense in it."

"Looky here, Jim; does a cat talk like we do?"

"No, a cat don't."

"Well, does a cow?"

"No, a cow don't, nuther."

"Does a cat talk like a cow, or a cow talk like a cat?"

"No, dey don't."

"It's natural and right for 'em to talk different from each other, ain't it?"

"'Course."

"And ain't it natural and right for a cat and a cow to talk different from *us?*"

"Why, mos' sholy it is."

if the baby's life was spared. This lesson reflects the earlier custody battle between pap Finn and the Widow Douglas over Huckleberry Finn.

11. *Dah's de stump.* There's the hard part.

12. *gumption.* Common sense.

13. *I knows him by de back.* I know him through and through, backward and forward. In Chapter 28 in *Life on the Mississippi*, Twain identified this phrase as gambling slang; it may refer to the ability to read another player's hand by the back of his cards.

14. *You take a man dat's got on'y one er two chillen.* Jim, for example; his love for his own children colors his opinion of Solomon's wisdom in offering to cut a baby in two.

15. *the dolphin.* The Dauphin, Louis Charles (1785–1795), survived the beheadings of his father, King Louis XVI, and mother, Marie Antoinette, to die of scrofula in prison. However, the mysterious circumstances of his burial gave rise to the legend that he escaped (just as

Louis Charles, the Dauphin.
Courtesy Library of Congress

"Well, then, why ain't it natural and right for a *Frenchman* to talk different from us? You answer me that."

"Is a cat a man, Huck?"

"No."

"Well, den, dey ain't no sense in a cat talkin' like a man. Is a cow a man?—er is a cow a cat?"

"No, she ain't either of them."

"Well, den, she ain' got no business to talk like either one er the yuther of 'em. Is a Frenchman a man?"

"Yes."

"*Well,* den! Dad blame it, why doan' he *talk* like a man? You answer me *dat!*"

I see it warn't no use wasting words—you can't learn a nigger to argue.[21] So I quit.

Anastasia, the daughter of Czar Nicholas and Czarina Alexandra, supposedly survived the Russian Revolution of 1917); and at least thirty-five impostors are known to have claimed the throne of France. So widely held was the speculation that even a monthly *Revue historique de la question Louis XVIII* was founded in 1905. And several of these pretenders came to the United States, as Twain learned in Horace W. Fuller's *Noted French Trials: Impostors and Adventurers* (1882). Blair and Fischer noted in the 1988 University of California edition that the Hannibal *Journal* reprinted an item about one of these frauds named "Aminidab Fitz-Louis Dolphin Bourbon," or the "Dolphin" for short. See Chapter 19, note 48.

Napoleon III. Illustration from *The Innocents Abroad*, 1869. *Private collection.*

16. *Some of them gets on the police.* Huck is referring to Napoléon III (1808–1873); Twain explained in *The Innocents Abroad* (Chapter 13) that when the Emperor of France was sent into exile, he "associated with the common herd in America, and . . . kept his faithful watch and walked his weary beat a common policeman of London," before returning to his homeland as President of France through a *coup d'etat*.

17. *some of them learns people how to talk French.* Blair and Fischer in the 1988 University of California edition suggested that Twain may have been recalling that Charles Darnay, a French nobleman in Charles Dickens's *A Tale of Two*

Cities, is "established in England as a higher teacher of the French language" before the French Revolution. "Princes that had been, and Kings that were to be, were not yet of the teacher class," noted Dickens (p. 393).

18. *you couldn't understand a word they said.* Twain himself struggled all his life with foreign languages, which were frequently the brunt of his jokes; *A Tramp Abroad* often refers to his frustrations with trying to master German. He had particular trouble with French; so much so that he referred to it in Chapter 68 of his *Autobiography* as "plainly a language likely to fail a person at the crucial moment."

19. Polly-voo franzy. *Parlez-vous français?*—Do you speak French? In Chapter 2 of the recently rediscovered *A Murder, a Mystery, and a Marriage*, a foreigner confounds a Missourian when he tries to communicate with him in several languages before trying English. "It ain't a Christian," thinks the American; "maybe it ain't human." This story was written in 1876, just as Twain was beginning *Huckleberry Finn*, but not published until 2001.

20. *I'd take en bust him over de head. . . . if he warn't white.* Jim amends his statement, because, according to Missouri law, any slave who lifted his hand against any person not a Negro or a mulatto unless "wantonly attacked" was liable to receive a maximum sentence of thirty lashes. Frederick Douglass revealed in Chapter 10 of his *Narrative* that in some areas "to strike a white man is death by Lynch law."

21. *you can't learn a nigger to argue.* Of course, Jim has won the argument in his own distinctive way, but Huck cannot bear to concede to an "inferior." Although Jim is no different from before, Huck's sympathies toward him have changed since he praised Jim for having "an uncommon level head for a nigger" earlier in the chapter. The boy's attitude toward the slave remains ambiguous, vacillating between admiration and contempt, as he struggles between theory and practice. "Huck's statement, despite the irony of Jim's actually having bested him in the argument, is damaging," argued Carmen Subryan in "Mark Twain and the Black Challenge," "because it portrays Jim as a fool and, at least superficially, supports a broader misconception of black people as incapable of reason (and thus not fully human)" (in James S. Leonard, Thomas A. Tenney, and Thadious M. Davis, *Satire or Evasion?*, 1992, p. 97). Perhaps that is so within the conventions of American society, but one of the themes of the novel is that one cannot look at things "superficially." "Readers must acknowledge," argued Jocelyn Chadwick-Joshua in *The Jim Dilemma: Reading Race in Huckleberry Finn* (1998), "what Jim is saying on the surface as well as below it in order to comprehend fully the deliberate language manipulation. The doubleness is particularly important with an African American audience. The relationship that emerges with this form of satire attempts to push the reader past the literal level to one that agitates the reader to rethink the occasion that caused the statement or scene" (p. 49). That is the function of irony. Jim, who speaks from the heart, relies on a higher good while Huck must use the Good Book to make his point. Often Huck says one thing, but Twain means another. "Huck's miseducation makes him the brunt of the humor here as much as Jim," complained Fredrick Woodard and Donnarae MacCann in "Minstrel Shackles and Nineteenth-Century 'Liberality' in *Huckleberry Finn*," "but the reader is shown many sides of Huck's character, whereas Jim is either the total fool or the overgrown child" (also in Leonard, Tenney, and Davis, *Satire or Evasion?*, p. 145). But it is not so simple. Jim is far more complex than that. "His position is based on his role as a man and a parent," explained Chadwick-Joshua. "Essentially, he speaks as an individual, a visible, worthwhile person speaking to an adolescent who honestly believes in the inherent ignorance of Jim's entire race. What makes Jim's significance important is how he does it" (pp. 47–48). Jim proves in this argument what Huck says grudgingly earlier in the chapter: "Well, he was right; he was most always right."

Chapter XV.

"WE WOULD SELL THE RAFT."

WE JUDGED that three nights more would fetch us to Cairo,[1] at the bottom of Illinois, where the Ohio River comes in, and that was what we was after. We would sell the raft and get on a steamboat and go way up the Ohio[2] amongst the free States, and then be out of trouble.[3]

Well, the second night a fog begun to come on, and we made for a tow-head to tie to, for it wouldn't do to try to run in fog; but when I paddled ahead in the canoe, with the line, to make fast, there warn't anything but little saplings to tie to. I passed the line around one of them right on the edge of the cut bank,[4] but there was a stiff current, and the raft come booming down so lively she tore it out by the roots and away she went. I see the fog closing down, and it made me so sick and scared I couldn't budge for most a half a minute it seemed to me—and then there warn't no raft in sight; you couldn't see twenty yards. I jumped into the canoe and run back to the stern and grabbed the paddle and set her back a stroke. But she didn't come. I was in such a hurry I hadn't untied her. I got up and tried to untie her, but I was so excited my hands shook so I couldn't hardly do anything with them.

As soon as I got started I took out after the raft, hot and heavy, right down the tow-head. That was all right as far as it

1. *Cairo*. Pronounced "Kay-ro," a town in Illinois at the junction of the Ohio and Mississippi rivers; it did not become a permanent settlement until the early 1850s. According to Chapter 12 of *American Notes* (1842), Charles Dickens found Cairo "a spot so much more desolate than any we had beheld, that the forlornest places we had passed, were, in comparison with it, full of interest. At the junction of the two rivers, on ground so flat and low and marshy, that at certain seasons of the year it is inundated to the house-tops, lies a breeding-place of fever, ague, and death. . . . A dismal swamp, on which the half-built houses rot away: cleared here and there for the space of a few yards; and teeming, then, with rank unwholesome vegetation, in whose baleful shade the wretched wanderers who are tempted hither, droop, and die, and lay their bones; the hateful Mississippi circling and eddying before it, and turning off upon its southern course a slimy monster

Cairo, Illinois. Color lithograph by Henry Lewis, *Das illustrirte Mississippithal*, 1857. *Courtesy Rare Books Division, New York Public Library, Astor, Lenox, and Tilden Foundations.*

went, but the tow-head warn't sixty yards long, and the minute I flew by the foot of it I shot out into the solid white fog, and hadn't no more idea which way I was going than a dead man.

Thinks I, it won't do to paddle; first I know I'll run into the bank or a tow-head or something; I got to set still and float, and yet it's mighty fidgety business to have to hold your hands still at such a time. I whooped and listened. Away down there, somewheres, I hears a small whoop, and up comes my spirits. I went tearing after it, listening sharp to hear it again. The next time it come, I see I warn't heading for it but heading away to the right of it. And the next time, I was heading away to the left of it—and not gaining on it much, either, for I was flying around, this way and that and 'tother, but it was going straight ahead all the time.

I did wish the fool would think to beat a tin pan, and beat it all the time, but he never did, and it was the still places between the whoops that was making the trouble for me. Well, I fought along, and directly I hears the whoop *behind* me. I was tangled good, now. That was somebody else's whoop, or else I was turned around.

I throwed the paddle down. I heard the whoop again; it was behind me yet, but in a different place; it kept coming, and kept changing its place, and I kept answering, till by-and-by it was in front of me again and I knowed the current had swung the canoe's head down stream and I was all right, if that was Jim and not some other raftsman hollering. I couldn't tell nothing about voices in a fog, for nothing don't look natural nor sound natural in a fog.

The whooping went on, and in about a minute I come a booming down on a cut bank with smoky ghosts of big trees on it, and the current throwed me off to the left and shot by, amongst a lot of snags that fairly roared, the current was tearing by them so swift.

In another second or two it was solid white and still again. I set perfectly still, then, listening to my heart thump, and I reckon I didn't draw a breath while it thumped a hundred.

I just give up, then I knowed what the matter was. That

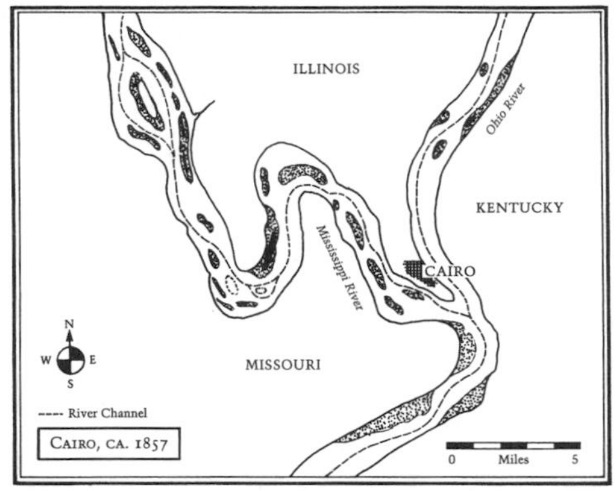

Map of Cairo, Illinois, circa 1857.
Reprinted with permission from the Mark Twain Project's Adventures of Huckleberry Finn, *edited by Victor Fischer and Lin Salamo (University of California, 2001). Copyright © 1985 and 2001 by the Regents of the University of California Press.*

hideous to behold; a hot bed of disease, an ugly sepulchre, a grave uncheered by any gleam of promise; a place without one single quality, in earth or air or water, to commend it." Dismal Cairo inspired "Eden," the miserable American settlement in *Martin Chuzzlewit* (1843).

2. *sell the raft and get on a steamboat and go way up the Ohio.* Travelers farther downstream on flatboats and rafts usually had to sell their crafts to get the passage on upbound steamboats.

3. *out of trouble.* The fugitives have had to change their plans: Because pro-slavery elements dominated the southern section of Illinois in the 1840s, the farther south Huck and Jim travel, the more dangerous their escape becomes. "Night after night they keep a sharp lookout for Cairo, where the Ohio river comes in," Twain explained in his notes for his 1895–1896 "Tour Around the World," "for there they would land and try to escape far north and east away from the domain of slavery" (University of California edition, 1988, p. 393). Not only was the Ohio River a convenient escape route, but there were plenty of abolitionists in Ohio to send him north on the Underground Railroad. But even if Jim does get to the free states, he will not automatically be a freeman. The Fugitive Slave Act of 1850 provided that a runaway was subject to arrest anywhere in the United States of America. The introduction to the 1881 edition of *Uncle Tom's Cabin* noted that even in

cut bank was an island, and Jim had gone down 'tother side of it. It warn't no tow-head, that you could float by in ten minutes. It had the big timber of a regular island; it might be five or six mile long and more than a half a mile wide.

I kept quiet, with my ears cocked, about fifteen minutes, I reckon. I was floating along, of course, four or five mile an hour; but you don't ever think of that. No, you *feel* like you are laying dead still on the water; and if a little glimpse of a snag slips by, you don't think to yourself how fast *you're* going, but you catch your breath and think, my! how that snag's tearing along. If you think it ain't dismal and lonesome out in a fog that way, by yourself, in the night, you try it once—you'll see.

Next, for about a half an hour, I whoops now and then; at last I hears the answer a long ways off, and tries to follow it,

AMONG THE SNAGS.

but I couldn't do it, and directly I judged I'd got into a nest of tow-heads, for I had little dim glimpses of them on both sides of me, sometimes just a narrow channel between; and some that I couldn't see, I knowed was there, because I'd hear the wash of the current against the old dead brush and trash that hung over the banks. Well, I warn't long losing the whoops, down amongst the tow-heads; and I only tried to chase them a little while, anyway, because it was worse

liberal Massachusetts the day-to-day reports of "the terror and despair which the law had occasioned to industrious, worthy colored people who had from time to time escaped to Boston. . . . She heard of families broken up and fleeing in the dead of winter to the frozen shores of Canada. But what seemed to her more inexplicable, more dreadful, was the apparent apathy of the Christian world of the free North to these proceedings. The pulpits that denounced them were exceptions; the voices raised to remonstrate few and far between. In New England, as in the West, professed abolitionists were a small, despised, unfashionable band, whose constant remonstrances from year to year had been disregarded as the voices of impracticable fanatics." Jim's only hope for complete freedom is to seek passage on the Underground Railroad and escape to Canada. However, Twain abandoned the plan to go north in the next chapter.

4. *the cut bank.* A precipitous hillside, formed by the river eroding the bank.

than chasing a Jack-o-lantern.[5] You never knowed a sound dodge around so, and swap places so quick and so much.

I had to claw away from the bank pretty lively, four or five times, to keep from knocking the islands out of the river; and so I judged the raft must be butting into the bank every now and then, or else it would get further ahead and clear out of hearing—it was floating a little faster than what I was.

Well, I seemed to be in the open river again, by-and-by, but I couldn't hear no sign of a whoop nowheres. I reckoned Jim had fetched up on a snag, maybe, and it was all up with him. I was good and tired, so I laid down in the canoe and said I wouldn't bother no more. I didn't want to go to sleep, of course; but I was so sleepy I couldn't help it; so I thought I would take just one little cat-nap.

But I reckon it was more than a cat-nap, for when I waked up the stars was shining bright, the fog was all gone, and I was spinning down a big bend stern first. First I didn't know where I was; I thought I was dreaming; and when things begun to come back to me, they seemed to come up dim out of last week.

It was a monstrous big river here, with the tallest and the thickest kind of timber on both banks; just a solid wall, as well as I could see, by the stars. I looked away down stream, and seen a black speck on the water. I took out after it; but when I got to it it warn't nothing but a couple of saw-logs made fast together. Then I see another speck, and chased that; then another, and this time I was right. It was the raft.

When I got to it Jim was setting there with his head down between his knees, asleep, with his right arm hanging over the steering oar. The other oar was smashed off, and the raft was littered up with leaves and branches and dirt. So she'd had a rough time.

I made fast and laid down under Jim's nose on the raft, and begun to gap, and stretch my fists out against Jim, and says:

"Hello, Jim, have I been asleep? Why didn't you stir me up?"

"Goodness gracious, is dat you, Huck? En you ain' dead—

5. *a Jack-o-lantern.* Huck is not referring to a carved Halloween pumpkin; this is another name for "will-o'-the-wisp," an elusive light, made by ignited methane gas or sulfurated hydrogen from clumps of bacteria, suspended over bodies of water at night and said to be carried by evil spirits.

6. *you ain' dead—you ain' drownded—you's back agin?* The second of Huck's "deaths" and "resurrections."

ASLEEP ON THE RAFT.

you ain' drownded—you's back agin?[6] It's too good for true, honey, it's too good for true. Lemme look at you, chile, lemme feel o' you. No, you ain' dead! you's back agin, 'live en soun', jis de same ole Huck—de same ole Huck, thanks to goodness!"

"What's the matter with you, Jim? You been a drinking?"

"Drinkin'? Has I ben a drinkin'? Has I had a chance to be a drinkin'?"

"Well, then, what makes you talk so wild?"

"How does I talk wild?"

"*How?* why, hain't you been talking about my coming back, and all that stuff, as if I'd been gone away?"

"Huck—Huck Finn, you look me in de eye; look me in de eye. *Hain't* you ben gone away?"

"Gone away? Why, what in the nation do you mean? *I* hain't been gone anywheres. Where would I go to?"

"Well, looky here, boss, dey's sumf'n wrong, dey is. Is I *me,* or who *is* I? Is I heah, or whah *is* I? Now dat's what I wants to know?"

"Well, I think you're here, plain enough, but I think you're a tangle-headed old fool, Jim."

"I is, is I? Well you answer me dis. Didn't you tote out de line in de canoe, fer to make fas' to de tow-head?"

"No, I didn't. What tow-head? I hain't seen no tow-head."

"You hain't seen no tow-head? Looky here—didn't de

line pull loose en de raf' go a hummin' down de river, en leave you en de canoe behine in de fog?"

"What fog?"

"Why *de* fog. De fog dat's ben aroun' all night. En didn't you whoop, en didn't I whoop, tell we got mix' up in de islands en one un us got los' en 'tother one was jis' as good as los', 'kase he didn' know whah he wuz? En didn't I bust up agin a lot er dem islands en have a turrible time en mos' git drownded? Now ain' dat so, boss—ain't it so? You answer me dat."

"Well, this is too many for me, Jim. I hain't seen no fog, nor no islands, nor no troubles, nor nothing. I been setting here talking with you all night till you went to sleep about ten minutes ago, and I reckon I done the same. You couldn't a got drunk in that time, so of course you've been dreaming."

"Dad fetch it, how is I gwyne to dream all dat in ten minutes?"[7]

"Well, hang it all, you did dream it, because there didn't any of it happen."

"But Huck, it's all jis' as plain to me as—"

"It don't make no difference how plain it is, there ain't nothing in it. I know, because I've been here all the time."

Jim didn't say nothing for about five minutes, but set there studying over it. Then he says:

"Well, den, I reck'n I did dream it, Huck; but dog my cats ef it ain't de powerfullest dream I ever see.[8] En I hain't ever had no dream b'fo' dat's tired me like dis one."

"Oh, well, that's all right, because a dream does tire a body like everything, sometimes. But this one was a staving[9] dream—tell me all about it, Jim."

So Jim went to work and told me the whole thing right through, just as it happened, only he painted it up considerable. Then he said he must start in and "'terpret" it, because it was sent for a warning.[10] He said the first towhead stood for a man that would try to do us some good, but the current was another man that would get us away from him. The whoops was warnings that would come to us every now and then, and if we didn't try hard to make out to

7. *how is I gwyne to dream all dat in ten minutes?* Actually, time is so distorted in dreams that one can experience a long string of events in a relatively short period.

8. *dog my cats ef it ain't de powerfullest dream I ever see.* "That was the dogonest plainest dream I ever did hev!" admits gullible Pike in in *History of the Big Bonanza* (1877) by Twain's friend "Dan De Quille" (William Wright), when Pike's friends play a prank as malicious as the one Huck pulls on Jim. To get even with Pike, Hank and their fellow prospectors fabricate an Indian attack on their Nevada mining camp so convincing that Pike rushes down the canyon "at the speed of an antelope." They come upon him next morning in town, and he is telling everyone about the terrible fight with the Indians. Certain that he left his friends for dead, Pike is understandably shocked to find them unharmed. They then confess that there were no Indians and that Pike must have dreamed the whole thing. Reluctant to believe at first, he finally admits that yes, it was all a dream, "sartain and sure . . . jist the same as bein' wide awake!" "Pike continued to tell his dream for some years," De Quille concluded, "constantly adding new matter, till at last it was a wonderful yarn." It makes no difference how hard the others try to convince him otherwise, Pike refuses to believe them. "Do you think . . . I was fool enough to believe sich things actually happened?" he asks. "No, it was all a dream from fust to last, and the biggest and plainest dream I ever had!" (pp. 547–55).

Although the two yarns follow much the same scheme, they differ significantly in each perpetrator's motivation: De Quille introduces the ruse of a dream to protect Pike from a suspicious and potentially violent crowd; Huck's is nothing more than a nasty practical joke on a "nigger" that takes advantage of the slave's deep affection and concern for the boy. But Jim is not so easily fooled as Pike. See also note 14.

9. *staving.* Strong, intense, vivid.

10. *it was sent for a warning.* Although the interpretation that follows at first seems as duplicitous as Jim's earlier prophecy with the hair ball (in Chapter 4, note 8), the boy and the runaway do encounter many "quarrelsome people and all kinds of mean folks" farther down the river.

understand them they'd just take us into bad luck, 'stead of keeping us out of it. The lot of tow-heads was troubles we was going to get into with quarrelsome people and all kinds of mean folks, but if we minded our business and didn't talk back and aggravate them, we would pull through and get out of the fog and into the big clear river,[11] which was the free States, and wouldn't have no more trouble.

It had clouded up pretty dark just after I got onto the raft, but it was clearing up again, now.

"Oh, well, that's all interpreted well enough, as far as it goes, Jim," I says; "but what does *these* things stand for?"

It was the leaves and rubbish on the raft, and the smashed oar. You could see them first rate, now.

Jim looked at the trash, and then looked at me, and back at the trash again. He had got the dream fixed so strong in his head that he couldn't seem to shake it loose and get the facts back into its place again, right away. But when he did get the thing straightened around, he looked at me steady, without ever smiling,[12] and says:

"What do dey stan' for? I's gwyne to tell you. When I got all wore out wid work, en wid de callin' for you, en went to sleep, my heart wuz mos' broke bekase you wuz los', en I didn' k'yer no mo' what become er me en de raf'. En when I wake up en fine you back agin', all safe en soun', de tears come en I could a got down on my knees en kiss' yo' foot I's so thankful. En all you wuz thinkin 'bout wuz how you could make a fool uv ole Jim wid a lie. Dat truck dah is *trash;* en trash is what people is dat puts dirt on de head er dey fren's en makes 'em ashamed."[13]

Then he got up slow, and walked to the wigwam, and went in there, without saying anything but that. But that was enough. It made me feel so mean[14] I could almost kissed *his* foot[15] to get him to take it back.

It was fifteen minutes before I could work myself up to go and humble myself to a nigger[16]—but I done it, and I warn't ever sorry for it afterwards, neither. I didn't do him no more mean tricks, and I wouldn't done that one if I'd a knowed it would make him feel that way.

11. *the big clear river*. The Ohio River, which (unlike the muddy lower Mississippi) is clear.

12. *he looked at me steady, without ever smiling*. Twain originally wrote the more humble "he was sort of sad" (**MS**) in the manuscript, but replaced it with the direct and defiant phrase. He also changed "Why dey mean dis" to "I's gwyne to tell you."

13. *trash is what people is dat puts dirt on de head er dey fren's en makes 'em ashamed*. Jim calls Huck by the most contemptuous term slaves had for white people—"white trash." "Jim's response is something my grandmother might have said," admitted David Bradley in *The New Yorker* (June 26/July 3, 1995, p. 133).

14. *It made me feel so mean*. And well it might. De Quille feels no better than Huck does when he sees Pike, terrified, dash down into the canyon and out of sight. "For my part," he admits in *History of the Big Bonanza*, "now that the fun was over, I began to feel quite miserable over the whole affair. . . . I firmly resolved never to take part in another affair of the kind" (pp. 551–52). De Quille worries that Pike might be hurt when he fails to return after he runs off. Huck learns a more devastating lesson: Jim's demonstration of his dignity awakens the boy's conscience. He will never feel the same again. Earlier, in Chapter 10, after putting the rattlesnake in Jim's bed that led its mate to bite him, the boy learned that the man feels pain just like anyone else; now Huck realizes that Jim has the same emotions as he and everyone else has. Huck was able to cover himself earlier by killing the snake and threw its skin away. After Jim calls him "trash," Huck feels guilt for his treatment of a slave probably for the first time in his life.

15. *kissed* his *foot*. Masters, overseers, and slave traders often forced disobedient slaves and recaptured runaways to kiss their boots to demonstrate submission.

16. *humble myself to a nigger*. "So," thought David Bradley when he first read the novel when a boy, "not all poor white trash are bigots. My responses might have been unsophisticated, but, reading *Huckleberry Finn*, I began to distinguish connotation from denotation, to judge intent by action rather than rhetoric"

(*New Yorker*, June 26/July 3, 1995, p. 133). Huck performs what must have been at the time the most degrading thing for a white person to do for a slave. "Jim violates the ethics of Jim Crow and *noblesse oblige* by reprimanding Huck for ridiculing him," Bernard W. Bell pointed out in "Twain's 'Nigger' Jim: The Tragic Face Behind the Minstrel Mask" (*Mark Twain Journal*, Spring 1985). "Here Jim's deep moral indignation surfaces from behind the comic mask which he wears defensively to conceal his true feelings and thoughts from Huck and other whites who pervert their humanity in demeaning or denying his" (p. 16). Huck and Jim are now equals.

"In many ways," Jocelyn Chadwick-Joshua argued in *The Jim Dilemma* (1998), "this section is the turning point of the novel. Jim is no longer invisible, and his 'silence' is clearly under his control. This decisive encounter signifies the redefining of the slave/master, white/black relationship to one of the caretaker-guardian/charge and adult/child, consequently amplifying Jim's manhood. Of equal significance is Huck's realization of this shift in their relationship" (p. 56). Toni Morrison suggested in her introduction to the 1996 "Oxford Mark Twain" edition of *Huckleberry Finn* that one "consider Huck's inability to articulate his true feelings for Jim to anybody other than the reader. When he 'humbles himself' in apology to Jim for the painful joke he plays on him, we are not given the words. . . . Until the hell-or-heaven choice, Huck can speak of the genuine affection and respect for Jim that blossoms throughout the narrative only aslant, or comically to the reader—never directly to any character or to Jim himself. While Jim repeatedly reiterates his love, the depth of Huck's feelings for Jim is stressed, underscored, and rendered unimpeachable by Twain's calculated use of speechlessness" (p. xxxvi). Huck cannot bear to say the simple word "friend" anywhere in the novel. And yet that is what Jim has been to him all along the Mississippi. T. S. Eliot in his 1950 introduction to the Cresset/Chanticleer edition pointed out a meaning in this passage which is often overlooked. "What is obvious, in it is the pathos and dignity of Jim, and this is moving enough," the poet explained, "but what I find still more disturbing, and still more unusual in literature, is the pathos and dignity of the boy, when reminded so humbly and humiliatingly, that his position in the world is not that of other boys, entitled from time to time to a practical joke; but that he must bear, and bear alone, the responsibility of a man."

Chapter XVI

1. *long sweeps*. Especially long oars for steering and propelling the craft.

2. *Jim said if the two big rivers joined together there, that would show*. "Ohio water didn't like to mix with Mississippi water," Twain explained in the "Raft Episode," a deleted section of *Huckleberry Finn* that was published in Chapter 3 of *Life on the Mississippi* (see Appendix B); "if you take the Mississippi on a rise when the Ohio is low, you'll find a wide band of clear water all the way down the east side of the Mississippi for a hundred mile or more, and the minute you get out a quarter of a mile from shore and pass the line, it is all thick and yaller the rest of the way across."

"IT *AMOUNTED* TO SOMETHING BEING A RAFTSMAN."

WE SLEPT most all day, and started out at night, a little ways behind a monstrous long raft that was as long going by as a procession. She had four long sweeps[1] at each end, so we judged she carried as many as thirty men, likely. She had five big wigwams aboard, wide apart, and an open camp fire in the middle, and a tall flag-pole at each end. There was a power of style about her. It *amounted* to something being a raftsman on such a craft as that.

We went drifting down into a big bend, and the night clouded up and got hot. The river was very wide, and was walled with solid timber on both sides; you couldn't see a break in it hardly ever, or a light. We talked about Cairo, and wondered whether we would know it when we got to it. I said likely we wouldn't, because I had heard say there warn't but about a dozen houses there, and if they didn't happen to have them lit up, how was we going to know we was passing a town? Jim said if the two big rivers joined together there, that would show.[2] But I said maybe we might think we was passing the foot of an island and coming into the same old river again. That disturbed Jim—and me too. So the question was, what to do? I said, paddle ashore the first time a light showed, and tell them pap was behind, coming along with a trading-scow, and was a green hand at the business,[3] and wanted to know how far it was to Cairo. Jim thought it was a good idea, so we took a smoke on it and waited.[4]

There warn't nothing to do, now, but to look out sharp for the town, and not pass it without seeing it. He said he'd be mighty sure to see it, because he'd be a free man the minute he seen it, but if he missed it he'd be in the slave country[5] again and no more show[6] for freedom. Every little while he jumps up and says:

"Dah she is!"

But it warn't. It was Jack-o-lanterns, or lightning-bugs;[7] so he set down again, and went to watching, same as before. Jim said it made him all over trembly and feverish to be so close to freedom. Well, I can tell you it made me all over trembly and feverish, too, to hear him, because I begun to get it through my head that he *was* most free—and who was to blame for it? Why, *me.* I couldn't get that out of my conscience,[8] no how nor no way. It got to troubling me so I couldn't rest; I couldn't stay still in one place. It hadn't ever come home to me before, what this thing was that I was doing. But now it did; and it staid with me, and scorched me more and more. I tried to make out to myself that *I* warn't to blame, because *I* didn't run Jim off from his rightful owner; but it warn't no use, conscience up and says, every time, "But you knowed he was running for his freedom, and you could a paddled ashore and told somebody." That was so—I couldn't get around that, noway. That was where it pinched. Conscience says to me, "What had poor Miss Watson done to you, that you could see her nigger go off right under your eyes and never say one single word? What did that poor old woman do to you, that you could treat her so mean? Why, she tried to learn you your book, she tried to learn you your manners,[9] she tried to be good to you every way she knowed how.[10] *That's* what she done."

I got to feeling so mean[11] and so miserable I most wished I was dead. I fidgeted up and down the raft, abusing

3. *pap . . . was a green hand at the business.* With some scorn toward his real father, Huck always describes the "pap" of his yarns along the river as unskilled and ineffectual.

4. *Jim thought it was a good idea, so we took a smoke on it and waited.* The deleted "Raft Episode" originally appeared at this point in the story. It was in the manuscript in 1876, before Twain pigeonholed it for several years. While expanding his *Atlantic Monthly* articles "Old Times on the Mississippi" into the subscription book *Life on the Mississippi*, Twain added this episode to Chapter 3 of the new book "by way of illustrating keelboat talk and manners, and that now-departed and hardly-remembered raft-life." He explained that in the fog, Huck and Jim "pass Cairo without knowing it. By-and-by they begin to suspect the truth, and Huck Finn is persuaded to end the dismal suspense by swimming down to the huge raft which they have seen in the distance ahead of them, creeping aboard under cover of the darkness, and gathering the needed information by eavesdropping."

When Twain finished *Huckleberry Finn* in 1883 as a sequel to *Tom Sawyer*, the "Raft Episode" was still part of the manuscript; he even considered including it on the program of his 1884–1885 public reading tour. But Charles L. Webster wrote him that he found the new book "so *much* larger than *Tom Sawyer*, would it not be better to omit that old Mississippi matter? I think it would improve it." Disregarding George W. Cable's suggestion to keep it in the novel, Twain readily agreed with Webster in a letter of April 22, 1884: "Yes, I think the raft chapter can be wholly left out, by heaving in a paragraph to say Huck visited the raft to find out how far it might be to Cairo, but got no satisfaction. Even *this* is not necessary unless that raft-visit is referred to later in the book. I think it is, but am not certain" (Samuel Charles Webster, *Mark Twain, Business Man*, 1946, pp. 249–50). Another consideration arose when Twain and Webster decided to publish *Huckleberry Finn* themselves rather than give it to James R. Osgood, the publisher of *Life on the Mississippi*. E. V. Lucas brought up the subject many years later when he met Twain at a *Punch* dinner in London. "I asked him why he had never incorporated in *Huckleberry Finn* the glorious chapters [*sic*] about the boasting bargemen which he dropped into *Life on the Mississippi*," Lucas told myself to myself, and Jim was fidgeting up and down past me. We neither of us could keep still. Every time he danced around and says, "Dah's Cairo!" it went through me like a shot,[12] and I thought if it *was* Cairo I reckoned I would die of miserableness.

Jim talked out loud all the time while I was talking to myself. He was saying how the first thing he would do when he got to a free State he would go to saving up money and never spend a single cent, and when he got enough he would buy his wife,[13] which was owned on a farm close to where Miss Watson lived; and then they would both work to buy the two children,[14] and if their master wouldn't sell them, they'd get an Ab'litionist to go and steal them.[15]

It most froze me to hear such talk. He wouldn't ever dared to talk such talk in his life before. Just see what a difference it made in him the minute he judged he was about free. It was according to the old saying, "give a nigger an inch and he'll take an ell."[16] Thinks I, this is what comes of my not thinking. Here was this nigger which I had as good as helped to run away, coming right out flat-footed and saying he would steal his children—children that belonged to a man I didn't even know; a man that hadn't ever done me no harm.

I was sorry to hear Jim say that, it was such a lowering of him. My conscience got to stirring me up hotter than ever, until at last I says to it, "Let up on me—it ain't too late, yet—I'll paddle ashore at the first light, and tell."[17] I felt easy, and happy, and light as a feather, right off. All my troubles was gone. I went to looking out sharp for a light, and sort of singing to myself. By-and-by one showed. Jim sings out:

"We's safe, Huck, we's safe! Jump up and crack yo' heels, dat's de good ole Cairo at las', I jis knows it!"[18]

I says:

"I'll take the canoe and go see, Jim. It mightn't be, you know."

He jumped and got the canoe ready, and put his old coat in the bottom for me to set on,[19] and give me the paddle; and as I shoved off, he says:

"Pooty soon I'll be a-shout'n for joy, en I'll say, it's all on

Cyril Clemens in "A Talk with Edward Verral Lucas" (*Canadian Bookman*, August/September 1938). "His reasons were not too understandable but I gather that some copyright question was involved" (p. 20). He never did add that paragraph explaining how Huck learns how far he and Jim are from Cairo. After he recovered all publishing rights to his books, including *Life on the Mississippi*, Twain had ample opportunity before he died in 1910 to restore the episode to *Huckleberry Finn*. He never did. Bernard DeVoto was the first one to return it to its proper place in the 1944 Limited Editions Club edition of *Huckleberry Finn*, followed by the *Portable Mark Twain* (1946). Because Twain never instructed that it be put back into the book, the "Raft Episode" is reprinted as Appendix B in this edition.

5. *the slave country*. Cairo was the point farthest south in free soil along the Mississippi; as they travel farther downstream, Huck and Jim are going deeper into slave country.

6. *no more show*. No more opportunity, not another chance.

7. *lightning-bugs*. Fireflies.

8. *my conscience*. When Twain included this internal debate in his "Tour Around the World," he revised this passage in his 1895–1896 public reading copy: "The thought struck me *cold*: I couldn't get that out of my conscience, no how nor no *way*. O, I had committed a *crime!*—I knowed it perfectly *well*—I could *see* it, *now*." Believing that "in a crucial moral emergency a sound heart is a safer guide than an ill-trained conscience," Twain prefaced an 1895–1896 reading of this episode by acknowledging Huck's moral struggle as an example in which "a sound heart and a deformed conscience come into collision and conscience suffers defeat" (Blair and Fischer, University of California edition, 1988, p. 806). By identifying the heart with one's natural responses and the conscience with conventional morality, Twain reintroduces the choice between the Widow Douglas's "Providence" and that of Miss Watson as discussed in Chapter 3, note 5. As Jim and Huck head closer to Cairo, the boy confronts the first crisis in which he must test these arguments; before this conflict, all questions of morality were merely theoretical.

accounts o' Huck; I's a free man, en I couldn't ever ben free ef it hadn' ben for Huck; Huck done it. Jim won't ever forgit you, Huck; you's de bes' fren' Jim's ever had; en you's de *only* fren' ole Jim's got now."[20]

I was paddling off, all in a sweat to tell on him; but when he says this, it seemed to kind of take the tuck all out of me.[21] I went along slow then, and I warn't right down certain whether I was glad I started or whether I warn't. When I was fifty yards off,[22] Jim says:

"Dah you goes, de ole true Huck; de on'y white genlman dat ever kep' his promise to ole Jim."

Well, I just felt sick. But I says, I *got* to do it—I can't get *out* of it. Right then, along comes a skiff with two men in it, with guns, and they stopped and I stopped. One of them says:

"What's that, yonder?"

"A piece of a raft," I says.

"Do you belong on it?"

"Yes, sir."

"Any men on it?"

"Only one, sir."

"Well, there's five niggers run off to-night, up yonder above the head of the bend. Is your man white or black?"

I didn't answer up prompt. I tried to, but the words wouldn't come. I tried, for a second or two, to brace up and out with it, but I warn't man enough—hadn't the spunk of a rabbit. I see I was weakening;[23] so I just give up trying, and up and says—

"He's white."[24]

"I reckon we'll go and see for ourselves."

"I wish you would," says I, "because it's pap that's there, and maybe you'd help me tow the raft ashore where the light is. He's sick—and so is mam and Mary Ann."[25]

"Oh, the devil! we're in a hurry, boy. But I s'pose we've got to. Come—buckle to your paddle,[26] and let's get along."

I buckled to my paddle[27] and they laid to their oars.[28] When we had made a stroke or two,[29] I says:

"Pap'll be mighty much obleeged to you, I can tell you.

In *What Is Man?* (1973), Twain suggested that within everyone there is the struggle between temperament, the disposition one is born with, and the conscience, "that independent Sovereign, that insolent absolute Monarch inside of a man who is the man's Master" (pp. 140–41). Huck is plagued by this "mysterious autocrat, lodged in a man, which compels the man to content its desires. It may be called the Master Passion—the hunger for Self-approval. . . . It is indifferent to the man's good; it never concerns itself about anything but the satisfying of its own desires" (p. 206). Education molds the conscience in accepting principles that the temperament might otherwise reject. "From the cradle to the grave, during all his waking hours," Twain continued in *What Is Man?*, "the human being is under training. In the very first rank of his trainers stands *association*. It is his human environment which influences his mind and his feelings, furnishes him his ideals, and sets him on his road and keeps him in it. If he leave that road he will find himself shunned by the people whom he most loves and esteems, and whose approval he most values" (p. 161). Huck already challenges public disapproval by helping the slave to run away. Training can make the conscience "prefer things which will be for the man's good, but it will prefer them only because it will content it better than other things would." It has no reason: "In *all* cases it seeks a *spiritual* contentment, let the *means* be what they may" (p. 206). Only the dictatorial temperament, which "is *born*, not made," can keep it in line, because it determines one's desires (p. 207). Thus Huck's conscience suffers another defeat in this particular battle.

Sam Clemens suffered from the same anxiety as Huck does. "Mine was a trained Presbyterian conscience," he explained in "Chapters from My Autobiography," "and knew but one duty—to hunt and harry its slave upon all pretexts and on all occasions; particularly when there was no sense or reason in it" (*North American Review*, May 3, 1907, p. 5). He admitted in "The Facts Concerning the Recent Carnival of Crime in Connecticut," published in *The Atlantic Monthly* (June 1876) one month before he began *Huckleberry Finn*, "All consciences *I* ever heard of were nagging, badgering, fault-finding, execrable savages! Yes; and always in a sweat about some poor little insignificant trifle or other—destruction catch the lot of them, *I* say! I would trade mine for the small-pox and seven kinds of consumption, and be glad of the chance" (p. 646). Therefore Twain agreed with W.E.H. Lecky's argument in *History of European Morals* (1869) that the conscience is indeed "the cause of more pain than pleasure. Its reproaches are felt more than its approval."

9. *your manners*. In his 1895–1896 public reading copy, Twain added an even more damning comment: "to be a Christian."

10. *she tried to be good to you every way she knowed how*. His cruel conscience seems to be confusing Widow Douglas with Miss Watson, who was *not* good to him. However, the irony of this battle between corrupted conscience and sound heart intensifies now that Huck *thinks* she was good to him.

11. *I got to feeling so mean*. "And treacherous," Twain added in his 1895–1896 public reading copy.

12. *shot*. "Sword" in Twain's 1895–1896 public reading copy, a slower and likely more painful process.

13. *when he got enough he would buy his wife*. Because they were legally chattel, families were often broken up according to the whims of their owners. "Don't you know a slave can't be married?" George reminds his wife in Chapter 3 of *Uncle Tom's Cabin* when his master decides to

A father sold from his family. Illustration from *The Child's Anti-Slavery Book*, 1859. *Courtesy Rare Book Room, Library of Congress.*

Everybody goes away when I want them to help me tow the raft ashore, and I can't do it by myself."

"Well, that's infernal mean. Odd, too. Say, boy, what's the matter with your father?"

"It's the—a—the—well, it ain't anything, much."

They stopped pulling. It warn't but a mighty little ways to the raft, now. One says:

"Boy, that's a lie. What *is* the matter with your pap? Answer up square, now, and it'll be the better for you."

"I will, sir, I will, honest[30]—but don't leave us, please. It's the—the—gentlemen, if you'll only pull ahead, and let me

"BOY, THAT'S A LIE."

heave you the head-line,[31] you won't have to come a-near the raft—please do."

"Set her back, John, set her back!" says one. They backed water.[32] "Keep away, boy—keep to looard.[33] Confound it, I just expect the wind has blowed it to us. Your pap's got the small-pox, and you know it precious well.[34] Why didn't you come out and say so? Do you want to spread it all over?"

"Well," says I, a-blubbering,[35] "I've told everybody before, and then they just went away and left us."

"Poor devil, there's something in that.[36] We are right down sorry for you, but we—well, hang it, we don't want the small-pox, you see. Look here, I'll tell you what to do. Don't you try to land by yourself, or you'll smash everything to pieces. You float along down about twenty miles and you'll come to a town on the left-hand side of the river. It will be long after sun-up, then, and when you ask for help, you tell them your folks are all down with chills and fever. Don't be a fool again, and let people guess what is the matter. Now we're trying to do you a kindness;[37] so you just put twenty miles between us, that's a good boy. It wouldn't do any good to land yonder where the light is—it's only a wood-yard.[38] Say—I reckon your father's poor, and I'm bound to say he's in pretty hard luck. Here—I'll put a twenty dollar gold piece on this board,[39] and you get it when it floats by. I feel mighty mean to leave you, but my kingdom! it won't do to fool with small-pox, don't you see?"

"Hold on, Parker," says the other man, "here's a twenty to put on the board for me. Good-bye, boy, you do as Mr. Parker told you, and you'll be all right."

"That's so, my boy—good-bye, good-bye. If you see any runaway niggers, you get help and nab them, and you can make some money by it."

"Good-bye, sir," says I, "I won't let no runaway niggers get by me if I can help it."

They went off, and I got aboard the raft,[40] feeling bad and low, because I knowed very well I had done wrong, and I see it warn't no use for me to try to learn to do right; a body that don't get *started* right when he's little, ain't got no show[41]—when the pinch comes there ain't nothing to back him up and keep him to his work, and so he gets beat. Then I thought a minute, and says to myself, hold on,—s'pose you'd a done right and give Jim up; would you felt better than what you do now? No, says I, I'd feel bad—I'd feel just the same way I do now.[42] Well, then, says I, what's the use you learning to do right, when it's troublesome to do right and ain't no trouble to do wrong, and the wages is just the same? I was stuck. I couldn't answer that. So I reckoned I wouldn't bother no more about it, but after this always do whichever come handiest at the time.[43]

I went into the wigwam; Jim warn't there. I looked all around; he warn't anywhere. I says:

"Jim!"

sell him down the river. "There is no law in the country for that; I can't hold you for my wife if he chooses to part us." She is Jim's wife in name only. "Marriage between negroes was prohibited by law," recalled Missourian David P. Dyer in *Autobiography and Reminiscences* (St. Louis: William Henry Miner Co., 1922), "and it was only by voluntary cohabitation that semblance was given to legality" (p. 69).

14. *they would both work to buy the two children.* The children of slaves legally belonged to the mother's, not the father's, owner. This law derived from the Bible, from the laws of Moses, that former Egyptian slave, in Exodus 21:24: "If a master has given him a wife, and she have borne him sons or daughters; the wife and her children shall be her master's, and he shall go out by himself." Huck does not indicate whether Jim's children live on the same farm with their mother. "It is a common custom, in the part of Maryland from which I ran away, to part children from their mothers at a very early age," Frederick Douglass revealed in Chapter 1 of his *Narrative*. Aunty Rachel describes what she went through in "A True Story" (*Atlantic Monthly*, November 1874): "An' dey sole my ole man, an' took him away, an' dey begin to sell my chil'en an' dey take *dem* away, an' I begin to cry; an' de man say, 'Shet up yo' dam blubberin',' an' hit me on de mouf wid his han'" (p. 592). It may have been the same with Jim's family.

Jim never does fulfill his promise to buy his wife and children in *Huckleberry Finn*. However, in the uncompleted "Tom Sawyer's Conspiracy" of 1898, "the Widow was hiring Jim for wages so he could buy his wife and children's freedom some time or other" (*Huck Finn and Tom Sawyer Among the Indians*, 1989, p. 134); and in a typewritten fragment in the Mark Twain Papers at the University of California at Berkeley, Tom and Huck present Jim with his wife and child (Twain evidently forgot that Jim has both a son and a daughter), with a bill of sale for $550 pinned to the woman's breast with the message "The Property of our Old Jim—Christmas gift from Tom and Huck."

15. *they'd get an Ab'litionist to go and steal them.* "It was *awful* to hear it," Huck adds in Twain's 1895–1896 public reading copy.

16. *the old saying, "Give a nigger an inch and he'll take an ell."* An ell was an old English measurement from the elbow to the tip of the middle finger, about forty-five inches. The current American equivalent of this saying is "Give a man an inch and he'll take a mile," from a popular English proverb which goes back as far as the sixteenth century. Frederick Douglass recalled in Chapter 6 of his *Narrative* how one of his masters used to say, "If you give a nigger an inch, he will take an ell."

17. *I'll paddle ashore at the first light, and tell.* "O! it was a *blessed* thought!" Huck goes on in Twain's 1895–1896 public reading copy, "I never can *tell* how *good* it made me feel—'cuz I *knowed* I was doing *right*, now."

18. *I jis knows it!* Jim continues in Twain's 1895–1896 public reading copy, "We's *safe*, Huck, we's *safe*, shore's you's *bawn*, we *safe!*"

19. *put his old coat in the bottom for me to set on.* This unnecessarily chivalrous act on Jim's part is worthy of Sir Walter Raleigh, who spread his coat over the mud for Queen Elizabeth to walk on; but Jim's generous gesture can only grate on Huck's guilty conscience.

20. *you's de* only *fren' ole Jim's got now.* "O bless de good old heart o' you, Huck!" Jim adds in Twain's 1895–1896 public reading copy. According to the Melbourne *Age* (September 30, 1895), when Twain read this chapter in Australia, "The audience fairly roared with laughter at Huck's naive remark, 'The truth is plenty good enough in ordinary places, but when you get into a tight place you can't rely on it,' just as they accentuated with their perfect silence in the pathos of the hunted slave's cry across the water, rendered with tears in his voice by the author, 'Dah you goes, de ole true Huck, de bes' frien' poor Jim ever had, de ony fren' poor Jim has now.'" Jim's cries are so plaintive, so urgent, because he knows who these men must be and what Huck might do.

21. *take the tuck all out of me.* Deflate me. "It kind of all *unsettled* me," Huck adds in Twain's 1895–1896 public reading copy, "and I couldn't seem to *tell* whether I was doing *right* or doing *wrong*."

22. *fifty yards off.* In his 1895–1896 public reading copy, Twain changed this to "one hundred or fifty yards off."

"HERE I IS, HUCK."

"Here I is, Huck. Is dey out o' sight yit? Don't talk loud."

He was in the river, under the stern oar, with just his nose out. I told him they was out of sight, so he come aboard. He says:

"I was a-listenin' to all de talk, en I slips into de river en was gwyne to shove for sho' if dey come aboard. Den I was gwyne to swim to de raf' agin when dey was gone. But lawsy, how you did fool 'em, Huck! Dat *wuz* de smartes' dodge![44] I tell you, chile, I 'speck it save' ole Jim—ole Jim ain't gwyne to forgit you for dat, honey."

Then we talked about the money. It was a pretty good raise, twenty dollars apiece. Jim said we could take deck passage[45] on a steamboat now, and the money would last us as far as we wanted to go in the free States. He said twenty mile more warn't far for the raft to go, but he wished we was already there.

Towards daybreak we tied up, and Jim was mighty particular about hiding the raft good. Then he worked all day fixing things in bundles, and getting all ready to quit rafting.

That night about ten we hove in sight of the lights of a town away down in a left-hand bend.

I went off in the canoe, to ask about it. Pretty soon I found a man out in the river with a skiff, setting a trot-line. I ranged up and says:

"Mister, is that town Cairo?"

"Cairo? no. You must be a blame' fool."

"What town is it, mister?"

"If you want to know, go and find out. If you stay here botherin' around me for about a half a minute longer, you'll get something you won't want."

I paddled to the raft. Jim was awful disappointed, but I said never mind, Cairo would be the next place, I reckoned.

We passed another town[46] before daylight, and I was going out again; but it was high ground, so I didn't go. No high ground about Cairo, Jim said. I had forgot it. We laid up for the day, on a tow-head tolerable close to the left-hand bank. I begun to suspicion something. So did Jim. I says:

"Maybe we went by Cairo in the fog that night."

He says:

"Doan' less' talk about it, Huck. Po' niggers can't have no luck. I awluz 'spected dat rattle-snake skin warn't done wid its work."

"I wish I'd never seen that snake-skin, Jim—I do wish I'd never laid eyes on it."

"It ain't yo' fault, Huck;[47] you didn' know. Don't you blame yo'self 'bout it."

When it was daylight, here was the clear Ohio water in shore, sure enough, and outside was the old regular Muddy![48] So it was all up with Cairo.[49]

We talked it all over. It wouldn't do to take to the shore; we couldn't take the raft up the stream, of course.[50] There warn't no way but to wait for dark, and start back in the canoe and take the chances. So we slept all day amongst the cotton-wood thicket, so as to be fresh for the work, and when we went back to the raft about dark the canoe was gone!

We didn't say a word for a good while. There warn't anything to say. We both knowed well enough it was some more work of the rattle-snake skin; so what was the use to talk about it? It would only look like we was finding fault, and that would be bound to fetch more bad luck—and keep on fetching it, too, till we knowed enough to keep still.

23. *I see I was weakening.* In his 1895–1896 public reading copy, Twain explained exactly what finally broke Huck's courage: While the slave hunter demands, "*Come*, answer *up*—is he *white* or black?" the frustrated boy hears the voice across the water, saying, "De good ole Huck, de good ole Huck!"

24. *He's white.* Twain gave Huck another observation in the 1895–1896 public reading copy: "It uz come time to lie; you always got to do that when you git in a close place. Facts ain't no good when a person is crowded." But Twain crossed it out and added another line: " 'It took you a good while to get it *out*.' "

25. *and so is mam and Mary Ann.* Huck lays it on a bit thick in Twain's 1895–1896 public reading copy by adding "and the baby."

26. *buckle to your paddle.* Begin paddling in earnest.

27. *I buckled to my paddle.* "Like Sam *Hill*, and says, 'I George! in luck at last!" Twain added to his 1895–1896 public reading copy

28. *they laid to their oars.* They proceeded.

29. *made a stroke or two.* "Gone about 100 yards" in Twain's 1895–1896 public reading copy.

30. *I will sir, I will, honest.* Twain noted in the copy of his 1895–1896 public reading copy the instruction to read this paragraph "blubbering."

31. *the head-line.* A line fastening the head of a vessel to the shore.

32. *They backed water.* They retreated.

33. *looard.* Critic Francis Dunham explained in his note to the 1962 Houghton Mifflin edition that *leeward* "means in the direction toward which the wind blows; as contrasted to *windward*, the direction from which it blows. If Huck stays to the leeward of the men, the wind cannot carry contagion to them."

34. *Your pap's got the small-pox, and you know it precious well.* Claude R. Flory suggested in "Huck, Sam and the Small-Pox" (*Mark Twain Journal*, Winter 1964–1965) that Twain likely knew a similar "dodge" in Harriet Beecher

Stowe's dialect collection *Sam Lawson's Oldtown Fireside Stories* (1872):

> They had a putty bad name, them Hokums. . . . Why, they got to owin' two dollars to Joe Gidger for butcher's meat . . . ; but he couldn't never get it out o' him. 'Member once Joe walked clean up to the cranberry-pond arter that 'are two dollars; but Mother Hokum she see him comin'. . . . She says to Hokum, "Get into bed old man, quick, and let me tell the story," says she. So she covered him up; and when Gidger come in she come up to him, and says she, "Why, Mr. Gidger, I'm jest ashamed to see ye: why, Mr. Hokum was jest a comin' down to pay ye that 'are money last week, but ye see he was took with the small-pox"—Joe didn't hear no more: he just turned round, and he streaked it out that 'are door with his coat-tails flyin' out straight ahind him; and old Mother Hokum she jest stood at the window holdin' her sides and laughin' fit to split, to see him turn. That 'are's jest a sample o' the ways them Hokums cut up.

In "Mark Twain and James W. C. Pennington: Huckleberry Finn's Smallpox Lie" (*Studies in American Fiction*, Spring 1981, pp. 103–12), William J. Andrews discussed another instance of this ruse in a slave narrative, James Pennington's *The Fugitive Blacksmith* (1849). When he was picked up as a runaway and asked who he belonged to and where he was from, quick-thinking Pennington replied, "I was sold from the eastern shore [of Maryland] to a slave-trader, who had a large gang, and set out for Georgia, but when he got to town in Virginia, he was taken sick, and died with the small-pox. Several of the gang also died with it, so that the people in the town became alarmed, and did not wish the gang to remain among them. No one claimed us or wished to have anything to do with us; I left the rest, and thought I would go somewhere and get work." His captors decided they had "better let the small-pox nigger go." But unlike Mother Hokum, Pennington suffered a "great moral dilemma" about telling a lie to save himself. "I never return to it," confessed this pastor and (like Sam Clemens) Presbyterian, "but with the most intense horror at a system which can put a man not only in peril of liberty, limb, and life itself, but which may even send him in haste to the bar of God with a lie on his lips." Stowe singled him out (along with Frederick Douglass) in her conclusion to *Uncle*

By-and-by we talked about what we better do, and found there warn't no way but just to go along down with the raft till we got a chance to buy a canoe to go back in. We warn't going to borrow it when there warn't anybody around, the way pap would do, for that might set people after us.

So we shoved out, after dark, on the raft.

Anybody that don't believe yet, that it's foolishness to handle a snake-skin, after all that that snake-skin done for us, will believe it now, if they read on and see what more it done for us.

The place to buy canoes is off of rafts laying up at shore. But we didn't see no rafts laying up; so we went along during three hours and more. Well, the night got gray, and ruther thick, which is the next meanest thing to fog. You can't tell the shape of the river, and you can't see no distance. It got to be very late and still, and then along comes a steamboat up the river. We lit the lantern, and judged she would see it. Up-stream boats didn't generly come close to us; they go out and follow the bars and hunt for easy water under the reefs; but nights like this they bull right up the channel against the whole river.

We could hear her pounding along, but we didn't see her good till she was close. She aimed right for us. Often they do that and try to see how close they can come without touching; sometimes the wheel bites off a sweep, and then the pilot sticks his head out and laughs, and thinks he's mighty smart. Well, here she comes, and we said she was going to try to shave us;[51] but she didn't seem to be sheering off a bit. She was a big one, and she was coming in a hurry, too, looking like a black cloud with rows of glow-worms around it; but all of a sudden she bulged out, big and scary, with a long row of wide-open furnace doors shining like red-hot teeth, and her monstrous bows and guards hanging right over us. There was a yell at us, and a jingling of bells to stop the engines, a pow-wow of cussing, and whistling of steam—and as Jim went overboard on one side and I on the other, she come smashing straight through the raft.

I dived—and I aimed to find the bottom, too, for a thirty-foot wheel had got to go over me,[52] and I wanted it to have plenty of room. I could always stay under water a minute; this time I reckon I staid under water a minute and a half. Then I bounced for the top in a hurry, for I was nearly busting. I popped out to my arm-pits and blowed the water out of my nose, and puffed a bit. Of course there was a booming current; and of course that boat started her engines again ten seconds after she stopped them, for they never cared much for raftsmen; so now she was churning along up the river, out of sight in the thick weather, though I could hear her.

I sung out for Jim about a dozen times, but I didn't get any answer; so I grabbed a plank that touched me while I was "treading water," and struck out for shore, shoving it ahead of me. But I made out to see that the drift of the current was towards the left-hand shore,[53] which meant that I was in a crossing; so I changed off and went that way.

It was one of these long, slanting, two-mile crossings;[54] so I was a good long time in getting over. I made a safe landing, and clum up the bank. I couldn't see but a little ways, but I went poking along over rough ground for a quarter of a mile or more, and then I run across a big old-fashioned double log house before I noticed it. I was going to rush by and get away, but a lot of dogs jumped out and went to howling and barking at me, and I knowed better than to move another peg.

CLIMBING UP THE BANK.

Tom's Cabin as famous examples of "men, but yesterday burst from the shackles of slavery, who, by a self-educating force . . . have risen to highly respectable stations in society."

35. *a-blubbering.* Twain changed this to "and then and there," since he had just used "blubbering" in his revisions for his 1895–1896 "Tour Around the World."

36. *Poor devil, there's something in that.* Twain reminded himself in his 1895–1896 public reading copy that the slave hunter "bellows" this paragraph.

37. *we're trying to do you a kindness.* Twain's slave hunters have some redeeming human qualities. "The great mass of Southerners, both in town and country," Twain explained in a suppressed passage of *Life on the Mississippi* (published in the 1944 Limited Editions Club edition), "are neighborly, friendly, hospitable, peaceable, and have an aversion for disagreements and embroilments; they belong to the church, and they frequent it; they are Sabbath-observers; they are promise-keepers; they are honorable and upright in their dealings; where their prejudices are not at the front, they are just, and they like to see justice done; they are able to reason, and they reason" (pp. 412–13). Only in their upholding of the peculiar institution of slavery were they different from other people. Even these gentlemen show sympathy for Huck's unfortunate "family" while hunting for fugitive slaves.

38. *only a wood-yard.* A rude settlement, which existed primarily as a spot for steamboats to stop and "wood up" with fuel.

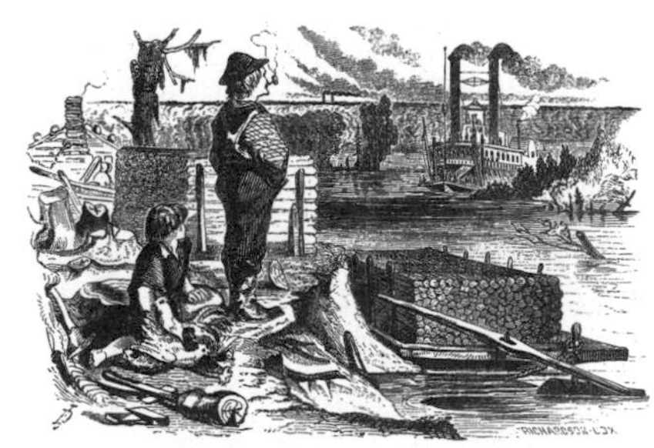

A wood-yard. Illustration from *Emerson's Magazine and Putnam's Monthly*, October 1857.
Courtesy Library of Congress.

39. *I'll put a twenty dollar gold piece on this board.* He tries to soothe *his* conscience by vainly offering the doomed family some money rather than to risk catching smallpox himself. Slave hunting must have been a lucrative business near Cairo, Illinois, for these men could easily spare $20 in gold, a considerable sum at the time.

40. *They went off, and I got aboard the raft.* Twain struggled with this passage almost as much as Huck did. He completely rewrote this paragraph, one of the few examples of his doing so in the entire manuscript. It originally read:

> They went off and I hopped aboard the raft, saying to myself, I've done wrong again, and was trying as hard as I could to do right, too; but when it come right down to telling them it was a nigger on the raft, and I opened my mouth a-purpose to do it, I couldn't. I am a mean, low coward, and it's the fault of them that brung me up. If I had been raised right, I wouldn't said anything about anybody being sick, but the more I try to do right, the more I can't. I reckon I won't ever try again, because it ain't no sort of use and only makes me feel bad. From this out I mean to do everything as wrong as I can do it, and just go straight to the dogs and done with it. I don't see why people's put here, anyway. (**MS**)

Originally, Huck says he is going straight to "the bad place," but Twain changed it because that is Miss Watson's phrase for Hell (see Chapter 1, note 24). Twain must have revised this passage when he realized that it is too early in the story for Huck to "*go* to hell" rather than to tell on Jim. For the time being, he will do only what seems most convenient.

And it still was not right. Twain introduced this chapter, called "Small-pox and a Lie Save Jim," as part of his "Morals Lecture" in Minneapolis on July 23, 1895, on his 1895–1896 "Tour Around the World." In an entry in his 1895 notebook he went back to his original conclusion: "Well, old Jim was *safe*. And as I set there floating along and thinking it over, my conscience was bitter sorry I had done *wrong*;—but as for *me*, I was awful *glad* I *hadn't* done *right*" (Blair and Fischer, University of California edition, 1988, p. 807). Twain kept it in the program for the next three months. "In telling the half humorous, half pathetic story of Huck Finn's dilemma in sheltering a runaway slave," the Melbourne *Age* reported on September 30, 1895, "the author gives us in greater detail than in the book the terrible struggle which goes on between Huck's sound heart and his 'deformed conscience.'" In April 1896, Twain again revised this particular passage; but it is not known if he ever read this version publicly. Gregg Campbell printed it in "'I Wouldn't Be as Ignorant as You for Wages': Huck Talks Back to His Conscience" (*Studies in American Fiction*, Autumn 1992):

> Old Jim was saved; and just as I was going to be glad, my conscience shoved in, just in the same old way and begun to skin me and scorch me and blister me because I'd done wrong, till I just couldn't *stand* it no more. So I just turned on it and says—Looky here I says, Things is gone jist a little too fur betwixt you and me, I says, and I'm gittin' powerful tired of it. In my opinion a conscience is just a *pin*cushion—and every time you ain't noticing you set *down* on it. Who asked you to come and take up with me? Nobody—you done it yourself. I don't want no such thing around as a conscience. . . . You ain't wanted, you ain't welcome, you ain't no use to me. I never see such a low-down troublesome cuss, I says. It don't make no difference what a person does, you ain't ever satisfied, and you mix in as free as if you owned the whole layout. If I'd a give Jim up you'd a kep me awake a week mournin' about it; and now you're gittin' ready to try to keep me awake another week because I *didn't* give him up. Now if you . . . want to stay with me, there's just one thing about it—You'll just mind your own business and I'll tend to mine—I don't want none of your help. I wouldn't be as ignorant as you for wages. You don't know right from wrong, you ain't got no judgement, you ain't got no sense about anything—you ain't no good but just to lazy around, find fault and keep a person in a sweat. I'd rather have any other kind of a character. I don't care *what*. I said them very words. I talked perfectly plain; I warn't in no humor to mince things. Them was my sentiments then, and they're my sentiments *yet*." (p. 171)

41. *a body that don't get* started *right when he's little, ain't got no show.* Blair and Fischer in the 1988 University of California edition pointed to the similar argument in a marginal note in Twain's hand in a copy of W.E.H. Lecky's *His-*

tory of European Morals (1869) that "all moral perceptions are acquired by the influences around us; these influences begin in infancy; we never get a chance to find out whether we have any that are innate or not" (p. 397).

42. *I'd feel just the same way I do now*. "As fur as *I* can see," Huck adds in Twain's 1895–1896 public reading copy, "a conscience is put in you just to *object* to whatever you *do* do, don't make no difference what it *is*."

43. *always do whichever come handiest at the time*. "And it's the best way, too," Twain added to his 1895–1896 public reading copy. Then he crossed it out. Rather than establish a moral code by which he must act in the future, Huck, like the slave hunter, chooses to do whatever seems the most expedient. "He is a chameleon," Twain argued in *What Is Man?*; "by a law of his nature he takes the color of his place of resort. The influences about him create his preferences, his aversions, his politics, his tastes, his morals, his religion. He creates none of these things for himself" (p. 161). However, Huck's heart conquers these influences; and because it is good, what seems most expedient is also the only moral decision to follow.

44. *dodge*. Ingenious contrivance.

45. *deck passage*. Steerage passage, the cheapest form of transport on a steamboat. "For every cabin passenger living in relative elegance of the upper deck on a typical Mississippi riverboat," John C. Gerber noted in the 1982 University of California edition of *Tom Sawyer Abroad/Tom Sawyer, Detective*, "there would be as many as four or five deck passengers crowded together below with no bed, no food other than what they brought aboard, no toilet facilities, often not even enough deck space on which to lie down. Deck passengers were not allowed on the upper deck except . . . to buy drinks at a carefully designated bar" (p. 185).

Deck passengers. Illustration for *Every Saturday*, September 2, 1871.
Courtesy Library of Congress.

46. *another town*. In Chapter 25 of *Life on the Mississippi*, Twain identified the two towns that Huck and Jim pass as Columbus and Hickman, Kentucky, the latter "a pretty town, perched on a handsome hill."

47. *It ain't yo' fault, Huck*. Of course the rattlesnake skin *was* Huck's fault, and Jim's denial is just another thing to grate on the boy's "deformed conscience."

48. *the old regular Muddy*. A popular name for the Mississippi River, describing both its color and consistency.

49. *So it was all up with Cairo*. Because Twain deleted the "Raft Episode" (Appendix B), the reader never learns the difference between the Ohio and Mississippi river water and so does not know how Huck knows they have passed Cairo. See note 2 above.

50. *we couldn't take the raft up the stream, of course*. Unlike steamboats, rafts were not self-propelled; they were always at the mercy of the river.

51. *she was going to try to shave us*. "Shaving" or bringing one boat as close as possible along the side of another one without touching was a popular and dangerous sport along the Mississippi, and a frequent cause of accidents. According to Chapters 10 and 11 of *Life on the Mississippi*, steamboat pilots were contemptuous of "small-fry craft" during the June rise; they thought they were an "intolerable nuisance" when they did not keep a light burning and were hard to see in the darkness. Twain recalled in Chapter 6 of *Life on the Mississippi* the time he was ordered, when a cub pilot, to "shave those steamboats as close as you'd peel an apple":

> I took the wheel, and my heart-beat fluttered up into the hundreds; for it seemed to me that we were about to scrape the side off every ship in the line, we were so close. I held my breath and began to claw the boat away from

"Shaving" a riverboat. Illustration from *Emerson's Magazine and Putnam's Monthly*, October 1857.
Courtesy Library of Congress.

the danger; and I had my opinion of the pilot who had known no better than to get us into such peril, but I was too wise to express it. In half a minute I had a wide margin of safety intervening between the *Paul Jones* and the ships; and within ten seconds more I was set aside in disgrace, and Mr. [Horace] Bixby [the pilot] was going into danger again and flaying me alive with abuse of my cowardice. I was stung, but I was obliged to admire the easy confidence with which my chief loafed from side to side of his wheel, and trimmed the ships so closely that disaster seemed ceaselessly imminent.

52. *I dived—and I aimed to find the bottom, too, for a thirty-foot wheel had got to go over me.* Blair and Fischer suggested in the 1988 University of California edition (p. 398) that Twain may have been recalling an incident described in "Old Times on the Mississippi" (*Atlantic Monthly*, May 1875, p. 570) of a cub pilot who saved himself when he dived under the paddlewheel as a steamboat collided with his sounding boat in the dark.

53. *the left-hand shore.* Although a running head of the next chapter in the first edition of *Huckleberry Finn* reads "The Farm in Arkansaw," Twain disclosed in the introduction to the next chapter in his 1895–1896 public reading copy, "Huck swam to the Kentucky side." But according to Blair and Fischer in the 1988 University of California Edition (p. 398), the river carries him near Darnall's Point, Tennessee, about two miles below Compromise Landing, Kentucky.

54. *It was one of those long, slanting, two-mile crossings.* In his 1895–1896 public reading copy, Twain revised this line to "The river was a mile and a quarter wide, and I made a long slanting [two-mile crossing]." Blair and Fischer in the 1988 University of California edition located this crossing at New Madrid Bend, "a notoriously dangerous part of the river" (p. 398).

Chapter XVII

"WHO'S THERE?"

IN ABOUT half a minute somebody spoke out of a window, without putting his head out, and says:

"Be done, boys! Who's there?"

I says:

"It's me."

"Who's me?"

"George Jackson,[1] sir."

"What do you want?"

"I don't want nothing, sir. I only want to go along by, but the dogs won't let me."

"What are you prowling around here this time of night, for—hey?"

"I warn't prowling around, sir; I fell overboard off of the steamboat."

"Oh, you did, did you? Strike a light there, somebody. What did you say your name was?"

"George Jackson, sir. I'm only a boy."

"Look here; if you're telling the truth, you needn't be afraid—nobody 'll hurt you. But don't try to budge; stand right where you are. Rouse out Bob and Tom, some of you, and fetch the guns. George Jackson, is there anybody with you?"

"No, sir, nobody."

I heard the people stirring around in the house, now, and see a light. The man sung out:

"Snatch that light away, Betsy, you old fool—ain't you got

1. *George Jackson.* In Chapter 49 of *Life on the Mississippi*, Twain himself employed a similar alias, "George Johnson," as he tried to travel incognito on the river. It did not work; Mark Twain was recognized immediately.

any sense? Put it on the floor behind the front door. Bob, if you and Tom are ready, take your places."

"All ready."

"Now, George Jackson, do you know the Shepherdsons?"[2]

"No, sir—I never heard of them."

"Well, that may be so, and it mayn't. Now, all ready. Step forward, George Jackson. And mind, don't you hurry—come mighty slow. If there's anybody with you, let him keep back—if he shows himself he'll be shot. Come along, now. Come slow; push the door open, yourself—just enough to squeeze in, d' you hear?"

I didn't hurry, I couldn't if I'd a wanted to. I took one slow step at a time, and there warn't a sound, only I thought I could hear my heart.[3] The dogs were as still as the humans, but they followed a little behind me. When I got to the three log door-steps, I heard them unlocking and unbarring and unbolting. I put my hand on the door and pushed it a little and a little more, till somebody said, "There, that's enough—put your head in." I done it, but I judged they would take it off.[4]

The candle was on the floor, and there they all was, looking at me, and me at them, for about a quarter of a minute. Three big men with guns pointed at me, which made me wince, I tell you; the oldest, gray and about sixty, the other two thirty or more[5]—all of them fine and handsome—and the sweetest old gray-headed lady, and back of her two young women which I couldn't see right well.[6] The old gentleman says:

"There—I reckon it's all right. Come in."

As soon as I was in, the old gentleman he locked the door and barred it and bolted it, and told the young men to come in with their guns, and they all went in a big parlor that had a new rag carpet[7] on the floor, and got together in a corner that was out of range of the front windows—there warn't none on the side. They held the candle, and took a good look at me, and all said, "Why *he* ain't a Shepherdson—no, there ain't any Shepherdson about him." Then the old man said he hoped I wouldn't mind being searched for arms,

2. *the Shepherdsons.* Huck's hosts and neighbors correspond to the Darnalls (also spelled "Darnells") of Tennessee and the Watsons of Kentucky in Chapter 26 of *Life on the Mississippi*. See Chapter 18, note 11.

3. *I could hear my heart.* "A-thumping" in Twain's 1895–1896 public reading copy.

4. *but I judged they would take it off.* In his 1895–1896 public reading copy, Twain changed this to "becuz I *had* to; but I reckoned t'uz the last I'd ever see of it."

5. *the other two thirty or more.* Twain changed this to "twenty-five or thirty or more," in the 1895–1896 public reading copy.

6. *two young women which I couldn't see right well.* Because, according to Twain's 1895–1896 public reading copy, "they was bundled up in quilts, anyway."

7. *rag carpet.* Homemade rug of strips of cloth knitted or sewn together; these carpets were the standard kind used by backwoods people of modest means throughout Missouri and the Southwest including Colonel Sellers in Chapter 5 of *The Gilded Age*. See note 21.

because he didn't mean no harm by it—it was only to make sure. So he didn't pry into my pockets, but only felt outside with his hands, and said it was all right. He told me to make myself easy and at home, and tell all about myself; but the old lady says:

"Why bless you, Saul, the poor thing's as wet as he can be; and don't you reckon it may be he's hungry?"

"True for you, Rachel—I forgot."

So the old lady says:

"Betsy" (this was a nigger woman), "you fly around and get him something to eat, as quick as you can, poor thing; and one of you girls go and wake up Buck and tell him—Oh, here he is himself. Buck, take this little stranger and get the wet clothes off from him and dress him up in some of yours that's dry."

"BUCK."

Buck looked about as old as me—thirteen or fourteen or along there,[8] though he was a little bigger than me. He hadn't on anything but a shirt,[9] and he was very frowsy-headed. He come in gaping and digging one fist into his eyes, and he was dragging a gun along with the other one. He says:

"Ain't they no Shepherdsons around?"

They said, no, 'twas a false alarm.

"Well," he says, "if they'd a ben some, I reckon I'd a got one."

They all laughed, and Bob says:

"Why, Buck, they might have scalped us all, you've been so slow in coming."

"Well, nobody come after me, and it ain't right. I'm always kep' down; I don't get no show."

8. *Buck looked about as old as me—thirteen or fourteen or along there.* Twain never gives Huck's exact age in the novel; as Blair and Fischer pointed out in the 1988 University of California edition (p. 398), he said that he "studiously avoided mentioning" the ages of the young heroes of *The Prince and the Pauper*. But Twain wrote in his notes for *Huckleberry Finn* that Huck is "a boy of 14." He observed in "Chapters from My Autobiography" (*North American Review*, January 4, 1907) that fourteen or fifteen is "the age at which a boy is willing to endure all things, suffer all things, short of death by fire, if thereby he may be conspicuous and show off before the public" (p. 5). That age had been the happiest of Twain's life. "Those were pleasant days," he confessed to a childhood friend on June 6, 1900; "none since have been so pleasant, none so well worth living over again. For the romance of life is the only part of it that is overwhelmingly valuable, and romance dies with youth. After that, life is a drudge, and indeed a sham. A sham, and likewise a failure. . . . I should greatly like to re-live my youth, and then get drowned. I should like to call back Will Bowen and John Garth and the others, and live the life, be as we were, and make holiday until 15, then all drown together" (*Mark Twain's Letters to Will Bowen*, 1941, p. 27). Kemble, however, depicts a boy younger than fourteen, maybe between ten and twelve.

9. *He hadn't on anything but a shirt.* "And not *much* of a shirt," Huck adds in the 1895–1896 public reading copy; "couldn't tell it from a *lamp-shade*."

"Never mind, Buck, my boy," says the old man, "you'll have show enough, all in good time, don't you fret about that. Go 'long with you now, and do as your mother told you."

When we got up stairs to his room, he got me a coarse shirt and a round-about[10] and pants of his, and I put them on. While I was at it he asked me what my name was, but before I could tell him, he started to telling me about a blue jay and a young rabbit he had catched in the woods day before yesterday, and he asked me where Moses was when the candle went out.[11] I said I didn't know; I hadn't heard about it before, no way.

"Well, guess," he says.

"How'm I going to guess," says I, "when I never heard tell about it before?"[12]

"But you can guess, can't you? It's just as easy."

"*Which* candle?" I says.

"Why, any candle," he says.

"I don't know where he was," says I; "where was he?"

"Why he was in the *dark!* That's where he was!"

"Well, if you knowed where he was, what did you ask me for?"[13]

"Why, blame it, it's a riddle, don't you see? Say, how long are you going to stay here?[14] You got to stay always. We can just have booming times—they don't have no school now.[15] Do you own a dog? I've got a dog—and he'll go in the river and bring out chips that you throw in. Do you like to comb up, Sundays, and all that kind of foolishness? You bet I don't, but ma she makes me. Confound these ole britches, I reckon I'd better put 'em on, but I'd ruther not, it's so warm. Are you all ready? All right—come along, old hoss."[16]

Cold corn-pone, cold corn-beef, butter and butter-milk—that is what they had for me down there, and there ain't nothing better that ever I've come across yet. Buck and his ma and all of them smoked cob pipes,[17] except the nigger woman, which was gone, and the two young women. They all smoked and talked, and I eat and talked. The young women had quilts around them, and their hair down their

10. *a round-about.* A short, close jacket; Twain also considered dressing him in a "blue jeans" or "yellow nankeen" jacket (**MS**) like the Obedstown loafers in Chapter 1 of *The Gilded Age*.

11. *where Moses was when the candle went out.* This old riddle inspired a popular "serio-comic song" by John Stamford, "Where Was Moses When the Lights Went Out?" (1878), beginning:

> *When I was but a child, I used to go to bed at eight each night,*
> *The nurse-girl to frighten me when she put out the light,*
> *She'd talk of ghosts and goblins in a very awful way,*
> *She'd then put out the candle, and to me she used to say*
>
> Chorus
> *Where was Moses when the lights went out?*
> *Where was Moses, what was he about?*
> *Now, my little man, tell me if you can,*
> *Where was Moses when the lights went out?*

12. *I never heard tell about it before?* "Never knowed it *happened* at *all*," Huck adds in the 1895–1896 public reading copy. This is one thing about Moses that the Widow Douglas never taught him.

13. *what did you ask me for?* Huck is far more vexed in the 1895–1896 public reading copy: "what the nation'd you ask *me* for?"

14. *Say, how long are you going to stay here?* This barrage of questions, littered with non sequiturs and gratuitous detail, is reminiscent of the soliloquies delivered by one of the Sellers twins in Chapter 7 of *The Gilded Age*:

> "She was my great-grandmother—and George's too; wasn't she, father? *You* never saw her, but Sis has seen her, when Sis was a baby—didn't you Sis? Sis has seen her most a hundred times. She was awful deef—she's dead, now. Ain't she, father! . . . It's our clock, now—and it's got wheels inside of it, and a thing that flutters every time she strikes—don't it, father! Great-grandmother died before hardly any of us was born—she was an Old-School Baptist and had warts all over her—you ask father if she didn't. She had an uncle once that was bald-headed and used to have fits; he wasn't *our* uncle, I don't know

backs. They all asked me questions, and I told them how pap and me and all the family was living on a little farm down at the bottom of Arkansaw, and my sister Mary Ann run off and got married[18] and never was heard of no more, and Bill went to hunt them and he warn't heard of no more, and Tom and Mort died, and then there warn't nobody but just me and pap left, and he was just trimmed down to nothing, on account of his troubles; so when he died I took what there was left, because the farm didn't belong to us, and started up the river, deck passage, and fell overboard; and that was how I come to be here. So they said I could have a home there as long as I wanted it. Then it was most daylight, and everybody went to bed, and I went to bed with Buck, and when I waked up in the morning, drat it all, I had forgot what my name was. So I laid there about an hour trying to think, and when Buck waked up, I says:

"Can you spell, Buck?"

"Yes," he says.

"I bet you can't spell my name," says I.

"I bet you what you dare I can," says he.

"All right," says I, "go ahead."

"G-o-r-g-e J-a-x-o-n[19]—there now," he says.

"Well," says I, "you done it, but I didn't think you could. It ain't no slouch[20] of a name to spell—right off without studying."

I set it down, private, because somebody might want *me* to spell it, next, and so I wanted to be handy with it and rattle it off like I was used to it.

It was a mighty nice family, and a mighty nice house,[21] too. I hadn't seen no house out in the country before that was so nice and had so much style. It didn't have an iron latch on the front door, nor a wooden one with a buckskin string, but a brass knob to turn, the same as houses in a town. There warn't no bed in the parlor, not a sign of a bed; but heaps of parlors in towns has beds in them. There was a big fireplace that was bricked on the bottom, and the bricks was kept clean and red by pouring water on them and scrubbing them with another brick; sometimes they washed them over with red water-paint that they call Span-

> what he was to us—some kin or another I reckon—father's seen him a thousand times—hain't you, father? We used to have a calf that et apples and just chawed up dishrags like nothing, and if you stay here you'll see lots of funerals—won't he, Sis? Did you see a horse afire? *I* have! . . ."

He is also reminiscent of "a bright, simple, guileless little darkey boy" who once waited on Twain in a hotel. "He did not tell me a single remarkable thing, or one that was worth remembering," Twain described the boy in "Sociable Jimmy" (*New York Times*, November 29, 1874); "and yet he was himself so interested in his small marvels, and they flowed so naturally and comfortably from his lips that his talk got the upper hand of my interest, too, and I listened to him as one who receives a revelation." Buck's vivid dialogue effectively introduces him, like Huck, as a typical and likable little boy; it only makes his fate in Chapter 18 all the more tragic.

15. *they don't have no school now.* Because, according to Chapter 9, it is June.

16. *old hoss.* A popular corruption of "horse," an affectionate, colloquial nickname Buck uses to make Huck feel at home.

17. *cob pipes.* Light, durable tobacco pipes, the bowls made out of corncobs; Twain himself was fond of these pipes, and often had himself photographed smoking one.

18. *my sister Mary Ann run off and got married.* Huck's "stretcher" is extraordinarily prescient: This is exactly what happens in the next chapter.

19. *G-o-r-g-e J-a-x-o-n.* In his 1895–1896 public reading copy, he further milked the phonetic humor of Buck's misspelling: "G-o-r-j-e G-a-x-o-n!" Susy Clemens too had trouble with the first name, spelling it "Jaurge" in a letter to her father of April 27, 1882 (*The Love Letters of Mark Twain*, p. 209).

20. *slouch.* Someone who is poor, indifferent, ineffectual; but when used in the negative as "no slouch," it is high praise.

21. *a mighty nice house.* A prototype for this mansion is the place Squire Hawkins erected with his new fortune, as described in Chapter 7 of *The Gilded Age*: "Hawkins fitted out his house with 'store' furniture from St. Louis, and the fame of its magnificence went abroad in the land. Even the parlor carpet was from St. Louis—though the other rooms were clothed in the 'rag' carpeting of the country. . . . His oil-cloth window-curtains had noble pictures on them of castles such as had never been seen anywhere but on window-curtains."

These homesteads are typical examples of "The House Beautiful" of this region, which Twain defined in Chapter 38 of *Life on the Mississippi*:

> Every town and village along that vast stretch of double river-frontage had a best dwelling, . . . the home of the wealthiest and most conspicuous citizen. It is easy to describe it: . . . iron knocker; brass door knob—discolored, for lack of polishing. Within, an uncarpeted hall, of planed boards; opening out of it, a parlor, fifteen feet by fifteen . . . ; ingrain carpet; mahogany center-table; lamp on it, with green

"The House Beautiful." Illustration from *Life on the Mississippi*, 1883. *Private collection*

ish-brown, same as they do in town. They had big brass dog-irons[22] that could hold up a saw-log. There was a clock on the middle of the mantel-piece, with a picture of a town painted on the bottom half of the glass front,[23] and a round place in the middle of it for the sun, and you could see the pendulum swing behind it. It was beautiful to hear that clock tick; and sometimes when one of these peddlers had been along and scoured her up and got her in good shape, she would start in and strike a hundred and fifty before she got tuckered out.[24] They wouldn't took any money for her.

Well, there was a big outlandish parrot on each side of the clock, made out of something like chalk,[25] and painted up gaudy. By one of the parrots was a cat made of crockery, and a crockery dog by the other; and when you pressed down on them they squeaked, but didn't open their mouths nor look different nor interested. They squeaked through underneath. There was a couple of big wild-turkey-wing fans spread out behind those things. On a table in the middle of the room was a kind of a lovely crockery basket that had apples and oranges and peaches and grapes piled up in it which was much redder and yellower and prettier than real ones is, but they warn't real[26] because you could see where pieces had got chipped off and showed the white chalk or whatever it was, underneath.

This table had a cover made out of beautiful oil-cloth, with a red and blue spread-eagle painted on it,[27] and a painted border all around. It come all the way from Philadelphia, they said.[28] There was some books[29] too, piled up perfectly exact, on each corner of the table. One was a big family Bible, full of pictures.[30] One was "Pilgrim's Progress,"[31] about a man that left his family it didn't say why. I read considerable in it now and then. The statements was interesting, but tough. Another was "Friendship's Offering,"[32] full of beautiful stuff and poetry; but I didn't read the poetry. Another was Henry Clay's Speeches,[33] and another was Dr. Gunn's Family Medicine,[34] which told you all about what to do if a body was sick or dead. There was a Hymn Book, and a lot of other books. And there was nice split-bottom chairs, and perfectly sound, too—not bagged down in the middle and busted, like an old basket.

They had pictures hung on the walls—mainly Washingtons[35] and Lafayettes,[36] and battles, and Highland Marys,[37] and one called "Signing the Declaration."[38] There was some that they called crayons,[39] which one of the daughters which was dead made her own self when she was only fifteen years old.[40] They was different from any pictures I ever see before; blacker, mostly, than is common. One was a woman in a slim black dress,[41] belted small under the arm-pits, with bulges like a cabbage in the middle of the sleeves,[42] and a large black scoop-shovel bonnet[43] with a black veil, and white slim ankles crossed about with black tape, and very wee black slippers, like a chisel,[44] and she was leaning pensive on a tombstone on her right elbow, under a weeping willow, and her other hand hanging down her side holding a white handkerchief and a reticule, and underneath the picture it said "Shall I Never See Thee More Alas." Another one was a young lady with her hair all combed up straight to the top of her head, and knotted there in front of a comb like a chair-back, and she was crying into a handkerchief and had a dead bird laying on its back in her other hand with its heels up, and underneath the picture it said "I Shall Never Hear Thy Sweet Chirrup More Alas."[45] There was one where a young lady was at a window looking up at the moon, and tears running down her cheeks; and she had an open letter in one hand with black sealing-wax showing on one edge of it,[46] and she was mashing a locket with a chain to it against her mouth, and underneath the picture it said "And Art Thou Gone Yes Thou Art Gone Alas." These was all nice pictures, I reckon, but I didn't somehow seem to take to them, because if ever I was down a little, they always give me the fan-tods. Everybody was sorry she died, because she had laid out a lot more of these pictures to do, and a body could see by what she had done what they had lost. But I reckoned, that with her disposition, she was having a better time in the graveyard. She was at work on what they said was her greatest picture when she took sick, and every day

paper shade—standing on a gridiron, so to speak, made of high-colored yarns, by the young ladies of the house, and called a lamp-mat; several books, piled and disposed, with cast-iron exactness; according to the inherited and unchangeable plan; among them, . . . *Friendship's Offering*, and *Affection's Wreath*, with their sappy inanities illustrated in die-away mezzotints; . . . maybe *Ivanhoe*; also *Album*, full of original "poetry" of Thou-hast-wounded-the-spirit-that-loved-thee breed; two or three goody-goody works . . . ; current number of the chaste and innocuous *Godey's Lady's Book* with painted fashion plate of wax-figure women with mouths all alike—lips and eyelids the same size. . . . On each end of the wooden mantel, over the fireplace, a large basket of peaches and other fruits, natural size, all double in plaster, rudely, or in wax, and painted to resemble the originals—which they don't. Over middle of mantel, engraving—Washington Crossing the Delaware; on the wall by the door, copy of it done in thunder-and-lightning crewels by one of the young ladies—work of art which would have made Washington hesitate about crossing. . . . Piano—kettle in disguise—with music, bound and unbound, piled on it, and a stand near by: "Battle of Prague"; "Bird Waltz"; "Arkansas Traveler"; . . . "The Last Link is Broken"; . . . "Go, forget me, Why should Sorrow o'er that Brow a Shadow fling"; . . . and spread open on the rack, where the plaintive singer has left it, *Ro*-holl on, silver *moo*-hoon, guide the *trav*-el-lerr his *way*, etc. . . . Framed in black moldings on the wall, other works of art, conceived and committed on the premises, by the young ladies; being grim black-and-white crayons; landscapes, mostly: lake, solitary sailboat, petrified clouds, pre-geological trees on shore, anthracite precipice; name of criminal conspicuous in the corner. . . . Other bric-a-brac: . . . painted toy-dog, seated upon bellows attachment—drops its jaw and squeaks when pressed upon. . . . Bracketed over whatnot—place of special sacredness—an outrage in water-color, done by the young niece that came on a visit long ago, and died. Pity, too; for she might have repented of this in time. Horse-hair chairs, horse-hair sofa which keeps sliding from under you. Window shades, of oil stuff, with milk-maids and ruined castles stencilled on them in fierce colors.

22. *dog-irons*. Andirons. These serve as another sign of this family's high place in backwoods and every night it was her prayer to be allowed to live till she got it done, but she never got the chance. It was a picture of a young woman in a long white gown,[47] standing on the rail of a bridge all ready to jump off,[48] with her hair all down her back, and looking up to the moon, with the tears running down her face, and she had two arms folded across her breast, and two arms stretched out in front, and two more reaching up towards the moon—and the idea was, to see which pair would look best[49] and then scratch out all

"IT MADE HER LOOK TOO SPIDERY."

the other arms; but, as I was saying, she died before she got her mind made up, and now they kept this picture over the head of the bed in her room, and every time her birthday come they hung flowers on it. Other times it was hid with a little curtain.[50] The young woman in the picture had a kind of a nice sweet face, but there was so many arms it made her look too spidery, seemed to me.

This young girl kept a scrap-book[51] when she was alive, and used to paste obituaries and accidents and cases of patient suffering in it out of the *Presbyterian Observer,*[52] and write poetry after them out of her own head. It was very

society. "When we first moved to Missouri," Ezra Ben Stiles Ely explained in Curtis Dahl, "Mark Twain and Ben Ely: Two Missouri Boyhoods" (*Missouri Historical Review*, July 1972), "the old-fashioned andirons with high brass stanchions were in use. This led to the circulation of the report among our neighbors that my father was marvelously wealthy, and not a few called at the house to see our gold andirons" (p. 554).

23. *a clock . . . with a picture of a town painted on the bottom half of the glass front*. Likely a variation of the Terry clock, named for its inventor, Eli Terry (1772–1852): an inexpensive clock with a glass front which was painted on the inside, popular from 1815 until 1840.

24. *she would start in and strike a hundred and fifty before she got tuckered out*. Just like the Sellers clock in Chapter 7 of *The Gilded Age*: "Remarkable clock!" Colonel Sellers says. "Ah . . . she's beginning again! Nineteen, twenty, twenty-one, twenty-two, twen—ah, that's all. . . . Now just listen at that. She'll strike a hundred and fifty, now, without stopping,—you'll see. There ain't another like that in Christendom." None, except this one in the Grangerford parlor.

25. *made out of something like chalk*. Plaster of Paris figurines were known as "chalkware" because they made marks like chalk when rubbed against a surface.

26. *much redder and yellower and prettier than real ones is, but they warn't real*. If the furnishings of a home reflect the character of the family who dwells within, then in this house, where the bricks are painted redder than they actually are, where the fancy clock cannot tell the correct time, where the crockery is fake china and the imitation fruit is not as fine as it is colored, artifice is treasured far above authenticity. Here live people who are not as noble as their wealth, manners, and ceremonies suggest. It is all surface style and no substance.

27. *a cover made out of beautiful oil-cloth, with a red and blue spread-eagle painted on it*. The center table of this parlor may sport the emblem of the United States of America, but the people who live here do not believe in democracy. Instead, they take the law into their own hands. Each and every detail in Huck's tight, meticulous good poetry. This is what she wrote about a boy by the name of Stephen Dowling Bots that fell down a well and was drownded:

ODE TO STEPHEN DOWLING BOTS, DEC'D.[53]

And did young Stephen sicken,
And did young Stephen die?
And did the sad hearts thicken,
And did the mourners cry?

No; such was not the fate of
Young Stephen Dowling Bots;
Though sad hearts round him thickened,
'Twas not from sickness' shots.

No whooping-cough did rack his frame,
Nor measles drear, with spots;
Not these impaired the sacred name
Of Stephen Dowling Bots.

Despised love struck not with woe
That head of curly knots,
Nor stomach troubles[54] laid him low,
Young Stephen Dowling Bots.

O no. Then list with tearful eye,
Whilst I his fate do tell.
His soul did from this cold world fly,
By falling down a well.

They got him out and emptied him;
Alas it was too late;
His spirit was gone for to sport aloft
In the realms of the good and great.[55]

If Emmeline[56] Grangerford[57] could make poetry like that before she was fourteen,[58] there ain't no telling what she could a done by-and-by. Buck said she could rattle off

THE FIRST SEAL (1782)
A spread eagle on the American National Seal.
Courtesy Library of Congress.

description of the decor of this house contributes to the satire of the entire picture just like a political cartoon. Nothing is gratuitous.

28. *It come all the way from Philadelphia, they said.* And it is important that they tell everyone that it comes from Philadelphia. This oilcloth is an example of what Richard Malcolm Johnson called in "Samuel Hele, Esq." (in Joseph G. Baldwin, *The Flush Times on the Mississippi*, 1853) "the Southern propensity of getting everything from abroad," from Yankeedom, "as if, as in the case of wines, the process of importing added to the value" (p. 290). But this custom was not limited to the South: Wealthy Yankees imported products from Europe and West Coasters from the East, not so much because the local articles were so inferior to foreign ones, but because the extravagance and expense of carting them by land, sea, or air increased their cachet and thus elevated the prestige of the purchasers within the community.

29. *some books.* "The literature of the country was mostly English—stolen, mainly," Twain admitted in a suppressed passage from Chapter 40 of *Life on the Mississippi*. "The manufactured articles used, were English" (Limited Editions Club edition, 1944, p. 406). Huck's selection from this library serves the same function as the volumes a porter left by Twain's bed in Chapter 57 of *The Innocents Abroad*, to cover "the whole range of legitimate literature"—theology, romance, poetry, law, and medicine. The titles perfectly reflect the religious, social, and political character of this part of the country. But being "piled up perfectly exact, on each corner of the table," they are there merely for decoration and do not appear ever to have been read.

30. *a big family Bible, full of pictures.* Maybe a Doré Bible, a big expensive edition full of engravings by French illustrator Gustave Doré (1833–1884). Twain referred to one in passing in Chapter 4 of *Tom Sawyer*.

31. *"Pilgrim's Progress."* John Bunyan's Calvinist allegory, issued in two parts in 1678 and 1684, was one of the most popular books ever published and a standard title in rural American homes of the nineteenth century. Twain wanted to call *The Innocents Abroad* "The New Pilgrim's Progress," but kept it for the subtitle. He once contemplated photographing people as Christian, Simple, Sloth, Presumption, and other characters in the book in modern dress and setting, believing that "this stereoptic panorama of Bunyan's *Pilgrim's Progress* could be exhibited in all countries at the same time and clear a fortune in a year" (*Mark Twain's Notebook*, 1935, p. 192). Although contemptuous of Bunyan's view of Paradise (which he parodied in *Captain Stormfield's Visit to Heaven*, 1909), Twain nevertheless owned several copies of the book, including an 1875 facsimile of the first edition.

32. *"Friendship's Offering."* One of a popular series of annuals, first published in England in 1841, designed as gifts for young ladies and filled with sentimental prints and literature; its poetry and pictures often dwelled on death and grief. Twain complained that James Fenimore Cooper's characters in *The Deerslayer* had a tendency to speak in the artificial style of "an illustrated, gilt-edged, tree-calf, hand-tooled, seven-dollar *Friendship's Offering*" ("Fenimore Cooper's Literary Offenses," *North American Review*, July 1895, p. 2).

33. *Henry Clay's Speeches.* Henry Clay (1777–1852) of Kentucky, one of the most powerful American politicians of the nineteenth century, served as congressman, senator, and secretary

"THEY GOT HIM OUT AND EMPTIED HIM."

poetry like nothing. She didn't ever have to stop to think. He said she would slap down a line, and if she couldn't find anything to rhyme with it she would just scratch it out and slap down another one, and go ahead. She warn't particular, she could write about anything you choose to give her to write about, just so it was sadful. Every time a man died, or a woman died, or a child died, she would be on hand with her "tribute"[59] before he was cold. She called them tributes. The neighbors said it was the doctor first, then Emmeline, then the undertaker—the undertaker never got in ahead of Emmeline but once, and then she hung fire[60] on a rhyme for the dead person's name, which was Whistler. She warn't ever the same, after that; she never complained, but she kind of pined away and did not live long. Poor thing, many's the time I made myself go up to the little room that used to be hers and get out her poor old scrap-book and read in it when her pictures had been aggravating me and I had soured on her a little. I liked all that family, dead ones and all, and warn't going to let anything come between us.

Poor Emmeline made poetry about all the dead people when she was alive, and it didn't seem right that there warn't nobody to make some about her, now she was gone; so I tried to sweat out a verse or two myself, but I couldn't seem to make it go, somehow. They kept Emmeline's room trim and nice and all the things fixed in it just the way she liked to have them when she was alive, and nobody ever slept there. The old lady took care of the room herself, though there was plenty of niggers, and she sewed there a good deal and read her Bible there, mostly.

Well, as I was saying about the parlor, there was beautiful curtains on the windows: white, with pictures painted on them, of castles with vines all down the walls, and cattle coming down to drink. There was a little old piano, too, that had tin pans in it,[61] I reckon, and nothing was ever so lovely as to hear the young ladies sing, "The Last Link is Broken"[62] and play "The Battle of Prague"[63] on it. The walls of all the rooms was plastered,[64] and most had carpets on the floors, and the whole house was whitewashed on the outside.

It was a double house,[65] and the big open place betwixt them was roofed and floored, and sometimes the table was set there in the middle of the day, and it was a cool, comfortable place. Nothing couldn't be better. And warn't the cooking good, and just bushels of it too!

THE HOUSE.

Henry Clay.
Courtesy General Collections, New York Public Library, Astor, Lenox, and Tilden Foundations.

of state and was an unsuccessful presidential candidate; he was also a slave owner, bane to abolitionists, and famous as "the Great Pacificator" for his part in the formulation of the Missouri Compromise of 1850, which strengthened the Fugitive Slave Law. His speeches were collected in 1842. Orion Clemens reported in Richard I. Holcombe's *History of Monroe County, Missouri* (1884) that his father, Judge Clemens, "believed strongly in Henry Clay" (p. 915). Orion did, too. "A great light has gone out," he wrote in the Hannibal *Journal* (July 1, 1852) on the occasion of Clay's death. "A sun has disappeared from the political universe. The world has lost a friend of liberty, and to our nation the depature of this mighty spirit, the stilling of his pure, and noble, and patriotic heart, is a calamity." R. Kent Rasmussen in *Mark Twain A to Z* (1995) identified the book of his speeches as "circumstantial evidence that the Grangerfords themselves live in Kentucky" (p. 75). See Chapter 16, note 53.

34. *Dr. Gunn's Family Medicine*. John C. Gunn's popular American household medical encyclopedia, originally titled *Domestic Medicine, or Poor Man's Friend, in the Hours of Affliction, Pain and*

Sickness (1830), was also one of the few books owned by backwoods physicians (see Henry Clay Lewis, *Odd Leaves from the Life of a Louisiana "Swamp Doctor,"* 1846, p. 23). Blair and Fischer in the 1988 University of California edition quoted Dr. Gunn's aims from the title page of the eighth edition (1836): "This book points out, in plain language, free from doctors' terms, the diseases of men, women, and children, and the latest and most approved means used in their cure, and is intended expressly for the benefit of families in the western and southern states. It also contains descriptions of the medicinal roots and herbs of the western and southern country, and how they are to be used in the cure of diseases. Arranged on a new and simple plan, by which the practice of medicine is reduced to principles of common sense" (p. 400). Leo Marx, in his notes to the 1967 Bobbs-Merrill edition of *Huckleberry Finn*, pointed to one chapter, "On the Passions," "a combination of psychology, ethics, and advice to the lovelorn," as of especial interest to the household of amateur artist Emmeline Grangerford.

35. *Washingtons*. Probably prints of the famous portrait of George Washington by Gilbert Stuart (1755–1828).

36. *Lafayettes*. Cheap portraits of the Marquis de Lafayette (1757–1834), French patriot who fought on the American side during the Revolutionary War.

37. *Highland Marys*. Popular prints of Mary Campbell, the first love of Scottish Romantic poet Robert Burns (1759–1796); she was a fitting subject for sentimental verse and painting, because she died young in 1786, inspiring several poems by Burns. Twain may or may not have known that the Darnalls of Tennessee, the models for this family, claimed direct descent from Robert Burns. See Twain's *The Grangerford–Shepherdson Feud*, 1985, p. 54.

38. *"Signing the Declaration."* Usually cheap prints after John Trumbull's 1820 painting then in the Rotunda of the United States Capitol. The family properly fills its home with the symbols of the American Revolution, but its members are as hypocritical in their politics as in their religion. They may be *patriotic* but not *democratic*.

Highland Mary. Colored lithograph by Sarony & Major, 1846.
Courtesy Library of Congress.

39. *crayons*. Pastels.

40. *one of the daughters which was dead . . . when she was only fifteen years old*. The girl was not much older than Huck. See Chapter 18, note 26.

41. *One was a woman in a slim black dress*. Huck describes a typical "mourning picture" of the

"The Declaration of Independence." Colored lithograph by N. Currier, 1840s.
Courtesy Library of Congress.

A mourning picture in an advertisement for a Hannibal marble works, Hannibal *Journal and Union*, November 13, 1851.
Courtesy Missouri Historical Society Collection.

period, with its tombstone, weeping willow, and stylish mourner, popular in America from the late eighteenth century until the Civil War; these folk paintings were generally the work of amateur lady artists who were encouraged to cultivate the "female arts" to help civilize and beautify the American wilderness.

42. *bulges like a cabbage in the middle of the sleeves.* Leg-of-mutton sleeves, popular in the 1830s.

43. *scoop-shovel bonnet.* A descriptive turn of phrase, the actual term being "scoop bonnet."

44. *white slim ankles crossed about with black tape, and very wee black slippers, like a chisel.* Huck's unabashed and innocent enthusiasm for such incompetent drawing adds considerably to Twain's satirical look at American folk art. He was a dilettante himself. As he traveled through Europe, all the museums crammed with the Old Masters wearied him. "Wherever you find a Raphael, a Rubens, a Michael Angelo, a Caracci, or a da Vinci (and we see them every day)," he observed in *The Innocents Abroad* (Chapter 19), "you find artists copying them, and the copies are always the handsomest. Maybe the originals were handsome when they were new, but they are not now." He was unimpressed with Leonardo da Vinci's *The Last Supper*: "The colors are dimmed with age; the countenances are scaled and marred, and nearly all expression is gone from them; the hair is a dead blur upon the wall, and there is no life in the eyes. Only the attitudes are certain. People come here from all parts of the world, and . . . stand entranced before it with bated breath and parted lips, and when they speak, it is only in the catchy ejections of rapture." But Twain saw nothing but a battered, scarred, stained, and discolored disaster on the wall. "It vexes me to hear people talk so glibly," he continued, "of 'feeling,' 'expression,' 'tone,' and those other easily acquired and inexpensive technicalities of art that make such a fine show in conversations concerning pictures."

45. *"I Shall Never Hear Thy Sweet Chirrup More Alas."* Mourning over dead pets was a theme of prints, paintings, and illustrations of the period. The false and petty pity lavished on this dead bird becomes less ridiculous and far more tragic when one learns of the vast carnage spread by the girl's family and neighbors in the following chapter. There it becomes clear why this sentimental young lady is so preoccupied with death.

46. *an open letter in one hand with black sealing-wax showing on one edge of it.* It was customary at the time, while in mourning, to seal one's letters (written on black-edged stationery) with black wax.

47. *It was a picture of a young woman in a long white gown.* American painter Grant Wood found this description to be a "revelation." "Having been born into a world of Victorian standards," he explained in "My Debt to Mark Twain" (*Mark Twain Quarterly*, Fall 1937), "I had accepted and admired the ornate, the lugubrious and the excessively sentimental naturally and without question. And this was my first intimation that there was something ridiculous about sentimentality" (p. 14). Wood's parodying of American taste in his art, as in his famous *American Gothic*, owes much to Twain's satire.

48. *standing on the rail of a bridge all ready to jump off.* Is it possible that the young artist was contemplating her own suicide before natural causes did her in?

49. *look best.* Twain changed this phrase to "be the most becoming" in his 1895–1896 public reading copy.

50. *they kept this picture over the head of the bed in her room, and every time her birthday come they hung flowers on it. Other times it was hid with a little curtain.* These people are so sentimental that they maintain a small shrine to the memory of their dead daughter, but this effluence of feeling is as false as their painted bricks, phony Staffordshire china, and chalk fruit. Mourning found various forms of expression in the nineteenth century: Queen Victoria similarly venerated Prince Albert's memory by keeping his room at Windsor Castle exactly as it was when he died in 1861; and Twain could not bear to live in his Hartford house after Susy Clemens died there, so he sold it.

51. *a scrap-book.* Nineteenth-century American households commonly kept scrapbooks of obituaries of family, friends, and famous people.

52. Presbyterian Observer. An anachronism: According to *The National Union Catalogue*, this journal did not commence publication until 1872, twenty or thirty years after the period of this story. Of course, there were plenty of other religious magazines at the time which would have been known to this family.

53. *ODE TO STEPHEN DOWLING BOTS, DEC'D.* "Dec'd" is the common abbreviation for "deceased." Twain was greatly amused by what he called "Post-Mortem Poetry." Sam Clemens was only seventeen when he wrote "a pretty crude parody" of Charles Wolfe's "The Burial of Sir John Moore after Corunna" (1817)" as "The Burial of Sir Abner Gilstrap, Editor of the Bloomington 'Republican'" (Hannibal *Daily Journal*, May 13, 1853), which reads in part:

Few and very *short were the* prayers *we said,*
And we felt not a pang of sorrow;
But we mused, as we gazed on the wretch now defunct—
Oh! where will he be to-morrow!

(The entire verse is reprinted in *Early Tales and Sketches*, 1979, vol. 1, pp. 108–9.) The next year he tried writing obituary verses while a compositor at the Philadelphia *Public Ledger*, but they were all summarily rejected. He got his revenge years later by publishing samples directly from the *Ledger* in *The Galaxy* (June 1870). Readers then sent him other examples of "those marvellous combinations of ostentatious and ghastly 'fine writing,'" clipped from various sources, that he published in *The Galaxy* in July, September, and November. "There is something so innocent, so guileless, so complacent, so unearthly serene and self-satisfied about this peerless 'hogwash,'" he said of one of them in November, "that the man must be made of stone who can read it without a dulcet ecstasy creeping along his backbone and quivering in his marrow" (p. 735). Despite his apparent disdain toward this kind of literature, Twain succumbed at least once to writing "post-mortum poetry" himself, a tribute to his daughter Susy on her death from spinal meningitis, "In Memoriam, Olivia Susan Clemens" (*Harper's Monthly*, November 1897, pp. 929–30).

Blair and Fischer in the 1988 University of California edition argued that Twain's poem "is a burlesque of a form, not a parody of any particular obituary verse or writer of such verse, and given his long acquaintance with such poems, it is unlikely that any single 'model' can be identified" (p. 403). But John R. Byers, Jr., in "Emmeline Grangerford's Hymn Book" (*American Literature*, May 1971) suggested that the first verse of the "Ode" may be a parody of "Submission at the Bleeding Cross" by Isaac Watts, first published as Hymn 311 in *Hymns and Spiritual Songs* (1707):

Alas! and did my Saviour bleed!
And did my sovereign die:
Did he devote that sacred head
For such a worm as I?

Another possible source is his "The Resurrection," Hymn 620:

And must this body die?
This mortal frame decay?
And must these active limbs of mine
Lie mould'ring in the clay?

The "Ode" was the sort of drivel written by "a shameless old idiot," Bloodgood Haviland Cutter (1817–1906), the "Poet Lariat" of *Innocents Abroad*. But the poet who likely most influenced Emmeline Grangerford was "The Sweet Singer of Michigan," Julia A. Moore (1847–1920), author of *The Sentimental Song Book* (1876). Twain admitted in Chapter 36 of *Following the Equator* that her alarming verse possessed that "subtle touch . . . that makes an intentionally humorous episode pathetic and an intentionally pathetic one funny." The majority of her "songs" concern early child death, the lamented fates of the late Little Susan, Little Minnie, Little Charley Hades, and all the others being as pathetic and funny as the

Julia A. Moore.
Courtesy Library of Congress.

sad history of Stephen Dowling Bots. Typical of Moore's tributes is "Little Andrew":

Andrew was a little infant,
And his life was two years old;
He was his parents' eldest boy
And he was drowned, I was told.
His parents never more can see him
In this world of grief and pain,
And Oh! they will not forget him
While on earth they do remain.

On one bright and pleasant morning
His uncle thought it would be nice
To take his dear little nephew
Down to play upon a raft,
Where he was to work upon it,
And this little child would company be—
The raft the water rushed around it,
Yet he the danger did not see.

This little child knew no danger—
Its little soul was free from sin—
He was looking in the water,
Where, alas, this child fell in.
Beneath the raft the water took him in,
For the current was strong,
And before they could rescue him
He was drowned and was gone.

Oh! how sad were his kind parents
When they saw their drowned child,
As they brought him from the water,
It almost made their hair grow wild.
Oh! how mournful was the parting
From that little infant son.
Friends, I pray you, all take warning,
Be careful of your little ones.

There are other fine examples of parodies of "mortuary poetry" in Midwestern and Southern literature by Eugene Field, Bill Nye, John Phoenix, and others. In Chapter 8 of *Out of the Hurly Burly* (1874) by "Max Adeler" (Charles Heber Clark), Colonel Bangs asks a poet to write somber uplifting verse to accompany newspaper obituaries, and he produces lines worthy of Emmeline Grangerford herself:

Willie had a purple monkey climbing on a yellow stick,
And when he sucked the paint all off it made him deathly sick;
And in his latest hours he clasped that monkey in his hand,
And bade good-bye to earth and went into a better land.

Oh! no more he'll shoot his sister with his little wooden gun;
And no more he'll twist the pussy's tail and make her yowl, for fun.
The pussy's tail now stands out straight; the gun is laid aside;
The monkey doesn't jump around since little Willie died.

But none of these other parodies is as famous as Emmeline Grangerford's effort. In a letter in *Mark Twain Quarterly* (Winter 1936), A. E. Housman confessed, "The inimitable ode to Stephen Dowling Bots is one of the poems I know by heart."

54. *stomach troubles*. Twain originally wrote "bowel trouble"(**MS**), but this indelicacy was replaced before the the book went to the printer.

55. *In the realms of the good and great*. Emmeline Grangerford's odious "ode" originally concluded with another verse:

Now all young people, come listen unto me:
So shape ye your variegated lots,
That you can all lie, when you come for to die,
Like the late sweet Stephen D. Bots. (**MS**)

56. *Emmeline*. Her name came from that of an "impressionist water color" by Daniele Ranzoni, "a head of a beautiful young girl, life size, because she looked just about like that." This picture, which the Clemenses bought in Italy in 1878, was one of various ornamental objects which stood on the mantel or hung near the fireplace in the parlor of Twain's Hartford, Connecticut, home; at the opposite end of *Emmeline* was an oil painting of a cat's head. "Every now and then," Twain recounted in "Chapters from My Autobiography" (*North American Review*, October 19, 1906), "the children required me to construct a romance—always impromptu—not a moment's preparation permitted—and into that romance I had to get all the bric-à-brac and the . . . pictures. I had to start always with the cat and finish with Emmeline" (p. 710). As these tales were always filled with gratuitous violence and bloodshed, it seems appropriate that Twain should name the ill-fated Grangerford girl after the equally tormented *Emmeline* on the Clemens parlor wall.

The fireplace in the library of the Clemens home in Hartford, Connecticut.
Negative Number 57720 © Collection of The New-York Historical Society.

57. *Grangerford*. Twain originally called the family "Peterson" (**MS**). He named the feuding clans Shepherdson and Grangerford probably to suggest the eternal animosity between farmers (grangers) and ranchers (shepherds). Note that the Shepherdsons always travel on horseback.

58. *before she was fourteen*. She was about Huck's age when she died. Sam Clemens was not much older when he suddenly got the urge like Emmeline to write some "pieces" for the local paper, a youthful desire that "went flaming and crashing through my system like the genuine lightning and thunder of originality. . . . I wrote them with that placid confidence and that happy facility which only want of practice and absence of literary experience can give. There was not one sentence in ten that cost half an hour's weighing and shaping and trimming and fixing. Indeed, it is possible that there was no one sentence whose mere wording cost even one-sixth of that time. If I remember rightly, there was not a single erasure or interlineation in all that chaste manuscript. (I have since lost that large belief in my powers, and likewise that marvellous perfection of execution.)" ("A General Reply," *Galaxy*, November 1870, p. 732)

59. *"tribute."* Encomium.

60. *hung fire*. Hesitated.

61. *a little old piano, too, that had tin pans in it*. "Perhaps the little piano . . . really had tin pans in it," Joseph Slater explained in "Notes and Queries: Music at Col. Grangerford's" (*American Literature*, March 1949). "Piano-makers of the early nineteenth century, responding to the programmatic demands of the battle-pieces and to the popularity of Turkish music and instruments, introduced devices for the production of a variety of unusual musical effects. Extra pedals were constructed which permitted the pianist to embellish his performance with the sound of cymbals, drums, and bells" (p. 111). Twain may have recalled the piano owned by Mrs. Richard T. Holliday, the model for the Widow Douglas, which had a drum attachment. See note 63 below.

62. *"The Last Link is Broken."* A popular song of "noble resignation," written by William Clifton, a composer of minstrel-songs, and published in 1840:

The last link is broken that bound me to thee,
And the words I have spoken have rendered me free;
That bright glance misleading on others may shine,
Those eyes smil'd unheeding when tears burst from mine,
If my love was deem'd boldness that error is o'er,
I've witnessed thy coldness and prize thee no more.

Chorus
I have not lov'd lightly, I'll think on thee yet,
I'll pray for thee nightly till life's sun is set.

The song was popular among the young people of Hannibal in the 1840s. In "Villagers of 1840–43" (1897), Twain included it among the songs that "tended to regrets for bygone days and vanished joys," like "Oft in the Stilly Night," "The Last Rose of Summer," "Bonny Doon," and "Old Dog Tray" (*Huck Finn and Tom Sawyer Among the Indians*, 1989, p. 99). It reappears in Chapter 38 of *Huckleberry Finn*, where Tom Sawyer calls it the kind of "painful music . . . that'll scoop a rat, quicker'n anything else."

63. *"The Battle of Prague."* A crude piano piece composed by Bohemian fiddler Franz Kotzwana (1730–1790), in 1788, to commemorate the 1757 skirmish between the armies of Prussia and Austria. It contains such novelties as three sharp staccato notes to represent "flying bullets" and sobbing treble figures to imitate "cries of the wounded." This ten-minute piece was well known to the boys and girls of Hannibal, when Sam Clemens was growing up there, through Mrs. Richard T. Holliday, the real Widow Douglas. "She owned a piano," Laura Hawkins (later Frazer), the model for Becky Thatcher, told Keene Abbott in "Tom Sawyer's Town" (*Harper's Weekly*, April 9, 1913), "and it was not merely a piano; it was a piano with a drum attachment. Oh, 'The Battle of Prague' executed with that marvelous drum attachment! It was our favorite selection because it had so much drum in it. I must have been about ten at the time, and Sam was two years older. As a result of those excursions of ours I remember that my greatest ambition was some day to have a piano with a drum attachment, and to be able to play 'The Battle of Prague'" (p. 17). In Chapter 21 of *Vanity Fair* (1847), William Makepeace Thackeray expressed his disdain for this piece of music: "The sisters began to play the Battle of Prague. 'Stop the d[amn] thing,' George [Osborne] howled out in a fury from the sofa. 'It makes me mad. *You* play us something, Miss Swartz, do. Sing something, anything but the Battle of Prague.'"

In 1878, according to Chapter 32 of *A Tramp Abroad*, an "Arkansaw" girl startled Twain with an energetic performance of the piece on the piano in the drawing room of the Jungfrau Hotel in Interlaken, Switzerland. "Without any preliminaries," he wrote, "she turned on all the horrors of the 'Battle of Prague,' that venerable shivaree, and waded chin deep in the blood of the slain. . . . The audience stood it with pretty fair grit for a while, but when the cannonade waxed hotter and fiercer, and the discord average rose to four in five, the procession began to move. A few stragglers held their ground ten minutes longer, but when the girl began to wring the true inwardness out of the 'cries of the wounded,' they struck their colors and retired in a kind of panic." It must have been unsettling for anyone to hear this musical blitzkrieg after the lugubrious "The Last Link Is Broken."

64. *The walls of all the rooms was plastered.* This domestic detail was a sign of high social status in the backwoods. In "A Big Thing" (Buffalo *Express*, March 12, 1870), Twain quoted a woman from Fentress County, Tennessee, discussing what her son and daughter-in-law have done to their house: "They've tuck 'n' gaumed the inside of theirn all over with some kind of nasty disgustin' truck which they say is all the go in Kaintuck amongst the upper hunky, and which they calls *plarsterin'!*" In Chapter 1 of *The Gilded Age*, Twain likewise recorded the following discussion of what Si Higgins has done to his house in Obedstown, East Tennessee:

"Si Higgins he's ben over to Kaintuck n' married a high-toned gal thar, outen the fust families, an' he's come back to the Forks with jist a hell's-mint o' whoop-jamboree notions, folks says. He's tuck an' fixed the ole house like they does in Kaintuck, he say, an' tha's ben folks come cler from Turpentine for to see it. He's tuck and gaumed it all over on the inside with plarsterin'."

"What's plarsterin'?"

"*I* dono. Hit's what *he* calls it. Ole Mam Higgins, she tole me. She say she warn't gwyne to hang out in no sich a dern hole like a hog. Says it's mud, or some sich kind o' nastiness that sticks on n' kivers up everything. Plarsterin', Si calls it."

65. *a double house*. Robert Montgomery Bird described a typical double log house of the period in Chapter 1 of vol. 2 of *Nick of the Woods* (1837): "It consisted of two separate cots, or wings, standing a little distance apart, but united by a common roof; which thus afforded shelter to the open hall, or passage, between them; while the roof being continued also from the eaves, both before and behind, in the pent-house fashion, it allowed space for wide porches, in which, and in the open passage, the summer traveller, resting in such a cabin, will always find the most agreeable quarters." The Grangerford homestead is like John and Patsy Quarles' place, near Florida, Missouri, where Sam Clemens spent much of his early boyhood. Twain reminded himself in his notes for the novel, "Describe aunt Patsy's house" (University of California edition, 1988, p. 728). "The house was a double log," he recalled in "Chapters from My Autobiography" (*North American Review*, March 1, 1907), "with a spacious floor (roofed in) connecting it with the kitchen. In the summer the table was set in the middle of that shady and breezy floor, and the sumptuous meals—well, it makes one cry to think of them" (p. 452). It also served as the model for the Phelps farm in Chapter 32.

Chapter XVIII.

COL. GRANGERFORD.

Col. Grangerford was a gentleman,[1] you see. He was a gentleman all over; and so was his family. He was well born, as the saying is, and that's worth as much in a man as it is in a horse, so the Widow Douglass said, and nobody ever denied that she was of the first aristocracy in our town;[2] and pap he always said it, too, though he warn't no more quality than a mud-cat,[3] himself. Col. Grangerford was very tall and very slim, and had a darkish-paly complexion, not a sign of red in it anywheres; he was clean-shaved every morning, all over his thin face, and he had the thinnest kind of lips, and the thinnest kind of nostrils, and a high nose, and heavy eyebrows, and the blackest kind of eyes, sunk so deep back that they seemed like they was looking out of caverns at you, as you may say. His forehead was high, and his hair was black and straight,[4] and hung to his shoulders. His hands was long and thin, and every day of his life he put on a clean shirt and a full suit from head to foot made out of linen so white it hurt your eyes to look at it;[5] and on Sundays he wore a blue tail-coat with brass buttons on it. He carried a mahogany cane with a silver head to it. There warn't no frivolishness about him, not a bit, and he warn't ever loud. He was as kind as he could be—you could feel that, you know,

1. *Col. Grangerford was a gentleman.* General Henry M. Darnall (also spelled "Darnell"; 1808–1880), who in part served as the inspiration for Colonel Saul Grangerford, was a typical Southern gentleman. Some friends described him in the Hickman (Ky.) *Courier* (August 31, 1877) as "a princely, chivalrous old gentleman, quick and courageous, but magnanimous, liberal hospitable, kind hearted and charitable." But the Memphis *Avalanche* (August 18, 1874) said that he was "a large planter . . . a gentleman of about sixty-five years of age, a man of large property and unbounded hospitality," who also possessed a "very vindictive temper," which "once aroused . . . was uncontrollable, and has figured in several deadly feuds." Also, like General Darnall, Colonel Grangerford has three boys and two daughters. He also shares some physical characteristics and habits with Sam's father, Judge John M. Clemens, but not his temperament. Twain thought that the Southern gentleman derived from Sir Walter Scott's "maudlin Middle-Age romanticism." He complained in Chapter 46 of *Life on the Mississippi* that the Scottish novelist and poet "made every gentleman in the South a Major or a Colonel or a General or a Judge, before the war; and it was he, also, that made these gentlemen value these bogus decorations. For it was he that created rank and caste down there, and also reverence for rank and caste, and pride and pleasure in them." Daniel R. Hundley, however, in *Social Relations in Our Southern States* (1860), argued that it was not the influence of Scott but rather a "military fever" that inspired these affectations. The Southern middle classes "are much given to a love of military titles, bestowed without regard to any sort of military service and upon all sorts of people. The young men, also, very much affect blue coats with brass buttons, and even sometimes sport veritable stripes

down the legs of their pantaloons. To such an extent does the military fever rage in some localities, a stranger would conclude at least every other male citizen to be either 'Captain, or Co-lo-nel, or Knight at arms' " (p. 127).

To those in Colonel Grangerford's class, pedigree determined "gentlemen." Judge Griswold, the Southern gentleman of the uncompleted "Simon Wheeler, Detective" (1877–1878), declared that "a man who came of gentle blood and fell to the ranks of scavengers and blacklegs, was still a gentleman and could not help it, since the word did not describe character but only birth; and a man who did not come of gentle blood might climb to the highest pinnacle of human grandeur but must still lack one thing—nothing could make him a gentleman; he might be called so by courtesy, but there an end" (*Mark Twain's Satires and Burlesques*, 1968, pp. 313–14).

But Twain believed that character, not accident of birth, determined a gentleman. "It seems to me," he said in his "Layman's Sermon," delivered at the New York YMCA on March 4, 1906, "that if any man has just, merciful and kindly instincts he would be a gentleman, for he would need nothing else in the world" (*Mark Twain's Speeches*, 1910, p. 138). If this were so, then Huckleberry Finn would be a gentleman but Colonel Grangerford would not be.

2. *nobody ever denied that she was of the first aristocracy in our town.* According to Chapter 5 of *Tom Sawyer*, the widow Douglas (like Colonel Grangerford) lives in the "best dwelling" around, a "hill mansion the only palace in the town, and the most hospitable and much the most lavish in the matter of festivities that St. Petersburg could boast."

3. *a mud-cat.* Popular name of the yellow catfish, generally considered an inferior species. This fish, according to Missourian Chester L. Davis in *The Twainian* (September/October 1961), "lives quite well in still water, in mud bottomed branches, in muddy ponds, it has a flat-shaped head as distinguished from that of the channel catfish which is more pointed, the meat is often more dark, the taste most often 'muddy'" (p. 4).

4. *his hair was black and straight.* Twain forgot that he had described Colonel Grangerford in

and so you had confidence. Sometimes he smiled, and it was good to see; but when he straightened himself up like a liberty-pole,[6] and the lightning begun to flicker out from under his eyebrows you wanted to climb a tree first, and find out what the matter was afterwards.[7] He didn't ever have to tell anybody to mind their manners—everybody was always good mannered where he was. Everybody loved to have him around, too; he was sunshine most always—I mean he made it seem like good weather. When he turned into a cloud-bank it was awful dark for a half a minute and that was enough; there wouldn't nothing go wrong again for a week.

When him and the old lady come down in the morning, all the family got up out of their chairs and give them good-day, and didn't set down again till they had set down. Then Tom and Bob went to the sideboard where the decanters was, and mixed a glass of bitters and handed it to him, and he held it in his hand and waited till Tom's and Bob's was mixed, and then they bowed and said "Our duty to you, sir, and madam;" and *they* bowed[8] the least bit in the world and said thank you, and so they drank, all three, and Bob and Tom poured a spoonful of water on the sugar and the mite of whisky or apple brandy in the bottom of their tumblers,[9] and give it to me and Buck, and we drank to the old people too.

Bob was the oldest, and Tom next. Tall, beautiful men with very broad shoulders and brown faces, and long black hair and black eyes. They dressed in white linen from head to foot, like the old gentleman, and wore broad Panama hats.

Then there was Miss Charlotte, she was twenty-five, and tall and proud and grand, but as good as she could be, when she warn't stirred up; but when she was, she had a look that would make you wilt in your tracks, like her father. She was beautiful.

So was her sister, Miss Sophia, but it was a different kind. She was gentle and sweet, like a dove, and she was only twenty.

Each person had their own nigger to wait on them—Buck, too. My nigger had a monstrous easy time, because I warn't used to having anybody do anything for me, but Buck's was on the jump most of the time.

This was all there was of the family, now; but there used to be more—three sons; they got killed; and Emmeline that died.

The old gentleman owned a lot of farms, and over a hundred niggers. Sometimes a stack of people would come there, horseback, from ten or fifteen mile around, and stay five or six days, and have such junketings[10] round about and on the river, and dances and picnics in the woods, daytimes, and balls at the house, nights. These people was mostly kin-folks of the family. The men brought their guns with them. It was a handsome lot of quality, I tell you.

There was another clan of aristocracy around there—five or six families—mostly of the name of Shepherdson.[11]

YOUNG HARNEY SHEPHERDSON.

They was as high-toned, and well born, and rich and grand, as the tribe of Grangerfords. The Shepherdsons and the Grangerfords used the same steamboat landing,[12] which

the previous chapter as "gray and about sixty"; the proofreader failed to catch it, too. Blair suggested in *Mark Twain and Huck Finn* (p. 214) that this error resulted from Twain's rephrasing his description of another Southern gentleman, Judge Griswold, in the uncompleted "Simon Wheeler, Detective":

> "Judge" [Griswold] had never been on the bench; but that was no matter; he was the first citizen of the place, he was a man of great personal dignity, therefore no power in this world could have saved him from the title. He had been dubbed Major, then Colonel, then Squire; but gradually the community settled upon "Judge," and Judge he remained, after that.
>
> He was sixty years old; very tall, very spare, with a long, thin, smooth-shaven, intellectual face, and long black hair that lay close to his head, was kept to the rear by his ears as one keeps curtains back by brackets, and fell straight to his coat collar without a single tolerant kink or relenting curve. He had an eagle's beak and an eagle's eye. He was a Kentuckian by birth and rearing. . . . Judge Griswold's manners and carriage were of the courtly old-fashioned sort; he had never worked; he was a gentleman." (*Mark Twain's Satires and Burlesques*, p. 313)

There are other similarities between "Simon Wheeler, Detective" and this chapter about the Grangerford house: there is a feud between the Griswolds and the Burnsides like that between the Grangerfords and the Shepherdsons; and the Burnsides have a "giddy and thoughtless, when . . . not sappy and sentimental" child named Hugh, who, like Emmeline Grangerford, is an amateur poet. "The world was hollow to him, then, and he was more than likely to shut himself up in his room and write some stuff about 'bruised hearts' or 'the despised and friendless,' and print it in one of the village journals under the impression that it was poetry" (p. 315).

5. *a full suit from head to foot made out of linen so white it hurt your eyes to look at it.* Twain himself got in the habit of wearing a full white suit in the manner of the Southern gentleman in December 1906; he often had himself photographed wearing this outfit until it became his most pervasive image. "He had always a relish for personal effect, which expressed itself in the white suit of complete serge which he wore in his last years," William Dean Howells recalled in *My Mark Twain* (1910). "That was not vanity in him, but a keen feeling for costume which the severity of our modern tailoring forbids men, though it flatters women to every excess in it; yet he also enjoyed the shock, the offence, the pang which it gave the sensibilities of others" (pp. 4–5). "I have found that when a man reaches the advanced age of 71 years as I have," he told Congress on December 7 (as was reported in the New York *Times* the following day), "the continual sight of dark clothing is likely to have a depressing effect upon him. Light-colored clothing is more pleasing to the eye and enlivens the spirit. Now, of course, I cannot compel every one to wear such clothing just for my especial benefit, so I do the next best thing and wear it myself."

6. *a liberty-pole*. A tall mast or staff with a Phrygian cap or some other symbol of liberty on top; a contradictory symbol for this Southern aristocrat, but here meaning merely "alone and erect."

7. *the lightning begun to flicker out from under his eyebrows you wanted to climb a tree first, and find out what the matter was afterwards*. Orion Clemens said in Richard I. Holcombe's *History of Marion County, Missouri* (1884) that his father, Judge Clemens, "had a grey eye of wonderful keenness, that seemed to pierce through you" (p. 915). "Besides being of faultless pedigree," Hundley explained in *Social Relations in Our Southern States*, "the Southern Gentleman is usually possessed of an equally faultless physical development. His average height is six feet, yet he is rarely gawky in his movements, or in the least clumsily put together; and his entire *physique* conveys to the mind an impression of firmness united with flexibility" (p. 28). But Hundley neglects to mention the violent mood swings of the stereotypical Southern gentleman, sunny one minute and dark the next.

Blair mentioned in *Mark Twain and Huck Finn* (pp. 216–17) other representative Southern gentleman in American literature, like Champ Effington, Esquire, of John Esten Cooke's *The Virginia Comedians* (1854) and Colonel Culpepper Starbottle of Bret Harte's *Gabriel Conroy* (1876). Frank Merriweather of John Pendleton Kennedy's *Swallow Barn; or, A Sojourn in the Old Dominion* (1832) is a kind and hospitable

was about two mile above our house; so sometimes when I went up there with a lot of our folks I used to see a lot of the Shepherdsons there, on their fine horses.

One day Buck and me was away out in the woods, hunting, and heard a horse coming. We was crossing the road. Buck says:

"Quick! Jump for the woods!"

We done it, and then peeped down the woods through the leaves. Pretty soon a splendid young man come galloping down the road, setting his horse easy and looking like a soldier. He had his gun across his pommel. I had seen him before. It was young Harney Shepherdson. I heard Buck's gun go off at my ear,[13] and Harney's hat tumbled off from his head. He grabbed his gun and rode straight to the place where we was hid. But we didn't wait. We started through the woods on a run. The woods warn't thick, so I looked over my shoulder, to dodge the bullet, and twice I seen Harney cover Buck with his gun; and then he rode away the way he come—to get his hat, I reckon, but I couldn't see. We never stopped running till we got home. The old gentleman's eyes blazed a minute—'twas pleasure, mainly, I judged—then his face sort of smoothed down, and he says, kind of gentle:

"I don't like that shooting from behind a bush.[14] Why didn't you step into the road, my boy?"

"The Shepherdsons don't, father. They always take advantage."

Miss Charlotte she held her head up like a queen while Buck was telling his tale, and her nostrils spread and her eyes snapped. The two young men looked dark, but never said nothing. Miss Sophia she turned pale, but the color come back when she found the man warn't hurt.[15]

Soon as I could get Buck down by the corn-cribs[16] under the trees by ourselves, I says:

"Did you want to kill him, Buck?"

"Well, I bet I did."

"What did he do to you?"

"Him? He never done nothing to me."

"Well, then, what did you want to kill him for?"

MISS CHARLOTTE.

"Why nothing—only it's on account of the feud."[17]

"What's a feud?"

"Why, where was you raised?[18] Don't you know what a feud is?"

"Never heard of it before—tell me about it."[19]

"Well," says Buck, "a feud is this way. A man has a quarrel with another man, and kills him; then that other man's brother kills *him;* then the other brothers, on both sides, goes for one another; then the *cousins* chip in—and by-and-by everybody's killed off, and there ain't no more feud. But it's kind of slow, and takes a long time."

"Has this one been going on long, Buck?"

"Well I should *reckon!* it started[20] thirty year ago,[21] or som'ers along there. There was trouble 'bout something[22] and then a lawsuit to settle it; and the suit went agin one of the men, and so he up and shot the man that won the suit—which he would naturally do, of course. Anybody would."

"What was the trouble about, Buck?—land?"

"I reckon maybe—I don't know."

"Well, who done the shooting?—was it a Grangerford or a Shepherdson?"

planter, but "always touchy on a point of honor"; and like the Grangerfords, the Merriweathers have two daughters (the elder high-spirited, the younger sweet and gentle) and a thirteen-year-old son who is full of mischief. The most likely prototype for Colonel Grangerford in contemporary literature was Peyton Beaumont of J. W. De Forest's *Kate Beaumont* (1872). Twain knew the book, and Howells said in *The Atlantic Monthly* (March 1872) that De Forest's novel described "the high-tone Southern society of the times before the war, as it was with slavery and chivalry, with hard drinking and easy shooting" (p. 363). The head of this household is, according to Howells, "a quivering mass of affection for his own flesh and blood, an impersonation of the highest and stupidest family pride, his hot blood afire with constant cocktails and his life always in his hand for the resentment of an insult, an impatient parent and an impenitent homicide." Howells was referring to the Beaumonts' feud with the McAlisters. See note 49 below.

8. *they bowed and said "Our duty to you, sir, and madam;" and* they *bowed.* The Grangerfords engage in a series of odd, empty formalities for an American backwoods family, courtesies probably picked up from Sir Walter Scott's chivalry. People in this part of the country were inclined to put on airs like European aristocrats. Twain recalled one particularly silly soul from Hannibal in "The Private History of a Campaign That Failed" (*Century Magazine*, December 1885): "He was young, ignorant, good-hearted, well-meaning, trivial, full of romance, and given to reading chivalric novels and singing forlorn love-ditties. He had some pathetic nickel-plated aristocratic instincts, and detested his name, which was Dunlap; detested it, partly because it was nearly as common in that region as Smith, but mainly because it had a plebean sound to his ear. So he tried to ennoble it by writing it in this way: *d'Unlap*" (p. 194). He could have been a Grangerford.

9. *a spoonful of water on the sugar and the mite of whiskey or apple brandy in the bottom of their tumblers.* An Old-Fashioned, said to be Twain's favorite drink. Franklin B. Sanborn reported in his review of *Huckleberry Finn*, in the Springfield (Mass.) *Daily Republican* (April 27, 1885), that that fine old Southern gentleman Andrew Jackson "used to drink his morning draught as described, and then hand the tumbler to one of his suite, who would pour in water and drink the heeltap." In 1874, Clemens wrote Olivia about his being introduced in London to a "cocktail" of "Scotch whiskey, a lemon, some crushed sugar, and . . . *Angostura bitters*" that he drank before breakfast, dinner, and going to bed. "To it I attribute the fact that up to this day my digestion has been wonderful—simply *perfect*," he reported. "It remains day after day and week after week as regular as a clock" (*The Love Letters of Mark Twain*, 1949, p. 190).

10. *junketings*. Pleasure excursions.

11. *another clan of aristocracy around there—five or six families—mostly of the name of Shepherdson*. Branch and Hirst suggested in *The Grangerford-Shepherdson Feud* (1985, p. 76) that Twain may well have known that the Watson clan also contained Beckhams, Starrs, and Dickinsons; Daniel Watson (1797–1865), the patriarch of the family, had six daughters, at least three of whom married and remained in the area.

12. *the same steamboat landing*. Compromise Landing, Kentucky; it lay on the border that divided Kentucky and Tennessee, hence its name.

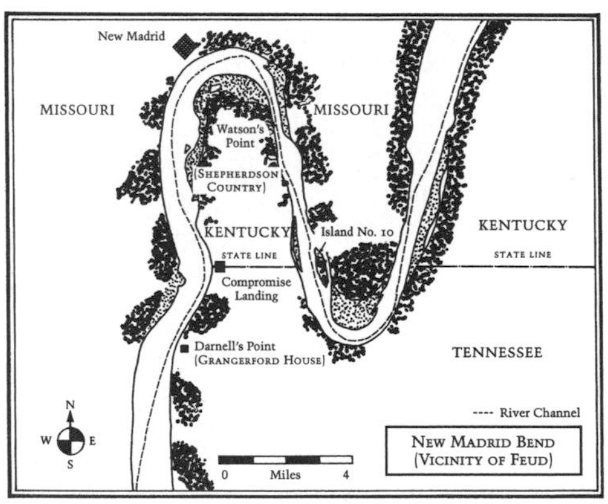

Map of the location of the Darnell–Watson feud.
Reprinted with permission from the Mark Twain Project's Adventures of Huckleberry Finn, *edited by Victor Fischer and Lin Salamo (University of California, 2001). Copyright © 1985 and 2001 by the Regents of the University of California Press.*

13. *I heard Buck's gun go off at my ear*. In the 1895–1896 public reading copy, Twain revised

"Laws, how do *I* know? it was so long ago."

"Don't anybody know?"

"Oh, yes, pa knows, I reckon, and some of the other old folks; but they don't know, now, what the row was about in the first place."

"Has there been many killed, Buck?"

"Yes—right smart chance of funerals. But they don't always kill. Pa's got a few buck-shot in him; but he don't mind it 'cuz he don't weigh much anyway.[23] Bob's been carved up some with a bowie,[24] and Tom's been hurt once or twice."

"Has anybody been killed this year, Buck?"

"Yes, we got one and they got one.[25] 'Bout three months ago, my cousin Bud, fourteen year old,[26] was riding through the woods, on t'other side of the river, and didn't have no weapon with him, which was blame' foolishness, and in a lonesome place he hears a horse a-coming behind him, and sees old Baldy Shepherdson a-linkin' after him[27] with his gun in his hand and his white hair a-flying in the wind; and 'stead of jumping off and taking to the brush, Bud 'lowed he could outrun him; so they had it, nip and tuck,[28] for five mile or more, the old man a-gaining all the time; so at last Bud seen it warn't any use,[29] so he stopped and faced around so as to have the bullet holes in front, you know, and the old man he rode up and shot him down. But he didn't git much chance to enjoy his luck, for inside of a week our folks laid *him* out."

"I reckon that old man was a coward, Buck."

"I reckon he *warn't* a coward. Not by a blame' sight. There ain't a coward amongst them Shepherdsons—not a one. And there ain't no cowards amongst the Grangerfords, either.[30] Why, that old man kep' up his end in a fight one day,[31] for a half an hour, against three Grangerfords, and come out winner. They was all a-horseback; he lit off of his horse and got behind[32] a little wood-pile, and kep' his horse before him to stop the bullets; but the Grangerfords staid on their horses and capered around the old man, and peppered away at him, and he peppered away at them. Him and his horse both went home pretty leaky and crippled, but the Grangerfords had to be *fetched* home—and one of 'em was dead, and another died the next day. No, sir, if a body's out hunting for cowards, he don't want to fool away any time amongst them Shepherdsons, becuz they don't breed any of that *kind*."

Next Sunday we all went to church, about three mile, everybody a-horseback. The men took their guns along, so did Buck, and kept them between their knees or stood them handy against the wall. The Shepherdsons done the same.[33] It was pretty ornery preaching—all about brotherly love, and such-like tiresomeness; but everybody said it was a good sermon, and they all talked it over going home,[34] and had such a powerful lot to say about faith, and good works, and free grace,[35] and preforeordestination,[36] and I don't know what all, that it did seem to me to be one of the roughest Sundays I had run across yet.

About an hour after dinner everybody was dozing around, some in their chairs and some in their rooms, and it got to be pretty dull. Buck and a dog was stretched out on the grass in the sun, sound asleep. I went up to our room, and judged I would take a nap myself. I found that sweet Miss Sophia standing in her door, which was next to ours, and she took me in her room and shut the door very soft, and asked me if I liked her, and I said I did; and she asked me if I would do something for her and not tell anybody, and I said I would. Then she said she'd forgot her Testament, and left it in the seat at church, between two other books and would I slip out quiet and go there and fetch it to her, and not say nothing to nobody. I said I would. So I slid out and slipped off up the road, and there warn't anybody at the church, except maybe a hog or two, for there warn't any lock on the door, and hogs likes a puncheon floor[37] in summer-time because it's cool. If you notice, most folks don't go to church only when they've got to; but a hog is different.[38]

Says I to myself something's up—it ain't natural for a girl to be in such a sweat about a Testament; so I give it a shake, and out drops a little piece of paper with *"Half-past two"* wrote on it with a pencil. I ransacked it, but couldn't find

this sentence for reading aloud to "Che-*bang!* Buck's gun went off at my ear."

14. *I don't like that shooting from behind a bush.* Unlike his sons and daughters, Colonel Grangerford is a Southern gentleman who follows a code of honor and does not believe that all is fair in love and war.

15. *Miss Sophia she turned pale, but the color come back when she found the man warn't hurt.* Twain expanded on this line in his 1895–1896 public reading copy: "Miss Sophia she turned pale—*I noticed that*, and judged it *meant* something;—but the color came *back* when she found the man warn't *hurt*,—and I noticed *that*, too."

16. *the corn-cribs.* Structures for drying corn; the air circulates freely through the open sides, either slats or latticework.

17. *the feud.* A vendetta, once characteristic of Scottish clans and Corsican families and associated with this part of the country. The names of the rival families suggest the long competition on the American frontier between farmers and herders; there is also a biblical prototype in the conflict between Cain the granger and Abel

Darnell *vs.* Watson. Illustration by A. B. Shute, *Life on the Mississippi*, 1883. *Private collection.*

the shepherd, which resulted in the first murder in Western history, that between two brothers. "In no part of the South," Twain wrote in Chapter 26 of *Life on the Mississippi*, "has the vendetta flourished more briskly, or held out longer between warring families," than in that area along the Kentucky–Tennessee border. Robert H. Sykes suggested in "A Source for Mark Twain's Feud" (*West Virginia History*, April 1967, pp. 191–98) that Twain may have been thinking in part of the most famous feud in American history, that between the Hatfields and McCoys of West Virginia. Loren K. Davidson in "The Darnell Watson Feud" (*Duquesne Review*, February 1968, pp. 76–95) and Edgar Marquess Branch and Robert H. Hirst in *The Grangerford–Shepherdson Feud* (1985) retrace the carnage left by both the Darnalls and Watsons over the years, but none of the accounts they have located exactly replicates the circumstances of the feud in either *Life on the Mississippi* or *Huckleberry Finn*. Twain may have taken such liberties with the facts to avoid offending either side of the feud.

"Every year or so somebody was shot, on one side or the other," Twain quoted a riverboat companion in *Life on the Mississippi*; "and as fast as one generation was laid out, their sons took up the feud and kept it a-going. And it's just as I say; they went on shooting each other year in and year out—making a kind of religion of it, you see—till they'd done forgot, long ago, what it was all about." Some people challenged the veracity of Twain's description of the Grangerford–Shepherdson feud, calling it "unnatural, unreasonable, ridiculous and absurd." But one reader, J. C. Fuller of Cincinnati, sent Twain a recent clipping from the Cincinnati *Enquirer*, "only one of many brought to the notice of the intelligent newspaper reader every year," with the suggestion that Twain "bring this knowledge to the attention of the *lunkheads* who disbelieve in the reality of the southern *vendetta*" (letter of August 10, 1885, Mark Twain Papers). When Reginald Cholmondeley, a friend in Shropshire, asked whether "blood-feuds really existed in Arkansas" at this time, Twain insisted on March 28, 1885, "Yes, indeed, feuds existed in Kentucky, Tennessee, and Arkansas, of the nature described, within my time and memory. I came very near being an eyewitness to the general engagement detailed in the book. The details are historical and correct" (quoted in Blair, *Mark Twain and Huck Finn*, 1960, p. 225).

"AND ASKED ME IF I LIKED HER."

anything else. I couldn't make anything out of that, so I put the paper in the book again, and when I got home and up stairs, there was Miss Sophia in her door waiting for me. She pulled me in and shut the door; then she looked in the Testament till she found the paper, and as soon as she read it she looked glad; and before a body could think, she grabbed me and give me a squeeze,[39] and said I was the best boy in the world, and not to tell anybody. She was mighty red in the face, for a minute, and her eyes lighted up and it made her powerful pretty. I was a good deal astonished, but when I got my breath I asked her what the paper was about, and she asked me if I had read it, and I said no, and she asked me if I could read writing, and I told her "no, only coarse-hand,"[40] and then she said the paper warn't anything but a book-mark to keep her place, and I might go and play now.

I went off down to the river, studying over this thing, and pretty soon I noticed that my nigger was following along behind. When we was out of sight of the house, he looked back and around a second, and then comes a-running, and says:

"Mars Jawge, if you'll come down into de swamp, I'll show you a whole stack o' water-moccasins."[41]

Thinks I, that's mighty curious; he said that yesterday. He oughter know a body don't love water-moccasins enough to go around hunting for them. What is he up to anyway? So I says—

"All right, trot ahead."

I followed a half a mile, then he struck out over the swamp and waded ankle deep as much as another half mile. We come to a little flat piece of land which was dry and very thick with trees and bushes and vines, and he says—

"You shove right in dah, jist a few steps, Mars Jawge, dah's whah dey is. I's seed 'm befo', I don't k'yer to see 'em no mo'."

Then he slopped right along and went away, and pretty soon the trees hid him. I poked into the place a-ways, and come to a little open patch as big as a bedroom, all hung around with vines, and found a man laying there asleep—and by jings it was my old Jim!

I waked him up, and I reckoned it was going to be a grand surprise to him to see me again, but it warn't. He nearly cried, he was so glad, but he warn't surprised. Said he swum along behind me, that night, and heard me yell every time, but dasn't answer, because he didn't want nobody to pick *him* up, and take him into slavery again. Says he—

"I got hurt a little, en couldn't swim fas', so I wuz a considable ways behine you, towards de las'; when you landed I reck'ned I could ketch up wid you on de lan' 'dout havin' to shout at you, but when I see dat house I begin to go slow. I 'uz off too fur to hear what dey say to you—I wuz 'fraid o' de dogs—but when it 'uz all quiet agin, I knowed you's in de house, so I struck out for de woods to wait for day. Early in de mawnin' some er de niggers come along, gwyne to de fields, en dey tuck me en showed me dis place,[42] whah de dogs can't track me on accounts o' de water, en dey brings me truck to eat every night, en tells me how you's a gitt'n along."

"Why didn't you tell my Jack[43] to fetch me here sooner, Jim?"

But Branch and Hirst proved in *The Grangerford–Shepherdson Feud* (1985) that Twain apparently combined at least two documented skirmishes between the Darnalls and the Watsons in *Huckleberry Finn* and *Life on the Mississippi*, neither of which he personally witnessed. The killing of the two boys later in the chapter corresponds to the gunfight at Compromise Landing on September 4, 1859, between Alexander F. Beckham and a relative named Starr, members of the Watson clan, and John Schultz, a friend and ally of General Darnall. The dispute arose over General Darnall's accusations in print that Jack, "a bad negro in our midst" owned by Beckham, had raped Beckham's sister-in-law Caroline Watson Dickinson; and then Beckham tried to cover it up by selling the slave south. General Darnall evidently heard the story from Schultz (Mrs. Dickinson's nephew), who pursued Jack to Beckham's place the night of the alleged rape.

A second incident occurred on March 17, 1869. A Yale graduate named Robert Lane married one of General Darnall's nieces, and the two reportedly conspired to forge the general's will and then kill him with an accomplice, Cullen C. Edwards. Lane's younger brother Clinton went to see Darnall and proceeded to insult him; in the fight that followed, Darnall shot Lane. On September 17, two of the Darnall boys and a cousin ambushed the Lane brothers and Edwards as they were coming from the steamboat *Belle of Memphis* at Island No. 10, near Watson's Landing; they shot and killed all three. They also fired on but missed Daniel Watson's son Randolph, who had accompanied the victims to the boat. "So history repeats itself," the St. Louis *Missouri Republican* added on March 19; "and the Vendetta, driven from the glens and mountains of far off Corsica, is revived in our own day in the Valley of the Mississippi." All three Darnalls were indited for murder, and Randolph Watson was called in as a state witness.

18. *where was you raised?* Aristocratic Buck puts down low-down Huck for being ignorant of the code of honor followed in this part of the country. He defends a system he believes in without really understanding it. Southern chivalry, like slavery, corrupted at even the tenderest age.

19. *Never heard of it before—tell me about it.* Twain suddenly stopped at this point in the manuscript in 1876; he had to put it aside and went on to other projects. He did not pick it up again until 1879, then dropped it again the next year; he did not finally finish the story until 1884. Perhaps he did not know how to handle the carnage left by a feud in what was intended to be a sequel to *Tom Sawyer*, his "bad boy" book. Satire was quickly slipping into brutal reality. Also, he may have not yet figured out just cause for the final confrontation between the warring families. He may have forgotten the reason for the 1859 tragedy, or he dared not describe in the novel the actual cause of the incident: One of Watson's slaves named Jack was accused of trying to rape of one of the Darnall women. He finally resorted to a romantic cliché cribbed from Shakespeare. See note 49 below.

Michael G. Miller observed in "Geography and Structure in *Huckleberry Finn*" (*Studies in the Novel,* Fall 1980) that "prior to the Grangerford–Shepherdson episode Twain supplies *The Adventures of Huckleberry Finn* with remarkable geographic realism and shows great if instinctive care that the raft's journey conform rigorously to the temporal and spatial limits of the actual Mississippi. After the feud, attention to geographic detail noticeably diminishes, and the awesome pilot's memory is much less employed than in the first part of the journey" (p. 203). Twain took his novel in another direction, for he had new themes to explore; the novel evolved into more a symbolic journey than an actual one down the Mississippi, contrasting bucolic life on the raft with chaos on the land. Jane Smiley complained in "Say It Ain't So, Huck" (*Harper's Magazine*, January 1996), "It is with the feud that the novel begins to fail, because from here on the episodes are mere distractions from the true subject of the work: Huck's affection for and responsibility to Jim. The signs of this failure are everywhere, as Jim is pushed to the side of the narrative, hiding on the raft and confined to it, while Huck follows the duke and the dauphin on the shore to the scenes of much simpler and much less philosophically taxing moral dilemmas, such as fraud" (p. 65). But Jim always hides in the background and is never far from Huck's thoughts and concerns as the boy confronts slave society on the riverbank. There is also the slap in the face of complacency in Chapter 23 when Jim recalls how he struck his deaf daughter; and the philosophical climax of the novel comes in Chapter 31 when Huck decides "to *go* to hell" to

"Well, 'twarn't no use to 'sturb you, Huck, tell we could do sumfn—but we's all right, now. I ben a-buyin' pots en pans en vittles,[44] as I got a chanst, en a patchin' up de raf', nights, when—"

"*What* raft, Jim?"

"Our ole raf'."

"You mean to say our old raft warn't smashed all to flinders?"[45]

"No, she warn't. She was tore up a good deal—one en' of her was—but dey warn't no great harm done, on'y our traps was mos' all los'. Ef we hadn' dive' so deep en swum so fur under water, en de night hadn' ben so dark, en we warn't so sk'yerd, en ben sich punkin-heads, as de sayin' is, we'd a seed de raf'. But it's jis' as well we didn't, 'kase now she's all fixed up agin mos' as good as new, en we's got a new lot o' stuff, too, in de place o' what 'uz los'."

"Why, how did you get hold of the raft again, Jim—did you catch her?"

"How I gwyne to ketch her, en I out in de woods? No, some er de niggers foun' her ketched on a snag, along heah in de ben', en dey hid her in a crick, 'mongst de willows, en dey wuz so much jawin'[46] 'bout which un 'um she b'long to de mos', dat I come to heah 'bout it pooty soon, so I ups en settles de trouble by tellin' 'um she don't b'long to none uv um, but to you en me; en I ast 'm if dey gwyne to grab a young white genlman's propaty, en git a hid'n for it? Den I gin 'm ten cents apiece, en dey 'uz mighty well satisfied, en wisht some mo' raf's 'ud come along en make 'm rich agin. Dey's mighty good to me, dese niggers is, en whatever I wants 'm to do fur me, I doan' have to ast 'm twice, honey. Dat Jack's a good nigger, en pooty smart."

"Yes, he is. He ain't ever told me you was here; told me to come, and he'd show me a lot of water-moccasins. If anything happens, *he* ain't mixed up in it.[47] He can say he never seen us together, and it'll be the truth."

I don't want to talk much about the next day.[48] I reckon I'll cut it pretty short. I waked up about dawn, and was agoing to turn over and go to sleep again, when I noticed how still it was—didn't seem to be anybody stirring. That warn't usual. Next I noticed that Buck was up and gone. Well, I gets up, a-wondering, and goes down stairs—nobody around; everything as still as a mouse. Just the same outside; thinks I, what does it mean? Down by the wood-pile I comes across my Jack, and says:

"What's it all about?"

Says he:

"Don't you know, Mars Jawge?"

"No," says I, "I don't."

"Well, den, Miss Sophia's run off! 'deed she has. She run off in de night, sometime—nobody don't know jis' when—run off to git married to dat young Harney Shepherdson,[49] you know—leastways, so dey 'spec. De fambly foun' it out, 'bout half an hour ago—maybe a little mo'—en' I *tell* you dey warn't no time los'. Sich another hurryin' up guns en hosses *you* never see! De women folks has gone for to stir up de relations, en ole Mars Saul en de boys tuck dey guns en rode up de river road for to try to ketch dat young man en kill him 'fo' he kin git acrost de river wid Miss Sophia.[50] I reck'n dey's gwyne to be mighty rough times."

"Buck went off 'thout waking me up."

"Well I reck'n he *did!* Dey warn't gwyne to mix you up in it. Mars Buck he loaded up his gun en 'lowed he's gwyne to fetch home a Shepherdson or bust. Well, dey'll be plenty un 'm dah, I reck'n, en you bet you he'll fetch one ef he gits a chanst."

I took up the river road as hard as I could put.[51] By-and-by I begin to hear guns a good ways off.[52] When I come in sight of the log store and the wood-pile where the steamboats lands, I worked along under the trees and brush till I got to a good place, and then I clumb up into the forks of a cotton-wood that was out of reach, and watched. There was a wood-rank[53] four foot high, a little ways in front of the tree, and first I was going to hide behind that; but maybe it was luckier I didn't.

There was four or five men cavorting around on their horses in the open place before the log store, cussing and yelling, and trying to get at a couple of young chaps that was behind the wood-rank alongside of the steamboat land-

free his friend. "If Huck and Jim had not passed Cairo, the last road to freedom for Jim," argued Jocelyn Chadwick-Joshua in *The Jim Dilemma* (1998), "the novel would necessarily have ended without any real, profound truths, and few southern and northern myths would be discovered. Passing Cairo gives Huck and Jim the opportunity to reexamine, and consequently reevaluate, a range of Old South myths and reject them. Rather than giving us one more romanticized fiction about mistreated slaves and the indomitable but silent spirit, Twain dodges logic by letting his characters continue in the wrong direction, flinging us into the paradoxes of the mythic South" (pp. 69–70). Huck and Jim must go south to expose the slave system in its pernicious practice and corruption of its people.

20. *it started.* Twain originally located it "in Ole Foginy" (old Virginia) in the manuscript (**MS**), the locale of the Hatfield–McCoy feud; West Virginia did not secede from Virginia until the Civil War. Twain probably dropped this detail to make the conflict less localized; it could have started any place in the South.

21. *thirty year ago.* "Thirty or forty or fifty year *ago*," in Twain's 1895–1896 public reading copy.

22. *trouble 'bout something.* Twain originally explained in the manuscript that the dispute was over "some land, or some cattle" (**MS**). According to Chapter 26 of *Life on the Mississippi*, the trouble between the Darnalls and Watsons was said to have started over a horse or a cow. Sykes explained in "A Source for Mark Twain's Feud" (pp. 193–94) that the catalyst for the Hatfield–McCoy feud was supposedly a dispute over a razorback hog; but by the time *Huckleberry Finn* came out, most people were really not quite sure exactly what caused all the trouble.

23. *but he don't mind it 'cuz he don't weigh much anyway.* "It's just *ballast*," Twain added in his 1895–1896 public reading copy.

24. *a bowie.* This formidable weapon was about a foot long in the blade, single-edged, very heavy, and with a sharp point; it was good for both cutting and stabbing; popular with hunters and desperadoes in the Southern backwoods. Although said to be named for Jim Bowie, the famous Indian fighter, it may have been invented by his brother Rezin P. Bowie, as a hunting knife rather than a deadly weapon. Sam Clemens learned on the streets of Hannibal the damage one could inflict, when "the young California emigrant . . . was stabbed with a bowie knife by a drunken comrade: I saw the red life gush from his breast" ("Chapters from My Autobiography," *North American Review*, May 3, 1907, p. 5). Sykes reported in "A Source for Mark Twain's Feud" (pp. 194–95) that during one altercation of the famous Hatfield–McCoy feud Tolbert McCoy slashed Bob Hatfield with a knife. "That the above implements are carried about the persons of so many of our citizens, is a disgrace and a reproach to our western country," complained the editorial "Bowie Knives and Pistols," reprinted in the Hannibal *Journal* (December 16, 1847). "If the opinion of civilized society is rapidly extending its power to the

A bowie knife. Illustration by A. B. Frost, "Tom Sawyer, Detective," *Harper's Monthly*, September 1896.

Courtesy Library of Congress.

suppression of duelling, how much more strongly should it be brought to bear on that thirst for human blood, unpalliated by what are called the rules of chivalry, which induces a man to walk abroad upon the earth, carrying about him *in anticipation*, the weapons of death, prepared to unsheath them on his fellow man, reckless of its consequences to the victim, or those connected with him." The author, like Twain, looked forward to the time "when the

"BEHIND THE WOOD-RANK."

ing—but they couldn't come it. Every time one of them showed himself on the river side of the wood-pile he got shot at. The two boys was squatting[54] back to back behind the pile, so they could watch both ways.

By-and-by the men stopped cavorting around and yelling. They started riding towards the store; then up gets one of the boys, draws a steady bead over the wood-rank, and drops one of them out of his saddle. All the men jumped off of their horses and grabbed the hurt one and started to carry him to the store; and that minute the two boys started on the run. They got half-way to the tree I was in before the men noticed. Then the men see them, and jumped on their horses and took out after them. They gained on the boys, but it didn't do no good, the boys had too good a start; they got to the wood-pile that was in front of my tree, and slipped in behind it, and so they had the bulge[55] on the men again. One of the boys was Buck, and the other was a slim young chap about nineteen years old.[56]

The men ripped around awhile, and then rode away. As soon as they was out of sight, I sung out to Buck and told him. He didn't know what to make of my voice coming out of the tree, at first. He was awful surprised. He told me to watch out sharp and let him know when the men come in sight again; said they was up to some devilment or other—wouldn't be gone long. I wished I was out of that tree, but I dasn't come down. Buck begun to cry and rip, and 'lowed that him and his cousin Joe (that was the other young chap) would make up for this day, yet. He said his father and his two brothers was killed, and two or three of the enemy. Said the Shepherdsons laid for them, in ambush. Buck said his father and brothers ought to waited for their relations—the Shepherdsons was too strong for them. I asked him what was become of young Harney and Miss Sophia. He said they'd got across the river and was safe. I was glad of that; but the way Buck did take on because he didn't manage to kill Harney that day he shot at him—I hain't ever heard anything like it.

All of a sudden, bang! bang! bang! goes three or four guns—the men had slipped around through the woods and come in from behind without their horses! The boys jumped for the river—both of them hurt—and as they swum down the current the men run along the bank shooting at them and singing out, "Kill them, kill them!" It made me so sick I most fell out of the tree. I ain't agoing to tell *all* that happened—it would make me sick again if I was to do that. I wished I hadn't ever come ashore that night, to see such things. I ain't ever going to get shut of[57] them—lots of times I dream about them.

I staid in the tree till it begun to get dark, afraid to come down. Sometimes I heard guns away off in the woods; and twice I seen little gangs of men gallop past the log store with guns; so I reckoned the trouble was still agoing on. I was mighty down-hearted; so I made up my mind I wouldn't ever go anear that house again, because I reckoned I was to blame, somehow. I judged that that piece of paper meant that Miss Sophia was to meet Harney somewheres at half-past two and run off; and I judged I ought to told her father about that paper and the curious way she acted, and then maybe he would a locked her up and this awful mess wouldn't ever happened.

When I got down out of the tree, I crept along down the

villain who arms himself systematically, and is constantly on the lookout for causes of quarrel, will be regarded as little better than a premeditate assassin, and be made to cower before the universal scorn and contempt of society."

"Buck and his father and brothers ought to have waited for their relations." Illustration by E. W. Kemble, "Autograph Edition" of *The Collected Works of Mark Twain*, 1899. *Private collection.*

25. *we got one and they got one.* Branch and Hirst suggested in *The Grangerford-Shepherdson Feud* (1985, p. 61) that Twain may have been familiar with an account of the March 17, 1869, Darnall ambush of the Lanes, Edwards, and Randolph Watson at Island No. 10 that was reprinted in Twain's paper the Buffalo *Express* on March 29. "Darnell and Watson were the names of two men whose families had kept up a long quarrel," Horace Bixby told Twain while he was gathering material for *Life on the Mississippi*. "The old man Darnell and his two sons came to the conclusion to leave that part of the country.

They started to take steamboat just above 'No. 10.' The Watsons got wind of it and as the young Darnells were walking up the companion way stairs with their wives on their arms they shot them in the back" (p. 68). Twain made use of this account in Chapter 26 of *Life on the Mississippi*. Of course, the Darnalls were the assailants in this instance.

26. *my cousin Bud, fourteen year old*. This boy is the same age as Huck and Buck. "Men would shoot boys, boys would shoot men," Twain quoted a travelling companion on the Darnell–Watson dispute in Chapter 26 of *Life on the Mississippi*. "A man shot a boy twelve years old—happened on him in the woods, and didn't give him no chance. If he *had* a' given him a chance, the boy'd shoot *him*." This was based on the account Twain's secretary wrote down in the notebook they used for this book: "Once a boy 12 years old connected with the Kentucky family was riding through the woods on the Missouri side. He was overtaken by a full-grown man and he shot that boy dead" (Branch and Hirst, *The Grangerford–Shepherdson Feud*, 1985, p. 41). Twain may well have heard it from the boy's father, between 1858 and 1861 when he was piloting on the Mississippi. But neither Davidson nor Branch and Hirst located any record of this particular incident in the press coverage of the Darnell–Watson feud.

27. *a-linkin' after him*. Tailing him.

28. *nip and tuck*. Neck and neck.

29. *so at last Bud seen it warn't any use*. Twain clarified exactly why in his 1895–1896 public reading copy: "so at last Bud hearn the horse so close behind he seen it warn't any use."

30. *There ain't a coward amongst them Shepherdsons—not a one. And there ain't no cowards amongst the Grangerfords, either*. So far the feud has been between equals, fought along the lines of chivalry, however mad its consequences. Buck expresses the flawed Southern thinking at the time. "The two greatest causes of the present lawless society in the South," Marryat argued in Chapter 8 of his 1840 diary, "are a mistaken notion of physical courage, and a total want of moral courage." These misconceptions led to the custom of settling disputes

river bank a piece, and found the two bodies laying in the edge of the water, and tugged at them till I got them ashore; then I covered up their faces, and got away as quick as I could. I cried a little when I was covering up Buck's face, for he was mighty good to me.

It was just dark, now. I never went near the house, but struck through the woods and made for the swamp. Jim warn't on his island, so I tramped off in a hurry for the crick, and crowded through the willows, red-hot to jump aboard and get out of that awful country—the raft was gone! My souls, but I was scared! I couldn't get my breath for most a minute. Then I raised a yell. A voice not twenty-five foot from me, says—

"Good lan'! is dat you, honey? Doan' make no noise."

It was Jim's voice—nothing ever sounded so good before. I run along the bank a piece and got aboard, and Jim he grabbed me and hugged me, he was so glad to see me. He says—

"Laws bless you, chile, I 'uz right down sho' you's dead agin. Jack's been heah, he say he reck'n you's ben shot, kase you didn' come home no mo'; so I's jes' dis minute a startin' de raf' down towards de mouf er de crick, so's to be all ready for to shove out en leave soon as Jack comes agin en tells me for certain you *is* dead. Lawsy, I's mighty glad to git you back agin, honey."

I says—

"All right—that's mighty good; they won't find me, and they'll think I've been killed, and floated down the river[58]—there's something up there that'll help them to think so—so don't you lose no time, Jim, but just shove off for the big water[59] as fast as ever you can."

I never felt easy till the raft was two mile below there and out in the middle of the Mississippi. Then we hung up our signal lantern, and judged that we was free and safe once more. I hadn't had a bite to eat since yesterday; so Jim he got out some corn-dodgers[60] and buttermilk, and pork and cabbage, and greens[61]—there ain't nothing in the world so good, when it's cooked right—and whilst I eat my supper we talked, and had a good time. I was powerful glad to get away from the feuds, and so was Jim to get away from the swamp. We said there warn't no home like a raft, after all. Other places do seem so cramped up and smothery, but a raft don't. You feel mighty free and easy and comfortable on a raft.

through duels and feuds in the antebellum South.

31. *that old man kep' up his end in a fight one day.* Davidson reported in "The Darnell–Watson Feud" (pp. 87–88) that on August 15, 1874, Colonel Darnall got shot in another gunfight near Darnall's Landing, sat down against a tree, and continued shooting back. He survived his wounds, and died of natural causes in his own bed in 1880. But the violence did not end there: His oldest son was killed by a tenant in 1874, the second by marauders in the Civil War, and the last was shot down in front of a post office in 1900.

32. *got behind.* "Backed up agin" in Twain's 1895–1896 public reading copy.

33. *we all went to church. . . . The Shepherdsons done the same.* "Both families belonged to the same church (everybody around there is religious)," Twain quoted his source on the Darnell–Watson feud in Chapter 26 of *Life on the Mississippi*; "through all this fifty or sixty years' fuss, both tribes was there every Sunday, to worship. They lived each side of the line, and the church was at a landing called Compromise. Half the church and half the aisle was in Kentucky, the other half in Tennessee. Sundays you'd see the families drive up, all in their Sunday clothes, men, women, and children, and file up the aisle, and set down, quiet and orderly, one lot on the Tennessee side of the church and the other on the Kentucky side; and the men and the boys would lean their guns up against the wall, handy, and then all hands would join in with prayer and praise; though they say the men next the aisle didn't kneel down, along with the rest of the family; kind of stood guard." But these details may have been Twain's invention, for Branch and Hirst in preparing *The Grangerford–Shepherdson Feud* found no proof that the Darnalls and the Watsons attended the same church (p. 71).

34. *they all talked it over going home.* "And talked it over and talked it over" in Twain's 1895–1896 public reading copy. But evidently it did no good. "The Gospel of Peace is always making a good deal of noise with its mouth," Twain complained on June 22, 1906; "always rejoicing in the progress it is making toward final perfection, and always diligently neglecting to furnish the statistics" ("Reflections on Religion," *Hudson Review*, Autumn 1963, p. 340).

35. *free grace.* The unmerited favor of God in disclosing to an individual the mystery of salvation.

36. *preforeordestination.* Huck has garbled two of the cardinal tenets of Presbyterianism: predestination and foreordination. These principles argue that all things are already planned by God and consequently He has already decided who will receive salvation. One would think that the blood feud would have damned their eternal souls, but being of "the first aristocracy," both the Grangerfords and Shepherdsons believe that they remain among God's elect. The "ornery" preaching only reinforces their immorality and hypocrisy.

37. *a puncheon floor.* "A puncheon floor is made of logs whose upper surfaces have been chopped flat with the adze," Twain explained in 1877. "The cracks between the logs were not filled; there was no carpet; consequently if you dropped anything smaller than a peach, it was likely to go through" (Blair and Fischer, University of California edition, 1988, p. 406). The Grangerford–Shepherdson church is the one Twain knew near his uncle John A. Quarles's farm, near Florida, Missouri, "perched upon short sections of logs, which elevated it two or three feet above ground. Hogs slept under there; and whenever the dogs got after them during services, the minister had to wait till the disturbance was over."

38. *most folks don't go to church only when they've got to; but a hog is different.* Considering how much the "ornery" sermon on brotherly love has affected the Grangerfords and their neighbors the Shepherdsons, one must agree with Huck's observation that the hogs get more out of the church than the congregation does.

39. *give me a squeeze.* Originally Twain had Sophia Grangerford "kiss me right on the mouth" (**MS**), apparently the boy's first kiss; but that is far too brazen for a young lady living in this place at this time, so he changed it to the more neutral but no less appreciative "squeeze." "I was reared in that atmosphere of reserve," Twain revealed in "Chapters from My Autobiography" (*North American Review*, October 5, 1906). "I never knew a member of my father's family to kiss another member of it except once, and that at a death-bed. And our village was not a kissing community. The kissing and caressing ended with courtship—along with the deadly piano-playing of that day" (p. 558).

40. *coarse-hand.* Block letters, printing.

41. *water-moccasins.* A species of venomous crotaline snake, native to the South.

42. *dey tuck me en showed me dis place.* There was enormous kinship among American slaves before the Civil War. "It is sometimes said that we slaves do not love and confide in each other," wrote Frederick Douglass in Chapter 10 of his *Narrative*. "In answer to this assertion, I can say, I never loved any or confided in any people more than my fellow-slaves. . . . I believe that we would have died for each other. We never undertook to do any thing, of any importance, without a mutual consultation. We never moved separately. We were one; and as much so by our tempers and dispositions, as by the mutual hardships to which we were necessarily subjected by our condition as slaves."

43. *Jack.* Branch and Hirst suggested in *The Grangerford–Shepherdson Feud* (p. 78) that Twain turned Jack, the "bad negro in our midst" of the 1859 Darnall–Watson clash, into Jack, the "good nigger," who brings Huck to Jim.

44. *I ben a-buyin' pots en pans en vittles.* "So Jim, with the assistance of the slave community, has been busy observing, orchestrating, and rebuilding their means of escape," noted Jocelyn Chadwick-Joshua in *The Jim Dilemma* (1998, p. 88). Although it is not indicated in the text, Huck apparently has enough respect for Jim to share some of the money they have gathered on the river, either the $8 found in the blanket overcoat in Chapter 10 or the gold from the slave hunters in Chapter 16. And he can be trusted to spend it wisely on necessities for their flight from "sivilization."

45. *our old raft warn't smashed all to flinders.* Twain had hit a snag in his plot when the steamboat rammed into the raft at the end of Chapter 16. How could Huck escape the Grangerford–Shepherdson feud and link up with Jim for more adventures if their sole means of transport was destroyed? Twain had no idea where his story was heading. While the actual course of the Mississippi determined the direction and certain events of the novel, the author was relying on improvisation in its composition. Then it hit him: "Back a little, *change*—raft only *crippled* by steamer" (Blair and Fischer, University of California edition, 1988, p. 730). With this ready means of escape now repaired and hidden by Jim in the creek among the willows, the story can continue.

46. *jawin'*. Quarreling.

47. *If anything happens,* he *ain't mixed up in it.* For self-preservation, the Southern slave like Huck's Jack was often a master of justifiable deception. "But I never see a nigger that *wouldn't* lie," Tom crudely reminds Huck in Chapter 6 of *Tom Sawyer*. When his wife asks why there did not seem to be any honest slaves, Augustine St. Clare, himself a slave owner, replies in Chapter 18 of *Uncle Tom's Cabin*, "From the mother's breast the colored child feels and sees that there are none but underhand ways open to it. It can get along no other way with its parents, its mistress, its young master and missie playfellows. Cunning and deception become necessary, inevitable habits. It isn't fair to expect anything else of him. He ought not to be punished for it. As to honesty, the slave is kept in the dependent, semi-childish state, that there is no making him realize the rights of property, or feel that his master's goods are not his own, if he can get them. For my part, I don't see how they can be honest." Frederick Douglass said in Chapter 3 of his *Narrative* that a common maxim among slaves was "a still tongue makes a wise head." He explained, "They suppress the truth rather than take the consequences of telling it." See also Chapter 26, note 15.

48. *I don't want to talk much about the next day.* "Well, one day—but I don't want to talk much about *that* day" in Twain's 1895–1896 public reading copy.

49. *Miss Sophia's run off . . . to git married to dat young Harney Shepherdson.* This backwoods version of Romeo and Juliet may have been suggested by the romance between the sweet younger daughter Kate Beaumont and Frank McAlister, members of feuding families in De Forest's *Kate Beaumont.* The fate of the fictitious sister of "George Jackson" in Chapter 17 may also have inspired this development; and Twain used this plot device in the unfinished "Simon Wheeler, Detective" (1877–1878), where Hale Dexter falls in love with Clara Burnside. According to Sykes, "A Source for Mark Twain's Feud" (p. 197), Roseanna McCoy ran off with a Hatfield, resulting in some of the worst bloodshed in the feud's fifty-year history. See also Chapter 21 for a burlesque of *Romeo and Juliet.*

50. *he kin git acrost de river wid Miss Sophia.* They will be safe in Missouri.

51. *as hard as I could put.* As fast as I could run.

52. *By-and-by I begin to hear guns a good ways off.* The climax of the Grangerford–Shepherdson feud too comes from the Darnell–Watson vendetta. Twain's secretary recorded the writer's saying: "I was on a Memphis packet and at a landing we made on the Kentucky side there was a row. Don't remember as there was anybody hurt then; but shortly afterwards there was another row at that place and a youth of 19 belonging to the Missouri tribe had wandered over there. Half a dozen of that Kentucky tribe got after him. He dodged among the wood piles and answered their shots. Presently he jumped into the river and they followed on after and peppered him and he had to make for the shore. By that time he was about dead—did shortly die" (Branch and Hirst, *The Grangerford–Shepherdson Feud*, 1985, p. 41).

Twain's riverboat companion gives a slightly different account in Chapter 26 of *Life on the Mississippi*; he cannot recall whether it concerned the Darnells and the Watsons, or possibly two other families. "Years ago," he says, "the Darnells was so thinned out that the old man and his two sons concluded they'd leave the country . . . ; but the Watsons got wind of it; and they arrived just as the two young Darnells was walking up the companion-way with their wives on their arms. The fight begun then, and they never got no further—both of them killed. After that, old Darnell got into trouble with the man that run the ferry, and the ferryman got the worst of it—and died. But his friends shot old Darnell through and through—filled him full of bullets, and ended him."

53. *wood-rank.* Stack of firewood.

54. *squatting.* "Stooping" in Twain's 1895–1896 public reading copy.

The Darnell–Watson feud. Illustration by A. B. Shute, *Life on the Mississippi*, 1883. *Private collection.*

55. *had the bulge*. Had the advantage, said to be mining slang.

56. *One of the boys was Buck, and the other was a slim young chap about nineteen years old*. "Twenty or twenty-five years ago," Twain's companion relates in Chapter 26 of *Life on the Mississippi*, "one of the feud families caught a young man of nineteen out and killed him. Don't remember whether it was the Darnells or Watsons, or one of the other feuds; but, anyway, this young man rode up—steamboat laying there at the time—and the first thing he saw was a whole gang of the enemy. He jumped down behind a wood-pile, but they rode around and begun on him, he firing back, and they galloping and cavorting and yelling and banging away with all their might. Think he wounded a couple of them; but they closed in on him and chased him into the river; and as he swum along down stream, they followed along the bank and kept on shooting at him; and when he struck shore he was dead." Twain said the source for this story was Captain John H. "Windy" Marshall, master of the mail-boat *John H. Dickey*, which often passed that way on the river. The Memphis *Daily Appeal* (September 6, 1859) reported that on September 4, words were exchanged between Schultz, Starr, and Beckham at Compromise Landing and a gunfight broke out; Beckham and Starr pursued the young man as he tried to escape in the river, and they shot him from the shore. The paper concluded that the tragedy "grew out of a dispute between Henry M. Darnall and A. F. Beckham in reference to certain outrages alleged to have been perpetrated by a negro belonging to Mr. Beckham."

57. *to get shut of*. To get rid of, to forget.

58. *they'll think I've been killed, and floated down the river*. Another of Huck's "deaths," here "George Jackson."

59. *the big water*. The Mississippi River, from the supposed Indian name.

60. *corn-dodgers*. Cornmeal cakes, baked until hard.

61. *greens*. Vegetables, usually boiled; often dandelion or beet leaves, or spinach.

Chapter XIX

HIDING DAY-TIMES.

Two or three days and nights went by; I reckon I might say they swum by, they slid along so quiet and smooth and lovely. Here is the way we put in the time.[1] It was a monstrous big river down there—sometimes a mile and a half wide; we run nights, and laid up and hid day-times; soon as night was most gone, we stopped navigating and tied up—nearly always in the dead water under a tow-head; and then cut young cotton-woods and willows and hid the raft with them. Then we set out the lines. Next we slid into the river and had a swim, so as to freshen up and cool off; then we set down on the sandy bottom where the water was about knee deep, and watched the daylight come. Not a sound, anywheres—perfectly still—just like the whole world was asleep, only sometimes the bull-frogs a-cluttering, maybe. The first thing to see,[2] looking away over the water, was a kind of dull line—that was the woods on t'other side—you couldn't make nothing else out; then a pale place in the sky; then more paleness, spreading around; then the river softened up, away off, and warn't black any more, but gray; you could see little dark spots drifting along, ever so far away—trading scows, and such things; and long black streaks—

1. *Here is the way we put in the time.* Here begins one of the most famous passages in *Huckleberry Finn*, the finest of the boy's descriptions of the beauty and power of Nature as observed along the journey down the river. What Thomas Wolfe found most memorable in his fellow Southerner's fiction was "how that huge river moves itself—not like a shining golden serpent of the day—but how it drinks from our continent—moves forever like a mighty, dark and secret river of the night" (quoted in Elizabeth Evans, "Thomas Wolfe: Some Echoes from Mark Twain," *Mark Twain Journal*, Summer 1976, p. 5).

Twain composed an early draft of this reverie in a letter to a twelve-year-old boy. David "Wattie" Bowser had written on March 16, 1880, in response to a school project "to select some man among the living great ones . . . with whom we would exchange place." "A few of us boys thought it would be a 'lark' to send our compositions to our favorites," he explained, "and ask them if they would be willing to change with us, and if their fame, riches, honors, and glory had made them perfectly happy—in fact ask them if they would be 'a boy again.'" Just the suggestion "to be a boy again" sent Twain into a rapturously nostalgic mood. He said he longed to be a "cub pilot" along the Mississippi again. "Summer always," he wrote; "the magnolias at Rifle Point always in bloom, so that the dreamy twilight should have the added charm of their perfume; the oleanders on the 'coast' always in bloom, likewise; the sugar cane always green . . . ; the river always bankful, so we could run all the chutes . . . ; we should see the thick banks of young willows dipping their leaves into the currentless water, and we could thrash right along against them without any danger of hurting anything; . . . and I would have the trips long, and the stays in port short" (quoted in Pascal Covici, Jr., "Dear Master Wattie," *Southwest Review*, Spring 1960, pp. 107–8).

To fully appreciate the flexibility and majesty of Huck Finn's voice, one need only compare this passage to similar ones in Twain's other writings. Chapter 14 of *Tom Sawyer* opens with another morning on the Mississippi, as Tom awakens on Jackson's Island:

> It was the cool gray dawn, and there was a delicious sense of repose and peace in the deep pervading calm and silence of the woods. Not a leaf stirred; not a sound obtruded upon great Nature's meditation. Beaded dew-drops stood upon the leaves and grasses. . . . Now, far away in the woods a bird called; another answered; presently the hammering of a woodpecker was heard. Gradually the cool dim gray of the morning whitened, and as gradually sounds multiplied and life manifested itself. The marvel of Nature shaking off sleep and going to work unfolded itself to the musing boy. . . . The birds were fairly rioting by this time. A cat-bird, the northern mocker, lit in a tree over Tom's head, and trilled out her imitations of her neighbors in a rapture of enjoyment; then a shrill jay swept down, a flash of blue flame, and stopped on a twig almost within the boy's reach, cocked his head to one side and eyed the stranger with a consuming curiosity; a gray squirrel and a big fellow of the "fox" kind came scurrying along, sitting up at intervals to inspect and chatter at the boys, for the wild things had probably never seen a human being before and scarcely knew whether to be afraid or not. All Nature was wide awake and stirring, now; long lances of sunlight pierced down through the dense foliage far and near, and a few butterflies came fluttering upon the scene.

But this is Sam Clemens speaking, not Huck Finn. Leaves "stir," sounds "obtrude," "long lances of sunlight pierced down through the dense foliage far and near." Consider another sunrise on the Mississippi on board the steamer *Gold Dust* in a letter to Olivia Clemens, April 25, 1882:

> There was a just a faint whitish suggestion in the east—the rest of the sky and the great river were wrapped in a sombre gloom. It was fascinating to see the day steal gradually upon

rafts; sometimes you could hear a sweep screaking;[3] or jumbled up voices, it was so still, and sounds come so far; and by-and-by you could see a streak on the water which you know by the look of the streak that there's a snag there in a swift current which breaks on it and makes that streak look that way; and you see the mist curl up off of the water,[4] and the east reddens up, and the river, and you make out a log cabin in the edge of the woods, away on the bank on t'other side of the river, being a wood-yard, likely, and piled by them cheats so you can throw a dog through it anywheres;[5] then the nice breeze springs up, and comes fanning you from over there, so cool and fresh, and sweet to smell, on account of the woods and the flowers; but sometimes not that way, because they've left dead fish laying around, gars, and such, and they do get pretty rank;[6] and next you've got the full day, and everything smiling in the sun, and the song-birds just going it!

A little smoke couldn't be noticed, now, so we would take some fish off of the lines, and cook up a hot breakfast. And afterwards we would watch the lonesomeness of the river, and kind of lazy along, and by-and-by lazy off to sleep.[7] Wake up, by-and-by, and look to see what done it, and maybe see a steamboat, coughing along up stream, so far off towards the other side you couldn't tell nothing about her only whether she was stern-wheel or side-wheel;[8] then for about an hour there wouldn't be nothing to hear nor nothing to see—just solid lonesomeness.[9] Next you'd see a raft sliding by, away off yonder, and maybe a galoot[10] on it chopping, because they're most always doing it on a raft; you'd see the ax flash, and come down—you don't hear nothing; you see that ax go up again, and by the time it's above the man's head, then you hear the *k'chunk!*[11]—it had took all that time to come over the water.[12] So we would put in the day, lazying around, listening to the stillness. Once there was a thick fog, and the rafts and things that went by was beating tin pans so the steamboats wouldn't run over them. A scow or a raft went by so close we could hear them talking and cussing[13] and laughing—heard them plain;[14] but we couldn't see no sign of them; it made you feel crawly, it was like spirits carrying on that way in the air.[15] Jim said he believed it was spirits; but I says:

"No, spirits wouldn't say, 'dern the dern fog.' "

Soon as it was night, out we shoved; when we got her out to about the middle, we let her alone, and let her float wherever the current wanted her to; then we lit the pipes, and dangled our legs in the water and talked about all kinds of things—we was always naked, day and night,[16] whenever the mosquitoes would let us—the new clothes Buck's folks made for me was too good to be comfortable, and besides I didn't go much on clothes, nohow.

Sometimes we'd have that whole river all to ourselves for the longest time. Yonder was the banks and the islands, across the water; and maybe a spark—which was a candle in a cabin window—and sometimes on the water you could see a spark or two—on a raft or a scow, you know; and maybe you could hear a fiddle or a song coming over from one of them crafts. It's lovely to live on a raft. We had the sky, up there, all speckled with stars, and we used to lay on our backs and look up at them, and discuss about whether they was made, or only just happened—Jim he allowed they was made, but I allowed they happened; I judged it would have took too long to *make* so many. Jim said the moon could a *laid* them; well, that looked kind of reasonable, so I didn't say nothing against it, because I've seen a frog lay most as many, so of course it could be done. We used to watch the stars that fell, too, and see them streak down. Jim allowed they'd got spoiled and was hove out of the nest.

Once or twice of a night we would see a steamboat slipping along in the dark, and now and then she would belch a whole world of sparks up out of her chimbleys, and they would rain down in the river and look awful pretty; then she would turn a corner and her lights would wink out and her pow-wow shut off and leave the river still again; and by-and-by her waves would get to us, a long time after she was gone, and joggle the raft a bit, and after that you wouldn't hear nothing for you couldn't tell how long, except maybe frogs or something.

> this vast silent world; and when the edge of the shorn sun pushed itself above the line of the forest, the marvels of shifting light and shade and color and dappled reflections, that followed, were bewitching to see. And the luxurious green walls of forest! and the jutting leafy capes! and the paling green of the far stretches! and the remote, shadowy, vanishing distances, away down the glistening highway under the horizon! *and* the riot of the singing birds!—it was all worth getting up for, I tell you. (*The Love Letters of Mark Twain*, 1949, p. 210)

Twain felicitously lards the language of this "scenery letter" with all the clichés of the guidebooks and *Tom Sawyer*: "sombre" instead of "somber," "the marvels of . . . dappled reflections . . . bewitching to see," "the riot of the singing birds." He made further use of a sunrise in Chapter 9 of *Life on the Mississippi*:

> A broad expanse of the river was turned to blood; in the middle distance the red hue brightened into gold, through which a solitary log came floating, black and conspicuous; in one place a long, slanting mark lay sparkling upon the water; in another the surface was broken by boiling, tumbling rings, that were as many-tinted as an opal; where the ruddy flush was faintest, was a smooth spot that was covered with graceful circles and radiating lines, ever so delicately traced; the shore on our left was densely wooded, and the sombre shadow that fell from this forest was broken in one place by a long, ruffled trail that shone like silver; and high above the forest wall a clean-stemmed dead tree waved a single leafy bough that glowed like a flame in the unobstructed splendor that was flowing from the sun. There were graceful curves, reflected images, woody heights, soft distances; and over the whole scene, far and near, the dissolving lights drifted steadily, enriching it, every passing moment, with new marvels of coloring.

The unexpected boldness of that first phrase ("A broad expanse of the river was turned to blood"), almost worthy of Stephen Crane, regresses into convention and cliché. While its style has its virtues, it still lacks the resonance of Huck's distinct voice. "When Mark Twain tried to write in a literary manner he produced, as in *Life on the Mississippi*, but indifferent journalese," W. Somerset Maugham complained in "The Classic Books of America" (*Saturday Evening Post*, January 6, 1940), "but in *Huckleberry Finn* he had the happy idea of writing in the person of his immortal hero and so produced a model of the vernacular style which has served as a foundation for some of the best and most characteristic writers of the present day. He showed them that a living manner of writing is not to be sought in the seventeenth and eighteenth century writers of England, but in the current speech of their own people" (p. 66).

Only in *Huckleberry Finn* does Twain's style reach great literary art. "Twain, at least in *Huckleberry Finn*," T. S. Eliot insisted in "American Literature and the American Language" (*Sewanee Review*, Winter 1965/1966), "reveals himself to be one of those writers, of whom there are not a great many in any literature, who have discovered a new way of writing, valid not only for themselves but for others. I should place him, in this respect, even with Dryden and Swift, as one of those rare writers who have brought their language up to date, and in so doing, 'purified the dialect of the tribe' " (p. 13). Through his careful selection of anxious, active vernacular expressions, the river emerges as a living force regardless of the vain attempts of men to tame it. "Nothing is fixed, absolute or perfect," Leo Marx observed in "The Pilot and the Passenger: Landscape Conventions and the Style of *Huckleberry Finn*" (*American Literature*, May 1956). "The passage gains immensely in verisimilitude from [Huck's] repeated approximations: 'soon as the night was *most* gone,' '*nearly always* in the dead water,' 'a *kind* of dull line,' '*sometimes* you can hear.' . . . Nature too is in process: 'the daylight *come*,' 'paleness, *spreading* around,' 'river *softened* up,' 'mist *curl* up,' 'east *reddens* up' . . . " (p. 139). "As with Conrad," Eliot wrote in his introduction to the 1950 Cresset/Chanticleer edition of *Huckleberry Finn*, "we were continually reminded of the power and terror of Nature, and the isolation and feebleness of Man." The Mississippi is the great American god whose only sin is its indifference. "The Book of Nature," Twain observed, "tells us distinctly that God cares not a rap for us—nor for any living creature. It tells us that His laws inflict pain and suffering and sorrow, but it does not say that this is done in order that He may get pleasure out of this misery" (*Mark Twain's Notebook*, 1935, p. 360).

But is Nature so terrible? Surely this passage serves as an idyllic interlude between the bru-

After midnight the people on shore went to bed, and then for two or three hours the shores was black—no more sparks in the cabin windows. These sparks was our clock—the first one that showed again meant morning was coming, so we hunted a place to hide and tie up, right away.

One morning about day-break, I found a canoe[17] and crossed over a chute[18] to the main shore—it was only two hundred yards—and paddled about a mile up a crick amongst the cypress woods, to see if I couldn't get some berries. Just as I was passing a place where a kind of a cow-path crossed the crick, here comes a couple of men tearing up the path as tight as they could foot it. I thought I was a goner, for whenever anybody was after anybody I judged it

"AND DOGS A-COMING."

was *me*—or maybe Jim. I was about to dig out from there in a hurry, but they was pretty close to me then, and sung out and begged me to save their lives—said they hadn't been doing nothing, and was being chased for it—said there was men and dogs a-coming. They wanted to jump right in, but I says—

"Don't you do it. I don't hear the dogs and horses yet; you've got time to crowd through the brush and get up the crick a little ways; then you take to the water and wade down to me and get in—that'll throw the dogs off the scent."

They done it, and soon as they was aboard I lit out for our tow-head, and in about five or ten minutes we heard the dogs and the men away off, shouting. We heard them come along towards the crick, but couldn't see them; they seemed to stop and fool around a while; then, as we got further and further away all the time, we couldn't hardly hear them at all; by the time we had left a mile of woods behind us and struck the river, everything was quiet, and we paddled over to the tow-head and hid in the cotton-woods and was safe.

One of these fellows[19] was about seventy, or upwards,[20] and had a bald head and very gray whiskers. He had an old battered-up slouch hat on, and a greasy blue woolen shirt, and ragged old blue jeans britches stuffed into his boot tops, and home-knit galluses—no, he only had one.[21] He had an old long-tailed blue jeans coat with slick brass buttons, flung over his arm, and both of them had big fat ratty-looking carpet-bags.[22]

The other fellow was about thirty and dressed about as ornery. After breakfast we all laid off and talked, and the first thing that come out was that these chaps didn't know one another.

"What got you into trouble?" says the baldhead to t'other chap.

"Well, I'd been selling an article to take the tartar off the teeth[23]—and it does take it off, too, and generly the enamel along with it—but I staid about one night longer than I ought to, and was just in the act of sliding out when I ran across you on the trail this side of town, and you told me they were coming, and begged me to help you to get off. So I told you I was expecting trouble myself and would scatter out *with* you. That's the whole yarn—what's yourn?"

"Well, I'd ben a-runnin' a little temperance revival[24] thar, 'bout a week, and was the pet of the women-folks, big and little, for I was makin' it mighty warm for the rummies, I *tell* you, and takin' as much as five or six dollars a night—ten cents a head, children and niggers free[25]—and busi-

talities committed in the Grangerford–Shepherdson feud and the introduction of those two scoundrels the duke and the king. The trouble lies not with Nature but with Man. The boy explores all five senses: sight (pale landscape); sound (bullfrogs' cluttering); smell (fragrant breezes); taste (fish breakfast); and touch (swimming nude). Man need only enjoy and stop fighting the river to discover its wonders. But those on the land cannot be bothered. They are too busy cheating their customers or killing gars or swearing to share Huck and Jim's communion with the Mississippi. Never on the raft are Huck and Jim entirely free of the threat of "sivilization." It lurks around every bend in the river. So long as the fugitives stay on water and away from land they are safe; they need not leave Eden.

2. *The first thing to see.* Notice the deft and dexterous unraveling of this long single run-on sentence which takes up most of this paragraph and nearly goes on for a page in the first edition as Huck's thoughts flow like the mighty Mississippi itself, each observation running effortlessly into the next. The river reveals its secrets as Huck reads the "signs" as expertly as young Sam Clemens did when he studied his trade on a steamboat. Twain explains its meaning in more mundane terms in Chapter 9 of *Life on the Mississippi*:

> This sun means that we are going to have a wind tomorrow; that floating log means that the river is rising, small thanks to it; that slanting mark on the river refers to a bluff reef which is going to kill somebody's steamboat one of these nights, if it keeps on stretching out like that; those tumbling 'boils" show a dissolving bar and a changing channel there; the lines and circles in the slick water over yonder are a warning that that troublesome place is shoaling up dangerously; that silver streak in the shadow of the first is the "break" from a new snag, and he has located himself in the very best place he could have found to fish for steamboats; that tall dead tree, with a single living branch, is not going to last long, and then how is a body going to get through this blind place at night without the friendly old landmark?

The river was losing its magic for the young cub pilot the more he learned how to "read" it. "All the value any feature of it had for me," he lamented in *Life on the Mississippi*, "now was the amount of usefulness it could furnish toward compassing the safe piloting of a steamboat." Nothing more, nothing less. Here was evidence the boy was growing up.

3. *screaking*. The sound of the oar's ungreased hinge or axle.

4. *you see the mist curl up off of the water*. Twain wisely revised the more self-consciously poetic "you would see the lightest and whitest mist curling up from the water" (**MS**).

5. *piled by them cheats so you can throw a dog through it anywheres*. "The yard's customers were cheated because stacks of wood were sold by volume, gaps included," explained the editors of the Norton Critical Edition.

6. *but sometimes not that way, because they've left dead fish laying around, gars, and such, and they do get pretty rank*. This phrase was an afterthought, inserted sometime between the manuscript and the finished book. "Gars" are large hard-scaled fish with sharp teeth and are generally considered inedible; fishermen kill them because they eat up the other fish. Because these pests cannot be eaten, men have left them lying about to rot in the sun. This is the one discordant detail of Huck's long litany on the beauty of the life on the river. The entrance of "sivilization" corrupts this American Eden. "Of the entire brood," Twain observed in "The Character of Man" of 1890, Man "is the only one—the solitary one—that possesses malice. That is the basest of all instincts, passions, vices—the most hateful. That one thing puts him below the rats, the grubs, the trichenae. He is the only creature that inflicts pain for sport, knowing it to *be* pain. . . . *all* creatures kill—there seems to be no exception; but of the whole list, man is the only one that kills for fun; he is the only one that kills in malice, the only one that kills for revenge" (*What Is Man?*, 1973, p. 60).

7. *And afterwards we would watch the lonesomeness of the river, and kind of lazy along, and by-and-by lazy off to sleep*. An improvement over the original "After we had had a smoke, we would watch the awful lonesomeness of the river, and kind of dream along, and be happy, not talking much, and by-and-by nod off to sleep" (**MS**). Having not yet entirely freed him-

ness a growin' all the time; when somehow or another a little report got around, last night, that I had a way of puttin' in my time with a private jug, on the sly. A nigger rousted me out this mornin',[26] and told me the people was getherin' on the quiet, with their dogs and horses, and they'd be along pretty soon and give me 'bout half an hour's start, and then run me down, if they could; and if they got me they'd tar and feather me and ride me on a rail,[27] sure. I didn't wait for no breakfast—I warn't hungry."

"Old man," says the young one, "I reckon we might double-team it[28] together; what do you think?"

"I ain't undisposed. What's your line—mainly?"[29]

"Jour printer,[30] by trade; do a little in patent medicines;[31] theatre-actor[32]—tragedy, you know; take a turn at mesmerism[33] and phrenology[34] when there's a chance; teach singing-geography school[35] for a change; sling a lecture,[36] sometimes—oh, I do lots of things—most anything that comes handy, so it ain't work. What's your lay?"[37]

"I've done considerable in the doctoring way[38] in my time. Layin' on o' hands[39] is my best holt[40]—for cancer, and paralysis, and sich things; and I k'n tell a fortune pretty good, when I've got somebody along to find out the facts for me.[41] Preachin's my line, too; and workin' camp-meetin's; and missionaryin' around."[42]

Nobody never said anything for a while; then the young man hove a sigh and says—

"Alas!"

"What 're you alassin' about?" says the baldhead.

"To think I should have lived to be leading such a life, and be degraded down into such company." And he begun to wipe the corner of his eye with a rag.

"Dern your skin, ain't the company good enough for you?" says the baldhead, pretty pert and uppish.

"Yes, it *is* good enough for me; it's as good as I deserve; for who fetched me so low, when I was so high? *I* did myself. I don't blame *you*, gentlemen—far from it; I don't blame anybody. I deserve it all. Let the cold world do its worst; one thing I know—there's a grave somewhere for me. The world may go on just as it's always done, and take everything from

"BY RIGHTS I AM A DUKE!"

me—loved ones, property, everything—but it can't take that. Some day I'll lie down in it and forget it all, and my poor broken heart will be at rest." He went on a-wiping.

"Drot your pore broken heart," says the baldhead; "what are you heaving your pore broken heart at *us* f'r? *We* hain't done nothing."

"No, I know you haven't. I ain't blaming you, gentlemen. I brought myself down—yes, I did it myself. It's right I should suffer—perfectly right—I don't make any moan."

"Brought you down from whar? Whar was you brought down from?"

"Ah, you would not believe me; the world never believes—let it pass—'tis no matter. The secret of my birth—"

"The secret of your birth? Do you mean to say—"

"Gentlemen," says the young man, very solemn, "I will reveal it to you, for I feel I may have confidence in you. By rights I am a duke!"[43]

Jim's eyes bugged out when he heard that; and I reckon mine did, too. Then the baldhead says: "No! you can't mean it?"

self from the idiom of the earlier books, Twain had to make extensive revisions of this paragraph to make it sound more like Huck Finn.

8. *stern-wheel or side-wheel.* The shallow waters of the Mississippi were navigated by small steamboats with the wheel in the rear rather

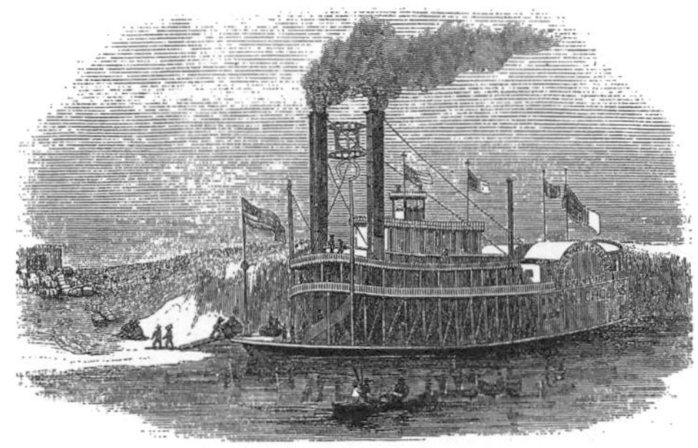

A stern-wheel steamboat.
Courtesy Picture Collection, New York Public Library, Astor, Lenox, and Tilden Foundations.

than at the sides as with the larger ships. The preference of one make over the other was based solely on tradition and not on practical technology; stern-wheelers were cheaper to build and cheaper to run, and yet they were less desirable and used primarily for transporting freight instead of passengers. They did not have as much "show" or style as the bigger, fancier side-wheelers.

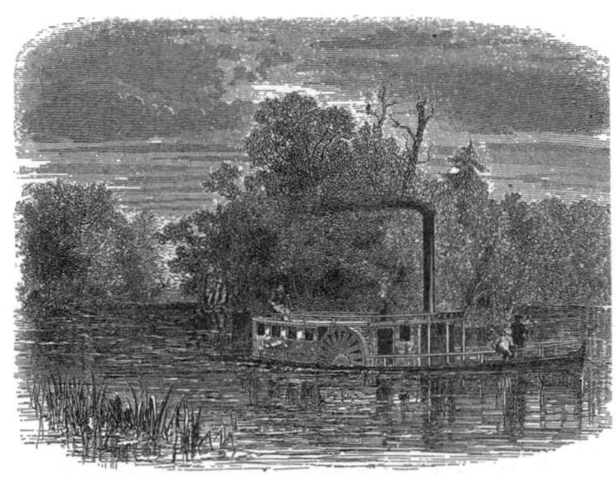

A side-wheel steamboat.
Courtesy Picture Collection, New York Public Library, Astor, Lenox, and Tilden Foundations.

"Yes. My great-grandfather, eldest son of the Duke of Bridgewater,[44] fled to this country about the end of the last century, to breathe the pure air of freedom; married here, and died, leaving a son, his own father dying about the same time. The second son of the late duke seized the title and estates—the infant real duke was ignored. I am the lineal descendant of that infant—I am the rightful Duke of Bridgewater; and here am I, forlorn, torn from my high estate, hunted of men, despised by the cold world, ragged, worn, heart-broken, and degraded to the companionship of felons on a raft!"

Jim pitied him ever so much, and so did I. We tried to comfort him, but he said it warn't much use, he couldn't be much comforted; said if we was a mind to acknowledge him, that would do him more good than most anything else; so we said we would, if he would tell us how. He said we ought to bow, when we spoke to him, and say "Your Grace," or "My Lord," or "Your Lordship"—and he wouldn't mind it if we called him plain "Bridgewater," which he said was a title, anyway, and not a name; and one of us ought to wait on him at dinner, and do any little thing for him he wanted done.

Well, that was all easy, so we done it. All through dinner Jim stood around and waited on him, and says, "Will yo' Grace have some o' dis, or some o' dat?" and so on, and a body could see it was mighty pleasing to him.

But the old man got pretty silent, by-and-by—didn't have much to say, and didn't look pretty comfortable over all that petting that was going on around that duke. He seemed to have something on his mind. So, along in the afternoon, he says:

"Looky here, Bilgewater,"[45] he says, "I'm nation sorry[46] for you, but you ain't the only person that's had troubles like that."

"No?"

"No, you ain't. You ain't the only person that's ben snaked down[47] wrongfully out'n a high place."

"Alas!"

"No, you ain't the only person that's had a secret of his birth." And by jings, *he* begins to cry.

9. *you couldn't tell nothing about her only whether she was stern-wheel or side-wheel; then for about an hour there wouldn't be nothing to hear nor nothing to see—just solid lonesomeness.* Originally "that she didn't seem to belong to this world at all, hardly; then for about an hour there wouldn't be a sound on the water, nor a solitary moving thing, as far as you could see—just solid Sunday and lonesomeness" (**MS**), but it had to be revised because it still sounded more like Sam Clemens ("solitary moving things") than Huckleberry Finn.

10. *a galoot.* Merely "a man" (**MS**) in the manuscript. "Galoot" may refer to an awkward uncouth person today; but Huck uses an earlier meaning, that of a young, unfledged sailor, a novice, usually given the menial work on a vessel.

11. *you don't hear nothing; you see that ax go up again, and by the time it's above the man's head, then you hear the* k'chunk! The original read "nary a sound any more than if it had sunk into butter; you'd see that ax go up again, and by the time it was above the man's head, then you'd hear the sound, sharp and clear" (**MS**); but Huck would never say "nary" and the rest sounds too much like that passage from *Life on the Mississippi*.

12. *it had took all that time to come over the water.* An acoustic mirage: The sound was actually made when the ax struck the wood; but because light travels faster than sound, it only seems that the "k'chunk" took a long time for Huck to hear it.

13. *and cussing.* An afterthought, not in the manuscript.

14. *heard them plain.* "As if they had been only five steps off" (**MS**) Twain explained in the manuscript.

15. *it made you feel crawly, it was like spirits carrying on that way in the air.* This does sound more like a backwoods boy than the original passage in the manuscript, "it was so like ghosts or spirits talking and laughing in the air; and the voices drifted off and faded out, just like the same as if they had been on the wing" (**MS**). Emmeline Grangerford might have said "on the wing," but never Huck Finn.

"Hold! What do you mean?"

"Bilgewater, kin I trust you?" says the old man, still sort of sobbing.

"To the bitter death!" He took the old man by the hand and squeezed it, and says, "The secret of your being: speak!"

"Bilgewater, I am the late Dauphin!"[48]

You bet you Jim and me stared, this time. Then the duke says:

"You are what?"

"Yes, my friend, it is too true—your eyes is lookin' at this very moment on the pore disappeared Dauphin, Looy the Seventeen, son of Looy the Sixteen and Marry Antonette."

"You! At your age![49] No! You mean you're the late Charlemagne;[50] you must be six or seven hundred years old, at the very least."

"Trouble has done it, Bilgewater, trouble has done it; trouble has brung these gray hairs and this premature balditude.[51] Yes, gentlemen, you see before you, in blue jeans and misery, the wanderin', exiled, trampled-on and sufferin' rightful King of France."

Well, he cried and took on so, that me and Jim didn't know hardly what to do, we was so sorry—and so glad and proud we'd got him with us, too. So we set in, like we done before with the duke, and tried to comfort *him.* But he said it warn't no use, nothing but to be dead and done with it all could do him any good; though he said it often made him feel easier and better for a while if people treated him according to his rights, and got down on one knee to speak to him, and always called him "Your Majesty," and waited on him first at meals, and didn't set down in his presence till he asked them.[52] So Jim and me set to majestying him, and doing this and that and t'other for him, and standing up till he told us we might set down. This done him heaps of good, and so he got cheerful and comfortable. But the duke kind of soured on him, and didn't look a bit satisfied with the way things was going; still, the king acted real friendly towards him, and said the duke's great-grandfather and all the other Dukes of Bilgewater was a good deal thought of by *his* father and was allowed to come to the palace consid-

16. *we was always naked, day and night.* "Criticism is a queer thing," Twain wrote, considering the conventions of nineteenth-century prudery in 1879, when he was working on this part of the novel. "If I print 'she was stark naked' and then proceed to describe her person in detail, what critic would not howl? Who would venture to leave the book on a parlor table? But the artist does this, and all ages gather around and look and talk and point. I can't say, 'They cut his head off, or stabbed him, etc.,' describe the blood and agony in his face" (*Mark Twain's Notebook*, 1935, p. 153). But this double standard for what was considered "decent" in contemporary art and literature took varying shapes: Victorian propriety forbade Kemble from depicting this detail of Twain's text in his illustrations; likewise Richard Watson Gilder dropped even the *mention* of Huck and Jim's being naked on the river in the excerpt "Royalty on the Mississippi: As Chronicled by Huckleberry Finn" (*Century Magazine*, February 1885). It may have been at Twain's (or Webster's) suggestion that Kemble

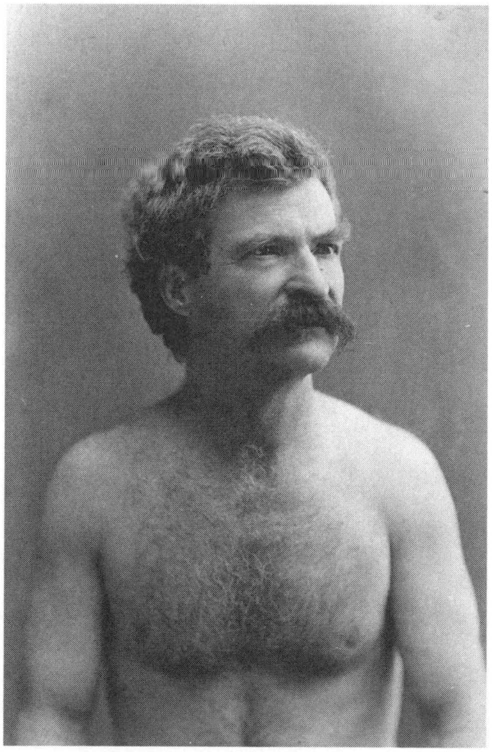

Mark Twain, circa 1883.
Courtesy Mark Twain Papers, Bancroft Library, University of California at Berkeley.

not depict them nude; and yet True W. Williams drew Huck, Tom, and Joe Harper skinny-dipping on Jackson's Island in Chapter 14 of *Tom Sawyer*, and John Harley showed Huck naked in his pictures for the "Raft Episode" in Chapter 3 of *Life on the Mississippi*, as A. B. Shute showed the Hannibal boys swimming in Chapter 54 of *Life on the Mississippi*.

Privately Twain expressed no sympathy for this moral hypocrisy. "The convention miscalled Modesty has no standard," he complained in "Letters to the Earth" of 1909, "and cannot have one, because, it is opposed to nature and reason, and is therefore an artificiality and subject to anybody's whim, anybody's diseased caprice" (*What Is Man?*, 1973, p. 417). Huck speaks for the author when he says in Chapter 8 of *Tom Sawyer Abroad*, "Clothes is well enough in school, and in towns, and at balls, too, but there ain't no sense in them when there ain't no civilization nor other kinds of bothers and fussiness around." Sam Clemens when a boy must have hated (and have frequently broken) an 1845 Hannibal ordinance forbidding anyone from swimming nude within the town's perimeter from one hour before sunrise until one hour after sunset; violators were subject to fines. "Man, with his soiled mind, covers himself," Twain observed in "Man's Place in the Animal World" of 1890. "He will not even enter a drawing room with his breast and back naked, so alive is he and his mates to indecent suggestion. . . . No—man is the Animal that Blushes. He is the only one that does it—or has occasion to" (*What Is Man?*, p. 83).

17. *I found a canoe.* Twain originally wrote "I took the canoe," but an alert copy editor noted while the novel was still in page proofs that the boat was lost when the raft was rammed at the end of Chapter 16, so Twain changed it. Evidently Huck and Jim (as well as Twain) have forgotten that they planned to buy a canoe and travel north to freedom. Twain did not know exactly what to do with Jim; at one point he wrote in his notes, "And Jim can be smuggled north on a ship?—no, a steamboat" (see Blair and Fischer, University of California edition, 1988, p. 752). As the two fugitives head deeper into slave country, they are entirely at the mercy of the river.

18. *a chute.* A French word for the narrow passage between an island and the mainland, complicated by a swift current and navigable only

"I AM THE LATE DAUPHIN!"

erable; but the duke staid huffy a good while, till by-and-by the king says:

"Like as not we got to be together a blamed long time, on this h-yer raft, Bilgewater, and so what's the use o' your bein' sour? It'll only make things oncomfortable. It ain't my fault I warn't born a duke, it ain't your fault you warn't born a king—so what's the use to worry? Make the best o' things the way you find 'em, says I—that's my motto. This ain't no bad thing that we've struck here—plenty grub and an easy life—come, give us your hand, Duke, and less all be friends."

The duke done it, and Jim and me was pretty glad to see it. It took away all the uncomfortableness, and we felt mighty good over it, because it would a been a miserable business to have any unfriendliness on the raft; for what you want, above all things, on a raft, is for everybody to be satisfied, and feel right and kind towards the others.

It didn't take me long to make up my mind that these liars warn't no kings nor dukes, at all, but just low-down humbugs and frauds. But I never said nothing, never let on; kept it to myself; it's the best way; then you don't have no quarrels, and don't get into no trouble. If they wanted us to call them kings and dukes, I hadn't no objections, 'long as it would keep peace in the family; and it warn't no use to tell Jim, so I didn't tell him. If I never learnt nothing else out of pap, I learnt that the best way to get along with his kind of people is to let them have their own way.

when the river is high enough. In Chapter 4 of *The Gilded Age*, Twain described how a steamboat entered such a waterway: "Sometimes she approached a solid wall of tall trees as if she meant to break through it, but all of a sudden a little crack would open just enough to admit her, and away she would go plowing through the 'chute' with just barely room enough between the island on one side and the mainland on the other."

19. *One of these fellows*. Blair and Fischer suggested in the 1988 University of California edition (p. 407) that Twain may have modeled the old man in part on Charles C. Duncan of the *Quaker City* and *The Innocents Abroad*; his baldness, gray whiskers, and coat with brass buttons were all characteristics of the captain of the ship Twain took to Europe in 1867. The two later quarreled while Twain was working on *Huckleberry Finn*. "I have known and observed Duncan for years," he told the New York *Times* in "Mr. Mark Twain Excited on Seeing the Name of Capt. C. C. Duncan in Print" (June 10, 1883), "and I think I have reason for believing him wholly without principle, without moral sense, without honor of any kind. I think I am justified in believing that he is cruel enough and heart-

Captain Charles C. Duncan of the *Quaker City*. Illustration from *The Innocents Abroad*, 1869.
Private collection.

less enough to rob any sailor or sailor's widow or orphan he can get his clutches upon, and I know him to be a coward enough. I know him to be a canting hypocrite, filled to the chin with sham godliness and forever oozing and dripping false piety and pharisaical prayers. I know his words to be worthless." He may well have recalled these accusations when he developed the king's "lay" in *Huckleberry Finn*.

20. *seventy, or upwards*. Twain originally wrote "fifty" (**MS**) in the manuscript but changed it when he decided to make the con artist much older; after all, Twain was just about to turn fifty himself.

21. *home-knit galluses—no, he had only one*. One suspender is all that is needed to hold up one's pants; two are worn for "style" and would suggest that this derelict is of a higher class than he really is. Note how carefully Kemble adhered to just one suspender for each of the backwoods characters in his pictures.

22. *carpet-bags*. Then the common luggage of the itinerant, being the cheapest and most convenient way of transporting one's goods while traveling; at one time they were actually made out of old carpets. Traveling salesmen, confidence men, and anyone else who had to move quickly from place to place carried them. They often contained all the material goods their owners possessed in the world and were the badge of an outsider with no house nor land nor shelter nor any other property to speak of. Not surprisingly, Southerners named Yankee speculators during Reconstruction "carpet-baggers."

23. *an article to take the tartar off the teeth*. Joseph Jones quoted in "The 'Duke's' Tooth-Powder Racket: A Note on *Huckleberry Finn*" (*Modern Language Notes*, November 1946) an article, "Tooth Destroyers" (New York *Weekly*, August 24, 1871), which describes exactly what line of business this gentleman is engaged in: "A boy is selected from a crowd gathered by the peddler's eloquence, and in an instant his teeth are cleansed. The staring spectators having thus seen a practical test of its virtue, purchase the tooth-powder, and use it on their own masticators until the acid and potash, of which it is composed, eats away the protecting enamel of the teeth rendering speedy decay certain" (pp. 468–69). The swindler once caught could have received up to a year in prison.

24. *a little temperance revival*. The old scoundrel has been lecturing on the evils of demon rum and recruiting converts to the temperance movement by having them swear off all intoxicating beverages. Temperance advocates argued that most social ills were the result of drinking and demanded the outlawing of the manufacture and sale of all alcoholic beverages. The movement grew tremendously in strength in the nineteenth century, its ranks consisting primarily of woman. Many of its followers were abolitionists, who pursued this cause as zealously as they did the eradication of slavery. One of the major forces behind the Woman's Christian Temperance Union was Francis B. Willard; in 1890 she joined forces with Susan B. Anthony (an old temperance advocate), Elizabeth Cady Stanton, and the National Woman Suffrage Association to form the National American Woman Suffrage Association. Willard did not live to see her dream fulfilled: The Nineteenth Amendment was passed in 1920, and Prohibition was introduced by the Twentieth Amendment the following year. President Franklin Delano Roosevelt repealed it when he took office in 1933.

25. *ten cents a head, children and niggers free*. A common admission price to a backwoods lecture at that time; Twain wrote in reference to another show, "Admission as usual: 25 cents, children and negroes half price" ("Chapters from My Autobiography," *North American Review*, January 4, 1907, p. 5). It is remarkable that the old fraud was able to draw between fifty and sixty people from so small a community for a temperance lecture. Because the speech is supposed to be educational and the lecturer wishes to induce as many people as possible to attend, boys and girls are admitted without charge. Slaves are considered no different from children, being no more than chattel; and because their masters may not trust them any more than their little ones to be left alone, slaves too are admitted free.

26. *A nigger rousted me out this mornin'*. The tip-off to the scoundrel is a remarkable act of magnanimity for the period and place. Jocelyn Chadwick-Joshua suggested in *The Jim Dilemma* (1998) that "the slave had acted out of his own experience, averting impending cruelty and suffering" (p. 96).

27. *tar and feather me and ride me on a rail*. A common backwoods punishment: The mob strips the offender bare, covers him in tar and feathers, and then drives him from town in disgrace on a wooden plank. " 'Riding on a rail' is an old custom, and originally Scandinavian," revealed Walter Besant in "My Favorite Novelist and His Best Book" (*Munsey's Magazine*, February 1898). "It was practised in the north of England within the memory of man, but is now discontinued" (p. 662). Chadwick Hansen in "The Character of Jim in the Ending of *Huckleberry Finn*" (*Massachusetts Review*, Autumn 1963) explained exactly why the king should be so terrified by the threat: "A rail was made by splitting a log length-wise, and then splitting the halves, so that the fence-rail was wedge-shaped at the ends, with a sharp and splintery edge. When a man was ridden on a rail, with nothing between his body and the rail but a coat of tar and feathers, there would be very little left of his groin, and the chances were that he would lose at least part of his genitals as well" (p. 63).

Tarring and feathering. Illustration by True W. Williams, *Mark Twain's Sketches, New and Old*, 1875.
Private collection.

Tarring and feathering is an ancient practice. Richard I of England approved it in 1185 as a punishment for theft; by the seventeenth century, English bishops administered it against incontinent nuns and friars; and the early settlers brought it with them to America. But it was illegal in Missouri and the rest of the country at the time of the story. It became one of the most frequently used forms of Lynch law justice. When Orion Clemens suggested in his Hannibal *Journal* that the husband in a local marital dispute should be tarred and feathered and ridden out of town on a rail, the rival *Missouri Courier* was quick to reply on May 26, 1853, "Does he forget that there is a law in this country—a law that protects the weak when oppressed by the strong, and insures the dispensation of justice to every one? Is he a champion of mob-ocracy and an advocate of 'higher law'? Or, acknowledging that every citizen should obey the law, would he take the execution of it from the hands of the legal authorities and place it in the hands of a mob? Take the sober second thought, neighbor, and unless your ideas of right and wrong are most woefully distorted, you will certainly arrive at the conclusion that the principle which you would teach . . . is unjust, fallacious, and if carried out would lead to ruinous circumstances."

28. *double-team it.* Work in concert, like a team of horses or oxen.

29. *What's your line—mainly?* The two gentlemen are by profession confidence men who deceive for profit. "There isn't anything so grotesque or so incredible that the average human being can't believe it," Twain said in June 22, 1906, in "Reflections on Religion" (*Hudson Review*, Autumn 1963, p. 343). Roving flimflam men were stock characters in Midwestern and Southern literature, two fine examples being the hero of Johnson Jones Hooper's *Adventures of Captain Simon Suggs* (1845), whose motto is "It is a good thing to be a *shifty* man in a new country," and the protagonist of Herman Melville's *The Confidence Man* (1857), who, like Twain's scoundrels, travels down the Mississippi in a series of disguises. Perhaps the best known example today is Harold Hill, the smooth-talking turn-of-the-century salesman in Meredith Wilson's famous musical *The Music Man* (1957). The con man was a new kind of thief, the old romantic desperado having been driven from the river by civilization. Melville astutely observed in Chapter 1 of his novel, "In new countries, where the wolves are killed off, the foxes increase." According to Donald H.

Welsh in "Sam Clemens' Hannibal, 1836–1838" (*Midcontinent American Studies Journal*, Spring 1962, p. 38), the situation was so bad in Hannibal that the *Gazette* (January 14, 1847) issued a warning for citizens to beware of "'*gentlemen*' of dubious character . . . about our town" and bar their doors at night. "Our friends from the country," it went on, "would do well to keep a sharp look out—and avoid all games with those who may ask them to play." It further advised readers on February 25 to be cautious of "a swarm of *gentleman black-legs*, who hang round the Coffee Houses, ready to pounce upon, and fleece any whom they can lure into their meshes"; and on September 2 reported that these scoundrels "will attempt to accomplish their purposes by *foul* means, if they cannot by *fair*." The two con artists are fitting companions for Huck Finn: He has been "conning" the public under alias after alias all along the river, but he does it to survive; this pair do it for money.

"There are surely no country places where such a ridiculous old fraud as the king could be believed," suggested Walter Besant in "My Favorite Novelist and His Best Book" (*Munsey's Magazine*, February 1898). "It may be objected that the characters are extravagant. Not so. They are all exactly and literally true; they are quite possible in a country so remote and so primitive" (p. 664). Just after *Huckleberry Finn* came out, Orion Clemens wrote his brother about two confidence men he had heard about recently. In a letter of June 8, 1885 (now in the Mark Twain Papers), he described how a man "bought some bars of common washing soap, . . . cut it up into small cakes, wrapped them in tissue paper, and sold them in the country in Iowa and Missouri villages at auction, for the cure of corns, to eradicate freckles, take out stains, and wash niggers white. He made $450 on a box or two of that soap." He also mentioned a factory worker who once put out a shingle as a lawyer, charging $100 a person to file a libel suit; he ran off with the money after paying another lawyer $40 to handle the case in court.

30. *jour printer*. Journeyman printer, one who works by the day at odd jobs and is not yet a master. In the talk "The Compositor," delivered at the New York Typothetæ Dinner on January 18, 1886, Twain described the typical " 'tramping' jour" as one "who flitted by in the summer and tarried a day, with his wallet stuffed with one shirt and a hatful of bills; for if he couldn't get any type to set he would do a temperance

A jour printer. Wood engraving from *Life and Sayings of Mrs. Partington* by B. P. Shillaber, 1854.
Courtesy Library of Congress.

lecture. His way of life was simple, his needs not complex; all he wanted was plate and bed and money enough to get drunk on, and he was satisfied" ("The Typothetæ," Hartford *Courant*, January 20, 1886). Sam Clemens himself traveled the country as a tramp printer in his youth, and he told Albert Bigelow Paine that he based this "jour printer" on one he knew in Virginia City, Nevada (*Mark Twain: A Biography*, vol. 2, 1912, p. 798). Twain originally considered making both men printers who "deliver temperance lectures, teach dancing, elocution, feel heads, distribute tracts, preach, fiddle, doctor (quack)" (University of California edition, 1988, p. 728). The one who remains possesses all the characteristics of another "jour printer" described by John S. Robb in *Streaks of Squatter Life, and Far-West Scenes* (1847): "intelligent, reckless, witty, improvident, competent, and unsteady" (p. 11).

31. *patent medicines*. Little federal legislation in the nineteenth century protected the public from bogus cure-alls; these medical frauds claimed to correct anything and everything from cold to cancer, but they often consisted of little more than a good dose of alcohol or laudanum mixed with some flavoring and sweet-

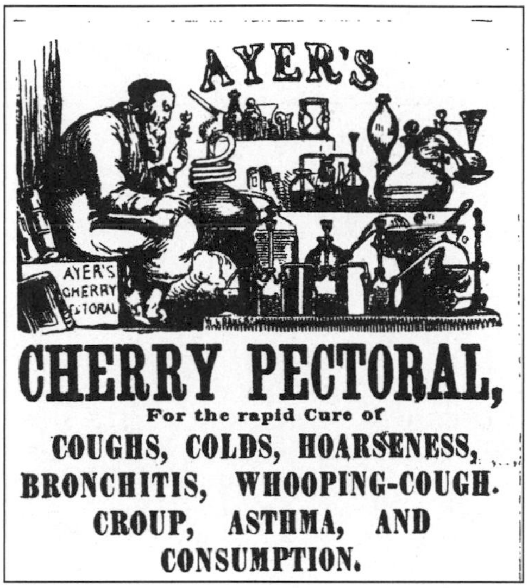

Patent medicine advertisement, Hannibal *Journal*, August 17, 1853.
Courtesy Missouri Historical Society Collection.

ener. Donald W. Welsh in "Sam Clemens' Hannibal, 1836–1838" (*Midcontinent American Studies Journal*, Spring 1962) listed assorted nostrums advertised in just one issue of the Hannibal *Gazette* (April 20, 1848), including Dr. Bragg's Sugar Coated Pills, an "improved treatment for Fever and Ague, and Bilious Fevers" and good for "all diseases prevalent in a western and southern climate"; Comstock's Concentrated Compound Fluid Extract of Sarsaparilla "for the cure of Scrofula, chronic rheumatism, general debility, cutaneous diseases, Scaly eruptions of the Skin, . . . Mercurial and Syphilis Disease, . . . pains and swelling of the bones, . . . [and] Costiveness in females and males"; and Dr. Connell's mixture for Gonorrhea and Gleet, Seminal effusions, and Weakness of Utera and Bladder, "equally good and certain for females" (pp. 40–41). Blair and Fischer noted in the 1988 University of California edition that in the summer of 1883, while working on *Huckleberry Finn*, Twain came across an advertisement for a remarkable compound for "Rheumatism, Dyspepsia, Liver Complaint, Constipation, Dropsy, Paralysis, St. Vitus' Dance, Delirium Tremens, Diabetes, Stone in the Bladder, Blood Diseases, Scrofula, Ulcers, Female Weakness and General Debility." He was so impressed that he wrote the manufacturer, Magnetic Rock Spring Company, in Colfax, Iowa, on August 1, to order a barrel. "I do believe that is what is the matter with me," he wrote. "It reads just like my symptoms" (p. 408). In the talk "The Compositor," delivered at the New York Typothetæ Dinner on January 18, 1886, Twain recalled that when he was one of several apprentices in the Hannibal *Missouri Courier* office, "Most of the yearly ads were patent medicine stereotypes, and we used to fence with them" ("The Typothetæ," Hartford *Courant*, January 21, 1886).

32. *theatre-actor*. At the time, acting was considered a particularly disgraceful profession; theaters were called "moral pest-houses." "Church members did not attend shows out there in those days," Twain recalled of his Hannibal childhood in 1906 (*Mark Twain in Eruption*, 1940, p. 111). Twain, however, harbored no such prejudice against the stage or its players. This former circuit lecturer and frustrated playwright had many theatrical friends, and some thought he would have made a fine actor himself. Twain supported his friend and neighbor William Gillette (and against the young man's family's wishes) when he took up a stage career; and Gillette became one of the most popular leading men and dramatists of his day, and created the role of Sherlock Holmes. Twain also founded with Edwin Booth, John Drew, and Joseph Jefferson the Players Club in New York City in 1888. The actor's parlance and lingo derive from nineteenth-century melodrama.

33. *mesmerism*. An early form of hypnotism, named for Franz Anton Mesmer (1734–1815). As a follower of occultism and a firm believer in the astrological influence on human behavior, this German physician developed the theory of "animal magnetism" as the life force which affected human health. To cure nervous disorders through magnetism, he held séances in which patients sat around a vat of dilute sulfuric acid while holding hands or grasping bars of iron protruding from the solution. The Viennese medical profession denounced him as a fraud, so he fled to Paris, where his sessions became fashionable; and although the French Academy (which included Antoine Lavoisier and Benjamin Franklin) too called him a quack, his theories gained wide acceptance throughout Europe and America. However, the form of hypnotism known as "mesmerism" was actually developed by his disciple Count Maxine de Puységur. The practice eventually regressed

Franz Anton Mesmer.
Courtesy Library of Congress.

into a sideshow attraction as it was best known throughout the United States before the Civil War. "These traveling 'Professors,' or many of them," James M. Field noted in *The Drama in Pokerville* (1847), "are charlatans, thus far, that they pretend to treat, *scientifically*, phenomena, the real nature of which they are, entirely ignorant of; and the study of which they are neither by education, habit, or *aim*, at all fitted for. They are charlatans, in that their superficial knowledge of mere *effects* is simply made available in the shape of *exhibition*; and the success of the *show* being their first object, they may be suspected, perhaps, in some cases, of a little *management*" (p. 129).

A memorable event of Sam Clemens's boyhood, when he was the same age as Huck Finn, was the arrival of the mesmerist in Hannibal. "Every night, for three nights," he recounted in "Chapters from My Autobiography" (*North American Review*, January 4, 1907), "I sat in the row of candidates on the platform, and held the magic disk in the palm of my hand, and gazed at it and tried to get sleepy, but it was a failure" (p. 5). He was, however, envious of how the spell affected another of the candidates, so on the fourth night he succumbed to the temptation to pretend to be sleepy while gazing at the whirling object. "Straightway came the professor," he recalled, "and made passes over my head and down my body and legs and arms, finishing each pass with a snap of his fingers in the air, to discharge the surplus electricity; then he began to 'draw' me with a disk, holding it in his fingers and telling me I couldn't take my eyes off it, try as I might; so I rose slowly, bent and gazing, and followed the disk all over the place, just as I had seen the others do. . . . Upon suggestion I fled from snakes; passed buckets at a fire; became excited over hot steamboat-races; made love to imaginary girls and kissed them; fished from the platform and landed mud-cats that outweighed me—and so on, all the customary marvels." Another part of the show demonstrated that the mesmerist had such command over the subject's mind that he felt no pain. "But I didn't wince," he confessed; "I only suffered, and shed tears on the inside. . . . They would stick a pin in my arm and bear on it until they drove it a third of its length in, and then be lost in wonder that by a mere exercise of will power the professor could turn my arm to iron and make it insensible to pain. Whereas it was not insensible to all; I was suffering agonies of pain." So convincing was his own display of

A mesmerist. Illustration by Farny,
A Boy's Town by William Dean Howells,
Harper's Young People, August 21, 1890.
Courtesy Library of Congress.

willpower that Clemens was never to convince his mother that it was just an act, that he was never hypnotized in the least, even after he confessed every detail of the fraud and insisted that he had been faking it all along that he was mesmerized. According to his working notes for *Huckleberry Finn*, published in the 1988 University of California edition (p. 730), Twain thought of recreating "the mesmeric foolishness" with Huck (and possibly the king) performing.

34. *phrenology*. The pseudoscience of studying the contours of the cranium to determine one's dispositions, characteristics, and talents. Viennese doctor Franz Joseph Gall (1758–1828) argued that the physical formation of the head was directly related to one's intelligence, religious belief, and propensity to crime. Banned in Austria as charlatanism, phrenology spread across Europe to Great Britain and finally the United States. Here it was popularized in 1832 by Johann Kaspar Spurzheim, and soon many American parlors displayed plaster phrenological heads which doubled as decorative sculptures. It eventually became a fortune-telling scheme run by con men as a sideshow attraction.

Franz Joseph Gall.
Courtesy Picture Collection, New York Public Library, Astor, Lenox, and Tilden Foundations.

Clemens first learned of phrenology as well as mesmerism while growing up in Missouri. "One of the most frequent arrivals in our village of Hannibal was the peripatetic phrenologist," he recalled in Chapter 13 of *The Autobiography of Mark Twain* (1959). "He gathered the people together and gave them a gratis lecture on the marvels of phrenology, then felt their bumps and made an estimate of the result, at twenty-five cents per head. . . . Phrenology found many a bump on a man's head and it labeled each bump with a formidable and outlandish name of its own." Clemens acquainted himself with the terminology of "the doctrine of temperaments" by reading George Sumner Weaver's *Lecture on Mental Science According to the Philosophy of Phrenology* (1852) and copying certain passages on "the physiology and general form of body and face, as indicating character" as they applied to his own features into his 1855 notebook. Several years later when in London, still fascinated and skeptical, he went under an assumed name to see Orson Fowler, then "the head of the phrenological industry." The writer subjected himself to a reading by the great Fowler himself, and he was amused until the phrenologist came upon one particular crevice: "He startled me by saying that the cavity represented the total absence of the sense of humor!" But three months later, when doubting Twain returned to be examined under his own name, that cavity had miraculously disappeared and in its place was "the loftiest bump of humor he had ever encountered in his lifelong experience!" See also Alan Gribben, "Mark Twain, Phrenology, and the 'Temperaments': A Study of Pseudoscientific Influence," *American Quarterly*, March 1972, pp. 45–68.

35. *singing-geography school*. According to Fischer and Salamo in the 2001 University of California edition, this method of instruction was invented by Benjamin Naylor of Philadelphia. "The teacher with a rod points out the various parts and repeats their names, grouping several together," explained *Naylor's System of Teaching Geography* (1851); "after they are somewhat familiarized with the names, they chant or sing them over repeatedly. . . . The children all join in the singing right merrily, keeping their eyes fixed upon the places on the map as he points them out." Instruction was often provided by itinerant teachers. Young Sam Clemens attended classes in Hannibal, Missouri: Hollister and Norman reported in *Five Famous Mis-*

sourians (1900, p. 17) that he once forgot his atlas and had to sit with the girls as punishment, and on another occasion he forgot the song and had to sit on the dunce-block.

36. *sling a lecture*. To deliver a lecture with ease or rapidity.

37. *What's your lay?* The old scoundrel gave a remarkably different reply in the manuscript:

> "Gospil-work mainly—most any kind of gospil work: boosting revivals along, or getting 'em up; working camp meetings; 'occupying' for a preacher that wants to take a week's rest; and missionarying. Thar's more money in missionarying than the others; folks will plank out cash for the heathen mighty free, if you only locate your heathen fur enough off. I've took in as much as seventeen dollars at one grist for the pore benighted Goojoos—invented 'em myself—located 'em away up jest back of the north pole. Seeing that that worked so good, I kind of strained myself, next time, and located some in a comet, expecting to jest simply bust the community—but it warn't a go. They wouldn't ante a red—and I come mighty near getting ducked, too." (**MS**)

The scorn for organized religion in this passage was perhaps more than Olivia Clemens or William Dean Howells could take, so Twain gave this old con artist a less offensive "line." "Occupying" for a preacher means substituting for him in prayer meetings. When Haley's Comet passed by Earth in 1835 (the year of Twain's birth), some religious sects believed that the end of the world was coming; but the public is not so "taken in" at the time of *Huckleberry Finn* as it was a few years earlier.

38. *the doctoring way*. Donald H. Welsh identified one of these backwoods quacks in "Sam Clemens' Hannibal, 1836–1838" (*Midcontinent American Studies Journal*, Spring 1962). According to the Hannibal *Journal* (October 21, 1847), "A scamp named Robinson, and calling himself Doctor, who has been *blowing* about the country for some months past, after managing to get smartly in our debt, left, a few days ago, for parts unknown." He advertised himself as a "Professor of diseases of the eye, from the London Ophthalmic Institution"; and the paper described him as "rather slender, pop-eyed, and had on when he left a gray frock coat with brass buttons. . . . he may infallibly be recognized by his cockney brogue, livery stable *gait*, vulgar manners, and a habit he has, when on horseback, of galloping as if the Devil or the constable was hard after him" (p. 41).

39. *Layin' on o' hands*. "Faith healing" was widely practiced in the backwoods, where there was a shortage of physicians. "When I was a boy," Twain wrote in "Christian Science" in 1907, "a farmer's wife who lived five miles from our village had great fame as a faith-doctor. . . . Sufferers came to her from all around, and she laid her hand upon them and said 'Have faith—it is all that is necessary,' and they went away well of their ailments. She was not a religious woman, and pretended to no occult powers. She said that the patient's faith in her did the work. Several times I saw her make immediate cures of severe tooth-aches. My mother was the patient" (*What Is Man?*, 1973, p. 232). See Chapter 41, note 8.

His wife likewise benefited from such treatment. A fall on the ice left Olivia L. Langdon an invalid when she was sixteen, and none of the prominent physicians brought to Elmira to treat her were of any help. Finally, her family sent for the famous Dr. Newton, denounced as a quack by the medical profession. Before he came to her, she could not even sit up without suffering severe nausea and exhaustion. After saying a short fervent prayer, he put an arm behind her shoulders and told her to sit up, which she did without any discomfort. He then helped her stand and walk a few steps; but he then confessed that although she would never be fully cured, she would be able to walk at least one or two hundred yards at a time for the rest of her life. "His charge was fifteen hundred dollars," Twain wrote in his *Autobiography* (1924), "and it was easily worth a hundred thousand" (vol. 2, p. 105). Years later the writer met Dr. Newton and asked him what his secret was. "He said he didn't know," Twain recalled, "but thought perhaps some subtle form of electricity proceeded from his body and wrought the cures."

Yet he was not entirely convinced, still suspicious of quackery in such treatments. Hank Morgan in Chapter 26 of *A Connecticut Yankee in King Arthur's Court* is particularly contemptuous of the ability of kings to cure the sick merely with their touch; it therefore seems appropriate that the second of the two scoundrels in *Huckleberry Finn* should be engaged in the fraudulent laying on of hands. See note 48 below.

40. *holt.* Hold, specialty.

41. *I k'n tell a fortune pretty good, when I've got somebody along to find out the facts for me.* Like the younger man's tooth powder and mesmerismic frauds, this trick requires an accomplice, if not the other con artist, then a boy. Obviously both men anticipate some profit in keeping Huck around.

42. *Preachin's my line, too; and workin' camp-meetin's; and missionaryin' around.* The scarcity of ordained preachers on the sparsely populated frontier required clergy to travel widely from congregation to congregation; and from colonial times, parishioners were frequently swindled by false circuit riders. This old scoundrel plays on different human frailties than does his new companion: The young man takes advantage of faith in current fads, the other of the faith in God and in one's fellow man. While the first profits on the profane instincts of man, on physical vanity, entertainment, and personal improvement, the other is the greater swindler in that he exploits both spiritual vanity and religion.

Albert Bigelow Paine explained in *Mark Twain: A Biography* (vol. 2, 1912) that "the king was created out of refuse from the whole human family—'all tears and flapdoodle,' the very ultimate of disrepute and hypocrisy." Robert P. Weeks argued in "The Captain, the Prophet, and the King" (*Mark Twain Journal*, Winter 1975–1976) for another source for the king in George J. Adams (1813–1880), a charismatic religious figure whom Twain described in *The Innocents Abroad* (Chapter 57) as "once an actor, then several other things, afterward a Mormon and a missionary, always an adventurer." He joined the Mormon Church in 1840; but after Adam Smith was murdered in 1844, Brigham Young expelled Adams, who went on to found his own Church of the Messiah. The greatest of Adams's swindles, as far as Twain was concerned, was his having convinced about 160 disciples—men, women, and children, many of them destitute—to sell all their worldly possessions, turn the proceeds over to him, and leave New England to establish a supposedly divinely inspired colony in the Holy Land. This ill-equipped Zionist utopia failed because of a combination of its leader's false promises and drunkenness and the resistance of the Turkish government. In Jaffa, the *Quaker City* took aboard about forty of Adams's weary pilgrims who had fled from the desert; they were "shamefully humbugged by their prophet, they felt humiliated and unhappy."

43. *By rights I am a duke!* The frontier must have been littered with American claimants to European titles. "In public we scoff at titles and hereditary privilege," Twain observed in "Chapters from My Autobiography" (*North American Review*, January 4, 1907), "but privately we hanker after them, and when we get a chance we buy them for cash and a daughter" (p. 4). He was referring to the then current fad of wealthy Americans' marrying their daughters to destitute European noblemen for their royal titles. Clemens himself was said to be descended from the earls of Durham on his mother's side. When a boy, he heard "the whole disastrous history of how the Lampton heir came to this country a hundred and fifty years or so ago, disgusted with that foolish fraud, hereditary aristocracy, and married, and shut himself away from the world in the remotenesses of the wilderness, and went to breeding ancestors of future American claimants, while at home in England he was given up as dead and his titles and estates turned over to his younger brother, usurper and personally responsible for the perverse and unseatable usurpers of our day" (*Autobiography*, 1924, vol. 1, p. 122).

The then "rightful Earl of Durham" was a distant cousin, Jesse Madison Leathers, a poor pitiful newspaper advertisement salesman and collections agent from Kentucky. Twain said that "all his time was taken up in trying to get me and others of the tribe to furnish him capital to fight his claim through the House of Lords with. He had all the documents, all the proofs; he knew he could win. And so he dreamed his life away, always in poverty, sometimes in actual want, and died at last, far from home, and was buried from a hospital by strangers who did not know that he was an earl, for he did not look it." There is a good deal of that "earl" in this "duke." So bombastic were Leathers's letters to him while he was working on *Huckleberry Finn* that Twain toyed with the idea of getting Leathers to write a book himself. Blair and Fischer quote from just two of his letters in the 1988 University of California edition: "Owing to my impecunious condition I have done nothing to assert the rights of the American heirs"; and "I . . . shall be only too happy if I can bring one little sunbeam to mingle with the pure light which brightens and cheers your humble hearth and home" (p. 408). This is also the idiom not only of the duke and king but of that other American flimflam man W. C. Fields.

Twain used his cousin as the model for Colonel Mulberry Sellers of *The Gilded Age*, and exploited the Lampton legend further in *The American Claimant* (1892) by having Sellers attempt to regain the earldom of Rossmore. Clemens did not particularly sympathize with the Lampton nobles; he preferred instead his father's ancestor Geoffrey Clement, who was a member of the court that condemned Charles I to death. He felt he himself belonged to another sort of aristocracy. "I reverence achievement, and that only," he once told Raymond Blathwait ("Mark Twain on Humor," New York *World*, May 31, 1891), "and so, it goes without saying that it isn't any matter to me whether achievement is the work of a person who wore a coronet or wooden shoes. I have no reverence for heredity of any kind. I should have had had I been educated to it, but I have not been so educated. I think that while the titles of Prince, Earl, Duke are high, yet they are not high enough yet to properly decorate men of prodigious achievement, as a recognition by the world of what they have done. I would furnish to such men all the gauds and titles they wanted or would take, but, I would give such things a real value by letting them perish with the winners of them."

And yet he must have secretly longed for some noble ancestry, for there are many other claimants to usurped titles and property in his books. He recalled in Chapter 5 of *Life on the Mississippi* a night watchman on the *Paul Jones* who "said he was the son of an English nobleman—either an earl or an alderman, he could not remember which, but believed was both. . . . It was a sore blight to find out that he was a low, vulgar, ignorant, sentimental, half-witted humbug, an untraveled native of the wilds of Illinois, who had absorbed wildcat literature and appropriated its marvels, until in time he had woven odds and ends of the mess into this yarn, and then gone on telling it to fledglings like me, until he had come to believe it himself." An early version of the duke is "Count Fontainebleau," the French impostor Jean Mercier, a barber's son, in the newly rediscovered *A Murder, A Mystery, and a Marriage*, written in 1876 but not published until 2001. But Twain introduced at least one true heir in his stories, Miles Hendon, the hero of *The Prince and the Pauper*; while fighting in Europe, Hendon is cheated out of his title, his estates, and his betrothed by a treacherous younger brother.

44. *the Duke of Bridgewater*. Twain took an actual English title that died out before he was born. W. G. Gaffney identified in "Mark Twain's 'Duke' and 'Dauphin'" (*Names*, September 1966, pp. 175–78) which one in particular Twain must have had in mind. Francis Egerton (1736–1803), the third Duke of Bridgewater, was said to be, in his time, the richest man in the world. But what makes the American "duke's" claim all the more outrageous is that Egerton died childless: Crushed by a thwarted love affair, he retired at age twenty-three from London society to devote the remainder of his life to the care and improvement of his vast estates; he never again associated with women in any capacity, whether social or menial, and so great was his bitterness that he refused to have any female servant wait on him. Therefore he could not have had any sons, legitimate or bastard; he was the third, the last, and the only bachelor

Francis Egerton, the Duke of Bridgewater.
Courtesy Library of Congress.

Duke of Bridgewater. Thus the American "duke" (as Twain well knew) could make any ludicrous claim to the title and property without any fear of legal action by a true direct descendant of this English nobleman.

The title of Bridgewater did survive Egerton, but by British law it was demoted from "duke" to "earl" when passed on to his cousin; and even this disappeared in 1829, when the eighth Earl of Bridgewater died in Paris. The last earl was almost as well known in his day as the great duke; this aristocrat was infamous for his eccentricities (supposedly he never wore the same pair of boots twice, and he fed all of his many dogs at the great dining table in his ancestral home) as well as being the author of an odd collection of "family anecdotes"; amusing stories about the peculiar Earl of Bridgewater circulated through anthologies of humor published in both Great Britain and the United States. Twain's readers would likely have recognized both the Duke and Earl of Bridgewater in his backwoods scoundrel.

Blair and Fischer reported in the 1988 University of California edition that Twain did know members of this family. While staying at the home of Reginald Cholmondeley in 1879, the American writer was introduced to his host's brother-in-law Lord Egerton of Tatton. Some people had publicly challenged his claim to the title of Bridgewater, but what offended Twain was how two American women were rudely excluded from the conversation when it turned to wills and other family matters. Cholmondeley read *Huckleberry Finn*, but was not insulted by the reference to his wife's family and offered to arrange for Twain to meet his brother-in-law the next time he was in England. Twain replied on March 28, 1885, that "*next* year maybe I can meet the original Bilgewater; and if he is in *your* company, I'll be mighty *glad* to" (pp. 408–9).

45. *Bilgewater*. The disgustingly foul and noxious water which collects in the bottom of a ship's "bilge," or hull; H. L. Mencken in *The American Language* (1963) defined "bilge" as "buncombe" (p. 750). Twain thought this a great comic name and used it frequently. "Bilgewater," he jotted in his notebook in 1865, for future use, "Good God what a name" (see the footnote to *Mark Twain's Notes and Journals*, vol. 1, 1975, pp. 76–77). There is a Mr. Bilgewater, of Benton, in the sketch "Female Suffrage" (New York *Sunday Mercury*, April 7, 1867) and a Colonel Bilgewater in Chapter 77 of *Roughing It*; one of the indelicate courtiers of the off-color "Date 1601" (1882) is "ye Duchess of Bilgewater, twenty-two yeres of age," who bears the distinction of having been "rog'red by four lords before she had a husband."

46. *nation sorry*. Extremely sorry, from "damnation"; sorry as hell.

47. *snaked down*. Dragged down.

48. *I am the late Dauphin!* A fine example of one-upmanship between scoundrels: Because the young man claims to be the true descendant of the once richest man in the world, the old swindler says that he is the rightful king of France! The legend that the son of Louis XVI had not died in prison but escaped inspired many false claimants on the American frontier. Twain was acquainted with tales of French pretenders through a chapter in Horace W. Fuller's *Noted French: Trials: Impostors and Adventurers* (1882), which described and debunked several of these phony dauphins; but there were many other sources for information on these bogus kings. At least one of them, the Duke of Normandy, came to the United States in 1804. But the strangest of these impostors was Eleazer Williams, who bore a striking resemblance to

Eleazer Williams.
Courtesy Picture Collection, New York Public Library, Astor, Lenox, and Tilden Foundations.

Louis XVIII, Lord Palmerston; born a deaf-mute, Williams miraculously began relating memories of the French court the day after he was hit on the head with a stone and then went on to swindle the Seneca into establishing a utopian society in the wilderness with himself in charge. Blair in *Mark Twain and Huck Finn* noted the similarly bombastic styles of the duke and Williams, as demonstrated in the latter's purported journal (quoted in *The Lost Prince*, 1853): "Is it true, that I am among the number, who are destined to . . . degradation—from a mighty power to a helpless prisoner of the state . . . to be exiled from one of the finest empires in Europe, and to be a wanderer in the wilds of America—from the society of the most polite and accomplished courtiers, to be associated with ignorant and degraded Indians?" (pp. 278–79).

John Ashmead suggested in "A Possible Hannibal Source for Mark Twain's Dauphin" (*American Literature*, March 1962, pp. 105–7) that Clemens likely knew "A Visit from Our Bourbon," an article in the Hannibal *Journal* (May 12, 1853) reprinted from a Philadelphia paper. Twain may have taken the name "Dolphin" from this article about another American claimant, "Aminidab Fitz-Louis X Dolphin Borebon." The author must have been thinking of Eleazar Williams when he insisted that this other "king" "is not one of the common Bourbons, such as spring up in Indian tribes."

Although he may claim to be of a higher rank than the younger man, the king is obviously from a lower class than the duke. Using such colloquialisms as "thar," "such," and "k'n" and littering his talk with mild curses, the king speaks a more extreme backwoods dialect than the duke does. Twain carefully went through the manuscript to change the duke's "hain't" to "haven't," "I done myself" to "I did myself" (**MS**), and to remove double negatives from his speech. He has an extensive vocabulary, uses proper syntax, and throws about complex and effective phrases; the king is basically ignorant with a vague and limited vocabulary and resorts to clumsy double-talk and phony words when pressed into tight situations. Although less original with words, the king is nevertheless slyer than the duke.

Twain had no use for the divine right of kings. "That the executive head of a nation should be a person of lofty character and extraordinary ability was manifest and indisputable," he noted in "Mark Twain and His Book" (New York *Times*, December 10, 1889); "that none but the deity could select that head unerringly was also manifest and indisputable; that the deity ought to make that selection, then was likewise manifest and indisputable; consequently, that He does make it, as claimed, was an unavoidable deduction." He called for irreverence for all royalties and all those titled creatures born into privilege. . . . Merit alone should be the only thing that should give a man title to eminence."

Having returned in 1879 from Europe, where he witnessed monarchy in action, Twain was newly inspired to briefly resume the manuscript of *Huckleberry Finn* that summer at Quarry Farm. "There are shams and shams," Twain observed; "there are frauds and frauds, but the transparentest of all is the sceptered one. We see monarchs meet and go through solemn ceremonies, farces, with straight countenances; but it is not possible to imagine them meeting in private and not laughing in each other's faces" (*Mark Twain's Notebook*, 1935, p. 196). Although in later years he was charmed by the queen of Romania, the emperor of Austria, the emperor and empress of Germany, and other royalty, Twain said he could not "find anything durable in the aristocracy of birth and privilege—it turns my stomach" (Item 195, *Catalogue of the Library and Manuscripts of Samuel L. Clemens*, 1911). Later, he wrote impassioned pamphlets denouncing the ruthless imperialism of King Leopold of Belgium in the Congo and the ruthless reprisals carried out by Czar Nicholas after the Revolution of 1905. The most contemptuous of all of Twain's characters toward monarchs is Hank Morgan, the Connecticut Yankee who speaks for the author when he says in Chapter 8 of *A Connecticut Yankee in King Arthur's Court* that "*any* kind of royalty, howsoever modified, *any* kind of aristocracy, however so pruned, is rightly an insult." On accepting his honorary Master of Arts degree from Yale University on June 27, 1888, Twain said that the trade of humorist in America, "with all its lightness and frivolity . . . has one serious purpose, one aim, one specialty, and it is constant to it—the deriding of shams, the exposure of pretentious falsities, the laughing of stupid superstitions out of existence; and that whoso is by instinct engaged in this sort of warfare is the natural enemy of royalties, nobilities, privileges and all kindred swindles, and the natural friend of human rights and human liberties" ("Mark Twain Accepts," Hartford *Courant*, June 29, 1888).

49. *At your age!* Had he lived, the dauphin would have been only in his mid-fifties.

50. *You mean you're the late Charlemagne.* The first great king of France, who died in 814.

51. *trouble has brung these gray hairs and this premature balditude.* Extreme grief can turn one's hair gray; that of Marie Antoinette, the young queen of France, turned white while she was in prison. Likewise, Byron in "The Prisoner of Chillon" noted:

My hair is gray, but not with tears,
Nor grew it white
In a single night,
As men's have grown from sudden fears.

52. *if people . . . didn't set down in his presence till he asked them.* Twain found this courtesy due monarchs particularly loathsome: Hank Morgan contemptuously mentions it in Chapter 8 of *A Connecticut Yankee in King Arthur's Court*; and in Chapter 12 of *The Prince and the Pauper*, when King Edward vows to grant in recognition of the man's service to him any privilege he wishes, Miles Hendon requests only that "I and my heirs, forever, *sit* in the presence of the majesty of England!"

Chapter XX

ON THE RAFT.

THEY ASKED us considerable many questions; wanted to know what we covered up the raft that way for, and laid by in the day-time instead of running—was Jim a runaway nigger? Says I—

"Goodness sakes, would a runaway nigger run *south*?"

No, they allowed he wouldn't. I had to account for things some way, so I says:

"My folks was living in Pike County, in Missouri,[1] where I was born, and they all died off but me and pa and my brother Ike.[2] Pa, he 'lowed he'd break up and go down and live with Uncle Ben, who's got a little one-horse place[3] on the river, forty-four mile below Orleans. Pa was pretty poor, and had some debts; so when he'd squared up[4] there warn't nothing left but sixteen dollars and our nigger, Jim. That warn't enough to take us fourteen hundred mile, deck passage nor no other way. Well, when the river rose, pa had a streak of luck one day; he ketched this piece of a raft; so we reckoned we'd go down to Orleans on it. Pa's luck didn't hold out; a steamboat run over the forrard corner of the raft, one night, and we all went overboard and dove under the wheel; Jim and me come up, all right, but pa was drunk, and Ike was only four years old, so they never come up no more. Well, for the next

1. *Pike County, in Missouri.* A county just down the river from Hannibal, and home of the typical "wandering gypsy-like, Southern poor white." See Explanatory, note 3. The duke and king could hardly be impressed by the boy's humble place of origin. While the two deadbeats elevate themselves to the rank of royalty, Huck puts himself on the lowest rung of Southern society. "This person often lives with his family in a wagon," John Russell Bartlett reported in his *Dictionary of Americanisms* (1877) under "Pike"; "he is frequently a squatter on other people's lands; 'he owns a rifle, a lot of children and dogs, a wife, and, if he can read, a law-book,' said a lawyer . . . ; he moves from place to place, as the humor seizes him, and is generally an injury to

Pike County in relation to Hannibal in Marion County, Missouri. Sketch by Mark Twain, "The Private History of a Campaign That Failed," *Century Magazine*, December 1885. *Private collection.*

day or two we had considerable trouble, because people was always coming out in skiffs and trying to take Jim away from me, saying they believed he was a runaway nigger. We don't run day-times no more, now; nights they don't bother us."

The duke says—

"Leave me alone to cipher out a way so we can run in the day-time if we want to. I'll think the thing over—I'll invent a plan that'll fix it. We'll let it alone for to-day, because of course we don't want to go by that town yonder in daylight—it mightn't be healthy."

Towards night it begun to darken up and look like rain; the heat lightning was squirting around, low down in the sky, and the leaves was beginning to shiver—it was going to be pretty ugly, it was easy to see that. So the duke and the king went to overhauling our wigwam, to see what the beds was like. My bed was a straw tick[5]—better than Jim's, which was a corn-shuck tick; there's always cobs around about in a shuck tick, and they poke into you and hurt; and when you roll over, the dry shucks sound like you was rolling over in a pile of dead leaves; it makes such a rustling that you wake up. Well, the duke allowed he would take my bed; but the king allowed he wouldn't.[6] He says—

"I should a reckoned the difference in rank would a sejested to you that a corn-shuck bed warn't just fitten for me to sleep on. Your Grace'll take the shuck bed yourself."

Jim and me was in a sweat again, for a minute, being afraid there was going to be some more trouble amongst them; so we was pretty glad when the duke says—

"'Tis my fate to be always ground into the mire under the iron heel of oppression. Misfortune has broken my once haughty spirit; I yield, I submit; 'tis my fate. I am alone in the world—let me suffer; I can bear it."

We got away as soon as it was good and dark. The king told us to stand well out towards the middle of the river, and not show a light till we got a long ways below the town. We come in sight of the little bunch of lights by-and-by—that was the town, you know—and slid by, about a half a

his neighbors. He will not work regularly; but he has a great tenacity of life, and is always ready for a law-suit." In contrast to the romantic duke and king, practical Huck invents a "yarn" that will fit his current circumstances. Even these con artists are conned. Also note Huck uses certain colloquial words (such as "'lowed" and "ketched") in this stretcher not employed elsewhere, to make his speech more authentically and extremely that of a "Piker."

2. *my brother Ike*. David Carkeet in "The Dialects of *Huckleberry Finn*" identified this as "the name of a forever undeveloped character in Pike County balladry, his sole claim to fame being his ability to rhyme with 'Pike'" (pp. 325–26). In Chapter 72 of Wright's *History of the Big Bonanza* appears the first stanza of the most famous traditional Pike County ballad, "Joe Bowers":

My name it is Joe Bowers, I've got a brother Ike,
I come from old Missouri, yes, all the way from Pike.

3. *a little one-horse place*. A contemptuous term for a town so small and insignificant that one horse is all that is needed to do all of its hauling and transporting.

4. *squared up*. Settled his debts.

5. *tick*. A mattress.

6. *the duke allowed he would take my bed; but the king allowed he wouldn't*. This heated dispute over the fine distinction between the two rude beds again points to the pettiness of protocol among royalty.

mile out, all right. When we was three-quarters of a mile below, we hoisted up our signal lantern; and about ten o'clock it come on to rain and blow and thunder and lighten like everything; so the king told us to both stay on watch till the weather got better; then him and the duke crawled into the wigwam and turned in for the night. It was my watch below, till twelve, but I wouldn't a turned in, anyway, if I'd had a bed; because a body don't see such a storm as that every day in the week, not by a long sight. My souls, how the wind did scream along! And every second or two there'd come a glare that lit up the white-caps[7] for a half a mile around, and you'd see the islands looking dusty through the rain, and the trees thrashing around in the wind; then comes a *h-wack!*—bum! bum! bumble-umble-um-bum-bum-bum-bum—and the thunder would go rumbling and grumbling away, and quit—and then *rip* comes another flash and another sockdolager.[8,9] The waves most washed me off the raft, sometimes, but I hadn't any clothes on, and didn't mind. We didn't have no trouble about snags; the lightning was glaring and flittering around so constant that we could see them plenty soon enough to throw her head this way or that and miss them.

I had the middle watch,[10] you know, but I was pretty sleepy by that time, so Jim he said he would stand the first half of it for me; he was always mighty good, that way, Jim was. I crawled into the wigwam, but the king and the duke had their legs sprawled around so there warn't no show for me; so I laid outside—I didn't mind the rain, because it was warm, and the waves warn't running so high, now. About two they come up again, though, and Jim was going to call me, but he changed his mind because he reckoned they warn't high enough yet to do any harm; but he was mistaken about that, for pretty soon all of a sudden along comes a regular ripper, and washed me overboard. It most killed Jim a-laughing. He was the easiest nigger[11] to laugh that ever was, anyway.

I took the watch, and Jim he laid down and snored away; and by-and-by the storm let up for good and all; and the

7. *white caps*. Rough waves.

8. *and you'd see the islands looking dusty . . . and another sockdolager*. An improvement on the original passage in the manuscript: "and made them look like whole armies of white worms squirming along on a march; and away beyond, you would see the dimmest kind of islands through the sheets of rain, and the trees waving and thrashing in the wind; then comes *h-whack!—bum! bum! bumble-umble-umble-bum-bum-bum*—and the thunder would slow down and go rumbling and tumbling down the sky, and taper off with a kind of muttering and grumbling, away yonder, and then die out—and then rip comes another flash and another jolting sockdolager. It was just beautiful" (**MS**).

9. *sockdolager*. In England, "slogdollager," literally a knockout punch, a "finisher"; said to be a perversion in spelling and pronunciation of "doxology" (see Chapter 25, note 10), the liturgy sung at the finish of a church service.

10. *the middle watch*. Traditionally that time between midnight and four in the morning that young Sam Clemens preferred when a pilot on the Mississippi. "The middle watch in summer moonlit nights is a gracious time," he admitted to David "Wattie" Bowser on March 16, 1880, "especially if the boat steers like a duck, and friends have staid up to keep one company, and sing, and smoke, and spin yarns, and blow the whistle when other boats are met" (in Pascal Covici, Jr., "Dear Master Wattie," *Southwest Review*, Spring 1960, pp. 107–8).

11. *nigger*. Twain originally wrote "fellow" (**MS**), but realized that no matter how much Huck may care for Jim he cannot quite call him anything else but "nigger" at this time and in this place. He knows no better; that is the term he has always heard.

first cabin-light that showed, I rousted him out and we slid the raft into hiding-quarters for the day.

The king got out an old ratty deck of cards, after breakfast, and him and the duke played seven-up[12] a while, five cents a game. Then they got tired of it, and allowed they would "lay out a campaign,"[13] as they called it. The duke went down into his carpet-bag and fetched up a lot of little printed bills, and read them out loud. One bill said "The celebrated Dr. Armand de Montalban of Paris,"[14] would "lecture on the Science of Phrenology" at such and such a place, on the blank day of blank, at ten cents admission, and "furnish charts of character[15] at twenty-five cents apiece." The duke said that was *him.* In another bill he was the "world renowned Shaksperean tragedian, Garrick the Younger, of Drury Lane, London."[16] In other bills he had a lot of other names and done other wonderful things, like finding water and gold with a "divining rod,"[17] "dissipating witch-spells,"[18] and so on. By-and-by he says—

"But the histrionic muse is the darling. Have you ever trod the boards,[19] Royalty?"

"No," says the king.

"You shall, then, before you're three days older, Fallen Grandeur," says the duke. "The first good town we come to, we'll hire a hall and do the sword-fight in Richard III.[20] and the balcony scene in Romeo and Juliet. How does that strike you?"

"I'm in, up to the hub,[21] for anything that will pay, Bilgewater, but you see I don't know nothing about play-actn', and hain't ever seen much of it. I was too small when pap used to have 'em at the palace. Do you reckon you can learn me?"

"Easy!"

"All right. I'm jist a-freezn' for something fresh,[22] anyway. Less commence, right away."

So the duke he told him all about who Romeo was, and who Juliet was, and said he was used to being Romeo, so the king could be Juliet.

"But if Juliet's such a young gal,[23] Duke, my peeled head

12. *seven-up*. Also called "Old Sledge" or "All Fours," popular trumping game of the backwoods won by the first player to get seven "chalks," or points.

13. *lay out a campaign.* Military slang, plan an attack.

14. *The celebrated Dr. Armand de Montalban of Paris.* Because phrenologists often came from Paris to practice in America, the duke appropriates a French alias.

15. *charts of character*. Large drawings of the subject's head in profile, divided into sections like a map on which were labeled human characteristics based upon the various contours of the skull.

16. *world renowned Shaksperean tragedian, Garrick the Younger, of Drury Lane, London.* This time the duke takes a British alias, and that of the most famous actor of late-eighteenth-century London, because, as Twain explained in a suppressed passage of *Life on the Mississippi*, "The stage was almost exclusively occupied by the English—very few native actors could 'draw' " (Limited Editions Club edition, 1944, p. 406). "Shakspere" was not a colloquial but an approved spelling of the bard's name at the time of the story. There was no David Garrick the Younger. See Chapter 21, note 11.

17. *like finding water and gold with a "divining rod."* It is still believed in certain parts of the world that some people (said to be those in the family with the most "devil" in them) were blessed with a sixth sense which enabled them to discover the best place to find water or gold. This "water witch" or "witch hazel professor" walked with a "divining rod" (a crotched witch hazel stick) held in front; and wherever it happened to point downward was the place to dig. "I have seen more than four hundred 'goldfinders,' first and last," Twain said in "A Big Thing" (Buffalo *Express*, March 12, 1870), "but I never saw anybody that ever heard of one ever finding anything. . . . I recall how four dreadful weeks I followed step by step in the track of a 'Professor' with a hazel stick in his hand,—a 'divining-rod'—which was to turn and tilt down and point to the gold whenever we came to any. But we never came to any, I suppose."

and my white whiskers is goin' to look oncommon odd on her, maybe."

"No, don't you worry—these country jakes won't ever think of that.[24] Besides, you know, you'll be in costume, and that makes all the difference in the world; Juliet's in a balcony, enjoying the moonlight before she goes to bed, and she's got on her night-gown and her ruffled night-cap. Here are the costumes for the parts."

THE KING AS JULIET.

He got out two or three curtain-calico[25] suits, which he said was meedyevil armor for Richard III.[26] and t'other chap,[27] and a long white cotton night-shirt and a ruffled night-cap to match. The king was satisfied; so the duke got out his book and read the parts over in the most splendid spread-eagle way,[28] prancing around and acting at the same time, to show how it had got to be done; then he give the book to the king and told him to get his part by heart.

There was a little one-horse town[29] about three mile down the bend, and after dinner the duke said he had ciphered out his idea about how to run in daylight without it being dangersome for Jim; so he allowed he would go down to the town and fix that thing. The king allowed he would go too, and see if he couldn't strike something. We was out of coffee, so Jim said I better go along with them in the canoe and get some.

When we got there, there warn't nobody stirring; streets empty, and perfectly dead and still, like Sunday. We found a sick nigger sunning himself in a back yard, and he said everybody that warn't too young or too sick or too old, was gone to camp-meeting, about two mile back in the woods.

18. *dissipating witch-spells.* Nervous disorders were once thought to be caused by witches, and "witch doctors" in the South were often called on to exorcise demons from the afflicted by administering various folk cures.

19. *Have you ever trod the boards.* Have you ever acted; theatrical cliché, the "boards" being the stage of a theater.

20. *sword-fight in Richard III.* Act V, scene v, the climax of Shakespeare's tragedy. *Richard III* was one of the most popular plays of American touring companies of the nineteenth century, no doubt largely because of the famous sword fight; even Tom Sawyer and Huckleberry Finn are familiar with it in Chapter 25 of *Tom Sawyer*. In Chapter 51 of *Life on the Mississippi*, Twain recalled that when he was a boy in Hannibal, "a couple of young Englishmen came to the town and sojourned a while; and one day they got themselves up in cheap royal finery and did the Richard III swordfight with maniac energy and prodigious powwow, in the presence of the village boys." Blair and Fischer reported in the 1988 University of California edition (p. 409) that actor Edmund King established the flamboyant way of staging this famous sword fight.

21. *up to the hub.* Deeply, no further; when a vehicle is stuck in the mud up to the hub of the wheels, it cannot move.

22. *a-freezn' for something fresh.* Intensely longing for something new.

23. *Juliet's such a young gal.* She is about Huck's age: Lady Capulet tells the Nurse, "She's not fourteen" (Act I, scene iii, line 12).

24. *these country jakes won't ever think of that.* According to Wecter's *Sam Clemens of Hannibal*, at this time (as in Shakespeare's day) in this part of the country, no woman could appear on the stage; all feminine roles were played by men. When the Thespian Society of Hannibal put on the play, Presley Minor played "Juliet" to James Minor's "Romeo"; by 1842, this troupe disbanded, supposedly because "the female impersonators had too large beards to perform well" (p. 186).

25. *curtain-calico.* A particularly gaudily printed cheap cloth.

The king got the directions, and allowed he'd go and work that camp-meeting for all it was worth, and I might go, too.

The duke said what he was after was a printing office. We found it; a little bit of a concern, up over a carpenter shop—carpenters and printers all gone to the meeting,[30] and no doors locked. It was a dirty, littered-up place, and had ink marks, and handbills with pictures of horses[31] and runaway niggers on them, all over the walls. The duke shed his coat and said he was all right, now. So me and the king lit out for the camp-meeting.[32]

We got there in about a half an hour,[33] fairly dripping,[34] for it was a most awful hot day. There was as much as a thousand people there, from twenty mile around.[35] The woods was full of teams and wagons, hitched everywheres, feeding out of the wagon troughs and stomping to keep off the flies. There was sheds made out of poles and roofed over with branches, where they had lemonade and gingerbread to sell, and piles of watermelons[36] and green corn and such-like truck.

The preaching was going on under the same kinds of sheds, only they was bigger and held crowds of people. The benches was made out of outside slabs of logs,[37] with holes bored in the round side to drive sticks into for legs. They didn't have no backs. The preachers had high platforms to stand on, at one end of the sheds. The women had on sun-bonnets; and some had linsey-woolsey frocks,[38] some gingham ones,[39] and a few of the young ones had on calico.[40] Some of the young men was barefooted, and some of the children didn't have on any clothes but just a tow-linen shirt.[41] Some of the old women was knitting, and some of the young folks was courting on the sly.[42]

The first shed we come to, the preacher was lining out a hymn.[43] He lined out two lines, everybody sung it, and it was kind of grand to hear it, there was so many of them and they done it in such a rousing way; then he lined out two more for them to sing—and so on. The people woke up more and more, and sung louder and louder; and towards the end, some begun to groan, and some begun to shout. Then the preacher begun to preach; and begun in earnest,

26. *meedyevil armor for Richard III.* The War of the Roses raged from 1455 to 1485; nineteenth-century "Richards" usually wore chainmail rather than the more cumbersome full armor.

27. *t'other chap.* "Richmond," or Henry, Earl of Richmond, afterward King Henry VII.

28. *spread-eagle way.* An extravagant, exaggerated, bombastic style of oratory, originally of a patriotic nature, referring to the eagle, the American national symbol.

29. *a little one-horse town.* Blair and Fischer in the 1988 University of California edition (p. 410) located this village somewhere between Compromise, Kentucky, and Napoleon, Arkansas; because Twain did not say which side of the river it is on, it is impossible to determine exactly which place he had in mind. His notes suggest that it is "Walnut Bend [in Arkansas] or some other wretched place."

30. *printers all gone to the meeting.* Young Sam Clemens and his fellow workers did just the same thing when they worked in the Hannibal *Missouri Courier* office. "Whenever there was a barbecue, or a circus, or a baptizing, we knocked off for half a day," he admitted in his talk "The Compositor," at a dinner at the Typothetæ in New York, on January 18, 1886 ("The Typothetæ," Hartford *Courier*, January 21, 1886).

31. *handbills with pictures of horses.* Twain originally said "stallions" (**MS**) in the manuscript. These cheap flyers advertising the sale of horses decorated the Hannibal *Missouri Courier* office, where Sam Clemens was apprenticed from 1853 to the summer of 1854. He fondly recalled them in his talk "The Compositor," delivered at the dinner of the Typothetæ, held in New York on January 18, 1886: "I can see the printing office of prehistoric times yet, with its

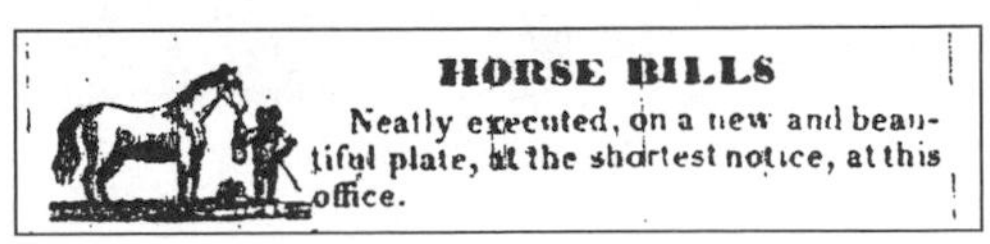

Advertisement for horse bills, Hannibal *Journal*, May 13, 1847.
Courtesy Missouri Historical Society Collection.

horse bills on the walls, the 'd' boxes clogged with tallow, because we always stood the candle in the 'k' box nights, its towel, which was not considered soiled until it could stand alone, and other signs and symbols that marked the establishment of that kind in the Mississippi valley" ("The Typothetæ," Hartford *Courant*, January 21, 1886). "Everybody is making a fortune out of blackness," quipped writer Ishmael Reed in an interview with Shamoon Zamir in *Callaloo* (Autumn 1974). "I finally discovered why in *Huckleberry Finn* the slaves and the horses are advertised on the same page in the newspapers, because we're natural resources. So I told my wife when I die, I want to be buried next to a horse" (p. 1149).

32. *the camp-meeting*. This open-air congress was known as a "revival," resulting from a sudden reemergence of intense religious feeling, often evangelical in intent and spreading far beyond the immediate community in its acquisition of new converts to its faith. "The country was so sparsely settled and the churches so far apart that they were the only means by which early settlers were enabled to enjoy the privileges of the sanctuary," Ben Ezra Stiles Ely explained in Curtis Dahl, "Mark Twain and Ben Ely: Two Missouri Boyhoods" (*Missouri Historical Review*, July 1972). "Those who attended often came thirty and even forty miles in their wagons or on horseback, sometimes two on one horse, bringing their bedding, cooking utensils and provisions, prepared to remain two or three weeks" (p. 556). Inspired by the Sermon on the

A camp meeting. Lithograph by A. Hervieu, *Domestic Manners of the Americans* by Frances Trollope, 1832.
Courtesy General Research and Humanities Division, New York Public Library, Astor, Lenox, and Tilden Foundations.

"COURTING ON THE SLY."

too; and went weaving first to one side of the platform and then the other, and then a leaning down over the front of it, with his arms and his body going all the time, and shouting his words out with all his might;[44] and every now and then he would hold up his Bible and spread it open, and kind of pass it around this way and that, shouting, "It's the brazen serpent in the wilderness![45] Look upon it and live!" And people would shout out, "Glory!—A-a-*men!*" And so he went on, and the people groaning and crying and saying amen:[46]

"Oh, come to the mourners' bench![47] come, black with sin! (*amen!*) come, sick and sore![48] (*amen!*) come, lame and halt, and blind! (*amen!*) come, pore and needy, sunk in shame! (*a-a-men!*) come all that's worn, and soiled, and suffering!—come with a broken spirit! come with a contrite heart! come in your rags and sin and dirt! the waters that cleanse is free, the door of heaven stands open—oh, enter in and be at rest!" (*a-a-men! glory, glory hallelujah!*)

And so on. You couldn't make out what the preacher said, any more, on account of the shouting and crying. Folks got up, everywheres in the crowd, and worked their way, just by main strength, to the mourners' bench, with the tears running down their faces; and when all the mourners had got up there to the front benches in a crowd,[49] they sung, and shouted, and flung themselves down on the straw, just crazy and wild.

Well, the first I knowed, the king got agoing;[50] and you could hear him over everybody;[51] and next he went a-charging up on to the platform[52] and the preacher he begged him to speak to the people, and he done it. He told them he was a pirate—been a pirate for thirty years, out in the Indian Ocean, and his crew was thinned out considerable, last spring, in a fight, and he was home now, to take out some fresh men, and thanks to goodness he'd been robbed last night, and put ashore off of a steamboat without a cent, and[53] he was glad of it, it was the blessedest thing that ever happened to him, because[54] he was a changed man now, and happy for the first time in his life; and poor as he was, he was going to start right off and work his way back to the Indian Ocean and put in the rest of his life trying to turn the pirates into the true path;[55] for he could do it better than anybody else, being acquainted with all the pirate crews in that ocean; and though it would take him a long time to get there, without money, he would get there

"A PIRATE FOR THIRTY YEARS."

Mount, these meetings gathered in the open so that as many people as possible could attend; most country churches were just too small to hold them all, and many communities did not have even that. They began in America in the early nineteenth century with the migration of Presbyterians from North Carolina to Tennessee and Kentucky; Methodists later adopted the camp meeting for their revivals. The direct and uninterrupted concentration on personal salvation through song and sermon for several days straight produced countless converts. The techniques of persuasion employed at these camp meetings survive in the hysteria of modern sects and self-help groups.

33. *We got there in about a half an hour*. Twain's fictional account follows closely Captain Marryat's description of a camp meeting he encountered on his trip to America as recorded in Chapter 32 of his 1839 diary, a work Twain read and extensively quoted in *Life on the Mississippi*:

> About an acre and a half was surrounded on the four sides by cabins built up of rough boards, the whole area in the centre was fitted up with planks, laid about a foot from the ground, as seats. At one end, but not close to the cabins, was a raised stand, which served as a pulpit for the preachers, one of them praying, while five or six others sat down behind him on benches. . . . At a farther distance were all the wagons and other vehicles which had conveyed the people to the meeting, whilst hundreds of horses were tethered under the trees, and plentifully provided with forage. . . . Fires were burning in every direction: pots boiling, chickens roasting, hams seething; indeed there appeared to be no want of creature comforts. . . .
>
> One of the preachers rose and gave out a hymn, which was sung by the congregation, amounting to about seven or eight hundred. . . . At last an elderly gentleman . . . knelt down in the center, and commenced a prayer . . . ; then another burst out into prayer, and another followed him; then their voices became all confused together; and then were heard the more silvery tones of woman's supplication. As the din increased so did their enthusiasm; handkerchiefs were raised to bright eyes, and sobs were intermingled with prayers and ejaculations. . . . One young man clung to the form, crying 'Satan tears at me, but I will hold fast. Help—help, he drags me

> down!" . . . when it was at its height, one of the preachers came in, and, raising his voice high, above the tumult, entreated the Lord to receive into his fold those who now repented and would fain return. . . . Groans, ejaculations, broken sobs, frantic motions and convulsions succeeded; some fell on their backs with their eyes closed, waving their hands with a slow motion, and crying out—"Glory, glory, glory!" I quitted the spot, and hastened into the forest, for the sight was too painful, too melancholy.

Marryat thought that the camp-meeting hysteria arose from "a fever created by collision and contact, of the same nature as that which stimulates a mob to deeds of blood and horror. Gregarious animals are by nature inoffensive. The cruel and the savage live apart, and in solitude; but the gregarious, upheld and stimulated by each other, become formidable. So it is with man." Further proof of Marryat's argument may be found in Chapter 21. Ely, however, gave a far more sympathetic picture of revivals in Hannibal in Dahl, "Mark Twain and Ben Ely" (*Missouri Historical Review*, July 1972). "Many of the pleasant memories of the early days in Missouri are associated with the camp meetings," he recalled. "The preaching of the Gospel and the devotional services were so sweet and solemn, and the singing of the old standard hymns and Psalms so fervent, that though these services often occupied two or three hours they were not wearisome and held the undivided attention of the worshippers" (pp. 556–57).

Twain did not share Ben Ely's fondness for such gatherings. He attended a Campbellite revival when a boy in Hannibal, where "farmers and their families drove or tramped into the village from miles around to get a sight of the illustrious Alexander Campbell and to have a chance to hear him preach" (quoted in Paine, *Mark Twain: A Biography*, vol. 2, 1912, p. 279). "All converted but me," he proudly recalled. "All sinners again in a week" (quoted in Wecter, *Sam Clemens of Hannibal*, 1952, p. 88). The king's "working the camp-meeting" must have been inspired by "The Captain Attends a Camp-Meeting" in Johnson Jones Hooper's *Adventures of Captain Simon Suggs* (1845). "The reader is requested to bear in mind, that the scenes described in this chapter are not *now* to be witnessed," Hooper added in a footnote. "Eight or ten years ago, all classes of population of the Creek country were very different from what

anyway, and every time he convinced a pirate he would say to him, "Don't you thank me, don't you give me no credit, it all belongs to them dear people in Pokeville[56] camp-meeting, natural brothers and benefactors of the race—and that dear preacher there, the truest friend a pirate ever had!"

And then he busted into tears, and so did everybody.[57] Then somebody sings out, "Take up a collection for him, take up a collection!" Well, a half a dozen made a jump to do it, but somebody sings out, "Let *him* pass the hat around!" Then everybody said it, the preacher too.

So the king went all through the crowd with his hat, swabbing his eyes, and blessing the people and praising them and thanking them for being so good to the poor pirates away off there; and every little while the prettiest kind of girls, with the tears running down their cheeks, would up and ask him would he let them kiss him, for to remember him by; and he always done it; and some of them he hugged and kissed as many as five or six times[58]—and he was invited to stay a week; and everybody wanted him to live in their houses, and said they'd think it was an honor; but he said as this was the last day of the camp-meeting he couldn't do no good, and besides he was in a sweat to get to the Indian Ocean right off and go to work on the pirates.

When we got back to the raft and he come to count up, he found he had collected eighty-seven dollars and seventy-five cents. And then he had fetched away a three-gallon jug of whisky, too, that he found under a wagon when we was starting home through the woods. The king said, take it all around, it laid over any day he'd ever put in in the missionarying line. He said it warn't no use talking, heathens don't amount to shucks, alongside of pirates, to work a camp-meeting with.

The duke was thinking *he'd* been doing pretty well, till the king come to show up, but after that he didn't think so so much. He had set up and printed off two little jobs for farmers, in that printing office—horse bills—and took the money, four dollars. And he had got in ten dollars worth of advertisements for the paper, which he said he would put in for four dollars if they would pay in advance—so they done it. The price of the paper was two dollars a year, but he took in three subscriptions for half a dollar apiece on condition of them paying him in advance; they were going to pay in cord-wood and onions, as usual,[59] but he said he had just bought the concern and knocked down the price as low as he could afford it, and was going to run it for cash. He set up a little piece of poetry, which he made, himself, out of his own head—three verses—kind of sweet and saddish—the name of it was, "Yes, crush, cold world, this breaking heart"[60]—and he left that all set up and ready to print in the paper and didn't charge nothing for it. Well, he took in nine dollars and a half, and said he'd done a pretty square day's work for it.

Then he showed us another little job he'd printed and hadn't charged for, because it was for us. It had a picture of a runaway nigger, with a bundle on a stick, over his shoul-

ANOTHER LITTLE JOB.

der,[61] and "$200 reward"[62] under it. The reading was all about Jim, and just described him to a dot.[63] It said he run away from St. Jacques' plantation, forty mile below New Orleans,[64] last winter, and likely went north, and whoever

they now are" (p. 122). See also notes 50 and 58 below.

34. *fairly dripping.* Originally "sweating like sin" (**MS**) in the manuscript.

35. *twenty mile around.* Twain also considered "*forty* mile around" (**MS**) in the manuscript.

36. *watermelons.* Changed from "watermillions" (**MS**) in the manuscript.

37. *The benches was made out of outside slabs of logs.* "A slab bench is made of the outside cut of a sawlog, with the bark side down," Twain recalled, drawing on his memory of those in the church not far from his Uncle John Quarles's farm, outside Florida, Missouri; "it is supported on four sticks driven into auger holes at the ends; it has no back and no cushions" (*Autobiography*, 1924, vol. 1, p. 8). Ely confirmed in Dahl, "Mark Twain and Ben Ely" (*Missouri Historical Review*, July 1972), that the congregation was provided "with backless seats made of boards, often of slabs hewn on one side with a broad axe" (p. 556).

38. *linsey-woolsey frocks.* Cheap dresses, made of a coarse homespun cloth, woven from a mixture of wool and flax or wool and cotton.

39. *gingham ones.* A cheap cotton cloth with the pattern woven in with colored threads.

40. *calico.* Huck can tell what class of backwoods society a woman belongs to by the kind of dress she wears: lower (linsey-woolsey), middle (gingham), and upper (calico).

41. *a tow-linen shirt.* Made of coarse-spun linen, often the only clothing worn by children of both races in the backwoods. See Chapter 32, note 8.

42. *some of the young folks was courting on the sly.* In a talk he delivered at the Players Club in 1894, Twain kidded about the "bundling courtships" at these gatherings and the resulting "camp-meeting babies." Marryat noted in Chapter 32 of his 1839 *Diary in America* that many people traveled as much as one hundred miles to attend camp meetings just "to indulge in the licentiousness which, it is said, but too often follows, when night has thrown her veil over the scene." Anniversaries and other events were often marked in the backwoods according to the dates of camp meetings; for example, a boy's age was said to be "twelve years old come next camp meeting." That shows how important these social gatherings were to the community, but that might also be a sarcastic reference to exactly when the child was conceived.

43. *the preacher was lining out a hymn.* The preacher says each line of the hymn and the congregation repeats it, because many of the penitents could not read themselves. Also hymn books were scarce and rather costly in the backwoods, so the preacher has to read the verses aloud line by line so that the crowd can join in the song of praise. Ely recalled in Dahl, "Mark Twain and Ben Ely" (*Missouri Historical Review*, July 1972), that the typical hymns sung at these gatherings were "Jesus Lover of My Soul," "Rock of Ages," and "There Is Nothing True but Heaven" (p. 557). Twain had been more specific in the manuscript, quoting "Am I a Soldier at the Cross" (1709) by Isaac Watts::

"Am I a soldier of the cross,
A follower of the Lamb,
And shall I fear to own his cause,
Or blush to speak his name?" (**MS**)

The minister reads the same verse "with relish" in Chapter 5 of *Tom Sawyer*.

44. *shouting his words out with all his might.* William Henry Milburn recalled in *Pioneers, Preachers and People of the Mississippi Valley* (1860) how camp-meeting sermons were delivered "in their loudest tone—and that was a very loud tone, for the lungs of the backwoods preachers were of the strongest. They roared like lions—their tones were absolutely like peals of lightning" (p. 388).

45. *It's the brazen serpent in the wilderness!* In Numbers 21, God sends snakes to plague the Israelites when they turn on Moses after he has led them out of Egypt and into the wilderness. When they repent and pray for them to go away, He commands Moses to put a bronze replica of a snake on a staff; anyone who has been bitten will recover by just looking at the brazen serpent.

46. *the people groaning and crying and saying amen.* Twain revised the sermon from the way it appeared in the manuscript:

would catch him and send him back, he could have the reward and expenses.

"Now," says the duke, "after to-night we can run in the daytime if we want to. Whenever we see anybody coming, we can tie Jim hand and foot with a rope, and lay him in the wigwam and show this handbill and say we captured him up the river, and were too poor to travel on a steamboat, so we got this little raft on credit from our friends and are going down to get the reward. Handcuffs and chains would look still better on Jim, but it wouldn't go well with the story of us being so poor.[65] Too much like jewelry. Ropes are the correct thing—we must preserve the unities,[66] as we say on the boards."

We all said the duke was pretty smart, and there couldn't be no trouble about running daytimes. We judged we could make miles enough that night to get out of the reach of the pow-wow we reckoned the duke's work in the printing office was going to make in that little town—then we could boom right along, if we wanted to.

We laid low and kept still, and never shoved out till nearly ten o'clock; then we slid by, pretty wide away from the town, and didn't hoist our lantern till we was clear out of sight of it.

When Jim called me to take the watch at four in the morning, he says—

"Huck, does you reck'n we gwyne to run acrost any mo' kings on dis trip?"

"No," I says, "I reckon not."

"Well," says he, "dat's all right, den. I doan' mine one er two kings, but dat's enough. Dis one's powerful drunk, en de duke ain' much better."

I found Jim had been trying to get him to talk French, so he could hear what it was like; but he said he had been in this country so long, and had so much trouble, he'd forgot it.

> . . . and next he would lay the Bible down and weave about the platform, and work back to the Bible again, pretty soon, and fetch it a bang with his fist and shout—"here it is! the rock of salvation—ah!" And so he went on a-raging, and the people groaning and crying, and jumping up and hugging one another, and *Amens* was popping off everywheres. Every little while he would preach right *at* the people that he saw was stirred up:
>
> "The sperrit's a workin' in you, brother—don't shake him off—ah!—Now is the accepted time—ah! (*A-a*-men!) The devil's holt is weakenin' on you, sister—shake him loose, shake him loose—ah! One more shake and the vict'ry's won—ah! (*Come* down, *Lord!*) Hell's a burning, the kingdom's a-coming—ah!—one more shake, sister, one more shake and your chains is broke—ah! (*Glory* hal-*lelu-jah!*) O, come to the mourner's bench! Come, black with sin! (*Amen*) come, sick and sore! (*Amen!*) come, pore and needy, sunk in shame! (*A-a*-men!) come all that's worn, and guilty and sufferin'!—come with a broken spirit! come with a contrite heart! come in your rags and sin and dirt! The waters that cleanse is free, the door of heaven stands open—O, enter into the everlasting rest!" (*A-a*-men! *Glo-o-ry! glory! Come* down, *Lord!*) (**MS**)

Twain went further than even Hooper in *Adventures of Captain Simon Suggs* dared in suggesting the underlying eroticism at a camp meeting. The preacher has worked up the penitents into an orgy of religious fervor that is not only blasphemous but almost obscene. The sexual innuendo of this sermon was not lost on the author of the infamous 1879 lecture "Some Thoughts on the Science of Onanism" to the Stomach Club in Paris as the unrelenting plea to "come" reaches climax ("The waters that cleanse is free, the door of heaven stands open—O, enter into the everlasting rest!"). Twain employs "ah!" in repetition as Molly Bloom does "yes" in her famous orgasmic soliloquy in James Joyce's *Ulysses* (1922). This was not the sort of thing one might read to Olivia Clemens and her little girls or publish in a book fit for the parlor. It had to be changed to a less urgent and more reverential version.

47. *the mourners' bench*. Or "anxious seat," front-row benches reserved for penitents who "mourned" for the absolution of their sins. Here seemed to be at least one place where slave and master were equal before God. "When we went to camp meeting we all went to de mourners bench," recalled former Missouri slave Richard Bruner. "De mourners bench stretch clear across de front of de Arbor; de whites and blacks, we all jest fell down at de mourners bench and got religion at de same time" (see Harris and Van Clief-Stefanon, *Adventures of Huckleberry Finn*, New Riverside Editions edition [Boston and New York: Houghton Mifflin, 2000], p. 25). See note 49 below.

48. *come, black with sin! . . . come, sick and sore!* John R. Byers, Jr., in "The Pokeville Preacher's Invitation in *Huckleberry Finn*" (*Mark Twain Journal*, Summer 1977), suggested that the preacher is paraphrasing the hymn "Come Ye Sinners" by Joseph Hart (1712–1768), No. 118 of his *Hymns Composed on Various Subjects* (1759), which begins:

> *Come, ye sinners, poor and needy,*
> *Weak and wounded, sick and sore,*
> *Jesus ready stands to save you,*
> *Full of pity, love and pow'r*
> *He is able, He is able,*
> *He is willing, doubt no more.* (p. 15)

Other stanzas begin "Come, ye thirsty, come and welcome," and "Come, ye weary, heavy-laden."

49. *a crowd*. Originally "a gang" (**MS**) in the manuscript. This was followed by a passage Twain finally dropped from the book:

> . . . they hugged one another, and shouted, and flung themselves down on the straw, and wallowed around, just plum crazy and wild. One fat nigger woman about forty, was the worst. The white mourners couldn't fend her off, no way—fast as one would get loose, she'd tackle the next one, and smother him. Next, down she went on the straw, along with the rest, and wallowed around, clawing dirt and shouting hallelujah same as they did. (**MS**)

Twain may have been recalling a similar scene in Hooper's *Adventures of Captain Simon Suggs:* "'Gl-o-*ree!*' yelled a huge, greasy negro woman, as in a fit of the jerks, she threw herself compulsively from her feet, and fell 'like a thousand of brick,' across a diminutive old man in a little round hat, who was speaking consolation to one of the mourners. 'Good Lord, have mercy!' ejaculated the little man earnestly and unaffectedly, as he strove to crawl from under the sable mass which was crushing him" (p. 121). Twain's crude image of an aggressive slave woman "wallowing around" at a religious service among white penitents (originally a forty-year-old "wench") was probably too suggestive for Olivia Clemens or Howells. And Twain himself may have had second thoughts on the propriety of this section.

But she was hardly the only one possessed by wild convulsions at these meetings. "The people were seized as by a sort of superhuman power," Milburn wrote of "strange manifestations" in *Pioneers, Preachers and People of the Mississippi Valley* (1860); "their physical energy was lost; their senses refused to perform their functions; all forms of manifesting consciousness were for the time annulled. Strong men fell upon the ground, utterly helpless; women were taken with a strange spasmodic motion, so that they were heaved to and fro, sometimes falling at length upon the floor, their hair dishevelled, and throwing their heads about with a quickness and violence so great as to make their hair crack against the floor as if it were a teamster's whip. Then they would rise up again under this strange power, fall on their faces, and the same violent movements and cracking noise would ensue" (p. 357).

50. *Well, the first I knowed, the king got agoing.* So too does Simon Suggs, "the very 'chief of sinners' in that region," confess his sins with crocodile tears before the revival's congregation, but minus the king's sillinesses. Hooper's swindler milks their sympathy by blubbering that divine grace aided him in his conquest of Satan, "the biggest, longest, rip-roarenest, blackest, scariest . . . Allegator!" (p. 139). And like Twain's king, Suggs runs off with the church's collection. Hooper's account is perhaps the sharper in its cynicism while Twain's is more sarcastic in his low view of society. After all, the king easily dupes the Pokeville congregation with an absurd tale of converting pirates of the Indian Ocean. Hooper felt compelled to apologize for any offense he might cause, perhaps at the request of his publisher. "Of course, no disrespect is intended to any denomination of Christianity," he said in a footnote. "We believe that camp-meetings are not peculiar to any church, though most usual in the Methodist—a denomination whose respectability in Alabama is attested to the fact, that *very many* of its worthy clergymen and lay members, hold honorable and profitable offices in the gift of the state legislature; of which, indeed, almost a controlling portion are themselves Methodists" (p. 134). But Twain published *Huckleberry Finn* himself as a subscription book which was sold from door to door, and he felt no need to cater to middle-class hypocrisy and he did not have to defend himself to anyone.

51. *you could hear him over everybody.* Twain had also said in the manuscript "for whooping and hugging and wallowing. And everything was just about its boomingest" (**MS**).

52. *next he went a-charging up on to the platform.* "And flung his arms around the preacher and went to hugging and kissing him, and crying all over him, and thanking him for saving him" (**MS**) in the manuscript.

53. *without a cent, and.* Here Twain took "glory hallelujah" (**MS**) from the manuscript, probably for sounding too blasphemous.

54. *it was the blessedest thing that ever happened to him, because.* "He'd got religion to-day" (**MS**) in the manuscript, but Twain dropped it probably to avoid offending good churchgoers like Olivia Clemens and Howells.

55. *back to the Indian Ocean and put in the rest of his life trying to turn the pirates into the true path.* The Indian Ocean was infamous for its pirates in the early nineteenth century; also, the influx of missionaries to this part of the world led to the Sepoy Rebellion of 1857 against foreign influence in India.

56. *Pokeville.* The name may have come from Joseph M. Field's *The Drama in Pokerville* (1847); it also suggests William Tappan Thompson's "Pineville" in Georgia.

57. *and so did everybody.* Twain eliminated another little bit of overindulgence from the manuscript, "and he hugged the preacher and cried on him again, and everybody hugged one another and sung out A-a-*men!* and all that sort of thing" (**MS**).

58. *he hugged and kissed as many as five or six times.* Twain vehemently opposed Kemble's drawing of "the lecherous old rascal kissing the girl at the camp-meeting." "It is powerful good," he admitted to Charley Webster, "but it mustn't go in—don't forget it. Let's not make *any* pictures of the camp-meeting. The subject won't *bear* illustrating. It is a disgusting thing, and pictures are sure to tell about it too plainly" (quoted in Webster, *Mark Twain, Business Man*, p. 260). Richard Watson Gilder agreed: He dropped this episode when "Royalty on the Mississippi" appeared in *Century* (February 1885). The Webster family eventually sold the suppressed sketch of the king at the camp meeting, but its whereabouts are unknown.

The king is as lecherous as the preacher in Hooper's *Adventures of Captain Simon Suggs* (1845). But Suggs sees right through the hypocrisy, saying, "Wonder what's the reason these here preachers never hugs up the old, ugly women? Never seed one do it in my life—the sperrit never moves 'em that way! It's nater tho'; and . . . I judge ef I was a preacher, I should save the purtiest souls fust, myself!" (pp. 134–35). Although he did introduce sexual hysteria veiled as religious inspiration at the Pikeville revival, Twain limited the overt goatishness to the king. Had he done otherwise, Olivia Clemens or Howells might likely have penciled it out.

59. *they were going to pay in cord-wood and onions, as usual.* Cash was scarce in the backwoods at this time, so bartering for services was common. Twain recalled in his talk "The Compositor" that when he was working in the Hannibal *Missouri Courier* office, "the town subscribers paid in groceries and the country ones in cabbages and cord-wood—when they paid at all, which was merely sometimes, and then we always stated the fact in the paper and gave them a puff; and if we forgot it they stopped the paper" ("The Typothetæ," Hartford *Courant*, January 21, 1886). Twain mentioned other produce in "Hannibal—By a Native Historian" (*Alta California*, May 26, 1867), when he recalled that the paper "bred a fierce spirit of enterprise in the neighboring farmers, because when they had any small potatoes left over that they couldn't sell, they didn't throw them away as they used to, but they took them to the editor and traded them off for subscriptions to his paper." According to Donald H. Welsh, "Sam Clemens' Hannibal, 1836–1838" (*Midcontinent American Studies Journal*, Spring 1962), the Hannibal *Gazette* (November 4, 1847) advertised that "we will take *wood, corn*, potatoes, or marketing, which a family can use, in exchange for the *Gazette*." But when they failed to pay, the paper published an announcement on November 26: "We would request such of our subscribers as have agreed to pay us in *wood*, to bring it on immediately, let it be seasoned, and split sticks. In this case, procrastination will not only be 'the thief of time,' but the cause of *red noses*!" (pp. 31–32).

60. *"Yes, crush, cold world, this breaking heart."* Sentimental Hugh Burnside, the amateur poet of the unfinished "Simon Wheeler, Detective" (*Mark Twain's Satires and Burlesques*, 1968), composes an equally mawkish verse, the "ten-line deformity, christened 'The Crushed Heart's Farewell,' and leading off with this couplet":

Tho' chill be the desert and bleak its aspect,
Far kinder its storms than this cold world's neglect. (p. 360)

Twain may also have been recalling the efforts of his first boss, Joseph Ament, editor of the Hannibal *Missouri Courier*. "He wrote with impressive flatulence and soaring confidence upon the vastest subjects," Twain said in his lecture "The Compositor." "He was always a poet . . . and whenever his intellect suppurated, and he read the result to the printers and asked for their opinion, they were very frank and straightforward about it. They generally scraped their rulers on the boxes all the time he was reading, and called it 'hogwash' when he got through" ("The Typothetæ," Hartford *Courant*, January 21, 1886). But young Sam Clemens was not one to talk: He too took to writing equally conventional love poems, two of which, "The Heart's Lament" and "Love Concealed," appeared in his brother Orion's Hannibal *Daily Journal*, and another, "Separation," in the rival *Missouri Courier*, all within a week's time in May 1853. Typical of this juvenilia is the opening stanza of "The Heart's Lament":

I know thou wilt forget me,
For that fond soul of thine
Turns boldly from the passionate,
And ardent love of mine.
It may be, that thou deemest it
A light and simple thing,
To strike with bold and nervous arm,
The heart's lone mystic string.

Such deathless doggerel is worthy of Emmeline Grangerford, Hugh Burnside, and the duke. All three verses appear in *Early Tales and Sketches* (vol. 1, 1979, pp. 89–90, 94, and 101).

61. *It had a picture of a runaway nigger, with a bundle on a stick, over his shoulder*. This was the stock wood engraving used on handbills and newspaper notices for fugitives. It was the same for women runaways: "The handbill had the usual rude woodcut of a turbaned negro woman running, with the customary bundle on a stick over her shoulder" (*Pudd'nhead Wilson*, Chapter 18). Young Sam Clemens may well have set some of them when he worked as a printer's apprentice in the offices of the Hannibal *Missouri Courier* and *Western Union*.

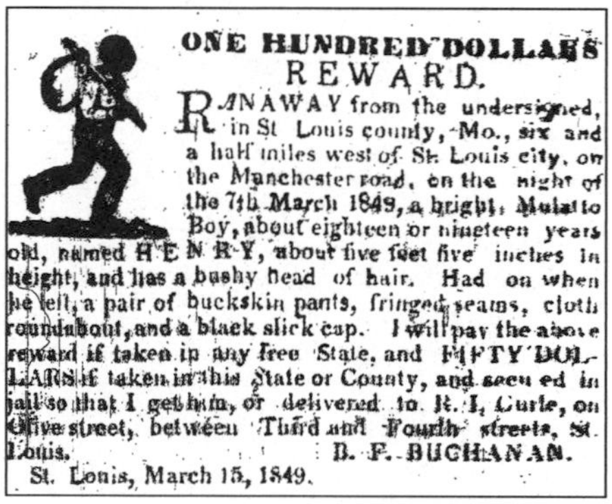

ONE HUNDRED DOLLARS
REWARD.

RANAWAY from the undersigned, in St Louis county, Mo., six and a half miles west of St. Louis city, on the Manchester road, on the night of the 7th March 1849, a bright Mulatto Boy, about eighteen or nineteen years old, named HENRY, about five feet five inches in height, and has a bushy head of hair. Had on when he left, a pair of buckskin pants, fringed seams, cloth roundabout, and a black slick cap. I will pay the above reward if taken in any free State, and FIFTY DOLLARS if taken in this State or County, and secured in jail so that I get him, or delivered to R. I. Curle, on Olive street, between Third and Fourth streets, St. Louis.

B. F. BUCHANAN.

St. Louis, March 15, 1849.

Notice of runaway slave, Hannibal *Western Union*, December 12, 1850.
Courtesy the Mark Twain Papers, Bancroft Library, University of California at Berkeley.

62. *"$200 reward."* All the Hannibal newspapers (even the Missouri *Western Union* that Orion Clemens owned) carried notices of runaways, but Jim commands in this bogus notice a slightly higher reward than the average one from the state. Although the *Missouri Courier* (August 28, 1851) carried an advertisement offering as much as $300 for a man who escaped from Lafayette County, the reward allowed by the statute of the state of Missouri for the apprehension of a fugitive slave was $100 if taken out of state, $50 if in the state, and $25 if in the county. The *Missouri Courier* (December 12, 1852) reported on a recent convention of slaveholders who recommended the formation of Slave Protection Societies, to provide funds for the recapture of runaways at rates "for a slave over 16 years old, $200, for younger ones, $100, and $50 for information which results in the capture of a fugitive." The reward for Roxy in Chapter 18 of *Pudd'nhead Wilson* is $100. Perhaps it is another grandiloquent gesture on the duke's part to claim Jim as more valuable than the usual slave.

63. *just described him to a dot*. "Needless to say," said Jocelyn Chadwick-Joshua in *The Jim Dilemma* (1998), "this scene is another source of anxiety for some African-American students and parents because of the very notion of replacing Jim into slavery. The bill itself and the wording, along with the emblematic image of the runaway slave, are the material of the horror of slavery itself. The [duke's] design is, however, accurate for the period, according to reprints of such announcements in the periodicals. In fact, many of the abolitionist periodicals and magazines, both African American and white, devoted space to reprinting runaway slave bills to further solidify their antislavery position and expose an unfavorable view of the South to others" (p. 98). Notices of runaways were often specific in their descriptions: "John is about 23 years of age, about 5 feet 8 inches high, dark mulatto color, very full face and broad teeth, and had on when he left a white wool hat, brown jeans clothing, and no shoes [and] Henry is about 21 years of age, 6 feet high, and color and clothing about the same of the other, with the exception he had on shoes, and a black, low-crowned hat; he has a habit of running his finger up his nostril, when spoken to or confused" (Hannibal *Missouri Courier*, October 4, 1849); "a negro boy who says his name is James, 5 feet six inches high, about 19 years of age, rather slender made, is of a dark copper color, and had on . . . a pair of old striped cassine pants, and blue cotton shirt, and an old cotton cap" (Hannibal *Western Union*, December 12, 1850); "a negro man named Louis, about 31 or 32 years of age, five feet five or six inches high, or rather below ordinary height of negro men; of copper or dark color; has lost one of the fore teeth from the upper jaw; is somewhat bow-legged, and at times limps in walking" (*Missouri Courier*, August 28, 1851). These notices emphasized two important details: the high value attached to the capture of a runaway, and the few clothes and other material goods possessed by slaves.

64. *St. Jacques' plantation, forty mile below New Orleans*. This notice provides Huck and Jim free passage all the way down the Mississippi to the fictitious Uncle Ben's place, forty miles below New Orleans. It also makes them vulnerable to the whims of the duke and the king.

65. *Handcuffs and chains would look still better on Jim, but it wouldn't go well with the story of us being so poor*. The duke originally suggested in the manuscript, "we can buy hand-cuffs and a chain at one of these towns along the river and they will still be better" (**MS**).

66. *we must preserve the unities*. We must follow the rules; theatrical slang, the "unities" referring to the three rigid principles of Aristotelian dramatic structure as adopted and expanded by French neoclassical playwrights, limiting Action, Time, and Place to one event occurring at one time and in one locale.

Chapter XXI.

PRACTICING.

IT WAS after sun-up, now, but we went right on, and didn't tie up. The king and the duke turned out, by-and-by, looking pretty rusty; but after they'd jumped overboard and took a swim, it chippered them up a good deal. After breakfast the king he took a seat on a corner of the raft, and pulled off his boots and rolled up his britches, and let his legs dangle in the water, so as to be comfortable, and lit his pipe, and went to getting his Romeo and Juliet by heart. When he had got it pretty good, him and the duke begun to practice it together. The duke had to learn him over and over again, how to say every speech; and he made him sigh, and put his hand on his heart, and after a while he said he done it pretty well; "only," he says, "you mustn't bellow out *Romeo!* that way, like a bull—you must say it soft, and sick, and languishy, so—R-o-o-meo! that is the idea; for Juliet's a dear sweet mere child of a girl, you know, and she don't bray like a jackass."

Well, next they got out a couple of long swords that the duke made out of oak laths, and begun to practice the sword-fight—the duke called himself Richard III.; and the way they laid on, and pranced around the raft was grand to see. But by-and-by the king tripped and fell overboard, and after that they took a rest, and had a talk about all kinds of

"The king tripped and fell overboard."
Illustration by E. W. Kemble,
New York *World*, December 10, 1899.
Private collection.

adventures they'd had in other times along the river.

After dinner, the duke says:

"Well, Capet,[1] we'll want to make this a first-class show, you know, so I guess we'll add a little more to it. We want a little something to answer encores with, anyway."

"What's onkores, Bilgewater?"

The duke told him, and then says:

"I'll answer by doing the Highland fling[2] or the sailor's hornpipe;[3] and you—well, let me see—oh, I've got it—you can do Hamlet's soliloquy."

"Hamlet's which?"

"Hamlet's soliloquy, you know; the most celebrated thing in Shakespeare. Ah, it's sublime, sublime! Always fetches the house. I haven't got it in the book—I've only got one volume[4]—but I reckon I can piece it out from memory. I'll just walk up and down a minute, and see if I can call it back from recollection's vaults."

So he went to marching up and down, thinking, and frowning horrible every now and then; then he would hoist

HAMLET'S SOLILOQUY.

up his eye-brows; next he would squeeze his hand on his forehead and stagger back and kind of moan; next he would

1. *Capet*. Family name of the French dynasty during the Middle Ages. After his arrest in 1792, King Louis XVI was called "Citizen Louis Capet" (although he was of the Bourbon dynasty). Twain may have learned this from Thomas Carlyle's *The French Revolution* (1837), one of his favorite books. According to "Mark Twain's Last Book" (*New York Times*, April 23, 1910), *The French Revolution* was the last one he read on his deathbed. See also Walter Blair, "The French Revolution and *Huckleberry Finn*," *Modern Philology*, August 1957, pp. 21–35.

2. *the Highland fling*. A spirited Scottish folk dance in which the performer stands on one foot, moving the other leg forward and back while alternating the arms in a stiff pose of one hand on the hip and the other over the head.

The Highland fling. Colored lithograph by Sarony & Major, 1846.
Courtesy Library of Congress.

3. *the sailor's hornpipe*. Originally the "Herne-pipe," a lively folk dance in honor of Herne, the pre-Saxon god of the harvest; by the eighteenth century, it was introduced on the popular stage as a solo dance in which the performer imitates certain shipboard tasks and gestures to a piper's tune. It and the Highland fling were often hauled out between acts of minstrel and other shows, so they could not have added much luster to a Shakespeare play, the duke's "first class show."

4. *I've only got one volume*. Traditionally Shakespeare's plays are arranged comedies, histories, and tragedies, so *Hamlet* is in a later volume.

sigh, and next he'd let on to drop a tear. It was beautiful to see him. By-and-by he got it. He told us to give attention. Then he strikes a most noble attitude,[5] with one leg shoved forwards, and his arms stretched away up, and his head tilted back, looking up at the sky; and then he begins to rip and rave and grit his teeth; and after that, all through his speech he howled, and spread around, and swelled up his chest, and just knocked the spots out of any acting ever *I* see before. This is the speech[6]—I learned it, easy enough, while he was learning it to the king:

To be, or not to be; that is the bare bodkin
That makes calamity of so long life;
For who would fardels bear, till Birnam Wood do come to Dunsinane,
But that the fear of something after death
Murders the innocent sleep,
Great nature's second course,
And makes us rather sling the arrows of outrageous fortune
Than fly to others that we know not of.
There's the respect must give us pause:[7]
Wake Duncan with thy knocking! I would thou couldst;
For who would bear the whips and scorns of time,
The oppressor's wrong, the proud man's contumely,
The law's delay,[8] and the quietus which his pangs might take,
In the dead waste and middle of the night, when churchyards yawn
In customary suits of solemn black,
But that the undiscovered country from whose bourne no traveler returns,
Breathes forth contagion on the world,
And thus the native hue of resolution, like the poor cat i' the adage,
Is sicklied o'er with care,
And all the clouds that lowered o'er our housetops,
With this regard their currents turn awry,

5. *a most noble attitude.* The duke seems to be following the acting techniques of the highly influential French teacher and theoretician François Delsarte (1811–1871). He tried to establish "a science of movement" to indicate emotions, attitudes, and ideas through expressive and often exaggerated gesture and pose. He opened his first school in 1839, and his system of acting became widely popular in the United States with both professional and amateur thespians. Although overly mechanized, it profoundly influenced American acting through the silent film era. However, by the end of the century some performers sought a less artificial means of expression; for example, Twain's friend William Gillette became famous for being able to smoke naturally on the stage. In Chapter 51 of *Life on the Mississippi*, Twain spoke about running into a sad "stage-struck" country jake who had left Hannibal to "trod the boards" in St. Louis, inspired by an amateur but energetic performance of the sword fight from *Richard III*. "He was standing musing on a street corner," Twain wrote, "with his right hand on his hip, the thumb of his left supporting his chin, face bowed and frowning, slouch hat pulled down over the forehead—imagining himself to be Othello or some other character, and imagining that the passing crowd marked his tragic bearing and were awe-struck." For thirty-four years, this man took walk-ons that rarely included even a line or two; and "yet, poor devil, he had been patiently studying the part of Hamlet for more than thirty years, and he lived and died in the belief that some day he would be invited to play it!"

6. *the speech.* Twain's burlesque of the most famous soliloquy in English drama is a hodgepodge of frequently quoted lines from *Hamlet* and *Macbeth* and one from *Richard III*: "And all the clouds that lowr'd on our house" (Act I, scene i, line 3). E. Bruce Kirkham argued in "Huck and Hamlet" (*Mark Twain Journal*, Summer 1969, pp. 17–19) that the duke's fractured soliloquy is not so foolish as it first sounds, but that its debate of whether to act or not to act reinforces the importance of the internal monologue as a dialectical device throughout the novel as Huck battles with his conscience.

Huck Finn is not the only person of the period so easily taken in by a phony *Hamlet*: In a passage he dropped from *Life on the Mississippi*, Twain told about an English troupe that played

And lose the name of action.
'Tis a consummation devoutly to be wished. But soft you,
the fair Ophelia:
Ope not thy ponderous and marble jaws,
But get thee to a nunnery—go!

Well, the old man he liked that speech, and he mighty soon got it so he could do it first rate. It seemed like he was just born for it; and when he had his hand in and was excited, it was perfectly lovely the way he would rip and tear and rair up behind when he was getting it off.

The first chance we got, the duke he had some show bills printed; and after that, for two or three days as we floated along, the raft was a most uncommon lively place, for there warn't nothing but sword-fighting and rehearsing—as the duke called it—going on all the time. One morning, when we was pretty well down the State of Arkansaw, we come in sight of a little one-horse town in a big bend;[9] so we tied up about three-quarters of a mile above it, in the mouth of a crick which was shut in like a tunnel by the cypress trees, and all of us but Jim took the canoe and went down there to see if there was any chance in that place for our show.

We struck it mighty lucky; there was going to be a circus there that afternoon, and the country people was already beginning to come in, in all kinds of old shackly wagons, and on horses. The circus would leave before night, so our show would have a pretty good chance. The duke he hired the court house, and we went around and stuck up our bills. They read like this:

Shaksperean Revival!!![10]
Wonderful Attraction!
For One Night Only!
The world renowned tragedians,
David Garrick the younger, of Drury Lane Theatre, London,
and
Edmund Kean the elder,[11] of the Royal Haymarket Theatre,
White-chapel, Pudding Lane, Piccadilly,[12] London,
and the Royal Continental Theatres, in their

Hamlet in Pittsburgh "one night, in the regulation way, and played a burlesque of it the next night; but they didn't *tell* the audience that it was a burlesque; so the women-folk went on crying while the roaring, gigantic Ophelia cavorted hither and thither, scattering her carrots and cabbages around, in lieu of rosemary and rue" (Limited Editions Club edition, 1944, pp. 404–5).

"Mutilations of Shakespeare," DeVoto noted in *Mark Twain's America* (1932), "can be met with everywhere in this literature but most often and most amusingly in the anecdotal recollections of Sol Smith" (pp. 254–55). Twain must have been familiar with the rambling amateur actors with makeshift props and costumes who (like the duke) garble *Richard III* in *Sol Smith's Theatrical Apprenticeship* (1845, pp. 61–62) and *Romeo and Juliet* in *The Theatrical Journey-Work and Anecdotal Recollections of Sol Smith* (1854, pp. 200–1). Twain wrote a tiresome "Burlesque Hamlet" in 1881, in which he added a modern character who comments on the action, anticipating not only *A Connecticut Yankee in King Arthur's Court* (1889) but Tom Stoppard's *Rosencrantz and Gildenstern Are Dead* (1966); he never finished it. It was first published in *Mark Twain's Satires and Burlesques* (1968, pp. 49–87). A parody, however, cannot work unless one knows what is being burlesqued. But, according to Alexis de Tocqueville in *Democracy in America* (vol. 2, 1835), the Bard could be found "in the recesses of the forests of the New World. There is hardly a pioneer's hut that does not contain a few odd volumes of Shakespeare. I remember that I read the feudal drama of *Henry V* for the first time in a log hut" (New York: Viking, 1961, p. 58). And perhaps the most widely burlesqued of all of Shakespeare's plays in both homegrown and foreign productions was *Hamlet*. "Audiences roared at the sight of Hamlet dressed in fur cap and collar, snowshoes and mittens," reported Lawrence W. Levine in *The Unpredictable Past: Explorations in American Culture* (1993); "they listened with amused surprise to his profanity when ordered by his father's ghost to 'swear' and commanding Ophelia, 'Get thee to a brewery'; they heard him recite his lines in black dialect or Irish brogue and sing his most famous soliloquy, 'To be, or not to be,' to the tune of 'Three Blind Mice'" (p. 141) But not everyone roared with laughter at these travesties. Some Americans took their Shakespeare seriously. "As to Dan Rice the

sublime Shaksperean Spectacle entitled
The Balcony Scene
in
Romeo and Juliet!!!

Romeo . . . . Mr. Garrick.
Juliet . . . . Mr. Kean.

Assisted by the whole strength of the company!
New costumes, new scenery, new appointments![13]
Also:
The thrilling, masterly, and blood-curdling
Broad-sword conflict
In Richard III.!!!

Richard III . . . . Mr. Garrick.
Richmond . . . . Mr. Kean.

also:
(by special request,)
Hamlet's Immortal Soliloquy!!
By the Illustrious Kean!
Done by him 300 consecutive nights in Paris!
For One Night Only,
On account of imperative European engagements!
Admission 25 cents; children and servants, 10 cents.

Then we went loafing around the town.[14] The stores and houses was most all old shackly dried-up frame concerns that hadn't ever been painted; they was set up three or four foot above ground on stilts, so as to be out of reach of the water when the river was overflowed. The houses had little gardens around them, but they didn't seem to raise hardly anything in them but jimpson weeds, and sunflowers,[15] and ash-piles, and old curled-up boots and shoes, and pieces of bottles, and rags, and played-out tin-ware. The fences was made of different kinds of boards, nailed on at different times; and they leaned every which-way, and had gates that didn't generly have but one hinge—a leather one.[16] Some of the fences had been whitewashed, some time or another, but the duke said it was in Clumbus's time, like enough. There was generly hogs in the garden, and people driving them out.

'great Sheakspearian [*sic*] clown,' we think the title Sheakspearian [*sic*] *blackguard* would suit him much better," complained the Hannibal *Journal* (June 29, 1848). "He is as perfectly devoid of true wit as he is of the principles of common decency, and every attempt he makes at anything of the kind is a mere slang drawling of the most repulsive obscenity. It is perfectly sickening to hear the most beautiful language and sublime ideas of the immortal 'Bard of Avon' prostituted and mingled up with the most common place dram-shop slang by the sacrilegious tongue of this brazen-faced traducer who, leper like, turns every thing he touches to moral filth and uncleanliness." Fischer and Salamo in the 2001 University of California edition mentioned a later burlesque in Albert W. Aiken's dime novel *Richard Talbot of Cinnabar* (1880): A traveling actor named J. Lysander Tubbs, "The Arkansaw Comedian," late of Drury Lane Theatre, prints a bombastic handbill featuring scenes from *Hamlet* and *Julius Caesar*; some boys come armed with various articles with which to pelt the performer.

7. *There's the respect must give us pause*. The line was different in Twain's first draft of this parody: "*There* lies the deep damnation of our taking off" (University of California edition, 1988, p. 761).

8. *The law's delay*. Originally "the insolence of office" (University of California edition, p. 761).

9. *a big bend*. Originally "Council Bend" (**MS**) in the manuscript.

10. *Shaksperean Revival!!!* A pun on religious "revival," as in the camp meeting in Chapter 20; a theatrical "revival" is the restoration of a play to the stage, but is not usually applied to standard works by standard authors like Shakespeare.

11. *David Garrick the younger . . . and Edmund Kean the elder*. David Garrick (1717–1779) was the most popular English actor of his day. He was also a producer and playwright, who rewrote Shakespeare; for example, he added his own death scene to *Romeo and Juliet* and let Ophelia live in *Hamlet*. Yet he raised the London stage to respectability. He gained his first fame in 1741 in *Richard III*; his farewell performance included scenes from *Hamlet* and *Richard III*.

All the stores was along one street. They had white-domestic awnings in front, and the country people hitched their horses to the awning-posts. There was empty dry-goods boxes under the awnings, and loafers[17] roosting on them all day long, whittling them with their Barlow knives; and chawing tobacco, and gaping and yawning and stretching—a mighty ornery lot. They generly had on yellow straw hats most as wide as an umbrella, but didn't wear no coats nor waistcoats; they called one another Bill, and Buck, and Hank, and Joe, and Andy, and talked lazy and drawly, and used considerable many cuss-words. There was as many as one loafer leaning up against every awning-post, and he most always had his hands in his britches pockets, except when he fetched them out to lend a chaw of tobacco or scratch. What a body was hearing amongst them, all the time was—

"Gimme a chaw 'v tobacker, Hank."

"Cain't—I hain't got but one chaw left. Ask Bill."

Maybe Bill he gives him a chaw; maybe he lies and says he

"GIMME A CHAW."

ain't got none. Some of them kinds of loafers never has a cent in the world, nor a chaw of tobacco of their own. They

David Garrick as Richard III. Engraving by William Hogarth.
Courtesy Prints and Drawings Division, New York Public Library, Astor, Lenox, and Tilden Foundations.

Edmund Kean (1789–1833) succeeded Garrick as England's greatest actor. Although his Romeo was thought laughable, he was famous for his Richard III, which likely inspired the duke and king's frantic sword fight. "Every per-

Edmund Kean as Richard III, supporting the Drury Lane Theatre, London. Caricature by George Cruikshank, 1814.
Private collection.

Charles Kean as Richard III.
Courtesy Picture Collection, New York Public Library, Astor, Lenox, and Tilden Foundations.

sonator of 'Richard' must fight like a madman, and fence on the ground, and when disarmed and wounded, thrust with savage impotence with his naked hand," reported a critic in *The Champion* (February 16, 1817). "Mr. Kean has passed this manner into law, and woe to him who breaks it." His son, Charles John Kean (1811–1868), succeeded him, but there was no Edmund Kean the younger; David Garrick died childless. By calling himself "the younger" and his partner "the elder," titles usually associated with members of the same dynasty within a profession, the duke is merely helping the frontier audience tell the difference between the two "stars"; and he is making another joke about the king's advanced age.

12. *Drury Lane Theatre . . . the Royal Haymarket Theatre, White-chapel, Pudding Lane, Piccadilly.* Garrick made the Drury Lane Theatre the most famous playhouse in London, where he played Hamlet and Romeo and Kean played Richard III. The Haymarket was another popular theater of the time; Whitechapel, Pudding Lane, and Piccadilly are all well-known sections of London. English touring companies that visited America in the nineteenth century were always advertising that they came straight from the Drury Lane or some other famous London the-

get all their chawing by borrowing[18]—they say to a fellow, "I wisht you'd len' me a chaw, Jack, I jist this minute give Ben Thompson the last chaw I had"—which is a lie, pretty much every time; it don't fool nobody but a stranger; but Jack ain't no stranger, so he says—

"*You* give him a chaw, did you? so did your sister's cat's grandmother. You pay me back the chaws you've awready borry'd off'n me, Lafe Buckner, then I'll loan you one or two ton of it, and won't charge you no back intrust,[19] nuther."

"Well, I *did* pay you back some of it wunst."

"Yes, you did—'bout six chaws. You borry'd store tobacker and paid back nigger-head."[20]

Store tobacco is flat black plug, but these fellows mostly chaws the natural leaf twisted. When they borrow a chaw, they don't generly cut it off with a knife, but they set the plug in between their teeth, and gnaw with their teeth and tug at the plug with their hands till they get it in two—then sometimes the one that owns the tobacco looks mournful at it when it's handed back, and says, sarcastic—

"Here, gimme the *chaw,* and you take the *plug.*"[21]

All the streets and lanes was just mud, they warn't nothing else *but* mud—mud as black as tar, and nigh about a foot deep in some places; and two or three inches deep in *all* the places. The hogs loafed and grunted around, everywheres. You'd see a muddy sow and a litter of pigs come lazying along the street and whollop herself right down in the way, where folks had to walk around her, and she'd stretch out, and shut her eyes, and wave her ears, whilst the pigs was milking her,[22] and look as happy as if she was on salary. And pretty soon you'd hear a loafer sing out, "Hi! *so* boy! sick him, Tige!" and away the sow would go, squealing most horrible, with a dog or two swinging to each ear, and three or four dozen more a-coming; and then you would see all the loafers get up and watch the thing out of sight, and laugh at the fun and look grateful for the noise. Then they'd settle back again till there was a dog-fight.[23] There couldn't anything wake them up all over, and make them happy all over, like a dog-fight—unless it might be putting turpentine on a stray dog and setting fire to him, or tying a tin pan to his tail and see him run himself to death.[24]

On the river front some of the houses was sticking out over the bank, and they was bowed and bent, and about ready to tumble in. The people had moved out of them. The bank was caved away under one corner of some others, and that corner was hanging over. People lived in them yet, but it was dangersome, because sometimes a strip of land as wide as a house caves in at a time. Sometimes a belt of land a quarter of a mile deep will start in and cave along and cave along till it all caves into the river in one summer. Such a town as that has to be always moving back, and back, and back, because the river's always gnawing at it.[25]

The nearer it got to noon that day, the thicker and thicker was the wagons and horses in the streets, and more coming all the time. Families fetched their dinners with them, from the country, and eat them in the wagons. There was considerable whisky drinking going on, and I seen three fights. By-and-by somebody sings out—

"Here comes old Boggs!—in from the country for his little old monthly drunk—here he comes, boys!"

All the loafers looked glad—I reckoned they was used to having fun out of Boggs. One of them says—

"Wonder who he's a gwyne to chaw up this time. If he'd a chawed up all the men he's ben a gwyne to chaw up in the last twenty year, he'd have considerble ruputation, now."

Another one says, "I wisht old Boggs 'd threaten me, 'cuz then I'd know I warn't gwyne to die for a thousan' year."

Boggs comes a-tearing along on his horse, whooping and yelling like an Injun, and singing out—

"Cler the track, thar. I'm on the waw-path, and the price uv coffins is a gwyne to raise."

He was drunk, and weaving about in his saddle; he was over fifty year old, and had a very red face. Everybody yelled at him, and laughed at him, and sassed him, and he sassed back, and said he'd attend to them and lay them out in their regular turns, but he couldn't wait now, because he'd come to town to kill old Colonel Sherburn,[26] and his motto was, "meat first, and spoon vittles to top off on."[27]

ater. Francis A. Durwige complained in "Newspaper Advertisements" in *Stray Subjects* (1848) that "the theatre-going man will find 'the small bill' . . . where he will believe, if he be sufficiently credulous, that all the characters down to the 'dummies' [nonspeaking roles], are supported by gentlemen from the Royal Theatres of London . . . after many a brilliant triumph at Drury Lane" (p. 148).

13. *appointments.* Properties, "props."

14. *the town.* Its name, Bricksville, is not revealed until Chapter 28; it is a particularly sarcastic one, because the town contains not a single brick building. At first glance, it seems to be Hannibal, Missouri, as recollected in Chapter 4 of *Life on the Mississippi*: "the white town drowsing in the sunshine of a summer's morning; the streets empty, or pretty nearly so; one or two clerks sitting in front of . . . stores, with their splint-bottomed chairs tilted back against the wall, chins on breasts, hats slouched over their faces, asleep—with shingle shavings enough around to show what broke them down; a sow and a litter of pigs loafing along the sidewalk, doing a good business in watermelon rinds and seeds."

Twain's notes, however, indicate that he was thinking of Napoleon, Arkansas, "town of innumerable fights—an inquest every day." But being the county seat, it was a far more impressive community than Bricksville. Twain looked for it in 1882 while he was gathering information for *Life on the Mississippi*; but as at Bricksville, the river was always gnawing at its banks and finally, as Twain was informed on his trip, "the Arkansas River burst through it, tore it all to rags, and emptied it into the Mississippi!" Twain observed in Chapter 32 that "it was an astonishing thing to see the Mississippi rolling between unpeopled shores and straight over the spot where I used to see a good big self-complacent town twenty years ago) . . . a town no more—swallowed up, vanished, gone to feed the fishes; nothing left but a fragment of a shanty and a crumbling brick chimney!"

But Twain probably intended Bricksville to be no more than a typical Mississippi River town. It is reminiscent of another fictional village, Pineville, Georgia, described in the well-known sketch "The Mystery Revealed" in William T. Thompson's *Chronicles of Pineville* (1844):

> Pineville awoke from the quiet slumber of a starless night. The . . . dense fog still rested upon the earth, involving houses and horse-blocks, shops and shanties, sign-posts and horse-racks, flower-gardens and duck-ponds, chimneys and fodder-stacks, objects conspicuous and objects out of sight, things elegant and things inelegant, (which in our villages are usually disposed in such pleasing contrast), in one general, indiscriminate obscurity. . . . The village swine were performing scavenger duty in the streets and yards . . . while a gang of vagabond goats were performing feats of agility about the courthouse steps. (pp. 59–60)

But Huck, in contrast to Twain in *Life on the Mississippi* or Thompson in *Chronicles of Pineville*, notes only the foul aspects of a sleepy Mississippi River town.

15. *jimpson weeds, and sunflowers.* Jimsonweed or Jamestown weed (said to be discovered at Jamestown, Virginia) is the thorn apple and a particularly ugly and poisonous plant. In Chapter 23 of *A Tramp Abroad*, Twain described a neglected garden as "thickly grown with the bloomy and villainous 'jimpson' weed and its common friend the stately sunflower." The miserable Bricksville gardens grow nothing else, because their owners are too lazy to tend them.

16. *gates that didn't generly have but one hinge—a leather one.* Because metal was scarce on the American frontier, settlers rarely used nails or any other iron in the construction of their homes and other buildings; doors and gates usually had only leather or wooden latches with leather straps as hinges. Recall back in Chapter 17 that the first thing that Huck notices about the Grangerford's house is its brass knob "the same as houses in town." Although few had secure metal locks, burglary was largely unknown in this part of the country. Perhaps there was nothing to steal.

17. *loafers.* The Bricksville loafer is the stereotypical "Southern Bully." Daniel R. Hundley described him in *Social Relations in Our Southern States* (1860) as "a swearing, tobacco-chewing, brandy drinking Bully, whose chief delight is to hang about the doors of groggeries and tavern tap-rooms, to fight chicken cocks, to play Old Sledge, or pitch-and-toss, chuck-a-luck, and the like, as well as to encourage dog-fights,

A LITTLE MONTHLY DRUNK.

He see me, and rode up and says—

"Whar'd you come f'm, boy? You prepared to die?"

Then he rode on. I was scared; but a man says—

"He don't mean nothing; he's always a carryin' on like that, when he's drunk. He's the best-naturedest old fool in Arkansaw—never hurt nobody, drunk nor sober."

Boggs rode up before the biggest store in town and bent his head down so he could see under the curtain of the awning, and yells—

"Come out here, Sherburn! Come out and meet the man you've swindled. You're the houn' I'm after, and I'm a gwyne to have you, too!"

And so he went on, calling Sherburn everything he could lay his tongue to, and the whole street packed with people listening and laughing and going on. By-and-by a proud-looking man about fifty-five—and he was a heap the best dressed man in that town, too—steps out of the store, and the crowd drops back on each side to let him come. He says to Boggs, mighty ca'm and slow—he says:

"I'm tired of this; but I'll endure it till one o'clock. Till one o'clock, mind—no longer. If you open your mouth against me only once, after that time, you can't travel so far but I will find you."[28]

Then he turns and goes in. The crowd looked mighty sober; nobody stirred, and there warn't no more laughing. Boggs rode off blackguarding Sherburn as loud as he could yell, all down the street; and pretty soon back he comes and stops before the store, still keeping it up. Some men crowded around him and tried to get him to shut up, but he wouldn't; they told him it would be one o'clock in about fifteen minutes, and so he *must* go home—he must go right away. But it didn't do no good. He cussed away, with all his might, and throwed his hat down in the mud and rode over it, and pretty soon away he went a-raging down the street again, with his gray hair a-flying. Everybody that could get a chance at him tried their best to coax him off of his horse so they could lock him up and get him sober; but it warn't no use—up the street he would tear again, and give Sherburn another cussing. By-and-by somebody says—

"Go for his daughter!—quick, go for his daughter; sometimes he'll listen to her. If anybody can persuade him, she can."

So somebody started on a run. I walked down street a ways, and stopped. In about five or ten minutes, here comes Boggs again—but not on his horse. He was a-reeling across the street towards me, bareheaded, with a friend on both sides of him aholt of his arms and hurrying him along. He was quiet, and looked uneasy; and he warn't hanging back any, but was doing some of the hurrying himself. Somebody sings out—

"Boggs!"

I looked over there to see who said it, and it was that Colonel Sherburn. He was standing perfectly still, in the street, and had a pistol raised in his right hand—not aiming it, but holding it out with the barrel tilted up towards the sky. The same second I see a young girl coming on the run, and two men with her. Boggs and the men turned round, to see who called him, and when they see the pistol the men jumped to one side, and the pistol barrel come down slow and steady to a level—both barrels cocked. Boggs throws up both of his hands, and says, "O Lord, don't shoot!" Bang! goes the first shot, and he staggers back clawing at the air—bang! goes the second one, and he tumbles backwards onto the ground, heavy and solid, with his arms spread out. That young girl screamed out, and comes rushing, and down she

Obedstown, Tennessee, loafers. Illustration by True W. Williams, *The Gilded Age*, 1874.
Private collection.

and occasionally to get up a little raw-head-and-bloody-bones affair on his own account" (pp. 223–24). And nowhere else was the Southern Bully more in evidence than in rough-and-tumble Arkansas: A popular joke of the period (reprinted in Shillaber's *Mrs. Partington's Carpet-Bag of Fun*, 1855) related how a tall, Arkansas-meat-ax-looking man sent a porter to fetch his luggage; and when the porter asked him to describe it, the fellow replied, "Why, three pistols, a pack of cards, a Bowie-knife, and one shirt. You'll find them all under my pillow" (p. 174). Twain too described "Mr. Arkansas" in Chapter 31 of *Roughing It* as "a stalwart ruffian . . . who carried two revolvers in his belt and a bowie knife projecting from his boot, and who was always drunk and always suffering for a fight."

An early version of the Bricksville loafers are the citizens of Obedstown, East Tennessee, in Chapter 1 of *The Gilded Age*: "Some wore vests, but few wore coats. . . . Every individual arrived with his hands in his pockets; a hand came out occasionally for a purpose, but it always went back again after service . . . ; many [dilapidated straw] hats were present . . . every individual was either chewing natural leaf tobacco prepared on his own premises, or smoking the same in a corn-cob pipe."

18. *They get all their chawing by borrowing.* Twain may have had in mind an exchange among the people of Pineville, Georgia, in "The Mystery Revealed," in Thompson's *Chronicles of Pineville* (1844):

Billy Wilder asked if anybody had any good tobacco; upon which Bob Echols pulled out a piece about the size of his hand . . . passed it to Billy, after which it passed through divers hands until the greater part found its way into the mouths of the bystanders, and not even the slightest moiety would have reached its owner again, had not some one in the outskirts of the crowd—who probably had a hole in his pocket—called out, 'Who's tobacco's this?' Bob owned the remnant, remarking that he "*bought* it at Harley's," and conversation and expectoration became brisk and general. (p. 61)

19. *I'll loan you one or two ton of it, and won't charge you no back intrust.* By suggesting that the sole capital of this one-horse town is chewing tobacco, Twain emphasizes the impoverishment and decay of Bricksville. Few other things were more revolting to Europeans, like Dickens and Mrs. Trollope, than the American habit of spitting tobacco juice in public. However, although the citizens of Obedstown in *The Gilded Age* are proficient in the art, Huck fails to mention any of the Bricksville chewers actually expectorating.

20. *nigger-head.* A strong black plug tobacco, often homemade and inferior to flat black plug.

21. *gimme the* chaw, *and you take the* plug. "The "chaw" is the mouthful, the "plug" the stick of tobacco. Cecil D. Eby, Jr., in "Mark Twain's 'Plug' and 'Chaw': An Anecdotal Parallel" (*Mark Twain Journal*, Summer 1960), discovered a similar joke recorded by David Hunter Strother ("Porte Crayon") in his Denver journal as an example of mining camp humor: "First loafer: 'Gimme a chaw of terbaccer, will ye?' The miner hands out his plug. Loafer helps himself. Miner says, 'Well, mister, if ye'll only gimme that chaw ye may keep the plug.' " Although Twain met Strother in 1876, he may well have first heard this joke during his mining days in Nevada rather than through Strother.

22. *milking her.* Originally the coarser "sucking her" (**MS**) in the first draft.

23. *a dog-fight.* The loafers of Obedstown, East Tennessee, are similarly distracted in Chapter 1 of *The Gilded Age*: "But presently there was a dog-fight over in the neighborhood of the blacksmith shop, and the visitors slid off their perch

THE DEATH OF BOGGS.

throws herself on her father, crying, and saying, "Oh, he's killed him, he's killed him!" The crowd closed up around them, and shouldered and jammed one another, with their necks stretched, trying to see, and people on the inside trying to shove them back, and shouting, "Back, back! give him air, give him air!"

Colonel Sherburn he tossed his pistol onto the ground, and turned around on his heels and walked off.

They took Boggs to a little drug store, the crowd pressing around, just the same, and the whole town following, and I rushed and got a good place at the window, where I was close to him and could see in. They laid him on the floor, and put one large Bible under his head, and opened another one and spread it on his breast[29]—but they tore open his shirt first, and I seen where one of the bullets went in. He made about a dozen long gasps, his breast lifting the Bible up when he drawed in his breath, and letting it down again when he breathed it out—and after that he laid still; he was dead. Then they pulled his daughter away from him, screaming and crying, and took her off. She was about sixteen, and very sweet and gentle-looking, but awful pale and scared.

Well, pretty soon the whole town was there, squirming and scrouging[30] and pushing and shoving to get at the window and have a look, but people that had the places wouldn't give them up, and folks behind them was saying all the time, "Say, now, you've looked enough, you fellows; 'taint right and 'taint fair, for you to stay thar all the time, and never give nobody a chance; other folks has their rights as well as you."[31]

There was considerable jawing back, so I slid out, thinking maybe there was going to be trouble. The streets was full, and everybody was excited. Everybody that seen the shooting was telling how it happened, and there was a big crowd packed around each one of these fellows, stretching their necks and listening. One long lanky man, with long hair and a big white fur stove-pipe hat on the back of his head, and a crooked-handled cane, marked out the places on the ground where Boggs stood, and where Sherburn stood, and the people following him around from one place to t'other and watching everything he done, and bobbing their heads to show they understood, and stooping a little and resting their hands on their thighs to watch him mark the places on the ground with his cane; and then he stood up straight and stiff where Sherburn had stood, frowning and having his hat-brim down over his eyes, and sung out, "Boggs!" and then fetched his cane down slow to a level, and says "Bang!" staggered backwards, says "Bang!" again, and fell down flat on his back. The people that had seen the thing said he done it perfect;[32] said it was just exactly the way it all happened. Then as much as a dozen people got out their bottles and treated him.

Well, by-and-by somebody said Sherburn ought to be lynched.[33] In about a minute everybody was saying it; so away they went, mad and yelling, and snatching down every clothes-line they come to, to do the hanging with.[34]

like so many turtles and strode to the battle-field with an interest bordering on eagerness."

24. *tying a tin pan to his tail and see him run himself to death.* Twain considered this trick "a practical joke of sufficiently poor quality." In Chapter 4 of *A Connecticut Yankee in King Arthur's Court*, to demonstrate how lacking in wit and good humor the court at Camelot is, Hank Morgan describes how Sir Dinadan the Humorist "tied some metal mugs to a dog's tail and turned him loose, and he tore round and around the place in a frenzy of fright, with all the other dogs bellowing after him and battering and crashing against everything that came in their way and making altogether a chaos of confusion and a most deafening din and turmoil; at which every man and woman of the multitude laughed till the tears flowed, and some fell out of their chairs and wallowed on the floor in ecstasy. It was just like so many children." It was bad enough when children engaged in such cruelty, but Twain had no patience for adults who also thought these jokes funny. "When grown-up persons indulge in a practical joke, the fact gauges them," Twain wrote in "Chapters from My Autobiography" (*North American Review*, February 1, 1907). "They have lived narrow, obscure, and ignorant lives, and at full manhood they still retain and cherish a job-lot of left-over standards and ideals that would have been discarded with their boyhood if they had then moved out into the world and a broader life" (pp. 229–30).

25. *the river's always gnawing at it.* The wearing away of the waterfront reinforces the town's complete indifference to its moral decay and the danger of eventual disappearance like Napoleon, Arkansas.

26. *he'd come to town to kill old Colonel Sherburn.* The following events reconstruct one of the first premeditated murders in Hannibal history: On January 24, 1845, William Perry Owsley shot Sam Smarr on the corner of Hill and Main Streets, just a few yards from the Clemens house. "Boggs represents Smarr in the book," Twain admitted in a letter of January 11, 1900 (University of California edition, 1988, p. 412). Nine-year-old Sam Clemens saw him die; and his father, as justice of the peace, took twenty-eight depositions from the witnesses. The murdered man was a beef farmer who, according to one witness, was "as honest a man as any in the

state"; but "when drinking . . . was a little turbulent and made a good deal of noise." No one thought he was really dangerous. Twain recalled in "Villagers of 1840–43" that Owsley was a "prosperous merchant" who "smoked fragrant cigars" (*Huck Finn and Tom Sawyer Among the Indians*, 1989, p. 101). He did not get along with others and was embroiled in several court cases. He was also a slave trader; and Smarr believed Owsley had cheated a friend out of $2,000. "I don't like him," Smarr said, "and don't want him to put himself in my way; if he ever does cross my path, I will kill him." A week before the killing, he was seen pacing up and down and shouting in front of Owsley's store, across the street from Judge Clemens's office. "O yes! O yes," he yelled five times, "here is Bill Owsley, has got a big stack of goods here, and stole two thousand dollars from Thompson in Palmyra." Owsley was also "a damned pickpocket" and "the damnedest rascal that lived ever in the county." Then Smarr's companion Tom Davis fired his pistol a couple times in the street. (Town drunkard Jimmy Finn remarked that the gun "would have made a hole in a man's belly.") One customer recalled that the commotion seemed to affect Owsley "a good deal, he had a kind of twitching, and turned white around the mouth, and said it was insufferable, and he could not stand it." But he did nothing at that time.

Smarr came back into town a few days later with a friend. They were walking down the street when Owsley came up behind them, shouting, "You Sam Smarr." Smarr turned around as Owsley drew a pistol from his pocket. "Mr. Owsley, don't fire," he cried. "Mr. Owsley was within about four paces of Mr. Smarr when he drew the pistol and fired twice in succession," recalled Smarr's companion; "after the second fire, Mr. Smarr fell, when Mr. Owsley turned on his heel and walked off." Smarr was carried into the drugstore, where he died half an hour later. See *Huck Finn and Tom Sawyer Among the Indians*, pp. 339–40, 348.

It was a year before Owsley came to trial. Although he did indeed kill Smarr, Owsley was acquitted. Some coercion was suspected. "But there was a cloud upon him—a social chill," Twain said, "and he presently moved away." Actually, Owsley stayed until 1849, when he sold his store and left for California; he came back to Hannibal in 1853, where he worked as a dry goods clerk. The "cloud," however, did not hover above the rest of his family: Clemens went to school with Owsley's daughters Elizabeth and Anna; according to "Mark Twain Going Home" (Hannibal *Morning Journal*, June 3, 1902), he dined with Elizabeth on his last visit to the town. Over a century after the murder, the Columbia (Mo.) *Daily Tribune* (October 2, 1989) reported in "Columbian Steps into Huck Finn" that a great-great-grandson of Sam Smarr, Robert Smarr, got together with Owsley's great-grandson Bernard Owsley to discuss the famous murder. Although each felt he had to defend his ancestor, there was no animosity between the two over the past. "It was a little before our time," admitted Owsley. "They'd've all been dead two or three times by now anyway," said Smarr.

27. *"Meat first, and spoon vittles to top off on."* Main course first, soup later.

28. *If you open your mouth against me only once, after that time, you can't travel so far but I will find you.* "Slander and detraction are the inseparable evils of a democracy," complained Marryat in Chapter 22 of his 1838 American diary; "and as neither public nor private characters are spared, and the law is impotent to protect them, men have no other resource than to defend their reputations with their lives, or to deter the defamer by the risk which he must incur." Europeans brought duels, feuds, and other lethal encounters to the New World as the correct way to settle questions of honor; despite laws forbidding them, they continued to flourish on the American frontier long after they had gone out of fashion in other parts of the country.

29. *They . . . put one large Bible under his head, and opened another one and spread it on his breast.* Here the "giver of life" is used to crush it out. It was the custom in this part of the country to place a Bible under the chin of the dead, but these people could have waited until Boggs had expired. "Bible on breast," Twain recalled Smarr's death in a note. "Gave him spiritual relief, no doubt, but crowded him physically" (Item 187, *Catalogue of the Library and Manuscripts of Samuel L. Clemens*, 1911). Although Wecter reported in *Sam Clemens of Hannibal* that no witness mentioned this detail in Judge Clemens's depositions, Twain confessed in "Chapters from My Autobiography" how his dreams were troubled for many nights after by "the grotesque closing picture—the great family Bible spread open on the profane man's breast by some thoughtful idiot, and rising and sinking to the labored breathings, and adding the torture of its leaden weight to the dying struggles. We are curiously made. In all the throng of gaping and sympathetic onlookers there was not one with common sense enough to perceive that an anvil would have been in better taste there than the Bible, less open to sarcastic criticism, and swifter in its atrocious work" (*North American Review*, May 3, 1907, p. 5). This detail of the murder was one of the most vivid and chilling memories of his childhood in Hannibal. "I can't ever forget Boggs," he admitted on January 11, 1900, "because I saw him die, with a family Bible spread open on his breast" (University of California edition, 1988, p. 412).

30. *scrouging*. Crowding, squeezing.

31. *other folks has their rights as well as you*. The crowd seems to think the shooting was arranged solely for its pleasure. But the Bricksville mob does not take any more delight in human suffering than anyone else might. Twain argued in the suppressed "The United States of Lyncherdom" that the public's interest in such ghastly scenes is because "each man is afraid of his neighbor's disapproval—a thing which, to the general run of the race, is more dreaded than wounds and death. When there is to be a lynching the people hitch up and come miles to see it, bringing their wives and children. Really to see it? No—they come only because they are afraid to stay at home, lest it be noticed and offensively commented upon" (*A Pen Warmed-Up in Hell*, 1972, p. 185).

32. *The people that had seen the thing said he done it perfect*. Alfred Kazin in his afterword to the 1981 Bantam Classic edition thought that this disturbing scene "shows Mark Twain the artist at his best," it being "one of the most powerful weapons ever directed at the complacency of democracy in America" (p. 292). The reconstruction of the murder in all its gory details by a prominent citizen seems to have been inspired by a scene Twain witnessed in Europe just before he resumed the manuscript of *Huckleberry Finn*. He described in Chapter 23 of *A Tramp Abroad* what happened after a boy was killed falling down a steep hillside and a crowd gathered: "All who had seen the catastrophe were describing it at once, and each trying to talk louder than his neighbor; and one youth of superior genius ran a little up the hill, called attention, tripped, fell, rolled down among us, and thus triumphantly showed exactly how the thing had been done." But Twain increased the bitterness of his satire by showing a man, not a boy, reenacting the murder in *Huckleberry Finn*.

33. *somebody said Sherburn ought to be lynched*. There is no record of anyone threatening to lynch Owsley after he murdered Boggs, so Twain probably picked up this idea from Thompson's "The Mystery Revealed" in *Chronicles of Pineville*. When a posse forms to capture some suspected bank robbers, "in less than five minutes, all of Pineville was in a commotion." As Thompson observed, "There are always some one or two persons in every small community, who lead the mass, and, as when some avant-swine breaks through the barrier that circumscribes the wanderings of the herd, the balance are sure to rush impetuously through the same hole, so the multitude are certain to give unanimous assent to the opinions of those whose lead they are accustomed to follow" (pp. 76–77).

Twain shared this cynical view of the public. "We are discreet sheep," he complained in "The Character of Man," written in 1885; "we wait to see how the drove is going, and then go with the drove. We have two opinions: one private, which we are afraid to express; and another one—the one we use—which we force ourselves to wear to please Mrs. Grundy, until habit makes us comfortable in it, and the custom of defending it presently makes us love it, adore it, and forget how pitifully we came by it" (*What Is Man?*, 1973, p. 62). Even good-hearted Huck is momentarily carried away with the excitement of a lynching party and joins the mob heading to Sherburn's house. However, the boy remains merely a spectator and not an active participant in the drama. The tragedy of mob rule lies not only in people being murdered, but in the fact that good ones stand by and do nothing to stop it.

34. *snatching down every clothes-line they come to, to do the hanging with*. "But they was too late," Twain originally concluded this chapter. "Sherburn's friends had got him away, long ago" (**MS**). Twain recorded in "Villagers of 1840–43" of 1897, that after Owsley was acquitted, "His party brought him huzzaing in from Palmyra at midnight" (*Huck Finn and Tom Sawyer Among the Indians*, 1989, p. 101). But Twain decided to take the novel in another direction: "No, let them lynch him" (**MS**).

Chapter XXII.

SHERBURN STEPS OUT.

They SWARMED up the street towards Sherburn's house, a-whooping and yelling and raging like Injuns, and everything had to clear the way or get run over and tromped to mush, and it was awful to see. Children was heeling it ahead of the mob, screaming and trying to get out of the way; and every window along the road was full of women's heads, and there was nigger boys in every tree, and bucks and wenches[1] looking over every fence; and as soon as the mob would get nearly to them they would break and skaddle back out of reach. Lots of the women and girls was crying and taking on, scared most to death.

They swarmed up in front of Sherburn's palings[2] as thick as they could jam together, and you couldn't hear yourself think for the noise. It was a little twenty-foot yard. Some sung out "Tear down the fence! tear down the fence!" Then there was a racket of ripping and tearing and smashing, and down she goes, and the front wall of the crowd begins to roll in like a wave.

Just then Sherburn steps out on to the roof of his little front porch, with a double-barrel gun in his hand, and takes his stand, perfectly ca'm and deliberate, not saying a word. The racket stopped, and the wave sucked back.

1. *bucks and wenches*. Young slave men and women. Chadwick-Joshua in *The Jim Dilemma* (1998) identified "wench" as "a common southern reference for African-American women slaves of breeding age" (p. 102). Sam Clemens knew well what this word implied. When he was working in the Hannibal *Courier* office, he noticed the distress that his employer's slave cook went through over the attentions another apprentice, Steve Wilkins, paid her daughter. Insensitive Sam thought it was hilarious how this huge young white man tormented the pretty and refined girl. But her mother had to use all her diplomatic skill to keep the situation from getting out of hand. "She quite well understood that by the customs of slaveholding communities it was Steve's right to make love to that girl if he wanted to," Twain wrote in "Chapters of My Autobiography" (*North American Review*, January 18, 1907, p. 119). As Chadwick-Joshua observed, as the mob heads for Sherburn's house, "the African American slaves are ever-watchful but at a safe and fearful distance."

2. *Sherburn's palings*. The erecting of a wooden fence around one's property was a high mark of social status in the backwoods; in Chapter 5 of *The Gilded Age*, one of the first things that Squire Hawkins does with his new wealth is to "put up the first 'paling' fence that had ever adorned the village; and he did not stop there, but whitewashed it."

Sherburn never said a word—just stood there, looking down. The stillness was awful creepy and uncomfortable.[3] Sherburn run his eye slow along the crowd;[4] and wherever it struck, the people tried a little to outgaze him, but they couldn't; they dropped their eyes and looked sneaky. Then pretty soon Sherburn sort of laughed; not the pleasant kind, but the kind that makes you feel like when you are eating bread that's got sand in it.[5]

Then he says, slow and scornful:

"The idea of *you* lynching anybody! It's amusing. The idea of you thinking you had pluck enough to lynch a *man!* Because you re brave enough to tar and feather poor friendless cast-out women that come along here,[6] did that make you think you had grit enough to lay your hands on a *man?* Why, a *man's* safe in the hands of ten thousand of your kind—as long as it's day-time and you're not behind him.

"Do I know you? I know you clear through. I was born and raised in the South, and I've lived in the North;[7] so I know the average all around. The average man's a coward.[8] In the North he lets anybody walk over him that wants to, and goes home and prays for a humble spirit to bear it. In the South one man, all by himself, has stopped a stage full of men, in the day-time, and robbed the lot.[9] Your newspapers call you a brave people so much that you think you *are* braver than any other people—whereas you're just *as* brave, and no braver. Why don't your juries hang murderers? Because they're afraid the man's friends will shoot them in the back, in the dark[10]—and it's just what they *would* do.

"So they always acquit; and then a *man* goes in the night, with a hundred masked cowards[11] at his back, and lynches the rascal. Your mistake is, that you didn't bring a man with you; that's one mistake, and the other is that you didn't come in the dark, and fetch your masks. You brought *part* of a man—Buck Harkness, there—and if you hadn't had him to start you, you'd a taken it out in blowing.

"You didn't want to come. The average man don't like trouble and danger.[12] *You* don't like trouble and danger. But if only *half* a man—like Buck Harkness, there—shouts 'Lynch him, lynch him!' you're afraid to back down—afraid

3. *The stillness was awful creepy and uncomfortable.* Huck was uncharacteristically wordy in the manuscript: "It seemed to me that the stillness was as awful, now, as the racket was before; and somehow it was more creepy and uncomfortable" (**MS**).

4. *Sherburn run his eye slow along the crowd.* "A Savonarola can quell and scatter a mob of lynchers with a mere glance of his eye," Twain argued in "The United States of Lyncherdom," referring to the Italian Renaissance religious reformer. "For no mob has any sand in the presence of a man known to be splendidly brave. Besides a lynching mob would *like* to be scattered, for of a certainty there are never ten men in it who would not prefer to be somewhere else—and would be if they had the courage to go" (*A Pen Warmed-Up in Hell*, 1972, p. 186). According to Blair and Fischer in the 1988 University of California edition, Twain was also familiar with accounts of French revolutionaries like Mirabeau, Marat, Robespierre, and Danton who were able to subdue mobs. Their defiance reinforced Twain's belief that "men in a crowd do not act as they would as individuals. In a crowd they don't think for themselves, but become impregnated by the contagious sentiment uppermost in the minds of all who happen to be en masse" (pp. 413–14). Twain admitted that he personally had met few such men of courage. "When I was a boy I saw a brave gentleman deride and insult a mob and drive it away," Twain recalled in "The United States of Lyncherdom"; but he never revealed who this gentleman was or the circumstances of the confrontation. He also said that while he was living in Nevada between 1861 and 1864, prospecting and writing for the *Territorial Enterprise*, "I saw a noted desperado make two hundred men sit still, with the house burning under them, until he gave them permission to retire." Twain mentioned another man in Virginia City, Nevada, who had this ability to quell a mob with just a glance: "The Major was a majestic creature, with a most stately and dignified military bearing, and he was by nature and training courteous, polite, graceful, winning; and he had that quality which I think I have encountered in only one other man—Bob Howland—a mysterious quality which resides in the eye; and when that eye turned upon an individual or a squad, in warning, that is enough" ("Chapters from My Autobiography," *North American Review*, December 21, 1906, p.

you'll be found out to be what you are—*cowards*—and so you raise a yell, and hang yourselves onto that half-a-man's coat tail, and come raging up here, swearing what big things you're going to do. The pitifulest thing out is a mob; that's what an army is—a mob; they don't fight with courage that's born in them, but with courage that's borrowed from their mass, and from their officers. But a mob without any *man* at the head of it, is *beneath* pitifulness. Now the thing for *you* to do, is to droop your tails and go home and crawl in a hole.[13] If any real lynching's going to be done, it will be

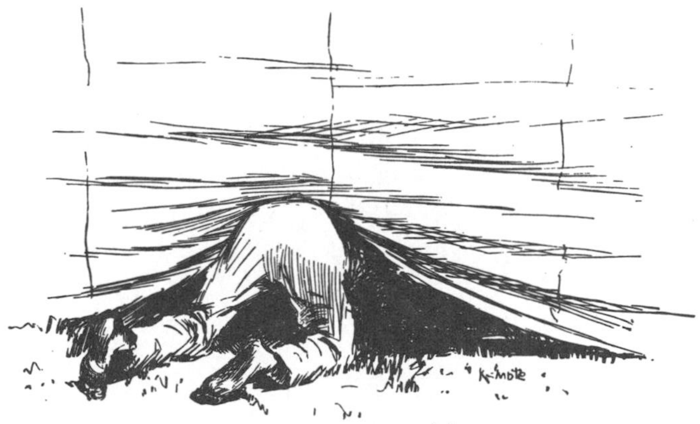

A DEAD HEAD.[14]

done in the dark, Southern fashion; and when they come they'll bring their masks, and fetch a *man* along. Now *leave*—and take your half-a-man with you"—tossing his gun up across his left arm and cocking it, when he says this.

The crowd washed back sudden,[15] and then broke all apart and went tearing off every which way, and Buck Harkness he heeled it after them, looking tolerable cheap. I could a staid, if I'd a wanted to, but I didn't want to.

I went to the circus, and loafed around the back side till the watchman went by, and then dived in under the tent. I had my twenty-dollar gold piece[16] and some other money, but I reckoned I better save it, because there ain't no telling how soon you are going to need it, away from home and amongst strangers, that way. You can't be too careful. I ain't opposed to spending money on circuses, when there ain't no other way, but there ain't no use in *wasting* it on them.

It was a real bully circus. It was the splendidest sight that

1219). Howland was "a slender, good-natured, amiable, gentle, kindly little skeleton of a man, with a sweet blue eye that would win your heart when it smiled upon you, or turn cold and freeze it, according to the nature of the occasion." Twain's remedy for lynchings in America was to "station a brave man in each affected community to encourage, support, and bring to light the deep disapproval of lynching hidden in the secret places of its heart—for it is there, beyond question. Then these communities will find something better to imitate—of course, being human, they must imitate something." Of brave men, Twain estimated that maybe "there are not three hundred of them in the earth." He agreed with Marryat (see Chapter 18, note 30) that *physical* courage was not the same as *moral* courage; and so, "upon reflection, the scheme will not work. There are not enough morally brave men in stock. We are out of moral-courage material; we are in a condition of profound poverty" (pp. 186–87).

5. *not the pleasant kind, but the kind that makes you feel like when you are eating bread that's got sand in it.* This excellent simile by this master of laughter was an afterthought; in the manuscript, Twain wrote the undistinguished phrase "not the kind of laugh you hear at the circus, but the kind that's fitten for a funeral—the kind that makes you feel crawly" (Ferguson, "Huck Finn Aborning," p. 174). Eating sand in bread would make anyone feel even more "crawly."

6. *poor friendless cast-out women that come along here.* Twain had added in the manuscript, "lowering themselves to your level to earn a bit of bitter bread to eat" (Wecter, *Sam Clemens of Hannibal*, p. 175); but it was dropped, evidently because it made their profession, prostitution, too explicit.

7. *I was born and raised in the South, and I've lived in the North.* Like the author himself. "I am a border-ruffian from the State of Missouri," Twain boasted in a talk, "Plymouth Rock and the Pilgrims," delivered in Philadelphia on December 22, 1881 (in *Mark Twain's Speeches*, 1910, pp. 19–20). "I am a Connecticut Yankee by adoption. In me, you have Missouri morals, Connecticut culture; this, gentleman, is the combination which makes the perfect man." This is also the voice of Satan in "The Chronicle of Young Satan" (1900), which became *The Mysterious Stranger* (1916): "I know your race. It

ever was,[17] when they all come riding in, two and two, a gentleman and lady, side by side, the men just in their drawers and under-shirts, and no shoes nor stirrups, and resting their hands on their thighs, easy and comfortable—there must a' been twenty of them—and every lady with a lovely complexion, and perfectly beautiful, and looking just like a gang of real sure-enough queens, and dressed in clothes that cost millions of dollars,[18] and just littered with diamonds. It was a powerful fine sight; I never see anything so lovely. And then one by one they got up and stood, and went a-weaving around the ring so gentle and wavy and graceful, the men looking ever so tall and airy and straight, with their heads bobbing and skimming along, away up there under the tent-roof, and every lady's rose-leafy dress flapping soft and silky around her hips, and she looking like the most loveliest parasol.

And then faster and faster they went, all of them dancing, first one foot stuck out in the air and then the other, the horses leaning more and more, and the ring-master going round and round the centre-pole, cracking his whip and shouting "hi!—hi!" and the clown cracking jokes behind him; and by-and-by all hands dropped the reins, and every lady put her knuckles on her hips and every gentleman folded his arms, and then how the horses did lean over and hump themselves! And so, one after the other they all skipped off into the ring, and made the sweetest bow I ever see, and then scampered out, and everybody clapped their hands and went just about wild.

Well, all through the circus they done the most astonishing things; and all the time that clown carried on so it most killed the people. The ring-master couldn't ever say a word to him but he was back at him quick as a wink with the funniest things a body ever said; and how he ever *could* think of so many of them, and so sudden and so pat, was what I couldn't noway understand. Why, I couldn't a thought of them in a year. And by-and-by a drunk man[19] tried to get into the ring—said he wanted to ride; said he could ride as well as anybody that ever was. They argued and tried to keep him out, but he wouldn't listen, and the whole show

is made up of sheep. It is governed by minorities, seldom or never by majorities. It suppresses its feelings and its beliefs and follows the handful that makes the most noise. Sometimes the noisy handful is right, sometimes wrong; but no matter, the crowd follows it. The vast majority of the race, whether savage or civilized, are secretly kind-hearted, and shrink from inflicting pain; but in the presence of the aggressive and pitiless minority they don't dare to assert themselves" (*A Pen Warmed-Up in Hell*, 1972, p. 59). Sherburn's speech has been criticized for being the most conspicuous part of *Huckleberry Finn* where the narrator has dropped his idiom; here the author does not speak in dialect but for himself. This is the same voice Twain employs when he denounces Southern violence in a suppressed portion of *Life on the Mississippi* (in the Limited Edition Club edition, 1944, pp. 412–16) as well as in the suppressed "The United States of Lyncherdom" (in *A Pen Warmed-Up in Hell*, 1972, pp. 180–81), which he suppressed as being too politically volatile. Alfred Kazin in his afterword to the 1981 Bantam edition considered "this terrifying scene" in *Huckleberry Finn* to be "one of the most powerful ever directed at the complacency of democracy in America" (p. 292).

8. *I know the average all around. The average man's a coward.* In the manuscript, Twain wrote, "I know the average man of the country, and the average man of the world. The average man of the world is a coward" (quoted in Blair, *Mark Twain and Huck Finn*, p. 337); but this knowledge may have been true of Mark Twain, world traveler, but not of Colonel Sherburn of the Arkansas backwoods, so the detail was deleted.

Twain believed moral courage to be "the rarest of human qualities" ("Chapters from My Autobiography," *North American Review*, May 17, 1907, p. 121). He said in "The United States of Lyncherdom" that moral cowardice "is the commanding feature of the make-up of 9,999 men in 10,000. . . . History will not allow us to forget or ignore this supreme trait of our character. It persistently and sardonically reminds us that from the beginning of the world no revolt against a public infamy or oppression has ever been begun but by the one daring man in 10,000, the rest timidly waiting, and slowly and reluctantly joining, under the influence of that man and his fellows from the other ten thousands. The abolitionists remember. Privately the public feeling was with them early, but each man was afraid to speak out until he got some hint that his neighbor was privately feeling as he privately felt himself. Then the boom followed. It always does" (*A Pen Warmed-Up in Hell*, 1972, p. 184).

9. *In the South one man, all by himself, has stopped a stage full of men, in the day-time, and robbed the lot.* In lamenting the want of personal courage in general humanity, in a suppressed passage of *Life on the Mississippi* (mentioned in note 7 above) Twain made much the same argument that Sherburn does: "The other day in Kentucky, a single highwayman, revolver in hand, stopped a stagecoach and robbed the passengers, some of whom were armed—and he got away unharmed. The unaverage Kentuckian, being plucky, is not afraid to attack half a dozen average Kentuckians; and his bold enterprise succeeds—probably because the average Kentuckian is like the average of the human race, not plucky, but timid" (Limited Editions Club edition, 1944, p. 415).

Colonel Sherburn's speech is largely a reworking of Twain's discussion of the myth of the fiery Southern temper in that suppressed passage of *Life on the Mississippi*:

> Now, in every community, North and South, there is one hot-head, or a dozen, or a hundred, according to distribution of population; the rest of the community are quiet folk. What do these hot-heads amount to in the North? Nothing. . . . Their heads never get so hot but that they retain cold sense enough to remind them that they are among a people who will not allow themselves to be walked over by their sort; a people who, although they will not insanely hang them upon suspicion and without trial, nor try them, convict them, and then let them go, but who will give them a fair and honest chance in the courts, and if conviction follow will punish them with imprisonment or the halter.
>
> In the South the case is very different. The one hot-head defies the hamlet. . . . Could he come North and be the terror of a town? Such a thing is impossible. Northern resolution, backing Northern law, was too much for even the "Mollie Maguires," powerful, numerous, and desperate as was that devilish secret organization. But it could have lived a long life in the South; for there it is not the rule for courts to hang murderers. (1944, pp. 413–14)

come to a standstill. Then the people begun to holler at him and make fun of him, and that made him mad, and he begun to rip and tear; so that stirred up the people, and a lot of men begun to pile down off of the benches and swarm towards the ring, saying, "Knock him down! throw him out!" and one or two women begun to scream. So, then, the ring-master he made a little speech, and said he hoped there wouldn't be no disturbance, and if the man would promise he wouldn't make no more trouble, he

HE SHED SEVENTEEN SUITS.

would let him ride, if he thought he could stay on the horse. So everybody laughed and said all right, and the man got on. The minute he was on, the horse begun to rip and tear and jump and cavort around, with two circus men hanging onto his bridle trying to hold him, and the drunk man hanging onto his neck, and his heels flying in the air every jump, and the whole crowd of people standing up shouting and laughing till the tears rolled down. And at last, sure enough, all the circus men could do, the horse broke loose, and away he went like the very nation,[20] round and round the ring, with that sot laying down on him and hanging to his neck, with first one leg hanging most to the ground on one side, and then t'other one on t'other side, and the people just crazy. It warn't funny to me, though;[21] I was all of a tremble to see his danger. But pretty soon he struggled up astraddle and grabbed the bridle, a-reeling this way and that; and the next minute he sprung up and dropped the bridle and stood! and the horse agoing like a house afire too. He just stood up there, a-sailing around as easy and comfortable as if he warn't ever drunk in his life—and then he begun to pull off his clothes and sling them. He shed them so thick they kind of clogged up the air, and altogether he shed seventeen suits. And then, there he was, slim and handsome, and dressed the gaudiest and prettiest you ever saw, and he lit into that horse with his whip and made him fairly hum—and finally skipped off, and made his bow and danced off to the dressing-room, and everybody just a-howling with pleasure and astonishment.

Then the ring-master he see how he had been fooled, and he *was* the sickest ring-master you ever see, I reckon. Why, it was one of his own men! He had got up that joke all out of his own head, and never let on to nobody. Well, I felt sheepish enough, to be took in so, but I wouldn't a been in that ring-master's place, not for a thousand dollars. I don't know; there may be bullier circuses than what that one was, but I never struck them yet. Anyways it was plenty good enough for *me;* and wherever I run across it, it can have all of *my* custom,[22] every time.

Well, that night we had *our* show; but there warn't only about twelve people there; just enough to pay expenses. And they laughed all the time, and that made the duke mad; and everybody left, anyway, before the show was over,[23] but one boy which was asleep. So the duke said these Arkansaw lunkheads couldn't come up to Shakspeare; what they wanted was low comedy[24]—and may be something ruther worse than low comedy, he reckoned. He said he could size their style. So next morning he got some big sheets of wrapping-paper and some black paint, and drawed off some handbills and stuck them up all over the village. The bills said:

The original intention of this suppressed chapter was to attack the idea of a "solid" South behind a single party; and it was probably not published because its conclusion would have offended Southern readers. "In one thing the average Northerner seems to be a step in advance of the average Southerner," Twain observed, "in that he bands himself with his timid fellows to support the law (at least in the matter of murder), protect judges, juries, and witnesses, and also to secure all citizens from personal danger and from obloquy or social ostracism on account of opinion, political or religious; whereas the average Southerners do not band themselves together in these high interests, but leave them to look out for themselves unsupported; the results being unpunished murder, against the popular approval, and the decay, and destruction of independent thought and action in politics" (p. 415).

Colonel Sherburn, however, does not make regional distinctions; he calls the average man *everywhere* a moral coward. Every person suffers from what Twain defined in "The United States of Lyncherdom" (1901) as "a man's commonest weakness, his aversion to being unpleasantly conspicuous, pointed at, shunned, as being on the unpopular side" (*A Pen Warmed-Up in Hell*, 1972, pp. 183–84).

10. *they're afraid the man's friends will shoot them in the back, in the dark*. The same was true of witnesses. "The other day in Kentucky," Twain wrote in the suppressed section of *Life on the Mississippi*, "a witness testified against a young man in court, and got him fined for a violation of a law. The young man went home and got his shot gun and made short work of that witness. He did not invent that method of correcting witnesses; it had been used before, in the South. Perhaps this detail accounts for the reluctance of witnesses, there, to testify; and also the reluctance for juries to convict; and perhaps, also, for the disposition of lynchers to go to their grewsome labors disguised" (1944, p. 414).

11. *a hundred masked cowards*. Here Twain was attacking his contemporaries as much as recalling antebellum vigilantes. Reconstruction had failed miserably to fulfill the promise of freedom for all; and magnolia-tinged novels of the period looked back nostalgically to the good old days of Southern plantations with their happy "darkies." Lynchings increased dramatically as

AT THE COURT HOUSE!

FOR 3 NIGHTS ONLY!

The World-Renowned Tragedians

DAVID GARRICK THE YOUNGER!

AND

EDMUND KEAN THE ELDER!

Of the London and Continental Theatres,

In their Thrilling Tragedy of

THE KING'S CAMELOPARD[25]

OR

THE ROYAL NONESUCH!!![26]

Admission 50 cents.[27]

Then at the bottom was the biggest line of all—which said:

LADIES AND CHILDREN NOT ADMITTED.

"There," says he, "if that line don't fetch them, I dont know Arkansaw!"

the century wore on. The Ku Klux Klan was just one of many secret societies that arose in the South after the Civil War, terrorizing all those they considered their enemies in the dark of night and behind masks. Twain angrily protested lynching in an unsigned editorial, "Only a Nigger," in the Buffalo *Express* (August 26, 1869). But it was not until 1901 that he penned his most impassioned attack on "The United States of Lyncherdom" when he learned of one in Missouri. Sadly, his essay was published posthumously and not until 1923, when Albert Bigelow Paine included it in *Europe and Elsewhere* (New York and London: Harper & Bros., pp. 239–49).

12. *The average man don't like trouble and danger.* Critic Vincent Freimack complained in "Mark Twain and 'Infelicities' of Southern Speech" (*American Speech*, October 1953) that this sentence is Colonel Sherburn's "only derivation from strictly grammatical English in the scornful words with which he cows the mob that has come to lynch him" (p. 234). However, the use of "don't" instead of "doesn't" was generally acceptable among Northern middle-class men and women (such as the de-Southernized Twain) during much of the nineteenth century.

13. *droop your tails and go home and crawl in a hole.* As other cowardly animals do.

14. *a dead head.* One who is admitted to a show without paying. Dan Rice's Circus and Great Hippodrome advertised in the Hannibal *Missouri Courier* (August 26, 1852) that "the price of admission will invariably be 50 cents; children half price."

15. *The crowd washed back sudden.* Much the same thing happens in Chapter 11 of *Tom Sawyer*: "The villagers had a strong desire to tar-and-feather Injun Joe and ride him on a rail, for body-snatching, but so formidable was his character that nobody could be found who was willing to take the lead in the matter, so it was dropped."

16. *I had my twenty-dollar gold piece.* Further proof that Huck must have given Jim the other gold piece the slave hunters passed to the boy back in Chapter 16.

17. *It was the splendidest sight that ever was.* In "Reading and Writing" (*New Republic*, May 1,

1944), critic George Mayberry praised Huck's description here as "prose that superbly fulfills its function; here of rendering the color, pageantry, and above all the movement of a circus performance as it works upon a boy's imagination" (p. 608). The cadences of the next two paragraphs "enforce the description of the several phases of action": "The preliminary easy riding is suggested by the balanced construction ('two and two, and gentleman and lady, side by side . . . drawers and undershirts . . . no shoes nor stirrups . . . their hands on their thighs easy and comfortable . . . '). When the performers stand up on their horses, the phrases expand to a rolling tripartite gait ('so gentle and wavy and graceful . . . so tall and airy and straight . . . their heads bobbing and skimming along, away up there under the tent-roof, and every lady's rose-leafy dress flapping soft and silky around her hips . . . "). Then the action accelerates to a rousing climax and drops to a close while 'everybody clapped their hands and went just about wild'—in an appropriate spondaic terminal." Although he thought "the most loveliest parasol" out of character for Huck, Mayberry concluded that this passage was "a notable example of a kind of writing by no means American, but marked in modern American writing at its best."

18. *clothes that cost millions of dollars.* Twain may have recalled that Dan Rice advertised his Circus and Great Hippodrome as costing $50,000, an enormous sum of money in 1852.

19. *a drunk man.* Huck witnesses one of the most popular circus acts of the time. Blair and Fischer suggested in the 1988 University of California edition (p. 414) that Sam Clemens may have first seen it when Dan Rice's Circus and Great Hippodrome came to Hannibal for two performances on August 31, 1852. Dressed as country bumpkin "Pete Jenkins, from Mud Corners," Rice staggered into the ring and tried several times to mount a horse without success; then miraculously, he was on top, shed coats, vests and trousers down to his circus tights, and performed extraordinary acrobatics on horseback as the steed continued to race around the ring. This act was also a popular subject of American comic writing of the period: William T. Thompson, William Wright, and George W. Harris all made use of the drunk-on-horseback trick; and Twain included Richard M. Johnston's "The Expensive Treat of Colonel Moses

The "drunk" rider. Illustration by Farny, *A Boy's Town* by William Dean Howells, *Harper's Young People*, June 3, 1890. *Courtesy Library of Congress.*

Grice" from *Dukesborough's Tales* (1881) in his *Library of Humor* (1888). William Dean Howells described the same act as he saw it as boy in "Circuses and Shows," Chapter 9 of *A Boy's Town* (1890):

> One of the most popular acts was that where a horse has been trained to misbehave, so that nobody can mount him; and after the actors have tried him, the ring-master turns to the audience, and asks if some gentleman among them wants to try it. Nobody stirs, till at last a tipsy country-jake is seen making his way down from one of the top-seats towards the ring. He can hardly walk, he is so drunk, and the clown has to help him across the ring-board, and even then he trips and rolls over on the sawdust, and has to be pulled to his feet. When they bring him up to the horse, he falls against it; and the little fellows think he will certainly get killed. . . . The ring-master and the clown manage to get the country-jake onto the broad platform on the horse's back, and then the ring-master cracks his whip, and the two supes who have been holding the horse's head let go, and the horse begins cantering round the ring. The little fellows are just sure the country-jake is going to fall off,

> he reels and totters so; . . . and pretty soon the country-jake begins to straighten up. He begins to unbutton his long gray overcoat, and then he takes it off and throws it into the ring, where one of the supes catches it. Then he sticks a short pipe into his mouth, and pulls on an old wool hat, and flourishes a stick that the supe throws to him, and you see that he is an Irishman just come across the sea; and then off goes another coat, and he comes out a British soldier in white duck trousers and red coat. That comes off, and he is an American sailor, with his hands on his hip, dancing a hornpipe. Suddenly away flash wig and beard and false-face, the pantaloons are stripped off with the same movement, the actor stoops for the reins lying on the horse's neck, and James Rivers, the greatest three-horse rider in the world nimbly capers on the broad pad, and kisses his hand to the shouting and cheering spectators as he dashes from the ring past the braying and bellowing brass-band into the dressing-room! (pp. 100–1)

This circus act seems appropriate for this story, because the trick rider turns out to be another con artist like the king and the duke—and Huck.

20. *like the very nation*. Like the very devil, from "damnation."

21. *It warn't funny to me, though*. What distinguishes Huck's description from other accounts of this famous circus act is the audience's reactions to the drunk's difficulties: They are disturbed, first by his disrupting the show and then by his angry words; they only laugh when it looks like he might fall off the horse and break his neck.

22. *it can have all of* my *custom*. It can have all of my business.

23. *everybody left, anyway, before the show was over*. The "broad-sword conflict in Richard III" must have seemed rather tame after the shooting of Boggs by Sherburn. The performance of *Romeo and Juliet* could not have been much better than one described in "The —— Troupe," which appeared in Orion Clemens's paper, the Hannibal *Journal* (March 18, 1852):

> All the little boys in town gazed on the groups of astonishing pictures which appeared on the . . . bills, and were thereby wrought up to the intense pitch of excitement. It was to be a real theatre, and the "troupe" (which nobody had ever heard of before) was so "celebrated." Well, the momentous evening came. Those who enjoyed the felicity of paying a quarter, to see the show, found a large man on the first story, who received the money, and a small man at the top of the second pair of steps, who received the tickets . . . the very persons who afterwards transformed into heros and soldiers by the power of paint. In the hall we found forty or fifty of our citizens, sitting in front of a striped curtain, behind which was all the mysterious paraphernalia of the theatre.
>
> When the curtain was pulled to one side, the first appearance on the stage was the large man. . . . He was evidently a novice, and acted his part about as you have seen boys, in a thespian society. He was intended to be a lover of the distinguished danseuse, who played the part of a miss in short dresses, though her apparent age would have justified her in wearing them longer, and we have seen spectacles on younger people. Then the small man . . . made up the third character in this burlesque of a farce, the dullness of which was not revealed even by the disgusting blackguardisms with which it is so profusely interlarded.

Apparently these backwoods audiences were not as dumb as they looked, but saw right through theatrical sham.

24. *low comedy*. In the manuscript, Twain wrote that the duke "judged he could cater to their baser instincts" (quoted in DeVoto, *Mark Twain at Work*, p. 84); but the phrase was probably too suggestive of the true nature of the return performance of "David Garrick the Younger" and "Edmund Kean the Elder." The audiences in Hannibal, Missouri, may not have been much better than those in Bricksville. When few people showed up for Dr. Hay's demonstrations of astronomy and the magnetic telegraph, the Hannibal *Journal* (June 15, 1848) noted that "the idea suggested itself to our mind, had it been a 'monkey show' or a 'Negro Congo Dance,' the house would have been full." It was impossible to get many people to attend local municipal meetings, too. "If some thimble-rigging buffoon, comes and advertises to edify the citizens of this great city with 'Dan Tucker' and the banjo, then *all go—none forget*," complained the Hannibal *Gazette* (November 26, 1846).

25. *THE KING'S CAMELOPARD.* Or "cameleopard," an archaic word for the giraffe; originally the name of a mythical beast the size of a camel and spotted like a leopard. Blair suggested in *Mark Twain and Huck Finn* (1960, pp. 319–20) that Twain knew Edgar Allan Poe's "Four Beasts in One; of the Homocameleopard" in *Tales of the Grotesque and Arabesque* (1845). The story describes a revolting public exhibition by Antiochus Epiphanes, Antiochus Illustrious, king of Syria, and the potent of potentates in the East. To celebrate his having slain one thousand Jews by his own hand, the tyrant appears before his barbaric people, who worship a baboon god, "ensconced in the hide of a beast, and . . . doing his best to play the part of a cameleopard; but this is done for the better sustaining his dignity as king." Poe bore as little respect for monarchy as Twain did: "With how superior a dignity, the monarch perambulates on all fours! His tail, you perceive, is held aloft by his two principal concubines . . . ; and his whole appearance would be infinitely prepossessing, were it not for the protuberance of his eyes, which will certainly start out of his head, and the queer color of his face, which has become nondescript from the quantity of wine he has swallowed." Twain did not care much for Poe as a writer; but he must have found this account of a bestial monarch amusing, enough to borrow from it for the king's "tragedy" in the next chapter.

26. *THE ROYAL NONESUCH.* A "nonesuch" is something unmatched and unrivaled. The original title of the duke's "thrilling tragedy" was "The Burning Shame"; but since it was such a notorious act, Twain thought it wise to call it something else. Miner Jim Gillis performed it for him up in his cabin on Jackass Hill in 1865. "In one of my books—*Huckleberry Finn*, I think—I have used one of Jim's impromptu tales, which he called 'The Tragedy of the Burning Shame,'" Twain recalled in 1907. "I had to modify it considerably to make it proper for print, and this was a great damage. As Jim told it—inventing it as he went along—I think it was one of the most outrageously funny things I have ever listened to. How mild it is in the book, and how pale; how extravagant and how gorgeous in its unprintable form!" (*Mark Twain in Eruption*, 1940, p. 361). As early as 1877, Twain thought of putting it in a novel he was planning about his brother Orion Clemens; but he never followed through with the idea. See Chapter 23, note 1.

27. Admission *50* cents. Note the sarcasm in charging twice the price of admission to the "Shaksperean Revival" for the "low comedy."

Chapter XXIII

TRAGEDY.

Well ALL day him and the king was hard at it, rigging up a stage, and a curtain, and a row of candles for foot-lights; and that night the house was jam full of men in no time. When the place couldn't hold no more, the duke he quit tending door and went around the back way and come onto the stage and stood up before the curtain, and made a little speech, and praised up this tragedy, and said it was the most thrillingest one that ever was; and so he went on a-bragging about the tragedy and about Edmund Kean the Elder, which was to play the main principal part in it; and at last when he'd got everybody's expectations up high enough, he rolled up the curtain, and the next minute the king come a-prancing out on all fours, naked; and he was painted all over, ring-streaked-and-striped, all sorts of colors, as splendid as a rainbow. And—but never mind the rest of his outfit, it was just wild,[1] but it was awful funny. The people most killed themselves laughing; and when the king got done capering, and capered off behind the scenes, they roared and clapped and stormed and haw-hawed till he come back and done it over again; and after that, they made him do it another time. Well, it would a made a cow laugh to see the shines that old idiot cut.

1. *wild.* Twain considered "scandalous" and "outrageous" before settling on this word. But what exactly was "The Burning Shame" (a.k.a. "The Royal Nonesuch")? Blair and Fischer in the 1988 University of California edition (pp. 414–15) located an Elizabethan variant of this hoax in W. Carew Hazlitt, *Studies in Jocular Literature* (1890), that dated back to the fifteenth or sixteenth century. But the London con artist absconds with the money before giving any performance. Robert Bridges in his review of the novel in *Life* (February 26, 1885) identified it as "a polite version of the 'Giascutus' story . . . a good chapter for lenten parlor entertainments and church festivals" (p. 119). Since it was already part of American folk culture by the publication of *Huckleberry Finn*, Twain could have come across versions of it in various books, newspapers, and magazines.

The Palmyra (Mo.) *Whig* (October 9, 1845) told how two broke Yankee clock peddlers, while roaming through the South, are "determined to take advantage of the passion for shows which possessed our people." To get some quick cash, they decide that one should "personate a rare best, for which they invented the name 'Gyascutus,' while the other was to be keeper or showman." In the next town, they tack up playbills that advertise their prey as "captured . . . in the wilds of the Arostook [in Maine] . . . more ferocious and terrible than the gnu, the hyena, or the ant-eater of the African desert! Admittance 25 cents, children and servants half price." An eager and curious crowd fills the house and watches beneath the curtain "four horrible feet, which to less excited fancies would have born a wonderful resemblance to the feet and hands of a live Yankee, with strips of coonskin sewed round his wrists and ankles." While the still hidden creature growls, the keeper begins to lecture on how ferocious and

Then the duke he lets the curtain down, and bows to the people, and says the great tragedy will be performed only two nights more, on accounts of pressing London engagements, where the seats is all sold aready for it in Drury Lane; and then he makes them another bow, and says if he has succeeded in pleasing them and instructing them, he will be deeply obleeged if they will mention it to their friends and get them to come and see it.

Twenty people sings out:

"What, is it over? Is that *all?*"

The duke says yes. Then there was a fine time. Everybody sings out "sold,"[2] and rose up mad, and was agoing for that stage and them tragedians. But a big fine-looking man jumps up on a bench, and shouts:

"Hold on! Just a word, gentlemen." They stopped to listen. "We are sold—mighty badly sold. But we don't want to be the laughing-stock of this whole town, I reckon, and never hear the last of this thing as long as we live. *No.* What we want, is to go out of here quiet, and talk this show up, and sell the *rest* of the town! Then we'll all be in the same boat. Ain't that sensible?" ("You bet it is!—the jedge[3] is right!" everybody sings out.) "All right, then—not a word about any sell.[4] Go along home, and advise everybody to come and see the tragedy."

Next day you couldn't hear nothing around that town but how splendid that show was. House was jammed again, that night, and we sold this crowd the same way. When me and the king and the duke got home to the raft, we all had a supper; and by-and-by, about midnight, they made Jim and me back her out and float her down the middle of the river and fetch her in and hide her about two mile below town.

The third night the house was crammed again—and they warn't new-comers, this time, but people that was at the show the other two nights. I stood by the duke at the door, and I see that every man that went in had his pockets bulging, or something muffled up under his coat—and I see it warn't no perfumery neither, not by a long sight. I smelt sickly eggs by the barrel, and rotten cabbages, and such things; and if I know the signs of a dead cat being around,

dangerous a beast it is, all the while poking at the curtain with a stick. Suddenly, it gives out a tremendous roar, and the man cries in horror, "Ladies and gentlemen—*save yourselves—the Gyascutus is loose!*" "Pell-mell, hurly-burly, screaming, leaping, crowding, the terrified spectators roll out"; and the two Yankees with their loot exit out the rear. See Wecter, *Sam Clemens of Hannibal*, 1952, pp. 187–88; and Blair, *Mark Twain and Huck Finn*, 1960, p. 318.

While this hoax has much in common with "The Royal Nonesuch," there is nothing in it that Twain need have censored. According to Francis Grose's *Dictionary of the Vulgar Tongue* (1785), a "burning shame" was "a lighted candle stuck into the private parts of a woman." In "'The Burning Shame' Broadside" (*Mark Twain Journal*, Fall 1991), Walter Kokernot reported locating in Houghton Library, Harvard University, a crude eighteenth-century broadside titled "The Burning Shame; or Covent-Garden Morning Frolick," describing the pranks three courtiers play on a washerwoman Peg Tear'em on her way to work. One of the wags suggests,

> "[L]et's see if this woman has not got good run-goods about her" and immediately began to rummage her apartments. Says Margery, "I assure you, gentlemen, you will find nothing there but what has been fairly enter'd, and if you will but put your noses to it, you will be convinc'd that I carry a wholesome British commodity about me. ["]We'll not take your word, you slut,["] says they, and immediately one of them gaug'd the cask. Upon his declaring all was right; they concluded among themselves to make Margery amends for the affront they had put upon her, in disputing the goodness of her ware. They said so good a thing ought to be properly ornamented, and turning Margery's smock and petticoat over her head, ty'd them close over it; they hung her candle and lanthorn in a string before Margery's dumb-glutton [private parts], and in that manner march'd in triumph with her to Bloomsbury Square, and knock'd at the gentleman's door she was going to, standing at a distance to see the event of their frolick. The first that came to the door was a West Country maid-servant, who seeing so strange a sight, and taking it for an apparition, immediately fainted away. The rest of the women-servants being afraid to go to the door, prevail'd on a blundering Irish footman to go to the spectre, and speak to it. Teague coming up, and seeing

so odd a figure, cries out, "O hu! by Jesus, but this is not an Irish ghost! I never saw before I was born an apparition with a candle and lanthorn stuck in her arse! In the name of Jesus who are you?[" "]Nobody but poor Margery, the washerwoman,["] cried the poor creature; ["]and for God's sake desire the maids to help undo me, and then I'll tell you how I've been serv'd.["] Teague bursting into a fit of laughter, runs and tells the maids who it was; "By Heavens,["] says he, ["]but they have made a pudding-bag of her petticoats to boil her head in; and they have cut a great gash in her belly and tied it round with a counsellor's perriwig. Upon my conscience but it is true; and they have hung a lighted candle and [lantern] before it, because nobody should see it. . . . ["]

After a deal of laughter on all sides, they untuck'd Margery, and on examining her pockets she found they had robb'd her of her pocket gin-bottle; but to comfort her for her loss, they left on the room of it three fine handkerchiefs, with a guinea in each, which Margery thinks a charming recompence for their fun. (p. 35)

This bit of ribaldry would have amused the author of the bawdy *Date, 1601* (1876), but it is probably more obscene than even Jim Gillis might have thought up. Daniel P. Mannix, the author of *Step Right Up!* (1951), described an act "for men only" he saw while working with a sideshow during the Depression:

A man comes out and explains he is going to present a trained dog act. Maybe they aren't interested in trained dogs? Well, they'll be interested in this one. He then calls. Off stage come barks and whines. Finally, the man exits and returns dragging a naked girl who is on all fours. She is generally painted in some way as with spots to represent a Dalmatian. The man tells her to sit up and beg, roll over, play dead, etc. Whenever he stops to address the "tip" (the crowd), the girl goes over and, raising one leg, pretends to urinate on him whereupon he indignantly kicks her away. This is used as a running gag throughout the show.

The girl goes through the motions of defecating, afterwards scratching with her hind legs. The man tells her there's a rat in the corner and she goes after it, wiggling her backside as she scratches in the corner. As the climax, the man calls on another dog which is

THEIR POCKETS BULGED.

and I bet I do,[5] there was sixty-four of them went in. I shoved in there for a minute, but it was too various[6] for me, I couldn't stand it. Well, when the place couldn't hold no more people, the duke he give a fellow a quarter and told him to tend door for him a minute, and then he started around for the stage door, I after him; but the minute we turned the corner and was in the dark, he says:

"Walk fast, now, till you get away from the houses, and then shin for the raft like the dickens was after you!"

I done it, and he done the same. We struck the raft at the same time, and in less than two seconds we was gliding down stream, all dark and still, and edging towards the middle of the river, nobody saying a word. I reckoned the poor king was in for a gaudy time of it with the audience; but nothing of the sort; pretty soon he crawls out from under the wigwam, and says:

"Well, how'd the old thing pan out this time, Duke?"

He hadn't been up town at all.

We never showed a light till we was about ten mile below that village. Then we lit up and had a supper, and the king and the duke fairly laughed their bones loose over the way they'd served them people. The duke says:

"Greenhorns, flatheads! *I* knew the first house would keep mum and let the rest of the town get roped in; and I knew they'd lay for us the third night, and consider it was *their* turn now. Well, it *is* their turn, and I'd give something to know how much they'd take for it. I *would* just like to know how they're putting in their opportunity. They can turn it into a picnic, if they want to—they brought plenty provisions."

Them rapscallions took in four hundred and sixty-five dollars in that three nights. I never see money hauled in by the wagon-load like that, before.

By-and-by, when they was asleep and snoring, Jim says:

"Don't it 'sprise you, de way dem kings carries on, Huck?"

"No," I says, "it don't."

"Why don't it, Huck?"

"Well, it don't, because it's in the breed. I reckon they're all alike."

"But, Huck, dese kings o' ourn is regular rapscallions; dat's jist what dey is; dey's regular rapscallions."

"Well, that's what I'm a-saying; all kings is mostly rapscallions, as fur as I can make out."

"Is dat so?"[7]

"You read about them once—you'll see. Look at Henry the Eight; this'n 's a Sunday-School Superintendent to *him*. And look at Charles Second, and Louis Fourteen, and Louis Fifteen, and James Second, and Edward Second, and Richard Third, and forty more; besides all them Saxon heptarchies[8] that used to rip around so in old times and raise Cain. My, you ought to seen old Henry the Eight when he was in bloom. He *was* a blossom. He used to marry a new wife every day, and chop off her head next morning.[9] And he would do it just as indifferent as if he was ordering up eggs. 'Fetch up Nell Gwynn,' he says. They fetch her up. Next morning, 'Chop off her head!' And they chop it off. 'Fetch up Jane Shore,' he says; and up she comes. Next morning 'Chop off her head'—and they chop it off. 'Ring up Fair Rosamun.'[10] Fair Rosamun answers the bell. Next morn-

> invisible. He says this one is female. The girl goes through the motions of sniffing the invisible dog's backside and then gets excited and pretends to mount her, going through the motions of breeding. The man tells her that that isn't nice and tries to get the invisible dog away from her but the girl holds on. In his efforts, the man falls to his hands and knees whereupon the girl mounts him and starts to breed him.

An old man could play the part as easily as a young woman; and such a show is indeed "something ruther worse than low comedy."

Critic Wallace Graves recorded in "Mark Twain's 'Burning Shame' " (*Nineteenth-Century Fiction*, June 1968) a less outrageous performance than this trained dog act, but Graves's version that he too heard in the 1930s closely follows the account in *Huckleberry Finn*:

> It was about two destitute traveling actors [in Sweden] who decided to raise some money by giving a performance in a small town. Women and children were not admitted; they rigged a stage with a curtain, and made sure that an escape door at the rear of the stage was open for a quick getaway after the show. One man collected money while the audience filed in, then came round and appeared before the curtain announcing that a great dramatic play called "The Burning Shame" was about to be shown. The curtain was then raised, and his partner, naked, came out on his hands and knees. The other said, "And now, gentlemen, you are about to see The Tragedy of the Burning Shame." He inserted a candle in the naked man's posterior, and lit it. When nothing further happened, the audience shouted for something more; the man said the performance was over; the viewers shouted, "You mean, that's all?" "Yes," the man said, "have you ever seen a better example of a 'Burning Shame'?" Then the two dashed out of town, the audience in hot pursuit. (p. 98)

However, Graves could not say whether this version preceded or was inspired by the famous unrevealed performance in *Huckleberry Finn*. But this, too, seems rather tame for what Twain called "one of the most outrageously funny things I have ever listened to."

2. *"sold."* Cheated, deceived, taken in. These rough backwoodsmen are so fired up for something even worse than the king's obscene performance that they feel they have not gotten their money's worth of entertainment from which women and children are barred.

3. *the jedge*. Even one of the most prominent men in this Arkansas town could not resist the biggest line of all, "LADIES AND CHILDREN NOT ADMITTED."

4. *not a word about any sell*. Seventeen-year-old Sam Clemens described a similar "sell" in one of the earliest sketches he ever wrote, "Historical Exhibition—a No. 1 Ruse" by "W. Epaminondus Adrastus Blab" (Hannibal *Daily Journal*, September 16, 1852): A store owner advertises a show called "Bonaparte crossing the Rhine" at "one dime per head, children half price"; but "everybody who saw the sight seemed seized with a sudden fit of melancholy immediately afterwards" and "the uninitiated could get nothing out of him on the subject; he was mum." Finally, a little boy named Jim C—— sees this spectacle of a hog's bone ("Bony-part") across a bacon rind (the "Rhine"). "Young man," the entrepreneur addresses him, "I am anxious . . . that you should be entirely satisfied with the exhibition . . . ; and if it has met with favor in your eyes, I shall hold myself under the greatest obligations (with a profound bow), if you will use your influence in forwarding the cause of learning and knowledge (another bow), by inciting your friends to step in when they pass this way. What, may I ask, is your opinion of the exhibition?" Slowly Jim replies, "Sold!—cheap . . . as . . . dirt!" And whenever any one brings up the subject, Jim says simply, "Bonaparte crossing—sold!" See *Early Tales and Sketches*, vol. 1, 1979, pp. 79–82.

5. *if I know the signs of a dead cat being around, and I bet I do*. Huck harks back to his introduction in Chapter 6 of *Tom Sawyer* as the "juvenile pariah of the village," dragging a dead cat for curing warts.

6. *too various*. Too many varieties of offensive odors; overwhelming. Richard Watson Gilder could not stand it either; he dropped the references to "dead cats" and "too various" from "Royalty on the Mississippi" when he published the excerpt in *Century Magazine* (February 1885). The foul smell tips off the duke to what the town has planned for the two con artists.

ing, 'Chop off her head.'[11] And he made every one of them tell him a tale every night; and he kept that up till he had hogged a thousand and one tales that way, and then he put them all in a book, and called it Domesday Book[12]—which was a good name and stated the case.[13] You don't know kings, Jim, but I know them; and this old rip of ourn is one of the cleanest I've struck in history. Well, Henry he takes a notion he wants to get up some trouble with this country. How does he go at it—give notice?—give the country a show? No. All of a sudden he heaves all the tea in Boston Harbor overboard, and whacks out a declaration of inde-

HENRY THE EIGHTH IN BOSTON HARBOR.

pendence, and dares them to come on. That was *his* style—he never give anybody a chance. He had suspicions of his father, the Duke of Wellington. Well, what did he do?—ask him to show up? No—drownded him in a butt of mamsey,[14] like a cat. Spose people left money laying around where he was—what did he do? He collared it. Spose he contracted to do a thing; and you paid him, and didn't set down there and see that he done it—what did he do? He always done the other thing. Spose he opened his mouth—what then? If he didn't shut it up powerful quick, he'd lose a lie, every time. That's the kind of a bug Henry was; and if we'd a had him along 'stead of our kings, he'd a fooled that town a heap worse than ourn done. I don't say that ourn is lambs, because they ain't, when you come right down to the cold facts; but they ain't nothing to *that* old ram, anyway. All I say is, kings is kings, and you got to make allowances. Take them all around, they're a mighty ornery lot. It's the way they're raised."

"But dis one do *smell* so like de nation, Huck."

"Well, they all do, Jim. *We* can't help the way a king smells; history don't tell no way."

"Now de duke, he's a tolerble likely man, in some ways."

"Yes, a duke's different. But not very different. This one's a middling hard lot, for a duke. When he's drunk, there ain't no near-sighted man could tell him from a king."

"Well, anyways, I doan' hanker for no mo' un um, Huck. Dese is all I kin stan'."

"It's the way I feel, too, Jim. But we've got them on our hands, and we got to remember what they are, and make allowances. Sometimes I wish we could hear of a country that's out of kings."

What was the use to tell Jim these warn't real kings and dukes? It wouldn't a done no good; and besides, it was just as I said; you couldn't tell them from the real kind.

I went to sleep, and Jim didn't call me when it was my turn. He often done that. When I waked up, just at day-break, he was setting there with his head down betwixt his knees, moaning and mourning to himself. I didn't take notice, nor let on. I knowed what it was about. He was thinking about his wife and his children, away up yonder, and he was low and homesick; because he hadn't ever been away from home before in his life; and I do believe he cared just as much for his people as white folks does for their'n.[15] It don't seem natural, but I reckon it's so. He was often moaning and mourning that way, nights, when he judged I was asleep, and saying, "Po' little 'Lizabeth! po' little Johnny! it mighty hard; I spec' I ain't ever gwyne to see you no mo', no mo'!" He was a mighty good nigger, Jim was.

But this time I somehow got to talking to him about his wife and young ones; and by-and-by he says:

"What makes me feel so bad dis time, 'uz bekase I hear

7. *Is dat so?* Here Huck and Jim are engaged in another minstrel-show debate, but the roles are reversed: Huck is the comic and Jim the straight man.

8. *Saxon heptarchies*. "Heptarchy" is the name for a government of seven persons or an alliance of seven kingdoms, each with its own ruler. Huck vaguely recollects the Anglo-Saxon heptarchy in England, 449–838 A.D.

9. *He used to marry a new wife every day, and chop off her head next morning*. Huck garbles Henry VIII with King Shariyar of *The Arabian Nights*, who daily marries a new wife and executes her the next morning—until he meets Scheherazade. "Somehow, the crochet got into [Shariyar's] skull that all women were faithless, and not to be trusted," explained Orion Clemens's Hannibal *Journal* (November 6, 1851); "and from the same skull sprung the original and brilliant idea, of marrying one of his subjects every day, and cutting off her head the next. This noble resolution he carried out, to great terror of all fathers and brothers in the kingdom. At last, a daughter of his grand vizier thought of the lucky expedient of amusing the monster by a series of stories." Henry VIII had only six wives, surely enough for any king, but had only two beheaded.

10. *Nell Gwynn. . . . Jane Shore. . . . Fair Rosamun*. Three of the most famous mistresses in English

Nell Gwynn.
Courtesy Picture Collection, New York Public Library, Astor, Lenox, and Tilden Foundations.

sumpn over yonder on de bank like a whack, er a slam, while ago, en it mine me er de time I treat my little 'Lizabeth so ornery.[16] She warn't on'y 'bout fo' year ole, en she tuck de sk'yarlet-fever, en had a powerful rough spell; but she got well, en one day she was a-stannin' aroun', en I says to her, I says:

"Shet de do'.'

"She never done it; jis' stood dah, kiner smilin' up at me. It make me mad; en I says agin, mighty loud, I says:

"'Doan' you hear me?—shet de do'!'

"She jis' stood de same way, kiner smilin' up. I was a-bilin'! I says:

"'I lay I *make* you mine!'

"En wid dat I fetch' her a slap side de head dat sont her a-sprawlin'. Den I went into de yuther room, en 'uz gone 'bout ten minutes; en when I come back, dah was dat do' a-stannin' open *yit,* en dat chile stannin' mos' right in it, a-lookin' down and mournin', en de tears runnin' down. My, but I *wuz* mad, I was agwyne for de chile, but jis' den—it was a do' dat open innerds—jis' den, 'long come de wind en slam it to, behine de chile, ker-*blam!*—en my lan', de chile never move'! My breff mos' hop outer me; en I feel so—so—I doan' know *how* I feel. I crope out, all a-tremblin', en crope aroun' en open de do' easy en slow, en poke my head in behine de chile, sof' en still, en all uv a sudden, I says *pow!* jis' as loud as I could yell. *She never budge!* Oh, Huck, I bust out a-cryin' en grab her up in my arms, en say, 'Oh, de po' little thing! de Lord God Amighty[17] forgive po' ole Jim, kaze he never gwyne to fogive hisself as long's he live!' Oh, she was plumb deef en dumb, Huck, plumb deef en dumb—en I'd ben a-treat'n her so!"

Jane Shore.
Courtesy Picture Collection, New York Public Library, Astor, Lenox, and Tilden Foundations.

"Fair Rosamund" Clifford.
Courtesy Picture Collection, New York Public Library, Astor, Lenox, and Tilden Foundations.

history, though none of them was the wife of King Henry VIII, who reigned from 1509 to 1547. Nell Gwynne was the concubine of Charles II (ruled 1660–1685); Jane Shore was that of Edward VI (1461–1470 and 1471–1483); and "Fair" Rosamund Clifford was said to be that of Henry II (1152–1189), whose jealous queen supposedly had her murdered.

11. *'Chop off her head.'* Twain deleted a grisly detail from the manuscript, "and next thing you see is the Chief of police with it in a rag" (**MS**). Twain may have been thinking of reports of how heads of decapitated noblemen during the French Revolution were held aloft in handkerchiefs before the mob like trophies after executions.

12. *he made every one of them tell him a tale every night . . . and then he put them all in a book, and called it Domesday Book.* A further misreading of *The Arabian Nights* (also known as *One Thousand and One Nights*), in which the king makes each of his new wives tell some diverting tale before retiring to bed and executes her the next day if she fails to enthrall him with her story; and all fail until Scheherazade so enchants him with her storytelling that after one thousand and one nights he finally decides not to kill her. The summer he completed *Huckleberry Finn*, Twain wrote a dull burlesque, "1002nd Arabian Night," which Howells advised him not to publish (but it was included in *Mark Twain's Satires and Burlesques*, 1968, pp. 91–133). The Domesday Book is the record of the Great Inquest, a census and land survey ordered by William the Conqueror in 1086.

13. *which was a good name and stated the case.* Huck seems to confuse "Domesday" with "Doomsday," the Day of Reckoning. Twain originally wrote in the manuscript: "and he kept it up til he had hogged a thousand one tales that way, and then he got out a copyright and published them in a book, and called it Domesday Book—which was a good name and stated the case. Of course most any publisher would do that, but you wouldn't think a king would" (Ferguson, "Huck Finn Aborning," p. 174). Twain may well have been recalling all his troubles with the piracy of his work. As an author, he was preoccupied with copyright questions; but that is an area of law Huck Finn would have no knowledge of. Of course, both *The Arabian Nights* and the Domesday Book were written long before copyright was an issue.

14. *the Duke of Wellington. . . . drownded him in a butt of mamsey.* Huck confuses the Duke of Wellington (1769–1852), the hero of the Battle of Waterloo in 1812, with George, Duke of Clarence (1449–1478), who was secretly killed in a butt of malmsey (a sweet, strong wine) by order of his brother Edward IV. Shakespeare comically reconstructed the murder in *Richard III* (Act I, scene iv, lines 84–280). And, of course, Henry VIII had nothing to do with the Boston Tea Party in 1773 or the signing of the Declaration of Independence in 1776.

15. *I do believe he cared just as much for his people as white folks does for their'n.* Mary Ann Cord, the cook at Quarry Farm in Elmira, New York, where the Clemenses spent their summers, told Twain as much back in 1874. "Well, sah, my ole man—dat's my husban'—he was lovin' an' kind to me, jist as kind as you is to yo' own wife," he quoted her in "A True Story" (*Atlantic Monthly*, November 1874.) "An' we had chil'en—seven chil'en. Dey was black, but de Lord can't make no chil'en so black but what dey mother loves 'em an' wouldn't give 'em up, no, not for anything dat's in dis whole world" (p. 591–92). Like Jim, Aunty Cord lost every member of her family when they were sold at auction. "A True Story," however brief it is, is a landmark in American literature. "The rugged truth of the sketch leaves all other stories of slave life infinitely far behind," William Dean Howells declared in *The Atlantic Monthly* (December 1875), "and reveals a gift in the author for the simple, dramatic report of reality which we have seen equalled in no other American writer" (pp. 750–51). Jim expresses the same unbridled love and agony for his family as "Aunty Rachel" does in "A True Story." And Twain recaptured its pathos in this chapter of *Huckleberry Finn*. Chadwick-Joshua argued in *The Jim Dilemma* (1998) that, despite the irony apparent in much of Huck's thinking, this realization that Jim loves his family just as other people do is "not a racist statement, as the opponents of the book have alleged, but rather a racial awakening by Huck as Jim eclipses Huck's own pap. It is a statement that denies one of the ugliest and most pervasive and pernicious stereotypes encouraged by slavemasters" (p. 107).

16. *de time I treat my little 'Lizabeth so ornery.* The source for this episode was an anecdote Twain jotted down in his notes for the novel in 1879 or 1880: "L. A. punished her child several days for refusing to answer and inattention (five year old) then while punishing discovered it was deaf and dumb! (from scarlet fever). It showed no reproachfulness for the whippings—kissed the punisher and showed non-comprehension of what it was all about" (University of California edition, 1988, p. 731). "L. A." has not been identified. Twain reminded himself in 1882 or 1883 to consider "some rhymes about the little child whose mother boxed its ears for inattention and presently when it did not notice the heavy slamming of a door, perceived that it was deaf" (*Mark Twain's Notebooks and Journals*, vol. 2, 1975, p. 510). So expertly did Twain handle this potentially maudlin scene that Jim earns the modern reader's full sympathy. "In one crystalline moment," observed Chadwick-Joshua in *The Jim Dilemma* (1998), "Jim's manhood emerges. Here is a man who has undertaken the most dangerous quest possible for a southern African American in the nineteenth century. Here is a man who can show emotion over the loss of his family. Here is a man who shares with his friend a dark truth about himself as a father. . . . We have seen Jim to be a man who can forgive others, but he cannot forgive himself for an unknowingly misguided act. He does not seek to displace blame and responsibility some place else: on whites, on fate" (pp. 105–7). In this chapter alone, Jim offers an extraordinary contrast as a man to the two white scoundrels asleep on their ticks.

17. *de Lord God Amighty*. Perhaps to divert Olivia Clemens or some pious proofreader, Twain wrote boldly in the margin of the manuscript, "This expression shall not be changed" (DeVoto, *Mark Twain at Work*, 1942, p. 82).

Chapter XXIV.

HARMLESS.

NEXT DAY, towards night, we laid up under a little willow tow-head out in the middle, where there was a village on each side of the river,[1] and the duke and the king begun to lay out a plan for working them towns. Jim he spoke to the duke, and said he hoped it wouldn't take but a few hours, because it got mighty heavy and tiresome to him when he had to lay all day in the wigwam tied with the rope. You see, when we left him all alone we had to tie him, because if anybody happened on him all by himself and not tied, it wouldn't look much like he was a runaway nigger, you know. So the duke said it *was* kind of hard to have to lay roped all day,[2] and he'd cipher out some way to get around it.

He was uncommon bright, the duke was, and he soon struck it. He dressed Jim up in King Lear's outfit—it was a long curtain-calico gown, and a white horse-hair wig and whiskers; and then he took his theatre-paint and painted Jim's face and hands and ears and neck all over a dead dull solid blue, like a man that's been drownded nine days. Blamed if he warn't the horriblest looking outrage I ever see. Then the duke took and wrote out a sign on a shingle so—

Sick Arab—but harmless when not out of his head.[3]

1. *a village on each side of the river*. They have drifted so far down the river that Arkansas is now on one side and the state of Mississippi on the other. Blair and Fischer in the 1988 University of California edition (p. 415) said that these two villages correspond to Columbia, Arkansas, and Greenville, Mississippi. "Napoleon [in Arkansas] had but small opinion of Greenville, Mississippi, in the old times," Twain reported in Chapter 33 of *Life on the Mississippi;* "but behold, Napoleon is gone to the cat-fishes, and here is Greenville full of life and activity, and making a considerable flourish in the Valley; having three thousand inhabitants, it is said, and doing a gross trade of $2,500,000 annually. A growing town."

2. *the duke said that it* was *kind of hard to have to lay roped all day*. "Jim continues to construct his own narrative," Chadwick-Joshua reminded the reader in *The Jim Dilemma* (1998). "It is he who expresses the need for another plan to conceal him during the day" (p. 108). The duke still seems to be "a tolerable likely man, in some ways," as Jim observed in the last chapter. Not so the king.

3. *Sick Arab—but harmless when not out of his head.* The duke may be thinking of Othello, Shakespeare's tragic Moor, who murders his wife in a jealous rage but is otherwise an admirable man; Jim is already dressed in the clothes of another mad monarch from Shakespeare, King Lear. This disguise is so outrageous that it is one of the least convincing elements in the novel, anticipating the more bizarre events in the "evasion" that concludes the novel. But Twain had to do something with Jim once he decided on the nature of the next confidence game in the story. The king and the

"Hop out of the wigwam and carry on a little." Illustration by E. W. Kemble, New York *World*, December 10, 1899.
Private collection.

duke cannot take him ashore with them, for it would be inconceivable for an English minister to be traveling with a slave. A valet is fine, but England long ago abolished slavery.

This disguise has also offended both Arab and African-American. Chadwick-Joshua noted in *The Jim Dilemma* (1998) that this episode is "often cited by *Huckleberry Finn* opponents as being the most clearly racist passage in the midsection of the novel" (p. 107). But this ruse may have a subtler significance than it has at first glance. "There is a tendency to accept blackness when it can be given a foreign air," explained Kenny J. Williams in "*Adventures of Huckleberry Finn*; or Mark Twain's Racial Ambiguity" (*Mark Twain Journal*, Fall 1984). "In the day before public accommodation laws, some blacks pretended to be exotic foreigners in order to stay in hotels and eat in restaurants. It was a joke that delighted blacks and fooled whites. Twain's duke and king are smart enough to know a dark-skinned foreigner is acceptable in the world of the Mississippi Valley" (p. 41). Jim can survive only by taking on this exotic mask, however silly and demeaning it may appear; it speaks more about the duke and king's opinion of the gullibility of the locals than it does about Jim. "Just how is it that Twain is negatively portraying Jim?" asked Chadwick-Joshua. "How is he completely marginalized? If Jim's goal is to find a way that better suits him for remaining on the raft alone, his actions can be understood, given that men with whom he and Huck must negotiate are themselves

And he nailed that shingle to a lath, and stood the lath up four or five foot in front of the wigwam. Jim was satisfied. He said it was a sight better than laying tied a couple of years every day and trembling all over every time there was a sound. The duke told him to make himself free and easy, and if anybody ever come meddling around, he must hop out of the wigwam, and carry on a little, and fetch a howl or two like a wild beast, and he reckoned they would light out and leave him alone. Which was sound enough judgment; but you take the average man, and he wouldn't wait for him to howl. Why, he didn't only look like he was dead, he looked considerable more than that.[4]

These rapscallions wanted to try the Nonesuch again, because there was so much money in it, but they judged it wouldn't be safe, because maybe the news might a worked along down by this time. They couldn't hit no project that suited, exactly; so at last the duke said he reckoned he'd lay off and work his brains an hour or two and see if he couldn't put up something on the Arkansaw village; and the king he allowed he would drop over to t'other village, without any plan, but just trust in Providence to lead him the profitable way—meaning the devil, I reckon. We had all bought store clothes where we stopped last; and now the king put his'n on, and he told me to put mine on. I done it, of course.[5] The king's duds was all black, and he did look real swell and starchy. I never knowed how clothes could change a body before. Why, before, he looked like the orneriest old rip that ever was; but now, when he'd take off his new white beaver[6] and make a bow and do a smile, he looked that grand and good and pious that you'd say he had walked right out of the ark, and maybe was old Leviticus himself.[7] Jim cleaned up the canoe, and I got my paddle ready. There was a big steamboat laying at the shore away up under the point, about three mile above town—been there a couple of hours, taking on freight.[8] Says the king:

"Seein' how I'm dressed, I reckon maybe I better arrive down from St. Louis or Cincinnati, or some other big place.

Go for the steamboat, Huckleberry; we'll come down to the village on her."

I didn't have to be ordered twice, to go and take a steamboat ride. I fetched the shore a half a mile above the village, and then went scooting along the bluff bank in the easy water. Pretty soon we come to a nice innocent-looking young country jake setting on a log swabbing the sweat off of his face, for it was powerful warm weather; and he had a couple of big carpet-bags by him.

"Run her nose in shore," says the king. I done it. "Wher' you bound for, young man?"

"For the steamboat; going to Orleans."

"Git aboard," says the king. "Hold on a minute, my servant 'll he'p you with them bags. Jump out and he'p the gentleman, Adolphus"—meaning me, I see.

I done so, and then we all three started on again. The young chap was mighty thankful; said it was tough work tot-

ADOLPHUS.

ing his baggage such weather. He asked the king where he was going, and the king told him he'd come down the river and landed at the other village this morning, and now he was going up a few mile to see an old friend on a farm up there. The young fellow says:

"When I first see you, I says to myself, 'It's Mr. Wilks, sure,

rogues. Jim never removes his eyes from the ultimate prize—freedom—even for a short time of comfort. His persistence says much in Jim's favor, not against him" (pp. 108–9). Remember also that the duke comes up with the wild disguise, keeping in character with his theatrical background.

4. *he looked considerable more than that.* The manuscript reveals exactly what Huck means: "He looked like he was mortified" (Ferguson, "Huck Finn Aborning," p. 179). An obvious pun on the term *rigor mortis*, the stiffening of the body after the point of death.

5. *I done it, of course.* "But it was because I had to; it warn't because I wanted to" (**MS**), Huck explained in the manuscript; but Twain struck it out.

6. *white beaver.* A tall hat, made of white beaver fur or felt in imitation of beaver; Kemble missed this detail, and gave the king a black slouch.

7. *you'd say he had walked right out of the ark, and maybe was old Leviticus himself.* Because the king now looks like a minister, Huck struggles to find the right biblical metaphor with which to describe him; instead, he garbles the story of Noah in Genesis 6:15–9:17 with the name of the third book of the Old Testament. The reference to the Ark was an afterthought; the manuscript reads, "He had walked right out of the Bible" (Ferguson, "Huck Finn Aborning," p. 179).

8. *taking on freight.* Originally "taking on cotton" in the manuscript. This indicated to Blair and Fischer in the 1988 University of California edition (p. 415) that Twain was thinking of Point Chicot, Arkansas, the sight of a well-known cotton plantation mentioned in *Life on the Mississippi*, Chapter 33.

and he come mighty near getting here in time.' But then I says again, 'No, I reckon it ain't him, or else he wouldn't be paddling up the river.' You *ain't* him, are you?"

"No, my name's Blodgett—Elexander Blodgett—*Reverend* Elexander Blodgett, I spose I must say, as I'm one o' the Lord's poor servants. But still I'm jist as able to be sorry for Mr. Wilks for not arriving in time, all the same, if he's missed anything by it—which I hope he hasn't."

"Well, he don't miss any property by it, because he'll get that all right; but he's missed seeing his brother Peter die—which he mayn't mind, nobody can tell as to that—but his brother would a give anything in this world to see *him* before he died; never talked about nothing else all these three weeks; hadn't seen him since they was boys together—and hadn't ever seen his brother William at all—that's the deef and dumb one—William ain't more than thirty or thirty-five. Peter and George was the only ones that come out here; George was the married brother; him and his wife both died last year. Harvey and William's the only ones that's left now; and, as I was saying, they haven't got here in time."

"Did anybody send 'em word?"

"Oh, yes; a month or two ago, when Peter was first took; because Peter said then that he sorter felt like he warn't going to get well this time. You see, he was pretty old, and George's g'yirls was too young to be much company for him, except Mary Jane the red-headed one; and so he was kinder lonesome after George and his wife died, and didn't seem to care much to live. He most desperately wanted to see Harvey—and William too, for that matter—because he was one of them kind that can't bear to make a will. He left a letter behind for Harvey, and said he'd told in it where his money was hid, and how he wanted the rest of the property divided up so George's g'yirls would be all right—for George didn't leave nothing. And that letter was all they could get him to put a pen to."

"Why do you reckon Harvey don't come? Wher' does he live?"

"Oh, he lives in England—Sheffield—preaches there—

hasn't ever been in this country. He hasn't had any too much time—and besides he mightn't a got the letter at all, you know."

"Too bad, too bad he couldn't a lived to see his brothers, poor soul. You going to Orleans, you say?"

"Yes, but that ain't only a part of it. I'm going in a ship, next Wednesday, for Ryo Janeero,[9] where my uncle lives."

"It's a pretty long journey. But it'll be lovely; I wisht I was agoing. Is Mary Jane the oldest? How old is the others?"

"Mary Jane's nineteen, Susan's fifteen, and Joanna's about fourteen[10]—that's the one that gives herself to good works and has a hare-lip."[11]

"Poor things! to be left alone in the cold world so."

"Well, they could be worse off. Old Peter had friends, and they ain't going to let them come to no harm. There's Hobson, the Babtis' preacher; and Deacon Lot Hovey, and Ben Rucker, and Abner Shackleford, and Levi Bell, the lawyer; and Dr. Robinson, and their wives, and the widow Bartley, and—well, there's a lot of them; but these are the ones that Peter was thickest with, and used to write about sometimes, when he wrote home; so Harvey'll know where to look for friends when he get's here."

Well, the old man he went on asking questions till he just fairly emptied that young fellow. Blamed if he didn't inquire about everybody and everything in that blessed

HE FAIRLY EMPTIED THAT YOUNG FELLOW.

9. *a ship . . . for Ryo Janeero.* Twain was likely referring to his own youthful ambitions when a "country jake" himself. "I had been reading Lieutenant Herndon's account of his explorations of the Amazon," he recalled in his *Autobiography* (vol. 2, 1924), "and had been mightily attracted by what he said of coca. I made up my mind that I would go to the headwaters of the Amazon and collect coca and trade in it and make a fortune. I left for New Orleans in the steamer *Paul Jones* with this great idea filling my mind" (p. 289). But he never did make it to Rio de Janeiro. "When I got to Orleans," he confessed, "I inquired about ships leaving for Pará and discovered that there weren't any and learned that there probably wouldn't be any during that century. It had not occurred to me to inquire about these particulars before leaving Cincinnati, so there I was. I couldn't get to the Amazon." Fortunately, he got to know the pilot of the *Paul Jones* and arranged in New Orleans to learn the trade under him.

10. *Joanna's about fourteen.* She was originally "twelve" (**MS**) in the manuscript, but Twain changed it to make her another child who is the same age as Huck Finn.

11. *the one that gives herself to good works and has a hare-lip.* A harelip is a congenitally deformed lip, usually the upper one, in which a vertical fissure makes it look like the cleft lip of a rabbit; it was once believed to be caused by the mother's having been scared by a rabbit when pregnant. The young man reverses cause and effect here: Because a harelip was considered unattractive on a girl, Joanna must devote her life to helping others, by visiting and praying for the sick and the unconverted, and by distributing religious tracts, medicines, and food. Today her harelip would probably be corrected by plastic surgery.

12. *a dissentering minister*. An English Protestant minister (usually Congregationalist, Baptist, or Presbyterian) who dissents from the tenets of the Church of England, the equivalent of the Episcopal Church in America.

13. *a big Orleans boat*. "The New Orleans steamboats are a very different description of vessels to any I had yet seen," wrote Thomas Hamilton in *Men and Manners in America* (vol. 2, 1833). "They are of great size, and the object being to carry as large a cargo as possible, the whole vessel . . . is devoted to this purpose, and the cabins for the passengers are raised in successive tiers above the main deck. . . . These vessels have very much the appearance of three-deckers, and many of them are upwards of 500 tons burden" (pp. 180–81).

A New Orleans steamboat. Lithograph by A. Hervieu, *Domestic Manners of the Americans* by Frances Trollope, 1832. *Courtesy General Research and Humanities Division, New York Public Library, Astor, Lenox, and Tilden Foundations.*

14. *I see what* he *was up to*. Blair in *Mark Twain and Huck Finn* suggested that the king's new confidence game was inspired in part by Fuller's *Noted French Trials: Impostors and Adventurers* (1882). The chapter "The Seven False Dauphins" describes the false claimant Mathurin Bruneau, who, on learning of his resemblance to a rich woman's missing son, "hastily acquired information in regard to the family, and at once presented himself to the widow as her returned son. Received with joy . . . he sustained for some time this deception, and then disappeared" (p. 327).

town, and all about all the Wilkses; and about Peter's business—which was a tanner; and about George's—which was a carpenter; and about Harvey's—which was a dissentering minister;[12] and so on, and so on. Then he says:

"What did you want to walk all the way up to the steamboat for?"

"Because she's a big Orleans boat,[13] and I was afeard she mightn't stop there. When they're deep they won't stop for a hail. A Cincinnati boat will, but this is a St. Louis one."

"Was Peter Wilks well off?"

"Oh, yes, pretty well off. He had houses and land, and it's reckoned he left three or four thousand in cash hid up som'ers."

"When did you say he died?"

"I didn't say, but it was last night."

"Funeral to-morrow, likely?"

"Yes, 'bout the middle of the day."

"Well, it's all terrible sad; but we've all got to go, one time or another. So what we want to do is to be prepared; then we're all right."

"Yes, sir, it's the best way. Ma used to always say that."

When we struck the boat, she was about done loading, and pretty soon she got off. The king never said nothing about going aboard, so I lost my ride, after all. When the boat was gone, the king made me paddle up another mile to a lonesome place, and then he got ashore, and says:

"Now hustle back, right off, and fetch the duke up here, and the new carpet-bags. And if he's gone over to t'other side, go over there and git him. And tell him to git himself up regardless. Shove along, now."

I see what *he* was up to;[14] but I never said nothing, of course. When I got back with the duke, we hid the canoe and then they set down on a log, and the king told him everything, just like the young fellow had said it—every last word of it. And all the time he was a doing it, he tried to talk like an Englishman;[15] and he done it pretty well too, for a slouch. I can't imitate him,[16] and so I ain't agoing to try to; but he really done it pretty good. Then he says:

"How are you on the deef and dumb,[17] Bilgewater?"

The duke said, leave him alone for that; said he had played a deef and dumb person on the histrionic boards. So then they waited for a steamboat.

About the middle of the afternoon a couple of little boats come along, but they didn't come from high enough up the river; but at last there was a big one, and they hailed her. She sent out her yawl,[18] and we went aboard, and she was from Cincinnati; and when they found we only wanted to go four or five mile, they was booming mad, and give us a cussing, and said they wouldn't land us. But the king was ca'm. He says:

"If gentlemen kin afford to pay a dollar a mile apiece, to be took on and put off in a yawl, a steamboat kin afford to carry 'em, can't it?"

So they softened down and said it was all right; and when we got to the village, they yawled us ashore. About two dozen men flocked down, when they see the yawl a coming; and when the king says—

"Kin any of you gentlemen tell me wher' Mr. Peter Wilks lives?" they give a glance at one another, and nodded their heads, as much as to say, "What d' I tell you?" Then one of them says, kind of soft and gentle:

"I'm sorry, sir, but the best we can do is to tell you where he *did* live yesterday evening."

Sudden as winking, the ornery old cretur went all to smash,[19] and fell up against the man, and put his chin on his shoulder, and cried down his back, and says:

"Alas, alas, our poor brother—gone, and we never got to see him; oh, it's too, *too* hard!"

Then he turns around, blubbering, and makes a lot of idiotic signs to the duke on his hands, and blamed if *he* didn't drop a carpet-bag and bust out a-crying. If they warn't the beatenest lot, them two frauds, that ever I struck.

Well, the men gethered around, and sympathized with them, and said all sorts of kind things to them, and carried their carpet-bags up the hill for them, and let them lean on them and cry, and told the king all about his brother's last

15. *he tried to talk like an Englishman*. One irony of the king and duke's scheme is that the duke with his Shakespearean background is the more qualified one for this impersonation, not the inexperienced and ignorant king. As Huck's account proves, he fails miserably in imitating the speech of an Englishman.

16. *I can't imitate him*. Twain originally wrote "with a pen" (**MS**), the only indication in the text that Huck is writing rather than dictating his story; but Twain struck it out of the manuscript.

17. *How are you on the deef and dumb*. The relatively simple deception of impersonating a deaf-mute was a common device in popular fiction and melodrama of the period; for example, Melville's Confidence-Man first appears on the steamboat disguised as both deaf and dumb. It seems to be a universal trick among Twain's impostors, including the Spaniard in Chapter 26 of *Tom Sawyer*; Simon Wheeler, the amateur detective, in an unpublished play of 1877; Brace Dunlap in "Tom Sawyer, Detective"; and the false slave in the uncompleted "Tom Sawyer's Conspiracy" of 1898. This fraud seems particularly insensitive and sarcastic coming so soon after Jim's lamentations for his deaf and dumb little girl.

18. *her yawl*. Steamboats were generally equipped with these small boats that transported passengers to shores that lacked a dock.

19. *Sudden as winking, the ornery old cretur went all to smash*. Twain had originally written, "The derned old cretur fell up against him; and put his chin on his shoulder and cried down" (**MS**). He then tried to make the king "kerflummoxed" before finally deciding on the far more expressive "went all to smash."

moments, and the king he told it all over again on his hands to the duke, and both of them took on about that dead tanner like they'd lost the twelve disciples. Well, if ever I struck anything like it, I'm a nigger. It was enough to make a body ashamed of the human race.[20]

"ALAS, OUR POOR BROTHER."

20. *It was enough to make a body ashamed of the human race.* One of the most famous and frequently quoted sentences in the novel. Twain expresses the same sentiment in Chapter 24 of *Tom Sawyer*, but in a more pedestrian fashion and with far less force: "Huck's confidence in the human race was well-nigh obliterated." Once he found the right words, Twain used them with some frequency in his work; for example, they are said by Hank Morgan in Chapter 20 of *A Connecticut Yankee in King Arthur's Court* and by Huck again in Chapter 12 of *Tom Sawyer Abroad*. However, the sincerity of this revelation is undercut by its being prefaced by one of the most offensive statements the boy ever makes: "Well, if ever I struck anything like it, I'm a nigger."

Chapter XXV

"YOU BET IT IS."

The news was all over town in two minutes, and you could see the people tearing down on the run, from every which way, some of them putting on their coats as they come.[1] Pretty soon we was in the middle of a crowd, and the noise of the tramping was like a soldier-march.[2] The windows and door-yards was full; and every minute somebody would say, over a fence:

"Is it *them?*"

And somebody trotting along with the gang would answer back and say,

"You bet it is."

When we got to the house, the street in front of it was packed, and the three girls was standing in the door. Mary Jane *was* red-headed, but that don't make no difference,[3] she was most awful beautiful, and her face and her eyes was all lit up like glory, she was so glad her uncles was come. The king he spread his arms,[4] and Mary Jane she jumped for them, and the hare-lip jumped for the duke, and there they *had* it! Everybody most, leastways women, cried for joy to see them meet again at last[5] and have such good times.

Then the king he hunched the duke, private—I see him do it—and then he looked around and see the coffin, over in the corner on two chairs; so then, him and the duke, with

1. *some of them putting on their coats as they come*. Blair and Fischer suggested in the 1988 University of California edition that Twain was likely recalling John W. Stavely, as he did in Chapter 55 of *Life on the Mississippi*, a saddler who "used to go tearing down the street, putting on his coat as he went; and then everybody knew a steamboat was coming." He was always there to greet the boats at the wharf, so Hannibal became known in the neighboring towns as "Stavely's Landing." See *Huck Finn and Tom Sawyer Among the Indians*, 1989, p. 341.

2. *the noise of the tramping was like a soldier-march*. Here Huck adopts Colonel Sherburn's sarcastic metaphor in Chapter 22 that a mob is an army.

3. *Mary Jane* was *red-headed, but that don't make no difference*. At this time in American history, red hair was considered unattractive. Typical of this attitude was a character's remark in Johnson Jones Hooper's *The Widow Rugby's Husband* (1851) that "this feller married a red-headed widow for her money—no man ever married sich for anything else" (p. 26). Clemens, who was a redhead himself, facetiously attacked this prejudice in one of his earliest sketches, "Oh She Has a Red Head!" (Hannibal *Daily Journal*, May 13, 1853): "Turn up your nose at red heads! What ignorance! I pity your lack of taste. Why, man, red is the natural color of beauty! What is there that is really beautiful or grand in Nature or Art, that is not tinted with this primordial color! . . . Most animals are fond of red—and *all children*, before their tastes are corrupted, and their judgements perverted, are fond of red. The Romans anciently regarded red hair as *necessary* to a beautiful lady!" (reprinted in *Early Tales and Sketches*, vol. 1, 1979, pp. 104–5).

a hand across each other's shoulder, and t'other hand to their eyes, walked slow and solemn over there, everybody dropping back to give them room, and all the talk and noise stopping, people saying "Sh!" and all the men taking their hats off and drooping their heads, so you could a heard a pin fall. And when they got there, they bent over and looked in the coffin, and took one sight, and then they bust out a crying so you could a heard them to Orleans, most; and then they put their arms around each other's necks, and hung their chins over each other's shoulders; and then for three minutes, or maybe four, I never see two men leak the way they done. And mind you, everybody was doing the same; and the place was that damp I never see anything like it. Then one of them got on one side of the coffin, and

LEAKING.

t'other on t'other side, and they kneeled down and rested their foreheads on the coffin, and let on to pray all to theirselves. Well, when it come to that, it worked the crowd like you never see anything like it, and so everybody broke down and went to sobbing right out loud—the poor girls, too; and every woman, nearly, went up to the girls, without saying a word, and kissed them, solemn, on the forehead,

4. *The king he spread his arms.* As Ferguson pointed out in "Huck Finn Aborning," the king and the duke were considerably more lecherous in the first draft of the novel: "Soon as he could, the king shook the hare-lip, and sampled Susan, which was better looking. After the king had kissed Mary Jane fourteen or fifteen times, he give the duke a show, and tapered off on the others" (p. 180). See Chapter 28, notes 3 and 9.

5. *to see them meet again at last.* An error: Blair and Fischer pointed out in the 1988 University of California edition (p. 531) that the Wilks girls have never met their uncles before.

and then put their hand on their head, and looked up towards the sky,[6] with the tears running down, and then busted out and went off sobbing and swabbing, and give the next woman[7] a show. I never see anything so disgusting.[8]

Well, by-and-by the king he gets up and comes forward a little, and works himself up and slobbers out a speech,[9] all full of tears and flapdoodle about its being a sore trial for him and his poor brother to lose the diseased, and to miss seeing diseased alive, after the long journey of four thousand mile, but it's a trial that's sweetened and sanctified to us by this dear sympathy and these holy tears, and so he thanks them out of his heart and out of his brother's heart, because out of their mouths they can't, words being too weak and cold, and all that kind of rot and slush, till it was just sickening; and then he blubbers out a pious goody-goody Amen, and turns himself loose and goes to crying fit to bust.

And the minute the words was out of his mouth somebody over in the crowd struck up the doxolojer,[10] and everybody joined in with all their might, and it just warmed you up and made you feel as good as church letting out. Music *is* a good thing; and after all that soul-butter[11] and hogwash,[12] I never see it freshen up things so, and sound so honest and bully.

Then the king begins to work his jaw again, and says how him and his nieces would be glad if a few of the main principal friends of the family would take supper here with them this evening, and help set up with the ashes of the diseased;[13] and says if his poor brother laying yonder could speak, he knows who he would name, for they was names that was very dear to him, and mentioned often in his letters; and so he will name the same, to-wit, as follows, vizz:—Rev. Mr. Hobson, and Deacon Lot Hovey, and Mr. Ben Rucker, and Abner Shackleford, and Levi Bell, and Dr. Robinson, and their wives, and the widow Bartley.

Rev. Hobson and Dr. Robinson was down to the end of the town, a-hunting together; that is, I mean the doctor was shipping a sick man to t'other world, and the preacher was pinting him right.[14] Lawyer Bell was away up to Louis-

6. *the sky*. Originally "the throne" (**MS**), meaning the Throne of God; but Twain may have feared it might be perceived as blasphemous, so he changed it.

"All full of tears and flapdoodle." Illustration by E. W. Kemble, "Autograph Edition" of *The Collected Works of Mark Twain*, 1899. *Private collection.*

7. *woman*. Originally the cruder and demeaning "heifer" (**MS**).

8. *I never see anything so disgusting*. Blair in *Mark Twain and Huck Finn* (p. 329) compared the duke and king's blubbering with that of another backwoods swindler, Simon Suggs, when he is mistaken for General Thomas Witherspoon, "the rich hog-drover from Kentucky," and "reunited" with the gentleman's nephew: "Young Mr. James Peyton and Captain Simon Suggs then embraced. Several of the bystanders laughed, but a large majority sympathized with the Captain. A few wept at the affecting sight,

ville[15] on some business. But the rest was on hand, and so they all come and shook hands with the king and thanked him and talked to him; and then they shook hands with the duke, and didn't say nothing but just kept a-smiling and bobbing their heads like a passel of sapheads[16] whilst he made all sorts of signs with his hands and said "Goo-goo—goo-goo-goo," all the time,[17] like a baby that can't talk.

So the king he blatted along, and managed to inquire about pretty much everybody and dog in town, by his name, and mentioned all sorts of little things that happened one time or another in the town, or to George's family, or to Peter; and he always let on that Peter wrote him the things, but that was a lie, he got every blessed one of them out of that young flathead that we canoed up to the steamboat.

Then Mary Jane she fetched the letter her father left behind,[18] and the king he read it out loud and cried over it. It give the dwelling-house and three thousand dollars, gold, to the girls; and it give the tanyard (which was doing a good business), along with some other houses and land (worth about seven thousand), and three thousand dollars in gold to Harvey and William, and told where the six thousand cash[19] was hid, down cellar. So these two frauds said they'd go and fetch it up, and have everything square and above-board; and told me to come with a candle. We shut the cellar door behind us, and when they found the bag they spilt it out on the floor, and it was a lovely sight, all them yaller-boys. My, the way the king's eyes did shine! He slaps the duke on the shoulder, and says:

"Oh, *this* ain't bully, nor noth'n! Oh, no, I reckon not! Why, Biljy, it beats the Nonesuch, *don't* it!"

The duke allowed it did. They pawed the yaller-boys,[20] and sifted them through their fingers and let them jingle down on the floor; and the king says:

"It ain't no use talkin'; bein' brothers to a rich dead man, and representatives of furrin heirs that's got left, is the line for you and me,[21] Bilge. Thish-yer comes of trust'n to Providence.[22] It's the best way, in the long run. I've tried 'em all, and ther' ain't no better way."

and one person expressed the opinion that nothing so soul-moving had ever before taken place in the city of Tuskaloosa. As for Simon, the tears rolled down his face, naturally as if they had been called forth by real emotion, instead of being pumped up mechanically to give effect to the scene" (Hooper, *Adventures of Captain Simon Suggs*, p. 62).

9. *the king . . . slobbers out a speech*. The king's pious rhetoric is the same as that used by another scoundrel, Senator Dilworthy, when he addresses the Cattleville Sunday School in Chapter 53 of *The Gilded Age*. The king's speech in the first draft of the novel was given exactly as delivered, but far less effectively in direct discourse:

> "Friends, good friends of the diseased, and ourn too, I trust—it's indeed a sore trial to lose him, and a sore trial to miss seeing of him alive, after the wearisome long journey of four thousand mile; but it's a trial that's sweetened and sanctified to us by this dear sympathy and those holy years; and so, out of our hearts we thank you, for out of our mouths we cannot, words being too weak and cold. May you find sech friends and sech sympathy, yourselves, when your own time of trial comes, and may this affliction be softened to you as ourn is today, by the soothing ba'm of earthly love and the healing of heavenly grace. Amen." (**MS**)

But this does not really sound like the king. "In this speech and its companion," Ferguson observed in "Huck Finn Aborning," "every phrase in the draft is carried over into the final text, but the indirect reporting, by implying compression from much greater length, immeasurably heightens the effect" (p. 175). Huck's editorializing ("all full of tears and flapdoodle") increases the absurdity and hypocrisy of it all and greatly sharpens the humor. But one detail has been dropped for propriety's sake, the point about "earthly love," a term usually applied to carnal desire and a Freudian slip of the tongue which reveals the king's true lecherous nature.

10. *the doxolojer*. The doxology, "Old One Hundred," the familiar hymn of Thomas Ken (1637–1711):

> *Praise God, from whom all blessings flow,*
> *Praise Him, all creatures here below,*

Most everybody would a been satisfied with the pile, and took it on trust; but no, they must count it. So they counts it, and it comes out four hundred and fifteen dollars short. Says the king:

"Dern him, I wonder what he done with that four hunderd and fifteen dollars?"

They worried over that a while, and ransacked all around for it. Then the duke says:

"Well, he was a pretty sick man, and likely he made a mistake—I reckon that's the way of it. The best way's to let it go, and keep still about it. We can spare it."

"Oh, shucks, yes, we can *spare* it. I don't k'yer noth'n 'bout that—it's the *count* I'm thinkin' about. We want to be awful square and open and above-board, here, you know. We want to lug this h-yer money up stairs and count it before everybody—then ther' ain't noth'n suspicious. But when the dead man says ther's six thous'n dollars, you know, we don't want to—"

"Hold on," says the duke. "Less make up the deffisit"—and he begun to haul out yaller-boys out of his pocket.

"It's a most amaz'n' good idea, duke—you *have* got a rat

MAKING UP THE "DEFFISIT."

Praise Him above, ye Heavenly Host,
Praise Father, Son, and Holy Ghost. Amen.

As demonstrated in Chapter 17 of *Tom Sawyer*, it is usually sung in unison at the close of a service as the final blessing. Apparently whoever "struck up the doxolojer" here wants to cut the meeting short. See Chapter 20, note 9.

11. *soul-butter*. Unctuous pious flattery. The famous phrase "soul-butter and hogwash" was an afterthought; the manuscript has the more prosaic "humbug and hogwash."

12. *hogwash*. According to Blair and Fischer in the 1988 University of California edition, Twain wrote John Horner of Belfast, Ireland, on January 12, 1906, that this word was "a term which was invented by the night foreman of the newspaper whereunto I was attached forty years ago, in the capacity of local reporter, to describe my literary efforts" (p. 416). According to his lecture "The Compositor," delivered at a dinner of the Typothetæ in New York on January 18, 1886, and printed in the Hartford *Courant* (January 21, 1886), Clemens and the others in the office also used "hogwash" to describe the editor's poetry. Of course, the word did not originate with them: Twain came across it in a letter written by one of his favorite writers, Horace Walpole, dated March 22, 1796. It appears frequently in Twain's writing; for example, he reprinted an example of "pointless imbecility and bathos," "the sickliest specimen of sham sentimentality," in *The Galaxy* (June 1870) under the heading "Hogwash" (p. 862).

13. *set up with the ashes of the diseased*. Because the spirit of the dead, like that of Jesus Christ, is believed to tarry near the unburied body for three days in wait for resurrection, the living must watch the body to keep away devils which lie in wait for the opportunity to seize the soul of the dear departed. It was believed in the South that one must also watch the corpse to keep cats from getting at it.

14. *the doctor was shipping a sick man to t'other world, and the preacher was pinting him right*. Doctors were not so venerated in nineteenth-century America as they are today, and were the frequent brunt of jokes. "He . . . has been a doctor a year now," says Laura Hawkins in Chapter 10 of *The Gilded Age*, "and he has had two patients—no, three, I think, yes it was three. I tlin' clever head on you," says the king. "Blest if the old Nonesuch ain't a heppin' us out agin"—and *he* begun to haul out yaller-jackets and stack them up.

It most busted them, but they made up the six thousand clean and clear.

"Say," says the duke, "I got another idea. Le's go up stairs and count this money, and then take and *give it to the girls.*"

"Good land, duke, lemme hug you! It's the most dazzling idea 'at ever a man struck. You have cert'nly got the most astonishin' head I ever see. Oh, this is the boss dodge,[23] ther' ain't no mistake 'bout it. Let 'em fetch along their suspicions now, if they want to—this'll lay 'em out."

When we got up stairs, everybody gethered around the table, and the king he counted it and stacked it up, three hundred dollars in a pile—twenty elegant little piles.[24] Everybody looked hungry at it, and licked their chops. Then they raked it into the bag again, and I see the king begin to swell himself up for another speech. He says:

"Friends all, my poor brother that lays yonder, has done generous by them that's left behind in the vale of sorrers.[25] He has done generous by these-yer poor little lambs that he loved and sheltered, and that's left fatherless and motherless. Yes, and we that knowed him, knows that he would a done *more* generous by 'em if he hadn't ben afeard o' woundin' his dear William and me. Now, *wouldn't* he? Ther' ain't no question 'bout it, in *my* mind. Well, then—what kind o' brothers would it be, that'd stand in his way at sech a time? And what kind o' uncles would it be that'd rob—yes, *rob*—sech poor sweet lambs as these 'at he loved so, at sech a time? If I know William—and I *think* I do—he—well, I'll jest ask him." He turns around and begins to make a lot of signs to the duke with his hands; and the duke he looks at him stupid and leather-headed[26] a while, then all of a sudden he seems to catch his meaning, and jumps for the king, goo-gooing with all his might for joy, and hugs him about fifteen times before he lets up. Then the king says, "I knowed it; I reckon *that*'ll convince anybody the way *he* feels about it. Here, Mary Jane, Susan, Joanner, take the money—take it *all.* It's the gift of him that lays yonder, cold but joyful."

attended their funerals." The preacher has come along to arrange the inevitable funeral and send him to heaven. Since their cures were often painful and of dubious scientific value, doctors were often as much the cause of death as diseases were. "The dull and ignorant physician day and night, and all the days and all the nights, drenched his patient with vast and hideous doses of the most repulsive drugs to be found in the store's stock," Twain wrote, detailing some old treatments in "Bible Teaching and Religious Practice" of 1890; "he bled him, cupped him, purged him, puked him, salivated him, never gave his system a chance to rally, nor nature a chance to help" (*Europe and Elsewhere*, 1923, p. 387).

15. *away up to Louisville*. Louisville, Kentucky, on the Ohio River, about seven hundred miles away.

16. *a passel of sapheads*. Or "parcel of sapheads," a pack of fools.

17. *he made all sorts of signs with his hands and said "Goo-goo—goo-goo-goo," all the time*. Brace Dunlap employs the same ruse when he disguises himself as a deaf-mute in Chapter 8 of "Tom Sawyer, Detective": "He smiled, and nodded his head several times, and made signs with his hands and says: 'Goo-goo,—goo-goo,' the way deef and dummies does."

18. *the letter her father left behind*. Blair and Fischer in the 1988 University of California edition (p. 531) pointed out that Huck has forgotten that according to "the country jake" in Chapter 24, Uncle Peter was the one who left this letter.

19. *the six thousand cash*. Evidently Twain thought this was a staggering sum of money at this time in this part of the country: Remember that Huck and Tom each have exactly the same amount back in St. Petersburg under Judge Thatcher's care. Twain originally said that the tanyard, houses, and land were worth "thirteen thousand" (**MS**), and Peter Wilks left "four thousand and thirty dollars in gold" (**MS**) to the brothers; Twain then realized that that was probably too much for the backwoodsman and reduced the value in the manuscript.

20. *yaller-boys*. Or "yellow-jackets," gold coins of any denomination in United States currency.

Mary Jane she went for him, Susan and the hare-lip went for the duke, and then such another hugging and kissing I never see yet. And everybody crowded up with the tears in their eyes, and most shook the hands off of them frauds, saying all the time:

"You *dear* good souls!—how *lovely!*—how *could* you!"

Well, then, pretty soon all hands got to talking about the diseased again, and how good he was, and what a loss he was, and all that; and before long a big iron-jawed man

GOING FOR HIM.

worked himself in there from outside, and stood a listening and looking, and not saying anything; and nobody saying anything to him either, because the king was talking and they was all busy listening. The king was saying—in the middle of something he'd started in on—

"—they bein' partickler friends o' the diseased. That's why they're invited here this evenin'; but to-morrow we want *all* to come—everybody; for he respected everybody, he liked everybody, and so it's fitten that his funeral orgies[27] sh'd be public."[28]

21. *representatives of furrin heirs that's got left, is the line for you and me.* The seemingly harmless ruse that they tried to pull on Huck and Jim, that they were the rightful long-lost heirs to European royal titles, has now turned a substantial profit.

22. *Thish-yer comes of trust'n to Providence.* The same cynical blasphemy is shared by Simon Suggs in Hooper's *Adventures of Captain Simon Suggs* (1845) after he too has pulled off a particularly profitable swindle: "Well! thar *is* a Providence that purvides; and ef a man will *only* stand squar' up to what's right, it *will* prosper his endeavors to make somethin' to feed his children on! Yes, thar *is* a Providence! . . . Ef a man says thar ain't no Providence, you may be sure thar's something wrong *here*," striking in the region of his vest pocket—"and *that* man will swindle you, ef he can—*certain!*" (p. 81).

Twain boosted the cynicism of this attitude by making the speaker a phony preacher. He knew well how all sorts of people, king, clergyman, and commoner alike, have twisted religious teachings to justify their own selfish ends. "The Christian's Bible is a drug-store," Twain observes in "Bible Teaching and Religious Practice" (*Europe and Elsewhere*, 1923). "Its contents remain the same; but the medical practice changes" (p. 287).

23. *the boss dodge.* The best trick.

24. *twenty elegant little piles.* They were originally only "thirteen or fourteen little piles" (**MS**) in the manuscript.

25. *the vale of sorrers.* "The Vale of Sorrows," a religious cliché for life on earth, which is said to be all transient and sorrowful.

26. *leather-headed.* Thick-headed, doltish.

27. *it's fitten that his funeral orgies.* "Orgies" is a fitting malapropism (and Freudian slip) for this lecherous old scoundrel. In the backwoods, one often attended funerals even if one did not know the deceased well. "Orgy" is actually from the Greek for "secret rites," referring particularly to the nocturnal festival in honor of Bacchus, the god of wine; in Latin it means "secret frantic reveling." The joke comes from "Death of a Princess" (Sacramento [Calif.], *Weekly Union*, July 21, 1866), in which Twain referred to "the funeral orgies of the dead King" of the

Hawaiian Islands. "The term is coarse," he admitted, "but perhaps it is a better one than a milder one would be."

Tom Sawyer has no clue what the word means in Chapter 33 of *Tom Sawyer* after he and Huck find Injun Joe's gold:

> "Now less fetch the guns and things," said Huck.
>
> "No, Huck—leave them there. They're just the tricks to have when we go to robbing. We'll keep them there all the time, and we'll hold our orgies there, too. It's an awful snug place for orgies."
>
> "What's orgies?"
>
> "*I* donno. But robbers always have orgies, and of course we've got to have them, too. . . . "

Wecter in *Sam Clemens of Hannibal* (1952) described a possible source for the king's fumbling exercise in etymology: The leading divines of Hannibal once participated in a debate of religious topics; but the program soon digressed into the tiresome discussion of a Greek derivative and whether "the active transitive *bap* is always *dip*" (p. 195). Blair suggested in *Mark Twain and Huck Finn* (1960) that a model for the double-talking king may have been Ephraim Jenkinson, "the greatest rascal under the canopy of heaven," in Chapter 14 of Oliver Goldsmith's *The Vicar of Wakefield* (1766): "Ay, Sir, the world is in its dotage, and yet the cosmogony or creation of the world has puzzled the philosophers of all ages. . . . Sancioniathon, Manetho, Borosus, and Ocellus Lucanus, have all attempted it in vain. The latter has these words, *Anarchon ara kai atelutaion to pan*, which imply that all things have neither beginning nor end. Manetho also, who lived about the time of old Nebuchadon-Asser, Asser being a Syriac word usually applied as a surname to the kings of that country, as Teglet Phael-Asser, Nabon-Asser, he, I say, formed a conjecture equally absurd; for we as we usually say, *ek to biblion kubernetes*, which implies that books will never teach the world; so he attempted to investigate—But, Sir, I ask pardon, I am straying from the question." Although he called *The Vicar of Wakefield* in Chapter 62 of *Following the Equator* (1897) "one long waste-pipe discharge of goody-goody puerilities and dreary moralities," Twain still must have been amused by the notion that "Asser" is usually applied to kings.

And so he went a-mooning on and on, liking to hear himself talk, and every little while he fetched in his funeral orgies again, till the duke he couldn't stand it no more; so he writes on a little scrap of paper, "*obsequies,* you old fool," and folds it up and goes to goo-gooing and reaching it over people's heads to him. The king he reads it, and puts it in his pocket, and says:

"Poor William, afflicted as he is, his *heart's* aluz right. Asks me to invite everybody to come to the funeral—wants me to make 'em all welcome. But he needn't a worried—it was jest what I was at."

Then he weaves along again, perfectly ca'm, and goes to dropping in his funeral orgies again every now and then, just like he done before. And when he done it the third time, he says:

"I say orgies, not because it's the common term, because it ain't—obsequies bein' the common term—but because orgies is the right term. Obsequies ain't used in England no more, now—it's gone out. We say orgies now, in England. Orgies is better, because it means the thing you're after, more exact. It's a word that's made up out'n the Greek *orgo,* outside, open, abroad; and the Hebrew *jeesum,* to plant, cover up; hence in*ter.* So, you see, funeral orgies is an open er public funeral."

THE DOCTOR.

He was the *worst* I ever struck. Well, the iron-jawed man he laughed right in his face. Everybody was shocked. Everybody says, "Why *doctor!*" and Abner Shackleford says:

"Why, Robinson, hain't you heard the news? This is Harvey Wilks."

The king he smiled eager, and shoved out his flapper,[29] and says:

"*Is* it my poor brother's dear good friend and physician? I—"

"Keep your hands off of me!" says the doctor. "*You* talk like an Englishman—*don't* you? It's the worse imitation I ever heard. *You* Peter Wilks's brother. You're a fraud, that's what you are!"

Well, how they all took on! They crowded around the doctor, and tried to quiet him down, and tried to explain to him, and tell him how Harvey'd showed in forty ways that he *was* Harvey, and knowed everybody by name, and the names of the very dogs, and begged and *begged* him not to hurt Harvey's feelings and the poor girls' feelings, and all that; but it warn't no use, he stormed right along, and said any man that pretended to be an Englishman and couldn't imitate the lingo no better than what he did, was a fraud and a liar. The poor girls was hanging to the king and crying; and all of a sudden the doctor ups and turns on *them*. He says:

"I was your father's friend, and I'm your friend; and I warn you *as* a friend, and an honest one, that wants to protect you and keep you out of harm and trouble, to turn your backs on that scoundrel, and have nothing to do with him, the ignorant tramp, with his idiotic Greek and Hebrew[30] as he calls it. He is the thinnest kind of an impostor[31]—has come here with a lot of empty names and facts which he has picked up somewheres, and you take them for *proofs*, and are helped to fool yourselves by these foolish friends here, who ought to know better. Mary Jane Wilks, you know me for your friend, and for your unselfish friend, too. Now listen to me; turn this pitiful rascal out—I *beg* you to do it. Will you?"

Mary Jane straightened herself up, and my, but she was handsome! She says:

"*Here* is my answer." She hove up the bag of money and put it in the king's hands, and says, "Take this six thousand dollars, and invest for me and my sisters any way you want to, and don't give us no receipt for it."

28. *sh'd be public*. It was customary, when someone died, to send a boy on horseback to spread the sad news from house to house; or an announcement might be published in the newspapers, describing the particulars of the service and whether the public was invited. Eager to take advantage of any opportunity for socializing, every man or woman in a community readily put aside the day's work, no matter how important, to pay last respects to the deceased.

29. *his flapper*. His hand.

30. *the ignorant tramp, with his idiotic Greek and Hebrew*. In the manuscript, Dr. Robinson was even more contemptuous of "the ignorant hog, with his putrid and idiotic Greek and Hebrew" (**MS**). The phony use of "orgies" has tipped off the doctor that the king and duke are frauds; nineteenth-century physicians were generally schooled in classical languages. The Rev. Hobson and Levi Bell, a clergyman and a lawyer, might also have spotted the swindle, for they too must have known Greek and Hebrew; but they both are conveniently called away on other business.

31. *He is the thinnest kind of an impostor*. Twain originally wrote the following:

> "He is the thinnest of thin impostors—has come here with a lot of empty names and facts which he picked up somewhere; and you weakly taken them for *proofs*, and are assisted in deceiving yourselves by these thoughtless unreasoning friends here, who ought to know better. Mary Jane Wilks, you know me for your friend, and your honest and unselfish friend. Now listen to me: cast this paltry villain out—I beg you, I beseech you to do it. Will you?"

But he wisely revised it. "As any reader of Victorian novels knows," Ferguson observed in "Huck Finn Aborning," "this was a natural idiom in the 1870s. But even if Dr. Robinson had really talked that way, it was not the natural idiom for Huck to report him in" (p. 175). "Cast this paltry villain out—I beg you, I beseech you to do it" sounds like Victorian melodrama. Dr. Robinson sounds more like Colonel Sherburn—or Mark Twain—than he does a typical Mississippi backwoodsman of the period. But his grammar becomes increasingly careless by the time he reappears in Chapter 29.

Then she put her arm around the king on one side, and Susan and the harelip done the same on the other. Everybody clapped their hands and stomped on the floor like a perfect storm, whilst the king held up his head and smiled proud. The doctor says:

"All right, I wash *my* hands of the matter. But I warn you all that a time's coming when you're going to feel sick whenever you think of this day"—and away he went.

"All right, doctor," says the king, kinder mocking him, "we'll try and get 'em to send for you"[32]—which made them all laugh, and they said it was a prime good hit.

THE BAG OF MONEY.

32. *"All right, doctor," says the king, kinder mocking him, "we'll try and get 'em to send for you."* The king's sarcasm increases when one considers the fate of the sick man whom the doctor and preacher were visiting: Obviously the patient died, for only Hobson stayed behind to officiate at the funeral.

Chapter XXVI

THE CUBBY.

WELL WHEN they was all gone, the king he asks Mary Jane how they was off for spare rooms, and she said she had one spare room,[1] which would do for Uncle William, and she'd give her own room to Uncle Harvey, which was a little bigger, and she would turn into the room with her sisters and sleep on a cot; and up garret was a little cubby, with a pallet in it. The king said the cubby would do for his valley—meaning me.

So Mary Jane took us up, and she showed them their rooms, which was plain but nice. She said she'd have her frocks and a lot of other traps took out of her room if they was in Uncle Harvey's way, but he said they warn't. The frocks was hung along the wall, and before them was a curtain made out of calico that hung down to the floor. There was an old hair trunk in one corner, and a guitar box in another, and all sorts of little knick-knacks and jimcracks[2] around, like girls brisken up[3] a room with. The king said it was all the more homely and more pleasanter for these fixings, and so don't disturb them. The duke's room was pretty small, but plenty good enough, and so was my cubby.

That night they had a big supper, and all them men and women was there, and I stood behind the king and the duke's chairs and waited on them, and the niggers waited

1. *she said she had one spare room.* Mary Jane originally arranged different accommodations for her guests:

> Well, when they was all gone the king asked Mary Jane how they was off for spare rooms, and she said they had two; so he said they *could* put *his* valley in the same bed with *him*—meaning me. He said in England it warn't unusual for a valley to sleep with his master, but in Rome he was always done the way the Romans done, and besides he warn't proud, and reckoned he could stand Adolphus very well. Maybe he could; but I couldn't a stood him, only I was long used to sleeping with the other kind of hogs. (Ferguson, "Huck Finn Aborning," p. 176)

Twain scrapped this delicious bit of sarcasm when he determined the final course of this chapter; the boy had to be given his own room to provide Huck some flexibility of movement. Unfortunately, in revising the passage, Twain dropped the explanation of what a "valley" (valet) is, as well as the boy's alias "Adolphus," which the King gave him when they met the country jake in Chapter 24.

2. *jimcracks.* "Gimcracks," cheap, showy, useless items.

3. *brisken up.* Smarten up, trim.

on the rest. Mary Jane she set at the head of the table, with Susan along side of her, and said how bad the biscuits was, and how mean the preserves was, and how ornery and tough the fried chickens was—and all that kind of rot, the way women always do for to force out compliments; and the people all knowed everything was tip-top, and said so—said "How *do* you get biscuits to brown so nice?" and "Where, for the land's sake *did* you get these amaz'n pickles?" and all that kind of hum-bug talky-talk, just the way people always does at a supper, you know.

And when it was all done, me and the hare-lip[4] had supper in the kitchen off of the leavings, whilst the others was helping the niggers clean up the things. The hare-lip she got to pumping me about England, and blest if I didn't think the ice was getting mighty thin, sometimes. She says:

SUPPER WITH THE HARE-LIP.

"Did you ever see the king?"

"Who? William Fourth? Well, I bet I have—he goes to our church." I knowed he was dead years ago,[5] but I never let on. So when I says he goes to our church, she says:

"What—regular?"

"Yes—regular. His pew's right over opposite ourn—on 'tother side the pulpit."

4. *me and the hare-lip.* Although the young man reported in Chapter 24 that Joanna was about fourteen, the same age as Huck, Kemble portrays her as a few years older than the boy.

5. *William Fourth? . . . I knowed he was dead years ago.* If the time of *Huckleberry Finn* was exactly fifty years ago as the subtitle suggests, then William IV (1765–1837) might actually have been living when the story took place. Queen Victoria succeeded him as monarch of Great Britain. Twain may have introduced this king here to continue his burlesque of royalty: William IV was a scoundrel and was said to have fathered eleven illegitimate children.

William IV of England.
Courtesy Picture Collection, New York Public Library, Astor, Lenox, and Tilden Foundations.

"I thought he lived in London?"

"Well, he does. Where *would* he live?"

"But I thought *you* lived in Sheffield?"[6]

I see I was up a stump. I had to let on to get choked with a chicken bone, so as to get time to think how to get down again. Then I says:

"I mean he goes to our church regular when he's in Sheffield. That's only in the summer-time, when he comes there to take the sea baths."[7]

"Why, how you talk—Sheffield ain't on the sea."

"Well, who said it was?"

"Why, you did."

"I *didn't,* nuther."

"You did!"

"I didn't."

"You did."

"I never said nothing of the kind."

"Well, what *did* you say, then?"

"Said he come to take the sea *baths*—that's what I said."

"Well, then! how's he going to take the sea baths if it ain't on the sea?"

"Looky here," I says; "did you ever see any Congress water?"[8]

"Yes."

"Well, did you have to go to Congress to get it?"

"Why, no."

"Well, neither does William Fourth have to go to the sea to get a sea bath."

"How does he get it, then?"

"Gets it the way people down here gets Congress-water—in barrels. There in the palace at Sheffield they've got furnaces, and he wants his water hot. They can't bile that amount of water away off there at the sea. They haven't got no conveniences for it."

"Oh, I see, now. You might a said that in the first place and saved time."

When she said that, I see I was out of the woods again, and so I was comfortable and glad. Next, she says:

"Do you go to church, too?"

6. *Sheffield.* Joanna knows her geography: Sheffield, famous for its steel and silver-plated cutlery, is located in South Yorkshire, about 158 miles north of London.

7. *he comes there to take the sea baths.* Huck is likely thinking of Bath, England, where wealthy men and women came to take advantage of its mineral springs as a health cure.

8. *Congress water.* Mineral water from the Congress Spring near Saratoga, New York, famous for its medicinal powers; as to Bath, people came to Saratoga to convalesce. But Twain was unaware that Congress Spring was not discovered until 1862.

Congress Spring, Saratoga Springs, New York. Illustration from *Every Saturday*, September 9, 1871. *Courtesy Library of Congress.*

"Yes—regular."

"Where do you set?"

"Why, in our pew."

"*Whose* pew?"

"Why, *ourn*—your Uncle Harvey's."

"His'n? What does *he* want with a pew?"

"Wants it to set in. What did you *reckon* he wanted with it?"

"Why, I thought he'd be in the pulpit."

Rot him, I forgot he was a preacher. I see I was up a stump again, so I played another chicken bone and got another think. Then I says:

"Blame it, do you suppose there ain't but one preacher to a church?"

"Why, what do they want with more?"

"What!—to preach before a king? I never see such a girl as you. They don't have no less than seventeen."

"Seventeen! My land! Why, I wouldn't set out such a string as that, not if I *never* got to glory. It must take 'em a week."

"Shucks, they don't *all* of 'em preach the same day—only *one* of 'em."

"Well, then, what does the rest of 'em do?"

"Oh, nothing much. Loll around, pass the plate—and one thing or another. But mainly they don't do nothing."

"Well, then, what are they *for?*"

"Why, they're for *style.* Don't you know nothing?"

"Well, I don't *want* to know no such foolishness as that. How is servants treated in England? Do they treat 'em better 'n we treat our niggers?"

"*No!* A servant ain't nobody there. They treat them worse than dogs."

"Don't they give 'em holidays, the way we do, Christmas and New Year's week, and Fourth of July?"[9]

"Oh, just listen! A body could tell *you* hain't ever been to England, by that. Why, Hare-l—why, Joanna, they never see a holiday from year's end to year's end; never go to the circus, nor theatre, nor nigger shows,[10] nor nowheres."

"Nor church?"

9. *Don't they give 'em holidays . . . Christmas and New Year's week, and Fourth of July?* At this time, Christmas and New Year's Day were not yet British bank holidays; recall that Bob Cratchit in *A Christmas Carol* (1843) has to ask Scrooge for Christmas off. Any holiday was left to the employer's discretion. Of course, the English did not celebrate July Fourth, America's Independence Day. It is with bitter irony that Twain notes that some slaves had that day off, too. "The days between Christmas and New Year's day are allowed as holidays," Frederick Douglass explained in Chapter 10 of his *Narrative*; "and, accordingly, we were not required to perform any labor, more than to feed and take care of stock. This time we regarded as our own, by the grace of our masters; and we therefore used or abused it nearly as we pleased. . . . These holidays serve as conductors, or safety-valves, to carry off the rebellious spirit of enslaved humanity. But for these, the slave would be forced up to the wildest desperation; and woe betide the slaveholder, the day he ventures to remove or hinder the operation of those conductors! . . . The holidays. . . . are professedly a custom established by the benevolence of the slaveholders; but I undertake to say, it is the result of selfishness, and one of the grossest frauds committed upon the down-trodden slave. They do not give the slaves this time because they would not like to have their work during its continuance, but because they know it would be unsafe to deprive them of it."

10. *nigger shows.* Minstrel shows. Nothing else delighted the boy Sam Clemens more than "the real nigger-show, the genuine nigger-show, the extravagant nigger-show,—the show which to me had no peer and whose peer has not yet arrived, in my experience" ("Chapters from My Autobiography," *North American Review*, June 7, 1907, p. 247). It would seem from his affectionate recollections of the minstrel show that Twain may have thought that African-Americans actually dominated these entertainments, rather than white singers and dancers in blackface: "The minstrels appeared with coal-black hands and faces and their clothing was a loud and extravagant burlesque of the clothing worn by the plantation slave of the time. . . . The minstrel used a very broad Negro dialect; he used it competently and with easy facility and it was funny—delightfully and satisfyingly funny. . . . 'Bones' and 'Banjo' were the prime jokers and whatever funniness was to be gotten out of

"Nor church."

"But *you* always went to church."

Well, I was gone up again. I forgot I was the old man's servant. But next minute I whirled in on a kind of an explanation how a valley was different from a common servant, and *had* to go to church whether he wanted to or not, and set with the family, on account of its being the law. But I didn't do it pretty good, and when I got done I see she warn't satisfied. She says:

"Honest injun, now, hain't you been telling me a lot of lies?"

"Honest injun," says I.

"None of it at all?"

"None of it at all. Not a lie in it," says I.

"Lay your hand on this book and say it."

I see it warn't nothing but a dictionary,[11] so I laid my hand on it and said it. So then she looked a little better satisfied, and says:

"Well, then, I'll believe some of it; but I hope to gracious if I'll believe the rest."

"HONEST INJUN."

A "nigger show." Illustration by True W. Williams, *The Adventures of Tom Sawyer*, 1876.
Private collection.

paint and exaggerated clothing they utilized to the limit. . . . The minstrel troupes had good voices and both their solos and their choruses were a delight to me. . . . The minstrel show was born in the early forties and it had a prosperous career for about thirty-five years; then it degenerated into a variety show and was nearly all variety show with a Negro act or two thrown in incidentally" (*Mark Twain in Eruption*, 1940, pp. 111–15). Anthony J. Berret suggested in "Huckleberry Finn and the Minstrel Show" (*American Studies*, Fall 1986, p. 38) that the structure of *Huckleberry Finn* follows the three sections of the traditional minstrel show: The opening chapters correspond to the comic dialogues and sentimental songs; the antics of the king and the duke represent the "olio" of novelty acts; and the "evasion" is just another one of the extravagant burlesques which closed a performance. But there was nothing equivalent in this tradition to the Grangerford–Shepherdson feud, the shooting of Boggs by Sherburn, or the murder of pap Finn in a brothel.

"Writing at a time when the blackfaced minstrel was still popular, and shortly after a war which left even the abolitionists weary of those problems associated with the Negro," Ralph Ellison argued in "Change the Joke and Slip the Yoke" (*Partisan Review*, Spring 1968), "Twain fitted Jim into the outlines of the minstrel tradition, and it is from behind this stereotype mask that we see Jim's dignity and human capacity—and Twain's complexity—emerge. Yet it is his source in this same tradition which creates that ambivalence between his identification as an adult and parent and his 'boyish'

"What is it you won't believe, Joe?" says Mary Jane, stepping in with Susan behind her. "It ain't right nor kind for you to talk so to him,[12] and him a stranger and so far from his people. How would you like to be treated so?"

"That's always your way, Maim—always sailing in to help somebody before they're hurt. I hain't done nothing to him. He's told some stretchers, I reckon; and I said I wouldn't swallow it all; and that's every bit and grain I *did* say. I reckon he can stand a little thing like that, can't he?"

"I don't care whether 'twas little or whether 'twas big, he's here in our house and a stranger, and it wasn't good of you to say it. If you was in his place, it would make you feel ashamed; and so you oughtn't to say a thing to another person that will make *them* feel ashamed."

"Why, Maim, he said—"

"It don't make no difference what he *said*—that ain't the thing. The thing is for you to treat him *kind*, and not be saying things to make him remember he ain't in his own country and amongst his own folks."

I says to myself, *this* is a girl that I'm letting that old reptle rob her of her money!

Then Susan *she* waltzed in; and if you'll believe me, she did give Hare-lip hark from the tomb![13]

Says I to myself, And this is *another* one that I'm letting him rob her of her money!

Then Mary Jane she took another inning, and went in sweet and lovely again—which was her way—but when she got done there warn't hardly anything left o' poor Hare-lip. So she hollered.

"All right, then," says the other girls, "you just ask his pardon."

She done it, too. And she done it beautiful. She done it so beautiful it was good to hear; and I wished I could tell her a thousand lies, so she could do it again.

I says to myself, this is *another* one that I'm letting him rob her of her money. And when she got through, they all jest laid theirselves out to make me feel at home and know I was amongst friends. I felt so ornery and low down and

naiveté, and which by contrast makes Huck, with his street-sparrow sophistication, seem more adult" (pp. 215–16). Other critics have accused Twain of just perpetuating minstrel-show stereotypes in *Huckleberry Finn*, but the form had so deteriorated by Reconstruction that it is now nearly impossible to know exactly what young Sam Clemens saw and so admired back in Hannibal. "Since minstrelsy was a national symbolic ritual of debasement of blacks for petty profit and for the psychological distancing of whites from their personal responsibility in the tragic perversion of American principles," argued Benard W. Bell in "Twain's 'Nigger' Jim: The Tragic Face Behind the Minstrel Mask" (*Mark Twain Journal*, Spring 1985), "Twain's taste in humor reveals his socialization as an American, not merely as a Southwesterner, in the ethics of white supremacy" (p. 12). But there is no indication that Twain was aware of any of that; he did feel that it was his personal responsibility to help compensate for what his race had done to another one, but he still saw no contradiction in loving the old minstrel show.

11. *I see it warn't nothing but a dictionary.* One usually swears on a Bible. Blair suggested in *Mark Twain and Huck Finn* that this pointless oath was likely inspired by another Twain observed on his first trip to England: The American consulate required that if one wanted to ship anything to the United States, the individual "must go there and swear to a great long rigmarole and *kiss the book* (years ago they found it was a dictionary)" (p. 415).

12. *It ain't right nor kind for you to talk so to him.* And, remember, Joanna is the sister who has devoted her life to good works!

13. *give . . . hark from the tomb.* A severe scolding, a shock; said to be from the popular hymn "A Funeral Thought," No. 614, by Isaac Watt:

Hark! from the tombs a doleful sound
My ears attend the cry:
"Ye living men, come view the ground
Where you must shortly lie!

"Princes, this clay must be your bed,
In spite of all your tow'rs;
The tall, the wise, the rev'red head,
Must lie as low as ours."

mean, that I says to myself, My mind's made up; I'll hive that money for them or bust.

So then I lit out—for bed, I said, meaning some time or another. When I got by myself, I went to thinking the thing over. I says to myself, shall I go to that doctor, private, and blow on these frauds? No—that won't do. He might tell who told him; then the king and the duke would make it warm for me. Shall I go, private, and tell Mary Jane? No—I dasn't do it. Her face would give them a hint, sure; they've got the money, and they'd slide right out and get away with it. If she was to fetch in help, I'd get mixed up in the business, before it was done with, I judge. No, there ain't no good way but one. I got to steal that money, somehow; and I got to steal it some way that they won't suspicion that I done it. They've got a good thing, here; and they ain't agoing to leave till they've played this family and this town for all they're worth, so I'll find a chance time enough. I'll steal it, and hide it; and by-and-by, when I'm away down the river, I'll write a letter and tell Mary Jane where it's hid. But I better hive it to-night, if I can, because the doctor maybe hasn't let up as much as he lets on he has; he might scare them out of here, yet.

So, thinks I, I'll go and search them rooms. Up stairs the hall was dark, but I found the duke's room, and started to paw around it with my hands; but I recollected it wouldn't be much like the king to let anybody else take care of that money but his own self; so then I went to his room and begun to paw around there. But I see I couldn't do nothing without a candle, and I dasn't light one, of course. So I judged I'd got to do the other thing—lay for them, and eavesdrop. About that time, I hears their footsteps coming, and was going to skip under the bed; I reached for it, but it wasn't where I thought it would be; but I touched the curtain that hid Mary Jane's frocks, so I jumped in behind that and snuggled in amongst the gowns, and stood there perfectly still.

They come in and shut the door; and the first thing the duke done was to get down and look under the bed. Then I

THE DUKE LOOKS UNDER THE BED.

was glad I hadn't found the bed when I wanted it. And yet, you know, it's kind of natural to hide under the bed when you are up to anything private. They sets down, then, and the king says:

"Well, what is it? and cut it middlin' short, because it's better for us to be down there a whoopin'-up the mournin', than up here givin' 'em a chance to talk us over."

"Well, this is it, Capet. I ain't easy; I ain't comfortable. That doctor lays on my mind. I wanted to know your plans. I've got a notion, and I think it's a sound one."

"What is it, duke?"

"That we better glide out of this, before three in the morning, and clip it down the river with what we've got. Specially, seeing we got it so easy—*given* back to us, flung at our heads, as you may say, when of course we allowed to have to steal it back. I'm for knocking off and lighting out."

That made me feel pretty bad. About an hour or two ago, it would a been a little different, but now it made me feel bad and disappointed. The king rips out and says:

"What! And not sell out the rest o' the property? March off like a passel o' fools and leave eight or nine thous'n' dollars' worth o' property layin' around jest sufferin' to be scooped in?—and all good salable stuff, too."

The duke he grumbled; said the bag of gold was enough,

and he didn't want to go no deeper—didn't want to rob a lot of orphans of *everything* they had.

"Why, how you talk!" says the king. "We shan't rob 'em of nothing at all but jest this money. The people that *buys* the property is the suff'rers; because as soon's it's found out 'at we didn't own it—which won't be long after we've slid—the sale won't be valid, and it'll all go back to the estate. These-yer orphans 'll git their house back agin, and that's enough for *them;* they're young and spry, and k'n easy earn a livin'. *They* ain't agoing to suffer. Why, jest think—there's thous'n's and thous'n's that ain't nigh so well off. Bless you, *they* ain't got noth'n to complain of."

Well, the king he talked him blind; so at last he give in, and said all right, but said he believed it was blame foolishness to stay, and that doctor hanging over them. But the king says:

"Cuss the doctor! What do we k'yer for *him?* Hain't we got all the fools in town on our side? and ain't that a big enough majority in any town?"

So they got ready to go down stairs again. The duke says:

"I don't think we put that money in a good place."

That cheered me up. I'd begun to think I warn't going to get a hint of no kind to help me. The king says:

"Why?"

"Because Mary Jane 'll be in mourning from this out; and first you know the nigger that does up the rooms will get an order to box these duds up and put 'em away;[14] and do you reckon a nigger can run across money and not borrow some of it?"[15]

"Your head's level, agin, duke," says the king; and he come a fumbling under the curtain two or three foot from where I was. I stuck tight to the wall, and kept mighty still, though quivery; and I wondered what them fellows would say to me if they catched me; and I tried to think what I'd better do if they did catch me. But the king he got the bag before I could think more than about a half a thought, and he never suspicioned I was around. They took and shoved the bag through a rip in the straw tick that was under the feather bed, and crammed it in a foot or two amongst the

14. *Mary Jane'll be in mourning from this out; and first you know the nigger that does up the rooms will get an order to box these duds up and put 'em away.* When she goes into "full mourning" for the funeral, Mary Jane must dress only in black for at least one year, so she will have no use for any of the other clothes up in the king's room.

15. *do you reckon a nigger can run across money and not borrow some of it?* It was once commonly assumed that all slaves were thieves, but Twain defended their actions in Chapter 2 of *Pudd'nhead Wilson*:

> They had an unfair show in the battle of life, and they held it no sin to take military advantage of the enemy—in a small way. . . . They would smouch provisions from the pantry whenever they got a chance; or a brass thimble, or a cake of wax, or an emery-bag, or a paper of needles, or a silver spoon, or a dollar bill, or small articles of clothing, or any other property of light value; and so far were they from considering such reprisals sinful, that they would go to church and shout and pray their loudest and sincerest with their plunder in their pockets. A farm smoke-house had to be kept heavily padlocked, for even the colored deacon himself could not resist a ham when Providence showed him in a dream, or otherwise, where such a thing hung. . . . perfectly sure that in taking this trifle from the man who daily robbed him of an inestimable treasure—his liberty—he was not committing any sin that God would remember against him in the Last Great Day.

straw and said it was all right, now, because a nigger only makes up the feather bed, and don't turn over the straw tick only about twice a year, and so it warn't in no danger of getting stole, now.

But I knowed better. I had it out of there before they was half-way down stairs. I groped along up to my cubby, and hid it there till I could get a chance to do better. I judged I better hide it outside of the house somewheres, because if they missed it they would give the house a good ransacking. I knowed that very well. Then I turned in, with my clothes all on; but I couldn't a gone to sleep, if I'd a wanted to, I was in such a sweat to get through with the business. By-and-by I heard the king and the duke come up; so I rolled off of my pallet and laid with my chin at the top of my ladder and waited to see if anything was going to happen. But nothing did.

So I held on till all the late sounds had quit and the early ones hadn't begun, yet; and then I slipped down the ladder.

HUCK TAKES THE MONEY.

Chapter XXVII

A CRACK IN THE DINING ROOM DOOR.

I crept to their doors and listened; they was snoring, so I tip-toed along, and got down stairs all right. There warn't a sound anywheres. I peeped through a crack of the dining-room door, and see the men that was watching the corpse all sound asleep on their chairs. The door was open into the parlor, where the corpse was laying, and there was a candle in both rooms. I passed along, and the parlor door was open; but I see there warn't nobody in there but the remainders of Peter; so I shoved on by; but the front door was locked, and the key wasn't there. Just then I heard somebody coming down the stairs, back behind me. I run in the parlor, and took a swift look around, and the only place I see to hide the bag was in the coffin. The lid was shoved along about a foot, showing the dead man's face down in there, with a wet cloth over it, and his shroud on. I tucked the money-bag in under the lid, just down beyond where his hands was crossed, which made me creep, they was so cold, and then I run back across the room and in behind the door.

The person coming was Mary Jane. She went to the coffin, very soft, and kneeled down and looked in; then she put up her handkerchief and I see she begun to cry, though I couldn't hear her, and her back was to me. I slid out, and as

1. *smouch*. Pilfer, one of Twain's favorite words.

I passed the dining-room I thought I'd make sure them watchers hadn't seen me; so I looked through the crack and everything was all right. They hadn't stirred.

I slipped up to bed, feeling ruther blue, on accounts of the thing playing out that way after I had took so much trouble and run so much resk about it. Says I, if it could stay where it is, all right; because when we get down the river a hundred mile or two, I could write back to Mary Jane, and she could dig him up again and get it; but that ain't the thing that's going to happen; the thing that's going to happen is, the money 'll be found when they come to screw on the lid. Then the king 'll get it again, and it 'll be a long day before he gives anybody another chance to smouch[1] it from him. Of course I *wanted* to slide down and get it out of there, but I dasn't try it. Every minute it was getting earlier, now, and pretty soon some of them watchers would begin to stir, and I might get catched—catched with six thousand dollars in my hands that nobody hadn't hired me to take care of. I don't wish to be mixed up in no such business as that, I says to myself.

When I got down stairs in the morning, the parlor was shut up, and the watchers was gone. There warn't nobody around but the family and the widow Bartley and our tribe. I watched their faces to see if anything had been happening, but I couldn't tell.

THE UNDERTAKER.

Towards the middle of the day the undertaker come, with his man, and they set the coffin in the middle of the room on a couple of chairs, and then set all our chairs in rows, and borrowed more from the neighbors till the hall and the parlor and the dining-room was full. I see the coffin lid was the way it was before, but I dasn't go to look in under it, with folks around.

Then the people begun to flock in, and the beats[2] and the girls took seats in the front row at the head of the coffin, and for a half an hour the people filed around slow, in single rank, and looked down at the dead man's face a minute, and some dropped in a tear, and it was all very still and solemn, only the girls and the beats holding handkerchiefs to their eyes and keeping their heads bent, and sobbing a little. There warn't no other sound but the scraping of the feet on the floor, and blowing noses—because people always blows them more at a funeral than they do at other places except church.

When the place was packed full, the undertaker he slid around in his black gloves with his softy soothering[3] ways, putting on the last touches, and getting people and things all ship-shape and comfortable, and making no more sound than a cat. He never spoke; he moved people around, he squeezed in late ones, he opened up passage-ways, and done it all with nods, and signs with his hands. Then he took his place over against the wall. He was the softest, glidingest, stealthiest man[4] I ever see; and there warn't no more smile to him than there is to a ham.

They had borrowed a melodeum[5]—a sick one; and when everything was ready, a young woman set down and worked it, and it was pretty skreeky[6] and colicky, and everybody joined in and sung, and Peter was the only one that had a good thing, according to my notion. Then the Reverend Hobson opened up, slow and solemn, and begun to talk; and straight off the most outrageous row busted out in the cellar a body ever heard; it was only one dog,[7] but he made a most powerful racket, and he kept it up, right along; the parson he had to stand there, over the coffin, and wait—you couldn't hear yourself think. It was right down awkward, and nobody didn't seem to know what to do. But pretty soon they see that long-legged undertaker make a sign to the preacher as much as to say, "Don't you worry—just depend on me." Then he stooped down and begun to glide along the wall, just his shoulders showing over the people's

2. *beats*. Deadbeats, cheats.

3. *soothering*. Flattering, coaxing, affectionate, a colloquial word from Ireland and Cumberland.

4. *the softest, glidingest, stealthiest man*. Howard G. Baetzhold suggested in *Mark Twain and John Bull* (1970) that Twain may be recalling Oliver Le Dain, the fawning barber and chief counsellor of Louis IX in Sir Walter Scott's *Quentin Durward* (1822), a Waverly novel which Twain actually liked and consulted while planning *The Prince and the Pauper*. In Chapter 8, Scott described this "little, pale, meagre man" who, "with the stealthy and quiet pace of a cat, . . . seemed modestly rather to glide than to walk through the apartment" (p. 95).

5. *melodeum*. Or "melodeon," an early form of the "American Organ," a small reed instrument with a keyboard and bellows, worked by foot pedals.

6. *skreeky*. " 'Skreeky' is a brilliantly created portmanteau word conveying, one assumes, a discordant combination of 'scream' and 'shriek,' " suggested Victor Doyno in "*Adventures of Huckleberry Finn*: The Growth of the Manuscript to Novel" (Sattelmayer and Crowley, *One Hundred Years of Huckleberry Finn*, 1985, p. 114).

7. *it was only one dog*. Blair noted in *Mark Twain and Huck Finn* the similarity between the ruckus at the Wilks funeral and that during a sermon delivered by the captain on the *Quaker City*, recorded by Twain in his journal: "In the midst of sermon, Capt. Duncan rushed madly out with one of those damned dogs, but didn't throw him overboard" (p. 331). Twain described in Chapter 5 of *Tom Sawyer* the disruption caused by a pinch-bug and a stray poodle during another church service: "The discourse was resumed presently, but it went lame and halting, all possibility of impressiveness being at an end; for even the gravest sentiments were constantly being received with a smothered burst of unholy mirth, under cover of some remote pew-back, as if the poor parson had said a rarely facetious thing."

heads. So he glided along, and the pow-wow and racket getting more and more outrageous all the time; and at last, when he had gone around two sides of the room, he disappears down cellar. Then, in about two seconds we heard a whack, and the dog he finished up with a most amazing howl or two, and then everything was dead still, and the parson begun his solemn talk where he left off. In a minute or two here comes this undertaker's back and shoulders gliding along the wall again; and so he glided, and glided, around three sides of the room, and then rose up, and shaded his mouth with his hands, and stretched his neck out towards the preacher, over the people's heads, and says, in a kind of a coarse whisper, *"He had a rat!"* [8] Then he drooped down and glided along the wall again to his place. You could see it was a great satisfaction to the people, because naturally they wanted to know. A little thing like

"*HE HAD A RAT!*"

that don't cost nothing, and it's just the little things that makes a man to be looked up to and liked. There warn't no more popular man in town than what that undertaker was.

Well, the funeral sermon was very good, but pison long[9] and tiresome; and then the king he shoved in and got off some of his usual rubbage, and at last the job was through, and the undertaker begun to sneak up on the coffin with his screw-driver. I was in a sweat then, and watched him pretty keen. But he never meddled at all; just slid the lid

8. "He had a rat!" The Hartford *Evening Post* (February 17, 1885) noted in its review of *Huckleberry Finn*, "The 'He had a rat' story put into a funeral scene, where it actually occurred in this city, will be recognized by a number of Hartford people, who have had many hearty laughs at it in its chrysalis period." As early as 1878, Twain jotted down the phrase "He had a rat!" several times in his notebook, in hope that he might be able to utilize it in his work one day.

9. *pison long*. Poisonously long.

along, as soft as mush, and screwed it down tight and fast. So there I was! I didn't know whether the money was in there, or not. So, says I, spose somebody has hogged that bag on the sly?—now how do *I* know whether to write to Mary Jane or not? Spose she dug him up and didn't find nothing—what would she think of me? Blame it, I says, I might get hunted up and jailed; I'd better lay low and keep dark, and not write at all; the thing's awful mixed, now; trying to better it, I've worsened it a hundred times, and I wish to goodness I'd just let it alone, dad fetch the whole business!

They buried him, and we come back home, and I went to watching faces again—I couldn't help it, and I couldn't rest easy. But nothing come of it; the faces didn't tell me nothing.

The king he visited around, in the evening, and sweetened every body up, and made himself ever so friendly; and he give out the idea that his congregration over in England would be in a sweat about him, so he must hurry and settle up the estate right away, and leave for home. He was very sorry he was so pushed, and so was everybody; they wished he could stay longer, but they said they could see it couldn't be done. And he said of course him and William would take the girls home with them; and that pleased everybody too, because then the girls would be well fixed, and amongst their own relations; and it pleased the girls, too—tickled them so they clean forgot they ever had a trouble in the world; and told him to sell out as quick as he wanted to, they would be ready. Them poor things was that glad and happy it made my heart ache to see them getting fooled and lied to so, but I didn't see no safe way for me to chip in and change the general tune.

Well, blamed if the king didn't bill[10] the house and the niggers and all the property for auction straight off—sale two days after the funeral; but anybody could buy private beforehand if they wanted to.

So the next day after the funeral, along about noontime, the girls' joy got the first jolt; a couple of nigger traders

10. *bill.* Advertised for sale, particularly on handbills.

come along, and the king sold them the niggers reasonable, for three-day drafts as they called it,[11] and away they went, the two sons up the river to Memphis, and their mother down the river to Orleans.[12] I thought them poor girls and them niggers would break their hearts for grief;[13] they cried around each other, and took on so it most made me down sick to see it. The girls said they hadn't ever dreamed of seeing the family separated or sold away from the town. I can't ever get it out of my memory,[14] the sight of them poor miserable girls and niggers hanging around each other's necks and crying; and I reckon I couldn't a stood it all but would a had to bust out and tell on our gang if I hadn't knowed the sale warn't no account and the niggers would be back home in a week or two.

The thing made a big stir in the town, too, and a good many come out flat-footed and said it was scandalous to separate the mother and the children that way.[15] It injured the frauds some; but the old fool he bulled right along, spite of all the duke could say or do, and I tell you the duke was powerful uneasy.

Next day was auction day. About broad-day in the morning, the king and the duke come up in the garret and woke me up, and I see by their look that there was trouble. The king says:

"Was you in my room night before last?"

"No, your majesty"—which was the way I always called him when nobody but our gang warn't around.

"Was you in there yisterday er last night?"

"No, your majesty."

"Honor bright, now—no lies."

"Honor bright, your majesty, I'm telling you the truth. I hain't been anear your room since Miss Mary Jane took you and the duke and showed it to you."

The duke says:

"Have you seen anybody else go in there?"

"No, your grace, not as I remember, I believe."

"Stop and think."

I studied a while, and see my chance, then I says:

11. *three-day drafts as they called it.* A bill of exchange allows the purchaser three dates on which to pay the money owed; and if either party fails to fulfill the agreement at any point between the first and last payment, then the contract becomes invalid.

12. *the two sons up the river to Memphis, and their mother down the river to Orleans.* In "A True Story" (*Atlantic Monthly*, November 1874), Twain records the grief suffered by a slave mother deprived of her children on the auction block, "repeated word for word" as Aunty Cord, a servant at Quarry Farm, near Elmira, New York, described it to him:

> "Dey put chains on us an' put us on a stan' as high as dis po'ch, . . . an' all de people stood aroun', crowds an' crowds. . . . An' dey sole my ole man, an' took him away, an' dey begin to sell my chil'en an' take *dem* away, an' I begin to cry; an' de man say, 'Shet up yo' dam blubberin,' an' hit me on de mouf wid his han'. An' when de las' one was gone but my little Henry, I grab' *him* clost up to my breas' so, an' I ris up an' says, 'You shan't take him away,' I says; 'I'll kill de man dat tetches him!' I says. . . . But dey got him—dey got him, de men did; but I took and tear de clo'es mos' off of 'em, an' beat 'em over de head wid my chain; an' *dey* give it to *me*, too, but I didn't mine dat." (p. 592)

A mother deprived of her children. Illustration by George Cruikshank, *Uncle Tom's Cabin* by Harriet Beecher Stowe, 1853. *Private collection.*

13. *I thought them poor girls and them niggers would break their hearts for grief.* The Wilks sis-

"WAS YOU IN MY ROOM?"

"Well, I see the niggers go in there several times."

Both of them give a little jump; and looked like they hadn't ever expected it, and then like they *had*. Then the duke says:

"What, *all* of them?"

"No—leastways not all at once. That is, I don't think I ever see them all come *out* at once but just one time."

"Hello—when was that?"

"It was the day we had the funeral. In the morning. It warn't early, because I overslept. I was just starting down the ladder, and I see them."

"Well, go on, *go* on—what did they do? How'd they act?"

"They didn't do nothing. And they didn't act anyway, much, as fur as I see. They tip-toed away; so I seen, easy enough, that they'd shoved in there to do up your majesty's room, or something, sposing you was up; and found you *warn't* up, and so they was hoping to slide out of the way of trouble without waking you up, if they hadn't already waked you up."

"Great guns, *this* is a go!" says the king; and both of them

ters and their slaves are not expressing false sentimentality. Because they raised them and were their playmates from earliest days, masters were often not only loyal to but also genuinely fond of their slaves and they of their owners. To Twain, "house servant of ours" was synonymous with "playmate of mine; for I was playmate to all the niggers, preferring their society to that of the elect, I being a person of low-down tastes from the start, notwithstanding my high birth, and ever ready to forsake the communion of high souls if I could strike anything nearer my grade" (*Huck Finn and Tom Sawyer Among the Indians*, 1989, pp. 90–91). When their fortunes change, the Hawkinses in Chapter 7 of *The Gilded Age* have to suffer the agony of having the sheriff sell their property: "The Hawkins hearts been torn to see Uncle Dan'l and his wife pass from the auction-block into the hands of a negro trader and depart for the remote South to be seen no more by the family. It had seemed like seeing their own flesh and blood sold into banishment."

The only slave his family owned that Sam Clemens ever knew was Jenny. "A woman who had been 'mammy'—that is, nurse—to several of us children, took a notion that she would like to change masters," he recalled in "Jane Lampton Clemens" in 1890. "She wanted to be sold to a Mr. [William B. Beebe], of our town. That was a sore trial, for the woman was almost like one of the family; but she pleaded hard—for that man had been beguiling her with all sorts of fine and alluring promises—and my mother yielded, and also persuaded my father" (*Huck Finn and Tom Sawyer Among the Indians*, 1989, p. 89). "He sold her down the river," Twain noted in "Villagers of 1840–43," written in 1897. "Was seen years later, chambermaid on a steamboat. Cried and lamented" (p. 104).

14. *I can't ever get it out of my memory*. "I have no recollection of ever seeing a slave auction in that town [Hannibal]," he said in a memorial essay about his mother, "Jane Lampton Clemens," in 1890; "but I am suspicious that that is because the thing was a common and commonplace spectacle, not an uncommon and impressive one. I vividly remember seeing a dozen black men and women chained to each other, once, and lying in a group on the pavement, awaiting shipment to the southern slave market. Those were the saddest faces I ever saw. Chained slaves could not have been a common sight, or this picture would not have taken so strong and lasting a hold upon me" (*Huck Finn and Tom Sawyer Among the Indians*, 1989, p. 88).

15. *it was scandalous to separate the mother and the children that way.* Twain is describing "the mild domestic slavery" of Hannibal, Missouri, and not the more severe kind of Arkansas in the Deep South. He recalled in "Jane Lampton Clemens" of 1890, "To separate and sell the members of a slave family to different masters was a thing not well liked by the people and so it was not often done, except in the settling of estates" (*Huck Finn and Tom Sawyer Among the Indians*, 1989, p. 88).

16. *He give me down the banks.* He gave me a good scolding or reprimand; an Irish expression.

17. *Quick sales* and *small profits!* Fischer and Salamo in the 2001 University of California edition identified this phrase as a popular nineteenth-century mercantile maxim, also known as "light gains make a heavy purse," meaning "small profits and a quick return, is the best way of getting wealthy."

looked pretty sick, and tolerable silly. They stood there a thinking and scratching their heads, a minute, and then the duke he bust into a kind of a little raspy chuckle, and says:

"It does beat all, how neat the niggers played their hand. They let on to be *sorry* they was going out of this region! and I believed they *was* sorry. And so did you, and so did everybody. Don't ever tell *me* any more that a nigger ain't got any histrionic talent. Why, the way they played that thing, it would fool *anybody*. In my opinion there's a fortune in 'em. If I had capital and a theatre, I wouldn't want a better lay out than that—and here we've gone and sold 'em for a song. Yes, and ain't privileged to sing the song, yet. Say, where *is* that song?—that draft."

"In the bank for to be collected. Where *would* it be?"

"Well, *that's* all right then, thank goodness."

Says I, kind of timid-like:

"Is something gone wrong?"

The king whirls on me and rips out:

"None o' your business! You keep your head shet, and mind y'r own affairs—if you got any. Long as you're in this town, don't you forgit *that,* you hear?" Then he says to the duke, "We got to jest swaller it, and say noth'n: mum's the word for *us.*"

As they was starting down the ladder, the duke he chuckles again, and says:

"Quick sales *and* small profits![17] It's a good business—yes."

The king snarls around on him and says,

"I was trying to do for the best, in sellin' 'm out so quick. If the profits has turned out to be none, lackin' considable, and none to carry, is it my fault any more'n it's yourn?"

"Well, *they'd* be in this house yet, and we *wouldn't* if I could a got my advice listened to."

The king sassed back, as much as was safe for him, and then swapped around and lit into *me* again. He give me down the banks[16] for not coming and *telling* him I see the niggers come out of his room acting that way—said any fool would a *knowed* something was up. And then waltzed in and cussed *himself* a while; and said it all come of him not laying late and taking his natural rest that morning, and he'd be blamed if he'd ever do it again. So they went off a jawing;[18] and I felt dreadful glad I'd worked it all off onto the niggers and yet hadn't done the niggers no harm by it.

JAWING.

18. *a jawing*. Oddly, Gilder changed the caption to the illustration from "Jawing" to "A Coolness between friends" when it appeared in "Royalty on the Mississippi" in *Century Magazine* (February 1885).

Chapter XXVIII

IN TROUBLE.

By and-by it was getting-up time; so I come down the ladder and started for down stairs, but as I come to the girls' room, the door was open, and I see Mary Jane setting by her old hair trunk, which was open and she'd been packing things in it—getting ready to go to England. But she had stopped now, with a folded gown in her lap, and had her face in her hands, crying. I felt awful bad to see it; of course anybody would. I went in there, and says:

"Miss Mary Jane, you can't abear to see people in trouble, and *I* can't—most always. Tell me about it."

So she done it. And it was the niggers—I just expected it. She said the beautiful trip to England was most about spoiled for her; she didn't know *how* she was ever going to be happy there, knowing the mother and the children warn't ever going to see each other no more—and then busted out bitterer than ever, and flung up her hands, and says:

"Oh, dear, dear, to think they ain't *ever* going to see each other any more!"

"But they *will*—and inside of two weeks—and I *know* it!" says I.

Laws it was out before I could think!—and before I could budge, she throws her arms around my neck, and told me to say it *again*, say it *again*, say it *again!*

I see I had spoke too sudden, and said too much, and was in a close place. I asked her to let me think a minute; and she set there, very impatient and excited, and handsome, but looking kind of happy and eased-up, like a person that's had a tooth pulled out. So I went to studying it out. I says to myself, I reckon a body that ups and tells the truth when he is in a tight place, is taking considerable many resks, though I ain't had no experience, and can't say for certain; but it looks so to me, anyway; and yet here's a case where I'm blest if it don't look to me like the truth is better, and actuly *safer*, than a lie. I must lay it by in my mind, and think it over some time or other, it's so kind of strange and unregular. I never see nothing like it. Well, I says to myself at last, I'm agoing to chance it; I'll up and tell the truth this time, though it does seem most like setting down on a kag of powder and touching it off just to see where you'll go to. Then I says:

"Miss Mary Jane, is there any place out of town a little ways, where you could go and stay three or four days?"

"Yes—Mr. Lothrop's. Why?"

"Never mind why, yet. If I'll tell you how I know the niggers will see each other again—inside of two weeks—here in this house—and *prove* how I know it—will you go to Mr. Lothrop's and stay four days?"

"Four days!" she says; "I'll stay a year!"

"All right," I says, "I don't want nothing more out of *you* than just your word—I druther have it than another man's kiss-the-Bible."[1] She smiled, and reddened up very sweet, and I says, "If you don't mind it, I'll shut the door—and bolt it."

Then I come back and set down again, and says:

"Don't you holler. Just set still, and take it like a man. I got to tell the truth, and you want to brace up, Miss Mary, because it's a bad kind, and going to be hard to take, but there ain't no help for it. These uncles of yourn ain't no uncles at all—they're a couples of frauds—regular deadbeats. There, now we're over the worst of it—you can stand the rest middling easy."

It jolted her up like everything, of course; but I was over

1. *kiss-the-Bible*. Sacred oath.

2. *I was over the shoal water now*. Safe and sound, like a riverboat leaving port and on its way.

3. *he kissed her sixteen or seventeen times*. Twain has forgotten that he had earlier deleted the king's lechery. See Chapter 25, note 4, as well as note 9 below.

4. *we'll have them tarred and feathered, and flung in the river*. Redheads were believed to be especially hotheaded, but sweet Mary Jane reacts just like any "man" in the novel. Her first reaction is to have them lynched.

5. *I'd be all right, but there'd be another person that you don't know about who'd be in big trouble*. Even in the most tense situation, Huck always looks out for Jim's welfare.

the shoal water now,[2] so I went right along, her eyes a blazing higher and higher all the time, and told her every blame thing, from where we first struck that young fool going up to the steamboat, clear through to where she flung herself onto the king's breast at the front door and he kissed her sixteen or seventeen times[3]—and then up she jumps, with her face afire like sunset, and says:

"The brute! Come—don't waste a minute—not a *second*—we'll have them tarred and feathered, and flung in the river!"[4]

Says I:

"Cert'nly. But do you mean, *before* you go to Mr. Lothrop's, or——"

"Oh," she says, "what am I *thinking* about!" she says, and set right down again. "Don't mind what I said—please don't—you *won't,* now, *will* you?" laying her silky hand on mine in that kind of a way that I said I would die first. "I never thought, I was so stirred up," she says; "now go on, and I won't do so any more. You tell me what to do, and whatever you say, I'll do it."

"Well," I says, "it's a rough gang, them two frauds, and I'm fixed so I got to travel with them a while longer, whether I want to or not—I druther not tell you why—and if you was to blow on them this town would get me out of their claws, and *I'd* be all right, but there'd be another person that you don't know about who'd be in big trouble.[5] Well, we got to save *him,* hain't we? Of course. Well, then, we won't blow on them."

INDIGNATION.

Saying them words put a good idea in my head. I see how maybe I could get me and Jim rid of the frauds; get them jailed here, and then leave. But I didn't want to run the raft in day-time, without anybody aboard to answer questions but me; so I didn't want the plan to begin working till pretty late to-night. I says:

"Miss Mary Jane, I'll tell you what we'll do—and you won't have to stay at Mr. Lothrop's so long, nuther. How fur is it?"

"A little short of four miles—right out in the country, back here."

"Well, that'll answer. Now you go along out there, and lay low till nine or half-past, to-night, and then get them to fetch you home again—tell them you've thought of something. If you get here before eleven, put a candle in this window, and if I don't turn up, wait *till* eleven, and *then* if I don't turn up it means I'm gone, and out of the way, and safe. Then you come out and spread the news around, and get these beats jailed."

"Good," she says, "I'll do it."

"And if it just happens so that I don't get away, but get took up along with them, you must up and say I told you the whole thing beforehand, and you must stand by me all you can."

"Stand by you, indeed I will. They sha'n't touch a hair of your head!" she says, and I see her nostrils spread and her eyes snap when she said it, too.

"If I get away, I sha'n't be here," I says, "to prove these rapscallions ain't your uncles, and I couldn't do it if I *was* here. I could swear they was beats and bummers, that's all; though that's worth something. Well, there's others can do that better than what I can—and they're people that ain't going to be doubted as quick as I'd be. I'll tell you how to find them. Gimme a pencil and a piece of paper. There—*'Royal Nonesuch, Bricksville.'* Put it away, and don't lose it. When the court wants to find out something about these two, let them send up to Bricksville and say they've got the men that played the Royal Nonesuch, and ask for some witnesses—why, you'll have that entire town down here before you can hardly wink, Miss Mary. And they'll come a-biling,[6] too."

I judged we had got everything fixed about right, now. So I says:

6. *a-biling*. Boiling, hot and bothered, furious.

7. *leather-face*. Expressionless, straight-faced, poker face. Throughout this confession, even before she has the chance to speak, Huck has been able to read Mary Jane's emotions through the changes in her facial expressions.

8. *coarse print*. Block letters, printing; like "coarse-hand" (see Chapter 18, note 40).

9. *Do you reckon you can go and face your uncles, when they come to kiss you good-morning*. The manuscript reads: "Do you reckon you can face your uncles, and take your regular three or four good-morning smacks?" (Ferguson, "Huck Finn Aborning," p. 180). But Twain changed the passage when he decided to make the frauds less lecherous. See Chapter 25, note 4.

HOW TO FIND THEM.

"Just let the auction go right along, and don't worry. Nobody don't have to pay for the things they buy till a whole day after the auction, on accounts of the short notice, and they ain't going out of this till they get that money—and the way we've fixed it the sale ain't going to count, and they ain't going to *get* no money. It's just like the way it was with the niggers—it warn't no sale, and the niggers will be back before long. Why, they can't collect the money for the *niggers*, yet—they're in the worst kind of a fix, Miss Mary."

"Well," she says, "I'll run down to breakfast now, and then I'll start straight for Mr. Lothrop's."

"'Deed, *that* ain't the ticket, Miss Mary Jane," I says, "by no manner of means; go *before* breakfast."

"Why?"

"What did you reckon I wanted you to go at all for, Miss Mary?"

"Well, I never thought—and come to think, I don't know. What was it?"

"Why, it's because you ain't one of these leather-face[7] people. I don't want no better book than what your face is. A body can set down and read it off like coarse print.[8] Do you reckon you can go and face your uncles, when they come to kiss you good-morning,[9] and never—"

"There, there, don't! Yes, I'll go before breakfast—I'll be glad to. And leave my sisters with them?"

"Yes—never mind about them. They've got to stand it yet a while. They might suspicion something if all of you was to go. I don't want you to see them, nor your sisters, nor nobody in this town—if a neighbor was to ask how is your uncles this morning, your face would tell something. No, you go right along, Miss Mary Jane, and I'll fix it with all of them. I'll tell Miss Susan to give your love to your uncles and say you've went away for a few hours for to get a little rest and change, or to see a friend, and you'll be back to-night or early in the morning."

"Gone to see a friend is all right, but I won't have my love given to them."

"Well, then, it sha'n't be." It was well enough to tell *her* so—no harm in it. It was only a little thing to do, and no trouble; and it's the little things that smoothes people's roads the most, down here below;[10] it would make Mary Jane comfortable, and it wouldn't cost nothing. Then I says: "There's one more thing—that bag of money."

"Well, they've got that; and it makes me feel pretty silly to think *how* they got it."

"No, you're out, there. They hain't got it."

"Why, who's got it?"

"I wish I knowed, but I don't. I *had* it, because I stole it from them: and I stole it to give to you; and I know where I hid it, but I'm afraid it ain't there no more. I'm awful sorry, Miss Mary Jane, I'm just as sorry as I can be; but I done the best I could; I did, honest. I come nigh getting caught, and I had to shove it into the first place I come to, and run—and it warn't a good place."

"Oh, stop blaming yourself—it's too bad to do it, and I won't allow it—you couldn't help it; it wasn't you fault. Where did you hide it?"

I didn't want to set her to thinking about her troubles again; and I couldn't seem to get my mouth to tell her what would make her see that corpse laying in the coffin with that bag of money on his stomach. So for a minute I didn't say nothing—then I says:

"I'd ruther not *tell* you where I put it, Miss Mary Jane, if you don't mind letting me off; but I'll write it for you on a piece of paper, and you can read it along the road to Mr. Lothrop's, if you want to. Do you reckon that'll do?"

"Oh, yes."

10. *it's the little things that smoothes people's roads the most, down here below.* Huck has fallen into the idiom of a Sunday-school superintendent; according to church teachings, Heaven expects Mary Jane to love everyone, especially "lost lambs" like the king and the duke.

HE WROTE.

So I wrote: "I put it in the coffin. It was in there when you was crying there, away in the night. I was behind the door, and I was mighty sorry for you, Miss Mary Jane."

It made my eyes water a little, to remember her crying there all by herself in the night, and them devils laying there right under her own roof, shaming her and robbing her; and when I folded it up and give it to her, I see the water come into her eyes, too; and she shook me by the hand, hard, and says:

"*Good*-bye—I'm going to do everything just as you've told me; and if I don't ever see you again, I sha'n't ever forget you, and I'll think of you a many and a many a time, and I'll *pray* for you, too!"—and she was gone.

Pray for me! I reckoned if she knowed me she'd take a job that was more nearer her size. But I bet she done it, just the same—she was just that kind. She had the grit to pray for Judus[11] if she took the notion—there warn't no back-down to her,[12] I judge. You may say what you want to, but in my opinion she had more sand in her[13] than any girl I ever see; in my opinion she was just full of sand. It sounds like flattery, but it ain't no flattery. And when it comes to beauty—and goodness too—she lays over them all. I hain't ever seen her since that time that I see her go out of that door;[14] no, I hain't ever seen her since, but I reckon I've thought of her a many and a many a million times, and of her saying she would pray for me; and if ever I'd a thought it would do any good for me to pray for *her*, blamed[15] if I wouldn't a done it or bust.

Well, Mary Jane she lit out the back way, I reckon; because nobody see her go. When I struck[16] Susan and the hare-lip, I says:

11. *She had the grit to pray for Judus*. She had the pluck to pray for anyone, even the greatest villain in Christian history; Twain originally wrote "Judas Iscariott," but that was too blasphemous and not likely something that Huck might say. In praising Mary Jane's courage, Huck unapologetically accuses her of going against conventional Christian morality. Twain once thought, as he wrote in "Jane Lampton Clemens" in 1890, that his mother "could be beguiled into saying a soft word for the devil himself" (*Huck Finn and Tom Sawyer Among the Indians*, 1989, p. 83).

12. *there warn't no back-down to her*. Huck originally added, "if *I* know a girl by the rake of her stern; and I think I do" (**MS**); but that was exactly the kind of knowledge this sexually inexperienced backwoods boy would *not* have known yet, so Twain deleted the reference.

13. *she had more sand in her*. See Chapter 8, note 16.

14. *that time that I see her go out of that door*. In the manuscript, he also saw her "turn at the stairs and kinder throw a kiss back at me" (**MS**); but this is too flirtatious, almost brazen, for Mary Jane. Then Twain wrote "like the light and comfort a-going out of a body's life" (**MS**); but he finally removed all hint of a budding romance between the innocent fourteen-year-old boy and the noble nineteen-year-old girl.

15. *blamed*. Originally the more blunt "I'm dam'd" (**MS**) in the manuscript.

16. *struck*. Encountered, ran into.

"What's the name of them people over on t'other side of the river that you all goes to see sometimes?"

They says:

"There's several; but it's the Proctors, mainly."

"That's the name," I says; "I most forgot it. Well, Miss Mary Jane she told me to tell you she's gone over there in a dreadful hurry—one of them's sick."

"Which one?"

"I don't know; leastways I kinder forget; but I think it's—"

"Sakes alive, I hope it ain't *Hanner?*"

"I'm sorry to say it," I says, "but Hanner's the very one."

"My goodness—and she so well only last week! Is she took bad?"

"It ain't no name for it. They set up with her all night, Miss Mary Jane said, and they don't think she'll last many hours."

"Only think of that, now! What's the matter with her!"

I couldn't think of anything reasonable, right off that way, so I says:

"Mumps."

"Mumps your granny! They don't set up with people that's got the mumps."

"They don't, don't they? You better bet they do with *these*

HANNER WITH THE MUMPS.

mumps. These mumps is different. It's a new kind, Miss Mary Jane said."

"How's it a new kind?"

"Because it's mixed up with other things."

"What other things?"

"Well, measles,[17] and whooping-cough, and erysiplas,[18] and consumption,[19] and yaller janders,[20] and brain fever,[21] and I don't know what all."

"My land! And they call it the *mumps?*"

"That's what Miss Mary Jane said."

"Well, what in the nation do they call it the *mumps* for?"

"Why, because it *is* the mumps. That's what it starts with."

"Well, ther' ain't no sense in it. A body might stump his toe, and take pison, and fall down the well, and break his neck, and bust his brains out, and somebody come along and ask what killed him, and some numskull up and say, 'Why, he stumped his *toe.*' [22] Would ther' be any sense in that? *No.* And ther' ain't no sense in *this,* nuther. Is it ketching?"

"Is it *ketching?* Why, how you talk. Is a *harrow* catching?—in the dark? If you don't hitch onto one tooth, you're bound to on another, ain't you? And you can't get away with that tooth without fetching the whole harrow along, can you? Well, these kind of mumps is a kind of a harrow, as you may say—and it ain't no slouch of a harrow, nuther, you come to get it hitched on good."

"Well, it's awful, *I* think," says the hare-lip. "I'll go to Uncle Harvey and—"

"Oh, yes," I says, "I *would.* Of *course* I would. I wouldn't lose no time."

"Well, why wouldn't you?"

"Just look at it a minute, and maybe you can see. Hain't your uncles obleeged to get along home to England as fast as they can? And do you reckon they'd be mean enough to go off and leave you to go all that journey by yourselves? *You* know they'll wait for you. So fur, so good. Your uncle Harvey's a preacher, ain't he? Very well, then; is a *preacher* going to deceive a steamboat clerk? is he going to deceive a

17. *measles.* Although now considered a relatively harmless common childhood disease in the United States, measles were once as deadly as any of the other ailments Huck mentions. "In 1845, when I was ten years old," Twain reported in "Chapters from My Autobiography" (*North American Review*, October 1907), "there was an epidemic of measles in the town and it made a most alarming slaughter among the little people. There was a funeral almost daily, and the mothers of the town were nearly demented with fright" (p. 168). This joke is a variant of one used by Billy Rogers in Twain's unpublished "Boy's Manuscript," written in 1868: "I've had the scarlet fever and the mumps, and the hoop'n cough, and ever so many things" (*Huck Finn and Tom Sawyer Among the Indians*, 1989, p. 7).

18. *erysiplas.* Erysipelas, or "St. Anthony's fire," a severe skin disease.

19. *consumption.* The common nineteenth-century name for tuberculosis, one of the most dreaded diseases of the nineteenth century. While still dangerous today, it can be cured.

20. *yaller janders.* Yellow jaundice, a liver ailment which discolors the skin.

21. *brain fever.* Equine encephalomyelitis, an inflammation of the brain or its members.

22. *"Why, he stumped his* toe." A nice malapropism confusing "stubbed" with a synonym for "baffled." This is a variant of a joke Twain used in the Buffalo *Express* (August 18, 1869): In Nevada, a man with consumption "took the smallpox from a negro, the cholera from a Chinaman, and the yellow fever and the erysipelas from other parties, and swallowed fifteen grains of strychnine, and fell out of the third story window and broke his neck. Verdict of the jury, 'Died by the visitation of God!' "

ship clerk?—so as to get them to let Miss Mary Jane go aboard? Now *you* know he ain't. What *will* he do, then? Why, he'll say, 'It's a great pity, but my church matters has got to get along the best way they can; for my niece has been exposed to the dreadful pluribus-unum mumps,[23] and so it's my bounden duty to set down here and wait the three months it takes to show on her if she's got it.' But never mind, if you think it's best to tell your uncle Harvey—"

"Shucks, and stay fooling around here when we could all be having good times in England whilst we was waiting to find out whether Mary Jane's got it or not? Why, you talk like a muggins."[24]

"Well, anyway, maybe you better tell some of the neighbors."

"Listen at that, now. You do beat all, for natural stupidness. Can't you *see* that *they'd* go and tell? Ther' ain't no way but just to not tell anybody at *all*."

"Well, maybe you're right—yes, I judge you *are* right."

"But I reckon we ought to tell Uncle Harvey she's gone out a while, anyway, so he wont be uneasy about her?"

"Yes, Miss Mary Jane she wanted you to do that. She says, 'Tell them to give Uncle Harvey and William my love and a kiss, and say I've run over the river to see Mr.—Mr.—what *is* the name of that rich family your uncle Peter used to think so much of?—I mean the one that—"

"Why, you must mean the Apthorps, ain't it?"

"Of course; bother them kind of names, a body can't ever seem to remember them, half the time, somehow. Yes, she said, say she has run over for to ask the Apthorps to be sure and come to the auction and buy this house, because she allowed her uncle Peter would ruther they had it than anybody else; and she's going to stick to them till they say they'll come, and then, if she ain't too tired, she's coming home; and if she is, she'll be home in the morning anyway. She said, don't say nothing about the Proctors, but only about the Apthorps—which'll be perfectly true, because she *is* going there to speak about their buying the house; I know it, because she told me so, herself."

23. *the dreadful pluribus-unum mumps*. Huck is trying to recall *E pluribus unum* ("One out of many"), the official motto of the United States of America that appears on the federal seal. Huck garbles probably the only Latin he has ever heard. It is an appropriate expression for a preacher who refers to "funeral orgies," and it summarizes all of Hannah's horrible afflictions as "one out of many." But almost any Latin might have done just as well; Huck uses it because it *sounds* impressive. "E Pluribus Unum" is the title of a minor item Twain published in the *Alta California* (November 22, 1868). "*E pluribus unum*!" Twain wrote Livy on March 6, 1869. "I do not know what *E pluribus unum* means, but it is a good word, anyway" (*The Love Letters of Mark Twain*, 1949, p. 80).

24. *a muggins*. A fool, a simpleton.

25. *pisonest.* A misprint: As both the manuscript and Kemble's illustration prove, this word should be "piousest."

THE AUCTION.

"All right," they said, and cleared out to lay for their uncles, and give them the love and the kisses, and tell them the message.

Everything was all right now. The girls wouldn't say nothing because they wanted to go to England; and the king and the duke would ruther Mary Jane was off working for the auction than around in reach of Doctor Robinson. I felt very good; I judged I had done it pretty neat—I reckoned Tom Sawyer couldn't a done it no neater himself. Of course he would a throwed more style into it, but I can't do that very handy, not being brung up to it.

Well, they held the auction in the public square, along towards the end of the afternoon, and it strung along, and strung along, and the old man he was on hand and looking his level pisonest,[25] up there longside of the auctioneer, and chipping in a little Scripture, now and then, or a little goody-goody saying, of some kind, and the duke he was around goo-gooing for sympathy all he knowed how, and just spreading himself generly.

But by-and-by the thing dragged through, and everything was sold. Everything but a little old trifling lot in the grave-yard. So they'd got to work *that* off—I never see such a giraft as the king was for wanting to swallow *everything*. Well, whilst they was at it, a steamboat landed, and in about two minutes up comes a crowd a whooping and yelling and laughing and carrying on, and singing out:

"*Here's* your opposition line! here's your two sets o' heirs[26] to old Peter Wilks—and you pays your money and you takes your choice!"

26. *two sets o' heirs.* Blair in *Mark Twain and Huck Finn* suggested that Twain must have had in mind the story of the false Martin Guerre, as described in Horace W. Fuller's *Noted French Trials: Impostors and Adventurers* (1882): A man returns to Normandy, claiming to be Martin Guerre, who left his wife many years before, but when his story is questioned, he is put on trial as an impostor; just as the judges "were about to give the accused the benefit of the doubt, there arrived . . . a new Martin Guerre. . . . he recognized . . . his neighbors, his relatives, his friends, as the other had done before him. . . . The newcomer arrived just in time to drag the judges back into uncertainty" (p. 328).

Chapter XXIX.

THE TRUE BROTHERS.

They was fetching a very nice looking old gentleman along, and a nice looking younger one, with his right arm in a sling. And my souls, how the people yelled, and laughed, and kept it up. But I didn't see no joke about it, and I judged it would strain the duke and the king some to see any. I reckoned they'd turn pale. But no, nary a pale did *they* turn. The duke he never let on he suspicioned what was up, but just went a goo-gooing around, happy and satisfied, like a jug that's googling out buttermilk; and as for the king, he just gazed and gazed down sorrowful on them new-comers like it give him the stomach-ache in his very heart to think there could be such frauds and rascals in the world. Oh, he done it admirable. Lots of the principal people gethered around the king, to let him see they was on his side. That old gentleman that had just come looked all puzzled to death. Pretty soon he begun to speak, and I see, straight off, he pronounced *like* an Englishman, not the king's way, though the king's *was* pretty good, for an imitation. I can't give the old gent's words, nor I can't imitate him;[1] but he turned around to the crowd, and says, about like this:

"This is a surprise to me which I wasn't looking for; and I'll acknowledge, candid and frank, I ain't very well fixed to

1. *I can't give the old gent's words, nor I can't imitate him.* And yet Huck has been able to reproduce the subtleties of the varying dialects of every other character in the story, from the Missouri Negro speech of Jim to the duke's "histrionic" jargon to Colonel Sherburn's eloquence. W. Keith Kraus in "*Huckleberry Finn*: A Final Irony" (*Mark Twain Journal*, Winter 1967–1968, pp. 18–19) suggested that Huck probably records the "Englishman's" words accurately, and that is only one clue that this new "Harvey Wilks" and his "brother" are just another pair of frauds. His manner of speaking is no more English than the king's is. There are perhaps too many convenient inconsistencies in their story. Also, they do not express any particular grief over the death of the late lamented Peter Wilks; they seem to be there only for the money. Not surprisingly then, the king and the duke do not betray any discomfort on the arrival of a second set of heirs; they see right through them as just another pair of impostors.

meet it and answer it; for my brother and me has had misfortunes, he's broke his arm, and our baggage got put off at a town above here, last night in the night by a mistake. I am Peter Wilks's brother Harvey, and this is his brother William, which can't hear nor speak—and can't even make signs to amount to much, now 't he's only got one hand to work them with. We are who we say we are; and in a day or two, when I get the baggage, I can prove it. But, up till then, I won't say nothing more, but go to the hotel and wait."

So him and the new dummy[2] started off; and the king he laughs, and blethers out:

"Broke his arm—*very* likely *ain't* it?—and very convenient, too, for a fraud that's got to make signs, and hain't learnt how. Lost their baggage! That's *mighty* good!—and mighty ingenious—under the *circumstances!*"

So he laughed again; and so did everybody else, except three or four, or maybe half a dozen. One of these was that doctor; another one was a sharp looking gentleman, with a carpet-bag of the old-fashioned kind made out of carpet-stuff, that had just come off of the steamboat and was talking to him in a low voice, and glancing towards the king now and then and nodding their heads—it was Levi Bell, the lawyer that was gone up to Louisville; and another one was a big rough husky that come along and listened to all the old gentleman said, and was listening to the king now. And when the king got done, this husky up and says:

"Say, looky here; if you are Harvey Wilks, when'd you come to this town?"

"The day before the funeral, friend," says the king.

"But what time o' day?"

"In the evenin'—'bout an hour er two before sundown."

"*How'd* you come?"

"I come down on the *Susan Powell*,[3] from Cincinnati."

"Well, then, how'd you come to be up at the Pint in the *mornin'*—in a canoe?"

"I warn't up at the Pint in the mornin'."

"It's a lie."

Several of them jumped for him and begged him not to talk that way to an old man and a preacher.

2. *dummy*. The common nineteenth-century term for a deaf-mute.

3. Susan Powell. Neither the ship nor the woman has been identified: No boat by that name is listed in William Lytle's *Merchant Steam Vessels of the United States 1807–1868* (Mystic, Conn.: Steamboat Historical Society of America, 1952); nor does "Susan Powell" appear in Twain's autobiography, journals, letters, or interviews. Twain may simply be recalling the custom of a riverboat being named after a lady, usually the captain's wife.

4. *It was nuts for the crowd.* It was very agreeable to the crowd.

"Preacher be hanged, he's a fraud and a liar. He was up at the Pint that mornin'. I live up there, don't I? Well, I was up there, and he was up there. I *see* him there. He come in a canoe, along with Tim Collins and a boy."

The doctor he up and says:

"Would you know the boy again if you was to see him, Hines?"

"I reckon I would, but I don't know. Why, yonder he is, now. I know him perfectly easy."

It was me he pointed at. The doctor says:

"Neighbors, I don't know whether the new couple is frauds or not; but if *these* two ain't frauds, I am an idiot, that's all. I think it's our duty to see that they don't get away from here till we've looked into this thing. Come along, Hines; come along, the rest of you. We'll take these fellows to the tavern and affront them with t'other couple, and I reckon we'll find out *something* before we get through."

It was nuts for the crowd,[4] though maybe not for the king's friends; so we all started. It was about sundown. The doctor he led me along by the hand, and was plenty kind enough, but he never let *go* my hand.

THE DOCTOR LEADS HUCK.

We all got in a big room in the hotel, and lit up some candles, and fetched in the new couple. First, the doctor says:

"I don't wish to be too hard on these two men, but *I* think they're frauds, and they may have complices that we don't know nothing about. If they have, won't the complices get away with that bag of gold Peter Wilks left? It ain't unlikely. If these men ain't frauds, they won't object to sending for that money and letting us keep it till they prove they're all right—ain't that so?"

Everybody agreed to that. So I judged they had our gang in a pretty tight place, right at the outstart. But the king he only looked sorrowful, and says:

"Gentlemen, I wish the money was there, for I ain't got no disposition to throw anything in the way of a fair, open, out-and-out investigation o' this misable business; but alas, the money ain't there; you k'n send and see, if you want to."

"Where is it, then?"

"Well, when my niece give it to me to keep for her, I took and hid it inside o' the straw tick o' my bed, not wishin' to bank it for the few days we'd be here, and considerin' the bed a safe place, we not bein' used to niggers, and suppos'n' 'em honest, like servants in England. The niggers stole it the very next mornin' after I had went down stairs; and when I sold 'em, I hadn't missed the money yit, so they got clean away with it. My servant here k'n tell you 'bout it gentlemen."

The doctor and several said "Shucks!" and I see nobody didn't altogether believe him. One man asked me if I see the niggers steal it. I said no, but I see them sneaking out of the room and hustling away, and I never thought nothing, only I reckoned they was afraid they had waked up my master and was trying to get away before he made trouble with them. That was all they asked me. Then the doctor whirls on me and says:

"Are *you* English too?"

I says yes; and him and some others laughed, and said, "Stuff!"

Well, then they sailed in on the general investigation, and there we had it, up and down, hour in, hour out, and nobody never said a word about supper, nor ever seemed to think about it—and so they kept it up, and kept it up; and it *was* the worst mixed-up thing you ever see. They made the king tell his yarn, and they made the old gentleman tell his'n; and anybody but a lot of prejudiced chuckleheads would a *seen* that the old gentleman was spinning truth and t'other one lies. And by-and-by they had me up to tell what I knowed. The king he give me a left-handed look[5] out of the corner of his eye, and so I knowed enough to talk on the right side. I begun to tell about Sheffield, and how we lived there, and all about the English Wilkses, and so on; but I didn't get pretty fur till the doctor begun to laugh; and Levi Bell, the lawyer, says:

"Set down, my boy, I wouldn't strain myself, if I was you. I reckon you ain't used to lying,[6] it don't seem to come handy; what you want is practice. You do it pretty awkward."

I didn't care nothing for the compliment, but I was glad to be let off, anyway.

The doctor he started to say something, and turns and says:

"If you'd been in town at first, Levi Bell—"

The king broke in and reached out his hand, and says:

"Why, is this my poor dead brother's old friend that he's wrote so often about?"

The lawyer and him shook hands, and the lawyer smiled and looked pleased, and they talked right along a while, and then got to one side and talked low; and at last the lawyer speaks up and says:

"That'll fix it. I'll take the order and send it, along with your brother's, and then they'll know it's all right."

So they got some paper and a pen, and the king he set down and twisted his head to one side, and chawed his tongue, and scrawled off something; and then they give the pen to the duke—and then for the first time, the duke looked sick. But he took the pen and wrote. So then the lawyer turns to the new old gentleman and says:

"You and your brother please write a line or two and sign your names."

5. *a left-handed look.* A sinister glance. The devil is said to linger on the left side of the body. See Chapter 4, notes 3 and 5.

6. *I reckon you ain't used to lying.* Actually Huck has been doing rather well for himself up to now; but here is the first time he has had to lie to educated men.

THE DUKE WROTE.

The old gentleman wrote, but nobody couldn't read it. The lawyer looked powerful astonished, and says:

"Well, it beats *me*"—and snaked a lot of old letters out of his pocket, and examined them, and then examined the old man's writing, and then *them* again; and then says: "These old letters is from Harvey Wilks; and here's *these* two's handwritings, and anybody can see *they* didn't write them" (the king and the duke looked sold and foolish, I tell you, to see how the lawyer had took them in), "and here's *this* old gentleman's handwriting, and anybody can tell, easy enough, *he* didn't write them—fact is, the scratches he makes ain't properly *writing*, at all. Now here's some letters from—"

The new old gentleman says:

"If you please, let me explain. Nobody can read my hand but my brother there—so he copies for me. It's *his* hand you've got there, not mine."

"Well!" says the lawyer, "this *is* a state of things. I've got some of William's letters too; so if you'll get him to write a line or so we can com—"

"He *can't* write with his left hand," says the old gentleman. "If he could use his right hand, you would see that he wrote his own letters and mine too. Look at both, please—they're by the same hand."

The lawyer done it, and says:

"I believe it's so—and if it ain't so, there's a heap stronger resemblance than I'd noticed before, anyway. Well, well, well! I thought we was right on the track of a slution, but it's gone to grass,[7] partly. But anyway, *one* thing is proved—*these* two ain't either of 'em Wilkses"—and he wagged his head towards the king and the duke.

Well, what do you think?—that muleheaded old fool wouldn't give in *then!* Indeed he wouldn't. Said it warn't no fair test. Said his brother William was the cussedest joker in the world, and hadn't *tried* to write—*he* see William was going to play one of his jokes the minute he put the pen to paper. And so he warmed up and went warbling and warbling right along, till he was actuly beginning to believe what he was saying, *himself*—but pretty soon the new old gentleman broke in, and says:

"I've thought of something. Is there anybody here that helped to lay out my br—helped to lay out the late Peter Wilks for burying?"

"Yes," says somebody, "me and Ab Turner done it. We're both here."

Then the old man turns towards the king, and says:

"Perhaps this gentleman can tell me what was tatooed on his breast?"[8]

Blamed if the king didn't have to brace up mighty quick, or he'd a squshed down like a bluff bank that the river has cut under,[9] it took him so sudden—and mind you, it was a thing that was calculated to make most *anybody* sqush to get fetched such a solid one[10] as that without any notice—because how was *he* going to know what was tatooed on the man? He whitened a little; he couldn't help it; and it was mighty still in there, and everybody bending a little forwards and gazing at him. Says I to myself, *Now* he'll throw up the sponge[11]—there ain't no more use. Well, did he? A body can't hardly believe it, but he didn't. I reckon he thought he'd keep the thing up till he tired them people out, so they'd thin out, and him and the duke could break loose and get away. Anyway, he set there, and pretty soon he begun to smile, and says:

"Mf! It's a *very* tough question, *ain't* it! *Yes,* sir, I k'n tell you what's tatooed on his breast. It's jest a small, thin, blue

7. *gone to grass*. Knocked to the ground or out, finished; prizefight slang, from the era when bouts were staged on open ground. According to Twain's burlesque "The Only True and Reliable Account of the Great Prize Fight" (San Francisco *Golden Era*, October 11, 1863), both candidates "went to grass" in the second round. Dan De Quille described in "Mark Twain Takes a Lesson in the Manly Art" (Virginia City [Nev.] *Territorial Enterprise*, April 1864) how a boxing instructor "busted" Twain in the "snoot," "sending him reeling—not exactly to grass, but across a bench." In Chapter 72 of *Roughing It,* Twain again uses the expression when writing of a Hawaiian king who went mad and challenged every man he met to box or wrestle: "Of course this pastime lost its novelty, inasmuch as it must necessarily have been the case when so powerful a deity sent a frail human opponent 'to grass' he never came back any more."

8. *what was tatooed on his breast*. According to DeVoto in *Mark Twain at Work*, Twain originally intended the distinguishing characteristic to be the more grotesque "glass eye with mark on the back of it" (p. 76).

9. *he'd a squshed down like a bluff bank that the river has cut under.* Originally "he'd a kerflummuxed" (**MS**), shown that he was perplexed; but fortunately, Twain came up with a more descriptive phrase that perfectly fits the personality of a boy who grew up along the Mississippi. "Squshed" is a vulgar word for "crushed."

10. *to get fetched such a solid one*. To be struck with such a powerful blow; appropriately, Huck describes this battle of wits in prize-ring slang.

11. *throw up the sponge*. Give in, acknowledge defeat like a fallen prizefighter (as in "The Only True and Reliable Account of the Great Prize Fight"; see note 7 above); today, "throw in the towel."

arrow—that's what it is; and if you don't look clost, you can't see it. *Now* what do you say—hey?"

Well, *I* never see anything like that old blister[12] for clean out-and-out cheek.

The new old gentleman turns brisk towards Ab Turner and his pard,[13] and his eye lights up like he judged he'd got the king *this* time, and says:

"There—you've heard what he said! Was there any such mark on Peter Wilks's breast?"

Both of them spoke up and says:

"We didn't see no such mark."

"Good!" says the old gentleman. "Now, what you *did* see on his breast was a small dim P, and a B (which is an initial he dropped when he was young), and a W, with dashes between them, so: P—B—W"—and he marked them that way on a piece of paper. "Come—ain't that what you saw?"

Both of them spoke up again, and says:

"No, we *didn't.* We never seen any marks at all."

Well, everybody *was* in a state of mind, now; and they sings out:

"The whole *bilin'* of 'm[14] 's frauds! Le's duck 'em![15] le's drown 'em! le's ride 'em on a rail!" and everybody was whooping at once, and there was a rattling pow-wow. But the lawyer he jumps on the table and yells, and says:

"Gentlemen—gentle*men!* Hear me just a word—just a *single* word—if you PLEASE! There's one way yet—let's go and dig up the corpse and look."

That took them.

"Hooray!" they all shouted, and was starting right off; but the lawyer and the doctor sung out:

"Hold on, hold on! Collar all these four men and the boy, and fetch *them* along, too!"

"We'll do it!" they all shouted: "and if we don't find them marks we'll lynch the whole gang!"

I *was* scared, now, I tell you. But there warn't no getting away, you know. They gripped us all, and marched us right along, straight for the graveyard, which was a mile and a half down the river, and the whole town at our heels, for we made noise enough, and it was only nine in the evening.

12. *blister.* An especially objectionable person.

13. *pard.* Partner, pal.

14. *The whole* bilin' *of 'm.* The whole boiling of them, a seething mass, usually of people; the whole lot, omitting nothing, as in "the whole kit and caboodle."

15. *Le's duck 'em!* Let's tar and feather them! It is astonishing how quickly this otherwise hospitable community can turn from affection for to hatred of these scoundrels.

16. *Goliar.* Goliath, the most famous giant in history, whom David slew in I Samuel 17.

"GENTLEMEN — GENTLE*MEN*!"

As we went by our house I wished I hadn't sent Mary Jane out of town; because now if I could tip her the wink, she'd light out and save me, and blow on our dead-beats.

Well, we swarmed along down the river road, just carrying on like wild-cats; and to make it more scary, the sky was darking up, and the lightning beginning to wink and flitter, and the wind to shiver amongst the leaves. This was the most awful trouble and most dangersome I ever was in; and I was kinder stunned; everything was going so different from what I had allowed for; stead of being fixed so I could take my own time, if I wanted to, and see all the fun, and have Mary Jane at my back to save me and set me free when the close-fit come, here was nothing in the world betwixt me and sudden death but just them tatoo-marks. If they didn't find them—

I couldn't bear to think about it; and yet, somehow, I couldn't think about nothing else. It got darker and darker, and it was a beautiful time to give the crowd the slip; but that big husky had me by the wrist—Hines—and a body might as well try to give Goliar[16] the slip. He dragged me right along, he was so excited; and I had to run to keep up.

When they got there they swarmed into the graveyard

and washed over it like an overflow. And when they got to the grave, they found they had about a hundred times as many shovels as they wanted, but nobody hadn't thought to fetch a lantern. But they sailed into digging, anyway, by the flicker of the lightning, and sent a man to the nearest house a half a mile off, to borrow one.

So they dug and dug, like everything; and it got awful dark, and the rain started, and the wind swished and swushed along, and the lightning come brisker and brisker, and the thunder boomed; but them people never took no notice of it, they was so full of this business; and one minute you could see everything and every face in that big crowd, and the shovelfuls of dirt sailing up out of the grave, and the next second the dark wiped it all out, and you couldn't see nothing at all.

At last they got out the coffin, and begun to unscrew the lid, and then such another crowding, and shouldering, and shoving as there was, to scrouge in and get a sight, you never see;[17] and in the dark, that way, it was awful. Hines he hurt my wrist dreadful, pulling and tugging so, and I reckon he clean forgot I was in the world, he was so excited and panting.

All of a sudden the lightning let go a perfect sluice of white glare,[18] and somebody sings out:

"By the living jingo, here's the bag of gold on his breast!"

Hines let out a whoop, like everybody else, and dropped my wrist and give a big surge to bust his way in and get a look, and the way I lit out and shinned for the road in the dark, there ain't nobody can tell.

I had the road all to myself, and I fairly flew—leastways I had it all to myself except the solid dark, and the now-and-then glares, and the buzzing of the rain, and the thrashing of the wind, and the splitting of the thunder; and sure as you are born I did clip it along!

When I struck the town, I see there warn't nobody out in the storm, so I never hunted for no back streets, but humped it straight through the main one; and when I begun to get towards our house I aimed my eye and set it. No light there; the house all dark—which made me feel sorry and

17. *get a sight, you never see.* Except in Chapter 21: This crowd acts exactly as the Bricksville mob did, "squirming and scrouging and pushing and shoving" to get a look at the dying Boggs.

18. *a perfect sluice of white glare.* A straight band of glaring light; from mining slang, referring to the jet of water in a trough while washing gold from clods of dirt.

disappointed, I didn't know why. But at last, just as I was sailing by, *flash* comes the light in Mary Jane's window! and my heart swelled up sudden, like to bust; and the same second the house and all was behind me in the dark, and wasn't ever going to be before me no more in this world. She *was* the best girl I ever see, and had the most sand.[19]

The minute I was far enough above the town to see I could make the towhead, I begun to look sharp for a boat to borrow; and the first time the lightning showed me one that wasn't chained, I snatched it and shoved. It was a canoe, and warn't fastened with nothing but a rope. The towhead was a rattling big distance off, away out there in the middle of the river, but I didn't lose no time; and when I struck the raft at last, I was so fagged I would a just laid down to blow and gasp if I could afforded it. But I didn't. As I sprung aboard I sung out:

"Out with you Jim, and set her loose! Glory be to goodness, we're shut of them!"

Jim lit out, and was a coming for me with both arms spread, he was so full of joy; but when I glimpsed him in the lightning, my heart shot up in my mouth, and I went over-

"JIM LIT OUT."

19. *She* was *the best girl I ever see, and had the most sand*. Twain originally wrote, "She *was* the best girl that ever was! and you could depend on her like the everlasting sun and the stars, every time"; but he changed it in proof, because, as Ferguson argued in "Huck Finn Aborning," "The speech might have fitted the mouth of the Playboy of the Western World, but not Huck's" (p. 174). As it stands, the terse statement is a fitting farewell to the boy's high regard for Mary Jane.

board backwards; for I forgot he was old King Lear and a drownded A-rab all in one, and it most scared the livers and lights out of me.[20] But Jim fished me out, and was going to hug me and bless me, and so on, he was so glad I was back and we was shut of the king and the duke, but I says:

"Not now—have it for breakfast,[21] have it for breakfast! Cut loose and let her slide!"

So, in two seconds, away we went, a sliding down the river, and it *did* seem so good to be free again and all by ourselves on the big river and nobody to bother us. I had to skip around a bit, and jump up and crack my heels a few times, I couldn't help it; but about the third crack, I noticed a sound that I knowed mighty well—and held my breath and listened and waited—and sure enough, when the next flash busted out over the water, here they come!—and just a laying to their oars and making their skiff hum! It was the king and the duke.

So I wilted right down onto the planks, then, and give up; and it was all I could do to keep from crying.

20. *scared the livers and lights out of me.* Scared the living daylights out of me.

21. *have it for breakfast.* "Put a lid on it"; wait until tomorrow.

Chapter XXX

1. *he had a boy about as big as me that died last year.* Again Huck invents a child who dies along the Mississippi. Death seems to lurk around every bend in the river, ready to grab some other little boy or girl.

THE KING SHAKES HUCK.

When THEY got aboard, the king went for me, and shook me by the collar, and says:

"Tryin' to give us the slip, was ye, you pup! Tired of our company—hey?"

I says:

"No, your majesty, we warn't—*please* don't, your majesty!"

"Quick, then, and tell us what *was* your idea, or I'll shake the insides out o' you!"

"Honest, I'll tell you everything, just as it happened, your majesty. The man that had aholt of me was very good to me, and kept saying he had a boy about as big as me that died last year,[1] and he was sorry to see a boy in such a dangerous fix; and when they was all took by surprise by finding the gold, and made a rush for the coffin, he lets go of me and whispers, 'Heel it, now, or they'll hang ye, sure!' and I lit out. It didn't seem no good for *me* to stay—*I* couldn't do nothing, and I didn't want to be hung if I could get away. So I never stopped running till I found the canoe; and when I got here I told Jim to hurry, or they'd catch me and hang me yet, and said I was afeard you and the duke wasn't alive, now, and I was awful sorry, and so was Jim, and was awful glad when we see you coming, you may ask Jim if I didn't."

Jim said it was so; and the king told him to shut up, and

said, "Oh, yes, it's *mighty* likely!" and shook me up again, and said he reckoned he'd drownd me. But the duke says:

"Leggo the boy, you old idiot![2] Would *you* a done any different? Did you inquire around for *him*, when you got loose? *I* don't remember it."

So the king let go of me, and begun to cuss that town and everybody in it. But the duke says:

"You better a blame sight give *yourself* a good cussing, for you're the one that's entitled to it most. You hain't done a thing, from the start, that had any sense in it, except coming out so cool and cheeky with that imaginary blue-arrow mark. That *was* bright—it was right down bully; and it was the thing that saved us. For if it hadn't been for that, they'd a jailed us till them Englishmen's baggage come—and then—the penitentiary, you bet! But that trick took 'em to the graveyard, and the gold done us a still bigger kindness; for if the excited fools hadn't let go all holts and made that rush to get a look, we'd a slept in our cravats to-night—cravats warranted to *wear*, too—longer than *we'd* need 'em."[3]

They was still a minute—thinking—then the king says, kind of absent-minded like:

"Mf! And we reckoned the *niggers* stole it!"

That made me squirm!

"Yes," says the duke, kinder slow, and deliberate, and sarcastic, "*We* did."

After about a half a minute, the king drawls out:

"Leastways—*I* did."

The duke says, the same way:

"On the contrary—*I* did."

The king kind of ruffles up, and says:

"Looky here, Bilgewater, what'r you referrin' to?"

The duke says, pretty brisk:

"When it comes to that, maybe you'll let me ask, what was *you* referring to?"

"Shucks!" says the king, very sarcastic; "but *I* don't know—maybe you was asleep, and didn't know what you was about."

The duke bristles right up, now, and says:

2. *Leggo the boy, you old idiot!* The duke is so mad that his mask drops, revealing his true origins as his pretentious actor's parlance gives way to a thick backwoods dialect.

3. *we'd a slept in our cravats to-night—cravats warranted to* wear, *too—longer than* we'd *need 'em.* The duke, employing traveling salesman's lingo, makes a rather grisly joke about their escape from a "necktie party"—from being lynched by the mob. Perhaps he speaks in such a roundabout way because it was bad luck to talk about getting hanged.

4. *to hook*. To steal cleverly.

THE DUKE WENT FOR HIM.

"Oh, let *up* on this cussed nonsense—do you take me for a blame' fool? Don't you reckon *I* know who hid that money in that coffin?"

"*Yes,* sir! I know you *do* know—because you done it yourself!"

"It's a lie!"—and the duke went for him. The king sings out:

"Take y'r hands off!—leggo my throat!—I take it all back!"

The duke says:

"Well, you just own up, first, that you *did* hide that money there, intending to give me the slip one of these days, and come back and dig it up, and have it all to yourself."

"Wait jest a minute, duke—answer me this one question, honest and fair; if you didn't put the money there, say it, and I'll b'lieve you, and take back everything I said."

"You old scoundrel, I didn't, and you know I didn't. There, now!"

"Well, then, I b'lieve you. But answer me only jest this one more—now *don't* git mad; didn't you have it in your *mind* to hook[4] the money and hide it?"

The duke never said nothing for a little bit; then he says:

"Well—I don't care if I *did,* I didn't *do* it, anyway. But you not only had it in mind to do it, but you *done* it."

"I wisht I may never die if I done it, duke, and that's honest. I won't say I warn't *goin'* to do it, because I *was;* but you—I mean somebody—got in ahead o' me."

"It's a lie! You done it, and you got to *say* you done it, or—"

The king begun to gurgle, and then he gasps out:

"'Nough!—*I own up!*"

I was very glad to hear him say that, it made me feel much more easier than what I was feeling before. So the duke took his hands off, and says:

"If you ever deny it again, I'll drown you. It's *well* for you to set there and blubber like a baby—it's fitten for you, after the way you've acted. I never see such an old ostrich for wanting to gobble everything[5]—and I a trusting you all the time, like you was my own father. You ought to been ashamed of yourself to stand by and hear it saddled onto a lot of poor niggers and you never say a word for 'em. It makes me feel ridiculous to think I was soft enough to *believe* that rubbage. Cuss you, I can see, now, why you was so anxious to make up the deffesit—you wanted to get what money I'd got out of the Nonesuch and one thing or another, and scoop it *all!*"[6]

The king says, timid, and still a snuffling:

"Why, duke, it was you that said make up the deffersit, it warn't me."

"Dry up! I don't want to hear no more *out* of you!" says the duke. "And *now* you see what you *got* by it. They've got all their own money back, and all of *ourn* but a shekel[7] or two, *besides.* G'long to bed—and don't you deffersit *me* no more deffersits, long 's *you* live!"

So the king sneaked into the wigwam, and took to his bottle for comfort; and before long the duke tackled *his* bottle; and so in about a half an hour they was as thick as thieves[8] again, and the tighter they got, the lovinger they got; and went off a snoring in each other's arms. They both got powerful mellow, but I noticed the king didn't get mellow enough to forget to remember to not deny about hiding the money-bag again. That made me feel easy and satisfied. Of course when they got to snoring, we had a long gabble,[9] and I told Jim everything.

5. *an old ostrich for wanting to gobble everything.* Supposedly ostriches will eat anything, even metal.

6. *and scoop it* all! And take it all. In the manuscript, the duke ends this outburst with a delicious epithet: "you unsatisfiable, tunnel-bellied old sewer!" (Ferguson, "Huck Finn Aborning," p. 180).

7. *a shekel.* An ancient Babylonian coin, which is metaphorically worthless.

8. *as thick as thieves.* An apt metaphor for these scoundrels, often used in Southwestern humor.

9. *a long gabble.* A rapid, continuous, and intimate conversation.

Chapter XXXI.

SPANISH MOSS.

We DASN'T stop again at any town, for days and days;[1] kept right along down the river. We was down south in the warm weather, now, and a mighty long ways from home. We begun to come to trees with Spanish moss[2] on them, hanging down from the limbs like long gray beards. It was the first I ever see it growing, and it made the woods look solemn and dismal. So now the frauds reckoned they was out of danger, and they begun to work the villages again.

First they done a lecture on temperance; but they didn't make enough for them both to get drunk on.[3] Then in another village they started a dancing school; but they didn't know no more how to dance than a kangaroo does; so the first prance they made, the general public jumped in and pranced them out of town. Another time they tried a go at yellocution;[4] but they didn't yellocute long till the audience got up and give them a solid good cussing and made them skip out. They tackled missionarying, and mesmerizering, and doctoring, and telling fortunes, and a little of everything; but they couldn't seem to have no luck. So at last they got just about dead broke, and laid around the raft, as she floated along, thinking, and thinking, and never say-

1. *for days and days.* Originally only "four or five days" (**MS**) in the manuscript.

2. *Spanish moss. Tillandsia usneoides*, also known as "longbeard" and native to the South; Frances Trollope wrote in *Domestic Manners of the Americans* (1832) that "it hangs gracefully from the boughs, converting the outline of all trees it hangs from into that of weeping willows" (p. 8). Although it grows on trees, it is not a parasite but an epiphyte; it takes no nourishment from the boughs from which it hangs. According to Blair and Fischer's note in the 1988 University of California edition, river guides of the period place the commencement of Spanish moss as "just below" Columbia, Chicot County, in the northeast corner of Arkansas, about thirty miles above the Louisiana border. But Twain wrote in Chapter 34 of *Life on the Mississippi* that Lake Providence, Louisiana, "is the first distinctly Southern-looking town you come to, downward-bound; lies level and low, shade-trees hung with venerable gray beards of Spanish moss."

3. *they done a lecture on temperance; but they didn't make enough for them both to get drunk on.* This paragraph is full of sarcastic puns as they drift past seven towns where the king and the duke "strike out."

4. *yellocution.* An onomatopoetic pun on elocution, the art of public speaking. Neither the king nor the duke said anything back in Chapter 19 about teaching elocution or dancing among their "lays," so they are trying anything that might help them "score" with the local rubes.

ing nothing, by the half a day at a time, and dreadful blue and desperate.

And at last they took a change, and begun to lay their heads together in the wigwam and talk low and confidential two or three hours at a time. Jim and me got uneasy. We didn't like the look of it. We judged they was studying up some kind of worse deviltry than ever. We turned it over and over, and at last we made up our minds they was going to break into somebody's house or store, or was going into the counterfeit-money business, or something. So then we was pretty scared, and made up an agreement that we wouldn't have nothing in the world to do with such actions, and if we ever got the least show we would give them the cold shake,[5] and clear out and leave them behind. Well, early one morning we hid the raft in a good safe place about two mile below a little bit of a shabby village, named Pikesville,[6] and the king he went ashore, and told us all to stay hid whilst he went up to town and smelt around to see if anybody had got any wind of the Royal Nonesuch there yet. ("House to rob, you *mean,*" says I to myself; "and when you get through robbing it you'll come back here and wonder what's become of me and Jim and the raft—and you'll have to take it out in wondering.") And he said if he warn't back by midday, the duke and me would know it was all right, and we was to come along.

So we staid where we was. The duke he fretted and sweated around, and was in a mighty sour way. He scolded us for everything, and we couldn't seem to do nothing right; he found fault with every little thing.[7] Something was a-brewing, sure. I was good and glad when midday come and no king; we could have a change, anyway—and maybe a chance for *the* change, on top of it. So me and the duke went up to the village, and hunted around there for the king, and by-and-by we found him in the back room of a little low doggery,[8] very tight, and a lot of loafers bullyragging him for sport, and he a cussing and threatening with all his might, and so tight he couldn't walk, and couldn't do nothing to them. The duke he begun to abuse him for an old

5. *give them the cold shake*. Give them the slip.

6. *Pikesville*. Another backwoods town in the tradition of James M. Field"s "Pokerville" and William Tappan Thompson's "Pineville." Blair and Fischer suggested in their notes to the 1988 University of California edition that Pikesville may be in the vicinity of Grand Lake Landing, Arkansas. But Sherwood Cummings suggested in "Mark Twain's Movable Farm and the Evasion" (*American Literature*, September 1991, p. 442) that Twain had in mind the now long-gone village of Point Coupee, Louisiana. See also note 21 below.

7. *he found fault with every little thing*. Twain originally expanded this passage in the manuscript: "and he cussed Jim for being a fool and keeping his blue paint and King Lear clothes on, and made him take them off and wash himself off; and yet it warn't no fault of Jim's, for nobody ever told him he might do it"; but when Twain crossed this out, he noted in the margin, "This is lugged—shove it back yonder to where they escape lynching and regain raft" (Ferguson, "Huck Finn Aborning," pp. 177–78). However, Twain forgot to make the change, so the novel never tells when or why Jim discards his "sick A-rab" costume. The deleted passage also indicates the duke's change of heart toward the runaway slave, which leads to betrayal in the next chapter.

8. *doggery*. Groggery, a rough drinking saloon.

fool, and the king begun to sass back; and the minute they was fairly at it, I lit out, and shook the reefs out of my hind legs,[9] and spun down the river road like a deer—for I see our chance; and I made up my mind that it would be a long day before they ever see me and Jim again. I got down there all out of breath but loaded up with joy, and sung out—

"Set her loose, Jim, we're all right, now!"

But there warn't no answer, and nobody come out of the wigwam. Jim was gone! I set up a shout—and then another—and then another one; and run this way and that in the woods, whooping and screeching; but it warn't no use—old Jim was gone. Then I set down and cried; I couldn't help it. But I couldn't set still long. Pretty soon I went out on the road, trying to think what I better do, and I run across a boy walking, and asked him if he'd seen a strange nigger, dressed so and so, and he says:

"Yes."

"Whereabouts?" says I.

"Down to Silas Phelps's place, two mile below here. He's a runaway nigger, and they've got him. Was you looking for him?"

"You bet I ain't! I run across him in the woods about an hour or two ago, and he said if I hollered he'd cut my livers out—and told me to lay down and stay where I was; and I done it. Been there ever since; afeard to come out."

"Well," he says, "you needn't be afeard no more, becuz they've got him. He run off f'm down South, som'ers."

"It's a good job they got him."

"Well, I *reckon!* There's two hunderd dollars reward on him. It's like picking up money out'n the road."

"Yes, it is—and *I* could a had it if I'd been big enough; I see him *first.* Who nailed him?"

"It was an old fellow—a stranger—and he sold out his chance in him for forty dollars, becuz he's got to go up the river and can't wait.[10] Think o' that, now! You bet *I'd* wait, if it was seven year."

"That's me, every time," says I. "But maybe his chance ain't worth no more than that, if he'll sell it so cheap. Maybe there's something ain't straight about it."

9. *shook the reefs out of my hind legs*. Loosened himself up to go running off; nautical slang.

10. *he sold out his chance in him for forty dollars, becuz he's got to go up the river and can't wait.* Twain was six years old in 1842 when his father had to go down the river to settle a long-standing debt owed him. Because the man did not have the cash, he paid the Judge with a slave named Charley; but to get the money to head back upstream, the Judge sold the man for ten barrels of tar worth only $40. Twain confessed in the brief memoir "Jane Lampton Clemens" (1890) that he thought his father was shockingly cool in his description of the impending transaction in a surviving letter, "poor Charley's approaching eternal exile from his home, and his mother, and his friends, and all things and creatures that make life dear and the heart to sing for joy, affecting him no more than if this humble comrade of his long pilgrimage had been an ox—and somebody else's ox. It makes a body homesick for Charley, even after fifty years" (*Huck Finn and Tom Sawyer Among the Indians*, 1989, p. 90). Just like Judge Clemens. Huck suffers the same agony for the sale of Jim for "forty dirty dollars" that Sam Clemens did for Charley. But Twain's distress may have been all in vain: Dahlia Armon and Walter Blair persuasively argued (pp. 277–78) that Charley may not have been a man but a horse; a horse might have fetched $40, but a slave was worth far more unless old or ill.

"WHO NAILED HIM?"

"But it *is,* though—straight as a string. I see the handbill myself. It tells all about him, to a dot—paints him like a picture, and tells the plantation he's frum, below New*leans.* No-sirree-*bob,* they ain't no trouble 'bout *that* speculation, you bet you. Say, gimme a chaw tobacker, won't ye?"

I didn't have none, so he left. I went to the raft, and set down in the wigwam to think. But I couldn't come to nothing. I thought till I wore my head sore, but I couldn't see no way out of the trouble. After all this long journey, and after all we'd done for them scoundrels, here was it all come to nothing, everything all busted up and ruined, because they could have the heart to serve Jim such a trick as that, and make him a slave again all his life, and amongst strangers, too, for forty dirty dollars.

Once I said to myself it would be a thousand times better for Jim to be a slave at home where his family was, as long as he'd *got* to be a slave, and so I'd better write a letter to Tom Sawyer and tell him to tell Miss Watson where he was. But I soon give up that notion, for two things: she'd be mad and disgusted at his rascality and ungratefulness for leaving her, and so she'd sell him straight down the river again; and if she didn't, everybody naturally despises an ungrateful nigger, and they'd make Jim feel it all the time, and so he'd feel ornery and disgraced. And then think of *me!* It would get all around, that Huck Finn helped a nigger to get his freedom; and if I was to ever see anybody from that town again, I'd be ready to get down and lick his boots for shame. That's just the way: a person does a low-down thing, and then he don't want to take no consequences of it. Thinks as long as he can hide it, it ain't no disgrace. That was my fix exactly. The more I studied about this, the more my conscience went to grinding me, and the more wicked and low-down and ornery I got to feeling. And at last, when it hit me all of a sudden that here was the plain hand of Providence slapping me in the face[11] and letting me know my wickedness was being watched all the time from up there in heaven, whilst I was stealing a poor old woman's nigger that hadn't ever done me no harm, and now was showing me there's One that's always on the lookout, and ain't agoing to allow no such miserable doings to go only just so fur and no further, I most dropped in my tracks I was so scared. Well, I tried the best I could to kinder soften it up somehow for myself, by saying I was brung up wicked, and so I warn't so much to blame; but something inside of me kept saying, "There was the Sunday school, you could a gone to it; and if you'd a done it they'd a learnt you, there, that people that acts as I'd been acting about that nigger goes to everlasting fire."[12]

It made me shiver. And I about made up my mind to pray; and see if I couldn't try to quit being the kind of a boy I was, and be better. So I kneeled down. But the words wouldn't come. Why wouldn't they? It warn't no use to try and hide it from Him. Nor from *me,* neither. I knowed very well why they wouldn't come. It was because my heart warn't right; it was because I warn't square; is was because I was playing double. I was letting *on* to give up sin, but away inside of me I was holding on to the biggest one of all. I was trying to make my mouth *say* I would do the right thing and the clean thing, and go and write to that nigger's owner and tell

11. *here was the plain hand of Providence slapping me in the face*. Huck's youthful arrogance that Heaven might be watching his every move is that of young Sam Clemens. He believed that all the horrible things that happened around him were there solely to teach *him* a lesson. "They were inventions of Providence to beguile me to a better life," he confessed in "Chapters from My Autobiography" (*North American Review*, May 3, 1907). "It sounds curiously innocent and conceited, now, but to me there was nothing strange about it; it was quite in accordance with the thoughtful and judicious ways of Providence as I understood them. . . . *Why* Providence should take such an anxious interest in such a property [as myself]—that idea never entered my head, and there was no one in that simple hamlet who would have dreamed of putting it there" (p. 6).

12. *everlasting fire*. It may be easy today to laugh at Huck Finn's literal interpretation of hellfire and damnation, but his honest fear should not be underestimated. It is no laughing matter to him. Whether he believes in the Widow Douglas and Miss Watson's vision of "the bad place" or just the superstitions he has picked up from pap, Jim, or the other slaves, Hell is a real place to the boy. "There is no reprieve, no appeal from hell," noted Chadwick-Joshua in *The Jim Dilemma* (1998); "once in, one is there forever, for eternity, and forever is a long time" (p. 114).

In spite of his upbringing, Twain himself did not believe in the hellfire-and-damnation vision of the next world. "If I am appointed to live again," he wrote of a then popular conception of Hell (in *What Is Man?*, 1973), "I feel sure it will be for some more sane and useful purpose than to flounder about for ages in a lake of fire and brimstone for having violated a confusion of ill-defined and contradictory rules said (but not evidenced) to be divine institution" (p. 57). Twain demanded a rational and just universe. Because he could not see how eternal punishment could serve any logical purpose, he refused to believe it might exist. "To chasten a man in order to perfect him might be reasonable enough," he continued; "to annihilate him when he shall have proved incapable of reaching perfection might be reasonable enough: but to roast him forever for a mere satisfaction of seeing him roast would not be reasonable—even the atrocious God imagined by the Jews would tire of the spectacle eventually." How-where he was; but deep down in me I knowed it was a lie—and He knowed it. You can't pray a lie—I found that out.

So I was full of trouble, full as I could be; and didn't know what to do. At last I had an idea; and I says, I'll go and write the letter—and *then* see if I can pray. Why, it was astonishing, the way I felt as light as a feather, right straight off, and my troubles all gone. So I got a piece of paper and a pencil, all glad and excited, and set down and wrote:

Miss Watson your runaway nigger Jim is down here two mile below Pikesville and Mr. Phelps has got him and he will give him up for the reward if you send.

HUCK FINN.

I felt good and all washed clean of sin for the first time I had ever felt so in my life, and I knowed I could pray now. But I didn't do it straight off, but laid the paper down and set there thinking—thinking how good it was all this happened so, and how near I come to being lost and going to hell. And went on thinking. And got to thinking over our trip down the river; and I see Jim before me, all the time, in the day, and in the night-time, sometimes moonlight, some-

THINKING.

ever, unlike his creator, Huck is a child of the society in which he was raised, superstitious and with a preoccupation with death; at this point in his education, he believes (and fears) only what he has been taught to be the truth.

13. *All right, then, I'll* go *to hell.* "Have you read *Huckleberry Finn?*" Robert Louis Stevenson asked J. A. Symonds in February 1885. "It contains many excellent things; above all, the whole story of a healthy boy's dealings with his conscience, incredibly well done" (*The Letters of Robert Louis Stevenson*, edited by Sidney Colvin, vol. 2, 1911, p. 268). Finally, in the famous crisis of conscience, Huck resolves the eternal battle between temperament and training; and if in following his instincts he defies society, then the public be damned. "We have arrived at a key point of the novel and, by an ironic reversal, of American fiction, a pivotal moment announcing the change of direction in the plot, a reversal as well as a recognition scene (like that in which Oedipus discovers his true identity) wherein a new definition of necessity is being formulated," argued Ralph Ellison in "Twentieth Century Fiction and the Black Mask of Humor" (*Confluence*, December 1953). "Huck has struggled with the problem poised by the clash between property rights and human rights, between what the community considered to be the proper attitude toward an escaped slave and his knowledge of Jim's humanity, gained through their adventures as fugitives together. He has made his decision on the side of humanity. In this passage Twain has stated the basic moral issue centering around Negroes and the white American's democratic ethics" (p. 9). Huck realizes that there is indeed a morality higher than that of social approval; abolitionists called it "higher law." It was this same duty to one's conscience which inspired Gandhi and Martin Luther King, Jr. If a law was unjust, then it was right to break it; one had the right to break it. Huck has grown greatly since he fled pap's shanty for Jackson's Island; and now that he has condemned himself, there is no turning back.

Huck's epiphany is the climax of the novel; and as is generally acknowledged, now begins the slow decline of the narrative. There are indeed certain lapses in Huck's character during subsequent events of the story; but never does the boy regret his having aided the runaway in his flight from slavery. He never apologizes and never does he weaken in his determination to set his friend free once and for all. Leo Marx pointed out in his notes to the 1967 Bobbs-Merrill edition that in pushing Huck the "wrong way" in his tug of war between conscience and temptation, Twain inverts a standard method of Christian rhetoric that goes back as far as the fourth century, to St. Augus-

times storms, and we a floating along, talking, and singing, and laughing. But somehow I couldn't seem to strike no places to harden me against him, but only the other kind. I'd see him standing my watch on top of his'n, stead of calling me, so I could go on sleeping; and see him how glad he was when I come back out of the fog; and when I come to him again in the swamp, up there where the feud was; and such-like times; and would always call me honey, and pet me, and do everything he could think of for me, and how good he always was; and at last I struck the time I saved him by telling the men we had small-pox aboard, and he was so grateful, and said I was the best friend old Jim ever had in the world, and the *only* one he's got now; and then I happened to look around, and see that paper.

It was a close place. I took it up, and held it in my hand. I was a trembling, because I'd got to decide, forever, betwixt two things, and I knowed it. I studied a minute, sort of holding my breath, and then says to myself:

"All right, then, I'll *go* to hell"[13]—and tore it up.

It was awful thoughts, and awful words, but they was said. And I let them stay said; and never thought no more about reforming. I shoved the whole thing out of my head; and said I would take up wickedness again, which was in my line, being brung up to it,[14] and the other warn't. And for a starter, I would go to work and steal Jim out of slavery again; and if I could think up anything worse, I would do that, too;[15] because as long as I was in, and in for good, I might as well go the whole hog.

Then I set to thinking over how to get at it, and turned over considerable many ways in my mind; and at last fixed up a plan that suited me. So then I took the bearings of a woody island that was down the river a piece, and as soon as it was fairly dark I crept out with my raft and went for it, and hid it there, and then turned in. I slept the night through, and got up before it was light, and had my breakfast, and put on my store clothes,[16] and tied up some others and one thing or another in a bundle, and took the canoe and cleared for shore. I landed below where I judged was Phelps's place, and hid my bundle in the woods, and then filled up the canoe with water, and loaded rocks into her and sunk her where I could find her again when I wanted her, about a quarter of a mile below a little steam sawmill that was on the bank.

Then I struck up the road, and when I passed the mill I see a sign on it, "Phelps's Sawmill," and when I come to the farm-houses, two or three hundred yards further along, I kept my eyes peeled, but didn't see nobody around, though it was good daylight, now. But I didn't mind, because I didn't want to see nobody just yet—I only wanted to get the lay of the land. According to my plan, I was going to turn up there from the village, not from below. So I just took a look, and shoved along, straight for town. Well, the very first man I see, when I got there, was the duke. He was sticking up a bill for the Royal Nonesuch—three-night performance—like that other time. *They* had the cheek, them frauds! I was right on him, before I could shirk. He looked astonished, and says:

"Hel-*lo!* Where'd *you* come from?" Then he says, kind of glad and eager, "Where's the raft?—got her in a good place?"

I says:

"Why, that's just what I was agoing to ask your grace."

Then he didn't look so joyful—and says:

"What was your idea for asking *me?*" he says.

"Well," I says, "when I see the king in that doggery yesterday, I says to myself, we can't get him home for hours, till he's soberer; so I went a loafing around town to put in the time, and wait. A man up and offered me ten cents to help him pull a skiff over the river and back to fetch a sheep, and so I went along; but when we was dragging him to the boat, and the man left me aholt of the rope and went behind him to shove him along, he was too strong for me, and jerked loose and run, and we after him. We didn't have no dog, and so we had to chase him all over the country till we tired him out. We never got him till dark, then we fetched him over, and I started down for the raft. When I got there and see it was gone, I says to myself, 'they've got into trouble and had to leave; and they've took my nigger, which is the only nig-

tine's *Confessions*. Make no mistake that Huck is breaking the law when he swears allegiance to Jim. He believes that he is breaking both man's and God's law. In vowing to help a slave escape, Huck denies his people, his country, and his God.

14. *I would take up wickedness again, which was in my line, being brung up to it.* Blair in *Mark Twain and Huck Finn* (1960) explored how Twain made extensive revisions in this passage, by enlarging it by almost 150 words and making it more serious and earnest. The earlier draft contained the facetious comment "What I had been getting ready for, and longing for and pining for, always, day and night and Sundays, was a career of crime. And just that thing was the thing I was a-starting in on, now, for good and all" (p. 353). So originally Twain wanted this section to return to the tone of the opening of the novel, to the discussion of Tom Sawyer's Gang; instead the final version became the classic argument of civil disobedience against conventional morality in nineteenth-century American fiction.

15. *if I could think up anything worse, I would do that, too.* This struggle within Huckleberry Finn inspired Twain's speech "Theoretical and Practical Morals." "As by the fires of experience, so by the commission of crime," he slyly argued here, "you learn real morals. Commit all the crimes, familiarize yourself with all sins, take them in rotation (there are only two or three thousand of them), stick to it, commit two or three every day, and by-and-by you will be proof against them. When you are through you will be proof against all sins and morally perfect" (*Mark Twain's Speeches*, 1910, p. 132). Although he never did anything so offensive as "nigger-stealing" back in Hannibal, Twain admitted having once pinched a watermelon; but the boy was justly punished—the watermelon was green.

16. *my store clothes.* The manuscript originally said "some old rough clothes" (see Ferguson, "Huck Finn Aborning," p. 178), but these would not have been convincing for Huck's mistaken identity of the subsequent chapter.

ger I've got in the world, and now I'm in a strange country, and ain't got no property no more, nor nothing, and no way to make my living;' so I set down and cried. I slept in the woods all night. But what *did* become of the raft then?—and Jim, poor Jim!"

"Blamed if *I* know—that is, what's become of the raft. That old fool had made a trade and got forty dollars, and when we found him in the doggery the loafers had matched half dollars[17] with him and got every cent but what he'd spent for whisky; and when I got him home late last night and found the raft gone, we said, 'That little rascal has stole our raft and shook us, and run off down the river.' "

"I wouldn't shake my *nigger,* would I?—the only nigger I had in the world, and the only property."

"We never thought of that. Fact is, I reckon we'd come to consider him *our* nigger; yes, we did consider him so—goodness knows we had trouble enough for him. So when we see the raft was gone, and we flat broke, there warn't anything for it but to try the Royal Nonesuch another shake. And I've pegged along[18] ever since, dry as a powder-horn.[19] Where's that ten cents? Give it here."

I had considerable money, so I give him ten cents, but begged him to spend it for something to eat, and give me some, because it was all the money I had, and I hadn't had nothing to eat since yesterday. He never said nothing. The next minute he whirls on me and says:

"Do you reckon that nigger would blow on us? We'd skin him if he done that!"

"How can he blow? Hain't he run off?"

"No! That old fool sold him, and never divided with me, and the money's gone."

"*Sold* him?" I says, and begun to cry; "why, he was *my* nigger, and that was my money. Where is he?—I want my nigger."

"Well, you can't *get* your nigger, that's all—so dry up your blubbering. Looky here—do you think *you'd* venture to blow on us? Blamed if I think I'd trust you. Why, if you *was* to blow on us—"

He stopped, but I never see the duke look so ugly out of his eyes before. I went on a-whimpering, and says:

17. *matched half dollars.* A popular gambling game in which the loser is determined by tossing coins.

18. *pegged along.* Worked on persistently.

19. *dry as a powder-horn.* He has not had a drop of liquor all this time; gunpowder is kept in powderhorns to protect it from moisture.

HE GAVE HIM TEN CENTS.

"I don't want to blow on nobody; and I ain't got no time to blow, nohow. I got to turn out and find my nigger."

He looked kinder bothered,[20] and stood there with his bills fluttering on his arm, thinking, and wrinkling up his forehead. At last he says:

"I'll tell you something. We got to be here three days. If you'll promise you won't blow, and won't let the nigger blow, I'll tell you where to find him."

So I promised, and he says:

"A farmer by the name of Silas Ph—" and then he stopped. You see he started to tell me the truth; but when he stopped, that way, and begun to study and think again, I reckoned he was changing his mind. And so he was. He wouldn't trust me; he wanted to make sure of having me out of the way the whole three days. So pretty soon he says: "The man that bought him is named Abram Foster—Abram G. Foster—and he lives forty miles back here in the country, on the road to Lafayette."[21]

"All right," I says, "I can walk it in three days. And I'll start this very afternoon."

20. *He looked kinder bothered.* And well he might, for he and the king could be arrested for "nigger stealing." But, of course, Huck does not dare "blow" on them for fear of exposing Jim as a runaway.

21. *Lafayette.* Blair and Fischer in the 1988 University of California edition (p. 418) identified this as Lafayette County, Arkansas, 135 miles away in the southwestern part of the state. But Sherwood Cummings pointed out in "Mark Twain's Movable Farm and the Evasion" (*American Literature*, September 1991, pp. 442–45) that there is no road there. He suggested instead that Twain was thinking of the highway from Point Coupee and Lafayette Parish, Louisiana.

"No you won't, you'll start *now;* and don't you lose any time about it, neither, nor do any gabbling by the way. Just keep a tight tongue in your head and move right along, and then you won't get into trouble with *us,* d'ye hear?"

That was the order I wanted, and that was the one I played for. I wanted to be left free to work my plans.

"So clear out," he says; "and you can tell Mr. Foster whatever you want to. Maybe you can get him to believe that Jim *is* your nigger—some idiots don't require documents—leastways I've heard there's such down South here.[22] And when you tell him the handbill and the reward's bogus, maybe he'll believe you when you explain to him what the idea was for getting 'em out. Go 'long, now, and tell him anything you want to; but mind you don't work your jaw any *between* here and there."

So I left, and struck for the back country.[23] I didn't look around, but I kinder felt like he was watching me. But I knowed I could tire him out at that. I went straight out in the country as much as a mile, before I stopped; then I doubled back through the woods towards Phelps's. I reckoned I better start in on my plan straight off, without fooling around, because I wanted to stop Jim's mouth till these fellows could get away. I didn't want no trouble with their kind. I'd seen all I wanted to of them, and wanted to get entirely shut of them.

STRIKING FOR THE BACK COUNTRY.

22. *some idiots don't require documents . . . down South here*. Apparently because any "person of color" who traveled through Arkansas at this time was naturally considered a slave; after March 1843, no freedman could emigrate to the state.

23. *the back country*. The interior and sparsely populated district.

Chapter XXXII

STILL AND SUNDAY-LIKE.

When I got there it was all still and Sunday-like, and hot and sunshiny—the hands was gone to the fields; and there was them kind of faint dronings of bugs and flies in the air that makes it seem so lonesome and like everybody's dead and gone; and if a breeze fans along and quivers the leaves, it makes you feel mournful, because you feel like it's spirits whispering—spirits that's been dead ever so many years—and you always think they're talking about *you.* As a general thing it makes a body wish *he* was dead, too, and done with it all.[1]

Phelps's was one of these little one-horse cotton plantations; and they all look alike.[2] A rail fence round a two-acre yard; a stile, made out of logs sawed off and up-ended, in steps, like barrels of a different length, to climb over the fence with, and for the women to stand on when they are going to jump onto a horse; some sickly grass-patches in the big yard, but mostly it was bare and smooth, like an old hat with the nap rubbed off; big double log house for the white folks—hewed logs, with the chinks stopped up with mud or mortar, and these mud-stripes been whitewashed some time or another; round-log kitchen, with a big broad, open but roofed passage joining it to the house; log smoke-house back of the kitchen; three little log nigger-cabins in a

1. *As a general thing it makes a body wish* he *was dead, too, and done with it all.* Here Huck suffers the same melancholy he described at the opening of the novel. "But it is right," argued T. S. Eliot in his introduction to the 1950 Cresset/Chanticleer Press edition, "that the mood of the end of the book should bring us back to that of the beginning." Although the boy was as yet not aware of it, he has in a sense returned to the society that he fled so long ago and so many miles up the river. He suffers the same sentiments in the opening of "Tom Sawyer, Detective."

2. *they all look alike.* This one looks just like the Grangerford house in Chapter 17, because both were based on Sam Clemens's Uncle John A. Quarles's place, four miles from Florida, Monroe County, Missouri. "It was a heavenly place for a boy," Twain recalled in "Chapters from My Autobiography" (*North American Review*, March 1, 1907). "The farmhouse stood in the middle of a very large yard, and the yard was fenced on three sides with rails and on the rear with high palings; against these stood the smokehouse; beyond the palings was the orchard; beyond the orchard were the negro quarter and the tobacco fields. The front yard was entered over a stile, made of sawed-off logs of graduated heights; I do not remember any gate. . . . Down a piece, abreast the house, stood a little log cabin against the rail fence; and there the woody hill fell sharply away, past the barns, the corn-crib, the stables and the tobacco-curing house, to a limpid brook" (pp. 452–53).

He spent his summers there until he was twelve years old, and these were some of the happiest times of his life. "We children had a mighty easy life," his cousin Tabitha "Puss" Quarles Greening recalled in the Palmyra (Mo.) *Spectator* (August 22, 1917). "You see the negroes did the work and we roamed the hills gathering flowers, picking nuts, tapping the trees for sugar and at night gathered around the fire place and heard the darkies tell their ghost stories. Sam just repeated those tales Uncle Dan'l and Uncle Ned told and the folks said he was smart." Twain admitted in "Chapters from My Autobiography" that his uncle's "farm has come in handy to me in literature, once or twice. In *Huck Finn* and 'Tom Sawyer, Detective,' I moved it down to Arkansas. It was all of six hundred miles, but it was no trouble, it was not a very large farm; five hundred acres, perhaps, but I could have done it if it had been twice as large" (pp. 451–52). But the resemblance ended with the farm: Twain added that he never consciously used his uncle or aunt in any of his books. Twain also mentioned the

"They peeped out from behind her."
Illustration by E. W. Kemble,
"Autograph Edition" of *The Collected Works of Mark Twain*, 1899.
Private collection.

row t'other side the smoke-house;[3] one little hut all by itself away down against the back fence; and some outbuildings down a piece the other side; ash-hopper,[4] and big kettle to bile soap in, by the little hut; bench by the kitchen door, with bucket of water and a gourd; hound asleep there, in the sun; more hounds asleep, round about; about three shade-trees away off in a corner; some currant bushes and gooseberry bushes in one place by the fence; outside of the fence a garden and a watermelon patch; then the cotton fields begins; and after the fields, the woods.

I went around and clumb over the back stile by the ash-hopper, and started for the kitchen. When I got a little ways, I heard the dim hum of a spinning-wheel wailing along up and sinking along down again; and then I knowed for certain I wished I was dead—for that *is* the lonesomest sound in the whole world.[5]

I went right along, not fixing up any particular plan, but just trusting to Providence to put the right words in my mouth when the time come; for I'd noticed that Providence always did put the right words in my mouth, if I left it alone.

When I got half-way, first one hound and then another got up and went for me, and of course I stopped and faced them, and kept still. And such another pow-wow as they made! In a quarter of a minute I was a kind of a hub of a wheel, as you may say—spokes made out of dogs[6]—circle of fifteen of them packed together around me, with their necks and noses stretched up towards me, a barking and howling; and more a coming; you could see them sailing over fences and around corners from everywheres.

A nigger woman come tearing out of the kitchen with a rolling-pin in her hand, singing out, "Begone! *you* Tige! you Spot! begone, sah!" and she fetched first one and then another of them a clip and sent him howling, and then the rest followed; and the next second, half of them come back, wagging their tails around me and making friends with me. There ain't no harm in a hound, nohow.[7]

And behind the woman comes a little nigger girl and two little nigger boys, without anything on but tow-linen shirts,[8] and they hung onto their mother's gown, and peeped out from behind her at me, bashful, the way they always do. And here comes the white woman running from the house, about forty-five or fifty year old, bareheaded, and her spinning-stick in her hand; and behind her comes her little white children,[9] acting the same way the little niggers was doing. She was smiling all over so she could hardly stand—and says:

"It's *you,* at last!—*ain't* it?"

I out with a "Yes'm," before I thought.

She grabbed me and hugged me tight; and then gripped me by both hands and shook and shook; and the tears come in her eyes, and run down over; and she couldn't seem to hug and shake enough, and kept saying, "You don't look as much like your mother as I reckoned you would, but law sakes,[10] I don't care for that, I'm *so* glad to see you! Dear, dear, it does seem like I could eat you up! Children, it's your cousin Tom!—tell him howdy."

SHE HUGGED HIM TIGHT.

But they ducked their heads, and put their fingers in their mouths, and hid behind her. So she run on:

"Lize, hurry up and get him a hot breakfast, right away—or did you get your breakfast on the boat?"

I said I had got it on the boat. So then she started for the

Phelps farm in the opening of the unfinished *Huck Finn and Tom Sawyer Among the Indians* (1989): "Me and Tom Sawyer and the nigger Jim . . . was away down in Arkansaw at Tom's aunt Sally's and uncle Silas'" (p. 33). See also Chapter 42, note 14.

3. *smoke-house.* As this was long before refrigeration, most Southern plantations had small huts where fish or meat was smoked for preservation.

4. *ash-hopper.* A lye cask, resembling a hopper in a mill and containing ashes, with which people made soap.

5. *the dim hum of a spinning-wheel wailing along up and sinking along down again . . . that* is *the lonesomest sound in the whole world.* Here Twain recalled the spinning wheel in the family room of his uncle's farmhouse, "a wheel whose rising and falling wail, heard from a distance, was the mournfulest of all sounds to me, and made me homesick and low-spirited, and filled my atmosphere with the wandering spirits of the dead" ("My Autobiography," *North American Review*, March 1, 1907, p. 455). The year he published *Huckleberry Finn* in America, Twain used almost the exact wording when he described the Mason farm in "The Private History of a Campaign That Failed" (*Century Magazine*, December 1885): "there was no sound but the plaintive wailing of the spinning-wheel, forever moaning out from some distant room,—the most lonesome sound in nature, a sound steeped and sodden with homesickness and the emptiness of life" (p. 201).

6. *dogs.* Twain also fondly recalled his uncle's farm for all the dogs he had for hunting. "A toot on a tin horn brought twice as many dogs as were needed," he mentioned in "Chapters from My Autobiography" (*North American Review*, March 1, 1907), "and in their happiness they raced and scampered about, and knocked small people down, and made no end of unnecessary noise. At the word, they vanished away toward the woods, and we drifted silently after them in the melancholy gloom" (pp. 462–63).

7. *There ain't no harm in a hound, nohow.* "There ain't any dog that's got a lovelier disposition than a bloodhound," Huck admits in Chapter 9 of "Tom Sawyer, Detective." But at

one time people thought them to be a savage breed, apparently because of nineteenth-century posters for touring companies of *Uncle Tom's Cabin*, advertising "real blood-hounds" tearing at Liza's flesh as she crossed the ice to freedom. Actually, these dogs are not considered vicious and do not attack their quarry.

8. *tow-linen shirts*. The general costume of little slave children, usually made by their mothers. Boys who wore them were known as "shirttails boys." According to Missouri slave Louis Hill, a tow-linen shirt was no more than "a straight slip like a gown and hit fastened round the neck. . . . Tah dis off an we was naked" (see Harris and Van Clief-Stefanon, *Adventures of Huckleberry Finn*, New Riverside Editions edition, p. 24). Frederick Douglass acknowledged in Chapter 2 of his *Narrative* (1841), "The children unable to work in the field had neither shoes, stockings, jackets, nor trousers, given to them; their clothing consisted of two coarse linen shirts per year. When these failed them, they went naked until the next allowance-day. Children from seven to ten years old, of both sexes, almost naked, might be seen at all seasons of the year." He admitted further in Chapter 5, "In hottest summer and coldest winter, I was kept almost naked—no shoes, no stockings, no jacket, no trousers, nothing on but a coarse tow linen shirt, reaching only to my knees." Twain noticed, during his tour of the Holy Land, in Chapter 47 of *The Innocents Abroad*, that the Arab children had "nothing on but a long coarse shirt like the 'tow-linen' shirts which used to form the only summer garment of little negro boys on Southern plantations."

9. *her little white children*. The manuscript introduced two of these children, named Mat and Phil and both about Huck's age; Twain dropped them to avoid further complicating the complicated plot of this sequence at the Phelps farm. "But," Ferguson explained in "Huck Finn Aborning," "he forgot to revise downward the ages of Silas and Sally (at first Ruth) Phelps, who therefore appear in the book somewhat elderly for the parents of so young a family" (p. 173). Kemble apparently followed the manuscript when he drew his picture. But no matter: Twain introduces another Phelps girl, eighteen-year-old Benny, as a central character in "Tom Sawyer, Detective."

10. *law sakes*. A mild version of "Lord's sake."

house, leading me by the hand, and the children tagging after. When we got there, she set me down in a split-bottomed chair, and set herself down on a little low stool in front of me, holding both of my hands, and says:[11]

"Now I can have a *good* look at you; and laws-a-me,[12] I've been hungry for it a many and a many a time, all these long years, and it's come at last! We been expecting you a couple of days and more. What's kep' you?—boat get aground?"

"Yes'm—she——"

"Don't say yes'm—say Aunt Sally. Where'd she get aground?"

I didn't rightly know what to say, because I didn't know whether the boat would be coming up the river or down. But I go a good deal on instinct; and my instinct said she would be coming up—from down towards Orleans. That didn't help me much, though; for I didn't know the names of bars[13] down that way. I see I'd got to invent a bar, or forget the name of the one we got aground on—or— Now I struck an idea, and fetched it out:

"It warn't the grounding—that didn't keep us back but a little. We blowed out a cylinder-head."

"Good gracious! anybody hurt?"

"No'm. Killed a nigger."

"Well, it's lucky; because sometimes people do get hurt.[14] Two years ago last Christmas, your uncle Silas was coming up from Newrleans on the old *Lally Rook*,[15] and she blowed out a cylinder-head and crippled a man.[16] And I think he died afterwards. He was a Baptist. Your uncle Silas knowed a family in Baton Rouge that knowed his people very well. Yes, I remember, now he *did* die. Mortification set in, and they had to amputate him. But it didn't save him. Yes, it was mortification—that was it. He turned blue all over, and died in the hope of a glorious resurrection. They say he was a sight to look at. Your uncle's been up to the town every day to fetch you. And he's gone again, not more'n an hour ago; he'll be back any minute, now. You must a met him on the road, didn't you?—oldish man, with a——"

"No, I didn't see nobody, Aunt Sally. The boat landed just

at daylight, and I left my baggage on the wharf-boat[17] and went looking around the town and out a piece in the country, to put in the time and not get here too soon; and so I come down the back way."

"Who'd you give the baggage to?"

"Nobody."

"Why, child, it'll be stole!"

"Not where *I* hid it I reckon it won't," I says.

"How'd you get your breakfast so early on the boat?"

It was kinder thin ice, but I says:

"The captain see me standing around, and told me I better have something to eat before I went ashore; so he took me in the texas to the officers' lunch,[18] and give me all I wanted."

I was getting so uneasy I couldn't listen good. I had my mind on the children all the time; I wanted to get them out to one side, and pump them a little, and find out who I was. But I couldn't get no show, Mrs. Phelps kept it up and run on so. Pretty soon she made the cold chills streak all down my back, because she says:

"But here we're a running on this way, and you hain't told me a word about Sis, nor any of them. Now I'll rest my works a little, and you start up yourn; just tell me *everything*—tell me all about 'm all—every one of 'm; and how they are, and what they're doing, and what they told you to tell me; and every last thing you can think of."

Well, I see I was up a stump—and up it good. Providence had stood by me this fur, all right, but I was hard and tight aground, now. I see it warn't a bit of use to try to go ahead—I'd *got* to throw up my hand.[19] So I says to myself, here's another place where I got to resk the truth. I opened my mouth to begin; but she grabbed me and hustled me in behind the bed, and says:

"Here he comes! stick your head down lower—there, that'll do; you can't be seen, now. Don't you let on you're here. I'll play a joke on him. Children, don't you say a word."

I see I was in a fix, now. But it warn't no use to worry; there warn't nothing to do but just hold still, and try and be

11. *she set me down . . . and says.* Aunt Sally's grilling of Huck has much in common with the embarrassing interview between Twain and a woman in Europe (mentioned in Chapter 11, note 9). Huck goes through the same discomfort Twain himself did ("It appeared to me that the ice was getting pretty thin here. . . . I sat still and let the cold sweat run down") as he is plied with questions that he has no idea how to answer.

12. *laws-a-me.* A mild version of "Lord help me."

13. *the names of bars.* Sandbars are dangerous deposits of dirt, gravel, and other earth which form shallow places or islands in the river; therefore steamboat pilots named them (often only with numbers) to help in the navigation around them.

14. *Well, it's lucky; because sometimes people do get hurt.* Aunt Sally's callous remark is perhaps Twain's most bitter comment on how good Christian men and women considered slaves to be less than human and thus undeserving of the compassion due any other people. Frederick Douglass revealed in Chapter 4 of his *Narrative* (1845) that "killing a slave, or any colored person . . . is not treated as a crime, either by the courts or the community. . . . It was a common saying, even among little white boys, that it was worth a half-cent to kill a 'nigger,' and a half-cent to bury one." Jane Clemens shared Aunt Sally's attitude. "Yet, kind-hearted and compassionate as she was," Twain recalled in the brief memoir "Jane Lampton Clemens" of 1890, "she was not conscious that slavery was a bald, grotesque, and unwarrantable usurpation. She had never heard it assailed in any pulpit but had heard it defended and sanctified in a thousand; her ears were familiar with Bible texts that approved it but if there were any that disapproved it they had not been quoted by her pastors; as far as her experience went, the wise and the good and the holy were unanimous in the conviction that slavery was right, righteous, sacred, the peculiar pet of the Deity, and a condition which the slave himself ought to be daily and nightly thankful for. Manifestly, training and association can accomplish strange miracles" (*Huck Finn and Tom Sawyer Among the Indians*, 1989, pp. 87–88).

Sam Clemens was only a boy when he observed this indifference firsthand in Hannibal. "When I was ten," he recalled, "I saw a man ready to stand from under when the lightning struck.

I had just one little glimpse of the old gentleman when he come in,[20] then the bed hid him. Mrs. Phelps she jumps for him and says:

"Has he come?"

"No," says her husband.

"Good-*ness* gracious!" she says, "what in the world *can* have become of him?"

"I can't imagine," says the old gentleman; "and I must say, it makes me dreadful uneasy."

"Uneasy!" she says, "I'm ready to go distracted! He *must* a come; and you've missed him along the road. I *know* it's so—something *tells* me so."

"Why Sally, I *couldn't* miss him along the road—*you* know that."

"But oh, dear, dear, what *will* Sis say! He must a come! You must a missed him. He—"

"Oh, don't distress me any more'n I'm already distressed. I don't know what in the world to make of it. I'm at my wit's end, and I don't mind acknowledging 't I'm right down scared. But there's no hope that he's come; for he *couldn't* come and me miss him. Sally, it's terrible—just terrible—something's happened to the boat, sure!"

"Why, Silas! Look yonder!—up the road!—ain't that somebody coming?"

He sprung to the window at the head of the bed, and that give Mrs. Phelps the chance she wanted. She stooped down quick, at the foot of the bed, and give me a pull, and out I come; and when he turned back from the window, there she stood, a-beaming and a-smiling like a house afire, and I standing pretty meek and sweaty alongside. The old gentleman stared, and says:

"Why, who's that?"

"Who do you reckon 't is?"[21]

"I haint no idea. Who *is* it?"

"It's *Tom Sawyer!*"

By jings, I most slumped though the floor. But there warn't no time to swap knives;[22] the old man grabbed me

fling a lump of iron ore at his slaveman in anger, for merely doing something awkwardly, as if that were a crime. It bounded from his skull and the man fell and never spoke again. He was dead in an hour. I knew the man had a right to kill his slave if he wanted to, and yet it seemed a pitiful thing, and somehow wrong. . . . Nobody in the village approved of that murder, but of course no one said much about it" (*Mark Twain's Notebook*, 1935, p. 271). The actual killing was shocking enough, but it especially distressed him that "everybody seemed indifferent about it—as regarded the slave—though considerable sympathy was felt for the slave's owner, who had been bereft of valuable property by a worthless person who was not able to pay for it" ("Jane Lampton Clemens," p. 89). This base disregard for human life hardly ceased with the Emancipation Proclamation. In an unsigned editorial titled "Only a Nigger" (Buffalo *Express*, August 26, 1869), Twain angrily responded to the recent lynching of an innocent man in Memphis: "Ah, well! Too bad, to be sure! A little blunder in the administration of justice by Southern mob-law; but nothing to speak of. Only 'a nigger' killed by mistake—that is all. Of course, every high-toned gentleman whose chivalric impulses were so unfortunately misled in this affair . . . is as sorry about it as a high-toned gentleman can be expected to be sorry about the unlucky fate of 'a nigger.' But mistakes will happen, even in the conduct of the best regulated and most high-toned mobs, and surely there is no good reason why Southern gentlemen should worry themselves with useless regrets, so long as only an innocent 'nigger' is hanged, or roasted or knotted to death, now and then."

But other people considered the death of a slave an economic catastrophe. An ironic reversal of Aunt Sally's response to the shipboard accident was recorded by John Habermehl in "Human Life Is Cheap" in his *Life on the Western Rivers* (1901): "Right here all of a sudden we hear an 'Oh,' and the next thing a splash; 'a man overboard, a man overboard.' The news of the accident soon reaches the ears of the owners of the boat and causes a palpitation of the hearts, until the anxious inquiry, 'Was it a nigger, a nigger?' is answered by 'No, he was white, one of the Dutch roustabouts tumbled in with a load on his back.' The assurance that it was a Dutchman and no nigger to pay for stopped the fluttering of the heart, leaving it as calm as a

"WHO DO YOU RECKON 'T IS?"

by the hand and shook, and kept on shaking; and all the time, how the woman did dance around and laugh and cry; and then how they both did fire off questions about Sid, and Mary, and the rest of the tribe.

But if they was joyful, it warn't nothing to what I was; for it was like being born again,[23] I was so glad to find out who I was. Well, they froze to me for two hours; and at last when my chin was so tired it couldn't hardly go, any more, I had told them more about my family—I mean the Sawyer family—than ever happened to any six Sawyer families. And I explained all about how we blowed out a cylinder-head at the mouth of White River[24] and it took us three days to fix it. Which was all right, and worked first rate; because *they* didn't know but what it would take three days to fix it. If I'd a called it a bolt-head it would a done just as well.

Now I was feeling pretty comfortable all down one side, and pretty uncomfortable all up the other. Being Tom Sawyer was easy and comfortable; and it stayed easy and comfortable till by-and-by I hear a steamboat coughing along down the river—then I says to myself, spose Tom Sawyer come down on that boat?—and spose he steps in

summer morning, with a deep sigh, 'Poor fellow!'" (p. 88).

This conversation between Huck and Aunt Sally deftly raises questions of the eternal conflict between property rights and human rights. "The irony here is surely plain to any literate reader," noted Charles H. Nichols in " 'A True Book with Some Stretchers': *Huck Finn* Today" (*Mark Twain Journal*, Fall 1984, p. 15). And yet it remains one of the most controversial passages in the entire novel. John H. Wallace mentioned it in "The Case Against *Huck Finn*" as proof that "*Huckleberry Finn* even suggests that blacks are not human beings" (Leonard, Tenney, and Davis, *Satire or Evasion?*, 1992, p. 21). Perhaps that would be true if one were meant to take the observation literally, but not everyone agrees. "There are many fine passages in *Huckleberry Finn*," argued E. Burleson Stevenson in "Mark Twain's Attitude Toward the Negro" (*Quarterly Review of Higher Education Among Negroes*, October 1945), "but the profoundest touch in all Mark Twain's writing on the race question is found in the lines just quoted. He seems to brood over the small value that is placed on the American Negro. He gives America something to think about" (p. 344). In *The Jim Dilemma* (1998), Chadwick-Joshua called Huck's remark "a visionary joke, a larger irony than any that has gone before in this comedy" (p. 117). It must be read in context: This boy has come to the woman's home specifically to steal a slave from her and her husband. "Huck has never met Aunt Sally prior to this scene," explained David L. Smith in "Huck, Jim, and American Racial Discourse" (*Mark Twain Journal*, Fall 1984), "and in spinning a lie which this stranger will find unobjectionable, he correctly assumes that the common notion of Negro subhumanity will be appropriate. Huck's off-hand remark is intended to exploit Aunt Sally's attitudes, not to express Huck's own. A nigger, Aunt Sally confirms, is not a person. Yet this exchange is hilarious, precisely because we know that Huck is playing upon her glib and conventional bigotry. We know that Huck's relationship to Jim has already invalidated for him such obtuse racial notions" (p. 5). To conceal his identity, Huck must tell this woman what he *thinks* she would like to hear. He cannot dare give her any suspicions that he is there to steal a slave.

15. *the old* Lally Rook. According to William Lytle's *Merchant Steam Vessels of the United*

States, 1807–1868 (1952), a side-wheeler named *Lallah Rookh* traveled from its home port of Mobile, Alabama, from 1838 until it was "abandoned" in 1847. It was named for the title heroine (literally "Lilly Cheek") of Thomas Moore's 1817 sentimental Near Eastern epic in imitation of Sir Walter Scott's medieval narrative poems.

16. *she blowed out a cylinder-head and crippled a man.* "Their engines are generally constructed on the high-pressure principle," Thomas Hamilton described the large New Orleans boats in *Men and Manners in America* (1833), "and one or two generally blow up every season, sending a score or two of parboiled passengers to an inconvenient altitude in the atmosphere" (vol. 2, p. 181). Twain recalled in Chapter 20 of *Life on the Mississippi* how his beloved younger brother Henry Clemens (the model for "Sid Sawyer") was severely injured when the *Pennsylvania*, the steamboat he was working on as a "mud clerk," exploded near Memphis in June 1858. Twain was there when his brother died.

17. *the wharf-boat.* "On the Western rivers," explained Bartlett in his *Dictionary of Americanisms*, "the height is so variable that a fixed wharf would be useless. In its place is used a rectangular float, in part covered, for the reception of goods, or for a dram-shop. It is generally aground on the shore side, and is entered by a plank or a movable platform." Edward Eggleston explained in his notes to the 1890 edition

A wharf-boat. Illustration from *Emerson's Magazine and Putnam's Monthly*, October 1857.
Courtesy Library of Congress.

here, any minute, and sings out my name before I can throw him a wink to keep quiet? Well, I couldn't *have* it that way—it wouldn't do at all. I must go up the road and waylay him. So I told the folks I reckoned I would go up to the town and fetch down my baggage. The old gentleman was for going along with me, but I said no, I could drive the horse myself, and I druther he wouldn't take no trouble about me.

of *The Hoosier School-Boy* that a wharf-boat is "a flat-boat with a roof, sometimes with a second-story cabin above, and kept lying near a village or landing place. Steamboats deposit freight and land their passengers on the wharf-boat, from which a wide moveable staging leads to the shore. The wharf-boat is moved as the water rises or falls" (p. 94).

18. *the officers' lunch.* The part of the boat where the officers were served their meals, now generally called the officers' mess.

19. *throw up my hand.* Drop out, as in a poker game.

20. *he come in.* In the manuscript, Silas Phelps originally came in with a little boy and girl named Phil and Mat who were about the same size as Huck; but they merely complicated the plot without adding much to it, so Twain dropped them from the story.

21. *"Who do you reckon 't is?"* When *Huckleberry Finn* was in the press the fall of 1884, the illustration for this line was maliciously changed perhaps by the printer's devil to show an unusual shape emerging from Uncle Silas's pants like an erect penis. Twain's salesmen were already canvasing the book when one of them noticed the offensive detail and reported it to Charles L. Webster. He immediately offered a reward of $500 for the apprehension and conviction of the person who altered the engraving as "to make it obscene." Apparently, no one was ever caught. Fortunately, although some of the salesman's "dummies" did contain the plate, Webster was able to call back all finished copies of the novel, excised the controversial page, and tipped in a corrected one. Unfortunately, the original publication date had to be postponed; and the book missed the important sales at Christmas 1884. But that was better than lose the estimated $25,000 in sales had the error not been discovered when it was.

22. *swap knives.* Change tactics.

23. *it was like being born again.* Another of Huck's "resurrections."

24. *White River.* A tributary of the Mississippi River, running from Missouri through Arkansas.

The suppressed obscene version of
"Who do you reckon 't is?"
Courtesy Library of Congress.

Chapter XXXIII.

1. *what you want to come back and ha'nt* me *for?* Doubting Tom Sawyer says almost the exact words that Jim did when he first encountered Huck on Jackson's Island in Chapter 8; here Tom repeats the popular belief that ghosts haunt only those who wronged them in life.

"IT WAS TOM SAWYER."

So I started for town, in the wagon, and when I was half-way I see a wagon coming, and sure enough it was Tom Sawyer, and I stopped and waited till he come along. I says "Hold on!" and it stopped alongside, and his mouth opened up like a trunk, and staid so; and he swallowed two or three times like a person that's got a dry throat, and then says:

"I hain't ever done you no harm. You know that. So then, what you want to come back and ha'nt *me* for?"[1]

I says:

"I hain't come back—I hain't been *gone.*"

When he heard my voice, it righted him up some, but he warn't quite satisfied yet. He says:

"Don't you play nothing on me, because I wouldn't on you. Honest injun, now, you ain't a ghost?"

"Honest injun, I ain't," I says.

"Well—I—I—well, that ought to settle it, of course; but I can't somehow seem to understand it, no way. Looky here, warn't you ever murdered *at all?*"

"No. I warn't ever murdered at all—I played it on them. You come in here and feel of me if you don't believe me."

So he done it; and it satisfied him; and he was that glad to see me again, he didn't know what to do. And he wanted to know all about it right off; because it was a grand adventure, and mysterious, and so it hit him where he lived.[2] But I said, leave it alone till by-and-by; and told his driver to wait, and we drove off a little piece, and I told him the kind of a fix I was in, and what did he reckon we better do? He said, let him alone a minute, and don't disturb him. So he thought and thought, and pretty soon he says:

"It's all right, I've got it. Take my trunk in your wagon, and let on it's your'n; and you turn back and fool along slow, so as to get to the house about the time you ought to; and I'll go towards town a piece, and take a fresh start, and get there a quarter or a half an hour after you; and you needn't let on to know me, at first."

I says:

"All right; but wait a minute. There's one more thing—a thing that *nobody* don't know but me. And that is, there's a nigger here that I'm a trying to steal out of slavery—and his name is *Jim*—old Miss Watson's Jim."

He says:

"What! Why Jim is—"

He stopped and went to studying. I says:

"*I* know what you'll say. You'll say it's dirty low-down business; but what if it is?—*I*'m low down; and I'm agoing to steal him, and I want you to keep mum and not let on. Will you?"

His eye lit up, and he says:

"I'll *help* you steal him!"

Well, I let go all holts then, like I was shot. It was the most astonishing speech I ever heard—and I'm bound to say Tom Sawyer fell, considerable, in my estimation.[3] Only I couldn't believe it. Tom Sawyer a *nigger stealer!*

"Oh, shucks," I says, "you're joking."

"I ain't joking, either."

"Well, then," I says, "joking or no joking, if you hear anything said about a runaway nigger, don't forget to remember that *you* don't know nothing about him, and *I* don't know nothing about him."

Then we took the trunk and put it in my wagon, and he drove off his way, and I drove mine. But of course I forgot all

2. *it hit him where he lived.* "Smote [him] sore with fear and dread," as Hank Morgan explains this expression in Chapter 14 of *A Connecticut Yankee in King Arthur's Court*.

3. *Tom Sawyer fell, considerable, in my estimation.* Tom finally has a chance to play at robbery, and not just anything. He is going to steal a slave! Huck, however, recognizes the seriousness of the situation. Although he has reconciled himself to "going to Hell," he cannot believe that Tom Sawyer, the great Tom Sawyer, of the "respectable" middle class, might lower himself to Huck's level, that of "poor white trash."

about driving slow, on accounts of being glad and full of thinking; so I got home a heap too quick for that length of a trip. The old gentleman was at the door, and he says:

"Why, this is wonderful. Who ever would a thought it was in that mare to do it. I wish we'd a timed her. And she hain't sweated a hair—not a hair. It's wonderful. Why, I wouldn't take a hunderd dollars for that horse now; I wouldn't, honest; and yet I'd a sold her for fifteen before, and thought 'twas all she was worth."

That's all he said. He was the innocentest, best old soul I ever see. But it warn't surprising; because he warn't only just a farmer, he was a preacher, too, and had a little one-horse log church[4] down back of the plantation, which he built it himself at his own expense, for a church and schoolhouse, and never charged nothing for his preaching, and it was worth it, too. There was plenty other farmer-preachers like that, and done the same way, down South.

In about half an hour Tom's wagon drove up to the front stile, and Aunt Sally she see it through the window because it was only about fifty yards, and says:

"Why, there's somebody come! I wonder who 'tis? Why, I do believe it's a stranger. Jimmy" (that's one of the children), "run and tell Lize to put on another plate for dinner."

Everybody made a rush for the front door, because, of course, a stranger don't come *every* year, and so he lays over the yaller fever,[5] for interest, when he does come. Tom was over the stile and starting for the house; the wagon was spinning up the road for the village, and we was all bunched in the front door. Tom had his store clothes on, and an audience—and that was always nuts for Tom Sawyer. In them circumstances it warn't no trouble to him to throw in an amount of style that was suitable. He warn't a boy to meeky along[6] up that yard like a sheep; no, he come ca'm and important, like the ram. When he got afront of us, he lifts his hat ever so gracious and dainty, like it was the lid of a box that had butterflies asleep in it and he didn't want to disturb them, and says:

"Mr. Archibald Nichols, I presume?"

4. *a little one-horse log church*. There was also one on the Quarles property, as Twain recalled in his *Autobiography* (vol. 1, 1924, p. 7). It was also the model for the Grangerford–Shepherdson church at Compromise, on the Kentucky–Tennessee border. See Chapter 18, note 33.

5. *lays over the yaller fever*. Yellow fever was one of the most feared and constant threats to the settlers in the Mississippi Valley. The swamps were especially conducive to disease during the summer, when it spread quickly from town to town along the river. In Chapter 29 of *Life on the Mississippi*, Twain quoted an account of a virulent outbreak in Memphis: "In August the yellow fever had reached its extremest height. Daily, hundreds fell a sacrifice to the terrible epidemic. The city was becoming a mighty graveyard, two-thirds of the population had deserted the place, and only the poor, the aged and the sick, remained behind, a sure prey for the insidious enemy. . . . On the street corners, and in the squares, lay sick men, suddenly overtaken by the disease; and even corpses, distorted and rigid. Food failed. Meat spoiled in a few hours in the fetid and pestiferous air, and turned black. . . . In the night stillness reigns. Only the physicians and the hearses hurry through the street; and out of the distance, at intervals, comes the muffled thunder of the railway train, which with the speed of the wind, and as if hunted by furies, flies by the pest-ridden city without halting."

6. *to meeky along*. To move meekly, skulk, sneak along.

"MR. ARCHIBALD NICHOLS, I PRESUME?"

"No, my boy," says the old gentleman, "I'm sorry to say 't your driver has deceived you; Nichols's place is down a matter of three mile more. Come in, come in."

Tom he took a look back over his shoulder, and says, "Too late—he's out of sight."

"Yes, he's gone, my son, and you must come in and eat your dinner with us; and then we'll hitch up and take you down to Nichols's."

"Oh, I *can't* make you so much trouble; I couldn't think of it. I'll walk—I don't mind the distance."

"But we won't *let* you walk—it wouldn't be Southern hospitality[7] to do it. Come right in."

"Oh, *do,*" says Aunt Sally; "it ain't a bit of trouble to us, not a bit in the world. You *must* stay. It's a long, dusty three mile, and we *can't* let you walk. And besides, I've already told 'em to put on another plate, when I see you coming; so you mustn't disappoint us. Come right in, and make yourself at home."

So Tom he thanked them very hearty and handsome, and let himself be persuaded, and come in; and when he was in,

7. *it wouldn't be Southern hospitality*. By this time, "Southern hospitality" was already legendary. Daniel R. Hundley expressed the current opinion in *Social Relations in Our Southern States* (1860) that nowhere else could one find "a much heartier welcome, a firmer shake of the hand, a greater desire to please, and less frigidity of deportment" than in the American South (p. 57).

8. *Hicksville, Ohio*. Founded in 1836 as a trading post, this town was in a lumbering district in northwestern Ohio, near the Indiana border.

he said he was a stranger from Hicksville, Ohio,[8] and his name was William Thompson—and he made another bow.

Well, he run on, and on, and on, making up stuff about Hicksville and everybody in it he could invent, and I getting a little nervious, and wondering how this was going to help me out of my scrape; and at last, still talking along, he reached over and kissed Aunt Sally right on the mouth, and then settled back again in his chair, comfortable, and was going on talking; but she jumped up and wiped it off with the back of her hand, and says:

"You owdacious puppy!"

He looked kind of hurt, and says:

"I'm surprised at you, m'am."

"You're s'rp—Why, what do you reckon *I* am? I've a good notion to take and—say, what do you mean by kissing me?"

He looked kind of humble, and says:

"I didn't mean nothing, m'am. I didn't mean no harm. I—I—thought you'd like it."

"Why, you born fool!" She took up the spinning-stick, and it looked like it was all she could do to keep from giving him a crack with it. "What made you think I'd like it?"

"Well, I don't know. Only, they—they—told me you would."

"*They* told you I would. Whoever told you 's *another* lunatic. I never heard the beat of it. Who's *they?*"

"Why—everybody. They all said so, m'am."

It was all she could do to hold in; and her eyes snapped, and her fingers worked like she wanted to scratch him; and she says:

"Who's 'everybody?' Out with their names—or ther'll be an idiot short."

He got up and looked distressed, and fumbled his hat, and says:

"I'm sorry, and I warn't expecting it. They told me to. They all told me to. They all said kiss her; and said she'll like it. They all said it—every one of them. But I'm sorry, m'am, and I won't do it no more—I won't, honest."

"You won't, won't you? Well, I sh'd *reckon* you won't!"

"No'm, I'm honest about it; I won't ever do it again. Till you ask me."

"Till I *ask* you! Well, I never see the beat of it in my born days! I lay you'll be the Methusalem-numskull of creation[9] before ever *I* ask you—or the likes of you."

"Well," he says, "it does surprise me so. I can't make it out, somehow. They said you would, and I thought you would. But—" He stopped and looked around slow, like he wished he could run across a friendly eye, somewhere's; and fetched up on the old gentleman's, and says, "Didn't *you* think she'd like me to kiss her, sir?"

"Why, no, I—I—well, no, I b'lieve I didn't."

Then he looks on around, the same way, to me—and says:

"Tom, didn't *you* think Aunt Sally 'd open out her arms and say, 'Sid Sawyer—' "

"My land!" she says, breaking in and jumping for him, "you impudent young rascal, to fool a body so—" and was going to hug him, but he fended her off, and says:

"No, not till you've asked me, first."

So she didn't lose no time, but asked him; and hugged him and kissed him, over and over again, and then turned him over to the old man, and he took what was left. And after they got a little quiet again, she says:

"Why, dear me, I never see such a surprise. We warn't looking for *you*, at all, but only Tom. Sis never wrote to me about anybody coming but him."

"It's because it warn't *intended* for any of us to come but Tom," he says; "but I begged and begged, and at the last minute she let me come, too; so, coming down the river, me and Tom thought it would be a first-rate surprise for him to come here to the house first, and for me to by-and-by tag along and drop in and let on to be a stranger. But it was a mistake, Aunt Sally. This ain't no healthy place for a stranger to come."

"No—not impudent whelps, Sid. You ought to had your jaws boxed; I hain't been so put out since I don't know when. But I don't care, I don't mind the terms—I'd be willing to stand a thousand such jokes to have you here. Well, to

9. *the Methusalem-numskull of creation.* The oldest fool who ever lived; according to Genesis 5:27, Methuselah lived 926 years, the longest life of anyone in the Bible. "Well—goodbye, and a short life and a merry one be yours," Twain closed a letter of February 9, 1879, to Howells. "Poor old Methusaleh, how did he manage to stand it so long?" (*Mark Twain–Howells Letters*, 1960, p. 257).

think of that performance! I don't deny it, I was most putrified[10] with astonishment when you give me that smack."

We had dinner out in that broad open passage betwixt the house and the kitchen; and there was things enough on that table for seven families—and all hot, too;[11] none of your flabby tough meat that's laid in a cupboard in a damp cellar all night and tastes like a hunk of old cold cannibal[12] in the morning. Uncle Silas he asked a pretty long blessing over it, but it was worth it; and it didn't cool it a bit, neither,

A PRETTY LONG BLESSING.

the way I've seen them kind of interruptions do, lots of times.

There was a considerable good deal of talk, all the afternoon, and me and Tom was on the lookout all the time, but it warn't no use, they didn't happen to say nothing about any runaway nigger, and we was afraid to try to work up to it. But at supper, at night, one of the little boys says:

"Pa, mayn't Tom and Sid and me go to the show?"

"No," says the old man, "I reckon there ain't going to be any; and you couldn't go if there was; because the runaway nigger told Burton and me all about that scandalous show, and Burton said he would tell the people; so I reckon they've drove the owdacious loafers out of town before this time."

So there it was!—but *I* couldn't help it. Tom and me was

10. *putrified.* An amusing portmanteau word combining "petrified" with "putrid," capturing both reactions Aunt Sally had to the boy's brazen behavior.

11. *enough on that table for seven families—and all hot, too.* In "Chapters from My Autobiography" (*North American Review*, March 1, 1907), Twain recalled the abundance served at the table at the Quarles farm: "Fried chicken, roast pig, wild and tame turkeys, ducks and geese; venison just killed; squirrels, rabbits, pheasants, partridges, prairie-chickens; biscuits, hot batter cakes, hot buckwheat cakes, hot 'wheat bread,' hot rolls; hot corn pone; fresh corn boiled on the ear, succotash, butter-beans, string-beans, tomatoes, pease, Irish potatoes, sweet-potatoes; buttermilk, sweet milk, 'clabber'; watermelons, muskmelons, cantaloupes—all fresh from the garden—apple pie, peach pie, pumpkin pie, apple dumplings, peach cobbler—I can't remember the rest" (p. 452). In "The Private History of a Campaign That Failed" (*Century Magazine*, December 1885), Twain described a "Missouri country breakfast" at the Masons which nearly duplicates the Arkansas dinner at the Phelpses, "and the world may be confidently challenged to furnish the equal to such a breakfast, as it is cooked in the South" (p. 201). As already seen in Chapter 18, the Grangerfords offered big meals, too, all part of Southern hospitality. But Huck should know by now that things are not always as wonderful as they first seem to be in these Southern homes.

12. *like a hunk of old cold cannibal.* Twain employed just as crude a simile in the manuscript, "like a hunk of your old cold grandfather" (Ferguson, "Huck Finn Aborning," p. 179); but the change hardly seems much of an improvement.

to sleep in the same room and bed; so, being tired, we bid good-night and went up to bed, right after supper, and clumb out of the window and down the lightning-rod,[13] and shoved for the town; for I didn't believe anybody was going to give the king and the duke a hint, and so, if I didn't hurry up and give them one they'd get into trouble sure.

On the road Tom he told me all about how it was reckoned I was murdered, and how pap disappeared, pretty soon, and didn't come back no more, and what a stir there was when Jim run away; and I told Tom all about our Royal Nonesuch rapscallions, and as much of the raft-voyage as I had time to; and as we struck into the town and up through the middle of it—it was as much as half after eight, then—here comes a raging rush of people, with torches, and an awful whooping and yelling, and banging tin pans and blowing horns; and we jumped to one side to let them go by; and as they went by, I see they had the king and the duke astraddle of a rail—that is, I knowed it *was* the king and the duke, though they was all over tar and feathers, and didn't look like nothing in the world that was human—just looked like a couple of monstrous big soldier-plumes.[14] Well, it made me sick to see it; and I was sorry for them poor pitiful rascals, it seemed like I couldn't ever feel any hardness against them any more in the world. It was a dreadful thing to see. Human beings *can* be awful cruel to one another.[15]

We see we was too late—couldn't do no good. We asked some stragglers about it, and they said everybody went to the show looking very innocent; and laid low and kept dark till the poor old king was in the middle of his cavortings on the stage; then somebody give a signal, and the house rose up and went for them.

So we poked along back home, and I warn't feeling so brash as I was before, but kind of ornery, and humble, and to blame, somehow—though *I* hadn't done nothing. But that's always the way; it don't make no difference whether you do right or wrong, a person's conscience ain't got no

13. *the lightning-rod.* Huck originally made his escape "into the branches of a tree" (**MS**), but then Twain recalled his own room at the Quarles farm. "It was a very satisfactory room," he admitted in "Chapters from My Autobiography" (*North American Review*, March 1, 1907), "and there was a lightning-rod which was reachable from the window, an adorable and skittish thing to climb up and down, summer nights, when there were duties on hand of a sort to make privacy desirable" (p. 462).

14. *like a couple of monstrous big soldier-plumes.* Describing the tarred-and-feathered scoundrels waving back and forth above the crowd like huge feathers on the hats or helmets of soldiers repeats Huck's observation that a mob is like an army.

15. *Human beings* can *be awful cruel to one another.* Although there have been constant threats throughout the story, this is first instance of anyone being lynched in the novel. Throughout this chapter, Twain explored a paradox in the Southern character: God-fearing people like the Phelpses and their neighbors can turn into a bloodthirsty mob at any minute and at the least provocation. Otherwise hospitable men and women are capable of enormous irrational cruelty.

sense, and just goes for him *anyway.* If I had a yaller dog that didn't know no more than a person's conscience does, I would pison him. It takes up more room than all the rest of a person's insides,[16] and yet ain't no good, nohow. Tom Sawyer he says the same.

TRAVELING BY RAIL.

16. *all the rest of a person's insides.* Huck was more contemptuous of his conscience in the manuscript, saying that it takes up "more room than a person's bowels" (Ferguson, "Huck Finn Aborning," p. 179).

Chapter XXXIV.

VITTLES.

We STOPPED talking, and got to thinking. By-and-by Tom says:

"Looky here, Huck, what fools we are, to not think of it before! I bet I know where Jim is."

"No! Where?"

"In that hut down by the ash-hopper. Why, looky here. When we was at dinner, didn't you see a nigger man go in there with some vittles?"

"Yes."

"What did you think the vittles was for?"

"For a dog."

"So'd I. Well, it wasn't for a dog."

"Why?"

"Because part of it was watermelon."

"So it was—I noticed it. Well, it does beat all, that I never thought about a dog not eating watermelon. It shows how a body can see and don't see at the same time."

"Well, the nigger unlocked the padlock when he went in, and he locked it again when he come out. He fetched uncle[1] a key, about the time we got up from table—same key, I bet. Watermelon shows man, lock shows prisoner; and it ain't likely there's two prisoners on such a little plantation, and where the people's all so kind and good. Jim's the prisoner. All right—I'm glad we found it out detective fash-

1. *uncle.* Twain explained in "Chapters from My Autobiography" (*North American Review*, March 1, 1907, p. 453) that it was "Southern fashion" to call older slave men and women "uncle" and "aunt."

ion;[2] I wouldn't give shucks for any other way. Now you work your mind and study out a plan to steal Jim, and I will study out one, too; and we'll take the one we like the best."

What a head for just a boy to have! If I had Tom Sawyer's head, I wouldn't trade it off to be a duke, nor mate of a steamboat, nor clown in a circus, nor nothing I can think of. I went to thinking out a plan, but only just to be doing something; I knowed very well where the right plan was going to come from. Pretty soon, Tom says:

"Ready?"

"Yes," I says.

"All right—bring it out."

"My plan is this," I says. "We can easy find out if it's Jim in there. Then get up my canoe to-morrow night, and fetch my raft over from the island. Then the first dark night that comes, steal the key out of the old man's britches, after he goes to bed, and shove off down the river on the raft, with Jim, hiding day-times and running nights, the way me and Jim used to do before. Wouldn't that plan work?"

"*Work?* Why cert'nly, it would work, like rats a fighting. But it's too blame' simple; there ain't nothing *to* it. What's the good of a plan that ain't no more trouble than that? It's as mild as goose-milk.[3] Why, Huck, it wouldn't make no more talk than breaking into a soap factory."

I never said nothing, because I warn't expecting nothing different; but I knowed mighty well that whenever he got *his* plan ready it wouldn't have none of them objections to it.

And it didn't. He told me what it was, and I see in a minute it was worth fifteen of mine, for style, and would make Jim just as free a man as mine would, and maybe get us all killed besides. So I was satisfied, and said we would waltz in on it. I needn't tell what it was, here, because I knowed it wouldn't stay the way it was.[4] I knowed he would be changing it around, every which way, as we went along, and heaving in new bullinesses wherever he got a chance. And that is what he done.

Well, one thing was dead sure; and that was, that Tom Sawyer was in earnest and was actuly going to help steal

2. *detective fashion.* Only in passing does Tom mention another source of his wild notions—detective stories. The genre was just coming into its own, but Twain had as little respect for this one as he did other romantic literature—and yet he was fascinated by it. A detective from St. Louis shows up briefly in Chapter 24 of *Tom Sawyer.* "What a curious thing a 'detective story' is," Twain wondered in 1896. "And was there ever one that the author needn't be ashamed of, except 'The Murders in the Rue Morgue'?" (Blair, *Mark Twain's Hannibal, Huck and Tom*, 1969, p. 158). And Twain did not care much for Edgar Allan Poe. Nevertheless, he wrote "Tom Sawyer, Detective" and began but never finished "Tom Sawyer's Conspiracy"; but this last was a parody of detective fiction as the last part of *Huckleberry Finn* burlesques escape literature. Tom is as irrational in "Tom Sawyer's Conspiracy" as he is here in trying to help Jim escape. "What's common sense got to do with detecting, you leatherhead?" Tom asks Huck. "It ain't got *anything* to do with it. What is wanted is genius and penetration and marvelousness. A detective that had common sense couldn't ever make a ruputation—couldn't even make his living" (*Huck Finn and Tom Sayer Among the Indians*, 1989, p. 117).

3. *mild as goose-milk.* Twain wrote in the manuscript "mild as Sunday School" (Ferguson, "Huck Finn Aborning," p. 179), a more apt simile than the published one, because it harks back to the attack on the Sunday school by Tom Sawyer and his gang in Chapter 3; but fear that it might be perceived as blasphemous might have demanded the change. See Chapter 35, note 2.

4. *I needn't tell what it was, here, because I knowed it wouldn't stay the way it was.* Huck is speaking as much for the author as he is for Tom Sawyer: It seems obvious that at this point in the story Twain had no idea where the novel was heading.

that nigger out of slavery. That was the thing that was too many for me. Here was a boy that was respectable, and well brung up; and had a character to lose; and folks at home that had characters; and he was bright and not leather-headed; and knowing and not ignorant; and not mean, but kind; and yet here he was, without any more pride, or rightness, or feeling, than to stoop to this business, and make himself a shame, and his family a shame, before everybody. I *couldn't* understand it, no way at all. It was outrageous, and I knowed I ought to just up and tell him so; and so be his true friend, and let him quit the thing right where he was, and save himself. And I *did* start to tell him; but he shut me up, and says:

"Don't you reckon I know what I'm about? Don't I generly know what I'm about?"

"Yes."

"Didn't I *say* I was going to help steal the nigger?"

"Yes."

"*Well* then."

That's all he said, and that's all I said. It warn't no use to say any more; because when he said he'd do a thing, he always done it. But *I* couldn't make out how he was willing to go into this thing; so I just let it go, and never bothered no more about it. If he was bound to have it so, *I* couldn't help it.

When we got home, the house was all dark and still; so we went on down to the hut by the ash-hopper, for to examine it. We went through the yard, so as to see what the hounds would do. They knowed us, and didn't make no more noise than country dogs is always doing when anything comes by in the night. When we got to the cabin, we took a look at the front and the two sides; and on the side I warn't acquainted with—which was the north side—we found a square window-hole, up tolerable high, with just one stout board nailed across it. I says:

"Here's the ticket. This hole's big enough for Jim to get through, if we wrench off the board."

Tom says:

"It's as simple as tit-tat-toe, three-in-a-row, and as easy as playing hooky. I should *hope* we can find a way that's a little more complicated than *that,* Huck Finn."

"Well then," I says, "how'll it do to saw him out, the way I done before I was murdered, that time?"

"That's more *like,*" he says. "It's real mysterious, and troublesome, and good," he says; "but I bet we can find a way that's twice as long. There ain't no hurry; le's keep on looking around."

Betwixt the hut and the fence, on the back side, was a lean-to, that joined the hut at the eaves, and was made out of plank. It was as long as the hut, but narrow—only about six foot wide. The door to it was at the south end, and was padlocked. Tom he went to the soap kettle, and searched around and fetched back the iron thing they lift the lid with; so he took it and prized out one of the staples. The chain fell down, and we opened the door and went in, and shut it, and struck a match, and see the shed was only built against the cabin and hadn't no connection with it; and there warn't no floor to the shed, nor nothing in it but some old rusty played-out hoes, and spades, and picks, and a crippled plow. The match went out, and so did we, and shoved

A SIMPLE JOB.

in the staple again, and the door was locked as good as ever. Tom was joyful. He says:

"Now we're all right. We'll *dig* him out. It'll take about a week!"

Then we started for the house, and I went in the back door—you only have to pull a buckskin latch-string, they don't fasten the doors[5]—but that warn't romantical enough for Tom Sawyer: no way would do him but he must climb up the lightning-rod. But after he got up half-way about three times, and missed fire and fell every time, and the last time most busted his brains out, he thought he'd got to give it up; but after he was rested, he allowed he would give her one more turn for luck, and this time he made the trip.

In the morning we was up at break of day, and down to the nigger cabins to pet the dogs and make friends with the nigger that fed Jim—if it *was* Jim that was being fed. The niggers was just getting through breakfast and starting for the fields; and Jim's nigger was piling up a tin pan with bread and meat and things; and whilst the others was leaving, the key come from the house.

This nigger had a good-natured, chuckleheaded face, and his wool was all tied up in little bunches with thread.[6] That was to keep witches off. He said the witches was pestering him awful, these nights, and making him see all kinds of strange things, and hear all kinds of strange words and noises, and he didn't believe he was ever witched so long, before, in his life. He got so worked up, and got to running on so about his troubles, he forgot all about what he'd been agoing to do. So Tom says:

"What's the vittles for? Going to feed the dogs?"

The nigger kind of smiled around graduly over his face, like when you heave a brickbat[7] in a mud puddle, and he says:

"Yes, Mars Sid, *a* dog. Cur'us dog, too. Does you want to go en look at 'im?"[8]

"Yes."

I hunched Tom, and whispers:

"You going, right here in the day-break? *That* warn't the plan."

5. *you only have to pull a buckskin latch-string, they don't fasten the doors.* See Chapter 21, note 16.

6. *his wool was all tied up . . . with thread.* To ward off witches. See Chapter 1, note 37.

7. *brickbat.* A piece of broken brick.

8. *Cur'us dog, too, Does you want to go en look at 'im?* Nat employs much the same trick that another slave, Jack, did back at the Grangerfords' in Chapter 18, to get Huck to see Jim.

"No, it warn't—but it's the plan *now.*"

So, drat him, we went along, but I didn't like it much. When we got in, we couldn't hardly see anything, it was so dark; but Jim was there, sure enough, and could see us; and he sings out:

"Why, *Huck!* En good *lan'!* ain' dat Misto Tom?"

I just knowed how it would be; I just expected it. *I* didn't know nothing to do; and if I had, I couldn't a done it; because that nigger busted in and says:

"Why, de gracious sakes! do he know you genlmen?"

We could see pretty well, now. Tom he looked at the nigger, steady and kind of wondering, and says:

"Does *who* know us?"

"Why, dish-yer runaway nigger."

"I don't reckon he does; but what put that into your head?"

"What *put* it dar? Didn' he jis' dis minute sing out like he knowed you?"

Tom says, in a puzzled-up kind of way:

"Well, that's mighty curious. *Who* sung out? *When* did he sing out? *What* did he sing out?" And turns to me, perfectly c'am, and says, "Did *you* hear anybody sing out?"

Of course there warn't nothing to be said but the one thing; so I says:

"No; *I* ain't heard nobody say nothing."

Then he turns to Jim, and looks him over like he never see him before; and says:

"Did you sing out?"

"No, sah," says Jim; "*I* hain't said nothing, sah."

"Not a word?"

"No, sah, I hain't said a word."

"Did you ever see us before?"

"No, sah; not as *I* knows on."

So Tom turns to

WITCHES.

the nigger, which was looking wild and distressed, and says, kind of severe:

"What do you reckon's the matter with you, anyway? What made you think somebody sung out?"

"Oh, it's de dad-blame' witches, sah, en I wisht I was dead, I do. Dey's awluz at it, sah, en dey do mos' kill me, dey sk'yers me so. Please to don't tell nobody 'bout it sah, er ole Mars Silas he'll scole me; 'kase he say dey *ain't* no witches. I jis' wish to goodness he was heah now—*den* what would he say! I jis' bet he couldn' fine no way to git aroun' it *dis* time. But it's awluz jis' so; people dat's *sot,* stays sot; dey won't look into noth'n en fine it out f'r deyselves, en when *you* fine it out en tell um 'bout it, dey doan' b'lieve you."

Tom give him a dime, and said we wouldn't tell nobody; and told him to buy some more thread to tie up his wool with; and then looks at Jim, and says:

"I wonder if Uncle Silas is going to hang this nigger. If I was to catch a nigger that was ungrateful enough to run away, *I* wouldn't give him up, I'd hang him." And whilst the nigger stepped to the door to look at the dime and bite it to see if it was good, he whispers to Jim, and says:

"Don't ever let on to know us. And if you hear any digging going on nights, it's us: we're going to set you free."

Jim only had time to grab us by the hand and squeeze it, then the nigger come back, and we said we'd come again some time if the nigger wanted us to; and he said he would, more particular if it was dark, because the witches went for him mostly in the dark, and it was good to have folks around then.

Chapter XXXV.

1. *fox-fire.* The phosphorescent glow emitted by decaying wood.

GETTING WOOD.

It WOULD be most an hour, yet, till breakfast, so we left, and struck down into the woods; because Tom said we got to have *some* light to see how to dig by, and a lantern makes too much, and might get us into trouble; what we must have was a lot of them rotten chunks that's called fox-fire[1] and just makes a soft kind of a glow when you lay them in a dark place. We fetched an armful and hid it in the weeds, and set down to rest, and Tom says, kind of dissatisfied:

"Blame it, this whole thing is just as easy and awkard as it can be. And so it makes it so rotten difficult to get up a difficult plan. There ain't no watchman to be drugged—now there *ought* to be a watchman. There ain't even a dog to give a sleeping-mixture to. And there's Jim chained by one leg, with a ten-foot chain, to the leg of his bed: why, all you got to do is to lift up the bedstead and slip off the chain. And Uncle Silas he trusts everybody; sends the key to the punkin-headed nigger, and don't send nobody to watch the nigger. Jim could a got out of that window hole before this, only there wouldn't be no use trying to travel with a ten-foot chain on his leg. Why, drat it, Huck, it's the stupidest arrangement I ever see. You got to invent *all* the difficulties.

Well, we can't help it, we got to do the best we can with the materials we've got. Anyhow, there's one thing—there's more honor in getting him out through a lot of difficulties and dangers, where there warn't one of them furnished to you by the people who it was their duty to furnish them, and you had to contrive them all out of your own head. Now look at just that one thing of the lantern. When you come down to the cold facts, we simply got to *let on* that a lantern's resky. Why, we could work with a torchlight procession if we wanted to, *I* believe. Now, whilst I think of it, we got to hunt up something to make a saw out of, the first chance we get."

"What do we want of a saw?"

"What do we *want* of it? Hain't we got to saw the leg of Jim's bed off, so as to get the chain loose?"

"Why, you just said a body could lift up the bedstead and slip the chain off."

"Well, if that ain't just like you, Huck Finn. You *can* get up the infant-schooliest ways[2] of going at a thing. Why, hain't you ever read any books at all?—Baron Trenck, nor Casanova, nor Benvenuto Chelleeny, nor Henri IV.,[3] nor none of them heroes? Whoever heard of getting a prisoner loose in such an old-maidy way as that? No; the way all the best authorities does, is to saw the bed-leg in two, and leave it just so, and swallow the sawdust, so it can't be found, and put some dirt and grease around the sawed place so the very keenest seneskal[4] can't see no sign of its being sawed, and thinks the bed-leg is perfectly sound. Then, the night you're ready, fetch the leg a kick, down she goes; slip off your chain, and there you are. Nothing to do but hitch your rope-ladder to the battle-ments, shin down it, break your leg in the moat—because a rope-ladder is nineteen foot too short,[5] you know—and there's your horses and your trusty vassles, and they scoop you up and fling you across a saddle and away you go, to your native Langudoc,[6] or Navarre,[7] or wherever it is. It's gaudy, Huck. I wish there was a moat to this cabin. If we get time, the night of the escape, we'll dig one."

I says:

2. *infant-schooliest ways*. "Sunday-schooliest ways" in the manuscript (Ferguson, "Huck Finn Aborning," p. 179); much of the original sarcasm is now lost in the final tame adjective.

3. *Baron Trenck . . . Casanova . . . Benvenuto Chelleeny . . . Henri IV*. Each of these men made daring prison escapes, but they were also famous rakes, which makes them as notorious as the mistresses of kings mentioned earlier (see Chapter 23, note 10). Their scandalous lives were hardly appropriate reading material for children of the period.

Baron Frederich von Trenck (1726–1794), a Prussian adventurer, and an officer in Frederick the Great's army, was imprisoned for an alleged liaison with the emperor's sister. He escaped from prison several times, and described these exploits in his memoirs, published in 1787. Not surprisingly, the book was an enormous success: Women of Paris, Belgium, and Vienna wore rings, necklaces, bonnets, and gowns à la

Baron von Trenck.
Courtesy Picture Collection, New York Public Library, Astor, Lenox, and Tilden Foundations.

Trenck; at least seven dramatizations of his life were staged. He went to France during the Revolution and was guillotined as a spy.

Giovanni Jacopo Casanova de Seingalt (1725–1798) was one of the most famous lovers in history; his name has come to mean libertine.

Casanova with a conquest.
Courtesy Picture Collection, New York Public Library, Astor, Lenox, and Tilden Foundations.

This Italian adventurer went from court to court and bed to bed, and wrote an infamous memoir, which was published posthumously in a truncated version. "The supremest charm of Casanova's Memoire," Twain wrote his brother Orion Clemens on February 26, 1880, "is, that he frankly, flowingly, and felicitously tells the dirtiest and vilest and most contemptible things on himself, without ever suspecting that they are other than things which the reader will admire and applaud" (quoted in Webster, *Mark Twain, Business Man*, 1946, pp. 143–44).

Benvenuto Cellini (1500–1771), "that rough-hewn saint" (as Hank Morgan calls him in Chapter 17 of *A Connecticut Yankee in King Arthur's Court*), was one of the greatest goldsmiths and sculptors of the Italian Renaissance; however, he is best remembered for his *Autobiography*, which he began in 1558, and in which he described his legendary escape from the Castel San Angelo in Rome. "That most entertaining of books," Twain wrote of the *Autobiography*, one of the most famous ever written and a model for Twain's. "It will last as long as his beautiful Perseus [his masterpiece]" (*Mark Twain's Notebook*, 1935, p. 144). Twain often referred to Cellini in his work, particularly the incident about the salamander.

Henry IV (1553–1610), the first Bourbon king of France (from whom the Dauphin descended),

"What do we want of a moat, when we're going to snake him out from under the cabin?"

But he never heard me. He had forgot me and everything else. He had his chin in his hand, thinking. Pretty soon, he sighs, and shakes his head; then sighs again, and says:

"No, it wouldn't do—there ain't necessity enough for it."

"For what?" I says.

"Why, to saw Jim's leg off," he says.

"Good land!" I says, "why, there ain't *no* necessity for it. And what would you want to saw his leg off for, anyway?"

"Well, some of the best authorities has done it. They couldn't get the chain off, so they just cut their hand off, and shoved. And a leg would be better still. But we got to let

ONE OF THE BEST AUTHORITIES.

that go. There ain't necessity enough in this case; and besides, Jim's a nigger and wouldn't understand the reasons for it, and how it's the custom in Europe; so we'll let it go. But there's one thing—he can have a rope-ladder; we can tear up our sheets and make him a rope-ladder[8] easy enough. And we can send it to him in a pie; it's mostly done that way. And I've et worse pies."

"Why, Tom Sawyer, how you talk," I says; "Jim ain't got no use for a rope-ladder."

"He *has* got use for it. How *you* talk, you better say; you don't know nothing about it. He's *got* to have a rope-ladder; they all do."

"What in the nation can he *do* with it?"

"*Do* with it? He can hide it in his bed, can't he? That's what they all do; and *he's* got to, too. Huck, you don't ever seem to want to do anything that's regular; you want to be starting something fresh all the time. Spose he *don't* do nothing with it? ain't it there in his bed, for a clew, after he's gone? and don't you reckon they'll want clews? Of course they will. And you wouldn't leave them any? That would be a *pretty* howdy-do, *wouldn't* it! I never heard of such a thing."

"Well," I says, "if it's in the regulations, and he's got to have it, all right, let him have it; because I don't wish to go back on no regulations; but there's one thing, Tom Sawyer—if we go to tearing up our sheets to make Jim a rope-ladder, we're going to get into trouble with Aunt Sally, just as sure as you're born. Now, the way I look at it, a hickry-bark ladder don't cost nothing, and don't waste nothing, and is just as good to load up a pie with, and hide in a straw tick, as any rag ladder you can start; and as for Jim, he ain't had no experience, and so *he* don't care what kind of a——"

"Oh, shucks, Huck Finn, if I was as ignorant as you, I'd keep still—that's what *I'd* do. Who ever heard of a state prisoner escaping by a hickry-bark ladder? Why, it's perfectly ridiculous."

"Well, all right, Tom, fix it your own way; but if you'll take my advice, you'll let me borrow a sheet off of the clothes-line."

He said that would do. And that give him another idea, and he says:

"Borrow a shirt, too."

"What do we want of a shirt, Tom?"

"Want it for Jim to keep a journal on."[9]

"Journal your granny—*Jim* can't write."[10]

Benevenuto Cellini.
Courtesy Picture Collection, New York Public Library, Astor, Lenox, and Tilden Foundations.

Henry IV of France.
Courtesy Picture Collection, New York Public Library, Astor, Lenox, and Tilden Foundations.

succeeded to the throne in 1589 upon the assassination of Henry III. He converted to Catholicism in 1589, and was himself assassinated in 1610. See note 7.

4. *seneskal*. Tom has a bit muddled the word "seneschal," the powerful steward to a medieval lord.

5. *break your leg in the moat—because a rope-ladder is nineteen foot too short*. Tom recalls that Cellini's rope ladder was too short, and he broke his leg when he fell into the moat of Castel San Angelo.

6. *Langudoc*. Tom's mispronunciation of "Languedoc," a southern province of medieval France.

7. *Navarre*. The ancient kingdom in the Pyrenees, where Henry IV fled after his escape.

8. *tear up our sheets and make him a rope-ladder*. Tom describes one of the clichés of escape literature; he refers to examples in fact (Baron von Trenck, Casanova, and Cellini) and fiction (Abbé Faria in *The Count of Monte Cristo*; see note 19 below).

9. *a shirt. . . . for Jim to keep a journal on*. Prisoners were often denied books, paper, pens, and ink. However, Abbé Faria wrote his *Traité sur la possibilité d'une monarchie en Italie* on two shirts; the Man in the Iron Mask (see note 14 below) wrote two letters on his shirts; and Count de Charney of J. X. Boniface's *Picciola* (see Chapter 38, note 18) wrote on handkerchiefs.

10. Jim *can't write*. According to Missouri law, passed on February 16, 1847, citizens were forbidden to teach freedmen and slaves to read and write; violators were subject to a $500 fine or six months in prison, or both, for each offense. Twain thought of playing it for laughs in some abandoned ideas for the story: "Takes history class among the niggers. . . . Teaches Jim to read and write—then uses dog-messenger. Had taught him a little before" (University of California edition, 1988, p. 753). In Chapter 22 of *Uncle Tom's Cabin*, Little Eva's mother callously explains in the cant of the day why slaves cannot read and write: "Because it is of no use for them to read. It don't help them to work any better, and they are not made for anything else." The Hannibal *Missouri Courier* (January 12,

"Spose he *can't* write—he can make marks on the shirt, can't he, if we make him a pen out of an old pewter spoon or a piece of an old iron barrel-hoop?"

"Why, Tom, we can pull a feather out of a goose and make him a better one; and quicker, too."

"*Prisoners* don't have geese running around the donjon-keep to pull pens out of, you muggins. They *always* make their pens out of the hardest, toughest, troublesomest piece of old brass candlestick or something like that they can get their hands on;[11] and it takes them weeks and weeks, and months and months to file it out, too, because they've got to do it by rubbing it on the wall. *They* wouldn't use a goose-quill if they had it. It ain't regular."

"Well, then, what'll we make him the ink out of?"

"Many makes it out of iron-rust and tears;[12] but that's the common sort and women; the best authorities uses their own blood.[13] Jim can do that; and when he wants to send any little common ordinary mysterious message to let the world know where he's captivated, he can write it on the bottom of a tin plate with a fork and throw it out of the window. The Iron Mask[14] always done that, and it's a blame' good way, too."

"Jim ain't got no tin plates. They feed him in a pan."

"That ain't anything; we can get him some."

"Can't nobody *read* his plates."

"That ain't got nothing to *do* with it, Huck Finn. All *he's* got to do is to write on the plate and throw it out. You don't *have* to be able to read it. Why, half the time you can't read anything a prisoner writes on a tin plate, or anywhere else."

"Well, then, what's the sense in wasting the plates?"

"Why, blame it all, it ain't the *prisoner's* plates."

"But it's *somebody's* plates, ain't it?"

"Well, spos'n it is? What does the *prisoner* care whose——"

He broke off there, because we heard the breakfast-horn blowing. So we cleared out for the house.

Along during that morning I borrowed a sheet and a white shirt off of the clothes-line; and I found an old sack and put them in it, and we went down and got the fox-fire, and put that in too. I called it borrowing, because that was

THE BREAKFAST HORN.

what pap always called it; but Tom said it warn't borrowing, it was stealing. He said we was representing prisoners; and prisoners don't care how they get a thing so they get it, and nobody don't blame them for it, either. It ain't no crime in a prisoner to steal the thing he needs to get away with, Tom said; it's his right; and so, as long as we was representing a prisoner, we had a perfect right to steal anything on this place we had the least use for, to get ourselves out of prison with. He said if we warn't prisoners it would be a very different thing, and nobody but a mean ornery person would steal when he warn't a prisoner. So we allowed we would steal everything there was that come handy. And yet he made a mighty fuss, one day, after that, when I stole a watermelon out of the nigger patch[15] and eat it; and he made me go and give the niggers a dime, without telling them what it was for. Tom said that what he meant was, we could steal anything we *needed.*[16] Well, I says, I needed the watermelon. But he said I didn't need it to get out of prison with, there's where the difference was. He said if I'd a wanted it to hide a knife in, and smuggle it to Jim to kill the seneskal

1854) warned that it was dangerous "to teach a negro slave how to read the Republican publications of the day, in which he is taught the 'degradation' of his condition, and the blessings of 'liberty,'—put into his hands a few incendiary abolition publications—teach him to write a pass—to read the finger-boards at the crossroads," because he or she would no longer be "the same obedient, happy, cheerful, contented slave as before. . . . Education and vigilance are essential to the preservation of liberty. Ignorance is an inseparable feature of slavery." The *Pike County Free Press* agreed that "that moment you begin to educate a slave, that moment you begin to loose his bonds. It may be a revolting truth to pro-slavery men, but it is no less a truth. For if a negro is educated, taught to think, to reflect, he ceases to be a slave mentally, and will soon cease to be one physically."

And Missourians meant it: Harriet Martineau reported in *Retrospect of Western Travel* (vol. 2, 1838, pp. 209–11) that two students of Marion College were "lynched" in Palmyra for teaching slaves to read and write; the mob gave them the choice of either taking twenty lashes each or leaving the state forever, and they took the latter. Frederick Douglass and other slaves had to go to great lengths to devise all sorts of clever ways to trick their masters and their children into teaching them how to read and write. Douglass recalled in Chapter 6 of his *Narrative* (1845) how one of his masters warned that "learning would *spoil* the best nigger in the world. . . . if you teach that nigger (speaking of myself) how to read, there would be no keeping him. It would forever unfit him to be a slave. He would at once become unmanageable, and of no value to his master." Those words only made his desire to educate himself all the greater. Douglass's story proves that knowledge is indeed power.

11. *pens out of the hardest, toughest, troublesomest piece of old brass candlestick or something like that they can get their hands on.* Casanova made a pen by gnawing a splinter off the door with his teeth; Abbé Faria made one out of the cartilage of the heads of hake; Count de Charney made a crowquill out of a toothpick; Dr. Alexandre Manette in Chapter 10 of Book Three of Charles Dickens's *A Tale of Two Cities* (1849) used a "rusty iron point." But Tom is probably recalling that Abbé Faria made a knife, "my masterpiece," out of an old candlestick.

12. *iron-rust and tears.* "Iron-rust and spit" in the manuscript (in DeVoto, *Mark Twain at Work*, 1942, p. 83).

13. *the best authorities uses their own blood.* Such as Baron von Trenck and Abbé Faria; Dr. Alexandre Manette in Chapter 10 of Book 3 of *A Tale of Two Cities* used "soot and charcoal from the chimney, mixed with blood."

14. *The Iron Mask.* Tom has been reading *The Man in the Iron Mask*, vol. 6 of the series known as the "D'Artagnon Romances," *Le Vicomte de Bragelonne* (1848–1850), by Alexandre Dumas the Elder. It is a fictionalized account of the legend of the prisoner in the Bastille who always wore an iron mask during his captivity.

The Man in the Iron Mask.
Courtesy Picture Collection, New York Public Library, Astor, Lenox, and Tilden Foundations.

The riddle of the man's true identity has never been solved. Dumas followed the legend that he was the twin brother of Louis XV; in Chapter 31, "The Silver Dish," he described how the prisoner scratched his name on the back of a plate with a knife and threw it out the window

with, it would a been all right. So I let it go at that, though I couldn't see no advantage in my representing a prisoner, if I got to set down and chaw over a lot of gold-leaf distinctions[17] like that, every time I see a chance to hog a watermelon.

Well, as I was saying, we waited that morning till everybody was settled down to business, and nobody in sight around the yard; then Tom he carried the sack into the lean-to whilst I stood off a piece to keep watch. By-and-by he come out, and we went and set down on the wood-pile, to talk. He says:

"Everything's all right, now, except tools: and that's easy fixed."

"Tools?" I says.

"Yes."

"Tools for what?"

"Why, to dig with. We ain't agoing to *gnaw* him out, are we?"

"Ain't them old crippled picks and things in there good enough to dig a nigger out with?" I says.

He turns on me looking pitying enough to make a body cry, and says:

"Huck Finn, did you *ever* hear of a prisoner having picks and shovels, and all the modern conveniences in his wardrobe to dig himself out with? Now I want to ask you—if you got any reasonableness in you at all—what kind of a show would *that* give him to be a hero? Why, they might as well lend him the key, and done with it. Picks and shovels—why they wouldn't furnish 'em to a king."

"Well, then," I says, "if we don't want the picks and shovels, what do we want?"

"A couple of case-knives."[18]

"To dig the foundations out from under that cabin with?"

"Yes."

"Confound it, it's foolish, Tom."

"It don't make no difference how foolish it is, it's the *right* way—and it's the regular way. And there ain't no *other* way, that ever *I* heard of, and I've read all the books that gives any information about these things. They always dig out with a case-knife—and not through dirt, mind you; generly it's through solid rock. And it takes them weeks and weeks and weeks, and for ever and ever. Why, look at one of them prisoners in the bottom dungeon of the Castle Deef,[19] in the harbor of Marseilles, that dug himself out that way; how long was *he* at it, you reckon?"

"I don't know."

"Well, guess."

"I don't know. A month and a half?"

"*Thirty-seven year*[20]—and he come out in China. *That's* the kind. I wish the bottom of *this* fortress was solid rock."

"*Jim* don't know nobody in China."

"What's *that* got to do with it? Neither did that other fellow. But you're always a-wandering off on a side issue. Why can't you stick to the main point?"

"All right—*I* don't care where he comes out, so he *comes* out; and Jim don't, either, I reckon. But there's one thing, anyway—Jim's too old[21] to be dug out with a case-knife. He won't last."

"Yes he will *last,* too. You don't reckon it's going to take thirty-seven years to dig out through a *dirt* foundation, do you?"

"How long will it take, Tom?"

"Well, we can't resk being as long as we ought to, because it mayn't take very long for Uncle Silas to hear from down there by New Orleans. He'll hear Jim ain't from there. Then his next move will be to advertise Jim, or something like that.[22] So we can't resk being as long digging him out as we ought to. By

SMOUCHING THE KNIVES.

of his cell. During the *Quaker City* excursion, Twain visited the sight of his imprisonment in the Castle d'If (see note 19 below), and described the place in Chapter 11 of *The Innocents Abroad*:

> They showed us the noisome cell where the celebrated "Iron Mask"—that ill-starred brother of a hard-hearted king of France—was confined for a season, before he was sent to hide the strange mystery of his life from the curious in the dungeons of St. Marguerite. The place had a far greater interest for us than it could have had if we had known beyond all question who the Iron Mask was, and what his history had been, and why this most unusual punishment had been meted out to him. Mystery! That was the charm. That speechless tongue, those prisoned features, that heart so frightened with unspoken troubles, and that breast so oppressed with its piteous secret, had been there. These dank walls had known the man whose dolorous story is a sealed book forever! There was fascination in the spot.

15. *the nigger patch.* On some plantations, slaves were allowed a certain amount of ground on which to grow food to supplement whatever their masters gave them; whatever else they produced could be sold at market to pay for clothes and other items. These gardens also benefited the slaveholders, who did not feel obligated to provide much beyond simple necessities.

16. *Tom said what he meant was, we could steal anything we* needed. This semantical debate between "borrowing" and "stealing" rephrases Huck and Jim's discussion of taking whatever provisions they needed for their survival as well as pap Finn's definition of the word "borrowing." See Chapter 12, note 10.

17. *gold-leaf distinctions.* Superciliously fine distinctions, as thin and flimsy as gold leaf.

18. *case-knives.* Large kitchen or table knives.

19. *one of them prisoners in the bottom dungeon of the Castle Deef.* Abbé Faria, a priest who was imprisoned for conspiracy to unite Italy, is one of the principal characters of Dumas's famous novel *The Count of Monte Cristo* (1844). He was incarcerated in the cell next to that of Edmond

Abbé Faria and Edmund Dantès from *Le Comte de Monte Cristo* by Alexandre Dumas, the Elder.
Courtesy Library of Congress.

Dantès in the infamous Chateau d'If, off Marseilles. "We hired a sailboat and a guide," Twain recounted in Chapter 11 of *The Innocents Abroad*, "and made an excursion to one of the islands to visit the Castle d'If. This ancient fortress has a melancholy history. It has been used as a prison for political offenders for two or three hundred years. . . . The walls of these dungeons are as thick as some bedchambers at home are wide—fifteen feet. We saw the damp, dismal cells in which two of Dumas' heroes passed their confinement—heroes of *Monte Cristo*. It was here that the brave Abbé wrote a book with his own blood; with a pen made of a piece of iron hoop, and by the light of a lamp made out of shreds of cloth soaked in grease obtained from his food; and then dug through the thick wall with some trifling instrument which he wrought himself out of a stray piece of iron or table cutlery, and freed Dantès from his chains. It was a pity that so many weeks of dreary labor have come to naught at last." A pity, indeed, that it took so long. Much of Tom's plot to rescue Jim is a parody of *The Count of Monte Cristo*, a particularly appropriate source because, like *Huckleberry Finn*, it tells the story of someone (like Huck himself) who is thought to be dead and then returns under a new name to steal back what is rightfully his.

20. *Thirty-seven year.* As usual, Tom exaggerates: Abbé Faria was imprisoned in the Castle d'If

rights I reckon we ought to be a couple of years; but we can't. Things being so uncertain, what I recommend is this: that we really dig right in, as quick as we can; and after that, we can *let on,* to ourselves, that we was at it thirty-seven years. Then we can snatch him out and rush him away the first time there's an alarm. Yes, I reckon that'll be the best way."

"Now, there's *sense* in that," I says. "Letting on don't cost nothing; letting on ain't no trouble; and if it's any object, I don't mind letting on we was at it a hundred and fifty year. It wouldn't strain me none, after I got my hand in. So I'll mosey along now, and smouch a couple of case-knives."

"Smouch three," he says; "we want one to make a saw out of."

"Tom, if it ain't unregular and irreligious to sejest it," I says, "there's an old rusty saw-blade around yonder sticking under the weatherboarding behind the smoke-house."

He looked kind of weary and discouraged-like, and says:

"It ain't no use to try to learn you nothing, Huck. Run along and smouch the knives—three of them." So I done it.

for no more than ten years; after three he dug his way into the cell of Edmond Dantès.

21. *Jim's too old.* There is some confusion as to how old Jim might be. Actors who have played him have been of various ages, from twenty-nine-year-old Antonio Fargas in the 1975 ABC-TV production to fifty-four-year-old Brock Peters in the 1981 NBC-TV production. Twain never indicated in the story exactly how old Jim is, but that is no surprise. "By far the larger part of the slaves know as little of their ages as horses know of theirs," Frederick Douglass explained in Chapter 1 of his *Narrative* (1845), "and it is the wish of most masters within my knowledge to keep their slaves that ignorant. I do not remember to have ever met a slave who could tell of his birthday." *St. James' Gazette* (May 22, 1894), in its review of *Tom Sawyer Abroad* (1894), referred to Jim as "an old nigger." In his tribute to Twain in *The North American Review* (June 1910), Booker T. Washington called Jim "the colored boy" (p. 829). In his introduction to his "Morals Lecture" (as quoted in the Cleveland *Plain Dealer*, July 19, 1895), Twain revealed that "a very particular friend" of Tom and Huck's was "a middle-aged slave, named Jim."

22. *to advertise Jim, or something like that.* Tom and Huck have only a year in which to release Jim or he will be sold at auction. See Chapter 42, note 4.

Chapter XXXVI ·

GOING DOWN
THE LIGHTNING ROD.

As soon as we reckoned everybody was asleep, that night, we went down the lightning-rod, and shut ourselves up in the lean-to, and got out our pile of fox-fire, and went to work. We cleared everything out of the way, about four or five foot along the middle of the bottom log. Tom said he was right behind Jim's bed now, and we'd dig in under it, and when we got through there couldn't nobody in the cabin ever know there was any hole there, because Jim's counterpin[1] hung down most to the ground, and you'd have to raise it up and look under to see the hole. So we dug and dug, with the case-knives, till most midnight; and then we was dog-tired, and our hands was blistered, and yet you couldn't see we'd done anything, hardly. At last I says:

"This ain't no thirty-seven year job, this is a thirty-eight year job, Tom Sawyer."

He never said nothing. But he sighed, and pretty soon he stopped digging, and then for a good little while I knowed he was thinking. Then he says:

"It ain't no use, Huck, it ain't agoing to work. If we was prisoners it would, because then we'd have as many years as we wanted, and no hurry; and we wouldn't get but a few minutes to dig, every day, while they was changing watches,

1. *counterpin*. Counterpane, bedspread.

and so our hands wouldn't get blistered, and we could keep it up right along, year in and year out, and do it right, and the way it ought to be done. But *we* can't fool along, we got to rush; we ain't got no time to spare. If we was to put in another night this way, we'd have to knock off for a week to let our hands get well—couldn't touch a case-knife with them sooner."

"Well, then, what we going to do, Tom?"

"I'll tell you. It ain't right, and it ain't moral, and I wouldn't like it to get out—but there ain't only just the one way; we got to dig him out with the picks, and *let on* it's case-knives."

"*Now* you're *talking!*" I says; "your head gets leveler and leveler all the time, Tom Sawyer," I says. "Picks is the thing, moral or no moral; and as for me, I don't care shucks for the morality of it, nohow. When I start in to steal a nigger, or a watermelon, or a Sunday-school book, I ain't no ways particular how it's done so it's done. What I want is my nigger; or what I want is my watermelon; or what I want is my Sunday-school book; and if a pick's the handiest thing, that's the thing I'm agoing to dig that nigger or that watermelon or that Sunday-school book out with; and I don't give a dead rat what the authorities thinks about it nuther."

"Well," he says, "there's excuse for picks and letting-on in a case like this; if it warn't so, I wouldn't approve of it, nor I wouldn't stand by and see the rules broke—because right is right, and wrong is wrong, and a body ain't got no business doing wrong when he ain't ignorant and knows better. It might answer for *you* to dig Jim out with a pick, *without* any letting-on, because you don't know no better; but it wouldn't for me, because I do know better. Gimme a case-knife."

He had his own by him, but I handed him mine. He flung it down, and says:

"Gimme a *case-knife.*"

I didn't know just what to do—but then I thought. I scratched around amongst the old tools, and got a pick-ax and give it to him, and he took it and went to work, and never said a word.

He was always just that particular. Full of principle.

So then I got a shovel, and then we picked and shoveled,

turn about, and made the fur fly. We stuck to it about a half an hour, which was as long as we could stand up; but we had a good deal of a hole to show for it. When I got up stairs, I looked out at the window and see Tom doing his level best with the lightning-rod, but he couldn't come it, his hands was so sore. At last he says:

"It ain't no use, it can't be done. What you reckon I better do? Can't you think up no way?"

"Yes," I says, "but I reckon it ain't regular. Come up the stairs, and let on it's a lightning-rod."

So he done it.

Next day Tom stole a pewter spoon and a brass candlestick in the house, for to make some pens for Jim out of, and six tallow candles; and I hung around the nigger cabins, and laid for a chance, and stole three tin plates. Tom said it wasn't enough; but I said nobody wouldn't ever see the plates that Jim throwed out, because they'd fall in the dog-fennel[2] and jimpson weeds under the window-hole—then we could tote them back and he could use them over again. So Tom was satisfied. Then he says:

"Now, the thing to study out is, how to get the things to Jim."

STEALING SPOONS.

2. *dog-fennel.* Or "stinking camomile," so called for its odor. Both dog fennel and jimsonweed are particularly miserable plants.

"Take them in through the hole," I says, "when we get it done."

He only just looked scornful, and said something about nobody ever heard of such an idiotic idea, and then he went to studying. By-and-by he said he had ciphered out two or three ways, but there warn't no need to decide on any of them yet. Said we'd got to post Jim first.

That night we went down the lightning-rod a little after ten, and took one of the candles along, and listened under the window-hole, and heard Jim snoring; so we pitched it in, and it didn't wake him. Then we whirled in with the pick and shovel, and in about two hours and a half the job was done. We crept in under Jim's bed and into the cabin, and pawed around and found the candle and lit it, and stood over Jim a while, and found him looking hearty and healthy, and then we woke him up gentle and gradual. He was so glad to see us he most cried; and called us honey, and all the pet names he could think of; and was for having us hunt up a cold chisel[3] to cut the chain off of his leg with, right away, and clearing out without losing any time. But Tom he showed him how unregular it would be, and set down and told him all about our plans, and how we could alter them in a minute any time there was an alarm; and not to be the least afraid, because we would see he got away, *sure.* So Jim he said it was all right, and we set there and talked over old times a while, and then Tom asked a lot of questions, and when Jim told him Uncle Silas come in every day or two to pray with him,[4] and Aunt Sally come in to see if he was comfortable and had plenty to eat, and both of them was kind as they could be, Tom says:

"*Now* I know how to fix it. We'll send you some things by them."

I said, "Don't do nothing of the kind; it's one of the most jackass ideas I ever struck;" but he never paid no attention to me; went right on. It was his way when he'd got his plans set.

So he told Jim how we'd have to smuggle in the rope-ladder pie, and other large things, by Nat, the nigger that fed him, and he must be on the lookout, and not be surprised, and not let Nat see him open them; and we would put small

3. *a cold chisel.* A strong, highly tempered iron or steel chisel that can cut through cold iron.

4. *Uncle Silas come in every day or two to pray with him.* Twain's notes indicate that he once considered introducing a struggle between Uncle Silas and his conscience over what to do with Jim: The farmer-preacher "wishes he would escape—if it warn't wrong, he'd set him free—but it's a gushy generosity with another man's property" (University of California edition, 1988, p. 756). Property rights win over human rights again. In making good-natured Uncle Silas largely indifferent toward the runaway's fate, Twain heightens the paradox of a man who preaches on Sunday and yet is blind to his fellow man's suffering the rest of the week.

"Tom Sawyer Detective" reveals other characteristics of Uncle Silas not evident in *Huckleberry Finn*: He may be as "gentle as mush" to Tom Sawyer, but the old man is so enraged by Brace Dunlap's attentions toward Benny Phelps that he strikes his neighbor to kill; when Dunlap is found dead, Uncle Silas is arrested for the crime. Uncle John Quarles, the model for Uncle Silas, may have been more like the character in "Tom Sawyer, Detective" than that in *Huckleberry Finn*. "Grandma [Jane Clemens] said he drank and was not kind to Patsy [his wife]," Annie Moffett Webster revealed to Dr. M.

Uncle Silas strikes to kill. Illustration by A. B. Frost, "Tom Sawyer, Detective," *Harper's Monthly*, September 1896.
Courtesy Library of Congress.

things in uncle's coat pockets and he must steal them out; and we would tie things to aunt's apron strings or put them in her apron pocket, if we got a chance; and told him what they would be and what they was for. And told him how to keep a journal on the shirt with his blood, and all that. He told him everything. Jim he couldn't see no sense in the most of it, but he allowed we was white folks and knowed better than him; so he was satisfied, and said he would do it all just as Tom said.

Jim had plenty corn-cob pipes and tobacco; so we had a right down good sociable time; then we crawled out through the hole, and so home to bed, with hands that looked like they'd been chawed.[5] Tom was in high spirits. He said it was the best fun he ever had in his life, and the most intellectural; and said if he only could see his way to it we would keep it up all the rest of our lives and leave Jim to our children to get out; for he believed Jim would come to like it better and better the more he got used to it. He said that in that way it could be strung out to as much as eighty year, and would be the best time on record. And he said it would make us all celebrated that had a hand in it.

In the morning we went out to the wood-pile and chopped up the brass candlestick into handy sizes, and Tom put them and the pewter spoon in his pocket. Then we went to the nigger cabins, and while I got Nat's notice off, Tom shoved a piece of candlestick into the middle of a corn-pone that was in Jim's pan, and we went along with Nat to see how it would work, and it just worked noble; when Jim bit into it it most mashed all his teeth out; and there warn't ever anything could a worked better. Tom said so himself. Jim he never let on but what it was only just a piece of rock or something like that that's always getting into bread, you know; but after that he never bit into nothing but what he jabbed his fork into it in three or four places, first.

And whilst we was a standing there in the dimmish light, here comes a couple of the hounds bulging in, from under Jim's bed; and they kept on piling in till there was eleven of them, and there warn't hardly room in there to get your breath. By jings, we forgot to fasten that lean-to door. The

M. Brashear in "Mark Twain's Niece, Daughter of His Sister, Pamela, Taking Keen Interest in Centennial" (Hannibal *Evening Courier-Post*, March 6, 1935). "Later when we were living in Fredonia . . . Grandma still suffered with her sister." According to Albert Bigelow Paine's *Mark Twain: A Biography* (vol. 1, 1912), John Quarles used to make the most horrible threats to his children for disobedience, such as "I will make you smell like a burnt horn" (p. 18). But he never followed them through. That part of his uncle's personality may have been what Twain recalled in "Tom Sawyer, Detective." His nephew Sam was probably unaware of their domestic troubles: Twain said of his uncle John Quarles in "Chapters from My Autobiography" (*North American Review*, March 1, 1907), "I have not come across a better man than he was" (p. 451).

5. *hands that looked like they'd been chawed.* Blair and Fischer explained in the 1988 University of California edition that Twain's typist evidently missed a crucial phrase in the margin of the manuscript, "by a dog" (p. 353).

nigger Nat he only just hollered "witches!" once, and keeled over onto the floor amongst the dogs, and begun to groan like he was dying. Tom jerked the door open and flung out a slab of Jim's meat, and the dogs went for it, and in two seconds he was out himself and back again and shut the door, and I knowed he'd fixed the other door too. Then he went to work on the nigger, coaxing him and petting him, and asking him if he'd been imagining he saw something again. He raised up, and blinked his eyes around, and says:

"Mars Sid, you'll say I's a fool, but if I didn't b'lieve I see most a million dogs, er devils, er some'n, I wisht I may die right heah in dese tracks. I did, mos' sholy. Mars Sid, I *felt* um—I *felt* um, sah; dey was all over me. Dad fetch it, I jis' wisht I could git my han's on one er dem witches jis' wunst—on'y jis' wunst—it's all *I*'d ast. But mos'ly I wisht dey'd lemme 'lone, I does."

Tom says:

"Well, I tell you what *I* think. What makes them come here just at this runaway nigger's breakfast-time? It's because they're hungry; that's the reason. You make them a witch pie; that's the thing for *you* to do."

"But my lan', Mars Sid, how's *I* gwyne to make 'm a witch

TOM ADVISES A WITCH PIE.

pie? I doan' know how to make it. I hain't ever hearn er sich a thing b'fo.'"

"Well, then, I'll have to make it myself."

"Will you do it, honey?—will you? I'll wusshup de groun' und' yo' foot, I will!"

"All right, I'll do it, seeing it's you, and you've been good to us and showed us the runaway nigger. But you got to be mighty careful. When we come around, you turn your back; and then whatever we've put in the pan, don't you let on you see it at all. And don't you look, when Jim unloads the pan—something might happen, I don't know what. And above all, don't you *handle* the witch-things."

"*Hannel* 'm Mars Sid? What *is* you a talkin' 'bout? I wouldn' lay de weight er my finger on um, not f'r ten hund'd thous'n' billion dollars, I wouldn't."

Chapter XXXVII

THE RUBBAGE PILE.

That was all fixed. So then we went away and went to the rubbage-pile in the back yard where they keep the old boots, and rags, and pieces of bottles, and wore-out tin things, and all such truck, and scratched around and found an old tin washpan and stopped up the holes as well as we could, to bake the pie in, and took it down cellar and stole it full of flour, and started for breakfast and found a couple of shingle-nails that Tom said would be handy for a prisoner to scrabble his name and sorrows on the dungeon walls with,[1] and dropped one of them in Aunt Sally's apron pocket which was hanging on a chair, and t'other we stuck in the band of Uncle Silas's hat, which was on the bureau, because we heard the children say their pa and ma was going to the runaway nigger's house this morning, and then went to breakfast, and Tom dropped the pewter spoon in Uncle Silas's coat pocket, and Aunt Sally wasn't come yet, so we had to wait a little while.

And when she come she was hot, and red, and cross, and couldn't hardly wait for the blessing; and then she went to sluicing out[2] coffee with one hand and cracking the handiest child's head with her thimble with the other, and says:

"I've hunted high, and I've hunted low, and it does beat all, what *has* become of your other shirt."

1. *a couple of shingle-nails that . . . would be handy for a prisoner to scrabble his name and sorrows on the dungeon walls with.* Twain observed in Chapter 11 of *The Innocents Abroad* that the walls of Castle d'If "are scarred with the rudely-carved names of many and many a captive who fretted his life away here, and left no record of himself but these sad epitaphs wrought with his own hands. How thick the names were! . . . Names everywhere!—some plebeian, some noble, some even princely. Plebeian, prince, and noble, had one solicitude in common—they would not be forgotten! They could suffer solitude, inactivity, and the horrors of a silence that

Inscriptions on the walls of the dungeon in the Castle d'If. Illustration by True W. Williams, *The Innocents Abroad*, 1869.
Courtesy Library of Congress.

no sound ever disturbed; but they could not bear the thought of being utterly forgotten by the world. Hence the carved names."

2. *sluicing out*. Pouring out quickly in a straight jet of liquid; mining slang. See Chapter 29, note 18.

3. *turned kinder blue around the gills*. Turned pale with fright.

My heart fell down amongst my lungs and livers and things, and a hard piece of corn-crust started down my throat after it and got met on the road with a cough and was shot across the table and took one of the children in the eye and curled him up like a fishing-worm, and let a cry out of him the size of a war-whoop, and Tom he turned kinder blue around the gills,[3] and it all amounted to a considerable state of things for about a quarter of a minute or as much as that, and I would a sold out for half price if there was a bidder. But after that we was all right again—it was the sudden surprise of it that knocked us so kind of cold. Uncle Silas he says:

"It's most uncommon curious, I can't understand it. I know perfectly well I took it *off*, because——"

"Because you hain't got but one *on*. Just *listen* at the man! *I* know you took it off, and know it by a better way than your wool-gathering memory, too, because it was on the clo'es-line yesterday—I see it there myself. But it's gone—that's the long and the short of it, and you'll just have to change to a red flann'l one till I can get time to make a new one. And it'll be the third I've made in two years; it just keeps a body on the jump to keep you in shirts; and whatever you do manage to *do* with 'm all, is more'n *I* can make out. A body'd think you *would* learn to take some sort of care of 'em, at your time of life."

"I know it, Sally, and I do try all I can. But it oughtn't to be altogether my fault, because you know I don't see them nor have nothing to do with them except when they're on me; and I don't believe I've ever lost one of them *off* of me."

"Well, it ain't *your* fault if you haven't, Silas—you'd a done it if you could, I reckon. And the shirt ain't all that's gone, nuther. Ther's a spoon gone; and *that* ain't all. There was ten, and now ther's only nine. The calf got the shirt I reckon, but the calf never took the spoon, *that's* certain."

"Why, what else is gone, Sally?"

"Ther's six *candles* gone—that's what. The rats could a got the candles, and I reckon they did; I wonder they don't walk off with the whole place, the way you're always going to stop their holes and don't do it; and if they warn't fools they'd sleep in your hair, Silas—*you'd* never find it out; but you can't lay the *spoon* on the rats, and that I *know*."

"Well, Sally, I'm in fault, and I acknowledge it; I've been remiss; but I won't let to-morrow go by without stopping up them holes."

"Oh, I wouldn't hurry, next year'll do. Matilda Angelina Araminta *Phelps!*"[4]

Whack comes the thimble, and the child snatches her claws out of the sugar-bowl without fooling around any. Just then, the nigger woman steps onto the passage, and says:

"Missus, dey's a sheet gone."

"A *sheet* gone! Well, for the land's sake!"

"I'll stop up them holes *to-day*," says Uncles Silas, looking sorrowful.

"Oh, *do* shet up!—spose the rats took the *sheet? Where's* it gone, Lize?"

"Clah to goodness I hain't no notion, Miss Sally. She wuz on de clo's-line yistiddy, but she done gone; she ain' dah no mo,' now."

"I reckon the world *is* coming to an end. I *never* see the beat of it, in all my born days. A shirt, and a sheet, and a spoon, and six can—"

"Missus," comes a young yaller wench,[5] "dey's a brass cannelstick miss'n."

"Cler out from here, you hussy, er I'll take a skillet to ye!"

"MISSUS, DEY'S A SHEET GONE."

Well, she was just a biling. I begun to lay for a chance; I reckoned I would sneak out and go for the woods till the weather moderated. She kept a raging right along, running

4. *Matilda Angelina Araminta* Phelps! "In those old days," Twain explained in a note to Chapter 11 of *The Gilded Age*, "the average man called his children after his most revered literary and historical idols; consequently there was hardly a family, at least in the West, but had a Washington in it—and also a Lafayette, a Franklin, and six or eight sounding names from Byron, Scott, and the Bible, if the offspring held out." Eggleston referred to the custom in *The Hoosier School-Boy* (1883) by naming a little boy Christopher Columbus George Washington Marquis de Lafayette Risdale, a "victim of that mania which some people have for 'naming after' great men" (p. 30). It was also burlesqued in minstrel shows: Anthony J. Berret mentioned in "Huckleberry Finn and the Minstrel Show" (*American Studies*, Fall 1986, pp. 40 and 44) two examples, George Washington Julius Caesar Andrew Jackson John Smith and the actor Edwin Forrest McKean Buchanan Davenport Booth. Blair and Fischer suggested in the 1988 University of California edition that the Phelps girl got her name from various romantic sources: Matilda from the heroine of Sir Walter Scott's poem *Rokeby* (1813); Angelina from Oliver Goldsmith's "The Hermit" in *The Vicar of Wakefield*; and Araminta from Congreve's *The Bachelor* (1693) or Moneytrap's wife in Vanburgh's *The Confederacy* (1705).

5. *a young yaller wench.* A young mulatto woman, the result of miscegenation often through the master himself; light-skinned female slaves were usually domestic servants who attended the mistress and her children. See Chapter 22, note 1.

her insurrection all by herself, and everybody else mighty meek and quiet; and at last Uncle Silas, looking kind of foolish, fishes up that spoon out of his pocket. She stopped, with her mouth open and her hands up; and as for me, I wished I was in Jeruslem or somewheres.[6] But not long; because she says:

"It's *just* as I expected. So you had it in your pocket all the time; and like as not you've got the other things there, too. How'd it get there?"

"I reely don't know, Sally," he says, kind of apologizing, "or you know I would tell. I was a-studying over my text in Acts Seventeen,[7] before breakfast, and I reckon I put it in there, not noticing, meaning to put my Testament in, and it must be so, because my Testament ain't in, but I'll go and see, and if the Testament is where I had it, I'll know I didn't put it in, and that will show that I laid the Testament down and took up the spoon, and—"

"Oh, for the land's sake! Give a body a rest! Go 'long now, the whole kit and biling of ye; and don't come nigh me again till I've got back my peace of mind."

I'd a heard her, if she'd a said it to herself, let alone speaking it out; and I'd a got up and obeyed her, if I'd a been dead. As we was passing through the setting-room, the old man he took up his hat, and the shingle-nail fell out on the floor, and he just merely picked it up and laid it on the mantel-shelf, and never said nothing, and went out. Tom see him do it, and remembered about the spoon, and says:

"Well, it ain't no use to send things by *him* no more, he ain't reliable." Then he says: "But he done us a good turn with the spoon, anyway, without knowing it, and so we'll go and do him one without *him* knowing it—stop up his rat-holes."

There was a noble good lot of them, down cellar, and it took us a whole hour, but we done the job tight and good, and ship-shape. Then we heard steps on the stairs, and blowed out our light, and hid; and here comes the old man, with a candle in one hand and a bundle of stuff in t'other, looking as absent-minded as year before last. He went a mooning around,[8] first to one rat-hole and then another,

6. *I wished I was in Jeruslem or somewheres.* Huck is trying to think of Jericho; see Chapter 3, note 31.

7. *Acts Seventeen.* The Arkansas preacher has been reading about his namesake, Silas, who accompanied Paul to the Thessalonians; but Uncle Silas remains unmoved by either the previous chapter, which told of Silas in prison, or by Paul's teaching in Acts 17:24–26: "God that made the world and all things therein . . . hath made of one blood all nations of men for to dwell on all the face of the earth." In Chapter 32 of *The Innocents Abroad*, Twain recounted his visit to Mars Hill in Athens, "where [St. Paul] 'disputed daily' with the gossip-loving Athenians. We climbed the stone steps St. Paul ascended, and stood in the square-cut place he stood in." After this pilgrimage to the spot of Acts 17, Twain and his fellow travelers tried to steal some grapes, but were thwarted by Greek farmers with guns; this incident may in part have inspired all the mayhem Tom and Huck cause in Chapter 40.

8. *He went a mooning around.* He wandered about stupidly, as if moonstruck or in a dream.

till he'd been to them all. Then he stood about five minutes, picking tallow-drip off of his candle and thinking. Then he turns off slow and dreamy towards the stairs, saying:

"Well, for the life of me I can't remember when I done it. I could show her now that I warn't to blame on account of the rats. But never mind—let it go. I reckon it wouldn't do no good."

And so he went on a mumbling up stairs, and then we left. He was a mighty nice old man. And always is.

Tom was a good deal bothered about what to do for a spoon, but he said we'd got to have it; so he took a think. When he had ciphered it out, he told me how we was to do; then we went and waited around the spoon-basket till we see Aunt Sally coming, and then Tom went to counting the spoons and laying them out to one side, and I slid one of them up my sleeve, and Tom says:

"Why, Aunt Sally, there ain't but nine spoons, *yet.*"

She says:

"Go 'long to your play, and don't bother me. I know better, I counted 'm myself."

"Well, I've counted them twice, Aunty, and *I* can't make but nine."

IN A TEARING WAY.

She looked out of all patience, but of course she come to count—anybody would.

"I declare to gracious ther' *ain't* but nine!" she says. "Why, what in the world—plague *take* the things, I'll count 'm again."

So I slipped back the one I had, and when she got done counting, she says:

"Hang the troublesome rubbage, ther's *ten,* now!" and she looked huffy and bothered both. But Tom says:

"Why, Aunty, *I* don't think there's ten."

"You numskull, didn't you see me *count* 'm?"

"I know, but—"

"Well, I'll count 'm *again.*"

So I smouched one, and they come out nine same as the other time. Well, she *was* in a tearing way—just a trembling all over, she was so mad. But she counted and counted, till she got that addled she'd start to count-in the *basket* for a spoon, sometimes; and so, three times they come out right, and three times they come out wrong. Then she grabbed up the basket and slammed it across the house and knocked the cat galley-west;[9] and she said cle'r out and let her have some peace, and if we come bothering around her again betwixt that and dinner, she'd skin us. So we had the odd spoon; and dropped it in her apron pocket whilst she was a giving us our sailing-orders,[10] and Jim got it all right, along with her shingle-nail, before noon. We was very well satisfied with this business, and Tom allowed it was worth twice the trouble it took, because he said *now* she couldn't ever count them spoons twice alike again to save her life; and wouldn't believe she'd counted them right, if she *did;* and said that after she'd about counted her head off, for the next three days, he judged she'd give it up and offer to kill anybody that wanted her to ever count them any more.

So we put the sheet back on the line, that night, and stole one out of her closet; and kept on putting it back and stealing it again, for a couple of days, till she didn't know how many sheets she had, any more, and said she didn't *care,* and warn't agoing to bullyrag[11] the rest of her soul out

9. *knocked the cat galley-west.* Knocked the cat head over heels, from "collyweston," dialectical English for "awry, askew, confused." Twain introduced this colloquialism in an amusing exchange in "Schoolhouse Hill" of 1898, an early draft of *The Mysterious Stranger*, in which Tom Sawyer struggles to get a stranger in town to understand him:

> "Galley west? . . . "
> "It's just a word, you know. Means you've knocked his props from under him."
> "Knocked his props from under him?"
> "Yes—trumped his ace."
> "Trumped his—"
> "Ace. That's it—pulled his leg."
> "I assure you this is in error. I have not pulled his leg."
> "But you don't understand. Don't you see? You've graveled him, and he's disgruntled."
> The new boy's face expressed his despair. Tom reflected a moment, then his eye lighted with hope, and he said, with confidence—
> "Now you'll get the idea. . . . Well, you've walked up to the captain's office with *your* Latin, now, and pulled in high, low, jack and the game, and it's taken the curl out of his tail. There—that's the idea."
> The new boy hesitated, passed his hand over his forehead, and began, haltingly—
> "It is still a little vague. It was but a poor dictionary—that French-English—and over-rich in omissions. . . . " (*Huck Finn and Tom Sawyer Among the Indians*, 1989, pp. 225–26)

10. *she was a giving us our sailing-orders.* She was telling them to get out.

11. *bullyrag.* Verbally abuse, scold.

about it, and wouldn't count them again not to save her life, she druther die first.

So we was all right now, as to the shirt and the sheet and the spoon and the candles, by the help of the calf and the rats and the mixed-up counting; and as to the candlestick, it warn't no consequence, it would blow over by-and-by.

But that pie was a job; we had no end of trouble with that pie. We fixed it up away down in the woods, and cooked it there; and we got it done at last, and very satisfactory, too; but not all in one day; and we had to use up three washpans full of flour, before we got through, and we got burnt pretty much all over, in places, and eyes put out with the smoke; because, you see, we didn't want nothing but a crust, and we couldn't prop it up right, and she would always cave in. But of course we thought of the right way at last; which was to cook the ladder, too, in the pie. So then we laid in with Jim, the second night, and tore up the sheet all in little strings, and twisted them together, and long before daylight we had a lovely rope, that you could a hung a person with. We let on it took nine months to make it.

And in the forenoon we took it down to the woods, but it wouldn't go in the pie. Being made of a whole sheet, that way, there was rope enough for forty pies, if we'd a wanted them, and plenty left over for soup, or sausage, or anything you choose. We could a had a whole dinner.

But we didn't need it. All we needed was just enough for the pie, and so we throwed the rest away. We didn't cook none of the pies in the washpan, afraid the solder would melt; but Uncle Silas he had a noble brass warming-pan[12] which he thought considerable of, because it belonged to one of his ancesters with a long wooden handle[13] that come over from England with William the Conqueror in the *Mayflower* or one of them early ships[14] and was hid away up garret with a lot of other old pots and things that was valuable, not on account of being any account because they warn't, but on account of them being relicts, you know, and we snaked her out, private, and took her down there, but she failed on the first pies, because we didn't know how,

12. *a noble brass warming-pan.* In colonial times, long before central heating, a person used a warming pan to warm the bed before climbing in at night; coals were placed into a lidded warming pan, which was then slipped under the covers at the foot of the bed to heat it up.

13. *it belonged to one of his ancesters with a long wooden handle.* Warming pans had long handles, but Kemble extended Twain's joke by literally interpreting Huck's misplaced modifier and giving Uncle Silas's ancestor (whom he depicts as a pilgrim from the *Mayflower*) a wooden leg.

14. *from England with William the Conqueror in the* Mayflower *or one of them early ships.* It is a wonder he did not say the *Nina*, the *Pinta*, and the *Santa Maria*, too! The joke pokes fun at American hero worship: When not claiming descent from shabby European royalty as the king and the duke do, Americans boast of having descended from the earliest settlers of this land. Even in a young country, traditions are greatly overrated. Again Huck has garbled his history: William the Conqueror crossed the English Channel from France into Britain in 1066, and the Pilgrims came over to America from Holland on the *Mayflower* in 1621. He has probably confused William the Conqueror with William Bradford, the first governor of Massachusetts Bay Colony.

15. *she come up smiling*. She succeeded admirably; from prize ring slang, usually applied to a boxer who, although badly beaten, comes out of defeat not only without complaint but also in good spirits; a good sport.

16. *cramp him down to business*. Put him in his place; originally riverboat slang, meaning to force a steamboat to go in the desired direction.

ONE OF HIS ANCESTERS.

but she come up smiling[15] on the last one. We took and lined her with dough, and set her in the coals, and loaded her up with rag-rope, and put on a dough roof, and shut down the lid, and put hot embers on top, and stood off five foot, with the long handle, cool and comfortable, and in fifteen minutes she turned out a pie that was a satisfaction to look at. But the person that et it would want to fetch a couple of kags of toothpicks along, for if that rope-ladder wouldn't cramp him down to business,[16] I don't know nothing what I'm talking about, and lay him in enough stomach-ache to last him till next time, too.

Nat didn't look, when we put the witch-pie in Jim's pan; and we put the three tin plates in the bottom of the pan under the vittles; and so Jim got everything all right, and as soon as he was by himself he busted into the pie and hid the rope-ladder inside of his straw tick, and scratched some marks on a tin plate and throwed it out of the window-hole.

Chapter XXXVIII

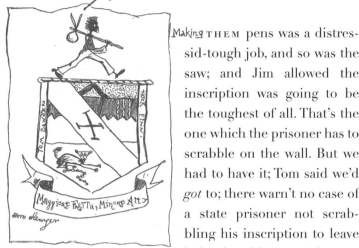

JIM'S COAT OF ARMS.

Making THEM pens was a distressid-tough job, and so was the saw; and Jim allowed the inscription was going to be the toughest of all. That's the one which the prisoner has to scrabble on the wall. But we had to have it; Tom said we'd *got* to; there warn't no case of a state prisoner not scrabbling his inscription to leave behind, and his coat of arms.

"Look at Lady Jane Grey," he says; "look at Gilford Dudley; look at old Northumberland![1] Why, Huck, spose it *is* considerble trouble?—what you going to do?—how you going to get around it? Jim's *got* to do his inscription and coat of arms.[2] They all do."

Jim says:

"Why, Mars Tom, I hain't got no coat o' arms; I hain't got nuffn but dish-yer ole shirt, en you knows I got to keep de journal on dat."

"Oh, you don't understand, Jim; a coat of arms is very different."

"Well," I says, "Jim's right, anyway, when he says he hain't got no coat of arms, because he hain't."

"I reckon *I* knowed that," Tom says, "but you bet he'll have one before he goes out of this—because he's going out *right*, and there ain't going to be no flaws in his record."

1. *Lady Jane Grey . . . Gilford Dudley . . . old Northumberland.* Tom has likely been reading William Harrison Ainsworth's popular romance *The Tower of London* (1840): The Duke of Northumberland (1502?–1553) treacherously persuades young King Edward VI to break his father King Henry VIII's will to change the line of succession in favor of the duke's Protestant daughter-in-law, Lady Jane Grey (1537–1554), instead of the king's Catholic sister, Mary Tudor. That would have shifted the power of the English throne from the Tudors to the Dudleys. Upon Edward's death, the sixteen-year-old girl ruled England for nine days before she was arrested with the duke and her husband, Lord Guildford Dudley (d. 1554); they were imprisoned in the Tower of London and all beheaded. Twain portrayed the doomed Lady Jane Grey sympathetically in *The Prince and the Pauper*.

Lady Jane Grey with Lord Guildford Dudley on her left and the Duke of Northumberland on her right.
Courtesy Picture Collection, New York Public Library, Astor, Lenox, and Tilden Foundations.

Northumberland's inscription in the Tower of London.
Courtesy Library of Congress.

So whilst me and Jim filed away at the pens on a brickbat apiece, Jim a making his'n out of the brass and I making mine out of the spoon, Tom set to work to think out the coat of arms. By-and-by he said he'd struck so many good ones he didn't hardly know which to take, but there was one which he reckoned he'd decide on. He says:

"On the scutcheon we'll have a bend *or* in the dexter base, a saltire *murrey* in the fess, with a dog, couchant, for common charge, and under his foot a chain embattled, for slavery, with a chevron *vert* in a chief engrailed, and three invected lines on a field *azure,* with the nombril points rampant on a dancette indented; crest, a runaway nigger, *sable,* with his bundle over his shoulder on a bar sinister: and a couple of gules for supporters,[3] which is you and me; motto, *Maggiore fretta, minore atto.* Got it out of a book—means, the more haste, the less speed."[4]

"Geewhillikins," I says, "but what does the rest of it mean?"

"We ain't got no time to bother over that," he says, "we got to dig in like all git-out."

"Well, anyway," I says, "what's *some* of it? What's a fess?"

"A fess—a fess is—*you* don't need to know what a fess is. I'll show him how to make it when he gets to it."

"Shucks, Tom," I says, "I think you might tell a person. What's a bar sinister?"

"Oh, *I* don't know. But he's got to have it. All the nobility does."[5]

That was just his way. If it didn't suit him to explain a thing to you, he wouldn't do it.[6] You might pump at him a week, it wouldn't make no difference.

He'd got all that coat of arms business fixed, so now he started in to finish up the rest of that part of the work, which was to plan out a mournful inscription—said Jim got to have one, like they all done. He made up a lot, and wrote them out on a paper, and read them off, so:

1. *Here a captive heart busted.*

2. *Here a poor prisoner, forsook by the world and friends, fretted out his sorrowful life.*

2. *Jim's* got *to do his inscription and coat of arms*. "Every room from roof to vault," Ainsworth described the Beauchamp Tower in Chapter 4 of Book II of *The Tower of London*, "is covered with melancholy memorials of its illustrious and unfortunate occupants. . . . In general, they are beautifully carved, ample time being allowed the writers for their melancholy employment." It was on one of these walls that the Duke of Northumberland carved his coat of arms. "This curious sculpture may still be seen on the right hand of the fire-place of the mess-room in the Beauchamp Tower," Ainsworth wrote in Chapter 7 of Book II, "and contains his cognizance, a bear and lion supporting a ragged staff surrounded by a border of roses, acorns, and flowers intermingled with foliage. Northumberland was employed upon the third line of the quatrain below his name, which remains unfinished to the present day, when he was interrupted by the entrance of a priest. . . ."

One of the worst manifestations of ancestor worship in America was the proliferation of phony coats of arms. "Distinctions of wealth and family, and those, too, well defined and strongly marked, have already appeared," observed Charles Augustus Murray in *Travels in North America* (1839), "accompanied by a criterion apparently trifling, but . . . bearing strong evidence, namely 'coats of arms,' and other heraldic anti-republican signs, which are daily gaining ground." Twain spoke as much for the

3. *Here a lonely heart broke, and a worn spirit went to its rest, after thirty-seven years of solitary captivity.*

4. *Here, homeless and friendless, after thirty-seven years of bitter captivity, perished a noble stranger, natural son of Louis XIV.*[7]

Tom's voice trembled, whilst he was reading them, and he most broke down. When he got done, he couldn't no way make up his mind which one for Jim to scrabble onto the wall, they was all so good; but at last he allowed he would let him scrabble them all on. Jim said it would take him a year to scrabble such a lot of truck onto the logs with a nail, and he didn't know how to make letters, besides; but Tom said he would block them out for him, and then he wouldn't have nothing to do but just follow the lines. Then pretty soon he says:

"Come to think, the logs ain't agoing to do; they don't have log walls in a dungeon: we got to dig the inscriptions into a rock. We'll fetch a rock."

Jim said the rock was worse than the logs; he said it would take him such a pison long time to dig them into a rock, he wouldn't ever get out. But Tom said he would let me help him do it. Then he took a look to see how me and Jim was getting along with the pens. It was most pesky tedious hard work and slow, and didn't give my hands no show to get well of the sores, and we didn't seem to make no headway, hardly. So Tom says:

"I know how to fix it. We got to have a rock for the coat of arms and mournful inscriptions, and we can kill two birds with that same rock. There's a gaudy big grindstone down at the mill, and we'll smouch it, and carve the things on it, and file out the pens and the saw on it, too."

It warn't no slouch of an idea; and it warn't no slouch of a grindstone nuther; but we allowed we'd tackle it. It warn't quite midnight, yet, so we cleared out for the mill, leaving Jim at work. We smouched the grindstone, and set out to roll her home, but it was a most nation tough job. Sometimes, do what we could, we couldn't keep her from falling over, and she come mighty near mashing us, every time.

present day as about the past: The American mania for European titles and other signs of royal descent increased steadily during the Gilded Age. And it has never gone out of fashion.

3. *scutcheon . . . supporters*. As James Birchfield discussed in "Jim's Coat of Arms" (*Mark Twain Journal*, Summer 1969, pp. 15–16), Tom generally uses the correct heraldic terms.

scutcheon. Escutcheon, the surface, usually shaped like a shield, on which the armorial emblems are depicted.

a bend or. A gold horizontal band, from top left to bottom right side across the shield from the top left to the bottom right.

the dexter base. An error: The dexter baston, which extends across the shield, could not be confined to the right-hand side of the bottom third of the design.

a saltire murrey *in the fess*. A mulberry-colored diagonal cross on its side, within a horizontal band across the shield.

a dog, couchant. A dog lying down but with the head erect.

for common charge. For whatever is on the base of the shield.

a chain embattled: A chain across the shield representing a row of battlements.

a chevron vert *in a chief engrailed*: A green band like an inverted V, usually at the base of the shield, but here within its top third, which

Missouri State seal.
Courtesy the Mark Twain Papers, Bancroft Library, University of California at Berkeley.

Tom said she was going to get one of us, sure, before we got through. We got her half way; and then we was plumb played out, and most drownded with sweat. We see it warn't no use, we got to go and fetch Jim. So he raised up his bed and slid the chain off of the bed-leg, and wrapt it round and round his neck, and we crawled out through our hole and down there, and Jim and me laid into that grindstone and walked her along like nothing; and Tom superintended. He could out-superintend any boy I ever see. He knowed how to do everything.

Our hole was pretty big, but it warn't big enough to get the grindstone through; but Jim he took the pick and soon made it big enough. Then Tom marked out them things on it with the nail, and set Jim to work on them, with the nail for a chisel and an iron bolt from the rubbage in the lean-to for a hammer, and told him to work till the rest of his candle quit on him, and then he could go to bed, and hide the grindstone under his straw tick and sleep on it. Then we helped him fix his chain back on the bed-leg, and was ready for bed ourselves. But Tom thought of something, and says:

"You got any spiders in here, Jim?"

"No, sah, thanks to goodness I hain't, Mars Tom."

"All right, we'll get you some."

A TOUGH JOB.

has scalloped edges, with the points downward.

invected lines on a field azure. Scalloped lines with the points downward and thus fitting within the engrailed edge, on a bright blue field.

the nombril points rampant. Generally the point situation between the fess point and the base of the shield, here pointing upward.

dancette indented. A zigzag band with edges notched toward the middle of the shield.

crest . . . sable. A black figure (Jim drawn in the fashion of the standard wood engraving of a runaway slave).

bar sinister. Actually "bend sinister," a band, generally smaller than the fess, which runs across the shield from the bottom left to the top right.

a couple of gules. Apparently a pun, for "gules" merely means red.

supporters. Figures placed at each side of the shield, usually applied to animals.

4. Maggiore fretta, minore atto . . . *the more haste, the less speed*. Actually "the more haste, the less action," an appropriate motto for Tom's cavalier attitude toward Jim's plight. This was a common textbook maxim of the period.

5. *a bar sinister. . . . he's got to have it. All the nobility does*. A sinister remark about aristocracy: A bar sinister is the mark of a bastard.

6. *If it didn't suit him to explain a thing to you, he wouldn't do it*. Tom's head is so full of empty romantic notions that he may know the names of all the rituals and symbols but he is ignorant of their meanings.

7. a noble stranger, natural son of Louis XIV. A "natural son" is a bastard; one theory about the Man in the Iron Mask was that he was the illegitimate child of Louis XIV and Mademoiselle de la Vallière.

"But bless you, honey, I doan' *want* none. I's afeard un um. I jis' 's soon have rattlesnakes aroun'."

Tom thought a minute or two, and says:

"It's a good idea. And I reckon it's been done. It *must* a been done; it stands to reason. Yes, it's a prime good idea. Where could you keep it?"

"Keep what, Mars Tom?"

"Why, a rattlesnake."

"De goodness gracious alive, Mars Tom! Why, if dey was a rattlesnake to come in heah, I'd take en bust right out thoo dat log wall, I would, wid my head."

"Why, Jim, you wouldn't be afraid of it, after a little. You could tame it."

"*Tame* it!"

"Yes—easy enough. Every animal is grateful for kindness and petting, and they wouldn't *think* of hurting a person that pets them. Any book will tell you that. You try—that's all I ask; just try for two or three days. Why, you can get him so, in a little while, that he'll love you; and sleep with you; and won't stay away from you a minute; and will let you wrap him round your neck and put his head in your mouth."

"*Please,* Mars Tom—*doan'* talk so! I can't *stan'* it! He'd *let* me shove his head in my mouf—fer a favor, hain't it? I lay he'd wait a pow'ful long time 'fo' I *ast* him. En mo' en dat, I doan' *want* him to sleep wid me."

"Jim, don't act so foolish. A prisoner's *got* to have some kind of a dumb pet,[8] and if a rattlesnake hain't ever been tried, why, there's more glory to be gained in your being the first to ever try it than any other way you could ever think of to save your life."

"Why, Mars Tom, I doan' *want* no sich glory. Snake take 'n bite Jim's chin off, den *whah* is de glory? No, sah, I doan' want no sich doin's."

"Blame it, can't you *try?* I only *want* you to try—you needn't keep it up if it don't work."

"But de trouble all *done,* ef de snake bite me while I's a tryin' him. Mars Tom, I's willin' to tackle mos' anything 'at ain't onreasonable, but ef you en Huck fetches a rattlesnake in heah for me to tame, I's gwyne to *leave,* dat's *shore.*"

8. *A prisoner's* got *to have some kind of a dumb pet.* Count de Charney made pets of spiders; Baron von Trenck trained a mouse. Byron's Prisoner of Chillon admits:

With spiders I had friendship made,
And watch'd them in their sullen trade,
Had seen the mice by moonlight play,
And why should I feel less than they?

"Well, then, let it go, let it go, if you're so bullheaded about it. We can get you some garter-snakes[9] and you can tie some buttons on their tails, and let on they're rattlesnakes,[10] and I reckon that'll have to do."

"I k'n stan' *dem,* Mars Tom,[11] but blame' 'f I couldn' get along widout um, I tell you dat. I never knowed b'fo', 't was so much bother and trouble to be a prisoner."

"Well, it *always* is, when it's done right. You got any rats around here?"

BUTTONS ON THEIR TAILS.

"No, sah, I hain't seed none."

"Well, we'll get you some rats."

"Why, Mars Tom, I doan' *want* no rats. Dey's de dad-blamedest creturs[12] to sturb a body, en rustle roun' over 'im, en bite his feet, when he's tryin' to sleep, I ever see. No, sah, gimme g'yarter-snakes, 'f I's got to have 'm, but doan' gimme no rats, I ain' got no use f'r um, skasely."

"But Jim, you *got* to have 'em—they all do. So don't make no more fuss about it. Prisoners ain't ever without rats. There ain't no instance of it. And they train them, and pet them, and learn them tricks, and they get to be as sociable as flies. But you got to play music to them. You got anything to play music on?"

"I ain' got nuffn but a coase comb en a piece o' paper,[13] en a juice-harp;[14] but I reck'n dey wouldn' take no stock in a juice-harp."

"Yes, they would. *They* don't care what kind of music 'tis. A jews-harp's plenty good enough for a rat. All animals

9. *garter-snakes*. Here the Quarles farm again. "Along outside of the front fence ran the country road," he reported in his autobiography (*North American Review*, March 1, 1907); "dusty in the summer-time, and a good place for snakes—they liked to lie in it and sun themselves; when they were rattlesnakes or puff adders, we killed them . . . when they were 'house snakes' or 'garters' we carried them home and put them in Aunt Patsy's work-basket for a surprise; for she was prejudiced against snakes, and always when she took the basket in her lap and they began to climb out of it it disordered her mind. She never could seem to get used to them; her opportunities went for nothing" (p. 456). As the next chapter discloses, Aunt Sally shares Aunt Patsy's "prejudice."

10. *you can tie some buttons on their tails, and let on they're rattlesnakes*. "Buttons" is a colloquial word for rattlesnake rattles.

11. *I k'n stan'* dem, *Mars Tom*. In his revision for the 1884–1885 "Twins of Genius" tour, Twain noted in the margin that Jim's lament should be "pathetic . . . almost tearful."

12. *dad-blamedest creturs*. For the 1884–1885 "Twins of Genius" tour, Twain wrote an alternative to this protest: "de troublesomest creturs bout gallopin and scramblin and carryin on over a pusson when he's tryin' to *res*—in de world!"

13. *a coase comb en a piece o' paper*. A "coarse comb" is a large, wide-toothed comb which can be made into a musical instrument by covering the teeth with a piece of paper and blowing a tune through it.

14. *a juice-harp*. A "Jew's harp" is made of an elastic metal tongue fastened at one end to a small lyre-shaped frame; it is played with the teeth. Both this and the coarse comb were simply made instruments played by slaves.

likes music—in a prison they dote on it. Specially, painful music; and you can't get no other kind out of a jews-harp. It always interests them; they come out to see what's the matter with you. Yes, you're all right; you're fixed very well. You want to set on your bed, nights, before you go to sleep, and early in the mornings, and play your jews-harp; play "The Last Link is Broken"[15]—that's the thing that'll scoop[16] a rat, quicker'n anything else: and when you've played about two minutes, you'll see all the rats, and the snakes, and spiders, and things begin to feel worried about you, and come. And they'll just fairly swarm over you, and have a noble good time."

"Yes, *dey* will, I reck'n, Mars Tom, but what kine er time is *Jim* havin'? Blest if I kin see de pint. But I'll do it ef I got to. I reck'n I better keep de animals satisfied, en not have no trouble in de house."

Tom waited to think over, and see if there wasn't nothing else; and pretty soon he says:

"Oh—there's one thing I forgot. Could you raise a flower here, do you reckon?"

"I doan' know but maybe I could, Mars Tom; but it's tolable dark in heah, en I ain' got no use f'r no flower, nohow, en she'd be a pow'ful sight o' trouble."

"Well, you try it, anyway. Some other prisoners has done it."

"One er dem big cat-tail-lookin' mullen-stalks[17] would grow in heah, Mars Tom, I reck'n, but she wouldn' be wuth half de trouble she'd coss."

"Don't you believe it. We'll fetch you a little one, and you plant it in the corner, over there, and raise it. And don't call it mullen, call it Pitchiola[18]—that's its right name, when it's in a prison. And you want to water it with your tears."

"Why, I got plenty spring water, Mars Tom."

"You don't *want* spring water; you want to water it with your tears. It's the way they always do."

"Why, Mars Tom, I lay I kin raise one er dem mullen-stalks twyste wid spring water whiles another man's a *start'n* one wid tears."

"That ain't the idea. You *got* to do it with tears."

15. *"The Last Link is Broken."* See Chapter 17, note 62.

16. *scoop.* Here catch, overpower.

17. *mullen-stalks.* Or "mullein"; a large wild plant with coarse leaves and yellow tubular flowers, of the same family as the North American foxglove.

18. *Pitchiola.* Tom has been reading the popular romance *Picciola, or Captivity Captive* (1836) by "M. D. Saintine" (Joseph Xavier Boniface). When Napoléon incarcerates the Count de Charney, the only thing that makes life worth living for the prisoner is a plant growing in his cell that his jailor calls "le picciola" (the stalk).

IRRIGATION.

"She'll die on my han's, Mars Tom, she sholy will; kase I doan' skasely ever cry."

So Tom was stumped. But he studied it over, and then said Jim would have to worry along the best he could with an onion. He promised he would go to the nigger cabins and drop one, private, in Jim's coffee-pot, in the morning. Jim said he would "jis' 's soon have tobacker in his coffee;" and found so much fault with it, and with the work and bother of raising the mullen, and jews-harping the rats, and petting and flattering up the snakes and spiders and things, on top of all the other work he had to do on pens, and inscriptions, and journals, and things, which made it more trouble and worry and responsibility to be a prisoner than anything he ever undertook, that Tom most lost all patience with him; and said he was just loadened down with more gaudier chances than a prisoner ever had in the world to make a name for himself, and yet he didn't know enough to appreciate them, and they was just about wasted on him. So Jim he was sorry, and said he wouldn't behave so no more, and then me and Tom shoved for bed.

Chapter XXXIX

KEEPING OFF DULL TIMES.

In THE morning we went up to the village and bought a wire rat trap and fetched it down, and unstopped the best rat hole, and in about an hour we had fifteen of the bulliest kind of ones; and then we took it and put it in a safe place under Aunt Sally's bed. But while we was gone for spiders, little Thomas Franklin Benjamin Jefferson Elexander Phelps[1] found it there, and opened the door of it to see if the rats would come out, and they did; and Aunt Sally she come in, and when we got back she was a standing on top of the bed raising Cain,[2] and the rats was doing what they could to keep off the dull times[3] for her. So she took and dusted us both with the hick'ry, and we was as much as two hours catching another fifteen or sixteen, drat that meddlesome cub, and they warn't the likeliest, nuther, because the first haul was the pick of the flock.[4] I never see a likelier lot of rats than what that first haul was.

We got a splendid stock of sorted spiders, and bugs, and frogs, and caterpillars, and one thing or another; and we like-to got a hornet's nest, but we didn't. The family was at home. We didn't give it right up, but staid with them as long as we could; because we allowed we'd tire them out or they'd got to tire us out, and they done it. Then we got ally-

1. *Thomas Franklin Benjamin Jefferson Elexander Phelps*. See Chapter 37, note 4.

2. *a standing on top of the bed raising Cain*. Twain was more detailed in his revision of this passage for his 1884–1885 "Twins of Genius" tour: "skippin' and a scallopin' around on her bed tryin' to turn herself inside out. You never *see* a body act so." And he wrote an alternative version in the margin: "a yelpin and screechin and a carryin on—perfect insurrection all by herself—well, you never see anything *like* it."

3. *keep off the dull times*. Twain changed this phrase to "make it sociable" for his 1884–1885 "Twins of Genius" tour.

4. *flock*. "Communion" in his revision for the 1884–1885 "Twins of Genius" tour. Huck disrespectfully compares a bunch of snakes with a church congregation.

cumpain[5] and rubbed on the places, and was pretty near all right again, but couldn't set down convenient.[6] And so we went for the snakes, and grabbed a couple of dozen garters and house-snakes, and put them in a bag, and put it in our room, and by that time it was supper time, and a rattling good honest day's work; and hungry?—oh, no, I reckon not! And there warn't a blessed snake up there, when we went back—we didn't half tie the sack, and they worked out, somehow, and left. But it didn't matter much, because they was still on the premises somewheres. So we judged we could get some of them again. No, there warn't no real scarcity of snakes about the house for a considerable spell. You'd see them dripping from the rafters and places, every now and then; and they generly landed[7] in your plate, or down the back of your neck, and most of the time[8] where you didn't want them. Well, they was handsome, and striped, and there warn't no harm in a million of them; but that never made no difference to Aunt Sally, she despised snakes, be the breed[9] what they might, and she couldn't stand them no way you could fix it; and every time one of them flopped down on her, it didn't make no difference what she was doing, she would just lay that work down and light out. I never see such a woman. And you could hear her whoop to Jericho. You couldn't get her to take aholt of one of them with the tongs. And if she turned over and found one in bed, she would scramble out and lift a howl that you would think the house was afire.[10] She disturbed the old man so, that he said he could most wish there hadn't ever been no snakes created. Why, after every last snake had been gone clear out of the house for as much as a week, Aunt Sally warn't over it yet; she warn't near over it; when she was setting thinking about something, you could[11] touch her on the back of her neck with a feather and she would jump right out of her stockings. It was very curious. But Tom said all women was just so. He said they was made that way; for some reason or other.

We got a licking every time one of our snakes come in her way; and she allowed these lickings warn't nothing to what she would do if we ever loaded up the place again with

5. *allycumpain*. Elecampane, a large coarse and bitter herb with yellow flowers, whose root was used as a remedy for pulmonary diseases.

6. *but couldn't set down convenient*. "That warn't no matter, didn't have time to set down" was added in the revisions for the 1884–1885 "Twins of Genius" tour.

7. *they generly landed*. "When you warn't expectin they'd come down ker-*whop*" was added in Twain's revisions for his 1884–1885 "Twins of Genius" tour.

8. *most of the time*. "Very often" in Twain's revisions for his 1884–1885 "Twins of Genius" tour.

9. *breed*. "Denomination" in Twain's revisions for his 1884–1885 "Twins of Genius" tour.

10. *a howl that you would think the house was afire*. Twain added in his revisions for the 1884–1885 "Twins of Genius" tour, "She *could* make more fuss over a little thing."

11. *when she was setting thinking about something, you could*. "Just take a frog or something cold" was added in Twain's revisions for his 1884–1885 "Twins of Genius" tour.

them. I didn't mind the lickings, because they didn't amount to nothing; but I minded the trouble we had, to lay in another lot. But we got them laid in, and all the other things; and you never see a cabin as blithesome as Jim's was when they'd all swarm out for music and go for him. Jim didn't like the spiders, and the spiders didn't like Jim; and so they'd lay for him and make it mighty warm for him.[12] And he said that between the rats, and the snakes, and the grindstone, there warn't no room in bed for him, skasely; and when there was, a body couldn't sleep, it was so lively, and it was always lively, he said, because *they* never all slept at one time, but took turn about, so when the snakes was asleep the rats was on deck, and when the rats turned in the snakes come on watch, so he always had one gang under him, in his way, and t'other gang having a circus over him, and if he got up to hunt a new place, the spiders would take a chance at him as he crossed over.[13] He said if he ever got out, this time, he wouldn't ever be a prisoner again, not for a salary.

Well, by the end of three weeks, everything was in pretty good shape.[14] The shirt was sent in early, in a pie, and every time a rat bit Jim he would get up and write a little in his journal whilst the ink was fresh; the pens was made, the

SAWDUST DIET.

12. *make it mighty warm for him*. "Sultry" instead of "warm" and "Well, it was beautiful to see" were added in the revisions for the 1884–1885 "Twins of Genius" tour.

13. *take a chance at him as he crossed over*. "Shy" instead of "chance" and "Well, he, well he was kinder disappointed" were added in the revisions for the 1884–1885 "Twins of Genius" tour.

14. *everything was in pretty good shape*. "For the escape" was added in the revisions for the 1884–1885 "Twins of Genius" tour.

inscriptions and so on was all carved on the grindstone; the bed-leg was sawed in two, and we had et up the sawdust, and it give us a most amazing stomach-ache. We reckoned we was all going to die, but didn't. It was the most undigestible sawdust I ever see; and Tom said the same. But as I was saying, we'd got all the work done, now, at last; and we was all pretty much fagged out, too, but mainly Jim. The old man had wrote a couple of times to the plantation below Orleans to come and get their runaway nigger, but hadn't got no answer, because there warn't no such plantation; so he allowed he would advertise Jim in the St. Louis and New Orleans papers; and when he mentioned the St. Louis ones, it give me the cold shivers, and I see we hadn't no time to lose. So Tom said, now for the nonnamous letters.

"What's them?" I says.

"Warnings to the people that something is up. Sometimes it's done one way, sometimes another.[15] But there's always somebody spying around, that gives notice to the governor of the castle. When Louis XVI. was going to light out of the Tooleries, a servant girl done it. It's a very good way, and so is the nonnamous letters. We'll use them both. And it's usual for the prisoner's mother to change clothes with him, and she stays in, and he slides out in her clothes. We'll do that too."

"But looky here, Tom, what do we want to *warn* anybody for, that something's up? Let them find it out for themselves[16]—it's their lookout."

"Yes, I know; but you can't depend on them. It's the way they've acted from the very start—left us to do *everything*. They're so confiding and mullet-headed[17] they don't take notice of nothing at all. So if we don't *give* them notice, there won't be nobody nor nothing to interfere with us, and so after all our hard work and trouble this escape 'll go off perfectly flat:[18] won't amount to nothing—won't be nothing *to* it."

"Well, as for me, Tom,[19] that's the way I'd like."

"Shucks," he says, and looked disgusted. So I says:

15. *Sometimes it's done one way, sometimes another*. Twain added "in the books" to "it's done one way" in the revisions for the 1884–1885 "Twins of Genius" tour. One of them was obviously Thomas Carlyle's *The French Revolution* (1838), because in Chapters 3 and 4 he described both ways: "a certain false Chambermaid of the Palace" betrayed Louis XVI to his enemies when the king tried to flee to the Tuileries, then the royal palace of France (now a park near the Louvre); and "a billet" warned "some Patriot Deputy" about the plans.

16. *Let them find it out for themselves*. "Let 'em take care of the nigger themselves" was added in the revisions for the 1884–1885 "Twins of Genius" tour.

17. *confiding and mullet-headed*. Trusting and stupid like the mullet, a fish.

18. *go off perfectly flat*. "Won't be no excitement" was added in Twain's revisions for his 1884–1885 "Twins of Genius" tour.

19. *as for me, Tom*. "Sawyer, when *I'm* settin' a runaway nigger free" was added in the revisions for the 1884–1885 "Twins of Genius" tour.

"But I ain't going to make no complaint. Any way that suits you suits me. What you going to do about the servant-girl?"

"You'll be her. You slide in, in the middle of the night, and hook that yaller girl's frock."

"Why, Tom, that'll make trouble next morning; because of course she prob'bly hain't got any but that one."

"I know; but you don't want it but fifteen minutes, to carry the nonnamous letter and shove it under the front door."

"All right, then, I'll do it; but I could carry it just as handy in my own togs."

"You wouldn't look like a servant-girl *then,* would you?"

"No, but there won't be nobody to see what I look like, *anyway.*"

"That ain't got nothing to do with it. The thing for us to do, is just to do our *duty,* and not worry about whether anybody *sees* us do it or not. Hain't you got no principle at all?"

"All right, I ain't saying nothing; I'm the servant-girl. Who's Jim's mother?"

"I'm his mother. I'll hook a gown from Aunt Sally."

"Well, then, you'll have to stay in the cabin when me and Jim leaves."

"Not much. I'll stuff Jim's clothes full of straw and lay it on his bed to represent his mother in disguise, and Jim 'll take the nigger woman's gown off of me and wear it,[20] and we'll all evade together. When a prisoner of style escapes, it's called an evasion.[21] It's always called so when a king escapes, frinstance. And the same with a king's son; it don't make no difference whether he's a natural one or an unnatural one."

So Tom he wrote the nonnamous letter, and I smouched the yaller wench's frock, that night, and put it on, and shoved it under the front door, the way Tom told me to. It said:

Beware. Trouble is brewing. Keep a sharp lookout.

UNKNOWN FRIEND.

20. *Jim'll take the nigger woman's gown off of me and wear it.* In his notes for the novel, Twain explained why he must escape in a dress: "Men won't shoot at women" (University of California edition, 1988, p. 756). "The nigger woman's gown" is an error: Tom means Aunt Sally's gown.

21. *an evasion.* A corruption of the French word *évasion*, or escape, as in Dumas's *L'évasion du duc de Beaufort*.

22. *bulge*. Scheme.

TROUBLE IS BREWING.

Next night we stuck a picture which Tom drawed in blood, of a skull and crossbones, on the front door; and next night another one of a coffin, on the back door. I never see a family in such a sweat. They couldn't a been worse scared if the place had a been full of ghosts laying for them behind everything and under the beds and shivering through the air. If a door banged, Aunt Sally she jumped, and said "ouch!" if anything fell, she jumped and said "ouch!" if you happened to touch her, when she warn't noticing, she done the same; she couldn't face noway and be satisfied, because she allowed there was something behind her every time—so she was always a whirling around, sudden, and saying "ouch," and before she'd get two-thirds around, she'd whirl back again, and say it again; and she was afraid to go to bed, but she dasn't set up. So the thing was working very well, Tom said; he said he never see a thing work more satisfactory. He said it showed it was done right.

So he said, now for the grand bulge![22] So the very next morning at the streak of dawn we got another letter ready, and was wondering what we better do with it, because we heard them say at supper they was going to have a nigger on watch at both doors all night. Tom he went down the lightning-rod to spy around; and the nigger at the back door was asleep, and he stuck it in the back of his neck and come back. This letter said:

> *Don't betray me, I wish to be your friend. There is a desprate gang of cutthroats from over in the Ingean Territory going to steal your runaway nigger*[23] *to-night, and they have been trying to scare you so as you will stay in the house and not bother them. I am one of the gang, but have got religgion and wish to quit it and lead a honest life again, and will betray the helish design. They will sneak down from northards, along the fence, at midnight exact, with a false key,*[24] *and go in the nigger's cabin to get him. I am to be off a piece and blow a tin horn if I see any danger; but stead of that, I will* BA *like a sheep soon as they get in and not blow at all; then whilst they are getting his chains loose, you slip there and lock them in, and can kill them at your leasure. Don't do anything but just the way I am telling you, if you do they will suspicion something and raise whoop-jamboreehoo.*[25] *I do not wish any reward but to know I have done the right thing.*
>
> UNKNOWN FRIEND.

23. *a desprate gang of cutthroats from over in the Ingean Territory going to steal your runaway nigger.* The Indian federal land grant of what is now Oklahoma was allocated by the federal government to certain Indian nations who were forced to relocate there in the 1820s and 1830s on the Trail of Tears; it later became a refuge for outlaws. Tom again seems to be emulating John Murrell, the famous land pirate, who, according to Chapter 29 of *Life on the Mississippi*, besides robbing, horse-stealing, counterfeiting, and murdering, stole slaves and planned an insurrection with them; but he was betrayed by a man named Stewart (like the "Unknown Friend"), who infiltrated his gang and informed on him to the authorities. See Chapter 2, note 21.

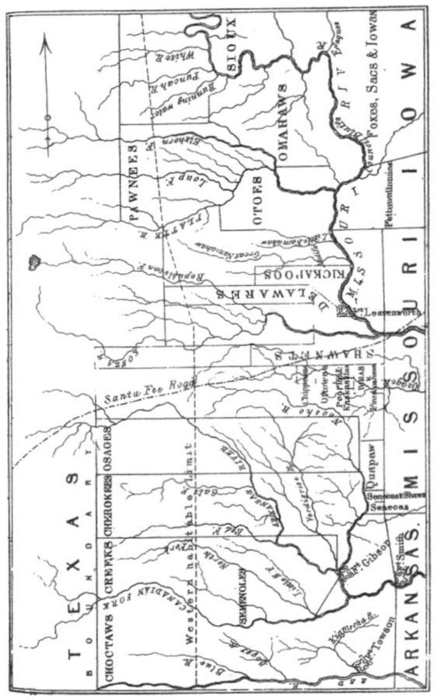

Map of the Indian Territory. Illustration from *The United States and Democratic Review*, February 1844.
Courtesy Library of Congress.

24. *a false key.* A copy of a key, usually made from a wax mold of the original.

25. *whoopjamboreehoo.* A noisy carousal.

Chapter XL.

FISHING.

We was feeling pretty good, after breakfast, and took my canoe and went over the river a fishing, with a lunch, and had a good time, and took a look at the raft and found her all right, and got home late to supper, and found them in such a sweat and worry they didn't know which end they was standing on, and made us go right off to bed the minute we was done supper, and wouldn't tell us what the trouble was, and never let on a word about the new letter, but didn't need to, because we knowed as much about it as anybody did, and as soon as we was half up stairs and her back was turned, we slid for the cellar cubboard and loaded up a good lunch and took it up to our room[1] and went to bed, and got up about half-past eleven, and Tom put on Aunt Sally's dress that he stole[2] and was going to start with the lunch, but says:

"Where's the butter?"

"I laid out a hunk of it," I says, "on a piece of a corn-pone."

"Well, you *left* it laid out, then—it ain't here."

"We can get along without it," I says.

"We can get along *with* it, too," he says; "just you slide down cellar and fetch it. And then mosey right down the lightning-rod and come along.[3] I'll go and stuff the straw

1. *as soon as we was half up stairs and her back was turned, we slid for the cellar cubboard and loaded up a good lunch and took it up to our room.* Twain replaced this in his revisions for the 1884–1885 "Twins of Genius" tour with "Tom told me to go sneak down cellar and hook a lunch."

2. *Tom put on Aunt Sally's dress that he stole.* "For a disguise" was added in the revisions for the 1884–1885 "Twins of Genius" tour.

3. *come along.* "To the cabin" was added in Twain's revisions for the 1884–1885 "Twins of Genius" tour.

into Jim's clothes to represent his mother[4] in disguise, and be ready to *ba* like a sheep and shove[5] soon as you get there."

So out he went, and down cellar went I. The hunk of butter, big as a person's fist, was where I had left it, so I took up the slab of corn-pone with it on, and blowed out my light, and started up stairs, very stealthy, and got up to the main floor all right, but here comes Aunt Sally with a candle, and I clapped the truck in my hat, and clapped my hat on my head, and the next second she see me; and she says:

"You been down cellar?"

"Yes'm."

"What you been doing down there?"

"Noth'n."

"Noth'n!"

"No'm."

"Well, then, what possessed you to go down there, this time of night?"

"I don't know'm."

"You don't *know?* Don't answer me that way, Tom, I want to know what you been *doing* down there?"

"I hain't been doing a single thing, Aunt Sally, I hope to gracious if I have."

I reckoned she'd let me go, now, and as a generl thing she would; but I spose there was so many strange things going on she was just in a sweat about every little thing that warn't yard-stick straight; so she says, very decided:[6]

"You just march into that setting-room and stay there till I come. You been up to something you no business to, and I lay I'll find out what it is before *I'm* done with you."

So she went away as I opened the door and walked into the setting-room. My, but there was a crowd there! Fifteen farmers, and every one of them had a gun.[7] I was most powerful sick, and slunk to a chair and set down. They was setting around, some of them talking a little, in a low voice, and all of them fidgety and uneasy, but trying to look like they warn't; but I knowed they was, because they was always taking off their hats, and putting them on, and scratching their

4. *to represent his mother*. "For a lay figure to leave behind" was added in Twain's revisions for the 1884–1885 "Twins of Genius" tour.

5. *and shove*. "With Jim" was added in Twain's revisions for the 1884–1885 "Twins of Genius" tour.

6. *The hunk of butter. . . . so she says, very decided*. In his revisions for the 1884–1885 "Twins of Genius" tour, Twain replaced this entire section with simply "and coming up I come ker-slam against Aunt Sally. She says."

7. *Fifteen farmers, and every one of them had a gun*. It was considered every man's business and duty in Arkansas to apprehend fugitive slaves and "nigger stealers." "Every crime increases in magnitude and proportion as it affects the welfare and interest of the community," Marryat explained "Lynch law" in his 1839 American diary. "Of punishments, it will be observed that society has awarded the most severe for crimes committed against it, rather than those that offend God. Upon this principle, in the Southern and Western States, you may murder *ten* white men and no one will arraign you or trouble himself about the matter; but *steal one nigger*, and the whole community are in arms, and express the most virtuous indignation against the sin of theft, although that of murder will be disregarded."

8. *all the same*. "'Count of the cargo in it" replaced this phrase in Twain's revisions for the 1884–1885 "Twins of Genius" tour.

9. *out of patience*. "Tired waiting for midnight" replaced this phrase in Twain's revisions for the 1884–1885 "Twins of Genius" tour.

EVERY ONE HAD A GUN.

heads, and changing their seats, and fumbling with their buttons. I warn't easy myself, but I didn't take my hat off, all the same.[8]

I did wish Aunt Sally would come, and get done with me, and lick me, if she wanted to, and let me get away and tell Tom how we'd overdone this thing, and what a thundering hornet's nest we'd got ourselves into, so we could stop fooling around, straight off, and clear out with Jim before these rips got out of patience[9] and come for us.

At last she come, and begun to ask me questions, but I *couldn't* answer them straight, I didn't know which end of me was up; because these men was in such a fidget now, that some was wanting to start right *now* and lay for them desperadoes, and saying it warn't but a few minutes to midnight; and others was trying to get them to hold on and wait for the sheep-signal; and here was aunty pegging away at the questions, and me a shaking all over and ready to sink down in my tracks I was that scared; and the place getting hotter and hotter, and the butter beginning to melt and run down my neck and behind my ears; and pretty soon, when one of them says, "*I'm* for going and getting in the cabin *first*, and right *now*, and catching them when they come," I most dropped; and a streak of butter come a trickling down my forehead, and Aunt Sally she see it, and turns white as a sheet, and says:

"For the land's sake what *is* the matter with the child!—

he's got the brain fever as shore as you're born, and they're oozing out!"

And everybody runs to see, and she snatches off my hat, and out comes the bread, and what was left of the butter, and she grabbed me, and hugged me, and says:

"Oh, what a turn you did give me! and how glad and grateful I am it ain't no worse; for luck's against us, and it never rains but it pours, and when I see that truck I thought we'd lost you, for I knowed by the color and all, it was just like your brains would be if—Dear, dear, whyd'nt you *tell* me that was what you'd been down there for, *I* wouldn't a cared. Now cler out to bed, and don't lemme see no more of you till morning!"[10]

I was up stairs in a second, and down the lightning-rod in another one, and shinning through the dark for the lean-to. I couldn't hardly get my words out, I was so anxious; but I told Tom as quick as I could, we must jump for it, now, and not a minute to lose—the house full of men, yonder, with guns!

His eyes just blazed; and he says:

"No!—is that so? *Ain't* it bully! Why, Huck, if it was to do over again, I bet I could fetch two hundred! If we could put it off till——"

"Hurry! *hurry!*" I says. "Where's Jim?"

"Right at your elbow; if you reach out your arm you can touch him. He's dressed, and everything's ready. Now we'll slide out and give the sheep-signal."

But then we heard the tramp of men, coming to the door, and heard them begin to fumble with the padlock; and heard a man say:

"I *told* you we'd be too soon; they haven't come—the door is locked. Here, I'll lock some of you into the cabin and you lay for 'em in the dark and kill 'em when they come; and the rest scatter around a piece, and listen if you can hear 'em coming."

So in they come, but couldn't see us in the dark, and most trod on us whilst we was hustling to get under the bed. But we got under all right, and out through the hole,[11] swift but soft—Jim first, me next, and Tom last, which was according to Tom's orders. Now we was in the lean-to, and

10. *most dropped. . . . of you till morning!* In his revisions for the 1884–1885 "Twins of Genius" tour, Twain replaced this section with simply "couldn't stand it no more, and I lit."

11. *out through the hole.* "Under the wall, and into the lean-to" was added in Twain's revisions for the 1884–1885 "Twins of Genius" tour.

heard trampings close by outside. So we crept to the door, and Tom stopped us there and put his eye to the crack, but couldn't make out nothing, it was so dark; and whispered and said he would listen for the steps to get further, and when he nudged us Jim must glide out first, and him last. So he set his ear to the crack and listened, and listened, and listened, and the steps a scraping around, out there, all the time;[12] and at last he nudged us, and we slid out, and stooped down, not breathing, and not making the least

TOM CAUGHT ON A SPLINTER.

noise, and slipped stealthy[13] towards the fence, in Injun file,[14] and got to it, all right, and me and Jim over it; but Tom's britches catched fast on a splinter on the top rail, and then he hear the steps coming, so he had to pull loose, which snapped the splinter and made a noise; and as he dropped in our tracks and started, somebody sings out:

"Who's that? Answer, or I'll shoot!"

But we didn't answer; we just unfurled our heels and shoved.[15] Then there was a rush, and a *bang, bang, bang!* and the bullets fairly whizzed around us! We heard them sing out:

12. *and the steps a scraping around, out there, all the time.* "For the steps to get further" replaced this phrase in Twain's revisions for the 1884–1885 "Twins of Genius" tour.

13. *slipped stealthy.* "Slip, slip, slip" replaced this phrase in Twain's revisions for the 1884–1885 "Twins of Genius" tour, with a notation that it was to be read "very slow."

14. *Injun file.* Single file; North American Indians generally traveled on a hunt or into battle one following the other by treading in the footsteps of the man in front of him to hide their number.

15. *unfurled our heels and shoved.* Or "showed our heels," to be off quickly; Twain changed "shoved" to "flew" in his revisions for the 1884–1885 "Twins of Genius" tour.

"Here they are! They've broke for the river! after 'em, boys! And turn loose the dogs!"

So here they come, full tilt. We could hear them, because they wore boots, and yelled, but we didn't wear no boots, and didn't yell. We was in the path to the mill;[16] and when they got pretty close onto us, we dodged into the bush and let them go by, and then dropped in behind them. They'd had all the dogs shut up, so they wouldn't scare off the robbers; but by this time somebody had let them loose, and here they come, making pow-wow enough for a million; but they was our dogs; so we stopped in our tracks till they catched up; and when they see it warn't nobody but us, and no excitement to offer them, they only just said howdy, and tore right ahead towards the shouting and clattering;[17] and then we up steam again and whizzed along after them till we was nearly to the mill, and then struck up through the bush to where my canoe was tied, and hopped in and pulled for dear life towards the middle of the river, but didn't make no more noise than we was obleeged to. Then we struck out, easy and comfortable, for the island where my raft was;[18] and we could hear them yelling and barking at each other all up and down the bank, till we was so far away the sounds got dim and died out. And when we stepped onto the raft, I says:

"*Now,* old Jim, you're a free man *again,* and I bet you won't ever be a slave no more."

"En a mighty good job it wuz, too, Huck. It 'uz planned beautiful, en it 'uz *done* beautiful; en dey ain't *nobody* kin git up a plan dat's mo' mixed-up en splendid den what dat one wuz."

We was all as glad as we could be, but Tom was the gladdest of all,[19] because he had a bullet in the calf of his leg.

When me and Jim heard that, we didn't feel so brash as what we did before. It was hurting him considerble, and bleeding; so we laid him in the wigwam and tore up one of the duke's shirts for to bandage him, but he says:

"Gimme the rags, I can do it myself. Don't stop, now; don't fool around here, and the evasion booming along so handsome; man the sweeps, and set her loose! Boys, we

16. *We was in the path to the mill.* "We was breakin for the mill" in Twain's revisions for the 1884–1885 "Twins of Genius" tour.

17. *they only just said howdy, and tore right ahead towards the shouting and clattering.* Fortunately, Twain avoided inserting into the novel some forced slapstick between Huck and the hounds he considered in his notes: "I fetched away a dog, part of the way—I had him by his teeth in my britches, behind" (University of California edition, 1988, p. 755).

18. *where my raft was.* "Hid" was added in Twain's revisions for the 1884–1885 "Twins of Genius" tour.

19. *Tom was the gladdest of all.* "And the proudest" was added in Twain's revisions for the 1884–1885 "Twins of Genius" tour.

done it elegant!—'deed we did. I wish *we'd* a had the handling of Louis XVI., there wouldn't a been no 'Son of Saint Louis, ascend to heaven!'[20] wrote down in *his* biography: no, sir, we'd a whooped him over the *border*—that's what we'd a done with *him*—and done it just as slick as nothing at all, too. Man the sweeps—man the sweeps!"

But me and Jim was consulting—and thinking. And after we'd thought a minute, I says:

"Say it, Jim."

So he says:

"Well, den, dis is de way it look to me, Huck. Ef it wuz *him* dat 'uz bein' sot free, en one er de boys wuz to git shot, would he say, 'Go on en save me, nemmine 'bout a doctor f'r to save dis one? Is dat like Mars Tom Sawyer? Would he say dat? You *bet* he wouldn't! *Well,* den, is *Jim* gwyne to say it? No, sah—I doan' budge a step out'n dis place, 'dout a *doctor;* not if it's forty year!"

I knowed he was white inside,[21] and I reckoned he'd say what he did say—so it was all right, now, and I told Tom I was agoing for a doctor. He raised considerble row about it, but me and Jim stuck to it and wouldn't budge; so he was

JIM ADVISES A DOCTOR.

20. *'Son of Saint Louis, ascend to heaven!'* Said to be the very last words heard by Louis XVI. In "Regicide: Place de la Révolution" in *The French Revolution*, Carlyle described the scene:

> The drums are beating: "*Taisez-vous*, Silence!" he cries "in a terrible voice, *d'une vois terrible*." He mounts the scaffold, not without delay. . . . He strips off the coat; stands disclosed in a sleeve-waistcoat of white flannel. The Executioners approach to bind him; he spurns,

"Son of Saint Louis, arise to Heaven." Eighteenth-century print.
Courtesy Picture Collection, New York Public Library, Astor, Lenox, and Tilden Foundations.

> resists; Abbé Edgeworth [the father confessor] has to remind him how the Saviour, in whom men trust, submitted to be bound. His hands are tied, his head bare; the fatal moment is come. He advances to the edge of the Scaffold, "his face very red," and says: "Frenchmen, I die innocent; I desire that France—" A General on horseback . . . prances out, with uplifted hand; "*Tambours!*" The drums drown the voice. "Executioners, do your duty!" The Executioners, desperate lest they be murdered . . . seize the hapless Louis: six of them desperate, him singly desperate, struggling there; and bind him to their plank. Abbé Edgeworth, stooping, bespeaks him: "Son of Saint Louis, ascend to Heaven." The Axe clanks down; a King's life is shorn away."

21. *I knowed he was white inside.* In his crude and now offensive way, Huck recognizes Jim to be just like him through and through. He praises Jim in probably the highest terms the for crawling out and setting the raft loose himself; but we wouldn't let him. Then he give us a piece of his mind—but it didn't do no good.

So when he see me getting the canoe ready, he says:

"Well, then, if you're bound to go, I'll tell you the way to do, when you get to the village. Shut the door, and blindfold the doctor tight and fast, and make him swear to be silent as the grave, and put a purse full of gold in his hand, and then take and lead him all around the back alleys and everywheres, in the dark, and then fetch him here in the canoe, in a roundabout way amongst the islands, and search him and take his chalk away from him, and don't give it back to him till you get him back to the village, or else he will chalk this raft so he can find it again. It's the way they all do."[22]

So I said I would, and left, and Jim was to hide in the woods when he see the doctor coming, till he was gone again.

boy is capable of expressing at that day and time. By his unselfish devotion to the wounded Tom, Jim demonstrates to Huck Finn another aspect of his deep humanity.

Julius Lester in "Morality and *Huckleberry Finn*" (*Mark Twain Journal*, Fall 1984) angrily accused Twain of presenting in Jim "a picture of the only kind of black that whites have ever truly liked—faithful, tending sick whites, not speaking, not causing trouble, and totally passive. He is the archetypal 'good nigger,' who lacks self-respect, dignity, and a sense of self separate from the one whites want him to have. A century of white readers have accepted this characterization because it permits their own 'humanity' to shine with more luster" (p. 44). But that is unfair. Lester seemed to expect Jim to conform to the expectations of African-Americans a century after the book's publication. Twain based the character on men he knew or thought he knew. He respected the great loyalty his butler had for the Clemenses; he said in "Chapters from My Autobiography" (*North American Review*, April 19, 1907) that he thought George Griffin "held the honor and credit of the family above his own" (p. 788). He was also impressed by the extraordinary bravery of John T. Lewis, a farmer who worked his in-laws' farm in Elmira, New York, and saved several people by stopping a runaway buggy. "But how this miracle was ever accomplished, by human strength, generalship and accuracy," Twain wrote Howells on June 25–27, 1879, "is clear beyond my comprehension—and grows more so the more I go and examine the ground and try to believe it was actually done. I know one thing, well; if Lewis had missed his aim he would have been killed on the spot in the trap he had made for himself, and we should have found the rest of the remains away down at the bottom of the steep ravine" (*Mark Twain–Howells Letters*, 1960, p. 197). The family gave the hero "a new sumptuous gold Swiss stem-winding stop-watch" (p. 198). "If Lewis chose to wear a town clock, who would become it better?" asked Twain. He told Howells that the modest man's thank-you note "contains a sentence which raises it to the dignity of literature: 'But I beg to say, humbly, that inasmuch as divine providence saw fit to use me as a instrument for the saving of those presshious lives, the honner conferd upon me was greater than the feat performed' " (p. 305). Howells urged Twain to write about the incident for *The Atlantic Monthly*, but he never did. Twain may well have been thinking of this modest man's courage when he had Jim sacrifice his own freedom to help the wounded Tom.

22. *It's the way they all do.* Tom is recalling "Ali Baba and the Forty Thieves" from *The Arabian Nights*. On discovering the drawn and quartered body of his brother Cassim strung up in the thieves' den, Ali Baba cuts the pieces down and returns home. To prepare the remains for proper burial, he sends a servant girl to fetch a cobbler to sew the parts together. She engages one named Mustapha by placing some gold in his palm; but to protect her master from discovery by his enemies, she blindfolds the cobbler before bringing him to the house. Meanwhile, the thieves have sent a spy to find out who has Cassim's body; and on interviewing Mustapha, he too blindfolds the cobbler, so he can lead the thief to Ali Baba's door, on which he marks an "X" with a piece of chalk. The shrewd servant sees the mark; and when the thieves arrive to search for the house, they come upon door after door chalked with X's. Hans Christian Andersen utilized this incident in "The Tinder Box": When the giant dog spirits away the princess to the soldier's room, her lady-in-waiting follows them and makes a mark on the soldier's door; however, the dog has seen her do it, and so he too goes from house to house, similarly making their doors.

This was one of the stories Sam Clemens used to read to the other Hannibal boys from his father's copy of *The Arabian Nights*; later he suggested that Harper & Brothers include it as one of his favorite fairy tales in their *Favorite Fairy Tales* (1907). Mention of this famous tale from *The Arabian Nights* returns the novel to the storybook atmosphere of the opening of *Huckleberry Finn*.

Chapter XLI

THE DOCTOR.

The DOCTOR was an old man; a very nice, kind-looking old man, when I got him up. I told him me and my brother was over on Spanish Island[1] hunting, yesterday afternoon, and camped on a piece of a raft we found, and about midnight he must a kicked his gun in his dreams, for it went off and shot him in the leg, and we wanted him to go over there and fix it and not say nothing about it, nor let anybody know, because we wanted to come home this evening, and surprise the folks.

"Who is your folks?" he says.

"The Phelpses, down yonder."

"Oh," he says. And after a minute, he says: "How'd you say he got shot?"

"He had a dream," I says, "and it shot him."

"Singular dream," he says.

So he lit up his lantern, and got his saddle-bags, and we started. But when he see the canoe, he didn't like the look of her—said she was big enough for one, but didn't look pretty safe for two. I says:

"Oh, you needn't be afeard, sir, she carried the three of us, easy enough."

"What three?"

"Why, me and Sid, and—and—and *the guns;* that's what I mean."

1. *Spanish Island.* A remnant of the time when Arkansas belonged to Spain; France annexed the territory in 1800, only to sell it to the United States as part of the Louisiana Purchase of 1804.

"Oh," he says.

But he put his foot on the gunnel, and rocked her; and shook his head, and said he reckoned he'd look around for a bigger one. But they was all locked and chained; so he took my canoe, and said for me to wait till he come back, or I could hunt around further, or maybe I better go down home and get them ready for the surprise, if I wanted to. But I said I didn't; so I told him just how to find the raft, and then he started.

I struck an idea, pretty soon. I says to myself, spos'n he can't fix that leg just in three shakes of a sheep's tail, as the saying is? spos'n it takes him three or four days? What are we going to do?—lay around there till he lets the cat out of the bag? No, sir, I know what *I'll* do. I'll wait, and when he comes back, if he says he's got to go any more, I'll get down there, too, if I swim; and we'll take and tie him, and keep him, and shove out down the river; and when Tom's done with him, we'll give him what it's worth, or all we got, and then let him get shore.

So then I crept into a lumber pile to get some sleep; and next time I waked up the sun was away up over my head! I

UNCLE SILAS IN DANGER.

shot out and went for the doctor's house, but they told me he'd gone away in the night, some time or other, and warn't back yet. Well, thinks I, that looks powerful bad for Tom, and I'll dig out for the island, right off. So away I shoved, and turned the corner, and nearly rammed my head into Uncle Silas's stomach! He says:

"Why, *Tom!* Where you been, all this time, you rascal?"

"*I* hain't been nowheres," I says, "only just hunting for the runaway nigger—me and Sid."

"Why, where ever did you go?" he says. "Your aunt's been mighty uneasy."

"She needn't," I says, "because we was all right. We followed the men and the dogs, but they out-run us, and we lost them; but we thought we heard them on the water, so we got a canoe and took out after them, and crossed over but couldn't find nothing of them; so we cruised along up-shore till we got kind of tired and beat out; and tied up the canoe and went to sleep, and never waked up till about an hour ago, then we paddled over here to hear the news, and Sid's at the post-office to see what he can hear,[2] and I'm a branching out to get something to eat for us, and then we're going home."

So then we went to the post-office to get "Sid"; but just as I suspicioned, he warn't there; so the old man he got a letter out of the office, and we waited a while longer but Sid didn't come; so the old man said come along, let Sid foot it home, or canoe-it, when he got done fooling around—but we would ride. I couldn't get him to let me stay and wait for Sid; and he said there warn't no use in it, and I must come along, and let Aunt Sally see we was all right.

When we got home, Aunt Sally was that glad to see me she laughed and cried both, and hugged me, and give me one of them lickings of hern that don't amount to shucks, and said she'd serve Sid the same when he come.

And the place was plumb full of farmers and farmers' wives, to dinner;[3] and such another clack[4] a body never heard. Old Mrs. Hotchkiss[5] was the worst; her tongue was agoing all the time. She says:

"Well, Sister[6] Phelps, I've ransacked that-air cabin over

2. *Sid's at the post-office to see what he can hear.* The local post office was both a source of information and a social center in these backwoods communities at the time. The arrival of the mail was an event, not so much for the letters (which were often few) but rather for the postman's news from other towns. "Presently the United States mail arrived, on horseback," Twain described a typical frontier scene in Chapter 1 of *The Gilded Age*. "There was but one letter, and it was for the postmaster. The long-legged youth who carried the mail tarried an hour to talk, for there was no hurry; and in a little while the male population of the village had assembled to help."

3. *And the place was plumb full of farmers and farmers' wives, to dinner.* "There is nothing just like this anywhere else in the story," noted Katherine Buxbaum in "Mark Twain and American Dialect" (*American Speech*, February 1927). "'S'I, 'sh-she,' and similar contractions are never used by Huckleberry" (p. 235). The reason is that the scene is based on a story by his friend Joel Chandler Harris, "At Teague Poteet's: A Sketch of the Hog Mountain Range" (*Century Magazine*, May and June 1883). David Carkeet noted in "The Source for the Arkansas Gossips in *Huckleberry Finn*" (*American Literary Realism*, Spring 1981) the similarity between Twain's passage and the following from the June issue:

> These women, living miles apart on the mountain and its spurs, had a habit of "picking up their work" and spending the day with each other. Upon one occasion it chanced that Mrs. Sue Parmalee and Mrs. Puritha Hightower rode ten miles to visit Mrs. Puss Poteet.
>
> "Don't lay the blame of it onter me, Puss," exclaimed Mrs. Hightower,—her shrill, thin voice in queer contrast with her fat and jovial appearance; "don't you lay the blame onter me. Dave, he's been a-complainin' bekaze they wa'n't no salsody in the house, an' I rid over to Sue's to borry some. Airter I got ther', Sue sez, se' she: 'Yess us pick up an' go an' light in on Puss,' se' she, 'an' fine out sump'n' nuther that's a-gwine on 'mongst folks,' se' she.
>
> "Yes, lay it all onter me," said Mrs. Parmalee, looking over her spectacles at Mrs. Poteet; "I sez to Purithy, s'I, 'Purithy, yess go down an' see Puss,' s'I; 'maybe we'll git a glimpse er that air new chap with the slick ha'r. Sid'll be a-

peddin' out airter awhile,' s'I, 'an' ef the new chap's ez purty ez I hear tell, maybe I'll set my cap fer 'im,' s'I." (p. 91)

Twain's notes for the episode (originally a "quilting" scene) confirm that he had Harris's recently published story in mind: "He must hear some Arkansas women, over their pipes and knitting (spitting from between teeth), swap reminiscences of Sister this and Brother that, and 'what become of so and so?—what was his first wife's name?. . . . s'I, sh-she, s-ze' " (University of California edition, 1988, p. 754). He also thought of having them carry on Twain's assault on royalty: "Let em drop in ignorant remarks about monarchs in Europe, and mix them up with Biblical monarchs." But he never followed through on this idea.

4. *clack*. Loud talk or chat.

5. *Hotchkiss*. Twain makes further use of both "Hotchkiss" and "Dunlap" in subsequent stories about Tom Sawyer and Huckleberry Finn: Mrs. Hotchkiss becomes "Hannah Hotchkiss" in "Schoolhouse Hill," an early draft of *The Mysterious Stranger*, and "Brace Dunlap" appears in "Tom Sawyer, Detective."

6. *Sister*. "'Sister' in the Methodist, or Presbyterian, or Baptist, or Campellite Church—nothing more," Twain explained in a note to Chapter 3 of "Schoolhouse Hill." "A common form, in those days" (*Huck Finn and Tom Sawyer Among the Indians*, 1989, p. 230). "Every man was expected to join one or another of the seventeen religious denominations," he recalled of the old days in a suppressed passage of *Life on the Mississippi* (published in the 1944 Limited Editions Club edition). "In the West and the South, and in portions of the East, people did not call each other Mr. Smith, and Mrs. Jones—no, it was 'Brother' Smith, and 'Sister' Jones—a phrase which survives in Uncle Remus' 'Ole Brer Fox' and 'Ole Brer Rabbit' " (pp. 406–7).

7. *crazy 's Nebokoodneezer*. Nebuchadnezzar was the heathen king of Babylon, whom, according to Daniel 4:1–37, God struck mad for seven years until he acknowledged the God of the Israelites: "He was driven from men, and did eat grass as oxen, and his body was wet with the dew of heaven, till his hairs were grown like eagle's feathers, and his nails like birds' claws."

an' I b'lieve the nigger was crazy. I says so to Sister Damrell—didn't I, Sister Damrell?—s'I, he's crazy, s'I—them's the very words I said. You all hearn me: he's crazy, s'I; everything shows it, s'I. Look at that-air grindstone, s'I; want to tell *me*'t any cretur 'ts in his right mind 's agoin' to scrabble all them crazy things onto a grindstone, s'I? Here sich 'n' sich a person busted his heart; 'n' here so 'n' so pegged along for thirty-seven year, 'n' all that—natcherl son o' Louis somebody, 'n' sich everlast'n rubbage. He's plumb crazy, s'I; it's what I says in the fust place, it's what I says in the middle, 'n' it's what I says last 'n' all the time—the nigger's crazy—crazy 's Nebokoodneezer,[7] s'I."

"An' look at that-air ladder made out'n rags, Sister Hotchkiss," says old Mrs. Damrell, "what in the name o' goodness *could* he ever want of—"

OLD MRS. HOTCHKISS.

"The very words I was a-sayin' no longer ago th'n this minute to Sister Utterback,[8] 'n' she'll tell you so herself. Sh-she, look at that-air rag ladder, sh-she; 'n' s'I, yes, *look* at it, s'I—what *could* he a wanted of it, s'I. Sh-she, Sister Hotchkiss, sh-she—"

"But how in the nation'd they ever *git* that grindstone *in* there, *any*-way? 'n' who dug that-air *hole?* 'n' who—"

"My very *words*, Brer Penrod! I was a-sayin'—pass that-air sasser o' m'lasses, won't ye?—I was a-sayin' to Sister Dunlap, jist this minute, how *did* they git that grindstone in there, s'I. Without *help*, mind you—'thout *help! Thar's* wher' 'tis. Don't tell *me*, s'I; there *wuz* help, s'I; 'n' ther' wuz a *plenty* help, too, s'I; ther's ben a *dozen* a-helpin' that nigger, 'n' I lay I'd skin every last nigger on this place, but *I'd* find out who done it, s'I; 'n' moreover, s'I—"

"A *dozen* says you!—*forty* couldn't a done everything that's been done. Look at them case-knife saws and things, how tedious they've been made; look at that bed-leg sawed off with 'm, a week's work for six men; look at that nigger made out'n straw on the bed; and look at—"

"You may *well* say it, Brer Hightower! It's jist as I was a-sayin' to Brer Phelps, his own self. S'e, what do *you* think of it, Sister Hotchkiss, s'e? think o' what, Brer Phelps, s'I? think o' that bed-leg sawed off that a way, s'e? *think* of it, s'I? I lay it never sawed *itself* off, s'I—somebody *sawed* it, s'I; that's my opinion, take it or leave it, it mayn't be no 'count, s'I, but sich as 't is, it's my opinion, s'I, 'n' if anybody k'n start a better one, s'I, let him *do* it, s'I, that's all. I says to Sister Dunlap, s'I—"

"Why, dog my cats, they must a ben a house-full o' niggers in there every night for four weeks, to a done all that work, Sister Phelps. Look at that shirt—every last inch of it kivered over with secret African writ'n done with blood! Must a ben a raft uv 'm at it right along, all the time, amost. Why, I'd give two dollars to have it read to me; 'n' as for the niggers that wrote it, I 'low I'd take 'n' lash 'm t'll—"

"People to *help* him, Brother Marples! Well, I reckon you'd *think* so, if you'd a been in this house for a while back. Why, they've stole everything they could lay their hands on—and we a watching, all the time, mind you. They stole that shirt right off o' the line! and as for that sheet they made the rag ladder out of ther' ain't no telling how many times they *didn't* steal that; and flour, and candles, and candlesticks, and spoons, and the old warming-pan, and most a thousand things that I disremember, now, and my new calico dress; and me, and Silas, and my Sid and Tom on the constant watch day *and* night, as I was a telling you, and not a one of us could catch hide nor hair, nor sight nor sound of

8. *Sister Utterback*. Sam Clemens knew a Mrs. Utterback, a "faith doctor" who lived five miles from Hannibal. "Her specialty was toothache," Twain recalled in "Chapters from My Autobiography" (*North American Review*, March 1, 1907). "She would lay her hand on the patient's jaw and say 'Believe!' and the cure was prompt. . . . Twice I rode out there behind my mother, horseback, and saw the cure performed. My mother was the patient" (p. 458).

them; and here at the last minute, lo and behold you, they slides right in under our noses, and fools us, and not only fools *us* but the Injun Territory robbers too, and actuly gets *away* with that nigger, safe and sound, and that with sixteen men and twenty-two dogs right on their very heels at that very time! I tell you, it just bangs anything I ever *heard* of. Why, *sperits* couldn't a done better, and been no smarter. And I reckon they must a *been* sperits[9]—because, *you* know our dogs, and ther' ain't no better; well, them dogs never even got on the *track* of 'm, once! You explain *that* to me, if you can!—*any* of you!"

"Well, it does beat——"

"Laws alive, I never——"

"So help me, I wouldn't a be——"

"*House*-thieves as well as——"

"Goodnessgracioussakes, I'd a ben afeard to *live* in sich a——"

"'Fraid to *live!*—why, I was that scared I das'nt hardly go to bed, or get up, or lay down, or *set* down, Sister Ridgeway. Why, they'd steal the very—why, goodness sakes, you can guess what kind of a fluster *I* was in by the time midnight come, last night. I hope to gracious if I warn't afraid they'd steal some o' the family! I was just to that pass, I didn't have no reasoning faculties no more. It looks foolish enough, *now*, in the day-time; but I says to myself, there's my two poor boys asleep, 'way up stairs in that lonesome room, and I declare to goodness I was that uneasy 't I crep' up there and locked 'em in! I *did*. And anybody would. Because, you know, when you get scared, that way, and it keeps running on, and getting worse and worse, all the time, and your wits gets to addling, and you get to doing all sorts o' wild things, and by-and-by you think to yourself, spos'n *I* was a boy, and was away up there, and the door ain't locked, and you——" She stopped, looking kind of wondering, and then she turned her head around slow, and when her eye lit on me—I got up and took a walk.

Says I to myself, I can explain better how we come to not be in that room this morning, if I go out to one side and

9. *I reckon they must a* been *sperits*. Howard Kerr suggested in *Mediums, and Spirit-Rappers, and Roaring Radicals* (Urbana: University of Illinois Press, 1972, pp. 172–81) that Twain may have taken some details of Tom and Huck's "evasion" from the 1850 "haunting" of the Rev. Eliakim Phelps's family in Stratford, Connecticut. "The Stratford ghost constructed life-size dummies by stuffing Eliakim's clothing with cloth and straw," Kerr explained. "Among other things, he dashed a brass candlestick to pieces; he dropped a key and a nail out of the air at the minister's feet; he repeatedly removed Mrs. Phelps' spoons from under lock and key, placing them on the table or bending them double and straightening them out again; and he took laundry from a locked cupboard, especially one sheet which reappeared each time Eliakim shut it away" (p. 174). There were also anonymous letters and mysterious messages in strange languages; among the requests the ghost rapped out was for pumpkin pie. While the gullible Rev. Phelps was convinced that the odd occurrences were the work of spirits, others believed that the perpetrators were no more than the minister's newly acquired and inventive stepchildren, an eleven-year-old boy and a sixteen-year-old girl.

study over it a little. So I done it. But I dasn't go fur, or she'd a sent for me. And when it was late in the day, the people all went, and then I come in and told her the noise and shooting waked up me and "Sid," and the door was locked, and we wanted to see the fun, so we went down the lightning-rod, and both of us got hurt a little, and we didn't never want to try *that* no more. And then I went on and told her all what I told Uncle Silas before; and then she said she'd forgive us, and maybe it was all right enough anyway, and about what a body might expect of boys, for all boys was a pretty harum-scarum[10] lot, as fur as she could see; and so, as long as no harm hadn't come of it, she judged she better put in her time being grateful we was alive and well and she had us still, stead of fretting over what was past and done. So then she kissed me, and patted me on the head, and dropped into a kind of a brown study;[11] and pretty soon jumps up, and says:

"Why, lawsamercy, it's most night, and Sid not come yet! What *has* become of that boy?"

I see my chance; so I skips up and says:

"I'll run right up to town and get him," I says.

"No you won't," she says. "You'll stay right wher' you are; *one's* enough to be lost at a time. If he ain't here to supper, your uncle 'll go."

Well, he warn't there to supper; so right after supper uncle went.

He come back about ten, a little bit uneasy; hadn't run across Tom's track. Aunt Sally was a good *deal* uneasy; but Uncle Silas he said there warn't no occasion to be—boys will be boys, he said, and you'll see this one turn up in the morning, all sound and right. So she had to be satisfied. But she said she'd set up for him a while, anyway, and keep a light burning, so he could see it.

And then when I went up to bed she come up with me and fetched her candle, and tucked me in, and mothered me so good I felt mean, and like I couldn't look her in the face; and she set down on the bed and talked with me a long time, and said what a splendid boy Sid was, and didn't

10. *harum-scarum.* Reckless, wild.

11. *a brown study.* Gloomy meditations; "miles and miles away," Huck explains in Chapter 11 of "Tom Sawyer, Detective."

12. *not for kingdoms*. Not for "Kingdom Come" or Heaven, not for anything.

AUNT SALLY TALKS TO HUCK.

seem to want to ever stop talking about him; and kept asking me every now and then, if I reckoned he could a got lost, or hurt, or maybe drownded, and might be laying at this minute, somewheres, suffering or dead, and she not by him to help him, and so the tears would drip down, silent, and I would tell her that Sid was all right, and would be home in the morning, sure; and she would squeeze my hand, or maybe kiss me, and tell me to say it again, and keep on saying it, because it done her good, and she was in so much trouble. And when she was going away, she looked down in my eyes, so steady and gentle, and says:

"The door ain't going to be locked, Tom; and there's the window and the rod; but you'll be good, *won't* you? And you won't go? For *my* sake."

Laws knows I *wanted* to go, bad enough, to see about Tom, and was all intending to go; but after that, I wouldn't a went, not for kingdoms.[12]

But she was on my mind, and Tom was on my mind; so I slept very restless. And twice I went down the rod, away in the night, and slipped around front, and see her setting there by her candle in the window with her eyes towards the road and the tears in them; and I wished I could do something for her, but I couldn't, only to swear that I wouldn't never do nothing to grieve her any more. And the third time, I waked up at dawn, and slid down, and she was there yet, and her candle was most out, and her old gray head was resting on her hand, and she was asleep.

Chapter XLII

TOM SAWYER WOUNDED.

The old man was up town again, before breakfast, but couldn't get no track of Tom; and both of them set at the table, thinking, and not saying nothing, and looking mournful, and their coffee getting cold, and not eating anything. And by-and-by the old man says:

"Did I give you the letter?"

"What letter?"

"The one I got yesterday out of the post-office."

"No, you didn't give me no letter."

"Well, I must a forgot it."

So he rummaged his pockets, and then went off somewheres where he had laid it down, and fetched it, and give it to her. She says:

"Why, it's from St. Petersburg—it's from Sis."

I allowed another walk would do me good; but I couldn't stir. But before she could break it open, she dropped it and run—for she see something. And so did I. It was Tom Sawyer on a mattress; and that old doctor; and Jim, in *her* calico dress, with his hands tied behind him; and a lot of people. I hid the letter behind the first thing that come handy, and rushed. She flung herself at Tom, crying, and says:

"Oh, he's dead, he's dead, I know he's dead!"

And Tom he turned his head a little, and muttered something or other, which showed he warn't in his right mind; then she flung up her hands, and says:

"He's alive, thank God! And that's enough!" and she snatched a kiss of him, and flew for the house to get the bed ready, and scattering orders right and left at the niggers and everybody else, as fast as her tongue could go, every jump of the way.

I followed the men to see what they was going to do with Jim; and the old doctor and Uncle Silas followed after Tom into the house. The men was very huffy, and some of them wanted to hang Jim, for an example to all the other niggers around there, so they wouldn't be trying to run away,[1] like Jim done, and making such a raft of trouble,[2] and keeping a whole family scared most to death for days and nights. But the others said, don't do it, it wouldn't answer at all, he ain't our nigger, and his owner would turn up and make us pay for him, sure. So that cooled them down a little, because the people that's always the most anxious for to hang a nigger that hain't done just right, is always the very ones that ain't the most anxious to pay for him when they've got their satisfaction out of him.[3]

They cussed Jim considerble, though, and give him a cuff or two, side the head, once in a while, but Jim never said nothing, and he never let on to know me, and they took him to the same cabin, and put his own clothes on him, and chained him again, and not to no bed-leg, this time, but to a big staple drove into the bottom log, and chained his hands, too, and both legs, and said he warn't to have nothing but bread and water to eat, after this, till his owner come or he was sold at auction, because he didn't come in a certain length of time,[4] and filled up our hole, and said a couple of farmers with guns must stand watch around about the cabin every night, and a bull-dog tied to the door in the day-time;[5] and about this time they was through with the job and was tapering off with a kind of generl good-bye cussing, and then the old doctor comes and takes a look, and says:

"Don't be no rougher on him than you're obleeged to, because he ain't a bad nigger.[6] When I got to where I found

1. *some of them wanted to hang Jim, for an example to all the other niggers around there, so they wouldn't be trying to run away.* A slave may have been considered valuable property at the time, but that hardly prevented cowardly, vindictive mobs from lynching them. The Hannibal *Missouri Courier* (June 16, 1853) reprinted an account from Richmond, Texas, concerning an elderly preacher convicted of conspiring with a boy to kill his master: "About midnight last night a party of some fifty men in disguise, entered the jail, tied the keepers, and took the negroes to the nearest tree and there hung them. They still hang there a warning to evil doers. Here was a real 'Uncle Tom.' "

The lynching of a fugitive slave. Illustration from *Archy Moore, the White Slave* by Richard Hildreth, 1855.
Courtesy Rare Book Room, Library of Congress.

An even more horrible incident occurred near Georgetown, Pettis County, where an accused man was burned at the stake by a mob for the rape and murder of a white woman. "The only excuse which can be offered for the awful retribution of burning this negro," the *Missouri Courier* (July 28, 1853) quoted a local account, "is the nature of the offense, and the frequent attempts of late years, of negroes to rape white women—several instances of which have occurred in this county—and the impression among the community that required such an example to protect them from the repetition of similar outrages."

But that justification for one crime against another one infuriated Twain. "Why has lynching, with various barbaric accompaniments," he lashed out in "The United States of Lyncherdom" (in *A Pen Warmed-Up in Hell*, 1972), "become a favorite regulator . . . in several parts of the country? Is it because men think a lurid and terrible punishment a more forcible object lesson and a more effective deterrent than sober and colorless hanging done privately in jail would be? Surely sane men do not think that. Even the average child should know better. It should know that any strange and much-talked-of event is always followed by imitations, the world being so well supplied with excitable people who only need a little stirring up to make them lose what is left of their heads and do mad things which they would not have thought of ordinarily" (p. 182).

2. *a raft of trouble.* A great deal of trouble, used disparagingly.

3. *the people that's always the most anxious for to hang a nigger . . . is always the very ones that ain't the most anxious to pay for him when they've got their satisfaction out of him.* A particularly cynical observation: The crowd backs down not for any moral reason; their cowardice results purely from economic considerations. Because they consider Jim chattel rather than a human being, his murderers would have to compensate his owner the market value of his property. Young Sam Clemens went through the same pangs when he and another boy rolled a big rock down a hill and just missed killing a slave in its path. He confessed to an old friend on visiting Hannibal in 1902, "If we had killed that man we'd have a dead nigger on our hands without a cent to pay for him" (quoted in Paine, *Mark Twain: A Biography*, 1912, vol. 3, p. 1170).

4. *till his owner come or he was sold at auction, because he didn't come in a certain length of time.* Twain has confused Missouri with Arkansas law: A slave captured in Missouri had to be committed to the local jail and then advertised on the courthouse door and later in the papers; if unclaimed after a year, he was then sold at auction. Orion Clemens published in the Hannibal *Western Union* (December 12, 1850) an announcement from the sheriff of St. Louis County, who said after identifying the fugitive and his rightful master:

> The owner of said slave is hereby required to make application to me for him, according to the statute, within three months from this date, pay charges, and take him away, otherwise I will on Monday, the ninth day of December, 1850, between the hours of nine and five o'clock of that day, at the east front

THE DOCTOR SPEAKS FOR JIM.

the boy, I see I couldn't cut the bullet out without some help, and he warn't in no condition for me to leave, to go and get help; and he got a little worse and a little worse, and after a long time he went out of his head, and wouldn't let me come anigh him, any more, and said if I chalked his raft he'd kill me, and no end of wild foolishness like that, and I see I couldn't do anything at all with him; so I says, I got to have *help,* somehow; and the minute I says it, out crawls this nigger from somewheres, and says he'll help, and he done it, too, and done it very well. Of course I judged he must be a runaway nigger, and there I *was!* and there I had to stick, right straight along all the rest of the day, and all night. It was a fix, I tell you! I had a couple of patients with the chills, and of course I'd of liked to run up to town and see them, but I dasn't, because the nigger might get away, and then I'd be to blame;[7] and yet never a skiff come close enough for me to hail. So there I had to stick, plumb till daylight this morning; and I never see a nigger that was a better nuss or faithfuller, and yet he was resking his freedom to do it, and was all tired out, too, and I see plain enough he'd been worked main hard, lately. I liked the nigger for that; I tell you, gentlemen, a nigger like that is worth a thousand dollars[8]—and kind treatment, too. I had everything I needed, and the boy was doing as well there as he would a done at home—better, maybe, because it was so quiet; but there I *was*, with both of 'm on my hands; and there I had to stick, till about dawn this morning; then some men in a skiff come by, and as good luck would have it, the nigger was setting by the pallet with his head propped on his knees, sound asleep; so I motioned them in, quiet, and they slipped up on him and grabbed him and tied him before he knowed what he was about, and we never had no trouble. And the boy being in a kind of a flighty sleep, too, we muffled the oars[9] and hitched the raft on, and towed her over very nice and quiet, and the nigger never made the least row nor said a word, from the start. He ain't no bad nigger, gentlemen; that's what I think about him."

Somebody says:

"Well, it sounds very good, doctor, I'm obleeged to say."

Then the others softened up a little, too, and I was mighty thankful to that old doctor for doing Jim that good turn; and I was glad it was according to my judgment of him, too; because I thought he had a good heart in him and was a good man, the first time I see him. Then they all agreed that Jim had acted very well, and was deserving to have some notice took of it, and reward. So every one of them promised, right out and hearty, that they wouldn't cuss him no more.

Then they come out and locked him up. I hoped they was going to say he could have one or two of the chains took off, because they was rotten heavy, or could have meat and greens with his bread and water, but they didn't think of it,[10] and I reckoned it warn't best for me to mix in, but I judged I'd get the doctor's yarn to Aunt Sally, somehow or other, as soon as I'd got through the breakers that was laying just ahead of me.[11] Explanations, I mean, of how I forgot to mention about Sid being shot, when I was telling how him and me put in that dratted night paddling around hunting the runaway nigger.

But I had plenty time. Aunt Sally she stuck to the sickroom all day and all night; and every time I see Uncle Silas mooning around, I dodged him.

door of the Court house, in the city and county of St. Louis, State of Missouri, sell the said negro boy, to the highest bidder for cash, pursuant to the statute in such case made and provided.

But in Arkansas the fugitive had to be kept in jail for six months, during which his capture had to be advertised in the papers; then he was transferred to the penitentiary for another six months, and if his owner still did not answer the announcements, the prisoner became the property of the state for life. It was not until 1861, after the commencement of the Civil War, that a runaway slave could be sold in Arkansas, and then only after two years in the penitentiary and after the sale was advertised for six weeks.

5. *a bull-dog tied to the door in the day-time.* Bulldogs are more vicious than hounds (see Chapter 32, note 7). Jim's captors are making sure that he does not escape again.

6. *a bad nigger.* Fischer and Salamo in the 2001 University of California edition explored the specific meaning of this antebellum expression. "Bad niggers," explained John W. Roberts in *From Trickster to Badman: The Black Folk Hero in Slavery and Freedom* (Philadelphia: University of Pennsylvania, 1989), were "bold individuals who refused to accept whippings, sauced masters and mistresses with impunity, ran away at the slightest provocation, and even killed masters and overseers who abused them" (p. 176). Therefore, they were, according to Alan Dundes in *Mother Wit from the Laughing Barrel* (Jackson: University Press of Mississippi, 1990), "Negroes with spirit, Negroes who were willing to fight the system" (p. 581).

7. *the nigger might get away, and then I'd be to blame.* The doctor was concerned because in the slave states, failure to report just seeing a runaway could result in arrest for aiding and abetting the flight of the fugitive.

8. *a nigger like that is worth a thousand dollars.* Not much of a compliment when one recalls that Miss Watson was willing to sell him for $800. Although Jim has more than proved his humanity, the good doctor cannot think of him as anything more than just another piece of property.

Next morning I heard Tom was a good deal better, and they said Aunt Sally was gone to get a nap. So I slips to the sick-room, and if I found him awake I reckoned we could put up a yarn for the family that would wash.[12] But he was sleeping, and sleeping very peaceful, too; and pale, not fire-faced the way he was when he come. So I set down and laid for him to wake. In about a half an hour, Aunt Sally comes gliding in, and there I was, up a stump again! She motioned me to be still, and set down by me, and begun to whisper, and said we could all be joyful now, because all the symptoms was first rate, and he'd been sleeping like that for ever so long, and looking better and peacefuller all the time, and ten to one he'd wake up in his right mind.

So we set there watching, and by-and-by he stirs a bit, and opened his eyes very natural, and takes a look, and says:

"Hello, why I'm at *home!* How's that? Where's the raft?"

"It's all right," I says.

"And *Jim?*"

"The same," I says, but couldn't say it pretty brash. But he never noticed, but says:

"Good! Splendid! *Now* we're all right and safe! Did you tell Aunty?"

I was going to say yes; but she chipped in and says:

"About what, Sid?"

"Why, about the way the whole thing was done."

"What whole thing?"

"Why, *the* whole thing. There ain't but one; how we set the runaway nigger free—me and Tom."

"Good land! Set the run— What *is* the child talking about! Dear, dear, out of his head again!"

"*No,* I ain't out of my HEAD; I know all what I'm talking about. We *did* set him free—me and Tom. We laid out to do it, and we *done* it. And we done it elegant, too." He'd got a start, and she never checked him up, just set and stared and stared, and let him clip along, and I see it warn't no use for *me* to put in. "Why, Aunty, it cost us a power of work—weeks of it—hours and hours, every night, whilst you was all asleep. And we had to steal candles, and the sheet, and the shirt, and your dress, and spoons, and tin plates, and case-knives, and the

9. *muffled the oars.* Covered them to deaden the sound.

10. *but they didn't think of it.* Despite their kind words, Jim's captors have not really changed their attitude toward the runaway.

11. *I'd got through the breakers that was laying just ahead of me.* Mississippi River slang for overcoming anticipated difficulties.

12. *put up a yarn for the family that would wash.* Come up with a story that the family would believe.

warming-pan, and the grindstone, and flour, and just no end of things, and you can't think what work it was to make the saws, and pens, and inscriptions, and one thing or another, and you can't think *half* the fun it was. And we had to make up the pictures of coffins and things, and nonnamous letters from the robbers, and get up and down the lightning-rod, and dig the hole into the cabin, and make the rope-ladder and send it in cooked up in a pie, and send in spoons and things to work with, in your apron pocket"—

"Mercy sakes!"

—"and load up the cabin with rats and snakes and so on, for company for Jim; and then you kept Tom here so long with the butter in his hat that you come near spiling the whole business, because the men come before we was out of the cabin, and we had to rush, and they heard us and let drive at us, and I got my share, and we dodged out of the path and let them go by, and when the dogs come they warn't interested in us, but went for the most noise, and we got our canoe, and made for the raft, and was all safe, and Jim was a free man, and we done it all by ourselves, and *wasn't* it bully, Aunty!"

"Well, I never heard the likes of it in all my born days! So it was *you,* you little rapscallions, that's been making all this trouble, and turned everybody's wits clean inside out and scared us all most to death. I've as good a notion as ever I had in my life, to take it out o' you this very minute. To think, here I've been, night after night, a—*you* just get well once, you young scamp, and I lay I'll tan the Old Harry[13] out o' both o' ye!"

But Tom, he *was* so proud and joyful, he just *couldn't* hold in, and his tongue just *went* it—she a-chipping in, and spitting fire all along, and both of them going it at once, like a cat-convention; and she says:

"*Well,* you get all the enjoyment you can out of it *now,* for mind I tell you if I catch you meddling with him again—"

"Meddling with *who?*" Tom says, dropping his smile and looking surprised.

"With *who?* Why, the runaway nigger, of course. Who'd you reckon?"

13. *the Old Harry*. The devil; like pious Miss Watson, Aunt Sally is such a good Christian that she cannot bear to say "Satan."

Tom looks at me very grave, and says:

"Tom, didn't you just tell me he was all right? Hasn't he got away?"

"Him?" says Aunt Sally; "the runaway nigger? 'Deed he hasn't. They've got him back, safe and sound, and he's in that cabin again, on bread and water, and loaded down with chains, till he's claimed or sold!"

Tom rose square up in bed, with his eye hot, and his nostrils opening and shutting like gills, and sings out to me:

"They hain't no *right* to shut him up! *Shove!*—and don't you lose a minute. Turn him loose! he ain't no slave; he's as free as any cretur that walks this earth!"

TOM ROSE SQUARE UP IN BED.

"What *does* the child mean?"

"I mean every word I *say*, Aunt Sally, and if somebody don't go, *I*'ll go. I've knowed him all his life, and so has Tom, there. Old Miss Watson died two months ago, and she was ashamed she ever was going to sell him down the river, and *said* so; and she set him free in her will."[14]

"Then what on earth did *you* want to set him free for, seeing he was already free?"

"Well, that *is* a question, I must say; and *just* like women! Why, I wanted the *adventure* of it; and I'd a waded neck-deep in blood to—goodness alive, AUNT POLLY!"

If she warn't standing right there, just inside the door,

14. *Old Miss Watson . . . set him free in her will.* It would seem that Twain committed the same literary offense he once accused James Fenimore Cooper of perpetuating in his novels, that "the personages of a tale shall confine themselves to possibilities and let miracles alone; or, if they venture a miracle, the author must so plausibly set it forth as to make it look possible and reasonable" ("Fenimore Cooper's Literary Offenses," *North American Review*, July 1895, p. 3). Fredrick Woodard and Donnarae MacCann in "Minstrel Shackles and Nineteenth-Century 'Liberality' in *Huckeberry Finn*" considered this slaver's freeing Jim in her will "an extraordinary sign of benevolence on Miss Watson's part since she has no way of knowing before she dies that Jim has not slain Huck, as many townsfolk believe and as evidence about Huck's disappearance indicates" (Leonard, Tenney, and Davis, *Satire or Evasion?*, 1992, p. 150). It was customary in certain classes of Southern society to free slaves in one's will. But, as Tom makes plain, guilt is Mrs. Watson's overriding reason. She does not suffer a miraculous change of heart; she must conform to local custom. Julius Lester complained in "Morality and *Adventures of Huckleberry Finn*" (*Mark Twain Journal*, Fall 1984) that "we are now to believe that an old white lady would free a black slave suspected of murdering a white child. White people might want to believe such fairy tales about themselves, but blacks know better" (p. 45). Guilt is a powerful force—even in white people.

looking as sweet and contented as an angel half-full of pie, I wish I may never!

Aunt Sally jumped for her, and most hugged the head off of her, and cried over her, and I found a good enough place for me under the bed, for it was getting pretty sultry for *us,* seemed to me. And I peeped out, and in a little while Tom's Aunt Polly shook herself loose and stood there looking across at Tom over her spectacles—kind of grinding him into the earth, you know. And then she says:

"Yes, you *better* turn y'r head away—I would if I was you, Tom."

"Oh, deary me!" says Aunt Sally; "*is* he changed so? Why, that ain't *Tom* it's Sid; Tom's—Tom's—why, where is Tom? He was here a minute ago."

"You mean where's Huck *Finn*—that's what you mean! I reckon I hain't raised such a scamp as my Tom all these years, not to know him when I *see* him. That *would* be a pretty howdy-do. Come out from under that bed, Huck Finn."

So I done it. But not feeling brash.

Aunt Sally she was one of the mixed-upest looking persons I ever see; except one, and that was Uncle Silas, when he come in, and they told it all to him. It kind of made him drunk, as you may say, and he didn't know nothing at all the rest of the day, and preached a prayer-meeting sermon that night that give him a rattling ruputation, because the oldest man in the world couldn't a understood it. So Tom's Aunt Polly, she told all about who I was, and what; and I had to up and tell how I was in such a tight place that when Mrs. Phelps took me for Tom Sawyer—she chipped in and says, "Oh, go on and call me Aunt Sally, I'm used to it, now, and 'tain't no need to change"—that when Aunt Sally took me for Tom Sawyer, I had to stand it—there warn't no other way, and I knowed he wouldn't mind, because it would be nuts for him, being a mystery, and he'd make an adventure out of it and be perfectly satisfied. And so it turned out, and he let on to be Sid, and made things as soft as he could for me.

And his Aunt Polly she said Tom was right about old Miss

Watson setting Jim free in her will; and so, sure enough, Tom Sawyer had gone and took all that trouble and bother to set a free nigger free! and I couldn't ever understand, before, until that minute and that talk, how he *could* help a body set a nigger free, with his bringing-up.

Well, Aunt Polly she said that when Aunt Sally wrote to her that Tom and *Sid* had come, all right and safe, she says to herself:

"Look at that, now! I might have expected it, letting him go off that way without anybody to watch him. So now I got to go and trapse all the way down the river, eleven hundred mile,[15] and find out what that creetur's up to, *this* time; as long as I couldn't seem to get any answer out of you about it."

"Why, I never heard nothing from you," says Aunt Sally.

"Well, I wonder! Why, I wrote to you twice, to ask you what you could mean by Sid being here."

"Well, I never got 'em, Sis."

Aunt Polly, she turns around slow and severe, and says:

"HAND OUT THEM LETERS."

"You, Tom!"

"Well—*what?*" he says, kind of pettish.

"Don't you what *me,* you impudent thing—hand out them letters."

"What letters?"

"*Them* letters. I be bound, if I have to take aholt of you I'll—"

"They're in the trunk. There, now. And they're just the same as they was when I got them out of the office. I hain't looked into them, I hain't touched them. But I knowed

15. *all the way down the river, eleven hundred mile.* Twain confirmed in Chapter 2 of "Tom Sawyer, Detective" that the distance between St. Petersburg and the Phelps farm in Arkansas is "not so very much short of a thousand miles." But according to Michael G. Miller's "Geography and the Structure of *Huckleberry Finn*" (*Studies in the Novel*, February 1980, p. 203), eleven hundred miles from Hannibal ("St. Petersburg") is Natchez, Mississippi, which would put the Phelps farm in either Mississippi or Louisiana, not Arkansas. Fischer and Salamo in the 2001 University of California edition estimated the distance between Hannibal and the Phelps farm as about than 820 miles. That would agree with Huck's recollection in Chapter 3 of *Tom Sawyer Abroad* that a two-weeks' journey down the Mississippi on the raft was "close onto eight hundred miles." See Chapter 32, note 2.

they'd make trouble, and I thought if you warn't in no hurry, I'd—"

"Well, you *do* need skinning, there ain't no mistake about it. And I wrote another one to tell you I was coming; and I spose he—"

"No, it come yesterday; I hain't read it yet, but *it's* all right, I've got that one."

I wanted to offer to bet two dollars she hadn't, but I reckoned maybe it was just as safe to not to. So I never said nothing.

Chapter the Last

1. *But I reckened it was about as well as the way it was*. But it does happen just as Tom hopes, if one is to believe the opening of *Tom Sawyer Abroad*: "You see, when we three come back up the river in glory, as you may say, from that long travel, and the village received us with a torchlight procession and speeches, and everybody hurrah'd and shouted, and some got drunk, it made us heroes, and that was what Tom Sawyer had always been hankerin' to be." But why would the entire town of St. Petersburg come out to greet a pair of phony "nigger stealers" and the former runaway? Perhaps, when writing *Tom Sawyer Abroad*, Twain took a quick glance at the end of *Huckleberry Finn* and misread what Tom hoped would happen as actually taking place.

OUT OF BONDAGE.

The FIRST time I catched Tom, private, I asked him what was his idea, time of the evasion?—what it was he'd planned to do if the evasion worked all right and he managed to set a nigger free that was already free before? And he said, what he had planned in his head, from the start, if we got Jim out all safe, was for us to run him down the river, on the raft, and have adventures plumb to the mouth of the river, and then tell him about his being free, and take him back up home on a steamboat, in style, and pay him for his lost time, and write word ahead and get out all the niggers around, and have them waltz him into town with a torchlight procession and a brass band, and then he would be a hero, and so would we. But I reckened it was about as well the way it was.[1]

We had Jim out of the chains in no time, and when Aunt Polly and Uncle Silas and Aunt Sally found out how good he helped the doctor nurse Tom, they made a heap of fuss over him, and fixed him up prime, and give him all he wanted to eat, and a good time, and nothing to do. And we had him up to the sick-room; and had a high talk; and Tom give Jim forty dollars for being prisoner for us so patient, and doing it up so good, and Jim was pleased most to death, and busted out, and says:

"*Dah,* now, Huck, what I tell you?—what I tell you up dah on Jackson islan'? I *tole* you I got a hairy breas', en what's de sign un it; en I *tole* you I ben rich wunst, en gwineter to be rich *agin;* en it's come true; en heah she *is! Dah,* now! doan' talk to *me*—signs is *signs,* mine I tell you; en I knowed jis' 's well 'at I 'uz gwineter be rich agin as I's a stannin' heah dis minute!"

And then Tom he talked along, and talked along, and says, le's all three slide out of here, one of these nights, and get an outfit, and go for howling adventures amongst the Injuns,[2] over in the Territory, for a couple of weeks or two; and I says, all right, that suits me, but I aint got no money for to buy the outfit,[3] and I reckon I couldn't get none from home, because it's likely pap's been back before now, and got it all away from Judge Thatcher and drunk it up.

"No he hain't," Tom says; "it's all there, yet—six thousand dollars and more; and your pap hain't ever been back since. Hadn't when I come away, anyhow."

Jim says, kind of solemn:

"He ain't a comin' back no mo', Huck."

I says:

"Why, Jim?"

TOM'S LIBERALITY.

2. *howling adventures amongst the Injuns.* In Chapter 13 of *A Boy's Town*, Howells described exactly what the romantic allure of the Indians was to young country boys at the time: Theirs was "a world where people spent their lives in hunting and fishing and ranging the woods, and never grew up into the toils and cares that can alone make men of boys. They wished to escape these, as many foolish persons do among civilized nations, and they thought if they could only escape then they would be happy; they did not know that they would be merely savage."

Once he had completed writing *Adventures of Huckleberry Finn*, Twain began in earnest in the summer of 1884 on the sequel "Huck Finn and Tom Sawyer Among the Indians." He never finished it. Just as he had burlesqued Sir Walter Scott and escape literature in the previous story, Twain took on James Fenimore Cooper's "noble savage" in the new one. Huck, Tom, and Jim head out for the Great Plains, and almost immediately encounter an Indian massacre. Evidently Twain just did not know how to honestly describe the rape of a white woman whom the Oglala have abducted, so he abandoned the story. It is probably just as well, because the fragment reeks of Twain's contempt for North American Indians.

3. *I ain't got no money for to buy the outfit.* And it could be a considerable expense, as indicated by the one described in the unfinished "Huck Finn and Tom Sawyer Among the Indians": five pack mules, matches, an almanac, a flask or two of liquor, "skillets and coffee pots and tin cups, and blankets, and three sacks of flour, and bacon and sugar and coffee, and fish hooks, and pipes and tobacco, and ammunition, and pistols, and three guns, and glass beads, and all such things" (*Huck Finn and Tom Sawyer Among the Indians*, 1989, p. 38).

"Nemmine why, Huck—but he ain't comin' back no mo'."

But I kept at him; so at last he says:

"Doan' you 'member de house dat was float'n down de river, en dey wuz a man in dah, kivered up, en I went in en unkivered him and didn' let you come in? Well, den, you k'n git yo' money when you wants it; kase dat wuz him."[4]

Tom's most well, now, and got his bullet around his neck on a watch-guard for a watch, and is always seeing what time it is, and so there ain't nothing more to write about, and I am rotten glad of it, because if I'd a knowed what a trouble it was to make a book I wouldn't a tackled it and ain't agoing to no more. But I reckon I got to light out for the Territory ahead of the rest, because Aunt Sally she's going to adopt me[5] and sivilize me and I can't stand it.[6] I been there before.

THE END. YOURS TRULY, HUCK FINN.

4. *kase dat wuz him*. Exactly why Jim held back this crucial information until the very last moment is never revealed in the story. "Though one of his motives for evading Huck's query about the dead man in the floating house may be his tender wish to spare Huck the knowledge of being an orphan," James M. Cox suggested in "A Hard Book to Take," "Jim has good reason to suspect that a Huck free of his pap might leave him high and dry" (Robert Sattelmeyer and Donald J. Crowley, editors, *One Hundred Years of Huckleberry Finn: The Boy, His Book, and American Culture*, 1985, p. 391). Considering how Jim has revealed his good heart on their adventures down the Mississippi, it seems unlikely that he would have withheld the fact of pap's death from Huck for any other reason than to spare the boy any pain. Jim has no knowledge of how Huck's father has abused him; Jim himself is a loving father.

5. *Aunt Sally she's going to adopt me*. But what about the Widow Douglas? Twain never fully resolves his story: It was Miss Watson, not Huck's guardian, who died, so the boy should return to St. Petersburg to his foster mother. Twain did get the women confused; he had to ask himself in his notes, "Widow Douglas—then who is 'Miss Watson'? Ah, she's Widow Douglas' *sister*—old spinster" (University of California edition, 1988, p. 735). Inexplicably, he raised Miss Watson from the dead in the unfinished "Tom Sawyer's Conspiracy" (*Huck Finn and Tom Sawyer Among the Indians*, 1989, pp. 134–213).

6. *and sivilize me and I can't stand it*. With the coming of the railroads, frontiersmen such as the legendary Mike Fink and Mick Shuck were

Autograph of "Mark Twain"/ Samuel L. Clemens.
Private collection.

forced to keep moving farther and farther west in search of freedom; so the Indian Territory was quickly becoming the last refuge from civilization in the country. Twain shared Huck's scorn for "sivilization" as mostly sham and hypocrisy. But one should not make too much of Huck's declaration of independence. Eugene McNamara argued in "Huck Lights Out for the Territory" (*University of Windsor Review*, Fall 1966, pp. 68–74) that it may only be a device to leave open the possibility of more adventures, particularly the unfinished "Huck Finn and Tom Sawyer Among the Indians."

Mark Twain on the lecture circuit, 1885.
Photograph by Falk, 1885.
Courtesy Central Children's Room,
New York Public Library, Astor, Lenox, and Tilden Foundations.

Appendix A

"*"Jim and the Dead Man"*"

The following *suppressed passage originally appeared after Huck and Jim take refuge in the cave during the storm in Chapter 9 of* Huckleberry Finn *(see note 5 of that chapter). It is not known exactly when it was deleted, whether Olivia objected to it or Twain dropped it when Charles L. Webster requested that Twain cut the text to make* Huckleberry Finn *uniform in size with* Tom Sawyer. *Although this incident reiterates Jim and Huck's fascination with ghosts and corpses, it was easily expendable, for it does not advance the plot. Twain never made use of the incident anywhere else in his writing, and it remained completely unknown until the first half of the holograph manuscript (now in the Buffalo and Erie County Public Library, Buffalo, New York) was discovered in 1990. It appeared first in* The New Yorker *(June 26/July 3, 1995) as "Jim and the Dead Man," and then as the "cadaver episode" in the 1996 Random House "Comprehensive Edition." It is reprinted with the permission of Random House and the Mark Twain Foundation.*

"I been in a storm here once before,[1] with Tom Sawyer and Jo Harper, Jim. It was a storm like this, too—last summer. We didn't know about this place and so we got soaked. The lightning tore a big tree all to flinders. Why don't lightning cast a shadow, Jim?"

"Well, I reckon it do, but I don't know."

"Well, it don't. *I* know. The sun does, and a candle does, but the lightning don't. Tom Sawyer says it don't, and it's so."

"Sho, child, I reckon you's mistaken 'bout dat. Gimme de gun—I's gwyne to see."

1. *I been in a storm here once before*. Huck is recalling Chapter 16 of *Tom Sawyer*, in which he, Tom, and Joe Harper escape to Jackson's Island on a raft after Becky Thatcher rejects Tom. On the third night away from home, a terrific storm strikes the island and the boys retreat to their tent. When the storm rips away their shelter, they seek refuge beneath a great oak. Examining the damage once it has passed, they discover that lightning destroyed the big sycamore under which they had set up their tent.

2. *Long time ago, when I was 'bout sixteen year old.* No subsequent reference to Jim's history prior to Miss Watson is ever made in the novel. Victor Doyno speculated in the 1996 Random House "Comprehensive Edition" that "Jim was not a field slave but was owned by a village family rich enough to pay for a son to be 'a student in a doctor college.' The knowledge of Jim's earlier, relatively high slave status makes his later desire to escape slavery even more urgent" (p. 372).

3. *a stugent in a doctor college.* Fischer and Salamo suggested in the 2001 University of California edition (pp. 463–64) that this episode was likely inspired by a story about Twain's mother's younger half-brother, James Andrew Hays Lampton (1824–1879). He lived next door to the Clemenses in Hannibal before going off to study at McDowell Medical College, the first medical college in St. Louis. Between 1866 and 1897, Twain reminded himself in several entries in his notebooks to write about "uncle Jim Lampton's adventure with the corpse in the dissecting room of McDowell's college at midnight." It was a big brick building in open ground like that described by Jim. Lampton gave up his practice because he could not stand the sight of blood.

Graduate student Vicky Raab suggested in a letter to the editor in *The New Yorker* (August 14, 1995, p. 6) that Twain may have based this anecdote on Frank Dumont's "Ethiopian sketch in one scene," "One Night in a Medical College," first performed by Duprez and Benedict's Minstrels in Gloucester, Massachusetts, on April 5, 1876, and later that month in Hartford, Connecticut, where Twain might have seen it. That summer he began *Huckleberry Finn*. If he was indeed familiar with this sketch, Twain borrowed little more than its locale and premise. Although a minstrel sketch, "One Night in a Medical College" was not written in dialect, perhaps so other groups might perform it. On a stormy night as turbulent as that on Jackson's Island, medical student Esculapius Scalpel is preparing to cut up a fresh corpse when an unexpected visitor, George Arrowroot, dives through his dissecting room to escape the lightning. George decides to sleep there, so the student cannot get on with his work. Scalpel warns him that ghosts will "seize you by the hair of the head, drag you all over the floor, spit flame and smoke into your eyes, yell into your ears until

So he stood up the gun in the door, and held it, and when it lightened the gun didn't cast any shadow. Jim says:

"Well, dat's mighty cur'us—dat's oncommon cur'us. Now dey say a ghos' don't cas' no shadder. Why is dat, you reckon? Of couse de reason is dat ghosts is made out'n lightnin', or else de lightnin' is made out'n ghosts—but I don't know which it is. I wisht I knowed which it is, Huck."

"Well I do, too; but I reckon there ain't no way to find out. Did you ever see a ghost, Jim?"

"Has I ever seed a ghos'? Well I reckon I has."

"O, tell me about it, Jim—tell me about it."

"De storm's a rippin' en a tearin', en a carryin' on so, a body can't hardly talk, but I reckon I'll try. Long time ago, when I was 'bout sixteen year old,[2] my young Mars. William, dat's dead, now, was a stugent in a doctor college[3] in de village whah we lived den. Dat college was a powerful big brick building, three stories high, en stood all by hersef in a big open place out to de edge er de village.—Well, one night in de middle of winter young Mars. William he tole me to go to de college, en go up stairs to de dissectin' room on de second flo', en warm up a dead man dat was dah on de table,[4] en git him soft so he can cut him up—"

"What for, Jim?"

"I don't know—see if can find sumfin in him, maybe. Anyways, dat's what he tole me. En he tole me to wait dah tell he come. So I takes a lantern[5] en starts out acrost de town. My, but it was a-blowin' en a-sleetin' en cold! Dey wan't nobody stirrin' in de streets en I could scasely shove along agin de wind. It was mos' midnight, en dreadful dark.

"I was mighty glad to git to de place, child. I onlocked de do' en went up stairs to de dissectin' room. Dat room was sixty foot long en twenty-five foot wide; en all along de wall, on bofe sides, was de long black gowns a-hangin', dat de stugents wears when dey's a-choppin' up de dead people. Well, I goes a swingin' de lantern along, en de shadders er dem gowns went to spreadin' out en drawin' in, along de wall, en it scairt me. It looked like dey was swinging' dey han's to git 'em warm. Well, I never looked at 'em no mo';

but it seemed like dey was a-doin' it behind my back jis' de same.

"Dey was a table 'bout forty foot long, down de middle er de room, wid fo' dead people on it, layin' on dey backs wid dey knees up[6] en sheets over 'em. You could see de shapes under de sheets. Well, Mars. William he tole me to warm up de big man wid de black whiskers.[7] So I unkivered one, en he didn't have no whiskers. But he had his eyes wide open, en I kivered him up quick, I bet you.—De next one was sich a gashly sight dat I mos' let de lantern drap. Well, I skipped one carcass, en went for de las' one. I raise' up de sheet en I says, all right, boss, you's de chap I's arter. He had de black whiskers en was a rattlin' big man, en looked wicked like a pirate. He was naked—dey all was. He was a layin' on round sticks—rollers. I took de sheet off'n him en rolled him along feet fust, to de en' er de table befo' de fire place. His laigs was apart en his knees was cocked up some; so when I upended him on de en' er de table, he sot up dah lookin pretty natural, wid his feet out en his big toes stickin' up like he was warmin' hissef. I propped him up wid de rollers, en den I spread de sheet over his back en over his head to help warm him, en den when I was a tyin' de corners under his chin, but jings he opened his eyes![8] I let go en stood off en looked at him, feelin' mighty shaky. Well, he didn't look at nuthin particular, en didn' do nuffin', so I knowed he was good en dead, yit.

"But I couldn't stan' dem eyes, you know. It made me feel all-overish, jis' to look at 'em. So I pulled de sheet cler down over his face en under his chin, en tied it hard—en den dah he sot, all naked in front, wid his head like a big snow-ball, en de sheet a-kiverin' his back en falling down on de table behind. So dah he sot, wid his laigs spread out, but blame it he didn't look no better'n what he did befo', his head was so awful, somehow.

"But dem eyes was kivered up, so I reckoned I'd let him stan' at dat, en not try to improve him up no mo'. Well, I stoop' down between his laigs on de hathstone, en took de candle out'n de lantern en hilt it in my han' so as to make

their unearthly screams freezes the blood in your veins and chills the marrow in your bones, making every hair upon your head stand like quills upon the fretful porcupine." But George refuses to budge, being more frightened of lightning than ghosts. Scalpel finally gives up, determined to teach George a lesson. While George is settling in, another unwanted guest, Peleg Venture, jumps through the window out of the storm. Just as Scalpel predicted, all hell breaks loose at midnight while ghosts and corpses attack the unwelcome visitors. Dumont himself played the "Subject" on the plank in the original production.

4. *a dead man dat was dah on de table.* As Doyno pointed out in the 1996 Random House "Comprehensive Edition," this anecdote "presents a relatively rare look at early medical school conditions. . . . Of course, because of religious opposition, these institutions often had a difficult time obtaining cadavers for instructional purposes. Grave robbery and body snatching were not unusual practices; in both fact and fiction—including Twain's—the practice was widely documented" (p. 374). One need only recall Dr. Robinson's murder in Chapter 9 of *Tom Sawyer*: Tom and Huck find Injun Joe, Muff Potter, and the young doctor in the graveyard, digging up a newly buried corpse. A graverobber named Slabside provides medical student Esculapius Scalpel with his cadaver in "One Night in a Medical College" (see note 3 above). "Many of these medical schools had an employee, usually a black male, who would work as a janitor and a body provider," Doyno explained. "These people were sarcastically called 'resurrectionists,' in a semiscientific mockery of religious beliefs." The corpses too were often African Americans. When Ruth Bolton attends medical school in Chapter 15 of *The Gilded Age*, she and another student talk the janitor into letting them into the college's dissecting room one night. The girls are repulsed when Ruth pulls the sheet off the head of "the new one"; and the scowl on the face seems to be saying, "Haven't you yet done with the outcast, persecuted black man, but you must now haul him from his grave, and send even your women to dismember his body?"

5. *a lantern.* Twain originally wrote "a candle," but that light would not have survived the storm.

6. *wid dey knees up.* "The raised knees suggest that the corpses were obtained illegally," explained Fischer and Salamo in the 2001 University of California edition, "for to avoid detection, grave robbers embalmed their corpses before shipping them, not in coffins, but in small boxes or barrels which required that the knees be flexed" (p. 465).

7. *de big man wid de black whiskers.* This corpse foreshadows the body Huck and Jim discover in the floating house later in Chapter 9. Doyno suggested in the 1996 Random House "Comprehensive Edition" (p. 373) that "Jim and the Dead Man" explains how Jim had the knowledge to determine that the murdered man had been dead for several days.

8. *he opened his eyes!* Some details of this episode may have been suggested by an incident with a corpse from Twain's childhood mentioned in Chapter 18 of *The Innocents Abroad*. Afraid of being whipped for having skipped school, Sam Clemens climbed through the window of his father's office late at night so he could sleep on the lounge. Little did he know that earlier in the day the body of a murdered man had been carried there and stretched out on the floor. "The pallid face of a man was there," he recalled, "with the corners of the mouth drawn down, and the eyes fixed and glassy in death! I raised to a sitting posture and glowered on that corpse till the light crept down the bare breast—line by line—inch by inch—past the nipple—and then it disclosed a ghastly stab!" He got out of there, and did not mind the whipping his father gave him back home. "I have slept in that the same room with him often since then—in my dreams," he said.

9. *dis feller's a-movin' his toes.* Doyno explained in the 1996 Random House "Comprehensive Edition" that "before brain-scanning machines—comatose people were occasionally presumed dead, and mourners were sometimes quite horrified when the 'corpse' revived" (pp. 374–75). Premature burial was a common fear during this period, and bodies were often affixed with bells or other alarms should the mistaken-for-dead person revive. In "A Dying Man's Confession" in Chapter 31 of *Life on the Mississippi*, Twain recounted the story of a morgue attendant who was dozing off "when sharp and suddenly that dead-bell rang out a blood-curdling

mo' light. Dey was some embers in de fire place, but de wood wass all to de yuther en' er de room. Whils' I was a stoopin' dah, gittin' ready to go arter de wood, de candle flickered, en I thought de ole man moved his laigs. It kinder made me shiver. I put out my han' en felt o' his laig dat was poked along pas' my lef' jaw, en it was cold as ice.—So I reckoned he didn't move. Den I felt o' de laig dat was poked pas' my right jaw, en it was powerful cold, too. You see I was a stoopin' down right betwix' 'em.

"Well, pretty soon I thought I see his toes move; dey was jis' in front er me, on bofe sides. I tell you, honey, I was gittin' oneasy. You see dat was a great big old ramblin' bildin' en nobody but me in it, en dat man over me wid dat sheet over his face, en de wind a wailin' roun' de place like sperits dat was in trouble, en de sleet a-drivin' agin' de glass; en den de clock struck twelve in de village, en it was so fur away, en de wind choke up de soun' so dat it only soun' like a moan—dat's all. Well, thinks I, I wisht I was out'n dis; what *is* gwyne to become er me?—en dis feller's a-movin' his toes,[9] I *knows* it—I kin *see* 'em move—en I kin jis' feel dem eyes er his'n en see dat ole dumplin' head done up in de sheet, en—

"Well, sir, jis' at dat minute, *down he comes*, right a-straddle er my neck wid his cold laigs, en kicked de candle out!"

"My! What did you do, Jim?"

"Do? Well I never done nuffin'; only I jis' got up en heeled it in de dark. *I* warn't gwyne to wait to fine out what he wanted. No sir; I jis' split down stairs en linked it home a-yelpin' every jump."

"What did your Mars. William say?"

"He said I was a fool. H went dah en found de dead man on de flo' all comfortable, en took en chopped him up. Dod rot him, I wisht I'd a had a hack at him."

"What made him hop on to your neck, Jim?"

"Well, Mars. William said I didn't prop him good wid de rollers.—But I don't know. It warn't no way for a dead man to act, nohow; it might a scairt some people to death."

"But Jim, he warn't rightly a ghost—he was only a dead man. Didn't you ever see a real sure-'nough ghost?"

"You bet I has—lots of 'em."

"Well, tell me about them, Jim."

"All right, I will, some time; but de storm's a-slackin' up, now, so we better go en tend to de lines en bait 'em agin."

alarum over my head!" When he went to investigate, he found that "a shrouded figure was sitting upright, wagging its head slowly from one side to the other—a grisly spectacle! . . . Think what it must have been to wake up in the midst of that voiceless hush, and look out over that grim congregation of the dead!"

Appendix B
The "Raft Episode"
Illustrated by John J. Harley

THE FOLLOWING *passage originally appeared after the second paragraph of Chapter 16 in* Huckleberry Finn *(see note 4 of that chapter). Having put aside that novel, "a book I have been working at, by fits and starts, during the past five or six years, and may possibly finish in the course of five or six more," Twain inserted it into Chapter 3 of* Life on the Mississippi *as a description of long-lost raft-life and keelboat manners and language. "The old-time flatboatmen and raftsmen—so famous in Mississippi history—are capitally drawn," said Lafcadio Hearn in his review of* Life on the Mississippi *in the New Orleans* Times-Democrat *(May 20, 1883). It was still part of* Huckleberry Finn *when Charles L. Webster objected to including this "old Mississippi matter" in the manuscript, and Twain left it out of the published work. He planned to read the "raftsman's fight" during the 1884–1885 "Twins of Genius" tour, and even revised the text for this presentation. But he never delivered it once it was decided not to put the section back into the book. Although he had ample opportunity, Twain himself never restored it in* Huckleberry Finn.

Although many critics (including Bernard DeVoto, who put it back into the 1944 Limited Editions Club edition) believe that the "Raft Episode" should be kept in the novel, this lengthy, highly detailed account of a particular part of long-lost American life is perhaps more suited to Life on the Mississippi *than to* Huckleberry Finn. *The vivid section may, as its defenders have argued, enlarge on themes established earlier in the story and provide Huck with information not disclosed elsewhere, but it suffers from what William Dean Howells in* Century Magazine *(September 1882, p. 782) said was true of portions of* Tom Sawyer, *"an excess of reality in portraying the characters and conditions" of the Southwest before the Civil War.*

But you know a young person can't wait very well when he is impatient to find a thing out. We talked it over, and by and by Jim said it was such a black night, now, that it wouldn't be no risk to swim down to the big raft and crawl aboard and listen,—they would talk about Cairo,[1] because they would be calculating to go ashore there for a spree, maybe, or anyway they would send boats ashore to buy whisky or fresh meat or something. Jim had a wonderful level head, for a nigger: he could most always start a good plan when you wanted one.

I stood up and shook my rags off and jumped into the river, and struck out for the raft's light. By and by, when I got down nearly to her, I eased up and went slow and cautious. But everything was all right—nobody at the sweeps. So I swum down along the raft till I was most abreast the camp fire in the middle, then I crawled aboard and inched along and got in amongst some bundles of shingles on the weather side of the fire.[2] There was thirteen men there—they was the watch on deck of course. And a mighty rough-looking lot, too. They had a jug, and tin cups, and they kept the jug moving. One man was singing—roaring, you may say; and it was n't a nice song—for a parlor anyway. He roared through his nose, and strung out the last word of every line very long. When he was done they all fetched a

"I SWUM DOWN ALONG THE RAFT."

1. *they would talk about Cairo*. Huck and Jim suspect that they have passed Cairo, Illinois, where the slave hopes to escape to the free states.

2. *on the weather side of the fire*. On the side away from where the wind is blowing, so the boy is out of the path of the smoke and light of the fire.

kind of Injun war-whoop, and then another was sung. It begun:—

"There was a woman in our towdn,[3]
In our towdn did dwed'l (dwell,)
She loved her husband dear-i-lee,
But another man twyste as wed'l.[4]

Singing too, riloo, riloo, riloo,
Ri-too, riloo, rilay - - - e,
She loved her husband dear-i-lee,
But another man twyste as we*d'l.*"

And so on—fourteen verses. It was kind of poor,[5] and when he was going to start on the next verse one of them said it was the tune the old cow died on;[6] and another one said, "Oh, give us a rest." And another one told him to take a walk.[7] They made fun of him till he got mad and jumped up and begun to cuss the crowd, and said he could lam any thief in the lot.

They was all about to make a break for him, but the biggest man there jumped up and says:—

"HE JUMPED UP IN THE AIR."

3. *There was a woman in our towdn*. Twain quoted only the first verse of a variant of a popular folk song. In Scotland, it is known as "The Wily Auld Carle" and "The Wife of Kelso"; in Maine as "The Old Woman of Dover"; in Kentucky as "Old Woman of London"; in Ohio as "Old Woman of Slapsadam"; in North Carolina as "The Old Woman's Blind Husband"; and in Missouri as "There was an Old Woman":

There was an old woman in our town,
In our town did dwell.
She loved her husband dearily,
But another man twice as well.

She went down to the doctor's shop
To see what she could find
To see if she could find anything
To make her old man blind.

She found six old beef bones
And made him chew them all.
He says, "Old woman, I am so blind
I can't see you at all."

He says, "Old woman, I'll drown myself
If I could find the way."
She says, "My dearest husband,
I'll go show you the way."

She took him by the hand
And led him to the brim.
He says, "Old woman, I'll drown myself
If you will push me in."

The old woman stepped a little one side
To give a sounding spring.
The old man stepped a little one side,
And she went bounding in.

The she bawled out, she squawled out,
As loud as she could bawl.
He says, "Old woman, I am so blind
I can't see you at all."

The old man being good-natured
And thought that she might swim,
He goes and gets a good long pole
And pushed her further in.

Some versions add the following:

Now my song is ended,
I'll sing you no more,
Wasn't she an old fool?
And he was seventy-four.

"Set whar you are, gentlemen. Leave him to me; he's my meat."[8]

Then he jumped up in the air three times and cracked his heels together every time. He flung off a buckskin coat that was all hung with fringes, and says, "You lay thar tell the chawin-up 's done;" and flung his hat down, which was all over ribbons, and says, "You lay thar tell his sufferins is over."

Then he jumped up in the air and cracked his heels together again and shouted out:—

"Whoo-oop! I'm the old original iron-jawed, brass-mounted, copper-bellied corpse-maker from the wilds of Arkansaw![9]—Look at me! I'm the man they call Sudden Death and General Desolation! Sired by a hurricane, dam'd by an earthquake, half-brother to the cholera, nearly related to the small-pox on the mother's side! Look at me! I take nineteen alligators and a bar'l of whisky for breakfast when I'm in robust health, and a bushel of rattlesnakes and a dead body when I'm ailing! I split the everlasting rocks with my glance, and I squench[10] the thunder when I speak! Whoo-oop! Stand back and give me room according to my strength! Blood's my natural drink, and the wails of the dying is music to my ear! Cast your eye on me, gentlemen!—and lay low and hold your breath, for I'm bout to turn myself loose!"

All the time he was getting this off, he was shaking his head and looking fierce, and kind of swelling around in a little circle, tucking up his wrist-bands, and now and then straightening up and beating his breast with his fist, saying,[11] "Look at me, gentlemen!" When he got through, he jumped up and cracked his heels together three times, and let off a roaring "whoo-oop! I'm the bloodiest son of a wild-cat that lives!"

Then the man that had started the row tilted his old slouch hat down over his right eye; then he bent stooping forward, with his back sagged and his south end[12] sticking out far, and his fists a-shoving out and drawing in in front of him, and so went around in a little circle about three times, swelling himself up and breathing hard. Then he

Or,

Now my song is ended,
I'll sing you no more.
Wasn't she an old fool
To trust her husband so?

This slightly improper ballad was one of Twain's favorite songs. Blair and Fischer noted in the 1988 University of California edition that Twain introduced the verse in a fragment of a play written in 1865, included in *Mark Twain's Satires and Burlesques* (1968, p. 211). According to Samuel Charles Webster's *Mark Twain, Business Man* (1946, p. 109), his sister-in-law recalled him singing it in the family's private railroad car on his wedding trip in 1870. Miles Hendon sings a few lines on Chapter 13 of *The Prince and the Pauper*, while sewing clothes for Edward Tudor.

4. *But another man twyste as wed'l.* While reading the proofs of *The Prince and the Pauper*, William Dean Howells objected to this line as "rather strong milk for babes," so Twain changed it to "But another man he loved she,—." However, when the author himself took the role of Miles Hendon in a private performance of the story put on by his daughters and their friends at Christmas in 1884, Twain sang it unexpurgated. (See *Mark Twain–Howells Letters*, 1960, pp. 375 and 874.) He deleted it when he revised the "raftsman's fight" for the 1884–1885 "Twins of Genius" public reading tour, and added merely "It was a long song—fourteen verses."

5. *poor*. "Stuff" added to his revisions for the 1884–1885 "Twins of Genius" public reading tour.

6. *the tune the old cow died on*. Ruth Ann Musick published this Missouri folk song in *Hoosier Folklore* (December 1948):

Farmer John from his work came home
One summer's afternoon,
And sat himself down by the maple grove
And sang himself this tune

Chorus:

Ri fol de ol, Di ri fol dal di
Tune the old cow died on.

The farmer's cows came running home
And round him formed a ring;
For they never heard good Farmer John
Before attempt to sing.

The oldest cow in the farmer's herd
Tried hard to join the song;
But she couldn't strike that melody—
Her voice was loud and strong.

The farmer laughed till the tears rolled down
His cheeks like apples red;
The cow got mad and tried to sing
Until she dropped down dead.

The farmer had an inquest held
To see what killed the cow,
The verdict of the jury was
What I mean to tell you now.

They said the cow would be living yet
To chew her cud with glee
If good Farmer John hadn't sung that song
Beneath the maple tree. (pp. 105–6)

7. *take a walk*. "Run to his mammy—she'd be uneasy to have him sing out so long" in the revisions for the 1884–1885 "Twins of Genius" public reading tour.

8. *my meat*. My quarry, my prey.

9. *I'm the old original iron-jawed, brass-mounted, copper-bellied corpse-maker from the wilds of Arkansaw!* "This long episode," noted Doyno in the 1996 Random House "Comprehensive Edition," "with its great emphasis on male competition, deceit, and distrust, paints a comical picture, but one strongly contrasting to our vision of Huck's and Jim's idyllic life isolated on their raft" (p. 378). Fighting was a common diversion of riverboatmen of the period. "The incredible strength of their pectoral muscles, growing out of their peculiar labor and manner of life," T. B. Thorpe explained in "Remembrances of the Mississippi" (*Harper's Monthly*, December 1855), "made fights with them a direful necessity—it was an appetite, and, like pressing hunger, had to be appeased. The keelboatman who boasted that he had never been whipped, stood upon a dangerous eminence, for every aspirant for fame was bound to dispute this claim to such distinction" (p. 30). Whenever two of these "ring-tailed squealers"

straightened, and jumped up and cracked his heels together three times before he lit again (that made them cheer), and he begun to shout like this:—

"WENT AROUND IN A LITTLE CIRCLE."

"Whoo-oop! bow your neck and spread,[13] for the kingdom of sorrow's a-coming! Hold me down to the earth, for I feel my powers a-working! whoo-oop! I'm a child of sin, *don't* let me get a start! Smoked glass,[14] here, for all! Don't attempt to look at me with the naked eye, gentlemen! When I'm playful I use the meridians of longitude and parallels of latitude for a seine, and drag the Atlantic Ocean for whales! I scratch my head with the lightning and purr myself to sleep with the thunder! When I'm cold, I bile the Gulf of Mexico and bathe in it; when I'm hot I fan myself with an equinoctial storm;[15] when I'm thirsty I reach up and suck a cloud dry like a sponge; when I range the earth hungry, famine follows in my tracks! Whoo-oop! Bow your neck and spread! I put my hand on the sun's face and make it night in the earth;[16] I bite a piece out of the moon and hurry the seasons;[17] I shake myself and crumble the mountains! Contemplate me through leather—*don't* use the naked eye![18] I'm the man with a petrified heart and biler-iron bowels![19] The massacre of isolated communities[20] is the pastime of my idle moments, the destruction of nationalities the serious business of my life! The boundless vastness of the great American desert is my enclosed property, and I bury my dead on my own premises!" He jumped up and cracked his heels together three times before he lit (they cheered him again), and as he come down he shouted out: "Whoo-oop! bow your neck and spread, for the pet child of calamity's a-coming!"[21]

Then the other one went to swelling around and blowing again—the first one—the one they called Bob; next, the Child of Calamity chipped in again, bigger than ever; then they both got at it at the same time, swelling round and round each other and punching their fists most into each other's faces, and whooping and jawing like Injuns; then Bob called the Child names, and the Child called him names back again: next, Bob called him a heap rougher names and the Child come back at him with the very worst kind of language; next, Bob knocked the Child's hat off, and the Child picked it up and kicked Bob's ribbony hat about six foot; Bob went and got it and said never mind, this warn't going to be the last of this thing, because he was a man that never forgot and never forgive, and so the Child better look out, for there was a time a-coming, just as sure as he was a living man, that he would have to answer to him with the best blood in his body. The Child said no man was willinger than he was for that time to come, and he would give Bob fair warning, *now,* never to cross his path again, for he could never rest till he had waded in his blood, for such was his nature, though he was sparing him now on account of his family, if he had one.

Both of them was edging away in different directions, growling and shaking their heads and going on[22] about what they was going to do; but a little black-whiskered chap skipped up and says:—

"Come back here, you couple of chicken-livered cowards, and I'll thrash the two of ye!"

And he done it, too. He snatched them, he jerked them this way and that, he booted them around, he knocked them sprawling faster than they could get up. Why, it warn't two minutes till they begged like dogs—and how the other lot did yell and laugh and clap their hands all the way through, and shout "Sail in, Corpse-Maker!" "Hi! at him again, Child of Calamity!" "Bully for you, little Davy!" Well, it was a perfect pow-wow for a while. Bob and the Child had

or "salt-water roarers" of the half-alligator variety" met, they would roll up their sleeves, crow like gaming cocks, and try to outboast each other. "I'm from the Lightning Forks of Roaring River. I'm all man, save what is a wild cat and extra lightning. I'm as hard to run against as a cypress snag—I never back water. . . . Cock-a-doodle-doo! I did hold down a bufferlo bull, and tar off his scalp with my teeth. . . . I'm the man that, single-handed, towed the broadhorn over a sandbar—the identical infant who girdled a hickory by smiling at the bark, and if any one denies it, let him make his will and pay the expenses of a funeral. I'm the genuine article, tough as bull's hide, keen as a rifle. . . . I'm painfully ferochus—I'm spiling for some one to whip me—if there's a creeter in this diggin' that wants to be disappointed in trying to do it, let him yell—whoop-hurra!"

The most famous of these riverboat boasters was Mike Fink, who challenged all comers with "Hurray for me, you scapegoats! I'm a land-screamer—I'm a water-dog—I'm a snapping turkle—I can lick five times my own weight in wild-cats. . . . I can out-run, out-dance, out-jump, out-dive, out-drink, out-holler, and out-lick any white thing in the shape o' 'human that's ever put foot within two thousand miles o' the big Mississip! Whoop!" (Emerson Bennett, *Mike Fink, A Legend of the Ohio*, 1852, p. 28).

These larger-than-life characters soon passed into American folklore as the railroads moved West, but their form of extravagant brag have survived in the taunts of Muhammad Ali and the World Wrestling Federation. American literature was full of these belligerent braggarts before the Civil War. There were Captain Roaring Ralph Stackpole and Bloody Ned in Robert Montgomery Bird's *Nick of the Woods*; Ned Jones in William Pauper Thompson's *Chronicles of Pineville*; Chunkey in William T. Porter's *The Big Bear of Arkansas*; but the combatants perhaps most like Twain's Child of Calamity and Big Bob were Mike Hooter and Arch Coony in Thomas Chandler Haliburton's *Traits of American Character* (1852, pp. 296–301), who exchange more cusses than cuffs. Twain changed "copper-bellied" to "copper-fastened" for the 1884–1885 "Twins of Genius" public reading tour.

10. *squench.* Suppress, quell.

11. *tucking up his wrist-bands, and now and then straightening up and beating his breast with his fist,* *saying*. "Then he skips into the air agin and says" in the revisions for the 1884–1885 'Twins of Genius" public reading tour.

12. *south end*. Twain originally wrote the cruder "back end" (**MS**) in the manuscript.

13. *Whoo-oop! bow your neck and spread*. Blair and Fischer noted in the 1988 University of California edition (p. 395) that this phrase came from Twain's childhood in Hannibal. Twain reminded his friend Will Bowen in a letter of February 6, 1870, how "old General Gaines used to say, 'Whoop! Bow your neck and spread' " (*Huck Finn and Tom Sawyer Among the Indians*, 1989, p. 20). Twain identified him as Hannibal's first town drunkard. Tom Blankenship's father "succeeded 'General' Gaines, and for a time he was sole and only incumbent of the office; but afterward Jimmy Finn proved competency and disputed the place with him, so we had two town drunkards at one time—and it made as much trouble in that village as Christendom experienced in the fourteenth century when there were two Popes at the same time" ("Chapters from My Autobiography," *North American Review*, August 2, 1907, pp. 691–92). Jim mentions "Gen'l Gaines" in "Huck Finn and Tom Sawyer Among the Indians" (p. 35).

14. *Smoked glass*. Tinted glass is worn to protect the eyes when looking directly into the sun, as in an eclipse. Child of Calamity upstages Big Bob in this battle of wits by suggesting that he is a god who can alter the universe while his opponent is just a mortal with superhuman strength.

15. *equinoctial storm*. In his revisions for the 1884–1885 "Twins of Genius" public reading tour, Twain changed this meteorological mouthful to simply "cyclone," a more likely term for a raftsman.

16. *I put my hand on the sun's face and make it night in the earth*. As in an eclipse; however, when the moon covers the sun in such an occurrence, it actually remains day while the light is blocked. In Chapter 6 of *A Connecticut Yankee in King Arthur's Court*, Hank Morgan, like Christopher Columbus, "played an eclipse as a saving trump on some savages," there King Arthur's court.

"He knocked them sprawling."

red noses and black eyes when they got through. Little Davy made them own up that they was sneaks and cowards and not fit to eat with a dog or drink with a nigger;[23] then Bob and the Child shook hands with each other, very solemn, and said they had always respected each other and was willing to let bygones be bygones. So then they washed their faces in the river; and just then there was a loud order to stand by for a crossing, and some of them went forward to man the sweeps there, and the rest went aft to handle the after-sweeps.

I laid still and waited for fifteen minutes, and had a smoke out of a pipe that one of them left in reach; then the crossing was finished, and they stumped back and had a drink around and went to talking and singing again. Next they got out an old fiddle, and one played, and another patted juba,[24] and the rest turned themselves loose on a regular old-fashioned keel-boat[25] breakdown.[26] They couldn't keep that up very long without getting winded, so by and by they settled around the jug again.

They sung "jolly, jolly raftsman's the life for me,"[27] with a rousing chorus, and then they got to talking about differences betwixt hogs, and their different kind of habits; and next about women and their different ways; and next about the best ways to put out houses that was afire; and next about what ought to be done with the Injuns; and next about what a king had to do, and how much he got; and next about how to make cats fight;[28] and next about what to do when a man has fits; and next about differences betwixt clear-water rivers and muddy-water ones. The man they called Ed said the muddy Mississippi water was wholesomer to drink than the clear water of the Ohio;[29] he said if you let a pint of this yaller Mississippi water settle, you

AN OLD-FASHIONED BREAK-DOWN.

would have about a half to three quarters of an inch of mud in the bottom, according to the stage of the river, and then it war n't no better then Ohio water—what you wanted to do was to keep it stirred up—and when the river was low, keep mud on hand to put in and thicken the water up the way it ought to be.

The Child of Calamity said that was so; he said there was nutritiousness in the mud, and a man that drunk Mississippi water could grow corn in his stomach if he wanted to. He says:—

"You look at the graveyards; that tells the tale. Trees won't

17. *I bite a piece out of the moon and hurry the seasons.* It was once believed that the phases of the moon altered the seasons, not that they actually follow the course of the earth's rotation around the sun.

18. don't *use the naked eye.* To condense the "raftsman's fight" for the 1884–1885 "Twins of Genius" public reading tour, Twain broke up this speech between the two combatants by adding a transitional sentence, "Then the first one he interrupted *him* and says 'Whoop! . . .' "

19. *bowels.* "Innards" (**MS**) in the manuscript. Somehow Twain's various censors missed "bowels" when *Life on the Mississippi* went to press; he changed it to "entrails" and finally "vitals" when he revised the passage for the 1884–1885 "Twins of Genius" pubic reading tour.

20. *isolated communities.* The New York *Tribune* (June 24, 1883), in a particularly sarcastic review of *Life on the Mississippi*, challenged the authenticity of the raftsman's talk: "What wealth of humor and what fidelity to nature! If one phrase more than another is typical of the vocabulary of a drunken rowdy on a Mississippi raft, that phrase is 'isolated communities'; and Mr. Clemens captures it like a bird."

21. *the pet child of calamity's a-coming!* In revising this passage for his 1884–1885 "Twins of Genius" public reading tour, Twain replaced the next paragraph with simply "And so they went on and on and on till they got plum out of breath."

22. *going on.* "Still blowing" in the revisions for the 1884–1885 "Twins of Genius" public reading tour.

23. *drink with a nigger.* At the time, considered by some whites as a habit only of the lowest of the low. In mentioning his ambivalent relationship with the slave Uncle Jake in Chapter 28 of *Tom Sawyer,* Huck Finn confesses, "Sometimes, I've set down and eat *with* him. But you needn't tell that. A body's got to do things when he's awful hungry he wouldn't do as a steady thing." Now he is eating regularly with Jim on the raft and liking it—and he does not have to apologize to anyone.

grow worth shucks in a Cincinnati graveyard, but in a Sent Louis graveyard they grow upwards of eight hundred foot high. It's all on account of the water the people drunk before they laid up. A Cincinnati corpse don't richen a soil any."

And they talked about how Ohio water didn't like to mix with Mississippi water. Ed said if you take the Mississippi on a rise when the Ohio is low, you'll find a wide band of clear water[30] all the way down the east side of the Mississippi for a hundred mile or more, and the minute you get out a quarter of a mile from shore and pass the line, it is all thick and yaller the rest of the way across. Then they talked about how to keep tobacco from getting mouldy, and from that they went into ghosts[31] and told about a lot that other folks had seen; but Ed says:—

"Why don't you tell something that you've seen yourselves? Now let me have a say. Five years ago I was on a raft as big as this, and right along here it was a bright moonshiny night, and I was on watch and boss of the stabboard oar forrard, and one of my pards was a man named Dick Allbright, and he come along to where I was sitting, forrard—gaping and stretching, he was—and stooped down on the edge of the raft and washed his face in the river, and come and set down by me and got out his pipe, and had just got it filled, when he looks up and says,—

"'Why looky-here,' he says, 'ain't that Buck Miller's place, over yander in the bend?'

"'Yes,' says I, 'it is—why?' He laid his pipe down and leant his head on his hand, and says,—

"'I thought we'd be furder down.' I says,—

"'I thought it too, when I went off watch'—we was standing six hours on and six off—'but the boys told me,' I says, 'that the raft didn't seem to hardly move, for the last hour,'—says I, 'though she's a slipping along all right, now,' says I. He give a kind of a groan, and says,—

"'I've seed a raft act so before, along here,' he says, ''pears to me the current has most quit above the head of this bend durin' the last two years,' he says.

24. *patted juba.* Or "patting Juba, or jubilee," a lively tap dance, accompanied by clapping hands and slapping knees, while singing:

Juba up and Juba down,
Juba all around the town,
Juba this and Juba that,
And Juba round the 'simmon vat.
  Hoe corn and hill tobacco,
Get over double trouble, Juba, boys, Juba!

This jig is said to be of African origin, Juba being an evil spirit. Despite their disdain for "niggers," these men think nothing of imitating their entertainments.

25. *keel-boat.* A large, long, slender, and light flatboat, propelled by either oars or sails, used in America primarily in low water on the Mississippi and Ohio Rivers.

26. *breakdown.* Any wild, boisterous, or riotous dance, a shuffling dance in rapid motions; it may be a juba, as in Chapter 16 of *The Gilded Age*, where "they saw two negroes . . . 'breaking down' in approved style, amid the 'hi, hi's' of the spectators." Blair and Fischer reported in the 1988 University of California edition (p. 96) that this dance had been observed among slaves as far back as 1700. Dickens described a spirited breakdown in Chapter 6 of his *American Notes* (1842) that he witnessed in the notorious Five Points area of New York City: "Single shuffle, cut and crosscut: snapping his fingers, rolling his eyes, turning in his knees, presenting the backs of his legs in front, spinning about his toes and heels . . . dancing with two left legs, two right legs, two wooden legs, two wire legs, two spring legs—all sorts of legs and no legs." Another white bigot's contradiction: He may not want to "drink with a nigger," but he does not mind dancing like one.

27. *"jolly, jolly, raftsman's the life for me."* Blair and Fischer, in the 1988 University of California edition (p. 396), identified this song as "The Jolly Raftsman" (also called "The Raftsman"), a minstrel song attributed to Daniel Emmett taken from an Italian air, first published in the second series of *Old Dan Emmit's* [sic] *Banjo Melodies* (1844); Emmett, billed as the "African Apollo," was a banjo-player and composer, best known for "Dixie," "Old Dan Tucker," "Turkey in

"Well, he raised up two or three times, and looked away off and around on the water. That started me at it, too. A body is always doing what he sees somebody else doing, though there may n't be no sense in it. Pretty soon I see a black something floating on the water away off to stabboard and quartering behind us. I see he was looking at it, too. I says,—

"'What's that?' He says, sort of pettish,—

"'Tain't nothing but an old empty bar'l.'

"'An empty bar'l!' says I, 'why,' says I, 'a spy-glass is a fool to *your* eyes. How can you tell it's an empty bar'l?' He says,—

"'I don't know; I reckon it ain't a bar'l, but I thought it might be,' says he.

"'Yes,' I says, 'so it might be, and it might be anything else, too; a body can't tell nothing about it, such a distance as that,' I says.

"We hadn't nothing else to do, so we kept on watching it. By and by I says,—

"'Why looky-here, Dick Allbright, that thing's a-gaining on us, I believe.'

"He never said nothing. The thing gained and gained, and I judged it must be a dog that was about tired out. Well, we swung down into the crossing, and the thing floated across the bright streak of the moonshine, and, by George, it *was* a bar'l. Says I,—

"'Dick Allbright, what made you think that thing was a bar'l, when it was a half a mile off,' says I. Says he,—

"'I don't know.' Says I,—

"'You tell me, Dick Allbright.' He says,—

"'Well, I knowed it was a bar'l; I've seen it before; lots has seen it; they says it's a hanted bar'l.'

"I called the rest of the watch, and they come and stood there, and I told them what Dick said. It floated right along abreast, now, and did n't gain any more. It was about twenty foot off. Some was for having it aboard, but the rest didn't want to. Dick Allbright said rafts that had fooled with it had got bad luck by it. The captain of the watch said he didn't

the Straw," and "The Blue Tail Fly." Andrew Evans wrote the words to "The Raftsman":

Oh, I was born in ole Virginny
And my little gal's name was Dine;
She always call'd me a prettier nigger
Than Dandy Jim ob Caroline

Chorus:
My Raft is by the shore
She's light and free
To be a jolly Raftsman's the life for me
And as we glide along
Our song shall be
Dearest Dine I love but thee.

Come, oh, come wid me my dearest lub,
I'll take you to the Northern states,
And you shall keep de oyster cellar,
Oh! you shall hurry up dem cakes.

I'll bid good-bye to old Virginny,
I now will take my last farewell,
If I marry you, my dearest Dine,
We will in peace and happiness dwell.

In spite of the crude dialect, this song seems particularly appropriate for the singer who, like Jim, longs to escape with his gal up North to freedom.

28. *how to make cats fight.* There was another subject in the manuscript but deleted from the story: "and next about why it was best to strap a razor toward the point end and a butcher knife toward the heel" (**MS**).

29. *the muddy Mississippi water was wholesomer to drink than the clear water of the Ohio.* "If you will let your glass stand half an hour," Twain advised in Chapter 22 of *Life on the Mississippi,* "you can separate the land from the water as easily as Genesis; and then you will find them both good: the one good to eat, the other good to drink. The land is very nourishing, the water is thoroughly wholesome. The one appeases hunger; the other, thirst. But the natives do not take them separately, but together, as nature mixed them. When they find an inch of mud in the bottom of a glass, they stir it up, and then take the draught as they would gruel." Charles Dickens tested this belief on his first American visit. "We drank the muddy water of this river while we were on it," he recorded in Chapter 12 believe in it. He said he reckoned the bar'l gained on us because it was in a little better current than what we was. He said it would leave by and by.

"So then we went to talking about other things, and we had a song, and then a breakdown; and after that the captain of the watch called for another song; but it was clouding up, now, and the bar'l stuck right thar in the same place, and the song didn't seem to have much warm-up to it, somehow, and so they didn't finish it, and there warn't any cheers, but it sort of dropped flat, and nobody said anything for a minute. Then everybody tried to talk at once, and one chap got off a joke, but it warn't no use, they didn't laugh, and even the chap that made the joke didn't laugh at it, which ain't usual. We all just settled down glum, and watched the bar'l, and was oneasy and oncomfortable. Well, sir, it shut down black and still, and then the wind begin to moan around, and next the lightning begin to play and the thunder to grumble. And pretty soon there was a regular storm, and in the middle of it a man that was running aft stumbled and fell and sprained his ankle so that he had to lay up.[32] This made the boys shake their heads. And every time the lightning come, there was that bar'l with the blue lights winking around it. We was always on the look-out for it. But by and by, towards dawn, she was gone. When the day come we couldn't see her anywhere, and we warn't sorry, neither.

THE MYSTERIOUS BARREL.

"But next night about half-past nine, when there was songs and high jinks going on, here she comes again, and took her old roost on the stabboard side. There warn't no more high jinks. Everybody got solemn; nobody talked; you

of *American Notes* (1842). "It is considered wholesome by the natives, and is something more opaque than gruel."

30. *a wide band of clear water*. Dickens recorded in Chapter 14 of *American Notes* how, at "the detestable morass called Cairo," travelers on the Mississippi "had the satisfaction of seeing that intolerable river dragging its slimy length and ugly freight abruptly off towards New Orleans; and passing a yellow line which stretched across the current, were again upon the clear Ohio, never, I trust, to see the Mississippi more saving in troubled dreams and nightmares. Leaving it for the company of its sparkling neighbor, was like the transition from pain to ease, or the awakening from a horrible vision to cheerful realities." Likewise, many a runaway like Jim must have shared these sentiments on passing from the treacherous Mississippi to the free Ohio.

31. *they went into ghosts*. Riverboatmen were superstitious and particularly fearful of ghosts. See Chapter 8, note 20.

32. *he had to lay up*. He had to take to his bed.

couldn't get anybody to do anything but set around moody and look at the bar'l. It begun to cloud up again. When the watch changed, the off watch stayed up, 'stead of turning in. The storm ripped and roared around all night, and in the middle of it another man tripped and sprained his ankle, and had to knock off. The bar'l left towards day, and nobody see it go.

"Everybody was sober and down in the mouth all day. I don't mean the kind of sober that comes of leaving liquor alone,—not that. They was quiet, but they all drunk more

"SOON THERE WAS A REGULAR STORM."

than usual,—not together,—but each man sidled off and took it private, by himself.

"After dark the off watch didn't turn in; nobody sung, nobody talked; the boys didn't scatter around, neither; they sort of huddled together, forrard; and for two hours they set there, perfectly still, looking steady in the one direction, and heaving a sigh once in a while. And then, here comes the bar'l again. She took up her old place. She staid there all night; nobody turned in. The storm come on again, after midnight. It got awful dark; the rain poured down; hail, too; the thunder boomed and roared and bellowed; the wind blowed a hurricane; and the lightning spread over everything in big sheets of glare, and showed the whole raft as

33. *jiggering*. Moving in succession of rapid jerks, fidgeting, as when attacked by chiggers.

"THE LIGHTNING KILLED TWO MEN."

plain as day; and the river lashed up white as milk as far as you could see for miles, and there was that bar'l jiggering[33] along, same as ever. The captain ordered the watch to man the after sweeps for a crossing, and nobody would go,—no more sprained ankles for them, they said. They wouldn't even *walk* aft. Well then, just then the sky split wide open, with a crash, and the lightning killed two men of the after watch, and crippled two more. Crippled them how, says you? Why, *sprained their ankles!*

"The bar'l left in the dark betwixt lightnings, towards dawn. Well, not a body eat a bite at breakfast that morning. After that the men loafed around, in twos and threes, and talked low together. But none of them herded with Dick Allbright. They all give him the cold shake. If he come around where any of the men was, they split up and sidled away. They wouldn't man the sweeps with him. The captain had all the skiffs hauled up on the raft, alongside of his wigwam, and wouldn't let the dead men be took ashore to be planted; he didn't believe a man that got ashore would come back; and he was right.

"After night come, you could see pretty plain that there was going to be trouble if that bar'l come again; there was such a muttering going on. A good many wanted to kill Dick Allbright, because he'd seen the bar'l on other trips, and that had an ugly look. Some wanted to put him ashore. Some said, let's all go ashore in a pile, if the bar'l comes again.

"This kind of whispers was still going on, the men being bunched together forrard watching for the bar'l, when, lo and behold you, here she comes again. Down she comes, slow and steady, and settles into her old tracks. You could a heard a pin drop. Then up comes the captain, and says:—

"'Boys, don't be a pack of children and fools; I don't want this bar'l to be dogging[34] us all the way to Orleans, and *you* don't; well, then, how's the best way to stop it? Burn it up,—that's the way. I'm going to fetch it aboard,' he says. And before anybody could say a word, in he went.

"He swum to it, and as he come pushing it to the raft, the men spread to one side. But the old man got it aboard and busted in the head, and there was a baby in it! Yes sir, a stark naked baby. It was Dick Allbright's baby; he owned up and said so.

"'Yes,' he says, a-leaning over it, 'yes, it is my own lamented darling, my poor lost Charles William Allbright deceased,' says he,—for he could curl his tongue around the bulliest words in the language when he was a mind to, and lay them before you without a jint started,[35] anywheres. Yes, he said he used to live up at the head of this bend, and one night he choked his child, which was crying, not intending to kill it,[36]—which was prob'ly a lie,—and then he was scared, and buried it in a bar'l, before his wife got home, and off he went, and struck the northern trail and went to rafting; and this was the third year that the bar'l had chased him. He said the bad luck always begun

"GRABBED THE LITTLE CHILD."

34. *dogging.* Following closely, persistently, as in tracking with dogs.

35. *without a jint started.* Without moving a single joint, effortlessly.

36. *one night he choked his child, which was crying, not intending to kill it.* Dick Allbright's "owning up" to his killing the baby foreshadows a similar confession, that of Jim's abuse of his deaf-and-dumb daughter in Chapter 23.

light, and lasted till four men was killed, and then the bar'l didn't come any more after that. He said if the men would stand it one more night,—and was a-going on like that,—but the men had got enough. They started to get out a boat to take him ashore and lynch him, but he grabbed the little child all of a sudden and jumped overboard with it hugged up to his breast and shedding tears, and we never see him again in this life, poor old suffering soul, nor Charles William neither."

"*Who* was shedding tears?" says Bob; "was it Allbright or the baby?"

"Why, Allbright, of course; didn't I tell you the baby was dead? Been dead three years—how could it cry?"

"Well, never mind how it could cry—how could it *keep* all that time?" says Davy. "You answer me that."

"I don't know how it done it," says Ed. "It done it though—that's all I know about it."

"Say—what did they do with the bar'l?" says the Child of Calamity.

"Why, they hove it overboard, and it sunk like a chunk of lead."

"Edward, did the child look like it was choked?" says one.

"Did it have its hair parted?" says another.

"What was the brand on that bar'l, Eddy?" says a fellow they called Bill.

"Have you got the papers for them statistics, Edmund?" says Jimmy.

"Say, Edwin,[37] was you one of the men that was killed by the lightning?" says Davy.

"Him? O, no, he was both of 'em," says Bob. Then they all haw-hawed.

"Say, Edward, don't you reckon you 'd better take a pill? You look bad—don't you feel pale?" says the Child of Calamity.

"O, come, now, Eddy," says Jimmy, "show up;[38] you must a kept part of that bar'l to prove the thing by. Show us the bunghole[39]—*do*—and we'll all believe you."

"Say, boys," says Bill, "less divide it up. Thar's thirteen of us. I can swaller a thirteenth of the yarn, if you can worry down the rest."[40]

37. *Edward . . . Edmund . . . Edwin*. His companions tease him with various proper names from which "Ed" is taken; in a sense, the shortened form is as much an alias as "Charles William Allbright," "Aleck James Hopkins," or "Mark Twain."

38. *show up*. Put up; provide the evidence.

39. *the bunghole*. The place in the barrel where the water or any other liquid is poured in or out.

40. *worry down the rest*. Force down the rest by dogged effort.

Ed got up mad and said they could all go to some place which he ripped out pretty savage, and then walked off aft cussing to himself, and they yelling and jeering at him, and roaring and laughing so you could hear them a mile.

"Boys, we'll split a watermelon on that," says the Child of Calamity; and he come rummaging around in the dark amongst the shingle bundles where I was, and put his hand on me. I was warm and soft and naked; so he says "Ouch!" and jumped back.

"ED GOT UP MAD."

"Fetch a lantern or a chunk of fire here, boys—there's a snake here as big as a cow!"

So they run there with a lantern and crowded up and looked in on me.

"Come out of that, you beggar!" says one.

"Who are you?" says another.

"What are you after here? Speak up prompt, or overboard you go."

"Snake him out, boys. Snatch him out by the heels."

I began to beg, and crept out amongst them trembling. They looked me over, wondering, and the Child of Calamity says:—

"A cussed thief! Lend a hand and less heave him overboard!"

"No," says Big Bob, "less get out the paint-pot and paint

41. *'Vast.* Avast, stop.

42. *Charles William Allbright.* Ironically, "dead" Huck is resurrected as the murdered baby. Another example of child death along the river.

him a sky blue all over from head to heel, and *then* heave him over!"

"Good! that's it. Go for the paint, Jimmy."

When the paint come, and Bob took the brush and was just going to

"WHO ARE YOU?"

begin, the others laughing and rubbing their hands, I begun to cry, and that sort of worked on Davy, and he says:—

"'Vast[41] there! He's nothing but a cub. I'll paint the man that tetches him!"

So I looked around on them, and some of them grumbled and growled, and Bob put down the paint, and the others didn't take it up.

"Come here to the fire, and less see what you're up to here," says Davy. "Now set down there and give an account of yourself. How long have you been aboard here?"

"Not over a quarter of a minute, sir," says I.

"How did you get dry so quick?"

"I don't know, sir. I'm always that way, mostly."

"Oh, you are, are you? What's your name?"

I warn't going to tell my name. I didn't know what to say, so I just says:

"Charles William Allbright,[42] sir."

Then they roared — the whole crowd; and I was mighty glad I said that, because maybe laughing would get them in a better humor.

When they got done laughing, Davy says:—

"It won't hardly do, Charles William. You couldn't have

growed this much in five year, and you was a baby when you come out of the bar'l, you know, and dead at that. Come, now, tell a straight story, and nobody'll hurt you, if you ain't up to anything wrong. What *is* your name?"

"Aleck Hopkins, sir. Aleck James Hopkins."

"Well, Aleck, where did you come from, here?"

"From a trading scow. She lays up the bend yonder. I was born on her. Pap has traded up and down here all his life; and he told me to swim off here, because when you went by he said he would like to get some of you to speak to a Mr. Jonas Turner, in Cairo, and tell him—"

"Oh, come!"

"Yes, sir, it's as true as the world; Pap he says—"

"Oh, your grandmother!"

They all laughed, and I tried again to talk, but they broke in on me and stopped me.

"Now, looky-here," says Davy; "you're scared, and so you talk wild. Honest, now, do you live in a scow, or is it a lie?"

"Yes, sir, in a trading scow. She lays up at the head of the bend. But I warn't born in her. It's our first trip."[43]

"CHARLES WILLIAM ALLBRIGHT, SIR."

43. *Yes, sir, in a trading scow. . . . It's our first trip.* In Chapter 16, Huck intended to stick to this "stretcher" by telling whomever he might meet on the shore that "pap was behind, coming along with a trading scow, and was a green hand at the business, and wanted to know how far it was to Cairo." He abandons this yarn when he encounters the slave hunters.

"Now you're talking! What did you come aboard here, for? To steal?"

"No, sir, I didn't.—It was only to get a ride on the raft. All boys does that."

"Well, I know that. But what did you hide for?"

"Sometimes they drive the boys off."

"So they do. They might steal. Looky-here; if we let you off this time, will you keep out of these kind of scrapes hereafter?"

"'Deed I will, boss. You try me."

"All right, then. You ain't but little ways from shore. Overboard with you, and don't you make a fool of yourself another time this way.—Blast it, boy, some raftsmen would rawhide you till you were black and blue!"

OVERBOARD.

I didn't wait to kiss good-bye, but went overboard and broke for shore. When Jim come along by and by, the big raft was away out of sight around the point. I swum out and got aboard, and was mighty glad to see home again.[44]

44. *mighty glad to see home again*. Two lines in the manuscript were dropped when Twain decided not to return this "old Mississippi matter" to *Huckleberry Finn*: "I had to tell Jim I didn't find out how far it was to Cairo. He was pretty sorry" (**MS**).

BIBLIOGRAPHY

BY MARK TWAIN

"The Dandy Frightening the Squatter." *The Carpet-Bag*, May 1, 1852.

"Historical Exhibition—A No. 1 Ruse." Hannibal *Journal*, September 16, 1852.

"Love Concealed: To Miss Katie of H——l." Hannibal *Daily Journal*, May 6, 1853.

"Oh, She Has a Red Head!" Hannibal *Daily Journal*, May 13, 1853.

"Story of a Bad Boy Who Didn't Come to Grief." San Francisco *Californian*, December 23, 1865.

"Reflections on the Sabbath." San Francisco *Golden Era*, March 18, 1866.

"A Complaint About Correspondents." San Francisco *Californian*, March 24, 1866.

"Morality and Huckleberries." San Francisco *Alta California*, September 8, 1868.

The Innocents Abroad. Illustrated by True W. Williams and others. Hartford, Conn.: American Publishing Co., 1869.

"Post-Mortum Poetry." *The Galaxy*, June 1870, pp. 864–65.

"The Indignity Put upon the Remains of George Holland." *The Galaxy*, February 1871, pp. 320–21.

Mark Twain's (Burlesque) Autobiography, and First Romance. Illustrated by Henry Louis Stephens. New York: Shelden & Co., 1871.

Roughing It. Illustrated by True W. Williams and others. Hartford, Conn.: American Publishing Co., 1872.

The Gilded Age. By Mark Twain and Charles Dudley Warner. Illustrated by Augustus Hoppin, Henry Louis Stephens, True W. Williams, and others. Hartford, Conn.: American Publishing Co., 1874.

"A True Story, Repeated Word for Word as I Heard It." *The Atlantic Monthly*, November 1874, pp. 591–94.

"Sociable Jimmy." New York *Times*, November 29, 1874.

Mark Twain's Sketches, New and Old. Illustrated by True W. Williams. Hartford, Conn.: American Publishing Co., 1875.

The Adventures of Tom Sawyer. Illustrated by True W. Williams. Hartford, Conn.: American Publishing Co., 1876.

"The Facts Concerning the Recent Carnival of Crime in Connecticut." *The Atlantic Monthly*, June 1876, pp. 641–50.

"Contributor's Club: The Boston Girl." *The Atlantic Monthly*, June 1880, pp. 851–60.

A Tramp Abroad. Illustrated by W. Fr. Brown, True W. Williams, B. Day, W. W. Denslow, and others. Hartford, Conn.: American Publishing Co., 1880.

Date, 1601. West Point, N.Y.: Academie Presse, 1882.

The Prince and the Pauper. Illustrated by Frank T. Merrill. Boston: James R. Osgood and Co., 1882.

Life on the Mississippi. Illustrated by E. H. Garrett, John J. Harley, A. B. Shute, and others. Boston: James R. Osgood and Co., 1883.

"An Adventure of Huckleberry Finn: With an Account of the Famous Grangerford–Shepherdson Feud." *Century Magazine*, December 1884, pp. 268–78.

"Jim's Investments, and King Sollermun." *Century Magazine*, January 1885, pp. 456–58.

"Royalty on the Mississippi: As Chronicled by Huckleberry Finn." *Century Magazine*, February 1885, pp. 544–67.

Adventures of Huckleberry Finn (Tom Sawyer's Comrade). Illustrated by Edward Windsor Kemble. New York: Charles L. Webster and Co., 1885.

"What Ought He to Have Done?" *The Christian Union*, July 16, 1885, pp. 4–5.

"The Private History of a Campaign That Failed." Illustrated by Edward Windsor Kemble. *Century Magazine*, December 1885, pp. 193–204.

"International Copyright." *Century Magazine*, February 1886, p. 634.

Mark Twain's Library of Humor. Edited by Mark Twain, William Dean Howells, and Charles Hopkins

Clark. Illustrated by Edward Windsor Kemble. New York: Charles L. Webster and Co., 1888.
A Connecticut Yankee in King Arthur's Court. Illustrated by Dan Beard. New York: Charles L. Webster and Co., 1889.
The American Claimant. Illustrated by Dan Beard. New York: Charles L. Webster and Co., 1892.
"Tom Sawyer Abroad." Illustrated by Dan Beard. *St. Nicholas*, November 1893 through April 1894.
Tom Sawyer Abroad. Illustrated by Dan Beard. New York: Charles L. Webster and Co., 1894.
The Tragedy of Pudd'nhead Wilson and the Comedy of Those Two Extraordinary Twins. Illustrated by F. N. Senior and C. H. Warren. Hartford, Conn.: American Publishing Co., 1894.
"Fenimore Cooper's Literary Offenses." *The North American Review*, July 1895, pp. 1–12.
"Tom Sawyer, Detective." Illustrated by Arthur Burdett Frost. *Harper's Monthly*, August and September 1896.
Tom Sawyer Abroad; Tom Sawyer, Detective; and Other Stories. Illustrated by Dan Beard and Arthur Burdett Frost. New York and London: Harper & Bros., 1896.
Following the Equator. Illustrated by Dan Beard, Arthur Burdett Frost, Peter Newell, and others, and with photographs. Hartford, Conn.: American Publishing Co., 1897.
"My First Lie and How I Got Out of It." New York *World*, December 10, 1899.
"John Hay and the Ballads." *Harper's Weekly*, October 21, 1905, p. 1530.
"Chapters from My Autobiography." *The North American Review*, September 7, 1906–December 1907.
Extract from Captain Stormfield's Visit to Heaven. Frontispiece by Albert Levering. New York and London: Harper & Bros., 1909.
Is Shakespeare Dead? New York and London: Harper & Bros., 1909.
Mark Twain's Speeches. Introduction by William Dean Howells. New York and London: Harper & Bros., 1910.
The Mysterious Stranger: A Romance. Edited by Albert Bigelow Paine and Frederick A. Duneka. Illustrated by Newell Convers Wyeth. New York and London: Harper & Bros., 1916.
Mark Twain's Letters. 2 vols. Edited by Albert Bigelow Paine. New York and London: Harper & Bros., 1917.
Europe and Elsewhere. Edited by Albert Bigelow Paine. New York and London: Harper & Bros., 1923.
Mark Twain's Speeches. Introduction by Albert Bigelow Paine, and an appreciation by William Dean Howells. New York and London: Harper & Bros., 1923.
Mark Twain's Autobiography. 2 vols. Edited by Albert Bigelow Paine. New York and London: Harper & Bros., 1924.
Mark Twain's Notebook. Edited by Albert Bigelow Paine. New York and London: Harper & Bros., 1935.
Mark Twain in Eruption: Hitherto Unpublished Pages About Men and Events. Edited by Bernard DeVoto. New York and London: Harper & Bros., 1940.
Mark Twain's Letters to Will Bowen. Edited by Theodore Hornberger. Austin: University of Texas Press, 1941.
Life on the Mississippi. Introduction by Edward Wagenknecht, with suppressed passages edited by Willis Wager. Illustrated by Thomas Hart Benton. New York: Limited Editions Club, 1944.
The Portable Mark Twain. Edited by Bernard DeVoto. New York: Viking, 1946.
The Love Letters of Mark Twain. Edited by Dixon Wecter. New York and London: Harper & Bros., 1949.
Mark Twain to Mrs. Fairbanks. Edited by Dixon Wecter. San Marino, Calif.: Huntington Library, 1949.
The Autobiography of Mark Twain. Edited by Charles Neider. New York: Harper & Row, 1959.
Mark Twain–Howells Letters. 2 vols. Edited by Henry Nash Smith, William M. Gibson, and Frederick Anderson. Cambridge, Mass.: Harvard University Press, 1960.
"Reflections on Religion." Edited by Charles Neider. *Hudson Review*, Autumn 1963, pp. 329–52.
Mark Twain's Letters to His Publishers. Edited by Hamlin Hill. Berkeley and Los Angeles: University of California Press, 1967.
Mark Twain's Which Was the Dream? and Other Symbolic Writings of Later Years. Edited by John S. Tuckey. Berkeley and Los Angeles: University of California Press, 1967.
Mark Twain's Satires and Burlesques. Edited by Franklin R. Rogers. Berkeley and Los Angeles: University of California Press, 1968.
"Huck Finn and Tom Sawyer Among the Indians." *Life*, December 20, 1968, pp. 33–38.
Mark Twain's Correspondence with Henry Huttleston Rogers 1893–1909. Edited by Lewis Leary. Berkeley and Los Angeles: University of California Press, 1969.
Mark Twain's Hannibal, Huck and Tom. Edited by Walter Blair. Berkeley and Los Angeles: University of California Press, 1969.
The Mysterious Stranger. Edited by William M. Gibson. Berkeley and Los Angeles: University of California Press, 1969.
Mark Twain's Fables of Man. Edited by John S. Tuckey. Berkeley and Los Angeles: University of California Press, 1972.

A Pen Warmed-Up in Hell. Edited by Frederick Anderson. New York: Harper & Row, 1972.
What Is Man? and Other Philosophical Writings. Edited by Paul Baender. Berkeley and Los Angeles: University of California Press, 1973.
Life As I See It. Edited by Charles Neider. New York: Harper & Row, 1975.
Mark Twain Speaks for Himself. Edited by Paul Fatout. West Lafayette, Ind.: Purdue University Press, 1978.
Early Tales and Sketches, vol. 1, 1851–1864. Edited by Edgar Marquess Branch, Robert H. Hirst, and Harriet Elinor Smith. Berkeley and Los Angeles: University of California Press, 1979.
Mark Twain's Notebooks and Journals, vol. 1. Edited by Frederick Anderson, Michael B. Frank, and Kenneth M. Sanderson. Berkeley and Los Angeles: University of California Press, 1975.
Mark Twain's Notebooks and Journals, vol. 2. Edited by Frederick Anderson, Lin Salamo, and Berend L. Stein. Berkeley and Los Angeles: University of California Press, 1979.
Mark Twain's Notebooks and Journals, vol. 3. Edited by Robert Park Browning, Michael B. Frank, and Lin Salamo. Berkeley and Los Angeles: University of California Press, 1979.
The Adventures of Tom Sawyer; Tom Sawyer Abroad; Tom Sawyer, Detective. Edited by John C. Gerber, Paul Baender, and Terry Firkins. Berkeley and Los Angeles: University of California Press, 1980.
Tom Sawyer; Tom Sawyer Abroad. Edited by John C. Gerber and Terry Firkins. Berkeley and Los Angeles: University of California Press, 1982.
The Grangerford–Shepherdson Feud. Edited by Edgar Marquess Branch and Robert H. Hirst. Berkeley: University of California, 1985.
Huck Finn and Tom Sawyer Among the Indians and Other Unfinished Stories. Edited by Dahlia Armon and Walter Blair. Berkeley: University of California Press, 1989.
"Jim and the Dead Man." *The New Yorker*, June 26/July 3, 1995, pp. 129–30.
A Murder, a Mystery, and a Marriage. Illustrated by Peter de Sève. New York: W. W. Norton, 2001.

NOTABLE EDITIONS OF *HUCKLEBERRY FINN*

According to the title page of the manuscript and the first American edition, the correct title of the novel is Adventures of Huckleberry Finn. *By error,* "The" *was added by the publishers to the running heads and by Kemble to the first chapter title illustration; consequently the cover and the title page of the first British edition, set by Chatto & Windus of London from the American sheets, reads* The Adventures of Huckleberry Finn. *Most subsequent editions retain the incorrect* The Adventures of Huckleberry Finn *to conform with* The Adventures of Tom Sawyer.

The Adventures of Huckleberry Finn (Tom Sawyer's Companion). Illustrated by E. W. Kemble. London: Chatto & Windus, 1884.
Adventures of Huckleberry Finn (Tom Sawyer's Comrade). Illustrated by E. W. Kemble. Montréal: Dawson, 1884.
Adventures of Huckleberry Finn (Tom Sawyer's Comrade). Illustrated by E. W. Kemble. New York: Charles L. Webster & Co., 1885.
The Adventures of Huckleberry Finn (Tom Sawyer's Comrade). Leipzig: B. Tauchnitz, 1885.
The Adventures of Huckleberry Finn. Illustrated by E. W. Kemble. New York and London: Harper & Bros., 1896.
The Adventures of Huckleberry Finn. "Autograph Edition." With four new halftone illustrations by E. W. Kemble. New York and London: Harper & Bros., 1899.
The Adventures of Huckleberry Finn. Introduction by Brander Matthews. New York and London: Harper & Bros., 1918.
The Adventures of Huckleberry Finn. Illustrated by Worth Brehm. New York and London: Harper & Bros., 1923.
The Adventures of Huckleberry Finn. Illustrated with stills from the 1920 Paramount motion picture. London: Eveleigh Nash & Crayson, 1923.
The Adventures of Huckleberry Finn. Introduction and notes by Eizo Ohashi. Tokyo: Kenkyusha, 1923.
The Adventures of Huckleberry Finn. Edited by Emily Fanning Barry and Herbert B. Bruner. New York and London: Harper & Bros., 1931.
The Adventures of Huckleberry Finn. Introduction by Booth Tarkington. Illustrated by E. W. Kemble. New York: Limited Editions Club, 1933.
The Adventures of Huckleberry Finn. Illustrated by A. S. Forrest. London: T. Nelson & Sons, 1935.
The Adventures of Huckleberry Finn. Introduction by John T. Winterich. Illustrated by Norman Rockwell. New York: Heritage Press, 1940.
The Adventures of Tom Sawyer and The Adventures of Huckleberry Finn. A Modern Library Giant Edition. New York: Random House, 1940.
The Adventures of Huckleberry Finn. Edited with an introduction by Bernard DeVoto. Illustrated by Thomas Hart Benton. New York and London: Limited Editions Club, 1942.

Tom Sawyer and Huckleberry Finn. Everyman's Library. Introduction by Christopher Morley. London: Dent; New York: E. P. Dutton, 1943.

The Adventures of Huckleberry Finn. Introduction by May Lamberton Becker. Illustrated by Baldwin Hawes. Cleveland: World Publishing Co., 1947.

The Adventures of Huckleberry Finn. Illustrated by Edward Burra. London: Paul Elek, 1948.

The Adventures of Huckleberry Finn. Illustrated by David McKay. New York: Grosset & Dunlap, 1948.

The Adventures of Huckleberry Finn. Introductions by Brander Matthews and Dixon Wecter. New York and London: Harper & Bros., 1948.

The Adventures of Huckleberry Finn. Introduction by Lionel Trilling. New York: Holt, Rinehart & Winston, 1948.

The Adventures of Tom Sawyer and The Adventures of Huckleberry Finn. Moscow: Foreign Publishing House, 1948.

The Adventures of Huckleberry Finn. Introduction by T. S. Eliot. London: Cresset Press; New York: Chanticleer Press, 1950.

The Adventures of Huckleberry Finn. Illustrated by Richard M. Powers. Garden City, New York: Doubleday, 1954.

The Adventures of Huckleberry Finn. Illustrated by C. Walter Hodges. London: Dent; New York: E. P. Dutton, 1955.

Huckleberry Finn. Illustrated by Geoffrey Whittam. London: Weidenfeld & Nicholson; Boston: Houghton Mifflin, 1958.

The Adventures of Huckleberry Finn. Illustrated by Logan MacFarland. London: Collins Clear-Type Press, 1960.

The Adventures of Huckleberry Finn. Illustrated by W. Mitchell Ireland. London: Collins, 1960.

The Adventures of Tom Sawyer and The Adventures of Huckleberry Finn. Preface by Clara Clemens. New York: Platt & Munk, 1960.

The Adventures of Huckleberry Finn. Illustrated by Edward Ardizzone. London: Heinemann, 1961.

Adventures of Huckleberry Finn. Introduction by Kenneth S. Lynn. Edited by Francis Dunham. Boston: Houghton Mifflin, 1962.

Adventures of Huckleberry Finn. Introduction and bibliography by Hamlin Hill. San Francisco: Chandler Publishing Co., 1962.

The Adventures of Huckleberry Finn. Afterword by Clifton Fadiman. Illustrated by John Falter. New York and London: Macmillan, 1962.

Huck Finn and His Critics. Edited by Richard Lettes, Robert F. McDonnell, and William E. Morris. New York: Macmillan, 1962.

The Adventures of Huckleberry Finn. Illustrated by Raymond Sheppard. London and Glasgow: Blackie, 1965.

The Adventures of Huckleberry Finn. Edited with an introduction and notes by Peter Coveney. Harmondsworth, England: Penguin, 1966.

The Adventures of Huckleberry Finn. Illustrated by Kamil Lhotak. London: Hamlyn, 1966.

The Adventures of Huckleberry Finn. Edited with an introduction and notes by Leo Marx. Indianapolis: Bobbs-Merrill, 1967.

The Art of Huckleberry Finn. Selected and edited by Hamlin Hill and Walter Blair. San Francisco: Chandler Publishing Co., 1969.

Adventures of Huckleberry Finn. Introduction by Edgar M. Branch. Edited by James K. Bowen and Richard Vanderbeets. Glenview, Ill.: Scott, Foresman, 1970.

Adventures of Huckleberry Finn. Edited by Sculley Bradley, Richmond Croom Beatty, E. Hudson Long, and Thomas Cooley. New York: Norton, 1977.

The Complete Adventures of Tom Sawyer and Huckleberry Finn. Illustrated by Warren Chappell. New York: Harper & Row, 1978.

The Adventures of Tom Sawyer and The Adventures of Huckleberry Finn. Introduction by James Dickey. New York and London: New American Library, 1979.

The Adventures of Huckleberry Finn. Afterword by Alfred Kazin. New York: Bantam Books, 1981.

The Annotated Huckleberry Finn. Introduction, notes, and bibliography by Michael Patrick Hearn. Illustrated by E. W. Kemble. New York: Clarkson N. Potter, 1981.

Adventures of Huckleberry Finn (Tom Sawyer's Comrade): A Facsimile of the Manuscript. Detroit: Gale Research Co., 1983.

The Adventures of Huckleberry Finn. Edited by G. P. Zlobin and A. I. Poltoratskii. Illustration by B. A. Alimov. Moscow: Raduga Publishers, 1984.

Adventures of Huckleberry Finn. Foreword by Henry Nash Smith. Illustrated by Barry Moser. West Hatfield, Mass.: Pennyroyal Press, 1985.

Adventures of Huckleberry Finn. Edited by Walter Blair and Victor Fischer. Berkeley and Los Angeles: University of California Press, 1988.

Adventures of Huckleberry Finn. "The Only Comprehensive Edition." Introduction by Justin Kaplan. Foreword and addendum by Victor Doyno. Illustrated by E. W. Kemble. New York: Random House, 1996.

Adventures of Huckleberry Finn. Foreword by Shelley Fisher Fishkin. Introduction by Toni Morrison. Afterword by Victor A. Doyno. New York: Oxford University Press, 1996.

Adventures of Huckleberry Finn. Oxford World Classics. Edited with an introduction and notes by Emory Eliott. Oxford and New York: Oxford University Press, 1999.

Adventures of Huckleberry Finn. New Riverside Editions. Edited by Susan K. Harris and Lyrae Van Clief-Stefanon. Illustrated by E. W. Kemble. Boston and New York: Houghton Mifflin, 2000.

Adventures of Huckleberry Finn. Edited by Victor Fischer and Lin Salamo with Harriet Elinor Smith and the late Walter Blair. Berkeley and Los Angeles: University of California Press, 2001.

About Mark Twain

Abbott, Keene. "Tom Sawyer's Town." *Harper's Weekly*, April 9, 1913, pp. 16–17.

Ade, George. "Mark Twain and the Old Time Subscription Book." *The American Review of Reviews*, June 1910, pp. 703–4.

Aldrich, Mrs. Thomas Bailey. *Crowding Memories*. Boston and New York: Houghton Mifflin, 1916.

Babcock, C. Merton. "Mark Twain, H. L. Mencken, and 'The Higher Goofyness.'" *American Quarterly*, Winter 1964, pp. 587–94.

Baetzhold, Howard G. *Mark Twain and John Bull: The British Connection*. Bloomington and London: Indiana University Press, 1970.

Baker, William. "Mark Twain and the Shrewd Ohio Audiences." *American Literary Realism*, Spring and Autumn 1985, pp. 14–30.

Beard, Daniel Carter. *Hardly a Man Is Now Alive*. New York: Doubleday, Doran, 1939.

Bennett, Arnold. "Arnold Bennett Considers Twain Was Divine Amateur." *The* (London) *Bookman*, June 1910, p. 118.

Blathwait, Raymond. "Mark Twain on Humor." New York *World*, May 31, 1891.

Borges, Jorge Luis. "Una Vindicacion de Mark Twain." *Sur*, November 1935, pp. 40–46.

Brashear, Dr. M. M. "Mark Twain's Niece, Daughter of His Sister, Pamela, Taking Keen Interest in Centennial." Hannibal *Evening Courier-Post*, March 6, 1935.

Brooks, Van Wyck. *The Ordeal of Mark Twain*. Revised edition. New York: E. P. Dutton, 1933.

Budd, Louis J., ed. *Mark Twain: The Contemporary Reviews*. Cambridge, England: Cambridge University Press, 1999.

Burnett, Adele Mehl. "Mark Twain in Critic's Role Guided E. W. Howe." Kansas City *Times*, October 17, 1961.

Cardwell, Guy. *Twins of Genius*. Michigan: Michigan State College Press, 1953.

Catalogue of the Library and Manuscripts of Samuel L. Clemens (Mark Twain). New York: Anderson Auction Co., 1911.

Chesterton, G. K. *A Handful of Authors*. Edited by Dorothy Collins. New York: Sheed & Ward, 1953.

Clemens, Clara. *My Father, Mark Twain*. New York: Harper & Bros., 1931.

——. *My Husband Gabrilowitsch.* New York: Harper & Bros., 1938.

Clemens, Cyril. "A Talk with Edward Verral Lucas." *Canadian Bookman*, August/September 1938, pp. 19–21.

Clemens, Will M. *Mark Twain, His Life and Work*. San Francisco: Clemens Publishing Co., 1892.

Clemens, Susy. *Papa, An Intimate Biography of Mark Twain*. Edited by Charles Neider. Garden City, N.Y.: Doubleday, 1985.

Covici, Pascal, Jr. "Dear Master Wattie: The Mark Twain—David Watt Bowser Letters." *Southwest Review*, Spring 1960, pp. 105–21.

Croy, Homer. "The Originals of Mark Twain's Characters." *The Bellman*, June 25, 1910, pp. 804–5.

DeVoto, Bernard. *Mark Twain at Work*. Cambridge, Mass.: Harvard University Press, 1942.

——. *Mark Twain's America*. Boston: Little, Brown, 1932.

Douglass, Jane, ed. *Trustable and Preshus Friends*. Foreword by Julie Harris. New York: Harcourt Brace Jovanovich, 1977.

Dreiser, Theodore. "Mark the Double Twain." *The English Review*, October 1935, pp. 615–27.

Eastman, Max. "Mark Twain's Elmira." *Harper's Monthly*, May 1938, pp. 620–32.

English, Thomas H. *Mark Twain to Uncle Remus*. Atlanta, Ga.: Emory University Press Library, 1953.

Faulkner, William. "The Art of Fiction." *Paris Review*, Spring 1956, pp. 46–47.

Fiedler, Elizabeth Davis. "Familiar Haunts of Mark Twain." *Harper's Weekly*, December 16, 1899, pp. 10–11.

Fisher, Henry W. *Abroad with Mark Twain and Eugene Field*. New York: Nichols L. Brown, 1922.

Fishkin, Shelley Fisher. *Lighting Out for the Territory: Reflections on Mark Twain and American Culture*. New York and Oxford: Oxford University Press, 1997.

Gabrilowitsch, Clara Clemens. "My Father." *The Mentor*, May 1924, pp. 21–23.

Gilder, Rosamund, ed. *Letters of Richard Watson Gilder*. Boston and New York: Houghton Mifflin, 1916.

Gillis, William R. *Memories of Mark Twain and Steve Gillis*. Sonora, Calif.: The Banner, 1924.
Graham, William A. "Mark Twain—Dean of Our Humorists." *Human Life*, May 1906, pp. 1–2.
Gribben, Alan. "Mark Twain, Phrenology, and the 'Temperaments.'" *American Quarterly*, March 1972, pp. 45–68.
Handford, Thomas W. *Pleasant Hours with Illustrious Men and Women with Many Personal Reminiscences*. Chicago, Philadelphia, and Cincinnati: R. G. Badoux & Co., 1885.
Harris, Helen L. "Mark Twain's Response to the Native American." *American Literature*, January 1975, pp. 495–505.
Harsnberger, Caroline Thomas. *Mark Twain's View of Religion*. Evanston, Ill.: Schori Press, 1961.
Hearn, Michael Patrick. "Like Old Man River, Mark Twain Just Keeps Rolling Along." *Teaching and Learning About Literature*, September/October 1995, pp. 38–48.
Hemminghaus, Edgar H. *Mark Twain in Germany*. New York: Columbia University Press, 1939.
Henderson, Archibold. *Mark Twain*. New York: Frederick A. Stokes, 1912.
"He Returns." Hannibal *Journal*, April 18, 1889.
Hollister, Wilfred R., and Harry Norman. *Five Famous Missourians*. Kansas City: Hudson-Kimberly Publishing Co., 1900.
Howells, William Dean. "Mark Twain." *Century Magazine*, September 1882, pp. 780–83.
———. "Mark Twain: An Inquiry." *North American Review*, February 1901, pp. 308–21.
———. *My Mark Twain*. New York: Harper & Bros., 1910.
———. "Recent Literature." *The Atlantic Monthly*, May 1876, pp. 621–22.
Johnson, Merle. *A Bibliography of the Works of Mark Twain*. Revised edition. New York: Harper & Bros., 1935.
Kaplan, Justin. *Mark Twain and His World*. New York: Simon & Schuster, 1974.
———. *Mr. Clemens and Mark Twain.* New York: Simon & Schuster, 1966.
Lang, Andrew. "The Art of Mark Twain." *Illustrated London News*, February 14, 1891, p. 222.
"Laura Hawkins Frazer Always Remembered as Idol of His Boyhood." Hannibal *Evening Courier-Post*, March 6, 1935.
Leary, Kate, with Mary Lawton. *A Lifetime with Mark Twain*. New York: Harcourt, Brace, 1925.
Leavis, F. R. "The Americanness of American Literature." *Commentary*, November 1952, pp. 466–74.
LeMaster, J. R., and James D. Wilson, editors. *The Mark Twain Encyclopedia*. New York and London: Garland, 1993.
Leonard, James S. *Making Mark Twain Work in the Classroom*. Durham, N.C.: Duke University Press, 1999.
Lorch, Fred W. "Mark Twain's 'Morals' Lecture During the American Phase of His World Tour in 1895–1896." *American Literature*, March 1954, pp. 52–66.
Lynn, Kenneth S. "Welcome Back to the Raft, Huck Honey!" *American Literature*, Summer 1977, pp. 338–47.
Macdonald, Dwight. "Mark Twain: An Unsentimental Journey." *The New Yorker*, April 9, 1960, pp. 160–96.
"Mark Twain and His Book: The Humorist and the Copyright Question." New York *Times*, December 10, 1889.
"Mark Twain as Lecturer: How He Feels When He Gets on the Stage Before an Audience." New York *World*, November 20, 1884.
"Mark Twain Brands a Fake: But It Does Not Irritate Him—Talk of Cable and Lecturing." Seattle *Post-Intelligencer*, August 14, 1895.
"Mark Twain Encountered." Rochester *Herald*, December 8, 1884.
"Mark Twain Interviewed." Calcutta *Englishman*, February 8, 1896.
"Mark Twain Is Here." Helena (Mont.) *Daily Herald*, August 3, 1895.
Mark Twain Journal, 1954–current.
Mark Twain Quarterly, 1936–1953.
"Mark Twain on Training That Pays: Speaks at a Supper of the Male Teachers' Association." New York *Times*, March 17, 1901.
"Mark Twain: The Lotus Club Dinner—His Speech and the Others—Those Present." New York *Times*, November 17, 1900.
"Mark Twain's Childhood Sweetheart Recalls Their Romance." *The Literary Digest*, March 23, 1918, pp. 70–75.
"Mark Twain's 70th Birthday." *Harper's Weekly*, December 23, 1905, pp. 1884–1914.
Masters, Edgar Lee. *Mark Twain: A Portrait*. New York and London: Charles Scribner's Sons, 1938.
Matthews, Brander. *The Tocsin of Revolt and Other Essays*. New York: Scribners, 1922.
———. "A Tribute to Mark Twain." New York *Times*, December 3, 1910.
Meltzer, Milton. *Mark Twain Himself*. New York: Thomas Y. Crowell Co., 1960.
Mencken, H. L. "Mark Twain." *The Smart Set*, October 1919, pp. 138–44.
———. "Oyez! Oyez! All Ye Who Read Books." *The Smart Set*, December 1908, pp. 153–60.

Moffett, Samuel E. "Mark Twain to Pay All: On His Way Around the World Now to Raise the Money." San Francisco *Examiner*, August 17, 1895.

Mumford, Lewis. *The Golden Day*. New York: Boni & Liveright, 1926.

Orians, G. Harrisdon. "Walter Scott, Mark Twain, and the Civil War." *The South Atlantic Quarterly*, October 1941, pp. 343–59.

Paine, Albert Bigelow. *Mark Twain: A Biography*. 3 vols. New York and London: Harper & Bros., 1912.

Park, Edwin J. "A Day with Mark Twain." Chicago *Tribune*, September 19, 1886.

Pattee, Fred Lewis. *A History of American Literature Since 1870*. New York: Century, 1915.

Pease, Lute. "Mark Twain Talks: The Famous Story-Teller Discusses Characters." Portland *Sunday Oregonian*, August 9, 1895.

Pettit, Arthur Gordon. "Mark Twain and the Negro, 1867–1869." *The Journal of Negro History*, April 1971, pp. 88–96.

———. *Mark Twain and the South*. Lexington: University of Kentucky Press, 1974.

———. "Mark Twain, Unreconstructed Southerner, and His View of the Negro, 1835–1860." *The Rocky Mountain Social Science Journal*, April 1970, pp. 17–27.

"Police Hustle Crowd Awaiting Mark Twain." New York *Times*, March 5, 1906.

Pond, James B. *Eccentricities of Genius*. New York: G. W. Dillingham Co., 1900.

Public Meeting under the Auspices of the American Academy and the National Institute of Arts and Letters at Carnegie Hall, New York, November 3, 1910, in Memory of Samuel Langhorne Clemens (Mark Twain). New York: American Academy of Arts and Letters, 1922.

Ramsay, Robert L., and Frances Guthrie Emberson. "A Mark Twain Lexicon." *University of Missouri Studies*, January 1, 1938, pp. 1–278.

Rasmussen, R. Kent. *Mark Twain A to Z*. New York and Oxford: Oxford University Press, 1995.

Roper, Gordon. "Mark Twain and His Canadian Publishers." *American Book Collector*, June 1960, pp. 13–29.

"Roosevelt's Speech at Twain Bridge." New York *Times*, September 5, 1936.

Rubin, Louis D., Jr. *George W. Cable*. New York: Pegasus, 1969.

Sanderlin, George. *Mark Twain: As Others Saw Him*. New York: Coward, McCann & Geoghegan, 1978.

Sinclair, Upton. *Mammonart: An Essay in Interpretation*. Pasadena, Calif.: privately printed, 1925.

Sosey, Frank S. "Palmyra and Its Historical Environment." *The Missouri Historical Review*, April 1929, pp. 361–62.

Stevenson, E. Burleson. "Mark Twain's Attitude Toward the Negro." *Quarterly Review of Higher Education Among Negroes*, October 1945, pp. 326–62.

Stronks, James B. "Mark Twain's Boston Stage Debut as Seen By Hamlin Garland." *The New England Quarterly*, March 1963, pp. 85–86.

Sweets, Henry H., III. *The Hannibal, Missouri Presbyterian Church: A Sesquicentennial History*. Hannibal: Presbyterian Church of Hannibal, 1984.

Turner, Arlin. *Mark Twain and G. W. Cable*. East Lansing: Michigan State University Press, 1960.

The Twainian, January 1939–December 1989, November 1993–current.

"The Typothetæ: Mark Twain Tells About the Primitive Newspaper." Hartford *Courant*, January 21, 1886.

Watts, Aretta L. "Mark Twain's Gay Mother." New York *Times*, February 5, 1928.

Webster, Samuel Charles. *Mark Twain, Business Man*. Boston: Little, Brown, 1946.

Wecter, Dixon. *Sam Clemens of Hannibal*. Boston: Houghton Mifflin, 1952.

Welland, Dennis. *Mark Twain in England*. London: Chatto & Windus, 1978.

Welsh, Donald H. "Sam Clemens' Hannibal, 1836–1838." *Midcontinent American Studies Journal*, Spring 1962, pp. 28–43.

Zinsser, William. *American Places: A Writer's Pilgrimage to 15 of This Country's Most Visited and Cherished Sites*. New York: HarperCollins, 1992.

ABOUT *HUCKLEBERRY FINN*

Adams, Lucille, editor. *Huckleberry Finn: A Descriptive Bibliography of the Huckleberry Finn Collection at the Buffalo Public Library*. Buffalo, N.Y.: Buffalo Public Library, 1950.

Allen, Margot. "*Huck Finn*: Two Generations of Pain." *Interracial Books for Children Bulletin*, no. 5, 1984, pp. 9–12.

Andrews, William L. "Mark Twain and James W. Pennington: Huckleberry Finn's Smallpox Lie." *Studies in American Fiction*, Spring 1981, pp. 103–12.

Arac, Jonathan. *Huckleberry Finn as Idol and Target: The Functions of Criticism in Our Times*. Madison: University of Wisconsin Press, 1997.

Ashmead, John. "A Possible Hannibal Source for Mark Twain's Dauphin." *American Literature*, March 1962, pp. 105–7.

Auden, W. H. "Huck and Oliver." *The Listener*, October 1, 1953, pp. 540–41.

Bailey, Roger. "Twain's *Adventures of Huckleberry Finn*,

Chapters 1 and 2." *The Explicator*, September 1967.
Baker, Russell. "The Only Gentleman." New York *Times*, April 14, 1982.
Baldanza, Frank. "The Structure of *Huckleberry Finn*." *American Literature*, November 1955, pp. 347–55.
Beaver, Harold. *Huckleberry Finn*. London: Allen & Unwin, 1987.
Belden, H. M. "Scyld Scefing and Huck Finn." *Modern Language Notes*, May 1918, p. 315.
Besant, Walter. "My Favorite Novelist and His Best Book." *Munsey's Magazine*, February 1898, pp. 659–64.
Birchfield, James. "Jim's Coat of Arms." *Mark Twain Journal*, Summer 1969, pp. 15–16.
Blair, Walter. "The French Revolution and *Huckleberry Finn*." *Modern Philology*, August 1957, pp. 21–35.
———. *Mark Twain and Huck Finn*. Berkeley and Los Angeles: University of California Press, 1960.
———. "The Reasons Mark Twain Did Not Finish His Story." *Life*, December 20, 1968, p. 50A.
Bloom, Harold, editor. *Major Literary Characters: Huck Finn.* New York: Chelsea House Publishers, 1990.
Boland, Sally, "The Seven Dialects in *Huckleberry Finn*." *North Dakota Quarterly*, Summer 1968, pp. 30–40.
Branch, Edgar M. "Mark Twain: Newspaper Reading and the Writer's Creativity." *Nineteenth-Century Fiction*, March 1983, pp. 576–603.
———. "The Two Providences: Thematic Form in *Huckleberry Finn*." *College English*, January 1950, pp. 188–95.
Bridges, Robert. "Mark Twain's Blood-Curdling Humor." *Life,* February 26, 1885, p. 119.
Brown, Sterling. *The Negro in American Fiction*. Washington, D. C.: Association of American Folk Education, 1937.
Budd, Louis J., editor. *New Essays on Adventures of Huckleberry Finn*. Cambridge, England: Cambridge University Press, 1985.
———. "The Recomposition of *Adventures of Huckleberry Finn*." *The Missouri Review*, vol. 10 (1987), pp. 113–29.
Byers, John R., Jr. "Miss Emmeline Grangerford's Hymn Book." *American Literature*, May 1971, pp. 259–63.
Carkeet, David. "The Dialects in Huckleberry Finn." *American Literature*, November 1979, pp. 315–32.
———. "The Source for the Arkansas Gossips in *Huckleberry Finn*." *American Literary Realism*, Spring 1981, pp. 90–92.
Carmody, Deidre. "What Huck and Jim Really Said in That Cave." New York *Times*, May 16, 1995.
Cecil, L. Moffitt. "The Historical Ending of *Adventures of Huckleberry Finn*: How Nigger Jim Was Set Free." *American Literary Realism*, Autumn 1980, pp. 280–83.
Chadwick-Joshua, Jocelyn. *The Jim Dilemma: Reading Race in Huckleberry Finn*. Jackson: University Press of Mississippi, 1998.
Champion, Laurie, editor. *The Critical Response to Mark Twain's Huckleberry Finn*. New York: Greenwood Press, 1991.
Clemens, Cyril. "Mark Twain's Favorite Book." *Overland Monthly*, May 1930, p. 157.
Colwell, James L. "Huckleberries and Humans: On the Naming of Huckleberry Finn." *PMLA*, January 1971, pp. 70–76.
Cummings, Sherwood. "Mark Twain's Moveable Farm and the Evasion." *American Literature*, September 1991, pp. 440–58.
Dahl, Curtis. "Mark Twain and Ben Ely: Two Missouri Boyhoods." *Missouri Historical Review*, July 1972, pp. 549–66.
Dawson, Hugh J. "The Ethnicity of Huck Finn—and the Difference It Makes." *American Literary Realism*, Winter 1998, pp. 1–16.
Dickinson, Asa Don. "Huckleberry Finn Is Fifty Years Old—Yes; But Is He Respectable?" *Wilson Bulletin for Librarians*, November 1935, pp. 180–85.
Doughty, Nanelia S. "Realistic Negro Characters in Postbellum Fiction." *Negro American Literature Forum*, Summer 1957, pp. 57–62.
Doyno, Victor A. *Writing Huckleberry Finn: Mark Twain's Creative Process*. Philadelphia: University of Pennsylvania Press, 1991.
Ellis, James. "The Bawdy Humor of 'The King's Cameleopard or The Royal Nonesuch.'" *American Literature*, December 1991, pp. 729–35.
Ferguson, De Lancey. "Huck Finn Aborning." *The Colophon*, Spring 1938, pp. 171–80.
Fiedler, Leslie A. "Come Back to the Raft Ag'in, Huck Honey!" In *An End to Innocence*. Boston: Beacon Press, 1955, pp. 142–51.
Fischer, Victor. "Huck Finn Reviewed: The Reception of *Huckleberry Finn* in the United States, 1884–1897." *American Literary Realism: 1870–1900*, Spring 1983, pp. 1–57.
Fishkin, Shelley Fisher. "Twain, In '85." New York *Times*, February 14, 1985.
———. *Was Huck Black? Mark Twain and African American Voices.* New York: Oxford University Press, 1993.
Gates, David. "Same Twain, Different Time." *Newsweek*, July 20, 1992, pp. 64–65.
Gelatt, Dorothy S. "Huck Finn Ms., Lost 100 Years,

Turns Up in Hollywood Attic." *Maine Antiques Digest*, April 1991, pp. 30A–31A.

Hearn, Michael Patrick. *The Annotated Huckleberry Finn.* New York: Clarkson N. Potter, 1981.

——. "Expelling Huck Finn." *The Nation*, August 7–14, 1982.

——. "Half-Baked Huckleberry Pie." San Jose *Mercury News*, May 5, 1996.

——. "Huck Finn: Watching His Language." *Washington Post Book World*, June 6, 1993, pp. 3, 7.

Hitchins, Christopher. "American Notes." *TLS*, March 8, 1985, p. 258.

Hutchinson, Stuart, editor. *Mark Twain: Tom Sawyer and Huckleberry Finn*. Columbia Critical Guides. New York: Columbia University Press, 1998.

Inge, M. Thomas, editor. *Huck Finn Among the Critics: A Centennial Selection*. Franklin, Md.: University Publications of America, 1985.

Johnson, Claudia D. *Understanding Adventures of Huckleberry Finn: A Student Casebook to Issues, Sources, and Historical Documents*. Westport, Conn.: Greenwood Press, 1996.

Jones, Charisse. "Library Threatens Legal Action over 'Huck' Manuscript." Los Angeles *Times*, April 20, 1991.

Kakutani, Michiko. "Adapting and Analyzing 'Huck Finn.' " New York *Times*, February 24, 1986.

Kaplan, Justin. *Born to Trouble: One Hundred Years of Huckleberry Finn.* The Center for the Book Viewpoint Series, no. 13. Washington, D. C.: Library of Congress, 1985.

——. "Selling 'Huck Finn' down the River." *The New York Times Book Review*, March 10, 1996, p. 27.

"Lee Arthur Has Converted 'Huckleberry Finn' into a Play." St. Louis *Republic*, October 12, 1902.

Leonard, James S., Thomas A. Tenney, and Thadious M. Davis, editors. *Satire or Evasion?: Black Perspectives on "Huckleberry Finn."* Durham, N.C., and London: Duke University Press, 1992.

Lorch, Fred W. "A Note on Tom Blankenship (Huckleberry Finn)." *American Literature*, November 1940, pp. 351–53.

Lucas, E. V. *Visibility Good*. Philadelphia: J. B. Lippincott, 1931.

McDowell, Edwin. "From Twain, a Letter on Debt to Blacks." New York *Times*, March 14, 1985.

McNamara, Brooks. "*Huckleberry Finn* on Stage: A Mark Twain Letter in the Shubert Archive." *The Passing Show*, Fall 1991, pp. 2–6.

Mailer, Norman. "Huckleberry Finn, Alive at 100." *The New York Times Book Review*, December 9, 1984, pp. 1, 36–37.

"Mark Twain on 'Huck Finn.' " *The Canadian Bookseller*, September 1902, p. 56.

Marschall, Richard. "An American Classic and a Classic Comic Strip." *Nemo*, December 1985, pp. 19–33.

Mason, Bobbie Ann, and others. "Huck, Continued." *The New Yorker*, June 26/July 3, 1995, pp. 130–33.

Meine, Franklin J. "Some Notes on the First Edition of *Huck Finn*." *American Book Collector*, June 1960, pp. 31–34.

Menaker, Donald. "The Phoenix-like Manuscript of *Adventures of Huckleberry Finn*." *At Random*, December 1995, pp. 45–47.

Miller, Michael G. "Geography and Structure in *Huckleberry Finn*." *Studies in the Novel*, Fall 1980, pp. 192–209.

Moran, Robert, and Connie Langland. "Pennsylvania NAACP Opposes 'Huck Finn' Requirement." Buffalo *News*, February 2, 1998.

Nadeau, Robert. " 'Huckleberry Finn' Is a Moral Story." Washington *Post*, April 11, 1982.

Osborn, Michelle. "Twain Tale Could Have $1M Ending." *USA Today*, April 16, 1991.

Puttock, Kay. "Many Responses to the Many Voices of *Huckleberry Finn*." *The Lion and the Unicorn*, June 1992, pp. 77–82.

Pearson, E. L. "The Children's Librarian *versus* Huckleberry Finn: A Brief for the Defense." *The Library Journal*, July 1907, pp. 312–14.

Pritchett, V. S. "America's First Truly Indigenous Masterpiece." *New Statesman and Nation*, August 2, 1941, p. 113.

Reif, Rita. "First Half of 'Huck Finn,' in Twain's Hand, Is Found." New York *Times*, February 14, 1991.

——. "How 'Huck Finn' Was Rescued." New York *Times*, March 17, 1991.

——. "More Huck Finn Adventures, to Buffalo via Hollywood." New York *Times*, August 2, 1992.

——. "30 Autographed Mark Twain Items for Sale." New York *Times*, January 29, 1988.

——. "Twain Manuscript Resolves Huck Finn Mysteries." New York *Times*, February 26, 1991.

Reigstad, Tom. " 'Huck Finn's' Buffalo Hideout." Buffalo *Courier-Express*, October 7, 1979.

Sager, Mike. "Mark Twain School Trying to Censor Huck." Washington *Post,* April 8, 1982.

Sattelmeyer, Robert, and J. Donald Crowley, editors. *One Hundred Years of Huckleberry Finn: The Boy, the Book, and American Culture: Centennial Essays*. Columbia: University of Missouri Press, 1985.

Smiley, Jane. "Say It Ain't So, Huck: Second Thoughts on Mark Twain's 'Masterpiece.'" *Harper's Magazine*, January 1996, pp. 61–67.

Strickland, Carol Colclough. "Emmeline Grangerford, Mark Twain's Folk Artist." *Bulletin of the New York Public Library*, Winter 1976, pp. 225–33.
Wallace, John H. "'Huckleberry Finn' Is Offensive." Washington *Post*, April 14, 1982.
Weaver, Thomas. "Mark Twain's Jim: An Identity as an Index to Cultural Attitudes." *American Literary Realism*, Spring 1980, pp. 19–29.
Weeks, Robert P. "The Captain, the Prophet, and the King." *Mark Twain Journal*, Winter 1975–1976, pp. 9–12.
Wieck, Carl F. *Refiguring Huckleberry Finn*. Athens (Ga.) and London: University of Georgia Press, 2000.
Wiley, B. J. "Guyuscutus, Royal Nonesuch, and Other Hoaxes." *Southern Folklore Quarterly*, December 1944, pp. 251–75.
Wilkinson, Tracy. "Missing Twain Manuscript Is Believed Found." Los Angeles *Times*, February 13, 1991.
——, and Jane Hall. "Library Apparently Will Get Twain Manuscript." Los Angeles *Times*, February 14, 1991.
Wood, Clement. *More Adventures of Huckleberry Finn*. New York and Cleveland: World, 1940.
Wood, Grant. "My Debt to Mark Twain." *Mark Twain Quarterly*, Fall 1937, pp. 6, 14, and 24.
Zamir, Shamoon. "An Interview with Ishmael Reed." *Callaloo*, Autumn 1994, pp. 1131–57.

ABOUT E. W. KEMBLE

Barclay, Donald A. "Interpreted Well Enough: Two Illustrators' Visions of *Adventures of Huckleberry Finn*." *The Horn Book*, May/June 1992, pp. 311–19.
Briden, Earl F. "Kemble's 'Specialty' and the Pictorial Countertext of *Huckleberry Finn*." *Mark Twain Journal*, Fall 1988, pp. 2–14.
Clemens, Cyril. "The Model for Huckleberry Finn." *Hobbies*, February 1955, pp. 106–7 and 109.
David, Beverly R. "Mark Twain and the Legends of *Huckleberry Finn*." *American Literary Realism*, Autumn 1982, pp. 155–64.
——. "The Pictorial *Huck Finn*: Mark Twain and His Illustrator E. W. Kemble." *American Quarterly*, October 1974, pp. 331–51.
——. "Visions of the South: Joel Chandler Harris and His Illustrators." *American Literary Realism*, Summer 1976, pp. 182–206.
Hearn, Michael Patrick. "Mark Twain, E. W. Kemble, and *Huckleberry Finn*." *American Book Collector*, November/December 1981, pp. 14–19.
Kemble, E. W. "Illustrating *Huckleberry Finn*." *The Colophon*, February 1930, pp. 45–52.
Martin, Francis, Jr. "Edward Windsor Kemble, A Master of Pen and Ink." *American Art Review*, January/February 1976, pp. 54–67.
——. "E. W. Kemble, 1861–1933: American Illustrator." *The Private Library*, Autumn, 1994, pp. 130–144.
Morris, Courtland. "The Model for Huck Finn." *Mark Twain Quarterly*, Fall 1938, pp. 22–23.
Obituary, New York *Times*, September 20, 1933.